Maps in a
Mirror

THE SHORT FICTION OF
ORSON SCOTT CARD

CENTURY
A LEGEND BOOK

LONDON   SYDNEY   AUCKLAND   JOHANNESBURG

First published in Great Britain in 1991 by Legend, an imprint of
Random Century Group
20 Vauxhall Bridge Road,
London SW1V 2SA

Century Hutchinson South Africa (Pty) Ltd
PO Box 337, Bergvlei 2012
South Africa

Random Century Australia Pty Ltd
20 Alfred Street, Milsons Point, Sydney, NSW 2061
Australia

Random Century New Zealand Ltd
PO Box 40–086, Glenfield, Auckland 10
New Zealand

British Library Cataloguing in Publication Data
Card, Orson Scott, *1951*—
Maps in a mirror.
I. Title
813.54

ISBN 0–7126–4544–2 Csd
0–7126–4855–0 Pbk

Printed and bound in Great Britain by
Mackays of Chatham PLC, Chatham, Kent

To Charlie Ben,
who can fly

CONTENTS

BOOK 1
THE HANGED MAN
Tales of Dread

BOOK 2
FLUX
Tales of Human Futures

BOOK 3

MAPS IN A MIRROR
Fables and Fantasies

BOOK 4

CRUEL MIRACLES
Tales of Death, Hope, and Holiness

BOOK 5

LOST SONGS
The Hidden Stories

BOOK 1

THE HANGED MAN

TALES OF DREAD

INTRODUCTION

I can't watch horror or suspense movies in the theatre. I've tried—but the tension becomes too much for me. The screen is too large, the figures are too real. I always end up having to get up, walk out, go home. It's more than I can bear.

You know where I end up watching those movies? At home. On cable TV. That little screen is so much *safer*. The familiar scenes of my home surround it. And when it gets too tense, I can flip away, watch reruns of *Dick Van Dyke* or *Green Acres* or some utterly lame depression-era movie until I calm down enough to flip back and see how things turned out.

That's how I watched *Aliens* and *The Terminator*—I never have watched them beginning-to-end. I realize that by doing this I'm subverting the filmmaker's art, which is linear. But then, my TV's remote control has turned viewing into a participatory art. I can now perform my own recutting on films that are too upsetting for my taste. For me, *Lethal Weapon* is much more pleasurable when intercut with fragments of *Wild and Beautiful on Ibiza* and *Life on Earth*.

Which brings us to the most potent tool of storytellers. Fear. And not just fear, but dread. *Dread* is the first and the strongest of the three kinds of fear. It is that tension, that waiting that comes when you know there is something to fear but you have not yet identified what it is. The fear that comes when you first realize that your spouse should have been home an hour ago; when you hear a strange sound in the baby's bedroom; when you realize that a window you are sure you closed is now open, the curtains billowing, and you're alone in the house.

Terror only comes when you see the thing you're afraid of. The intruder is coming at you with a knife. The headlights coming toward you are clearly in your lane. The klansmen have emerged from the bushes and one of them is holding a rope. This is when all the muscles of your body, except perhaps the sphincters, tauten and you stand rigid; or you scream; or you run. There is a frenzy to this moment, a climactic power—but it is the power of release, not the power of tension. And bad as it is, it is better than dread in this respect: Now, at least, you know the face of the thing you fear. You know its borders, its dimensions. You know what to expect.

Horror is the weakest of all. After the fearful thing has happened, you see its remainder, its relics. The grisly, hacked-up corpse. Your emotions range from nausea to pity for the victim. And even your pity is tinged with revulsion and disgust; ultimately you reject the scene and deny its humanity; with repetition, horror loses its ability to move you and, to some degree, dehumanizes the victim and therefore dehumanizes you. As the sonderkommandos in the death camps learned, after you move enough naked murdered corpses, it stops making you want to weep or puke. You just do it. They've stopped being people to you.

This is why I am depressed by the fact that contemporary storytellers of fear have moved almost exclusively toward horror and away from dread. The slasher movies almost don't bother anymore with creating the sympathy for character that is required to fill an audience with dread. The moments of terror are no longer terrifying because we empathize with the victim, but are rather fascinating because we want to see what creative new method of mayhem the writer and art director have come up with. Ah— murder by shish-ka-bob! Oh, cool—the monster poked the guy's eye out from *inside* his head!

Obsessed with the desire to film the unfilmable, the makers of horror flicks now routinely show the unspeakable, in the process dehumanizing their audience by turning human suffering into pornographically escalating "entertainment." This is bad enough, but to my regret, too many writers of the fiction of fear are doing the same thing. They failed to learn the real lesson of Stephen King's success. It isn't the icky stuff that makes King's stories work. It's how much he makes you care about his characters before the icky stuff ever happens. And his best books are the ones like *The Dead Zone* and *The Stand* in which not that much horror ever happens at all. Rather the stories are suffused with dread leading up to cathartic moments of terror and pain. Most important, the suffering that characters go through *means something*.

That is the artistry of fear. To make the audience so empathize with a character that we fear what he fears, for his reasons. We don't stand outside, looking at a gory slime cover him or staring at his gaping wounds. We stand inside him, anticipating the terrible things that might or will happen. Anybody can hack a fictional corpse. Only a storyteller can make you hope the character will live.

So: I don't write horror stories. True, bad things happen to my characters. Sometimes terrible things. But I don't show it to you in living color. I don't have to. I don't *want* to. Because, caught up in dread, you'll imagine far worse things happening than I could ever think up to show you myself.

EUMENIDES IN THE FOURTH
FLOOR LAVATORY

L iving in a fourth-floor walkup was part of his revenge, as if to say to Alice,
"Throw me out of the house, will you? Then I'll live in squalor in a
Bronx tenement, where the toilet is shared by four apartments! My shirts
will go unironed, my tie will be perpetually awry. *See what you've done
to me?*"

But when he told Alice about the apartment, she only laughed bitterly and said,
"Not anymore, Howard. I won't play those games with you. You win every damn time."

She pretended not to care about him anymore, but Howard knew better. He knew
people, knew what they wanted, and Alice wanted *him*. It was his strongest card in
their relationship—that she wanted him more than he wanted her. He thought of this
often: at work in the offices of Humboldt and Breinhardt, Designers; at lunch in a cheap
lunchroom (part of the punishment); on the subway home to his tenement (Alice had
kept the Lincoln Continental). He thought and thought about how much she wanted
him. But he kept remembering what she had said the day she threw him out: If you
ever come near Rhiannon again I'll kill you.

He could not remember why she had said that. Could not remember and did not
try to remember because that line of thinking made him uncomfortable and one thing
Howard insisted on being was comfortable with himself. Other people could spend
hours and days of their lives chasing after some accommodation with themselves, but
Howard was accommodated. Well adjusted. At ease. I'm OK, I'm OK, I'm OK. Hell
with you. "If you let them make you feel uncomfortable," Howard would often say,
"you give them a handle on you and they can run your life." Howard could find other
people's handles, but they could never find Howard's.

It was not yet winter but cold as hell at three A.M. when Howard got home from
Stu's party. A must attend party, if you wished to get ahead at Humboldt and Breinhardt.
Stu's ugly wife tried to be tempting, but Howard had played innocent and made her
feel so uncomfortable that she dropped the matter. Howard paid careful attention to

office gossip and knew that several earlier departures from the company had got caught with, so to speak, their pants down. Not that Howard's pants were an impenetrable barrier. He got Dolores from the front office into the bedroom and accused her of making life miserable for him. "In little ways," he insisted. "I know you don't mean to, but you've got to stop."

"What ways?" Dolores asked, incredulous yet (because she honestly tried to make other people happy) uncomfortable.

"Surely you knew how attracted I am to you."

"No. That hasn't—that hasn't even crossed my mind."

Howard looked tongue-tied, embarrassed. He actually was neither. "Then—well, then, I was—I was wrong, I'm sorry, I thought you were doing it deliberately—"

"Doing what?"

"Snub—snubbing me—never mind, it sounds adolescent, just little things, hell, Dolores, I had a stupid schoolboy crush—"

"Howard, I didn't even know I was hurting you."

"God, how insensitive," Howard said, sounding even more hurt.

"Oh, Howard, do I mean that much to you?"

Howard made a little whimpering noise that meant everything she wanted it to mean. She looked uncomfortable. She'd do anything to get back to feeling right with herself again. She was so uncomfortable that they spent a rather nice half hour making each other feel comfortable again. No one else in the office had been able to get to Dolores. But Howard could get to anybody.

He walked up the stairs to his apartment feeling very, very satisfied. Don't need you, Alice, he said to himself. Don't need nobody, and nobody's who I've got. He was still mumbling the little ditty to himself as he went into the communal bathroom and turned on the light.

He heard a gurgling sound from the toilet stall, a hissing sound. Had someone been in there with the light off? Howard went into the toilet stall and saw nobody. Then looked closer and saw a baby, probably about two months old, lying in the toilet bowl. Its nose and eyes were barely above the water; it looked terrified, its legs and hips and stomach were down the drain. Someone had obviously hoped to kill it by drowning— it was inconceivable to Howard that anyone could be so moronic as to think it would fit down the drain.

For a moment he thought of leaving it there, with the big-city temptation to mind one's own business even when to do so would be an atrocity. Saving this baby would mean inconvenience: calling the police, taking care of the child in his apartment, perhaps even headlines, certainly a night of filling out reports. Howard was tired. Howard wanted to go to bed.

But he remembered Alice saying, "You aren't even human, Howard. You're a goddam selfish monster." I am not a monster, he answered silently, and reached down into the toilet bowl to pull the child out.

The baby was firmly jammed in—whoever had tried to kill it had meant to catch it tight. Howard felt a brief surge of genuine indignation that anyone could think to solve his problems by killing an innocent child. But thinking of crimes committed on children was something Howard was determined not to do, and besides, at that moment he suddenly acquired other things to think about.

As the child clutched at Howard's arm, he noticed the baby's fingers were fused together into flipperlike flaps of bone and skin at the end of the arm. Yet the flippers gripped his arms with an unusual strength as, with two hands deep in the toilet bowl, Howard tried to pull the baby free.

At last, with a gush, the child came up and the water finished its flushing action. The legs, too, were fused into a single limb that was hideously twisted at the end. The child was male; the genitals, larger than normal, were skewed off to one side. And Howard noticed that where the feet should be were two more flippers, and near the tips were red spots that looked like putrefying sores. The child cried, a savage mewling that reminded Howard of a dog he had seen in its death throes. (Howard refused to be reminded that it had been he who killed the dog by throwing it out in the street in front of a passing car, just to watch the driver swerve; the driver hadn't swerved.)

Even the hideously deformed have a right to live, Howard thought, but now, holding the child in his arms, he felt a revulsion that translated into sympathy for whoever, probably the parents, had tried to kill the creature. The child shifted its grip on him, and where the flippers had been Howard felt a sharp, stinging pain that quickly turned to agony as it was exposed to the air. Several huge, gaping sores on his arm were already running with blood and pus.

It took a moment for Howard to connect the sores with the child, and by then the leg flippers were already pressed against his stomach, and the arm flippers already gripped his chest. The sores on the child's flippers were not sores; they were powerful suction devices that gripped Howard's skin so tightly that it ripped away when the contact was broken. He tried to pry the child off, but no sooner was one flipper free than it found a new place to hold even as Howard struggled to break the grip of another.

What had begun as an act of charity had now become an intense struggle. This was not a child, Howard realized. Children could not hang on so tightly, and the creature had teeth that snapped at his hands and arms whenever they came near enough. A human face, certainly, but not a human being. Howard threw himself against the wall, hoping to stun the creature so it would drop away. It only clung tighter, and the sores where it hung on him hurt more. But at last Howard pried and scraped it off by levering it against the edge of the toilet stall. It dropped to the ground, and Harold backed quickly away, on fire with the pain of a dozen or more stinging wounds.

It had to be a nightmare. In the middle of the night, in a bathroom lighted by a single bulb, with a travesty of humanity writhing on the floor, Howard could not believe that it had any reality.

Could it be a mutation that had somehow lived? Yet the thing had far more purpose, far more control of its body than any human infant. The baby slithered across the floor as Howard, in pain from the wounds on his body, watched in a panic of indecision. The baby reached the wall and cast a flipper onto it. The suction held and the baby began to inch its way straight up the wall. As it climbed, it defecated, a thin drool of green tracing down the wall behind it. Howard looked at the slime following the infant up the wall, looked at the pus-covered sores on his arms.

What if the animal, whatever it was, did not die soon of its terrible deformity? What if it lived? What if it were found, taken to a hospital, cared for? What if it became an adult?

It reached the ceiling and made the turn, clinging tightly to the plaster, not falling off as it hung upside down and inched across toward the light bulb.

The thing was trying to get directly over Howard, and the defecation was still dripping. Loathing overcame fear, and Howard reached up, took hold of the baby from the back, and, using his full weight, was finally able to pry it off the ceiling. It writhed and twisted in his hands, trying to get the suction cups on him, but Howard resisted with all his strength and was able to get the baby, this time headfirst, into the toilet bowl. He held it there until the bubbles stopped and it was blue. Then he went back to his apartment for a knife. Whatever the creature was, it had to disappear from the face of the earth. It had to die, and there had to be no sign left that could hint that Howard had killed it.

He found the knife quickly, but paused for a few moments to put something on his wounds. They stung bitterly, but in a while they felt better. Howard took off his shirt; thought a moment and took off all his clothes, then put on his bathrobe and took a towel with him as he returned to the bathroom. He didn't want to get any blood on his clothes.

But when he got to the bathroom, the child was not in the toilet. Howard was alarmed. Had someone found it drowning? Had they, perhaps, seen him leaving the bathroom—or worse, returning with his knife? He looked around the bathroom. There was nothing. He stepped back into the hall. No one. He stood a moment in the doorway, wondering what could have happened.

Then a weight dropped onto his head and shoulders from above, and he felt the suction flippers tugging at his face, at his head. He almost screamed. But he didn't want to arouse anyone. Somehow the child had not drowned after all, had crawled out of the toilet, and had waited over the door for Howard to return.

Once again the struggle resumed, and once again Howard pried the flippers away with the help of the toilet stall, though this time he was hampered by the fact that the child was behind and above him. It was exhausting work. He had to set down the knife so he could use both hands, and another dozen wounds stung bitterly by the time he had the child on the floor. As long as the child lay on its stomach, Howard could seize it from behind. He took it by the neck with one hand and picked up the knife with the other. He carried both to the toilet.

He had to flush twice to handle the flow of blood and pus. Howard wondered if the child was infected with some disease—the white fluid was thick and at least as great in volume as the blood. Then he flushed seven more times to take the pieces of the creature down the drain. Even after death, the suction pads clung tightly to the porcelain; Howard pried them off with the knife.

Eventually, the child was completely gone. Howard was panting with the exertion, nauseated at the stench and horror of what he had done. He remembered the smell of his dog's guts after the car hit it, and he threw up everything he had eaten at the party. Got the party out of his system, felt cleaner; took a shower, felt cleaner still. When he was through, he made sure the bathroom showed no sign of his ordeal.

Then he went to bed.

It wasn't easy to sleep. He was too keyed up. He couldn't take out of his mind the thought that he had committed murder (not murder, not murder, simply the elimination of something too foul to be alive). He tried thinking of a dozen, a hundred other things. Projects at work—but the designs kept showing flippers. His children—but their faces turned to the intense face of the struggling monster he had killed. Alice—ah, but Alice was harder to think of than the creature.

At last he slept, and dreamed, and in his dream remembered his father, who had died when he was ten. Howard did not remember any of his standard reminiscences. No long walks with his father, no basketball in the driveway, no fishing trips. Those things had happened, but tonight, because of the struggle with the monster, Howard remembered darker things that he had long been able to keep hidden from himself.

"We can't afford to get you a ten-speed bike, Howie. Not until the strike is over."

"I know, Dad. You can't help it." Swallow bravely. "And I don't mind. When all the guys go riding around after school, I'll just stay home and get ahead on my homework."

"Lots of boys don't have ten-speed bikes, Howie."

Howie shrugged, and turned away to hide the tears in his eyes. "Sure, lot of them. Hey, Dad, don't you worry about me. Howie can take care of himself."

Such courage. Such strength. He had got a ten-speed within a week. In his dream, Howard finally made a connection he had never been able to admit to himself before. His father had a rather elaborate ham radio setup in the garage. But about that time he had become tired of it, he said, and he sold it off and did a lot more work in the yard and looked bored as hell until the strike was over and he went back to work and got killed in an accident in the rolling mill.

Howard's dream ended madly, with him riding piggy-back on his father's shoulders as the monster had ridden on *him*, tonight—and in his hand was a knife, and he was stabbing his father again and again in the throat.

He awoke in early morning light, before his alarm rang, sobbing weakly and whimpering, "I killed him, I killed him, I killed him."

And then he drifted upward out of sleep and saw the time. Six-thirty. "A dream," he said. And the dream had woken him early, too early, with a headache and sore eyes from crying. The pillow was soaked. "A hell of a lousy way to start the day," he mumbled. And, as was his habit, he got up and went to the window and opened the curtain.

On the glass, suction cups clinging tightly, was the child.

It was pressed close, as if by sucking very tightly it would be able to slither through the glass without breaking it. Far below were the honks of early morning traffic, the roar of passing trucks: but the child seemed oblivious to its height far above the street, with no ledge to break its fall. Indeed, there seemed little chance it would fall. The eyes looked closely, piercingly at Howard.

Howard had been prepared to pretend that the night before had been another terribly realistic nightmare.

He stepped back from the glass, watched the child in fascination. It lifted a flipper, planted it higher, pulled itself up to a new position where it could stare at Howard eye to eye. And then, slowly and methodically, it began beating on the glass with its head.

The landlord was not generous with upkeep on the building. The glass was thin, and Howard knew that the child would not give up until it had broken through the glass so it could get to Howard.

He began to shake. His throat tightened. He was terribly afraid. Last night had been no dream. The fact that the child was here today was proof of that. Yet he had cut the child into small pieces. It could not possibly be alive. The glass shook and rattled with every blow the child's head struck.

The glass slivered in a starburst from where the child had hit it. The creature was coming in. And Howard picked up the room's one chair and threw it at the child, threw it at the window. Glass shattered and the sun dazzled on the fragments as they exploded outward like a glistening halo around the child and the chair.

Howard ran to the window, looked out, looked down and watched as the child landed brutally on the top of a large truck. The body seemed to smear as it hit, and fragments of the chair and shreds of glass danced around the child and bounced down into the street and the sidewalk.

The truck didn't stop moving; it carried the broken body and the shards of glass and the pool of blood on up the street, and Howard ran to the bed, knelt beside it, buried his face in the blanket, and tried to regain control of himself. He had been seen. The people in the street had looked up and seen him in the window. Last night he had gone to great lengths to avoid discovery, but today discovery was impossible to avoid. He was ruined. And yet he could not, could never have let the child come into the room.

Footsteps on the stairs. Stamping up the corridor. Pounding on the door. "Open up! Hey in there!"

If I'm quiet long enough, they'll go away, he said to himself, knowing it was a lie. He must get up, must answer the door. But he could not bring himself to admit that he ever had to leave the safety of his bed.

"Hey, you son-of-a-bitch—" The imprecations went on but Howard could not move until, suddenly, it occurred to him that the child could be under the bed, and as he thought of it he could feel the tip of the flipper touching his thigh, stroking and ready to fasten itself—

Howard leaped to his feet and rushed for the door. He flung it wide, for even if it was the police come to arrest him, they could protect him from the monster that was haunting him.

It was not a policeman at the door. It was the man on the first floor who collected rent. "You son-of-a-bitch irresponsible pig-kisser!" the man shouted, his toupee only approximately in place. "That chair could have hit somebody! That window's expensive! Out! Get out of here, right now, I want you out of this place, I don't care how the hell drunk you are—"

"There was—there was this thing on the window, this creature—"

The man looked at him coldly, but his eyes danced with anger. No, not anger. Fear. Howard realized the man was afraid of him.

"This is a decent place," the man said softly. "You can take your creatures and your booze and your pink stinking elephants and that's a hundred bucks for the window, a hundred bucks right now, and you can get out of here in an hour, an hour, you hear? Or I'm calling the police, you hear?"

"I hear." He heard. The man left when Howard counted out five twenties. The man seemed careful to avoid touching Howard's hands, as if Howard had become, somehow, repulsive. Well, he had. To himself, if to no one else. He closed the door as soon as the man was gone. He packed the few belongings he had brought to the apartment in two suitcases and went downstairs and called a cab and rode to work. The cabby looked at him sourly, and wouldn't talk. It was fine with Howard, if only the driver hadn't kept looking at him through the mirror—nervously, as if he was afraid of what Howard might do or try. I won't try anything, Howard said to himself, I'm a decent man. Howard tipped the cabby well and then gave him twenty to take his bags to his house in Queens, where Alice could damn well keep them for a while. Howard was through with the tenement—that one or any other.

Obviously it had been a nightmare, last night and this morning. The monster was only visible to him, Howard decided. Only the chair and the glass had fallen from the fourth floor, or the manager would have noticed.

Except that the baby had landed on the truck, and might have been real, and might be discovered in New Jersey or Pennsylvania later today.

Couldn't be real. He had killed it last night and it was whole again this morning. A nightmare. I didn't really kill anybody, he insisted. (Except the dog. Except Father, said a new, ugly voice in the back of his mind.)

Work. Draw lines on paper, answer phone calls, dictate letters, keep your mind off your nightmares, off your family, off the mess your life is turning into. "Hell of a good party last night." Yeah, it was, wasn't it? "How are you today, Howard?" Feel fine, Dolores, fine—thanks to you. "Got the roughs on the IBM thing?" Nearly, nearly. Give me another twenty minutes. "Howard, you don't look well." Had a rough night. The party, you know.

He kept drawing on the blotter on his desk instead of going to the drawing table and producing real work. He doodled out faces. Alice's face, looking stern and terrible. The face of Stu's ugly wife. Dolores's face, looking sweet and yielding and stupid. And Rhiannon's face.

But with his daughter Rhiannon, he couldn't stop with the face.

His hand started to tremble when he saw what he had drawn. He ripped the sheet off the blotter, crumpled it, and reached under the desk to drop it in the wastebasket. The basket lurched, and flippers snaked out to seize his hand in an iron grip.

Howard screamed, tried to pull his hand away. The child came with it, the leg flippers grabbing Howard's right leg. The suction pad stung, bringing back the memory of all the pain last night. He scraped the child off against a filing cabinet, then ran for the door, which was already opening as several of his co-workers tumbled into his office demanding, "What is it! What's wrong! Why did you scream like that!"

Howard led them gingerly over to where the child should be. Nothing. Just an overturned wastebasket, Howard's chair capsized on the floor. But Howard's window was open, and he could not remember opening it. "Howard, what is it? Are you tired, Howard? What's wrong?"

I don't feel well. I don't feel well at all.

Dolores put her arm around him, led him out of the room. "Howard, I'm worried about you."

I'm worried, too.

"Can I take you home? I have my car in the garage downstairs. Can I take you home?"

Where's home? Don't have a home, Dolores.

"My home, then. I have an apartment, you need to lie down and rest. Let me take you home."

Dolores's apartment was decorated in early Holly Hobby, and when she put records on the stereo it was old Carpenters and recent Captain and Tennille. Dolores led him to the bed, gently undressed him, and then, because he reached out to her, undressed herself and made love to him before she went back to work. She was naively eager. She whispered in his ear that he was only the second man she had ever loved, the first in five years. Her inept lovemaking was so sincere it made him want to cry.

When she was gone he did cry, because she thought she meant something to him and she did not.

Why am I crying? he asked himself. Why should I care? It's not my fault she let me get a handle on her. . . .

Sitting on the dresser in a curiously adult posture was the child, carelessly playing with itself as it watched Howard intently. "No," Howard said, pulling himself up to the head of the bed. "You don't exist," he said. "No one's ever seen you but me." The child gave no sign of understanding. It just rolled over and began to slither down the front of the dresser.

Howard reached for his clothes, took them out of the bedroom. He put them on in the living room as he watched the door. Sure enough, the child crept along the carpet to the living room; but Howard was dressed by then, and he left.

He walked the streets for three hours. He was coldly rational at first. Logical. The creature does not exist. There is no reason to believe in it.

But bit by bit his rationality was worn away by constant flickers of the creature at the edges of his vision. On a bench, peering over the back at him; in a shop window; staring from the cab of a milk truck. Howard walked faster and faster, not caring where he went, trying to keep some intelligent process going on in his mind, and failing utterly as he saw the child, saw it clearly, dangling from a traffic signal.

What made it even worse was that occasionally a passerby, violating the unwritten law that New Yorkers are forbidden to look at each other, would gaze at him, shudder, and look away. A short European-looking woman crossed herself. A group of teenagers looking for trouble weren't looking for him—they grew silent, let him pass in silence, and in silence watched him out of sight.

They may not be able to see the child, Howard realized, but they see something.

And as he grew less and less coherent in the ramblings of his mind, memories began flashing on and off, his life passing before his eyes like a drowning man is supposed to see, only, he realized, if a drowning man saw this he would gulp at the water, breathe it deeply just to end the visions. They were memories he had been unable to find for years; memories he would never have wanted to find.

His poor, confused mother, who was so eager to be a good parent that she read everything, tried everything. Her precocious son Howard read it, too, and understood it better. Nothing she tried ever worked. And he accused her several times of being too demanding, of not demanding enough; of not giving him enough love, of drowning him in phony affection; of trying to take over with his friends, of not liking his friends enough. Until he had badgered and tortured the woman until she was timid every time she spoke to him, careful and longwinded and she phrased everything in such a way that it wouldn't offend, and while now and then he made her feel wonderful by giving her a hug and saying, "Have I got a wonderful Mom," there were far more times when he put a patient look on his face and said, "That again, Mom? I thought we went over that years ago." A failure as a parent, that's what you are, he reminded her again and again, though not in so many words, and she nodded and believed and died inside with every contact they had. He got everything he wanted from her.

And Vaughn Robles, who was just a little bit smarter than Howard and Howard wanted very badly to be valedictorian and so Vaughn and Howard became best friends and Vaughn would do anything for Howard and whenever Vaughn got a better grade than Howard he could not help but notice that Howard was hurt, that Howard wondered if he was really worth anything at all. "Am I really worth anything at all, Vaughn? No matter how well I do, there's always someone ahead of me, and I guess it's just that before my father died he told me and told me, Howie, be better than your Dad. Be the top. And I promised him I'd be the top but hell, Vaughn, I'm just not cut out for it—" and once he even cried. Vaughn was proud of himself as he sat there and listened to Howard give the valedictory address at high school graduation. What were a few grades, compared to a true friendship? Howard got a scholarship and went away to college and he and Vaughn almost never saw each other again.

And the teacher he provoked into hitting him and losing his job; and the football player who snubbed him and Howard quietly spread the rumor that the fellow was gay and he was ostracized from the team and finally quit; and the beautiful girls he stole from their boyfriends just to prove that he could do it and the friendships he destroyed just because he didn't like being excluded and the marriages he wrecked and the co-workers he undercut and he walked along the street with tears streaming down his face, wondering where all these memories had come from and why, after such a long time in hiding, they had come out now. Yet he knew the answer. The answer was slipping behind doorways, climbing lightpoles as he passed, waving obscene flippers at him from the sidewalk almost under his feet.

And slowly, inexorably, the memories wound their way from the distant past through a hundred tawdry exploitations because he could find people's weak spots without even trying until finally memory came to the one place where he knew it could not, could not ever go.

He remembered Rhiannon.

Born fourteen years ago. Smiled early, walked early, almost never cried. A loving child from the start, and therefore easy prey for Howard. Oh, Alice was a bitch in her own right—Howard wasn't the only bad parent in the family. But it was Howard who manipulated Rhiannon most. "Daddy's feelings are hurt, Sweetheart," and Rhiannon's eyes would grow wide, and she'd be sorry, and whatever Daddy wanted, Rhiannon would do. But this was normal, this was part of the pattern, this would have fit easily into all his life before, except for last month.

And even now, after a day of grief at his own life, Howard could not face it. Could not but did. He unwillingly remembered walking by Rhiannon's almost-closed door, seeing just a flash of cloth moving quickly. He opened the door on impulse, just on impulse, as Rhiannon took off her brassiere and looked at herself in the mirror. Howard had never thought of his daughter with desire, not until that moment, but once the desire formed Howard had no strategy, no pattern in his mind to stop him from trying to get what he wanted. He was *uncomfortable*, and so he stepped into the room and closed the door behind him and Rhiannon knew no way to say no to her father. When Alice opened the door Rhiannon was crying softly, and Alice looked and after a moment Alice screamed and screamed and Howard got up from the bed and tried to smooth it all over but Rhiannon was still crying and Alice was still screaming, kicking at his crotch, beating him, raking at his face, spitting at him, telling him he was a monster, a monster, until at last he was able to flee the room and the house and, until now, the memory.

He screamed now as he had not screamed then, and threw himself against a plate-glass window, weeping loudly as the blood gushed from a dozen glass cuts on his right arm, which had gone through the window. One large piece of glass stayed embedded in his forearm. He deliberately scraped his arm against the wall to drive the glass deeper. But the pain in his arm was no match for the pain in his mind, and he felt nothing.

They rushed him to the hospital, thinking to save his life, but the doctor was surprised to discover that for all the blood there were only superficial wounds, not dangerous at all. "I don't know why you didn't reach a vein or an artery," the doctor said. "I think the glass went everywhere it could possibly go without causing any important damage."

After the medical doctor, of course, there was the psychiatrist, but there were many suicidals at the hospital and Howard was not the dangerous kind. "I was insane for a moment, Doctor, that's all. I don't want to die, I didn't want to die then, I'm all right now. You can send me home." And the psychiatrist let him go home. They bandaged his arm. They did not know that his real relief was that nowhere in the hospital did he see the small, naked, child-shaped creature. He had purged himself. He was free.

Howard was taken home in an ambulance, and they wheeled him into the house and lifted him from the stretcher to the bed. Through it all Alice hardly said a word except to direct them to the bedroom. Howard lay still on the bed as she stood over him, the two of them alone for the first time since he left the house a month ago.

"It was kind of you," Howard said softly, "to let me come back."

"They said there wasn't room enough to keep you, but you needed to be watched and taken care of for a few weeks. So lucky me, I get to watch you." Her voice was a low monotone, but the acid dripped from every word. It stung.

"You were right, Alice," Howard said.

"Right about what? That marrying you was the worst mistake of my life? No, Howard. *Meeting* you was my worst mistake."

Howard began to cry. Real tears that welled up from places in him that had once been deep but that now rested painfully close to the surface. "I've been a monster, Alice. I haven't had any control over myself. What I did to Rhiannon—Alice, I wanted to die, I wanted to die!"

Alice's face was twisted and bitter. "And I wanted you to, Howard. I have never been so disappointed as when the doctor called and said you'd be all right. You'll never be all right, Howard, you'll always be—"

"Let him be, Mother."

Rhiannon stood in the doorway.

"Don't come in, Rhiannon," Alice said.

Rhiannon came in. "Daddy, it's all right."

"What she means," Alice said, "is that we've checked her and she isn't pregnant. No little monster is going to be born."

Rhiannon didn't look at her mother, just gazed with wide eyes at her father. "You didn't need to—hurt yourself, Daddy. I forgive you. People lose control sometimes. And it was as much my fault as yours, it really was, you don't need to feel bad, Father."

It was too much for Howard. He cried out, shouted his confession, how he had manipulated her all his life, how he was an utterly selfish and rotten parent, and when it was over Rhiannon came to her father and laid her head on his chest and said, softly, "Father, it's all right. We are who we are. We've done what we've done. But it's all right now. I forgive you."

When Rhiannon left, Alice said, "You don't deserve her."

I know.

"I was going to sleep on the couch, but that would be stupid. Wouldn't it, Howard?"

I deserve to be left alone, like a leper.

"You misunderstand, Howard. I need to stay here to make sure you don't do anything else. To yourself or to anyone."

Yes. Yes, please. I can't be trusted.

"Don't wallow in it, Howard. Don't enjoy it. Don't make yourself even more disgusting than you were before."

All right.

They were drifting off to sleep when Alice said, "Oh, when the doctor called he wondered if I knew what had caused those sores all over your arms and chest."

But Howard was asleep, and didn't hear her. Asleep with no dreams at all, the sleep of peace, the sleep of having been forgiven, of being clean. It hadn't taken that much, after all. Now that it was over, it was easy. He felt as if a great weight had been taken from him.

He felt as if something heavy was lying on his legs. He awoke, sweating even though the room was not hot. He heard breathing. And it was not Alice's low-pitched, slow breath, it was quick and high and hard, as if the breather had been exerting himself.

Itself.

Themselves.

One of them lay across his legs, the flippers plucking at the blanket. The other two lay on either side, their eyes wide and intent, creeping slowly toward where his face emerged from the sheets.

Howard was puzzled. "I thought you'd be gone," he said to the children. "You're supposed to be gone now."

Alice stirred at the sound of his voice, mumbled in her sleep.

He saw more of them stirring in the gloomy corners of the room, another writhing slowly along the top of the dresser, another inching up the wall toward the ceiling.

"I don't need you anymore," he said, his voice oddly high-pitched.

Alice started breathing irregularly, mumbling, "What? What?"

And Howard said nothing more, just lay there in the sheets, watching the creatures carefully but not daring to make a sound for fear Alice would wake up. He was terribly afraid she would wake up and not see the creatures, which would prove, once and for all, that he had lost his mind.

He was even more afraid, however, that when she awoke she *would* see them. That was the one unbearable thought, yet he thought it continuously as they relentlessly approached with nothing at all in their eyes, not even hate, not even anger, not even contempt. We are with you, they seemed to be saying, we will be with you from now on. We will be with you, Howard, forever.

And Alice rolled over and opened her eyes.

QUIETUS

I t came to him suddenly, a moment of blackness as he sat working late at his desk. It was as quick as an eye-blink, but before the darkness the papers on his desk had seemed terribly important, and afterward he stared at them blankly, wondering what they were and then realizing that he didn't really give a damn what they were and he ought to be going home now.

Ought definitely to be going home now. And C. Mark Tapworth of CMT Enterprises, Inc., arose from his desk without finishing all the work that was on it, the first time he had done such a thing in the twelve years it had taken him to bring the company from nothing to a multi-million-dollar-a-year business. Vaguely it occurred to him that he was not acting normally, but he didn't really care, it didn't really matter to him a bit whether any more people bought—bought—

And for a few seconds C. Mark Tapworth could not remember what it was that his company made.

It frightened him. It reminded him that his father and his uncles had all died of strokes. It reminded him of his mother's senility at the fairly young age of sixty-eight. It reminded him of something he had always known and never quite believed, that he was mortal and that all the works of all his days would trivialize gradually until his death, at which time his life would be his only act, the forgotten stone whose fall had set off ripples in the lake that would in time reach the shore having made, after all, no difference.

I'm tired, he decided. MaryJo is right. I need a rest.

But he was not the resting kind, not until that moment standing by his desk when again the blackness came, this time a jog in his mind and he remembered nothing, saw nothing, heard nothing, was falling interminably through nothingness.

Then, mercifully, the world returned to him and he stood trembling, regretting now the many, many nights he had stayed far too late, the many hours he had not spent with MaryJo, had left her alone in their large but childless house; and he imagined her waiting for him forever, a lonely woman dwarfed by the huge living room, waiting patiently for a husband who would, who must, who always had come home.

Is it my heart? Or a stroke? he wondered. Whatever it was, it was enough that he saw the end of the world lurking in the darkness that had visited him, and like the prophet returning from the mount things that once had mattered overmuch mattered not at all, and things he had long postponed now silently importuned him. He felt a terrible urgency that there was something he must do before—

Before what? He would not let himself answer. He just walked out through the large room full of ambitious younger men and women trying to impress him by working later than he; noticed but did not care that they were visibly relieved at their reprieve from another endless night. He walked out into the night and got in his car and drove home through a thin mist of rain that made the world retreat a comfortable distance from the windows of his car.

The children must be upstairs, he realized. No one ran to greet him at the door. The children, a boy and a girl half his height and twice his energy, were admirable creatures who ran down stairs as if they were skiing, who could no more hold completely still than a hummingbird in midair. He could hear their footsteps upstairs, running lightly across the floor. They hadn't come to greet him at the door because their lives, after all, had more important things in them than mere fathers. He smiled, set down his attaché case, and went to the kitchen.

MaryJo looked harried, upset. He recognized the signals instantly—she had cried earlier today.

"What's wrong?"

"Nothing," she said, because she always said Nothing. He knew that in a moment she would tell him. She always told him everything, which had sometimes made him impatient. Now as she moved silently back and forth from counter to counter, from cupboard to stove, making another perfect dinner, he realized that she was not going to tell him. It made him uncomfortable. He began to try to guess.

"You work too hard," he said. "I've offered to get a maid or a cook. We can certainly afford them."

MaryJo only smiled thinly. "I don't want anyone else mucking around in the kitchen," she said. "I thought we dropped that subject years ago. Did you—did you have a hard day at the office?"

Mark almost told her about his strange lapses of memory, but caught himself. This would have to be led up to gradually. MaryJo would not be able to cope with it, not in the state she was already in. "Not too hard. Finished up early."

"I know," she said. "I'm glad."

She didn't sound glad. It irritated him a little. Hurt his feelings. But instead of going off to nurse his wounds, he merely noticed his emotions as if he were a dispassionate observer. He saw himself; important self-made man, yet at home a little boy who can be hurt, not even by a word, but by a short pause of indecision. Sensitive, sensitive, and he was amused at himself: for a moment he almost saw himself standing a few inches away, could observe even the bemused expression on his own face.

"Excuse me," MaryJo said, and she opened a cupboard door as he stepped out of the way. She pulled out a pressure cooker. "We're out of potato flakes," she said. "Have to do it the primitive way." She dropped the peeled potatoes into the pan.

"The children are awfully quiet today," he said. "Do you know what they're doing?"

MaryJo looked at him with a bewildered expression.

"They didn't come meet me at the door. Not that I mind. They're busy with their own concerns, I know."

"Mark," MaryJo said.

"All right, you see right through me so easily. But I was only a little hurt. I want to look through today's mail." He wandered out of the kitchen. He was vaguely aware that behind him MaryJo had started to cry again. He did not let it worry him much. She cried easily and often.

He wandered into the living room, and the furniture surprised him. He had expected to see the green sofa and chair that he had bought from Deseret Industries, and the size of the living room and the tasteful antiques looked utterly wrong. Then his mind did a quick turn and he remembered that the old green sofa and chair were fifteen years ago, when he and MaryJo had first married. Why did I expect to see them? he wondered, and he worried again; worried also because he had come into the living room expecting to find the mail, even though for years MaryJo had put it on his desk every day.

He went into his study and picked up the mail and started sorting through it until he noticed out of the corner of his eye that something large and dark and massive was blocking the lower half of one of the windows. He looked. It was a coffin, a rather plain one, sitting on a rolling table from a mortuary.

"MaryJo," he called. "MaryJo."

She came into the study, looking afraid. "Yes?"

"Why is there a coffin in my study?" he asked.

"Coffin?" she asked.

"By the window, MaryJo. How did it get here?"

She looked disturbed. "Please don't touch it," she said.

"Why not?"

"I can't stand seeing you touch it. I told them they could leave it here for a few hours. But now it looks like it has to stay all night." The idea of the coffin staying in the house any longer was obviously repugnant to her.

"Who left it here? And why us? It's not as if we're in the market. Or do they sell these at parties now, like Tupperware?"

"The bishop called and asked me—asked me to let the mortuary people leave it here for the funeral tomorrow. He said nobody could get away to unlock the church and so could we take it here for a few hours—"

It occurred to him that the mortuary would not have parted with a funeral-bound coffin unless it were full.

"MaryJo, is there a body in this?"

She nodded, and a tear slipped over her lower eyelid. He was aghast. He let himself show it. "They left a corpse in a coffin here in the house with you all day? With the kids?"

She buried her face in her hands and ran from the room, ran upstairs.

Mark did not follow her. He stood there and regarded the coffin with distaste. At least they had the good sense to close it. But a coffin! He went to the telephone at his desk, dialed the bishop's number.

"He isn't here." The bishop's wife sounded irritated at his call.

"He has to get this body out of my office and out of my house tonight. This is a terrible imposition."

"I don't know where to reach him. He's a doctor, you know, Brother Tapworth.

He's at the hospital. Operating. There's no way I can contact him for something like this."

"So what am I supposed to do?"

She got surprisingly emotional about it. "Do what you want! Push the coffin out in the street if you want! It'll just be one more hurt to the poor man!"

"Which brings me to another question. Who is he, and why isn't his family—"

"He doesn't have a family, Brother Tapworth. And he doesn't have any money. I'm sure he regrets dying in our ward, but we just thought that even though he had no friends in the world someone might offer him a little kindness on his way out of it."

Her intensity was irresistible, and Mark recognized the hopelessness of getting rid of the box that night. "As long as it's gone tomorrow," he said. A few amenities, and the conversation ended. Mark sat in his chair staring angrily at the coffin. He had come home worried about his health. And found a coffin to greet him when he came. Well, at least it explained why poor MaryJo had been so upset. He heard the children quarreling upstairs. Well, let MaryJo handle it. Their problems would take her mind off this box, anyway.

And so he sat and stared at the coffin for two hours, and had no dinner, and did not particularly notice when MaryJo came downstairs and took the burnt potatoes out of the pressure cooker and threw the entire dinner away and lay down on the sofa in the living room and wept. He watched the patterns of the grain of the coffin, as subtle as flames, winding along the wood. He remembered having taken naps at the age of five in a makeshift bedroom behind a plywood partition in his parents' small home. The wood grain there had been his way of passing the empty sleepless hours. In those days he had been able to see shapes: clouds and faces and battles and monsters. But on the coffin, the wood grain looked more complex and yet far more simple. A road map leading upward to the lid. An engineering drawing describing the decomposition of the body. A graph at the foot of the patient's bed, saying nothing to the patient but speaking death into the trained physician's mind. Mark wondered, briefly, about the bishop, who was even now operating on someone who might very well end up in just such a box as this.

And finally his eyes hurt and he looked at the clock and felt guilty about having spent so long closed off in his study on one of his few nights home early from the office. He meant to get up and find MaryJo and take her up to bed. But instead he got up and went to the coffin and ran his hands along the wood. It felt like glass, because the varnish was so thick and smooth. It was as if the living wood had to be kept away, protected from the touch of a hand. But the wood was not alive, was it? It was being put into the ground also to decompose. The varnish might keep it alive longer. He thought whimsically of what it would be like to varnish a corpse, to preserve it. The Egyptians would have nothing on us then, he thought.

"Don't," said a husky voice from the door. It was MaryJo, her eyes red-rimmed, her face looking slept in.

"Don't what?" Mark asked her. She didn't answer, just glanced down at his hands. To his surprise, Mark noticed that his thumbs were under the lip of the coffin lid, as if to lift it.

"I wasn't going to open it," he said.

"Come upstairs," MaryJo said.

"Are the children asleep?"

He had asked the question innocently, but her face was immediately twisted with pain and grief and anger.

"Children?" she asked. "What is this? And why tonight?"

He leaned against the coffin in suprise. The wheeled table moved slightly.

"We don't have any children," she said.

And Mark remembered with horror that she was right. On the second miscarriage, the doctor had tied her tubes because any further pregnancies would risk her life. There were no children, none at all, and it had devastated her for years; it was only through Mark's great patience and utter dependability that she had been able to stay out of the hospital. Yet when he came home tonight—he tried to remember what he had heard when he came home. Surely he had heard the children running back and forth upstairs. Surely—

"I haven't been well," he said.

"If it was a joke, it was sick."

"It wasn't a joke—it was—" But again he couldn't, at least didn't tell her about the strange memory lapses at the office, even though this was even more proof that something was wrong. He had never had any children in his home, their brothers and sisters had all been discreetly warned not to bring children around poor MaryJo, who was quite distraught to be—the Old Testament word?—barren.

And he had talked about having children all evening.

"Honey, I'm sorry," he said, trying to put his whole heart into the apology.

"So am I," she answered, and went upstairs.

Surely she isn't angry at me, Mark thought. Surely she realizes something is wrong. Surely she'll forgive me.

But as he climbed the stairs after her, taking off his shirt as he did, he again heard the voice of a child.

"I want a drink, Mommy." The voice was plaintive, with the sort of whine only possible to a child who is comfortable and sure of love. Mark turned at the landing in time to see MaryJo passing the top of the stairs on the way to the children's bedroom, a glass of water in her hand. He thought nothing of it. The children always wanted extra attention at bedtime.

The children. The children, of course there were children. This was the urgency he had felt in the office, the reason he had to get home. They had always wanted children and so there were children. C. Mark Tapworth always got what he set his heart on.

"Asleep at last," MaryJo said wearily when she came into the room.

Despite her weariness, however, she kissed him good night in the way that told him she wanted to make love. He had never worried much about sex. Let the readers of Reader's Digest worry about how to make their sex lives fuller and richer, he always said. As for him, sex was good, but not the best thing in his life; just one of the ways that he and MaryJo responded to each other. Yet tonight he was disturbed, worried. Not because he could not perform, for he had never been troubled by even temporary impotence except when he had a fever and didn't feel like sex anyway. What bothered him was that he didn't exactly care.

He didn't not care, either. He was just going through the motions as he had a thousand times before, and this time, suddenly, it all seemed so silly, so redolent of petting in the backseat of a car. He felt embarrassed that he should get so excited over a little stroking. So he was almost relieved when one of the children cried out. Usually he would say to ignore the cry, would insist on continuing the lovemaking. But this time he pulled away, put on a robe, went into the other room to quiet the child down.

There was no other room.

Not in this house. He had, in his mind, been heading for their hopeful room filled with crib, changing table, dresser, mobiles, cheerful wallpaper—but that room had been years ago, in the small house in Sandy, not here in the home in Federal Heights with its magnificent view of Salt Lake City, its beautiful shape and decoration that spoke of taste and shouted of wealth and whispered faintly of loneliness and grief. He leaned against a wall. There were no children. There were no children. He could still hear the child's cry ringing in his mind.

MaryJo stood in the doorway to their bedroom, naked but holding her nightgown in front of her. "Mark," she said. "I'm afraid."

"So am I," he answered.

But she asked him no questions, and he put on his pajamas and they went to bed and as he lay there in darkness listening to his wife's faintly rasping breath he realized that it didn't really matter as much as it ought. He was losing his mind, but he didn't much care. He thought of praying about it, but he had given up praying years ago, though of course it wouldn't do to let anyone else know about his loss of faith, not in a city where it's good business to be an active Mormon. There'd be no help from God on this one, he knew. And not much help from MaryJo, either, for instead of being strong as she usually was in an emergency, this time she would be, as she said, afraid.

"Well, so am I," Mark said to himself. He reached over and stroked his wife's shadowy cheek, realized that there were some creases near the eye, understood that what made her afraid was not his specific ailment, odd as it was, but the fact that it was a hint of aging, of senility, of imminent separation. He remembered the box downstairs, like death appointed to watch for him until at last he consented to go. He briefly resented them for bringing death to his home, for so indecently imposing on them; and then he ceased to care at all. Not about the box, not about his strange lapses of memory, not about anything.

I am at peace, he realized as he drifted off to sleep. I am at peace, and it's not all that pleasant.

"Mark," said MaryJo, shaking him awake. "Mark, you overslept."

Mark opened his eyes, mumbled something so the shaking would stop, then rolled over to go back to sleep.

"Mark," MaryJo insisted.

"I'm tired," he said in protest.

"I know you are," she said. "So I didn't wake you any sooner. But they just called. There's something of an emergency or something—"

"They can't flush the toilet without someone holding their hands."

"I wish you wouldn't be crude, Mark," MaryJo said. "I sent the children off to school without letting them wake you by kissing you good-bye. They were very upset."

"Good children."

"Mark, they're expecting you at the office."

Mark closed his eyes and spoke in measured tones. "You can tell them and tell them I'll come in when I damn well feel like it and if they can't cope with the problem themselves I'll fire them all as incompetents."

MaryJo was silent for a moment. "Mark, I can't say that."

"Word for word. I'm tired. I need a rest. My mind is doing funny things to me." And with that Mark remembered all the illusions of the day before, including the illusion of having children.

"There aren't any children," he said.

Her eyes grew wide. "What do you mean?"

He almost shouted at her, demanded to know what was going on, why she didn't just tell him the truth for a moment. But the lethargy and disinterest clamped down and he said nothing, just rolled back over and looked at the curtains as they drifted in and out with the air conditioning. Soon MaryJo left him, and he heard the sound of machinery starting up downstairs. The washer, the dryer, the dishwasher, the garbage disposer: it seemed that all the machines were going at once. He had never heard the sounds before—MaryJo never ran them in the evenings or on weekends, when he was home.

At noon he finally got up, but he didn't feel like showering and shaving, though any other day he would have felt dirty and uncomfortable until those rituals were done with. He just put on his robe and went downstairs. He planned to go in to breakfast, but instead he went into his study and opened the lid of the coffin.

It took him a bit of preparation, of course. There was some pacing back and forth before the coffin, and much stroking of the wood, but finally he put his thumbs under the lid and lifted.

The corpse looked stiff and awkward. A man, not particularly old, not particularly young. Hair of a determinedly average color. Except for the grayness of the skin color the body looked completely natural and so utterly average that Mark felt sure he might have seen the man a million times without remembering he had seen him at all. Yet he was unmistakably dead, not because of the cheap satin lining the coffin rather slackly, but because of the hunch of the shoulders, the jut of the chin. The man was not comfortable.

He smelled of embalming fluid.

Mark was holding the lid open with one hand, leaning on the coffin with the other. He was trembling. Yet he felt no excitement, no fear. The trembling was coming from his body, not from anything he could find within his thoughts. The trembling was because it was cold.

There was a soft sound or absence of sound at the door. He turned around abruptly. The lid dropped closed behind him. MaryJo was standing in the door, wearing a frilly housedress, her eyes wide with horror.

In that moment years fell away and to Mark she was twenty, a shy and somewhat awkward girl who was forever being surprised by the way the world actually worked. He waited for her to say, "But Mark, you cheated him." She had said it only once, but ever since then he had heard the words in his mind whenever he was closing a deal. It was the closest thing to a conscience he had in his business dealings. It was enough to get him a reputation as a very honest man.

"Mark," she said softly, as if struggling to keep control of herself, "Mark, I couldn't go on without you."

She sounded as if she were afraid something terrible was going to happen to him, and her hands were shaking. He took a step toward her. She lifted her hands, came to him, clung to him, and cried in a high whimper into his shoulder. "I couldn't. I just couldn't."

"You don't have to," he said, puzzled.

"I'm just not," she said between gentle sobs, "the kind of person who can live alone."

"But even if I, even if something happened to me, MaryJo, you'd have the—" He was going to say the children. Something was wrong with that, though, wasn't there? They loved no one better in the world than their children; no parents had ever been happier than they had been when their two were born. Yet he couldn't say it.

"I'd have what?" MaryJo asked. "Oh, Mark, I'd have nothing."

And then Mark remembered again (what's happening to me!) that they were childless, that to MaryJo, who was old-fashioned enough to regard motherhood as the main purpose for her existence, the fact that they had no hope of children was God's condemnation of her. The only thing that had pulled her through after the operation was Mark, was her fussing over his meaningless and sometimes invented problems at the office or telling him endlessly the events of her lonely days. It was as if he were her anchor to reality, and only he kept her from going adrift in the eddies of her own fears. No wonder the poor girl (for at such times Mark could not think of her as completely adult) was distraught as she thought of Mark's death, and the damned coffin in the house did no good at all.

But I'm in no position to cope with this, Mark thought. I'm falling apart, I'm not only forgetting things, I'm remembering things that didn't happen. And what if I died? What if I suddenly had a stroke like my father had and died on the way to the hospital? What would happen to MaryJo?

She'd never lack for money. Between the business and the insurance, even the house would be paid off, with enough money to live like a queen on the interest. But would the insurance company arrange for someone to hold her patiently while she cried out her fears? Would they provide someone for her to waken in the middle of the night because of the nameless terrors that haunted her?

Her sobs turned into frantic hiccoughs and her fingers dug more deeply into his back through the soft fabric of his robe. See how she clings to me, he thought. She'll never let me go, he thought, and then the blackness came again and again he was falling backward into nothing and again he did not care about anything. Did not even know there was anything to care about.

Except for the fingers pressing into his back and the weight he held in his arms. I do not mind losing the world, he thought. I do not mind losing even my memories of the past. But these fingers. This woman. I cannot lay this burden down because there is no one who can pick it up again. If I mislay her she is lost.

And yet he longed for the darkness, resented her need that held him. Surely there is a way out of this, he thought. Surely a balance between two hungers that leaves both satisfied. But still the hands held him. All the world was silent and the silence was peace except for the sharp, insistent fingers and he cried out in frustration and the sound was still ringing in the room when he opened his eyes and saw MaryJo standing against a wall, leaning against the wall, looking at him in terror.

"What's wrong?" she whispered.

"I'm losing," he answered. But he could not remember what he had thought to win.

And at that moment a door slammed in the house and Amy came running with little loud feet through the kitchen and into the study, flinging herself on her mother and bellowing about the day at school and the dog that chased her for the second time and how the teacher told her she was the *best* reader in the second grade but Darrel had spilled milk on her and could she have a sandwich because she had dropped hers and stepped on it accidentally at lunch—

MaryJo looked at Mark cheerfully and winked and laughed. "Sounds like Amy's had a busy day, doesn't it, Mark?"

Mark could not smile. He just nodded as MaryJo straightened Amy's disheveled clothing and led her toward the kitchen.

"MaryJo," Mark said. "There's something I have to talk to you about."

"Can it wait?" MaryJo asked, not even pausing. Mark heard the cupboard door opening, heard the lid come off the peanut butter jar, heard Amy giggle and say, "Mommy, not so *thick*."

Mark didn't understand why he was so confused and terrified. Amy had had a sandwich after school ever since she had started going—even as an infant she had had seven meals a day, and never gained an ounce of fat. It wasn't what was happening in the kitchen that was bothering him, couldn't be. Yet he could not stop himself from crying out, "MaryJo! MaryJo, come here!"

"Is Daddy mad?" he heard Amy ask softly.

"No," MaryJo answered, and she bustled back into the room and impatiently said, "What's wrong, dear?"

"I just need—just need to have you in here for a minute."

"Really, Mark, that's not your style, is it? Amy needs to have a lot of attention right after school, it's the way she is. I wish you wouldn't stay home from work with nothing to do, Mark, you become quite impossible around the house." She smiled to show that she was only half serious and left again to go back to Amy.

For a moment Mark felt a terrible stab of jealousy that MaryJo was far more sensitive to Amy's needs than to his.

But that jealousy passed quickly, like the memory of the pain of MaryJo's fingers pressing into his back, and with a tremendous feeling of relief Mark didn't care about anything at all, and he turned around to the coffin, which fascinated him, and he opened the lid again and looked inside. It was as if the poor man had no face at all, Mark realized. As if death stole faces from people and made them anonymous even to themselves.

He ran his fingers back and forth across the satin and it felt cool and inviting. The rest of the room, the rest of the world receded into deep background. Only Mark and the coffin and the corpse remained and Mark felt very tired and very hot, as if life itself were a terrible friction making heat within him, and he took off his robe and pajamas and awkwardly climbed on a chair and stepped over the edge into the coffin and knelt and then lay down. There was no other corpse to share the slight space with him; nothing between his body and the cold satin, and as he lay on it it didn't get any warmer because at last the friction was slowing, was cooling, and he reached up and pulled down the lid and the world was dark and silent and there was no odor and no taste and no feel but the cold of the sheets.

"Why is the lid closed?" asked little Amy, holding her mother's hand.

"Because it's not the body we must remember," MaryJo said softly, with careful control, "but the way Daddy always was. We must remember him happy and laughing and loving us."

Amy looked puzzled. "But I remember he spanked me."

MaryJo nodded, smiling, something she had not done recently. "It's all right to remember that, too," MaryJo said, and then she took her daughter from the coffin back into the living room, where Amy, not realizing yet the terrible loss she had sustained, laughed and climbed on Grandpa.

David, his face serious and tear-stained because he did understand, came and put his hand in his mother's hand and held tightly to her. "We'll be fine," he said.

"Yes," MaryJo answered. "I think so."

And her mother whispered in her ear, "I don't know how you can stand it so bravely, my dear."

Tears came to MaryJo's eyes. "I'm not brave at all," she whispered back. "But the children. They depend on me so much. I can't let go when they're leaning on me."

"How terrible it would be," her mother said, nodding wisely, "if you had no children."

Inside the coffin, his last need fulfilled, Mark Tapworth heard it all, but could not hold it in his mind, for in his mind there was space or time for only one thought: consent. Everlasting consent to his life, to his death, to the world, and to the everlasting absence of the world. For now there were children.

DEEP BREATHING EXERCISES

If Dale Yorgason weren't so easily distracted, he might never have noticed the breathing. But he was on his way upstairs to change clothes, noticed the headline on the paper, and got deflected; instead of climbing the stairs, he sat on them and began to read. He could not even concentrate on that, however. He began to hear all the sounds of the house. Brian, their two-year-old son, was upstairs, breathing heavily in sleep. Colly, his wife, was in the kitchen, kneading bread and also breathing heavily.

Their breath was exactly in unison. Brian's rasping breath upstairs, thick with the mucus of a child's sleep; Colly's deep breaths as she labored with the dough. It set Dale to thinking, the newspapers forgotten. He wondered how often people did that—breathed perfectly together for minutes on end. He began to wonder about coincidence.

And then, because he was easily distracted, he remembered that he had to change his clothes and went upstairs. When he came down in his jeans and sweatshirt, ready for a good game of outdoor basketball now that it was spring, Colly called to him. "I'm out of cinnamon, Dale!"

"I'll get it on the way home!"

"I need it *now!*" Colly called.

"We have two cars!" Dale yelled back, then closed the door. He briefly felt bad about not helping her out, but reminded himself that he was already running late and it wouldn't hurt her to take Brian with her and get outside the house; she never seemed to get out of the house anymore.

His team of friends from Allways Home Products, Inc., won the game, and he came home deliciously sweaty. No one was there. The bread dough had risen impossibly, was spread all over the counter and dropping in large chunks onto the floor. Colly had obviously been gone too long. He wondered what could have delayed her.

Then came the phone call from the police, and he did not have to wonder anymore. Colly had a habit of inadvertently running stop signs.

*   *   *

The funeral was well attended because Dale had a large family and was well liked at the office. He sat between his own parents and Colly's parents. The speakers droned on, and Dale, easily distracted, kept thinking of the fact that of all the mourners there, only a few were there in private grief. Only a few had actually known Colly, who preferred to avoid office functions and social gatherings; who stayed home with Brian most of the time being a perfect housewife and reading books and being, in the end, solitary. Most of the people at the funeral had come for Dale's sake, to comfort him. Am I comforted? he asked himself. Not by my friends—they had little to say, were awkward and embarrassed. Only his father had had the right instinct, just embracing him and then talking about everything except Dale's wife and son who were dead, so mangled in the incident that the coffin was never opened for anyone. There was talk of the fishing in Lake Superior this summer; talk of the bastards at Continental Hardware who thought that the 65-year retirement rule ought to apply to the president of the company; talk of nothing at all. But it was good enough. It distracted Dale from his grief.

Now, however, he wondered whether he had really been a good husband for Colly. Had she really been happy, cooped up in the house all day? He had tried to get her out, get to meet people, and she had resisted. But in the end, as he wondered whether he knew her at all, he could not find an answer, not one he was sure of. And Brian —he had not known Brian at all. The boy was smart and quick, speaking in sentences when other children were still struggling with single words; but what had he and Dale ever had to talk about? All Brian's companionship had been with his mother; all Colly's companionship had been with Brian. In a way it was like their breathing—the last time Dale had heard them breathe—in unison, as if even the rhythms of their bodies were together. It pleased Dale somehow to think that they had drawn their last breath together, too, the unison continuing to the grave; now they would be lowered into the earth in perfect unison, sharing a coffin as they had shared every day since Brian's birth.

Dale's grief swept over him again, surprising him because he had thought he had cried as much as he possibly could, and now he discovered there were more tears waiting to flow. He was not sure whether he was crying because of the empty house he would come home to, or because he had always been somewhat closed off from his family; was the coffin, after all, just an expression of the way their relationship had always been? It was not a productive line of thought, and Dale let himself be distracted. He let himself notice that his parents were breathing together.

Their breaths were soft, hard to hear. But Dale heard, and looked at them, watched their chests rise and fall together. It unnerved him—was unison breathing more common than he had thought? He listened for others, but Colly's parents were not breathing together, and certainly Dale's breaths were at his own rhythm. Then Dale's mother looked at him, smiled, and nodded to him in an attempt at silent communication. Dale was not good at silent communication; meaningful pauses and knowing looks always left him baffled. They always made him want to check his fly. Another distraction, and he did not think of breathing again.

Until at the airport, when the plane was an hour late in arriving because of technical difficulties in Los Angeles. There was not much to talk to his parents about; even his father's chatter failed him, and they sat in silence most of the time, as did most of the other passengers. Even a stewardess and the pilot sat near them, waiting silently for the plane to arrive.

It was in one of the deeper silences that Dale noticed that his father and the pilot were both swinging their crossed legs in unison. Then he listened, and realized there was a strong sound in the gate waiting area, a rhythmic soughing of many of the passengers inhaling and exhaling together. Dale's mother and father, the pilot, the stewardess, several other passengers, all were breathing together. It unnerved him. How could this be? Brian and Colly had been mother and son; Dale's parents had been together for years. But why should half the people in the waiting area breathe together?

He pointed it out to his father.

"Kind of strange, but I think you're right," his father said, rather delighted with the odd event. Dale's father loved odd events.

And then the rhythm broke, and the plane taxied close to the windows, and the crowd stirred and got ready to board, even though the actual boarding was surely half an hour off.

The plane broke apart at landing. About half the people in the airplane survived. However, the entire crew and several passengers, including Dale's parents, were killed when the plane hit the ground.

It was then that Dale realized that the breathing was not a result of coincidence, or the people's closeness during their lives. It was a messenger of death; they breathed together *because* they were going to draw their last breath together. He said nothing about this thought to anyone else, but whenever he got distracted from other things, he tended to speculate on this. It was better than dwelling on the fact that he, a man to whom family had been very important, was now completely without family; that the only people with whom he was completely himself, completely at ease, were gone, and there was no more ease for him in the world. Much better to wonder whether his knowledge might be used to save lives. After all, he often thought, reasoning in a circular pattern that never seemed to end, if I notice this again, I should be able to alert someone, to warn someone, to save their lives. Yet if I were going to save their lives, would they then breathe in unison? If my parents had been warned, and changed flights, he thought, they wouldn't have died, and therefore wouldn't have breathed together, and so I wouldn't have been able to warn them, and so they *wouldn't* have changed flights, and so they *would* have died, and so they *would* have breathed in unison, and so I would have noticed and warned them. . . .

More than anything that had ever passed through his mind before, this thought engaged him, and he was not easily distracted from it. It began to hurt his work; he slowed down, made mistakes, because he concentrated only on breathing, listening constantly to the secretaries and other executives in his company, waiting for the fatal moment when they would breathe in unison.

He was eating alone in a restaurant when he heard it again. The sighs of breath came all together, from every table near him. It took him a few moments to be sure; then he leaped from the table and walked briskly outside. He did not stop to pay, for the breathing was still in unison at every table to the door of the restaurant.

The maître d', predictably, was annoyed at his leaving without paying, and called out to him. Dale did not answer. "Wait! You didn't pay!" cried the man, following Dale out into the street.

Dale did not know how far he had to go for safety from whatever danger faced everyone in the restaurant; he ended up having no choice in the matter. The maître d' stopped him on the sidewalk, only a few doors down from the restaurant, tried to pull him back toward the place, Dale resisting all the way.

"You can't leave without paying! What do you think you're doing?"

"I can't go back," Dale shouted. "I'll pay you! I'll pay you right here!" And he fumbled in his wallet for the money as a huge explosion knocked him and the maître d' to the ground. Flame erupted from the restaurant, and people screamed as the building began crumbling from the force of the explosion. It was impossible that anyone still inside the building could be alive.

The maître d', his eyes wide with horror, stood up as Dale did, and looked at him with dawning understanding. "You knew!" the maître d' said. "You knew!"

Dale was acquitted at the trial—phone calls from a radical group and the purchase of a large quantity of explosives in several states led to indictment and conviction of someone else. But at the trial enough was said to convince Dale and several psychiatrists that something was seriously wrong with him. He was voluntarily committed to an institution, where Dr. Howard Rumming spent hours in conversation with Dale, trying to understand his madness, his fixation on breathing as a sign of coming death.

"I'm sane in every other way, aren't I, Doctor?" Dale asked, again and again.

And repeatedly the doctor answered, "What is sanity? Who has it? How can *I* know?"

Dale soon found that the mental hospital was not an unpleasant place to be. It was a private institution, and a lot of money had gone into it; most of the people there were voluntary commitments, which meant that conditions had to remain excellent. It was one of the things that made Dale grateful for his father's wealth. In the hospital he was safe; the only contact with the outside world was on the television. Gradually, meeting people and becoming attached to them in the hospital, he began to relax, to lose his obsession with breathing, to stop listening quite so intently for the sound of inhalation and exhalation, the way that different people's breathing rhythms fit together. Gradually he began to be his old, distractable self.

"I'm nearly cured, Doctor," Dale announced one day in the middle of a game of backgammon.

The doctor sighed. "I know it, Dale. I have to admit it—I'm disappointed. Not in your cure, you understand. It's just that you've been a breath of fresh air, you should pardon the expression." They both laughed a little. "I get so tired of middle-aged women with fashionable nervous breakdowns."

Dale was gammoned—the dice were all against him. But he took it well, knowing that next time he was quite likely to win handily—he usually did. Then he and Dr. Rumming got up from their table and walked toward the front of the recreation room, where the television program had been interrupted by a special news bulletin. The people around the television looked disturbed; news was never allowed on the hospital television, and only a bulletin like this could creep in. Dr. Rumming intended to turn if off immediately, but then heard the words being said.

". . . from satellites fully capable of destroying every major city in the United States. The President was furnished with a list of fifty-four cities targeted by the orbiting missiles. One of these, said the communique, will be destroyed immediately to show that the threat is serious and will be carried out. Civil defense authorities have been notified, and citizens of the fifty-four cities will be on standby for immediate evacuation." There followed the normal parade of special reports and deep background, but the reporters were all afraid.

Dale's mind could not stay on the program, however, because he was distracted by something far more compelling. Every person in the room was breathing in perfect unison, including Dale. He tried to break out of the rhythm, and couldn't.

It's just my fear, Dale thought. Just the broadcast, making me think that I hear the breathing.

A Denver newsman came on the air then, overriding the network broadcast. "Denver, ladies and gentlemen, is one of the targeted cities. The city has asked us to inform you that orderly evacuation is to begin immediately. Obey all traffic laws, and drive east from the city if you live in the following neighborhoods. . . ."

Then the newsman stopped, and, breathing heavily, listened to something coming through his earphone.

The newsman was breathing in perfect unison with all the people in the room.

"Dale," Dr. Rumming said.

Dale only breathed, feeling death poised above him in the sky.

"Dale, can you hear the breathing?"

Dale heard the breathing.

The newsman spoke again. "Denver is definitely the target. The missiles have already been launched. Please leave immediately. Do not stop for any reason. It is estimated that we have less than—less than three minutes. My God," he said, and got up from his chair, breathing heavily, running out of the range of the camera. No one turned any equipment off in the station—the tube kept on showing the local news set, the empty chairs, the tables, the weather map.

"We can't get out in time," Dr. Rumming said to the inmates in the room. "We're near the center of Denver. Our only hope is to lie on the floor. Try to get under tables and chairs as much as possible." The inmates, terrified, complied with the voice of authority.

"So much for my cure," Dale said, his voice trembling. Rumming managed a half-smile. They lay together in the middle of the floor, leaving the furniture for everyone else because they knew that the furniture would do no good at all.

"You definitely don't belong here," Rumming told him. "I never met a saner man in all my life."

Dale was distracted, however. Instead of his impending death he thought of Colly and Brian in their coffin. He imagined the earth being swept away in a huge wind, and the coffin being ashed immediately in the white explosion from the sky. The barrier is coming down at last, Dale thought, and I will be with them as completely as it is possible to be. He thought of Brian learning to walk, crying when he fell; he remembered Colly saying, "Don't pick him up every time he cries, or he'll just learn that crying gets results." And so for three days Dale had listened to Brian cry and cry, and never lifted a hand to help the boy. Brian learned to walk quite well, and quickly. But now, suddenly, Dale felt again that irresistible impulse to pick him up, to put his pathetically red and weeping face on his shoulder, to say, That's all right, Daddy's holding you.

"That's all right, Daddy's holding you," Dale said aloud, softly. Then there was a flash of white so bright that it could be seen as easily through the walls as through the window, for there were no walls, and all the breath was drawn out of their bodies at once, their voices robbed from them so suddenly that they all involuntarily shouted and then, forever, were silent. Their shout was taken up in a violent wind that swept the sound, wrung from every throat in perfect unison, upward into the clouds forming over what had once been Denver.

And in the last moment, as the shout was drawn from his lungs and the heat took his eyes out of his face, Dale realized that despite all his foreknowledge, the only life he had ever saved was that of a maître d'hôtel, whose life, to Dale, didn't mean a thing.

FAT FARM

The receptionist was surprised that he was back so soon.

"Why, Mr. Barth, how glad I am to see you," she said.

"Surprised, you mean," Barth answered. His voice rumbled from the rolls of fat under his chin.

"Delighted."

"How long has it been?" Barth asked.

"Three years. How time flies."

The receptionist smiled, but Barth saw the awe and revulsion on her face as she glanced over his immense body. In her job she saw fat people every day. But Barth knew he was unusual. He was proud of being unusual.

"Back to the fat farm," he said, laughing.

The effort of laughing made him short of breath, and he gasped for air as she pushed a button and said, "Mr. Barth is back."

He did not bother to look for a chair. No chair could hold him. He did lean against a wall, however. Standing was a labor he preferred to avoid.

Yet it was not shortness of breath or exhaustion at the slightest effort that had brought him back to Anderson's Fitness Center. He had often been fat before, and he rather relished the sensation of bulk, the impression he made as crowds parted for him. He pitied those who could only be slightly fat—short people, who were not able to bear the weight. At well over two meters, Barth could get gloriously fat, stunningly fat. He owned thirty wardrobes and took delight in changing from one to another as his belly and buttocks and thighs grew. At times he felt that if he grew large enough, he could take over the world, be the world. At the dinner table he was a conqueror to rival Genghis Khan.

It was not his fatness, then, that had brought him in. It was that at last the fat was interfering with his other pleasures. The girl he had been with the night before had tried and tried, but he was incapable—a sign that it was time to renew, refresh, reduce.

"I am a man of pleasure," he wheezed to the receptionist, whose name he never bothered to learn. She smiled back.

"Mr. Anderson will be here in a moment."

"Isn't it ironic," he said, "that a man such as I, who is capable of fulfilling every one of his desires, is never satisfied!" He gasped with laughter again. "Why haven't we ever slept together?" he asked.

She looked at him, irritation crossing her face. "You always ask that, Mr. Barth, on your way in. But you never ask it on your way out."

True enough. When he was on his way out of the Anderson Fitness Center, she never seemed as attractive as she had on his way in.

Anderson came in, effusively handsome, gushingly warm, taking Barth's fleshy hand in his and pumping it with enthusiasm.

"One of my best customers," he said.

"The usual," Barth said.

"Of course," Anderson answered. "But the price *has* gone up."

"If you ever go out of business," Barth said, following Anderson into the inner rooms, "give me plenty of warning. I only let myself go this much because I know you're here."

"Oh," Anderson chuckled. "We'll never go out of business."

"I have no doubt you could support your whole organization on what you charge *me*."

"You're paying for much more than the simple service we perform. You're also paying for privacy. Our, shall we say, lack of government intervention."

"How many of the bastards do you bribe?"

"Very few, very few. Partly because so many high officials also need our service."

"No doubt."

"It isn't just weight gains that bring people to us, you know. It's cancer and aging and accidental disfigurement. You'd be surprised to learn who has had our service."

Barth doubted that he would. The couch was ready for him, immense and soft and angled so that it would be easy for him to get up again.

"Damn near got married this time," Barth said, by way of conversation.

Anderson turned to him in surprise.

"But you didn't?"

"Of course not. Started getting fat, and she couldn't cope."

"Did you tell her?"

"That I was getting fat? It was obvious."

"About us, I mean."

"I'm not a fool."

Anderson looked relieved. "Can't have rumors getting around among the thin and young, you know."

"Still, I think I'll look her up again, afterward. She did things to me a woman shouldn't be able to do. And I thought I was jaded."

Anderson placed a tight-fitting rubber cap over Barth's head.

"Think your key thought," Anderson reminded him.

Key thought. At first that had been such a comfort, to make sure that not one iota of his memory would be lost. Now it was boring, almost juvenile. Key thought. Do you have your own Captain Aardvark secret decoder ring? Be the first on your block. The only thing Barth had been the first on his block to do was reach puberty. He had also been the first on his block to reach one hundred fifty kilos.

How many times have I been here? he wondered as the tingling in his scalp began. *This is the eighth time. Eight times, and my fortune is larger than ever, the kind of wealth that takes on a life on its own. I can keep this up forever,* he thought, with relish. Forever at the supper table with neither worries nor restraints. "It's dangerous to gain so much weight," Lynette had said. "Heart attacks, you know." But the only things that Barth worried about were hemorrhoids and impotence. The former was a nuisance, but the latter made life unbearable and drove him back to Anderson.

Key thought. What else? Lynette, standing naked on the edge of the cliff with the wind blowing. She was courting death, and he admired her for it, almost hoped that she would find it. She despised safety precautions. Like clothing, they were restrictions to be cast aside. She had once talked him into playing tag with her on a construction site, racing along the girders in the darkness, until the police came and made them leave. That had been when Barth was still thin from his last time at Anderson's. But it was not Lynette on the girders that he held in his mind. It was Lynette, fragile and beautiful Lynette, daring the wind to snatch her from the cliff and break up her body on the rocks by the river.

Even that, Barth thought, *would be a kind of pleasure. A new kind of pleasure, to taste a grief so magnificently, so admirably earned.*

And then the tingling in his head stopped. Anderson came back in.

"Already?" Barth asked.

"We've streamlined the process." Anderson carefully peeled the cap from Barth's head, helped the immense man lift himself from the couch.

"I can't understand why it's illegal," Barth said. "Such a simple thing."

"Oh, there are reasons. Population control, that sort of thing. This is a kind of immortality, you know. But it's mostly the repugnance most people feel. They can't face the thought. You're a man of rare courage."

But it was not courage, Barth knew. It was pleasure. He eagerly anticipated seeing, and they did not make him wait.

"Mr. Barth, meet Mr. Barth."

It nearly broke his heart to see his own body young and strong and beautiful again, as it never had been the first time through his life. It was unquestionably himself, however, that they led into the room. Except that the belly was firm, the thighs well muscled but slender enough that they did not meet, even at the crotch. They brought him in naked, of course. Barth insisted on it.

He tried to remember the last time. Then *he* had been the one coming from the learning room, emerging to see the immense fat man that all his memories told him was himself. Barth remembered that it had been a double pleasure, to see the mountain he had made of himself, yet to view it from inside this beautiful young body.

"Come here," Barth said, his own voice arousing echoes of the last time, when it had been the other Barth who had said it. And just as that other had done the last time, he touched the naked young Barth, stroked the smooth and lovely skin, and finally embraced him.

And the young Barth embraced him back, for that was the way of it. No one loved Barth as much as Barth did, thin or fat, young or old. Life was a celebration of Barth; the sight of himself was his strongest nostalgia.

"What did I think of?" Barth asked.

The young Barth smiled into his eyes. "Lynette," he said. "Naked on a cliff. The wind blowing. And the thought of her thrown to her death."

"Will you go back to her?" Barth asked his young self eagerly.

"Perhaps. Or to someone like her." And Barth saw with delight that the mere thought of it had aroused his young self more than a little.

"He'll do," Barth said, and Anderson handed him the simple papers to sign—papers that would never be seen in a court of law because they attested to Barth's own compliance in and initiation of an act that was second only to murder in the lawbooks of every state.

"That's it, then," Anderson said, turning from the fat Barth to the young, thin one. "You're Mr. Barth now, in control of his wealth and his life. Your clothing is in the next room."

"I know where it is," the young Barth said with a smile, and his footsteps were buoyant as he left the room. He would dress quickly and leave the Fitness Center briskly, hardly noticing the rather plain-looking receptionist, except to take note of her wistful look after him, a tall, slender, beautiful man who had, only moments before, been lying mindless in storage, waiting to be given a mind and a memory, waiting for a fat man to move out of the way so he could fill his space.

In the memory room Barth sat on the edge of the couch, looking at the door, and then realized, with surprise, that he had no idea what came next.

"My memories run out here," Barth said to Anderson. "The agreement was—what was the agreement?"

"The agreement was tender care of you until you passed away."

"Ah, yes."

"The agreement isn't worth a damn thing," Anderson said, smiling.

Barth looked at him with surprise. "What do you mean?"

"There are two options, Barth. A needle within the next fifteen minutes. Or employment."

"What are you talking about?"

"You didn't think we'd waste time and effort feeding you the ridiculous amounts of food you require, did you?"

Barth felt himself sink inside. This was not what he had expected, though he had not honestly expected anything. Barth was not the kind to anticipate trouble. Life had never given him much trouble.

"A needle?"

"Cyanide, if you insist, though we'd rather be able to vivisect you and get as many useful body parts as we can. Your body's still fairly young. We can get incredible amounts of money for your pelvis and your glands, but they have to be taken from you alive."

"What are you talking about? This isn't what we agreed."

"I agreed to nothing with *you*, my friend," Anderson said, smiling. "I agreed with Barth. And Barth just left the room."

"Call him back! I insist—"

"Barth doesn't give a damn what happens to you."

And he knew that it was true.

"You said something about employment."

"Indeed."

"What kind of employment?"

Anderson shook his head. "It all depends," he said.

"On what?"

"On what kind of work turns up. There are several assignments every year that must be performed by a living human being, for which no volunteer can be found. No person, not even a criminal, can be compelled to do them."

"And I?"

"Will do them. Or one of them, rather, since you rarely get a second job."

"How can you do this? I'm a human being!"

Anderson shook his head. "The law says that there is only one possible Barth in all the world. And you aren't it. You're just a number. And a letter. The letter *H*."

"Why *H*?"

"Because you're such a disgusting glutton, my friend. Even our first customers haven't got past *C* yet."

Anderson left then, and Barth was alone in the room. Why hadn't he anticipated this? *Of course, of course,* he shouted to himself now. Of course they wouldn't keep him pleasantly alive. He wanted to get up and try to run. But walking was difficult for him; running would be impossible. He sat there, his belly pressing heavily on his thighs, which were spread wide by the fat. He stood, with great effort, and could only waddle because his legs were so far apart, so constrained in their movement.

This has happened every time, Barth thought. *Every damn time I've walked out of this place young and thin, I've left behind someone like me, and they've had their way, haven't they?* His hands trembled badly.

He wondered what he had decided before and knew immediately that there was no decision to make at all. Some fat people might hate themselves and choose death for the sake of having a thin version of themselves live on. But not Barth. Barth could never choose to cause himself any pain. And to obliterate even an illegal, clandestine version of himself—impossible. Whatever else he might be, he was still Barth. The man who walked out of the memory room a few minutes before had not taken over Barth's identity. He had only duplicated it. *They've stolen my soul with mirrors,* Barth told himself. *I have to get it back.*

"Anderson!" Barth shouted. "Anderson! I've made up my mind."

It was not Anderson who entered, of course. Barth would never see Anderson again. It would have been too tempting to try to kill him.

"Get to work, H!" the old man shouted from the other side of the field.

Barth leaned on his hoe a moment more, then got back to work, scraping weeds from between the potato plants. The calluses on his hands had long since shaped themselves to fit the wooden handle, and his muscles knew how to perform the work without Barth's having to think about it at all. Yet that made the labor no easier. When he first realized that they meant him to be a potato farmer, he had asked, "Is this my assignment? Is this *all*?" And they had laughed and told him no. "It's just preparation," they said, "to get you in shape." So for two years he had worked in the potato fields, and now he began to doubt that they would ever come back, that the potatoes would ever end.

The old man was watching, he knew. His gaze always burned worse than the sun. The old man was watching, and if Barth rested too long or too often, the old man would come to him, whip in hand, to scar him deeply, to hurt him to the soul.

He dug into the ground, chopping at a stubborn plant whose root seemed to cling to the foundation of the world. "Come up, damn you," he muttered. He thought his arms were too weak to strike harder, but he struck harder anyway. The root split, and the impact shattered him to the bone.

He was naked and brown to the point of blackness from the sun. The flesh hung loosely on him in great folds, a memory of the mountain he had been. Under the loose skin, however, he was tight and hard. It might have given him pleasure, for every muscle had been earned by hard labor and the pain of the lash. But there was no pleasure in it. The price was too high.

I'll kill myself, he often thought and thought again now with his arms trembling with exhaustion. *I'll kill myself so they can't use my body and can't use my soul.*

But he would never kill himself. Even now, Barth was incapable of ending it.

The farm he worked on was unfenced, but the time he had gotten away he had walked and walked and walked for three days and had not once seen any sign of human habitation other than an occasional jeep track in the sagebrush-and-grass desert. Then they found him and brought him back, weary and despairing, and forced him to finish a day's work in the field before letting him rest. And even then the lash had bitten deep, the old man laying it on with a relish that spoke of sadism or a deep, personal hatred.

But why should the old man hate me? Barth wondered. *I don't know him.* He finally decided that it was because he had been so fat, so obviously soft, while the old man was wiry to the point of being gaunt, his face pinched by years of exposure to the sunlight. Yet the old man's hatred had not diminished as the months went by and the fat melted away in the sweat and sunlight of the potato field.

A sharp sting across his back, the sound of slapping leather on skin, and then an excruciating pain deep in his muscles. He had paused too long. The old man had come to him.

The old man said nothing. Just raised the lash again, ready to strike. Barth lifted the hoe out of the ground, to start work again. It occurred to him, as it had a hundred times before, that the hoe could reach as far as the whip, with as good effect. But, as a hundred times before, Barth looked into the old man's eyes, and what he saw there, while he did not understand it, was enough to stop him. He could not strike back. He could only endure.

The lash did not fall again. Instead he and the old man just looked at each other. The sun burned where blood was coming from his back. Flies buzzed near him. He did not bother to brush them away.

Finally the old man broke the silence.

"H," he said.

Barth did not answer. Just waited.

"They've come for you. First job," said the old man.

First job. It took Barth a moment to realize the implications. The end of the potato fields. The end of the sunlight. The end of the old man with the whip. The end of the loneliness or, at least, of the boredom.

"Thank God," Barth said. His throat was dry.

"Go wash," the old man said.

Barth carried the hoe back to the shed. He remembered how heavy the hoe had seemed when he first arrived. How ten minutes in the sunlight had made him faint. Yet they had revived him in the field, and the old man had said, "Carry it back." So he had carried back the heavy, heavy hoe, feeling for all the world like Christ bearing his cross. Soon enough the others had gone, and the old man and he had been alone together, but the ritual with the hoe never changed. They got to the shed, and the old man carefully took the hoe from him and locked it away, so that Barth couldn't get it in the night and kill him with it.

And then into the house, where Barth bathed painfully and the old man put an excruciating disinfectant on his back. Barth had long since given up on the idea of an anesthetic. It wasn't in the old man's nature to use an anesthetic.

Clean clothes. A few minutes' wait. And then the helicopter. A young, businesslike man emerged from it, looking unfamiliar in detail but very familiar in general. He was an echo of all the businesslike young men and women who had dealt with him before. The young man came to him, unsmilingly, and said, "H?"

Barth nodded. It was the only name they used for him.

"You have an assignment."

"What is it?" Barth asked.

The young man did not answer. The old man, behind him, whispered, "They'll tell you soon enough. And then you'll wish you were back here, H. They'll tell you, and you'll pray for the potato fields."

But Barth doubted it. In two years there had not been a moment's pleasure. The food was hideous, and there was never enough. There were no women, and he was usually too tired to amuse himself. Just pain and labor and loneliness, all excruciating. He would leave that now. Anything would be better, anything at all.

"Whatever they assign you, though," the old man said, "it can't be any worse than my assignment."

Barth would have asked him what his assignment had been, but there was nothing in the old man's voice that invited the question, and there was nothing in their relationship in the past that would allow the question to be asked. Instead, they stood in silence as the young man reached into the helicopter and helped a man get out. An immensely fat man, stark-naked and white as the flesh of a potato, looking petrified. The old man strode purposefully toward him.

"Hello, I," the old man said.

"My name's Barth," the fat man answered, petulantly. The old man struck him hard across the mouth, hard enough that the tender lip split and blood dripped from where his teeth had cut into the skin.

"I," said the old man. "Your name is I."

The fat man nodded pitiably, but Barth—H—felt no pity for him. Two years this time. Only two damnable years and he was already in this condition. Barth could vaguely remember being proud of the mountain he had made of himself. But now he felt only contempt. Only a desire to go to the fat man, to scream in his face, "Why did you do it! Why did you let it happen again!"

It would have meant nothing. To I, as to H, it was the first time, the first betrayal. There had been no others in his memory.

Barth watched as the old man put a hoe in the fat man's hands and drove him out into the field. Two more young men got out of the helicopter. Barth knew what they would do, could almost see them helping the old man for a few days, until I finally learned the hopelessness of resistance and delay.

But Barth did not get to watch the replay of his own torture of two years before. The young man who had first emerged from the copter now led him to it, put him in a seat by a window, and sat beside him. The pilot speeded up the engines, and the copter began to rise.

"The bastard," Barth said, looking out the window at the old man as he slapped I across the face brutally.

The young man chuckled. Then he told Barth his assignment.

Barth clung to the window, looking out, feeling his life slip away from him even as the ground receded slowly. "I can't do it."

"There are worse assignments," the young man said.

Barth did not believe it.

"If I live," he said, "if I live, I want to come back here."

"Love it that much?"

"To kill him."

The young man looked at him blankly.

"The old man," Barth explained, then realized that the young man was ultimately incapable of understanding anything. He looked back out the window. The old man looked very small next to the huge lump of white flesh beside him. Barth felt a terrible loathing for I. A terrible despair in knowing that nothing could possibly be learned, that again and again his selves would replay this hideous scenario.

Somewhere, the man who would be J was dancing, was playing polo, was seducing and perverting and being delighted by every woman and boy and, God knows, sheep that he could find; somewhere the man who would be J dined.

I bent immensely in the sunlight and tried, clumsily, to use the hoe. Then, losing his balance, he fell over into the dirt, writhing. The old man raised his whip.

The helicopter turned then, so that Barth could see nothing but sky from his window. He never saw the whip fall. But he imagined the whip falling. Imagined and relished it, longed to feel the heaviness of the blow flowing from his own arm. *Hit him again!* he cried out inside himself. *Hit him for me!* And inside himself he made the whip fall a dozen times more.

"What are you thinking?" the young man asked, smiling, as if he knew the punch line of a joke.

"I was thinking," Barth said, "that the old man can't possibly hate him as much as I do."

Apparently that was the punch line. The young man laughed uproariously. Barth did not understand the joke, but somehow he was certain that he was the butt of it. He wanted to strike out but dared not.

Perhaps the young man saw the tension in Barth's body, or perhaps he merely wanted to explain. He stopped laughing but could not repress his smile, which penetrated Barth far more deeply than the laugh.

"But don't you see?" the young man asked. "Don't you know who the old man is?"

Barth didn't know.

"What do you think we did with A?" And the young man laughed again.

There are worse assignments than mine, Barth realized. And the worst of all would be to spend day after day, month after month, supervising that contemptible animal that he could not deny was himself.

The scar on his back bled a little, and the blood stuck to the seat when it dried.

CLOSING THE TIMELID

Gemini lay back in his cushioned chair and slid the box over his head. It was pitch black inside, except the light coming from down around his shoulders.

"All right, I'm pulling us over," said Orion. Gemini braced himself. He heard the clicking of a switch (or someone's teeth clicking shut in surprise?) and the timelid closed down on him, shut out the light, and green and orange and another, nameless color beyond purple danced at the edges of his eyes.

And he stood, abruptly, in thick grass at the side of a road. A branch full of leaves brushed heavily against his back with the breeze. He moved forward, looking for—

The road, just as Orion had said. About a minute to wait, then.

Gemini slid awkwardly down the embankment, covering his hands with dirt. To his surprise it was moist and soft, clinging. He had expected it to be hard. That's what you get for believing pictures in the encyclopedia, he thought. And the ground gave gently under his feet.

He glanced behind him. Two furrows down the bank showed his path. I have a mark in this world after all, he thought. It'll make no difference, but there is a sign of me in this time when men could still leave signs.

Then dazzling lights far up the road. The truck was coming. Gemini sniffed the air. He couldn't smell anything—and yet the books all stressed how smelly gasoline engines had been. Perhaps it was too far.

Then the lights swerved away. The curve. In a moment it would be here, turning just the wrong way on the curving mountain road until it would be too late.

Gemini stepped out into the road, a shiver of anticipation running through him. Oh, he had been under the timelid several times before. Like everyone, he had seen the major events. Michelangelo doing the Sistine Chapel. Handel writing the *Messiah* (everyone strictly forbidden to hum *any* tunes). The premiere performance of *Love's Labour's Lost*. And a few offbeat things that his hobby of history had sent him to: the assassination of John F. Kennedy, a politician; the meeting between Lorenzo d'Medici and the King of Naples; Jeanne d'Arc's death by fire—grisly.

And now, at last, to experience in the past something he was utterly unable to live through in the present.

Death.

And the truck careened around the corner, the lights sweeping the far embankment and then swerving in, brilliantly lighting Gemini for one instant before he leaped up and in, toward the glass (how horrified the face of the driver, how bright the lights, how harsh the metal) and then

agony. Ah, agony in a tearing that made him feel, for the first time, every particle of his body as it screamed in pain. Bones shouting as they splintered like old wood under a sledgehammer. Flesh and fat slithering like jelly up and down and sideways. Blood skittering madly over the surface of the truck. Eyes popping open as the brain and skull crushed forward, demanding to be let through, let by, let fly. No no no no no, cried Gemini inside the last fragment of his mind. No no no no no, make it stop!

And green and orange and more-than-purple dazzled the sides of his vision. A twist of his insides, a shudder of his mind, and he was back, snatched from death by the inexorable mathematics of the timelid. He felt his whole, unmarred body rushing back, felt every particle, yes, as clearly as when it had been hit by the truck, but now with pleasure—pleasure so complete that he didn't even notice the mere orgasm his body added to the general symphony of joy.

The timelid lifted. The box was slid back. And Gemini lay gasping, sweating, yet laughing and crying and longing to sing.

What was it like? The others asked eagerly, crowding around. What is it like, what is it, is it like—

"It's like nothing. It's." Gemini had no words. "It's like everything God promised the righteous and Satan promised the sinners rolled into one." He tried to explain about the delicious agony, the joy passing all joys, the—

"Is it better than fairy dust?" asked one man, young and shy, and Gemini realized that the reason he was so retiring was that he was undoubtedly dusting tonight.

"After this," Gemini said, "dusting is no better than going to the bathroom."

Everyone laughed, chattered, volunteered to be next ("Orion knows how to throw a party"), as Gemini left the chair and the timelid and found Orion a few meters away at the controls.

"Did you like the ride?" Orion asked, smiling gently at his friend.

Gemini shook his head. "Never again," he said.

Orion looked disturbed for a moment, worried. "That bad for you?"

"Not bad. Strong. I'll never forget it, I've never felt so—alive, Orion. Who would have thought it. Death being so—"

"Bright," Orion said, supplying the word. His hair hung loosely and clean over his forehead—he shook it out of his eyes. "The second time is better. You have more time to appreciate the dying."

Gemini shook his head. "Once is enough for me. Life will never be bland again." He laughed. "Well, time for somebody else, yes?"

Harmony had already lain down on the chair. She had removed her clothing, much to the titillation of the other party-goers, saying, "I want nothing between me and the cold metal." Orion made her wait, though, while he corrected the setting. While he worked, Gemini thought of a question. "How many times have you done this, Orion?"

"Often enough," the man answered, studying the holographic model of the timeclip. And Gemini wondered then if death could not, perhaps, be as addictive as fairy dust, or cresting, or pitching in.

Rod Bingley finally brought the truck to a halt, gasping back the shock and horror. The eyes were still resting there in the gore on the windshield. Only they seemed real. The rest was road-splashing, mud flipped by the weather and the tires.

Rod flung open the door and ran around the front of the truck, hoping to do— what? There was no hope that the man was alive. But perhaps some identification. A nuthouse freak, turned loose in weird white clothes to wander the mountain roads? But there was no hospital near here.

And there was no body on the front of his truck.

He ran his hand across the shiny metal, the clean windshield. A few bugs on the grill.

Had this dent in the metal been there before? Rod couldn't remember. He looked all around the truck. Not a sign of anything. Had he imagined it?

He must have. But it seemed so real. And he hadn't drunk anything, hadn't taken any uppers—no trucker in his right mind *ever* took stay-awakes. He shook his head. He felt creepy. *Watched.* He glanced back over his shoulder. Nothing but the trees bending slightly in the wind. Not even an animal. Some moths already gathering in the headlights. That's all.

Ashamed of himself for being afraid at nothing, he nevertheless jumped into the cab quickly and slammed the door shut behind him and locked it. The key turned in the starter. And he had to force himself to look up through that windshield. He half-expected to see those eyes again.

The windshield was clear. And because he had a deadline to meet, he pressed on. The road curved away infinitely before him.

He drove more quickly, determined to get back to civilization before he had another hallucination.

And as he rounded a curve, his lights sweeping the trees on the far side of the road, he thought he glimpsed a flash of white to the right, in the middle of the road.

The lights caught her just before the truck did, a beautiful girl, naked and voluptuous and eager. Madly eager, standing there, legs broadly apart, arms wide. She dipped, then jumped up as the truck caught her, even as Rod smashed his foot into the brake, swerved the truck to the side. Because he swerved she ended up, not centered, but caught on the left side, directly in front of Rod, one of her arms flapping crazily around the edge of the cab, the hand rapping on the glass of the side window. She, too, splashed.

Rod whimpered as the truck again came to a halt. The hand had dropped loosely down to the woman's side, so it no longer blocked the door. Rod got out quickly, swung himself around the open door, and touched her.

Body warm. Hand real. He touched the buttock nearest him. It gave softly, sweetly, but under it Rod could feel that the pelvis was shattered. And then the body slopped free of the front of the truck, slid to the oil-and-gravel surface of the road
and disappeared.

Rod took it calmly for a moment. She fell from the front of the truck, and then there was nothing there. Except a faint (and new, definitely new!) crack in the windshield, there was no sign of her.

Rodney screamed.

The sound echoed from the cliff on the other side of the chasm. The trees seemed to swell the sound, making it louder among the trunks. An owl hooted back.

And finally, Rod got back into the truck and drove again, slowly, but erratically, wondering what, please God tell me what the hell's the matter with my mind.

Harmony rolled off the couch, panting and shuddering violently.

"Is it better than sex?" one of the men asked her. One who had doubtless tried, but failed, to get into her bed.

"It *is* sex," she answered. "But it's better than sex with *you*."

Everyone laughed. What a wonderful party. Who could top this? The would-be hosts and hostesses despaired, even as they clamored for a chance at the timelid.

But the crambox opened then, buzzing with the police override. "We're busted!" somebody shrieked gaily, and everyone laughed and clapped.

The policeman was young, and she seemed unused to the forceshield, walking awkwardly as she stepped into the middle of the happy room.

"Orion Overweed?" she asked, looking around.

"I," answered Orion, from where he sat at the controls, looking wary, Gemini beside him.

"Officer Mercy Manwool, Los Angeles Timesquad."

"Oh no," somebody muttered.

"You have no jurisdiction here," Orion said.

"We have a reciprocal enforcement agreement with the Canadian Chronospot Corporation. And we have reason to believe you are interfering with timetracks in the eighth decade of the twentieth century." She smiled curtly. "We have witnessed two suicides, and by making a careful check of your recent use of your private timelid, we have found several others. Apparently you have a new way to pass the time, Mr. Overweed."

Orion shrugged. "It's merely a passing fancy. But I am not interfering with timetracks."

She walked over to the controls and reached unerringly for the coldswitch. Orion immediately snagged her wrist with his hand. Gemini was surprised to see how the muscles of his forearm bulged with strength. Had he been playing some kind of *sport?* It would be just like Orion, of course, behaving like one of the lower orders—

"A warrant," Orion said.

She withdrew her arm. "I have an official complaint from the Timesquad's observation team. That is sufficient. I must interrupt your activity."

"According to law," Orion said, "you must show cause. Nothing we have done tonight will in any way change history."

"That truck is not robot-driven," she said, her voice growing strident. "There's a man in there. You are changing his life."

Orion only laughed. "Your observers haven't done their homework. I have. Look."

He turned to the control and played a speeded-up sequence, focused always on the shadow image of a truck speeding down a mountain road. The truck made turn after turn, and since the hologram was centered perpetually on the truck, it made the surrounding scenery dance past in a jerky rush, swinging left and right, up and down as the truck banked for turns or struck bumps.

And then, near the bottom of the chasm, between mountains, the truck got on a long, slow curve that led across the river on a slender bridge.

But the bridge wasn't there.

And the truck, unable to stop, skidded and swerved off the end of the truncated road, hung in the air over the chasm, then toppled, tumbled, banging against first this side, then that side of the ravine. It wedged between two outcroppings of rock more than ten meters above the water. The cab of the truck was crushed completely.

"He dies," Orion said. "Which means that anything we do with him before his death and after his last possible contact with another human being is legal. According to the code."

The policeman turned red with anger.

"I saw your little games with airplanes and sinking ships. But this is cruelty, Mr. Overweed."

"Cruelty to a dead man is, by definition, not cruelty. I don't change history. And Mr. Rodney Bingley is dead, has been for more than four centuries. I am doing no harm to any living man. And you owe me an apology."

Officer Mercy Manwool shook her head. "I think you're as bad as the Romans, who threw people into circuses to be torn by lions—"

"I know about the Romans," Orion said coldly, "and I know whom they threw. In this case, however, I am throwing my friends. And retrieving them very safely through the full retrieval and reassembly feature of the Hamburger Safety Device built inextricably into every timelid. And you owe me an apology."

She drew herself erect. "The Los Angeles Timesquad officially apologizes for making improper allegations about the activities of Orion Overweed."

Orion grinned. "Not exactly heartfelt, but I accept it. And while you're here, may I offer you a drink?"

"Nonalcoholic," she said instantly, and then looked away from him at Gemini, who was watching her with sad but intent eyes. Orion went for glasses and to try to find something nonalcoholic in the house.

"You performed superbly," Gemini said.

"And you, Gemini," she said softly (voicelessly), "were the first subject to travel."

Gemini shrugged. "Nobody said anything about my not taking part."

She turned her back on him. Orion came back with the drink. He laughed. "Coca-Cola," he said. "I had to import it all the way from Brazil. They still drink it there, you know. Original recipe." She took it and drank.

Orion sat back at the controls.

"Next!" he shouted, and a man and woman jumped on the couch together, laughing as the others slid the box over their heads.

Rod had lost count. At first he had tried to count the curves. Then the white lines in the road, until a new asphalt surface covered them. Then stars. But the only number that stuck in his head was nine.

9

NINE

Oh God, he prayed silently, what is happening to me, what is happening to me, change this night, let me wake up, whatever is happening to me make it *stop*.

A gray-haired man was standing beside the road, urinating. Rod slowed to a crawl. Slowed until he was barely moving. Crept past the man so slowly that if he had even twitched Rod could have stopped the truck. But the gray-haired man only finished, dropped his robe, and waved gaily to Rod. At that moment Rod heaved a sigh of relief and sped up.

Dropped his robe. The man was wearing a robe. Except for this gory night men

did not wear *robes*. And at that moment he caught through his side mirror the white
flash of the man throwing himself under the rear tires. Rod slammed on the brake and
leaned his head against the steering wheel and wept loud, wracking sobs that shook the
whole cab, that set the truck rocking slightly on its heavy-duty springs.

For in every death Rod saw the face of his wife after the traffic accident (not my
fault!) that had killed her instantly and yet left Rod to walk away from the wreck without
a scratch on him.

I was not supposed to live, he thought at the time, and thought now. I was not
supposed to live, and now God is telling me that I am a murderer with my wheels and
my motor and my steering wheel.

And he looked up from the wheel.

Orion was still laughing at Hector's account of how he fooled the truck driver into
speeding up.

"He thought I was conking into the bushes at the side of the road!" he howled
again, and Orion burst into a fresh peal of laughter at his friend.

"And then a backflip into the road, under his tires! How I wish I could see it!"
Orion shouted. The other guests were laughing, too. Except Gemini and Officer Manwool.

"You can see it, of course," Manwool said softly.

Her words penetrated through the noise, and Orion shook his head. "Only on the
holo. And that's not very good, not a good image at all."

"It'll do," she said.

And Gemini, behind Orion, murmured, "Why not, Orry?"

The sound of the old term of endearment was startling to Orion, but oddly com-
forting. Did Gemini, then, treasure those memories as Orion did? Orion turned slowly,
looked into Gemini's sad, deep eyes. "Would you like to see it on the holo?" he asked.

Gemini only smiled. Or rather, twitched his lips into that momentary piece of a
smile that Orion knew from so many years before (only forty years, but forty years was
back into my childhood, when I was only thirty and Gemini was—what?—fifteen.
Helot to my Spartan; Slav to my Hun) and Orion smiled back. His fingers danced over
the controls.

Many of the guests gathered around, although others, bored with the coming and
going in the timelid, however extravagant it might be as a party entertainment ("Enough
energy to light all of Mexico for an hour," said the one with the giddy laugh who had
already promised her body to four men and a woman and was now giving it to another
who would not wait), occupied themselves with something decadent and delightful and
distracting in the darker corners of the room.

The holo flashed on. The truck crept slowly down the road, its holographic image
flickering.

"Why does it do that?" someone asked, and Orion answered mechanically, "There
aren't as many chronons as there are photons, and they have a lot more area to cover."

And then the image of a man flickering by the side of the road. Everyone laughed
as they realized it was Hector, conking away with all his heart. Then another laugh as
he dropped his robe and waved. The truck sped up, and then a backflip by the manfigure,
under the wheels. The body flopped under the doubled back tires, then lay limp and
shattered in the road as the truck came to a stop only a few meters ahead. A few moments
later, the body disappeared.

"Brilliantly done, Hector!" Orion shouted again. "Better than you told it!" Everyone applauded in agreement, and Orion reached over to flip off the holo. But Officer Manwool stopped him.

"Don't turn it off, Mr. Overweed," she said. "Freeze it, and move the image."

Orion looked at her for a moment, then shrugged and did as she said. He expanded the view, so that the truck shrank. And then he suddenly stiffened, as did the guests close enough and interested enough to notice. Not more than ten meters in front of the truck was the ravine, where the broken bridge waited.

"He can see it," somebody gasped. And Officer Manwool slipped a lovecord around Orion's wrist, pulled it taut, and fastened the loose end to her workbelt.

"Orion Overweed, you're under arrest. That man can see the ravine. He will not die. He was brought to a stop in plenty of time to notice the certain death ahead of him. He will live—with a knowledge of whatever he saw tonight. And already you have altered the future, the present, and all the past from his time until the present."

And for the first time in all his life, Orion realized that he had reason to be afraid.

"But that's a capital offense," he said lamely.

"I only wish it included torture," Officer Manwool said heatedly, "the kind of torture you put that poor truck driver through!"

And then she started to pull Orion out of the room.

Rod Bingley lifted his eyes from the steering wheel and stared uncomprehendingly at the road ahead. The truck's light illuminated the road clearly for many meters. And for five seconds or thirty minutes or some other length of time that was both brief and infinite he did not understand what it meant.

He got out of the cab and walked to the edge of the ravine, looking down. For a few minutes he felt relieved.

Then he walked back to the truck and counted the wounds in the cab. The dents on the grill and the smooth metal. Three cracks in the windshield.

He walked back to where the man had been urinating. Sure enough, though there was no urine, there was an indentation in the ground where the hot liquid had struck, speckles in the dirt where it had splashed.

And in the fresh asphalt, laid, surely, that morning (but then why no warning signs on the bridge? Perhaps the wind tonight blew them over), his tire tracks showed clearly. Except for a manwidth stretch where the left rear tires had left no print at all.

And Rodney remembered the dead, smashed faces, especially the bright and livid eyes among the blood and broken bone. They all looked like Rachel to him. Rachel who had wanted him to—to what? Couldn't even remember the dreams anymore?

He got back into the cab and gripped the steering wheel. His head spun and ached, but he felt himself on the verge of a marvelous conclusion, a simple answer to all of this. There was evidence, yes, even though the bodies were gone, there was evidence that he had hit those people. He had not imagined it.

They must, then, be (he stumbled over the word, even in his mind, laughed at himself as he concluded:) angels. Jesus sent them, he knew it, as his mother had taught him, destroying angels teaching him the death that he had brought to his wife while daring, himself, to walk away scatheless.

It was time to even up the debt.

He started the engine and drove, slowly, deliberately toward the end of the road. And as the front tires bumped off and a sickening moment passed when he feared that the truck would be too heavy for the driving wheels to push along the ground, he clasped his hands in front of his face and prayed, aloud: "Forward!"

And then the truck slid forward, tipped downward, hung in the air, and fell. His body pressed into the back of the truck. His clasped hands struck his face. He meant to say, "Into thy hands I commend my spirit," but instead he screamed, "No no no no no," in an infinite negation of death that, after all, didn't do a bit of good once he was committed into the gentle, unyielding hands of the ravine. They clasped and enfolded him, pressed him tightly, closed his eyes and pillowed his head between the gas tank and the granite.

"Wait," Gemini said.

"Why the hell should we?" Officer Manwool said, stopping at the door with Orion following docilely on the end of the lovecord. Orion, too, stopped, and looked at the policeman with the adoring expression all lovecord captives wore.

"Give the man a break," Gemini said.

"He doesn't deserve one," she said. "And neither do you."

"I say give the man a break. At least wait for the proof."

She snorted. "What more proof does he need, Gemini? A signed statement from Rodney Bingley that Orion Overweed is a bloody hitler?"

Gemini smiled and spread his hands. "We didn't actually *see* what Rodney did next, did we? Maybe he was struck by lightning two hours later, before he saw anybody—I mean, you're required to show that damage did happen. And I don't feel any change to the present—"

"You know that changes aren't felt. They aren't even known, since we wouldn't remember anything other than how things actually happened!"

"At least," Gemini said, "watch what happens and see whom Rodney tells."

So she led Orion back to the controls, and at her instructions Orion lovingly started the holo moving again.

And they all watched as Rodney Bingley walked to the edge of the ravine, then walked back to the truck, drove it to the edge and over into the chasm, and died on the rocks.

As it happened, Hector hooted in joy. "He died after all! Orion didn't change a damned thing, not one damned thing!"

Manwool turned on him in disgust. "You make me sick," she said.

"The man's dead," Hector said in glee. "So get that stupid string off Orion or I'll sue for a writ of—"

"Go pucker in a corner," she said, and several of the women pretended to be shocked. Manwool loosened the lovecord and slid it off Orion's wrist. Immediately he turned on her, snarling. "Get out of here! Get out! Get out!"

He followed her to the door of the crambox. Gemini was not the only one who wondered if he would hit her. But Orion kept his control, and she left unharmed.

Orion stumbled back from the crambox rubbing his arms as if with soap, as if trying to scrape them clean from contact with the lovecord. "That thing ought to be outlawed. I actually loved her. I actually loved that stinking, bloody, son-of-a-bitching cop!" And he shuddered so violently that several of the guests laughed and the spell was broken.

Orion managed a smile and the guests went back to amusing themselves. With the sensitivity that even the insensitive and jaded sometimes exhibit, they left him alone with Gemini at the controls of the timelid.

Gemini reached out and brushed a strand of hair out of Orion's eyes. "Get a comb someday," he said. Orion smiled and gently stroked Gemini's hand. Gemini slowly removed his hand from Orion's reach. "Sorry, Orry," Gemini said, "but not anymore."

Orion pretended to shrug. "I know," he said. "Not even for old times' sake." He laughed softly. "That stupid string made me love her. They shouldn't even do that to criminals."

He played with the controls of the holo, which was still on. The image zoomed in; the cab of the truck grew larger and larger. The chronons were too scattered and the image began to blur and fade. Orion stopped it.

By ducking slightly and looking through a window into the cab, Orion and Gemini could see the exact place where the outcropping of rock crushed Rod Bingley's head against the gas tank. Details, of course, were indecipherable.

"I wonder," Orion finally said, "if it's any different."

"What's any different?" Gemini asked.

"Death. If it's any different when you don't wake up right afterward."

A silence.

Then the sound of Gemini's soft laughter.

"What's funny?" Orion asked.

"You," the younger man answered. "Only one thing left that you haven't tried, isn't there?"

"How could I do it?" Orion asked, half-seriously (only half?). "They'd only clone me back."

"Simple enough," Gemini said. "All you need is a friend who's willing to turn off the machine while you're on the far end. Nothing is left. And you can take care of the actual suicide yourself."

"Suicide," Orion said with a smile. "Trust you to use the policeman's term."

And that night, as the other guests slept off the alcohol in beds or other convenient places, Orion lay on the chair and pulled the box over his head. And with Gemini's last kiss on his cheek and Gemini's left hand on the controls, Orion said, "All right. Pull me over."

After a few minutes Gemini was alone in the room. He did not even pause to reflect before he went to the breaker box and shut off all the power for a critical few seconds. Then he returned, sat alone in the room with the disconnected machine and the empty chair. The crambox soon buzzed with the police override, and Mercy Manwool stepped out. She went straight to Gemini, embraced him. He kissed her, hard.

"Done?" she asked.

He nodded.

"The bastard didn't deserve to live," she said.

Gemini shook his head. "You didn't get your justice, my dear Mercy."

"Isn't he dead?"

"Oh yes, that. Well, it's what he wanted, you know. I told him what I planned. And he asked me to do it."

She looked at him angrily. "You would. And then tell *me* about it, so I wouldn't get any joy out of this at all." Gemini only shrugged.

Manwool turned away from him, walked to the timelid. She ran her fingers along the box. Then she detached her laser from her belt and slowly melted the timelid until it was a mass of hot plastic on a metal stand. The few metal components had even melted a little, bending to be just a little out of shape.

"Screw the past anyway," she said. "Why can't it stay where it belongs?"

FREEWAY GAMES

Except for Donner Pass, everything on the road between San Francisco and Salt Lake City was boring. Stanley had driven the road a dozen deadly times until he was sure he knew Nevada by heart: an endless road winding among hills covered with sagebrush. "When God got through making scenery," Stanley often said, "there was a lot of land left over in Nevada, and God said, 'Aw, to hell with it,' and that's where Nevada's been ever since."

Today Stanley was relaxed, there was no rush for him to get back to Salt Lake, and so, to ease the boredom, he began playing freeway games.

He played Blue Angels first. On the upslope of the Sierra Nevadas he found two cars riding side by side at fifty miles an hour. He pulled his Datsun 260Z into formation beside them. At fifty miles an hour they cruised along, blocking all the lanes of the freeway. Traffic began piling up behind them.

The game was successful—the other two drivers got into the spirit of the thing. When the middle car drifted forward, Stanley eased back to stay even with the driver on the right, so that they drove down the freeway in an arrowhead formation. They made diagonals, funnels; danced around each other for half an hour; and whenever one of them pulled slightly ahead, the frantically angry drivers behind them jockeyed behind the leading car.

Finally, Stanley tired of the game, despite the fun of the honks and flashing lights behind them. He honked twice, and waved jauntily to the driver beside him, then pressed on the accelerator and leaped forward at seventy miles an hour, soon dropping back to sixty as dozens of other cars, their drivers trying to make up for lost time (or trying to compensate for long confinement), passed by going much faster. Many paused to drive beside him, honking, glaring, and making obscene gestures. Stanley grinned at them all.

He got bored again east of Reno.

This time he decided to play Follow. A yellow AM Hornet was just ahead of him on the highway, going fifty-eight to sixty miles per hour. A good speed. Stanley settled in behind the car, about three lengths behind, and followed. The driver was a woman, with dark hair that danced in the erratic wind that came through her open windows. Stanley wondered how long it would take her to notice that she was being followed.

Two songs on the radio (Stanley's measure of time while traveling), and halfway through a commercial for hair spray—and she began to pull away. Stanley prided himself on quick reflexes. She didn't even gain a car length; even when she reached seventy, he stayed behind her.

He hummed along with an old Billy Joel song even as the Reno radio station began to fade. He hunted for another station, but found only country and western, which he loathed. So in silence he followed as the woman in the Hornet slowed down.

She went thirty miles an hour, and still he didn't pass. Stanley chuckled. At this point, he was sure she was imagining the worst. A rapist, a thief, a kidnapper, determined to destroy her. She kept on looking in her rearview mirror.

"Don't worry, little lady," Stanley said, "I'm just a Salt Lake City boy who's having fun." She slowed down to twenty, and he stayed behind her; she sped up abruptly until she was going fifty, but her Hornet couldn't possibly out-accelerate his Z.

"I made forty thousand dollars for the company," he sang in the silence of his car, "and that's six thousand dollars for me."

The Hornet came up behind a truck that was having trouble getting up a hill. There was a passing lane, but the Hornet didn't use it at first, hoping, apparently, that Stanley would pass. Stanley didn't pass. So the Hornet pulled out, got even with the nose of the truck, then rode parallel with the truck all the rest of the way up the hill.

"Ah," Stanley said, "playing Blue Angels with the Pacific Intermountain Express." He followed her closely.

At the top of the hill, the passing lane ended. At the last possible moment the Hornet pulled in front of the truck—and stayed only a few yards ahead of it. There was no room for Stanley, and now on a two-lane road a car was coming straight at him.

"What a bitch!" Stanley mumbled. In a split second, because when angry Stanley doesn't like to give in, he decided that she wasn't going to outsmart *him*. He nosed into the space between the Hornet and the truck anyway.

There wasn't room. The truck driver leaned on his horn and braked; the woman, afraid, pulled forward. Stanley got out of the way just as the oncoming car, its driver a father with a wife and several rowdy children looking petrified at the accident that had nearly happened, passed on the left.

"Think you're smart, don't you, bitch? But Stanley Howard's feeling rich." Nonsense, nonsense, but it sounded good and he sang it in several keys as he followed the woman, who was now going a steady sixty-five, two car-lengths behind. The Hornet had Utah plates—she was going to be on that road a long time.

Stanley's mind wandered. From thoughts of Utah plates to a memory of eating at Alioto's and on to his critical decision that no matter how close you put Alioto's to the wharf, the fish there wasn't any better than the fish at Bratten's in Salt Lake. He decided that he would have to eat there soon, to make sure his impression was correct; he wondered whether he should bother taking Liz out again, since she so obviously wasn't interested; speculated on whether Genevieve would say yes if he asked her.

And the Hornet wasn't in front of him anymore.

He was only going forty-five, and the PIE truck was catching up to him on a straight section of the road. There were curves into a mountain pass up ahead—she must have gone faster when he wasn't noticing. But he sped up, sped even faster, and didn't see her. She must have pulled off somewhere, and Stanley chuckled to think of her panting, her heart beating fast, as she watched Stanley drive on by. What a relief that must have been, Stanley thought. Poor lady. What a nasty game. And he giggled with delight, silently, his chest and stomach shaking but making no sound.

He stopped for gas in Elko, had a package of cupcakes from the vending machine in the gas station, and was leaning on his car when he watched the Hornet go by. He waved, but the woman didn't see him. He did notice, however, that she pulled into an Amoco station not far up the road.

It was just a whim. I'm taking this too far, he thought, even as he waited in his car for her to pull out of the gas station. She pulled out. For just a moment Stanley hesitated, decided not to go on with the chase, then pulled out and drove along the main street of Elko a few blocks behind the Hornet. The woman stopped at a light. When it turned green, Stanley was right behind her. He saw her look in her rearview mirror again, stiffen; her eyes were afraid.

"Don't worry, lady," he said. "I'm not following you this time. Just going my own sweet way home."

The woman abruptly, without signalling, pulled into a parking place. Stanley calmly drove on. "See?" he said. "Not following. Not following."

A few miles outside Elko, he pulled off the road. He knew why he was waiting. He denied it to himself. Just resting, he told himself. Just sitting here because I'm in no hurry to get back to Salt Lake City. But it was hot and uncomfortable, and with the car stopped, there wasn't the slightest breeze coming through the windows of the Z. This is stupid, he told himself. Why persecute the poor woman anymore? he asked himself. Why the hell am I still sitting here?

He was still sitting there when she passed him. She saw him. She sped up. Stanley put the car in gear, drove out into the road from the shoulder, caught up with her quickly, and settled in behind her. "I am a shithead," he announced to himself. "I am the meanest asshole on the highway. I ought to be shot." He meant it. But he stayed behind her, cursing himself all the way.

In the silence of his car (the noise of the wind did not count as sound; the engine noise was silent to his accustomed ears), he recited the speeds as they drove. "Fifty-five, sixty, sixty-five on a curve, are we out of our minds, young lady? Seventy—ah, ho, now, look for a Nevada state trooper anywhere along here." They took curves at ridiculous speeds; she stopped abruptly occasionally; always Stanley's reflexes were quick, and he stayed a few car lengths behind her.

"I really am a nice person, young lady," he said to the woman in the car, who was pretty, he realized as he remembered the face he saw when she passed him back in Elko. "If you met me in Salt Lake City, you'd like me. I might ask you out for a date sometime. And if you aren't some tight-assed little Mormon girl, we might get it on. You know? I'm a nice person."

She was pretty, and as he drove along behind her ("What? Eighty-five? I never thought a Hornet could go eighty-five"), he began to fantasize. He imagined her running out of gas, panicking because now, on some lonely stretch of road, she would be at the mercy of the crazy man following her. But in his fantasy, when he stopped it was she who had a gun, she who was in control of the situation. She held the gun on him, forced him to give her his car keys, and then she made him strip, took his clothes and stuffed them in the back of the Z, and took off in his car. "It's you that's dangerous, lady," he said. He replayed the fantasy several times, and each time she spent more time with him before she left him naked by the road with an out-of-gas Hornet and horny as hell.

Stanley realized the direction his fantasies had taken him. "I've been too lonely too long," he said. "Too lonely too long, and Liz won't unzip anything without a license." The word *lonely* made him laugh, thinking of tacky poetry. He sang: "Bury me not on the lone prairie where the coyotes howl and wind blows free."

For hours he followed the woman. By now he was sure she realized it was a game. By now she must know he meant no harm. He had done nothing to try to get her to pull over. He was just tagging along. "Like a friendly dog," he said. "Arf. Woof. Growrrr." And he fantasized again until suddenly the lights of Wendover were dazzling, and he realized it was dark. He switched on his lights. When he did, the Hornet sped up, its taillights bright for a moment, then ordinary among the lights and signs saying that this was the last chance to lose money before getting to Utah.

Just inside Wendover, a police car was pulled to the side of the road, its lights flashing. Some poor sap caught speeding. Stanley expected the woman to be smart, to pull over behind the policeman, while Stanley moved on over the border, out of Nevada jurisdiction.

The Hornet, however, went right by the policeman, sped up, in fact, and Stanley was puzzled for a moment. Was the woman crazy? She must be scared out of her wits by now, and here was a chance for relief and rescue, and she ignored it. Of course, Stanley reasoned, as he followed the Hornet out of Wendover and down to the long straight stretch of the highway over the Salt Flats, of course she didn't stop. Poor lady was so conscious of having broken the law speeding that she was *afraid* of cops.

Crazy. People do crazy things under pressure, Stanley decided.

The highway stretched out straight in the blackness. No moon. Some starlight, but there were no landmarks on either side of the road, and so the cars barreled on as if in a tunnel, with only a hypnotic line to the left and headlights behind and taillights ahead.

How much gas would the tank of a Hornet hold? The Salt Flats went a long way before the first gas station, and what with daylight saving time it must be ten-thirty, eleven o'clock, maybe only ten, but some of those gas stations would be closing up now. Stanley's Z could get home to Salt Lake with gas to spare after a fill-up in Elko, but the Hornet might run out of gas.

Stanley remembered his daydreams of the afternoon and now translated them into night, into her panic in the darkness, the gun flashing in his headlights. This lady was armed and dangerous. She was carrying drugs into Utah, and thought he was from the mob. She probably thought he was planning to get her on the lonely Salt Flats, miles from anywhere. She was probably checking the clip of her gun.

Eight-five, said the speedometer.

"Going pretty fast, lady," he said.

Ninety, said the speedometer.

Of course, Stanley realized. She *is* running out of gas. She wants to get going as fast as she can, outrun me, but at least have enough momentum to coast when she runs out.

Nonsense, thought Stanley. It's dark, and the poor lady is scared out of her wits. I've got to stop this. This is dangerous. It's dark and it's dangerous and this stupid game has gone on for four hundred miles. I never meant it to go on this long.

Stanley passed the road signs that told him, habituated as he was to this drive, that the first big curve was coming up. A lot of people unfamiliar with the Salt Flats thought it went straight as an arrow all the way. But there was a curve where there was no reason to have a curve, before the mountains, before anything. And in typical Utah Highway Department fashion, the Curve sign was posted right in the middle of the turn. Instinctively, Stanley slowed down.

The woman in the Hornet did not.

In his headlights Stanley saw the Hornet slide off the road. He screeched on his brakes; as he went past, he saw the Hornet bounce on its nose, flip over and bounce on its tail, then topple back and land flat on the roof. For a moment the car lay there. Stanley got his car stopped, looked back over his shoulder. The Hornet erupted in flames.

Stanley stayed there for only a minute or so, gasping, shuddering. In horror. In horror, he insisted to himself, saying, "What have I done! My God, what have I done," but knowing even as he pretended to be appalled that he was having an orgasm, that the shuddering of his body was the most powerful ejaculation he had ever had, that he had been trying to get up the Hornet's ass all the way from Reno and finally, finally, he had come.

He drove on. He drove for twenty minutes and came to a gas station with a pay phone. He got out of the car stiffly, his pants sticky and wet, and fumbled in his sticky pocket for a sticky dime, which he put in the phone. He dialed the emergency number.

"I—I passed a car on the Salt Flats. In flames. About fifteen miles before this Chevron station. Flames."

He hung up. He drove on. A few minutes later he saw a patrol car, lights whirling, speeding past going the other way. From Salt Lake City out into the desert. And still later he saw an ambulance and a fire truck go by. Stanley gripped the wheel tightly. They would know. They would see his skid marks. Someone would tell about the Z that was following the Hornet from Reno until the woman in the Hornet died in Utah.

But even as he worried, he knew that no one would know. He hadn't touched her. There wasn't a mark on his car.

The highway turned into a six-lane street with motels and shabby diners on either side. He went under the freeway, over the railroad tracks, and followed North Temple street up to Second Avenue, the school on the left, the Slow signs, everything normal, everything as he had left it, everything as it always had been when he came home from a long trip. To L Street, to the Chateau LeMans apartments; he parked in the underground garage, got out. All the doors opened to his key. His room was undisturbed.

What the hell do I expect? he asked himself. Sirens heading my way? Five detectives in my living room waiting to grill me?

The woman, the woman had died. He tried to feel terrible. But all that he could remember, all that was important in his mind, was the shuddering of his body, the feeling that the orgasm would never end. There was nothing. Nothing like that in the world.

He went to sleep quickly, slept easily. Murderer? he asked himself as he drifted off.

But the word was taken by his mind and driven into a part of his memory where Stanley could not retrieve it. Can't live with that. Can't live with that. And so he didn't.

Stanley found himself avoiding looking at the paper the next morning, and so he forced himself to look. It wasn't front-page news. It was buried back in the local news section. Her name was Alix Humphreys. She was twenty-two and single, working as a secretary to some law firm. Her picture showed her as a young, attractive girl.

"The driver apparently fell asleep at the wheel, according to police investigators. The vehicle was going faster than eighty miles per hour when the mishap occurred."

Mishap.

Hell of a word for the flames.

Yet, Stanley went to work just as he always did, flirted with the secretaries just as he always did, and even drove his car, just as he always did, carefully and politely on the road.

It wasn't long, however, before he began playing freeway games again. On his way up to Logan, he played Follow, and a woman in a Honda Civic smashed head-on into a pickup truck as she foolishly tried to pass a semitruck at the crest of a hill in Sardine Canyon. The police reports didn't mention (and no one knew) that she was trying to get away from a Datsun 260Z that had relentlessly followed her for eighty miles. Her name was Donna Weeks, and she had two children and a husband who had been expecting her back in Logan that evening. They couldn't get all her body out of the car.

On a hop over to Denver, a seventeen-year-old skier went out of control on a snowy road, her VW smashing into a mountain, bouncing off, and tumbling down a cliff. One of the skis on the back of her bug, incredibly enough, was unbroken. The other was splintered into kindling. Her head went through the windshield. Her body didn't.

The roads between Cameron trading post and Page, Arizona, were the worst in the world. It surprised no one when an eighteen-year-old blond model from Phoenix was killed when she smashed into the back of a van parked beside the road. She had been going more than a hundred miles an hour, which her friends said did not surprise them, she had always sped, especially when driving at night. A child in the van was killed in his sleep, and the family was hospitalized. There was no mention of a Datsun with Utah plates.

And Stanley began to remember more often. There wasn't room in the secret places of his mind to hold all of this. He clipped their faces out of the paper. He dreamed of them at night. In his dreams they always threatened him, always deserved the end they got. Every dream ended with orgasm. But never as strong a convulsion as the ecstacy when the collision came on the highway.

Check. And mate.

Aim, and fire.

Eighteen, seven, twenty-three, hike.

Games, all games, and the moment of truth.

"I'm sick." He sucked the end of his Bic four-color pen. "I need help."

The phone rang.

"Stan? It's Liz."

Hi, Liz.

"Stan, aren't you going to answer me?"

Go to hell, Liz.

"Stan, what kind of game is this? You don't call for nine months, and now you just sit there while I'm trying to talk to you?"

Come to bed, Liz.

"That *is* you, isn't it?"

"Yeah, it's me."

"Well, why didn't you answer me? Stan, you scared me. That really scared me."

"I'm sorry."

"Stan, what happened? Why haven't you called?"

"I needed you too much." Melodramatic, melodramatic. But true.

"Stan, I know. I was being a bitch."

"No, no, not really. I was being too demanding."

"Stan, I miss you. I want to be with you."

"I miss you, too, Liz. I've really needed you these last few months."

She droned on as Stanley sang silently, "Oh, bury me not on the lone prairie, where the coyotes howl—"

"Tonight? My apartment?"

"You mean you'll let me past the sacred chain lock?"

"Stanley. Don't be mean. I miss you."

"I'll be there."

"I love you."

"Me, too."

After this many months, Stanley was not sure, not sure at all. But Liz was a straw to grasp at. "I drown," Stanley said. "I die. *Morior. Moriar. Mortuus sum.*"

Back when he had been dating Liz, back when they had been together, Stanley hadn't played these freeway games. Stanley hadn't watched these women die. Stanley hadn't had to hide from himself in his sleep. "*Caedo. Caedam. Cecidi.*"

Wrong, wrong. He had been dating Liz the first time. He had only stopped after —after. Liz had nothing to do with it. Nothing would help. "*Despero. Desperabo. Desperavi.*"

And because it was the last thing he wanted to do, he got up, got dressed, went out to his car, and drove out onto the freeway. He got behind a woman in a red Audi. And he followed her.

She was young, but she was a good driver. He tailed her from Sixth South to the place where the freeway forks, I-15 continuing south, I-80 veering east. She stayed in the right-hand lane until the last moment, then swerved across two lanes of traffic and got onto I-80. Stanley did not think of letting her go. He, too, cut across traffic. A bus honked loudly; there was a screeching of brakes; Stanley's Z was on two wheels and he lost control; a lightpost loomed, then passed.

And Stanley was on I-80, following a few hundred yards behind the Audi. He quickly closed the gap. This woman was smart, Stanley said to himself. "You're smart, lady. You won't let me get away with anything. Nobody today. Nobody today." He meant to say nobody dies today, and he knew that was what he was really saying (hoping; denying), but he did not let himself say it. He spoke as if a microphone hung over his head, recording his words for posterity.

The Audi wove through traffic, averaging seventy-five. Stanley followed close behind. Occasionally, a gap in the traffic closed before he could use it; he found another. But he was a dozen cars behind when she cut off and took the last exit before I-80 plunged upward into Parley's Canyon. She was going south on I-215, and Stanley followed, though he had to brake violently to make the tight curve that led from one freeway to the other.

She drove rapidly down I-215 until it ended, turned into a narrow two-lane road winding along the foot of the mountain. As usual, a gravel truck was going thirty miles an hour, shambling along shedding stones like dandruff onto the road. The Audi pulled behind the gravel truck, and Stanley's Z pulled behind the Audi.

The woman was smart. She didn't try to pass. Not on that road.

When they reached the intersection with the road going up Big Cottonwood Canyon to the ski resorts (closed now in the spring, so there was no traffic), she seemed to be planning to turn right, to take Fort Union Boulevard back to the freeway. Instead, she turned left. But Stanley had been anticipating the move, and he turned left, too.

They were not far up the winding canyon road before it occurred to Stanley that this road led to nowhere. At Snowbird it was a dead end, a loop that turned around and headed back down. This woman, who had seemed so smart, was making a very stupid move.

And then he thought, I might catch her. He said, "I might catch you, girl. Better watch out."

What he would do if he caught her he wasn't sure. She must have a gun. She must be armed, or she wouldn't be daring him like this.

She took the curves at ridiculous speeds, and Stanley was pressed to the limit of his driving skills to stay up with her. This was the most difficult game of Follow he had ever played. But it might end too quickly—on any of these curves she might smash up, might meet a car coming the other way. Be careful, he thought. Be careful, be careful, it's just a game, don't be afraid, don't panic.

Panic? The moment this woman had realized she was being followed, she had sped and dodged, leading him on a merry chase. None of the confusion the others had shown. This was a live one. When he caught her, she'd know what to do. She'd know. "*Veniebam. Veniam. Venies.*" He laughed at his joke.

Then he stopped laughing abruptly, swung the wheel hard to the right, jamming on the brake. He had seen just a flash of red going up a side road. Just a flash, but it was enough. This bitch in the red Audi thought she'd fool him. Thought she could ditch into a side road and he'd go on by.

He skidded in the gravel of the shoulder, but regained control and charged up the narrow dirt road. The Audi was stopped a few hundred yards from the entrance.

Stopped.

At last.

He pulled in behind her, even had his fingers on the door handle. But she had not meant to stop, apparently. She had only meant to pull out of sight till he went by. He had been too smart for her. He had seen. And now she was caught on a terribly lonely mountain road, still moist from the melting snow, with only trees around, in weather too warm for skiers, too cold for hikers. She had thought to trick him, and now he had trapped her.

She drove off. He followed. On the bumpy dirt road, twenty miles an hour was uncomfortably fast. She went thirty. His shocks were being shot to hell, but this was one that wouldn't get away. She wouldn't get away from Stanley. Her Audi was voluptuous with promises.

After interminable jolting progress up the side canyon, the mountains suddenly opened out into a small valley. The road, for a while, was flat, though certainly not straight. And the Audi sped up to forty incredible miles an hour. She wasn't giving up. And she was a damned good driver. But Stanley was a damned good driver, too. "I should quit now," he said to the invisible microphone in his car. But he didn't quit. He didn't quit and he didn't quit.

The road quit.

He came around a tree-lined curve and suddenly there was no road. Just a gap in the trees and, a few hundred yards away, the other side of a ravine. To the right, out of the corner of his eye, he saw where the road made a hairpin turn, saw the Audi stopped there, saw, he thought, a face looking at him in horror. And because of that face he turned to look, tried to look over his shoulder, desperate to see the face, desperate not to watch as the trees bent gracefully toward him and the rocks rose up and enlarged and engorged, and he impaled himself, himself and his Datsun 260Z on a rock that arched upward and shuddered as he swallowed its tip.

She sat in the Audi, shaking, her body heaving in great sobs of relief and shock at what had happened. Relief and shock, yes. But by now she knew that the shuddering was more than that. It was also ecstacy.

This has to stop, she cried out silently to herself. Four, four, four. "Four is enough," she said, beating on the steering wheel. Then she got control of herself, and the orgasm passed except for the trembling in her thighs and occasional cramps, and she jockeyed the car until it was turned around, and she headed back down the canyon to Salt Lake City, where she was already an hour late.

A SEPULCHRE OF SONGS

She was losing her mind during the rain. For four weeks it came down nearly every day, and the people at the Millard County Rest Home didn't take any of the patients outside. It bothered them all, of course, and made life especially hellish for the nurses, everyone complaining to them constantly and demanding to be entertained.

Elaine didn't demand entertainment, however. She never seemed to demand much of anything. But the rain hurt her worse than anyone. Perhaps because she was only fifteen, the only child in an institution devoted to adult misery. More likely because she depended more than most on the hours spent outside; certainly she took more pleasure from them. They would lift her into her chair, prop her up with pillows so her body would stay straight, and then race down the corridor to the glass doors, Elaine calling, "Faster, faster," as they pushed her until finally they were outside. They told me she never really said anything out there. Just sat quietly in her chair on the lawn, watching everything. And then later in the day they would wheel her back in.

I often saw her being wheeled in—early, because I was there, though she never complained about my visits' cutting into her hours outside. As I watched her being pushed toward the rest home, she would smile at me so exuberantly that my mind invented arms for her, waving madly to match her childishly delighted face; I imagined legs pumping, imagined her running across the grass, breasting the air like great waves. But there were the pillows where arms should be, keeping her from falling to the side, and the belt around her middle kept her from pitching forward, since she had no legs to balance with.

It rained four weeks, and I nearly lost her.

My job was one of the worst in the state, touring six rest homes in as many counties, visiting each of them every week. I "did therapy" wherever the rest home administrators thought therapy was needed. I never figured out how they decided—all the patients were mad to one degree or another, most with the helpless insanity of age, the rest with the anguish of the invalid and the crippled.

You don't end up as a state-employed therapist if you had much ability in college. I sometimes pretend that I didn't distinguish myself in graduate school because I marched to a different drummer. But I didn't. As one kind professor gently and brutally told me, I wasn't cut out for science. But I was sure I was cut out for the art of therapy. Ever since I comforted my mother during her final year of cancer I had believed I had a knack for helping people get straight in their minds. I was everybody's confidant.

Somehow I had never supposed, though, that I would end up trying to help the hopeless in a part of the state where even the healthy didn't have much to live for. Yet that's all I had the credentials for, and when I (so maturely) told myself I was over the initial disappointment, I made the best of it.

Elaine was the best of it.

"Raining raining raining," was the greeting I got when I visited her on the third day of the wet spell.

"Don't I know it?" I said. "My hair's soaking wet."

"Wish mine was," Elaine answered.

"No, you don't. You'd get sick."

"Not me," she said.

"Well, Mr. Woodbury told me you're depressed. I'm supposed to make you happy."

"Make it stop raining."

"Do I look like God?"

"I thought maybe you were in disguise. *I'm* in disguise," she said. It was one of our regular games. "I'm really a large Texas armadillo who was granted one wish. I wished to be a human being. But there wasn't enough of the armadillo to make a full human being; so here I am." She smiled. I smiled back.

Actually, she had been five years old when an oil truck exploded right in front of her parents' car, killing both of them and blowing her arms and legs right off. That she survived was a miracle. That she had to keep on living was unimaginable cruelty. That she managed to be a reasonably happy person, a favorite of the nurses—that I don't understand in the least. Maybe it was because she had nothing else to do. There aren't many ways that a person with no arms or legs can kill herself.

"I want to go outside," she said, turning her head away from me to look out the window.

Outside wasn't much. A few trees, a lawn, and beyond that a fence, not to keep the inmates in but to keep out the seamier residents of a rather seamy town. But there were low hills in the distance, and the birds usually seemed cheerful. Now, of course, the rain had driven both birds and hills into hiding. There was no wind, and so the trees didn't even sway. The rain just came straight down.

"Outer space is like the rain," she said. "It sounds like that out there, just a low drizzling sound in the background of everything."

"Not really," I said. "There's no sound out there at all."

"How do *you* know?" she asked.

"There's no air. Can't be any sound without air."

She looked at me scornfully. "Just as I thought. You don't *really* know. You've never *been* there, have you?"

"Are you trying to pick a fight?"

She started to answer, caught herself, and nodded. "Damned rain."

"At least you don't have to drive in it," I said. But her eyes got wistful, and I knew I had taken the banter too far. "Hey," I said. "First clear day I'll take you out driving."

"It's hormones," she said.

"What's hormones?"

"I'm fifteen. It always bothered me when I had to stay in. But I want to scream. My muscles are all bunched up, my stomach is all tight, I want to go outside and *scream*. It's hormones."

"What about your friends?" I asked.

"Are you kidding? They're all out there, playing in the rain."

"A*ll* of them?"

"Except Grunty, of course. He'd dissolve."

"And where's Grunty?"

"In the freezer, of course."

"Someday the nurses are going to mistake him for ice cream and serve him to the guests."

She didn't smile. She just nodded, and I knew that I wasn't getting anywhere. She really was depressed.

I asked her whether she wanted something.

"No pills," she said. "They make me sleep all the time."

"If I gave you uppers, it would make you climb the walls."

"Neat trick," she said.

"It's that strong. So do you want something to take your mind off the rain and these four ugly yellow walls?"

She shook her head. "I'm trying not to sleep."

"Why not?"

She just shook her head again. "Can't sleep. Can't let myself sleep too much."

I asked again.

"Because," she said, "I might not wake up." She said it rather sternly, and I knew I shouldn't ask anymore. She didn't often get impatient with me, but I knew this time I was coming perilously close to overstaying my welcome.

"Got to go," I said. "You *will* wake up." And then I left, and I didn't see her for a week, and to tell the truth I didn't think of her much that week, what with the rain and a suicide in Ford County that really got to me, since she was fairly young and had a lot to live for, in my opinion. She disagreed and won the argument the hard way.

Weekends I live in a trailer in Piedmont. I live alone. The place is spotlessly clean because cleaning is something I do religiously. Besides, I tell myself, I might want to bring a woman home with me one night. Some nights I even do, and some nights I even enjoy it, but I always get restless and irritable when they start trying to get me to change my work schedule or take them along to the motels I live in or, once only, get the trailer-park manager to let them into my trailer when I'm gone. To keep things cozy for me. I'm not interested in "cozy." This is probably because of my mother's death; her cancer and my responsibilities as housekeeper for my father probably explain why I am a neat housekeeper. Therapist, therap thyself. The days passed in rain and highways and depressing people depressed out of their minds; the nights passed in television and sandwiches and motel bedsheets at state expense; and then it was time to go to the Millard County Rest Home again, where Elaine was waiting. It was then that I thought of her and realized that the rain had been going on for more than a week, and the poor girl must be almost out of her mind. I bought a cassette of Copland conducting Copland. She insisted on cassettes, because they stopped. Eight-tracks went on and on until she couldn't think.

"Where have you been?" she demanded.

"Locked in a cage by a cruel duke in Transylvania. It was only four feet high, suspended over a pond filled with crocodiles. I got out by picking the lock with my teeth. Luckily, the crocodiles weren't hungry. Where have *you* been?"

"I mean it. Don't you keep a schedule?"

"I'm right on my schedule, Elaine. This is Wednesday. I was here last Wednesday. This year Christmas falls on a Wednesday, and I'll be here on Christmas."

"It feels like a year."

"Only ten months. Till Christmas. Elaine, you aren't being any fun."

She wasn't in the mood for fun. There were tears in her eyes. "I can't stand much more," she said.

"I'm sorry."

"I'm afraid."

And she *was* afraid. Her voice trembled.

"At night, and in the daytime, whenever I sleep. I'm just the right size."

"For what?"

"What do you mean?"

"You said you were just the right size."

"I did? Oh, I don't know what I meant. I'm going crazy. That's what you're here for, isn't it? To keep me sane. It's the rain. I can't do anything, I can't see anything, and all I can hear most of the time is the hissing of the rain."

"Like outer space," I said, remembering what she had said the last time.

She apparently didn't remember our discussion. She looked startled. "How did you know?" she asked.

"You told me."

"There isn't any sound in outer space," she said.

"Oh," I answered.

"There's no air out there."

"I knew that."

"Then why did you say, 'Oh, of course'? The engines. You can hear them all over the ship. It's a drone, all the time. That's just like the rain. Only after a while you can't hear it anymore. It becomes like silence. Anansa told me."

Another imaginary friend. Her file said that she had kept her imaginary friends long after most children give them up. That was why I had first been assigned to see her, to get rid of the friends. Grunty, the ice pig; Howard, the boy who beat up everybody; Sue Ann, who would bring her dolls and play with them for her, making them do what Elaine said for them to do; Fuchsia, who lived among the flowers and was only inches high. There were others. After a few sessions with her I saw that she knew that they weren't real. But they passed time for her. They stepped outside her body and did things she could never do. I felt they did her no harm at all, and destroying that imaginary world for her would only make her lonelier and more unhappy. She was sane, that was certain. And yet I kept seeing her, not entirely because I liked her so much. Partly because I wondered whether she had been pretending when she told me she knew her friends weren't real. Anansa was a new one.

"Who's Anansa?"

"Oh, you don't want to know." She didn't want to talk about her; that was obvious.

"I want to know."

She turned away. "I can't make you go away, but I wish you would. When you get nosy."

"It's my job."

"Job!" She sounded contemptuous. "I see all of you, running around on your healthy legs, doing all your *jobs*."

What could I say to her? "It's how we stay alive," I said. "I do my best."

Then she got a strange look on her face; *I've got a secret,* she seemed to say, *and I want you to pry it out of me.* "Maybe I can get a job, too."

"Maybe," I said. I tried to think of something she could do.

"There's always music," she said.

I misunderstood. "There aren't many instruments you can play. That's the way it is." Dose of reality and all that.

"Don't be stupid."

"Okay. Never again."

"I meant that there's always the music. On my job."

"And what job is this?"

"Wouldn't you like to know?" she said, rolling her eyes mysteriously and turning toward the window. I imagined her as a normal fifteen-year-old girl. Ordinarily I would have interpreted this as flirting. But there was something else under all this. A feeling of desperation. She was right. I really would like to know. I made a rather logical guess. I put together the two secrets she was trying to get me to figure out today.

"What kind of job is Anansa going to give you?"

She looked at me, startled. "So it's true then."

"What's true?"

"It's so frightening. I keep telling myself it's a dream. But it isn't, is it?"

"What, Anansa?"

"You think she's just one of my friends, don't you. But they're not in my dreams, not like this. Anansa—"

"What about Anansa?"

"She sings to me. In my sleep."

My trained psychologist's mind immediately conjured up mother figures. "Of course," I said.

"She's in space, and she sings to me. You wouldn't believe the songs."

It reminded me. I pulled out the cassette I had bought for her.

"Thank you," she said.

"You're welcome. Want to hear it?"

She nodded. I put it on the cassette player. *Appalachian Spring.* She moved her head to the music. I imagined her as a dancer. She felt the music very well.

But after a few minutes she stopped moving and started to cry.

"It's not the same," she said.

"You've heard it before?"

"Turn it off. Turn it *off!*"

I turned it off. "Sorry," I said. "Thought you'd like it."

"Guilt, nothing but guilt," she said. "You always feel guilty, don't you?"

"Pretty nearly always," I admitted cheerfully. A lot of my parents threw psychological jargon in my face. Or soap-opera language.

"*I'm* sorry," she said. "It's just—it's just not the music. Not *the* music. Now that

I've heard it, everything is so dark compared to it. Like the rain, all gray and heavy and dim, as if the composer is trying to see the hills but the rain is always in the way. For a few minutes I thought he was getting it right."

"Anansa's music?"

She nodded. "I know you don't believe me. But I hear her when I'm asleep. She tells me that's the only time she can communicate with me. It's not talking. It's all her songs. She's out there, in her starship, singing. And at night I hear her."

"Why you?"

"You mean, Why only me?" She laughed. "Because of what I am. You told me yourself. Because I can't run around, I live in my imagination. She says that the threads between minds are very thin and hard to hold. But mine she can hold, because I live completely in my mind. She holds on to me. When I go to sleep, I can't escape her now anymore at all."

"Escape? I thought you liked her."

"I don't know what I like. I like—I like the music. But Anansa wants me. She wants to have me—she wants to give me a job."

"What's the singing like?" When she said *job*, she trembled and closed up; I referred back to something that she had been willing to talk about, to keep the floundering conversation going.

"It's not like anything. She's there in space, and it's black, just the humming of the engines like the sound of rain, and she reaches into the dust out there and draws in the songs. She reaches out her—out her fingers, or her ears, I don't know; it isn't clear. She reaches out and draws in the dust and the songs and turns them into the music that I hear. It's powerful. She says it's her songs that drive her between the stars."

"Is she alone?"

Elaine nodded. "She wants me."

"Wants you. How can she have you, with you here and her out there?"

Elaine licked her lips. "I don't want to talk about it," she said in a way that told me she was on the verge of telling me.

"I wish you would. I really wish you'd tell me."

"She says—she says that she can take me. She says that if I can learn the songs, she can pull me out of my body and take me there and give me arms and legs and fingers and I can run and dance and—"

She broke down, crying.

I patted her on the only place that she permitted, her soft little belly. She refused to be hugged. I had tried it years before, and she had screamed at me to stop it. One of the nurses told me it was because her mother had always hugged her, and Elaine wanted to hug back. And couldn't.

"It's a lovely dream, Elaine."

"It's a terrible dream. Don't you see? I'll be like *her*."

"And what's she like?"

"She's the ship. She's the starship. And she wants me with her, to be the starship with her. And sing our way through space together for thousands and thousands of years."

"It's just a dream. Elaine. You don't have to be afraid of it."

"They did it to her. They cut off her arms and legs and put her into the machines."

"But no one's going to put you into a machine."

"I want to go outside," she said.

"You can't. It's raining."

"Damn the rain."

"I do, every day."

"I'm not joking! She pulls me all the time now, even when I'm awake. She keeps pulling at me and making me fall asleep, and she sings to me, and I feel her pulling and pulling. If I could just go outside, I could hold on. I feel like I could hold on, if I could just—"

"Hey, relax. Let me give you a—"

"No! I don't want to sleep!"

"Listen, Elaine. It's just a dream. You can't let it get to you like this. It's just the rain keeping you here. It makes you sleepy, and so you keep dreaming this. But don't fight it. It's a beautiful dream in a way. Why not go with it?"

She looked at me with terror in her eyes.

"You don't mean that. You don't want me to go."

"No. Of course I don't want you to go anywhere. But you won't, don't you see? It's a dream, floating out there between the stars—"

"She's not floating. She's ramming her way through space so fast it makes me dizzy whenever she shows me."

"Then be dizzy. Think of it as your mind finding a way for you to run."

"You don't understand, Mr. Therapist. I thought you'd understand."

"I'm trying to."

"If I go with her, then I'll be dead."

I asked her nurse, "Who's been reading to her?"

"We all do, and volunteers from town. They like her. She always has someone to read to her."

"You'd better supervise them more carefully. Somebody's been putting ideas in her head. About spaceships and dust and singing between the stars. It's scared her pretty bad."

The nurse frowned. "We approve everything they read. She's been reading that kind of thing for years. It's never done her any harm before. Why now?"

"The rain, I guess. Cooped up in here, she's losing touch with reality."

The nurse nodded sympathetically and said, "I know. When she's asleep, she's doing the strangest things now."

"Like what? What kind of things?"

"Oh, singing these horrible songs."

"What are the words?"

"There aren't any words. She just sort of hums. Only the melodies are awful. Not even like music. And her voice gets funny and raspy. She's completely asleep. She sleeps a lot now. Mercifully, I think. She's always gotten impatient when she can't go outside."

The nurse obviously liked Elaine. It would be hard not to feel sorry for her, but Elaine insisted on being liked, and people liked her, those that could get over the horrible flatness of the sheets all around her trunk. "Listen," I said. "Can we bundle her up or something? Get her outside in spite of the rain?"

The nurse shook her head. "It isn't just the rain. It's cold out there. And the explosion that made her like she is—it messed her up inside. She isn't put together right. She doesn't have the strength to fight off any kind of disease at all. You understand—there's a good chance that exposure to that kind of weather would kill her eventually. And I won't take a chance on that."

"I'm going to be visiting her more often, then," I said. "As often as I can. She's got something going on in her head that's scaring her half to death. She thinks she's going to die."

"Oh, the poor darling," the nurse said. "Why would she think that?"

"Doesn't matter. One of her imaginary friends may be getting out of hand."

"I thought you said they were harmless."

"They were."

When I left the Millard County Rest Home that night, I stopped back in Elaine's room. She was asleep, and I heard her song. It was eerie. I could hear, now and then, themes from the bit of Copland music she had listened to. But it was distorted, and most of the music was unrecognizable—wasn't even music. Her voice was high and strange, and then suddenly it would change, would become low and raspy, and for a moment I clearly heard in her voice the sound of a vast engine coming through walls of metal, carried on slender metal rods, the sound of a great roar being swallowed up by a vast cushion of nothing. I pictured Elaine with wires coming out of her shoulders and hips, with her head encased in metal and her eyes closed in sleep, like her imaginary Anansa, piloting the starship as if it were her own body. I could see that this would be attractive to Elaine, in a way. After all, she hadn't been born this way. She had memories of running and playing, memories of feeding herself and dressing herself, perhaps even of learning to read, of sounding out the words as her fingers touched each letter. Even the false arms of a spaceship would be something to fill the great void.

Children's centers are not inside their bodies; their centers are outside, at the point where the fingers of the left hand and the fingers of the right hand meet. What they touch is where they live; what they see is their self. And Elaine had lost herself in an explosion before she had the chance to move inside. With this strange dream of Anansa she was getting a self back.

But a repellent self, for all that. I walked in and sat by Elaine's bed, listening to her sing. Her body moved slightly, her back arching a little with the melody. High and light; low and rasping. The sounds alternated, and I wondered what they meant. What was going on inside her to make this music come out?

If I go with her, then I'll be dead.

Of course she was afraid. I looked at the lump of flesh that filled the bed shapelessly below where her head emerged from the covers. I tried to change my perspective, to see her body as she saw it, from above. It almost disappeared then, with the foreshortening and the height of her ribs making her stomach and hint of hips vanish into insignificance. Yet this was all she had, and if she believed—and certainly she seemed to—that surrendering to the fantasy of Anansa would mean the death of this pitiful body, is death any less frightening to those who have not been able to fully live? I doubt it. At least for Elaine, what life she had lived had been joyful. She would not willingly trade it for a life of music and metal arms, locked in her own mind.

Except for the rain. Except that nothing was so real to her as the outside, as the trees and birds and distant hills, and as the breeze touching her with a violence she permitted to no living person. And with that reality, the good part of her life, cut off from her by the rain, how long could she hold out against the incessant pulling of Anansa and her promise of arms and legs and eternal song?

I reached up, on a whim, and very gently lifted her eyelids.

Her eyes remained open, staring at the ceiling, not blinking.

I closed her eyes, and they remained closed.

I turned her head, and it stayed turned. She did not wake up. Just kept singing as if I had done nothing to her at all.

Catatonia, or the beginning of catalepsy. *She's losing her mind,* I thought, *and if I don't bring her back, keep her here somehow, Anansa will win, and the rest home will be caring for a lump of mindless flesh for the next however many years they can keep this remnant of Elaine alive.*

"I'll be back on Saturday," I told the administrator.

"Why so soon?"

"Elaine is going through a crisis of some kind," I explained. An imaginary woman from space wants to carry her off—that I didn't say. "Have the nurses keep her awake as much as they can. Read to her, play with her, talk to her. Her normal hours at night are enough. Avoid naps."

"Why?"

"I'm afraid for her, that's all. She could go catatonic on us at any time, I think. Her sleeping isn't normal. I want to have her watched all the time."

"This is really serious?"

"This is really serious."

On Friday it looked as if the clouds were breaking, but after only a few minutes of sunshine a huge new bank of clouds swept down from the northwest, and it was worse than before. I finished my work rather carelessly, stopping a sentence in the middle several times. One of my patients was annoyed with me. She squinted at me. "You're not paid to think about your woman troubles when you're talking to me." I apologized and tried to pay attention. She was a talker; my attention always wandered. But she was right in a way. I couldn't stop thinking of Elaine. And my patient's saying that about woman troubles must have triggered something in my mind. After all, my relationship with Elaine was the longest and closest I had had with a woman in many years. If you could think of Elaine as a woman.

On Saturday I drove back to Millard County and found the nurses rather distraught. They didn't realize how much she was sleeping until they tried to stop her, they all said. She was dozing off for two or three naps in the mornings, even more in the afternoons. She went to sleep at night at seven-thirty and slept at least twelve hours. "Singing all the time. It's awful. Even at night she keeps it up. Singing and singing."

But she was awake when I went in to see her.

"I stayed awake for you."

"Thanks," I said.

"A Saturday visit. I must really be going bonkers."

"Actually, no. But I don't like how sleepy you are."

She smiled wanly. "It isn't my idea."

I think my smile was more cheerful than hers. "And I think it's all in your head."

"Think what you like, Doctor."

"I'm not a doctor. My degree says I'm a master."

"How deep is the water outside?"

"Deep?"

"All this rain. Surely it's enough to keep a few dozen arks afloat. Is God destroying the world?"

"Unfortunately, no. Though He has killed the engines on a few cars that went a little fast through the puddles."

"How long would it have to rain to fill up the world?"

"The world is round. It would all drip off the bottom."

She laughed. It was good to hear her laugh, but it ended too abruptly, and she looked at me fearfully. "I'm going, you know."

"You are?"

"I'm just the right size. She's measured me, and I'll fit perfectly. She has just the place for me. It's a good place, where I can hear the music of the dust for myself, and learn to sing it. I'd have the directional engines."

I shook my head. "Grunty the ice pig was cute. This isn't cute, Elaine."

"Did I ever say I thought Anansa was cute? Grunty the ice pig was real, you know. My father made him out of crushed ice for a luau. He melted before they got the pig out of the ground. I don't make my friends up."

"Fuchsia the flower girl?"

"My mother would pinch blossoms off the fuchsia by our front door. We played with them like dolls in the grass."

"But not Anansa."

"Anansa came into my mind when I was asleep. She found me. I didn't make her up."

"Don't you see, Elaine, that's how the real hallucinations come? They feel like reality."

She shook her head. "I know all that. I've had the nurses read me psychology books. Anansa is—Anansa is other. She couldn't come out of my head. She's something else. She's real. I've heard her music. It isn't plain, like Copland. It isn't false."

"Elaine, when you were asleep on Wednesday, you were becoming catatonic."

"I know."

"You know?"

"I felt you touch me. I felt you turn my head. I wanted to speak to you, to say good-bye. But she was singing, don't you see? She was singing. And now she lets me sing along. When I sing with her, I can feel myself travel out, like a spider along a single thread, out into the place where she is. Into the darkness. It's lonely there, and black, and cold, but I know that at the end of the thread there she'll be, a friend for me forever."

"You're frightening me, Elaine."

"There aren't any trees on her starship, you know. That's how I stay here. I think of the trees and the hills and the birds and the grass and the wind, and how I'd lose all of that. She gets angry at me, and a little hurt. But it keeps me here. Except now I can hardly remember the trees at all. I try to remember, and it's like trying to remember the face of my mother. I can remember her dress and her hair, but her face is gone forever. Even when I look at a picture, it's a stranger. The trees are strangers to me now."

I stroked her forehead. At first she pulled her head away, then slid it back.

"I'm sorry," she said. "I usually don't like people to touch me there."

"I won't," I said.

"No, go ahead. I don't mind."

So I stroked her forehead again. It was cool and dry, and she lifted her head almost imperceptibly, to receive my touch. Involuntarily I thought of what the old woman had said the day before. *Woman troubles.* I was touching Elaine, and I thought of making love to her. I immediately put the thought out of my mind.

"Hold me here," she said. "Don't let me go. I want to go so badly. But I'm not meant for that. I'm just the right size, but not the right shape. Those aren't my arms. I know what my arms felt like."

"I'll hold you if I can. But you have to help."

"No drugs. The drugs pull my mind away from my body. If you give me drugs, I'll die."

"Then what can I do?"

"Just keep me here, any way you can."

Then we talked about nonsense, because we had been so serious, and it was as if she weren't having any problems at all. We got on to the subject of the church meetings.

"I didn't know you were religious," I said.

"I'm not. But what else is there to do on Sunday? They sing hymns, and I sing with them. Last Sunday there was a sermon that really got to me. The preacher talked about Christ in the sepulchre. About Him being there three days before the angel came to let Him go. I've been thinking about that, what it must have been like for Him, locked in a cave in the darkness, completely alone."

"Depressing."

"Not really. It must have been exhilarating for Him, in a way. If it was true, you know. To lie there on that stone bed, saying to Himself, 'They thought I was dead, but I'm here. I'm not dead.' "

"You make Him sound smug."

"Sure. Why not? I wonder if I'd feel like that, if I were with Anansa."

Anansa again.

"I can see what you're thinking. You're thinking, 'Anansa again.' "

"Yeah," I said. "I wish you'd erase her and go back to some more harmless friends."

Suddenly her face went angry and fierce.

"You can believe what you like. Just leave me alone."

I tried to apologize, but she wouldn't have any of it. She insisted on believing in this star woman. Finally I left, redoubling my cautions against letting her sleep. The nurses looked worried, too. They could see the change as easily as I could.

That night, because I was in Millard on a weekend, I called up Belinda. She wasn't married or anything at the moment. She came to my motel. We had dinner, made love, and watched television. She watched television, that is. I lay on the bed, thinking. And so when the test pattern came on and Belinda at last got up, beery and passionate, my mind was still on Elaine. As Belinda kissed and tickled me and whispered stupidity in my ear, I imagined myself without arms and legs. I lay there, moving only my head.

"What's the matter, you don't want to?"

I shook off the mood. No need to disappoint Belinda—I was the one who had called *her*. I had a responsibility. Not much of one, though. That was what was nagging at me. I made love to Belinda slowly and carefully, but with my eyes closed. I kept superimposing Elaine's face on Belinda's. Woman troubles. Even though Belinda's fingers played up and down my back, I thought I was making love to Elaine. And the stumps of arms and legs didn't revolt me as much as I would have thought. Instead, I only felt sad. A deep sense of tragedy, of loss, as if Elaine were dead and I could have saved her, like the prince in all the fairy tales; a kiss, so symbolic, and the princess awakens and lives happily ever after. And I hadn't done it. I had failed her. When we were finished, I cried.

"Oh, you poor sweetheart," Belinda said, her voice rich with sympathy. "What's wrong—you don't have to tell me." She cradled me for a while, and at last I went to sleep with my head pressed against her breasts. She thought I needed her. I suppose that, briefly, I did.

I did not go back to Elaine on Sunday as I had planned. I spent the entire day almost going. Instead of walking out the door, I sat and watched the incredible array of terrible Sunday morning television. And when I finally did go out, fully intending to go to the rest home and see how she was doing, I ended up driving, luggage in the back of the car, to my trailer, where I went inside and again sat down and watched television.

Why couldn't I go to her?

Just keep me here, she had said. Any way you can, she had said.

And I thought I knew the way. That was the problem. In the back of my mind all this was much too real, and the fairy tales were wrong. The prince didn't wake her with a kiss. He wakened the princess with a promise: In his arms she would be safe forever. She awoke for the happily ever after. If she hadn't known it to be true, the princess would have preferred to sleep forever.

What was Elaine asking of me?

Why was I afraid of it?

Not my job. Unprofessional to get emotionally involved with a patient.

But then, when had I ever been a professional? I finally went to bed, wishing I had Belinda with me again, for whatever comfort she could bring. Why weren't all women like Belinda, soft and loving and undemanding?

Yet as I drifted off to sleep, it was Elaine I remembered, Elaine's face and hideous, reproachful stump of a body that followed me through all my dreams.

And she followed me when I was awake, through my regular rounds on Monday and Tuesday, and at last it was Wednesday, and still I was afraid to go to the Millard County Rest Home. I didn't get there until afternoon. Late afternoon, and the rain was coming down as hard as ever, and there were lakes of standing water in the fields, torrents rushing through the unprepared gutters of the town.

"You're late," the administrator said.

"Rain," I answered, and he nodded. But he looked worried.

"We hoped you'd come yesterday, but we couldn't reach you anywhere. It's Elaine."

And I knew that my delay had served its damnable purpose, exactly as I expected.

"She hasn't woken up since Monday morning. She just lies there, singing. We've got her on an IV. She's asleep."

She was indeed asleep. I sent the others out of the room.

"Elaine," I said.

Nothing.

I called her name again, several times. I touched her, rocked her head back and forth. Her head stayed wherever I placed it. And the song went on, softly, high and then low, pure and then gravelly. I covered her mouth. She sang on, even with her mouth closed, as if nothing were the matter.

I pulled down her sheet and pushed a pin into her belly, then into the thin flesh at her collarbone. No response. I slapped her face. No response. She was gone. I saw her again, connected to a starship, only this time I understood better. It wasn't her body that was the right size; it was her mind. And it was her mind that had followed the slender spider's thread out to Anansa, who waited to give her a body.

A job.

Shock therapy? I imagined her already-deformed body leaping and arching as the electricity coursed through her. It would accomplish nothing, except to torture un-thinking flesh. Drugs? I couldn't think of any that could bring her back from where she had gone. In a way, I think, I even believed in Anansa, for the moment. I called her name. "Anansa, let her go. Let her come back to me. Please. I need her."

Why had I cried in Belinda's arms? Oh, yes. Because I had seen the princess and let her lie there unawakened, because the happily ever after was so damnably much work.

I did not do it in the fever of the first realization that I had lost her. It was no act of passion or sudden fear or grief. I sat beside her bed for hours, looking at her weak and helpless body, now so empty. I wished for her eyes to open on their own, for her to wake up and say, "Hey, would you believe the dream *I* had!" For her to say, "Fooled you, didn't I? It was really hard when you poked me with pins, but I fooled you."

But she hadn't fooled me.

And so, finally, not with passion but in despair, I stood up and leaned over her, leaned my hands on either side of her and pressed my cheek against hers and whispered in her ear. I promised her everything I could think of. I promised her no more rain forever. I promised her trees and flowers and hills and birds and the wind for as long as she liked. I promised to take her away from the rest home, to take her to see things she could only have dreamed of before.

And then at last, with my voice harsh from pleading with her, with her hair wet with my tears, I promised her the only thing that might bring her back. I promised her me. I promised her love forever, stronger than any songs Anansa could sing.

And it was then that the monstrous song fell silent. She did not awaken, but the song ended, and she moved on her own; her head rocked to the side, and she seemed to sleep normally, not catatonically. I waited by her bedside all night. I fell asleep in the chair, and one of the nurses covered me. I was still there when I was awakened in the morning by Elaine's voice.

"What a liar you are! It's still raining."

It was a feeling of power, to know that I had called someone back from places far darker than death. Her life was painful, and yet my promise of devotion was enough, apparently, to compensate. This was how I understood it, at least. This was what made me feel exhilarated, what kept me blind and deaf to what had really happened.

I was not the only one rejoicing. The nurses made a great fuss over her, and the administrator promised to write up a glowing report. "Publish," he said.

"It's too personal," I said. But in the back of my mind I was already trying to figure out a way to get the case into print, to gain something for my career. I was ashamed of myself for twisting what had been an honest, heartfelt commitment into personal advancement. But I couldn't ignore the sudden respect I was receiving from people to whom, only hours before, I had been merely ordinary.

"It's too personal," I repeated firmly. "I have no intention of publishing."

And to my disgust I found myself relishing the administrator's respect for that decision. There was no escape from my swelling self-satisfaction. Not as long as I stayed around those determined to give me cheap payoffs. Ever the wise psychologist, I returned to the only person who would give me gratitude instead of admiration. *The gratitude I had earned*, I thought. I went back to Elaine.

"Hi," she said. "I wondered where you had gone."

"Not far," I said. "Just visiting with the Nobel Prize committee."

"They want to reward you for bringing me here?"

"Oh, no. They had been planning to give me the award for having contacted a genuine alien being from outer space. Instead, I blew it and brought you back. They're quite upset."

She looked flustered. It wasn't like her to look flustered—usually she came back with another quip. "But what will they do to you?"

"Probably boil me in oil. That's the usual thing. Though, maybe they've found a way to boil me in solar energy. It's cheaper." A feeble joke. But she didn't get it.

"This isn't the way she said it was—she said it was—"

She. I tried to ignore the dull fear that suddenly churned in my stomach. *Be analytical*, I thought. *She could be anyone.*

"She said? Who said?" I asked.

Elaine fell silent. I reached out and touched her forehead. She was perspiring.

"What's wrong?" I asked. "You're upset."

"I should have known."

"Known what?"

She shook her head and turned away from me.

I knew what it was, I thought. I knew what it was, but we could surely cope. "Elaine," I said, "you aren't completely cured, are you? You haven't got rid of Anansa, have you? You don't have to hide it from me. Sure, I would have loved to think you'd been completely cured, but that would have been too much of a miracle. Do I look like a miracle worker? We've just made progress, that's all. Brought you back from catalepsy. We'll free you of Anansa eventually."

Still she was silent, staring at the rain-gray window.

"You don't have to be embarrassed about pretending to be completely cured. It was very kind of you. It made me feel very good for a little while. But I'm a grown-up. I can cope with a little disappointment. Besides, you're awake, you're back, and that's all that matters." Grown-up, hell! I was terribly disappointed, and ashamed that I wasn't more sincere in what I was saying. No cure after all. No hero. No magic. No great achievement. Just a psychologist who was, after all, not extraordinary.

But I refused to pay too much attention to those feelings. Be a professional, I told myself. She needs your help.

"So don't go feeling guilty about it."

She turned back to face me, her eyes full. "Guilty?" She almost smiled. "Guilty." Her eyes did not leave my face, though I doubted she could see me well through the tears brimming her lashes.

"You tried to do the right thing," I said.

"Did I? Did I really?" She smiled bitterly. It was a strange smile for her, and for a terrible moment she no longer looked like my Elaine, my bright young patient. "I meant to stay with her," she said. "I wanted her with me, she was so alive, and when she finally joined herself to the ship, she sang and danced and swung her arms, and I said, 'This is what I've needed; this is what I've craved all my centuries lost in the songs.' But then I heard *you*."

"Anansa," I said, realizing at that moment who was with me.

"I heard *you*, crying out to her. Do you think I made up my mind quickly? She heard you, but she wouldn't come. She wouldn't trade her new arms and legs for anything. They were so new. But I'd had them for long enough. What I'd never had was—you."

"Where is she?" I asked.

"Out there," she said. "She sings better than I ever did." She looked wistful for a moment, then smiled ruefully. "And I'm here. Only I made a bad bargain, didn't I? Because I didn't fool you. You won't want me, now. It's Elaine you want, and she's gone. I left her alone out there. She won't mind, not for a long time. But then—then she will. Then she'll know I cheated her."

The voice was Elaine's voice, the tragic little body her body. But now I knew I had not succeeded at all. Elaine was gone, in the infinite outer space where the mind hides to escape from itself. And in her place—Anansa. A stranger.

"You cheated her?" I said. "How did you cheat her?"

"It never changes. In a while you learn all the songs, and they never change. Nothing moves. You go on forever until all the stars fail, and yet nothing ever moves."

I moved my hand and put it to my hair. I was startled at my own trembling touch on my head.

"Oh, God," I said. They were just words, not a supplication.

"You hate me." she said.

Hate her? Hate my little, mad Elaine? Oh, no. I had another object for my hate. I hated the rain that had cut her off from all that kept her sane. I hated her parents for not leaving her home the day they let their car drive them on to death. But most of all I remembered my days of hiding from Elaine, my days of resisting her need, of pretending that I didn't remember her or think of her or need her, too. She must have wondered why I was so long in coming. Wondered and finally given up hope, finally realized that there was no one who would hold her. And so she left, and when I finally came, the only person waiting inside her body was Anansa, the imaginary friend who had come, terrifyingly, to life. I knew whom to hate. I thought I would cry. I even buried my face in the sheet where her leg would have been. But I did not cry. I just sat there, the sheet harsh against my face, hating myself.

Her voice was like a gentle hand, a pleading hand touching me. "I'd undo it if I could," she said. "But I can't. She's gone, and I'm here. I came because of you. I came to see the trees and the grass and the birds and your smile. The happily ever after. That was what she had lived for, you know, all she lived for. Please smile at me."

I felt warmth on my hair. I lifted my head. There was no rain in the window. Sunlight rose and fell on the wrinkles of the sheet.

"Let's go outside," I said.

"It stopped raining," she said.

"A bit late, isn't it?" I answered. But I smiled at her.

"You can call me Elaine," she said. "You won't tell, will you?"

I shook my head. No, I wouldn't tell. She was safe enough. I wouldn't tell because then they would take her away to a place where psychiatrists reigned but did not know enough to rule. I imagined her confined among others who had also made their escape from reality and I knew that I couldn't tell anyone. I also knew I couldn't confess failure, not now.

Besides, I hadn't really completely failed. There was still hope. Elaine wasn't really gone. She was still there, hidden in her own mind, looking out through this imaginary person she had created to take her place. Someday I would find her and bring her home. After all, even Grunty the ice pig had melted.

I noticed that she was shaking her head. "You won't find her," she said. "You won't bring her home. I won't melt and disappear. She *is* gone and you couldn't have prevented it."

I smiled. "Elaine," I said.

And then I realized that she had answered thoughts I hadn't put into words.

"That's right," she said, "Let's be honest with each other. You might as well. You can't lie to me."

I shook my head. For a moment, in my confusion and despair, I had believed it all, believed that Anansa was real. But that was nonsense. Of course Elaine knew what I was thinking. She knew me better than I knew myself. "Let's go outside," I said. A failure and a cripple, out to enjoy the sunlight, which fell equally on the just and the unjustifiable.

"I don't mind," she said. "Whatever you want to believe: Elaine or Anansa. Maybe it's better if you still look for Elaine. Maybe it's better if you let me fool you after all."

The worst thing about the fantasies of the mentally ill is that they're so damned consistent. They never let up. They never give you any rest.

"I'm Elaine," she said, smiling. "I'm Elaine, pretending to be Anansa. You love me. That's what I came for. You promised to bring me home, and you did. Take me outside. You made it stop raining for me. You did everything you promised, and I'm home again, and I promise I'll never leave you."

She hasn't left me. I come to see her every Wednesday as part of my work, and every Saturday and Sunday as the best part of my life. I take her driving with me sometimes, and we talk constantly, and I read to her and bring her books for the nurses to read to her. None of them know that she is still unwell—to them she's Elaine, happier than ever, pathetically delighted at every sight and sound and smell and taste and every texture that they touch against her cheek. Only I know that she believes she is not Elaine. Only I know that I have made no progress at all since then, that in moments of terrible honesty I call her Anansa, and she sadly answers me.

But in a way I'm content. Very little has changed between us, really. And after a few weeks I realized, with certainty, that she was happier now than she had ever been before. After all, she had the best of all possible worlds, for her. She could tell herself that the real Elaine was off in space somewhere, dancing and singing and hearing songs, with arms and legs at last, while the poor girl who was confined to the limbless body at the Millard County Rest Home was really an alien who was very, very happy to have even that limited body.

And as for me, I kept my commitment to her, and I'm happier for it. I'm still human—I still take another woman into my bed from time to time. But Anansa doesn't mind. She even suggested it, only a few days after she woke up. "Go back to Belinda somtimes," she said. "Belinda loves you, too, you know. I won't mind at all." I still can't remember when I spoke to her of Belinda, but at least she didn't mind, and so there aren't really any discontentments in my life. Except.

Except that I'm not God. I would like to be God. I would make some changes.

When I go to the Millard County Rest Home, I never enter the building first. She is never in the building. I walk around the outside and look across the lawn by the trees. The wheelchair is always there; I can tell it from the others by the pillows, which glare white in the sunlight. I never call out. In a few moments she always sees me, and the nurses wheel her around and push the chair across the lawn.

She comes as she has come hundreds of times before. She plunges toward me, and I concentrate on watching her, so that my mind will not see my Elaine surrounded by blackness, plunging through space, gathering dust, gathering songs, leaping and dancing with her new arms and legs that she loves better than me. Instead I watch the wheelchair, watch the smile on her face. She is happy to see me, so delighted with the world outside that her body cannot contain her. And when my imagination will not be restrained, I am God for a moment. I see her running toward me, her arms waving. I give her a left hand, a right hand, delicate and strong; I put a long and girlish left leg on her, and one just as sturdy on the right.

And then, one by one, I take them all away.

Prior Restraint

I met Doc Murphy in a writing class taught by a mad Frenchman at the University of Utah in Salt Lake City. I had just quit my job as a coat-and-tie editor at a conservative family magazine, and I was having a little trouble getting used to being a slob student again. Of a shaggy lot, Doc was the shaggiest and I was prepared to be annoyed by him and ignore his opinions. But his opinions were not to be ignored. At first because of what he did to me. And then, at last, because of what had been done to him. It has shaped me; his past looms over me whenever I sit down to write.

Armand the teacher, who had not improved on his French accent by replacing it with Bostonian, looked puzzled as he held up my story before the class. "This is commercially viable," he said. "It is also crap. What else can I say?"

It was Doc who said it. Nail in one hand, hammer in the other, he crucified me and the story. Considering that I had already decided not to pay attention to him, and considering how arrogant I was in the lofty position of being the one student who had actually sold a novel, it is surprising to me that I listened to him. But underneath the almost angry attack on my work was something else: A basic respect, I think, for what a good writer should be. And for that small hint in my work that a good writer might be hiding somewhere in me.

So I listened. And I learned. And gradually, as the Frenchman got crazier and crazier, I turned to Doc to learn how to write. Shaggy though he was, he had a far crisper mind than anyone I had ever known in a business suit.

We began to meet outside class. My wife had left me two years before, so I had plenty of free time and a pretty large rented house to sprawl in; we drank or read or talked, in front of a fire or over Doc's convincing veal parmesan or out chopping down an insidious vine that wanted to take over the world starting in my backyard. For the first time since Denae had gone I felt at home in my house—Doc seemed to know by instinct what parts of the house held the wrong memories, and he soon balanced them by making me feel comfortable in them again.

Or uncomfortable. Doc didn't always say nice things.

"I can see why your wife left you," he said once.

"You don't think I'm good in bed, either?" (This was a joke—neither Doc nor I had any unusual sexual predilections.)

"You have a neanderthal way of dealing with people, that's all. If they aren't going where you want them to go, club 'em a good one and drag 'em away."

It was irritating. I didn't like thinking about my wife. We had only been married three years, and not good years either, but in my own way I had loved her and I missed her a great deal and I hadn't wanted her to go when she left. I didn't like having my nose rubbed in it. "I don't recall clubbing *you*."

He just smiled. And, of course, I immediately thought back over the conversation and realized that he was right. I hated his goddam smile.

"OK," I said, "you're the one with long hair in the land of the last surviving crew cuts. Tell me why you like 'Swap' Morris."

"I don't like Morris. I think Morris is a whore selling someone else's freedom to win votes."

And I *was* confused, then. I had been excoriating good old "Swap" Morris, Davis County Commissioner, for having fired the head librarian in the county because she had dared to stock a "pornographic" book despite his objections. Morris showed every sign of being illiterate, fascist, and extremely popular, and I would gladly have hit the horse at his lynching.

"So you don't like Morris either—what did I say wrong?"

"Censorship is never excusable for any reason, says you."

"You *like* censorship?"

And then the half-serious banter turned completely serious. Suddenly he wouldn't look at me. Suddenly he only had eyes for the fire, and I saw the flames dancing in tears resting on his lower eyelids, and I realized again that with Doc I was out of my depth completely.

"No," he said. "No, I don't *like* it."

And then a lot of silence until he finally drank two full glasses of wine, just like that, and went out to drive home; he lived up Emigration Canyon at the end of a winding, narrow road, and I was afraid he was too drunk, but he only said to me at the door, "I'm not drunk. It takes half a gallon of wine just to get up to normal after an hour with you, you're so damn sober."

One weekend he even took me to work with him. Doc made his living in Nevada. We left Salt Lake City on Friday afternoon and drove to Wendover, the first town over the border. I expected him to be an employee of the casino we stopped at. But he didn't punch in, just left his name with a guy; and then he sat in a corner with me and waited.

"Don't you have to work?" I asked.

"I'm working," he said.

"I used to work just the same way, but I got fired."

"I've got to wait my turn for a table. I told you I made my living with poker."

And it finally dawned on me that he was a freelance professional—a player—a cardshark.

There were four guys named Doc there that night. Doc Murphy was the third one called to a table. He played quietly, and lost steadily but lightly for two hours. Then, suddenly, in four hands he made back everything he had lost and added nearly fifteen hundred dollars to it. Then he made his apologies after a decent number of losing hands and we drove back to Salt Lake.

"Usually I have to play again on Saturday night," he told me. Then he grinned. "Tonight I was lucky. There was an idiot who thought he knew poker."

I remembered the old saw: Never eat at a place called Mom's, never play poker with a man named Doc, and never sleep with a woman who's got more troubles than you. Pure truth. Doc memorized the deck, knew all the odds by heart, and it was a rare poker face that Doc couldn't eventually see through.

At the end of the quarter, though, it finally dawned on me that in all the time we were in class together, I had never seen one of his own stories. He hadn't written a damn thing. And there was his grade on the bulletin board—A.

I talked to Armand.

"Oh, Doc writes," he assured me. "Better than you do, and you got an A. God knows how, you don't have the talent for it."

"Why doesn't he turn it in for the rest of the class to read?"

Armand shrugged. "Why should he? Pearls before swine."

Still it irritated me. After watching Doc disembowel more than one writer, I didn't think it was fair that his own work was never put on the chopping block.

The next quarter he turned up in a graduate seminar with me, and I asked him. He laughed and told me to forget it. I laughed back and told him I wouldn't. I wanted to read his stuff. So the next week he gave me a three-page manuscript. It was an unfinished fragment of a story about a man who honestly thought his wife had left him even though he went home to find her there every night. It was some of the best writing I've ever read in my life. No matter how you measure it. The stuff was clear enough and exciting enough that any moron who likes Harold Robbins could have enjoyed it. But the style was rich enough and the matter of it deep enough even in a few pages that it made most other "great" writers look like chicken farmers. I reread the fragment five times just to make sure I got it all. The first time I had thought it was metaphorically about me. The third time I knew it was about God. The fifth time I knew it was about everything that mattered, and I wanted to read more.

"Where's the rest?" I asked.

He shrugged. "That's it," he said.

"It doesn't feel finished."

"It isn't."

"Well, finish it! Doc, you could sell this anywhere, even the *New Yorker*. For them you probably don't even *have* to finish it."

"Even the *New Yorker*. Golly."

"I can't believe you think you're too good for *anybody*, Doc. Finish it. I want to know how it ends."

He shook his head. "That's all there is. That's all there ever will be."

And that was the end of the discussion.

But from time to time he'd show me another fragment. Always better than the one before. And in the meantime we became closer, not because he was such a good writer—I'm not so self-effacing I like hanging around with people who can write me under the table—but because he was Doc Murphy. We found every decent place to get a beer in Salt Lake City—not a particular time-consuming activity. We saw three good movies and another dozen that were so bad they were fun to watch. He taught me to play poker well enough that I broke even every weekend. He put up with my succession of girlfriends and prophesied that I would probably end up married again. "You're just weak willed enough to try to make a go of it," he cheerfully told me.

At last, when I had long since given up asking, he told me why he never finished anything.

I was two and a half beers down, and he was drinking a hideous mix of Tab and tomato juice that he drank whenever he wanted to punish himself for his sins, on the theory that it was even worse than the Hindu practice of drinking your own piss. I had just got a story back from a magazine I had been sure would buy it. I was thinking of giving it up. He laughed at me.

"I'm serious," I said.

"Nobody who's any good at all needs to give up writing."

"Look who's talking. The king of the determined writers." He looked angry. "You're a paraplegic making fun of a one-legged man," he said.

"I'm sick of it."

"Quit then. Makes no difference. Leave the field to the hacks. You're probably a hack, too."

Doc hadn't been drinking anything to make him surly, not drunk-surly, anyway. "Hey, Doc, I'm asking for encouragement."

"If you need encouragement, you don't deserve it. There's only one way a good writer can be stopped."

"Don't tell me you have a selective writer's block. Against endings."

"Writer's block? Jesus, I've never been blocked in my life. Blocks are what happen when you're not good enough to write the thing you know you have to write."

I was getting angry. "And *you*, of course, are always good enough."

He leaned forward, looked at me in the eyes. "I'm the best writer in the English language."

"I'll give you this much. You're the best who never finished anything."

"I finish everything," he said. "I finish everything, beloved friend, and then I burn all but the first three pages. I finish a story a week, sometimes. I've written three complete novels, four plays. I even did a screenplay. It would've made millions of dollars and been a classic."

"Says who?"

"Says—never mind who says. It was bought, it was cast, it was ready for filming. It had a budget of thirty million. The studio believed in it. Only intelligent thing I've ever heard of them doing."

I couldn't believe it. "You're joking."

"If I'm joking, who's laughing? It's true."

I'd never seen him looked so poisoned, so pained. It was true, if I knew Doc Murphy, and I think I did. Do. "Why?" I asked.

"The Censorship Board."

"What? There's no such thing in America."

He laughed. "Not full-time anyway."

"Who the hell is the Censorship Board?"

He told me:

When I was twenty-two I lived on a rural road in Oregon, he said, outside of Portland. Mailboxes out on the road. I was writing, I was a playwright, I thought there'd be a career in that; I was just starting to try fiction. I went out one morning after the mailman had gone by. It was drizzling slightly. But I didn't much care. There was an envelope there from my Hollywood agent. It was a contract. Not an option—a sale. A hundred thousand dollars. It had just occurred to me that I was getting wet and I ought to go in when two men came out of the bushes—yeah, I know, I guess they go for dramatic entrances. They were in business suits. God, I hate men who wear business suits. The one guy just held out his hand. He said, "Give it to me now and save yourself a lot of trouble." Give it to him? I told him what I thought of his suggestion. They looked like the mafia, or like a comic parody of the mafia, actually.

They were about the same height, and they seemed almost to be the same person, right down to a duplicate glint of fierceness in the eyes; but then I realized that my first impression had been deceptive. One was blond, one dark-haired; the blond had a slightly receding chin that gave his face a meek look from the nose down; the dark one had once had a bad skin problem and his neck was treeish, giving him an air of stupidity, as if a face had been pasted on the front of the neck with no room for a head at all. Not mafia at all. Ordinary people.

Except the eyes. That glint in the eyes was not false, and that was what had made me see them wrong at first. Those eyes had seen people weep, and had cared, and had hurt them again anyway. It's a look that human eyes should never have.

"It's just the *contract*, for Christ's sake," I told them, but the dark one with acne scars only told me again to hand it over.

By now, though, my first fear had passed; they weren't armed, and so I might be able to get rid of them without violence. I started back to the house. They followed me.

"What do you want my contract for?" I asked.

"That film will never be made," says Meek, the blond one with the missing chin. "We won't allow it to be made."

I'm thinking who writes their dialogue for them, do they crib it from Fenimore Cooper? "Their hundred thousand dollars says they want to try. I want them to."

"You'll never get the money, Murphy. And this contract and that screenplay will pass out of existence within the next four days. I promise you that."

I ask him, "What are you, a critic?"

"Close enough."

By now I was inside the door and they were on the other side of the threshold. I should have closed the door, probably, but I'm a gambler. I had to stay in this time because I had to know what kind of hand they had. "Plan to take it by force?" I asked.

"By inevitability," Tree says. And then he says, "You see, Mr. Murphy, you're a dangerous man; with your IBM Self-Correcting Selectric II typewriter that has a sluggish return so that you sometimes get letters printed a few spaces in from the end. With your father who once said to you, 'Billy, to tell you the honest-to-God truth, I don't know if I'm your father or not. I wasn't the only guy your Mom had been seeing when I married her, so I really don't give a damn if you live or die.' "

He had it right down. *Word for word*, what my father told me when I was four years old. I'd never told anybody. And he had it word for word.

CIA, Jesus. That's pathetic.

No, they weren't CIA. They just wanted to make sure that I didn't write. Or rather, that I didn't publish.

I told them I wasn't interested in their suggestions. And I was right—they weren't muscle types. I closed the door and they just went away.

And then the next day as I was driving my old Galaxy along the road, under the speed limit, a boy on a bicycle came right out in front of me. I didn't even have a chance to brake. One second he wasn't there, and the next second he was. I hit him.

The bicycle went under the car, but he mostly came up the top. His foot stuck in the bumper, jammed in by the bike. The rest of him slid up over the hood, pulling his hip apart and separating his spine in three places. The hood ornament disemboweled him and the blood flowed up the windshield like a heavy rainstorm, so that I couldn't see anything except his face, which was pressed up against the glass with the eyes open. He died on the spot, of course. And I wanted to.

He had been playing Martians or something with his brother. The brother was standing there near the road with a plastic ray gun in his hand and a stupid look on his face. His mother came out of the house screaming. I was screaming, too. There were two neighbors who saw the whole thing. One of them called the cops and ambulance. The other one tried to control the mother and keep her from killing me. I don't remember where I was going. All I remember is that the car had taken an unusually long time starting that morning. Another minute and a half, I think—a long time, to start a car. If it had started up just like usual, I wouldn't have hit the kid. I kept thinking that—it was all just a coincidence that I happened to be coming by just at that moment. A half-second sooner and he would have seen me and swerved. A half-second later and I would have seen him. Just coincidence. The only reason the boy's father didn't kill me when he came home ten minutes later was because I was crying so damn hard. It never went to court because the neighbors testified that I hadn't a chance to stop, and the police investigator determined that I hadn't been speeding. Not even negligence. Just terrible, terrible chance.

I read the article in the paper. The boy was only nine, but he was taking special classes at school and was very bright, a good kid, ran a paper route and always took care of his brothers and sisters. A real tear-jerker for the consumption of the subscribers. I thought of killing myself. And then the men in the business suits came back. They had four copies of my script, my screenplay. Four copies is all I had ever made—the original was in my file.

"You see, Mr. Murphy, we have every copy of the screenplay. You will give us the original."

I wasn't in the mood for this. I started closing the door.

"You have so much taste," I said. I didn't care how they got the script, not then. I just wanted to find a way to sleep until when I woke up the boy would still be alive.

They pushed the door open and came in. "You see, Mr. Murphy, until we altered your car yesterday, your path and the boy's never did intersect. We had to try four times to get the timing right, but we finally made it. It's the nice thing about time travel. If you blow it, you can always go back and get it right the next time."

I couldn't believe anyone would want to take credit for the boy's death. "What for?" I asked.

And they told me. Seems the boy was even more talented than anyone thought. He was going to grow up and be a writer. A journalist and critic. And he was going to cause a lot of problems for a particular government some forty years down the line. He was especially going to write three books that would change the whole way of thinking of a large number of people. The wrong way.

"We're all writers ourselves," Meek says to me. "It shouldn't surprise you that we take our writing very seriously. More seriously than *you* do. Writers, the good writers, can change people. And some of the changes aren't very good. By killing that boy yesterday, you see, you stopped a bloody civil war some sixty years from now. We've already checked and there are some unpleasant side effects, but nothing that can't be coped with. Saved seven million lives. You shouldn't feel bad about it."

I remembered the things they had known about me. Things that nobody could have known. I felt stupid because I began to believe they might be for real. I felt afraid because they were calm when they talked of the boy's death. I asked, "Where do I come in? Why me?"

"Oh, it's simple. You're a very good writer. Destined to be the best of your age. Fiction. And this screenplay. In three hundred years they're going to compare you to Shakespeare and the poor old bard will lose. The trouble is, Murphy, you're a godawful hedonist and a pessimist to boot, and if we can just keep you from publishing anything, the whole artistic mood of two centuries will be brightened considerably. Not to mention the prevention of a famine in seventy years. History makes strange connections, Murphy, and you're at the heart of a lot of suffering. If you never publish, the world will be a much better place for everyone."

You weren't there, you didn't hear them. You didn't see them, sitting on my couch, legs crossed, nodding, gesturing like they were saying the most natural thing in the world. From them I learned how to write genuine insanity. Not somebody frothing at the mouth; just somebody sitting there like a good friend, saying impossible things, cruel things, and smiling and getting excited and—Jesus, you don't know. Because I believed them. They knew, you see. And they were *too* insane, even a madman could have come up with a better hoax than that. And I'm making it sound as if I believed them logically, but I didn't, I don't think I can persuade you, either, but trust me—if I know when a man is bluffing or telling the truth, and I do, these two were not bluffing. A child had died, and they knew how many times I had turned the key in the ignition. And there was truth in those terrible eyes when Meek said, "If you willingly refrain from publishing, you will be allowed to live. If you refuse, then you will die within three days. Another writer will kill you—accidently, of course. We only have authority to work through authors."

I asked them why. The answer made me laugh. It seems they were from the Authors' Guild. "It's a matter of responsibility. If you refuse to take responsibility for the future consequences of your acts, we'll have to give the responsibility to somebody else."

And so I asked them why they didn't just kill me in the first place instead of wasting time talking to me.

It was Tree who answered, and the bastard was crying, and he says to me, "Because we love you. We love everything you write. We've learned everything we know about writing from you. And we'll lose it if you die."

They tried to console me by telling me what good company I was in. Thomas Hardy—they made him give up novels and stick to poetry which nobody read and so it was safe. Meek tells me, "Hemingway decided to kill himself instead of waiting for us to do it. And there are some others who only had to refrain from writing a particular book. It hurt them, but Fitzgerald was still able to have a decent career with the other books he could write, and Perelman gave it to us in laughs, since he couldn't be allowed to write his real work. We only bother with great writers. Bad writers aren't a threat to anybody."

We struck a sort of bargain. I could go on writing. But after I had finished everything, I had to burn it. All but the first three pages. "If you finish it at all," says Meek, "we'll have a copy of it here. There's a library here that—uh, I guess the easiest way to say it is that it exists outside time. You'll be published, in a way. Just not in your own time. Not for about eight hundred years. But at least you can write. There are others who have to keep their pens completely still. It breaks our hearts, you know."

I knew all about broken hearts, yes sir, I knew all about it. I burned all but the first three pages.

There's only one reason for a writer to quit writing, and that's when the Censorship Board gets to him. Anybody else who quits is just a gold-plated jackass. "Swap" Morris doesn't even know what real censorship is. It doesn't happen in libraries. It happens on the hoods of cars. So go on, become a real estate broker, sell insurance, follow Santa Claus and clean up the reindeer poo, I don't give a damn. But if you give up something that I will never have, I'm through with you. There's nothing in you for me.

So I write. And Doc reads it and tears it to pieces; everything except this. This he'll never see. This he'd probably kill me for, but what the hell? It'll never get published. No, no I'm too vain. You're reading it, aren't you? See how I put my ego on the line? If I'm really a good enough writer, if my work is important enough to change the world, then a couple of guys in business suits will come make me a proposition I can't refuse, and you won't read this at all, but you are reading it, aren't you? Why am I doing this to myself? Maybe I'm hoping they'll come and give me an excuse to quit writing now, before I find out that I've already written as well as I'm ever going to. But here I thumb my nose at those goddam future critics and they ignore me, they tell exactly what my work is worth.

Or maybe not. Maybe I really *am* good, but my work just happens to have a positive effect, happens not to make any unpleasant waves in the future. Maybe I'm one of the lucky ones who can accomplish something powerful that doesn't need to be censored to protect the future.

Maybe pigs have wings.

The Changed Man and the
King of Words

Once there was a man who loved his son more than life. Once there was a boy who loved his father more than death.

They are not the same story, not really. But I can't tell you one without telling you the other.

The man was Dr. Alvin Bevis, and the boy was his son, Joseph, and the only woman that either of them loved was Connie, who in 1977 married Alvin, with hope and joy, and in 1978 gave birth to Joe on the brink of death and adored them both accordingly. It was an affectionate family. This made it almost certain that they would come to grief.

Connie could have no more children after Joe. She shouldn't even have had *him*. Her doctor called her a damn fool for refusing to abort him in the fourth month when the problems began. "He'll be born retarded. You'll die in labor." To which she answered, "I'll have one child, or I won't believe that I ever lived." In her seventh month they took Joe out of her, womb and all. He was scrawny and little, and the doctor told her to expect him to be mentally deficient and physically uncoordinated. Connie nodded and ignored him. She was lucky. She had Joe, alive, and silently she said to any who pitied her, *I am more a woman than any of you barren ones who still have to worry about the phases of the moon.*

Neither Alvin nor Connie ever believed Joe would be retarded. And soon enough it was clear that he wasn't. He walked at eight months. He talked at twelve months. He had his alphabet at eighteen months. He could read at a second-grade level by the time he was three. He was inquisitive, demanding, independent, disobedient, and exquisitely beautiful, with a shock of copper-colored hair and a face as smooth and deep as a coldwater pool.

His parents watched him devour learning and were sometimes hard pressed to feed him with what he needed. *He will be a great man*, they both whispered to each other in the secret conversations of night. It made them proud; it made them afraid to know that his learning and his safety had, by chance or the grand design of things, been entrusted to them.

Out of all the variety the Bevises offered their son in the first few years of his life, Joe became obsessed with stories. He would bring books and insist that Connie or Alvin read to him, but if it was not a storybook, he quickly ran and got another, until at last they were reading a story. Then he sat imprisoned by the chain of events as the tale unfolded, saying nothing until the story was over. Again and again "Once upon a time," or "There once was a," or "One day the king sent out a proclamation," until Alvin and Connie had every storybook in the house practically memorized. Fairy tales were Joe's favorites, but as time passed, he graduated to movies and contemporary stories and even history.

The problem was not the thirst for tales, however. The conflict began because Joe had to live out his stories. He would get up in the morning and announce that Mommy was Mama Bear, Daddy was Papa Bear, and he was Baby Bear. When he was angry, he would be Goldilocks and run away. Other mornings Daddy would be Rumpelstiltskin, Mommy would be the Farmer's Daughter, and Joe would be the King. Joe was Hansel, Mommy was Gretel, and Alvin was the Wicked Witch.

"Why can't I be Hansel's and Gretel's father?" Alvin asked. He resented being the Wicked Witch. Not that he thought it *meant* anything. He told himself it merely annoyed him to have his son constantly assigning him dialogue and action for the day's activities. Alvin never knew from one hour to the next who he was going to be in his own home.

After a time, mild annoyance gave way to open irritation; if it was a phase Joe was going through, it ought surely to have ended by now. Alvin finally suggested that the boy be taken to a child psychologist. The doctor said it was a phase.

"Which means that sooner or later he'll get over it?" Alvin asked. "Or that you just can't figure out what's going on?"

"Both," said the psychologist cheerfully. "You'll just have to live with it."

But Alvin did not like living with it. He wanted his son to call him Daddy. He *was* the father, after all. Why should he have to put up with his child, no matter how bright the boy was, assigning him silly roles to play whenever he came home? Alvin put his foot down. He refused to answer to any name but Father. And after a little anger and a lot of repeated attempts, Joe finally stopped trying to get his father to play a part. Indeed, as far as Alvin knew, Joe entirely stopped acting out stories.

It was not so, of course. Joe simply acted them out with Connie after Alvin had gone for the day to cut up DNA and put it back together creatively. That was how Joe learned to hide things from his father. He wasn't *lying*; he was just biding his time. Joe was sure that if only he found good enough stories, Daddy would play again.

So when Daddy was home, Joe did not act out stories. Instead he and his father played number and word games, studied elementary Spanish as an introduction to Latin, plinked out simple programs on the Atari, and laughed and romped until Mommy came in and told her boys to calm down before the roof fell in on them. *This is being a father*, Alvin told himself. *I am a good father*. And it was true. It was true, even though every now and then Joe would ask his mother hopefully, "Do you think that Daddy will want to be in *this* story?"

"Daddy just doesn't like to pretend. He likes your stories, but not acting them out."

In 1983 Joe turned five and entered school; that same year Dr. Bevis created a bacterium that lived on acid precipitation and neutralized it. In 1987 Joe left school, because he knew more than any of his teachers; at precisely that time Dr. Bevis began earning royalties on commercial breeding of his bacterium for spot cleanup in acidized bodies of water. The university suddenly became terrified that he might retire and live on his income and take his name away from the school. So he was given a laboratory and twenty assistants and secretaries and an administrative assistant, and from then on Dr. Bevis could pretty well do what he liked with his time.

What he liked was to make sure the research was still going on as carefully and methodically as was proper and in directions that he approved of. Then he went home and became the faculty of one for his son's very private academy.

It was an idyllic time for Alvin.

It was hell for Joe.

Joe loved his father, mind you. Joe played at learning, and they had a wonderful time reading *The Praise of Folly* in the original Latin, duplicating great experiments and then devising experiments of their own—too many things to list. Enough to say that Alvin had never had a graduate student so quick to grasp new ideas, so eager to devise newer ones of his own. How could Alvin have known that Joe was starving to death before his eyes?

For with Father home, Joe and Mother could not play.

Before Alvin had taken him out of school Joe used to read books with his mother. All day at home she would read *Jane Eyre* and Joe would read it in school, hiding it behind copies of *Friends and Neighbors*. Homer. Chaucer. Shakespeare. Twain. Mitchell. Galsworthy. Elswyth Thane. And then in those precious hours after school let out and before Alvin came home from work they would be Ashley and Scarlett, Tibby and Julian, Huck and Jim, Walter and Griselde, Odysseus and Circe. Joe no longer assigned the parts the way he did when he was little. They both knew what book they were reading and they would live within the milieu of that book. Each had to guess from the other's behavior what role had been chosen that particular day; it was a triumphant moment when at last Connie would dare to venture Joe's name for the day, or Joe call Mother by hers. In all the years of playing the games never once did they choose to be the same person; never once did they fail to figure out what role the other played.

Now Alvin was home, and that game was over. No more stolen moments of reading during school. Father frowned on stories. History, yes; lies and poses, no. And so, while Alvin thought that joy had finally come, for Joe and Connie joy was dead.

Their life became one of allusion, dropping phrases to each other out of books, playing subtle characters without ever allowing themselves to utter the other's name. So perfectly did they perform that Alvin never knew what was happening. Just now and then he'd realize that something was going on that he didn't understand.

"What sort of weather is this for January?" Alvin said one day looking out the window at heavy rain.

"Fine," said Joe, and then, thinking of "The Merchant's Tale," he smiled at his mother. "In May we climb trees."

"What?" Alvin asked. "What does that have to do with anything?"

"I just like tree climbing."

"It all depends," said Connie, "on whether the sun dazzles your eyes."

When Connie left the room. Joe asked an innocuous question about teleology, and Alvin put the previous exchange completely out of his mind.

Or rather tried to put it out of his mind. He was no fool. Though Joe and Connie were very subtle, Alvin gradually realized he did not speak the native language of his own home. He was well enough read to catch a reference or two. Turning into swine. Sprinkling dust. "Frankly, I don't give a damn." Remarks that didn't quite fit into the conversation, phrases that seemed strangely resonant. And as he grew more aware of his wife's and his son's private language, the more isolated he felt. His lessons with Joe began to seem not exciting but hollow, as if they were both acting a role. Taking parts in a story. The story of the loving father-teacher and the dutiful, brilliant student-son. It had been the best time of Alvin's life, better than any life he had created in the lab, but that was when he had believed it. Now it was just a play. His son's real life was somewhere else.

I didn't like playing the parts he gave me, years ago, Alvin thought. *Does he like playing the part that I have given him?*

"You've gone as far as I can take you," Alvin said at breakfast one day, "in everything, except biology of course. So I'll guide your studies in biology, and for everything else I'm hiring advanced graduate students in various fields at the university. A different one each day."

Joe's eyes went deep and distant. "You won't be my teacher anymore?"

"Can't teach you what I don't know." Alvin said. And he went back to the lab. Went back and with delicate cruelty tore apart a dozen cells and made them into something other than themselves, whether they would or not.

Back at home. Joe and Connie looked at each other in puzzlement. Joe was thirteen. He was getting tall and felt shy and awkward before his mother. They had been three years without stories together. With Father there, they had played at being prisoners, passing messages under the guard's very nose. Now there was no guard, and without the need for secrecy there was no message anymore. Joe took to going outside and reading or playing obsessively at the computer; more doors were locked in the Bevis home than had ever been locked before.

Joe dreamed terrifying, gentle nightmares, dreamed of the same thing, over and over; the setting was different, but always the story was the same. He dreamed of being on a boat, and the gunwale began to crumble wherever he touched it, and he tried to warn his parents, but they wouldn't listen, they leaned, it broke away under their hands, and they fell into the sea, drowning. He dreamed that he was bound up in a web, tied like a spider's victim, but the spider never, never, never came to taste of him, left him there to desiccate in helpless bondage, though he cried out and struggled. How could he explain such dreams to his parents? He remembered Joseph in Genesis, who spoke too much of dreams; remembered Cassandra; remembered Iocaste, who thought to slay her child for fear of oracles. *I am caught up in a story,* Joe thought, *from which I cannot escape. Each change is a fall; each fall tears me from myself. If I cannot be the people of the tales, who am I then?*

Life was normal enough for all that. Breakfast lunch dinner, sleep wake sleep, work earn spend own, use break fix. All the cycles of ordinary life played out despite the shadow of inevitable ends. One day Alvin and his son were in a bookstore, the Gryphon, which had the complete Penguin Classics. Alvin was browsing through the titles to see what might be of some use when he noticed Joe was no longer following him.

His son, all the slender five feet nine inches of him, was standing half the store away bent in avid concentration over something on the counter. Alvin felt a terrible yearning for his son. He was so beautiful and yet somehow in these dozen and one years of Joe's life. Alvin had lost him. Now Joe was nearing manhood and very soon it would be too late. *When did he cease to be mine?* Alvin wondered. *When did he become so much his mother's son? Why must he be as beautiful as she and yet have the mind he has? He is Apollo.* Alvin said to himself.

And in that moment he knew what he had lost. By calling his son Apollo he had told himself what he had taken from his son. A connection between stories the child acted out and his knowledge of who he was. The connection was so real it was almost tangible and yet Alvin could not put it into words could not bear the knowledge and so and so and so.

Just as he was sure he had the truth of things it slipped away. Without words his memory could not hold it, lost the understanding the moment it came. *I knew it all and I have already forgotten.* Angry at himself, Alvin strode to his son and realized that Joe was not doing anything intelligent at all. He had a deck of tarot cards spread before him. He was doing a reading.

"Cross my palms with silver" said Alvin. He thought he was making a joke but his anger spoke too loudly in his voice Joe looked up with shame on his face. Alvin cringed inside himself. *Just by speaking to you I wound you.* Alvin wanted to apologize but he had no strategy for that so he tried to affirm that it had been a joke by making another. "Discovering the secrets of the universe?"

Joe half-smiled and quickly gathered up the cards and put them away.

No Alvin said "No, you were interested: you don't have to put them away."

"It's just nonsense." Joe said.

You're lying. Alvin thought.

"All the meanings are so vague they could fit just about anything." Joe laughed mirthlessly.

"You looked pretty interested."

"I was just you know wondering how to program a computer for this wondering whether I could do a program that would make it make some sense. Not just the random fall of the cards you know. A way to make it respond to who a person really is. Cut through all the

"Yes?

"Just wondering"

"Cut through all the ?"

"Stories we tell ourselves. All the lies that we believe about ourselves. About who we really are."

Something didn't ring true in the boy's words, Alvin knew. Something was wrong. And because in Alvin's world nothing could long exist unexplained he decided the boy seemed awkward because his father had made him ashamed of his own curiosity. *I am ashamed that I have made you ashamed*, Alvin thought. *So I will buy you the cards.*

"I'll buy the cards. And the book you were looking at."

"No Dad." said Joe.

"No it's all right Why not? Play around with the computer. See if you can turn this nonsense into something. What the hell, you might come up with some good graphics and sell the program for a bundle." Alvin laughed. So did Joe. Even Joe's *laugh* was a lie.

What Alvin didn't know was this: Joe was not ashamed. Joe was merely afraid. For he had laid out the cards as the book instructed, but he had not needed the explanations, had not needed the names of the faces. He had known their names at once, had known their faces. It was Creon who held the sword and the scales. Ophelia, naked wreathed in green, with man and falcon, bull and lion around. Ophelia who danced in her madness. And I was once the boy with the starflower in the sixth cup, giving to my child-mother, when gifts were possible between us. The cards were not dice, they were names, and he laid them out in stories drawing them in order from the deck in a pattern that he knew was largely the story of his life. All the names that he had borne were in these cards, and all the shapes of past and future dwelt here, waiting to be dealt. It was this that frightened him. He had been deprived of stories for so long, his own story of father, mother, son was so fragile now that he was madly grasping at anything; Father mocked, but Joe looked at the story of the cards, and he believed. *I do not want to take these home. It puts myself wrapped in a silk in my own hands.* "Please don't," he said to his father.

But Alvin, who knew better, bought them anyway, hoping to please his son.

Joe stayed away from the cards for a whole day. He had only touched them the once; surely he need not toy with this fear again. It was irrational, mere wish fulfillment, Joe told himself. *The cards mean nothing. They are not to be feared. I can touch them and learn no truth from them.* And yet all his rationalism, all his certainty that the cards were meaningless, were, he knew, merely lies he was telling to persuade himself to try the cards again, and this time seriously.

"What did you bring *those* home for?" Mother asked in the other room.

Father said nothing. Joe knew from the silence that Father did not want to make any explanation that might be overheard.

"They're silly," said Mother. "I thought you were a scientist and a skeptic. I thought you didn't believe in things like this."

"It was just a lark," Father lied. "I bought them for Joe to plink around with. He's thinking of doing a computer program to make the cards respond somehow to people's personalities. The boy has a right to play now and then."

And in the family room, where the toy computer sat mute on the shelf, Joe tried not to think of Odysseus walking away from the eight cups, treading the lip of the ocean's basin, his back turned to the wine. *Forty-eight kilobytes and two little disks. This isn't computer enough for what I mean to do,* Joe thought. *I will not do it, of course. But with Father's computer from his office upstairs, with the hard disk and the right type of interface, perhaps there is space and time enough for all the operations. Of course I will not do it. I do not care to do it. I do not dare to do it.*

At two in the morning he got up from his bed, where he could not sleep, went downstairs, and began to program the graphics of the tarot deck upon the screen. But in each picture he made changes, for he knew that the artist, gifted as he was, had made mistakes. Had not understood that the Page of Cups was a buffoon with a giant phallus, from which flowed the sea. Had not known that the Queen of Swords was a statue and it was her throne that was alive, an angel groaning in agony at the stone burden she had to bear. The child at the Gate of Ten Stars was being eaten by the old man's dogs. The man hanging upside down with crossed legs and peace upon his face, he wore no halo; his hair was afire. And the Queen of Pentacles had just given birth to a bloody star, whose father was not the King of Pentacles, that poor cuckold.

And as the pictures and their stories came to him, he began to hear the echoes of all the other stories he had read. Cassandra, Queen of Swords, flung her bladed words, and people batted them out of the air like flies, when if they had only caught them and used them, they would not have met the future unarmed. For a moment Odysseus bound to the mast was the Hanged Man; in the right circumstances. Macbeth could show up in the ever-trusting Page of Cups, or crush himself under the ambitious Queen of Pentacles, Queen of Coins if she crossed him. The cards held tales of power, tales of pain, in the invisible threads that bound them to one another. Invisible threads, but Joe knew they were there, and he had to make the pictures right, make the program right, so that he could find true stories when he read the cards.

Through the night he labored until each picture was right: the job was only begun when he fell asleep at last. His parents were worried on finding him there in the morning, but they hadn't the heart to waken him. When he awoke, he was alone in the house, and he began again immediately, drawing the cards on the TV screen, storing them in the computer's memory; as for his own memory, he needed no help to recall them all, for he knew their names and their stories and was beginning to understand how their names changed every time they came together.

By evening it was done, along with a brief randomizer program that dealt the cards. The pictures were right. The names were right. But this time when the computer spread the cards before him—This is you, this covers you, this crosses you—it was meaningless. The computer could not do what hands could do. It could not understand and unconsciously deal the cards. It was not a randomizer program that was needed at all, for the shuffling of the tarot was not done by chance.

"May I tinker a little with your computer?" Joe asked.

"The hard disk?" Father looked doubtful. "I don't want you to open it, Joe. I don't want to try to come up with another ten thousand dollars this week if something goes wrong." Behind his words was a worry: *This business with the tarot cards has gone far enough, and I'm sorry I bought them for you, and I don't want you to use the computer, especially if it would make this obsession any stronger.*

"Just an interface, Father. You don't use the parallel port anyway, and I can put it back afterward."

"The Atari and the hard disk aren't even compatible."

"I know," said Joe.

But in the end there really couldn't be much argument. Joe knew computers better than Alvin did, and they both knew that what Joe took apart, Joe could put together. It took days of tinkering with hardware and plinking at the program. During that time Joe did nothing else. In the beginning he tried to distract himself. At lunch he told Mother about books they ought to read; at dinner he spoke to Father about Newton and Einstein until Alvin had to remind him that he was a biologist, not a mathematician. No one was fooled by these attempts at breaking the obsession. The tarot program drew Joe back after every meal, after every interruption, until at last he began to refuse meals and ignore the interruptions entirely.

"You have to eat. You can't die for this silly game," said Mother.

Joe said nothing. She set a sandwich by him, and he ate some of it.

"Joe, this had gone far enough. Get yourself under control," said Father.

Joe didn't look up. "I'm under control," he said, and he went on working.

After six days Alvin came and stood between Joe and the television set. "This nonsense will end now," Alvin said. "You are behaving like a boy with serious problems. The most obvious cure is to disconnect the computer, which I will do if you do not stop working on this absurd program at once. We try to give you freedom, Joe, but when you do this to us and to yourself, then—"

"That's all right," said Joe. "I've mostly finished it anyway." He got up and went to bed and slept for fourteen hours.

Alvin was relieved. "I thought he was losing his mind."

Connie was more worried than ever. "What do you think he'll do if it doesn't work?"

"Work? How could it work? Work at what? Cross my palm with silver and I'll tell your future."

"Haven't you been *listening* to him?"

"He hasn't said a word in days."

"He believes in what he's doing. He thinks his program will tell the truth."

Alvin laughed. "Maybe your doctor, what's-his-name, maybe he was right. Maybe there was brain damage after all."

Connie looked at him in horror. "God, Alvin."

"A joke, for Christ's sake."

"It wasn't funny."

They didn't talk about it, but in the middle of the night, at different times, each of them got up and went into Joe's room to look at him in his sleep.

Who are you? Connie asked silently. *What are you going to do if this project of yours is a failure? What are you going to do if it succeeds?*

Alvin, however, just nodded. He refused to be worried. Phases and stages of life. Children go through times of madness as they grow.

Be a lunatic thirteen-year-old, Joe, if you must. You'll return to reality soon enough. You're my son, and I know that you'll prefer reality in the long run.

The next evening Joe insisted that his father help him test the program. "It won't work on me," Alvin said. "I don't believe in it. It's like faith healing and taking vitamin C for colds. It never works on skeptics."

Connie stood small near the refrigerator. Alvin noticed the way she seemed to retreat from the conversation.

"Did you try it?" Alvin asked her.

She nodded.

"Mom did it four times for me," Joe said gravely.

"Couldn't get it right the first time?" Father asked. It was a joke.

"Got it right every time," Joe said.

Alvin looked at Connie. She met his gaze at first, but then looked away in—what? Fear? Shame? Embarrassment? Alvin couldn't tell. But he sensed that something painful had happened while he was at work. "Should I do it?" Alvin asked her.

"No," Connie whispered.

"Please," Joe said. "How can I test it if you won't help? I can't tell if it's right or wrong unless I know the people doing it."

"What kind of fortuneteller are you?" Alvin asked. "You're supposed to be able to tell the future of strangers."

"I don't tell the future," Joe said. "The program just tells the truth."

"Ah, truth!" said Alvin. "Truth about what?"

"Who you really are."

"Am I in disguise?"

"It tells your names. It tells your story. Ask Mother if it doesn't."

"Joe," Alvin said, "I'll play this little game with you. But don't expect me to regard it as *true*. I'll do almost anything for you, Joe, but I won't lie for you."

"I know."

"Just so you understand."

"I understand."

Alvin sat down at the keyboard. From the kitchen came a sound like the whine a cringing hound makes, back in its throat. It was Connie, and she was terrified. Her fear, whatever caused it, was contagious. Alvin shuddered and then ridiculed himself for letting this upset him. He was in control, and it was absurd to be afraid. He wouldn't be snowed by his own son.

"What do I do?"

"Just type things in."

"What things?"

"Whatever comes to mind."

"Words? Numbers? How do I know what to write if you don't tell me?"

"It doesn't matter what you write. Just so you write whatever you feel like writing."

I don't feel like writing anything. Alvin thought. *I don't feel like humoring this nonsense another moment.* But he could not say so, not to Joe; he had to be the patient father, giving this absurdity a fair chance. He began to come up with numbers, with words. But after a few moments there was no randomness, no free association in his choice. It was not in Alvin's nature to let chance guide his choices. Instead he began reciting on the keyboard the long strings of genetic-code information on his most recent bacterial subjects, fragments of names, fragments of numeric data, progressing in order through the DNA. He knew as he did it that he was cheating his son, that Joe wanted something of himself. But he told himself, *What could be more a part of me than something I made?*

"Enough?" he asked Joe.

Joe shrugged. "Do you think it is?"

"I could have done five words and you would have been satisfied?"

"If you think you're through, you're through," Joe said quietly.

"Oh, you're very good at this," Alvin said. "Even the hocus-pocus."

"You're through then?"

"Yes."

Joe started the program running. He leaned back and waited. He could sense his father's impatience, and he found himself relishing the wait. The whirring and clicking of the disk drive. And then the cards began appearing on the screen. This is you. This covers you. This crosses you. This is above you, below you, before you, behind you. Your foundation and your house, your death and your name. Joe waited for what had come before, what had come so predictably, the stories that had flooded in upon him when he read for his mother and for himself a dozen times before. But the stories did not come. Because the cards were the same. Over and over again, the King of Swords.

Joe looked at it and understood at once. Father had lied. Father had consciously controlled his input, had ordered it in some way that told the cards that they were being forced. The program had not failed. Father simply would not be read. The King of Swords, by himself, was power, as all the Kings were power. The King of Pentacles was the power of money, the power of the bribe. The King of Wands was the power of life, the power to make new. The King of Cups was the power of negation and obliteration, the power of murder and sleep. And the King of Swords was the power of words that others would believe. Swords could say, "I will kill you," and be believed, and so be obeyed. Swords could say, "I love you," and be believed, and so be adored. Swords could lie. And all his father had given him was lies. What Alvin didn't know was that even the choice of lies told the truth.

"Edmund," said Joe. Edmund was the lying bastard in *King Lear*.

"What?" asked Father.

"We are only what nature makes us. And nothing more."

"You're getting this from the cards?"

Joe looked at his father, expressing nothing.

"It's all the same card," said Alvin.

"I know," said Joe.

"What's this supposed to be?"

"A waste of time," said Joe. Then he got up and walked out of the room.

Alvin sat there, looking at the little tarot cards laid out on the screen. As he watched, the display changed, each card in turn being surrounded by a thin line and then blown up large, nearly filling the screen. The King of Swords every time. With the point of his sword coming out of his mouth, and his hands clutching at his groin. *Surely,* Alvin thought, *that was not what was drawn on the Waite deck.*

Connie stood near the kitchen doorway, leaning on the refrigerator. "And that's all?" she asked.

"Should there be more?" Alvin asked.

"God," she said.

"What happened with you?"

"Nothing," she said, walking calmly out of the room. Alvin heard her rush up the stairs. And he wondered how things got out of control like this.

Alvin could not make up his mind how to feel about his son's project. It was silly, and Alvin wanted nothing to do with it, wished he'd never bought the cards for him. For days on end Alvin would stay at the laboratory until late at night and rush back again in the morning without so much as eating breakfast with his family. Then, exhausted from lack of sleep, he would get up late, come downstairs, and pretend for the whole day that nothing unusual was going on. On such days he discussed Joe's readings with him, or his own genetic experiments; sometimes, when the artificial cheer had been maintained long enough to be believed, Alvin would even discuss Joe's tarot program. It was at such times that Alvin offered to provide Joe with introductions, to get him better computers to work with, to advise him on the strategy of development and publication. Afterward Alvin always regretted having helped Joe, because what Joe was doing was a shameful waste of a brilliant mind. It also did not make Joe love him any more.

Yet as time passed, Alvin realized that other people were taking Joe seriously. A group of psychologists administered batteries of tests to hundreds of subjects—who had also put random data into Joe's program. When Joe interpreted the tarot readouts for these people, the correlation was statistically significant. Joe himself rejected those results, because the psychological tests were probably invalid measurements themselves. More important to him was the months of work in clinics, doing readings with people the doctors knew intimately. Even the most skeptical of the participating psychologists had to admit that Joe knew things about people that he could not possibly know. And most of the psychologists said openly that Joe not only confirmed much that they already knew but also provided brilliant new insights. "It's like stepping into my patient's mind," one of them told Alvin.

"My son is brilliant, Dr. Fryer, and I want him to succeed, but surely this mumbo jumbo can't be more than luck."

Dr. Fryer only smiled and took a sip of wine. "Joe tells me that you have never submitted to the test yourself."

Alvin almost argued, but it was true. He never had *submitted,* even though he went through the motions. "I've seen it in action." Alvin said.

"Have you? Have you seen his results with someone you know well?"

Alvin shook his head, then smiled. "I figured that since I didn't believe in it, it wouldn't work around me."

"It isn't magic."

"It isn't science, either," said Alvin.

"No, you're right. Not science at all. But just because it isn't science doesn't mean it isn't true."

"Either it's science or it isn't."

"What a clear world you live in," said Dr. Fryer. "All the lines neatly drawn. We've run double-blind tests on his program, Dr. Bevis. Without knowing it, he has analyzed data taken from the same patient on different days, under different circumstances: the patient has even been given different instructions in some of the samples so that it wasn't random. And you know what happened?"

Alvin knew but did not say so.

"Not only did his program read substantially the same for all the different random inputs for the same patient, but the program also spotted the ringers. Easily. And then it turned out that the ringers were a consistent result for the woman who wrote the test we happened to use for the non-random input. Even when it shouldn't have worked, it worked."

"Very impressive," said Alvin, sounding as unimpressed as he could.

"It *is* impressive."

"I don't know about that," said Alvin. "So the cards are consistent. How do we know that they *mean* anything, or that what they mean is *true*?"

"Hasn't it occurred to you that your *son* is why it's true?"

Alvin tapped his spoon on the tablecloth, providing a muffled rhythm.

"Your son's computer program objectifies random input. But only your son can read it. To me that says that it's his *mind* that makes his method work, not his program. If we could figure out what's going on inside your son's head, Dr. Bevis, then his method would be science. Until then it's an art. But whether it is art or science, he tells the truth."

"Forgive me for what might seem a slight to your profession," said Alvin, "but how in God's name do *you* know whether what he says is true?"

Dr. Fryer smiled and cocked his head. "Because I can't conceive of it being wrong. We can't test his interpretations the way we tested his program. I've tried to find objective tests. For instance, whether his findings agree with my notes. But my notes mean nothing, because until your son reads my patients, I really don't understand them. And after he reads them, I can't conceive of any other view of them. Before you dismiss me as hopelessly subjective, remember please, Dr. Bevis, that I have every reason to fear and fight against your son's work. It undoes everything that I have believed in. It undermines my own life's work. And Joe is just like you. He doesn't think psychology is a science, either. Forgive *me* for what might seem a slight to your son, but he is troubled and cold and difficult to work with. I don't like him much. So why do I believe him?"

"That's your problem, isn't it?"

"On the contrary, Dr. Bevis. Everyone who's seen what Joe does, believes it. Except for you. I think that most definitely makes it *your* problem."

Dr. Fryer was wrong. Not everyone believed Joe.

"No," said Connie.

"No what?" asked Alvin. It was breakfast. Joe hadn't come downstairs yet. Alvin and Connie hadn't said a word since "Here's the eggs" and "Thanks."

Connie was drawing paths with her fork through the yolk stains on her plate. "Don't do another reading with Joe."

"I wasn't planning on it."

"Dr. Fryer told you to believe it, didn't he?" She put her fork down.

"But I didn't believe Dr. Fryer."

Connie got up from the table and began washing the dishes. Alvin watched her as she rattled the plates to make as much noise as possible. Nothing was normal anymore. Connie was angry as she washed the dishes. There was a dishwasher, but she was scrubbing everything by hand. Nothing was as it should be. Alvin tried to figure out why he felt such dread.

"You will do a reading with Joe," said Connie, "*because* you don't believe Dr. Fryer. You always insist on verifying everything for yourself. If you believe, you must question your belief. If you doubt, you doubt your own disbelief. Am I not right?"

"No." *Yes.*

"And I'm telling you this once to have faith in your doubt. There is no truth whatever in his God-*damned* tarot."

In all these years of marriage, Alvin could not remember Connie using such coarse language. But then she hadn't said *god-damn*; she had said God-*damned*, with all the theological overtones.

"I mean," she went on, filling the silence. "I mean how can anyone take this seriously? The card he calls Strength—a woman closing a lion's mouth, yes, fine, but then he makes up a God-*damned* story about it, how the lion wanted her baby and she *fed it to him*." She looked at Alvin with fear. "It's sick, isn't it?"

"He said that?"

"And the Devil, forcing the lovers to stay together. He's supposed to be the firstborn child, chaining Adam and Eve together. That's why Iocaste and Laios tried to kill Oedipus. Because they hated each other, and the baby would force them to stay together. But then they stayed together anyway because of shame at what they had done to an innocent child. And then they told everyone that asinine lie about the oracle and her prophecy."

"He's read too many books."

Connie trembled. "If he does a reading of you, I'm afraid of what will happen."

"If he feeds me crap like that, Connie, I'll just bite my lip. No fights, I promise."

She touched his chest. Not his shirt, his chest. It felt as if her finger burned right through the cloth. "I'm not worried that you'll fight," she said. "I'm afraid that you'll believe him."

"Why would I believe him?"

"We don't live in the Tower, Alvin!"

"Of course we don't."

"I'm not Iocaste, Alvin!"

"Of course you aren't."

"Don't believe him. Don't believe anything he says."

"Connie, don't get so upset." Again: "Why would I believe him?"

She shook her head and walked out of the room. The water was still running in the sink. She hadn't said a word. But her answer rang in the room as if she had spoken: "Because it's true."

*   *   *

Alvin tried to sort it out for hours. Oedipus and Iocaste. Adam, Eve, and the Devil. The mother feeding her baby to the lion. As Dr. Fryer had said, it isn't the cards, it isn't the program, it's Joe. Joe and the stories in his head. Is there a story in the world that Joe hasn't read? All the tales that man has told himself, all the visions of the world, and Joe knew them. Knew and believed them. Joe the repository of all the world's lies, and now he was telling the lies back, and they believed him, every one of them believed him.

No matter how hard Alvin tried to treat this nonsense with the contempt it deserved, one thing kept coming back to him. Joe's program had known that Alvin was lying, that Alvin was playing games, not telling the truth. Joe's program was valid at least that far. *If his method can pass that negative test, how can I call myself a scientist if I disbelieve it before I've given it the* positive test *as well?*

That night while Joe was watching M*A*S*H reruns, Alvin came into the family room to talk to him. It always startled Alvin to see his son watching normal television shows, especially old ones from Alvin's own youth. The same boy who had read *Ulysses* and made sense of it without reading a single commentary, and he was laughing out loud at the television.

It was only after he had sat beside his son and watched for a while that Alvin realized that Joe was not laughing at the places where the laugh track did. He was not laughing at the jokes. He was laughing at Hawkeye himself.

"What was so funny?" asked Alvin.

"Hawkeye," said Joe.

"He was being serious."

"I know," said Joe. "But he's so sure he's *right*, and everybody believes him. Don't you think that's funny?"

As a matter of fact, no, I don't. "I want to give it another try, Joe," said Alvin.

Even though it was an abrupt change of subject, Joe understood at once, as if he had long been waiting for his father to speak. They got into the car, and Alvin drove them to the university. The computer people immediately made one of the full-color terminals available. This time Alvin allowed himself to be truly random, not thinking at all about what he was choosing, avoiding any meaning as he typed. When he was sick of typing, he looked at Joe for permission to be through. Joe shrugged. Alvin entered one more set of letters and then said, "Done."

Alvin entered a single command that told the computer to start analyzing the input, and father and son sat together to watch the story unfold.

After a seemingly eternal wait, in which neither of them said a word, a picture of a card appeared on the screen.

"This is you," said Joe. It was the King of Swords.

"What does it mean?" asked Alvin.

"Very little by itself."

"Why is the sword coming out of his mouth?"

"Because he kills by the words of his mouth."

Father nodded. "And why is he holding his crotch?"

"I don't know."

"I thought you knew," said Father.

"I don't know until I see the other cards." Joe pressed the return key, and a new card almost completely covered the old one. A thin blue line appeared around it, and then it was blown up to fill the screen. It was Judgment, an angel blowing a trumpet, awakening the dead, who were gray with corruption, standing in their graves. "This covers you," said Joe.

"What does it mean?"

"It's how you spend your life. Judging the dead."

"Like God? You're saying I think I'm God?"

"It's what you do, Father," said Joe. "You judge everything. You're a scientist. I can't help what the cards say."

"I study life."

"You break life down into its pieces. Then you make your judgment. Only when it's all in fragments like the flesh of the dead."

Alvin tried to hear anger or bitterness in Joe's voice, but Joe was calm, matter-of-fact, for all the world like a doctor with a good bedside manner. Or like a historian telling the simple truth.

Joe pressed the key, and on the small display another card appeared, again on top of the first two, but horizontally. "This crosses you," said Joe. And the card was outlined in blue, and zoomed close. It was the Devil.

"What does it mean, crossing me?"

"Your enemy, your obstacle. The son of Laios and Iocaste."

Alvin remembered that Connie had mentioned Iocaste. "How similar is this to what you told Connie?" he asked.

Joe looked at him impassively. "How can I know after only three cards?"

Alvin waved him to go on.

A card above. "This crowns you." The Two of Wands, a man holding the world in his hands, staring off into the distance, with two small saplings growing out of the stone parapet beside him. "The crown is what you think you are, the story you tell yourself about yourself. Lifegiver, the God of Genesis, the Prince whose kiss awakens Sleeping Beauty and Snow White."

A card below. "This is beneath you, what you most fear to become." A man lying on the ground, ten swords piercing him in a row. He did not bleed.

"I've never lain awake at night afraid that someone would stab me to death."

Joe looked at him placidly. "But, Father, I told you, swords are words as often as not. What you fear is death at the hands of storytellers. According to the cards, you're the sort of man who would have killed the messenger who brought bad news."

According to the cards, or according to you? But Alvin held his anger and said nothing.

A card to the right. "This is behind you, the story of your past." A man in a sword-studded boat, poling the craft upstream, a woman and child sitting bowed in front of him. "Hansel and Gretel sent into the sea in a leaky boat."

"It doesn't look like a brother and sister," said Alvin. "It looks like a mother and child."

"Ah," said Joe. A card to the left. "This is before you, where you know your course will lead." A sarcophagus with a knight sculpted in stone upon it, a bird resting on his head.

Death, thought Alvin. Always a safe prediction. And yet not safe at all. The cards themselves seemed malevolent. They all depicted situations that cried out with agony or fear. That was the gimmick, Alvin decided. Potent enough pictures will seem to be important whether they really mean anything or not. Heavy with meaning like a pregnant woman, they can be made to bear anything.

"It isn't death," said Joe.

Alvin was startled to have his thoughts so appropriately interrupted.

"It's a monument after you're dead. With your words engraved on it and above it. Blind Homer. Jesus. Mahomet. To have your words read like scripture."

And for the first time Alvin was genuinely frightened by what his son had found. Not that this future frightened him. Hadn't he forbidden himself to hope for it, he wanted it so much? No, what he feared was the way he felt himself say, silently, *Yes, yes, this is True. I will not be flattered into belief,* he said to himself. But underneath every layer of doubt that he built between himself and the cards he believed. Whatever Joe told him, he would believe, and so he denied belief now, not because of disbelief but because he was afraid. Perhaps that was why he had doubted from the start.

Next the computer placed a card in the lower right-hand corner. "This is your house." It was the Tower, broken by lightning, a man and a woman falling from it, surrounded by tears of flame.

A card directly above it. "This answers you." A man under a tree, beside a stream, with a hand coming from a small cloud, giving him a cup. "Elijah by the brook, and the ravens feed him."

And above that a man walking away from a stack of eight cups, with a pole and traveling cloak. The pole is a wand, with leaves growing from it. The cups are arranged so that a space is left where a ninth cup had been. "This saves you."

And then, at the top of the vertical file of four cards, Death. "This ends it." A bishop, a woman, and a child kneeling before Death on a horse. The horse is trampling the corpse of a man who had been a king. Beside the man lie his crown and a golden sword. In the distance a ship is foundering in a swift river. The sun is rising between pillars in the east. And Death holds a leafy wand in his hand, with a sheaf of wheat bound to it at the top. A banner of life over the corpse of the king. "This ends it," said Joe definitively.

Alvin waited, looking at the cards, waiting for Joe to explain it. But Joe did not explain. He just gazed at the monitor and then suddenly got to his feet. "Thank you, Father," he said. "It's all clear now."

"To you it's clear," Alvin said.

"Yes," said Joe. "Thank you very much for not lying this time." Then Joe made as if to leave.

"Hey, wait," Alvin said. "Aren't you going to explain it to me?"

"No," said Joe.

"Why not?"

"You wouldn't believe me."

Alvin was not about to admit to anyone, least of all himself, that he did believe. "I still want to know. I'm curious. Can't I be curious?"

Joe studied his father's face. "I told Mother, and she hasn't spoken a natural word to me since."

So it was not just Alvin's imagination. The tarot program had driven a wedge between Connie and Joe. He'd been right. "I'll speak a natural word or two every day, I promise," Alvin said.

"That's what I'm afraid of," Joe said.

"Son," Alvin said. "Dr. Fryer told me that the stories you tell, the way you put things together, is the closest thing to truth about people that he's ever heard. Even if I don't believe it, don't I have the right to hear the truth?"

"I don't know if it *is* the truth. Or if there is such a thing."

"There is. The way things *are,* that's truth."

"But how *are* things, with people? What causes me to feel the way I do or act the way I do? Hormones? Parents? Social patterns? All the causes or purposes of all our acts are just stories we tell ourselves, stories we believe or disbelieve, changing all the time. But still we live, still we act, and all those acts have *some* kind of cause. The patterns all fit together into a web that connects everyone who's ever lived with everyone else. And every new person changes the web, adds to it, changes the connections, makes it all different. That's what I find with this program, how you believe you fit into the web."

"Not how I *really* fit?"

Joe shrugged. "How can I know? How can I measure it? I discover the stories that you believe most secretly, the stories that control your acts. But the very telling of the story changes the way you believe. Moves some things into the open, changes who you *are*. I undo my work by doing it."

"Then undo your work with me, and tell me the truth."

"I don't want to."

"Why not?"

"Because I'm in your story."

Alvin spoke then more honestly than he ever meant to. "Then for God's sake tell me the story, because I don't know who the hell you are."

Joe walked back to his chair and sat down. "I am Goneril and Regan, because you made me act out the lie that you needed to hear. I am Oedipus, because you pinned my ankles together and left me exposed on the hillside to save your own future."

"I have loved you more than life."

"You were always afraid of me, Father. Like Lear, afraid that I wouldn't care for you when I was still vigorous and you were enfeebled by age. Like Laios, terrified that my power would overshadow you. So you took *control*; you put me out of my place."

"I gave years to educating you—"

"Educating me in order to make me forever your shadow, your student. When the only thing that I really loved was the one thing that would free me from you—all the stories."

"Damnable stupid fictions."

"No more stupid than the fiction *you* believe. Your story of little cells and DNA, your story that there is such a thing as reality that can be objectively perceived. God, what an idea, to see with inhuman eyes, without interpretation. That's exactly how stones see, without interpretation, because without interpretation there isn't any *sight*."

"I think I know that much at least," Alvin said, trying to feel as contemptuous as he sounded. "I never said I was objective."

"*Scientific* was the word. What could be verified was scientific. That was all that you would ever let me study, what could be verified. The trouble is, Father, that nothing in the world that matters at all is verifiable. What makes us who we are is forever tenuous, fragile, the web of a spider eaten and remade every day. I can never see out of your eyes. Yet I can never see any other way than through the eyes of every storyteller who ever taught me how to see. That was what you did to me, Father. You forbade me to hear any storyteller but you. It was *your* reality I had to surrender to. *Your* fiction I had to believe."

Alvin felt his past slipping out from under him. "If I had know those games of make-believe were so important to you, I wouldn't have—"

"You knew they were that important to me," Joe said coldly. "Why else would you have bothered to forbid me? But my mother dipped me into the water, all but my heel, and I got all the power you tried to keep from me. You see, Mother was not Griselde. She wouldn't kill her children for her husband's sake. When you exiled me, you exiled her. We lived the stories together as long as we were free."

"What do you mean?"

"Until you came home to teach me. We were free until then. We acted out all the stories that we could. Without you."

It conjured for Alvin the ridiculous image of Connie playing Goldilocks and the Three Bears day after day for years. He laughed in spite of himself, laughed sharply, for only a moment.

Joe took the laugh all wrong. Or perhaps took it exactly right. He took his father by the wrist and gripped him so tightly that Alvin grew afraid. Joe was stronger than Alvin had thought. "Grendel feels the touch of Beowulf on his hand," Joe whispered, "and he thinks, Perhaps I should have stayed at home tonight. Perhaps I am not hungry after all."

Alvin tried for a moment to pull his arm away but could not. *What have I done to you, Joe?* he shouted inside himself. Then he relaxed his arm and surrendered to the tale. "Tell me my story from the cards," he said. "Please."

Without letting go of his father's arm, Joe began. "You are Lear, and your kingdom is great. Your whole life is shaped so that you will live forever in stone, in memory. Your dream is to create life. You thought I would be such life, as malleable as the little worlds you make from DNA. But from the moment I was born you were afraid of me. I couldn't be taken apart and recombined like all your little animals. And you were afraid that I would steal the swords from your sepulchre. You were afraid that you would live on as Joseph Bevis's father, instead of me forever being Alvin Bevis's son."

"I was jealous of my child," said Alvin, trying to sound skeptical.

"Like the father rat that devours his babies because he knows that someday they will challenge his supremacy, yes. It's the oldest pattern in the world, a tale older than teeth."

"Go on, this is quite fascinating." *I refuse to care.*

"All the storytellers know how this tale ends. Every time a father tries to change the future by controlling his children, it ends the same. Either the children lie, like Goneril and Regan, and pretend to be what he made them, or the children tell the truth, like Cordelia, and the father casts them out. I tried to tell the truth, but then together Mother and I lied to you. It was so much easier, and it kept me alive. She was Grim the Fisher, and she saved me alive."

Iocaste and Laios and Oedipus. "I see where this is going," Alvin said. "I thought you were bright enough not to believe in that Freudian nonsense about the Oedipus complex."

"Freud thought he was telling the story of all mankind when he was only telling his own. Just because the story of Oedipus isn't true for everyone doesn't mean that it isn't true for me. But don't worry, Father. I don't have to kill you in the forest in order to take possession of your throne."

"I'm not worried." It was a lie. It was a truthful understatement.

"Laios died only because he would not let his son pass along the road."

"Pass along any road you please."

"And I am the Devil. You and Mother were in Eden until I came. Because of me you were cast out. And now you're in hell."

"How neatly it all fits."

"For you to achieve your dream, you had to kill me with your story. When I lay there with your blades in my back, only then could you be sure that your sepulchre was safe. When you exiled me in a boat I could not live in, only then could you be safe, you thought. But I am the Horn Child, and the boat bore me quickly across the sea to my true kingdom."

"This isn't anything coming from the computer," said Alvin. "This is just you being a normal resentful teenager. Just a phase that everyone goes through."

Joe's grip on Alvin's arm only tightened. "I didn't die, I didn't wither, I have my power now, and you're not safe. Your house is broken, and you and Mother are being thrown from it to your destruction, and you know it. Why did you come to me, except that you knew you were being destroyed?"

Again Alvin tried to find a way to fend off Joe's story with ridicule. This time he could not. Joe had pierced through shield and armor and cloven him, neck to heart. "In the name of God, Joe, how do we end it all?" He barely kept from shouting.

Joe relaxed his grip on Alvin's arm at last. The blood began to flow again, painfully; Alvin fancied he could measure it passing through his calibrated arteries.

"Two ways," said Joe. "There is one way you can save yourself."

Alvin looked at the cards on the screen. "Exile."

"Just leave. Just go away for a while. Let us alone for a while. Let me pass you by, stop trying to rule, stop trying to force your story on me, and then after a while we can see what's changed."

"Oh, excellent. A son divorcing his father. Not too likely."

"Or death. As the deliverer. As the fulfillment of your dream. If you die now, you defeat me. As Laios destroyed Oedipus at last."

Alvin stood up to leave. "This is rank melodrama. Nobody's going to die because of this."

"Then why can't you stop trembling?" asked Joe.

"Because I'm angry, that's why," Alvin said. "I'm angry at the way you choose to look at me. I love you more than any other father I know loves his son, and this is the way you choose to view it. How sharper than a serpent's tooth—"

"How sharper than a serpent's tooth it is to have a thankless child. Away, away!"

"Lear, isn't it? You gave me the script, and now I'm saying the goddamn lines."

Joe smiled a strange, sphinxlike smile. "It's a good exit line, though, isn't it?"

"Joe, I'm not going to leave, and I'm not going to drop dead, either. You've told me a lot. Like you said, not the truth, not *reality*, but the way you see things. That helps, to know how you see things."

Joe shook his head in despair. "Father, you don't understand. It was *you* who put those cards up on the screen. Not I. My reading is completely different. Completely different, but no better."

"If I'm the King of Swords, who are you?"

"The Hanged Man," Joe said.

Alvin shook his head. "What an ugly world you choose to live in."

"Not neat and pretty like yours, not bound about by rules the way yours is. Laws and principles, theories and hypotheses, may they cover your eyes and keep you happy."

"Joe, I think you need help," said Alvin.

"Don't we all," said Joe.

"So do I. A family counselor maybe. I think we need outside help."

"I've told you what you can do."

"I'm not going to run away from this, Joe, no matter how much you want me to."

"You already have. You've been running away for months. These are *your* cards, Father, not mine."

"Joe, I want to help you out of this—unhappiness."

Joe frowned. "Father, don't you understand? The Hanged Man is smiling. The Hanged Man has won."

Alvin did not go home. He couldn't face Connie right now, did not want to try to explain what he felt about what Joe had told him. So he went to the laboratory and lost himself for a time in reading records of what was happening with the different subject organisms. Some good results. If it all held up, Alvin Bevis would have taken mankind a long way toward being able to read the DNA chain. There was a Nobel in it. More important still, there was real change. *I will have changed the world,* he thought. And then there came into his mind the picture of the man holding the world in his hands, looking off into the distance. The Two of Wands. His dream. Joe was right about that. Right about Alvin's longing for a monument to last forever.

And in a moment of unusual clarity Alvin saw that Joe was right about everything. Wasn't Alvin even now doing just what the cards called for him to do to save himself, going into hiding with the Eight of Cups? His house was breaking down, all was being undone, and he was setting out on a long journey that would lead him to solitude. Greatness, but solitude.

There was one card that Joe hadn't worked into his story, however. The Four of Cups. "This answers you," he had said. The hand of God coming from a cloud. Elijah by the brook. *If God were to whisper to me, what would He say?*

He would say, Alvin thought, that there is something profoundly wrong, something circular in all that Joe has done. He has synthesized things that no other mind in the world could have brought together meaningfully. He is, as Dr. Fryer said, touching on the borders of Truth. But, by God, there is something wrong, something he has over-looked. Not a *mistake,* exactly. Simply a place where Joe has not put two true things together in his own life: Stories make us who we are: the tarot program identifies the stories we believe: by hearing the tale of the tarot, we have changed who we are: therefore—

Therefore, no one knows how much of Joe's tarot story is believed because it is true, and how much becomes true because it is believed. Joe is not a scientist. Joe is a tale-teller. But the gifted, powerful teller of tales soon lives in the world he has created, for as more and more people believe him, his tales become true.

We do not have to be the family of Laios. I do not have to play at being Lear. I can say no to this story, and make it false. Not that Joe could tell any other story, because this is the one that he believes. But I can change what he believes by changing what the cards say, and I can change what the cards say by being someone else.

King of Swords. Imposing my will on others, making them live in the world that my words created. And now my son, too, doing the same. But I can change, and so can he, and then perhaps his brilliance, his insights can shape a better world than the sick one he is making us live in.

And as he grew more excited, Alvin felt himself fill with light, as if the cup had poured into him from the cloud. He believed, in fact, that he had already changed. That he was already something other than what Joe said he was.

The telephone rang. Rang twice, three times, before Alvin reached out to answer it. It was Connie.

"Alvin?" she asked in a small voice.

"Connie," he said.

"Alvin, Joe called me." She sounded lost, distant.

"Did he? Don't worry, Connie, everything's going to be fine."

"Oh, I know," Connie said. "I finally figured it out. It's the thing that Helen never figured out. It's the thing that Iocaste never had the guts to do. Enid knew it, though, Enid could do it. I love you, Alvin." She hung up.

Alvin sat with his hand on the phone for thirty seconds. That's how long it took him to realize that Connie sounded *sleepy*. That Connie was trying to change the cards, too. By killing herself.

All the way home in the car, Alvin was afraid that he was going crazy. He kept warning himself to drive carefully, not to take chances. He wouldn't be able to save Connie if he had an accident on the way. And then there would come a voice that sounded like Joe's, whispering, That's the story you tell yourself, but the truth is you're driving slowly and carefully, hoping she will die so everything will be simple again. It's the best solution. Connie has solved it all, and you're being *slow* so she can succeed, but telling yourself you're being *careful* so you can live with yourself after she's dead.

No, said Alvin again and again, pushing on the accelerator, weaving through the traffic, then forcing himself to slow down, not to kill himself to save two seconds. Sleeping pills weren't *that* fast. And maybe he was wrong; maybe she hadn't taken pills. Or maybe he was thinking that in order to slow himself down so that Connie would die and everything would be simple again—

Shut up, he told himself. *Just get there*, he told himself.

He got there, fumbled with the key, and burst inside. "Connie!" he shouted.

Joe was standing in the archway between the kitchen and the family room.

"It's all right," Joe said. "I got here when she was on the phone to you. I forced her to vomit, and most of the pills hadn't even dissolved yet."

"She's awake?"

"More or less."

Joe stepped aside, and Alvin walked into the family room. Connie sat on a chair, looking catatonic. But as he came nearer, she turned away, which at once hurt him and relieved him. At least she was not hopelessly insane. So it was not too late for change.

"Joe," Alvin said, still looking at Connie. "I've been thinking. About the reading."

Joe stood behind him, saying nothing.

"I believe it. You told the truth. The whole thing, just as you said."

Still Joe did not answer. *Well, what can he say, anyway?* Alvin asked himself. *Nothing. At least he's listening.* "Joe, you told the truth. I really screwed up the family. I've had to have the whole thing my way, and it really screwed things up. Do you hear me, Connie? I'm telling both of you, I agree with Joe about the past. But not the future. There's nothing magical about those cards. They don't tell the future. They just tell the outcome of the pattern, the way things will end if the pattern isn't changed. But we can change it, don't you see? That's what Connie was trying to do with the pills, change the way things turn out. Well, *I'm* the one who can really change, by changing me. Can you see that? I'm changed already. As if I drank from the cup that came to me out of the cloud, Joe. I don't have to control things the way I did. It's all going to be better now. We can build up from, up from—"

The ashes, those were the next words. But they were the wrong words, Alvin could sense that. All his words were wrong. It had seemed true in the lab, when he thought of it; now it sounded dishonest. Desperate. Ashes in his mouth. He turned around to Joe. His son was not listening silently. Joe's face was contorted with rage, his hands trembling, tears streaming down his cheeks.

As soon as Alvin looked at him, Joe screamed at him. "You can't just let it be, can you! You have to do it again and again and again, don't you!"

Oh, I see, Alvin thought. *By wanting to change things, I was just making them more the same. Trying to control the world they live in. I didn't think it through well enough. God played a dirty trick on me, giving me that cup from the cloud.*

"I'm sorry," Alvin said.

"No!" Joe shouted. "There's nothing you can say!"

"You're right," Alvin said, trying to calm Joe. "I should just have—"

"Don't say *anything!*" Joe screamed, his face red.

"I won't, I won't," said Alvin. "I won't say another—"

"*Nothing! Nothing! Nothing!*"

"I'm just agreeing with you, that's—"

Joe lunged forward and screamed it in his father's face. "God damn you, don't talk at all!"

"I see," said Alvin, suddenly realizing. "I see—as long as I try to put it in words, I'm forcing my view of things on the rest of you, and if I—"

There were no words left for Joe to say. He had tried every word he knew that might silence his father, but none would. Where words fail, there remains the act. The only thing close at hand was a heavy glass dish on the side table. Joe did not mean to grab it, did not mean to strike his father across the head with it. He only meant his father to be still. But all his incantations had failed, and still his father spoke, still his father stood in the way, refusing to let him pass, and so he smashed him across the head with the glass dish.

But it was the dish that broke, not his father's head. And the fragment of glass in Joe's hand kept right on going after the blow, followed through with the stroke, and the sharp edge of the glass cut neatly through the fleshy, bloody, windy part of Alvin's throat. All the way through, severing the carotid artery, the veins, and above all the trachea, so that no more air flowed through Alvin's larynx. Alvin was wordless as he fell backward, spraying blood from his throat, clutching at the pieces of glass imbedded in the side of his face.

"Uh-oh," said Connie in a high and childish voice.

Alvin lay on his back on the floor, his head propped up on the front edge of the couch. He felt a terrible throbbing in his throat and a strange silence in his ears where the blood no longer flowed. He had not know how noisy the blood in the head could be, until now, and now he could not tell anyone. He could only lie there, not moving, not turning his head, watching.

He watched as Connie stared at his throat and slowly tore at her hair; he watched as Joe carefully and methodically pushed the bloody piece of glass into his right eye and then into his left. *I see now,* said Alvin silently. *Sorry I didn't understand before. You found the answer to the riddle that devoured us, my Oedipus. I'm just not good at riddles, I'm afraid.*

MEMORIES OF MY HEAD

E ven with the evidence before you, I'm sure you will not believe my account of my own suicide. Or rather, you'll believe that I wrote it, but not that I wrote it after the fact. You'll assume that I wrote this letter in advance, perhaps not yet sure that I would squeeze the shotgun between my knees, then balance a ruler against the trigger, pressing downward with a surprisingly steady hand until the hammer fell, the powder exploded, and a tumult of small shot at close range blew my head off, embedding brain, bone, skin, and a few carbonized strands of hair in the ceiling and wall behind me. But I assure you that I did not write in anticipation, or as an oblique threat, or for any other purpose than to report to you, after I did it, why the deed was done.

You must already have found my raggedly decapitated body seated at my rolltop desk in the darkest corner of the basement where my only source of light is the old pole lamp that no longer went with the decor when the living room was redecorated. But picture me, not as you found me, still and lifeless, but rather as I am at this moment, with my left hand neatly holding the paper. My right hand moves smoothly across the page, reaching up now and then to dip the quill in the blood that has pooled in the ragged mass of muscle, veins, and stumpy bone between my shoulders.

Why do I, being dead, bother to write to you now? If I didn't choose to write before I killed myself, perhaps I should have abided by that decision after death; but it was not until I had actually carried out my plan that I finally had something to say to you. And having something to say, writing became my only choice, since ordinary diction is beyond one who lacks larynx, mouth, lips, tongue, and teeth. All my tools of articulation have been shredded and embedded in the plasterboard. I have achieved utter speechlessness.

Do you marvel that I continue to move my arms and hands after my head is gone? I'm not surprised: My brain has been disconnected from my body for many years. All my actions long since became habits. Stimuli would pass from nerves to spinal cord and rise no further. You would greet me in the morning or lob your comments at me for hours in the night and I would utter my customary responses without these exchanges provoking a single thought in my mind. I scarcely remember being alive for the last years—or, rather, I remember being alive, but can't distinguish one day from another, one Christmas from any other Christmas, one word you said from any other word you might have said. Your voice has become a drone, and as for my own voice, I haven't listened to a thing I said since the last time I humiliated myself before you, causing you to curl your lip in distaste and turn over the next three cards in your solitaire game. Nor can I remember which of the many lip-curlings and card-turnings in my memory was the particular one that coincided with my last self-debasement before you. Now my habitual body continues as it has for all these years, writing this memoir of my suicide as one last, complex, involuntary twitching of the muscles in my arm and hand and fingers.

I'm sure you have detected the inconsistency. You have always been able to evade my desperate attempts at conveying meaning. You simply wait until you can catch some seeming contradiction in my words, then use it as a pretext to refuse to listen to anything else I say because I am not being logical, and therefore am not rational, and you refuse to speak to someone who is not being rational. The inconsistency you have noticed is: If I am completely a creature of habit, how is it that I committed suicide in the first place, since that is a new and therefore non-customary behavior?

But you see, this is no inconsistency at all. You have schooled me in all the arts of self-destruction. Just as the left hand will sympathetically learn some measure of a skill practiced only with the right, so I have made such a strong habit of subsuming my own identity in yours that it was almost a reflex finally to perform the physical annihilation of myself.

Indeed, it is merely the culmination of long custom that when I made the most powerful statement of my life, my most dazzling performance, my finest hundredth of a second, in that very moment I lost my eyes and so will not be able to witness the response of my audience. I write to you, but you will not write or speak to me, or if you do, I shall not have eyes to read or ears to hear you. Will you scream? (Will someone else find me, and will *that* person scream? But it *must* be you.) I imagine disgust, perhaps. Kneeling, retching on the old rug that was all we could afford to use in my basement corner.

And later, who will peel the ceiling plaster? Rip out the wallboard? And when the wall has been stripped down to the studs, what will be done with those large slabs of drywall that have been plowed with shot and sown with bits of my brain and skull? Will there be fragments of drywall buried with me in my grave? Will they even be displayed in the open coffin, neatly broken up and piled where my head used to be? It would be appropriate, I think, since a significant percentage of my corpse is there, not attached to the rest of my body. And if some fragment of your precious house were buried with me, perhaps you would come occasionally to shed some tears on my grave.

I find that in death I am not free of worries. Being speechless means I cannot correct misinterpretations. What if someone says, "It wasn't suicide: The gun fell and discharged accidentally"? Or what if *murder* is supposed? Will some passing vagrant be apprehended? Suppose he heard the shot and came running, and then was found, holding the shotgun and gibbering at his own blood-covered hands; or, worse, going through my clothes and stealing the hundred-dollar bill I always carry on my person. (You remember how I always joked that I kept it as busfare in case I ever decided to leave you, until you forbade me to say it one more time or you would not be responsible for what you did to me. I have kept my silence on that subject ever since—have you noticed?—for I want you always to be responsible for what you do.)

The poor vagrant could not have administered first aid to me—I'm quite sure that nowhere in the Boy Scout Handbook would he have read so much as a paragraph on caring for a person whose head has been torn away so thoroughly that there's not enough neck left to hold a tourniquet. And since the poor fellow couldn't help me, why shouldn't he help himself? I don't begrudge him the hundred dollars—I hereby bequeath him all the money and other valuables he can find on my person. You can't charge him with stealing what I freely give to him. I also hereby affirm that he did not kill me, and did not dip my drawing pen into the blood in the stump of my throat and then hold my hand, forming the letters that appear on the paper you are reading. You are also witness of this, for you recognize my handwriting. No one should be punished for my death who was not involved in causing it.

But my worst fear is not sympathetic dread for some unknown body-finding stranger, but rather that no one will discover me at all. Having fired the gun, I have now had sufficient time to write all these pages. Admittedly I have been writing with a large hand and much space between the lines, since in writing blindly I must be careful not to run words and lines together. But this does not change the fact that considerable time has elapsed since the unmissable sound of a shotgun firing. Surely some neighbor must have heard; surely the police have been summoned and even now are hurrying to investigate the anxious reports of a gunshot in our picturebook home. For all I know the sirens even now are sounding down the street, and curious neighbors have gathered on their lawns to see what sort of burden the police carry forth. But even when I wait for a few moments, my pen hovering over the page, I feel no vibration of heavy footfalls on the stairs. No hands reach under my armpits to pull me away from the page. Therefore I conclude that there has been no phone call. No one has come, no one will come, unless you come, *until* you come.

Wouldn't it be ironic if you chose this day to leave me? Had I only waited until your customary homecoming hour, you would not have come, and instead of transplanting a cold rod of iron into my lap I could have walked through the house for the first time as if it were somewhat my own. As the night grew later and later, I would have become more certain you were not returning; how daring I would have been then! I might have kicked the shoes in their neat little rows on the closet floor. I might have jumbled up my drawers without dreading your lecture when you discovered it. I might have read the newspaper in the holy of holies, and when I needed to get up to answer a call of nature, I could have left the newspaper spread open on the coffee table instead of folding it neatly just as it came from the paperboy and when I came back there it would be, wide open, just as I left it, without a tapping foot and a scowl and a rosary of complaints about people who are unfit to live with civilized persons.

But you have not left me. I know it. You will return tonight. This will simply be one of the nights that you were detained at the office and if I were a productive human being I would know that there are times when one cannot simply drop one's work and come home because the clock has struck such an arbitrary hour as five. You will come in at seven or eight, after dark, and you will find the cat is not indoors, and you will begin to seethe with anger that I have left the cat outside long past its hour of exercise on the patio. But I couldn't very well kill myself with the cat in here, could I? How could I write you such a clear and eloquent missive as this, my sweet, with your beloved feline companion climbing all over my shoulders trying to lick at the blood that even now I use as ink? No, the cat had to remain outdoors, as you will see; I actually had a valid reason for having violated the rules of civilized living.

Cat or no cat, all the blood is gone and now I am using my ballpoint pen. Of course, I can't actually see whether the pen is out of ink. I remember the pen running out of ink, but it is the memory of many pens running out of ink many times, and I can't recall how recent was the most recent case of running-out-of-ink, and whether the most recent case of pen-buying was before or after it.

In fact it is the issue of memory that most troubles me. How is it that, headless, I remember anything at all? I understand that my fingers might know how to form the alphabet by reflex, but how is it that I remember how to spell these words, how has so much language survived within me, how can I cling to these thoughts long enough to write them down? Why do I have the shadowy memory of all that I am doing now, as if I had done it all before in some distant past?

I removed my head as brutally as possible, yet memory persists. This is especially ironic for, if I remember correctly, memory is what I most hoped to kill. Memory is a parasite that dwells within me, a mutant creature that has climbed up my spine and now perches atop my ragged neck, taunting me as it spins a sticky thread out of its own belly like a spider, then weaves it into shapes that harden in the air and become bone. I am being cheated; human bodies are not supposed to be able to regrow body parts that are any more complex than fingernails or hair, and here I can feel with my fingers that the bone has changed. My vertebrae are once again complete, and now the base of my skull has begun to form again.

How quickly? Too fast! And inside the bone grow softer things, the terrible small creature that once inhabited my head and refuses even now to die. This little knob at the top of my spine is a new limbic node; I recognize it, for when I squeeze it lightly with my fingers I feel strange passions, half-forgotten passions. Soon, though, such animality will be out of reach, for the tissues will swell outward to form a cerebellum, a folded gray cerebrum; and then the skull will close around it, sheathed in wrinkled flesh and scanty hair.

My undoing is undone, and far too quickly. What if my head is fully restored to my shoulders before you come home? Then you will find me in the basement with a bloody mess and no rational explanation for it. I can imagine you speaking of it to your friends. You can't leave me alone for a single hour, you poor thing, it's just a constant burden living with someone who is constantly making messes and then lying about them. Imagine, you'll say to them, a whole letter, so many pages, explaining how I killed myself—it would be funny if it weren't so sad.

You will expose me to the scorn of your friends; but that changes nothing. Truth is truth, even when it is ridiculed. Still, why should I provide entertainment for those wretched soulless creatures who live only to laugh at one whose shoe-latchets they are not fit to unlace? If you cannot find me headless, I refuse to let you know what I have done at all. You will not read this account until some later day, after I finally succeed in dying and am embalmed. You'll find these pages taped on the bottom side of a drawer in my desk, where you will have looked, not because you hoped for some last word from me, but because you are searching for the hundred-dollar bill, which I will tape inside it.

And as for the blood and brains and bone embedded in the plasterboard, even that will not trouble you. I will scrub; I will sand; I will paint. You will come home to find the basement full of fumes and you will wear your martyr's face and take the paint away and send me to my room as if I were a child caught writing on the walls. You will have no notion of the agony I suffered in your absence, of the blood I shed solely in the hope of getting free of you. You will think this was a day like any other day. But I will know that on this day, this one day like the marker between B.C. and A.D., I found the courage to carry out an abrupt and terrible plan that I did not first submit for your approval.

Or has this, too, happened before? Will I, in the maze of memory, be unable to recall which of many head-explodings was the particular one that led me to write this message to you? Will I find, when I open the drawer, that on its underside there is already a thick sheaf of papers tied there around a single hundred-dollar bill? There is nothing new under the sun, said old Solomon in Ecclesiastes. Vanity of vanities; all is vanity. Nothing like that nonsense from King Lemuel at the end of Proverbs: Many daughters have done virtuously, but thou excellest them all.

Let her own works praise her in the gates, ha! I say let her own head festoon the walls.

LOST BOYS

I've worried for a long time about whether to tell this story as fiction or fact. Telling it with made-up names would make it easier for some people to take. Easier for me, too. But to hide my own lost boy behind some phony made-up name would be like erasing him. So I'll tell it the way it happened, and to hell with whether it's easy for either of us.

Kristine and the kids and I moved to Greensboro on the first of March, 1983. I was happy enough about my job—I just wasn't sure I wanted a job at all. But the recession had the publishers all panicky, and nobody was coming up with advances large enough for me to take a decent amount of time writing a novel. I suppose I could whip out 75,000 words of junk fiction every month and publish them under a half dozen pseudonyms or something, but it seemed to Kristine and me that we'd do better in the long run if I got a job to ride out the recession. Besides, my Ph.D. was down the toilet. I'd been doing good work at Notre Dame, but when I had to take out a few weeks in the middle of a semester to finish *Hart's Hope*, the English Department was about as understanding as you'd expect from people who prefer their authors dead or domesticated. Can't feed your family? So sorry. You're a writer? Ah, but not one that anyone's written a scholarly essay about. So long, boy-oh!

So sure, I was excited about my job, but moving to Greensboro also meant that I had failed. I had no way of knowing that my career as a fiction writer wasn't over. Maybe I'd be editing and writing books about computers for the rest of my life. Maybe fiction was just a phase I had to go through before I got a *real* job.

Greensboro was a beautiful town, especially to a family from the western desert. So many trees that even in winter you could hardly tell there was a town at all. Kristine and I fell in love with it at once. There were local problems, of course—people bragged about Greensboro's crime rate and talked about racial tension and what-not—but we'd just come from a depressed northern industrial town with race riots in the high schools, so to us this was Eden. There were rumors that several child disappearances were linked to some serial kidnapper, but this was the era when they started putting pictures of missing children on milk cartons—those stories were in every town.

It was hard to find decent housing for a price we could afford. I had to borrow from the company against my future earnings just to make the move. We ended up in the ugliest house on Chinqua Drive. You know the house—the one with cheap wood siding in a neighborhood of brick, the one-level rambler surrounded by split-levels and two-stories. Old enough to be shabby, not old enough to be quaint. But it had a big fenced yard and enough bedrooms for all the kids and for my office, too—because we hadn't given up on my writing career, not yet, not completely.

The little kids—Geoffrey and Emily—thought the whole thing was really exciting, but Scotty, the oldest, he had a little trouble with it. He'd already had kindergarten and half of first grade at a really wonderful private school down the block from our house in South Bend. Now he was starting over in mid-year, losing all his friends. He had to ride a school bus with strangers. He resented the move from the start, and it didn't get better.

Of course, *I* wasn't the one who saw this. I was at work—and I very quickly learned that success at Compute! Books meant giving up a few little things like seeing your children. I had expected to edit books written by people who couldn't write. What astonished me was that I was editing books about computers written by people who couldn't *program*. Not all of them, of course, but enough that I spent far more time rewriting programs so they made sense—so they even *ran*—than I did fixing up people's language. I'd get to work at 8:30 or 9:00, then work straight through till 9:30 or 10:30 at night. My meals were Three Musketeers bars and potato chips from the machine in the employee lounge. My exercise was typing. I met deadlines, but I was putting on a pound a week and my muscles were all atrophying and I saw my kids only in the mornings as I left for work.

Except Scotty. Because he left on the school bus at 6:45 and I rarely dragged out of bed until 7:30, during the week I never saw Scotty at all.

The whole burden of the family had fallen on Kristine. During my years as a freelancer from 1978 till 1983, we'd got used to a certain pattern of life, based on the fact that Daddy was *home*. She could duck out and run some errands, leaving the kids, because I was home. If one of the kids was having discipline problems, I was there. Now if she had her hands full and needed something from the store; if the toilet clogged; if the xerox jammed, then she had to take care of it herself, somehow. She learned the joys of shopping with a cartful of kids. Add to this the fact tha she was pregnant and sick half the time, and you can understand why sometimes I couldn't tell whether she was ready for sainthood or the funny farm.

The finer points of child-rearing just weren't within our reach at that time. She knew that Scotty wasn't adapting well at school, but what could she do? What could I do?

Scotty had never been the talker Geoffrey was—he spent a lot of time just keeping to himself. Now, though, it was getting extreme. He would answer in monosyllables, or not at all. Sullen. As if he were angry, and yet if he was, he didn't know it or wouldn't admit it. He'd get home, scribble out his homework (did they give homework when *I* was in first grade?), and then just mope around.

If he had done more reading, or even watched TV, then we wouldn't have worried so much. His little brother Geoffrey was already a compulsive reader at age five, and Scotty used to be. But now Scotty'd pick up a book and set it down again without reading it. He didn't even follow his mom around the house or anything. She'd see him sitting in the family room, go in and change the sheets on the beds, put away a load of clean clothes, and then come back in and find him sitting in the same place, his eyes open, staring at *nothing*.

I tried talking to him. Just the conversation you'd expect:

"Scotty, we know you didn't want to move. We had no choice."

"Sure. That's OK."

"You'll make new friends in due time."

"I know."

"Aren't you ever happy here?"

"I'm OK."

Yeah, right.

But we didn't have *time* to fix things up, don't you see? Maybe if we'd imagined this was the last year of Scotty's life, we'd have done more to right things, even if it meant losing the job. But you never know that sort of thing. You always find out when it's too late to change anything.

And when the school year ended, things *did* get better for a while.

For one thing, I saw Scotty in the mornings. For another thing, he didn't have to go to school with a bunch of kids who were either rotten to him or ignored him. And he didn't mope around the house all the time. Now he moped around outside.

At first Kristine thought he was playing with our other kids, the way he used to before school divided them. But gradually she began to realize that Geoffrey and Emily always played together, and Scotty almost never played with them. She'd see the younger kids with their squirtguns or running through the sprinklers or chasing the wild rabbit who lived in the neighborhood, but Scotty was never with them. Instead, he'd be poking a twig into the tent-fly webs on the trees, or digging around at the open skirting around the bottom of the house that kept animals out of the crawl space. Once or twice a week he'd come in so dirty that Kristine had to heave him into the tub, but it didn't reassure her that Scotty was acting normally.

On July 28th, Kristine went to the hospital and gave birth to our fourth child. Charlie Ben was born having a seizure, and stayed in intensive care for the first weeks of his life as the doctors probed and poked and finally figured out that they didn't know what was wrong. It was several months later that somebody uttered the words "cerebral palsy," but our lives had already been transformed by then. Our whole focus was on the child in the greatest need—that's what you *do*, or so we thought. But how do you measure a child's need? How do you compare those needs and decide who deserves the most?

When we finally came up for air, we discovered that Scotty had made some friends. Kristine would be nursing Charlie Ben, and Scotty'd come in from outside and talk about how he'd been playing army with Nicky or how he and the guys had played pirate. At first she thought they were neighborhood kids, but then one day when he talked about building a fort in the grass (I didn't get many chances to mow), she happened to remember that she'd seen him building that fort all by himself. Then she got suspicious and started asking questions. Nicky who? I don't know, Mom. Just Nicky. Where does he live? Around. I don't know. Under the house.

In other words, imaginary friends.

How long had he known them? Nicky was the first, but now there were eight names—Nicky, Van, Roddy, Peter, Steve, Howard, Rusty, and David. Kristine and I had never heard of anybody having more than one imaginary friend.

"The kid's going to be more successful as a writer than I am," I said. "Coming up with eight fantasies in the same series."

Kristine didn't think it was funny. "He's so *lonely*, Scott," she said. "I'm worried that he might go over the edge."

It *was* scary. But if he was going crazy, what then? We even tried taking him to a clinic, though I had no faith at all in psychologists. Their fictional explanations of human behavior seemed pretty lame, and their cure rate was a joke—a plumber or barber who performed at the same level as a psychotherapist would be out of business in a month. I took time off work to drive Scotty to the clinic every week during August, but Scotty didn't like it and the therapist told us nothing more than what we already knew—that Scotty was lonely and morose and a little bit resentful and a little bit afraid. The only difference was that she had fancier names for it. We were getting a vocabulary lesson when we needed help. The only thing that seemed to be helping was the therapy we came up with ourselves that summer. So we didn't make another appointment.

Our homegrown therapy consisted of keeping him from going outside. It happened that our landlord's father, who had lived in our house right before us, was painting the house that week, so that gave us an excuse. And I brought home a bunch of video games, ostensibly to review them for *Compute!*, but primarily to try to get Scotty involved in something that would turn his imagination away from these imaginary friends.

It worked. Sort of. He didn't complain about not going outside (but then, he never complained about anything), and he played the video games for hours a day. Kristine wasn't sure she loved *that*, but it was an improvement—or so we thought.

Once again, we were distracted and didn't pay much attention to Scotty for a while. We were having insect problems. One night Kristine's screaming woke me up. Now, you've got to realize that when Kristine screams, that means everything's pretty much OK. When something really terrible is going on, she gets cool and quiet and *handles* it. But when it's a little spider or a huge moth or a stain on a blouse, then she screams. I expected her to come back into the bedroom and tell me about this monstrous insect she had to hammer to death in the bathroom.

Only this time, she didn't stop screaming. So I got up to see what was going on. She heard me coming—I was up to 230 pounds by now, so I sounded like Custer's whole cavalry—and she called out, "Put your shoes on first!"

I turned on the light in the hall. It was hopping with crickets. I went back into my room and put on my shoes.

After enough crickets have bounced off your naked legs and squirmed around in your hands you stop wanting to puke—you just scoop them up and stuff them into a garbage bag. Later you can scrub yourself for six hours before you feel clean and have nightmares about little legs tickling you. But at the time your mind goes numb and you just do the job.

The infestation was coming out of the closet in the boys' room, where Scotty had the top bunk and Geoffrey slept on the bottom. There were a couple of crickets in Geoff's bed, but he didn't wake up even as we changed his top sheet and shook out his blanket. Nobody but us even saw the crickets. We found the crack in the back of the closet, sprayed Black Flag into it, and then stuffed it with an old sheet we were using for rags.

Then we showered, making jokes about how we could have used some seagulls to eat up our invasion of crickets, like the Mormon pioneers got in Salt Lake. Then we went back to sleep.

It wasn't just crickets, though. That morning in the kitchen Kristine called me again: There were dead June bugs about three inches deep in the window over the sink, all down at the bottom of the space between the regular glass and the storm window. I opened the window to vacuum them out, and the bug corpses spilled all over the kitchen counter. Each bug made a nasty little rattling sound as it went down the tube toward the vacuum filter.

The next day the window was three inches deep again, and the day after. Then it tapered off. Hot fun in the summertime.

We called the landlord to ask whether he'd help us pay for an exterminator. His answer was to send his father over with bug spray, which he pumped into the crawl space under the house with such gusto that we had to flee the house and drive around all that Saturday until a late afternoon thunderstorm blew away the stench or drowned it enough that we could stand to come back.

Anyway, what with that and Charlie's continuing problems, Kristine didn't notice what was happening with the video games at all. It was on a Sunday afternoon that I happened to be in the kitchen, drinking a Diet Coke, and heard Scotty laughing out loud in the family room.

That was such a rare sound in our house that I went and stood in the door to the family room, watching him play. It was a great little video game with terrific animation: Children in a sailing ship, battling pirates who kept trying to board, and shooting down giant birds that tried to nibble away the sail. It didn't look as mechanical as the usual video game, and one feature I really liked was the fact that the player wasn't alone— there were other computer-controlled children helping the player's figure to defeat the enemy.

"Come on, Sandy!" Scotty said. "Come on!" Whereupon one of the children on the screen stabbed the pirate leader through the heart, and the pirates fled.

I couldn't wait to see what scenario this game would move to then, but at that point Kristine called me to come and help her with Charlie. When I got back, Scotty was gone, and Geoffrey and Emily had a different game in the Atari.

Maybe it was that day, maybe later, that I asked Scotty what was the name of the game about children on a pirate ship. "It was just a game, Dad," he said.

"It's got to have a name."

"I don't know."

"How do you find the disk to put it in the machine?"

"I don't know." And he sat there staring past me and I gave up.

Summer ended. Scotty went back to school. Geoffrey started kindergarten, so they rode the bus together. Most important, things settled down with the newborn, Charlie—there wasn't a cure for cerebral palsy, but at least we knew the bounds of his condition. He wouldn't get *worse*, for instance. He also wouldn't get well. Maybe he'd talk and walk someday, and maybe he wouldn't. Our job was just to stimulate him enough that if it turned out he wasn't retarded, his mind would develop even though his body was so drastically limited. It was do-able. The fear was gone, and we could breathe again.

Then, in mid-October, my agent called to tell me that she'd pitched my Alvin Maker series to Tom Doherty at TOR Books, and Tom was offering enough of an advance that we could live. That plus the new contract for *Ender's Game*, and I realized that for us, at least, the recession was over. For a couple of weeks I stayed on at Compute! Books, primarily because I had so many projects going that I couldn't just leave them in the lurch. But then I looked at what the job was doing to my family and to my body, and I realized the price was too high. I gave two weeks' notice, figuring to wrap up the projects that only I knew about. In true paranoid fashion, they refused to accept the two weeks—they had me clean my desk out that afternoon. It left a bitter taste, to have them act so churlishly, but what the heck. I was free. I was home.

You could almost feel the relief. Geoffrey and Emily went right back to normal; I actually got acquainted with Charlie Ben; Christmas was coming (I start playing Christmas music when the leaves turn) and all was right with the world. Except Scotty. Always except Scotty.

It was then that I discovered a few things that I simply hadn't known. Scotty never played any of the video games I'd brought home from *Compute!* I knew that because when I gave the games back, Geoff and Em complained bitterly—but Scotty didn't even know what the missing games *were*. Most important, that game about kids in a pirate ship wasn't there. Not in the games I took back, and not in the games that belonged to us. Yet Scotty was still playing it.

He was playing one night before he went to bed. I'd been working on *Ender's Game* all day, trying to finish it before Christmas. I came out of my office about the third time I heard Kristine say, "Scotty, go to bed *now!*"

For some reason, without yelling at the kids or beating them or anything, I've always been able to get them to obey when Kristine couldn't even get them to acknowledge her existence. Something about a fairly deep male voice—for instance, I could always sing insomniac Geoffrey to sleep as an infant when Kristine couldn't. So when I stood in the doorway and said, "Scotty, I think your mother asked you to go to bed," it was no surprise that he immediately reached up to turn off the computer.

"*I'll* turn it off," I said. "Go!"

He still reached for the switch.

"Go!" I said, using my deepest voice-of-God tones.

He got up and went, not looking at me.

I walked to the computer to turn it off, and saw the animated children, just like the ones I'd seen before. Only they weren't on a pirate ship, they were on an old steam locomotive that was speeding along a track. What a game, I thought. The single-sided Atari disks don't even hold a 100K, and here they've got two complete scenarios and all this animation and—

And there wasn't a disk in the disk drive.

That meant it was a game that you upload and then remove the disk, which meant it was completely RAM resident, which meant all this quality animation fit into a mere 48K. I knew enough about game programming to regard that as something of a miracle.

I looked around for the disk. There wasn't one. So Scotty had put it away, thought I. Only I looked and looked and couldn't find any disk that I didn't already know.

I sat down to play the game—but now the children were gone. It was just a train. Just speeding along. And the elaborate background was gone. It was the plain blue screen behind the train. No tracks, either. And then no train. It just went blank, back to the ordinary blue. I touched the keyboard. The letters I typed appeared on the screen. It took a few carriage returns to realize what was happening—the Atari was in memo-pad mode. At first I thought it was a pretty terrific copy-protection scheme, to end the game by putting you into a mode where you couldn't access memory, couldn't do anything without turning off the machine, thus erasing the program code from RAM. But then I realized that a company that could produce a game so good, with such tight code, would surely have some kind of sign-off when the game ended. And why did it end? Scotty hadn't touched the computer after I told him to stop. I didn't touch it, either. Why did the children leave the screen? Why did the train disappear? There was no way the computer could "know" that Scotty was through playing, especially since the game *had* gone on for a while after he walked away.

Still, I didn't mention it to Kristine, not till after everything was over. She didn't know anything about computers then except how to boot up and get WordStar on the Altos. It never occurred to her that there was anything weird about Scotty's game.

It was two weeks before Christmas when the insects came again. And they shouldn't have—it was too cold outside for them to be alive. The only thing we could figure was that the crawl space under our house stayed warmer or something. Anyway, we had another exciting night of cricket-bagging. The old sheet was still wadded up in the crack in the closet—they were coming from under the bathroom cabinet this time. And the next day it was daddy longlegs spiders in the bathtub instead of June bugs in the kitchen window.

"Just don't tell the landlord," I told Kristine. "I couldn't stand another day of that pesticide."

"It's probably the landlord's father *causing* it," Kristine told me. "Remember he was here painting when it happened the first time? And today he came and put up the Christmas lights."

We just lay there in bed chuckling over the absurdity of that notion. We had thought it was silly but kind of sweet to have the landlord's father insist on putting up Christmas lights for us in the first place. Scotty went out and watched him the whole time. It was the first time he'd ever seen lights put up along the edge of the roof—I have enough of a case of acrophobia that you couldn't get me on a ladder high enough to do the job, so our house always went undecorated except the tree lights you could see through the window. Still, Kristine and I are both suckers for Christmas kitsch. Heck, we even play the Carpenters' Christmas album. So we thought it was great that the landlord's father wanted to do that for us. "It was my house for so many years," he said. "My wife and I always had them. I don't think this house'd look *right* without lights."

He was such a nice old coot anyway. Slow, but still strong, a good steady worker. The lights were up in a couple of hours.

Christmas shopping. Doing Christmas cards. All that stuff. We were busy.

Then one morning, only about a week before Christmas, I guess, Kristine was reading the morning paper and she suddenly got all icy and calm—the way she does when something *really* bad is happening. "Scott, read this," she said.

"Just *tell* me," I said.

"This is an article about missing children in Greensboro."

I glanced at the headline: CHILDREN WHO WON'T BE HOME FOR CHRISTMAS. "I don't want to hear about it," I said. I can't read stories about child abuse or kidnappings. They make me crazy. I can't sleep afterward. It's always been that way.

"You've got to," she said. "Here are the names of the little boys who've been reported missing in the last three years. Russell DeVerge, Nicholas Tyler—"

"What are you getting at?"

"Nicky. Rusty. David. Roddy. Peter. Are these names ringing a bell with you?"

I usually don't remember names very well. "No."

"Steve, Howard, Van. The only one that doesn't fit is the last one, Alexander Booth. He disappeared this summer."

For some reason the way Kristine was telling me this was making me very upset. *She* was so agitated about it, and she wouldn't get to the point. "So *what?*" I demanded.

"Scotty's imaginary friends," she said.

"Come on," I said. But she went over them with me—she had written down all the names of his imaginary friends in our journal, back when the therapist asked us to keep a record of his behavior. The names matched up, or seemed to.

"Scotty must have read an earlier article," I said. "It must have made an impression on him. He's always been an empathetic kid. Maybe he started identifying with them because he felt—I don't know, like maybe he'd been abducted from South Bend and carried off to Greensboro." It sounded really plausible for a moment there—the same moment of plausibility that psychologists live on.

Kristine wasn't impressed. "This article says that it's the first time anybody's put all the names together in one place."

"Hype. Yellow journalism."

"Scott, he got *all* the names right."

"Except one."

"I'm so relieved."

But I wasn't. Because right then I remembered how I'd heard him talking during the pirate video game. Come on Sandy. I told Kristine. Alexander, Sandy. It was as good a fit as Russell and Rusty. He hadn't matched a mere eight out of nine. He'd matched them all.

You can't put a name to all the fears a parent feels, but I can tell you that I've never felt any terror for myself that compares to the feeling you have when you watch your two-year-old run toward the street, or see your baby go into a seizure, or realize that somehow there's a connection between kidnappings and your child. I've never been on a plane seized by terrorists or had a gun pointed to my head or fallen off a cliff, so maybe there are worse fears. But then, I've been in a spin on a snowy freeway, and I've clung to the handles of my airplane seat while the plane bounced up and down in mid-air, and still those weren't like what I felt then, reading the whole article. Kids who just disappeared. Nobody saw anybody pick up the kids. Nobody saw anybody lurking around their houses. The kids just didn't come home from school, or played outside and never came in when they were called. Gone. And Scotty knew all their names. Scotty had played with them in his imagination. How did he know who they were? Why did he fixate on these lost boys?

We watched him, that last week before Christmas. We saw how distant he was. How he shied away, never let us touch him, never stayed with a conversation. He was aware of Christmas, but he never asked for anything, didn't seem excited, didn't want to go shopping. He didn't even seem to sleep. I'd come in when I was heading for bed—at one or two in the morning, long after he'd climbed up into his bunk—and he'd be lying there, all his covers off, his eyes wide open. His insomnia was even worse than Geoffrey's. And during the day, all Scotty wanted to do was play with the computer or hang around outside in the cold. Kristine and I didn't know what to do. Had we already lost him somehow?

We tried to involve him with the family. He wouldn't go Christmas shopping with us. We'd tell him to stay inside while we were gone, and then we'd find him outside anyway. I even unplugged the computer and hid all the disks and cartridges, but it was only Geoffrey and Emily who suffered—I still came into the room and found Scotty playing his impossible game.

He didn't ask for anything until Christmas Eve.

Kristine came into my office, where I was writing the scene where Ender finds his way out of the Giant's Drink problem. Maybe I was so fascinated with computer games for children in that book because of what Scotty was going through—maybe I was just trying to pretend that computer games made sense. Anyway, I still know the very sentence that was interrupted when she spoke to me from the door. So very calm. So very frightened.

"Scotty wants us to invite some of his friends in for Christmas Eve," she said.

"Do we have to set extra places for imaginary friends?" I asked.

"They're aren't imaginary," she said. "They're in the backyard, waiting."

"You're kidding," I said. "It's *cold* out there. What kind of parents would let their kids go outside on Christmas Eve?"

She didn't say anything. I got up and we went to the back door together. I opened the door.

There were nine of them. Ranging in age, it looked like, from six to maybe ten. All boys. Some in shirt sleeves, some in coats, one in a swimsuit. I've got no memory for faces, but Kristine does. "They're the ones," she said softly, calmly, behind me. "That one's Van. I remembered him."

"Van?" I said.

He looked up at me. He took a timid step toward me.

I heard Scotty's voice behind me. "Can they come in, Dad? I told them you'd let them have Christmas Eve with us. That's what they miss the most."

I turned to him. "Scotty, these boys are all reported missing. Where have they been?"

"Under the house," he said.

I thought of the crawl space. I thought of how many times Scotty had come in covered with dirt last summer.

"How did they get there?" I asked.

"The old guy put them there," he said. "They said I shouldn't tell anybody or the old guy would get mad and they never wanted him to be mad at them again. Only I said it was OK, I could tell *you*."

"That's right," I said.

"The landlord's father," whispered Kristine.

I nodded.

"Only how could he keep them under there all this time? When does he feed them? When—"

She already knew that the old guy didn't feed them. I don't want you to think Kristine didn't guess that immediately. But it's the sort of thing you deny as long as you can, and even longer.

"They can come in," I told Scotty. I looked at Kristine. She nodded. I knew she would. You don't turn away lost children on Christmas Eve. Not even when they're dead.

Scotty smiled. What that meant to us—Scotty smiling. It had been so long. I don't think I really saw a smile like that since we moved to Greensboro. Then he called out to the boys. "It's OK! You can come in!"

Kristine held the door open, and I backed out of the way. They filed in, some of them smiling, some of them too shy to smile. "Go on into the living room," I said. Scotty led the way. Ushering them in, for all the world like a proud host in a magnificent new mansion. They sat around on the floor. There weren't many presents, just the ones from the kids; we don't put out the presents from the parents till the kids are asleep. But the tree was there, lighted, with all our homemade decorations on it—even the old needlepoint decorations that Kristine made while lying in bed with desperate morning sickness when she was pregnant with Scotty, even the little puff-ball animals we glued together for that first Christmas tree in Scotty's life. Decorations older than he was. And not just the tree—the whole room was decorated with red and green tassels and little wooden villages and a stuffed Santa hippo beside a wicker sleigh and a large chimney-sweep nutcracker and anything else we hadn't been able to resist buying or making over the years.

We called in Geoffrey and Emily, and Kristine brought in Charlie Ben and held him on her lap while I told the stories of the birth of Christ—the shepherds and the wise men, and the one from the Book of Mormon about a day and a night and a day without darkness. And then I went on and told what Jesus lived for. About forgiveness for all the bad things we do.

"Everything?" asked one of the boys.

It was Scotty who answered. "No!" he said. "Not killing."

Kristine started to cry.

"That's right," I said. "In our church we believe that God doesn't forgive people who kill on purpose. And in the New Testament Jesus said that if anybody ever hurt a child, it would be better for him to tie a huge rock around his neck and jump into the sea and drown."

"Well, it *did* hurt, Daddy," said Scotty. "They never told me about that."

"It was a secret," said one of the boys. Nicky, Kristine says, because she remembers names and faces.

"You should have told me," said Scotty. "I wouldn't have let him touch me."

That was when we knew, really knew, that it was too late to save him, that Scotty, too, was already dead.

"I'm sorry, Mommy," said Scotty. "You told me not to play with them anymore, but they were my friends, and I wanted to be with them." He looked down at his lap. "I can't even cry anymore. I used it all up."

It was more than he'd said to us since we moved to Greensboro in March. Amid all the turmoil of emotions I was feeling, there was this bitterness: All this year, all our worries, all our efforts to reach him, and yet nothing brought him to speak to us except death.

But I realized now it wasn't death. It was the fact that when he knocked, we opened the door; that when he asked, we let him and his friends come into our house that night. He had trusted us, despite all the distance between us during that year, and we didn't disappoint him. It was trust that brought us one last Christmas Eve with our boy.

But we didn't try to make sense of things that night. They were children, and needed what children long for on a night like that. Kristine and I told them Christmas stories and we told about Christmas traditions we'd heard of in other countries and other times, and gradually they warmed up until every one of the boys told all about his own family's Christmases. They were good memories. They laughed, they jabbered, they joked. Even though it was the most terrible of Christmases, it was also the best Christmas of our lives, the one in which every scrap of memory is still precious to us, the perfect Christmas in which being together was the only gift that mattered. Even though Kristine and I don't talk about it directly now, we both remember it. And Geoffrey and Emily remember it, too. They call it "the Christmas when Scotty brought his friends." I don't think they ever really understood, and I'll be content if they never do.

Finally, though, Geoffrey and Emily were both asleep. I carried each of them to bed as Kristine talked to the boys, asking them to help us. To wait in our living room until the police came, so they could help us stop the old guy who stole them away from their families and their futures. They did. Long enough for the investigating officers to get there and see them, long enough for them to hear the story Scotty told.

Long enough for them to notify the parents. They came at once, frightened because the police had dared not tell them more over the phone than this: that they were needed in a matter concerning their lost boy. They came: with eager, frightened eyes they stood on our doorstep, while a policeman tried to help them understand. Investigators were bringing ruined bodies out from under our house—there was no hope. And yet if they came inside, they would see that cruel Providence was also kind, and *this* time there would be what so many other parents had longed for but never had: a chance to say good-bye. I will tell you nothing of the scenes of joy and heartbreak inside our home that night—those belong to other families, not to us.

Once their families came, once the words were spoken and the tears were shed, once the muddy bodies were laid on canvas on our lawn and properly identified from the scraps of clothing, then they brought the old man in handcuffs. He had our landlord and a sleepy lawyer with him, but when he saw the bodies on the lawn he brokenly confessed, and they recorded his confession. None of the parents actually had to look at him; none of the boys had to face him again.

But they knew. They knew that it was over, that no more families would be torn apart as theirs—as ours—had been. And so the boys, one by one, disappeared. They were there, and then they weren't there. With that the other parents left us, quiet with grief and awe that such a thing was possible, that out of horror had come one last night of mercy and of justice, both at once.

Scotty was the last to go. We sat alone with him in our living room, though by the lights and talking we were aware of the police still doing their work outside. Kristine and I remember clearly all that was said, but what mattered most to us was at the very end.

"I'm sorry I was so mad all the time last summer," Scotty said. "I knew it wasn't really your fault about moving and it was bad for me to be so angry but I just was."

For him to ask *our* forgiveness was more than we could bear. We were full of far deeper and more terrible regrets, we thought, as we poured out our remorse for all that we did or failed to do that might have saved his life. When we were spent and silent at last, he put it all in proportion for us. "That's OK. I'm just glad that you're not mad at me." And then he was gone.

We moved out that morning before daylight; good friends took us in, and Geoffrey and Emily got to open the presents they had been looking forward to for so long. Kristine's and my parents all flew out from Utah and the people in our church joined us for the funeral. We gave no interviews to the press; neither did any of the other families. The police told only of the finding of the bodies and the confession. We didn't agree to it; it's as if everybody who knew the whole story also knew that it would be wrong to have it in headlines in the supermarket.

Things quieted down very quickly. Life went on. Most people don't even know we had a child before Geoffrey. It wasn't a secret. It was just too hard to tell. Yet, after all these years, I thought it *should* be told, if it could be done with dignity, and to people who might understand. Others should know how it's possible to find light shining even in the darkest place. How even as we learned of the most terrible grief of our lives, Kristine and I were able to rejoice in our last night with our firstborn son, and how together we gave a good Christmas to those lost boys, and they gave as much to us.

AFTERWORD

In August 1988 I brought this story to the Sycamore Hill Writers Workshop. That draft of the story included a disclaimer at the end, a statement that the story was fiction, that Geoffrey is my oldest child and that no landlord of mine has ever done us harm. The reaction of the other writers at the workshop ranged from annoyance to fury.

Karen Fowler put it most succinctly when she said, as best I can remember her words, "By telling this story in first person with so much detail from your own life, you've appropriated something that doesn't belong to you. You've pretended to feel the grief of a parent who has lost a child, and you don't have a right to feel that grief."

When she said that, I agreed with her. While this story had been rattling around in my imagination for years, I had only put it so firmly in first person the autumn before, at a Halloween party with the students of Watauga College at Appalachian State. Everybody was trading ghost stories that night, and so on a whim I tried out this one; on a whim I made it highly personal, partly because by telling true details from my own life I spared myself the effort of inventing a character, partly because ghost stories are most powerful when the audience half-believes they might be true. It worked better than any tale I'd ever told out loud, and so when it came time to write it down, I wrote it the same way.

Now, though, Karen Fowler's words made me see it in a different moral light, and I resolved to change it forthwith. Yet the moment I thought of revising the story, of stripping away the details of my own life and replacing them with those of a made-up character, I felt a sick dread inside. Some part of my mind was rebelling against what Karen said. No, it was saying, she's wrong, you *do* have a right to tell this story, to claim this grief.

I knew at that moment what this story was *really* about, why it had been so important to me. It wasn't a simple ghost story at all; I hadn't written it just for fun. I should have known—I never write anything just for fun. This story wasn't about a fictional eldest child named "Scotty." It was about my real-life youngest child, Charlie Ben.

Charlie, who in the five and a half years of his life has never been able to speak a word to us. Charlie, who could not smile at us until he was a year old, who could not hug us until he was four, who still spends his days and nights in stillness, staying wherever we put him, able to wriggle but not to run, able to call out but not to speak, able to understand that he cannot do what his brother and sister do, but not to ask us why. In short, a child who is not dead and yet can barely taste life despite all our love and all our yearning.

Yet in all the years of Charlie's life, until that day at Sycamore Hill, I had never shed a single tear for him, never allowed myself to grieve. I had worn a mask of calm and acceptance so convincing that I had believed it myself. But the lies we live will always be confessed in the stories that we tell, and I am no exception. A story that I had fancied was a mere lark, a dalliance in the quaint old ghost-story tradition, was the most personal, painful story of my career—and, unconsciously, I had confessed as much by making it by far the most autobiographical of all my works.

Months later, I sat in a car in the snow at a cemetery in Utah, watching a man I dearly love as he stood, then knelt, then stood again at the grave of his eighteen-year-old daughter. I couldn't help but think of what Karen had said; truly I had no right to pretend that I was entitled to the awe and sympathy we give to those who have lost a child. And yet I knew that I couldn't leave this story untold, for that would also be a kind of lie. That was when I decided on this compromise: I would publish the story as I knew it had to be written, but then I would write this essay as an afterword, so that you would know exactly what was true and what was not true in it. Judge it as you will; this is the best that I know how to do.

AFTERWORD

Authors have no more story ideas than anyone else. We all live through or hear about thousands of story ideas a day. Authors are simply more practiced at recognizing them as having the potential to become stories.

The real challenge is to move from the idea through the process of inventing the characters and their surroundings, structuring the tale, and discovering the narrative voice and the point of view, and finally writing it all down in a way that will be clear and effective for the reader. That's the part that separates people who wish they were writers or intend someday to write a book, and those of us who actually put the words down on paper and send them out in hope of finding an audience.

To the best of my memory, here are the origins of each of the stories in this book:

"EUMENIDES IN THE FOURTH FLOOR LAVATORY"

I was working at *The Ensign* magazine as an assistant editor and sometime staff writer. Jay A. Parry was copy editor there, as he had been at Brigham Young University Press, where my editorial career began. In fact, Jay was the one who alerted me to the possibility of applying for a position at *The Ensign* and helped shepherd me through the process.

He and I and another editor, Lane Johnson, all had dreams of being writers. I had already had something of a career as a playwright, but when it came to prose fiction we were all new. We started taking lunch together down in the cafeteria of the LDS Church Office Building in Salt Lake City, riding the elevators down from the twenty-third floor, grabbing a quick salad, and then hunching over a table talking stories.

Naturally, when we actually wrote the stories down, we showed them to each other. In many ways we were the blind leading the blind—none of us had sold anything when we began. Yet we were all professional editors; we all worked in a daily mill of taking badly written articles, restructuring them, and then rewriting them smoothly and clearly. We might not have known how to sell fiction, but we certainly knew how to *write*. And we also knew how to see other people's work clearly and search for the soul of their story, in order to preserve that soul through any number of incarnations as text.

(Indeed, that may be the reason I have always been so skeptical of the whole contemporary critical scene, in which the text is regarded as some immutable miracle, to be worshipped or dissected as if it were the story itself. What anyone trained as an editor and rewriter knows is that the text is *not* the story—the text is merely one attempt to place the story inside the memory of the audience. The text can be replaced by an infinite number of other attempts. Some will be better than others, but no text will be "right" for all audiences, nor will any one text be "perfect." The story exists only in the memory of the reader, as an altered version of the story intended (consciously or not) by the author. It is possible for the audience to create for themselves a better story than the author could ever have created in the text. Thus audiences have taken to their hearts miserably-written stories like *Tarzan of the Apes* by Edgar Rice Burroughs, because what they received transcended the text; while any number of beautifully written texts have been swallowed up without a trace, because the text, however lovely, did a miserable job of kindling a living story within the readers' memories.)

How other stories in this collection grew out of that friendship, those lunchtime meetings, will be recounted in their place. This story came rather late in that time. I had already left *The Ensign* magazine and was beginning my freelance career. I still had much contact with the *Ensign* staff because I was supposed to be finishing a project that I had not yet completed when I resigned my position as of 1 January 1978. In one conversation I had with Jay Parry, he mentioned a terrible dream he had had. "You can use it for a story if you want," he said. "I think there's a story in it, but it would be too terrible for me to write."

Jay lacks my vicious streak, you see; or perhaps it's just that he was already a father and I wasn't. I'm not altogether sure I could write this story after Kristine and I started having kids. At the time, though, Jay's nightmare image of a child with flipper arms drowning in a toilet seemed fascinating, even poignant.

I had recently read whatever story collection of Harlan Ellison's was current at the time, and I had discerned a pattern in his toughest, meanest tales—a sin-and-punishment motif in which terrible things only seemed to happen to the most appropriate people. It seemed obvious to me that the way to develop this deformed baby into a story was to have it come into the life of someone who deserved to be confronted with a twisted child.

After my first draft, however, I submitted the story to Francois Camoin, by then my teacher in writing classes at the University of Utah. I had taken writing classes before, and except for occasional helpful comments had found that their primary value was that they provided me with deadlines so I *had* to produce stories. Francois was different—he actually understood, not only how to write, but also how to *teach* writing, a skill that is almost completely missing among teachers of creative writing in America today. He didn't know everything—no one does—but compared to what I knew at the time he might as well have known everything! Even though I was selling my science fiction quite regularly, I still didn't understand, except in the vaguest way, why some of my stories worked and others didn't. Francois helped open up my own work to me, both its strengths and weaknesses.

As a playwright I had learned that I have a tendency to write in epigrams; as one critical friend put it, all my characters said words that were meant to be carved in stone over the entrance of a public building. That tendency toward clever didacticism was still showing up in my fiction (and probably still does). It was Francois who helped me understand that while the events of the story should be clear—what happened and why—the *meaning* of the story should be subtle, arcane; it should be left lying about for readers to discover, but never forced upon them. "This story is *about* guilt," said Francois. "In fact, the child, the tiny Fury, *is* guilt. When you have a word embodied in a story, the word itself should never appear. So don't ever say the word 'guilt' in this story."

I knew at once that he was right. It wasn't just a matter of removing the word, of course. It meant removing most sentences that had the word in it, and occasionally even whole paragraphs had to come out. It was a pleasurable process, though not without some pain—rather like peeling away dead skin after a bad sunburn. What was left was much stronger.

It appeared in a rather obscure place—Roy Torgeson's *Chrysalis* anthology series from Zebra books. But Terry Carr picked it up for his best-of-the-year fantasy anthology, so it got a little better exposure. My name is on it, but much of this story is owed to others: Jay, for the seminal image; Harlan, for the basic structure; and Francois, for the things that *aren't* in the text here printed.

"QUIETUS"

Like "Eumenides," this story began with someone else's nightmare. My wife woke up one morning upset by a strange lingering dream. We lived at the time in a rented Victorian house on J Street in the Avenues district of Salt Lake City. We were only a bit more than a block from the Emigration Ward LDS meetinghouse, where we attended church. In Kristine's dream, the bishop of our ward had called us up and told us that they were holding a funeral for a stranger the next day, but that tonight there was no place to keep the coffin. Would we be willing to let them bring it by and leave it in our living room until morning?

Kristine isn't in the habit of saying no to requests for help, even in her dreams, and so she agreed. She woke up from her dream just as she was opening the coffin lid.

That was all—a stranger's coffin in the living room. But I knew at once that there was a story in it, and what the story had to be. A coffin in your own living room can only have one body in it: your own. And so I sat down to write a story of a man who was haunting his own house without realizing it, until he finally opened the coffin and climbed in, accepting death.

What I *didn't* know when I started writing was *why* he was left outside his coffin for a while, and why he then reconciled himself to death. So I started writing as much of the story as I knew, hoping something would come to me. I told of the moment of his death in his office, though he didn't realize it was death; I wrote of his homecoming; but the ultimate meaning of the story came by accident. I can't remember now what my mistake was in the first draft. Something like this: During the office scene I had written that he had no children, but by the time I wrote his homecoming, I had forgotten his childlessness and had him hear children's voices or see their drawings on the refrigerator—or something to that effect. Only when I showed the first draft of the story's opening to Kristine did we (probably she) notice the contradiction.

It was one of those silly dumb authorial lapses that every writer commits. My first thought was simply to change one or the other reference so they were reconciled.

However, as I sat there, preparing to revise, I had an intuition that my "mistake" was no mistake at all, but rather my unconscious answer to the fundamental question in the story: Why couldn't he accept death at first? Instead of eliminating the contradiction, I enhanced it, switching back and forth. Now they have children, now they don't. He could not accept death until their childlessness was replaced with children.

If you want to get psychological about it, Kristine was pregnant with our first child at the time. My "mistake" may have been a traditional freudian slip, revealing my ambivalence about entering onto the irrevocable step of having and raising children. What matters more, however, is not the personal source of the feeling, but what I learned about the process of writing: Trust your mistakes. Over and over again since then, I have found that when I do something "wrong" in an early draft of the story, I should not eliminate it immediately. I should instead explore it and see if there's some way that the mistake can be justified, amplified, made part of the story. I have come to believe that a storyteller's best work comes, not from his conscious plans, but from his impulses and errors. That is where his unconscious mind wells up to the surface. That is how stories become filled, not with what the writer believes that he believes, or thinks he ought to care about, but rather with what he believes without question and cares about most deeply. That is how a story acquires its truth.

"DEEP BREATHING EXERCISES"

The idea for this story came simply enough. My son, Geoffrey, was a born insomniac. It took him hours to fall asleep every night, and we learned that the most effective way to get him to sleep was for me to hold him and sing to him. (For some reason he responded more to a baritone than a mezzo-soprano.) This would continue until he was four or five years old; by that time I was spending a couple of hours a night lying by his bed, reading in the dim light from the hall while humming the tune to "Away in a Manger." When he was a baby, though, I stood in his room, rocking back and forth, singing, nonsense songs that included tender lyrics like, "Go to sleep, you little creep, Daddy's about to die." Even when he finally seemed to have drifted off I learned that he was only faking, and if I laid him down too soon he'd immediately scream. I appreciate a call for an encore as much as the next guy, but enough is enough. Especially since Kristine was asleep in the other room. Most of the time I didn't begrudge her that—she would be up in the morning taking care of Geoffrey (always an early riser no matter how late he dropped off) while I slept in, so it all evened out. Still, there were many nights when I stood there, rocking back and forth, listening to both of them breathing during the breaks in my lullaby.

One night I realized that Geoffrey's breath on my shoulder was exactly in rhythm with my wife's breath as she slept in the other room. The two of them inhaling and exhaling in perfect unison. My mind immediately began to take the idea and wander with it. I thought: It doesn't matter how long Daddy stands here singing to the kid, the bond with his mother is always the strongest one, right down to the level of their breathing. Mother and child share the same breath so long together—it's no surprise that out of the womb the child still seeks to breathe with her, to cling to the rhythms of his first and best home. From there my thoughts wandered to the fact that the unborn child is so tied to the mother that if she dies, he dies with her.

Before Geoffrey fell asleep, the story was written in my mind: Breathing in unison is a sign, not that people were born together, but that they were now irrevocably doomed to die together.

"FAT FARM"

My life can be viewed as one long struggle with my own body. I wasn't hopelessly uncoordinated as a kid. If I tried, I could swing a bat or get a ball through a hoop. And I suppose that if I had worked at it, I could have held my own in childhood athletics. But some are born nerds, some choose nerdhood, and some have nerdiness thrust upon them. I chose. I just didn't *care* about sports or physical games of any kind. As a child, given the choice, I would always rather read a book. Soon enough, however, I learned that this was a mistake. By the time I got to junior high, I realized that young male Americans are valued only for their contribution to athletic contests—or so it seemed to me. The result was that to avoid abuse, I avoided athletic situations.

Then, when I was about fifteen, I passed some sort of metabolic threshold. I had always been an outrageously skinny kid—you could count my ribs through my shirt. All of a sudden, though, without any change that I was aware of in my eating habits, I began to gain weight. Not a lot—just enough that I softened in the belly. Began to get that faintly pudgy wormlike look that is always so attractive and fashionable, especially in teenage boys. As the years passed, I gained a little more weight and began to discover that the abuse heaped upon nerds in childhood is nothing like the open, naked bigotry displayed toward adults who are overweight. People who would never dream of mocking a cripple or making racial or ethnic slurs feel no qualms about poking or pinching a fat person's midriff and making obscenely personal remarks. My hatred of such people was limitless. Some of my acquaintances in those days had no notion how close they came to immediate death.

The only thing that keeps fat people from striking back is that, in our hearts, most of us fear that our tormentors are right, that we somehow deserve their contempt, their utter despite for us as human beings. Their loathing for us is only surpassed by our loathing for ourselves.

I had my ups and downs. I weighed 220 pounds when I went on my LDS mission to Brazil in 1971. Through much walking and exercise, and relatively little eating (though Brazilian ice cream is exquisite) I came home two years later weighing 176 pounds. I looked and felt great. And the weight stayed off, mostly, for several years. I became almost athletic. My first two summers home, I operated a summer repertory theatre at an outdoor amphitheatre, the Castle, on the hill behind the state mental hospital. We weren't allowed to drive right up to the Castle, so at the beginning of every rehearsal we would walk up a switchback road. Within a few weeks I was in good enough shape that I was running up the steepest part of the hill right among the younger kids, and reaching the stage of the Castle without being out of breath. We had a piano that we stored in a metal box at the base of the amphitheatre and carried—not rolled —up a stony walkway to the stage for rehearsals and performances of musicals (*Camelot, Man of La Mancha*, and my own *Father, Mother, Mother, and Mom*). Soon I was carrying one end of the piano alone. I reveled in the fact that my body could be slender and well-muscled, not wormlike at all.

But then I began my editorial career and my theatre company folded, leaving me with heavy debts. I spent every day then sedentary and tense, with a candy machine just around the corner. My only exercise was pushing quarters into the machine. By the time I got married in 1977 I was back up to 220 pounds. Freelance writing made things even worse. Whenever I needed a break, I'd get up, walk thirty feet into the kitchen, make some toast and pour some orange juice. All very healthy. And only about a billion calories a day. I was near 265 pounds when I wrote "Fat Farm." It was an exercise in self-loathing and desperate hope. I knew that I was capable of having a strong, healthy body, but lacked the discipline to create it for myself. I had actually gone through the experience of trading bodies—it just took me longer than it took the hero of the story. In a way, I suppose the story was a wish that someone would *make* me change.

Ironically, within a few months after writing "Fat Farm," our lives went through a transition. We were moving to a larger house. The first thing I did was take all my old thin clothes and give them away to charity. I knew that I would never be thin again. It was no longer an issue. I was going to be a fat person for the rest of my life. Orson Welles was my hero.

Then I began packing up our thousands of books and carrying and stacking the boxes. The exercise began to take up more and more of each day. I ate less and less, since I wasn't constantly looking for breaks from writing. By the time we got into our new place, I had dropped ten pounds. Just like that, without even trying.

So I kept it up. Eating little—I now followed a thousand-calorie balanced diet—and exercising more and more, within a year I was 185 pounds and was riding a bicycle many miles a day. And I stayed thin for several years. Not until I moved to North Carolina and got a sedentary job under extreme tension did I put the weight back on again. I sit here writing this with a current weight of 255 pounds. But that's down almost ten pounds from my holiday high, and I'm riding an exercise bike and enjoying the sensation of being hungry most of the time and—who knows?

In short, "Fat Farm" isn't fiction. It's my physical autobiography.

And it's no accident that the story ends with our hero set up to fulfill ugly violent assignments. The undercurrent of violence is real. I hereby warn all those who think it's all right to greet a friend by saying, "Put on a little weight, haven't you!" You would never dream of greeting a friend by saying, "Wow, that's quite an enormous pimple you've got on your nose there," or, "Can't you afford to buy clothes that look good or do you just have no taste?" If you did, you would expect to lose the friend. Well, be prepared. Some of us are about to run out of patience with your criminal boorishness. Someday one of you is going to glance down at our waistline, grin, and then—before you can utter one syllable of your offensive slur—we're going to break you into a pile of skinny little matchsticks. No jury of fat people would convict us.

"CLOSING THE TIMELID"

I think it was in a conversation with Jay and Lane that we began wondering what death might feel like. Maybe, after all our fear of it, the actual moment of death—not the injuries leading up to it, but the moment itself—was the most sublime pleasure imaginable. After a few months of letting this idea gel in the back of my mind, I hit on the device of using time travel as a way to let people experience death without dying.

Time travel is one of those all-purpose science fictional devices. You can do *anything* with it, depending on how you set up the rules. In this case, I made it so that the time-traveler's body *does* materialize in the past, and can be injured—but upon return the body is restored to its condition when it left, though still feeling whatever feelings it had just before the return. It's a fun exercise for science fiction writers, to think up new variations on the rules of time travel. Each variation opens up thousands of possible stories. That's why it's so discouraging to see how many time-travel stories use the same old tired clichés. These writers are like tourists with cameras. They don't actually come to experience a strange land. They just take snapshots of each other and move on. Snapshot science fiction might as well not be written. Why write a time-travel story if you don't think through the mechanics of your fantasy and find the implications of the particular rules of your time-travel device? As long as we're dealing in impossibilities, why not make them interesting and fresh?

But I digress. Being a preacher at heart, I found that with this story I had written a homily of hedonism as self-destruction. Absurd as these people may seem, their obsession with a perverse pleasure is no stranger than any other pleasure that seduces its seekers from the society of normal human beings. Drug users, homosexuals, corporate takeover artists, steroid-popping bodybuilders and athletes—all such groups have, at some time or another, constructed societies whose whole purpose is celebrating the single pleasure whose pursuit dominates their lives, while it separates them from the rest of the world, whose rules and norms they resent and despise. Furthermore, they pursue their pleasure at the constant risk of self-destruction. And then they wonder why so many other people look at them with something between horror and distaste.

"FREEWAY GAMES"

The origin of this idea is simple enough. I learned to drive a car only in my early twenties (the state of Utah required that you take driver's ed. before you could get a license, my high school didn't offer it, and I never had time to take it on my own), and so went through my aggressive teenage driving period when I was over twenty-one. Thus even as I went through my bouts of naked competitiveness and aggression on the highway, I was intellectually mature enough to recognize the madness of my behavior. And, rarely, that intellectual awareness curbed some of my stupidest impulses. For instance, long before freeway shootings in California, I realized that when you flash your brights at some bozo you're taking your life in your hands. No, the way to punish a freeway offender was to do it passively. Follow them. Just—follow. Not tailgating. Just—following. If they squirt ahead in traffic, don't leap out to follow. Just work your way up until a few minutes later, there you are again, following. If they really deserve a scare, take a little bit of time out of your life and take their exit with them. Follow them along residential streets. Watch them panic.

I never actually went to that extreme—never actually followed somebody off the freeway. But I did follow a couple of bozos long enough that it clearly made them nervous; yet I never did anything aggressive enough to make them mad. They could never *really* be sure that they were being followed. It was the cruelest thing I can remember doing.

I thought for a while of writing a humor piece about freeway games—ways to pass the time while on long commutes. But when I showed my first draft to Kristine, she said, "That isn't funny, that's *horrible*." So I set it aside.

Later, taking a writing course from Francois Camoin, I decided to write a story that had no science fiction or fantasy element in it. While trying to think of something to write about, I hit on that "freeway games" essay and realized that when Kristine said it was horrible, I should have realized that she really meant that the idea was *horror*. A horror story with no monster except the human being behind the wheel. Somebody who didn't know when to stop. Who kept pushing and pushing until somebody died. In short, me—only out of control. So I wrote a story about a normal nice person who suddenly discovers one day that he's a monster after all.

"A SEPULCHRE OF SONGS"

I remember reading a spate of stories about human beings who had been cyborgized —their brains put into machinery so that moving an arm actually moved a cargo bay door and walking actually fired up a rocket engine, that sort of thing. It seemed that almost all of these stories—and a lot of robot and android stories as well—ended up being rewrites of "Pinocchio." They always wish they could be a real boy.

In years since then, the fashion has changed and more sf writers celebrate rather than regret the body mechanical. Still, at the time the issue interested me. Couldn't there be someone for whom a mechanical body would be liberating? So I wrote a story that juxtaposed two characters, one a pinocchio of a spaceship, a cyborg that wished for the sensations of real life; the other a hopelessly crippled human being, trapped in a body that can never *act*, longing for the power that would come from a mechanical replacement. They trade places, and both are happy.

A simple enough tale, but I couldn't tell it quite that way. Perhaps because I wanted it to be truer than a fantasy, I told the story from the point of view of a human observer who could never know whether a *real* trade had taken place or whether the story was just a fantasy that made life livable for a young girl with no arms or legs. Thus it became a story about the stories we tell ourselves that make it possible to live with *anything*.

All this was many years before my third son, Charlie, was born. I never really believed that someday I would have a child who lies on his bed except when we put him in a chair, who stays indoors unless we take him out. In some ways his condition is better than that of the heroine of "Sepulchre of Songs"—he has learned to grasp things and can manipulate his environment a little, since his limbs are not utterly useless. In some ways his condition is worse—so far he cannot speak, and so he is far more lonely, far more helpless than one who can at least have conversation with others. And sometimes when I hold him or sit and look at him, I think back to this story and realize that the fundamental truth of it is something quite unrelated to the issue of whether a powerful mechanical body would be preferable to a crippled one of flesh and bone.

The truth is this: The girl in the story brought joy and love into the lives of others, and when she left her body (however you interpret her leaving), she lost the power to do that. I would give almost anything to see my Charlie run; I wake up some mornings full of immeasurable joy because in the dream that is just fading Charlie spoke to me and I heard the words of his mouth; yet despite these longings I recognize something else: You don't measure whether a life is worth living except by measuring whether that life is giving any good to other people and receiving any joy from them. Plenty of folks with healthy bodies are walking minuses, subtracting from the joy of the world wherever they go, never able to receive much satisfaction either. But Charlie gives and receives many delights, and our family would be far poorer if he weren't a part of us. It teaches us something of goodness when we are able to earn his smile, his laughter. And nothing delights him more than when he earns our smiles, our praise, and our joy in his company. If some cyborg starship passed by, imaginary or otherwise, offering to trade bodies with my little boy, I would understand it if he chose to go. But I hope that he would not, and I would miss him terribly if he ever left.

"PRIOR RESTRAINT"

This story is a bit of whimsy, based in part on some thoughts about censorship and in part on the experience of knowing Doc Murdock, a fellow writing student in Francois Camoin's class. Doc really did support himself at times by gambling, though the last I heard he was making money hand-over-fist as a tech writer. Couldn't happen to a nicer guy.

I almost never consciously base characters on real people or stories on real events. Part of the reason is that the person involved will almost always be offended, unless you treat him as a completely romantic figure, the way I did with Doc Murdock. But the most important reason is that you don't really *know* any of the people you know in real life—that is, you never, ever, *ever* know *why* they do what they do. Even if they tell you why, that's no help because they never understand themselves the complete cause of anything they do. So when you try to follow a real person that you actually know, you will constantly run into vast areas of ignorance and misunderstanding. I find that I tell much more truthful and powerful stories when I work with fully fictional characters, because *them* I can know right down to the core, and am never hampered by thinking, "Oh, he'd never do that," or, worse yet, "I'd better not show him doing *that* or so-and-so will kill me."

And, in a way, "Prior Restraint" is proof that for me, at least, modeling characters on real people is a bad idea. Because, while I think the story is fun, it's also one of my shallower works. Scratch the surface and there's nothing there. It was never much deeper than the conscious idea.

By the way, this story was a *long* time making it into print. I wrote the first version of it very early in my career; Ben Bova rejected it, in part on the grounds that it's not a good idea to write stories about people writing stories, if only because it reminds the reader that he's reading a story. His advice was mostly right, though sometimes you *want* to remind readers they're reading. Still, I liked this idea, flaws and all, and so I sent it off to Charlie Ryan at *Galileo*. He accepted it—but then *Galileo* folded. Charlie wrote to me and offered to send the story back. I knew, however, that I wouldn't be able to sell it to Ben Bova or, probably, anybody else. So when Charlie suggested that he'd like to hang onto it in case someday he was able to restart *Galileo* or some other magazine, I agreed.

It was almost a decade later that a letter came out of the blue, telling me that Charlie was going to edit *Aboriginal SF*, and could he please use "Prior Restraint"? By then I was well aware of the relative weakness of the story, particularly considering the things I'd learned about storytelling since then. It might be a bit embarrassing to have such a primitive work come out now, in the midst of much more mature stories. But Charlie had taken the story back in the days when most editors didn't return my phone calls and some sent me insulting rejections; why shouldn't he profit from it now that things had changed? As long as the story wasn't too embarrassing. So I asked him to send me a copy and let me see if I still liked it.

I did. It wasn't a subtle piece, but it was still a decent idea and, with a bit of revision to get rid of my stylistic excesses from those days, I felt that it could be published without embarrassing me. I don't know whether to be chagrined or relieved that nobody seemed to be able to tell the difference—that nobody said, " 'Prior Restraint' feels like *early* Card." Maybe I haven't learned as much in the intervening years as I thought!

"THE CHANGED MAN AND THE KING OF WORDS"

The genesis of this story is easy enough. I was living in South Bend, Indiana, where I was working on a doctorate at Notre Dame. One of my professors was Ed Vasta, one of the great teachers that come along only a few times in one's life. We both loved Chaucer, and he was receptive to my quirky ideas about literature; he also wrote science fiction, so that there was another bond between us. One night I was at a party at his house. After an hour of everybody grousing about the stupidity of Hesburgh's choosing a high school teacher named Gerry Faust as the football coach, we got on the subject of tarot. Ed was a semi-believer—that is, he didn't really believe in any occult phenomena, but he did think that the cards provided a focus, a framework for bringing intuitive understanding into the open.

Kristine and I are both very uncomfortable around any occult dealings, partly because we are very uncomfortable with the sort of people who believe in the occult. But this was Ed Vasta, a very rational man, and so I consented to a reading. I remember thinking that the process was fascinating, precisely because nothing happened that could not be explained by Vasta's own personal knowledge of me; and yet the cards did provide a way of relating that previous knowledge together in surprising and illuminating patterns.

The experience led me to write a story, combining tarot with my then-new obsession with computers. The story itself is a cliché, a deliberately oedipal story by an author who thinks Freud's notion of an Oedipus complex is an utter crock. It's one of the few times that I've ever mechanically followed a symbolic structure, and for that reason it remains unsatisfying to me. What I really cared about were the ideas—the computer and the tarot cards—and I have since explored the interrelationship between storytelling computers and human beings in such works as my novels *Ender's Game* and *Speaker for the Dead*.

"MEMORIES OF MY HEAD"

This story began very recently when Lee Zacharias, my writing teacher at the University of North Carolina at Greensboro, mentioned that suicide stories were common enough among young writers that she despaired of ever seeing a good one. I remembered that when I was teaching at Elon College the semester before I had gotten enough of those suicide endings to make the pronouncement to my students that I hereby *forbade* them to end a story with suicide. It was a cop-out, said I—it was a confession that the writer had no idea how the story *really* ought to end.

Now, though, I was feeling a bit defiant. I had said that suicide stories were dumb, and now Lee was saying the same thing. Why not see if I could write one that was any good? And why not make it even more impossible by making it first person present tense, just because I detest present tense and have declared that first person is usually a bad choice?

The result is one of the strangest stories I've ever written. But I *like* it. I enjoyed using this epistolary form to tell the tale of a hideously malformed relationship between a couple who had lived together far longer than they had any reason to.

"LOST BOYS"

This story came with its own afterword. Let me only add that since its publication, it has been criticized somewhat for its supposed cheating—I promise at the beginning to tell the truth, and then I lie. I can only say that it is a long tradition in ghost stories to pretend to be telling the truth; part of the pleasure in the tale is to keep the reader wondering whether *this* time the story might not be real. The ghost stories *I've* enjoyed most and remember the best have been the ones told as if they were true and had really happened to the teller. I tip my hat to Jack McLaughlin, a wonderful grad student in the theatre department at BYU, who spooked a whole bunch of us undergrad acting students with a really hair-raising poltergeist story that Actually Happened To Him.

I also enjoy the fact that criticisms of my story for violating expectations have all come from the more literary, "experimental" wing of the science fiction community. It seems that they love experimentation and literary flamboyance—but only if it follows the correct line. If somebody dares to do something that is *surprisingly* shocking instead of *predictably* shocking, well, fie on them. Thus do the radicals reveal their orthodoxy.

The fact remains that *Lost Boys* is the most autobiographical, personal, and painful story I've ever written. I wrote it in the absolutely only way *I* could have written it. So even if the manner of its writing is a literary crime, as these critics say, I can only answer, "So shoot me." I'm in the business of telling true stories as well as I possibly can. I've never yet found any of their rules that helped me tell a story better; and if I had followed their rules on this story, I never could have told it at all.

BOOK 2

FLUX

TALES OF HUMAN FUTURES

INTRODUCTION

Never mind the question of why anybody would ever become a writer at all. The sheer arrogance of thinking that other people ought to pay to read my words should be enough to mark all us writers as unfit for decent society. But then, few indeed are the communities that reward proper modesty and disdain those who thrust themselves into the limelight. All human societies hunger for storytellers, and those whose tales we like, we reward well. In the meantime, the storytellers are constantly reinventing and redefining their society. We are paid to bite the hand that feeds us. We are birds that keep tearing down and rebuilding every nest in the tree.

So never mind the question of why I became a writer. Instead let's ask an easy one. Why did I choose to write science fiction?

The glib answer is to say that I didn't. Some are born to science fiction, some choose science fiction, and some have science fiction thrust upon them. Surely I belong to the last category. I was a playwright by choice. Oh, I entered college as an archaeology major, but I soon discovered that being an archaeologist didn't mean being Thor Heyerdahl or Yigael Yadin. It meant sorting through eight billion potsherds. It meant moving a mountain with a teaspoon. In short, it meant work. Therefore it was not for me.

During the two semesters it took for me to make this personal discovery, I had already taken four theatre classes for every archaeology class I signed up for, and it was in theatre that I spent all my time. Because I attended Brigham Young High School, I was already involved with the BYU theatre program before I officially started college. In fact, I had already been in a student production, and continued acting almost continuously through all my years at the university. I was no great shakes as an actor —too cerebral, not able to use my body well enough to look comfortable or right on stage. But I gave great cold readings at auditions, so I kept getting cast. And when I gave up on archaeology, it was theatre that was there waiting for me. It was the first time I consciously made a decision based on autobiography. Instead of examining my feelings (which change hourly anyway) or making those ridiculous pro-and-con lists that always look so rational, I simply looked back at the last few years of my life and saw that the only thing I did that I really followed through on, the only thing I did over and over again regardless of whether it profited me in any way, was theatre. So I changed majors, thereby determining much of my future.

One obvious result was that I lost my scholarship. I was at BYU on a full-ride presidential scholarship—tuition, books, housing. But I had to maintain a high grade point average, and while that was easy enough in academic subjects, it was devilishly hard in the subjective world of the arts. The matter hadn't come up before—presidential scholars hadn't ever gone into the arts before me. So there was no mechanism for dealing with the subjective grades that came out of theatre. If I worked my tail off in an academic subject, I got an A. Period. No question. But I could work myself half to death on a play, do my very best, and still get a C because the teacher didn't agree with my interpretation or didn't like my blocking or just plain didn't like *me*, and who could argue? There was nothing quantifiable. So choosing the arts cost me money. It also taught me that you can never please a critic determined to detest your work. I had to choose my professors carefully, or reconcile myself to low grades. I did both.

But if I wasn't working for grades and I wasn't trying to change myself to fit professors' preconceived notions of what my work ought to be, what *was* I working for? The answer came to me gradually, but once I understood it I never wavered. I rejected the notion, put forth by one English professor, that one should write for oneself. Indeed, his own life was a clear refutation of his lofty sentiment that "I write for myself and God." In fact he spent half his life pressing his writings on anyone who would hold still long enough to read or listen. He showed me what I was already becoming aware of: Art is a dialogue with the audience. There is no reason to create art except to present it to other people; and you present it to other people in order to change them. The world must be changed by what I create, I decided, or it isn't worth doing.

Within a year of becoming a theatre major, I was writing plays. I didn't plan it. Writing wasn't something I thought of as a career. In my family, writing was simply something that you *did*. My dad often bought *Writer's Digest*; I entered their contest a couple of times in my teens. But mostly I thought of writing as coming up with skits or assemblies at school or roadshows at church (Mormons have a longstanding commitment to theatre); it also meant that I could usually ace an essay exam if I knew even a little bit about the subject. It wasn't a *career*.

But as a fledgling director, I had run into the frustration of directing inadequate scripts. When I was assistant director of a college production of *Flowers for Algernon*, I finally got a professor—the director—to agree with me. The second act was terrible. I had read and loved the story, and so I was particularly frustrated by some bad choices made by the adapter. With the director's permission, I went home and rewrote the second act. We used my script.

About the same time (I think), I was taking a course in advanced interpretation, which included reader's theatre. I loved the whole concept of stripping the stage and letting the actors, in plain clothes, with no sets and minimal movements, act out the story for the audience. As part of the course, I wrote an adaptation of Marjorie Kellogg's *Tell Me That You Love Me, Junie Moon*. I had loved the book, and my adaptation was (and still is) one of my best works, because it preserved both the story and the madcap flavor of the writing. I asked for permission to direct it. I was told that advanced interp wasn't a course for which students were allowed to direct. There was only *one* course undergraduates could take that allowed them to direct a play, and I had taken it and received a C, and that was that.

No it wasn't. My professor in that course, Preston Gledhill, was sympathetic, and so he arranged to bend the rules and I got my performance. Two nights in the Experimental Theatre, doing reader's theatre as it had never been done before. The audience laughed in all the right places. They sobbed at the end. The standing ovation was earned. The actors still remember, as I do, that it was something remarkable. I may have been using someone else's story, but that student production told me, for the first time, that I could produce a script and a performance that audiences would take into themselves. I had changed people.

Because of those two adaptations, I resolved to try playwriting in a more serious way. Charles Whitman, who was the favorite among us undergraduates in those days (the late 1960s), was also the playwriting teacher and a fervent advocate of Mormon theatre. He thought that young Mormon theatre people ought to be producing plays for their own people, and I agreed—and still agree, enough that I have never stopped producing Mormon art throughout my career, often allowing it to take precedence over my more visible (and lucrative) career in "the world." Taking Whitman's class opened the floodgates. I wrote dozens of plays. I tried my hand at realism, comedy, verse drama, vignettes, anything that would hold still long enough for me to write it. I adapted stories from Mormon history and the Book of Mormon; I took personal stories out of my life and my parents' lives; and through all this writing, I *still* thought of myself as primarily an actor and director.

I mean, just because I wrote a lot of plays didn't mean I *was* a playwright. I also designed costumes and did makeup and composed music and designed and built stage sets. The only reason I didn't do lighting was because of a healthy case of acrophobia. No, I wasn't a playwright, I was an all-around theatre person. I didn't make the decision that I was a writer until one day I was sitting in the Theatre Department office with a group—some meeting, I don't remember what—and a professor happened to say to me, "So you're going to be a playwright." I found something about his statement to be offensive. It flashed through my mind that I had already written a dozen plays that had been produced to sold-out houses. I was at least as much a writer as he was an actor or director or teacher—because I had done it to the satisfaction of an audience. So I answered, rather coldly, "I'm not *going* to be a playwright. I *am* a playwright."

A short while later, I happened to be sitting in on a class he was teaching, and he referred to that conversation in front of his class. "Some of you are going to be actors and some directors and some playwrights," he said. Then, pointing at me, he said, "Except for Scott Card, there, who already *is* a playwright." It was a great laugh line. The mockery I thought I heard in his words left me angry and frustrated. Later I would learn that he had intended his comments as a kind of respect; and we have worked together well on other projects. But I interpreted things then with the paranoia normal to "sensitive" adolescents, and took his words as a challenge. I brooded on them for days. Weeks. And at the end of that time, in my own mind I *was* a playwright, and all my other theatrical enterprises were secondary. I could succeed or fail at them without it making much difference—my future was tied to my writing.

Skip a few years now. Years in which I started a repertory theatre company, which by some measures was a resounding success; but at the end of that time I found myself $20,000 in debt on an annual income of about $5,000. My own scripts had been quite successful in the company, but some bad business decisions—*my* decisions, I must add—had made a good thing go sour. I folded the company, and probably should have declared personal and corporate bankruptcy, but instead decided to pay it all off.

How? My income as an editor at BYU Press would never be enough to make a dent in what I owed. I had to make money on the side. Doing what? The only thing I knew how to do was write, and because my plays were all aimed at the Mormon audience, there was no way that a script of mine would bring in that kind of money—not from royalties. There just weren't enough warm bodies with dollars in their pockets to bring me what I needed. I thought of writing plays for the New York audience, but that would be so chancy and require so much investment in time that I rejected it. Instead, I thought of writing fiction.

In a way, that was as scary as trying to write plays for the American audience at large. The difference was that with fiction, you find out much sooner whether you've failed. You can take years flogging a few scripts around in New York and regional theatre and end up with nothing—no audience, no money, no future. But you can find yourself in exactly that condition after only a few months of mailing out fiction manuscripts.

And when considering what kind of fiction to write, science fiction was an easy choice. I wanted to start with short stories, and when it comes to short fiction, science fiction was then and is now the most open market there is. First, because the money is fairly low, the established novelists generally stay out of the short fiction market, making it more open to new names. Second, because science fiction thrives on strangeness, new writers are more welcome in this field than any other. True strangeness is the product of genius, but a good substitute is the strangeness inherent in every writer's unique voice, so that when a science fiction writer is both competent and new, he gives off the luster of an ersatz kind of genius, and the field welcomes him with open arms. (Others might say that the field chews you up, swallows you, and pukes you back, but that would be crude and unkind, and it doesn't *always* happen that way.)

So for purely commercial reasons, deep in debt, I chose science fiction. I was lucky enough that the second story I sent out sold after only a couple of tries (told about elsewhere) and went on to come in second for a Hugo and win me the Campbell Award for best new writer. So as long as people were paying me to write science fiction why should I stop?

That's the colorful, devil-may-care answer. It's also a crock.

Because during that whole time that I "was" a playwright, I was also writing science fiction. I had not yet written a play when at sixteen I first came up with the story idea that eventually became "Ender's Game." I was taking fiction-writing courses at BYU right along with my playwriting courses, and, although I had brains enough not to turn in sci-fi for class credit, my heart went into the Worthing stories I was already writing before my first play was produced. Like my plays, my stories were all written on narrow-ruled paper in spiral notebooks, and at first my mother typed them for me. Then I mailed them out and treasured the very kind rejection notes I got. Not many—only a couple of submissions, only a couple of rejections. But between rejections—and between plays—I worked on my fiction as assiduously as I ever worked on anything else in my life.

So now, glib answers aside, why science fiction? Why is it that, left to myself, the stories I am drawn to write are all science fiction and fantasy? It wasn't because sci-fi was all I read. On the contrary, while I went through several science fiction binges, during high school and college I usually read only the sci-fi and fantasy that were making the rounds. I read *Dune* when everybody read *Dune*; the same with *Lord of the Rings* and *Foundation* and *I Sing the Body Electric* and *Dandelion Wine*. At the same time, I was reading Hersey's *The Wall* and *White Lotus*, Ayn Rand's *Fountainhead*, Rod McKuen's *Stanyan Street and Other Sorrows*. Hell, I even read Khalil Gibran. I may not have dropped acid, but I wasn't totally cut off from my generation. (Fortunately, by the time *Jonathan Livingston Seagull* came out I had matured enough to recognize it immediately as drivel.) I never, not once, not for a moment, thought of myself as a "science fiction reader." Some science fiction books came to me like revelations, yes, but so did many other books—and none had anything like the influence on me that came from Shakespeare and Joseph Smith, the two writers who, more than any others, formed the way I think and write.

If I wasn't a science fiction reader, per se, why did my impulse toward storytelling come out in science fictional forms? I think it was the same reason that my playwriting impulses always expressed themselves in stories aimed at and arising from the Mormon audience. The possibility of the transcendental is part of it. More important, though —for Mormonism is *not* a transcendental religion—is the fact that science fiction, like Mormonism, offered a vocabulary for rationalizing the transcendental. That is, within science fiction it is possible to find the meaning of life without resorting to Mystery. I detest Mystery (though I love mysteries); I think it is the name we put on our decision to stop trying to understand. From Joseph Smith I learned to reject any philosophy that requires you to swallow paradox as if it were profound; if it makes no sense, it's probably hogwash. Within the genre of science fiction, I could shuck off the shackles of realism and make up worlds in which the issues I cared about were clear and powerful. The tale could be told direct. It could be *about something*.

Since then I have learned ways to make more realistic fiction be *about something* as well—but not the ways my literature professors tried to teach me. The oblique methods used by contemporary American literateurs are bankrupt because they have forsaken the audience. But there are writers doing outside of science fiction the things that I thought, at the age of twenty-three, could only be done within it. I think of Olive Ann Burns's *Cold Sassy Tree* as the marker that informed me that all the so-called Mysteries could still be reached through stories that told of love and sex and death; the need to belong, the hungers of the body, and the search for individual worth; Community, Carnality, Identity. Ultimately, that triad is what all stories are about. The great stories are simply the ones that do it better for a particular audience at a particular place and time. So I'm gradually reaching out to write other stories, outside of both the Mormon and the science fiction communities. But the fact remains that it was in science fiction that I first found it possible to speak to non-Mormons about the things that mattered most to me. That's why I wrote science fiction, and write science fiction, and will write it for many years to come.

A Thousand Deaths

"Y̲ou will make no speeches," said the prosecutor.

"I didn't expect they'd let me," Jerry Crove answered, affecting a confidence he didn't feel. The prosecutor was not hostile; he seemed more like a high school drama coach than a man who was seeking Jerry's death.

"They not only won't let you," the prosecutor said, "but if you try anything, it will go much worse for you. We have you cold, you know. We don't need anywhere near as much proof as we have."

"You haven't proved anything." "We've proved you knew about it," the prosecutor insisted mildly. "No point arguing now. Knowing about treason and not reporting it is exactly equal to committing treason."

Jerry shrugged and looked away.

The cell was bare concrete. The door was solid steel. The bed was a hammock hung from hooks on the wall. The toilet was a can with a removable plastic seat. There was no conceivable way to escape. Indeed, there was nothing that could conceivably occupy an intelligent person's mind for more than five minutes. In the three weeks he had been here, he had memorized every crack in the concrete, every bolt in the door. He had nothing to look at, except the prosecutor. Jerry reluctantly met the man's gaze.

"What do you say when the judge asks you how you plead to the charges?"

"Nolo contendere."

"Very good. It would be much nicer if you'd consent to say 'guilty'," the prosecutor said.

"I don't like the word."

"Just remember. Three cameras will be pointing at you. The trial will be broadcast live. To America, you represent all Americans. You must comport yourself with dignity, quietly accepting the fact that your complicity in the assassination of Peter Anderson—"

"Andreyevitch—"

"*Anderson* has brought you to the point of death, where all depends on the mercy of the court. And now I'll go have lunch. Tonight we'll see each other again. And remember. No speeches. Nothing embarrassing."

Jerry nodded. This was not the time to argue. He spent the afternoon practicing conjugations of Portuguese irregular verbs, wishing that somehow he could go back and undo the moment when he agreed to speak to the old man who had unfolded all the plans to assassinate Andreyevitch. "Now I must trust you," said the old man. "*Temos que confiar no senhor americano.* You love liberty, *né?*"

Love liberty? Who knew anymore? What was liberty? Being free to make a buck? The Russians had been smart enough to know that if they let Americans make money, they really didn't give a damn which language the government was speaking. And, in fact, the government spoke English anyway.

The propaganda that they had been feeding him wasn't funny. It was too true. The United States had never been so peaceful. It was more prosperous than it had been since the Vietnam War boom thirty years before. And the lazy, complacent American people were going about business as usual, as if pictures of Lenin on buildings and billboards were just what they had always wanted.

I was no different, he reminded himself. I sent in my work application, complete with oath of allegiance. I accepted it meekly when they opted me out for a tutorial with a high Party official. I even taught his damnable little children for three years in Rio.

When I should have been writing plays.

But what do I write about? Why not a comedy—*The Yankee and the Commissar,* a load of laughs about a woman commissar who marries an American blue blood who manufactures typewriters. There are no women commissars, of course, but one must maintain the illusion of a free and equal society.

"Bruce, my dear," says the commissar in a thick but sexy Russian accent, "your typewriter company is suspiciously close to making a profit."

"And if it were running at a loss, you'd turn me in, yes, my little noodle?" (Riotous laughs from the Russians in the audience; the Americans are not amused, but then, they speak English fluently and don't need broad humor. Besides, the reviews are all approved by the Party, so we don't have to worry about the critics. Keep the Russians happy, and screw the American audience.) Dialogue continues:

"All for the sake of Mother Russia."

"Screw Mother Russia."

"Please do," says Natasha. "Regard me as her personal incarnation."

Oh, but the Russians do love onstage sex. Forbidden in Russia, of course, but Americans are *supposed* to be decadent.

I might as well have been a ride designer for Disneyland, Jerry thought. Might as well have written shtick for vaudeville. Might as well go stick my head in an oven. But with my luck, it would be electric.

He may have slept. He wasn't sure. But the door opened, and he opened his eyes with no memory of having heard footsteps approach. The calm before the storm: and now, the storm.

The soldiers were young, but unSlavic. Slavish, but definitely American. Slaves to the Slavs. Put that in a protest poem sometime, he decided, if only there were someone who wanted to read a protest poem.

The young American soldiers (But the uniforms were wrong. I'm not old enough to remember the old ones, but these are not made for American bodies.) escorted him down corridors, up stairs, through doors, until they were outside and they put him into a heavily armored van. What did they think, he was part of a conspiracy and his fellows would come to save him? Didn't they know that a man in his position would have no friends by now?

Jerry had seen it at Yale. Dr. Swick had been very popular. Best damn professor in the department. He could take the worst drivel and turn it into a *play*, take terrible actors and make them look good, take apathetic audiences and make them, of all things, enthusiastic and hopeful. And then one day the police had broken into his home and found Swick with four actors putting on a play for a group of maybe a score of friends. What was it—*Who's Afraid of Virginia Woolf?* Jerry remembered. A sad script. A despairing script. But a sharp one, nonetheless, one that showed despair as being an ugly, destructive thing, one that showed lies as suicide, one that, in short, made the audience feel that, by God, something was *wrong* with their lives, that the peace was illusion, that the prosperity was a fraud, that America's ambitions had been cut off and that so much that was good and proud was still undone—

And Jerry realized that he was weeping. The soldiers sitting across from him in the armored van were looking away. Jerry dried his eyes.

As soon as news got out that Swick was arrested, he was suddenly unknown. Everyone who had letters or memos or even class papers that bore his name destroyed them. His name disappeared from address books. His classes were empty as no one showed up. No one even hoping for a substitute, for the university suddenly had no record that there had ever been such a class, ever been such a professor. His house had gone up for sale, his wife had moved, and no one said good-bye. And then, more than a year later, the CBS news (which always showed official trials then) had shown ten minutes of Swick weeping and saying, "Nothing has ever been better for America than Communism. It was just a foolish, immature desire to prove myself by thumbing my nose at authority. It meant nothing. I was wrong. The government's been kinder to me than I deserve." And so on. The words were silly. But as Jerry had sat, watching, he had been utterly convinced. However meaningless the words were, Swick's face was meaningful: he was utterly sincere.

The van stopped, and the doors in the back opened just as Jerry remembered that he had burned his copy of Swick's manual on playwriting. Burned it, but not until he had copied down all the major ideas. Whether Swick knew it or not, he had left something behind. But what will I leave behind? Jerry wondered. Two Russian children who now speak fluent English and whose father was blown up in their front yard right in front of them, his blood spattering their faces, because Jerry had neglected to warn him? What a legacy.

For a moment he was ashamed. A life is a life, no matter whose or how lived.

Then he remembered the night when Peter Andreyevitch (no—Anderson. Pretending to be American is fashionable nowadays, so long as everyone can tell at a glance that you're *really* Russian) had drunkenly sent for Jerry and demanded, as Jerry's employer (i.e., owner), that Jerry recite his poems to the guests at the party. Jerry had tried to laugh it off, but Peter was not that drunk: he insisted, and Jerry went upstairs and got his poems and came down and read them to a group of men who could not understand the poems, to a group of women who understood them and were merely amused. Little Andre said afterward, "The poems were good, Jerry," but Jerry felt like a virgin who had been raped and then given a two-dollar tip by the rapist.

In fact, Peter had given him a bonus. And Jerry had spent it.

Charlie Ridge, Jerry's defense attorney, met him just inside the doors of the courthouse. "Jerry, old boy, looks like you're taking all this pretty well. Haven't even lost any weight."

"On a diet of pure starch, I've had to run around my cell all day just to stay thin." Laughter. Ha ho, what a fun time we're having. What jovial people we are.

"Listen, Jerry, you've got to do this right, you know. They have audience response measurements. They can judge how sincere you seem. You've got to really *mean* it."

"Wasn't there once a time when defense attorneys tried to get their clients off?" Jerry asked.

"Jerry, that kind of attitude isn't going to get you anywhere. These aren't the good old days when you could get off on a technicality and a lawyer could delay trial for five years. You're guilty as hell, and so if you cooperate, they won't do anything to you. They'll just deport you."

"What a pal," Jerry said. "With you on my side, I haven't a worry in the world."

"Exactly right," said Charlie. "And don't you forget it."

The courtroom was crowded with cameras. (Jerry had heard that in the old days of freedom of the press, cameras had often been barred from courtrooms. But then, in those days the defendant didn't usually testify and in those days the lawyers didn't both work from the same script. Still, there was the press, looking for all the world as if they thought they were free.)

Jerry had nothing to do for nearly half an hour. The audience (Are they paid? Jerry wondered. In America, they must be.) filed in, and the show began at exactly eight o'clock. The judge came in looking impressive in his robes, and his voice was resonant and strong, like a father on television remonstrating his rebellious son. Everyone who spoke faced the camera with the red light on the top. And Jerry felt very tired.

He did not waver in his determination to try to turn this trial to his own advantage, but he seriously wondered what good it would do. And was it to his own advantage? They would certainly punish him more severely. Certainly they would be angry, would cut him off. But he had written his speech as if it were an impassioned climactic scene in a play (*Crove Against the Communists* or perhaps *Liberty's Last Cry*), and he the hero who would willingly give his life for the chance to instill a little bit of patriotism (a little bit of intelligence, who gives a damn about patriotism!) in the hearts and minds of the millions of Americans who would be watching.

"Gerald Nathan Crove, you have heard the charges against you. Please step forward and state your plea."

Jerry stood up and walked with, he hoped, dignity to the taped X on the floor where the prosecutor had insisted that he stand. He looked for the camera with the red light on. He stared into it intently, sincerely, and wondered if, after all, it wouldn't be better just to say *nolo contendere* or even *guilty* and have an easier time of it.

"Mr. Crove," intoned the judge, "America is watching. How do you plead?"

America was watching indeed. And Jerry opened his mouth and said not the Latin but the English he had rehearsed so often in his mind:

"There is a time for courage and a time for cowardice, a time when a man can give in to those who offer him leniency and a time when he must, instead, resist them for the sake of a higher goal. America was once a free nation. But as long as they pay our salaries, we seem content to be slaves! I plead not guilty, because any act that serves to weaken Russian domination of any nation in the world is a blow for all the things that make life worth living and against those to whom power is the only god worth worshiping!"

Ah. Eloquence. But in his rehearsals he had never dreamed he would get even this far, and yet they still showed no sign of stopping him. He looked away from the camera. He looked at the prosecutor, who was taking notes on a yellow pad. He looked at Charlie, and Charlie was resignedly shaking his head and putting his papers back in his briefcase. No one seemed to be particularly worried that Jerry was saying these things over live television. And the broadcasts *were* live—they had stressed that, that he must be careful to do everything correctly the first time because it was all live—

They were lying, of course. And Jerry stopped his speech and jammed his hands into his pockets, only to discover that the suit they had provided for him had no pockets (Save money by avoiding nonessentials, said the slogan), and his hands slid uselessly down his hips.

The prosecutor looked up in surprise when the judge cleared his throat. "Oh, I beg your pardon," he said. "The speeches usually go on much longer. I congratulate you, Mr. Crove, on your brevity."

Jerry nodded in mock acknowledgment, but he felt no mockery.

"We always have a dry run," said the prosecutor, "just to catch you last-chancers."

"Everyone knew that?"

"Well, everyone but you, of course, Mr. Crove. All right, everybody, you can go home now."

The audience arose and quietly shuffled out.

The prosecutor and Charlie got up and walked to the bench. The judge was resting his chin on his hands, looking not at all fatherly now, just a little bored. "How much do you want?" the judge asked.

"Unlimited," said the prosecutor.

"Is he really that important?" Jerry might as well have not been there. "After all, they're doing the actual bombers in Brazil."

"Mr. Crove is an American," said the prosecutor, "who chose to let a Russian ambassador be assassinated."

"All right, all right," said the judge, and Jerry marveled that the man hadn't the slightest trace of a Russian accent.

"Gerald Nathan Crove, the court finds you guilty of murder and treason against the United States of America and its ally, the Union of Soviet Socialist Republics. Do you have anything to say before sentence is pronounced?"

"I just wondered," said Jerry, "why you all speak English."

"Because," said the prosecutor icily, "we are in America."

"Why do you even bother with trials?"

"To stop other imbeciles from trying what you did. He just wants to argue, Your Honor."

The judge slammed down his gavel. "The court sentences Gerald Nathan Crove to be put to death by every available method until such time as he convincingly apologizes for his action to the American people. Court stands adjourned. Lord in heaven, do I have a headache."

They wasted no time. At five o'clock in the morning, Jerry had barely fallen asleep. Perhaps they monitored this, because they promptly woke him up with a brutal electric shock across the metal floor where Jerry was lying. Two guards—this time Russians—came in and stripped him and then dragged him to the execution chamber even though, had they let him, he would have walked.

The prosecutor was waiting. "I have been assigned your case," he said, "because you promise to be a challenge. Your psychological profile is interesting, Mr. Crove. You long to be a hero."

"I wasn't aware of that."

"You displayed it in the courtroom, Mr. Crove. You are no doubt aware—your middle name implies it—of the last words of the American Revolutionary War espionage agent named Nathan Hale. 'I regret that I have but one life to give for my country,' he said. You shall discover that he was mistaken. He should be very glad he had but one life.

"Since you were arrested several weeks ago in Rio de Janeiro, we have been growing a series of clones for you. Development is quite accelerated, but they have been kept in zero-sensation environments until the present. Their minds are blank.

"You are surely aware of somec, yes, Mr. Crove?"

Jerry nodded. The starship sleep drug.

"We don't need it in this case, of course. But the mind-taping technique we use on interstellar flights—that is quite useful. When we execute you, Mr. Crove, we shall be continuously taping your brain. All your memories will be rather indecorously dumped into the head of the first clone, who will immediately become *you*. However, he will clearly remember all your life up to and including the moment of death.

"It was so easy to be a hero in the old days, Mr. Crove. Then you never knew for sure what death was like. It was compared to sleep, to great emotional pain, to quick departure of the soul from the body. None of these, of course, is particularly accurate."

Jerry was frightened. He had heard of multiple death before, of course—it was rumored to exist because of its deterrent value. "They resurrect you and kill you again and again," said the horror story, and now he knew that it was true. Or they wanted him to believe it was true.

What frightened Jerry was the way they planned to kill him. A noose hung from a hook in the ceiling. It could be raised and lowered, but there didn't seem to be the slightest provision for a quick, sharp drop to break his neck. Jerry had once almost choked to death on a salmon bone. The sensation of not being able to breathe terrified him.

"How can I get out of this?" Jerry asked, his palms sweating.

"The first one, not at all," said the prosecutor. "So you might as well be brave and use up your heroism this time around. Afterward we'll give you a screen test and see how convincing your repentance is. We're fair, you know. We try to avoid putting anyone through this unnecessarily. Please sit."

Jerry sat. A man in a lab coat put a metal helmet on his head. A few needles pricked into Jerry's scalp.

"Already," said the prosecutor, "your first clone is becoming aware. He already has all your memories. He is right now living through your panic—or shall we say your attempts at courage. Make sure you concentrate carefully on what is about to happen to you, Jerry. You want to make sure you remember every detail."

"Please," Jerry said.

"Buck up, my man," said the prosecutor with a grin. "You were wonderful in the courtroom. Let's have some of that noble resistance now."

Then the guards led him to the noose and put it around his neck, being careful not to dislodge the helmet. They pulled it tight and then tied his hands behind his back. The rope was rough on his neck. He waited, his neck tingling, for the sensation of being lifted in the air. He flexed his neck muscles, trying to keep them rigid, though he knew the effort would be useless. His knees grew weak, waiting for them to raise the rope.

The room was plain. There was nothing to see, and the prosecutor had left the room. There was, however, a mirror on a wall beside him. He could barely see into it without turning his entire body. He was sure it was an observation window. They would watch, of course.

Jerry needed to go to the bathroom.

Remember, he told himself, I won't really die. I'll be awake in the other room in just a moment.

But his body was not convinced. It didn't matter a bit that a new Jerry Crove would be ready to get up and walk away when this was over. *This* Jerry Crove would die.

"What are you waiting for?" he demanded, and as if that had been their cue the guards pulled the rope and lifted him into the air.

From the beginning it was worse than he had thought. The rope had an agonizingly tight grip on his neck; there was no question of resisting at all. The suffocation was nothing, at first. Like being under water holding your breath. But the rope itself was painful, and his neck hurt, and he wanted to cry out with the pain; but nothing could escape his throat.

Not at first.

There was some fumbling with the rope, and it jumped up and down as the guards tied it to the hook on the wall. Once Jerry's feet even touched the floor.

By the time the rope held still, however, the effects of the strangling were taking over and the pain was forgotten. The blood was pounding inside Jerry's head. His tongue felt thick. He could not shut his eyes. And now he wanted to breathe. He had to breathe. His body demanded a breath.

His body was not under control. Intellectually, he knew that he could not possibly reach the floor, knew that this death would be temporary, but right now his mind was not having much influence over his body. His legs kicked and struggled to reach the ground. His hands strained at the rope behind him. And all the exertion only made his eyes bulge more with the pressure of the blood that could not get past the rope; only made him need air more desperately.

There was no help for him, but now he tried to scream for help. The sound now escaped his throat—but at the cost of air. He felt as if his tongue were being pushed up into his nose. His kicking grew more violent, though every kick was agony. He spun on the rope; he caught a glimpse of himself in the mirror. His face was turning purple.

How long will it be? Surely not much longer!

But it was much longer.

If he had been underwater, holding his breath, he would now have given up and drowned.

If he had a gun and a free hand, he would kill himself now to end this agony and the sheer physical terror of being unable to breathe. But he had no gun, and there was no question of inhaling, and the blood throbbed in his head and made his eyes see everything in shades of red, and finally he saw nothing at all.

Saw nothing, except what was going through his mind, and that was a jumble, as if his consciousness were madly trying to make some arrangement that would eliminate the strangulation. He kept seeing himself in the creek behind his house, where he had fallen in when he was a child, and someone was throwing him a rope, but he couldn't and he couldn't and he couldn't catch it, and then suddenly it was around his neck and dragging him under.

Spots of black stabbed at his eyes. His body felt bloated, and then it erupted, his bowel and bladder and stomach ejecting all that they contained, except that his vomit was stopped at his throat, where it burned.

The shaking of his body turned into convulsive jerks and spasms, and for a moment Jerry felt himself reaching the welcome state of unconsciousness. Then, suddenly, he discovered that death is not so kind.

There is no such thing as slipping off quietly in your sleep. No such thing as being "killed immediately" or having death mercifully end the pain.

Death woke him from his unconsciousness, for perhaps a tenth of a second. But that tenth of a second was infinite, and in it he experienced the infinite agony of impending nonexistence. His life did not flash before his eyes. The lack of life instead exploded, and in his mind he experienced far greater pain and fear than anything he had felt from the mere hanging.

And then he died.

For an instant he hung in limbo, feeling and seeing nothing. Then a light stabbed at his eyes and soft foam peeled away from his skin and the prosecutor stood there, watching as he gasped and retched and clutched at his throat. It seemed incredible that he could now breathe, and if he had experienced only the strangling, he might now sigh with relief and say, "I've been through it once, and now I'm not afraid of death." But the strangling was nothing. The strangling was a prelude. And he was afraid of death.

They forced him to come into the room where he had died. He saw his body hanging, black-faced, from the ceiling, the helmet still on the head, the tongue protruding.

"Cut it down," the prosecutor said, and for a moment Jerry waited for the guards to obey. Instead, a guard handed Jerry a knife.

With death still heavy in his mind, Jerry swung around and lunged at the prosecutor. But a guard caught his hand in an irresistible grip, and the other guard held a pistol pointed at Jerry's head.

"Do you want to die again so soon?" asked the prosecutor, and Jerry whimpered and took the knife and reached up to cut himself down from the noose. In order to reach above the knot, he had to stand close enough to the corpse to touch it. The stench was incredible. And the fact of death was unavoidable. Jerry trembled so badly he could hardly control the knife, but eventually the rope parted and the corpse slumped to the ground, knocking Jerry down as it fell. An arm lay across Jerry's legs. The face looked at Jerry eye-to-eye.

Jerry screamed.

"You see the camera?"

Jerry nodded, numbly.

"You will look at the camera and you will apologize for having done anything against the government that has brought peace to the earth."

Jerry nodded again, and the prosecutor said, "Roll it."

"Fellow Americans," Jerry said, "I'm sorry. I made a terrible mistake. I was wrong. There's nothing wrong with the Russians. I let an innocent man be killed. Forgive me. The government has been kinder to me than I deserve." And so on. For an hour Jerry babbled, insisting that he was craven, that he was guilty, that he was worthless, that the government was vying with God for respectability.

And when he was through, the prosecutor came back in, shaking his head.

"Mr. Crove, you can do better than that.

"Nobody in the audience believed you for one minute. Nobody in the test sample, not one person, believed that you were the least bit sincere. You still think the government ought to be deposed. And so we have to try the treatment again."

"Let me try to confess again."

"A screen test is a screen test, Mr. Crove. We have to give you a little more experience with death before we can permit you to have any involvement with life."

This time Jerry screamed right from the beginning. He made no attempt at all to bear it well. They hung him by the armpits over a long cylinder filled with boiling oil. They slowly lowered him. Death came when the oil was up to his chest—by then his legs had been completely cooked and the meat was falling off the bones in large chunks.

They made him come in and, when the oil had cooled enough to touch, fish out the pieces of his own corpse.

He wept all through his confession this time, but the test audience was completely unconvinced. "The man's a phony," they said. "He doesn't believe a word of what he's saying."

"We have a problem," said the prosecutor. "You seem so willing to cooperate after your death. But you have reservations. You aren't speaking from the heart. We'll have to help you again."

Jerry screamed and struck out at the prosecutor. When the guards had pulled him away (and the prosecutor was nursing an injured nose), Jerry shouted, "Of course I'm lying! No matter how often you kill me it won't change the fact that this is a government of fools by vicious, lying bastards!"

"On the contrary," said the prosecutor, trying to maintain his good manners and cheerful demeanor despite the blood pouring out of his nose, "if we kill you enough, you'll completely change your mind."

"You can't change the truth!"

"We've changed it for everyone else who's gone through this. And you are far from being the first who had to go to a third clone. But this time, Mr. Crove, do try to forget about being a hero."

They skinned him alive, arms and legs first, and then, finally, they castrated him and ripped the skin off his belly and chest. He died silently when they cut his larynx out —no, not silently. Just voiceless. He found that without a voice he could still whisper a scream that rang in his ears when he awoke and was forced to go in and carry his bloody corpse to the disposal room. He confessed again, and the audience was not convinced.

They slowly crushed him to death, and he had to scrub the blood out of the crusher when he awoke, but the audience only commented. "Who does the jerk think he's fooling?"

They disemboweled him and burned his guts in front of him. They infected him with rabies and let his death linger for two weeks. They crucified him and let exposure and thirst kill him. They dropped him a dozen times from the roof of a one-story building until he died.

Yet the audience knew that Jerry Crove had not repented.

"My God, Crove, how long do you think I can keep doing this?" asked the prosecutor. He did not seem cheerful. In fact, Jerry thought he looked almost desperate.

"Getting a little tough on you?" Jerry asked, grateful for the conversation because it meant there would be a few minutes between deaths.

"What kind of man do you think I am? We'll bring him back to life in a minute anyway, I tell myself, but I didn't get into this business in order to find new, hideous ways of killing people."

"You don't like it? And yet you have such a natural talent for it."

The prosecutor looked sharply at Crove. "Irony? Now you can joke? Doesn't death mean anything to you?"

Jerry did not answer, only tried to blink back the tears that these days came unbidden every few minutes.

"Crove, this is not cheap. Do you think it's cheap? We've spent literally billions of rubles on you. And even with inflation, that's a hell of a lot of money."

"In a classless society there's no need for money."

"What is this, dammit! *Now* you're getting rebellious? *Now* you're trying to be a hero?"

"No."

"No wonder we've had to kill you eight times! You keep thinking up clever arguments against us!"

"I'm sorry. Heaven knows I'm sorry."

"I've asked to be released from this assignment. I obviously can't crack you."

"Crack me! As if I didn't long to be cracked."

"You're costing too much. There's a definite benefit in having criminals convincingly recant on television. But you're getting too expensive. The cost-benefit ratio is ridiculous now. There's a limit to how much we can spend on you."

"I have a way for you to save money."

"So do I. Convince the damned audience!"

"Next time you kill me, don't put a helmet on my head."

The prosecutor looked absolutely shocked. "That would be final. That would be capital punishment. We're a humane government. We never kill anybody permanently."

They shot him in the gut and let him bleed to death. They threw him from a cliff into the sea. They let a shark eat him alive. They hung him upside down so that just his head was under water, and when he finally got too tired to hold his head out of the water he drowned.

But through all this, Jerry had become more inured to the pain. His mind had finally learned that none of these deaths was permanent after all. And now when the moment of death came, though it was still terrible, he endured it better. He screamed less. He approached death with greater calm. He even hastened the process, deliberately inhaling great draughts of water, deliberately wriggling to attract the shark. When they had the guards kick him to death he kept yelling, "Harder," until he couldn't yell anymore.

And finally when they set up a screen test, he fervently told the audience that the Russian government was the most terrifying empire the world had ever known, because this time they were efficient at keeping their power, because this time there was no outside for barbarians to come from, and because they had seduced the freest people in history into loving slavery. His speech was from the heart—he loathed the Russians and loved the memory that once there had been freedom and law and a measure of justice in America.

And the prosecutor came into the room ashen-faced.

"You bastard," he said.

"Oh. You mean the audience was live this time?"

"A hundred loyal citizens. And you corrupted all but three of them."

"Corrupted?"

"Convinced them."

Silence for a moment, and then the prosecutor sat down and buried his head in his hands.

"Going to lose your job?" Jerry asked.

"Of course."

"I'm sorry. You're good at it."

The prosecutor looked at him with loathing. "No one ever failed at this before. And I had never had to take anyone beyond a second death. You've died a dozen times, Crove, and you've got used to it."

"I didn't mean to."

"How did you do it?"

"I don't know."

"What kind of animal are you, Crove? Can't you make up a lie and *believe* it?"

Crove chuckled. (In the old days, at this level of amusement he would have laughed uproariously. But inured to death or not, he had scars. And he would never laugh loudly again.) "It was my business. As a playwright. The willing suspension of disbelief."

The door opened and a very important looking man in a military uniform covered with medals came in, followed by four Russian soldiers. The prosecutor sighed and stood up. "Good-bye, Crove."

"Good-bye," Jerry said.

"You're a very strong man."

"So," said Jerry, "are you." And the prosecutor left.

The soldiers took Jerry out of the prison to a different place entirely. A large complex of buildings in Florida. Cape Canaveral. They were exiling him, Jerry realized.

"What's it like?" he asked the technician who was preparing him for the flight.

"Who knows?" the technician asked. "No one's ever come back. Hell, no one's ever arrived yet."

"After I sleep on somec, will I have any trouble waking up?"

"In the labs, here on earth, no. Out there, who knows?"

"But you think we'll live?"

"We send you to planets that look like they might be habitable. If they aren't, so sorry. You take your chances. The worst that can happen is you die."

"Is that all?" Jerry murmured.

"Now lie down and let me tape your brain."

Jerry lay down and the helmet, once again, recorded his thoughts. It was irresistible, of course: when you are conscious that your thoughts are being taped, Jerry realized, it is impossible not to try to think something important. As if you were performing. Only the audience would consist of just one person. Yourself when you woke up.

But he thought this: That this starship and the others that would be and had been sent out to colonize in prison worlds were not really what the Russians thought they were. True, the prisoners sent in the Gulag ships would be away from earth for centuries before they landed, and many or most of them would not survive. But some would survive.

I will survive, Jerry thought as the helmet picked up his brain pattern and transferred it to tape.

Out there the Russians are creating their own barbarians. I will be Attila the Hun. My child will be Mohammed. My grandchild will be Genghis Khan.

One of us, someday, will sack Rome.

Then the somec was injected, and it swept through him, taking consciousness with it, and Jerry realized with a shock of recognition that this, too, was death: but a welcome death, and he didn't mind. Because this time when he woke up he would be free.

He hummed cheerfully until he couldn't remember how to hum, and then they put his body with hundreds of others on a starship and pushed them all out into space, where they fell upward endlessly into the stars. Going home.

CLAP HANDS AND SING

On the screen the crippled man screamed at the lady, insisting that she must not run away. He waved a certificate. "I'm a registered rapist, damnit!" he cried. "Don't run so fast! You have to make allowances for the handicapped!" He ran after her with an odd, left-heavy lope. His enormous prosthetic phallus swung crazily, like a clumsy propeller that couldn't quite get started. The audience laughed madly. Must be a funny, funny scene!

Old Charlie sat slumped in his chair, feeling as casual and permanent as glacial debris. *I am here only by accident, but I'll never move.* He did not switch off the television set. The audience roared again with laughter. Canned or live? After more than eight decades of watching television, Charlie couldn't tell anymore. Not that the canned laughter had got any more real: It was the real laughter that had gone tinny, premeditated. As if the laughs were timed to come *now*, no matter what, and the poor actors could strain to get off their gags in time, but always they were just *this* much early, *that* much late.

"It's late," the television said, and Charlie started awake, vaguely surprised to see that the program had changed: Now it was a demonstration of a convenient electric breast pump to store up natural mother's milk for those times when you just can't be with baby. "It's late."

"Hello, Jock," Charlie said.

"Don't sleep in front of the television again, Charlie."

"Leave me alone, swine," Charlie said. And then: "Okay, turn it off."

He hadn't finished giving the order when the television flickered and went white, then settled down into its perpetual springtime scene that meant *off*. But in the flicker Charlie thought he saw—who? Name? From the distant past. A girl. Before the name came to him, there came another memory: a small hand resting lightly on his knee as they sat together, as light as a long-legged fly upon a stream. In his memory he did not turn to look at her; he was talking to others. But he knew just where she would be if he turned to look. Small, with mousy hair, and yet a face that was always the child Juliet. But that was not her name. Not Juliet, though she was Juliet's age in that memory. *I am Charlie*, he thought. *She is—Rachel.*

Rachel Carpenter. In the flicker on the screen hers was the face the random light had brought him, and so he remembered Rachel as he pulled his ancient body from the chair; thought of Rachel as he peeled the clothing from his frail skeleton, delicately, lest some rough motion strip away the wrinkled skin like cellophane.

And Jock, who of course did not switch himself off with the television, recited: "An aged man is a paltry thing, a tattered coat upon a stick."

"Shut up," Charlie ordered.

"Unless Soul clap its hands."

"I said shut up!"

"And sing, and louder sing, for every tatter in its mortal dress."

"Are you finished?" Charlie asked. He knew Jock was finished. After all, Charlie had programmed him to recite—*it* to recite—just that fragment every night when his shorts hit the floor.

He stood naked in the middle of the room and thought of Rachel, whom he had not thought of in years. It was a trick of being old, that the room he was in now so easily vanished, and in its place a memory could take hold. *I've made my fortune from time machines*, he thought, *and now I discover that every aged person is his own time machine.* For now he stood naked. No, that was a trick of memory; memory had these damnable tricks. He was not naked. He only felt naked, as Rachel sat in the car beside him. Her voice—he had almost forgotten her voice—was soft. Even when she shouted, it got more whispery, so that if she shouted, it would have all the wind of the world in it and he wouldn't hear it at all, would only feel it cold on his naked skin. That was the voice she was using now, saying yes. I loved you when I was twelve, and when I was thirteen, and when I was fourteen, but when you got back from playing God in São Paulo, you didn't call me. All those letters, and then for three months you didn't call me and I knew that you thought I was just a child and I fell in love with—Name? Name gone. Fell in love with a *boy*, and ever since then you've been treating me like. Like. No, she'd never say *shit*, not in that voice. And take some of the anger out, that's right. Here are the words . . . here they come: You could have had me, Charlie, but now all you can do is try to make me miserable. It's too late, the time's gone by, the time's over, so stop criticizing me. Leave me *alone*.

First to last, all in a capsule. The words are nothing, Charlie realized. A dozen women, not least his dear departed wife, had said exactly the same words to him since, and it had sounded just as maudlin, just as unpleasantly uninteresting every time. The difference was that when the others said it, Charlie felt himself insulated with a thousand layers of unconcern. But when Rachel said it to his memory, he stood naked in the middle of his room, a cold wind drying the parchment of his ancient skin.

"What's wrong?" asked Jock.

Oh, yes, dear computer, a change in the routine of the habitbound old man, and you suspect what, a heart attack? Incipient death? Extreme disorientation?

"A name," Charlie said. "Rachel Carpenter."

"Living or dead?"

Charlie winced again, as he winced every time Jock asked that question; yet it was an important one, and far too often the answer these days was Dead. "I don't know."

"Living and dead, I have two thousand four hundred eighty in the company archives alone."

"She was twelve when I was—twenty. Yes, twenty. And she lived then in Provo, Utah. Her father was a pianist. Maybe she became an actress when she grew up. She wanted to."

"Rachel Carpenter. Born 1959. Provo, Utah. Attended—"

"Don't show off, Jock. Was she ever married?"

"Thrice."

"And don't imitate my mannerisms. Is she still alive?"

"Died ten years ago."

Of course. Dead, of course. He tried to imagine her—where? "Where did she die?"

"Not pleasant."

"Tell me anyway. I'm feeling suicidal tonight."

"In a home for the mentally incapable."

It was not shocking; people often outlived their minds these days. But sad. For she had always been bright. Strange perhaps, but her thoughts always led to something worth the sometimes-convoluted path. He smiled even before he remembered what he was smiling at. Yes. Seeing through your knees. She had been playing Helen Keller in *The Miracle Worker*, and she told him how she had finally come to understand blindness. "It isn't seeing the red insides of your eyelids, I knew that. I knew it isn't even seeing black. It's like trying to see where you never had eyes at all. Seeing through your knees. No matter how hard you try, there just isn't any *vision* there." And she had liked him because he hadn't laughed. "I told my brother, and he laughed," she said. But Charlie had not laughed.

Charlie's affection for her had begun then, with a twelve-year-old girl who could never stay on the normal, intelligible track, but rather had to stumble her own way through a confusing underbrush that was thick and bright with flowers. "I think God stopped paying attention long ago." she said. "Any more than Michelangelo would want to watch them whitewash the Sistine Chapel."

And he knew that he would do it even before he knew what it was that he would do. She had ended in an institution, and he, with the best medical care that money could buy, stood naked in his room and remembered when passion still lurked behind the lattices of chastity and was more likely to lead to poems than to coitus.

You overtold story, he said to the wizened man who despised him from the mirror. You are only tempted because you're bored. Making excuses because you're cruel. Lustful because your dim old dong is long past the exercise.

And he heard the old bastard answer silently, You *will* do it, because you can. Of all the people in the world, *you* can.

And he thought he saw Rachel look back at him, bright with finding herself beautiful at fourteen, laughing at the vast joke of knowing she was admired by the very man whom she, too, wanted. Laugh all you like, Charlie said to his vision of her. I was too kind to you then. I'm afraid I'll undo my youthful goodness now.

"I'm going back," he said aloud. "Find me a day."

"For what purpose?" Jock asked.

"My business."

"I have to know your purpose, or how can I find you a day?"

And so he had to name it. "I'm going to have her if I can."

Suddenly a small alarm sounded, and Jock's voice was replaced by another. "Warning. Illegal use of THIEF for possible present-altering manipulation of the past."

Charlie smiled. "Investigation has found that the alteration is acceptable. Clear." And the program release: "Byzantium."

"You're a son of a bitch," said Jock.

"Find me a day. A day when the damage will be least—when I can. . ."

"Twenty-eight October 1973."

That was after he got home from São Paulo, the contracts signed, already a capitalist before he was twenty-three. That was during the time when he had been afraid to call her, because she was only fourteen, for God's sake.

"What will it do to her, Jock?"

"How should I know?" Jock answered. "And what difference would it make to you?"

He looked in the mirror again. "A difference."

I won't do it, he told himself as he went to the THIEF that was his most ostentatious sign of wealth, a private THIEF in his own rooms. I won't do it, he decided again as he set the machine to wake him in twelve hours, whether he wished to return or not. Then he climbed into the couch and pulled the shroud over his head, despairing that even this, even doing it to *her*, was not beneath him. There was a time when he had automatically held back from doing a thing because he knew that it was wrong. *Oh, for that time!* he thought, but knew as he thought it that he was lying to himself. He had long since given up on right and wrong and settled for the much simpler standards of effective and ineffective, beneficial and detrimental.

He had gone in a THIEF before, had taken some of the standard trips into the past. Gone into the mind of an audience member at the first performance of Handel's *Messiah* and listened. The poor soul whose ears he used wouldn't remember a bit of it afterward. So the future would not be changed. That was safe, to sit in a hall and listen. He had been in the mind of a farmer resting under a tree on a country lane as Wordsworth walked by and had hailed the poet and asked his name, and Wordsworth had smiled and been distant and cold, delighting in the countryside more than in those whose tillage made it beautiful. But those were legal trips—Charlie had done nothing that could alter the course of history.

This time, though. This time he would change Rachel's life. Not his own, of course. That would be impossible. But Rachel would not be blocked from remembering what happened. She would remember, and it would turn her from the path she was meant to take. Perhaps only a little. Perhaps not importantly. Perhaps just enough for her to dislike him a little sooner, or a little more. But too much to be legal, if he were caught.

He would not be caught. Not Charlie. Not the man who owned THIEF and therefore could have owned the world. It was all too bound up in secrecy. Too many agents had used his machines to attend the enemy's most private conferences. Too often the Attorney General had listened to the most perfect of wiretaps. Too often politicians who were willing to be in Charlie's debt had been given permission to lead their opponents into blunders that cost them votes. All far beyond what the law allowed; who would dare complain now if Charlie also bent the law to his own purpose?

No one but Charlie. *I can't do this to Rachel*, he thought. And then the THIEF carried him back and put him in his own mind, in his own body, on 28 October 1973, at ten o'clock, just as he was going to bed, weary because he had been wakened that morning by a six A.M. call from Brazil.

As always, there was the moment of resistance, and then peace as his self of that time slipped into unconsciousness. Old Charlie took over and saw, not the past, but the now.

*   *   *

A moment before, he was standing before a mirror, looking at his withered, hanging face; now he realizes that this gazing into a mirror before going to bed is a lifelong habit. *I am Narcissus*, he tells himself, *an unbeautiful idolator at my own shrine*. But now he is not unbeautiful. At twenty-two, his body still has the depth of young skin. His belly is soft, for he is not athletic, but still there is a litheness to him that he will never have again. And now the vaguely remembered needs that had impelled him to this find a physical basis; what had been a dim memory has him on fire.

He will not be sleeping tonight, not soon. He dresses again, finding with surprise the quaint print shirts that once had been in style. The wide-cuffed pants. The shoes with inch-and-a-half heels. *Good God, I wore that!* he thinks, and then wears it. No questions from his family; he goes quietly downstairs and out to his car. The garage reeks of gasoline. It is a smell as nostalgic as lilacs and candlewax.

He still knows the way to Rachel's house, though he is surprised at the buildings that have not yet been built, which roads have not yet been paved, which intersections still don't have the lights he knows they'll have soon, should surely have already. He looks at his wristwatch; it must be a habit of the body he is in, for he hasn't worn a wristwatch in decades. The arm is tanned from Brazilian beaches, and it has no age spots, no purple veins drawing roadmaps under the skin. The time is ten-thirty. *She'll doubtless be in bed.*

He almost stops himself. Few things are left in his private catalog of sin, but surely this is one. He looks into himself and tries to find the will to resist his own desire solely because its fulfillment will hurt another person. He is out of practice—so far out of practice that he keeps losing track of the reason for resisting.

The lights are on, and her mother—Mrs. Carpenter, dowdy and delightful, scatterbrained in the most attractive way—her mother opens the door suspiciously until she recognizes him. "Charlie," she cries out.

"Is Rachel still up?"

"Give me a minute and she will be!"

And he waits, his stomach trembling with anticipation. *I am not a virgin*, he reminds himself, *but this body does not know that*. This body is alert, for it has not yet formed the habits of meaningless passion that Charlie knows far too well. At last she comes down the stairs. He hears her running on the hollow wooden steps, then stopping, coming slowly, denying the hurry. She turns the corner, looks at him.

She is in her bathrobe, a faded thing that he does not remember ever having seen her wear. Her hair is tousled, and her eyes show that she had been asleep.

"I didn't mean to wake you."

"I wasn't really asleep. The first ten minutes don't count anyway."

He smiles. Tears come to his eyes. Yes, he says silently. This is Rachel, yes. The narrow face; the skin so translucent that he can see into it like jade; the slender arms that gesture shyly, with accidental grace.

"I couldn't wait to see you."

"You've been home three days. I thought you'd phone."

He smiles. In fact he will not phone her for months. But he says, "I hate the telephone. I want to talk to you. Can you come out for a drive?"

"I have to ask my mother."

"She'll say yes."

She does say yes. She jokes and says that she trusts Charlie. And the Charlie she knows was trustworthy. *But not me,* Charlie thinks. You are putting your diamonds into the hands of a thief.

"Is it cold?" Rachel asks.

"Not in the car." And so she doesn't take a coat. It's all right. The night breeze isn't bad.

As soon as the door closes behind them, Charlie begins. He puts his arm around her waist. She does not pull away or take it with indifference. He has never done this before, because she's only fourteen, just a child, but she leans against him as they walk, as if she had done this a hundred times before. As always, she takes him by surprise.

"I've missed you," he says.

She smiles, and there are tears in her eyes. "I've missed you, too," she says.

They talk of nothing. It's just as well. Charlie does not remember much about the trip to Brazil, does not remember anything of what he's done in the three days since getting back. No problem, for she seems to want to talk only of tonight. They drive to the Castle, and he tells her its history. He feels an irony about it as he explains. She, after all, is the reason he knows the history. A few years from now she will be part of a theater company that revives the Castle as a public amphitheater. But now it is falling into ruin, a monument to the old WPA, a great castle with turrets and benches made of native stone. It is on the property of the state mental hospital, and so hardly anyone knows it's there. They are alone as they leave the car and walk up the crumbling steps to the flagstone stage.

She is entranced. She stands in the middle of the stage, facing the benches. He watches as she raises her hand, speech waiting at the verge of her lips. He remembers something. Yes, that is the gesture she made when she bade her nurse farewell in *Romeo and Juliet*. No, not *made*. Will make, rather. The gesture must already be in her, waiting for this stage to draw it out.

She turns to him and smiles because the place is strange and odd and does not belong in Provo, but it does belong to her. She should have been born in the Renaissance, Charlie says softly. She hears him. He must have spoken aloud. "You belong in an age when music was clean and soft and there was no makeup. No one would rival you then."

She only smiles at the conceit. "I missed you," she says.

He touches her cheek. She does not shy away. Her cheek presses into his hand, and he knows that she understands why he brought her here and what he means to do.

Her breasts are perfect but small, her buttocks are boyish and slender, and the only hair on her body is that which tumbles onto her shoulders, that which he must brush out of her face to kiss her again. "I love you," she whispers. "All my life I love you."

And it is exactly as he would have had it in a dream, except that the flesh is tangible, the ecstasy is real, and the breeze turns colder as she shyly dresses again. They say nothing more as he takes her home. Her mother has fallen asleep on the living room couch, a jumble of the *Daily Herald* piled around her feet. Only then does he remember that for her there will be a tomorrow, and on that tomorrow Charlie will not call. For three months Charlie will not call, and she'll hate him.

He tries to soften it. He tries by saying, "Some things can happen only once." It is the sort of thing he might then have said. But she only puts her finger on his lips and says, "I'll never forget." Then she turns and walks toward her mother, to waken her. She turns and motions for Charlie to leave, then smiles again and waves. He waves back and goes out of the door and drives home. He lies awake in this bed that feels like childhood to him, and he wishes it could have gone on forever like this. *It should have gone on like this*, he thinks. *She is no child. She* was *no child*, he should have thought, for THIEF was already transporting him home.

"What's wrong, Charlie?" Jock asked.

Charlie awoke. It had been hours since THIEF brought him back. It was the middle of the night, and Charlie realized that he had been crying in his sleep. "Nothing," he said.

"You're crying, Charlie. I've never seen you cry before."

"Go plug into a million volts, Jock. I had a dream."

"What dream?"

"I destroyed her."

"No, you didn't."

"It was a goddamned selfish thing to do."

"You'd do it again. But it didn't hurt her."

"She was only fourteen."

"No, she wasn't."

"I'm tired. I was asleep. Leave me alone."

"Charlie, remorse isn't your style."

Charlie pulled the blanket over his head, feeling petulant and wondering whether this childish act was another proof that he was retreating into senility after all.

"Charlie, let me tell you a bedtime story."

"I'll erase you."

"Once upon a time, ten years ago, an old woman named Rachel Carpenter petitioned for a day in her past. And it was a day *with* someone, and it was a day with *you*. So the routine circuits called me, as they always do when your name comes up, and I found her a day. She only wanted to visit, you see, only wanted to relive a good day. I was surprised, Charlie. I didn't know you ever had good days."

This program had been with Jock too long. It knew too well how to get under his skin.

"And in fact there were no days as good as she thought," Jock continued. "Only anticipation and disappointment. That's all you ever gave anybody, Charlie. Anticipation and disappointment."

"I can count on you."

"This woman was in a home for the mentally incapable. And so I gave her a day. Only instead of a day of disappointment, or promises she knew would never be fulfilled, I gave her a day of answers. I gave her a night of answers, Charlie."

"You couldn't know that I'd have you do this. You couldn't have known it ten years ago."

"That's all right, Charlie. Play along with me. You're dreaming anyway, aren't you?"

"And don't wake me up."

"So an old woman went back into a young girl's body on twenty-eight October 1973, and the young girl never knew what had happened; so it didn't change her life, don't you see?"

"It's a lie."

"No, it isn't. I can't lie, Charlie. You programmed me not to lie. Do you think I would have let you go back and *harm* her?"

"She was the same. She was as I remembered her."

"Her body was."

"She hadn't changed. She wasn't an old woman, Jock. She was a girl. She was a girl, Jock."

And Charlie thought of an old woman dying in an institution, surrounded by yellow walls and pale gray sheets and curtains. He imagined young Rachel inside that withered form, imprisoned in a body that would not move, trapped in a mind that could never again take her along her bright, mysterious trails.

"I flashed her picture on the television," Jock said.

And yet, Charlie thought, *how is it less bearable than that beautiful boy who wanted so badly to do the right thing that he did it all wrong, lost his chance, and now is caught in the sum of all his wrong turns? I got on the road they all wanted to take, and I reached the top, but it wasn't where I should have gone. I'm still that boy. I did not have to lie when I went home to her.*

"I know you pretty well, Charlie," Jock said. "I knew that you'd be enough of a bastard to go back. And enough of a human being to do it right when you got there. She came back happy, Charlie. She came back satisfied."

His night with a beloved child was a lie then; it wasn't young Rachel any more than it was young Charlie. He looked for anger inside himself but couldn't find it. For a dead woman had given him a gift, and taken the one he offered, and it still tasted sweet.

"Time for sleep, Charlie. Go to sleep again. I just wanted you to know that there's no reason to feel any remorse for it. No reason to feel anything bad at all."

Charlie pulled the covers tight around his neck, unaware that he had begun that habit years ago, when the strange shadowy shapes hid in his closet and only the blanket could keep him safe. Pulled the covers high and tight, and closed his eyes, and felt her hand stroke him, felt her breast and hip and thigh, and heard her voice as breath against his cheek.

"O chestnut tree," Jock said, as he had been taught to say, ". . . great rooted blossomer,

"Are you the leaf, the blossom, or the bole?

"O body swayed to music, O brightening glance,

"How can we know the dancer from the dance?"

The audience applauded in his mind while he slipped into sleep, and he thought it remarkable that they sounded genuine. He pictured them smiling and nodding at the show. Smiling at the girl with her hand raised so; nodding at the man who paused forever, then came on stage.

DOGWALKER

I was an innocent pedestrian. Only reason I got in this in the first place was I got a vertical way of thinking and Dogwalker thought I might be useful, which was true, and also he said I might enjoy myself, which was a prefabrication, since people done a lot more enjoying on me than I done on them.

When I say I think vertical, I mean to say I'm metaphysical, that is, simular, which is to say, I'm dead but my brain don't know it yet and my feet still move. I got popped at age nine just lying in my own bed when the goat next door shot at his lady and it went through the wall and into my head. Everybody went to look at them cause they made all the noise, so I was a quart low before anybody noticed I been poked.

They packed my head with supergoo and light pipe, but they didn't know which neutron was supposed to butt into the next so my alchemical brain got turned from rust to diamond. Goo Boy. The Crystal Kid.

From that bright electrical day I never grew another inch, anywhere. Bullet went nowhere near my gonadicals. Just turned off the puberty switch in my head. Saint Paul said he was a eunuch for Jesus, but who am I a eunuch for?

Worst thing about it is here I am near thirty and I still have to take barkeepers to court before they'll sell me beer. And it ain't hardly worth it even though the judge prints out in my favor and the barkeep has to pay costs, because my corpse·is so little I get toxed on six ounces and pass out pissing after twelve. I'm a lousy drinking buddy. Besides, anybody hangs out with me looks like a pederast.

No, I'm not trying to make you drippy-drop for me—I'm used to it, OK? Maybe the homecoming queen never showed me True Love in a four-point spread, but I got this knack that certain people find real handy and so I always made out. I dress good and I ride the worm and I don't pay much income tax. Because I am the Password Man. Give me five minutes with anybody's curriculum vitae, which is to say their autopsychoscopy, and nine times out of ten I'll spit out their password and get you into their most nasty sticky sweet secret files. Actually it's usually more like three times out of ten, but that's still a lot better odds than having a computer spend a year trying to push out fifteen characters to make just the right P-word, specially since after the third wrong try they string your phone number, freeze the target files, and call the dongs.

Oh, do I make you sick? A cute little boy like me, engaged in critical unspecified dispopulative behaviors? I may be half glass and four feet high, but I can simulate you better than your own mama, and the better I know you, the deeper my hooks. I not only know your password *now*, I can write a word on a paper, seal it up, and then you go home and *change* your password and then open up what I wrote and there it'll be, your *new* password, three times out of ten. I am *vertical*, and Dogwalker knowed it. Ten percent more supergoo and I wouldn't even be legally human, but I'm still under the line, which is more than I can say for a lot of people who are a hundred percent zoo inside their head.

Dogwalker comes to me one day at Carolina Circle, where I'm playing pinball standing on a stool. He didn't say nothing, just gave me a shove, so naturally he got my elbow in his balls. I get a lot of twelve-year-olds trying to shove me around at the arcades, so I'm used to teaching them lessons. Jack the Giant Killer. Hero of the fourth graders. I usually go for the stomach, only Dogwalker wasn't a twelve-year-old, so my elbow hit low.

I knew the second I hit him that this wasn't no kid. I didn't know Dogwalker from God, but he gots the look, you know, like he been hungry before, and he don't care what he eats these days.

Only he got no ice and he got no slice, just sits there on the floor with his back up against the Eat Shi'ite game, holding his boodle and looking at me like I was a baby he had to diaper. "I hope you're Goo Boy," he says, "cause if you ain't, I'm gonna give you back to your mama in three little tupperware bowls." He doesn't sound like he's making a threat, though. He sounds like he's chief weeper at his own funeral.

"You want to do business, use your mouth, not your hands," I says. Only I say it real apoplectic, which is the same as apologetic except you are also still pissed.

"Come with me," he says. "I got to go buy me a truss. You pay the tax out of your allowance."

So we went to Ivey's and stood around in children's wear while he made his pitch. "One P-word," he says, "only there can't be no mistake. If there's a mistake, a guy loses his job and maybe goes to jail."

So I told him no. Three chances in ten, that's the best I can do. No guarantees. My record speaks for itself, but nobody's perfect, and I ain't even close.

"Come on," he says, "you got to have ways to make sure, right? If you can do three times out of ten, what if you find out more about the guy? What if you meet him?"

"OK, maybe fifty-fifty."

"Look, we can't go back for seconds. So maybe you can't get it. But do you *know* when you ain't got it?"

"Maybe half the time when I'm wrong, I know I'm wrong."

"So we got three out of four that you'll know whether you got it?"

"No," says I. "Cause half the time when I'm right, I don't know I'm right."

"Shee-it," he says. "This is like doing business with my baby brother."

"You can't afford me anyway," I says. "I pull two dimes minimum, and you barely got breakfast on your gold card."

"I'm offering a cut."

"I don't want a cut. I want cash."

"Sure thing," he says. He looks around, real careful. As if they wired the sign that said Boys Briefs Sizes 10–12. "I got an inside man at Federal Coding," he says.

"That's nothing," I says. "I got a bug up the First Lady's ass, and forty hours on tape of her breaking wind."

I got a mouth. I know I got a mouth. I especially know it when he jams my face into a pile of shorts and says, "Suck on this, Goo Boy."

I hate it when people push me around. And I know ways to make them stop. This time all I had to do was cry. Real loud, like he was hurting me. Everybody looks when a kid starts crying. "I'll be good." I kept saying it. "Don't hurt me no more! I'll be good."

"Shut up," he says. "Everybody's looking."

"Don't you ever shove me around again," I says. "I'm at least ten years older than you, and a hell of a lot more than ten years smarter. Now I'm leaving this store, and if I see you coming after me, I'll start screaming about how you zipped down and showed me the pope, and you'll get yourself a child-molesting tag so they pick you up every time some kid gets jollied within a hundred miles of Greensboro." I've done it before, and it works, and Dogwalker was no dummy. Last thing he needed was extra reasons for the dongs to bring him in for questioning. So I figured he'd tell me to get poked and that'd be the last of it.

Instead he says, "Goo Boy, I'm sorry, I'm too quick with my hands."

Even the goat who shot me never said he was sorry. My first thought was, what kind of sister is he, abjectifying right out like that. Then I reckoned I'd stick around and see what kind of man it is who emulsifies himself in front of a nine-year-old-looking kid. Not that I figured him to be purely sorrowful. He still just wanted me to get the P-word for him, and he knew there wasn't nobody else to do it. But most street pugs aren't smart enough to tell the right lie under pressure. Right away I knew he wasn't your ordinary street hook or low arm, pugging cause they don't have the sense to stick with any kind of job. He had a deep face, which is to say his head was more than a hairball, by which I mean he had brains enough to put his hands in his pockets without seeking an audience with the pope. Right then was when I decided he was my kind of no-good lying son-of-a-bitch.

"What are you after at Federal Coding?" I asked him. "A record wipe?"

"Ten clean greens," he says. "Coded for unlimited international travel. The whole ID, just like a real person."

"The President has a green card," I says. "The Joint Chiefs have clean greens. But that's all. The U.S. Vice-President isn't even cleared for unlimited international travel."

"Yes he is," he says.

"Oh, yeah, you know everything."

"I need a P. My guy could do us reds and blues, but a clean green has to be done by a burr-oak rat two levels up. My guy knows how it's done."

"They won't just have it with a P-word," I says. "A guy who can make green cards, they're going to have his finger on it."

"I know how to get the finger," he says. "It takes the finger *and* the password."

"You take a guy's finger, he might report it. And even if you persuade him not to, somebody's gonna notice that it's gone."

"Latex," he says. "We'll get a mold. And don't start telling me how to do my part of the job. You get P-words, I get fingers. You in?"

"Cash," I says.

"Twenty percent," says he.

"Twenty percent of pus."

"The inside guy gets twenty, the girl who brings me the finger, she gets twenty, and I damn well get forty."

"You can't just sell these things on the street, you know."

"They're worth a meg apiece," says he, "to certain buyers." By which he meant Orkish Crime, of course. Sell ten, and my twenty percent grows up to be two megs. Not enough to be rich, but enough to retire from public life and maybe even pay for some high-level medicals to sprout hair on my face. I got to admit that sounded good to me.

So we went into business. For a few hours he tried to do it without telling me the baroque rat's name, just giving me data he got from his guy at Federal Coding. But that was real stupid, giving me secondhand face like that, considering he needed me to be a hundred percent sure, and pretty soon he realized that and brought me in all the way. He hated telling me anything, because he couldn't stand to let go. Once I knew stuff on my own, what was to stop me from trying to go into business for myself? But unless he had another way to get the P-word, he had to get it from me, and for me to do it right, I had to know everything I could. Dogwalker's got a brain in his head, even if it is all biodegradable, and so he knows there's times when you got no choice but to trust somebody. When you just got to figure they'll do their best even when they're out of your sight.

He took me to his cheap condo on the old Guilford College campus, near the worm, which was real congenital for getting to Charlotte or Winston or Raleigh with no fuss. He didn't have no soft floor, just a bed, but it was a big one, so I didn't reckon he suffered. Maybe he bought it back in his old pimping days, I figured, back when he got his name, running a string of bitches with names like Spike and Bowser and Prince, real hydrant leg-lifters for the tweeze trade. I could see that he used to have money, and he didn't anymore. Lots of great clothes, tailor-tight fit, but shabby, out of sync. The really old ones, he tore all the wiring out, but you could still see where the diodes used to light up. We're talking neanderthal.

"Vanity, vanity, all is profanity," says I, while I'm holding out the sleeve of a camisa that used to light up like an airplane coming in for a landing.

"They're too comfortable to get rid of," he says. But there's a twist in his voice so I know he don't plan to fool nobody.

"Let this be a lesson to you," says I. "This is what happens when a walker don't walk."

"Walkers do steady work," says he. "But me, when business was good, it felt bad, and when business was bad, it felt good. You walk cats, maybe you can take some pride in it. But you walk dogs, and you know they're getting hurt every time—"

"They got a built-in switch, they don't feel a thing. That's why the dongs don't touch you, walking dogs, cause nobody gets hurt."

"Yeah, so tell me, which is worse, somebody getting tweezed till they scream so some old honk can pop his pimple, or somebody getting half their brain replaced so when the old honk tweezes her she can't feel a thing? I had these women's bodies around me and I knew that they used to be people."

"You can be glass," says I, "and still be people."

He saw I was taking it personally. "Oh hey," says he, "you're under the line."

"So are dogs," says I.

"Yeah well," says he. "You watch a girl come back and tell about some of the things they done to her, and she's *laughing*, you draw your own line."

I look around his shabby place. "Your choice," says I.

"I wanted to feel clean," says he. "That don't mean I got to stay poor."

"So you're setting up this grope so you can return to the old days of peace and propensity."

"Propensity," says he. "What the hell kind of word is that? Why do you keep using words like that?"

"Cause I know them," says I.

"Well you *don't* know them," says he, "because half the time you get them wrong."

I showed him my best little-boy grin. "I know," says I. What I don't tell him is that the fun comes from the fact that almost nobody ever *knows* I'm using them wrong. Dogwalker's no ordinary pimp. But then the ordinary pimp doesn't bench himself halfway through the game because of a sprained moral qualm, by which I mean that Dogwalker had some stray diagonals in his head, and I began to think it might be fun to see where they all hooked up.

Anyway we got down to business. The target's name was Jesse H. Hunt, and I did a real job on him. The Crystal Kid really plugged in on this one. Dogwalker had about two pages of stuff—date of birth, place of birth, sex at birth (no changes since), education, employment history. It was like getting an armload of empty boxes. I just laughed at it. "You got a jack to the city library?" I asked him, and he shows me the wall outlet. I plugged right in, visual onto my pocket sony, with my own little crystal head for ee-i-ee-i-oh. Not every goo-head can think clear enough to do this, you know, put out clean type just by thinking the right stuff out my left ear interface port.

I showed Dogwalker a little bit about research. Took me ten minutes. I know my way right through the Greensboro Public Library. I have P-words for every single librarian and I'm so ept that they don't even guess I'm stepping upstream through their access channels. From the Public Library you can get all the way into North Carolina Records Division in Raleigh, and from there you can jumble into federal personnel records anywhere in the country. Which meant that by nightfall on that most portentous day we had hardcopy of every document in Jesse H. Hunt's whole life, from his birth certificate and first grade report card to his medical history and security clearance reports when he first worked for the feds.

Dogwalker knew enough to be impressed. "If you can do all that," he says, "you might as well pug his P-word straight out."

"No puedo, putz," says I as cheerful as can be. "Think of the fed as a castle. Personnel files are floating in the moat—there's a few alligators but I swim real good. Hot data is deep in the dungeon. You can get in there, but you can't get out clean. And P-words—P-words are kept up the queen's ass."

"No system is unbeatable," he says.

"Where'd you learn that, from graffiti in a toilet stall? If the P-word system was even a little bit breakable, Dogwalker, the gentlemen you plan to sell these cards to would already be inside looking out at us, and they wouldn't need to spend a meg to get clean greens from a street pug."

Trouble was that after impressing Dogwalker with all the stuff I could find out about Jesse H., I didn't know that much more than before. Oh, I could guess at some P-words, but that was all it was—guessing. I couldn't even pick a P most likely to succeed. Jesse was one ordinary dull rat. Regulation good grades in school, regulation good evaluations on the job, probably gave his wife regulation lube jobs on a weekly schedule.

"You don't really think your girl's going to get his finger," says I with sickening scorn.

"You don't know the girl," says he. "If we needed his flipper she'd get molds in five sizes."

"You don't know this guy," says I. "This is the straightest opie in Mayberry. I don't see him cheating on his wife."

"Trust me," says Dogwalker. "She'll get his finger so smooth he won't even know she took the mold."

I didn't believe him. I got a knack for knowing things about people, and Jesse H. wasn't faking. Unless he started faking when he was five, which is pretty unpopulated. He wasn't going to bounce the first pretty girl who made his zipper tight. Besides which he was smart. His career path showed that he was always in the right place. The right people always seemed to know his name. Which is to say he isn't the kind whose brain can't run if his jeans get hot. I said so.

"You're really a marching band," says Dogwalker. "You can't tell me his P-word, but you're obliquely sure that he's a limp or a wimp."

"Neither one," says I. "He's hard and straight. But a girl starts rubbing up to him, he isn't going to think it's because she heard that his crotch is cantilevered. He's going to figure she wants something, and he'll give her string till he finds out what."

He just grinned at me. "I got me the best Password Man in the Triass, didn't I? I got me a miracle worker named Goo-Boy, didn't I? The ice-brain they call Crystal Kid. I got him, didn't I?"

"Maybe," says I.

"I got him or I kill him," he says, showing more teeth than a primate's supposed to have.

"You got me," says I. "But don't go thinking you can kill me."

He just laughs. "I got you and you're so good, you can bet I got me a girl who's at least as good at what she does."

"No such," says I.

"Tell me his P-word and then I'll be impressed."

"You want quick results? Then go ask him to give you his password himself."

Dogwalker isn't one of those guys who can hide it when he's mad. "I want quick results," he says. "And if I start thinking you can't deliver, I'll pull your tongue out of your head. Through your nose."

"Oh, that's good," says I. "I always do my best thinking when I'm being physically threatened by a client. You really know how to bring out the best in me."

"I don't want to bring out the best," he says. "I just want to bring out his password."

"I got to meet him first," says I.

He leans over me so I can smell his musk, which is to say I'm very olfactory and so I can tell you he reeked of testosterone, by which I mean ladies could fill up with babies just from sniffing his sweat. "Meet him?" he asks me. "Why don't we just ask him to fill out a job application?"

"I've read all his job applications," says I.

"How's a glass-head like you going to meet Mr. Fed?" says he. "I bet you're always getting invitations to the same parties as guys like him."

"I don't get invited to *grown-up* parties," says I. "But on the other hand, grown-ups don't pay much attention to sweet little kids like me."

He sighed. "You really have to meet him?"

"Unless fifty-fifty on a P-word is good enough odds for you."

All of a sudden he goes nova. Slaps a glass off the table and it breaks against the wall, and then he kicks the table over, and all the time I'm thinking about ways to get out of there unkilled. But it's me he's doing the show for, so there's no way I'm leaving, and he leans in close to me and screams in my face. "That's the last of your fifty-fifty and sixty-forty and three times in ten I want to hear about, Goo Boy, you hear me?"

And I'm talking real meek and sweet, cause this boy's twice my size and three times my weight and I don't exactly have no leverage. So I says to him, "I can't help talking in odds and percentages, Dogwalker, I'm vertical, remember? I've got glass channels in here, they spit out percentages as easy as other people sweat."

He slapped his hand against his own head. "This ain't exactly a sausage biscuit, either, but you know and I know that when you give me all them exact numbers it's all guesswork anyhow. You don't know the odds on this beakrat anymore than I do."

"I don't know the odds on *him*, Walker, but I know the odds on *me*. I'm sorry you don't like the way I sound so precise, but my crystal memory has every P-word I ever plumbed, which is to say I can give you exact to the third decimal percentages on when I hit it right on the first try after meeting the subject, and how many times I hit it right on the first try just from his curriculum vitae, and right now if I don't meet him and I go on just what I've got here you have a 48.838 percent chance I'll be right on my P-word first time and a 66.667 chance I'll be right with one out of three."

Well that took him down, which was fine I must say because he loosened up my sphincters with that glass-smashing table-tossing hot-breath-in-my-face routine he did. He stepped back and put his hands in his pockets and leaned against the wall. "Well I chose the right P-man, then, didn't I," he says, but he doesn't smile, no, he *says* the back-down words but his eyes don't back down, his eyes say don't try to flash my face because I see through you, I got most excellent inward shades all polarized to keep out your glitz and see you straight and clear. I never saw eyes like that before. Like he knew me. Nobody ever knew me, and I didn't think he *really* knew me either, but I didn't like him looking at me as if he *thought* he knew me cause the fact is I didn't know me all that well and it worried me to think he might know me better than I did, if you catch my drift.

"All I have to do is be a little lost boy in a store," I says.

"What if he isn't the kind who helps little lost boys?"

"Is he the kind who lets them cry?"

"I don't know. What if he is? What then? Think you can get away with meeting him a second time?"

"So the lost boy in the store won't work. I can crash my bicycle on his front lawn. I can try to sell him cable magazines."

But he was ahead of me already. "For the cable magazines he slams the door in your face, if he even comes to the door at all. For the bicycle crash, you're out of your little glass brain. I got my inside girl working on him right now, very complicated, because he's not the playing around kind, so she has to make this a real emotional come-on, like she's breaking up with a boyfriend and he's the only shoulder she can cry on, and his wife is so lucky to have a man like him. This much he can believe. But then suddenly he has this little boy crashing in his yard, and because he's paranoid, he begins to wonder if some weird rain isn't falling, right? I know he's paranoid because you don't get to his level in the fed without you know how to watch behind you and kill the enemy even before *they* know they're out to get you. So he even suspects, for one instant, that somebody's setting him up for something, and what does he do?"

I knew what Dogwalker was getting at now, and he was right, and so I let him have his victory and I let the words he wanted march out all in a row. "He changes all his passwords, all his habits, and watches over his shoulder all the time."

"And my little project turns into compost. No clean greens."

So I saw for the first time why this street boy, this ex-pimp, why he was the one to do this job. He wasn't vertical like me, and he didn't have the inside hook like his fed boy, and he didn't have bumps in his sweater so he couldn't do the girl part, but he had eyes in his elbows, ears in his knees, by which I mean he noticed everything there was to notice and then he thought of new things that weren't even noticeable yet and noticed them. He earned his forty percent. And he earned part of my twenty, too.

Now while we waited around for the girl to fill Jesse's empty aching arms and get a finger off him, and while we were still working on how to get me to meet him slow and easy and sure, I spent a lot of time with Dogwalker. Not that he ever asked me, but I found myself looping his bus route every morning till he picked me up, or I'd be eating at Bojangle's when he came in to throw cajun chicken down into his ulcerated organs. I watched to make sure he didn't mind, cause I didn't want to piss this boy, having once beheld the majesty of his wrath, but if he wanted to shiver me he gave me no shiv.

Even after a few days, when the ghosts of the cold hard street started haunting us, he didn't shake me, and that includes when Bellbottom says to him, "Looks like you stopped walking dogs. Now you pimping little boys, right? Little catamites, we call you Catwalker now, that so? Or maybe you just keep him for private use, is that it? You be Boypoker now?" Well like I always said, someday somebody's going to kill Bellbottom just to flay him and use his skin for a convertible roof, but Dogwalker just waved and walked on by while I made little pissy bumps at Bell. Most people shake me right off when they start getting splashed on about liking little boys, but Doggy, he didn't say we were friends or nothing, but he didn't give me no Miami howdy, neither, which is to say I didn't find myself floating in the Bermuda Triangle with my ass pulled down around my ankles, by which I mean he wasn't ashamed to be seen with me on the street, which don't sound like a six-minute orgasm to you but to me it was like a breeze in August, I didn't ask for it and I don't trust it to last but as long as it's there I'm going to like it.

How I finally got to meet Jesse H. was dervish, the best I ever thought of. Which made me wonder why I never thought of it before, except that I never before had Dogwalker like a parrot saying "stupid idea" every time I thought of something. By the time I finally got a plan that he didn't say "stupid idea," I was almost drowned in the deepest lightholes of my lucidity. I mean I was going at a hundred watts by the time I satisfied him.

First we found out who did babysitting for them when Jesse H. and Mrs. Jesse went out on the town (which for Nice People in G-boro means walking around the mall wishing there was something to do and then taking a piss in the public john). They had two regular teenage girls who usually came over and ignored their children for a fee, but when these darlettes were otherwise engaged, which meant they had a contract to get squeezed and poked by some half-zipped boy in exchange for a humbuger and a vid, they called upon Mother Hubbard's Homecare Hotline. So I most carefully assinuated myself into Mother Hubbard's estimable organization by passing myself off as a lamentably prepubic fourteen-year-old, specializing in the northwest section of town and on into the county. All this took a week, but Walker was in no hurry. Take the time to do it right, he said, if we hurry somebody's going to notice the blur of motion and look our way and just by looking at us they'll undo us. A horizontal mind that boy had.

Came a most delicious night when the Hunts went out to play, and both their diddle-girls were busy being squeezed most delectably (and didn't we have a lovely time persuading two toddle-boys to do the squeezing that very night). This news came to Mr. and Mrs. Jesse at the very last minute, and they had no choice but to call Mother Hubbard's, and isn't it lovely that just a half hour before, sweet little Stevie Queen, being *moi*, called in and said that he was available for baby-stomping after all. Ein and ein made zwei, and there I was being dropped off by a Mother Hubbard driver at the door of the Jesse Hunt house, whereupon I not only got to look upon the beatific face of Mr. Fed himself, I also got to have my dear head patted by Mrs. Fed, and then had the privilege of preparing little snacks for fussy Fed Jr. and foul-mouthed Fedene, the five-year-old and the three-year-old, while Microfed, the one-year-old (not yet human and, if I am any judge of character, not likely to live long enough to become such) sprayed uric acid in my face while I was diapering him. A good time was had by all.

Because of my heroic efforts, the small creatures were in their truckle beds quite early, and being a most fastidious baby-tucker, I browsed the house looking for burglars and stumbling, quite by chance, upon the most useful information about the beak-rat whose secret self-chosen name I was trying to learn. For one thing, he had set a watchful hair upon each of his bureau drawers, so that if I had been inclined to steal, he would know that unlawful access of his drawers had been attempted. I learned that he and his wife had separate containers of everything in the bathroom, even when they used the same brand of toothpaste, and it was he, not she, who took care of all their prophylactic activities (and not a moment too soon, thought I, for I had come to know their children). He was not the sort to use lubrificants or little pleasure-giving ribs, either. Only the regulation government-issue hard-as-concrete rubber rafts for him, which suggested to my most pernicious mind that he had almost as much fun between the sheets as me.

I learned all kinds of joyful information, all of it trivial, all of it vital. I never know which of the threads I grasp are going to make connections deep within the lumens of my brightest caves. But I never before had the chance to wander unmolested through a person's own house when searching for his P-word. I saw the notes his children brought home from school, the magazines his family received, and more and more I began to see that Jesse H. Hunt barely touched his family at any point. He stood like a waterbug on the surface of life, without ever getting his feet wet. He could die, and if nobody tripped over the corpse it would be weeks before they noticed. And yet this was not because he did not care. It was because he was so very very careful. He examined everything, but through the wrong end of the microscope, so that it all became very small and far away. I was a sad little boy by the end of that night, and I whispered to Microfed that he should practice pissing in male faces, because that's the only way he would ever sink a hook into his daddy's face.

"What if he wants to take you home?" Dogwalker asked me, and I said, "No way he would, nobody does that," but Dogwalker made sure I had a place to go all the same, and sure enough, it was Doggy who got voltage and me who went limp. I ended up riding in a beak-rat buggy, a genuine made-in-America rattletrap station wagon, and he took me to the for-sale house where Mama Pimple was waiting crossly for me and made Mr. Hunt go away because he kept me out too late. Then when the door was closed Mama Pimple giggled her gig and chuckled her chuck, and Walker himself wandered out of the back room and said, "That's one less favor you owe me, Mama Pimple," and she said, "No, my dear boyoh, that's one more favor *you* owe *me*" and then they kissed a deep passionate kiss if you can believe it. Did you imagine anybody ever kissed Mama Pimple that way? Dogwalker is a boyful of shocks.

"Did you get all you needed?" he asks me.

"I have P-words dancing upward," says I, "and I'll have a name for you tomorrow in my sleep."

"Hold onto it and don't tell me," says Dogwalker. "I don't want to hear a name until after we have his finger."

That magical day was only hours away, because the girl—whose name I never knew and whose face I never saw—was to cast her spell over Mr. Fed the very next day. As Dogwalker said, this was no job for lingeree. The girl did not dress pretty and pretended to be lacking in the social graces, but she was a good little clerical who was going through a most distressing period in her private life, because she had undergone a premature hysterectomy, poor lass, or so she told Mr. Fed, and here she was losing her womanhood and she had never really felt like a woman at all. But he was so kind to her, for weeks he had been so kind, and Dogwalker told me afterward how he locked the door of his office for just a few minutes, and held her and kissed her to make her feel womanly, and once his fingers had all made their little impressions on the thin electrified plastic microcoating all over her lovely naked back and breasts, she began to cry and most gratefully informed him that she did not want him to be unfaithful to his wife for her sake, that he had already given her such a much of a lovely gift by being so kind and understanding, and she felt better thinking that a man like him could bear to touch her knowing she was defemmed inside, and now she thought she had the confidence to go on. A very convincing act, and one calculated to get his hot naked handprints without giving him a crisis of conscience that might change his face and give him a whole new set of possible Ps.

The microsheet got all his fingers from several angles, and so Walker was able to dummy out a finger mask for our inside man within a single night. Right index. I looked at it most skeptically, I fear, because I had my doubts already dancing in the little lightpoints of my inmost mind. "Just one finger?"

"All we get is one shot," said Dogwalker. "One single try."

"But if he makes a mistake, if my first password isn't right, then he could use the middle finger on the second try."

"Tell me, my vertical pricket, whether you think Jesse H. Hunt is the sort of burr oak rat who makes mistakes?"

To which I had to answer that he was not, and yet I had my misgivings and my misgivings all had to do with needing a second finger, and yet I am vertical, not horizontal, which means that I can see the present as deep as you please but the future's not mine to see, que sera, sera.

From what Doggy told me, I tried to imagine Mr. Fed's reaction to this nubile flesh that he had pressed. If he had poked as well as peeked, I think it would have changed his P-word, but when she told him that she would not want to compromise his un-compromising virtue, it reinforced him as a most regular or even regulation fellow and his name remained pronouncedly the same, and his P-word also did not change. "InvictusXYZrwr," quoth I to Dogwalker, for that was his veritable password, I knew it with more certainty than I had ever had before.

"Where in hell did you come up with that?" says he.

"If I knew how I did it, Walker, I'd never miss at all," says I. "I don't even know if it's in the goo or in the zoo. All the facts go down, and it all gets mixed around, and up come all these dancing P-words, little pieces of P."

"Yeah but you don't just make it up, what does it mean?"

"Invictus is an old poem in a frame stuck in his bureau drawer, which his mama gave him when he was still a little fed-to-be. XYZ is his idea of randomizing, and rwr is the first U.S. President that he admired. I don't know why he chose these words now. Six weeks ago he was using a different P-word with a lot of numbers in it, and six weeks from now he'll change again, but right now—"

"Sixty percent sure?" asked Doggy.

"I give no percents this time," says I. "I've never roamed through the bathroom of my subject before. But this or give me an assectomy, I've never been more sure."

Now that he had the P-word, the inside guy began to wear his magic finger every day, looking for a chance to be alone in Mr. Fed's office. He had already created the preliminary files, like any routine green card requests, and buried them within his work area. All he needed was to go in, sign on as Mr. Fed, and then if the system accepted his name and P-word and finger, he could call up the files, approve them, and be gone within a minute. But he had to have that minute.

And on that wonderful magical day he had it. Mr. Fed had a meeting and his secretary sprung a leak a day early, and in went Inside Man with a perfectly legitimate note to leave for Hunt. He sat before the terminal, typed name and P-word and laid down his phony finger, and the machine spread wide its lovely legs and bid him enter. He had the files processed in forty seconds, laying down his finger for each green, then signed off and went on out. No sign, no sound that anything was wrong. As sweet as summertime, as smooth as ice, and all we had to do was sit and wait for green cards to come in the mail.

"Who you going to sell them to?" says I.

"I offer them to no one till I have clean greens in my hand," says he. Because Dogwalker is careful. What happened was not because he was not careful.

Every day we walked to the ten places where the envelopes were supposed to come. We knew they wouldn't be there for a week—the wheels of government grind exceeding slow, for good or ill. Every day we checked with Inside Man, whose name and face I have already given you, much good it will do, since both are no doubt different by now. He told us every time that all was the same, nothing was changed, and he was telling the truth, for the fed was most lugubrious and palatial and gave no leaks that anything was wrong. Even Mr. Hunt himself did not know that aught was amiss in his little kingdom.

Yet even with no sign that I could name, I was jumpy every morning and sleepless every night. "You walk like you got to use the toilet," says Walker to me, and it is verily so. Something is wrong, I say to myself, something is most deeply wrong, but I cannot find the name for it even though I know, and so I say nothing, or I lie to myself and try to invent a reason for my fear. "It's my big chance," says I. "To be twenty percent of rich."

"Rich," says he, "not just a fifth."

"Then you'll be double rich."

And he just grins at me, being the strong and silent type.

"But then why don't you sell nine," says I, "and keep the other green? Then you'll have the money to pay for it, and the green to go where you want in all the world."

But he just laughs at me and says, "Silly boy, my dear sweet pinheaded lightbrained little friend. If someone sees a pimp like me passing a green, he'll tell a fed, because he'll know there's been a mistake. Greens don't go to boys like me."

"But you won't be dressed like a pimp," says I, "and you won't stay in pimp hotels."

"I'm a low-class pimp," he says again, "and so however I dress that day, that's just the way pimps dress. And whatever hotel I go to, that's a low-class pimp hotel until I leave."

"Pimping isn't some disease," says I. "It isn't in your gonads and it isn't in your genes. If your daddy was a Kroc and your mama was an Iacocca, you wouldn't be a pimp."

"The hell I wouldn't," says he. "I'd just be a high-class pimp, like my mama and my daddy. Who do you think gets green cards? You can't sell no virgins on the street."

I thought that he was wrong and I still do. If anybody could go from low to high in a week, it's Dogwalker. He could be anything and do anything, and that's the truth. Or almost anything. If he could do *anything* then his story would have a different ending. But it was not his fault. Unless you blame pigs because they can't fly. *I* was the vertical one, wasn't I? I should have named my suspicions and we wouldn't have passed those greens.

I held them in my hands, there in his little room, all ten of them when he spilled them on the bed. To celebrate he jumped up so high he smacked his head on the ceiling again and again, which made them ceiling tiles dance and flip over and spill dust all over the room. "I flashed just one, a single one," says he, "and a cool million was what he said, and then I said what if ten? And he laughs and says fill in the check yourself."

"We should test them," says I.

"We can't test them," he says. "The only way to test it is to use it, and if you use it then your print and face are in its memory forever and so we could never sell it."

"Then sell one, and make sure it's clean."

"A package deal," he says. "If I sell one, and they think I got more by I'm holding out to raise the price, then I may not live to collect for the other nine, because I might have an accident and lose these little babies. I sell all ten tonight at once, and then I'm out of the green card business for life."

But more than ever that night I am afraid, he's out selling those greens to those sweet gentlebodies who are commonly referred to as Organic Crime, and there I am on his bed, shivering and dreaming because I know that something will go most deeply wrong but I still don't know what and I still don't know why. I keep telling myself, You're only afraid because nothing could ever go so right for you, you can't believe that anything could ever make you rich and safe. I say this stuff so much that I believe that I believe it, but I don't really, not down deep, and so I shiver again and finally I cry, because after all my body still believes I'm nine, and nine-year-olds have tear ducts very easy of access, no password required. Well he comes in late that night, and I'm asleep he thinks, and so he walks quiet instead of dancing, but I can hear the dancing in his little sounds, I know he has the money all safely in the bank, and so when he leans over to make sure if I'm asleep, I say, "Could I borrow a hundred thou?"

So he slaps me and he laughs and dances and sings, and I try to go along, you bet I do, I know I should be happy, but then at the end he says, "You just can't take it, can you? You just can't handle it," and then I cry all over again, and he just puts his arm around me like a movie dad and gives me play-punches on the head and says, "I'm gonna marry me a wife, I am, maybe even Mama Pimple herself, and we'll adopt you and have a little spielberg family in Summerfield, with a riding mower on a real grass lawn."

"I'm older than you *or* Mama Pimple," says I, but he just laughs. Laughs and hugs me until he thinks that I'm all right. Don't go home, he says to me that night, but home I got to go, because I know I'll cry again, from fear or something, anyway, and I don't want him to think his cure wasn't permanent. "No thanks," says I, but he just laughs at me. "Stay here and cry all you want to, Goo Boy, but don't go home tonight.

I don't want to be alone tonight, and sure as hell you don't either." And so I slept between his sheets, like with a brother, him punching and tickling and pinching and telling dirty jokes about his whores, the most good and natural night I spent in all my life, with a true friend, which I know you don't believe, snickering and nickering and ickering your filthy little thoughts, there was no holes plugged that night because nobody was out to take pleasure from nobody else, just Dogwalker being happy and wanting me not to be so sad.

And after he was asleep, I wanted so bad to know who it was he sold them to, so I could call them up and say, "Don't use those greens, cause they aren't clean. I don't know how, I don't know why, but the feds are onto this, I know they are, and if you use those cards they'll nail your fingers to your face." But if I called would they believe me? They were careful too. Why else did it take a week? They had one of their nothing goons use a card to make sure it had no squeaks or leaks, and it came up clean. Only then did they give the cards to seven big boys, with two held in reserve. Even Organic Crime, the All-seeing Eye, passed those cards same as we did.

I think maybe Dogwalker was a little bit vertical too. I think he knew same as me that something was wrong with this. That's why he kept checking back with the inside man, cause he didn't trust how good it was. That's why he didn't spend any of his share. We'd sit there eating the same old schlock, out of his cut from some leg job or my piece from a data wipe, and every now and then he'd say, "Rich man's food sure tastes good." Or maybe even though he wasn't vertical he still thought maybe I was right when I thought something was wrong. Whatever he thought, though, it just kept getting worse and worse for me, until the morning when we went to see the inside man and the inside man was gone.

Gone clean. Gone like he never existed. His apartment for rent, cleaned out floor to ceiling. A phone call to the fed, and he was on vacation, which meant they had him, he wasn't just moved to another house with his newfound wealth. We stood there in his empty place, his shabby empty hovel that was ten times better than anywhere we ever lived, and Doggy says to me, real quiet, he says, "What was it? What did I do wrong? I thought I was like Hunt, I thought I never made a single mistake in this job, in this one job."

And that was it, right then I knew. Not a week before, not when it would do any good. Right then I finally knew it all, knew what Hunt had done. Jesse Hunt never made *mistakes*. But he was also so paranoid that he haired his bureau to see if the babysitter stole from him. So even though he would never *accidentally* enter the wrong P-word, he was just the kind who would do it *on purpose*. "He doublefingered every time," I says to Dog. "He's so damn careful he does his password wrong the first time every time, and then comes in on his second finger."

"So one time he comes in on the first try, so what?" He says this because he doesn't know computers like I do, being half-glass myself.

"The system knew the pattern, that's what. Jesse H. is so precise he never changed a bit, so when *we* came in on the first try, that set off alarms. It's my fault, Dog, I knew how crazy paranoidical he is, I knew that something was wrong, but not till this minute I didn't know what it was. I should have known it when I got his password, I should have known, I'm sorry, you never should have gotten me into this, I'm sorry, you should have listened to me when I told you something was wrong, I should have known, I'm sorry."

What I done to Doggy that I never meant to do. What I done to him! Anytime, I could have thought of it, it was all there inside my glassy little head, but no, I didn't think of it till after it was way too late. And maybe it's because I didn't want to think of it, maybe it's because I really wanted to be wrong about the green cards, but however it flew, I did what I do, which is to say I'm not the pontiff in his fancy chair, by which I mean I can't be smarter than myself.

Right away he called the gentlebens of Ossified Crime to warn them, but I was already plugged into the library sucking news as fast as I could and so I knew it wouldn't do no good, cause they got all seven of the big boys and their nitwit taster, too, locked up good and tight for card fraud.

And what they said on the phone to Dogwalker made things real clear. "We're dead," says Doggy.

"Give them time to cool," says I.

"They'll never cool," says he. "There's no chance, they'll never forgive this even if they know the whole truth, because look at the names they gave the cards to, it's like they got them for their biggest boys on the borderline, the habibs who bribe presidents of little countries and rake off cash from octopods like Shell and ITT and every now and then kill somebody and walk away clean. Now they're sitting there in jail with the whole life story of the organization in their brains, so they don't care if we meant to do it or not. They're hurting, and the only way they know to make the hurt go away is to pass it on to somebody else. And that's us. They want to make us hurt, and hurt real bad, and for a long long time."

I never saw Dog so scared. That's the only reason we went to the feds ourselves. We didn't ever want to stool, but we needed their protection plan, it was our only hope. So we offered to testify how we did it, not even for immunity, just so they'd change our faces and put us in a safe jail somewhere to work off the sentence and come out alive, you know? That's all we wanted.

But the feds, they laughed at us. They had the inside guy, see, and he was going to get immunity for testifying. "We don't need you," they says to us, "and we don't care if you go to jail or not. It was the big guys we wanted."

"If you let us walk," says Doggy, "then they'll think we set them up."

"Make us laugh," says the feds. "Us work with street poots like you? They know that we don't stoop so low."

"They bought from us," says Doggy. "If we're big enough for them, we're big enough for the dongs."

"Do you believe this?" says one fed to his identical junior officer. "These jollies are begging us to take them into jail. Well listen tight, my jolly boys, maybe we don't want to add you to the taxpayers' expense account, did you think of that? Besides, all we'd give you is time, but on the street, those boys will give you time and a half, and it won't cost us a dime."

So what could we do? Doggy just looks like somebody sucked out six pints, he's so white. On the way out of the fedhouse, he says, "Now we're going to find out what it's like to die."

And I says to him, "Walker, they stuck no gun in your mouth yet, they shove no shiv in your eye. We still breathing, we got legs, so let's *walk* out of here."

"Walk!" he says. "You walk out of G-boro, glasshead, and you bump into trees."

"So what?" says I. "I can plug in and pull out all the data we want about how to live in the woods. Lots of empty land out there. Where do you think the marijuana grows?"

"I'm a city boy," he says. "I'm a city boy." Now we're standing out in front, and he's looking around. "In the city I got a chance, I know the city."

"Maybe in New York or Dallas," says I, "but G-boro's just too small, not even half a million people, you can't lose yourself deep enough here."

"Yeah well," he says, still looking around. "It's none of your business now anyway, Goo Boy. They aren't blaming *you*, they're blaming *me*."

"But it's my fault," says I, "and I'm staying with you to tell them so."

"You think they're going to stop and listen?" says he.

"I'll let them shoot me up with speakeasy so they know I'm telling the truth."

"It's nobody's fault," says he. "And I don't give a twelve-inch poker whose fault it is anyway. You're clean, but if you stay with me you'll get all muddy, too. I don't need you around, and you sure as hell don't need me. Job's over. Done. Get lost."

But I couldn't do that. The same way he couldn't go on walking dogs, I couldn't just run off and leave him to eat my mistake. "They know I was your P-word man," says I. "They'll be after me, too."

"Maybe for a while, Goo Boy. But you transfer your twenty percent into Bobby Joe's Face Shop, so they aren't looking for you to get a refund, and then stay quiet for a week and they'll forget all about you."

He's right but I don't care. "I was in for twenty percent of rich," says I. "So I'm in for fifty percent of trouble."

All of a sudden he sees what he's looking for. "There they are, Goo Boy, the dorks they sent to hit me. In that Mercedes." I look but all I see are electrics. Then his hand is on my back and he gives me a shove that takes me right off the portico and into the bushes, and by the time I crawl out, Doggy's nowhere in sight. For about a minute I'm pissed about getting scratched up in the plants, until I realize he was getting me out of the way, so I wouldn't get shot down or hacked up or lased out, whatever it is they planned to do to him to get even.

I was safe enough, right? I should've walked away, I should've ducked right out of the city. I didn't even have to refund the money. I had enough to go clear out of the country and live the rest of my life where even Occipital Crime couldn't find me.

And I thought about it. I stayed the night in Mama Pimple's flophouse because I knew somebody would be watching my own place. All that night I thought about places I could go. Australia. New Zealand. Or even a foreign place, I could afford a good vocabulary crystal so picking up a new language would be easy.

But in the morning I couldn't do it. Mama Pimple didn't exactly ask me but she looked so worried and all I could say was, "He pushed me into the bushes and I don't know where he is."

And she just nods at me and goes back to fixing breakfast. Her hands are shaking she's so upset. Because she knows that Dogwalker doesn't stand a chance against Orphan Crime.

"I'm sorry," says I.

"What can you do?" she says. "When they want you, they get you. If the feds don't give you a new face, you can't hide."

"What if they didn't want him?" says I.

She laughs at me. "The story's all over the street. The arrests were in the news, and now everybody knows the big boys are looking for Walker. They want him so bad the whole street can smell it."

"What if they knew it wasn't his fault?" says I. "What if they knew it was an accident? A mistake?"

Then Mama Pimple squints at me—not many people can tell when she's squinting, but I can—and she says, "Only one boy can tell them that so they'll believe it."

"Sure, I know," says I.

"And if that boy walks in and says, Let me tell you why you don't want to hurt my friend Dogwalker—"

"Nobody said life was safe," I says. "Besides, what could they do to me that's worse than what already happened to me when I was nine?"

She comes over and just puts her hand on my head, just lets her hand lie there for a few minutes, and I know what I've got to do.

So I did it. Went to Fat Jack's and told him I wanted to talk to Junior Mint about Dogwalker, and it wasn't thirty seconds before I was hustled on out into the alley and driven somewhere with my face mashed into the floor of the car so I couldn't tell where it was. Idiots didn't know that somebody as vertical as me can tell the number of wheel revolutions and the exact trajectory of every curve. I could've drawn a freehand map of where they took me. But if I let them know that, I'd never come home, and since there was a good chance I'd end up dosed with speakeasy, I went ahead and erased the memory. Good thing I did—that was the first thing they asked me as soon as they had the drug in me.

Gave me a grown-up dose, they did, so I practically told them my whole life story and my opinion of them and everybody and everything else, so the whole session took hours, felt like forever, but at the end they knew, they absolutely knew that Dogwalker was straight with them, and when it was over and I was coming up so I had some control over what I said, I asked them, I begged them, Let Dogwalker live. Just let him go. He'll give back the money, and I'll give back mine, just let him go.

"OK," says the guy.

I didn't believe it.

"No, you can believe me, we'll let him go."

"You got him?"

"Picked him up before you even came in. It wasn't hard."

"And you didn't kill him?"

"Kill him? We had to get the money back first, didn't we, so we needed him alive till morning, and then you came in, and your little story changed our minds, it really did, you made us feel all sloppy and sorry for that poor old pimp."

For a few seconds there I actually believed that it was going to be all right. But then I knew from the way they looked, from the way they acted, I knew the same way I know about passwords.

They brought in Dogwalker and handed me a book. Dogwalker was very quiet and stiff and he didn't look like he recognized me at all. I didn't even have to look at the book to know what it was. They scooped out his brain and replaced it with glass, like me only way over the line, way way over, there was nothing of Dogwalker left inside his head, just glass pipe and goo. The book was a User's Manual, with all the instructions about how to program him and control him.

I looked at him and he was Dogwalker, the same face, the same hair, everything. Then he moved or talked and he was dead, he was somebody else living in Dogwalker's body. And I says to them, "Why? Why didn't you just kill him, if you were going to do this?"

"This one was too big," says the guy. "Everybody in G-boro knew what happened, everybody in the whole country, everybody in the world. Even if it was a mistake, we couldn't let it go. No hard feelings, Goo Boy. He *is* alive. And so are you. And you both stay that way, as long as you follow a few simple rules. Since he's over the line, he has to have an owner, and you're it. You can use him however you want—rent out data storage, pimp him as a jig or a jaw—but he stays with you always. Every day, he's on the street here in G-boro, so we can bring people here and show them what happens to boys who make mistakes. You can even keep your cut from the job, so you don't have to scramble at all if you don't want to. That's how much we like you, Goo Boy. But if he leaves this town or doesn't come out, even one single solitary day, you'll be very sorry for the last six hours of your life. Do you understand?"

I understood. I took him with me. I bought this place, these clothes, and that's how it's been ever since. That's why we go out on the street every day. I read the whole manual, and I figure there's maybe ten percent of Dogwalker left inside. The part that's Dogwalker can't ever get to the surface, can't even talk or move or anything like that, can't ever remember or even consciously think. But maybe he can still wander around inside what used to be his head, maybe he can sample the data stored in all that goo. Maybe someday he'll even run across this story and he'll know what happened to him, and he'll know that I tried to save him.

In the meantime this is my last will and testament. See, I have us doing all kinds of research on Orgasmic Crime, so that someday I'll know enough to reach inside the system and unplug it. Unplug it all, and make those bastards lose everything, the way they took everything away from Dogwalker. Trouble is, some places there ain't no way to look without leaving tracks. Goo is as goo do, I always say. I'll find out I'm not as good as I think I am when somebody comes along and puts a hot steel putz in my face. Knock my brains out when it comes. But there's this, lying in a few hundred places in the system. Three days after I don't lay down my code in a certain program in a certain place, this story pops into view. The fact you're reading this means I'm dead.

Or it means I paid them back, and so I quit suppressing this because I don't care anymore. So maybe this is my swan song, and maybe this is my victory song. You'll never know, will you, mate?

But you'll wonder. I like that. You wondering about us, whoever you are, you thinking about old Goo Boy and Dogwalker, you guessing whether the fangs who scooped Doggy's skull and turned him into self-propelled property paid for it down to the very last delicious little drop.

And in the meantime, I've got this goo machine to take care of. Only ten percent a man, he is, but then I'm only forty percent myself. All added up together we make only half a human. But that's the half that counts. That's the half that still wants things. The goo in me and the goo in him is all just light pipes and electricity. Data without desire. Lightspeed trash. But I have some desires left, just a few, and maybe so does Dogwalker, even fewer. And we'll get what we want. Every speck. Every sparkle. Believe it.

But We Try Not to Act Like It

There was no line. Hiram Cloward commented on it to the pointy-faced man behind the counter. "There's no line."

"This is the complaint department. We pride ourselves on having few complaints." The pointy-faced man had a prim little smile that irritated Hiram. "What's the matter with your television?"

"It shows nothing but soaps, that's what's the matter. And asinine gothics."

"Well—that's programming, sir, not mechanical at all."

"It's mechanical. I can't turn the damn set off."

"What's your name and social security number?"

"Hiram Cloward. 528-80-693883-7."

"Address?"

"ARF-487-U7b."

"That's singles, sir. Of course you can't turn off your set."

"You mean because I'm not married I can't turn off my television?"

"According to congressionally authorized scientific studies carried out over a three-year period from 1989 to 1991, it is imperative that persons living alone have the constant companionship of their television sets."

"I like solitude. I also like silence."

"But the Congress passed a *law*, sir, and we can't disobey the *law*—"

"Can't I talk to somebody intelligent?"

The pointy-faced man flared a moment, his eyes burning. But he instantly regained his composure, and said in measured tones, "As a matter of fact, as soon as any complainant becomes offensive or hostile, we immediately refer them to section A-6."

"What's that, the hit squad?"

"It's behind that door."

And Hiram followed the pointing finger to the glass door at the far end of the waiting room. Inside was an office, which was filled with comfortable, homey knickknacks, several chairs, a desk, and a man so offensively nordic that even Hitler would have resented him. "Hello," the Aryan said, warmly.

"Hi."

"Please, sit down." Hiram sat, the courtesy and warmth making him feel even more resentful—did they think they could fool him into believing he was not being grossly imposed upon?

"So you don't like something about your programming," said the Aryan.

"*Your* programming, you mean. It sure as hell isn't mine. I don't know why Bell Television thinks it has the right to impose its idea of fun and entertainment on me twenty-four hours a day, but I'm fed up with it. It was bad enough when there was some variety, but for the last two months I've been getting nothing but soaps and gothics."

"It took you two months to notice?"

"I try to ignore the set. I like to *read*. You can bet that if I had more than my stinking little pension from our loving government, I could pay to have a room where there wasn't a TV so I could have some *peace*."

"I really can't help your financial situation. And the law's the law."

"Is that all I'm going to hear from you? The law? I could have heard that from the pointy-faced jerk out there."

"Mr. Cloward, looking at your records, I can certainly see that soaps and gothics are not appropriate for you."

"They aren't appropriate," Hiram said, "for anyone with an IQ over eight."

The Aryan nodded. "You feel that people who enjoy soaps and gothics aren't the intellectual equals of people who don't."

"Damn right. I have a Ph.D. in *literature*, for heaven's sake!"

The Aryan was all sympathy. "Of *course* you don't like soaps! I'm sure it's a mistake. We try not to make mistakes, but we're only human—except the computers, of course." It was a joke, but Hiram didn't laugh. The Aryan kept up the small talk as he looked at the computer terminal that he could see and Hiram could not. "We may be the only television company in town, you know, but—"

"But you try not to act like it."

"Yes. Ha. Well, you must have heard our advertising."

"Constantly."

"Well, let's see now. Hiram Cloward, Ph.D. Nebraska 1981. English literature, twentieth century, with a minor in Russian literature. Dissertation on Dostoevski's influence on English-language novelists. A near-perfect class attendance record, and a reputation for arrogance and competence."

"How much do you *know* about me?"

"Only the standard consumer research data. But we do have a bit of a problem."

Hiram waited, but the Aryan merely punched a button, leaned back, and looked at Hiram. His eyes were kindly and warm and intense. It made Hiram uncomfortable.

"Mr. Cloward."

"Yes?"

"You are unemployed."

"Not willingly."

"Few people are willingly unemployed, Mr. Cloward. But you have no job. You also have no family. You also have no friends."

"That's consumer research? What, only people with friends buy Rice Krispies?"

"As a matter of fact, Rice Krispies are favored by solitary people. We have to know who is more likely to be receptive to advertising, and we direct our programming accordingly."

Hiram remembered that he ate Rice Krispies for breakfast almost every morning. He vowed on the spot to switch to something else. Quaker Oats, for instance. Surely they were more gregarious.

"You understand the importance of the Selective Programming Broadcast Act of 1985, yes?"

"Yes."

"It was deemed unfair by the Supreme Court for all programming to be geared to the majority. Minorities were being slighted. And so Bell Television was given the assignment of preparing an individually selected broadcast system so that each individual, in his own home, would have the programming perfect for him."

"I know all this."

"I must go over it again anyway, Mr. Cloward, because I'm going to have to help you understand why there can be no change in your programming."

Hiram stiffened in his chair, his hands flexing. "I knew you bastards wouldn't change."

"Mr. Cloward, we bastards would be delighted to change. But we are very closely regulated by the government to provide the most healthful programming for every American citizen. Now, I will continue my review."

"I'll just go home, if you don't mind."

"Mr. Cloward, we are directed to prepare programming for minorities as small as ten thousand people—but no smaller. Even for minorities of ten thousand the programming is ridiculously expensive—a program seen by so few costs far more per watching-minute to produce than one seen by thirty or forty million. However, you belong to a minority even smaller than ten thousand."

"That makes me feel so special."

"Furthermore, the Consumer Protection Broadcast Act of 1989 and the regulations of the Consumer Broadcast Agency since then have given us very strict guidelines. Mr. Cloward, we cannot show you any program with overt acts of violence."

"Why not?"

"Because you have tendencies toward hostility that are only exacerbated by viewing violence. Similarly, we cannot show you any programs with sex."

Cloward's face turned red.

"You have no sex life whatsoever, Mr. Cloward. Do you realize how dangerous that is? You don't even masturbate. The tension and hostility inside you must be tremendous."

Cloward leaped to his feet. There were limits to what a man had to put up with. He headed for the door.

"Mr. Cloward, I'm sorry." The Aryan followed him to the door. "I don't make these things up. Wouldn't you rather know *why* these decisions are reached?"

Hiram stopped at the door, his hand on the knob. The Aryan was right. Better to know why than to hate them for it.

"How," Hiram asked. "How do they know what I do and do not do within the walls of my home?"

"We don't *know*, of course, but we're pretty sure. We've studied people for years. We know that people who have certain buying patterns and certain living patterns behave in certain ways. And, unfortunately, you have strong destructive tendencies. Repression and denial are your primary means of adaptation to stress, that and, unfortunately, occasional acting out."

"What the hell does all that mean?"

"It means that you lie to yourself until you can't anymore, and then you attack somebody."

Hiram's face was packed with hot blood, throbbing. I must look like a tomato, he told himself, and deliberately calmed himself. I don't care, he thought. They're wrong anyway. Damn scientific tests.

"Aren't there any movies you could program for me?"

"I am sorry, no."

"Not all movies have sex and violence."

The Aryan smiled soothingly. "The movies that don't wouldn't interest you anyway."

"Then turn the damn thing off and let me read!"

"We can't do that."

"Can't you turn it *down*?"

"No."

"I am so sick of hearing all about Sarah Wynn and her damn love life!"

"But isn't Sarah Wynn attractive?" asked the Aryan.

That stopped Hiram cold. He dreamed about Sarah Wynn at night. He said nothing. He had no attraction to Sarah Wynn.

"Isn't she?" the Aryan insisted.

"Isn't who what?"

"Sarah Wynn."

"Who was talking about Sarah Wynn? What about documentaries?"

"Mr. Cloward, you would become extremely hostile if the news programs were broadcast to you. You know that."

"Walter Cronkite's dead. Maybe I'd like them better now."

"You don't care about the news of the real world, Mr. Cloward, do you?"

"No."

"Then you see where we are. Not one iota of our programming is really appropriate for you. But ninety percent of it is downright harmful to you. And we can't turn the television off, because of the Solitude Act. Do you see our dilemma?"

"Do you see mine?"

"Of course, Mr. Cloward. And I sympathize completely. Make some friends, Mr. Cloward, and we'll turn off your television."

And so the interview was over.

For two days Cloward brooded. All the time he did, Sarah Wynn was grieving over her three-days' husband who had just been killed in a car wreck on Wiltshire Boulevard, wherever the hell that was. But now the body was scarcely cold and already her old suitors were back, trying to help her, trying to push their love on her. "Can't you let yourself depend on me, just a little?" asked Teddy, the handsome one with lots of money.

"I don't like depending on people," Sarah answered.

"You depended on George." George was the husband's name. The dead one.

"I know," she said, and cried for a moment. Sarah Wynn was good at crying. Hiram Cloward turned another page in *The Brothers Karamazov*.

"You need friends," Teddy insisted.

"Oh, Teddy, I know it," she said, weeping. "Will you be my friend?"

"Who writes this stuff?" Hiram Cloward asked aloud. Maybe the Aryan in the television company offices had been right. Make some friends. Get the damn set turned off whatever the cost.

He got up from his chair and went out into the corridor in the apartment building. Clearly posted on the walls were several announcements:

Chess club 5–9 wed

Encounter groups nightly at 7

Learn to knit 6:30 bring yarn and needles

Games games games in game room (basement)

Just want to chat? Friends of the Family 7:30 to 10:30 nightly

Friends of the Family? Hiram snorted. Family was his maudlin mother and her constant weeping about how hard life was and how no one in her right mind would ever be born a woman if anybody had any choice but there was no choice and marriage was a trap men sprung on women, giving them a few minutes of pleasure for a lifetime of drudgery, and I swear to God if it wasn't for my little baby Hiram I'd ditch that bastard for good, it's for your sake I don't leave, my little baby, because if I leave you'll grow up into a macho bastard like your beerbelly father.

And friends? What friends ever come around when good old Dad is boozing and belting the living crap out of everybody he can get his hands on?

I read. That's what I do. *The Prince and the Pauper. Connecticut Yankee. Pride and Prejudice.* Worlds within worlds within worlds, all so pretty and polite and funny as hell.

Friends of the Family. Worth a shot, anyway.

Hiram went to the elevator and descended eighteen floors to the Fun Floor. Friends of the Family were in quite a large room with alcohol at one end and soda pop at the other. Hiram was surprised to discover that the term *soda pop* had been revived. He walked to the cola sign and asked the woman for a Coke.

"How many cups of coffee have you had today?" she asked.

"Three."

"Then I'm so sorry, but I can't give you a soda pop with caffeine in it. May I suggest Sprite?"

"You may not," Hiram said, clenching his teeth. "We're too damn overprotected."

"Exactly how I feel," said a woman standing beside him, Sprite in hand. "They protect and protect and protect, and what good does it do? People still die, you know."

"I suspected as much," Hiram said, struggling for a smile, wondering if his humor sounded funny or merely sarcastic. Apparently funny. The woman laughed.

"Oh, you're a gem, you are," she said. "What do you do?"

"I'm a detached professor of literature at Princeton."

"But how can you live *here* and work *there*?"

He shrugged. "I don't work there. I said detached. When the new television teaching came in, my PQ was too low. I'm not a screen personality."

"So few of us are," she said sagely, nodding and smiling. "Oh, how I long for the good old days. When ugly men like David Brinkley could deliver the news."

"You remember Brinkley?"

"Actually, no," she said, laughing. "I just remember my mother talking about him." Hiram looked at her appreciatively. Nose not very straight, of course—but that seemed to be the only thing keeping her off TV. Nice voice. Nice nice face. Body.

She put her hand on his thigh.

"What are you doing tonight?" she asked.

"Watching television," he grimaced.

"Really? What do you have?"

"Sarah Wynn."

She squealed in delight. "Oh, how wonderful! We must be kindred spirits then! I have Sarah Wynn, too!"

Hiram tried to smile.

"Can I come up to your apartment?"

Danger signal. Hand moving up thigh. Invitation to apartment. Sex.

"No."

"Why not?"

And Hiram remembered that the only way he could ever get rid of the television was to prove that he wasn't solitary. And fixing up his sex life—i.e., having one—would go a long way toward changing their damn profiles. "Come on," he said, and they left the Friends of the Family without further ado.

Inside the apartment she immediately took off her shoes and blouse and sat down on the old-fashioned sofa in front of the TV. "Oh," she said, "so many books. You really are a professor, aren't you?"

"Yeah," he said, vaguely sensing that the next move was up to him, and not having the faintest idea of that the next move was. He thought back to his only fumbling attempt at sex when he was (what?) thirteen? (no) fourteen and the girl was fifteen and was doing it on a lark. She had walked with him up the creekbed (back when there were creeks and open country) and suddenly she had stopped and unzipped his pants (back when there were zippers) but he was finished before she had hardly started and gave up in disgust and took his pants and ran away. Her name was Diana. He went home without his pants and had no rational explanation and his mother had treated him with loathing and brought it up again and again for years afterward, how a man is a man no matter how you treat him and he'll still get it when he can, who cares about the poor girl. But Hiram was used to that kind of talk. It rolled off him. What haunted him was the uncontrolled shivering of his body, the ecstacy of it, and then the look of disgust on the girl's face. He had thought it was because—well, never mind. Never mind, he thought. I don't think of this anymore.

"Come on," said the woman.

"What's your name?" Hiram asked.

She looked at the ceiling. "Agnes, for heaven's sake, come on."

He decided that taking off his shirt might be a good idea. She watched, then decided to help.

"No," he said.

"What?"

"Don't touch me."

"Oh, for pete's sake. What's wrong? Impotent?"

Not at all. Not at all. Just uninterested. Is that all right?

"Look, I don't want to play around with a psycho case, all right? I've got better things to do. I make a hundred a whack, that's what I charge, that's standard, right?"

Standard what? Hiram nodded because he didn't dare ask what she was talking about.

"But you obviously, heaven knows how, buddy, you sure as hell obviously don't know what's going on in the world. Twenty bucks. Enough for the ten minutes you've screwed up for me. Right?"

"I don't have twenty," Hiram said.

Her eyes got tight. "A fairy *and* a deadbeat. What a pick. Look, buddy, next time you try a pickup, figure out what you want to do with her first, right?"

She picked up her shoes and blouse and left. Hiram stood there.

"Teddy, no," said Sarah Wynn.

"But I need you. I need you so desperately," said Teddy on the screen.

"It's only been a few days. How can I sleep with another man only a few days after George was killed? Only four days ago we—oh, no, Teddy. Please."

"Then when? How soon? I love you so much."

Drivel, George thought in his analytical mind. But nevertheless obviously based on the Penelope story. No doubt her George, her Odysseus, would return, miraculously alive, ready to sweep her back into wedded bliss. But in the meantime, the suitors: enough suitors to sell fifteen thousand cars and a hundred thousand boxes of tampax and four hundred thousand packages of Cap'n Crunch.

The nonanalytical part of his mind, however, was not the least bit concerned with Penelope. For some reason he was clasping and unclasping his hands in front of him. For some reason he was shaking. For some reason he fell to his knees at the couch, his hands clasping and unclasping around *Crime and Punishment*, as his eyes strained to cry but could not.

Sarah Wynn wept.

But she can cry easily, Hiram thought. It's not fair, that she should cry so easily. Spin flax, Penelope.

The alarm went off, but Hiram was already awake. In front of him the television was singing about Dove with lanolin. The products haven't changed, Hiram thought. Never change. They were advertising Dove with lanolin in the little market carts around the base of the cross while Jesus bled to death, no doubt. For softer skin.

He got up, got dressed, tried to read, couldn't, tried to remember what had happened last night to leave him so upset and nervous, but couldn't, and at last he decided to go back to the Aryan at the Bell Television offices.

"Mr. Cloward," said the Aryan.

"You're a psychiatrist, aren't you?" Hiram asked.

"Why, Mr. Cloward, I'm an A-6 complaint representative from Bell Television. What can I do for you?"

"I can't stand Sarah Wynn anymore," Hiram said.

"That's a shame. Things are finally going to work out for her starting in about two weeks."

And in spite of himself, Hiram wanted to ask what was going to happen. It isn't fair for this nordic uberman to know what sweet little Sarah is going to be doing weeks before I do. But he fought down the feeling, ashamed that he was getting caught up in the damn soap.

"Help me," Hiram said.

"How can I help you?"

"You can change my life. You can get the television out of my apartment."

"Why, Mr. Cloward?" the Aryan asked. "It's the one thing in life that's absolutely free. Except that you get to watch commercials. And you know as well as I do that the commercials are downright entertaining. Why, there are people who actually choose to have double the commercials in their personal programming. We get a thousand requests a day for the latest McDonald's ad. You have no idea."

"I have a very good idea. I want to read. I want to be alone."

"On the contrary, Mr. Cloward, you long not to be alone. You desperately need a friend."

Anger. "And what makes you so damn sure of that?"

"Because, Mr. Cloward, your response is completely typical of your group. It's a group we're very concerned about. We don't have a budget to program for you—there are only about two thousand of you in the country—but a budget wouldn't do us much good because we really don't know what kind of programming you *want*."

"I am not part of any group."

"Oh, you're so much a part of it that you could be called typical. Dominant mother, absent and/or hostile father, no long-term relationships with anybody. No sex life."

"I have a sex life."

"If you have in fact attempted any sexual activity it was undoubtedly with a prostitute and she expected too high a level of sophistication from you. You are easily ashamed, you couldn't cope, and so you have not had intercourse. Correct?"

"What are you! What are you trying to do to me!"

"I *am* a psychoanalyst, of course. Anybody whose complaints can't be handled by our bureaucratic authority figure out in front obviously needs help, not another bureaucrat. I want to help you. I'm your friend."

And suddenly the anger was replaced by the utter incongruity of this nordic masterman wanting to help little Hiram Cloward. The unemployed professor laughed.

"Humor! Very healthy!" said the Aryan.

"What is this? I thought shrinks were supposed to be subtle."

"With some people—notably paranoids, which you are not, and schizoids, which you are not either."

"And what am I?"

"I told you. Denial and repression strategies. Very unhealthy. Acting out—less healthy yet. But you're extremely intelligent, able to do many things. I personally think it's a damn shame you can't teach."

"I'm an excellent teacher."

"Tests with randomly selected students showed that you had an extremely heavy emphasis on esoterica. Only people like you would really enjoy a class from a person like you. There aren't many people like you. You don't fit into many of the normal categories."

"And so I'm being persecuted."

"Don't try to pretend to be paranoid." The Aryan smiled. Hiram smiled back. This is insane. Lewis Carroll, where are you now that we really need you?

"If you're a shrink, then I should talk freely to you."

"If you like."

"I don't like."

"And why not?"

"Because you're so godutterlydamn Aryan, that's why."

The Aryan leaned forward with interest. "Does that bother you?"

"It makes me want to throw up."

"And why is that?"

The look of interest was too keen, too delightful. Hiram couldn't resist. "You don't know about my experiences in the war, then, is that it?"

"What war? There hasn't been a war recently enough—"

"I was very, very young. It was in Germany. My parents aren't really my parents, you know. They were in Germany with the American embassy. In Berlin in 1938, before the war broke out. My real parents were there, too—German Jews, or half Jews, anyway. My real father—but let that pass, you don't need my whole genealogy. Let's just say that when I was only eleven days old, totally unregistered, my real Jewish father took me to his friend, Mr. Cloward in the American embassy, whose wife had just had a miscarriage. 'Take my child,' he said.

" 'Why?' Cloward asked.

" 'Because my wife and I have a perfect, utterly foolproof plan to kill Hitler. But there is no way for us to survive it.' And so Cloward, my adopted father, took me in.

"And then, the next day, he read in the papers about how my real parents had been killed in an 'accident' in the street. He investigated—and discovered that just by chance, while my parents were on their way to carry out their foolproof plan, some brown shirts in the street had seen them. Someone pointed them out as Jews. They were bored— so they attacked them. Had no idea they were saving Hitler's life, of course. These nordic mastermen started beating my mother, forcing my father to watch as they stripped her and raped her and then disemboweled her. My father was then subjected to ex- perimental use of the latest model testicle-crusher until he bit off his own tongue in agony and bled to death. I don't like nordic types." Hiram sat back, his eyes full of tears and emotion, and realized that he had actually been able to cry—not much, but it was hopeful.

"Mr. Cloward," said the Aryan, "you were born in Missouri in 1951. Your parents of record are your natural parents."

Hiram smiled. "But it was one hell of a Freudian fantasy, wasn't it? My mother raped, my father emasculated to death, myself divorced from my true heritage, etc., etc."

The Aryan smiled. "You should be a writer, Mr. Cloward."

"I'd rather read. Please, let me read."

"I can't stop you from reading."

"Turn off Sarah Wynn. Turn off the mansions from which young girls flee from the menace of a man who turns out to be friendly and loving. Turn off the commercials for cars and condoms."

"And leave you alone to wallow in cataleptic fantasies among your depressing Russian novels?"

Hiram shook his head. Am I begging? he wondered. Yes, he decided. "I'm begging. My Russian novels aren't depressing. They're exalting, uplifting, overwhelming."

"It's part of your sickness, Mr. Cloward, that you long to be overwhelmed."

"Every time I read Dostoevski, I feel fulfilled."

"You have read everything by Dostoevski twenty times over. And everything by Tolstoy a dozen times."

"Every time I read Dostoevski is the first time!"

"We can't leave you alone."

"I'll kill myself!" Hiram shouted. "I can't live like this much longer!"

"Then make friends," the Aryan said simply. Hiram gasped and panted, gathering his rage back under control. This is not happening. I am not angry. Put it away, put it back, get control, smile. Smile at the Aryan.

"You're my friend, right?" Hiram asked.

"If you'll let me," the Aryan answered.

"I'll let you," Hiram said. Then he got up and left the office.

On the way home he passed a church. He had often seen the church before. He had little interest in religion—it had been too thoroughly dissected for him in the novels. What Twain had left alive, Dostoevski had withered and Pasternak had killed. But his mother was a passionate Presbyterian. He went into the church.

At the front of the building was a huge television screen. On it a very charismatic young man was speaking. The tones were subdued—only those in the front could hear it. Those in the back seemed to be mediating. Cloward knelt at a bench to meditate, too.

But he couldn't take his eyes off the screen. The young man stepped aside, and an older man took his place, intoning something about Christ. Hiram could hear the word *Christ*, but no others.

The walls were decorated with crosses. Row on row of crosses. This was a Protestant church—none of the crosses contained a figure of Jesus bleeding. But Hiram's imagination supplied him nonetheless. Jesus, his hands and wrists nailed to the cross, his feet pegged to the cross, his throat at the intersection of the beams.

Why the cross, after all? The intersection of two utterly opposite lines, perpendiculars that can only touch at one point. The epitome of the life of man, passing through eternity without a backward glance at those encountered along the way, each in his own, endlessly divergent direction. The cross. But not at all the symbol of today, Hiram decided. Today we are in spheres. Today we are curves, not lines, bending back on ourselves, touching everybody again and again, wrapped up inside little balls, none of us daring to be at the outside. Pull me in, we cry, pull me and keep me safe, don't let me fall out, don't let me fall off the edge of the world.

But the world has an edge now, and we can all see it, Hiram decided. We know where it is, and we can't bear to let anyone find his own way of staying on top.

Or do I want to stay on top?

The age of crosses is over. Now the age of spheres. Balls.

"We are your friends," said the old man on the screen. "We can help you."

There is a grandeur, Hiram answered silently, about muddling through alone.

"Why be alone when Jesus can take your burden?" said the man on the screen.

If I were alone, Hiram answered, there would be no burden to bear.

"Pick up your cross, fight the good fight," said the man on the screen.

If only, Hiram answered, I could find my cross to pick it up.

Then Hiram realized that he still could not hear the voice from the television. Instead he had been supplying his own sermon, out loud. Three people near him in the back of the church were watching him. He smiled sheepishly, ducked his head in apology, and left. He walked home whistling.

Sarah Wynn's voice greeted him. "Teddy. Teddy! What have we done? Look what we've done."

"It was beautiful," Teddy said. "I'm glad of it."

"Oh, Teddy! How can I ever forgive myself?" And Sarah wept.

Hiram stood transfixed, watching the screen. Penelope had given in. Penelope had left her flax and fornicated with a suitor! This is wrong, he thought.

"This is wrong," he said.

"I love you, Sarah," Teddy said.

"I can't bear it, Teddy," she answered. "I feel that in my heart I have murdered George! I have betrayed him!"

Penelope, is there no virtue in the world? Is there no Artemis, hunting? Just Aphrodite, bedding down every hour on the hour with every man, god, or sheep that promised forever and delivered a moment. The bargains are never fulfilled, never, Hiram thought.

At that moment on the screen, George walked in. "My dear," he exclaimed. "My dear Sarah! I've been wandering with amnesia for days! It was a hitchhiker who was burned to death in my car! I'm home!"

And Hiram screamed and screamed and screamed.

The Aryan found out about it quickly, at the same time that he got an alarming report from the research teams analyzing the soaps. He shook his head, a sick feeling in the pit of his stomach. Poor Mr. Cloward. Ah, what agony we do in the name of protecting people, the Aryan thought.

"I'm sorry," he said to Hiram. But Hiram paid him no attention. He just sat on the floor, watching the television set. As soon as the report had come in, of course, all the soaps—especially Sarah Wynn's—had gone off the air. Now the game shows were on, a temporary replacement until errors could be corrected.

"I'm so sorry," the Aryan said, but Hiram tried to shrug him away. A black woman had just traded the box for the money in the envelope. It was what Hiram would have done, and it paid off. Five thousand dollars instead of a donkey pulling a cart with a monkey in it. She had just avoided being zonked.

"Mr. Cloward, I thought the problem was with you. But it wasn't at all. I mean, you were marginal, all right. But we didn't realize what Sarah Wynn was doing to people."

Sarah schmarah, Hiram said silently, watching the screen. The black woman was bounding up and down in delight.

"It was entirely our fault. There are thousands of marginals just like you who were seriously damaged by Sarah Wynn. We had no idea how powerful the identification was. We had no idea."

Of course not, thought Hiram. You didn't read enough. You didn't know what the myths do to people. But now was the Big Deal of the Day, and Hiram shook his head to make the Aryan go away.

"Of course the Consumer Protection Agency will pay you a lifetime compensation. Three times your present salary and whatever treatment is possible."

At last Hiram's patience ended. "Go away!" he said. "I have to see if the black woman there is going to get the car!"

"I just can't decide," the black woman said.

"Door number three!" Hiram shouted. "Please, God, door number three!"

The Aryan watched Hiram silently.

"Door number two!" the black woman finally decided. Hiram groaned. The announcer smiled.

"Well," said the announcer. "Is the car behind door number *two*? Let's just see!"

The curtain opened, and behind it was a man in a hillbilly costume strumming a beat-up looking banjo. The audience moaned. The man with the banjo sang "Home on the Range." The black woman sighed.

They opened the curtains, and there was the car behind door number three. "I knew it," Hiram said, bitterly. "They never listen to me. Door number three, I say, and they never do it."

The Aryan turned to leave.

"I told you, didn't I?" Hiram asked, weeping.

"Yes," the Aryan said.

"I knew it. I knew it all along. I was *right*." Hiram sobbed into his hands.

"Yeah," the Aryan answered, and then he left to sign all the necessary papers for the commitment. Now Cloward fit into a category. No one can exist outside one for long, the Aryan realized. We are creating a new man. *Homo categoricus*. The classified man.

But the papers didn't have to be signed after all. Instead Hiram went into the bathroom, filled the tub, and joined the largest category of all.

"Damn," the Aryan said, when he heard about it.

I PUT MY BLUE GENES ON

*I*t had taken three weeks to get there—longer than any man in living memory
had been in space, and there were four of us crammed into the little Hunter
III skipship. It gave us a hearty appreciation for the pioneers, who had had
to crawl across space at a tenth of the speed of light. No wonder only three
colonies ever got founded. Everybody else must have eaten each other alive after the
first month in space.

Harold had taken a swing at Amauri the last day, and if we hadn't hit the homing
signal I would have ordered the ship turned around to go home to Núncamais, which
was mother and apple pie to everybody but me—I'm from Pennsylvania. But we got
the homing signal and set the computer to scanning the old maps, and after a few hours
found ourselves in stationary orbit over Prescott, Arizona.

At least that's what the geologer said, and computers can't lie. It didn't look like
what the old books *said* Arizona should look like.

But there was the homing signal, broadcasting in Old English: "God bless America,
come in, safe landing guaranteed." The computer assured us that in Old English the
word *guarantee* was *not* obscene, but rather had something to do with a statement being
particularly trustworthy—we had a chuckle over that one.

But we were excited, too. When great-great-great-great to the umpteenth power
grandpa and grandma upped their balloons from old Terra Firma eight hundred years
ago, it had been to escape the ravages of microbiological warfare that was just beginning
(a few germs in a sneak attack on Madagascar, quickly spreading to epidemic proportions,
and South Africa holding the world ransom for the antidote; quick retaliation with
virulent cancer; you guess the rest). And even from a couple of miles out in space, it
was pretty obvious that the war hadn't stopped there. And yet there was this homing
signal.

"Obviamente automática," Amauri observed.

"*Que* máquina, que ñāo pofa em tantos anos, bichinha! Não acredito!" retorted Harold, and I was afraid I might have a rerun of the day before.

"English," I said. "Might as well get used to it. We'll have to speak it for a few days, at least."

Vladimir sighed. "Merda."

I laughed. "All right, you can keep your scatological comments in lingua deporto."

"Are you so sure there's anybody alive down there?" Vladimir asked.

What could I say? That I felt it in my bones? So I just threw a sponge at him, which scattered drinking water all over the cabin, and for a few minutes we had a waterfight. I know, discipline, discipline. But we're not a land army up here, and what the hell. I'd rather have my crew acting like crazy children than like crazy grown-ups.

Actually, I didn't believe that at the level of technology our ancestors had reached in 1992 they could build a machine that would keep running until 2810. Somebody had to be alive down there—or else they'd gotten smart. Again, the surface of old Terra didn't give many signs that anybody had gotten smart.

So somebody was alive down there. And that was exactly what we had been sent to find out.

They complained when I ordered monkeysuits.

"That's old Mother *Earth* down there!" Harold argued. For a halibut with an ike of 150 he sure could act like a baiano sometimes.

"Show me the cities," I answered. "Show me the millions of people running around taking the sun in their rawhide summer outfits."

"And there may be germs," Amauri added, in his snottiest voice, and immediately I had another argument going between two men brown enough to know better.

"We will follow," I said in my nasty captain's voice, "standard planetary procedure, whether it's Mother Earth or mother—"

And at that moment the monotonous homing signal changed.

"Please respond, please identify, please respond, or we'll blast your asses out of the sky."

We responded. And soon afterward found ourselves in monkeysuits wandering around in thick pea soup up to our navels (if we could have located our navels without a map, surrounded as they were with lifesaving devices) waiting for somebody to open a door.

A door opened and we picked ourselves up off a very hard floor. Some of the pea soup had fallen down the hatch with us. A gas came into the sterile chamber where we waited, and pretty soon the pea soup settled down and turned into mud.

"Mariajoseijesus!" Amauri muttered. "Aquela merda *vivia!*"

"English," I muttered into the monkey mouth, "and clean up your language."

"That crap was alive," Amauri said, rephrasing and cleaning up his language.

"And now it isn't, but we are." It was hard to be patient.

For all we knew, what passed for humanity here liked eating spacemen. Or sacrificing them to some local deity. We passed a nervous four hours in that cubicle. And I had already laid about five hopeless escape plans—when a door opened, and a person appeared.

He was dressed in a white farmersuit, or at least close to it. He was very short, but smiled pleasantly and beckoned. Proof positive. Living human beings. Mission successful. *Now* we know there was no cause for rejoicing, but at that moment we rejoiced. Backslapping, embracing our little host (afraid of crushing him for a moment), and then into the labyrinth of U.S. MB Warfare Post 004.

They were all very small—not more than 140 centimeters tall—and the first thought that struck me was how much humanity had grown since then. The stars must agree with us, I thought.

Till quiet, methodical Vladimir, looking, as always, white as a ghost, pointedly turned a doorknob and touched a lightswitch (it actually was *mechanical*). They were both above eye level for our little friends. So it wasn't us colonists who had grown—it was our cousins from old Gaea who had shrunk.

We tried to catch them up on history, but all they cared about was their own politics. "Are you American?" they kept asking.

"I'm from Pennsylvania," I said, "but these humble-butts are from Núncamais."

They didn't understand.

"Núncamais. It means 'never again.' In lingua deporto."

Again puzzled. But they asked another question.

"Where did your colony *come from?*" One-track minds.

"Pennsylvania was settled by Americans from Hawaii. We lay no bets as to why they named the damned planet Pennsylvania."

One of the little people piped up, "That's obvious. Cradle of liberty. And *them?*"

"From Brazil," I said.

They conferred quietly on that one, and then apparently decided that while Brazilian ancestry wasn't a capital offense, it didn't exactly confer human status. From then on, they made no attempt to talk to my crew. Just watched them carefully, and talked to me.

Me they loved.

"God bless America," they said.

I felt agreeable. "God bless America," I answered.

Then, again in unison, they made an obscene suggestion as to what I should do with the Russians. I glanced at my compatriots and fellow travelers and shrugged. I repeated the little folks' wish for the Russian's sexual bliss.

Fact time. I won't bore by repeating all the clever questioning and probing that elicited the following information. Partly because it didn't take any questioning. They seemed to have been rehearsing for years what they would say to any visitors from outer space, particularly the descendants of the long-lost colonists. It went this way:

Germ warfare had begun in earnest about three years after we left. Three very cleverly designed cancer viruses had been loosed on the world, apparently by no one at all, since both the Russians and the Americans denied it and the Chinese were all dead. That was when the scientists knuckled down and set to work.

Recombinant DNA had been a rough enough science when my ancestors took off for the stars—and we hadn't developed it much since then. When you're developing raw planets you have better things to do with your time. But under the pressure of warfare, the science of do-it-yourself genetics had a field day on planet Earth.

"We are constantly developing new strains of viruses and bacteria," they said. "And constantly we are bombarded by the Russians' latest weapons." They were hard-pressed. There weren't many of them in that particular MB Warfare Post, and the enemy's assaults were clever.

And finally the picture became clear. To all of us at once. It was Harold who said, "Fossa-me, mãe! You mean for eight hundred *years* you bunnies've been down here?"

They didn't answer until I asked the question—more politely, too, since I had noticed a certain set to those inscrutable jaws when Harold called them bunnies. Well, they *were* bunnies, white as white could be, but it was tasteless for Harold to call them that, particularly in front of Vladimir, who had more than a slight tendency toward white skin himself.

"Have you Americans been trapped down here ever since the war began?" I asked, trying to put awe into my voice, and succeeding. Horror isn't that far removed from awe, anyway.

They beamed with what I took for pride. And I was beginning to be able to interpret some of their facial expressions. As long as I had good words for America, I was all right.

"Yes, Captain Kane Kanea, we and our ancestors have been here from the beginning."

"Doesn't it get a little cramped?"

"Not for American soldiers, Captain. For the right to life, liberty, and the pursuit of happiness we would sacrifice anything." I didn't ask how much liberty and happiness-pursuing were possible in a hole in the rock. Our hero went on: "We fight on that millions may live, free, able to breathe the clean air of America unoppressed by the lashes of Communism."

And then they broke into a few choice hymns about purple mountains and yellow waves with a rousing chorus of God blessing America. It all ended with a mighty shout: "Better dead than red." When it was over we asked them if we could sleep, since according to our ship's time it was well past bedding-down hour.

They put us in a rather small room with three cots in it that were far too short for us. Didn't matter. We couldn't possibly be comfortable in our monkeysuits anyway.

Harold wanted to talk in lingua deporto as soon as we were alone, but I managed to convince him without even using my monkeysuit's discipliner button that we didn't want them to think we were trying to keep any secrets. We all took it for granted that they were monitoring us.

And so our conversation was the sort of conversation that one doesn't mind having overheard by a bunch of crazy patriots.

Amauri: "I am amazed at their great love for America, persisting so many centuries." Translation: "What the hell got these guys so nuts about something as dead as the ancient U.S. empire?"

Me: "Perhaps it is due to such unwavering loyalty to the flag, God, country, and liberty" (I admit I was laying it on thick, but better to be safe, etc.) "that they have been able to survive so long." Translation: "Maybe being crazy fanatics is all that's kept them alive in this hole."

Harold: "I wonder how long we can stay in this bastion of democracy before we must reluctantly go back to our colony of the glorious American dream." Translation: "What are the odds they don't let us go? After all, they're so loony they might think we're spies or something."

Vladimir: "I only hope we can learn from them. Their science is infinitely beyond anything we have hitherto developed with our poor resources." Translation: "We're not going anywhere until I have a chance to do *my* job and check out the local flora and fauna. Eight hundred years of recombining DNA has got to have something we can take back home to Núncamais."

And so the conversation went until we were sick of the flowers and perfume that kept dropping out of our mouths. Then we went to sleep.

The next day was guided tour day, Russian attack day, and damn near good-bye to the crew of the good ship Pollywog.

The guided tour kept us up hill and down dale for most of the morning. Vladimir was running the tracking computer from his monkeysuit. Mine was too busy analyzing the implications of all their comments while Amauri was absorbing the science and Harold was trying to figure out how to pick his nose with mittens on. Harold was along for the ride—a weapons expert, just in case. Thank God.

We began to be able to tell one little person from another. George Washington Steiner was our usual guide. The big boss, who had talked to us through most of the history lesson the day before, was Andrew Jackson Wallichinsky. And the guy who led the singing was Richard Nixon Dixon. The computer told us those were names of beloved American presidents, with surnames added.

And my monkeysuit's analysis also told us that the music leader was the *real* big boss, while Andy Jack Wallichinsky was merely the director of scientific research. Seems that the politicians ran the brains, instead of vice versa.

Our guide, G.W. Steiner, was very proud of his assignment. He showed us everything. I mean, even with the monkeysuit keeping three-fourths of the gravity away from me, my feet were sore by lunchtime (a quick sip of recycled xixi and cocó). And it was impressive. Again, I give it unto you in abbreviated form:

Even though the installation was technically airtight, in fact the enemy viruses and bacteria could get in quite readily. It seems that early in the twenty-first century the Russians had stopped making any kind of radio broadcasts. (I know, that sounds like a non sequitur. Patience, patience.) At first the Americans in 004 had thought they had won. And then, suddenly, a new onslaught of another disease. At this time the 004 researchers had never been *personally* hit by any diseases—the airtight system was working fine. But their commander at that time, Rodney Fletcher, had been very suspicious.

"He thought it was a commie trick," said George Washington Steiner. I began to see the roots of superpatriotism in 004's history.

So Rodney Fletcher set the scientists to working on strengthening the base personnel's antibody system. They plugged away at it for two weeks and came up with three new strains of bacteria that selectively devoured practically anything that wasn't supposed to be in the human body. Just in time, too, because then that new disease hit. It wasn't stopped by the airtight system, because instead of being a virus, it was just two little amino acids and a molecule of lactose, put together *just so*. It fit right through the filters. It sailed right through the antibiotics. It entered right into the lungs of every man, woman, and child in 004. And if Rodney Fletcher hadn't been a paranoid, they all would have died. As it was, only about half lived.

Those two amino acids and the lactose molecule had the ability to fit right into *that* spot on a human DNA and then make the DNA replicate that way. Just one little change—and pretty soon nerves just stopped working.

Those two amino acids and the lactose molecule system worked just well enough to slow down the disease's progress until a plug could be found that fit even better into that spot on the DNA, keeping the Russians' little devices out. (Can they be called viruses? Can they be called alive? I'll leave it to the godcallers and the philosophers to decide that.)

Trouble was, the plugs also caused all the soldiers' babies to grow up to be very short with a propensity for having their teeth fall out and their eyes go blind at the age of thirty. G.W. Steiner was very proud of the fact that they had managed to correct for the eyes after four generations. He smiled and for the first time we really noticed that his teeth weren't like ours.

"We make them out of certain bacteria that gets very hard when a particular virus is exposed to it. My own great-great-grandmother invented it," Steiner said. "We're always coming up with new and useful tools."

I asked to see how they did this trick, which brings us full circle to what we saw on the guided tour that day. We saw the laboratories where eleven researchers were playing clever little games with DNA. I didn't understand any of it, but my monkeysuit assured me that the computer was getting it all.

We also saw the weapons delivery system. It was very clever. It consisted of setting a culture dish full of a particular nasty weapon in a little box, closing the door to the box, and then pressing a button that opened another door to the box that led outside.

"We let the wind take it from there," said Steiner. "We figure it takes about a year for a new weapon to reach Russia. But by then it's grown to a point that it's irresistible."

I asked him what the bacteria lived on. He laughed. "Anything," he said. It turns out that their basic breeding stock is a bacterium that can photosynthesize and dissolve any form of iron, both at the same time. "Whatever else we change about a particular weapon, we don't change that," Steiner said. "Our weapons can travel anywhere without hosts. Quarantines don't do any good."

Harold had an idea. I was proud of him. "If these little germs can dissolve steel, George, why the hell aren't they in here dissolving this whole installation?"

Steiner looked like he had just been hoping we'd ask that question.

"When we developed our basic breeder stock, we also developed a mold that inhibits the bacteria from reproducing and eating. The mold only grows on metal and the spores die if they're away from both mold and metal for more than one-seventy-seventh of a second. That means that the mold grows all the way around this installation—and nowhere else. My fourteenth great-uncle William Westmoreland Hannamaker developed the mold."

"Why," I asked, "do you keep mentioning your blood relationship to these inventors? Surely after eight hundred years here everybody's related?"

I thought I was asking a simple question. But G.W. Steiner looked at me coldly and turned away, leading us to the next room.

We found bacteria that processed other bacteria that processed still other bacteria that turned human excrement into very tasty, nutritious food. We took their word for the tasty. I know, we were still eating recycled us through the tubes in our suit. But at least we knew where *ours* had been.

They had bacteria that without benefit of sunlight processed carbon dioxide and water back into oxygen and starch. So much for photosynthesis.

And we got a list of what shelf after shelf of weapons could do to an unprepared human body. If somebody ever broke all those jars on Núncamais or Pennsylvania or Kiev, everybody would simply disappear, completely devoured and incorporated into the life-systems of bacteria and viruses and trained amino-acid sets.

No sooner did I think of that, than I said it. Only I didn't get any farther than the word *Kiev.*

"Kiev? One of the colonies is named Kiev?"

I shrugged. "There are only three planets colonized. Kiev, Pennsylvania, and Núncamais."

"*Russian* ancestry?"

Oops, I thought. Oops is an all-purpose word standing for every bit of profanity, blasphemy, and pornographic and scatological exculpation I could think of.

The guided tour ended right then.

Back in our bedroom, we became aware that we had somehow dissolved our hospitality. After a while, Harold realized that it was my fault.

"Captain, by damn, if you hadn't told them about Kiev we wouldn't be locked in here like this!"

I agreed, hoping to pacify him, but he didn't calm down until I used the discipliner button in my monkeysuit.

Then we consulted the computers.

Mine reported that in all we had been told, two areas had been completely left out: While it was obvious that in the past the little people had done extensive work on human DNA, there had been no hint of any work going on in that field today. And though we had been told of all kinds of weapons that had been flung among the Russians on the other side of the world, there had been no hint of any kind of limited effect antipersonnel weapon *here*.

"Oh," Harold said. "There's nothing to stop us from walking out of here anytime we can knock the door down. And I can knock the door down anytime I want to," he said, playing with the buttons on his monkeysuit. I urged him to wait until all the reports were done.

Amauri informed us that he had gleaned enough information from their talk and his monkeyeyes that we could go home with the entire science of DNA recombination hidden away in our computer.

And then Vladimir's suit played out a holomap of Post 004.

The bright green, infinitesimally thin lines marked walls, doors, passages. We immediately recognized the corridors we had walked in throughout the morning, located the laboratories, found where we were imprisoned. And then we noticed a rather larger area in the middle of the holomap that seemed empty.

"Did you see a room like that?" I asked. The others shook their heads. Vladimir asked the holomap if we had been in it. The suit answered in its whispery monkeyvoice: "No. I have only delineated the unpenetrated perimeter and noted apertures that perhaps give entry."

"So they didn't let us in there," Harold said. "I knew the bastards were hiding something."

"And let's make a guess," I said. "That room either has something to do with antipersonnel weapons, or it has something to do with human DNA research."

We sat and pondered the revelations we had just had, and realized they didn't add up to much. Finally Vladimir spoke up. Trust a half-bunny to come up with the idea where three browns couldn't. Just goes to show you that a racial theory is a bunch of waggy-woggle.

"Antipersonnel hell," Vladimir said. "They don't need antipersonnel. All they have to do is open a little hole in our suits and let the germs come through."

"Our suits close immediately," Amauri said, but then corrected himself. "I guess it doesn't take long for a virus to get through, does it?"

Harold didn't get it. "Let one of those bunnies try to lay a knife on me, and I'll split him from ass to armpit."

We ignored him.

"What makes you think there are germs in here? Our suits don't measure that," I pointed out.

Vladimir had already thought of that. "Remember what they said. About the Russians getting those little amino-acid monsters in here."

Amauri snorted. "Russians."

"Yeah, right," Vladimir said, "but keep the voice down, viado."

Amauri turned red, started to say, "Quem é que cê chama de viado!"—but I pushed the discipliner button. No time for any of that crap.

"Watch your language, Vladimir. We got enough problems."

"Sorry, Amauri, Captain," Vladimir said. "I'm a little wispy, you know?"

"So's everybody."

Vladimir took a breath and went on. "Once those bugs got in here, 004 must have been pretty thoroughly permeable. The, uh, Russians must've kept pumping more variations on the same into Post 004."

"So why aren't they all dead?"

"What I think is that a lot of these people *have* been killed—but the survivors are ones whose bodies took readily to those plugs they came up with. The plugs are regular parts of their body chemistry now. They'd have to be, wouldn't they? They told us they were passed on in the DNA transmitted to the next generation."

I got it. So did Amauri, who said, "So they've had seven or eight centuries to select for adaptability."

"Why not?" Vladimir asked. "Didn't you notice? Eleven researchers on developing new weapons. And only two on developing new defenses. They can't be *too* worried."

Amauri shook his head. "Oh, Mother Earth. Whatever got into you?"

"Just caught a cold," Vladimir said, and then laughed. "A virus. Called humanity."

We sat around looking at the holomap for a while. I found four different routes from where we were to the secret area—if we wanted to get there. I also found three routes to the exit. I pointed them out to the others.

"Yeah," Harold said. "Trouble is, who knows if those doors really lead into that unknown area? I mean, what the hell, three of the four doors might lead to the broom closets or service stations."

A good point.

We just sat there, wondering whether we should head for the Pollywog or try to find out what was in the hidden area, when the Russian attack made up our minds for us. There was a tremendous bang. The floor shook, as if some immense dog had just picked up Post 004 and given it a good shaking. When it stopped the lights flickered and went out.

"Golden opportunity," I said into the monkeymouth. The others agreed. So we flashed on the lights from our suits and pointed them at the door. Harold suddenly felt very important. He went to the door and ran his magic flipper finger all the way around the door. Then he stepped back and flicked a lever on his suit.

"Better turn your backs," he said. "This can flash pretty bright."

Even looking at the back wall the explosion blinded me for a few seconds. The world looked a little green when I turned around. The door was in shreds on the floor, and the doorjamb didn't look too healthy.

"Nice job, Harold," I said.

"Graças a deus," he answered, and I had to laugh. Odd how little religious phrases refused to die, even with an irreverent filho de punta like Harold.

Then I remembered that I was in charge of order-giving. So I gave.

The second door we tried led into the rooms we wanted to see. But just as we got in, the lights came on.

"Damn. They've got the station back in order," Amauri said. But Vladimir just pointed down the corridor.

The pea soup had gotten in. It was oozing sluggishly toward us.

"Whatever the Russians did, it must have opened up a big hole in the station." Vladimir pointed his laser finger at the mess. Even on full power, it only made a little spot steam. The rest just kept coming.

"Anyone for swimming?" I asked. No one was. So I hustled them all into the not-so-hidden room.

There were some little people in there, cowering in the darkness. Harold wrapped them in cocoons and stuck them in a corner. So we had time to look around.

There wasn't that much to see, really. Standard lab equipment, and then thirty-two boxes, about a meter square. They were under sunlamps. We looked inside.

The animals were semisolid looking. I didn't touch one right then, but the sluggish way it sent out pseudopodia, I concluded that the one I was watching, at least, had a rather crusty skin—with jelly inside. They were all a light brown—even lighter than Vladimir's skin. But there were little green spots here and there. I wondered if they photosynthesized.

"Look what they're floating in," Amauri said, and I realized that it was pea soup.

"They've developed a giant amoeba that lives on all other microorganisms, I guess," Vladimir said. "Maybe they've trained it to carry bombs. Against the Russians."

At that moment Harold began firing his arsenal, and I noticed that the little people were gathered at the door to the lab, looking agitated. A few at the front were looking dead.

Harold probably would have killed all of them, except that we were still standing next to a box with a giant amoeba in it. When he screamed, we looked and saw the creature fastened against his leg. Even as we watched, Harold fell, the bottom half of his leg dropping away as the amoeba continued eating up his thigh.

We watched just long enough for the little people to grab hold of us in sufficient numbers that resistance would have been ridiculous. Besides, we couldn't take our eyes off Harold.

At about the groin, the amoeba stopped eating. It didn't matter. Harold was dead anyway—we didn't know what disease got him, but as soon as his suit had cracked he started vomiting into his suit. There were pustules all over his face. In short, Vladimir's guess about the virus content of Post 004 had been pretty accurate.

And now the amoeba formed itself into a pentagon. Five very smooth sides, the creature sitting in a clump on the gaping wound that had once been a pelvis. Suddenly, with a brief convulsion, all the sides bisected, forming sharp angles, so that now there were ten sides to the creature. A hairline crack appeared down the middle. And then, like jelly sliced in the middle and finally deciding to split, the two halves slumped away on either side. They quickly formed into two new pentagons, and then they relaxed into pseudopodia again, and continued devouring Harold.

"Well," Amauri said. "They *do* have an antipersonnel weapon."

When he spoke, the spell of stillness was broken, and the little people had us spread on tables with sharp-pointed objects pointed at us. If any one of those punctured a suit even for a moment, we would be dead. We held very still.

Richard Nixon Dixon, the top halibut, interrogated us himself. It all started with a lot of questions about the Russians, when we had visited them, why we had decided to serve them instead of the Americans, etc. We kept insisting that they were full of crap.

But when they threatened to open a window into Vladimir's suit, I decided enough was enough.

"Tell 'em!" I shouted into the monkeymouth, and Vladimir said, "All right," and the little people leaned back to listen.

"There *are* no Russians," Vladimir said.

The little people got ready to carve holes.

"No, wait, it's true! After we got your homing signal, before we landed, we made seven orbital passes over the entire planet. There is absolutely no human life anywhere but here!"

"Commie lies," Richard Nixon Dixon said.

"God's own truth!" I shouted. "Don't touch him, man! He's telling the truth! The only thing out there over this whole damn planet is that pea soup! It covers every inch of land and every inch of water, except a few holes at the poles."

Dixon began to feel a little confused, and the little people murmured. I guess I sounded sincere.

"If there aren't any people," Dixon said, "where do the Russian attacks come from?"

Vladimir answered that one. For a bunny, he was quick on the uptake. "Spontaneous recombination! You and the Russians got new strains of every microbe developing like crazy. All the people, all the animals, all the *plants* were killed. And only the microbes lived. But you've been introducing new strains constantly, tough competitors for all those beasts out there. The ones that couldn't adapt died. And now that's all that's left—the ones who adapt. Constantly."

Andrew Jackson Wallichinsky, the head researcher, nodded. "It sounds plausible."

"If there's anything we've learned about commies in the last thousand years," Richard Nixon Dixon said, "it's that you can't trust 'em any farther than you can spit."

"Well," Andy Jack said, "it's easy enough to test them."

Dixon nodded. "Go ahead."

So three of the little people went to the boxes and each came back with an amoeba. In a minute it was clear that they planned to set them on us. Amauri screamed. Vladimir turned white. I would have screamed but I was busy trying to swallow my tongue.

"Relax," Andy Jack said. "They won't hurt you."

"Acredito!" I shouted. "Like it didn't hurt Harold!"

"Harold was killing people. These won't harm you. Unless you were lying."

Great, I thought. Like the ancient test for witches. Throw them in the water, if they drown they're innocent, if they float they're guilty so kill 'em.

But *maybe* Andy Jack was telling the truth and they wouldn't hurt us. And if we refused to let them put those buggers on us they'd "know" we had been lying and punch holes in our monkeysuits.

So I told the little people to put one on me only. They didn't need to test us all.

And then I put my tongue between my teeth, ready to bite down hard and inhale the blood when the damn thing started eating me. Somehow I thought I'd feel better about going honeyduck if I helped myself along.

They set the thing on my shoulder. It didn't penetrate my monkeysuit. Instead it just oozed up toward my head.

It slid over my faceplate and the world went dark.

"Kane Kanea," said a faint vibration in the faceplate.

"Meu deus," I muttered.

The amoeba could talk. But I didn't have to speak to answer it. A question would come through the vibration of the faceplate. And then I would lie there and—it knew my answer. Easy as pie. I was so scared I urinated twice during the interview. But my imperturbable monkeysuit cleaned it all up and got it ready for breakfast, just like normal.

And at last the interview was over. The amoeba slithered off my faceplate and returned to the waiting arms of one of the little people, who carried it back to Andy Jack and Ricky Nick. The two men put their hands on the thing, and then looked at us in surprise.

"You're telling the truth. There are no Russians."

Vladimir shrugged. "Why would we lie?"

Andy Jack started toward me, carrying the writhing monster that had interviewed me.

"I'll kill myself before I let that thing touch me again."

Andy Jack stopped in surprise. "You're still afraid of that?"

"It's intelligent," I said. "It read my mind."

Vladimir looked startled, and Amauri muttered something. But Andy Jack only smiled. "Nothing mysterious about that. It can read and interpret the electromagnetic fields of your brain, coupled with the amitron flux in your thyroid gland."

"What *is* it?" Vladimir asked.

Andy Jack looked very proud. "This one is my son."

We waited for the punch line. It didn't come. And suddenly we realized that we had found what we had been looking for—the result of the little people's research into recombinant human DNA.

"We've been working on these for years. Finally we got it right about four years ago," Andy Jack said. "They were our last line of defense. But now that we know the Russians are dead—well, there's no reason for them to stay in their nests."

And the man reached down and laid the amoeba into the pea soup that was now about sixty centimeters deep on the floor. Immediately it flattened out on the surface until it was about a meter in diameter. I remembered the whispering voice through my faceplate.

"It's too flexible to have a brain," Vladimir said.

"It doesn't have one," Andy Jack answered. "The brain functions are distributed throughout the body. If it were cut in forty pieces, each piece would have enough memory and enough mindfunction to continue to live. It's indestructible. And when several of them get together, they set up a sympathetic field. They become very bright, then."

"Head of the class and everything, I'm sure," Vladimir said. He couldn't hide the loathing in his voice. Me, I was trying not to be sick.

So this is the next stage of evolution, I thought. Man screws up the planet till it's fit for nothing but microbes—and then changes himself so that he can live on a diet of bacteria and viruses.

"It's really the perfect step in evolution," Andy Jack said. "This fellow can adapt to new species of parasitic bacteria and viruses almost by reflex. Control the makeup of his own DNA consciously. Manipulate the DNA of other organisms by absorbing them through the semipermeable membranes of specialized cells, altering them, and setting them free again."

"Somehow it doesn't make me want to feed it or change its diapers."

Andy Jack laughed lightly. "Since they reproduce by fission, they're never infant. Oh, if the piece were too small, it would take a while to get back to adult competence again. But otherwise, in the normal run of things, it's always an adult."

Then Andy Jack reached down, let his son wrap itself around his arm, and then walked back to where Richard Nixon Dixon stood watching. Andy Jack put the arm that held the amoeba around Dixon's shoulder.

"By the way, sir," Andy Jack said. "With the Russians dead, the damned war is over, sir."

Dixon looked startled. "And?"

"We don't need a commander anymore."

Before Dixon could answer, the amoeba had eaten through his neck and he was quite dead. Rather an abrupt coup, I thought, and looked at the other little people for a reaction. No one seemed to mind. Apparently their superpatriotic militarism was only skin deep. I felt vaguely relieved. Maybe they had something in common with me after all.

They decided to let us go, and we were glad enough to take them up on the offer. On the way out, they showed us what had caused the explosion in the last "Russian" attack. The mold that protected the steel surface of the installation had mutated slightly in one place, allowing the steel-eating bacteria to enter into a symbiotic relationship. It just happened that the mutation occurred at the place where the hydrogen storage tanks rested against the wall. When a hole opened, one of the first amino-acid sets that came through with the pea soup was one that combines radically with raw hydrogen. The effect was a three-second population explosion. It knocked out a huge chunk of Post 004.

We were glad, when we got back to our skipship, that we had left dear old Pollywog floating some forty meters off the ground. Even so, there had been some damage. One of the airborne microbes had a penchant for lodging in hairline cracks and reproducing rapidly, widening microscopic gaps in the structure of the ship. Nevertheless, Amauri judged us fit for takeoff.

We didn't kiss anybody good-bye.

So now I've let you in on the true story of our visit to Mother Earth back in 2810. The parallel with our current situation should be obvious. If we let Pennsylvania get soaked into this spongy little war between Kiev and Núncamais, we'll deserve what we get. Because those damned antimatter convertors will do things that make germ warfare look as pleasant as sniffing pinkweeds.

And if anything human survives the war, it sure as hell won't look like anything we call human now.

And maybe that doesn't matter to anybody these days. But it matters to me. I don't like the idea of amoebas for grandchildren, and having an antimatter great-nephew thrills me less. I've been human all my life, and I like it.

So I say, turn on our repressors and sit out the damned war. Wait until they've disappeared each other, and then go about the business of keeping humanity alive— and human.

So much for the political tract. If you vote for war, though, I can promise you there'll be more than one skipship heading for the wild black yonder. We've colonized before, and we can do it again. In case no one gets the hint, that's a call for volunteers, if, as, and when. Over.

Not over. On the first printing of this program, I got a lot of inquiries as to why we didn't report all this when we got back home. The answer's simple. On Núncamais it's a capital crime to alter a ship's log. But we had to.

As soon as we got into space from Mother Earth, Vladimir had the computer present all its findings, all its data, and all its conclusions about recombinant DNA. And then he erased it all.

I probably would have stopped him if I'd known what he was doing in advance.

But once it was done, Amauri and I realized that he was right. That kind of merda didn't belong in the universe. And then we systematically covered our tracks. We erased all reference to Post 004, eradicated any hint of a homing signal. All we left in the computer was the recording of our overflight, showing nothing but pea soup from sea to soupy sea. It was tricky, but we also added a serious malfunction of the EVA lifesupport gear on the way home—which cost us the life of our dear friend and comrade, Harold.

And then we recorded in the ship's log, "Planet unfit for human occupancy. No human life found."

Hell. It wasn't even a lie.

IN THE DOGHOUSE
(WITH JAY A. PARRY)

As Mklikluln awoke, he felt the same depression that he had felt as he went to sleep ninety-seven years ago. And though he knew it would only make his depression worse, he immediately scanned backward as his ship decelerated, hunting for the star that had been the sun. He couldn't find it. Which meant that even with acceleration and deceleration time, the light from the nova—or supernova—had not yet reached the system he was heading for.

Sentimentality be damned, he thought savagely as he turned his attention to the readouts on the upcoming system. So the ice cliffs will melt, and the sourland will turn to huge, planet-spanning lakes. So the atmosphere will fly away in the intense heat. Who cares? Humanity was safe.

As safe as bodiless minds can be, resting in their own supporting mindfields somewhere in space, waiting for the instantaneous message that *here* is a planet with bodies available, *here* is a home for the millions for whom there had been no spaceships, *here* we can once again—

Once again what?

No matter how far we search, Mklikluln reminded himself, we have no hope of finding those graceful, symmetrical, hexagonally delicate bodies we left behind to burn.

Of course, Mklikluln still had his, but only for a while.

Thirteen true planetary bodies, two of which co-orbited as binaries in the third position. Ignoring the gas giants and the crusty pebbles outside the habitable range, Mklikluln got increasingly more complex readouts on the binary and the single in the fourth orbit, a red midget.

The red was dead, the smaller binary even worse, but the blue-green larger binary was ideal. Not because it matched the conditions on Mklikluln's home world—that would be impossible. But because it had life. And not only life—intelligent life.

Or at least fairly bright life. Energy output in the sub- and supravisible spectra exceeded reflection from the star (No, I must try to think of it as the *sun*) by a significant degree. Energy clearly came from a breakdown of carbon compounds, just what current theory (current? ninety-seven-year-old) had assumed would be the logical energy base of a developing world in this temperature range. The professors would be most gratified.

And after several months of maneuvering his craft, he was in stationary orbit around the larger binary. He began monitoring communications on the supravisible wavelengths. He learned the language quickly, though of course he couldn't have produced it with his own body, and sighed a little when he realized that the aliens, like his own people, called their little star "the sun," their minor binary "the moon," and their own humble, overhot planet "earth" (terra, mund, etc.). The array of languages was impressive—to think that people would go to all the trouble of thinking out hundreds of completely different ways of communicating for the sheer love of the logical exercise was amazing—what minds they must have!

For a moment he fleetingly thought of taking over for his people's use the bipedal bodies of the dominant intelligent race; but law was law, and his people would commit mass suicide if they realized—as they would surely realize—that they had gained their bodies at the expense of another intelligent race. One could think of such bipedals as being almost human, right down to the whimsical sense of humor that so reminded Mklikluln of his wife (Ah, Glundnindn, and you the pilot who volunteered to plunge into the sun, scooping out the sample that killed you, but saved us!); but he refused to mourn.

The dominant race was out. Similar bipedals were too small in population, too feared or misunderstood by the dominant race. Other animals with appropriate populations didn't have body functions that could easily support intelligence without major revisions—and many were too weak to survive unaided, too short of lifespan to allow civilization.

And so he narrowed down the choices to two quadrupeds, of very different sorts, of course, but well within the limits of choice: both had full access to the domiciles of the dominant race; both had adequate body structure to support intellect; both had potential means of communicating; both had sufficient population to hold all the encapsulated minds waiting in the space between the stars.

Mklikluln did the mental equivalent of flipping a coin—would have flipped a coin, in fact, except that he had neither hand nor coin nor adequate gravity for flipping.

The choice made—for the noisy one of greater intelligence that already had the love of most members of the master race—he set about making plans on how to introduce the transceivers that would call his people. (The dominant race must not know what is happening; and it can't be done without the cooperation of the dominant race.)

Mklikluln's six points vibrated just a little as he thought.

Abu was underpaid, underfed, underweight, and within about twelve minutes of the end of his lifespan. He was concentrating on the first problem, however, as the fourth developed.

"Why am I being paid less than Faisel, who sits on his duff by the gate while I walk back and forth in front of the cells all day?" he righteously said—under his breath, of course, in case his supervisor should overhear him. "Am I not as good a Muslim? Am I not as smart? Am I not as loyal to the Party?"

And as he was immersed in righteous indignation at man's inhumanity, not so much to mankind as to Abu ibn Assur, a great roaring sound tore through the desert prison, followed by a terrible, hot, dry, sand-stabbing wind. Abu screamed and covered his eyes—too late, however, and the sand ripped them open, and the hot air dried them out.

That was why he didn't see the hole in the outside wall of cell 23, which held a political prisoner condemned to die the next morning for having murdered his wife—normally not a political crime, except when the wife was also the daughter of somebody who could make phone calls and get people put in prison.

That was why he didn't see his supervisor come in, discover cell 23 empty, and then aim his submachine gun at Abu as the first step to setting up the hapless guard as the official scapegoat for this fiasco. Abu did, however, hear and feel the discharge of the gun, and wondered vaguely what had happened as he died.

Mklikluln stretched the new arms and legs (the fourness of the body, the two-sidedness, the overwhelming sexuality of it—all were amazing, all were delightful) and walked around his little spacecraft. And the fiveness and tenness of the fingers and toes! (What we could have done with fingers and toes! except that we might not have developed thoughttalk, then, and would have been tied to the vibration of air as are these people.) Inside the ship he could see his own body melting as the hot air of the Kansas farmland raised the temperature above the melting point of ice.

He had broken the law himself, but could see no way around it. Necessary as his act had been, and careful as he had been to steal the body of a man doomed anyway to die, he knew that his own people would try him, convict him, and execute him for depriving an intelligent being of life.

But in the meantime, it was a new body and a whole range of sensations. He moved the tongue over the teeth. He made the buzzing in his throat that was used for communication. He tried to speak.

It was impossible. Or so it seemed, as the tongue and lips and jaw tried to make the Arabic sounds the reflex pathways were accustomed to, while Mklikluln tried to speak in the language that had dominated the airwaves.

He kept practicing as he carefully melted down his ship (though it was transparent to most electromagnetic spectra, it might still cause comment if found) and by the time he made his way into the nearby city, he was able to communicate fairly well. Well enough, anyway, to contract with the Kansas City Development Corporation for the manufacture of the machine he had devised; with Farber, Farber, and Maynard to secure patents on every detail of the machinery; and with Sidney's carpentry shop to manufacture the doghouses.

He sold enough diamonds to pay for the first 2,000 finished models. And then he hit the road, humming the language he had learned from the radio. "It's the real thing, Coke is," he sang to himself. "Mr. Transmission will put in commission the worst transmissions in town."

The sun set as he checked into a motel outside Manhattan, Kansas. "How many?" asked the clerk.

"One," said Mklikluln.

"Name?"

"Robert," he said, using a name he had randomly chosen from among the many thousands mentioned on the airwaves. "Robert Redford."

"Ha-ha," said the clerk. "I bet you get teased about that a lot."

"Yeah. But I get in to see a lot of important people."

The clerk laughed. Mklikluln smiled. Speaking was fun. For one thing, you could lie. An art his people had never learned to cultivate.

"Profession?"

"Salesman."

"Really, Mr. Redford? What do you sell?"

Mklikluln shrugged, practicing looking mildly embarrassed. "Doghouses," he said.

Royce Jacobsen pulled open the front door of his swelteringly hot house and sighed. A salesman.

"We don't want any," he said.

"Yes you do," said the man, smiling.

Royce was a little startled. Salesmen usually didn't argue with potential customers —they usually whined. And those that did argue rarely did it with such calm self-assurance. The man was an ass, Royce decided. He looked at the sample case. On the side were the letters spelling out: "Doghouses Unlimited."

"We don't got a dog," Royce said.

"But you *do* have a very warm house, I believe," the salesman said.

"Yeah. Hotter'n Hades, as the preachers say. Ha." The laugh would have been bigger than one *Ha*, but Royce was hot and tired and it was only a salesman.

"But you have an air conditioner."

"Yeah," Royce said. "What I don't have is a permit for more than a hundred bucks worth of power from the damnpowercompany. So if I run the air conditioner more than one day a month, I get the refrigerator shut down, or the stove, or some other such thing."

The salesman looked sympathetic.

"It's guys like me," Royce went on, "who always get the short end of the stick. You can bet your boots that the mayor gets all the air conditioning he wants. You can bet your boots *and* your overalls, as the farmers say, ha ha, that the president of the damnpowercompany takes three hot showers a day and three cold showers a night and leaves his windows open in the winter, too, you can bet on it."

"Right," said the salesman. "The power companies own this whole country. They own the whole world, you know? Think it's any different in England? In Japan? They got the gas, and so they get the gold."

"Yeah," Royce agreed. "You're my kind of guy. You come right in. House is hot as Hades, as the preachers say, ha ha ha, but it sure beats standing in the sun."

They sat on a beat-up looking couch and Royce explained exactly what was wrong with the damnpowercompany and what he thought of the damnpowercompany's executives and in what part of their anatomy they should shove their quotas, bills, rates, and periods of maximum and minimum use. "I'm sick to death of having to take a shower at 2:00 A.M.!" Royce shouted.

"Then do something about it!" the salesman rejoindered.

"Sure. Like what?"

"Like buy a doghouse from me."

Royce thought that was funny. He laughed for a good long while.

But then the salesman started talking very quietly, showing him pictures and diagrams and cost analysis papers that proved—what?

"That the solar energy utilizer built into this doghouse can power your entire house, all day every day, with four times as much power as you could use if you turned on all your home appliances all day every day, for exactly zero once you pay me this simple one-time fee."

Royce shook his head, though he coveted the doghouse. "Can't. Illegal. I think they passed a law against solar energy thingies back in '85 or '86, to protect the power companies."

The salesman laughed. "How much protection do the power companies need?"

"Sure," Royce answered, "it's me that needs protection. But the meter reader—if I stop using power, he'll report me, they'll investigate—"

"That's why we don't put your whole house on it. We just put the big power users on it, and gradually take more off the regular current until you're paying what, maybe fifteen dollars a month. Right? Only instead of fifteen dollars a month and cooking over a fire and sweating to death in a hot house, you've got the air conditioner running all day, the heater running all day in the winter, showers whenever you want them, and you can open the refrigerator as often as you like."

Royce still wasn't sure.

"What've you got to lose?" the salesman asked.

"My sweat," Royce answered. "You hear that? My sweat. Ha ha ha ha."

"That's why we build them into doghouses—so that nobody'll suspect anything."

"Sure, why not?" Royce asked. "Do it. I'm game. I didn't vote for the damncongressman who voted in that stupid law anyway."

The air conditioner hummed as the guests came in. Royce and his wife, Junie, ushered them into the living room. The television was on in the family room and the osterizer was running in the kitchen. Royce carelessly flipped on a light. One of the women gasped. A man whispered to his wife. Royce and Junie carelessly began their conversation—as Royce *left the door open.*

A guest noticed it—Mr. Detweiler from the bowling team. He said, "Hey!" and leaped from the chair toward the door.

Royce stopped him, saying, "Never mind, never mind, I'll get it in a minute. Here, have some peanuts." And the guests all watched the door in agony as Royce passed the peanuts around, then (finally!) went to the door to close it.

"Beautiful day outside," Royce said, holding the door open a few minutes longer.

Somebody in the living room mentioned a name of the deity. Somebody else countered with a one word discussion of defecation. Royce was satisfied that the point had been made. He shut the door.

"Oh, by the way," he said. "I'd like you to meet a friend to mine. His name is Robert Redford."

Gasp, gasp, of course you're joking, Robert Redford, what a laugh, sure.

"Actually, his name *is* Robert Redford, but he isn't, of course, the all time greatest star of stage, screen, and the Friday Night Movie, as the disc jockeys say, ha ha. He is, in short, my friends, a doghouse salesman."

Mklikluln came in then, and shook hands all around.

"He looks like an Arab," a woman whispered.

"Or a Jew," her husband whispered back. "Who can tell?"

Royce beamed at Mklikluln and patted him on the back. "Redford here is the best salesman I ever met."

"Must be, if he sold you a doghouse, and you not even got a dog," said Mr. Detweiler of the bowling league, who could sound patronizing because he was the only one in the bowling league who had ever had a perfect game.

"Neverthemore, as the raven said, ha ha ha, I want you all to see my doghouse." And so Royce led the way past a kitchen where all the lights were on, where the refrigerator was standing open ("Royce, the fridge is open!" "Oh, I guess one of the kids left it that way." "I'd kill one of my kids that did something like that!"), where the stove *and* microwave *and* osterizer *and* hot water were all running at once. Some of the women looked faint.

And as the guests tried to rush through the back door all at once, to conserve energy, Royce said, "Slow down, slow down, what's the panic, the house on fire? Ha ha ha." But the guests still hurried through.

On the way out to the doghouse, which was located in the dead center of the backyard, Detweiler took Royce aside.

"Hey, Royce, old buddy. Who's your touch with the damnpowercompany? How'd you get your quota upped?"

Royce only smiled, shaking his head. "Quota's the same as ever, Detweiler." And then, raising his voice just a bit so that everybody in the backyard could hear, he said, "I only pay fifteen bucks a month for power as it is."

"Woof woof," said a small dog chained to the hook on the doghouse.

"Where'd the dog come from?" Royce whispered to Mklikluln.

"Neighbor was going to drown 'im," Mklikluln answered. "Besides, if you don't have a dog the power company's going to get suspicious. It's cover."

Royce nodded wisely. "Good idea, Redford. I just hope this party's a good idea. What if somebody talks?"

"Nobody will," Mklikluln said confidently.

And then Mklikluln began showing the guests the finer points of the doghouse.

When they finally left, Mklikluln had twenty-three appointments during the next two weeks, checks made out to Doghouses Unlimited for $221.23, including taxes, and many new friends. Even Mr. Detweiler left smiling, his check in Mklikluln's hand, even though the puppy had pooped on his shoe.

"Here's your commission," Mklikluln said as he wrote out a check for three hundred dollars to Royce Jacobsen. "It's more than we agreed, but you earned it," he said.

"I feel a little funny about this," Royce said. "Like I'm conspiring to break the law or something."

"Nonsense," Mklikluln said. "Think of it as a Tupperware party."

"Sure," Royce said after a moment's thought. "It's not as if I actually did any selling myself, right?"

Within a week, however, Detweiler, Royce, and four other citizens of Manhattan, Kansas, were on their way to various distant cities of the United States, Doghouses Unlimited briefcases in their hands.

And within a month, Mklikluln had a staff of three hundred in seven cities, building doghouses and installing them. And into every doghouse went a frisky little puppy. Mklikluln did some figuring. In about a year, he decided. One year and I can call my people.

"What's happened to power consumption in Manhattan, Kansas?" asked Bill Wilson, up-and-coming young executive in the statistical analysis section of Central Kansas Power, otherwise known as the damnpowercompany.

"It's gotten lower," answered Kay Block, relic of outdated affirmative action programs in Central Kansas Power, who had reached the level of records examiner before the ERA was repealed to make our bathrooms safe for mankind.

Bill Wilson sneered, as if to say, "That much I knew, woman." And Kay Block simpered, as if to say, "Ah, the boy has an IQ after all, eh?"

But they got along well enough, and within an hour they had the alarming statistic that power consumption in the city of Manhattan, Kansas, was down by forty percent.

"What was consumption in the previous trimester?"

Normal. Everything normal.

"Forty percent is ridiculous," Bill fulminated.

"Don't fulminate at me," Kay said, irritated at her boss for raising his voice. "Go yell at the people who unplugged their refrigerators!"

"No," Bill said. "*You* go yell at people who unplugged their refrigerators. Something's gone wrong there, and if it isn't crooked meter readers, it's people who've figured out a way to jimmy the billing system."

After two weeks of investigation, Kay Block sat in the administration building of Kansas State University (9–2 last football season, coming *that* close to copping the Plains Conference pennant for '98) refusing to admit that her investigation had turned up a big fat zero. A random inspection of thirty-eight meters showed no tampering at all. A complete audit of the local branch office's books showed no doctoring at all. And a complete examination of KSU's power consumption figures showed absolutely nothing. No change in consumption—no change in billing system—and yet a sharp drop in electricity use.

"The drop in power use may be localized," Kay suggested to the white-haired woman from the school who was babysitting her through the process. "The stadium surely uses as much light as ever—so the drop must be somewhere else, like in the science labs."

The white-haired woman shook her head. "That may be so, but the figures you see are the figures we've got."

Kay sighed and looked out the window. Down from the window was the roof of the new Plant Science Building. She looked at it as her mind struggled vainly to find something meaningful in the data she had. Somebody was cheating—but how?

There was a doghouse on the roof of the Plant Science Building.

"What's a doghouse doing on the roof of that building?" asked Kay.

"I would assume," said the white-haired woman, "for a dog to live in."

"On the roof?"

The white-haired woman smiled. "Fresh air, perhaps," she said.

Kay looked at the doghouse awhile longer, telling herself that the only reason she was suspicious was because she was hunting for *anything* unusual that could explain the anomalies in the Manhattan, Kansas, power usage pattern.

"I want to see that doghouse," she said.

"Why?" asked the white-haired lady. "Surely you don't think a generator could hide in a doghouse! Or solar-power equipment! Why, those things take whole buildings!"

Kay looked carefully at the white-haired woman and decided that she protested a bit too much. "I insist on seeing the doghouse," she said again.

The white-haired woman smiled again. "Whatever you want, Miss Block. Let me call the custodian so he can unlock the door to the roof."

After the phone call they went down the stairs to the main floor of the administration building, across the lawns, and then up the stairs to the roof of the Plant Science Building. "What's the matter, no elevators?" Kay asked sourly as she panted from the exertion of climbing the stairs.

"Sorry," the white-haired woman said. "We don't build elevators into buildings anymore. They use too much power. Only the power company can afford elevators these days."

The custodian was at the door of the roof, looking very apologetic.

"Sorry if old Rover's been causin' trouble ladies. I keep him up on the roof nowadays, ever since the break-in attempt through the roof door last spring. Nobody's tried to jimmy the door since."

"Arf," said a frisky, cheerful looking mix between an elephant and a Labrador retriever (just a quick guess, of course) that bounded up to them.

"Howdy, Rover old boy," said the custodian. "Don't bite nobody."

"Arf," the dog answered, trying to wiggle out of his skin and looking as if he might succeed. "Gurrarf."

Kay examined the roof door from the outside. "I don't see any signs of anyone jimmying at the door," she said.

"Course not," said the custodian. "The burglars was seen from the administration building before they could get to the door."

"Oh," said Kay. "Then why did you need to put a dog up here?"

"Cause what if the burglars hadn't been seen?" the custodian said, his tone implying that only a moron would have asked such a question.

Kay looked at the doghouse. It looked like every other doghouse in the world. It looked like cartoons of doghouses, in fact, it was so ordinary. Simple arched door. Pitched roof with gables and eaves. All it lacked was a water dish and piles of doggy-do and old bones. No doggy-do?

"What a talented dog," Kay commented. "He doesn't even go to the bathroom."

"Uh," answered the custodian, "he's really housebroken. He just won't go until I take him down from here to the lawn, will ya Rover?"

Kay surveyed the wall of the roof-access building they had come through. "Odd. He doesn't even mark the walls."

"I told you. He's really housebroken. He wouldn't think of mucking up the roof here."

"Arf," said the dog as it urinated on the door and then defecated in a neat pile at Kay's feet. "Woof woof woof," he said proudly.

"All that training," Kay said, "and it's all gone to waste."

Whether the custodian's answer was merely describing what the dog had done or had a more emphatic purpose was irrelevant. Obviously the doghouse was not normally used for a dog. And if that was true, what was a doghouse doing on the roof of the Plant Science Building?

The damnpowercompany brought civil actions against the city of Manhattan, Kansas, and a court injunction insisted that all doghouses be disconnected from all electric wiring systems. The city promptly brought countersuit against the damnpowercompany (a very popular move) and appealed the court injunction.

The damnpowercompany shut off all the power in Manhattan, Kansas.

Nobody in Manhattan, Kansas, noticed, except the branch office of the damnpowercompany, which now found itself the only building in the city without electricity.

The "Doghouse War" got quite a bit of notoriety. Feature articles appeared in magazines about Doghouses Unlimited and its elusive founder, Robert Redford, who refused to be interviewed and in fact could not be found. All five networks did specials on the cheap energy source. Statistics were gathered showing that not only did seven percent of the American public *have* doghouses, but also that 99.8 percent of the American public *wanted* to have doghouses. The 0.2 percent represented, presumably, power company stockholders and executives. Most politicians could add, or had aides who could, and the prospect of elections coming up in less than a year made the result clear.

The antisolar power law was repealed.

The power companies' stock plummeted on the stock market.

The world's most unnoticed depression began.

With alarming rapidity an economy based on expensive energy fell apart. The OPEC monolith immediately broke up, and within five months petroleum had fallen to 38¢ a barrel. Its only value was in plastics and as a lubricant, and the oil producing nations had been overproducing for those needs.

The reason the depression wasn't much noticed was because Doghouses Unlimited easily met the demand for their product. Scenting a chance for profit, the government slapped a huge export tax on the doghouses. Doghouses Unlimited retaliated by publishing the complete plans for the doghouse and declaring that foreign companies would not be used for manufacturing it.

The U.S. government just as quickly removed the huge tax, whereupon Doghouses Unlimited announced that the plans it had published were not complete, and continued to corner the market around the world.

As government after government, through subterfuge, bribery, or, in a few cases, popular revolt, were forced to allow Doghouses Unlimited into their countries, Robert Redford (the doghouse one) became even more of a household word than Robert Redford (the old-time actor). Folk legends which had formerly been ascribed to Kuan Yu, Paul Bunyan, or Gautama Buddha became, gradually, attached to Robert Doghouse Redford.

And, at last, every family in the world that wanted one had a cheap energy source, an unlimited energy source, and everybody was happy. So happy that they shared their newfound plenty with all God's creatures, feeding birds in the winter, leaving bowls of milk for stray cats, and putting dogs in the doghouses.

Mklikluln rested his chin in his hands and reflected on the irony that he had, quite inadvertently, saved the world for the bipedal dominant race, solely as a byproduct of his campaign to get a good home for every dog. But good results are good results, and humanity—either his own or the bipedals—couldn't condemn him completely for his murder of an Arab political prisoner the year before.

"What will happen when you come?" he asked his people, though of course none of them could hear him. "I've saved the world—but when these creatures, bright as they are, come in contact with our infinitely superior intelligence, won't it destroy them? Won't they suffer in humiliation to realize that we are so much more powerful than they; that we can span galactic distances at the speed of light, communicate telepathically, separate our minds and allow our bodies to die while we float in space unscathed, and then, at the beck of a simple machine, come instantaneously and inhabit the bodies of animals completely different from our former bodies?"

He worried—but his responsibility to his own people was clear. If this bipedal race was so proud they could not cope with inferiority, that was not Mklikluln's problem.

He opened the top drawer of his desk in the San Diego headquarters of Doghouses Unlimited, his latest refuge from the interview seekers, and pushed a button on a small box.

From the box, a powerful burst of electromagnetic energy went out to the eighty million doghouses in southern California. Each doghouse relayed the same signal in an unending chain that gradually spread all over the world—wherever doghouses could be found.

When the last doghouse was linked to the network, all the doghouses simultaneously transmitted something else entirely. A signal that only sneered at lightspeed and that crossed light-years almost instantaneously. A signal that called millions of encapsulated minds that slept in their mindfields until they heard the call, woke, and followed the signal back to its source, again at speeds far faster than poor pedestrian light.

They gathered around the larger binary in the third orbit from their new sun, and listened as Mklikluln gave a full report. They were delighted with his work, and commended him highly, before convicting him of murder of an Arabian political prisoner and ordering him to commit suicide. He felt very proud, for the commendation they had given him was rarely awarded, and he smiled as he shot himself.

And then the minds slipped downward toward the doghouses that still called to them.

"Argworfgyardworfl," said Royce's dog as it bounded excitedly through the backyard.

"Dog's gone crazy," Royce said, but his two sons laughed and ran around with the dog as it looped the yard a dozen times, only to fall exhausted in front of the doghouse.

"Griffwigrofrf," the dog said again, panting happily. It trotted up to Royce and nuzzled him.

"Cute little bugger," Royce said.

The dog walked over to a pile of newspapers waiting for a paper drive, pulled the top newspaper off the stack, and began staring at the page.

"I'll be humdingered," said Royce to Junie, who was bringing out the food for their backyard picnic supper. "Dog looks like he's readin' the paper."

"Here, Robby!" shouted Royce's oldest son, Jim. "Here, Robby! Chase a stick."

The dog, having learned how to read and write from the newspaper, chased the stick, brought it back, and instead of surrendering it to Jim's outstretched hand, began to write with it in the dirt.

"Hello, man," wrote the dog. "Perhaps you are surprised to see me writing."

"Well," said Royce, looking at what the dog had written. "Here, Junie, will you look at that. This is some dog, eh?" And he patted the dog's head and sat down to eat. "Now I wonder, is there anybody who'd pay to see a dog do that?"

"We mean no harm to your planet," wrote the dog.

"Jim," said Junie, slapping spoonfuls of potato salad onto paper plates, "you make sure that dog doesn't start scratching around in the petunias."

"C'mere, Robby," said Jim. "Time to tie you up."

"Wrowrf," the dog answered, looking a bit perturbed and backing away from the chain.

"Daddy," said Jim, "the dog won't come when I call anymore."

Impatiently, Royce got up from his chair, his mouth full of chicken salad sandwich. "Doggonit, Jim, if you don't control the dog we'll just have to get rid of it. We only got it for you kids anyway!" And Royce grabbed the dog by the collar and dragged it to where Jimmy held the other end of the chain.

Clip.

"Now you learn to obey, dog, cause if you don't I don't care what tricks you can do, I'll sell ya."

"Owrf."

"Right. Now you remember that."

The dog watched them with sad, almost frightened eyes all through dinner. Royce began to feel a little guilty, and gave the dog a leftover ham.

That night Royce and Junie seriously discussed whether to show off the dog's ability to write, and decided against it, since the kids loved the dog and it was cruel to use animals to perform tricks. They were, after all, very enlightened people.

And the next morning they discovered that it was a good thing they'd decided that way—because all anyone could talk about was their dog's newfound ability to write, or unscrew garden hoses, or lay and start an entire fire from a cold empty fireplace to a bonfire. "I got the most talented dog in the world," crowed Detweiler, only to retire into grim silence as everyone else in the bowling team bragged about his own dog.

"Mine goes to the bathroom in the toilet now, and flushes it, too!" one boasted.

"And mine can fold an entire laundry, after washing her little paws so nothing gets dirty."

The newspapers were full of the story, too, and it became clear that the sudden intelligence of dogs was a nationwide—a worldwide—phenomenon. Aside from a few superstitious New Guineans, who burned their dogs to death as witches, and some Chinese who didn't let their dogs' strange behavior stop them from their scheduled appointment with the dinnerpot, most people were pleased and proud of the change in their pets.

"Worth twice as much to me now," boasted Bill Wilson, formerly an up-and-coming executive with the damnpowercompany. "Not only fetches the birds, but plucks 'em and cleans 'em and puts 'em in the oven."

And Kay Block smiled and went home to her mastiff, which kept her good company and which she loved very, very much.

"In the five years since the sudden rise in dog intelligence," said Dr. Wheelwright to his class of graduate students in animal intelligence, "we have learned a tremendous amount about how intelligence arises in animals. The very suddenness of it has caused us to take a second look at evolution. Apparently mutations can be much more complete than we had supposed, at least in the higher functions. Naturally, we will spend much of this semester studying the research on dog intelligence, but for a brief overview:

"At the present time it is believed that dog intelligence surpasses that of the dolphin, though it still falls far short of man's. However, while the dolphin's intelligence is nearly useless to us, the dog can be trained as a valuable, simple household servant, and at last it seems that man is no longer alone on his planet. To which animal such a rise in intelligence will happen next, we cannot say, any more than we can be certain that such a change *will* happen to any other animal."

Question from the class.

"Oh, well, I'm afraid it's like the big bang theory. We can guess and guess at the cause of certain phenomena, but since we can't repeat the event in a laboratory, we will never be quite sure. However, the best guess at present is that some critical mass of total dog population in a certain ratio to the total mass of dog brain was reached that pushed the entire species over the edge into a higher order of intelligence. This change, however, did not affect *all* dogs equally—primarily it affected dogs in civilized areas, leading many to speculate on the possibility that continued exposure to man was a contributing factor. However, the very fact that many dogs, mostly in uncivilized parts of the world, were *not* affected destroys completely the idea that cosmic radiation or some other influence from outer space was responsible for the change. In the first place, any such influence would have been detected by the astronomers constantly watching every wavelength of the night sky, and in the second place, such an influence would have affected all dogs equally."

Another question from a student.

"Who knows? But I doubt it. Dogs, being incapable of speech, though many have learned to write simple sentences in an apparently mnemonic fashion somewhere between the blind repetition of parrots and the more calculating repetition at high speeds by dolphins—um, how did I get into this sentence? I can't get out!"

Student laughter.

"Dogs, I was saying, are incapable of another advance in intelligence, particularly an advance bringing them to equal intellect with man, because they cannot communicate verbally and because they lack hands. They are undoubtedly at their evolutionary peak. It is only fortunate that so many circumstances combined to place man in the situation he has reached. And we can only suppose that somewhere, on some other planet, some other species might have an even more fortunate combination leading to even higher intelligence. But let us hope not!" said the professor, scratching the ears of his dog, B. F. Skinner. "Right, B. F.? Because man may not be able to cope with the presence of a more intelligent race!"

Student laughter.

"Owrowrf," said B. F. Skinner, who had once been called Hihiwnkn on a planet where white hexagons had telepathically conquered time and space; hexagons who had only been brought to this pass by a solar process they had not quite learned how to control. What he wished he could say was, "Don't worry, professor. Humanity will never be fazed by a higher intelligence. It's too damn proud to notice."

But instead he growled a little, lapped some water from a bowl, and lay down in a corner of the lecture room as the professor droned on.

It snowed in September in Kansas in the autumn of the year 2000, and Jim (Don't call me Jimmy anymore, I'm grown up) was out playing with his dog Robby as the first flakes fell.

Robby had been uprooting crabgrass with his teeth and paws, a habit much encouraged by Royce and Junie, when Jim yelled, "Snow!" and a flake landed on the grass in front of the dog. The flake melted immediately, but Robby watched for another, and another, and another. And he saw the whiteness of the flakes, and the delicate six-sided figures so spare and strange and familiar and beautiful, and he wept.

"Mommy!" Jim called out. "It looks like Robby's crying!"

"It's just water in his eyes," Junie called back from the kitchen, where she stood washing radishes in front of an open window. "Dogs don't cry."

But the snow fell deep all over the city that night, and many dogs stood in the snow watching it fall, sharing an unspoken reverie.

"Can't we?" again and again the thought came from a hundred, a thousand minds.

"No, no, no," came the despairing answer. For without fingers of *some* kind, how could they ever build the machines that would let them encapsulate again and leave this planet?

And in their despair, they cursed for the millionth time that fool Mklikluln, who had got them into this.

"Death was too good for the bastard," they agreed, and in a worldwide vote they removed the commendation they had voted him. And then they all went back to having puppies and teaching them everything they knew.

The puppies had it easier. They had never known their ancestral home, and to them snowflakes were merely fun, and winter was merely cold. And instead of standing out in the snow, they curled up in the warmth of their doghouses and slept.

THE ORIGINIST

*L*eyel Forska sat before his lector display, reading through an array of recently published scholarly papers. A holograph of two pages of text hovered in the air before him. The display was rather larger than most people needed their pages to be, since Leyel's eyes were no younger than the rest of him. When he came to the end he did not press the PAGE key to continue the article. Instead he pressed NEXT.

The two pages he had been reading slid backward about a centimeter, joining a dozen previously discarded articles, all standing in the air over the lector. With a soft beep, a new pair of pages appeared in front of the old ones.

Deet spoke up from where she sat eating breakfast. "You're only giving the poor soul *two pages* before you consign him to the wastebin?"

"I'm consigning him to oblivion," Leyel answered cheerfully. "No, I'm consigning him to hell."

"What? Have you rediscovered religion in your old age?"

"I'm creating one. It has no heaven, but it has a terrible everlasting hell for young scholars who think they can make their reputation by attacking my work."

"Ah, you have a theology," said Deet. "Your work is holy writ, and to attack it is blasphemy."

"I welcome *intelligent* attacks. But this young tube-headed professor from—yes, of course, Minus University—"

"Old Minus U?"

"He thinks he can refute me, destroy me, lay me in the dust, and all he has bothered to cite are studies published within the last thousand years."

"The principle of millennial depth is still widely used—"

"The principle of millennial depth is the confession of modern scholars that they are not willing to spend as much effort on research as they do on academic politics. I shattered the principle of millennial depth thirty years ago. I proved that it was—"

"Stupid and outmoded. But my dearest darling sweetheart Leyel, you did it by spending part of the immeasurably vast Forska fortune to search for inaccessible and forgotten archives in every section of the Empire."

"Neglected and decaying. I had to reconstruct half of them."

"It would take a thousand universities' library budgets to match what you spent on research for 'Human Origin on the Null Planet.' "

"But once I spent the money, all those archives were open. They *have* been open for three decades. The *serious* scholars all use them, since millennial depth yields nothing but predigested, preexcreted muck. They search among the turds of rats who have devoured elephants, hoping to find ivory."

"So colorful an image. My breakfast tastes much better now." She slid her tray into the cleaning slot and glared at him. "Why are you so snappish? You used to read me sections from their silly little papers and we'd laugh. Lately you're just nasty."

Leyel sighed. "Maybe it's because I once dreamed of changing the galaxy, and every day's mail brings more evidence that the galaxy refuses to change."

"Nonsense. Hari Seldon has promised that the Empire will fall any day now."

There. She had said Hari's name. Even though she had too much tact to speak openly of what bothered him, she was hinting that Leyel's bad humor was because he was still waiting for Hari Seldon's answer. Maybe so—Leyel wouldn't deny it. It *was* annoying that it had taken Hari so long to respond. Leyel had expected a call the day Hari got his application. At least within the week. But he wasn't going to give her the satisfaction of admitting that the waiting bothered him. "The Empire will be killed by its own refusal to change. I rest my case."

"Well, I hope you have a wonderful morning, growling and grumbling about the stupidity of everyone in origin studies—except your esteemed self."

"Why are you teasing me about my vanity today? I've always been vain."

"I consider it one of your most endearing traits."

"At least I make an effort to live up to my own opinion of myself."

"That's nothing. You even live up to *my* opinion of you." She kissed the bald spot on the top of his head as she breezed by, heading for the bathroom.

Leyel turned his attention to the new essay at the front of the lector display. It was a name he didn't recognize. Fully prepared to find pretentious writing and puerile thought, he was surprised to find himself becoming quite absorbed. This woman had been following a trail of primate studies—a field so long neglected that there simply *were* no papers within the range of millennial depth. Already he knew she was his kind of scholar. She even mentioned the fact that she was using archives opened by the Forska Research Foundation. Leyel was not above being pleased at this tacit expression of gratitude.

It seemed that the woman—a Dr. Thoren Magolissian—had been following Leyel's lead, searching for the *principles* of human origin rather than wasting time on the irrelevant search for one particular planet. She had uncovered a trove of primate research from three millennia ago, which was based on chimpanzee and gorilla studies dating back to seven thousand years ago. The earliest of these had referred to original research so old it may have been conducted before the founding of the Empire—but those most ancient reports had not yet been located. They probably didn't exist any more. Texts abandoned for more than five thousand years were very hard to restore; texts older than eight thousand years were simply unreadable. It was tragic, how many texts had been "stored" by librarians who never checked them, never refreshed or recopied them. Presiding over vast archives that had lost every scrap of readable information. All neatly catalogued, of course, so you knew *exactly* what it was that humanity had lost forever.

Never mind.

Magolissian's article. What startled Leyel was her conclusion that primitive language capability seemed to be inherent in the primate mind. Even in primates incapable of speech, other symbols could easily be learned—at least for simple nouns and verbs—and the nonhuman primates could come up with sentences and ideas that had never been spoken to them. This meant that mere production of language, per se, was prehuman, or at least not the determining factor of humanness.

It was a dazzling thought. It meant that the difference between humans and nonhumans—the real origin of humans in recognizably human form—was postlinguistic. Of course this came as a direct contradiction of one of Leyel's own assertions in an early paper—he had said that "since language is what separates human from beast, historical linguistics may provide the key to human origins"—but this was the sort of contradiction he welcomed. He wished he could shout at the other fellow, make him look at Magolissian's article. See? This is how to do it! Challenge my assumption, not my conclusion, and do it with new evidence instead of trying to twist the old stuff. Cast a light in the darkness, don't just churn up the same old sediment at the bottom of the river.

Before he could get into the main body of the article, however, the house computer informed him that someone was at the door of the apartment. It was a message that crawled along the bottom of the lector display. Leyel pressed the key that brought the message to the front, in letters large enough to read. For the thousandth time he wished that sometime in the decamillennia of human history, somebody had invented a computer capable of *speech*.

"Who is it?" Leyel typed.

A moment's wait, while the house computer interrogated the visitor.

The answer appeared on the lector: "Secure courier with a message for Leyel Forska."

The very fact that the courier had got past house security meant that it was genuine—and important. Leyel typed again. "From?"

Another pause. "Hari Seldon of the Encyclopedia Galactica Foundation."

Leyel was out of his chair in a moment. He got to the door even before the house computer could open it, and without a word took the message in his hands. Fumbling a bit, he pressed the top and bottom of the black glass lozenge to prove by fingerprint that it was he, by body temperature and pulse that he was alive to receive it. Then, when the courier and her bodyguards were gone, he dropped the message into the chamber of his lector and watched the page appear in the air before him.

At the top was a three-dimensional version of the logo of Hari's Encyclopedia Foundation. Soon to be my insignia as well, thought Leyel. Hari Seldon and I, the two greatest scholars of our time, joined together in a project whose scope surpasses anything ever attempted by any man or group of men. The gathering together of all the knowledge of the Empire in a systematic, easily accessible way, to preserve it through the coming time of anarchy so that a new civilization can quickly rise out of the ashes of the old. Hari had the vision to foresee the need. And I, Leyel Forska, have the understanding of all the old archives that will make the Encyclopedia Galactica possible.

Leyel started reading with a confidence born of experience; had he ever really desired anything and been denied?

My dear friend:

I was surprised and honored to see an application from you and insisted on writing your answer personally. It is gratifying beyond measure that you believe in the Foundation enough to apply to take part. I can truthfully tell you that we have received no application from any other scholar of your distinction and accomplishment.

Of course, thought Leyel. There *is* no other scholar of my stature, except Hari himself, and perhaps Deet, once her current work is published. At least we have no equals by the standards that Hari and I have always recognized as valid. Hari created the science of psychohistory. I transformed and revitalized the field of originism.

And yet the tone of Hari's letter was wrong. It sounded like—flattery. That was it. Hari was softening the coming blow. Leyel knew before reading it what the next paragraph would say.

Nevertheless, Leyel, I must reply in the negative. The Foundation on Terminus is designed to collect and preserve knowledge. Your life's work has been devoted to expanding it. You are the opposite of the sort of researcher we need. Far better for you to remain on Trantor and continue your inestimably valuable studies, while lesser men and women exile themselves on Terminus.

Your servant,

Hari

Did Hari imagine Leyel to be so vain he would read these flattering words and preen himself contentedly? Did he think Leyel would believe that this was the real reason his application was being denied? Could Hari Seldon misknow a man so badly?

Impossible. Hari Seldon, of all people in the Empire, knew how to know other people. True, his great work in psychohistory dealt with large masses of people, with populations and probabilities. But Hari's fascination with populations had grown out of his interest in and understanding of individuals. Besides, he and Hari had been friends since Hari first arrived on Trantor. Hadn't a grant from Leyel's own research fund financed most of Hari's original research? Hadn't they held long conversations in the early days, tossing ideas back and forth, each helping the other hone his thoughts? They may not have seen each other much in the last—what, five years? Six?—but they were adults, not children. They didn't need constant visits in order to remain friends. And this was not the letter a true friend would send to Leyel Forska. Even if, doubtful as it might seem, Hari Seldon really meant to turn him down, he would not suppose for a moment that Leyel would be content with a letter like *this*.

Surely Hari would have known that it would be like a taunt to Leyel Forska. "Lesser men and women," indeed! The Foundation on Terminus was so valuable to Hari Seldon that he had been willing to risk death on charges of treason in order to launch the project. It was unlikely in the extreme that he would populate Terminus with second-raters. No, this was the form letter sent to placate prominent scholars who were judged unfit for the Foundation. Hari would have known Leyel would immediately recognize it as such.

There was only one possible conclusion. "Hari could not have written this letter," Leyel said.

"Of course he could," Deet told him, blunt as always. She had come out of the bathroom in her dressing gown and read the letter over his shoulder.

"If *you* think so then I truly *am* hurt," said Leyel. He got up, poured a cup of peshat, and began to sip it. He studiously avoided looking at Deet.

"Don't pout, Leyel. Think of the problems Hari is facing. He has so little time, so much to do. A hundred thousand people to transport to Terminus, most of the resources of the Imperial Library to duplicate—"

"He already *had* those people—"

"All in six months since his trial ended. No wonder we haven't seen him, socially or professionally, in—years. A decade!"

"You're saying that he no longer knows me? Unthinkable."

"I'm saying that he knows you very well. He knew you would recognize his message as a form letter. He also knew that you would understand at once what this meant."

"Well, then, my dear, he overestimated me. I do *not* understand what it means, unless it means he did not send it himself."

"Then you're getting old, and I'm ashamed of you. I shall deny we are married and pretend you are my idiot uncle whom I allow to live with me out of charity. I'll tell the children they were illegitimate. They'll be very sad to learn they won't inherit a bit of the Forska estate."

He threw a crumb of toast at her. "You are a cruel and disloyal wench, and I regret raising you out of poverty and obscurity. I only did it for pity, you know."

This was an old tease of theirs. She had commanded a decent fortune in her own right, though of course Leyel's dwarfed it. And, technically, he *was* her uncle, since her stepmother was Leyel's older half sister Zenna. It was all very complicated. Zenna had been born to Leyel's mother when she was married to someone else—before she married Leyel's father. So while Zenna was well dowered, she had no part in the Forska fortune. Leyel's father, amused at the situation, once remarked, "Poor Zenna. Lucky you. My semen flows with gold." Such are the ironies that come with great fortune. Poor people don't have to make such terrible distinctions between their children.

Deet's father, however, assumed that a Forska was a Forska, and so, several years after Deet had married Leyel, he decided that it wasn't enough for his daughter to be married to uncountable wealth, he ought to do the same favor for himself. He *said*, of course, that he loved Zenna to distraction, and cared nothing for fortune, but only Zenna believed him. Therefore she married him. Thus Leyel's half sister became Deet's stepmother, which made Leyel his wife's stepuncle—and his own stepuncle-in-law. A dynastic tangle that greatly amused Leyel and Deet.

Leyel of course compensated for Zenna's lack of inheritance with a lifetime stipend that amounted to ten times her husband's income each year. It had the happy effect of keeping Deet's old father in love with Zenna.

Today, though, Leyel was only half teasing Deet. There were times when he needed her to confirm him, to uphold him. As often as not she contradicted him instead. Sometimes this led him to rethink his position and emerge with a better understanding—thesis, antithesis, synthesis, the dialectic of marriage, the result of being espoused to one's intellectual equal. But sometimes her challenge was painful, unsatisfying, infuriating.

Oblivious to his underlying anger, she went on. "Hari assumed that you would take his form letter for what it is—a definite, final no. He isn't hedging, he's not engaging in some bureaucratic deviousness, he isn't playing politics with you. He isn't stringing you along in hopes of getting more financial support from you—if that were it you know he'd simply ask."

"I already know what he *isn't* doing."

"What he *is* doing is turning you down with finality. An answer from which there is no appeal. He gave you credit for having the wit to understand that."

"How convenient for you if I believe that."

Now, at last, she realized he was angry. "What's that supposed to mean?"

"You can stay here on Trantor and continue your work with all your bureaucratic friends."

Her face went cold and hard. "I told you. I am quite happy to go to Terminus with you."

"Am I supposed to believe that, even now? Your research in community formation within the Imperial bureaucracy cannot possibly continue on Terminus."

"I've already done the most important research. What I'm doing with the Imperial Library staff is a test."

"Not even a scientific one, since there's no control group."

She looked annoyed. "I'm the one who told *you* that."

It was true. Leyel had never even heard of control groups until she taught him the whole concept of experimentation. She had found it in some very old child-development studies from the 3100s G.E. "Yes, I was just agreeing with you," he said lamely.

"The point is, I can write my book as well on Terminus as anywhere else. And yes, Leyel, you *are* supposed to believe that I'm happy to go with you, because I said it, and therefore it's so."

"I believe that you believe it. I also believe that in your heart you are very glad that I was turned down, and you don't want me to pursue this matter any further so there'll be no chance of your having to go to the godforsaken end of the universe."

Those had been her words, months ago, when he first proposed applying to join the Seldon Foundation. "We'd have to go to the godforsaken end of the universe!" She remembered now as well as he did. "You'll hold that against me forever, won't you! I think I deserve to be forgiven my first reaction. I did consent to go, didn't I?"

"Consent, yes. But you never wanted to."

"Well, Leyel, that's true enough. I never *wanted* to. Is that your idea of what our marriage means? That I'm to subsume myself in you so deeply that even your desires become my own? I thought it was enough that from time to time we consent to sacrifice for each other. I never expected you to *want* to leave the Forska estates and come to Trantor when I needed to do my research here. I only asked you to *do* it—whether you wanted to or not—because *I* wanted it. I recognized and respected your sacrifice. I am very angry to discover that *my* sacrifice is despised."

"*Your* sacrifice remains unmade. We are still on Trantor."

"Then by all means, go to Hari Seldon, plead with him, humiliate yourself, and then realize that what I told you is true. He doesn't want you to join his Foundation and he will not allow you to go to Terminus."

"Are you so certain of that?"

"No, I'm not *certain*. It merely seems likely."

"I *will* go to Terminus, if he'll have me. I hope I don't have to go alone."

He regretted the words as soon as he said them. She froze as if she had been slapped, a look of horror on her face. Then she turned and ran from the room. A few moments later, he heard the chime announcing that the door of their apartment had opened. She was gone.

No doubt to talk things over with one of her friends. Women have no sense of discretion. They cannot keep domestic squabbles to themselves. She will tell them all the awful things I said, and they'll cluck and tell her it's what she must expect from a husband, husbands demand that their wives make all the sacrifices, you poor thing, poor poor Deet. Well, Leyel didn't begrudge her this barnyard of sympathetic hens. It was part of human nature, he knew, for women to form a perpetual conspiracy against the men in their lives. That was why women have always been so certain that men also formed a conspiracy against *them*.

How ironic, he thought. Men have no such solace. Men do not bind themselves so easily into communities. A man is always aware of the possibility of betrayal, of conflicting loyalties. Therefore when a man *does* commit himself truly, it is a rare and sacred bond, not to be cheapened by discussing it with others. Even a marriage, even a *good* marriage like theirs—*his* commitment might be absolute, but he could never trust hers so completely.

Leyel had buried himself within the marriage, helping and serving and loving Deet with all his heart. She was wrong, completely wrong about his coming to Trantor. He hadn't come as a sacrifice, against his will, solely because she wanted to come. On the contrary: because she wanted so much to come, he *also* wanted to come, changing even his desires to coincide with hers. She commanded his very heart, because it was impossible for him not to desire anything that would bring her happiness.

But she, no, she could not do that for him. If *she* went to Terminus, it would be as a noble sacrifice. She would never let him forget that she hadn't wanted to. To him, their marriage was his very soul. To Deet, their marriage was just a friendship with sex. Her soul belonged as much to these other women as to him. By dividing her loyalties, she fragmented them; none were strong enough to sway her deepest desires. Thus he discovered what he supposed all faithful men eventually discover—that no human relationship is ever anything but tentative. There is no such thing as an unbreakable bond between people. Like the particles in the nucleus of the atom. They are bound by the strongest forces in the universe, and yet they can be shattered, they can break.

Nothing can last. Nothing is, finally, what it once seemed to be. Deet and he had had a perfect marriage until there came a stress that exposed its imperfection. Anyone who thinks he has a perfect marriage, a perfect friendship, a perfect trust of any kind, he only believes this because the stress that will break it has not yet come. He might die with the illusion of happiness, but all he has proven is that sometimes death comes before betrayal. If you live long enough, betrayal will inevitably come.

Such were the dark thoughts that filled Leyel's mind as he made his way through the maze of the city of Trantor. Leyel did not seal himself inside a private car when he went about in the planet-wide city. He refused the trappings of wealth; he insisted on experiencing the life of Trantor as an ordinary man. Thus his bodyguards were under strict instructions to remain discreet, interfering with no pedestrians except those carrying weapons, as revealed by a subtle and instantaneous scan.

It was much more expensive to travel through the city this way, of course—every time he stepped out the door of his simple apartment, nearly a hundred high-paid bribeproof employees went into action. A weaponproof car would have been much cheaper. But Leyel was determined not to be imprisoned by his wealth.

So he walked through the corridors of the city, riding cabs and tubes, standing in lines like anyone else. He felt the great city throbbing with life around him. Yet such was his dark and melancholy mood today that the very life of the city filled him with a sense of betrayal and loss. Even you, great Trantor, the Imperial City, even you will be betrayed by the people who made you. Your empire will desert you, and you will become a pathetic remnant of yourself, plated with the metal of a thousand worlds and asteroids as a reminder that once the whole galaxy promised to serve you forever, and now you are abandoned. Hari Seldon had seen it. Hari Seldon understood the change-ability of humankind. He knew that the great empire would fall, and so—unlike the government, which depended on things remaining the same forever—Hari Seldon could actually take steps to ameliorate the Empire's fall, to prepare on Terminus a womb for the rebirth of human greatness. Hari was creating the future. It was unthinkable that he could mean to cut Leyel Forska out of it.

The Foundation, now that it had legal existence and Imperial funding, had quickly grown into a busy complex of offices in the four-thousand-year-old Putassuran Building. Because the Putassuran was originally built to house the Admiralty shortly after the great victory whose name it bore, it had an air of triumph, of monumental optimism about it—rows of soaring arches, a vaulted atrium with floating bubbles of light rising and dancing in channeled columns of air. In recent centuries the building had served as a site for informal public concerts and lectures, with the offices used to house the Museum Authority. It had come empty only a year before Hari Seldon was granted the right to form his Foundation, but it seemed as though it had been built for this very purpose. Everyone was hurrying this way and that, always seeming to be on urgent business, and yet also happy to be part of a noble cause. There had been no noble causes in the Empire for a long, long time.

Leyel quickly threaded his way through the maze that protected the Foundation's director from casual interruption. Other men and women, no doubt, had tried to see Hari Seldon and failed, put off by this functionary or that. Hari Seldon is a very busy man. Perhaps if you make an appointment for later. Seeing him today is out of the question. He's in meetings all afternoon and evening. Do call before coming next time.

But none of this happened to Leyel Forska. All he had to do was say, "Tell Mr. Seldon that Mr. Forska wishes to continue a conversation." However much awe they might have of Hari Seldon, however they might intend to obey his orders not to be disturbed, they all knew that Leyel Forska was the universal exception. Even Linge Chen would be called out of a meeting of the Commission of Public Safety to speak with Forska, especially if Leyel went to the trouble of coming in person.

The ease with which he gained entry to see Hari, the excitement and optimism of the people, of the building itself, had encouraged Leyel so much that he was not at all prepared for Hari's first words.

"Leyel, I'm surprised to see you. I thought you would understand that my message was final."

It was the worst thing that Hari could possibly have said. Had Deet been right after all? Leyel studied Hari's face for a moment, trying to see some sign of change. Was all that had passed between them through the years forgotten now? Had Hari's friendship never been real? No. Looking at Hari's face, a bit more lined and wrinkled now, Leyel saw still the same earnestness, the same plain honesty that had always been there. So instead of expressing the rage and disappointment that he felt, Leyel answered carefully, leaving the way open for Hari to change his mind. "I understood that your message was deceptive, and therefore could not be final."

Hari looked a little angry. "Deceptive?"

"I know which men and women you've been taking into your Foundation. They are not second-raters."

"Compared to you they are," said Hari. "They're academics, which means they're clerks. Sorters and interpreters of information."

"So am I. So are all scholars today. Even *your* inestimable theories arose from sorting through a trillion bytes of data and interpreting it."

Hari shook his head. "I didn't just sort through data. I had an idea in my head. So did you. Few others do. You and I are expanding human knowledge. Most of the rest are only digging it up in one place and piling it in another. That's what the Encyclopedia Galactica *is*. A new pile."

"Nevertheless, Hari, you know and I know that this is not the real reason you turned me down. And don't tell me that it's because Leyel Forska's presence on Terminus would call undue attention to the project. You already have so much attention from the government that you can hardly breathe."

"You are unpleasantly persistent, Leyel. I don't like even having this conversation."

"That's too bad, Hari. I want to be part of your project. I would contribute to it more than any other person who might join it. I'm the one who plunged back into the oldest and most valuable archives and exposed the shameful amount of data loss that had arisen from neglect. I'm the one who launched the computerized extrapolation of shattered documents that your Encyclopedia—"

"Absolutely depends on. Our work would be impossible without your accomplishments."

"And yet you turned me down, and with a crudely flattering note."

"I didn't mean to give offense, Leyel."

"You also didn't mean to tell the truth. But you *will* tell me, Hari, or I'll simply go to Terminus anyway."

"The Commission of Public Safety has given my Foundation absolute control over who may or may not come to Terminus."

"Hari. You know perfectly well that all I have to do is hint to some lower-level functionary that I want to go to Terminus. Chen will hear of it within minutes, and within an hour he'll grant me an exception to your charter. If I did that, and if you fought it, you'd lose your charter. You *know* that. If you want me not to go to Terminus, it isn't enough to forbid me. You must persuade me that I ought not to be there."

Hari closed his eyes and sighed. "I don't think you're willing to be persuaded, Leyel. Go if you must."

For a moment Leyel wondered if Hari was giving in. But no, that was impossible, not so easily. "Oh, yes, Hari, but then I'd find myself cut off from everybody else on Terminus except my own serving people. Fobbed off with useless assignments. Cut out of the real meetings."

"That goes without saying," said Hari. "You are not part of the Foundation, you will not be, you cannot be. And if you try to use your wealth and influence to force your way in, you will succeed only in annoying the Foundation, not in joining it. Do you understand me?"

Only too well, thought Leyel in shame. Leyel knew perfectly well the limitations of power, and it was beneath him to have tried to bluster his way into getting something that could only be given freely. "Forgive me, Hari. I wouldn't have tried to force you. You know I don't do that sort of thing."

"I know you've never done it since we've been friends, Leyel. I was afraid that I was learning something new about you." Hari sighed. He turned away for a long moment, then turned back with a different look on his face, a different kind of energy in his voice. Leyel knew that look, that vigor. It meant Hari was taking him more deeply into his confidence. "Leyel, you have to understand, I'm not just creating an encyclopedia on Terminus."

Immediately Leyel grew worried. It had taken a great deal of Leyel's influence to persuade the government not to have Hari Seldon summarily exiled when he first started disseminating copies of his treatises about the impending fall of the Empire. They were sure Seldon was plotting treason, and had even put him on trial, where Seldon finally persuaded them that all he wanted to do was create the Encyclopedia Galactica, the repository of all the wisdom of the Empire. Even now, if Seldon confessed some ulterior motive, the government would move against him. It was to be assumed that the Pubs —Public Safety Office—were recording this entire conversation. Even Leyel's influence couldn't stop them if they had a confession from Hari's own mouth.

"No, Leyel, don't be nervous. My meaning is plain enough. For the Encyclopedia Galactica to succeed, I have to create a thriving city of scholars on Terminus. A colony full of men and women with fragile egos and unstemmable ambition, all of them trained in vicious political infighting at the most dangerous and terrible schools of bureaucratic combat in the Empire—the universities."

"Are you actually telling me you won't let me join your Foundation because I never attended one of those pathetic universities? My self-education is worth ten times their lockstep force-fed pseudolearning."

"Don't make your antiuniversity speech to me, Leyel. I'm saying that one of my most important concerns in staffing the Foundation is compatibility. I won't bring anyone to Terminus unless I believe he—or *she*—would be happy there."

The emphasis Hari put on the word *she* suddenly made everything clearer. "This isn't about me at all, is it?" Leyel said. "It's about Deet."

Hari said nothing.

"You know she doesn't want to go. You know she prefers to remain on Trantor. And that's why you aren't taking me! Is that it?"

Reluctantly, Hari conceded the point. "It does have something to do with Deet, yes."

"Don't you know how much the Foundation means to me?" demanded Leyel. "Don't you know how much I'd give up to be part of your work?"

Hari sat there in silence for a moment. Then he murmured, "Even Deet?"

Leyel almost blurted out an answer. Yes, of course, even Deet, anything for this great work.

But Hari's measured gaze stopped him. One thing Leyel had known since they first met at a conference back in their youth was that Hari would not stand for another man's self-deception. They had sat next to each other at a presentation by a demographer who had a considerable reputation at the time. Leyel watched as Hari destroyed the poor man's thesis with a few well-aimed questions. The demographer was furious. Obviously he had not seen the flaws in his own argument—but now that they had been shown to him, he refused to admit that they were flaws at all.

Afterward, Hari had said to Leyel, "I've done him a favor."

"How, by giving him someone to hate?" said Leyel.

"No. Before, he believed his own unwarranted conclusions. He had deceived himself. Now he doesn't believe them."

"But he still propounds them."

"So—now he's more of a liar and less of a fool. I have improved his private integrity. His public morality I leave up to him."

Leyel remembered this and knew that if he told Hari he could give up Deet for any reason, even to join the Foundation, it would be worse than a lie. It would be foolishness.

"It's a terrible thing you've done," said Leyel. "You know that Deet is part of myself. I can't give her up to join your Foundation. But now for the rest of our lives together I'll know that I could have gone, if not for her. You've given me wormwood and gall to drink, Hari."

Hari nodded slowly. "I hoped that when you read my note you'd realize I didn't want to tell you more. I hoped you wouldn't come to me and ask. I can't lie to you, Leyel. I wouldn't if I could. But I did withhold information, as much as possible. To spare us both problems."

"It didn't work."

"It isn't Deet's fault, Leyel. It's who she is. She belongs on Trantor, not on Terminus. And you belong with her. It's a fact, not a decision. We'll never discuss this again."

"No," said Leyel.

They sat there for a long minute, gazing steadily at each other. Leyel wondered if he and Hari would ever speak again. No. Never again. I don't ever want to see you again, Hari Seldon. You've made me regret the one unregrettable decision of my life —Deet. You've made me wish, somewhere in my heart, that I'd never married her. Which is like making me wish I'd never been born.

Leyel got up from his chair and left the room without a word. When he got outside, he turned to the reception room in general, where several people were waiting to see Seldon. "Which of you are mine?" he asked.

Two women and one man stood up immediately.

"Fetch me a secure car and a driver."

Without a glance at each other, one of them left on the errand. The others fell in step beside Leyel. Subtlety and discretion were over for the moment. Leyel had no wish to mingle with the people of Trantor now. He only wanted to go home.

Hari Seldon left his office by the back way and soon found his way to Chandrakar Matt's cubicle in the Department of Library Relations. Chanda looked up and waved, then effortlessly slid her chair back until it was in the exact position required. Hari picked up a chair from the neighboring cubicle and, again without showing any particular care, set it exactly where it had to be.

Immediately the computer installed inside Chanda's lector recognized the configuration. It recorded Hari's costume of the day from three angles and superimposed the information on a long-stored holoimage of Chanda and Hari conversing pleasantly. Then, once Hari was seated, it began displaying the hologram. The hologram exactly matched the positions of the real Hari and Chanda, so that infrared sensors would show no discrepancy between image and fact. The only thing different was the faces—the movement of lips, blinking of eyes, the expressions. Instead of matching the words Hari and Chanda were actually saying, they matched the words being pushed into the air outside the cubicle—a harmless, randomly chosen series of remarks that took into account recent events so that no one would suspect that it was a canned conversation.

It was one of Hari's few opportunities for candid conversation that the Pubs would not overhear, and he and Chanda protected it carefully. They never spoke long enough or often enough that the Pubs would wonder at their devotion to such empty conversations. Much of their communication was subliminal—a sentence would stand for a paragraph, a word for a sentence, a gesture for a word. But when the conversation was done, Chanda knew where to go from there, what to do next; and Hari was reassured that his most important work was going on behind the smokescreen of the Foundation.

"For a moment I thought he might actually leave her."

"Don't underestimate the lure of the Encyclopedia."

"I fear I've wrought too well, Chanda. Do you think someday the Encyclopedia Galactica might actually exist?"

"It's a good idea. Good people are inspired by it. It wouldn't serve its purpose if they weren't. What should I tell Deet?"

"Nothing, Chanda. The fact that Leyel is staying, that's enough for her."

"If he changes his mind, will you actually let him go to Terminus?"

"If he changes his mind, then he *must* go, because if he would leave Deet, he's not the man for us."

"Why not just tell him? Invite him?"

"He must become part of the Second Foundation without realizing it. He must do it by natural inclination, not by a summons from me, and above all not by his own ambition."

"Your standards are so high, Hari, it's no wonder so few measure up. Most people in the Second Foundation don't even know that's what it is. They think they're librarians. Bureaucrats. They think Deet is an anthropologist who works among them in order to study them."

"Not so. They once thought that, but now they think of Deet as one of them. As one of the *best* of them. She's defining what it means to be a librarian. She's making them proud of the name."

"Aren't you ever troubled, Hari, by the fact that in the practice of your art—"

"My *science*."

"Your meddlesome magical *craft*, you old wizard, you don't fool *me* with all your talk of science. I've seen the scripts of the holographs you're preparing for the vault on Terminus."

"That's all a pose."

"I can just imagine you saying those words. Looking perfectly satisfied with yourself. 'If you care to smoke, I wouldn't mind . . . Pause for chuckle . . . Why should I? I'm not really here.' Pure showmanship."

Hari waved off the idea. The computer quickly found a bit of dialogue to fit his gesture, so the false scene would not seem false. "No, I'm *not* troubled by the fact that in the practice of my *science* I change the lives of human beings. Knowledge has always changed people's lives. The only difference is that I *know* I'm changing them—and the changes I introduce are planned, they're under control. Did the man who invented the first artificial light—what was it, animal fat with a wick? A light-emitting diode?—did he realize what it would do to humankind, to be given power over night?"

As always, Chanda deflated him the moment he started congratulating himself. "In the first place, it was almost certainly a woman, and in the second place, she knew exactly what she was doing. It allowed her to find her way through the house at night. Now she could put her nursing baby in another bed, in another room, so she could get some sleep at night without fear of rolling over and smothering the child."

Hari smiled. "If artificial light was invented by a woman, it was certainly a prostitute, to extend her hours of work."

Chanda grinned. He did not laugh—it was too hard for the computer to come up with jokes to explain laughter. "We'll watch Leyel carefully, Hari. How will we know when he's ready, so we can begin to count on him for protection and leadership?"

"When you already count on him, then he's ready. When his commitment and loyalty are firm, when the goals of the Second Foundation are already in his heart, when he acts them out in his life, then he's ready."

There was a finality in Hari's tone. The conversation was nearly over.

"By the way, Hari, you were right. No one has even questioned the omission of any important psychohistorical data from the Foundation library on Terminus."

"Of course not. Academics never look outside their own discipline. That's another reason why I'm glad Leyel isn't going. *He* would notice that the only psychologist we're sending is Bor Alurin. Then I'd have to explain more to him than I want. Give my love to Deet, Chanda. Tell her that her test case is going very well. She'll end up with a husband *and* a community of scientists of the mind."

"Artists. Wizards. Demigods."

"Stubborn misguided women who don't know science when they're doing it. All in the Imperial Library. Till next time, Chanda."

If Deet had asked him about his interview with Hari, if she had commiserated with him about Hari's refusal, his resentment of her might have been uncontainable, he might have lashed out at her and said something that could never be forgiven. Instead, she was perfectly herself, so excited about her work and so beautiful, even with her face showing all the sag and wrinkling of her sixty years, that all Leyel could do was fall in love with her again, as he had so many times in their years together.

"It's working beyond anything I hoped for, Leyel. I'm beginning to hear stories that I created months and years ago, coming back as epic legends. You remember the time I retrieved and extrapolated the accounts of the uprising at Misercordia only three days before the Admiralty needed them?"

"Your finest hour. Admiral Divart still talks about how they used the old battle plots as a strategic guideline and put down the Tellekers' strike in a single three-day operation without loss of a ship."

"You have a mind like a trap, even if you *are* old."

"Sadly, all I can remember is the past."

"Dunce, that's all *anyone* can remember."

He prompted her to go on with her account of today's triumph. "It's an epic legend now?"

"It came back to me without my name on it, and bigger than life. As a reference. Rinjy was talking with some young librarians from one of the inner provinces who were on the standard interlibrary tour, and one of them said something about how you could stay in the Imperial Library on Trantor all your life and never see the real world at all."

Leyel hooted. "Just the thing to say to Rinjy!"

"Exactly. Got her dander up, of course, but the important thing is, she immediately told them the story of how a librarian, *all on her own,* saw the similarity between the Misercordia uprising and the Tellekers' strike. She knew no one at the Admiralty would listen to her unless she brought them all the information at once. So she delved back into the ancient records and found them in deplorable shape—the original data had been stored in glass, but that was forty-two centuries ago, and no one had refreshed the data. None of the secondary sources actually showed the battle plots or ship courses— Misercordia had mostly been written about by biographers, not military historians—"

"Of course. It was Pol Yuensau's first battle, but he was just a pilot, not a commander—"

"I know *you* remember, my intrusive pet. The point is what Rinjy *said* about this mythical librarian."

"You."

"I was standing right there. I don't think Rinjy knew it was me, or she would have said something—she wasn't even in the same division with me then, you know. What matters is that Rinjy heard a version of the story and by the time she told it, it was transformed into a magic hero tale. The prophetic librarian of Trantor."

"What does *that* prove? You *are* a magic hero."

"The way she told it, I did it all on my own initiative—"

"You did. You were assigned to do document extrapolation, and you just happened to start with Misercordia."

"But in Rinjy's version, I had *already* seen its usefulness with the Tellekers' strike. She said the librarian sent it to the Admiralty and only then did they realize it was the key to bloodless victory."

"Librarian saves the Empire."

"Exactly."

"But you did."

"But I didn't *mean* to. And Admiralty requested the information—the only really extraordinary thing was that I had already finished two weeks of document restoration —"

"Which you did brilliantly."

"Using programs you had helped design, thank you very much, O Wise One, as you indirectly praise yourself. It was sheer coincidence that I could give them exactly what they wanted within five minutes of their asking. But now it's a hero story within the community of librarians. In the Imperial Library itself, and now spreading outward to all the other libraries."

"This is so anecdotal, Deet. I don't see how you can publish this."

"Oh, I don't intend to. Except perhaps in the introduction. What matters to me is that it proves my theory."

"It has no statistical validity."

"It proves it to *me*. I know that my theories of community formation are true. That the vigor of a community depends on the allegiance of its members, and the allegiance can be created and enhanced by the dissemination of epic stories."

"She speaks the language of academia. I should be writing this down, so you don't have to think up all those words again."

"Stories that make the community seem more important, more central to human life. Because Rinjy could tell this story, it made her more proud to be a librarian, which increased her allegiance to the community and gave the community more power within her."

"You are possessing their souls."

"And they've got mine. Together our souls are possessing each other."

There was the rub. Deet's role in the library had begun as applied research—joining the library staff in order to confirm her theory of community formation. But that task was impossible to accomplish without in fact becoming a committed part of the library community. It was Deet's dedication to serious science that had brought them together. Now that very dedication was stealing her away. It would hurt her more to leave the library than it would to lose Leyel.

Not true. Not true at all, he told himself sternly. Self-pity leads to self-deception. Exactly the opposite is true—it would hurt her more to lose Leyel than to leave her community of librarians. That's why she consented to go to Terminus in the first place. But could he blame her for being glad that she didn't have to choose? Glad that she could have both?

Yet even as he beat down the worst of the thoughts arising from his disappointment, he couldn't keep some of the nastiness from coming out in his conversation. "How will you know when your experiment is over?"

She frowned. "It'll never be *over*, Leyel. They're all really librarians—I don't pick them up by the tails like mice and put them back in their cages when the experiment's done. At some point I'll simply stop, that's all, and write my book."

"Will you?"

"Write the book? I've written books before, I think I can do it again."

"I meant, will you stop?"

"When, now? Is this some test of my love for you, Leyel? Are you jealous of my friendships with Rinjy and Animet and Fin and Urik?"

No! Don't accuse me of such childish, selfish feelings!

But before he could snap back his denial, he knew that his denial would be false.

"Sometimes I am, yes, Deet. Sometimes I think you're happier with them."

And because he had spoken honestly, what could have become a bitter quarrel remained a conversation. "But I *am*, Leyel," she answered, just as frankly. "It's because when I'm with them, I'm creating something new, I'm creating something *with them*. It's exciting, invigorating, I'm discovering new things every day, in every word they say, every smile, every tear someone sheds, every sign that being one of *us* is the most important thing in their lives."

"I can't compete with that."

"No, you can't, Leyel. But you complete it. Because it would all mean nothing, it would be more frustrating than exhilarating if I couldn't come back to you every day and tell you what happened. You always understand what it means, you're always excited for me, you validate my experience."

"I'm your audience. Like a parent."

"Yes, old man. Like a husband. Like a child. Like the person I love most in all the world. You are my root. I make a brave show out there, all branches and bright leaves in the sunlight, but I come here to suck the water of life from your soil."

"Leyel Forska, the font of capillarity. You are the tree, and I am the dirt."

"Which happens to be full of fertilizer." She kissed him. A kiss reminiscent of younger days. An invitation, which he gladly accepted.

A softened section of floor served them as an impromptu bed. At the end, he lay beside her, his arm across her waist, his head on her shoulder, his lips brushing the skin of her breast. He remembered when her breasts were small and firm, perched on her chest like small monuments to her potential. Now when she lay on her back they were a ruin, eroded by age so they flowed off her chest to either side, resting wearily on her arms.

"You are a magnificent woman," he whispered, his lips tickling her skin.

Their slack and flabby bodies were now capable of greater passion than when they were taut and strong. Before, they were all potential. That's what we love in youthful bodies, the teasing potential. Now hers is a body of accomplishment. Three fine children were the blossoms, then the fruit of this tree, gone off and taken root somewhere else. The tension of youth could now give way to a relaxation of the flesh. There were no more promises in their lovemaking. Only fulfillment.

She murmured softly in his ear, "That was a ritual, by the way. Community maintenance."

"So I'm just another experiment?"

"A fairly successful one. I'm testing to see if this little community can last until one of us drops."

"What if you drop first? Who'll write the paper then?"

"You will. But you'll sign my name to it. I want the Imperial medal for it. Post-humously. Glue it to my memorial stone."

"I'll wear it myself. If you're selfish enough to leave all the real work to me, you don't deserve anything better than a cheap replica."

She slapped his back. "You are a nasty selfish old man, then. The real thing or nothing."

He felt the sting of her slap as if he deserved it. A nasty selfish old man. If she only knew how right she was. There had been a moment in Hari's office when he'd almost said the words that would deny all that there was between them. The words that would cut her out of his life. Go to Terminus without her! I would be more myself if they took my heart, my liver, my brain.

How could I have thought I wanted to go to Terminus, anyway? To be surrounded by academics of the sort I most despise, struggling with them to get the encyclopedia properly designed. They'd each fight for their petty little province, never catching the vision of the whole, never understanding that the encyclopedia would be valueless if it were compartmentalized. It would be a life in hell, and in the end he'd lose, because the academic mind was incapable of growth or change.

It was here on Trantor that he could still accomplish something. Perhaps even solve the question of human origin, at least to his own satisfaction—and perhaps he could do it soon enough that he could get his discovery included in the Encyclopedia Galactica before the Empire began to break down at the edges, cutting Terminus off from the rest of the Galaxy.

It was like a shock of static electricity passing through his brain; he even saw an afterglow of light around the edges of his vision, as if a spark had jumped some synaptic gap.

"What a sham," he said.

"Who, you? Me?"

"Hari Seldon. All this talk about his Foundation to create the Encyclopedia Galactica."

"Careful, Leyel." It was almost impossible that the Pubs could have found a way to listen to what went on in Leyel Forska's own apartments. Almost.

"He told me twenty years ago. It was one of his first psychohistorical projections. The Empire will crumble at the edges first. He projected it would happen within the next generation. The figures were crude then. He must have it down to the year now. Maybe even the month. Of course he put his Foundation on Terminus. A place so remote that when the edges of the Empire fray, it will be among the first threads lost. Cut off from Trantor. Forgotten at once!"

"What good would *that* do, Leyel? They'd never hear of any new discoveries then."

"What you said about us. A tree. Our children like the fruit of that tree."

"I never said that."

"I thought it, then. He is dropping his Foundation out on Terminus like the fruit of Empire. To grow into a new Empire by and by."

"You frighten me, Leyel. If the Pubs ever heard you say that—"

"That crafty old fox. That sly, deceptive—he never actually lied to me, but of course he couldn't send me there. If the Forska fortune was tied up with Terminus, the Empire would never lose track of the place. The edges might fray elsewhere, but never there. Putting me on Terminus would be the undoing of the *real* project." It was such a relief. Of course Hari couldn't tell him, not with the Pubs listening, but it had nothing to do with him or Deet. It wouldn't have to be a barrier between them after all. It was just one of the penalties of being the keeper of the Forska fortune.

"Do you really think so?" asked Deet.

"I was a fool not to see it before. But Hari was a fool too if he thought I wouldn't guess it."

"Maybe he expects you to guess everything."

"Oh, nobody could ever come up with *everything* Hari's doing. He has more twists and turns in his brain than a hyperpath through core space. No matter how you labor to pick your way through, you'll always find Hari at the end of it, nodding happily and congratulating you on coming this far. He's ahead of us all. He's already planned everything, and the rest of us are doomed to follow in his footsteps."

"Is it doom?"

"Once I thought Hari Seldon was God. Now I know he's much less powerful than that. He's merely Fate."

"No, Leyel. Don't say that."

"Not even Fate. Just our guide through it. He sees the future, and points the way."

"Rubbish." She slid out from under him, got up, pulled her robe from its hook on the wall. "My old bones get cold when I lie about naked."

Leyel's legs were trembling, but not with cold. "The future is his, and the present is yours, but the past belongs to me. I don't know how far into the future his probability curves have taken him, but I can match him, step for step, century for century into the past."

"Don't tell me you're going to solve the question of origin. You're the one who proved it wasn't worth solving."

"I proved that it wasn't important or even possible to find the planet of origin. But I also said that we could still discover the natural laws that accounted for the origin of man. Whatever forces created us as human beings must still be present in the universe."

"I did read what you wrote, you know. You said it would be the labor of the next millennium to find the answer."

"Just now. Lying here, just now, I saw it, just out of reach. Something about your work and Hari's work, and the tree."

"The tree was about me needing you, Leyel. It wasn't about the origin of humanity."

"It's gone. Whatever I saw for a moment there, it's gone. But I can find it again. It's there in your work, and Hari's Foundation, and the fall of the Empire, and the damned pear tree."

"I never said it was a pear tree."

"I used to play in the pear orchard on the grounds of the estate in Holdwater. To me the word 'tree' always means a pear tree. One of the deep-worn ruts in my brain."

"I'm relieved. I was afraid you were reminded of pears by the shape of these ancient breasts when I bend over."

"Open your robe again. Let me see if I think of pears."

Leyel paid for Hari Seldon's funeral. It was not lavish. Leyel had meant it to be. The moment he heard of Hari's death—not a surprise, since Hari's first brutal stroke had left him half-paralyzed in a wheelchair—he set his staff to work on a memorial service appropriate to honor the greatest scientific mind of the millennium. But word arrived, in the form of a visit from Commissioner Rom Divart, that any sort of public services would be . . .

"Shall we say, inappropriate?"

"The man was the greatest genius I've ever heard of! He virtually invented a branch of science that clarified things that—he made a science out of the sort of thing that soothsayers and—and—*economists* used to do!"

Rom laughed at Leyel's little joke, of course, because he and Leyel had been friends forever. Rom was the only friend of Leyel's childhood who had never sucked up to him or resented him or stayed cool toward him because of the Forska fortune. This was, of course, because the Divart holdings were, if anything, slightly greater. They had played together unencumbered by strangeness or jealousy or awe.

They even shared a tutor for two terrible, glorious years, from the time Rom's father was murdered until the execution of Rom's grandfather, which caused so much outrage among the nobility that the mad Emperor was stripped of power and the Imperium put under the control of the Commission of Public Safety. Then, as the youthful head of one of the great families, Rom had embarked on his long and fruitful career in politics.

Rom said later that for those two years it was Leyel who taught him that there was still some good in the world; that Leyel's friendship was the only reason Rom hadn't killed himself. Leyel always thought this was pure theatrics. Rom was a born actor. That's why he so excelled at making stunning entrances and playing unforgettable scenes on the grandest stage of all—the politics of the Imperium. Someday he would no doubt exit as dramatically as his father and grandfather had.

But he was not all show. Rom never forgot the friend of his childhood. Leyel knew it, and knew also that Rom's coming to deliver this message from the Commission of Public Safety probably meant that Rom had fought to make the message as mild as it was. So Leyel blustered a bit, then made his little joke. It was his way of surrendering gracefully.

What Leyel didn't realize, right up until the day of the funeral, was exactly *how* dangerous his friendship with Hari Seldon had been, and how stupid it was for him to associate himself with Hari's name now that the old man was dead. Linge Chen, the Chief Commissioner, had not risen to the position of greatest power in the Empire without being fiercely suspicious of potential rivals and brutally efficient about eliminating them. Hari had maneuvered Chen into a position such that it was more dangerous to kill the old man than to give him his Foundation on Terminus. But now Hari was dead, and apparently Chen was watching to see who mourned.

Leyel did—Leyel and the few members of Hari's staff who had stayed behind on Trantor to maintain contact with Terminus up to the moment of Hari's death. Leyel should have known better. Even alive, Hari wouldn't have cared who came to his funeral. And now, dead, he cared even less. Leyel didn't believe his friend lived on in some ethereal plane, watching carefully and taking attendance at the services. No, Leyel simply felt he had to be there, felt he had to speak. Not for Hari, really. For himself. To continue to be himself, Leyel had to make some kind of public gesture toward Hari Seldon and all he had stood for.

Who heard? Not many. Deet, who thought his eulogy was too mild by half. Hari's staff, who were quite aware of the danger and winced at each of Leyel's list of Hari's accomplishments. Naming them—and emphasizing that only Seldon had the vision to do these great works—was inherently a criticism of the level of intelligence and integrity in the Empire. The Pubs were listening, too. They noted that Leyel clearly agreed with Hari Seldon about the certainty of the Empire's fall—that in fact as a galactic empire it had probably already fallen, since its authority was no longer coextensive with the Galaxy.

If almost anyone else had said such things, to such a small audience, it would have been ignored, except to keep him from getting any job requiring a security clearance. But when the head of the Forska family came out openly to affirm the correctness of the views of a man who had been tried before the Commission of Public Safety—that posed a greater danger to the Commission than Hari Seldon.

For, as head of the Forska family, if Leyel Forska wanted, he could be one of the great players on the political stage, could have a seat on the Commission along with Rom Divart and Linge Chen. Of course, that would also have meant constantly watching for assassins—either to avoid them or to hire them—and trying to win the allegiance of various military strongmen in the farflung reaches of the Galaxy. Leyel's grandfather had spent his life in such pursuits, but Leyel's father had declined, and Leyel himself had thoroughly immersed himself in science and never so much as inquired about politics.

Until now. Until he made the profoundly political act of paying for Hari Seldon's funeral and then *speaking* at it. What would he do next? There were a thousand would-be warlords who would spring to revolt if a Forska promised what would-be emperors so desperately needed: a noble sponsor, a mask of legitimacy, and *money*.

Did Linge Chen really believe that Leyel meant to enter politics at his advanced age? Did he really think Leyel posed a threat?

Probably not. If he *had* believed it, he would surely have had Leyel killed, and no doubt all his children as well, leaving only one of his minor grandchildren, whom Chen would carefully control through the guardians he would appoint, thereby acquiring control of the Forska fortune as well as his own.

Instead, Chen only believed that Leyel *might* cause trouble. So he took what were, for him, mild steps.

That was why Rom came to visit Leyel again, a week after the funeral.

Leyel was delighted to see him. "Not on somber business this time, I hope," he said. "But such bad luck—Deet's at the library again, she practically lives there now, but she'd want to—"

"Leyel." Rom touched Leyel's lips with his fingers.

So it *was* somber business after all. Worse than somber. Rom recited what had to be a memorized speech.

"The Commission of Public Safety has become concerned that in your declining years—"

Leyel opened his mouth to protest, but again Rom touched his lips to silence him.

"That in your declining years, the burdens of the Forska estates are distracting you from your exceptionally important scientific work. So great is the Empire's need for the new discoveries and understanding your work will surely bring us, that the Commission of Public Safety has created the office of Forska Trustee to oversee all the Forska estates and holdings. You will, of course, have unlimited access to these funds for your scientific work here on Trantor, and funding will continue for all the archives and libraries you have endowed. Naturally, the Commission has no desire for you to thank us for what is, after all, our duty to one of our noblest citizens, but if your well-known courtesy required you to make a brief public statement of gratitude it would not be inappropriate."

Leyel was no fool. He knew how things worked. He was being stripped of his fortune and being placed under arrest on Trantor. There was no point in protest or remonstrance, no point even in trying to make Rom feel guilty for having brought him such a bitter message. Indeed, Rom himself might be in great danger—if Leyel so much as hinted that he expected Rom to come to his support, his dear friend might also fall. So Leyel nodded gravely, and then carefully framed his words of reply.

"Please tell the Commissioners how grateful I am for their concern on my behalf. It has been a long, long time since anyone went to the trouble of easing my burdens. I accept their kind offer. I am especially glad because this means that now I can pursue my studies unencumbered."

Rom visibly relaxed. Leyel wasn't going to cause trouble. "My dear friend, I will sleep better knowing that you are always here on Trantor, working freely in the library or taking your leisure in the parks."

So at least they weren't going to confine him to his apartment. No doubt they would never let him off-planet, but it wouldn't hurt to ask. "Perhaps I'll even have time now to visit my grandchildren now and then."

"Oh, Leyel, you and I are both too old to enjoy hyperspace any more. Leave that for the youngsters—they can come visit you whenever they want. And sometimes they can stay home, while their parents come to see you."

Thus Leyel learned that if any of his children came to visit him, *their* children would be held hostage, and vice versa. Leyel himself would never leave Trantor again.

"So much the better," said Leyel. "I'll have time to write several books I've been meaning to publish."

"The Empire waits eagerly for every scientific treatise you publish." There was a slight emphasis on the word "scientific." "But I hope you won't bore us with one of those tedious autobiographies."

Leyel agreed to the restriction easily enough. "I *promise*, Rom. You know better than anyone else exactly how boring my life has always been."

"Come now. My life's the boring one, Leyel, all this government claptrap and bureaucratic bushwa. You've been at the forefront of scholarship and learning. Indeed, my friend, the Commission hopes you'll honor us by giving us first look at every word that comes out of your scriptor."

"Only if you promise to read it carefully and point out any mistakes I might make." No doubt the Commission intended only to censor his work to remove political material—which Leyel had never included anyway. But Leyel had already resolved never to publish anything again, at least as long as Linge Chen was Chief Commissioner. The safest thing Leyel could do now was to disappear, to let Chen forget him entirely—it would be egregiously stupid to send occasional articles to Chen, thus reminding him that Leyel was still around.

But Rom wasn't through yet. "I must extend that request to Deet's work as well. We really want first look at it—do tell her so."

"Deet?" For the first time Leyel almost let his fury show. Why should Deet be punished because of Leyel's indiscretion? "Oh, she'll be too shy for that, Rom—she doesn't think her work is *important* enough to deserve any attention from men as busy as the Commissioners. They'll think you only want to see her work because she's my wife—she's always annoyed when people patronize her."

"You must insist, then, Leyel," said Rom. "I assure you, her studies of the functions of the Imperial bureaucracy have long been interesting to the Commission for their own sake."

Ah. Of course. Chen would never have allowed a report on the workings of government to appear without making sure it wasn't dangerous. Censorship of Deet's writings wouldn't be Leyel's fault after all. Or at least not entirely.

"I'll tell her that, Rom. She'll be flattered. But won't you stay and tell her yourself? I can bring you a cup of peshat, we can talk about old times—"

Leyel would have been surprised if Rom had stayed. No, this interview had been at least as hard on Rom as it had been on him. The very fact that Rom had been forced into being the Commission's messenger to his childhood friend was a humiliating reminder that the Chens were in the ascendant over the Divarts. But as Rom bowed and left, it occurred to Leyel that Chen might have made a mistake. Humiliating Rom this way, forcing him to place his dearest friend under arrest like this—it might be the straw to break the camel's back. After all, though no one had ever been able to find out who hired the assassin who killed Rom's father, and no one had ever learned who denounced Rom's grandfather, leading to his execution by the paranoid Emperor Wassiniwak, it didn't take a genius to realize that the House of Chen had profited most from both events.

"I wish I could stay," said Rom. "But duty calls. Still, you can be sure I'll think of you often. Of course, I doubt I'll think of you as you are *now*, you old wreck. I'll remember you as a boy, when we used to tweak our tutor—remember the time we recoded his lector, so that for a whole week explicit pornography kept coming up on the display whenever the door of his room opened?"

Leyel couldn't help laughing. "You never forget anything, do you!"

"The poor fool. He never figured out that it was us! Old times. Why couldn't we have stayed young forever?" He embraced Leyel and then swiftly left.

Linge Chen, you fool, you have reached too far. Your days are numbered. None of the Pubs who were listening in on their conversation could possibly know that Rom and Leyel had never teased their tutor—and that they had never done anything to his lector. It was just Rom's way of letting Leyel know that they were still allies, still keeping secrets together—and that someone who had authority over both of them was going to be in for a few nasty surprises.

It gave Leyel chills, thinking about what might come of all this. He loved Rom Divart with all his heart, but he also knew that Rom was capable of biding his time and then killing swiftly, efficiently, coldly. Linge Chen had just started his latest six-year term of office, but Leyel knew he'd never finish it. And the next Chief Commissioner would not be a Chen.

Soon, though, the enormity of what had been done to him began to sink in. He had always thought that his fortune meant little to him—that he would be the same man with or without the Forska estates. But now he began to realize that it wasn't true, that he'd been lying to himself all along. He had known since childhood how despicable rich and powerful men could be—his father had made sure he saw and understood how cruel men became when their money persuaded them they had a right to use others however they wished. So Leyel had learned to despise his own birthright, and, starting with his father, had pretended to others that he could make his way through the world solely by wit and diligence, that he would have been exactly the same man if he had grown up in a common family, with a common education. He had done such a good job of acting as if he didn't care about his wealth that he came to believe it himself.

Now he realized that Forska estates had been an invisible part of himself all along, as if they were extensions of his body, as if he could flex a muscle and cargo ships would fly, he could blink and mines would be sunk deep into the earth, he could sigh and all over the Galaxy there would be a wind of change that would keep blowing until everything was exactly as he wanted it. Now all those invisible limbs and senses had been amputated. Now he was crippled—he had only as many arms and legs and eyes as any other human being.

At last he was what he had always pretended to be. An ordinary, powerless man. He hated it.

For the first hours after Rom left, Leyel pretended he could take all this in stride. He sat at the lector and spun through the pages smoothly—without anything on the pages registering in his memory. He kept wishing Deet were there so he could laugh with her about how little this hurt him; then he would be glad that Deet was not there, because one sympathetic touch of her hand would push him over the edge, make it impossible to contain his emotion.

Finally he could not help himself. Thinking of Deet, of their children and grand-children, of all that had been lost to them because he had made an empty gesture to a dead friend, he threw himself to the softened floor and wept bitterly. Let Chen listen to recordings of what the spy beam shows of this! Let him savor his victory! I'll destroy him somehow, my staff is still loyal to me, I'll put together an army, I'll hire assassins of my own, I'll make contact with Admiral Sipp, and then Chen will be the one to sob, crying out for mercy as I disfigure him the way he has mutilated me—

Fool.

Leyel rolled over onto his back, dried his face on his sleeve, then lay there, eyes closed, calming himself. No vengeance. No politics. That was Rom's business, not Leyel's. Too late for him to enter the game now—and who would help him, anyway, now that he had already lost his power? There was nothing to be done.

Leyel didn't really want to do anything, anyway. Hadn't they guaranteed that his archives and libraries would continue to be funded? Hadn't they guaranteed him un-limited research funds? And wasn't that all he had cared about anyway? He had long since turned over all the Forska operations to his subordinates—Chen's trustee would simply do the same job. And Leyel's children wouldn't suffer much—he had raised them with the same values that he had grown up with, and so they all pursued careers unrelated to the Forska holdings. They were true children of their father and mother —they wouldn't have any self-respect if they didn't earn their own way in the world. No doubt they'd be disappointed by having their inheritance snatched away. But they wouldn't be destroyed.

I am not ruined. All the lies that Rom told are really true, only they didn't realize it. All that matters in my life, I still have. I really *don't* care about my fortune. It's just the *way* I lost it that made me so furious. I can go on and be the same person I always was. This will even give me an opportunity to see who my true friends are—to see who still honors me for my scientific achievements, and who despises me for my poverty.

By the time Deet got home from the library—late, as was usual these days—Leyel was hard at work, reading back through all the research and speculation on protohuman behavior, trying to see if there was anything other than half-assed guesswork and pompous babble. He was so engrossed in his reading that he spent the first fifteen minutes after she got home telling her of the hilarious stupidities he had found in the day's reading, and then sharing a wonderful, impossible thought he had had.

"What if the human species isn't the only branch to evolve on our family tree? What if there's some other primate species that looks exactly like us, but can't interbreed with us, that functions in a completely different way, and we don't even know it, we all think everybody's just like us, but here and there all over the Empire there are whole towns, cities, maybe even worlds of people who secretly aren't human at all."

"But Leyel, my overwrought husband, if they look just like us and act just like us, then they *are* human."

"But they *don't* act exactly like us. There's a difference. A completely different set of rules and assumptions. Only they don't know that we're different, and we don't know that *they're* different. Or even if we suspect it, we're never sure. Just two different species, living side by side and never guessing it."

She kissed him. "You poor fool, that isn't speculation, it already exists. You have just described the relationship between males and females. Two completely different species, completely unintelligible to each other, living side by side and thinking they're really the same. The fascinating thing, Leyel, is that the two species persist in marrying each other and having babies, sometimes of one species, sometimes of the other, and the whole time they can't understand why they can't understand each other."

He laughed and embraced her. "You're right, as always, Deet. If I could once understand women, then perhaps I'd know what it is that makes men human."

"Nothing could possibly make men human," she answered. "Every time they're just about to get it right, they end up tripping over the damned Y chromosome and turning back into beasts." She nuzzled his neck.

It was then, with Deet in his arms, that he whispered to her what had happened when Rom visited that day. She said nothing, but held him tightly for the longest time. Then they had a very late supper and went about their nightly routines as if nothing had changed.

Not until they were in bed, not until Deet was softly snoring beside him, did it finally occur to Leyel that Deet was facing a test of her own. Would she still love him, now that he was merely Leyel Forska, scientist on a pension, and not Lord Forska, master of worlds? Of course she would *intend* to. But just as Leyel had never been aware of how much he depended on his wealth to define himself, so also she might not have realized how much of what she loved about him was his vast power; for even though he didn't flaunt it, it had always been there, like a solid platform underfoot, hardly noticed except now, when it was gone, when their footing was unsure.

Even before this, she had been slipping away into the community of women in the library. She would drift away even faster now, not even noticing it as Leyel became less and less important to her. No need for anything as dramatic as divorce. Just a little gap between them, an empty space that might as well be a chasm, might as well be the abyss. My fortune was a part of me, and now that it's gone, I'm no longer the same man she loved. She won't even know that she doesn't love me any more. She'll just get busier and busier in her work, and in five or ten years when I die of old age, she'll grieve—and then suddenly she'll realize that she isn't half as devastated as she thought she'd be. In fact, she won't be devastated at all. And she'll get on with her life and won't even remember what it was like to be married to me. I'll disappear from all human memory then, except perhaps for a few scientific papers and the libraries.

I'm like the information that was lost in all those neglected archives. Disappearing bit by bit, unnoticed, until all that's left is just a little bit of noise in people's memories. Then, finally, nothing. Blank.

Self-pitying fool. That's what happens to everyone, in the long run. Even Hari Seldon—someday he'll be forgotten, sooner rather than later, if Chen has his way. We all die. We're all lost in the passage of time. The only thing that lives on after us is the new shape we've given to the communities we lived in. There are things that are known because I said them, and even though people have forgotten who said it, they'll go on knowing. Like the story Rinjy was telling—she had forgotten, if she ever knew it, that Deet was the librarian in the original tale. But still she remembered the tale. The community of librarians was different because Deet had been among them. They would be a little different, a little braver, a little stronger, because of Deet. She had left traces of herself in the world.

And then, again, there came that flash of insight, that sudden understanding of the answer to a question that had long been troubling him.

But in the moment that Leyel realized that he held the answer, the answer slipped away. He couldn't remember it. You're asleep, he said silently. You only dreamed that you understood the origin of humanity. That's the way it is in dreams—the truth is always so beautiful, but you can never hold on to it.

"How is he taking it, Deet?"

"Hard to say. Well, I think. He was never much of a wanderer anyway."

"Come now, it can't be that simple."

"No. No, it isn't."

"Tell me."

"The social things—those were easy. We rarely went anyway, but now people don't invite us. We're politically dangerous. And the few things we had scheduled got canceled or, um, postponed. You know—we'll call you as soon as we have a new date."

"He doesn't mind this?"

"He *likes* that part. He always hated those things. But they've canceled his speeches. And the lecture series on human ecology."

"A blow."

"He pretends not to mind. But he's brooding."

"Tell me."

"Works all day, but he doesn't read it to me any more, doesn't make me sit down at the lector the minute I get home. I think he isn't writing anything."

"Doing nothing?"

"No. Reading. That's all."

"Maybe he just needs to do research."

"You don't know Leyel. He *thinks* by writing. Or talking. He isn't doing either."

"Doesn't talk to you?"

"He answers. I try to talk about things here at the library, his answers are—what? Glum. Sullen."

"He resents your work?"

"That's not possible. Leyel has always been as enthusiastic about my work as about his own. And he won't talk about his own work, either. I ask him, and he says nothing."

"Not surprising."

"So it's all right?"

"No. It's just not surprising."

"What is it? Can't you tell me?"

"What good is telling you? It's what we call ILS—Identity Loss Syndrome. It's identical to the passive strategy for dealing with loss of body parts."

"ILS. What happens in ILS?"

"Deet, come on, you're a scientist. What do you expect? You've just described Leyel's behavior, I tell you that it's called ILS, you want to know what ILS is, and what am I going to do?"

"Describe Leyel's behavior back to me. What an idiot I am."

"Good, at least you can laugh."

"Can't you tell me what to expect?"

"Complete withdrawal from you, from everybody. Eventually he becomes completely antisocial and starts to strike out. Does something self-destructive—like making public statements against Chen, that'd do it."

"No!"

"Or else he severs his old connections, gets away from you, and reconstructs himself in a different set of communities."

"This would make him happy?"

"Sure. Useless to the Second Foundation, but happy. It would also turn you into a nasty-tempered old crone, not that you aren't one already, mind you."

"Oh, you think Leyel's the only thing keeping me human?"

"Pretty much, yes. He's your safety valve."

"Not lately."

"I know."

"Have I been so awful?"

"Nothing that we can't bear. Deet, if we're going to be fit to govern the human race someday, shouldn't we first learn to be good to each other?"

"Well, I'm glad to provide you all with an opportunity to test your patience."

"You should be glad. We're doing a fine job so far, wouldn't you say?"

"Please. You were teasing me about the prognosis, weren't you?"

"Partly. Everything I said was true, but you know as well as I do that there are as many different ways out of a B-B syndrome as there are people who have them."

"Behavioral cause, behavioral effect. No little hormone shot, then?"

"Deet. He doesn't know who he is."

"Can't I help him?"

"Yes."

"What? What can I do?"

"This is only a guess, since I haven't talked to him."

"Of course."

"You aren't home much."

"I can't *stand* it there, with him brooding all the time."

"Fine. Get him out with you."

"He won't go."

"Push him."

"We barely talk. I don't know if I even have any leverage over him."

"Deet. You're the one who wrote, 'Communities that make few or no demands on their members cannot command allegiance. All else being equal, members who feel most needed have the strongest allegiance.' "

"You memorized that?"

"Psychohistory *is* the psychology of populations, but populations can only be quantified as communities. Seldon's work on statistical probabilities only worked to predict the future within a generation or two until you first published your community theories. That's because statistics *can't* deal with cause and effect. Stats tell you what's happening, never why, never the result. Within a generation or two, the present statistics evaporate, they're meaningless, you have whole new populations with new configurations. Your community theory gave us a way of predicting which communities would survive, which would grow, which would fade. A way of looking across long stretches of time and space."

"Hari never told me he was using community theory in any important way."

"How could he tell you that? He had to walk a tightrope—publishing enough to get psychohistory taken seriously, but not so much that anybody outside the Second

Foundation could ever duplicate or continue his work. Your work was a key—but he couldn't say so."

"Are you just saying this to make me feel better?"

"Sure. That's why I'm saying it. But it's also true—since lying to you wouldn't make you feel better, would it? Statistics are like taking cross sections of the trunk of a tree. It can tell you a lot about its history. You can figure how healthy it is, how much volume the whole tree has, how much is root and how much is branch. But what it *can't* tell you is where the tree will branch, and which branches will become major, which minor, and which will rot and fall off and die."

"But you can't *quantify* communities, can you? They're just stories and rituals that bind people together—"

"You'd be surprised what we can quantify. We're very good at what we do, Deet. Just as you are. Just as Leyel is."

"*Is* his work important? After all, human origin is only a historical question."

"Nonsense, and you know it. Leyel has stripped away the historical issues and he's searching for the scientific ones. The principles by which human life, as we understand it, is differentiated from nonhuman. If he finds that—don't you see, Deet? The human race is re-creating itself all the time, on every world, in every family, in every individual. We're born animals, and we teach each other how to be human. Somehow. It matters that we find out how. It matters to psychohistory. It matters to the Second Foundation. It matters to the human race."

"So—you aren't just being kind to Leyel."

"Yes, we are. You are, too. Good people are kind."

"Is that all? Leyel is just one man who's having trouble?"

"We need him. He isn't important just to you. He's important to *us.*"

"Oh. Oh."

"Why are you crying?"

"I was so afraid—that I was being selfish—being so worried about him. Taking up your time like this."

"Well, if that doesn't—I thought you were beyond surprising me."

"Our problems were just—our problems. But now they're not."

"Is that so important to you? Tell me, Deet—do you really value this community so much?"

"Yes."

"More than Leyel?"

"No! But enough—that I felt *guilty* for caring so much about him."

"Go home, Deet. Just go home."

"What?"

"That's where you'd rather be. It's been showing up in your behavior for two months, ever since Hari's death. You've been nasty and snappish, and now I know why. You *resent* us for keeping you away from Leyel."

"No, it was my choice, I—"

"Of course it was your choice! It was your *sacrifice* for the good of the Second Foundation. So now I'm telling you—healing Leyel is more important to Hari's plan than keeping up with your day-to-day responsibilities here."

"You're not removing me from my position, are you?"

"No. I'm just telling you to ease up. And get Leyel out of the apartment. Do you understand me? Demand it! Reengage him with *you,* or we've all lost him."

"Take him *where?*"

"I don't know. Theater. Athletic events. Dancing."

"We don't *do* those things."

"Well, what *do* you do?"

"Research. And then talk about it."

"Fine. Bring him here to the library. Do research with him. Talk about it."

"But he'll meet people here. He'd certainly meet *you*."

"Good. Good. I like that. Yes, let him come here."

"But I thought we had to keep the Second Foundation a secret from him until he's ready to take part."

"I didn't say you should introduce me as First Speaker."

"No, no, of course you didn't. What am I thinking of? Of course he can meet you, he can meet everybody."

"Deet, listen to me."

"Yes, I'm listening."

"It's all right to love him, Deet."

"I know that."

"I mean, it's all right to love him more than you love us. More than you love any of us. More than you love all of us. There you are, crying again."

"I'm so—"

"Relieved."

"How do you understand me so well?"

"I only know what you show me and what you tell me. It's all we ever know about each other. The only thing that helps is that nobody can ever lie for long about who they really are. Not even to themselves."

For two months Leyel followed up on Magolissian's paper by trying to find some connection between language studies and human origins. Of course this meant weeks of wading through old, useless point-of-origin studies, which kept indicating that Trantor was the focal point of language throughout the history of the Empire, even though *nobody* seriously put forth Trantor as the planet of origin. Once again, though, Leyel rejected the search for a particular planet; he wanted to find out regularities, not unique events.

Leyel hoped for a clue in the fairly recent work—only two thousand years old—of Dagawell Kispitorian. Kispitorian came from the most isolated area of a planet called Artashat, where there were traditions that the original settlers came from an earlier world named Armenia, now uncharted. Kispitorian grew up among mountain people who claimed that long ago, they spoke a completely different language. In fact, the title of Kispitorian's most interesting book was *No Man Understood Us*; many of the folk tales of these people began with the formula "Back in the days when no man understood us . . ."

Kispitorian had never been able to shake off this tradition of his upbringing, and as he pursued the field of dialect formation and evolution, he kept coming across evidence that at one time the human species spoke not one but many languages. It had always been taken for granted that Galactic Standard was the up-to-date version of the language of the planet of origin—that while a few human groups might have developed dialects, civilization was impossible without mutually intelligible speech. But Kispitorian had begun to suspect that Galactic Standard did not become the universal human language until *after* the formation of the Empire—that, in fact, one of the first labors of the Imperium was to stamp out all other competing languages. The mountain people of

Artashat believed that their language had been stolen from them. Kispitorian eventually devoted his life to proving they were right.

He worked first with names, long recognized as the most conservative aspect of language. He found that there were many separate naming traditions, and it was not until about the year 6000 GE that all were finally amalgamated into one Empire-wide stream. What was interesting was that the farther back he went, the *more* complexity he found.

Because certain worlds tended to have unified traditions, and so the simplest explanation of this was the one he first put forth—that humans left their home world with a unified language, but the normal forces of language separation caused each new planet to develop its own offshoot, until many dialects became mutually unintelligible. Thus, different languages would not have developed until humanity moved out into space; this was one of the reasons why the Galactic Empire was necessary to restore the primeval unity of the species.

Kispitorian called his first and most influential book *Tower of Confusion*, using the widespread legend of the Tower of Babble as an illustration. He supposed that this story might have originated in that pre-Empire period, probably among the rootless traders roaming from planet to planet, who had to deal on a practical level with the fact that no two worlds spoke the same language. These traders had preserved a tradition that when humanity lived on one planet, they all spoke the same language. They explained the linguistic confusion of their own time by recounting the tale of a great leader who built the first "tower," or starship, to raise mankind up into heaven. According to the story, "God" punished these upstart people by confusing their tongues, which forced them to disperse among the different worlds. The story presented the confusion of tongues as the *cause* of the dispersal instead of its result, but cause-reversal was a commonly recognized feature of myth. Clearly this legend preserved a historical fact.

So far, Kispitorian's work was perfectly acceptable to most scientists. But in his forties he began to go off on wild tangents. Using controversial algorithms—on calculators with a suspiciously high level of processing power—he began to tear apart Galactic Standard itself, showing that many words revealed completely separate phonetic traditions, incompatible with the mainstream of the language. They could not comfortably have evolved within a population that regularly spoke either Standard or its primary ancestor language. Furthermore, there were many words with clearly related meanings that showed they had once diverged according to standard linguistic patterns and then were brought together later, with different meanings or implications. But the time scale implied by the degree of change was far too great to be accounted for in the period between humanity's first settlement of space and the formation of the Empire. Obviously, claimed Kispitorian, there had been many different languages *on the planet of origin*; Galactic Standard was the *first* universal human language. Throughout all human history, separation of language had been a fact of life; only the Empire had had the pervasive power to unify speech.

After that, Kispitorian was written off as a fool, of course—his own Tower of Babble interpretation was now used against him as if an interesting illustration had now become a central argument. He very narrowly escaped execution as a separatist, in fact, since there was an unmistakable tone of regret in his writing about the loss of linguistic diversity. The Imperium did succeed in cutting off all his funding and jailing him for a while because he had been using a calculator with an illegal level of memory and processing power. Leyel suspected that Kispitorian got off easy at that—working with language as he did, getting the results he got, he might well have developed a calculator so intelligent that it could understand and produce human speech, which, if discovered, would have meant either the death penalty or a lynching.

No matter now. Kispitorian insisted to the end that his work was pure science, making no value judgments on whether the Empire's linguistic unity was a Good Thing or not. He was merely reporting that the natural condition of humanity was to speak many different languages. And Leyel believed that he was right.

Leyel could not help but feel that by combining Kispitorian's language studies with Magolissian's work with language-using primates he could come up with something important. But what was the connection? The primates had never developed their *own* languages—they only learned nouns and verbs presented to them by humans. So they could hardly have developed diversity of language. What connection could there be? Why would diversity ever have developed? Could it have something to do with why humans became human?

The primates used only a tiny subset of Standard. For that matter, so did most people—most of the two million words in Standard were used only by a few professionals who actually needed them, while the common vocabulary of humans throughout the Galaxy consisted of a few thousand words.

Oddly, though, it was that small subset of Standard that was the *most* susceptible to change. Highly esoteric scientific or technical papers written in 2000 GE were still easily readable. Slangy, colloquial passages in fiction, especially in dialogue, became almost unintelligible within five hundred years. The language shared by the most different communities was the language that changed the most. But over time, that mainstream language always changed *together*. It made no sense, then, for there ever to be linguistic diversity. Language changed most when it was most unified. Therefore when people were most divided, their language should remain most similar.

Never mind, Leyel. You're out of your discipline. Any competent linguist would know the answer to that.

But Leyel knew that wasn't likely to be true. People immersed in one discipline rarely questioned the axioms of their profession. Linguists all took for granted the fact that the language of an isolated population is invariably more archaic, less susceptible to change. Did they understand why?

Leyel got up from his chair. His eyes were tired from staring into the lector. His knees and back ached from staying so long in the same position. He wanted to lie down, but knew that if he did, he'd fall asleep. The curse of getting old—he could fall asleep so easily, yet could never stay asleep long enough to feel well rested. He didn't *want* to sleep now, though. He wanted to think.

No, that wasn't it. He wanted to *talk*. That's how his best and clearest ideas always came, under the pressure of conversation, when someone else's questions and arguments forced him to think sharply. To make connections, invent explanations. In a contest with another person, his adrenaline flowed, his brain made connections that would never otherwise be made.

Where was Deet? In years past, he would have been talking this through with Deet all day. All week. She would know as much about his research as he did, and would constantly say "Have you thought of this?" or "How can you possibly think that!" And he would have been making the same challenges to *her* work. In the old days.

But these weren't the old days. She didn't need him any more—she had her friends on the library staff. Nothing wrong with that, probably. After all, she wasn't *thinking* now, she was putting old thoughts into practice. She needed *them*, not *him*. But he still needed *her*. Did she ever think of that? I might as well have gone to Terminus—damn Hari for refusing to let me go. I stayed for Deet's sake, and yet I don't have her after all, not when I need her. How *dare* Hari decide what was right for Leyel Forska!

Only Hari hadn't decided, had he? He would have let Leyel go—without Deet. And Leyel hadn't stayed with Deet so she could help him with his research. He had stayed with her because . . . because . . .

He couldn't remember why. Love, of course. But he couldn't think why that had been so important to him. It wasn't important to *her*. Her idea of love these days was to urge him to come to the library. "You can do your research there. We could be together more during the days."

The message was clear. The only way Leyel could remain part of Deet's life was if he became part of her new "family" at the library. Well, she could forget that idea. If she chose to get swallowed up in that place, fine. If she chose to leave him for a bunch of—*indexers* and *cataloguers*—fine. Fine.

No. It wasn't fine. He wanted to *talk* to her. Right now, at this moment, he wanted to tell her what he was thinking, wanted her to question him and argue with him until she made him come up with an answer, or lots of answers. He needed her to see what he wasn't seeing. He needed her a lot more than *they* needed her.

He was out amid the thick pedestrian traffic of Maslo Boulevard before he realized that this was the first time since Hari's funeral that he'd ventured beyond the immediate neighborhood of his apartment. It was the first time in months that he'd had anyplace to go. That's what I'm doing here, he thought. I just need a change of scenery, a sense of destination. That's the only reason I'm heading to the library. All that emotional nonsense back in the apartment, that was just my unconscious strategy for making myself get out among people again.

Leyel was almost cheerful when he got to the Imperial Library. He had been there many times over the years, but always for receptions or other public events—having his own high-capacity lector meant that he could get access to all the library's records by cable. Other people—students, professors from poorer schools, lay readers—they actually *had* to come here to read. But that meant that they knew their way around the building. Except for finding the major lecture halls and reception rooms, Leyel hadn't the faintest idea where anything was.

For the first time it dawned on him how very large the Imperial Library was. Deet had mentioned the numbers many times—a staff of more than five thousand, including machinists, carpenters, cooks, security, a virtual city in itself—but only now did Leyel realize that this meant that many people here had never met each other. Who could possibly know *five thousand* people by name? He couldn't just walk up and ask for Deet by name. What was the department Deet worked in? She had changed so often, moving through the bureaucracy.

Everyone he saw was a patron—people at lectors, people at catalogues, even people reading books and magazines printed on paper. Where were the librarians? The few staff members moving through the aisles turned out not to be librarians at all—they were volunteer docents, helping newcomers learn how to use the lectors and catalogues. They knew as little about library staff as he did.

He finally found a room full of real librarians, sitting at calculators preparing the daily access and circulation reports. When he tried to speak to one, she merely waved a hand at him. He thought she was telling him to go away until he realized that her hand remained in the air, a finger pointing to the front of the room. Leyel moved toward the elevated desk where a fat, sleepy-looking middle-aged woman was lazily paging through long columns of figures, which stood in the air before her in military formation.

"Sorry to interrupt you," he said softly.

She was resting her cheek on her hand. She didn't even look at him when he spoke. But she answered. "I pray for interruptions."

Only then did he notice that her eyes were framed with laugh lines, that her mouth even in repose turned upward into a faint smile.

"I'm looking for someone. My wife, in fact. Deet Forska."

Her smile widened. She sat up. "You're the beloved Leyel."

It was an absurd thing for a stranger to say, but it pleased him nonetheless to realize that Deet must have spoken of him. Of course everyone would have known that Deet's husband was *the* Leyel Forska. But this woman hadn't said it that way, had she? Not as *the* Leyel Forska, the celebrity. No, here he was known as "the beloved Leyel." Even if this woman meant to tease him, Deet must have let it be known that she had some affection for him. He couldn't help but smile. With relief. He hadn't known that he feared the loss of her love so much, but now he wanted to laugh aloud, to move, to dance with pleasure.

"I imagine I am," said Leyel.

"I'm Zay Wax. Deet must have mentioned me, we have lunch every day."

No, she hadn't. She hardly mentioned anybody at the library, come to think of it. These two had lunch every day, and Leyel had never heard of her. "Yes, of course," said Leyel. "I'm glad to meet you."

"And I'm relieved to see that your feet actually touch the ground."

"Now and then."

"She works up in Indexing these days." Zay cleared her display.

"Is that on Trantor?"

Zay laughed. She typed in a few instructions and her display now filled with a map of the library complex. It was a complex pile of rooms and corridors, almost impossible to grasp. "This shows only this wing of the main building. Indexing is these four floors."

Four layers near the middle of the display turned to a brighter color.

"And here's where you are right now."

A small room on the first floor turned white. Looking at the labyrinth between the two lighted sections, Leyel had to laugh aloud. "Can't you just give me a ticket to guide me?"

"Our tickets only lead you to places where patrons are allowed. But this isn't really hard, Lord Forska. After all, you're a genius, aren't you?"

"Not at the interior geography of buildings, whatever lies Deet might have told you."

"You just go out this door and straight down the corridor to the elevators—can't miss them. Go up to fifteen. When you get out, turn as if you were continuing down the same corridor, and after a while you go through an archway that says 'Indexing.' Then you lean back your head and bellow 'Deet' as loud as you can. Do that a few times and either she'll come or security will arrest you."

"That's what I was going to do if I *didn't* find somebody to guide me."

"I was hoping you'd ask me." Zay stood up and spoke loudly to the busy librarians. "The cat's going away. The mice can play."

"About time," one of them said. They all laughed. But they kept working.

"Follow me, Lord Forska."

"Leyel, please."

"Oh, you're such a flirt." When she stood, she was even shorter and fatter than she had looked sitting down. "Follow me."

They conversed cheerfully about nothing much on the way down the corridor. Inside the elevator, they hooked their feet under the rail as the gravitic repulsion kicked in. Leyel was so used to weightlessness after all these years of using elevators on Trantor that he never noticed. But Zay let her arms float in the air and sighed noisily. "I *love* riding the elevator," she said. For the first time Leyel realized that weightlessness must be a great relief to someone carrying as many extra kilograms as Zay Wax. When the elevator stopped, Zay made a great show of staggering out as if under a great burden. "My idea of heaven is to live forever in gravitic repulsion."

"You can get gravitic repulsion for your apartment, if you live on the top floor."

"Maybe *you* can," said Zay. "But *I* have to live on a librarian's salary."

Leyel was mortified. He had always been careful not to flaunt his wealth, but then, he had rarely talked at any length with people who couldn't afford gravitic repulsion. "Sorry," he said. "I don't think I could either, these days."

"Yes, I heard you squandered your fortune on a real bang-up funeral."

Startled that she would speak so openly of it, he tried to answer in the same joking tone. "I suppose you could look at it that way."

"I say it was worth it," she said. She looked slyly up at him. "I knew Hari, you know. Losing him cost humanity more than if Trantor's sun went nova."

"Maybe," said Leyel. The conversation was getting out of hand. Time to be cautious.

"Oh, don't worry. I'm not a snitch for the Pubs. Here's the Golden Archway into Indexing. The Land of Subtle Conceptual Connections."

Through the arch, it was as though they had passed into a completely different building. The style and trim were the same as before, with deeply lustrous fabrics on the walls and ceiling and floor made of the same smooth sound-absorbing plastic, glowing faintly with white light. But now all pretense at symmetry was gone. The ceiling was at different heights, almost at random; on the left and right there might be doors or archways, stairs or ramps, an alcove or a huge hall filled with columns, shelves of books and works of art surrounding tables where indexers worked with a half-dozen scriptors and lectors at once.

"The form fits the function," said Zay.

"I'm afraid I'm rubbernecking like a first-time visitor to Trantor."

"It's a strange place. But the architect was the daughter of an indexer, so she knew that standard, orderly, symmetrical interior maps are the enemy of freely connective thought. The finest touch—and the most expensive too, I'm afraid—is the fact that from day to day the layout is rearranged."

"Rearranged! The rooms move?"

"A series of random routines in the master calculator. There are rules, but the program isn't afraid to waste space, either. Some days only one room is changed, moved off to some completely different place in the Indexing area. Other days, everything is changed. The only constant is the archway leading in. I really wasn't joking when I said you should come here and bellow."

"But—the indexers must spend the whole morning just finding their stations."

"Not at all. Any indexer can work from any station."

"Ah. So they just call up the job they were working on the day before."

"No. They merely pick up on the job that is already in progress on the station they happen to choose that day."

"Chaos!" said Leyel.

"Exactly. How do you think a good hyperindex is made? If one person alone indexes a book, then the only connections that book will make are the ones that person knows about. Instead, each indexer is forced to skim through what his predecessor did the day before. Inevitably he'll add some new connections that the other indexer didn't think of. The environment, the work pattern, everything is designed to break down habits of thought, to make everything surprising, everything *new*."

"To keep everybody off balance."

"Exactly. Your mind works quickly when you're running along the edge of the precipice."

"By that reckoning, acrobats should all be geniuses."

"Nonsense. The whole labor of acrobats is to learn their routines so perfectly they *never* lose balance. An acrobat who improvises is soon dead. But indexers, when they lose their balance, they fall into wonderful discoveries. That's why the indexes of the Imperial Library are the only ones worth having. They startle and challenge as you read. All the others are just—clerical lists."

"Deet never mentioned this."

"Indexers rarely discuss what they're doing. You can't really explain it anyway."

"How long has Deet been an indexer?"

"Not long, really. She's still a novice. But I hear she's very, very good."

"Where *is* she?"

Zay grinned. Then she tipped her head back and bellowed. "Deet!"

The sound seemed to be swallowed up at once in the labyrinth. There was no answer.

"Not nearby, I guess," said Zay. "We'll have to probe a little deeper."

"Couldn't we just *ask* somebody where she is?"

"Who would know?"

It took two more floors and three more shouts before they heard a faint answering cry. "Over here!"

They followed the sound. Deet kept calling out, so they could find her.

"I got the flower room today, Zay! Violets!"

The indexers they passed along the way all looked up—some smiled, some frowned.

"Doesn't it interfere with things?" asked Leyel. "All this shouting?"

"Indexers *need* interruption. It breaks up the chain of thought. When they look back down, they have to rethink what they were doing."

Deet, not so far away now, called again. "The smell is so intoxicating. Imagine— the same room twice in a month!"

"Are indexers often hospitalized?" Leyel asked quietly.

"For what?"

"Stress."

"There's no stress on this job," said Zay. "Just play. We come up here as a *reward* for working in other parts of the library."

"I see. This is the time when librarians actually get to *read* the books in the library."

"We all chose this career because we love books for their own sake. Even the old inefficient corruptible paper ones. Indexing is like—writing in the margins."

The notion was startling. "Writing in someone *else's* book?"

"It used to be done all the time, Leyel. How can you possibly engage in dialogue with the author without writing your answers and arguments in the margins? Here she is." Zay preceded him under a low arch and down a few steps.

"I heard a man's voice with you, Zay," said Deet.

"Mine," said Leyel. He turned a corner and saw her there. After such a long journey to reach her, he thought for a dizzying moment that he didn't recognize her. That the library had randomized the librarians as well as the rooms, and he had happened upon a woman who merely resembled his long-familiar wife; he would have to reacquaint himself with her from the beginning.

"I thought so," said Deet. She got up from her station and embraced him. Even this startled him, though she usually embraced him upon meeting. It's only the setting that's different, he told himself. I'm only surprised because usually she greets me like this at home, in familiar surroundings. And usually it's Deet arriving, not me.

Or was there, after all, a greater warmth in her greeting here? As if she loved him more in this place than at home? Or, perhaps, as if the new Deet were simply a warmer, more comfortable person?

I thought that she was comfortable with me.

Leyel felt uneasy, shy with her. "If I'd known my coming would cause so much trouble," he began. Why did he need so badly to apologize?

"What trouble?" asked Zay.

"Shouting. Interrupting."

"Listen to him, Deet. He thinks the world has stopped because of a couple of shouts."

In the distance they could hear a man bellowing someone's name.

"Happens all the time," said Zay. "I'd better get back. Some lordling from Mahagonny is probably fuming because I haven't granted his request for access to the Imperial account books."

"Nice to meet you," said Leyel.

"Good luck finding your way back," said Deet.

"Easy this time," said Zay. She paused only once on her way through the door, not to speak, but to slide a metallic wafer along an almost unnoticeable slot in the doorframe, above eye level. She turned back and winked at Deet. Then she was gone.

Leyel didn't ask what she had done—if it were his business, something would have been said. But he suspected that Zay had either turned on or turned off a recording system. Unsure of whether they had privacy here from the library staff, Leyel merely stood for a moment, looking around. Deet's room really was filled with violets, real ones, growing out of cracks and apertures in the floor and walls. The smell was clear but not overpowering. "What is this room *for?*"

"For *me*. Today, anyway. I'm so glad you came."

"You never told me about this place."

"I didn't know about it until I was assigned to this section. Nobody talks about Indexing. We never tell outsiders. The architect died three thousand years ago. Only our own machinists understand how it works. It's like—"

"Fairyland."

"Exactly."

"A place where all the rules of the universe are suspended."

"Not all. We still stick with good old gravity. Inertia. That sort of thing."

"This place is right for you, Deet. This room."

"Most people go years without getting the flower room. It isn't always violets, you know. Sometimes climbing roses. Sometimes periwinkle. They say there's really a dozen flower rooms, but never more than one at a time is accessible. It's been violets for me both times, though."

Leyel couldn't help himself. He laughed. It was funny. It was delightful. What did this have to do with a library? And yet what a marvelous thing to have hidden away in the heart of this somber place. He sat down on a chair. Violets grew out of the top of the chairback, so that flowers brushed his shoulders.

"You finally got tired of staying in the apartment all day?" asked Deet.

Of course she would wonder why he finally came out, after all her invitations had been so long ignored. Yet he wasn't sure if he could speak frankly. "I needed to talk with you." He glanced back at the slot Zay had used in the doorframe. "Alone," he said.

Was that a look of dread that crossed her face?

"We're alone," Deet said quietly. "Zay saw to that. Truly alone, as we can't be even in the apartment."

It took Leyel a moment to realize what she was asserting. He dared not even speak the word. So he mouthed his question: Pubs?

"They never bother with the library in their normal spying. Even if they set up something special for you, there's now an interference field blocking out our conversation. Chances are, though, that they won't bother to monitor you again until you leave here."

She seemed edgy. Impatient. As if she didn't like having this conversation. As if she wanted him to get on with it, or maybe just get it over with.

"If you don't mind," he said. "I haven't interrupted you here before, I thought that just this once—"

"Of course," she said. But she was still tense. As if she feared what he might say.

So he explained to her all his thoughts about language. All that he had gleaned from Kispitorian's and Magolissian's work. She seemed to relax almost as soon as it became clear he was talking about his research. What did she dread, he wondered. Was she afraid I came to talk about our relationship? She hardly needed to fear *that*. He had no intention of making things more difficult by whining about things that could not be helped.

When he was through explaining the ideas that had come to him, she nodded carefully—as she had done a thousand times before, after he explained an idea or argument. "I don't know," she finally said. As so many times before, she was reluctant to commit herself to an immediate response.

And, as he had often done, he insisted. "But what do you *think*?"

She pursed her lips. "Just offhand—I've never tried a serious linguistic application of community theory, beyond jargon formation, so this is just my first thought—but try this. Maybe small isolated populations *guard* their language—jealously, because it's part of who they are. Maybe language is the most powerful ritual of all, so that people who have the same language are one in a way that people who can't understand each other's speech never are. We'd never know, would we, since everybody for ten thousand years has spoken Standard."

"So it isn't the size of the population, then, so much as—"

"How much they *care* about their language. How much it defines them as a community. A large population starts to think that everybody talks like them. They want to *distinguish* themselves, form a separate identity. Then they start developing jargons and slangs to separate themselves from others. Isn't that what happens to common speech? Children try to find ways of talking that their parents don't use. Professionals talk in private vocabularies so laymen won't know the passwords. All rituals for community definition."

Leyel nodded gravely, but he had one obvious doubt.

Obvious enough that Deet knew it, too. "Yes, yes, I know, Leyel. I immediately interpreted your question in terms of my own discipline. Like physicists who think that everything can be explained by physics."

Leyel laughed. "I thought of that, but what you said makes sense. And it would explain why the natural tendency of communities is to diversify language. We want a common tongue, a language of open discourse. But we also want private languages. Except a *completely* private language would be useless—whom would we talk to? So wherever a community forms, it creates at least a few linguistic barriers to outsiders, a few shibboleths that only insiders will know."

"And the more allegiance a person has to a community, the more fluent he'll become in that language, and the more he'll speak it."

"Yes, it makes sense," said Leyel. "So easy. You see how much I need you?"

He knew that his words were a mild rebuke—why weren't you home when I needed you—but he couldn't resist saying it. Sitting here with Deet, even in this strange and redolent place, felt right and comfortable. How could she have withdrawn from him? To him, her presence was what made a place home. To her, this place was home whether he was there or not.

He tried to put it in words—in abstract words, so it wouldn't sting. "I think the greatest tragedy is when one person has more allegiance to his community than any of the other members."

Deet only half smiled and raised her eyebrows. She didn't know what he was getting at.

"He speaks the community language all the time," said Leyel. "Only nobody else ever speaks it to him, or not enough anyway. And the more he speaks it, the more he alienates the others and drives them away, until he's alone. Can you imagine anything more sad? Somebody who's filled up with a language, hungry to speak, to hear it spoken, and yet there's no one left who understands a word of it."

She nodded, her eyes searching him. Does she understand what I'm saying? He waited for her to speak. He had said all he dared to say.

"But imagine this," she finally said. "What if he left that little place where no one understood him, and went over a hill to a new place, and all of a sudden he heard a hundred voices, a thousand, speaking the words he had treasured all those lonely years. And then he realized that he had never really known the language at all. The words had hundreds of meanings and nuances he had never guessed. Because each speaker changed the language a little just by speaking it. And when he spoke at last, his own voice sounded like music in his ears, and the others listened with delight, with rapture, his music was like the water of life pouring from a fountain, and he knew that he had never been home before."

Leyel couldn't remember hearing Deet sound so—rhapsodic, that was it, she herself was singing. She is the person she was talking about. In this place, her voice is different, that's what she meant. At home with me, she's been alone. Here in the library she's found others who speak her secret language. It isn't that she didn't want our marriage to succeed. She hoped for it, but I never understood her. These people did. Do. She's home here, that's what she's telling me.

"I understand," he said.

"Do you?" She looked searchingly into his face.

"I think so. It's all right."

She gave him a quizzical look.

"I mean, it's fine. It's good. This place. It's fine."

She looked relieved, but not completely. "You shouldn't be so *sad* about it, Leyel. This is a happy place. And you could do everything here that you ever did at home."

Except love you as the other part of me, and have you love me as the other part of you. "Yes, I'm sure."

"No, I mean it. What you're working on—I can see that you're getting close to something. Why not work on it *here*, where we can talk about it?"

Leyel shrugged.

"You *are* getting close, aren't you?"

"How do I know? I'm thrashing around like a drowning man in the ocean at night. Maybe I'm close to shore, and maybe I'm just swimming farther out to sea."

"Well, what do you have? Didn't we get closer just now?"

"No. This language thing—if it's just an aspect of community theory, it can't be the answer to human origin."

"Why not?"

"Because many primates have communities. A lot of other animals. Herding animals, for instance. Even schools of *fish*. Bees. Ants. Every multicelled organism is a community, for that matter. So if linguistic diversion grows out of community, then it's inherent in prehuman animals and therefore isn't part of the definition of humanity."

"Oh. I guess not."

"Right."

She looked disappointed. As if she had really hoped they would find the answer to the origin question right there, that very day.

Leyel stood up. "Oh well. Thanks for your help."

"I don't think I helped."

"Oh, you did. You showed me I was going up a dead-end road. You saved me a lot of wasted—thought. That's progress, in science, to know which answers aren't true."

His words had a double meaning, of course. She had also shown him that their marriage was a dead-end road. Maybe she understood him. Maybe not. It didn't matter—he had understood *her*. That little story about a lonely person finally discovering a place where she could be at home—how could he miss the point of that?

"Leyel," she said. "Why not put your question to the indexers?"

"Do you think the library researchers could find answers where *I* haven't?"

"Not the research department. *Indexing*."

"What do you mean?"

"Write down your questions. All the avenues you've pursued. Linguistic diversity. Primate language. And the other questions, the old ones. Archaeological, historical approaches. Biological. Kinship patterns. Customs. Everything you can think of. Just put it together as questions. And then we'll have them index it."

"Index my *questions*?"

"It's what we do—we read things and think of other things that might be related somehow, and we connect them. We don't say what the connection means, but we know that it means something, that the connection is real. We won't give you answers, Leyel, but if you follow the index, it might help you to think of connections. Do you see what I mean?"

"I never thought of that. Do you think a couple of indexers might have the time to work on it?"

"Not a couple of us. *All* of us."

"Oh, that's absurd, Deet. I wouldn't even ask it."

"*I* would. We aren't supervised up here, Leyel. We don't meet quotas. Our job is to read and think. Usually we have a few hundred projects going, but for a day we could easily work on the same document."

"It would be a waste. I can't publish anything, Deet."

"It doesn't have to be published. Don't you understand? Nobody but us knows what we do here. We can take it as an unpublished document and work on it just the same. It won't ever have to go online for the library as a whole."

Leyel shook his head. "And then if they lead me to the answer—what, will we publish it with two hundred bylines?"

"It'll be *your* paper, Leyel. We're just indexers, not authors. You'll still have to make the connections. Let us try. Let us be *part* of this."

Suddenly Leyel understood why she was so insistent on this. Getting him involved with the library was her way of pretending she was still part of his life. She could believe she hadn't left him, if he became part of her new community.

Didn't she know how unbearable that would be? To see her here, so happy without him? To come here as just one friend among many, when once they had been—or he had thought they were—one indivisible soul? How could he possibly do such a thing?

And yet she wanted it, he could see it in the way she was looking at him, so girlish, so pleading that it made him think of when they were first in love, on another world —she would look at him like that whenever he insisted that he had to leave. Whenever she thought she might be losing him.

Doesn't she know who has lost whom?

Never mind. What did it matter if she didn't understand? If it would make her happy to have him pretend to be part of her new home, part of these librarians—if she wanted him to submit his life's work to the ministrations of these absurd indexers, then why not? What would it cost him? Maybe the process of writing down all his questions in some coherent order would help him. And maybe she was right—maybe a Trantorian index would help him solve the origin question.

Maybe if he came here, he could still be a small part of her life. It wouldn't be like marriage. But since that was impossible, then at least he could have enough of her here that he could remain himself, remain the person that he had become because of loving her for all these years.

"Fine," he said. "I'll write it up and bring it in."

"I really think we can help."

"Yes," he said, pretending to more certainty than he felt. "Maybe." He started for the door.

"Do you have to leave already?"

He nodded.

"Are you sure you can find your way out?"

"Unless the rooms have moved."

"No, only at night."

"Then I'll find my way out just fine." He took a few steps toward her, then stopped.

"What?" she asked.

"Nothing."

"Oh." She sounded disappointed. "I thought you were going to kiss me good-bye." Then she puckered up like a three-year-old child.

He laughed. He kissed her—like a three-year-old—and then he left.

* * *

For two days he brooded. Saw her off in the morning, then tried to read, to watch the vids, anything. Nothing held his attention. He took walks. He even went topside once, to see the sky overhead—it was night, thick with stars. None of it engaged him. Nothing *held*. One of the vid programs had a moment, just briefly, a scene on a semiarid world, where a strange plant grew that dried out at maturity, broke off at the root, and then let the wind blow it around, scattering seeds. For a moment he felt a dizzying empathy with the plant as it tumbled by—am I as dry as that, hurtling through dead land? But no, he knew even that wasn't true, because the tumbleweed had life enough left in it to scatter seeds. Leyel had no seed left. That was scattered years ago.

On the third morning he looked at himself in the mirror and laughed grimly. "Is this how people feel before they kill themselves?" he asked. Of course not—he knew that he was being melodramatic. He felt no desire to die.

But then it occurred to him that if this feeling of uselessness kept on, if he never found anything to engage himself, then he might as well be dead, mightn't he, because his being alive wouldn't accomplish much more than keeping his clothes warm.

He sat down at the scriptor and began writing down questions. Then, under each question, he would explain how he had already pursued that particular avenue and why it didn't yield the answer to the origin question. More questions would come up then —and he was right, the mere process of summarizing his own fruitless research made answers seem tantalizingly close. It was a good exercise. And even if he never found an answer, this list of questions might be of help to someone with a clearer intellect— or better information—decades or centuries or millennia from now.

Deet came home and went to bed with Leyel still typing away. She knew the look he had when he was fully engaged in writing—she did nothing to disturb him. He noticed her enough to realize that she was carefully leaving him alone. Then he settled back into writing.

The next morning she awoke to find him lying in bed beside her, still dressed. A personal message capsule lay on the floor in the doorway from the bedroom. He had finished his questions. She bent over, picked it up, took it with her to the library.

"His questions aren't academic after all, Deet."

"I told you they weren't."

"Hari was right. For all that he seemed to be a dilettante, with his money and his rejection of the universities, he's a man of substance."

"Will the Second Foundation benefit, then, if he comes up with an answer to his question?"

"I don't know, Deet. Hari was the fortune-teller. Presumably mankind is already human, so it isn't as if we have to start the process over."

"Do you think not?"

"What, should we find some uninhabited planet and put some newborns on it and let them grow up feral, and then come back in a thousand years and try to turn them human?"

"I have a better idea. Let's take ten thousand worlds filled with people who live their lives like animals, always hungry, always quick with their teeth and their claws, and let's strip away the veneer of civilization to expose to them what they really are. And then, when they see themselves clearly, let's come back and teach them how to be *really* human this time, instead of only having bits and flashes of humanity."

"All right. Let's do that."

"I knew you'd see it my way."

"Just make sure your husband finds out *how* the trick is done. Then we have all the time in the world to set it up and pull it off."

When the index was done, Deet brought Leyel with her to the library when she went to work in the morning. She did not take him to Indexing, but rather installed him in a private research room lined with vids—only instead of giving the illusion of windows looking out onto an outside scene, the screens filled all the walls from floor to ceiling, so it seemed that he was on a pinnacle high above the scene, without walls or even a railing to keep him from falling off. It gave him flashes of vertigo when he looked around—only the door broke the illusion. For a moment he thought of asking for a different room. But then he remembered Indexing, and realized that maybe he'd do better work if he too felt a bit off balance all the time.

At first the indexing seemed obvious. He brought the first page of his questions to the lector display and began to read. The lector would track his pupils, so that whenever he paused to gaze at a word, other references would begin to pop up in the space beside the page he was reading. Then he'd glance at one of the references. When it was uninteresting or obvious, he'd skip to the next reference, and the first one would slide back on the display, out of the way, but still there if he changed his mind and wanted it.

If a reference engaged him, then when he reached the last line of the part of it on display, it would expand to full-page size and slide over to stand in front of the main text. Then, if this new material had been indexed, it would trigger new references— and so on, leading him farther and farther away from the original document until he finally decided to go back and pick up where he left off.

So far, this was what any index could be expected to do. It was only as he moved farther into reading his own questions that he began to realize the quirkiness of this index. Usually, index references were tied to important words, so that if you just wanted to stop and think without bringing up a bunch of references you didn't want, all you had to do was keep your gaze focused in an area of placeholder words, empty phrases like "If this were all that could be . . ." Anyone who made it a habit to read indexed works soon learned this trick and used it till it became reflex.

But when Leyel stopped on such empty phrases, references came up anyway. And instead of having a clear relationship to the text, sometimes the references were perverse or comic or argumentative. For instance, he paused in the middle of reading his argument that archaeological searches for "primitiveness" were useless in the search for origins because all "primitive" cultures represented a decline from a star-going culture. He had written the phrase "All this primitivism is useful only because it predicts what we might become if we're careless and don't preserve our fragile links with civilization." By habit his eyes focused on the empty words "what we might become if." Nobody could index a phrase like that.

Yet they had. Several references appeared. And so instead of staying within his reverie, he was distracted, drawn to what the indexers had tied to such an absurd phrase.

One of the references was a nursery rhyme that he had forgotten he knew:

Wrinkly Grandma Posey
Rockets all are rosy.
Lift off, drift off,
All fall down.

Why in the world had the indexer put *that* in? The first thought that came to Leyel's mind was himself and some of the servants' children, holding hands and walking in a circle, round and round till they came to the last words, whereupon they threw themselves to the ground and laughed insanely. The sort of game that only little children could possibly think was fun.

Since his eyes lingered on the poem, it moved to the main document display and new references appeared. One was a scholarly article on the evolution of the poem, speculating that it might have arisen during the early days of starflight on the planet of origin, when rockets may have been used to escape from a planet's gravity well. Was that why this poem had been indexed to his article? Because it was tied to the planet of origin?

No, that was too obvious. Another article about the poem was more helpful. It rejected the early-days-of-rockets idea, because the earliest versions of the poem never used the word "rocket." The oldest extant version went like this:

> *Wrinkle down a rosy,*
> *Pock-a fock-a posy,*
> *Lash us, dash us,*
> *All fall down.*

Obviously, said the commentator, these were mostly nonsense words—the later versions had arisen because children had insisted on trying to make sense of them.

And it occurred to Leyel that perhaps this was why the indexer had linked this poem to his phrase—because the poem had once been nonsense, but we insisted on making sense out of it.

Was this a comment on Leyel's whole search for origins? Did the indexer think it was useless?

No—the poem had been tied to the empty phrase "what we might become if." Maybe the indexer was saying that human beings are like this poem—our lives make no sense, but we insist on making sense out of them. Didn't Deet say something like that once, when she was talking about the role of storytelling in community formation? The universe resists causality, she said. But human intelligence demands it. So we tell stories to impose causal relationships among the unconnected events of the world around us.

That includes ourselves, doesn't it? Our own lives are nonsense, but we impose a story on them, we sort our memories into cause-and-effect chains, forcing them to make sense even though they don't. Then we take the sum of our stories and call it our "self." This poem shows us the process—from randomness to meaning—and then we think our meanings are "true."

But somehow all the children had come to agree on the new version of the poem. By the year 2000 G.E., only the final and current version existed in all the worlds, and it had remained constant ever since. How was it that all the children on every world came to agree on the same version? How did the change spread? Did ten thousand kids on ten thousand worlds happen to make up the same changes?

It had to be word of mouth. Some kid somewhere made a few changes, and his version spread. A few years, and all the children in his neighborhood use the new version, and then all the kids in his city, on his planet. It could happen very quickly, in fact, because each generation of children lasts only a few years—seven-year-olds might take the new version as a joke, but repeat it often enough that five-year-olds think it's the true version of the poem, and within a few years there's nobody left among the children who remembers the old way.

A thousand years is long enough for the new version of the poem to spread. Or for five or a dozen new versions to collide and get absorbed into each other and then spread back, changed, to worlds that had revised the poem once or twice already.

And as Leyel sat there, thinking these thoughts, he conjured up an image in his mind of a network of children, bound to each other by the threads of this poem, extending from planet to planet throughout the Empire, and then back through time, from one generation of children to the previous one, a three-dimensional fabric that bound all children together from the beginning.

And yet as each child grew up, he cut himself free from the fabric of that poem. No longer would he hear the words "Wrinkly Grandma Posey" and immediately join hands with the child next to him. He wasn't part of the song any more.

But his own children were. And then his grandchildren. All joining hands with each other, changing from circle to circle, in a never-ending human chain reaching back to some long-forgotten ritual on one of the worlds of mankind—maybe, maybe on the planet of origin itself.

The vision was so clear, so overpowering, that when he finally noticed the lector display it was as sudden and startling as waking up. He had to sit there, breathing shallowly, until he calmed himself, until his heart stopped beating so fast.

He had found some part of his answer, though he didn't understand it yet. That fabric connecting all the children, that was part of what made us human, though he didn't know why. This strange and perverse indexing of a meaningless phrase had brought him a new way of looking at the problem. Not that the universal culture of children was a new idea. Just that he had never thought of it as having anything to do with the origin question.

Was this what the indexer meant by including this poem? Had the indexer also seen this vision?

Maybe, but probably not. It might have been nothing more than the idea of becoming something that made the indexer think of transformation—becoming old, like wrinkly Grandma Posey? Or it might have been a general thought about the spread of humanity through the stars, away from the planet of origin, that made the indexer remember how the poem seemed to tell of rockets that rise up from a planet, drift for a while, then come down to settle on a planet. Who knows what the poem meant to the indexer? Who knows why it occurred to her to link it with his document on that particular phrase?

Then Leyel realized that in his imagination, he was thinking of Deet making that particular connection. There was no reason to think it was her work, except that in his mind she was all the indexers. She had joined them, become one of them, and so when indexing work was being done, she was part of it. That's what it meant to be part of a community—all its works became, to a degree, your works. All that the indexers did, Deet was a part of it, and therefore Deet had done it.

Again the image of a fabric came to mind, only this time it was a topologically impossible fabric, twisted into itself so that no matter what part of the edge of it you held, you held the entire edge, and the middle, too. It was all one thing, and each part held the whole within it.

But if that was true, then when Deet came to join the library, so did Leyel, because she contained Leyel within her. So in coming here, she had not left him at all. Instead, she had woven him into a new fabric, so that instead of losing something he was gaining.

He was part of all this, because *she* was, and so if he lost her it would only be because he rejected her.

Leyel covered his eyes with his hands. How did his meandering thoughts about the origin question lead him to thinking about his marriage? Here he thought he was on the verge of profound understanding, and then he fell back into self-absorption.

He cleared away all the references to "Wrinkly Grandma Posey" or "Wrinkle Down a Rosy" or whatever it was, then returned to reading his original document, trying to confine his thoughts to the subject at hand.

Yet it was a losing battle. He could not escape from the seductive distraction of the index. He'd be reading about tool use and technology, and how it could not be the dividing line between human and animal because there were animals that made tools and taught their use to others.

Then, suddenly, the index would have him reading an ancient terror tale about a man who wanted to be the greatest genius of all time, and he believed that the only thing preventing him from achieving greatness was the hours he lost in sleep. So he invented a machine to sleep for him, and it worked very well until he realized that the machine was having all his dreams. Then he demanded that his machine tell him what it was dreaming.

The machine poured forth the most astonishing, brilliant thoughts ever imagined by any man—far wiser than anything this man had ever written during his waking hours. The man took a hammer and smashed the machine, so that he could have his dreams back. But even when he started sleeping again, he was never able to come close to the clarity of thought that the machine had had.

Of course he could never publish what the machine had written—it would be unthinkable to put forth the product of a machine as if it were the work of a man. After the man died—in despair—people found the printed text of what the machine had written, and thought the man had written it and hidden it away. They published it, and he was widely acclaimed as the greatest genius who had ever lived.

This was universally regarded as an obscenely horrifying tale because it had a machine stealing part of a man's mind and using it to destroy him, a common theme. But why did the indexer refer to it in the midst of a discussion of tool-making?

Wondering about that led Leyel to think that this story itself was a kind of tool. Just like the machine the man in the story had made. The storyteller gave his dreams to the story, and then when people heard it or read it, his dreams—his nightmares—came out to live in their memories. Clear and sharp and terrible and true, those dreams they received. And yet if he tried to *tell* them the same truths, directly, not in the form of a story, people would think his ideas were silly and small.

And then Leyel remembered what Deet had said about how people absorb stories from their communities and take them into themselves and use these stories to form their own spiritual autobiography. They remember doing what the heroes of the stories did, and so they continue to act out each hero's character in their own lives, or, failing that, they measure themselves against the standard the story set for them. Stories become the human conscience, the human mirror.

Again, as so many other times, he ended these ruminations with his hands pressed over his eyes, trying to shut out—or lock in?—images of fabrics and mirrors, worlds and atoms, until finally, finally, he opened his eyes and saw Deet and Zay sitting in front of him.

No, leaning over him. He was on a low bed, and they knelt beside him.

"Am I ill?" he asked.

"I hope not," said Deet. "We found you on the floor. You're exhausted, Leyel. I've been telling you—you have to eat, you have to get a normal amount of sleep. You're not young enough to keep up this work schedule."

"I've barely started."

Zay laughed lightly. "Listen to him, Deet. I told you he was so caught up in this that he didn't even know what day it was."

"You've been doing this for three weeks, Leyel. For the last week you haven't even come home. I bring you food, and you won't eat. People talk to you, and you forget that you're in a conversation, you just drift off into some sort of—trance. Leyel, I wish I'd never brought you here, I wish I'd never suggested indexing—"

"No!" Leyel cried. He struggled to sit up.

At first Deet tried to push him back down, insisting he should rest. It was Zay who helped him sit. "Let the man talk," she said. "Just because you're his wife doesn't mean you can stop him from talking."

"The index is wonderful," said Leyel. "Like a tunnel opened up into my own mind. I keep seeing light just *that* far out of reach, and then I wake up and it's just me alone on a pinnacle except for the pages up on the lector. I keep losing it—"

"No, Leyel, we keep losing *you*. The index is poisoning you, it's taking over your mind—"

"Don't be absurd, Deet. You're the one who suggested this, and you're right. The index keeps surprising me, making me think in new ways. There are some answers already."

"Answers?" asked Zay.

"I don't know how well I can explain it. What makes us human. It has to do with communities and stories and tools and—it has to do with you and me, Deet."

"I should hope we're human," she said. Teasing him, but also urging him on.

"We lived together all those years, and we formed a community—with our children, till they left, and then just us. But we were like animals."

"Only sometimes," she said.

"I mean like herding animals, or primate tribes, or any community that's bound together only by the rituals and patterns of the present moment. We had our customs, our habits. Our private language of words and gestures, our dances, all the things that flocks of geese and hives of bees can do."

"Very primitive."

"Yes, that's right, don't you see? That's a community that dies with each generation. When we die, Deet, it will all be gone with us. Other people will marry, but none of them will know our dances and songs and language and—"

"Our children will."

"No, that's my point. They knew us, they even think they *know* us, but they were never part of the community of our marriage. Nobody is. Nobody *can* be. That's why, when I thought you were leaving me for this—"

"When did you think that I—"

"Hush, Deet," said Zay. "Let the man babble."

"When I thought you were leaving me, I felt like I was dead, like I was losing everything, because if you weren't part of our marriage, then there was nothing left. You see?"

"I don't see what that has to do with human origins, Leyel. I only know that I would never leave you, and I can't believe that you could think—"

"Don't distract him, Deet."

"It's the children. All the children. They play Wrinkly Grandma Posey, and then they grow up and don't play anymore, so the actual community of these particular five or six children doesn't exist any more—but other kids are still doing the dance. Chanting the poem. For ten thousand years!"

"This makes us human? Nursery rhymes?"

"They're all part of the same community! Across all the empty space between the stars, there are still connections, they're still somehow the *same kids*. Ten thousand years, ten thousand worlds, quintillions of children, and they all knew the poem, they all did the dance. Story and ritual—it doesn't die with the tribe, it doesn't stop at the border. Children who never met face-to-face, who lived so far apart that the light from one star still hasn't reached the other, they belonged to the same community. We're human because we conquered time and space. We conquered the barrier of perpetual ignorance between one person and another. We found a way to slip my memories into your head, and yours into mine."

"But these are the ideas you already rejected, Leyel. Language and community and—"

"No! No, not just language, not just tribes of chimpanzees chattering at each other. *Stories*, epic tales that define a community, mythic tales that teach us how the world works, we use them to create each other. We became a different species, we became *human*, because we found a way to extend gestation beyond the womb, a way to give each child ten thousand parents that he'll never meet face-to-face."

Then, at last, Leyel fell silent, trapped by the inadequacy of his words. They couldn't tell what he had seen in his mind. If they didn't already understand, they never would.

"Yes," said Zay. "I think indexing your paper was a very good idea."

Leyel sighed and lay back down on the bed. "I shouldn't have tried."

"On the contrary, you've succeeded," said Zay.

Deet shook her head. Leyel knew why—Deet was trying to signal Zay that she shouldn't attempt to soothe Leyel with false praise.

"Don't hush me, Deet. I know what I'm saying. I may not know Leyel as well as you do, but I know truth when I hear it. In a way, I think Hari knew it instinctively. That's why he insisted on all his silly holodisplays, forcing the poor citizens of Terminus to put up with his pontificating every few years. It was his way of continuing to create them, of remaining alive within them. Making them feel like their lives had purpose behind them. Mythic and epic story, both at once. They'll all carry a bit of Hari Seldon within them just the way that children carry their parents with them to the grave."

At first Leyel could only hear the idea that Hari would have approved of his ideas of human origin. Then he began to realize that there was much more to what Zay had said than simple affirmation.

"You knew Hari Seldon?"

"A little," said Zay.

"Either tell him or don't," said Deet. "You can't take him this far in, and not bring him the rest of the way."

"I knew Hari the way you know Deet," said Zay.

"No," said Leyel. "He would have mentioned you."

"Would he? He never mentioned his students."

"He had thousands of students."

"I know, Leyel. I saw them come and fill his lecture halls and listen to the half-baked fragments of psychohistory that he taught them. But then he'd come away, here to the library, into a room where the Pubs never go, where he could speak words that the Pubs would never hear, and there he'd teach his real students. Here is the only place where the science of psychohistory lives on, where Deet's ideas about the formation of community actually have application, where your own vision of the origin of humanity will shape our calculations for the next thousand years."

Leyel was dumbfounded. "In the Imperial Library? Hari had his own college here in the library?"

"Where else? He had to leave us at the end, when it was time to go public with his predictions of the Empire's fall. Then the Pubs started watching him in earnest, and in order to keep them from finding us, he couldn't ever come back here again. It was the most terrible thing that ever happened to us. As if he died, for us, years before his body died. He was part of us, Leyel, the way that you and Deet are part of each other. She knows. She joined us before he left."

It stung. To have had such a great secret, and not to have been included. "Why Deet, and not me?"

"Don't you know, Leyel? Our little community's survival was the most important thing. As long as you were Leyel Forska, master of one of the greatest fortunes in history, you couldn't possibly be part of this—it would have provoked too much comment, too much attention. Deet could come, because Commissioner Chen wouldn't care that much what she did—he never takes spouses seriously, just one of the ways he proves himself to be a fool."

"But Hari always meant for you to be one of us," said Deet. "His worst fear was that you'd go off half-cocked and force your way into the First Foundation, when all along he wanted you in this one. The Second Foundation."

Leyel remembered his last interview with Hari. He tried to remember—did Hari ever lie to him? He told him that Deet couldn't go to Terminus—but now that took on a completely different meaning. The old fox! He never lied at all, but he never told the truth, either.

Zay went on. "It was tricky, striking the right balance, encouraging you to provoke Chen just enough that he'd strip away your fortune and then forget you, but not so much that he'd have you imprisoned or killed."

"You were making that happen?"

"No, no, Leyel. It was going to happen anyway, because you're who you are and Chen is who he is. But there was a range of possibility, somewhere between having you and Deet tortured to death on the one hand, and on the other hand having you and Rom conspire to assassinate Chen and take control of the Empire. Either of those extremes would have made it impossible for you to be part of the Second Foundation. Hari was convinced—and so is Deet, and so am I—that you belong with us. Not dead. Not in politics. Here."

It was outrageous, that they should make such choices for him, without telling him. How could Deet have kept it secret all this time? And yet they were so obviously correct. If Hari had told him about this Second Foundation, Leyel would have been eager, proud to join it. Yet Leyel couldn't have been told, couldn't have joined them until Chen no longer perceived him as a threat.

"What makes you think Chen will ever forget me?"

"Oh, he's forgotten you, all right. In fact, I'd guess that by tonight he'll have forgotten everything he ever knew."

"What do you mean?"

"How do you think we've dared to speak so openly today, after keeping silence for so long? After all, we aren't in Indexing now."

Leyel felt a thrill of fear run through him. "They can hear us?"

"If they were listening. At the moment, though, the Pubs are very busy helping Rom Divart solidify his control of the Commission of Public Safety. And if Chen hasn't been taken to the radiation chamber, he soon will be."

Leyel couldn't help himself. The news was too glorious—he sprang up from his bed, almost danced at the news. "Rom's doing it! After all these years—overthrowing the old spider!"

"It's more important than mere justice or revenge," said Zay. "We're absolutely certain that a significant number of governors and prefects and military commanders will refuse to recognize the overlordship of the Commission of Public Safety. It will take Rom Divart the rest of his life just to put down the most dangerous of the rebels. In order to concentrate his forces on the great rebels and pretenders close to Trantor, he'll grant an unprecedented degree of independence to many, many worlds on the periphery. To all intents and purposes, those outer worlds will no longer be part of the Empire. Imperial authority will not touch them, and their taxes will no longer flow inward to Trantor. The Empire is no longer Galactic. The death of Commissioner Chen—today—will mark the beginning of the fall of the Galactic Empire, though no one but us will notice what it means for decades, even centuries to come."

"So soon after Hari's death. Already his predictions are coming true."

"Oh, it isn't just coincidence," said Zay. "One of our agents was able to influence Chen just enough to ensure that he sent Rom Divart in person to strip you of your fortune. That was what pushed Rom over the edge and made him carry out this coup. Chen would have fallen—or died—sometime in the next year and a half no matter what we did. But I'll admit we took a certain pleasure in using Hari's death as a trigger to bring him down a little early, and under circumstances that allowed us to bring you into the library."

"We also used it as a test," said Deet. "We're trying to find ways of influencing individuals without their knowing it. It's still very crude and haphazard, but in this case we were able to influence Chen with great success. We had to do it—your life was at stake, and so was the chance of your joining us."

"I feel like a puppet," said Leyel.

"Chen was the puppet," said Zay. "You were the prize."

"That's all nonsense," said Deet. "Hari loved you, *I* love you. You're a great man. The Second Foundation had to have you. And everything you've said and stood for all your life made it clear that you were hungry to be part of our work. Aren't you?"

"Yes," said Leyel. Then he laughed. "The index!"

"What's so funny?" asked Zay, looking a little miffed. "We worked very hard on it."

"And it was wonderful, transforming, hypnotic. To take all these people and put them together as if they were a single mind, far wiser in its intuition than anyone could ever be alone. The most intensely unified, the most powerful human community that's ever existed. If it's our capacity for storytelling that makes us human, then perhaps our capacity for indexing will make us something better than human."

Deet patted Zay's hand. "Pay no attention to him, Zay. This is clearly the mad enthusiasm of a proselyte."

Zay raised an eyebrow. "*I'm* still waiting for him to explain why the index made him *laugh*."

Leyel obliged her. "Because all the time, I kept thinking—how could librarians have done this? Mere librarians! And now I discover that these librarians are all of Hari Seldon's prize students. My questions were indexed by psychohistorians!"

"Not exclusively. Most of us *are* librarians. Or machinists, or custodians, or whatever—the psychologists and psychohistorians are rather a thin current in the stream of the library. At first they were seen as outsiders. Researchers. *Users* of the library, not members of it. That's what Deet's work has been for these last few years—trying to bind us all together into one community. She came here as a researcher too, remember? Yet now she has made everyone's allegiance to the library more important than any other loyalty. It's working beautifully too, Leyel, you'll see. Deet is a marvel."

"We're *all* creating it together," said Deet. "It helps that the couple of hundred people I'm trying to bring in are so knowledgeable and understanding of the human mind. They understand exactly what I'm doing and then try to help me make it work. And it *isn't* fully successful yet. As years go by, we have to see the psychology group teaching and accepting the children of librarians and machinists and medical officers, in full equality with their own, so that the psychologists don't become a ruling caste. And then intermarriage between the groups. Maybe in a hundred years we'll have a truly cohesive community. This is a democratic city-state we're building, not an academic department or a social club."

Leyel was off on his own tangent. It was almost unbearable for him to realize that there were hundreds of people who knew Hari's work, while Leyel didn't. "You have to teach me!" Leyel said. "Everything that Hari taught you, all the things that have been kept from me—"

"Oh, eventually, Leyel," said Zay. "At present, though, we're much more interested in what you have to teach *us*. Already, I'm sure, a transcription of the things you said when you first woke up is being spread through the library."

"It was recorded?" asked Leyel.

"We didn't know if you were going to go catatonic on us at any moment, Leyel. You have no idea how you've been worrying us. Of course we recorded it—they might have been your last words."

"They won't be. I don't feel tired at all."

"Then you're not as bright as we thought. Your body is dangerously weak. You've been abusing yourself terribly. You're not a young man, and we insist that you stay away from your lector for a couple of days."

"What, are you now my doctor?"

"Leyel," Deet said, touching him on his shoulder the way she always did when he needed calming. "You *have* been examined by doctors. And you've got to realize— Zay is First Speaker."

"Does that mean she's commander?"

"This isn't the Empire," said Zay, "and I'm not Chen. All that it means to be First Speaker is that I speak first when we meet together. And then, at the end, I bring together all that has been said and express the consensus of the group."

"That's right," said Deet. "*Everybody* thinks you ought to rest."

"*Everybody* knows about me?" asked Leyel.

"Of course," said Zay. "With Hari dead you're the most original thinker we have. Our work needs you. Naturally we care about you. Besides, Deet loves you so much, and we love *Deet* so much, we feel like we're all a little bit in love with you ourselves."

She laughed, and so did Leyel, and so did Deet. Leyel noticed, though, that when he asked whether they all *knew* of him, she had answered that they cared about him and loved him. Only when Zay said this did he realize that she had answered the question he really meant to ask.

"And while you're recuperating," Zay continued, "Indexing will have a go at your new theory—"

"Not a theory, just a proposal, just a *thought*—"

"—and a few psychohistorians will see whether it can be quantified, perhaps by some variation on the formulas we've been using with Deet's laws of community development. Maybe we can turn origin studies into a real science yet."

"Maybe," Leyel said.

"Feel all right about this?" asked Zay.

"I'm not sure. Mostly. I'm very excited, but I'm also a little angry at how I've been left out, but mostly I'm—I'm so relieved."

"Good. You're in a hopeless muddle. You'll do your best work if we can keep you off balance forever." With that, Zay led him back to the bed, helped him lie down, and then left the room.

Alone with Deet, Leyel had nothing to say. He just held her hand and looked up into her face, his heart too full to say anything with words. All the news about Hari's byzantine plans and a Second Foundation full of psychohistorians and Rom Divart taking over the government—that receded into the background. What mattered was this: Deet's hand in his, her eyes looking into his, and her heart, her self, her soul so closely bound to his that he couldn't tell and didn't care where he left off and she began.

How could he ever have imagined that she was leaving him? They had created each other through all these years of marriage. Deet was the most splendid accomplishment of his life, and he was the most valued creation of hers. We are each other's parent, each other's child. We might accomplish great works that will live on in this other community, the library, the Second Foundation. But the greatest work of all is the one that will die with us, the one that no one else will ever know of, because they remain perpetually outside. We can't even explain it to them. They don't have the language to understand us. We can only speak it to each other.

AFTERWORD

"A THOUSAND DEATHS"

My early fiction won me a reputation for cruelty. The most memorable line was from a review in *Locus:* "Reading Card is like playing pattycake with Baby Huey." This sort of comment, however well-phrased, worried me more than a little. Clearly my fiction was giving the impression of being bloodier than most writers' stories, and yet that was never my intent. I'm an innately nonviolent person. I have almost never struck another person in anger; my custom in school when the subject of fighting came up was to talk my way out when I couldn't simply run. I never tortured animals. I don't enjoy pain. So why was I writing fiction that made grown men gag?

This story, "A Thousand Deaths," was one of a pair (the other is "Kingsmeat") that did most to earn me that reputation. It is the one story I've written that was so sickening that my wife couldn't finish reading it—she never has, as far as I know. And yet I couldn't see at the time—and still can't—how it could be written any other way.

The story is about noncompliance. It was triggered in part by a line in Robert Bolt's *A Man for All Seasons,* which dwells in my memory in this form: "I do none harm, I think none harm, and if this be not enough to keep a man alive, then in faith I long not to live." There are times when a government, to stay in power, requires that certain people be broken, publicly. Their noncompliance with the will of the government is a constant refreshment to the enemies of the state. One thinks of Nelson Mandela, who, to be set free, has only to sign a statement renouncing violence as a means of obtaining the rights of his people. One thinks of the wonderful line from the movie *Gandhi* (which had not been made when I wrote this story, though the line expresses the theme of this story almost perfectly): "They can even kill me. What will they have then? My dead body. Not my obedience." It is the power of passive resistance, even in the face of a government that has the power to inflict the ultimate penalty, that eventually breaks the power of that government.

With "A Thousand Deaths" I simply did what satiric science fiction always does— I set up a society that exaggerates the point in question. In this case, it was the power of the state to inflict punishment in order to control the behavior of others, and my *what-if* was, "What if a government could, not just threaten to kill you, but actually kill you over and over until it finally got the confession it needed?" The mechanism was easy enough—I had already developed the drug somec and had stolen the idea of brain-taping from many other writers years before, for my *Worthing Chronicle* series. What mattered to me, though, was to focus on the point where coercion ultimately breaks down, and that is on the rock of truth. The government kills the story's hero, trying to break him to the point where he will confess his wrong, and confess the rightness of the government. The trouble is that the government will only measure his confession against a standard too high for him to meet. It isn't enough that his confession be passionate. It must also be *believed*. And that is the one thing that the hero cannot deliver—a believable confession. He can't believe it himself; neither can anyone else. That is what coercion cannot do. It can win compliance from fearful people. But it cannot win belief. The heart is an unstormable citadel.

How, tell me please, could I possibly have told this story without making you, the reader, believe absolutely in the hero's deaths? You have to experience some shadow of the suffering in order to understand the impossibility of his confession. If you find the story unbearable, remember that there have been far more deaths than this, and more terrible ones as well, in the same struggle in the real world.

A footnote: In the late seventies, I set this story in a United States ruled by a Soviet government. In this I was not seriously predicting something I believed likely to happen. But I was trying to place the story of a totalitarian state within the United States if only to bring home the idea to American readers, who, outside of the experience of American blacks in many a Southern town, are ignorant of the suffering and terror of totalitarianism. Once the decision to set the story here was made, I had two choices: to show an America ruled by a homegrown demagogue, or to show an America ruled by an foreign conqueror. I rejected the former, in part because at that time it had lately become a cliché of American literateurs to pretend that the only danger to the U.S. was from conservative extremists. I preferred to show America ruled by the most cruel and efficient totalitarian system ever to exist on the face of the Earth: the Stalinist version of the Communist Party.

The events of 1989 in eastern Europe do not change this; it was the very unwillingness of Gorbachev to play Stalin that led to the unshackling of the captive nations. Had he been willing to resort to the machine gun and the tank, as his predecessors did, there would be no more Solidarity, no second Prague Spring, no holes in the Berlin Wall, no bullet-riddled body of Ceausescu, no Hungarian border open to Austria. Or would there? Gorbachev was the man who brought Russia over that moral cusp—but I think it would have had to come eventually, with him or someone else. "A Thousand Deaths" is a true story, and I used the Soviets in it because they are the most recent world power to prove that it is true.

"CLAP HANDS AND SING"

Once, back in the mid-1970s, I had a conversation with a young woman I had once thought myself to be in love with. "I had such a crush on you before you went on your mission," she said. "And the poems you wrote me while you were gone . . . I thought something would come of it when you got home. But when you returned from Brazil, I waited and waited and you never even called."

"I thought of calling," I said. "Often."

"But you never did. And on the rebound from you I fell in love with someone else."

Here's the funny thing: I never guessed how *she* felt. One reason I never called her was because I thought she might think I was weird to try to convert a friendship to something more. Thus do adolescents manage to work at cross-purposes often enough to make romantic tragedies possible.

In the years since, I have found a much deeper love and stronger commitment than anything I ever imagined in those days. But when I was exploring the idea of time travel, and thought of an ironic story in which two people, unknown to each other, both journey back in time to have a perfect night together, my mind naturally turned to that moment of impotent frustration when I realized that this young lady and I, had I but acted a bit differently, might have ended up together. Since it's much easier to use real events than to make up phony ones, I stole from my own life to find, I hoped, that sense of bittersweet memory that is the stuff of movie romances.

"DOGWALKER"

Cyberpunk was all the rage, and I was driving home from ArmadilloCon, the science fiction convention held in Austin, the see of the bishop of cyberpunk, Bruce Sterling. I had long had an ambivalent feeling toward cyberpunk. Bruce Sterling's ideas about science fiction fascinated me greatly, if only because he was the one person I could hear talking about science fiction in terms that weren't either warmed-over James Blish and Damon Knight or stolen from the mouldering corpse of Modernism that still stinks to high heaven in the English departments of American universities. In short, Sterling actually had Ideas instead of Echoes.

At the same time, I could not help but be a bit disgusted at what was being done in the name of cyberpunk. William Gibson, though quite talented, seemed to be writing the same story over and over again. Furthermore, it was the same self-serving story that was being churned out in every creative writing course in America and published in every little literary magazine at least once an issue: the suffering artist who is alienated from his society and is struggling to find out a reason to live. My answer is easy enough: An artist who is alienated from his society *has* no reason to live—as an artist, anyway. You can only live as an artist when you're firmly connected to the community to whom you offer your art.

But the worst thing about cyberpunk was the shallowness of those who imitated it. Splash some drugs onto brain-and-microchip interface, mix it up with some vague sixties-style counterculture, and then use really self-conscious, affected language, and you've got cyberpunk. Never mind that the actual stories being told were generally clichés that were every bit as stupid and derivative as the worst of the stuff Bruce Sterling had initially rebelled against. Even if the underlying stories had been highly original, stylistic imitation and affectation are crimes enough to make a literary movement worthy of the death sentence.

So, being the perverse and obnoxious child that I am, I challenged myself: Is the derivativeness of cyberpunk the source or a symptom of its emptiness? Is it possible to write a good story that uses all the clichés of cyberpunk? The brain-microchip interface, the faked-up slang, the drugs, the counterculture . . . Could I, a good Mormon boy who watched the sixties through the wrong end of the binoculars, write a convincing story in that mode—and also tell a tale that would satisfy *me* as good fiction?

One thing was certain—I couldn't imitate anybody else's *story*. It was the language, the *style* that I was imitating. So I had to violate my own custom and start, not with the story, but with the voice. With a monologue. The first two paragraphs of *Dogwalker* were the first two I wrote, pretty much as they stand now. The plot came only after I had the voice and the character of the narrator pretty well established.

I got the thing done soon after returning home, and sent it off to Gardner Dozois at *Asimov's*. I expected the story to get bounced. I had a mental picture of Gardner staggering out into the hall at Davis Publications, gagging and choking, holding out the manuscript as if it were a bag of burning dog dung. "Look at this. *Card* is trying to write cyberpunk now." Instead, Gardner sent me a contract. It rather spoiled my plans—I expected to use the story as my entry at Sycamore Hill that summer, but since it had sold I couldn't do that. The result was that I ended up writing my novella "Pageant Wagon" during that workshop, so it wasn't a total loss.

In the meantime, however, Gardner never published "Dogwalker." He held it two-and-a-half years before I finally sent a note pointing out that our contract had expired and if they didn't have immediate plans to publish it, I wanted it back to sell it elsewhere. At that point they seemed to have suddenly remembered that they had it, and it was scheduled and published barely in time to be included in this book.

In a way, though, Gardner did me a favor—perhaps on purpose. By holding the story so long, he had seen to it that "Dogwalker" appeared in print *after* the spate of cyberpunk imitations was over. The story was not so clearly pegged as derivative. And though it was clearly not like a "typical Card story" on its surface, it could more easily be received as my work than as pale-imitation Gibson. Thus was I spared the fate of appearing as pathetic as, say, Barbra Streisand singing disco with the BeeGees.

"BUT WE TRY NOT TO ACT LIKE IT"

For a short time, Kristine's and my favorite restaurant in Salt Lake City was the Savoy, a purportedly English restaurant that nevertheless had wonderful food. We brought friends, we went alone—we did everything we could to make that restaurant succeed. Furthermore it was always crowded. And six months later, it was out of business.

It happens over and over. TV shows I like are doomed to cancellation. Authors I fall in love with stop writing the kind of book I loved. (Come on, Mortimer and Rendell! Rumpole and Wexford are the reason you were born! As for you, Gregory McDonald, write Fletch or die!) Trends in science fiction and fantasy that I applaud quickly vanish; the ones that make me faintly sick seem to linger like herpes. For one reason or another, my tastes are just not reflected in the real world.

That's what gave rise to this story. Unfortunately, I never let the story rise above its origin. I have learned since then that I shouldn't write a story from a single idea, but rather should wait for a second, unrelated idea, so that out of their confluence can come something truly alive. The result is that this story bears the curse of most of science fiction—it is idea-driven rather than character-driven, which means that it is ultimately forgettable. That doesn't mean it's valueless—I hope it's kind of fun to read it once. But you'll certainly not be rewarded for reading it again. You already received everything it had to offer on the first reading.

"I PUT MY BLUE GENES ON"

Jim Baen wrote an editorial in *Galaxy* magazine in which he called on science fiction writers to stop writing the same old "futures" and take a look at what science was doing *now*. Where, for example, were the stories extrapolating on current research in recombinant DNA?

I was still working at *The Ensign* magazine then, and Jay and Lane and I took this as a personal challenge. Naturally, in the tradition of young sci-fi writers, I mechanically took the idea of gene-splicing (I'd been reading *Scientific American* like a good boy, so I could fake it up pretty well), carried it to an extreme, and served it up in a stereotypical plot about two nations in a life-and-death struggle—only one of the nations doesn't realize that the other one was wiped out long ago and that its struggle is now against the very world they have destroyed. As a let's-stop-messing-up-the-world polemic, I think the story still holds up pretty well. As an artful story, it's definitely a work of my youth. Recombining DNA has been treated far better since then, both in my own stories (*Wyrms*, *Speaker for the Dead*) and in the works of writers who've done the subject more justice. (I think particularly of the magnificent work Octavia Butler has done with *Dawn*, *Adulthood Rites*, and *Imago*.) If you want proof that I was but an adolescent playing at fiction-writing, you have only to look at the title, a bad pun on a fun-but-dumb popular song that was, I believe, written as the theme music for a jeans ad.

I notice now, however, that some later interests of mine were already cropping up in "I Put My Blue Genes On." For one thing, I actually put Brazilians in space. I was not the first to do it, but it was the beginning of my deliberate effort to try to get American sci-fi writers to realize that the future probably does *not* belong to America. Science fiction of the pre–World War I era always seemed to put Englishmen and Frenchmen into space; now, in this post-imperialist world, we think of that as a rather quaint idea. I firmly believe that in fifty years the idea of Americans leading the world anywhere will be just as anachronistic, and only those of us who put Brazilians, Thais, Chinese, and Mexicans into space will look at all prescient.

Of course, maybe I'm wrong about the specific prediction I'm making. But there's another reason to open up science fiction to other cultures, and that is that science fiction is the one lasting American contribution to prose literature. In every other area, we're derivative to the—well, not to the core, because in those areas we *have* no core. Nobody in other countries aspires to write Westerns, and nobody in Russia or Germany or Japan looks to Updike or Bellow to teach them how to write "serious" fiction. They already have literary traditions older and better than our so-called best. But in science fiction, they *all* look to us. They want to write science fiction, too, because those who read it in every nation see it as the fiction of possibility, the fiction of strangeness. It's the one genre now that allows the writer to do satire that isn't recognized as satire, to do metaphysical fiction that isn't seen as philosophical or religious proselytizing. In short, it is the freest, most open literature in the world today, and it is the one literature that foreign writers are learning first and foremost from Americans.

Why, then, do science fiction writers persist in imagining only American futures? Our audience is much broader than these shores. And there are countries where our words are taken far more seriously than they are here. If we actually aspire to change the world with our fiction—and I can't think of any other reason for ever setting pen to paper—then we ought to be talking to the world. And one sure way to let the world know we are talking to them is to put them—citizens of other countries, children of other cultures—into our futures. To do otherwise is to slap them in the face and say, "I have seen the future, and you aren't there." Well, I *have* seen the future, and they *are* there—in great numbers, with great power. I want my voice to have been one of the voices they listened to on their way up to be king of the hill. And, in "I Put My Blue Genes On," I took my first step along that road.

"IN THE DOGHOUSE" (with Jay A. Parry)

What if the aliens don't come to us in alien form? What if they come in a form we already recognize, that we already think we understand? Jay Parry and I toyed with the idea of telling this story differently—with the aliens coming in the form of an oppressed minority. American Indians or blacks, we thought. But the problems at the time seemed insurmountable—particularly the political problems. It's a very tricky business, for a white writer to try to express the black point of view without being politically incorrect. It seemed to me then that there were things that black writers could say about and on behalf of blacks that white writers couldn't, not without the message being taken wrong. In the years since then, I've learned that a writer of any race or sex or religion or nation can write about any other race or sex or religion or nation; he only needs to:

1. Do enough research that he doesn't make an ass of himself.
2. Tell the truth as he sees it without pandering or condescending to any group.
3. Have a thick enough skin to accept the fact that he'll be impaled with a thousand darts no matter how well he does at 1 and 2.

Being timid, Jay and I worked out the plot using animals that have been as firmly pegged in our human prejudices as any human group. Faithful, beloved dogs. Man's best friend. All the same possibilities were there—the White Man's Burden, the condescending affection (some of my best friends are dogs), and, above all, the rigid determination to keep them in their place.

"THE ORIGINIST"

In my review column in *The Magazine of Fantasy and Science Fiction*, I wrote a diatribe deploring the 1980s trend of trying to turn sci-fi authors' private worlds into generic brand name universes where other writers can romp. It began with *Star Trek*, and it was not part of anybody's grand design. There were these *Star Trek* fans, you see, who got impatient with Paramount's neglect of their heroes and began to write their *own* stories about the crew of the starship Enterprise. (In a way this was singularly appropriate: The original series was written and performed like somebody's garage production anyway, so why not continue the tradition?) Legend has it that Paramount at first intended to sue, until it dawned on them that there might be *money* in publishing never-filmed stories about Kirk, Spock, and the other crew members of *Wagon Train among the Cheap Interplanetary Sets*. They were right, to the tune of many readers and many dollars. A new industry was born: Science fiction written in somebody else's poorly imagined but passionately studied universe.

I suppose it was inevitable that publishers who weren't getting any of those *Star Trek* bucks would try to turn other successful imagined futures into equally lucrative backdrops where one writer's work would be as good as any others'. There ensued in the late 1980s a spate of novels set "in the world of———," in which journeyman writers who often didn't have a clue about the inner truth that led the Old Pro to create his or her world tried to set their own stories in it. The result was stories that nobody was proud of and nobody cared about.

What was unspoken (I hope) was the true premise of all these worlds-as-brand-names books: The readers won't be able to tell the difference. Here's what they found out: Unlike the *Star Trek* audience, the readers of most science fiction *can* tell the difference and they care very much. Written science fiction has an author-driven audience. The *real* science fiction audience doesn't want to read John Varley's Dune novel or Lisa Goldstein's Lensman novel or Howard Waldrop's Dragonworld novel. (Well, actually, I would *love* to read Howard Waldrop's Dragonworld novel, but not for any reason I'm proud of.)

So I laid down the law in my column: Writers should not waste their time or talent trying to tell stories in someone else's universe. Furthermore, established writers should not cooperate in the wasting of younger writers' talent by allowing their worlds to be franchised.

As soon as that column hit print, Martin Harry Greenberg mentioned to me that he was preparing a festschrift anthology commemorating Isaac Asimov's fiftieth year in publishing, a book called *Foundation's Friends*. And for this one anthology, Dr. Asimov was allowing the participants to set stories within his own closely-held fictional universes, using his own established characters. We could actually write robot stories using the three laws and positronic brains and Susan Calvin. We could actually write Foundation stories using Hari Seldon and Trantor and Terminus and the Mule.

Suddenly I was sixteen years old again and I remembered the one story I wanted so badly to read, the one that Asimov had never written—the story of how the Second Foundation actually got started in the library at Trantor.

Did I forget that I had just gotten through banning the franchising of universes for all time? No. I simply have a perverse streak in me that says that whenever somebody lays down a law, that law is meant to be broken—even when I was the lawgiver. So I wrote "The Originist" as both a tribute to and, perhaps, a sidelight on Asimov's masterwork.

This doesn't mean that I think the law I stated isn't true. In fact, I stand by it as firmly as ever. It's just that, like all laws, this one *can* be circumvented if you work hard enough. The reason why franchised worlds generally don't work is because the junior writers don't understand the original world well enough, don't know what it is about the original writer's work that made his stories work, and don't feel enough personal responsibility to do their best work under these circumstances. Well, in my arrogance, I thought I *did* know the Foundation universe well enough—not in the trivial details, but in the overall sweep of the story, in what it *means* (Yes, I've read *Decline and Fall*, too, but that isn't the foundation of Foundation, either.) Also, I thought I understood something of how the stories worked—the delight of discovering that no matter how many curtains you peel back, you never find the *real* curtain or the *real* man behind it in Asimov's Oz. There are always plans underlying plans, causes hidden behind plausible causes.

And, finally, I had a compelling story of my own to tell. I had already made a stab at it, with a fragment of a novel that was to be called *Genesis*—a book I may still write someday. In it I was trying to show the borderline between human and animal, the exact comma in the punctuational model of evolution that marked the transition between non-human and human. For me, that borderline is the human universal of storytelling; that is what joins a community together across time; that is what preserved a human identity after death and defines it in life. Without stories, we aren't human; with them, we are. But *Genesis* became impossible to write, in part because to do it properly I had to visit Kashmir and Ethiopia, two places where it is not terribly safe to travel these days.

But I *could* develop many of the same themes, though at a greater distance, in my story of "The Originist." Moreover, Asimov himself had broached a related question in *Foundation*, when he presented a character who was searching through libraries in order to find the planet of origin of the human species. I was able to take a purely Asimovian point—the futility of secondary research—and interlayer it with my own point—the fundamental role of storytelling in shaping human individuals and communities. I went further in my effort to make "The Originist" a true Foundation story. I also used a form that Asimov has perfected, but I had never tried before: the story in which almost nothing happens except dialogue. Asimov can make this work because of the piercing clarity of his writing and the sublime intelligence of his ideas—it is never boring listening to his characters discuss ideas, because you are never lost and the ideas are always worth hearing. The challenge was to come as close as I could to matching that clarity; I had to trust that others would find my ideas as interesting as I had always found Asimov's.

So it was that, even though I knew "The Originist" would never be received as standing on its own, I poured a novel's worth of love and labor into it. In the long run, I proved my own law—I wrote this story at the expense of a purely Orson Scott Card novel that will probably never be written. Yet I think it was worth doing—once—partly to prove it could be done well (if in fact I did it well), and partly because I'm proud of the story itself: because of the achievement of it, because of what the story says, and because it is a tribute to the writer that I firmly believe is the finest writer of American prose in our time, bar none.

BOOK 3

Maps in a Mirror

FABLES AND FANTASIES

INTRODUCTION

I don't believe in the "collective unconscious," not in the Jungian way I've seen it used. But I do believe that it is in large part through shared stories that communities create themselves and bind themselves together.

It begins with the way we establish our identity, which is intimately tied to our discovery of causality. All of nature relies on mechanical causation: Stimulus A causes response B. But almost as soon as we acquire language, we are taught an entirely different system: purposive causation, in which a person engaged in behavior B in order to accomplish result A. Never mind that it was X and Y, not A, that resulted. When it comes to evaluating human behavior, we quickly learn that it is the story we believe about a person's *purpose* that counts most.

You know the phrases of moral evaluation: "Why did you do that?" "I didn't mean to." "I was just trying to surprise you." "Do you want me to be humiliated in front of everybody?" "I don't work my fingers to the bone so you can go out and . . ." All of these sentences contain or invite stories; it is the stories we believe about our behavior that give them their moral value. Even the cruelest or weakest among us must find stories that excuse—or even ennoble—their own character flaws. On the day I'm writing this, the mayor of a major American city, arrested for using cocaine, actually stood before the cameras and said, in effect, "I guess I've just been working so hard serving the people that I didn't have time to take care of my own needs." What a story—smoking crack as an altruistic, selfless endeavor. The point is not whether the story is true; the point is that all human beings engage in storytelling about themselves, creating the story they want to believe about themselves, the story they actually believe about themselves, the story they want *others* to believe about them, the stories they believe about others, and the stories that they are afraid *might* be true about themselves and others.

Our very identity is a collection of the stories we have come to believe about ourselves. We are bombarded with the stories of others about us; even our memories of our own lives are filtered through the stories we have constructed to interpret those past events. We revise our identity by revising our self-story. Traditional psychotherapies rely heavily on this process: You *thought* you were trying to do X, but in fact your unconscious purpose was Y. Ah, now I understand myself! But I think not—I think that in the moment of believing the new story you simply *revised* your identity. I am no longer a person who tries to do X. I am a person who was being driven to do Y, without even realizing it. You remain the same person, who performed the same acts. Only the story has been changed.

All this deals with individual identities, and the tragedy of the individual is that the true cause of his behavior remains forever unknowable. And if we cannot know ourselves, true understanding of any other human being is permanently out of reach. Other people's behavior must be, in that case, completely unpredictable. And yet no human community could ever exist if we had no mechanism to enable us to feel safe in trusting other people's behavior to follow certain predictable patterns. And these predictable patterns can't arise solely from personal experience—we must know, with some certainty, *before* we have observed another member of the community for any length of time, what he or she is likely to do in most situations.

There are two kinds of stories that not only give us the illusion of understanding other people's behavior, but also go a long way toward making that illusion true. Each community has its own epic: a complex of stories about what it means to be a member of that community. These stories can arise from shared experience: Have you ever heard two Catholics reminisce about catechism or being taught in Catholic school by nuns? Or they can arise from what is perceived to be a common heritage, spreading a sense of community identity across space and time. Thus it is that Americans feel there is nothing incongruous about referring to Washington as "our" first president, even though no living American was present for his administration and most Americans have precious few ancestors who lived here during that time. Thus it is that an American living in Los Angeles can hear of something that happened in Springfield, Illinois, or Springfield, Massachusetts, and say, "Only here in America . . ."

Of course, membership in communities is never absolute. The same person could just as easily say, "We sure aren't like that here in California" or "here in L.A.," thus asserting the epic of another community. But the more important a community is to us, the more power its stories have in forming our view of the world—and in shaping our own behavior. I don't think my children are the only ones who've heard prescriptive epic stories like this one: "I don't care what other people's children do. In *our* family we . . ." Every community's epic includes shibboleth stories—stories that define what members do and do not do. "No good Baptist would ever . . ." ". . . just like a true American." And the stories that define a person's individual identity are often interpreted by the role that person plays within the community. "You make us all so proud of you, son." "An outstanding role model for young ———s." "I just wish other young people would be more like you." "I hope you're proud of the example you're setting for the other kids." "Now everybody's going to think all us blacks/Rotarians/Jews/Americans are like you!" Thus we not only are defined by the epic stories of the communities we belong to, but also help revise the community's epic stories by our behavior. (If I were going into this in detail, I'd talk about the role of outsiders in shaping a community's epic, and also about negative epic. But this is an essay, not a book in itself.)

The second category of story that shapes human behavior so that we can live together is not perceived as being tied to a particular community. It is mythic; those who believe in the story believe that it defines the way *human beings* behave. These stories are not really about how this character or that character behaved in a certain situation. They are about how *people* behave in such situations.

All storytelling contains elements of the particular, the epic, and the mythic. Fiction and scripture are both uniquely suited to telling mythic tales, however, because by definition fiction is *not* tied to particular people in the real world, and by definition scripture is perceived by its believers to be the universal truth rather than being merely and particularly true, the way history is usually received. That fiction and scripture are also inevitably epic, reflecting values and assumptions of the community out of which they arose, is true but not terribly important, for their audience *believes* mythic stories to be universal and, over time, comes to behave as if they *were* universal.

But fiction is not all equally mythic. Some fiction is quite particular, tied to a time and place and even characters in the real world. Thus historical fiction or contemporary realistic fiction with a strong sense of place can lead the reader to say, "Those people certainly were/are strange," rather than the more mythic response, "People certainly are strange," or the even more mythic response, "I never knew people were like that," or the ultimate mythic response, "Yes, that's how people are."

It might seem then that fiction becomes more mythic as it is divorced from identifiable real-world patterns, but it is not really the disconnection from reality that makes fiction mythic—if that were so, our myths would all be of madmen. Rather a story becomes more mythic as it connects to things that transcend reality. Tolkien's Middle Earth is so thoroughly created in *The Lord of the Rings* that the wealth of detail makes readers feel as though they had visited in a real place; but it is a place where human behavior takes on enormous importance, so that moral issues (the goodness or evil of a person's choices and actions) and causal issues (why things happen; the way the world works) take on far greater clarity. We find in Aragorn, not just that he is noble, but Nobility. We find in Frodo, not just that he is willing to bear a difficult burden, but Acceptance. And Samwise is not just a faithful servant, but also the personification of Service.

Thus it is in fantasy that we can most easily explore, not human behaviors, but Humanity. And in exploring it, we also define it; and in defining, invent it. Those of us who have received a story and believed in its truth (even if we don't believe in its factuality) carry those memories inside us and, if we care enough about the tale, act out the script it provides us. Because I remember standing at the Cracks of Doom, and because I remember experiencing it through Sam Gamgee's eyes, I clearly remember seeing that those who reach for power are possessed by it, and if they are not utterly destroyed by it, they lose part of themselves in getting free. I doubt that in crucial situations I'll summon up the memory of *Lord of the Rings* and consciously use it as a guide to my behavior—who has time for such involved mental processes when a choice is urgent, anyway? But unconsciously I remember being a person who made certain choices, and at that unconscious level I don't believe that I—or anyone—distinguishes between personal and community memories. They are all stories, and we act out the ones we believe in and care about most, the ones that have become part of us.

While I have been speaking about what fantasy *can* be—a particularly powerful source of mythic stories—it is worth pointing out that most fantasy, like most other kinds of fiction, doesn't live up to its potential. Furthermore, because it is to be received and acted upon unconsciously, the most successful fantasy is not often that which *looks* most mythic; often the most powerful fantasies are those that seem to be very realistic and particular. I think this is part of the reason that Tolkien shunned allegory. Consciously figured storytelling is received intellectually; it is never as powerful as stories whose symbols and figures—whose mythic connections—are received unconsciously. And I've come to believe that the most successful mythic writing is that storytelling in which the author was unconscious of his or her most powerful mythic elements.

So, while the best fantasy will have a powerful mythic effect, the most successful fantasists are not those who set out to write myth. Rather, the best fantasies come, I think, from storytellers who strive to create a particular story very well—but who use settings and events that give great freedom to their imagination, so that mythic elements can arise from their unconscious and play a strong role in the story. A fantasist who works from a deliberate plan will almost never achieve as much as the fantasist who is constantly surprised by the best moments in his or her stories.

You can see, then, that I'm not defining *fantasy* the way the word is used in contemporary publishing. When publishers speak of *fantasy* they generally mean stories set in a kind of pseudo-medieval world in which some kind of magic plays a role. Certainly good mythic fantasy can still be written in that kind of setting; but since such a world has been a staple of romance since before Chaucer, one can hardly credit most authors who work in it with having allowed their imagination to play a large role in their writing. Most such "fantasists" tuck their imagination away somewhere before they enter the mythic marketplace; they have come to buy, not to sell.

It's worth pointing out that works of derivative fantasists often sell very well; there is a large audience that buys fantasy in order to have their pre-existing vision of The Way Things Work reaffirmed. And some quite brilliant fantasists remain obscure, because their mythic universe is so challenging that few readers are happy to dwell in it. But when a fantasist imagines well—and writes evocatively—many people drink in the story as if it were water, and their lives till then a vast desert in which they wandered without ever realizing how much they thirsted.

The real fantasists are not content to echo other writers' myths. They must discover their own. They venture into the most dangerous, uncharted places in the human soul, where existing stories don't yet explain what people think and feel and do. In that frightening place they find a mirror that lets them glimpse a true image. Then they return and hold up the mirror, and unlike mirrors in the real world, this one holds the storyteller's image for just a fleeting moment, just long enough for us also to glimpse the long-shadowed soul that brightly lingers there. In that moment we make the mythic connection; for that moment we *are* another person; and we carry that rare and precious understanding with us until we die.

And what am I? Like most who attempt fantasy, I imagine that I am doing true Imagining; like most, I am usually echoing other people's visions. There's always the hope, though, that at least some readers will dip into the old dry well and find new water there, seeped in from an undiscovered spring.

UNACCOMPANIED SONATA

TUNING UP

When Christian Haroldsen was six months old, preliminary tests showed a predisposition toward rhythm and a keen awareness of pitch. There were other tests, of course, and many possible routes still open to him. But rhythm and pitch were the governing signs of his own private zodiac, and already the reinforcement began. Mr. and Mrs. Haroldsen were provided with tapes of many kinds of sound, and instructed to play them constantly, waking or sleeping.

When Christian Haroldsen was two years old, his seventh battery of tests pinpointed the future he would inevitably follow. His creativity was exceptional, his curiosity insatiable, his understanding of music so intense that the top of all the tests said "Prodigy."

Prodigy was the word that took him from his parents' home to a house in a deep deciduous forest where winter was savage and violent and summer a brief desperate eruption of green. He grew up cared for by unsinging servants, and the only music he was allowed to hear was birdsong, and windsong, and the cracking of winter wood; thunder, and the faint cry of golden leaves as they broke free and tumbled to the earth; rain on the roof and the drip of water from icicles; the chatter of squirrels and the deep silence of snow falling on a moonless night.

These sounds were Christian's only conscious music; he grew up with the symphonies of his early years only a distant and impossible-to-retrieve memory. And so he learned to hear music in unmusical things—for he had to find music, even when there was none to find.

He found that colors made sounds in his mind; sunlight in summer a blaring chord; moonlight in winter a thin mournful wail; new green in spring a low murmur in almost (but not quite) random rhythms; the flash of a red fox in the leaves a gasp of startlement.

And he learned to play all those sounds on his Instrument.

In the world were violins, trumpets, clarinets and krumhorns, as there had been for centuries. Christian knew nothing of that. Only his Instrument was available. It was enough.

One room in Christian's house, which he had alone most of the time, he lived in: a bed (not too soft), a chair and table, a silent machine that cleaned him and his clothing, and an electric light.

The other room contained only his Instrument. It was a console with many keys and strips and levers and bars, and when he touched any part of it, a sound came out. Every key made a different sound; every point on the strips made a different pitch; every lever modified the tone; every bar altered the structure of the sound.

When he first came to the house, Christian played (as children will) with the Instrument, making strange and funny noises. It was his only playmate; he learned it well, could produce any sound he wanted to. At first he delighted in loud, blaring tones. Later he began to play with soft and loud, and to play two sounds at once, and to change those two sounds together to make a new sound, and to play again a sequence of sounds he had played before.

Gradually, the sounds of the forest outside his house found their way into the music he played. He learned to make winds sing through his Instrument; he learned to make summer one of the songs he could play at will; green with its infinite variations was his most subtle harmony; the birds cried out from his Instrument with all the passion of Christian's loneliness.

And the word spread to the licensed Listeners:

"There's a new sound north of here, east of here; Christian Haroldsen, and he'll tear out your heart with his songs."

The Listeners came, a few to whom variety was everything first, then those to whom novelty and vogue mattered most, and at last those who valued beauty and passion above everything else. They came, and stayed out in Christian's woods, and listened as his music was played through perfect speakers on the roof of his house. When the music stopped, and Christian came out of his house, he could see the Listeners moving away; he asked, and was told why they came; he marveled that the things he did for love on his Instrument could be of interest to other people.

He felt, strangely, even more lonely to know that he could sing to the Listeners and yet would never be able to hear their songs.

"But they have no songs," said the woman who came to bring him food every day. "They are listeners. You are a Maker. You have songs, and they listen."

"Why?" asked Christian, innocently.

The woman looked puzzled. "Because that's what they want most to do. They've been tested, and they are happiest as Listeners. You are happiest as a Maker. Aren't you happy?"

"Yes," Christian answered, and he was telling the truth. His life was perfect, and he wouldn't change anything, not even the sweet sadness of the backs of the Listeners as they walked away at the end of his songs.

Christian was seven years old.

FIRST MOVEMENT

For the third time the short man with glasses and a strangely inappropriate mustache dared to wait in the underbrush for Christian to come out. For the third time he was overcome by the beauty of the song that had just ended, a mournful symphony that made the short man with glasses feel the pressure of the leaves above him even though it was summer and they had months left before they would fall. The fall is still inevitable, said Christian's song; through all their life the leaves hold within them the power to die, and that must color their life. The short man with glasses wept—but when the song ended and the other Listeners moved away, he hid in the brush and waited.

This time his wait was rewarded. Christian came out of his house, and walked among the trees, and came toward where the short man with glasses waited. The short man admired the easy, unpostured way that Christian walked. The composer looked to be about thirty, yet there was something childish in the way he looked around him, the way his walk was aimless, and prone to stop just so he could touch (not break) a fallen twig with his bare toes.

"Christian," said the short man with glasses.

Christian turned, startled. In all these years, no Listener had ever spoken to him. It was forbidden. Christian knew the law.

"It's forbidden," Christian said.

"Here," the short man with glasses said, holding out a small black object.

"What is it?"

The short man grimaced. "Just take it. Push the button and it plays."

"Plays?"

"Music."

Christian's eyes went wide. "But that's forbidden. I can't have my creativity polluted by hearing other musicians' work. That would make me imitative and derivative instead of original."

"Reciting," the man said. "You're just reciting that. This is the music of Bach." There was reverence in his voice.

"I can't," Christian said.

And then the short man shook his head. "You don't know. You don't know what you're missing. But I heard it in your song when I came here years ago, Christian. You want this."

"It's forbidden," Christian answered, for to him the very fact that a man who knew an act was forbidden still wanted to perform it was astounding, and he couldn't get past the novelty of it to realize that some action was expected of him.

There were footsteps and words being spoken in the distance, and the short man's face became frightened. He ran at Christian, forced the recorder into his hands, then took off toward the gate of the preserve.

Christian took the recorder and held it in a spot of sunlight through the leaves. It gleamed dully. "Bach," Christian said. Then, "Who is Bach?"

But he didn't throw the recorder down. Nor did he give the recorder to the woman who came to ask him what the short man with glasses had stayed for. "He stayed for at least ten minutes."

"I only saw him for thirty seconds," Christian answered.

"And?"

"He wanted me to hear some other music. He had a recorder."

"Did he give it to you?"

"No," Christian said. "Doesn't he still have it?"

"He must have dropped it in the woods."

"He said it was Bach."

"It's forbidden. That's all you need to know. If you should find the recorder, Christian, you know the law."

"I'll give it to you."

She looked at him carefully. "You know what would happen if you listened to such a thing."

Christian nodded.

"Very well. We'll be looking for it, too. I'll see you tomorrow, Christian. And next time somebody stays after, don't talk to him. Just come back in the house and lock the doors."

"I'll do that," Christian said.

When she left, he played his Instrument for hours. More Listeners came, and those who had heard Christian before were surprised at the confusion in his song.

There was a summer rainstorm that night, wind and rain and thunder, and Christian found that he could not sleep. Not from the music of the weather—he'd slept through a thousand such storms. It was the recorder that lay behind the Instrument against the wall. Christian had lived for nearly thirty years surrounded only by this wild, beautiful place and the music he himself made. But now.

Now he could not stop wondering. Who was Bach? Who *is* Bach? What is his music? How it is different from mine? Has he discovered things that I don't know?

What is his music?

What is his music?

What is his music?

Until at dawn, when the storm was abating and the wind had died, Christian got out of his bed, where he had not slept but only tossed back and forth all night, and took the recorder from its hiding place and played it.

At first it sounded strange, like noise, odd sounds that had nothing to do with the sounds of Christian's life. But the patterns were clear, and by the end of the recording, which was not even a half-hour long, Christian had mastered the idea of fugue and the sound of the harpsichord preyed on his mind.

Yet he knew that if he let these things show up in his music, he would be discovered. So he did not try a fugue. He did not attempt to imitate the harpsichord's sound.

And every night he listened to the recording, for many nights, learning more and more until finally the Watcher came.

The Watcher was blind, and a dog led him. He came to the door and because he was a Watcher the door opened for him without his even knocking.

"Christian Haroldsen, where is the recorder?" the Watcher asked.

"Recorder?" Christian asked, then knew it was hopeless, and took the machine and gave it to the Watcher.

"Oh, Christian," said the Watcher, and his voice was mild and sorrowful. "Why didn't you turn it in without listening to it?"

"I meant to," Christian said. "But how did you know?"

"Because suddenly there are no fugues in your work. Suddenly your songs have lost the only Bachlike thing about them. And you've stopped experimenting with new sounds. What were you trying to avoid?"

"This," Christian said, and he sat down and on his first try duplicated the sound of the harpsichord.

"Yet you've never tried to do that until now, have you?"

"I thought you'd notice."

"Fugues and harpsichord, the two things you noticed first—and the only things you didn't absorb into your music. All your other songs for these last weeks have been tinted and colored and influenced by Bach. Except that there was no fugue, and there was no harpsichord. You have broken the law. You were put here because you were a genius, creating new things with only nature for your inspiration. Now, of course, you're derivative, and truly new creation is impossible for you. You'll have to leave."

"I know," Christian said, afraid yet not really understanding what life outside his house would be like.

"We'll train you for the kinds of jobs you can pursue now. You won't starve. You won't die of boredom. But because you broke the law, one thing is forbidden to you now."

"Music."

"Not all music. There is music of a sort, Christian, that the common people, the ones who aren't Listeners, can have. Radio and television and record music. But living music and new music—those are forbidden to you. You may not sing. You may not play an instrument. You may not tap out a rhythm."

"Why not?"

The Watcher shook his head. "The world is too perfect, too at peace, too happy for us to permit a misfit who broke the law to go about spreading discontent. The common people make casual music of a sort, knowing nothing better because they haven't the aptitude to learn it. But if you—never mind. It's the law. And if you make more music, Christian, you will be punished drastically. Drastically."

Christian nodded, and when the Watcher told him to come, he came, leaving behind the house and the woods and his Instrument. At first he took it calmly, as the inevitable punishment for his infraction; but he had little concept of punishment, or of what exile from his Instrument would mean.

Within five hours he was shouting and striking out at anyone who came near him, because his fingers craved the touch of the Instrument's keys and levers and strips and bars, and he could not have them, and now he knew that he had never been lonely before.

It took six months before he was ready for normal life. And when he left the Retraining Center (a small building, because it was so rarely used), he looked tired, and years older, and he didn't smile at anyone. He became a delivery truck driver, because the tests said that this was a job that would least grieve him, and least remind him of his loss, and most engage his few remaining aptitudes and interests.

He delivered doughnuts to grocery stores.

And at night he discovered the mysteries of alcohol, and the alcohol and the doughnuts and the truck and his dreams were enough that he was, in his way, content. He had no anger in him. He could live the rest of his life this way, without bitterness.

He delivered fresh doughnuts and took the stale ones away with him.

SECOND MOVEMENT

"With a name like Joe," Joe always said, "I had to open a bar and grill, just so I could put up a sign saying Joe's Bar and Grill." And he laughed and laughed, because after all Joe's Bar and Grill was a funny name these days.

But Joe was a good bartender, and the Watcher had put him in the right kind of place. Not in a big city, but in a smaller town; a town just off the freeway, where truck drivers often came; a town not far from a large city, so that interesting things were nearby to be talked about and worried about and bitched about and loved.

Joe's Bar and Grill was, therefore, a nice place to come, and many people came there. Not fashionable people, and not drunks, but lonely people and friendly people in just the right mixture. "My clients are like a good drink, just enough of this and that to make a new flavor that tastes better than any of the ingredients." Oh, Joe was a poet, he was a poet of alcohol and like many another person these days, he often said, "My father was a lawyer, and in the old days I would have probably ended up a lawyer, too, and I never would have known what I was missing."

Joe was right. And he was a damn good bartender, and he didn't wish he were anything else, and so he was happy.

One night, however, a new man came in, a man with a doughnut delivery truck and a doughnut brand name on his uniform. Joe noticed him because silence clung to the man like a smell—wherever he walked, people sensed it, and though they scarcely looked at him, they lowered their voices, or stopped talking at all, and they got reflective and looked at the walls and the mirror behind the bar. The doughnut delivery man sat in a corner and had a watered-down drink that meant he intended to stay a long time and didn't want his alcohol intake to be so rapid that he was forced to leave early.

Joe noticed things about people, and he noticed that this man kept looking off in the dark corner where the piano stood. It was an old, out-of-tune monstrosity from the old days (for this had been a bar for a long time) and Joe wondered why the man was fascinated by it. True, a lot of Joe's customers had been interested, but they had always walked over and plunked on the keys, trying to find a melody, failing with the out-of-tune keys, and finally giving up. This man, however, seemed almost afraid of the piano, and didn't go near it.

At closing time, the man was still there, and then, on a whim, instead of making the man leave, Joe turned off the piped-in music and turned off most of the lights, and then went over and lifted the lid and exposed the grey keys.

The doughnut delivery man came over to the piano. *Chris*, his nametag said. He sat and touched a single key. The sound was not pretty. But the man touched all the keys one by one, and then touched them in different orders, and all the time Joe watched, wondering why the man was so intense about it.

"Chris," Joe said.

Chris looked up at him.

"Do you know any songs?"

Chris's face went funny.

"I mean, some of those old-time songs, not those fancy ass-twitchers on the radio, but *songs*. 'In a Little Spanish Town.' My mother sang that one to me." And Joe began to sing, "In a little Spanish town, 'twas on a night like this. Stars were peek-a-booing down, 'twas on a night like this."

Chris began to play as Joe's weak and toneless baritone went on with the song. But it wasn't an accompaniment, not anything Joe could call an accompaniment. It was instead an opponent to his melody, an enemy to it, and the sounds coming out of the piano were strange and unharmonious and by God beautiful. Joe stopped singing and listened. For two hours he listened, and when it was over he soberly poured the man a drink, and poured one for himself, and clinked glasses with Chris the doughnut delivery man who could take that rotten old piano and make the damn thing sing.

Three nights later Chris came back, looking harried and afraid. But this time Joe knew what would happen (had to happen) and instead of waiting until closing time, Joe turned off the piped-in music ten minutes early. Chris looked up at him pleadingly.

Joe misunderstood—he went over and lifted the lid to the keyboard and smiled. Chris walked stiffly, perhaps reluctantly, to the stool and sat.

"Hey, Joe," one of the last five customers shouted, "closing early?"

Joe didn't answer. Just watched as Chris began to play. No preliminaries this time; no scales and wanderings over the keys. Just power, and the piano was played as pianos aren't meant to be played; the bad notes, the out-of-tune notes were fit into the music so that they sounded right, and Chris's fingers, ignoring the strictures of the twelve-tone scale, played, it seemed to Joe, in the cracks.

None of the customers left until Chris finished an hour and a half later. They all shared that final drink, and went home shaken by the experience.

The next night Chris came again, and the next, and the next. Whatever private battle had kept him away for the first few days after his first night of playing, he had apparently won it or lost it. None of Joe's business. What Joe cared about was the fact that when Chris played the piano, it did things to him that music had never done, and he wanted it.

The customers apparently wanted it, too. Near closing time people began showing up, apparently just to hear Chris play. Joe began starting the piano music earlier and earlier, and he had to discontinue the free drinks after the playing because there were so many people it would have put him out of business.

It went on for two long, strange months. The delivery van pulled up outside, and people stood aside for Chris to enter. No one said anything to him; no one said anything at all, but everyone waited until he began to play the piano. He drank nothing at all. Just played. And between songs the hundreds of people in Joe's Bar and Grill ate and drank.

But the merriment was gone. The laughter and the chatter and the camaraderie were missing, and after a while Joe grew tired of the music and wanted to have his bar back the way it was. He toyed with the idea of getting rid of the piano, but the customers would have been angry at him. He thought of asking Chris not to come anymore, but he could not bring himself to speak to the strange silent man.

And so finally he did what he knew he should have done in the first place. He called the Watchers.

They came in the middle of a performance, a blind Watcher with a dog on a leash, and a Watcher with no ears who walked unsteadily, holding to things for balance. They came in the middle of a song, and did not wait for it to end. They walked to the piano and closed the lid gently, and Chris withdrew his fingers and looked at the closed lid.

"Oh, Christian," said the man with the seeing-eye dog.

"I'm sorry," Christian answered. "I tried not to."

"Oh, Christian, how can I bear doing to you what must be done?"

"Do it," Christian said.

And so the man with no ears took a laser knife from his coat pocket and cut off Christian's fingers and thumbs, right where they rooted into his hands. The laser cauterized and sterilized the wound even as it cut, but still some blood spattered on Christian's uniform. And, his hands now meaningless palms and useless knuckles, Christian stood and walked out of Joe's Bar and Grill. The people made way for him again, and they listened intently as the blind Watcher said, "That was a man who broke the law and was forbidden to be a Maker. He broke the law a second time, and the law insists that he be stopped from breaking down the system that makes all of you so happy."

The people understood. It grieved them, it made them uncomfortable for a few hours, but once they had returned to their exactly-right homes and got back to their exactly-right jobs, the sheer contentment of their lives overwhelmed their momentary sorrow for Chris. After all, Chris had broken the law. And it was the law that kept them all safe and happy.

Even Joe. Even Joe soon forgot Chris and his music. He knew he had done the right thing. He couldn't figure out, though, why a man like Chris would have broken the law in the first place, or what law he would have broken. There wasn't a law in the world that wasn't designed to make people happy—and there wasn't a law Joe could think of that he was even mildly interested in breaking.

Yet. Once Joe went to the piano and lifted the lid and played every key on the piano. And when he had done that he put his head down on the piano and cried, because he knew that when Chris lost that piano, lost even his fingers so he could never play again—it was like Joe losing his bar. And if Joe ever lost his bar, his life wouldn't be worth living.

As for Chris, someone else began coming to the bar driving the same doughnut delivery van, and no one ever knew Chris again in that part of the world.

THIRD MOVEMENT

"Oh what a beautiful mornin'!" sang the road crew man who had seen *Oklahoma!* four times in his home town.

"Rock my soul in the bosom of Abraham!" sang the road crew man who had learned to sing when his family got together with guitars.

"Lead, kindly light, amid the encircling gloom!" sang the road crew man who believed.

But the road crew man without hands, who held the signs telling the traffic to Stop or go Slow, listened but never sang.

"Whyn't you never sing?" asked the road crew man who liked Rodgers and Hammerstein; asked all of them, at one time or another.

And the man they called Sugar just shrugged. "Don't feel like singin'," he'd say, when he said anything at all.

"Why they call him Sugar?" a new guy once asked. "He don't look sweet to me."

And the man who believed said, "His initials are *C H*. Like the sugar. C&H, you know." And the new guy laughed. A stupid joke, but the kind of gag that makes life easier on the road-building crew.

Not that life was that hard. For these men, too, had been tested, and they were in the job that made them happiest. They took pride in the pain of sunburn and pulled muscles, and the road growing long and thin behind them was the most beautiful thing in the world. And so they sang all day at their work, knowing that they could not possibly be happier than they were this day.

Except Sugar.

Then Guillermo came. A short Mexican who spoke with an accent, Guillermo told everyone who asked, "I may come from Sonora, but my heart belongs in Milano!" And when anyone asked why (and often when no one asked anything) he'd explain. "I'm an Italian tenor in a Mexican body," and he proved it by singing every note that Puccini and Verdi ever wrote. "Caruso was nothing," Guillermo boasted. "Listen to this!"

Guillermo had records, and sang along with them, and at work on the road crew he'd join in with any man's song and harmonize with it, or sing an obligato high above the melody, a soaring tenor that took the roof off his head and filled the clouds. "I can sing," Guillermo would say, and soon the other road crew men answered. "Damn right, Guillermo! Sing it again!"

But one night Guillermo was honest, and told the truth. "Ah, my friends, I'm no singer."

"What do you mean? Of course you are!" came the unanimous answer.

"Nonsense!" Guillermo cried, his voice theatrical. "If I am this great singer, why do you never see me going off to record songs? Hey? This is a great singer? Nonsense! Great singers they raise to be great singers. I'm just a man who loves to sing, but has no talent! I'm a man who loves to work on the road crew with men like you, and sing his guts out, but in the opera I could never be! Never!"

He did not say it sadly. He said it fervently, confidently. "Here is where I belong! I can sing to you who like to hear me sing! I can harmonize with you when I feel a harmony in my heart. But don't be thinking that Guillermo is a great singer, because he's not!"

It was an evening of honesty, and every man there explained why it was he was happy on the road crew, and didn't wish to be anywhere else. Everyone, that is, except Sugar.

"Come on, Sugar. Aren't you happy here?"

Sugar smiled. "I'm happy. I like it here. This is good work for me. And I love to hear you sing."

"Then why don't you sing with us?"

Sugar shook his head. "I'm not a singer."

But Guillermo looked at him knowingly. "Not a singer, ha! Not a singer. A man without hands who refuses to sing is not a man who is not a singer. Hey?"

"What the hell does that mean?" asked the man who sang folksongs.

"It means that this man you call Sugar, he's a fraud. Not a singer! Look at his hands. All his fingers gone! Who is it who cuts off men's fingers?"

The road crew didn't try to guess. There were many ways a man could lose fingers, and none of them were anyone's business.

"He loses his fingers because he breaks the law and the Watchers cut them off! That's how a man loses fingers. What was he doing with his fingers that the Watchers wanted him to stop? He was breaking the law, wasn't he?"

"Stop," Sugar said.

"If you want," Guillermo said, but for once the others would not respect Sugar's privacy.

"Tell us," they said.

Sugar left the room.

"Tell us," and Guillermo told them. That Sugar must have been a Maker who broke the law and was forbidden to make music anymore. The very thought that a Maker was working on the road crew with them—even a lawbreaker—filled the men with awe. Makers were rare, and they were the most esteemed of men and women.

"But why his fingers?"

"Because," Guillermo said, "he must have tried to make music again afterward. And when you break the law a second time, the power to break it a third time is taken away from you." Guillermo spoke seriously, and so to the road crew men Sugar's story sounded as majestic and terrible as an opera. They crowded into Sugar's room, and found the man staring at the wall.

"Sugar, is it true?" asked the man who loved Rodgers and Hammerstein.

"Were you a Maker?" asked the man who believed.

"Yes," Sugar said.

"But Sugar," the man who believed said, "God can't mean for a man to stop making music, even if he broke the law."

Sugar smiled. "No one asked God."

"Sugar," Guillermo finally said, "There are nine of us on the crew, nine of us, and we're miles from any human beings. You know us, Sugar. We swear on our mother's graves, every one of us, that we'll never tell a soul. Why should we? You're one of us. But sing, dammit man, sing!"

"I can't," Sugar said. "You don't understand."

"It isn't what God intended," said the man who believed. "We're all doing what we love best, and here you are, loving music and not able to sing a note. Sing for us! Sing with us! And only you and us and God will know!"

They all promised. They all pleaded.

And the next day as the man who loved Rodgers and Hammerstein sang "Love, Look Away," Sugar began to hum. As the man who believed sang "God of Our Fathers" Sugar sang softly along. And as the man who loved folksongs sang "Swing Low, Sweet Chariot," Sugar joined in with a strange, piping voice and all the men laughed and cheered and welcomed Sugar's voice to the songs.

Inevitably Sugar began inventing. First harmonies, of course, strange harmonies that made Guillermo frown and then, after a while, grin as he joined in, sensing as best he could what Sugar was doing to the music.

And after harmonies, Sugar began singing his own melodies, with his own words. He made them repetitive, the word simple and the melodies simpler still. And yet he shaped them into odd shapes, and built them into songs that had never been heard of before, that sounded wrong and yet were absolutely right. It was not long before the man who loved Rodgers and Hammerstein and the man who sang folksongs and the man who believed were learning Sugar's songs and singing them joyously or mournfully or angrily or gaily as they worked along the road.

Even Guillermo learned the songs, and his strong tenor was changed by them until his voice, which had, after all, been ordinary, became something unusual and fine. Guillermo finally said to Sugar one day, "Hey, Sugar, your music is all wrong, man. But I like the way it feels in my nose! Hey, you know? I like the way it feels in my mouth!"

Some of the songs were hymns: "Keep me hungry, Lord," Sugar sang, and the road crew sang it too.

Some of the songs were love songs: "Put your hands in someone else's pockets," Sugar sang angrily; "I hear your voice in the morning," Sugar sang tenderly; "Is it summer yet?" Sugar sang sadly; and the road crew sang it, too.

Over the months the road crew changed, one man leaving on Wednesday and a new man taking his place on Thursday, as different skills were needed in different places. Sugar was silent when each newcomer came, until the man had given his word and the secret was sure to be kept.

What finally destroyed Sugar was the fact that his songs were so unforgettable. The men who left would sing the songs with their new crews, and those crews would learn them, and teach them to others. Crewmen taught the songs in bars and on the road; people learned them quickly, and loved them; and one day a blind Watcher heard the songs and knew, instantly, who had first sung them. They were Christian Haroldsen's music, because in those melodies, simple as they were, the wind of the north woods still whistled and the fall of leaves still hung oppressively over every note and—and the Watcher sighed. He took a specialized tool from his file of tools and boarded an airplane and flew to the city closest to where a certain road crew worked. And the blind Watcher took a company car with a company driver up the road and at the end of it, where the road was just beginning to pierce a strip of wilderness, the blind Watcher got out of the car and heard singing. Heard a piping voice singing a song that made even an eyeless man weep.

"Christian," the Watcher said, and the song stopped.

"You," said Christian.

"Christian, even after you lost your fingers?"

The other men didn't understand—all the other men, that is, except Guillermo.

"Watcher," said Guillermo. "Watcher, he done no harm."

The Watcher smiled wryly. "No one said he did. But he broke the law. You, Guillermo, how would you like to work as a servant in a rich man's house? How would you like to be a bank teller?"

"Don't take me from the road crew, man," Guillermo said.

"It's the law that finds where people will be happy. But Christian Haroldsen broke the law. And he's gone around ever since making people hear music they were never meant to hear."

Guillermo knew he had lost the battle before it began, but he couldn't stop himself. "Don't hurt him, man. I was meant to hear his music. Swear to God, it's made me happier."

The Watcher shook his head sadly. "Be honest, Guillermo. You're an honest man. His music's made you miserable, hasn't it? You've got everything you could want in life, and yet his music makes you sad. All the time, sad."

Guillermo tried to argue, but he was honest, and he looked into his own heart, and he knew that the music was full of grief. Even the happy songs mourned for something; even the angry songs wept; even the love songs seemed to say that everything dies and contentment is the most fleeting thing. Guillermo looked in his own heart and all Sugar's music stared back up at him and Guillermo wept.

"Just don't hurt him, please," Guillermo murmured as he cried.

"I won't," the blind Watcher said. Then he walked to Christian, who stood passively waiting, and he held the special tool up to Christian's throat. Christian gasped.

"No," Christian said, but the word only formed with his lips and tongue. No sound came out. Just a hiss of air. "No."

The road crew watched silently as the Watcher led Christian away. They did not sing for days. But then Guillermo forgot his grief one day and sang an aria from *La Bohème*, and the songs went on from there. Now and then they sang one of Sugar's songs, because the songs could not be forgotten.

In the city, the blind Watcher furnished Christian with a pad of paper and a pen. Christian immediately gripped the pencil in the crease of his palm and wrote: "What do I do now?"

The driver read the note aloud, and the blind Watcher laughed. "Have we got a job for you! Oh, Christian, have we got a job for you!" The dog barked loudly, to hear his master laugh.

APPLAUSE

In all the world there were only two dozen Watchers. They were secretive men, who supervised a system that needed little supervision because it actually made nearly everybody happy. It was a good system, but like even the most perfect of machines, here and there it broke down. Here and there someone acted madly, and damaged himself, and to protect everyone and the person himself, a Watcher had to notice the madness and go to fix it.

For many years the best of the Watchers was a man with no fingers, a man with no voice. He would come silently, wearing the uniform that named him with the only name he needed—Authority. And he would find the kindest, easiest, yet most thorough way of solving the problem and curing the madness and preserving the system that made the world, for the first time in history, a very good place to live. For practically everyone.

For there were still a few people—one or two each year—who were caught in a circle of their own devising, who could neither adjust to the system nor bear to harm it, people who kept breaking the law despite their knowledge that it would destroy them.

Eventually, when the gentle maimings and deprivations did not cure their madness and set them back into the system, they were given uniforms and they, too, went out. Watching.

The keys of power were placed in the hands of those who had most cause to hate the system they had to preserve. Were they sorrowful?

"I am," Christian answered in the moments when he dared to ask himself that question.

In sorrow he did his duty. In sorrow he grew old. And finally the other Watchers, who reverenced the silent man (for they knew he had once sung magnificent songs), told him he was free. "You've served your time," said the Watcher with no legs, and he smiled.

Christian raised an eyebrow, as if to say, "And?"

"So wander."

Christian wandered. He took off his uniform, but lacking neither money nor time he found few doors closed to him. He wandered where in his former lives he had once lived. A road in the mountains. A city where he had once known the loading entrance of every restaurant and coffee shop and grocery store. And at last to a place in the woods where a house was falling apart in the weather because it had not been used in forty years.

Christian was old. The thunder roared and it only made him realize that it was about to rain. All the old songs. All the old songs, he mourned inside himself, more because he couldn't remember them than because he thought his life had been particularly sad.

As he sat in a coffee shop in a nearby town to stay out of the rain, he heard four teenagers who played the guitar very badly singing a song that he knew. It was a song he had invented while the asphalt poured on a hot summer day. The teenagers were not musicians and certainly were not Makers. But they sang the song from their hearts, and even though the words were happy, the song made everyone who heard it cry.

Christian wrote on the pad he always carried, and showed his question to the boys. "Where did that song come from?"

"It's a Sugar song," the leader of the group answered. "It's a song by Sugar."

Christian raised an eyebrow, making a shrugging motion.

"Sugar was a guy who worked on a road crew and made up songs. He's dead now, though," the boy answered.

"Best damn songs in the world," another boy said, and they all nodded.

Christian smiled. Then he wrote (and the boys waited impatiently for this speechless old man to go away): "Aren't you happy? Why sing sad songs?"

The boys were at a loss for an answer. The leader spoke up, though, and said, "Sure I'm happy. I've got a good job, a girl I like, and man, I couldn't ask for more. I got my guitar. I got my songs. And my friends."

And another boy said, "These songs aren't sad, Mister. Sure, they make people cry, but they aren't sad."

"Yeah," said another. "It's just that they were written by a man who knows."

Christian scribbled on his paper. "Knows what?"

"He just knows. Just knows, that's all. Knows it all."

And then the teenagers turned back to their clumsy guitars and their young, untrained voices, and Christian walked to the door to leave because the rain had stopped and because he knew when to leave the stage. He turned and bowed just a little toward the singers. They didn't notice him, but their voices were all the applause he needed. He left the ovation and went outside where the leaves were just turning color and would soon, with a slight inaudible sound, break free and fall to the earth.

For a moment he thought he heard himself singing. But it was just the last of the wind, coasting madly through the wires over the street. It was a frenzied song, and Christian thought he recognized his voice.

A CROSS-COUNTRY TRIP TO KILL RICHARD NIXON

S iggy wasn't the killer type. Nor did he have delusions of grandeur. In fact, if he had any delusions, they were delusions of happiness. When he was thirty, he gave up a good job as a commercial artist and went down in the world, deliberately downward in income, prestige, and tension. He bought a cab.

"Who is going to drive this cab, Siggy?" his mother asked. She was a German of the old school, well-bred with contempt for the servant class.

"I am," Siggy answered mildly. He endured the tirade that followed, but from then on his sole source of income was the cab. He didn't work every day. But whenever he felt like working or getting out of the apartment or picking up some money, he would take his cab out in Manhattan. His cab was spotless. He gave excellent service. He enjoyed himself immensely. And when he came home, he sat down at the easel or with a sketchpad on his knees, and did art. He wasn't very good. His talents had been best suited for commercial art. Anything more difficult than the back of a Cheerios box, and Siggy was out of his element. He never sold any of his paintings. But he didn't really care. He loved everything he did and everything he was.

So did his wife, Marie. She was French, he was German; they married and moved to America on the eve of World War II, bringing their families with them, and they were exquisitely well matched and happy through both of Siggy's careers. In 1978, at the age of fifty-seven, she died of a heart attack, and Siggy took the cab out and drove for eleven hours without picking up a single fare. At four o'clock in the morning, he finally made his decision and drove home. He would go on living. And sooner than he expected, he was happy again.

He had never dreamed of conquering the world or of getting rich or even of getting into bed with a movie star or a high-class prostitute. So it was not in his nature to imagine himself doing impossible things. It took him rather by surprise when he was chosen to save America.

She was a Disney fairy godmother, and she came in the craziest dream he had ever had. "You, Siegfried Reinhardt, are the lucky winner of exactly one wish," she said, sounding like the lady from Magic Carpet Land the last time she called to offer a free carpet cleaning.

"One?" Siggy answered in his dream, thinking this was rather below standard for godmothers.

"And you have a choice," the fairy godmother answered. "You may either use the wish on your own behalf, or you may use it to save America."

"America's going to hell and needs all the wishes it can get." Siggy said. "On the other hand, I don't really need anything I haven't got already. So it's America."

"Very well," she answered, and turned to go.

"Wait a minute," he said in his dream. "Is that all?"

"You asked for a wish for America, you get a wish for America. Which is a waste of a perfectly good wish, if you ask me, for thirty years America hasn't been worth *scheisse*. Try not to mess things up too badly, Siggy. This wish business is pretty complicated, and you're a simple type fellow." And then she was gone, and Siggy woke up, the dream impressed on his memory as dreams so rarely were.

Crazy, crazy, he thought, laughing it off. I'm getting old, Marie dragged me to too many Disney movies, I'm too lonely. But for all that he knew the dream was nonsense, he could not forget it.

I mean, what *if*, he told himself. What *if* I had a wish. Just one thing I could change, to make everybody in America happier. What would it be?

"What's wrong with America?" his mother asked, rolling her eyes and rocking back and forth in her wheelchair. To Siggy's knowledge she had never had a rocking chair in her life, and compensated by moving in every other kind of chair as if it were a rocker. "Everything's wrong with America," she said.

"But one thing, Mother. Just the worst thing to fix."

"It's too late, nothing can fix it. It all started with *him*. If there is such a thing as reincarnation, may he be reincarnated as a fly that I can swat. May he come back as a fire hydrant for all the dogs to pee against." Siggy's mother was impeccably polite in German, but in English she was crude, and, as so often before, Siggy wondered why she still lingered on at a ridiculous ninety-two when Marie, who was delicate and sensitive, was dead. "Don't be crude, Mother."

"I'm an American, I have the papers, I can be crude. Nineteen sixty-eight, that's when everything went to Hell."

"You can't blame everything on one man."

"What do you know? You drive a cab."

"One man doesn't make that big a difference."

"What about Adolf Hitler!" his mother said triumphantly, slapping the arms of the wheelchair and rocking back and forth. "Adolf Hitler! One man! Just like Richard Nixon, may his electric razor short-circuit and fry his face."

She was still laughing and cursing Nixon when Siggy finally left. Fairy godmother, he said to himself. What do I need a fairy godmother for? I have Mom.

But the dream wouldn't go away. The fairy godmother kept flitting in and out, hovering on the edges of all his dreams, wordlessly saying, "Hurry and make up your mind, Siggy. Fairy godmothers are busy, you're wasting my time."

"Don't push me," he said. "I'm being careful."

"I've got other clients, give me a break."

"I resent being pushed around by figments of my imagination," he said. "I get one wish, I want to use it right." When he woke up, he was vaguely embarrassed that he was taking the fairy godmother so seriously in his dreams. "Just a dream," he said to himself. But dream or not, he started doing research.

He took a poll. He kept a notebook beside him in the cab, and asked people, "Just out of curiosity what's the worst thing wrong with America? What's the one thing you'd change if you could?"

There were quite a few suggestions, but they always came back to Richard Nixon. "It all started with Nixon," they'd say. Or, "It's Carter. But if it hadn't been for Nixon, Carter would never have been elected."

"It's the unions, driving up prices," said a woman. And then, after a little thought, "If Nixon hadn't screwed up we might have kept some *control* in this country."

It wasn't just that his name kept coming up. It was the way people *said* it. With loathing, with contempt, with fear. It was an emotional word. It sounded evil. They said *Nixon* the way they might say *slime*. Or *spider*.

Siggy sat one night staring at the results of his poll, unable to get out of his cab because of the thoughts that had taken over his head. I'm crazy, he thought to himself, but his thoughts ignored him and went right on, the fairy godmother giggling in the background. Richard Nixon, said the thoughts. If there could be one wish, it must be used to eliminate Richard Nixon.

But I voted for him, dammit, Siggy said silently. He *thought* it would be silent, but the words echoed inside the cab after all. "I voted for him. And I thought he did a damn good job sometimes." He was almost embarrassed saying the words—they weren't the kind of sentiment that made a cabby popular with his paying passengers. But thinking of Nixon made him remember the triumphant moment when Nixon said Up Yours to the North Vietnamese and bombed the hell out of them and got them to the negotiating table that one last time. And the wonderful landslide election that kept the crazy man from South Dakota out of the White House. And the trip to China, and the trip to Russia, and the feeling that America was maybe strong like it had been under Roosevelt when Hitler got his ass kicked up into his throat. Siggy remembered that, remembered that it felt good, remembered being angry as the press attacked and attacked and attacked and finally Nixon fell apart and turned out to be exactly as rotten a person as the papers said he was.

And the feeling of betrayal that he had felt all through 1973 came back, and Siggy said, "Nixon," and inside the cab his voice sounded even more poisonous than the passengers'.

If there was something wrong with America, Siggy knew then, it was Richard Nixon. Whether a person had ever liked him or not. Because those who liked him had been betrayed, and those who hated him had not been appeased, and there he was out in California breeding the hatred that surpassed even the hatred for the phone company and the unions and the oil companies and the Congress.

I will wish him dead, Siggy thought. And inside his mind he could hear the fairy godmother cheering. "Make the wish," she said.

"Not yet," Siggy said. "I've got to be fair."

"Fair, schmair. Make the wish, I've got work to do."

"I've got to talk to him first," Siggy said. "I can't wish him dead without he has a chance to say his piece."

Siggy had planned to travel alone. Who would understand his purpose, when he didn't really understand it himself? He told no one he was going, just pulled five hundred dollars out of the bank and got in his cab and started driving. New Jersey, Pennsylvania; found himself on I-70 and decided what the hell, I-70 goes most of the way, that's my highway. He stopped at Richmond, Indiana, to go to the bathroom and get something to eat, then decided to spend the night in a cheap motel.

It was his first night in unfamiliar surroundings in years. It bothered him; things were out of place, and the sheets were rough and harsh, and there weren't a hundred reminders of Marie and happiness. He slept badly (but, thank heaven, without the fairy godmother), and when he left in the morning he realized that he was lonelier then he thought possible. He wasn't used to driving without conversation. He wasn't used to driving without a fare.

So he picked up a hitchhiker waiting by the on-ramp to the freeway. It was a boy —no, in his own eyes doubtless a man—in his early twenties. Hair fairly long, but cleaner than the usual scruffy roadside bum, and he'd be somebody to talk to, and if there was any trouble, well, Siggy had always carried a tire iron beside the seat, though he was not quite sure what he would ever do with it, or when. It made him feel safe. Safe enough to pull over and pick up the boy.

Siggy reached over and opened the car door as the boy ran up.

"Hey, uh," the boy said, leaning into the car. "I don't need a cab, I need a free ride."

"Don't we all," Siggy said, smiling. "I'm from New York City. In Indiana, I give free rides. I'm on vacation."

The boy nodded and got in beside him. Siggy moved out and was on the freeway in moments, going at a steady fifty-five. He put on the cruise control and glanced at the boy. He was looking out the front window, his face glum.

"Where are you going?" Siggy asked.

"West."

"There's lots of west in the world. Wherever you go, there's still more west on ahead."

"They put an ocean at the end, I stop before I get wet, OK?"

"*I'm* going to Los Angeles," Siggy offered.

The boy said nothing. Obviously didn't want to talk. That was all right. Lots of customers liked silence, and Siggy had no objection to giving it to them. Enough that there was someone breathing in the car. It gave Siggy a feeling of legitimacy. It was all right to drive as long as someone else was in the car.

But this couldn't go on all the way, of course, Siggy realized. When he picked the boy up, he figured on St. Louis, maybe Kansas City, then the boy gets out and Siggy's alone again. He'd have to stop for the night, Denver, maybe. Did the boy think a motel room went along with the ride?

"Where you from?"

The boy seemed to wake up, as if he had dozed off with his eyes wide open. Looking out on Indiana as it went by.

"What do you mean, from?" the boy asked.

"I mean *from*, the opposite of *to*. I mean, where were you born, where do you live?"

"I was born in Rochester. I don't think I live anywhere."

"Rochester. What's it like in Rochester?"

"I lived in a Mafia neighborhood. Everybody kept their yards neat and nobody ever broke into the houses."

"A lot of factories?"

"Eastman Kodak and Xerox Corporation. There's a lot of shit in the world, and Rochester exists by making copies of it." The boy said it bitterly, but Siggy laughed. It was funny, after all. The boy finally smiled, too.

"What are you going to do in California?" Siggy asked.

"Find a place to sleep and maybe a job."

"Want to be an actor?"

The boy looked at Siggy with contempt. "An *actor?* Like Jane Fonda?" He said the name like poison. The tone of voice was familiar. Siggy decided to try him out on the Name.

"What do you think of Richard Nixon?" Siggy asked.

"I don't," said the boy.

And then, madly, knowing it could ruin everything, Siggy blurted, "I'm going to get him."

"What?" the boy asked.

Siggy recovered his senses. Some of them, anyway. "I'm going to meet him. At San Clemente."

The boy laughed. "What do you want to meet him for?"

Siggy shrugged.

"They won't let you near him anyway. You think he wants to see people like us? Nixon." And there it was. The tone of voice. The contempt. Siggy was reassured. He was doing the right thing.

The hours passed and so did the states. Illinois came and went, and they crossed the Mississippi at St. Louis. Not as big as Siggy had expected, but still a hell of a lot of water, when you thought about it. Then Missouri, which was too wide and too dull. And because it was dull, they kept talking. The boy had a bitter streak a mile wide—everything seemed to lead to it. Siggy found it more comfortable to do the talking himself, and since the boy kept listening and saying something now and then, it seemed OK. They were beginning to pass signs that promised Kansas City as if it were a prize when Siggy got on the subject of Marie. Remembered things about her. How she loved wine—a French vice that Siggy loved in her.

"When she was a little drunk," he told the boy, "her eyes would get big. Sometimes full of tears, but she'd still smile. And she'd lift up her chin and stretch her neck. Like a deer."

Maybe the boy was getting tired of the conversation. Maybe he just resented hearing about a love that actually worked. He answered snappishly. "When you ever seen a deer, Manhattan cabdriver? The zoo?"

Siggy refused to be offended. "She was like a deer."

"I think she sounds like a giraffe." The boy smirked a little, as if saying this were somehow a victory over Siggy. Well, it was. It had worn down his patience.

"It's my wife we're talking about. She died two years ago."

"What do I care? I mean what makes you think I give a pink shit about it? You want to cry? You want to get all weepy about it? Then do it quiet. Jesus, give a guy a break, will you?"

Siggy kept his eyes on the road. There was a bitter feeling in his stomach. For a moment his hands felt violent, and he gripped the wheel. Then the feeling passed, and he got his curiosity back again.

"Hey, what're you so mad about?"

"Mad? What says I'm mad?"

"You sounded mad."

"I sounded mad!"

"Yeah, I wondered if maybe you wanted to talk about it."

The boy laughed acidly. "What, the seat reclines? It becomes maybe a couch? I stuck my thumb out because I wanted a ride. I want psychoanalysis, I stick out a different finger, you understand?"

"Hey, fine, relax."

"I'm not tense, shithead." He gripped the door handle so tightly that Siggy was afraid the door would crumple like tinfoil and fall away from the car.

"I'm sorry," the boy said finally, still looking forward. He didn't let go of the door.

"It's OK," Siggy answered.

"About your wife, I mean. I'm not like that. I don't just go around making fun of people's dead wives."

"Yeah."

"And you're right. I'm mad."

"At me?"

"You? What're you? A piss-ant. One of twelve million piss-ants in New York City. We're all piss-ants."

"What're you mad at?" Siggy could not resist adding the figures to his checklist. "Inflation? Oil companies? Nuclear plants?"

"What is this, the Gallup poll?"

"Maybe yeah. People get mad at a lot of the same things. Nuclear plants then?"

"I'm mad at nuclear plants, yeah."

"You want 'em all shut down, right?"

"Wrong, turkey. I want 'em to build a million of 'em. I want 'em to build 'em everywhere, and then on the count of three they all blow up, they wipe out this whole country."

"America?"

"From sea to shitting sea."

Then silence again. Siggy thought he could feel the whole car trembling with the young man's anger. It made Siggy sad. He kept glancing at the boy's face. It wasn't old. There were some acne scars; the beard was thin in quite a few places. Siggy tried to imagine the face without the beard. Without the anger. Without the too many drugs and too many bottles. The face when it was childish and innocent.

"You know," Siggy said, "I can't believe—I look at you, I can't believe that somebody loved you once."

"Nobody asked you to believe it."

"But they must have, right? Somebody taught you to walk. And talk. And ride a bicycle. You had a father, right?"

Suddenly the boy's fist shot out and slammed into the glove compartment door, which popped open with a crash. Siggy was startled, afraid. The boy showed no sign of pain, though it seemed he had hit hard enough to break a finger.

"Hey, careful," Siggy said.

"You want me to be careful? You tell me to be careful, asshole?" The boy grabbed the steering wheel, jerked on it. The taxi swung into another lane; a car behind them squealed on its brakes and honked.

"Are you crazy? Do you want to get us killed? Get mad, wreck the car, but don't kill us!" Siggy was screaming in anger, and the boy sat there, trembling, his eyes not quite focused. Then the car that had honked at them pulled up beside them on the right. The driver was yelling something with his window down. His face looked ugly with anger. The boy held up his middle finger. The man made the same gesture back again.

And suddenly the boy rolled down the window. "Hey, don't get us in trouble," Siggy said. The boy ignored him. He yelled a string of obscenities out the window. Siggy sped up, trying to pull away from the other car. The driver of the other car kept pace with him, yelled back his own curses.

And then the boy pulled a revolver out of his pocket, a big, mean-looking black pistol, and aimed it out the window at the driver of the other car. The man suddenly looked terrified. Siggy slammed on the brakes, but so did the other driver, and they stayed nearly parallel.

"Don't!" Siggy screamed, and he sped up, leaving the other car in the distance. The boy pulled the gun back into the car and laid it on his lap, the cock still back, his finger still on the trigger.

"It isn't loaded, right?" Siggy asked. "It was just a joke, right? Would you take your finger off the trigger?"

But it was as if the boy didn't hear him. As if he didn't even remember the last few minutes. "You wanted to know if I had a father, right? I have a father."

At the moment Siggy didn't much care whether the boy had been born in a test tube. But better he should talk about his father than wave the gun around.

"My father," said the boy, "spends his life making sure enough Xerox machines are getting sold and putting more ads in the magazines when they aren't."

They crossed the border into Kansas, and Siggy hoped the incident with the pistol wouldn't get reported across state lines.

"My father never taught me to ride a bike. My brother did. My brother was killed in Mr. President Nixon's war. You know?"

"That was a long time ago," Siggy said.

The boy looked at him coldly. "It was yesterday, asshole. You don't believe those calendars, do you? All lies, so we'll think it's OK to forget about it. Maybe your wife died years ago, Mr. Cabdriver, but I thought you loved her better than that."

Then the boy looked down at the pistol in his lap, still cocked, still ready to fire. "I thought I left this home," he said in surprise. "What's it doing here?"

"I should know?" Siggy asked. "Do me a favor, uncock the thing and put it away."

"OK," the boy said. But he didn't do anything.

"Hey, please," Siggy said. "You scare me, that thing sitting there ready to shoot."

The boy bowed his head over the pistol for a few moments. "Let me out," he said. "Let me get out."

"Hey, come on, just put the gun away, you don't have to get out, I won't be mad, just put the gun away."

The boy looked up at him and there were tears in his eyes, spilling out onto his cheeks. "You think I brought this gun by accident? I don't want to kill you."

"Then why'd you bring it?"

"I don't know. Jesus, man, let me out."

"You want to go to California, I'm going to California."

"I'm dangerous," the boy said.

Damn right you're dangerous, Siggy thought. Damn right. And I'm a doubledamned fool not to let you out of here right this second, right this minute, very next off-ramp I'll pull over and let him off.

"Not to me," Siggy said, wondering why he wasn't more afraid.

"To you. I'm dangerous to you."

"Not to me." And Siggy realized why he was so confident. It was the fairy godmother, sitting inside the back of his head. "You think I'm going to let anything happen to you, *dummkopf?*" she asked him silently. "If you knock off before you make your wish, it ruins my life. The clerical work alone would take years." I'm crazy, thought Siggy. This boy is nuts, but I'm crazy.

"Yeah," the boy said finally, gently letting down the hammer and putting the gun back into the pocket of his jacket. "Not to you."

They drove in silence for a while, as the plains flattened out and the sky went even flatter and the sun went dim behind the gray overcast. "Richard Nixon, huh?" the boy asked.

"Yeah."

"You really think they'll let us get near him?"

"I'll see to it," Siggy said. And it occurred to him for the first time that fairy godmothers might fulfill wishes in unpleasant ways. Wish him dead? I should wish Nixion dead, and this boy goes to prison forever for killing him? Watch it, fairy godmother, he warned. I won't let you trick me. I have a plan, and I won't let you trick me into hurting this boy.

"Hungry, Son?" Siggy asked. "Or can you hold out till Denver?"

"Denver's fine," said the boy. "But don't call me Son."

It was hot in Los Angeles, but as Siggy neared the sea the breezes became steadily cooler. He was tired. He was used to driving, but not so long a stretch, not so far. In a way the freeways were restful—no traffic, no guesswork about where the car to the right would be a few minutes later. People actually paid attention to the lines between lanes. But the freeways went on, relentlessly, mile after mile, until he felt like he was standing still and the road and the scenery played swiftly past him and under him. At last they had brought Los Angeles to him, and here the scenery would stop for him and wait for him to act. San Clemente. Richard Nixon's house. He found them easily, as if he had always known the way. The boy, asleep beside him for the last few hundred miles, woke up when Siggy brought the cab to a halt.

"What?" asked the boy, sleepily.

"Go back to sleep," Siggy said, getting out of the car. The boy got out, too. "This is it?"

"Yes," Siggy said, already walking toward the entrance.

"I gotta pee," the boy said. But Siggy ignored him, and kept on walking. The boy followed, ran a little, caught up, saying softly, "Shit can't you even wait a minute?"

Secret Service men were everywhere, of course, but by now Siggy's madness was complete. He knew that they could not stop him. He had to meet Richard Nixon, and so he would. He had parked a long way from the mansion, and he just walked in, the boy at his heels. He didn't climb fences or do anything extraordinary. Just walked up the drive, around the house, and out onto the beach. No one saw him. No one called out to him. Secret Servicemen seemed always to have their backs to him, or to be on an urgent errand somewhere else. He would have his meeting with Richard Nixon. He would use his wish.

And he was standing where the water charged up the sand, always falling short of its last achievement as the tide ebbed. The boy stood beside him. Siggy watched the house, but the boy watched Siggy. "I thought they had us," the boy said. "I can't believe we got in here."

"Sh," Siggy answered softly. "Sh."

Siggy felt as nervous as a virgin at her wedding, more dreading than longing for what was to come. What if Nixon thinks I'm a fool? he thought. He needn't have worried. As he stood in the sand, Nixon emerged from the house, came down to the beach, and stopped at the waterline, staring out to sea. He was alone.

Taking a deep breath, Siggy walked to him. The sand kept slipping under his feet, so that every step forward tried to turn him out of his path. He persevered, and stood beside Richard Nixon. It was the face, the nose, at once the heavily shadowed evil face of the Herblock cartoons and the hopeful, strong face of the man Siggy had voted for three times.

"Mr. Nixon," Siggy said.

Nixon did not turn at first. He just said, "How did you get here?"

Siggy shrugged. "I had to see you."

Then Nixon turned to him, his face set to smile. Siggy watched as Nixon's eyes met his, then glanced over his shoulder at the boy, who was walking up, who stopped just behind Siggy.

The boy spoke. "We've come to kill you," he said.

And the boy had his hand in his pocket, where the gun was, and Siggy felt a moment of panic. But the voice of the fairy godmother sounded gently in his ear. "Don't worry," she said. "Take your time."

So Siggy shook his head at the boy, who frowned but did not shoot, and then Siggy turned back to Nixon. The former president was still smiling, his eyes narrowed a bit, but not showing any fear. Siggy felt a moment of satisfaction. This was the Nixon he had admired, the man with such great physical courage, who had faced mobs of Communists in Venezuela and Peru without flinching.

"You wouldn't be the first to want to," Nixon said.

"Oh, but I don't want to," Siggy said. "I have to. For America."

"Ah." Nixon nodded, knowingly. "We all do the most unpleasant things, don't we, for America."

Siggy felt a stab of relief. He understood, which would make it all so much easier.

"You're lucky," Nixon said. "I came out here alone, this once. To say good-bye. I'm leaving here. Tomorrow I would have been gone." He shook his head slightly, slowly, from side to side. "Well, get on with it. I can't stop you."

"Oh," Siggy said. "I'm not going to shoot you. All I have to do is *wish* you dead." Behind him Siggy heard the boy gasp a little. And Nixon sighed slightly. For a moment it sounded to Siggy like disappointment. Then he realized it was relief. And the smile returned to Nixon's face.

"But not today," Siggy went on. I can't just wish for you to be assassinated now, Mr. Nixon. Or for you to die in bed or in an accident. The damage is done. So I'll have to have you die in the past."

The boy made a soft noise behind him.

.   Nixon nodded wisely. "That will be much better, I think."

"So I've decided that the best time will be right after you're sworn into office the second time. In 1972, before the Watergate thing got out of hand, right after you got a peace treaty from the Vietnamese and right after your landslide victory. Then an assassin picks you off, and you're a bigger hero and a greater legend than Kennedy."

"And everything since then?" Nixon asked.

"Changed. They won't keep after you, you see, after you're dead. You'll be a pleasant memory to almost everybody. Their hate will be gone, mostly."

Nixon shook his head. "You said your wish was supposed to be for the good of America, didn't you?"

Siggy nodded.

"Well, if I had been assassinated then, Spiro Agnew would have become president."

Siggy had forgotten. Spiro Agnew. What a bum. There was no way that could be good for the country. "You're right," Siggy said. "So it'll have to be before. Right before the election. It'll be almost as good then, you were leading in the polls."

"But then," Nixon said, "George McGovern would have been president."

Worse and worse. Siggy began to realize the difficulties involved in carrying out his responsibility. Everything he changed would have consequences. How could he fix the country's woes, if he kept increasing them with the changes he made?

"And if you have me killed in 1968, it's either Spiro Agnew or Hubert Humphrey," Nixon added. "Maybe you'll just have to wish for me to win in 1960."

Siggy thought of that. Thought very carefully. "No," he said. "That would be good for *you*. It would have made you a better president, not to have those bad experiences first. But would you have taken us to the moon? Would you have kept the Vietnam War as small as it was?"

"Smaller," Nixon said. "I would have won it by 1964."

Siggy shook his head. "And been at war with Red China, and the world might have been destroyed, and millions of people killed. I don't think the wrong man won in 1960."

Nixon's face went kind of sad. "Then maybe it would be kindest of all if you simply wished for me to lose every election I ever tried. Keep me out of Congress, out of the vice-presidency. Let me be a used car salesman." And he smiled a twisted, sad smile.

Siggy reached out and touched the man's shoulder. "Maybe I should," he said, and the boy behind him made another soft sound.

"But no," Nixon said. "You wanted to save America. And it wouldn't make any difference to keep me out of government. If it hadn't been me, it would have been someone else. There would have been a Richard Nixon anyway. If they hadn't wanted me, I wouldn't have been there. If Richard Nixon hadn't existed, they would have made one."

Siggy sighed. "Then I don't know what to do," he said.

Nixon turned and looked out over the water. "I only did what they wanted me to do. And when they changed their minds, they were surprised at what I was." The beach was cold and damp between waves. The breeze from the land carried the air of Los Angeles with it, and it made the beach smell slimy and old. "Maybe," Nixon said, "there's nothing you can wish for that will save America. Maybe there's nothing you can do at all."

And the noise the boy made was loud enough that Siggy at last turned to look at him. To his surprise, the boy was no longer standing up. He was sitting cross-legged in the sand, bowed over, his hands gripping each other behind his neck. His body shook.

"What's wrong, Son?" Nixon asked. He sounded concerned.

The boy looked up, anger and grief in his face. "You," he said, and his voice shook. "*You* can call me Son."

Nixon knelt in the sand, painfully as if his leg hurt, and touched the boy's shoulder. "What's wrong, Son?"

"His brother was killed in Vietnam," Siggy said, as if that explained anything.

"I'm sorry," Nixon said. "I'm really sorry."

The boy threw off Nixon's hand. "Do you think that matters? Do you think it makes any difference how *sorry* you are?" The words stung Nixon, clearly. He shuddered as if his face had been slapped.

"I don't know what else I can do," Nixon said softly.

The boy's hand shot out and grabbed him by the lapels of his suit, pulling him down until they were face to face, and the boy screamed, "You can pay for it! You can pay and pay and pay—" and the boy's lips and teeth were almost touching Nixon's face, and Nixon looked pathetic and helpless in the boy's grip, flecks of the boy's spit beginning to dot his cheeks and lips. Siggy watched, and realized there was nothing that Nixon could do that would pay it all, that would give the boy back what he had lost, realized that Nixon had not really taken it from the boy. Had not taken it, could not return it, was as much a victim as anyone else. How could Siggy, with a single wish, set it all right? How could he even up all the scales?

"Think, idiot," said the fairy godmother. "I'm losing patience."

"I don't know what to do," he said to her.

"And you're the one with the plan," she answered contemptuously.

The boy was still screaming, again and again, and Nixon was weeping now, silently letting the tears flow to join the spittle on his face, as if to agree, as if to make it unanimous.

"I wish," said Siggy, "for everyone to forgive you, Mr. Nixon. For everyone in America to stop hating you, little by little, until all the hate is gone."

The fairy godmother danced in his mind, waving her wand around and turning everything pink.

And the boy stopped screaming and let go of Nixon, gazed wonderingly into the old man's eyes at the tears there, and said, "I'm sorry for you," and meant it with all his heart. Then Siggy helped the boy to his feet and they turned away, leaving Nixon on the beach. The world was tinged with pink and Siggy put his arm around the boy and they smiled at each other. And they headed back to the cab. Siggy saw the fairy godmother flying away ahead of them, north and east from San Clemente, trailing stars behind her as she flew.

"Bibbity bobbity boo," she cried, and she was gone.

THE PORCELAIN SALAMANDER

T hey called their country the Beautiful Land, and they were right. It perched on the edge of the continent. Before the Beautiful Land stretched the broad ocean, which few dared to cross; behind it stood the steep Rising, a cliff so high and sheer that few dared to climb. And in such isolation the people, who called themselves, of course, the Beautiful People, lived splendid lives.

Not all were rich, of course. And not all were happy. But there was such a majesty to living in the Beautiful Land that the poverty could easily be missed by the undiscerning eye, and misery seemed so very fleeting.

Except to Kiren.

To Kiren, misery was the way of life. For though she lived in a rich house with servants and had, it seemed, anything she could possibly want, she was deeply miserable most of the time. For this was a land where cursing and blessing and magic worked— not always, and not always in the way the person doing it might have planned—but sometimes the cursing worked, and in her case it had.

Not that she had done anything to deserve it; she had been as innocent as any other child in her cradle. But her mother had been a weak woman, and the pain and terror of giving birth had killed her. And Kiren's father loved his wife so much that when he learned of the news, and saw the baby that had been born even as her mother died, he cried out, "You killed her! You killed her! May you never move a muscle in your life, until you lose someone you love as much as I loved her!" It was a terrible curse, and the nurse wept when she heard it, and the doctors stopped Kiren's father's mouth so that he could say no more in his madness.

But his curse took hold, and though he regretted it a million times during Kiren's infancy and childhood, there was nothing he could do. Oh, the curse was not all *that* strong. Kiren did learn to walk, after a fashion. And she could stand for as much as two minutes at a time. But most of the times she sat or lay down, because she grew so weary, and her muscles only weakly did what she told them to. She could lift a spoon to her mouth, but soon became tired, and had to be fed. She scarcely had the energy to chew.

And every time her father saw her, he wanted to weep, and often did weep. And sometimes he even thought of killing himself to finally wipe away his guilt. But he knew that this would only injure poor Kiren even more, and she had done nothing to deserve injury.

When his guilt grew too much for him to bear, however, he did escape. He put a bag of fine fruits and clever handwork from the Beautiful Land on his back, and set out for the Rising. He would be gone for months, and no one knew when he would return, or whether the Rising would this time prove too much for him and send him plunging to his death. But when he returned, he always brought something for Kiren. And for a while she would smile, and she would say, "Father, thank you." And things would go well, for a time, until she again became despondent and her father again suffered from watching the results of his ill-thought curse.

It was late spring in the year Kiren turned eleven when her father came home even happier than he usually was after a trip up the Rising. He rushed to his daughter where she lay wanly on the porch listening to the birds.

"Kiren!" he cried. "Kiren! I've brought you a gift!"

And she smiled, though even the muscles for smiling were weak, which made her smile sad. Her father reached into his bag (which was full of all kinds of wonders, which he would, being a careful man, sell to those with money to pay, not just for goods, but for rarity) and he pulled out his gift and handed it to Kiren.

It was a box, and the box lurched violently this way and that.

"There's something alive in there," Kiren said.

"No, my dear Kiren, there is not. But there's something moving, and it's yours. And before I help you open it, I'll tell you the story. I came one day in my wanderings to a town I had never visited before, and in the town were many merchants. And I asked a man, 'Who has the rarest and best merchandise in town?' He told me that I had to see Irvass. So I found the man in a humble and poor-looking shop. But inside were wonders such as you've never seen. I tell you, the man understands the bright magic from over the sky. And he asked, 'What do you want most in the world?' and of course I said to him, 'I want my daughter to be healed.' "

"Oh, Father," said Kiren. "You don't mean—"

"I do mean. I mean it very much. I told him exactly how you are and exactly how you got that way, and he said, 'Here is the cure,' and now let's open the box so you can see."

So Kiren opened the box, with more than a little help from her father, but she dared not reach inside. "You get it out, Father," she suggested, and he reached inside and pulled out a porcelain salamander. It was shiny yet deep with fine enameling, and though it was white—not at all the normal color for salamanders—the shape was unmistakable.

It was, in fact, a perfect model of a salamander. And it moved.

The legs raced madly in the air; the tongue darted in and out of the lips; the head turned; the eyes rolled. And Kiren cried out and laughed and said, "Oh, Father, what did he do to make it move so wonderfully!"

"Well," said her father, "he told me that he had given it the gift of movement— but not the gift of life. And if it ever *stops* moving, it will immediately become like any other porcelain. Stiff and hard and cold."

"How it races," she said, and it became the delight of her life.

When she awoke in the morning the salamander danced on her bed. At mealtimes it raced around the table. Wherever she lay or sat, the salamander was forever chasing after something or exploring something or trying to get away from something. She watched him constantly, and he in turn never got out of sight. And then at night, while she slept, he raced around and around in her room, the porcelain feet hitting the carpet silently, only occasionally making a slight tinkling sound as it ran lightly across the brick of the hearth.

Her father watched for a cure, and slowly but surely it began to come. For one thing, Kiren was no longer miserable. The salamander was too funny not to laugh at. It never went away. And so she felt better. Feeling better was not all of it, though. She began to walk a bit more often, and stay standing more, and sit when ordinarily she would have lain. She began to go from one room to another by her own choice.

By the end of the summer she even took walks into the woods. Though she often had to stop and rest, she enjoyed the journey, and grew a little stronger.

What she never told anyone (partly because she was afraid that it might be her imagination) was that the salamander could also speak.

"You can speak," she said in surprise one day, when the salamander ran across her foot and said, "Excuse me."

"Of course," he said. "To *you*."

"Why not anyone else?"

"Because I'm here for *you*," he answered, as he ran along the top of the garden wall, then leaped down near her. "It's the way I am. Movement and speech. Best I can do, you know. Can't have life. Doesn't work that way."

And so on their long walks in the forest they also talked, and Kiren fancied that the salamander had grown as fond of her as she had grown of him. In fact, she told the salamander one day, "I love you."

"Love love love love love love love," he answered, scampering up and down a tree.

"Yes," Kiren said. "More than life. More than anything at all."

"More than your father?" asked the salamander.

It was hard. Kiren was not a disloyal child, and really had forgiven her father for the curse years before. Yet she had to be honest to her salamander. "Yes," she said. "More than Father. More than—more than my dream of my mother. For you love me and can play with me and talk to me all the time."

"Love love love," said the salamander. "Unfortunately, I'm porcelain. Love love love love love. It's a word. Two consonants and a vowel. Like sap sap sap sap sap. Lovely sound." And he leaped across a small brook in the way.

"Don't—don't you love me?"

"I can't. It's an emotion, you know. I'm porcelain. Beg your pardon," and he clambered down her back as she leaned her shoulder on a tree. "Can't love. So sorry."

She was terribly, terribly hurt. "Don't you feel anything toward me at all?"

"Feel? Feel? Don't confuse things. Emotions come and go. Who can trust them? Isn't it enough that I spend every moment with you? Isn't it enough that I talk only to you? Isn't it enough that I would—that I would—"

"Would what?"

"I was about to start making foolish predictions. I was about to say, isn't it enough that I would die for you? But of course that's nonsense, because I'm not I'm not alive. Just porcelain. Watch out for the spider."

She stepped out of the path of a little green hunting spider that could fell a horse with one bite. "Thank you," she said. "And thank you." The first was for saving her life, but that was his job. The second was for telling her that, in his own way, he loved her after all. "So I'm not foolish for loving you, am I?"

"Foolish you are. Foolish indeed. Foolish as the moons are foolish, to dance endlessly in the sky and never never never go home together."

"I love you," said Kiren, "better than I love the hope of being whole."

And, you see, it was because she said that that the odd man came to the door of her father's house the very next day.

"I'm sorry," said the servant. "You haven't an appointment."

"Just tell him," said the odd man, "that Irvass has come."

Kiren's father came running down the stairs. "Oh, you can't take the salamander back!" he cried. "The cure has only begun!"

"Which I know much better than you do," said Irvass. "The girl is in the woods?"

"With the salamander. What marvelous changes—but why are you here?"

"To finish the cure," said Irvass.

"What?" asked Kiren's father. "Isn't the salamander itself the cure?"

"What were the words of your curse?" Irvass asked, instead of answering.

Kiren's father's face grew dour, but he forced himself to quietly say the very words. "May you never move a muscle in your life, until you lose someone you love as much as I loved her."

"Well then," said Irvass. "She now loves the salamander exactly as much as you loved your wife."

It took only a moment for Kiren's father to realize. "No!" he cried out. "I can't let her suffer what I suffered!"

"It's the only cure. Isn't it better with a little piece of porcelain than if she had come to love *you* that much?"

And Kiren's father shuddered, and then wept, for he alone knew exactly how much pain she would suffer.

Irvass said nothing more, though the look he gave to Kiren's father might have been a pitying one. All he did was draw a rectangle in the soil of the garden, and place two stones within it, and mumble a few words.

And at that moment, out in the wood, the salamander said, "Very odd. Wasn't a wall here ever before. Never before. Here's a wall." And it was a wall. It was just high enough that when Kiren reached as high as she could, her fingers were one inch short of touching the top.

The salamander tried to climb it, but found it slippery—though he had always been able to climb every other wall he found. "Magic. Must be magic," The porcelain salamander mumbled.

So they circled the wall, hunting for a gate. There was none. It was all around them, though they had never entered it. And at no point did a tree limb cross the wall. They were trapped.

"I'm afraid," said Kiren. "There's good magic and bad magic, but how could such a thing as this be a blessing? It must be a curse." And the thought of a curse caused too much of the old misery to return, and she fought back the tears.

Fought back the tears until night, and then in the darkness, as the salamander scampered here and there, she could fight no longer.

"No," wailed the salamander.

"I can't help crying," she answered.

"I can't bear it," he said. "It makes me cold."

"I'll try to stop," she said, and she tried, and she pretty much stopped except for a few whimpers and sniffles until morning brought the light, and she saw that the wall was exactly where it had been.

No, not exactly. For behind her the wall had crept up in the night, and was only a few feet away. Her prison was now not even a quarter the size it had been the day before.

"Not good," said the salamander. "Oh, it could be dangerous."

"I know," she answered.

"You must get out," said the salamander.

"And you," she answered. "But how?"

And throughout the morning the wall played vicious taunting games with them, for whichever way neither of them was looking, the wall would creep up a foot or two. Since the salamander was faster, and moved constantly, he watched three sides. "And you hold the other in place." But Kiren couldn't help blinking, and anytime the salamander looked away the wall twitched, and by noon their prison was only ten feet square.

"Getting pretty tight here," said the salamander.

"Oh, salamander, can't I throw you over the wall?"

"We could try that, and I could run and get help—"

And so they tried. But though she used every ounce of strength she had, the wall seemed to leap up and catch him and send him sliding back down to the ground. Inside.

Soon she was exhausted, and the salamander said, "No more." Even as they had been trying, the walls had shrunk, and now the space was only five feet square. "Getting cramped," said the salamander as he raced around the tiny space remaining. "But I know the only solution."

"Tell me!" Kiren cried.

"I think," said the salamander, "that if you had something you could stand on, you could climb out."

"How could I?" she asked. "The wall won't let anything out!"

"I think," said the salamander, "that the wall only won't let *me* out. Because the birds are flying back and forth, and the wall doesn't catch them." It was true. A bird was singing in a nearby tree; it flew across just afterward, as if to prove the salamander's point. "I'm not alive, you see," said the salamander. "I'm moving only by magic. So you *could* get out."

"But what would I stand on?"

"Me," said the salamander.

"You?" she asked. "But you move so quickly—"

"For you," he said, "I'll hold still."

"No!" she cried. "No, no!" she screamed.

But the salamander stood at the edge of the wall, and he was only a statue in porcelain, hard and stiff and cold.

Kiren only wept for a moment, for then the wall behind her began to push at her, and her prison was only three feet square. The salamander had given his life so she could climb out. She ought at least to try.

So she tried. Standing on the salamander, she could reach the top of the wall. By standing tiptoe, she could get a grip on the top. And by using every bit of strength she had in her, she was able to force her body to the top and gradually heave herself over.

She fell in a heap on the ground. And in that moment, that very moment, two things happened. The walls shrank quickly until they were only a pillar, and then they disappeared completely, taking the salamander with them. And all the normal, natural strength of an eleven-year-old child came to Kiren, and she was able to run. She was able to leap. She was able to swing from the tree branches.

The strength was in her as suddenly as strong wine, and she could not lie on the ground. She jumped to her feet, and the movement was so strong she nearly fell over. She ran, leaped over brooks, clambered up into the trees as high as she could climb. The curse had ended. She was free.

But even normal children grow tired. And as she slowed down, she was no longer caught up in her own strength. And she remembered the porcelain salamander, and what he had done for her.

They found her that afternoon, weeping miserably into a pile of last year's leaves.

"You see," said Irvass, who had insisted on leading the way in the search—which is why they found her immediately—"You see, she has her strength, and the curse is ended."

"But her heart is broken," said her father as he gathered his little girl into his arms.

"Broken?" asked Irvass. "It should not be. For the porcelain salamander was never alive."

"Yes he was!" she shouted. "He spoke to me! He gave his life for me!"

"He did all that," said Irvass. "But think. For all the time the magic was on him, he could never, never rest. Do you think he never got tired?"

"Of course he didn't."

"Yes he did," said Irvass. "Now he can rest. But more than rest. For when he stopped moving and froze forever in one position, what was going through his mind?"

Irvass stood up and turned to leave. But only a few steps away, he turned back. "Kiren," he said.

"I want my salamander," she answered, her voice an agony of sobs.

"Oh, he would have become boring by and by," said Irvass. "He would have ceased to amuse you, and you would have avoided him. But now he is a memory. And, speaking of memory, remember that he also has memory, frozen as he is."

It was scant comfort then, for eleven-year-olds are not very philosophical. But when she grew older, Kiren remembered. And she knew that wherever the porcelain salamander was, he lived in one frozen, perfect moment—the moment when his heart was so full of love—

No, not love. The moment when he decided, without love, that it would be better for his life, such as it was, to end than to have to watch Kiren's life end.

It is a moment that can be lived with for eternity. And as Kiren grew older, she knew that such moments come rarely to people, and last only a moment, while the porcelain salamander would never lose it.

And as for Kiren—she became known, though she never sought fame, as the most Beautiful of the Beautiful People, and more than one of the rare wanderers from across the sea or from beyond Rising came only to see her, and talk to her, and draw her face in their minds to keep it with them forever.

And when she talked, her hands always moved, always danced in the air. Never stopped moving at all, it seemed, and they were white and lustrous as deep-enameled porcelain, and her smile was as bright as the moons, and came back to her face as constantly as the sea, and those who knew her well could almost see her gaze keep flickering about the room or about the garden, as if she watched a bright, quick animal scamper by.

MIDDLE WOMAN

A h-Cheu was a woman of the great kingdom of Ch'in, a land of hills and valleys, a land of great wealth and dire poverty. But Ah-Cheu was a middle person, neither rich nor poor, neither old nor young, and her husband's farm was half in the valley and half on the hill. Ah-Cheu had a sister older than her, and a sister younger than her, and one lived thirty leagues to the north, and the other thirty leagues to the south. "I am a middle woman," Ah-Cheu boasted once, but her husband's mother rebuked her, saying, "Evil comes to the middle, and good goes out to the edges."

Every year Ah-Cheu put a pack on her back and journeyed for a visit either to the sister to the north or to the sister to the south. It took her three days to make the journey, for she did not hurry. But one year she did not make the journey, for she met a dragon on the road.

The dragon was long and fine and terrible, and Ah-Cheu immediately knelt and touched her forehead to the road and said, "Oh, dragon, spare my life!"

The dragon only chuckled deep in his throat and said, "Woman, what do they call you?"

Not wishing to tell her true name to the dragon, she said, "I am called Middle Woman."

"Well, Middle Woman, I will give you a choice. The first choice is to have me eat you here in the road. The second choice is to have me grant you three wishes."

Surprised, Ah-Cheu raised her head. "But of course I take the second choice. Why do you set me a problem with such an easy solution?"

"It is more amusing," said the dragon, "to watch human beings destroy themselves than to overpower them quickly."

"But how can three wishes destroy me?"

"Make a wish, and see."

Ah-Cheu thought of many things she might wish for, but was soon ashamed of her greed. "I wish," she finally said, having decided to ask for only what she truly needed, "for my husband's farm to always produce plenty for all my family to eat."

"It shall be done," said the dragon, and he vanished, only to reappear a moment later, smiling and licking his lips. "I have done," he said, "exactly what you asked—I have eaten all your family, and so your husband's farm, even if it produces nothing, will always produce plenty for *them* to eat."

Ah-Cheu wept and mourned and cursed herself for being a fool, for now she saw the dragon's plan. Any wish, however innocent, would be turned against her.

"Think all you like," said the dragon, "but it will do you no good. I have had lawyers draw up legal documents eight feet long, but I have found the loopholes."

Then Ah-Cheu knew what she had to ask for. "I wish for all the world to be exactly as it was one minute before I left my home to come on this journey."

The dragon looked at her in surprise. "That's all? That's all you want to wish for?"

"Yes," said Ah-Cheu. "And you must do it now."

And suddenly she found herself in her husband's house, putting on her pack and bidding good-bye to her family. Immediately she set down the pack.

"I have changed my mind," she said. "I am not going."

Everyone was shocked. Everyone was surprised. Her husband berated her for being a changeable woman. Her mother-in-law denounced her for having forgotten her duty to her sisters. Her children pouted because she had always brought them each a present from her journeys to the north and south. But Ah-Cheu was firm. She would not risk meeting the dragon again.

And when the furor died down, Ah-Cheu was far more cheerful than she had ever been before, for she knew that she had one wish left, the third wish, the unused wish. And if there were ever a time of great need, she could use it to save herself and her family.

One year there was a fire, and Ah-Cheu was outside the house, with her youngest child trapped within. Almost she used her wish, but then thought, Why use the wish, when I can use my arms? And she ducked low, and ran into the house, and saved the boy, though it singed off all her hair. And she still had her son, and she still had her wish.

One year there was a famine, and it looked like all the world would starve. Ah-Cheu almost used her wish, but then thought, Why use the wish, when I can use my feet? And she wandered up into the hills, and came back with a basket of roots and leaves, and with such food she kept her family alive until the Emperor's men came with wagons full of rice. And she still had her family, and she still had her wish.

And in another year there was a great flood, and all the homes were swept away, and as Ah-Cheu and her son's baby sat upon the roof, watching the water eat away the walls of the house, she almost used her wish to get a boat so she could escape. But then she thought, Why use the wish, when I can use my head? And she took up the boards from the roof and walls, and with her skirts she tied them into a raft large enough for the baby, and setting the child upon it she swam away, pushing the raft until they reached high ground and safety. And when her son found her alive, he wept with joy, and said, "Mother Ah-Cheu, never has a son loved his mother more!"

And Ah-Cheu had her posterity, and yet still she had her wish.

And then it was time for Ah-Cheu to die, and she lay sick and frail upon a bed of honor in her son's house, and the women and children and old men of the village came to keen for her and honor her as she lay dying. "Never has there been a more fortunate woman than Ah-Cheu," they said. "Never has there been a kinder, a more generous, a more godfavored woman!" And she was content to leave the world, because she had been so happy in it.

And on her last night, as she lay alone in darkness, she heard a voice call her name.

"Middle Woman," said the voice, and she opened her eyes, and there was the dragon.

"What do you want with me?" she asked. "I'm not much of a morsel to eat now, I'm afraid."

But then she saw the dragon looked terrified, and she listened to what he had to say.

"Middle Woman," said the dragon, "you have not used your third wish."

"I never needed it."

"Oh, cruel woman! What a vengeance you take! In the long run, I never did you any harm! How can you do this to me?"

"But what am I doing?" she asked.

"If you die, with your third wish unused, then I, too, will die!" he cried. "Maybe that doesn't seem so bad to you, but dragons are usually immortal, and so you can believe me when I say my death would cut me off with most of my life unlived."

"Poor dragon," she said. "But what have I to wish for?"

"Immortality," he said. "No tricks. I'll let you live forever."

"I don't want to live forever," she said. "It would make the neighbors envious."

"Great wealth, then, for your family."

"But they have all they need right now."

"Any wish!" he cried. "Any wish, or I will die!"

And so she smiled, and reached out a frail old hand and touched his supplicating claw, and said, "Then I wish a wish, dragon. I wish that all the rest of your life should be nothing but happiness for you and everyone you meet."

The dragon looked at her in surprise, and then in relief, and then he smiled and wept for joy. He thanked her many times, and left her home rejoicing.

And that night Ah-Cheu also left her home, more subtly than the dragon, and far less likely to return, but no less merrily for all that.

THE BULLY AND THE BEAST

The page entered the Count's chamber at a dead run. He had long ago given up sauntering—when the Count called, he expected a page to appear immediately, and any delay at all made the Count irritable and likely to assign a page to stable duty.

"My lord," said the page.

"My lord indeed," said the Count. "What kept you?" The Count stood at the window, his back to the boy. In his arms he held a velvet gown, incredibly embroidered with gold and silver thread. "I think I need to call a council," said the Count. "On the other hand, I haven't the slightest desire to submit myself to a gaggle of jabbering knights. They'll be quite angry. What do you think?"

No one had ever asked the page for advice before, and he wasn't quite sure what was expected of him. "Why should they be angry, my lord?"

"Do you see this gown?" the Count asked, turning around and holding it up.

"Yes, my lord."

"What do you think of it?"

"Depends, doesn't it, my lord, on who wears it."

"It cost eleven pounds of silver."

The page smiled sickly. Eleven pounds of silver would keep the average knight in arms, food, women, clothing, and shelter for a year with six pounds left over for spending money.

"There are more," said the Count. "Many more."

"But who are they for? Are you going to marry?"

"None of your business!" roared the Count. "If there's anything I hate, it's a meddler!" The Count turned again to the window and looked out. He was shaded by a huge oak tree that grew forty feet from the castle walls. "What's today?" asked the Count.

"Thursday, my lord."

"The day, the day!"

"Eleventh past Easter Feast."

"The tribute's due today," said the Count. "Due on Easter, in fact, but today the Duke will be certain I'm not paying."

"Not paying the tribute, my lord?"

"How? Turn me upside down and shake me, but I haven't a farthing. The tribute money's gone. The money for new arms is gone. The travel money is gone. The money for new horses is gone. Haven't got any money at all. But gad, boy, what a wardrobe." The Count sat on the sill of the window. "The Duke will be here very quickly, I'm afraid. And he has the latest in debt collection equipment."

"What's that?"

"An army." The Count sighed. "Call a council, boy. My knights may jabber and scream, but they'll fight. I know they will."

The page wasn't sure. "They'll be very angry, my lord. Are you sure they'll fight?"

"Oh, yes," said the Count. "If they don't, the Duke will kill them."

"Why?"

"For not honoring their oath to me. Do go now, boy, and call a council."

The page nodded. Kind of felt sorry for the old boy. Not much of a Count, as things went, but he could have been worse, and it was pretty plain the castle would be sacked and the Count imprisoned and the women raped and the page sent off home to his parents. "A council!" he cried as he left the Count's chamber. "A council!"

In the cold cavern of the pantry under the kitchen, Bork pulled a huge keg of ale from its resting place and lifted it, not easily, but without much strain, and rested it on his shoulders. Head bowed, he walked slowly up the stairs. Before Bork worked in the kitchen, it used to take two men most of an afternoon to move the huge kegs. But Bork was a giant, or what passed for a giant in those days. The Count himself was of average height, barely past five feet. Bork was nearly seven feet tall, with muscles like an ox. People stepped aside for him.

"Put it there," said the cook, hardly looking up. "And don't drop it."

Bork didn't drop the keg. Nor did he resent the cook's expecting him to be clumsy. He had been told he was clumsy all his life, ever since it became plain at the age of three that he was going to be immense. Everyone knew that big people were clumsy. And it was true enough. Bork was so strong he kept doing things he never meant to do, accidentally. Like the time the swordmaster, admiring his strength, had invited him to learn to use the heavy battleswords. Bork hefted them easily, of course, though at the time he was only twelve and hadn't reached his full strength.

"Hit me," the swordmaster said.

"But the blade's sharp," Bork told him.

"Don't worry. You won't come near me." The swordmaster had taught a hundred knights to fight. None of them had come near him. And, in fact, when Bork swung the heavy sword the swordmaster had his shield up in plenty of time. He just hadn't counted on the terrible force of the blow. The shield was battered aside easily, and the blow threw the sword upward, so it cut off the swordmaster's left arm just below the shoulder, and only narrowly missed slicing deeply into his chest.

Clumsy, that was all Bork was. But it was the end of any hope of his becoming a knight. When the swordmaster finally recovered, he consigned Bork to the kitchen and the blacksmith's shop, where they needed someone with enough strength to skewer a cow end to end and carry it to the fire, where it was convenient to have a man who, with a double-sized ax, could chop down a large tree in half an hour, cut it into logs, and carry a month's supply of firewood into the castle in an afternoon.

A page came into the kitchen. "There's a council, cook. The Count wants ale, and plenty of it."

The cook swore profusely and threw a carrot at the page. "Always changing the schedule! Always making me do extra work." As soon as the page had escaped, the cook turned on Bork. "All right, carry the ale out there, and be quick about it. Try not to drop it."

"I won't," Bork said.

"He won't," the cook muttered. "Clever as an ox, he is."

Bork manhandled the cask into the great hall. It was cold, though outside the sun was shining. Little light and little warmth reached the inside of the castle. And since it was spring, the huge logpile in the pit in the middle of the room lay cold and damp.

The knights were beginning to wander into the great hall and sit on the benches that lined the long, pock-marked slab of a table. They knew enough to carry their mugs—councils were always well-oiled with ale. Bork had spent years as a child watching the knights practice the arts of war, but the knights seemed more natural carrying their cups than holding their swords at the ready. They were more dedicated to their drinking than to war.

"Ho, Bork the Bully," one of the knights greeted him. Bork managed a half-smile. He had learned long since not to take offense.

"How's Sam the stableman?" asked another, tauntingly.

Bork blushed and turned away, heading for the door to the kitchen.

The knights were laughing at their cleverness. "Twice the body, half the brain," one of them said to the others. "Probably hung like a horse," another speculated, then quipped, "Which probably accounts for those mysterious deaths among the sheep this winter." A roar of laughter, and cups beating on the table. Bork stood in the kitchen trembling. He could not escape the sound—the stones carried it echoing to him wherever he went.

The cook turned and looked at him. "Don't be angry, boy," he said. "It's all in fun."

Bork nodded and smiled at the cook. That's what it was. All in fun. And besides, Bork deserved it, he knew. It was only fair that he be treated cruelly. For he had earned the title Bork the Bully, hadn't he? When he was three, and already massive as a ram, his only friend, a beautiful young village boy named Winkle, had hit upon the idea of becoming a knight. Winkle had dressed himself in odds and ends of leather and tin, and made a makeshift lance from a hog prod.

"You're my destrier," Winkle cried as he mounted Bork and rode him for hours. Bork thought it was a fine thing to be a knight's horse. It became the height of his ambition, and he wondered how one got started in the trade. But one day Sam, the stableman's son, had taunted Winkle for his make-believe armor, and it had turned into a fist fight, and Sam had thoroughly bloodied Winkle's nose. Winkle screamed as if he were dying, and Bork sprang to his friend's defense, walloping Sam, who was three years older, along the side of his head.

Ever since then Sam spoke with a thickness in his voice, and often lost his balance; his jaw, broken in several places, never healed properly, and he had problems with his ear.

It horrified Bork to have caused so much pain, but Winkle assured him that Sam deserved it. "After all, Bork, he was twice my size, and he was picking on me. He's a bully. He had it coming."

For several years Winkle and Bork were the terror of the village. Winkle would constantly get into fights, and soon the village children learned not to resist him. If Winkle lost a fight, he would scream for Bork, and though Bork was never again so harsh as he was with Sam, his blows still hurt terribly. Winkle loved it. Then one day he tired of being a knight, dismissed his destrier, and became fast friends with the other children. It was only then that Bork began to hear himself called Bork the Bully; it was Winkle who convinced the other children that the only villain in the fighting had been Bork. "After all," Bork overheard Winkle say one day, "he's twice as strong as anyone else. Isn't fair for him to fight. It's a cowardly thing for him to do, and we mustn't have anything to do with him. Bullies must be punished."

Bork knew Winkle was right, and ever after that he bore the burden of shame. He remembered the frightened looks in the other children's eyes when he approached them, the way they pleaded for mercy. But Winkle was always screaming and writhing in agony, and Bork always hit the child despite his terror, and for that bullying Bork was still paying. He paid in the ridicule he accepted from the knights; he paid in the solitude of all his days and nights; he paid by working as hard as he could, using his strength to serve instead of hurt.

But just because he knew he deserved the punishment did not mean he enjoyed it. There were tears in his eyes as he went about his work in the kitchen. He tried to hide them from the cook, but to no avail. "Oh, no, you're not going to cry, are you?" the cook said. "You'll only make your nose run and then you'll get snot in the soup. Get out of the kitchen for awhile!"

Which is why Bork was standing in the doorway of the great hall watching the council that would completely change his life.

"Well, where's the tribute money gone to?" demanded one of the knights. "The harvest was large enough last year!"

It was an ugly thing, to see the knights so angry. But the Count knew they had a right to be upset—it was they who would have to fight the Duke's men, and they had a right to know why.

"My friends," the Count said. "My friends, some things are more important than money. I invested the money in something more important than tribute, more important than peace, more important than long life. I invested the money in beauty. Not to create beauty, but to perfect it." The knights were listening now. For all their violent preoccupations, they all had a soft spot in their hearts for true beauty. It was one of the requirements for knighthood. "I have been entrusted with a jewel, more perfect than any diamond. It was my duty to place that jewel in the best setting money could buy. I can't explain. I can only show you." He rang a small bell, and behind him one of the better-known secret doors in the castle opened, and a wizened old woman emerged. The Count whispered in her ear, and the woman scurried back into the secret passage.

"Who's she?" asked one of the knights.

"She is the woman who nursed my children after my wife died. My wife died in childbirth, you remember. But what you don't know is that the child lived. My two sons you know well. But I have a third child, my last child, whom you know not at all, and this one is not a son."

The Count was not surprised that several of the knights seemed to puzzle over this riddle. Too many jousts, too much practice in full armor in the heat of the afternoon.

"My child is a daughter."

"Ah," said the knights.

"At first, I kept her hidden away because I could not bear to see her—after all, my most beloved wife had died in bearing her. But after a few years I overcame my grief, and went to see the child in the room where she was hidden, and lo! She was the most beautiful child I had ever seen. I named her Brunhilda, and from that moment on I loved her. I was the most devoted father you could imagine. But I did not let her leave the secret room. Why, you may ask?"

"Yes, why!" demanded several of the knights.

"Because she was so beautiful I was afraid she would be stolen from me. I was terrified that I would lose her. Yet I saw her every day, and talked to her, and the older she got, the more beautiful she became, and for the last several years I could no longer bear to see her in her mother's cast-off clothing. Her beauty is such that only the finest cloths and gowns and jewels of Flanders, of Venice, of Florence would do for her. You'll see! The money was not ill spent."

And the door opened again, and the old woman emerged, leading forth Brunhilda.

In the doorway, Bork gasped. But no one heard him, for all the knights gasped, too.

She was the most perfect woman in the world. Her hair was a dark red, flowing behind her like an auburn stream as she walked. Her face was white from being indoors all her life, and when she smiled it was like the sun breaking out on a stormy day. And none of the knights dared look at her body for very long, because the longer they looked the more they wanted to touch her, and the Count said, "I warn you. Any man who lays a hand on her will have to answer to me. She is a virgin, and when she marries she shall be a virgin, and a king will pay half his kingdom to have her, and still I'll feel cheated to have to give her up."

"Good morning, my lords," she said, smiling. Her voice was like the song of leaves dancing in the summer wind, and the knights fell to their knees before her.

None of them was more moved by her beauty than Bork, however. When she entered the room he forgot himself; there was no room in his mind for anything but the great beauty he had seen for the first time in his life. Bork knew nothing of courtesy. He only knew that, for the first time in his life, he had seen something so perfect that he could not rest until it was his. Not his to own, but his to be owned by. He longed to serve her in the most degrading ways he could think of, if only she would smile upon him; longed to die for her, if only the last moment of his life were filled with her voice saying, "You may love me."

If he had been a knight, he might have thought of a poetic way to say such things. But he was not a knight, and so his words came out of his heart before his mind could find a way to make them clever. He strode blindly from the kitchen door, his huge body casting a shadow that seemed to the knights like the shadow of death passing over them. They watched with uneasiness that soon turned to outrage as he came to the girl, reached out, and took her small white hands in his.

"I love you," Bork said to her, and tears came unbidden to his eyes. "Let me marry you."

At that moment several of the knights found their courage. They seized Bork roughly by the arms, meaning to pull him away and punish him for his effrontery. But Bork effortlessly tossed them away. They fell to the ground yards from him. He never saw them fall; his gaze never left the lady's face.

She looked wonderingly into his eyes. Not because she thought him attractive, because he was ugly and she knew it. Not because of the words he had said, because she had been taught that many men would say those words, and she was to pay no attention to them. What startled her, what amazed her, was the deep truth in Bork's face. That was something she had never seen, and though she did not recognize it for what it was, it fascinated her.

The Count was furious. Seeing the clumsy giant holding his daughter's small white hands in his was outrageous. He would not endure it. But the giant had such great strength that to tear him away would mean a full-scale battle, and in such a battle Brunhilda might be injured. No, the giant had to be handled delicately, for the moment.

"My dear fellow," said the Count, affecting a joviality he did not feel. "You've only just met."

Bork ignored him. "I will never let you come to harm," he said to the girl.

"What's his name?" the Count whispered to a knight. "I can't remember his name."

"Bork," the knight answered.

"My dear Bork," said the Count. "All due respect and everything, but my daughter has noble blood, and you're not even a knight."

"Then I'll become one," Bork said.

"It's not that easy, Bork, old fellow. You must do something exceptionally brave, and then I can knight you and we can talk about this other matter. But in the meantime, it isn't proper for you to be holding my daughter's hands. Why don't you go back to the kitchen like a good fellow?"

Bork gave no sign that he heard. He only continued looking into the lady's eyes. And finally it was she who was able to end the dilemma.

"Bork," she said, "I will count on you. But in the meantime, my father will be angry with you if you don't return to the kitchen."

Of course, Bork thought. Of course, she is truly concerned for me, doesn't want me to come to harm on her account. "For your sake," he said, the madness of love still on him. The he turned and left the room.

The Count sat down, sighing audibly. "Should have got rid of him years ago. Gentle as a lamb, and then all of a sudden goes crazy. Get rid of him—somebody take care of that tonight, would you? Best to do it in his sleep. Don't want any casualties when we're likely to have a battle at any moment."

The reminder of the battle was enough to sober even those who were on their fifth mug of ale. The wizened old woman led Brunhilda away again. "But not to the secret room, now. To the chamber next to mine. And post a double guard outside her door, and keep the key yourself," said the Count.

When she was gone, the Count looked around at the knights. "The treasury has been emptied in a vain attempt to find clothing to do her justice. I had no other choice."

And there was not a knight who would say the money had been badly spent.

The Duke came late that afternoon, much sooner than he was expected. He demanded the tribute. The Count refused, of course. There was the usual challenge to come out of the castle and fight, but the Count, outnumbered ten to one, merely replied, rather saucily, that the Duke should come in and get him. The messenger who delivered the sarcastic message came back with his tongue in a bag around his neck. The battle was thus begun grimly: and grimly it continued.

The guard watching on the south side of the castle was slacking. He paid for it.

The Duke's archers managed to creep up to the huge oak tree and climb it without any alarm being given, and the first notice any of them had was when the guard fell from the battlements with an arrow in his throat.

The archers—there must have been a dozen of them—kept up a deadly rain of arrows. They wasted no shots. The squires dropped dead in alarming numbers until the Count gave orders for them to come inside. And when the human targets were all under cover, the archers set to work on the cattle and sheep milling in the open pens. There was no way to protect the animals. By sunset, all of them were dead.

"Dammit," said the cook. "How can I cook all this before it spoils?"

"Find a way," said the Count. "That's our food supply. I refuse to let them starve us out."

So all night Bork worked, carrying the cattle and sheep inside, one by one. At first the villagers who had taken refuge in the castle tried to help him, but he could carry three animals inside the kitchen in the time it took them to drag one, and they soon gave it up.

The Count saw who was saving the meat. "Don't get rid of him tonight," he told the knights. "We'll punish him for his effrontery in the morning."

Bork only rested twice in the night, taking naps for an hour before the cook woke him again. And when dawn came, and the arrows began coming again, all the cattle were inside, and all but twenty sheep.

"That's all we can save," the cook told the Count.

"Save them all."

"But if Bork tries to go out there, he'll be killed!"

The Count looked the cook in the eyes. "Bring in the sheep or have him die trying."

The cook was not aware of the fact that Bork was under sentence of death. So he did his best to save Bork. A kettle lined with cloth and strapped onto the giant's head; a huge kettle lid for a shield. "It's the best we can do," the cook said.

"But I can't carry sheep if I'm holding a shield," Bork said.

"What can I do? The Count commanded it. It's worth your life to refuse."

Bork stood and thought for a few moments, trying to find a way out of his dilemma. He saw only one possibility. "If I can't stop them from hitting me, I'll have to stop them from shooting at all."

"How!" the cook demanded, and then followed Bork to the blacksmith's shop, where Bork found his huge ax leaning against the wall.

"Now's not the time to cut firewood," said the blacksmith.

"Yes it is," Bork answered.

Carrying the ax and holding the kettle lid between his body and the archers, Bork made his way across the courtyard. The arrows pinged harmlessly off the metal. Bork got to the drawbridge. "Open up!" he shouted, and the drawbridge fell away and dropped across the moat. Bork walked across, then made his way along the moat toward the oak tree.

In the distance the Duke, standing in front of his dazzling white tent with his emblem of yellow on it, saw Bork emerge from the castle. "Is that a man or a bear?" he asked. No one was sure.

The archers shot at Bork steadily, but the closer he got to the tree, the worse their angle of fire and the larger the shadow of safety the kettle lid cast over his body. Finally, holding the lid high over his head, Bork began hacking one-handed at the trunk. Chips of wood flew with each blow; with his right hand alone he could cut deeper and faster than a normal man with both hands free.

But he was concentrating on cutting wood, and his left arm grew tired holding his makeshift shield, and an archer was able to get off a shot that slipped past the shield and plunged into his left arm, in the thick muscle at the back.

He nearly dropped the shield. Instead, he had the presence of mind to let go of the ax and drop to his knees, quickly balancing the kettle lid between the tree trunk, his head, and the top of the ax handle. Gently he pulled at the arrow shaft. It would not come backward. So he broke the arrow and pushed the stub the rest of the way through his arm until it was out the other side. It was excruciatingly painful, but he knew he could not quit now. He took hold of the shield with his left arm again, and despite the pain held it high as he began to cut again, girdling the tree with a deep white gouge. The blood dripped steadily down his arm, but he ignored it, and soon enough the bleeding stopped and slowed.

On the castle battlements, the Count's men began to realize that there was a hope of Bork's succeeding. To protect him, they began to shoot their arrows into the tree. The archers were well hidden, but the rain of arrows, however badly aimed, began to have its effect. A few of them dropped to the ground, where the castle archers could easily finish them off; the others were forced to concentrate on finding cover.

The tree trembled more and more with each blow, until finally Bork stepped back and the tree creaked and swayed. He had learned from his lumbering work in the forest how to make the tree fall where he wanted it; the oak fell parallel to the castle walls, so it neither bridged the moat nor let the Duke's archers scramble from the tree too far from the castle. So when the archers tried to flee to the safety of the Duke's lines, the castle bowmen were able to kill them all.

One of them, however, despaired of escape. Instead, though he already had an arrow in him, he drew a knife and charged at Bork, in a mad attempt to avenge his own death on the man who had caused it. Bork had no choice. He swung his ax through the air and discovered that men are nowhere near as sturdy as a tree.

In the distance, the Duke watched with horror as the giant cut a man in half with a single blow. "What have they got!" he said. "What is this monster?"

Covered with the blood that had spurted from the dying man, Bork walked back toward the drawbridge, which opened again as he approached. But he did not get to enter. Instead the Count and fifty mounted knights came from the gate on horseback, their armor shining in the sunlight.

"I've decided to fight them in the open," the Count said. "And you, Bork, must fight with us. If you live through this, I'll make you a knight!"

Bork knelt. "Thank you, my Lord Count," he said.

The Count glanced around in embarrassment. "Well, then. Let's get to it. Charge!" he bellowed.

Bork did not realize that the knights were not even formed in a line yet. He simply followed the command and charged, alone, toward the Duke's lines. The Count watched him go, and smiled.

"My Lord Count," said the nearest knight. "Aren't we going to attack with him?"

"Let the Duke take care of him," the Count said.

"But he cut down the oak and saved the castle, my lord."

"Yes," said the Count. "An exceptionally brave act. Do you want him to try to claim my daughter's hand?"

"But my lord," said the knight, "if he fights beside us, we might have a chance of winning. But if he's gone, the Duke will destroy us."

"Some things," said the Count, with finality, "are more important than victory.

Would you want to go on living in a world where perfection like Brunhilda's was possessed by such a man as that?"

The knights were silent, then, as they watched Bork approach the Duke's army, alone.

Bork did not realize he was alone until he stood a few feet away from the Duke's lines. He had felt strange as he walked across the fields, believing he was marching into battle with the knights he had long admired in their bright armor and deft instruments of war. Now the exhilaration was gone. Where were the others? Bork was afraid.

He could not understand why the Duke's men had not shot any arrows at him. Actually, it was a misunderstanding. If the Duke had known Bork was a commoner and not a knight at all, Bork would have had a hundred arrows bristling from his corpse. As it was, however, one of the Duke's men called out, "You, sir! Do you challenge us to single combat?"

Of course. That was it—the Count did not intend Bork to face an army, he intended him to face a single warrior. The whole outcome of the battle would depend on him alone! It was a tremendous honor, and Bork wondered if he could carry it off.

"Yes! Single combat!" he answered. "Your strongest, bravest man!"

"But you're a giant!" cried the Duke's man.

"But I'm wearing no armor." And to prove his sincerity, Bork took off his helmet, which was uncomfortable anyway, and stepped forward. The Duke's knights backed away, making an opening for him, with men in armor watching him pass from both sides. Bork walked steadily on, until he came to a cleared circle where he faced the Duke himself.

"Are you the champion?" asked Bork.

"I'm the Duke," he answered. "But I don't see any of my knights stepping forward to fight you."

"Do you refuse the challenge, then?" Bork asked, trying to sound as brave and scornful as he imagined a true knight would sound.

The Duke looked around at his men, who, if the armor had allowed, would have been shuffling uncomfortably in the morning sunlight. As it was, none of them looked at him.

"No," said the Duke. "I accept your challenge myself." The thought of fighting the giant terrified him. But he was a knight, and known to be a brave man; he had become Duke in the prime of his youth, and if he backed down before a giant now, his duchy would be taken from him in only a few years; his honor would be lost long before. So he drew his sword and advanced upon the giant.

Bork saw the determination in the Duke's eyes, and marvelled at a man who would go himself into a most dangerous battle instead of sending his men. Briefly Bork wondered why the Count had not shown such courage; he determined at that moment that if he could help it the Duke would not die. The blood of the archer was more than he had ever wanted to shed. Nobility was in every movement of the Duke, and Bork wondered at the ill chance that had made them enemies.

The Duke lunged at Bork with his sword flashing. Bork hit him with the flat of the ax, knocking him to the ground. The Duke cried out in pain. His armor was dented deeply; there had to be ribs broken under the dent.

"Why don't you surrender?" asked Bork.

"Kill me now!"

"If you surrender, I won't kill you at all."

The Duke was surprised. There was a murmur from his men.

"I have your word?"

"Of course. I swear it."

It was too startling an idea.

"What do you plan to do, hold me for ransom?"

Bork thought about it. "I don't think so."

"Well, what then? Why not kill me and have done with it?" The pain in his chest now dominated the Duke's voice, but he did not spit blood, and so he began to have some hope.

"All the Count wants you to do is go away and stop collecting tribute. If you promise to do that, I'll promise that not one of you will be harmed."

The Duke and his men considered in silence. It was too good to believe. So good it was almost dishonorable even to consider it. Still—there was Bork, who had broken the Duke's body with one blow, right through the armor. If he chose to let them walk away from the battle, why argue?

"I give my word that I'll cease collecting tribute from the Count, and my men and I will go in peace."

"Well, then, that's good news," Bork said. "I've got to tell the Count." And Bork turned away and walked into the fields, heading for where the Count's tiny army waited.

"I can't believe it," said the Duke. "A knight like that, and he turns out to be generous. The Count could have his way with the King, with a knight like that."

They stripped the armor off him, carefully, and began wrapping his chest with bandages.

"If he were mine," the Duke said, "I'd use him to conquer the whole land."

The Count watched, incredulous, as Bork crossed the field.

"He's still alive," he said, and he began to wonder what Bork would have to say about the fact that none of the knights had joined his gallant charge.

"My Lord Count!" cried Bork, when he was within range. He would have waved, but both his arms were exhausted now. "They surrender!"

"What?" the Count asked the knights near him. "Did he say they surrender?"

"Apparently," a knight answered. "Apparently he won."

"Damn!" cried the Count. "I won't have it!"

The knights were puzzled. "If anybody's going to defeat the Duke, *I* am! Not a damnable commoner! Not a giant with the brains of a cockroach! Charge!"

"What? several of the knights asked.

"I said charge!" And the Count moved forward, his warhorse plodding carefully through the field, building up momentum.

Bork saw the knights start forward. He had watched enough mock battles to recognize a charge. He could only assume that the Count hadn't heard him. But the charge had to be stopped—he had given his word, hadn't he? So he planted himself in the path of the Count's horse.

"Out of the way, you damned fool!" cried the Count. But Bork stood his ground. The Count was determined not to be thwarted. He prepared to ride Bork down.

"You can't charge!" Bork yelled. "They surrendered!"

The Count gritted his teeth and urged the horse forward, his lance prepared to cast Bork out of the way.

A moment later the Count found himself in midair, hanging to the lance for his life. Bork held it over his head, and the knights laboriously halted their charge and wheeled to see what was going on with Bork and the Count.

"My Lord Count," Bork said respectfully. "I guess you didn't hear me. They surrendered. I promised them they could go in peace if they stopped collecting tribute."

From his precarious hold on the lance, fifteen feet off the ground, the Count said, "I didn't hear you."

"I didn't think so. But you *will* let them go, won't you?"

"Of course. Could you give a thought to letting me down, old boy?"

And so Bork let the Count down, and there was a peace treaty between the Duke and the Count, and the Duke's men rode away in peace, talking about the generosity of the giant knight.

"But he isn't a knight," said a servant to the Duke.

"What? Not a knight?"

"No. Just a villager. One of the peasants told me, when I was stealing his chickens."

"Not a knight," said the Duke, and for a moment his face began to turn the shade of red that made his knights want to ride a few feet further from him—they knew his rage too well already.

"We were tricked, then," said a knight, trying to fend off his lord's anger by anticipating it.

The Duke said nothing for a moment. Then he smiled. "Well, if he's not a knight, he should be. He has the strength. He has the courtesy. Hasn't he?"

The knights agreed that he had.

"He's the moral equivalent of a knight," said the Duke. Pride assuaged, for the moment, he led his men back to his castle. Underneath, however, even deeper than the pain in his ribs, was the image of the Count perched on the end of a lance held high in the air by the giant, Bork, and he pondered what it might have meant, and what, more to the point, it might mean in the future.

Things were getting out of hand, the Count decided. First of all, the victory celebration had not been his idea, and yet here they were, riotously drunken in the great hall, and even villagers were making free with the ale, laughing and cheering among the knights. That was bad enough, but worse was the fact that the knights were making no pretense about it—the party was in honor of Bork.

The Count drummed his fingers on the table. No one paid any attention. They were too busy—Sir Alwishard trying to keep two village wenches occupied near the fire, Sir Silwiss pissing in the wine and laughing so loud that the Count could hardly hear Sir Braig and Sir Umlaut as they sang and danced along the table, kicking plates off with their toes in time with the music. It was the best party the Count had ever seen. And it wasn't for him, it was for that damnable giant who had made an ass of him in front of all his men and all the Duke's men and, worst of all, the Duke. He heard a strange growling sound, like a savage wolf getting ready to spring. In a lull in the bedlam he suddenly realized that the sound was coming from his own throat.

Get control of yourself, he thought. The real gains, the solid gains were not Bork's—they were mine. The Duke is gone, and instead of paying him tribute from now on, he'll be paying me. Word would get around, too, that the Count had won a battle with the Duke. After all, that was the basis of power—who could beat whom in battle. A duke was just a man who could beat a count, a count someone who could beat a baron, a baron someone who could beat a knight.

But what was a person who could beat a duke?

"You should be king," said a tall, slender young man standing near the throne.

The Count looked at him, making a vague motion with his hidden hand. How had the boy read his thoughts?

"I'll pretend I didn't hear that."

"You heard it," said the young man.

"It's treason."

"Only if the king beats you in battle. If *you* win, it's treason *not* to say so."

The Count looked the boy over. Dark hair that looked a bit too carefully combed for a villager. A straight nose, a pleasant smile, a winning grace when he walked. But something about his eyes gave the lie to the smile. The boy was vicious somehow. The boy was dangerous.

"I like you," said the Count.

"I'm glad." He did not sound glad. He sounded bored.

"If I'm smart, I'll have you strangled immediately."

The boy only smiled more.

"Who are you?"

"My name is Winkle. And I'm Bork's best friend."

Bork. There he was again, that giant sticking his immense shadow into everything tonight. "Didn't know Bork the Bully had any friends."

"He has one. Me. Ask him."

"I wonder if a friend of Bork's is really a friend of mine," the Count said.

"I said I was his best friend. I didn't say I was a good friend." And Winkle smiled.

A thoroughgoing bastard, the Count decided, but he waved to Bork and beckoned for him to come. In a moment the giant knelt before the Count, who was irritated to discover that when Bork knelt and the Count sat, Bork still looked down on him.

"This man," said the Count, "claims to be your friend."

Bork looked up and recognized Winkle, who was beaming down at him, his eyes filled with love, mostly. A hungry kind of love, but Bork wasn't discriminating. He had the admiration and grudging respect of the knights, but he hardly knew them. This was his childhood friend, and at the thought that Winkle claimed to be his friend Bork immediately forgave all the past slights and smiled back. "Winkle," he said. "Of course we're friends. He's my *best* friend."

The Count made the mistake of looking in Bork's eyes and seeing the complete sincerity of his love for Winkle. It embarrassed him, for he knew Winkle all too well already, from just the moments of conversation they had had. Winkle was nobody's friend. But Bork was obviously blind to that. For a moment the Count almost pitied the giant, had a glimpse of what his life must be like, if the predatory young villager was his best friend.

"Your majesty," said Winkle.

"Don't call me that."

"I only anticipate what the world will know in a matter of months."

Winkle sounded so confident, so sure of it. A chill went up the Count's spine. He shook it off. "I won one battle, Winkle. I still have a huge budget deficit and a pretty small army of fairly lousy knights."

"Think of your daughter, even if *you* aren't ambitious. Despite her beauty she'll be lucky to marry a duke. But if she were the daughter of a king, she could marry anyone in all the world. And her own lovely self would be a dowry—no prince would think to ask for more."

The Count thought of his daughter, the beautiful Brunhilda, and smiled.

Bork also smiled, for he was also thinking of the same thing.

"Your majesty," Winkle urged, "with Bork as your right-hand man and me as your counselor, there's nothing to stop you from being king within a year or two. Who would be willing to stand against an army with the three of us marching at the head?"

"Why three?" asked the Count.

"You mean, why me. I thought you would already understand that—but then, that's what you need me for. You see, your majesty, you're a good man, a godly man, a paragon of virtue. You would never think of seeking power and conniving against your enemies and spying and doing repulsive things to people you don't like. But kings *have* to do those things or they quickly cease to be kings."

Vaguely the Count remembered behaving in just that way many times, but Winkle's words were seductive—they *should* be true.

"Your majesty, where you are pure, I am polluted. Where you are fresh, I am rotten. I'd sell my mother into slavery if I had a mother and I'd cheat the devil at poker and win hell from him before he caught on. And I'd stab any of your enemies in the back if I got the chance."

"But what if my enemies aren't your enemies?" the Count asked.

"Your enemies are *always* my enemies. I'll be loyal to you through thick and thin."

"How can I trust you, if you're so rotten?"

"Because you're going to pay me a lot of money." Winkle bowed deeply.

"Done," said the Count.

"Excellent," said Winkle, and they shook hands. The Count noticed that Winkle's hands were smooth—he had neither the hard horny palms of a village workingman nor the slick calluses of a man trained to warfare.

"How have you made a living, up to now?" the Count asked.

"I steal," Winkle said, with a smile that said I'm joking and a glint in his eye that said I'm not.

"What about me?" asked Bork.

"Oh, you're in it, too," said Winkle. "You're the king's strong right arm."

"I've never met the king," said Bork.

"Yes you have," Winkle retorted. "That is the king."

"No he's not," said the giant. "He's only a count."

The words stabbed the Count deeply. *Only* a count. Well, that would end. "Today I'm only a count," he said patiently. "Who knows what tomorrow will bring? But Bork—I shall knight you. As a knight you must swear absolute loyalty to me and do whatever I say. Will you do that?"

"Of course I will," said Bork. "Thank you, my Lord Count." Bork arose and called to his new friends throughout the hall in a voice that could not be ignored. "My Lord Count has decided I will be made a knight!" There were cheers and applause and stamping of feet. "And the best thing is," Bork said, "that now I can marry the Lady Brunhilda."

There was no applause. Just a murmur of alarm. Of course. If he became a knight, he was eligible for Brunhilda's hand. It was unthinkable—but the Count himself had said so.

The Count was having second thoughts, of course, but he knew no way to back out of it, not without looking like a word-breaker. He made a false start at speaking, but couldn't finish. Bork waited expectantly. Clearly he believed the Count would confirm what Bork had said.

It was Winkle, however, who took the situation in hand. "Oh, Bork," he said sadly—but loudly, so that everyone could hear. "Don't you understand? His majesty is making you a knight out of gratitude. But unless you're a king or the son of a king, you have to do something exceptionally brave to earn Brunhilda's hand."

"But, wasn't I brave today?" Bork asked. After all, the arrow wound in his arm still hurt, and only the ale kept him from aching unmercifully all over from the exertion of the night and the day just past.

"You were brave. But since you're twice the size and ten times the strength of an ordinary man, it's hardly fair for you to win Brunhilda's hand with ordinary bravery. No, Bork—it's just the way things work. It's just the way things are done. Before you're worthy of Brunhilda, you have to do something ten times as brave as what you did today."

Bork could not think of something ten times as brave. Hadn't he gone almost unprotected to chop down the oak tree? Hadn't he attacked a whole army all by himself, and won the surrender of the enemy? What could be ten times as brave?

"Don't despair," the Count said. "Surely in all the battles ahead of us there'll be *something* ten times as brave. And in the meantime, you're a knight, my friend, a great knight, and you shall dine at my table every night! And when we march into battle, there you'll be, right beside me—"

"A few steps ahead," Winkle whispered discreetly.

"A few steps ahead of me, to defend the honor of my country—"

"Don't be shy," whispered Winkle.

"No, not my country. My kingdom. For from today, you men no longer serve a count! You serve a king!"

It was a shocking declaration, and might have caused sober reflection if there had been a sober man in the room. But through the haze of alcohol and torchlight and fatigue, the knights looked at the Count and he did indeed seem kingly. And they thought of the battles ahead and were not afraid, for they had won a glorious victory today and not one of them had shed a drop of blood. Except, of course, Bork. But in some corner of their collected opinions was a viewpoint they would not have admitted to holding, if anyone brought the subject out in the open. The opinion so well hidden from themselves and each other was simple: Bork is not like me. Bork is not one of us. Therefore, Bork is expendable.

The blood that still stained his sleeve was cheap. Plenty more where that came from.

And so they plied him with more ale until he fell asleep, snoring hugely on the table, forgetting that he had been cheated out of the woman he loved; it was easy to forget, for the moment, because he was a knight, and a hero, and at last he had friends.

It took two years for the Count to become King. He began close to home, with other counts, but soon progressed to the great dukes and earls of the kingdom. Wherever he went, the pattern was the same. The Count and his fifty knights would ride their horses, only lightly armored so they could travel with reasonable speed. Bork would walk, but his long legs easily kept up with the rest of them. They would arrive at their victim's castle, and three squires would hand Bork his new steel-handled ax. Bork, covered with impenetrable armor, would wade the moat, if there was one, or simply walk up to the gates, swing the ax, and begin chopping through the wood. When the gates collapsed, Bork would take a huge steel rod and use it as a crow, prying at the portcullis, bending the heavy iron like pretzels until there was a gap wide enough for a mounted knight to ride through.

Then he would go back to the Count and Winkle.

Throughout this operation, not a word would have been said; the only activity from the Count's other men would be enough archery that no one would be able to pour boiling oil or hot tar on Bork while he was working. It was a precaution, and nothing more—even if they set the oil on the fire the moment the Count's little army approached, it would scarcely be hot enough to make water steam by the time Bork was through.

"Do you surrender to his Majesty the King?" Winkle would cry.

And the defenders of the castle, their gate hopelessly breached and terrified of the giant who had so easily made a joke of their defenses, would usually surrender. Occasionally there was some token resistance—when that happened, at Winkle's insistence, the town was brutally sacked and the noble's family was held in prison until a huge ransom was paid.

At the end of two years, the Count and Bork and Winkle and their army marched on Winchester. The King—the real king—fled before them and took up his exile in Anjou, where it was warmer anyway. The Count had himself crowned king, accepted the fealty of every noble in the country, and introduced his daughter Brunhilda all around. Then, finding Winchester not to his liking, he returned to his castle and ruled from there. Suitors for his daughter's hand made a constant traffic on the roads leading into the country; would-be courtiers and nobles vying for positions filled the new hostelries that sprang up on the other side of the village. All left much poorer than they had arrived. And while much of that money found its way into the King's coffers, much more of it went to Winkle, who believed that skimming off the cream meant leaving at least a quarter of it for the King.

And now that the wars were done, Bork hung up his armor and went back to normal life. Not quite normal life, actually. He slept in a good room in the castle, better than most of the knights. Some of the knights had even come to enjoy his company, and sought him out for ale in the evenings or hunting in the daytime—Bork could always be counted on to carry home two deer himself, and was much more convenient than a packhorse. All in all, Bork was happier than he had ever thought he would be.

Which is how things were going when the dragon came and changed it all forever.

Winkle was in Brunhilda's room, a place he had learned many routes to get to, so that he went unobserved every time. Brunhilda, after many gifts and more flattery, was on the verge of giving in to the handsome young advisor to the King when strange screams and cries began coming from the fields below. Brunhilda pulled away from Winkle's exploring hands and, clutching her half-open gown around her, rushed to the window to see what was the matter.

She looked down, to where the screams were coming from, and it wasn't until the dragon's shadow fell across her that she looked up. Winkle, waiting on the bed, only saw the claws reach in and, gently but firmly, take hold of Brunhilda and pull her from the room. Brunhilda fainted immediately, and by the time Winkle got to where he could see her, the dragon had backed away from the window and on great flapping wings was carrying her limp body off toward the north whence he had come.

Winkle was horrified. It was so sudden, something he could not have foreseen or planned against. Yet still he cursed himself and bitterly realized that his plans might be ended forever. A dragon had taken Brunhilda who was to be his means of legitimately becoming king; now the plot of seduction, marriage, and inheritance was ruined.

Ever practical, Winkle did not let himself lament for long. He dressed himself quickly and used a secret passage out of Brunhilda's room, only to reappear in the corridor outside it a moment later. "Brunhilda!" he cried, beating on the door. "Are you all right?"

The first of the knights reached him, and then the King, weeping and wailing and smashing anything that got in his way. Brunhilda's door was down in a moment, and the King ran to the window and cried out after his daughter, now a pinpoint speck in the sky many miles away. "Brunhilda! Brunhilda! Come back!" She did not come back. "Now," cried the King, as he turned back into the room and sank to the floor, his face twisted and wet with grief, "Now I have nothing, and all is in vain!"

My thoughts precisely, Winkle thought, but I'm not weeping about it. To hide his contempt he walked to the window and looked out. He saw, not the dragon, but Bork, emerging from the forest carrying two huge logs.

"Sir Bork," said Winkle.

The King heard a tone of decision in Winkle's voice. He had learned to listen to whatever Winkle said in that tone of voice. "What about him?"

"Sir Bork could defeat a dragon," Winkle said, "if any man could."

"That's true," the King said, gathering back some of the hope he had lost. "Of course that's true."

"But will he?" asked Winkle.

"Of course he will. He loves Brunhilda, doesn't he?"

"He said he did. But Your Majesty, is he really loyal to you? After all, why wasn't he here when the dragon came? Why didn't he save Brunhilda in the first place?"

"He was cutting wood for the winter."

"Cutting wood? When Brunhilda's life was at stake?"

The King was outraged. The illogic of it escaped him—he was not in a logical mood. So he was furious when he met Bork at the gate of the castle.

"You've betrayed me!" the King cried.

"I have?" Bork was smitten with guilt. And he hadn't even meant to.

"You weren't here when we needed you. When *Brunhilda* needed you!"

"I'm sorry," Bork said.

"Sorry, sorry, sorry. A lot of good it does to say you're sorry. You swore to protect Brunhilda from any enemy, and when a really dangerous enemy comes along, how do you repay me for everything I've done for you? You hide out in the forest!"

"What enemy?"

"A dragon," said the King, "as if you didn't see it coming and run out into the woods."

"Cross my heart, Your Majesty, I didn't know there was a dragon coming." And then he made the connection in his mind. "The dragon—it took Brunhilda?"

"It took her. Took her half-naked from her bedroom when she leaped to the window to call to you for help."

Bork felt the weight of guilt, and it was a terrible burden. His face grew hard and angry, and he walked into the castle, his harsh footfalls setting the earth to trembling. "My armor!" he cried. "My sword!"

In minutes he was in the middle of the courtyard, holding out his arms as the heavy mail was draped over him and the breastplate and helmet were strapped and screwed into place. The sword was not enough—he also carried his huge ax and a shield so massive two ordinary men could have hidden behind it.

"Which way did he go?" Bork asked.

"North," the King answered.

"I'll bring back your daughter, Your Majesty, or die in the attempt."

"Damn well better. It's all your fault."

The words stung, but the sting only impelled Bork further. He took the huge sack of food the cook had prepared for him and fastened it to his belt, and without a backward glance strode from the castle and took the road north.

"I almost feel sorry for the dragon," said the King.

But Winkle wondered. He had seen how large the claws were as they grasped Brunhilda—she had been like a tiny doll in a large man's fingers. The claws were razor sharp. Even if she were still alive, could Bork really best the dragon? Bork the Bully, after all, had made his reputation picking on men smaller than he, as Winkle had ample reason to know. How would he do facing a dragon at least five times his size? Wouldn't he turn coward? Wouldn't he run as other men had run from *him*?

He might. But Sir Bork the Bully was Winkle's only hope of getting Brunhilda and the kingdom. If he could do anything to ensure that the giant at least *tried* to fight the dragon, he would do it. And so, taking only his rapier and a sack of food, Winkle left the castle by another way, and followed the giant along the road toward the north.

And then he had a terrible thought.

Fighting the dragon was surely ten times as brave as anything Bork had done before. If he won, wouldn't he have a claim on Brunhilda's hand himself?

It was not something Winkle wished to think about. Something would come to him, some way around the problem when the time came. Plenty of opportunity to plan something—*after* Bork wins and rescues her.

Bork had not rounded the second turn in the road when he came across the old woman, waiting by the side of the road. It was the same old woman who had cared for Brunhilda all those years that she was kept in a secret room in the castle. She looked wizened and weak, but there was a sharp look in her eyes that many had mistaken for great wisdom. It was not great wisdom. But she did know a few things about dragons.

"Going after the dragon, are you?" she asked in a squeaky voice. "Going to get Brunhilda back, are you?" She giggled darkly behind her hand.

"I am if anyone can," Bork said.

"Well, anyone can't," she answered.

"*I* can."

"Not a prayer, you big bag of wind!"

Bork ignored her and started to walk past.

"Wait!" she said, her voice harsh as a dull file taking rust from armor. "Which way will you go?"

"North," he said. "That's the way the dragon took her."

"A quarter of the world is north, Sir Bork the Bully, and a dragon is small compared to all the mountains of the earth. But I know a way you can find the dragon, if you're really a knight.

"Light a torch, man. Light a torch, and whenever you come to a fork in the way, the light of the torch will leap the way you ought to go. Wind or no wind, fire seeks fire, and there is a flame at the heart of every dragon."

"They *do* breathe fire, then?" he asked. He did not know how to fight fire.

"Fire is light, not wind, and so it doesn't come from the dragon's mouth or the dragon's nostrils. If he burns you, it won't be with his breath." The old woman cackled like a mad hen. "No one knows the truth about dragons anymore!"

"Except you."

"I'm an old wife," she said. "And I know. They don't eat human beings, either. They're strict vegetarians. But they kill. From time to time they kill."

"Why, if they aren't hungry for meat?"

"You'll see," she said. She started to walk away, back into the forest.

"Wait!" Bork called. "How far will the dragon be?"

"Not far," she said. "Not far, Sir Bork. He's waiting for you. He's waiting for you and all the fools who come to try to free the virgin." Then she melted away into the darkness.

Bork lit a torch and followed it all night, turning when the flame turned, unwilling to waste time in sleep when Brunhilda might be suffering unspeakable degradation at the monster's hands. And behind him, Winkle forced himself to stay awake, determined not to let Bork lose him in the darkness.

All night, and all day, and all night again Bork followed the light of the torch, through crooked paths long unused, until he came to the foot of a dry, tall hill, with rocks and crags along the top. He stopped, for here the flame leaped high, as if to say, "Upward from here." And in the silence he heard a sound that chilled him to the bone. It was Brunhilda, screaming as if she were being tortured in the cruelest imaginable way. And the screams were followed by a terrible roar. Bork cast aside the remnant of his food and made his way to the top of the hill. On the way he called out, to stop the dragon from whatever it was doing.

"Dragon! Are you there!"

The voice rumbled back to him with a power that made the dirt shift under Bork's feet. "Yes indeed."

"Do you have Brunhilda?"

"You mean the little virgin with the heart of an adder and the brain of a gnat?"

In the forest at the bottom of the hill, Winkle ground his teeth in fury, for despite his designs on the kingdom, he loved Brunhilda as much as he was capable of loving anyone.

"Dragon!" Bork bellowed at the top of his voice. "Dragon! Prepare to die!"

"Oh dear! Oh dear!" cried out the dragon. "Whatever shall I do?"

And then Bork reached the top of the hill, just as the sun topped the distant mountains and it became morning. In the light Bork immediately saw Brunhilda tied to a tree, her auburn hair glistening. All around her was the immense pile of gold that the dragon, according to custom, kept. And all around the gold was the dragon's tail.

Bork looked at the tail and followed it until finally he came to the dragon, who was leaning on a rock chewing on a tree trunk and smirking. The dragon's wings were clad with feathers, but the rest of him was covered with tough gray hide the color of weathered granite. His teeth, when he smiled, were ragged, long, and pointed. His claws were three feet long and sharp as a rapier from tip to base. But in spite of all this armament, the most dangerous thing about him was his eyes. They were large and soft and brown, with long lashes and gently arching brows. But at the center each eye held a sharp point of light, and when Bork looked at the eyes that light stabbed deep into him, seeing his heart and laughing at what it found there.

For a moment, looking at the dragon's eyes, Bork stood transfixed. Then the dragon reached over one wing toward Brunhilda, and with a great growling noise he began to tickle her ear.

Brunhilda was unbearably ticklish, and she let off a bloodcurdling scream.

"Touch her not!" Bork cried.

"Touch her what?" asked the dragon, with a chuckle. "I will not."

"Beast!" bellowed Bork. "I am Sir Bork the Big! I have never been defeated in battle! No man dares stand before me, and the beasts of the forest step aside when I pass!"

"You must be awfully clumsy," said the dragon.

Bork resolutely went on. He had seen the challenges and jousts—it was obligatory to recite and embellish your achievements in order to strike terror into the heart of the enemy. "I can cut down trees with one blow of my ax! I can cleave an ox from head to tail, I can skewer a running deer, I can break down walls of stone and doors of wood!"

"Why can't I ever get a handy servant like that?" murmured the dragon. "Ah well, you probably expect too large a salary."

The dragon's sardonic tone might have infuriated other knights; Bork was only confused, wondering if this matter was less serious than he had thought. "I've come to free Brunhilda, dragon. Will you give her up to me, or must I slay you?"

At that the dragon laughed long and loud. Then it cocked its head and looked at Bork. In that moment Bork knew that he had lost the battle. For deep in the dragon's eyes he saw the truth.

Bork saw himself knocking down gates and cutting down trees, but the deeds no longer looked heroic. Instead he realized that the knights who always rode behind him in these battles were laughing at him, that the King was a weak and vicious man, that Winkle's ambition was the only emotion he had room for; he saw that all of them were using him for their own ends, and cared nothing for him at all.

Bork saw himself asking for Brunhilda's hand in marriage, and he was ridiculous, an ugly, unkempt, and awkward giant in contrast to the slight and graceful girl. He saw that the King's hints of the possibility of their marriage were merely a trick, to blind him. More, he saw what no one else had been able to see—that Brunhilda loved Winkle, and Winkle wanted her.

And at last Bork saw himself as a warrior, and realized that in all the years of his great reputation and in all his many victories, he had fought only one man—an archer who ran at him with a knife. He had terrorized the weak and the small, but never until now had he faced a creature larger than himself. Bork looked in the dragon's eyes and saw his own death.

"Your eyes are deep," said Bork softly.

"Deep as a well, and you are drowning."

"Your sight is clear." Bork's palms were cold with sweat.

"Clear as ice, and you will freeze."

"Your eyes," Bork began. Then his mouth was suddenly so dry that he could barely speak. He swallowed. "Your eyes are filled with light."

"Bright and tiny as a star," the dragon whispered. "And see; your heart is afire."

Slowly the dragon stepped away from the rock, even as the tip of his tail reached behind Bork to push him into the dragon's waiting jaws. But Bork was not in so deep a trance that he could not see.

"I see that you mean to kill me," Bork said. "But you won't have me as easily as that." Bork whirled around to hack at the tip of the dragon's tail with his ax. But he was too large and slow, and the tail flicked away before the ax was fairly swung.

The battle lasted all day. Bork fought exhaustion as much as he fought the dragon, and it seemed the dragon only toyed with him. Bork would lurch toward the tail or a wing or the dragon's belly, but when his ax or sword fell where the dragon had been, it only sang in the air and touched nothing.

Finally Bork fell to his knees and wept. He wanted to go on with the fight, but his body could not do it. And the dragon looked as fresh as it had in the morning.

"What?" asked the dragon. "Finished already?"

Then Bork felt the tip of the dragon's tail touch his back, and the sharp points of the claws pressed gently on either side. He could not bear to look up at what he knew he would see. Yet neither could he bear to wait, not knowing when the blow would come. So he opened his eyes, and lifted his head, and saw.

The dragon's teeth were nearly touching him, poised to tear his head from his shoulders.

Bork screamed. And screamed again when the teeth touched him, when they pushed into his armor, when the dragon lifted him with teeth and tail and talons until he was twenty feet above the ground. He screamed again when he looked into the dragon's eyes and saw, not hunger, not hatred, but merely amusement.

And then he found his silence again, and listened as the dragon spoke through clenched teeth, watching the tongue move massively in the mouth only inches from his head.

"Well, little man. Are you afraid?"

Bork tried to think of some heroic message of defiance to hurl at the dragon, some poetic words that might be remembered forever so that his death would be sung in a thousand songs. But Bork's mind was not quick at such things; he was not that accustomed to speech, and had no ear for gallantry. Instead he began to think it would be somehow cheap and silly to die with a lie on his lips.

"Dragon," Bork whispered, "I'm frightened."

To Bork's surprise, the teeth did not pierce him then. Instead, he felt himself being lowered to the ground, heard a grating sound as the teeth and claws let go of his armor. He raised his visor, and saw that the dragon was now lying on the ground, laughing, rolling back and forth, slapping its tail against the rocks, and clapping its claws together.

"Oh, my dear tiny friend," said the dragon. "I thought the day would never dawn."

"What day?"

"Today," answered the dragon. It had stopped laughing, and it once again drew near to Bork and looked him in the eye. "I'm going to let you live."

"Thank you," Bork said, trying to be polite.

"Thank me? Oh no, my midget warrior. You won't thank me. Did you think my teeth were sharp? Not half so pointed as the barbs of your jealous, disappointed friends."

"I can go?"

"You can go, you can fly, you can dwell in your castle for all I care. Do you want to know why?"

"Yes."

"Because you were afraid. In all my life, I have only killed brave knights who knew no fear. You're the first, the very first, who was afraid in that final moment. Now go."

And the dragon gave Bork a push and sent him down the hill.

Brunhilda, who had watched the whole battle in curious silence, now called after him. "Some kind of knight you are! Coward! I hate you! Don't leave me!" The shouts went on until Bork was out of earshot.

Bork was ashamed.

Bork went down the hill and, as soon as he entered the cool of the forest, he lay down and fell asleep.

Hidden in the rocks, Winkle watched him go, watched as the dragon again began to tickle Brunhilda, whose gown was still open as it had been when she was taken by the dragon. Winkle could not stop thinking of how close he had come to having her. But now, if even Bork could not save her, her cause was hopeless, and Winkle immediately began planning other ways to profit from the situation.

All the plans depended on his reaching the castle before Bork. Since Winkle had dozed off and on during the day's battle, he was able to go farther—to a village, where he stole an ass and rode clumsily, half-asleep, all night and half the next day and reached the castle before Bork awoke.

The King raged. The King swore. The King vowed that Bork would die.

"But Your Majesty," said Winkle, "you can't forget that it is Bork who inspires fear in the hearts of your loyal subjects. You can't kill him—if he were dead, how long would you be king?"

That calmed the old man down. "Then I'll let him live. But he won't have a place in this castle, that's certain. I won't have him around here, the coward. Afraid! Told the dragon he was afraid! Pathetic. The man has no gratitude." And the King stalked from the court.

When Bork got home, weary and sick at heart, he found the gate of the castle closed to him. There was no explanation—he needed none. He had failed the one time it mattered most. He was no longer worthy to be a knight.

And now it was as it had been before. Bork was ignored, despised, feared, he was completely alone. But still, when it was time for great strength, there he was, doing the work of ten men, and not thanked for it. Who would thank a man for doing what he must to earn his bread.

In the evenings he would sit in his hut, staring at the fire that pushed a column of smoke up through the hole in the roof. He remembered how it had been to have friends, but the memory was not happy, for it was always poisoned by the knowledge that the friendship did not outlast Bork's first failure. Now the knights spat when they passed him on the road or in the fields.

The flames did not let Bork blame his troubles on them, however. The flames constantly reminded him of the dragon's eyes, and in their dance he saw himself, a buffoon who dared to dream of loving a princess, who believed that he was truly a knight. Not so, not so. I was never a knight, he thought. I was never worthy. Only now am I receiving what I deserve. And all his bitterness turned inward, and he hated himself far more than any of the knights could hate him.

He had made the wrong choice. When the dragon chose to let him go, he should have refused. He should have stayed and fought to the death. He should have died.

Stories kept filtering into the village, stories of the many heroic and famous knights who accepted the challenge of freeing Brunhilda from the dragon. All of them went as heroes. All of them died as heroes. Only Bork had returned alive from the dragon, and with every knight who died Bork's shame grew. Until he decided that he would go back. Better to join the knights in death than to live his life staring into the flames and seeing the visions of the dragon's eyes.

Next time, however, he would have to be better prepared. So after the spring plowing and planting and lambing and calving, where Bork's help was indispensable to the villagers, the giant went to the castle again. This time no one barred his way, but he was wise enough to stay as much out of sight as possible. He went to the one-armed swordmaster's room. Bork hadn't seen him since he accidentally cut off his arm in sword practice years before.

"Come for the other arm, coward?" asked the swordmaster.

"I'm sorry," Bork said. "I was younger then."

"You weren't any smaller. Go away."

But Bork stayed, and begged the swordmaster to help him. They worked out an arrangement. Bork would be the swordmaster's personal servant all summer, and in exchange the swordmaster would try to teach Bork how to fight.

They went out into the fields every day, and under the swordmaster's watchful eye he practiced sword-fighting with bushes, trees, rocks—anything but the swordmaster, who refused to let Bork near him. Then they would return to the swordmaster's rooms, and Bork would clean the floor and sharpen swords and burnish shields and repair broken practice equipment. And always the swordmaster said, "Bork, you're too stupid to do anything right!" Bork agreed. In a summer of practice, he never got any better, and at the end of the summer, when it was time for Bork to go out in the fields and help with the harvest and the preparations for winter, the swordmaster said, "It's hopeless, Bork. You're too slow. Even the bushes are more agile than you. Don't come back. I still hate you, you know."

"I know," Bork said, and he went out into the fields, where the peasants waited impatiently for the giant to come carry sheaves of grain to the wagons.

Another winter looking at the fire, and Bork began to realize that no matter how good he got with the sword, it would make no difference. The dragon was not to be defeated that way. If excellent swordplay could kill the dragon, the dragon would be dead by now—the finest knights in the kingdom had already died trying.

He had to find another way. And the snow was still heavy on the ground when he again entered the castle and climbed the long and narrow stairway to the tower room where the wizard lived.

"Go away," said the wizard, when Bork knocked at his door. "I'm busy."

"I'll wait," Bork answered.

"Suit yourself."

And Bork waited. It was late at night when the wizard finally opened the door. Bork had fallen asleep leaning on it—he nearly knocked the magician over when he fell inside.

"What the devil are you—you waited!"

"Yes," said Bork, rubbing his head where it had hit the stone floor.

"Well, I'll be back in a moment." The wizard made his way along a narrow ledge until he reached the place where the wall bulged and a hole opened onto the outside of the castle wall. In wartime, such holes were used to pour boiling oil on attackers. In peacetime, they were even more heavily used. "Go on inside and wait," the wizard said.

Bork looked around the room. It was spotlessly clean, the walls were lined with books, and here and there a fascinating artifact hinted at hidden knowledge and arcane powers—a sphere with the world on it, a skull, an abacus, beakers and tubes, a clay pot from which smoke rose, though there was no fire under it. Bork marvelled until the wizard returned.

"Nice little place, isn't it?" the wizard asked. "You're Bork, the bully, aren't you?"

Bork nodded.

"What can I do for you?"

"I don't know," Bork asked. "I want to learn magic. I want to learn magic powerful enough that I can use it to fight the dragon."

The wizard coughed profusely.

"What's wrong?" Bork asked.

"It's the dust," the wizard said.

Bork looked around and saw no dust. But when he sniffed the air, it felt thick in his nose, and a tickling in his chest made him cough, too.

"Dust?" asked Bork. "Can I have a drink?"

"Drink," said the wizard. "Downstairs—"

"But there's a pail of water right here. It looks perfectly clean—"

"Please don't—"

But Bork put the dipper in the pail and drank. The water sloshed into his mouth, and he swallowed, but it felt dry going down, and his thirst was unslaked. "What's wrong with the water?" Bork asked.

The wizard sighed and sat down. "It's the problem with magic, Bork old boy. Why do you think the King doesn't call on me to help him in his wars? He knows it, and now you'll know it, and the whole world probably will know it by Thursday."

"You don't know any magic?"

"Don't be a fool! I know all the magic there is! I can conjure up monsters that would make your dragon look tame! I can snap my fingers and have a table set with food to make the cook die of envy. I can take an empty bucket and fill it with water, with wine, with gold—whatever you want. But try spending the gold, and they'll hunt you down and kill you. Try drinking the water and you'll die of thirst."

"It isn't real."

"All illusion. Handy, sometimes. But that's all. Can't create anything except in your head. That pail, for instance—" And the wizard snapped his fingers. Bork looked, and the pail was filled, not with water, but with dust and spider webs. That wasn't all. He looked around the room, and was startled to see that the bookshelves were gone, as were the other trappings of great wisdom. Just a few books on a table in a corner, some counters covered with dust and papers and half-decayed food, and the floor inches deep in garbage.

"The place is horrible," the wizard said. "I can't bear to look at it." He snapped his fingers, and the old illusion came back. "Much nicer, isn't it?"

"Yes."

"I have excellent taste, haven't I? Now, you wanted me to help you fight the dragon, didn't you? Well, I'm afraid it's out of the question. You see, my illusions only work on human beings, and occasionally on horses. A dragon wouldn't be fooled for a moment. You understand?"

Bork understood, and despaired. He returned to his hut and stared again at the flames. His resolution to return and fight the dragon again was undimmed. But now he knew that he would go as badly prepared as he had before, and his death and defeat would be certain. Well, he thought, better death than life as Bork the coward, Bork the bully who only has courage when he fights people smaller than himself.

The winter was unusually cold, and the snow was remarkably deep. The firewood ran out in February, and there was no sign of an easing in the weather.

The villagers went to the castle and asked for help, but the King was chilly himself, and the knights were all sleeping together in the great hall because there wasn't enough firewood for their barracks and the castle, too. "Can't help you," the King said.

So it was Bork who led the villagers—the ten strongest men, dressed as warmly as they could, yet still cold to the bone in the wind—and they followed in the path his body cut in the snow. With his huge ax he cut down tree after tree; the villagers set the wedges and Bork split the huge logs; the men carried what they could but it was

Bork who made seven trips and carried most of the wood home. The village had enough to last until spring—more than enough, for, as Bork had expected, as soon as the stacks of firewood were deep in the village, the King's men came and took their tax of it.

And Bork, exhausted and frozen from the expedition, was carefully nursed back to health by the villagers. As he lay coughing and they feared he might die, it occurred to them how much they owed to the giant. Not just the firewood, but the hard labor in the farming work, and the fact that Bork had kept the armies far from their village, and they felt what no one in the castle had let himself feel for more than a few moments—gratitude. And so it was that when he had mostly recovered, Bork began to find gifts outside his door from time to time. A rabbit, freshly killed and dressed; a few eggs; a vast pair of hose that fit him very comfortably; a knife specially made to fit his large grip and to ride with comfortable weight on his hip. The villagers did not converse with him much. But then, they were not talkative people. The gifts said it all.

Throughout the spring, as Bork helped in the plowing and planting, with the villagers working alongside, he realized that this was where he belonged—with the villagers, not with the knights. They weren't rollicking good company, but there was something about sharing a task that must be done that made for stronger bonds between them than any of the rough camaraderie of the castle. The loneliness was gone.

Yet when Bork returned home and stared into the flames in the center of his hut, the call of the dragon's eyes became even stronger, if that were possible. It was not loneliness that drove him to seek death with the dragon. It was something else, and Bork could not think what. Pride? He had none—he accepted the verdict of the castle people that he was a coward. The only guess he could make was that he loved Brunhilda and felt a need to rescue her. The more he tried to convince himself, however, the less he believed it.

He had to return to the dragon because, in his own mind, he knew he should have died in the dragon's teeth, back when he fought the dragon before. The common folk might love him for what he did for them, but he hated himself for what he was.

He was nearly ready to head back for the dragon's mountain when the army came.

"How many are there?" the King asked Winkle.

"I can't get my spies to agree," Winkle said. "But the lowest estimate was two thousand men."

"And we have a hundred and fifty here in the castle. Well, I'll have to call on my dukes and counts for support."

"You don't understand, Your Majesty. These *are* your dukes and counts. This isn't an invasion. This is a rebellion."

The King paled. "How do they dare?"

"They dare because they heard a rumor, which at first they didn't believe was true. A rumor that your giant knight had quit, that he wasn't in your army anymore. And when they found out for sure that the rumor was true, they came to cast you out and return the old King to his place."

"Treason!" the King shouted. "Is there no loyalty?"

"I'm loyal," Winkle said, though of course he had already made contact with the other side in case things didn't go well. "But it seems to me that your only hope is to prove the rumors wrong. Show them that Bork is still fighting for you."

"But he isn't. I threw him out two years ago. The coward was even rejected by the dragon."

"Then I suggest you find a way to get him back into the army. If you don't, I doubt you'll have much luck against that crowd out there. My spies tell me they're placing wagers about how many pieces you can be cut into before you die."

The King turned slowly and stared at Winkle, glared at him, gazed intently in his eyes. "Winkle, after all we've done to Bork over the years, persuading him to help us now is a despicable thing to do."

"True."

"And so it's your sort of work, Winkle. Not mine. You get him back in the army."

"I can't do it. He hates me worse than anyone, I'm sure. After all, I've betrayed him more often."

"You get him back in the army within the next six hours, Winkle, or I'll send pieces of you to each of the men in that traitorous group that you've made friends with in order to betray me."

Winkle managed not to looked startled. But he *was* surprised. The King had somehow known about it. The King was not quite the fool he had seemed to be.

"I'm sending four knights with you to make sure you do it right."

"You misjudge me, Your Majesty," Winkle said.

"I hope so, Winkle. Persuade Bork for me, and you live to eat another breakfast."

The knights came, and Winkle walked with them to Bork's hut. They waited outside.

"Bork, old friend," Winkle said. Bork was sitting by the fire, staring in the flames. "Bork, you aren't the sort who holds grudges, are you?"

Bork spat into the flames.

"Can't say I blame you," Winkle said. "We've treated you ungratefully. We've been downright cruel. But you rather brought it on yourself, you know. It isn't *our* fault you turned coward in your fight with the dragon. Is it?"

Bork shook his head. "My fault, Winkle. But it isn't my fault the army has come, either. I've lost my battle. You lose yours."

"Bork, we've been friends since we were three—"

Bork looked up so suddenly, his face so sharp and lit with the glow of the fire, that Winkle could not go on.

"I've looked in the dragon's eyes," Bork said, "and I know who you are."

Winkle wondered if it was true, and was afraid. But he had courage of a kind, a selfish courage that allowed him to dare anything if he thought he would gain by it.

"Who I am? No one knows anything as it is, because as soon as it's known it changes. You looked in the dragon's eyes years ago, Bork. Today I am not who I was then. Today you are not who you were then. And today the King needs you."

"The King is a petty count who rode to greatness on my shoulders. He can rot in hell."

"The other knights need you, then. Do you want them to die?"

"I've fought enough battles for them. Let them fight their own."

And Winkle stood helplessly, wondering how he could possibly persuade this man, who would not be persuaded.

It was then that a village child came. The knights caught him lurking near Bork's hut; they roughly shoved him inside. "He might be a spy," a knight said.

For the first time since Winkle came, Bork laughed. "A spy? Don't you know your own village, here? Come to me, Laggy." And the boy came to him, and stood near him as if seeking the giant's protection. "Laggy's a friend of mine," Bork said. "Why did you come, Laggy?"

The boy wordlessly held out a fish. It wasn't large, but it was still wet from the river.

"Did you catch this?" Bork said.

The boy nodded.

"How many did you catch today?"

The boy pointed at the fish.

"Just the one? Oh, then I can't take this, if it's all you caught."

But as Bork handed the fish back, the boy retreated, refused to take it. He finally opened his mouth and spoke. "For you," he said, and then he scurried out of the hut and into the bright morning sunlight.

And Winkle knew he had his way to get Bork into the battle.

"The villagers," Winkle said.

Bork looked at him quizzically.

And Winkle *almost* said, "If you don't join the army, we'll come out here and burn the village and kill all the children and sell the adults into slavery in Germany." But something stopped him; a memory, perhaps, of the fact that he was once a village child himself. No, not that. Winkle was honest enough with himself to know that what stopped him from making the threat was a mental picture of Sir Bork striding into battle, not in front of the King's army, but at the head of the rebels. A mental picture of Bork's ax biting deep into the gate of the castle, his huge crow prying the portcullis free. This was not the time to threaten Bork.

So Winkle took the other tack. "Bork, if they win this battle, which they surely will if you aren't with us, do you think they'll be kind to this village? They'll burn and rape and kill and capture these people for slaves. They hate us, and to them these villagers are part of us, part of their hatred. If you don't help us, you're killing them."

"I'll protect them," Bork said.

"No, my friend. No, if you don't fight with us, as a knight, they won't treat you chivalrously. They'll fill you full of arrows before you get within twenty feet of their lines. You fight with us, or you might as well not fight at all."

Winkle knew he had won. Bork thought for several minutes, but it was inevitable. He got up and returned to the castle, strapped on his old armor, took his huge ax and his shield, and, with his sword belted at his waist, walked into the courtyard of the castle. The other knights cheered, and called out to him as if he were their dearest friend. But the words were hollow and they knew it, and when Bork didn't answer they soon fell silent.

The gate opened and Bork walked out, the knights on horseback behind him.

And in the rebel camp, they knew that the rumors were a lie—the giant still fought with the King, and they were doomed. Most of the men slipped away into the woods. But the others, particularly the leaders who would die if they surrendered as surely as they would die if they fought, stayed. Better to die valiantly than as a coward, they each thought, and so as Bork approached he still faced an army—only a few hundred men, but still an army.

They came out to meet Bork one by one, as the knights came to the dragon on his hill. And one by one, as they made their first cut or thrust, Bork's ax struck, and their heads flew from their bodies, or their chests were cloven nearly in half, or the ax reamed them end to end, and Bork was bright red with blood and a dozen men were dead and not one had touched him.

So they came by threes and fours, and fought like demons, but still Bork took them, and when even more than four tried to fight him at once they got in each other's way and he killed them more easily.

And at last those who still lived despaired. There was no honor in dying so pointlessly. And with fifty men dead, the battle ended, and the rebels laid down their arms in submission.

Then the King emerged from the castle and rode to the battleground, and paraded triumphantly in front of the defeated men.

"You are all sentenced to death at once," the King declared.

But suddenly he found himself pulled from his horse, and Bork's great hands held him. The King gasped at the smell of gore; Bork rubbed his bloody hands on the King's tunic, and took the King's face between his sticky palms.

"No one dies now. No one dies tomorrow. These men will all live, and you'll send them home to their lands, and you'll lower their tribute and let them dwell in peace forever."

The King imagined his own blood mingling with that which already covered Bork, and he nodded. Bork let him go. The King mounted his horse again, and spoke loudly, so all could hear. "I forgive you all. I pardon you all. You may return to your homes. I confirm you in your lands. And your tribute is cut in half from this day forward. Go in peace. If any man harms you, I'll have his life."

The rebels stood in silence.

Winkle shouted at them "Go! You heard the king! You're free! Go home!"

And they cheered, and long-lived-the-King, and then bellowed their praise to Bork.

But Bork, if he heard them, gave no sign. He stripped off his armor and let it lie in the field. He carried his great ax to the stream, and let the water run over the metal until it was clean. Then he lay in the stream himself, and the water carried off the last of the blood, and when he came out he was clean.

Then he walked away, to the north road, ignoring the calls of the King and his knights, ignoring everything except the dragon who waited for him on the mountain. For this was the last of the acts Bork wold perform in his life for which he would feel shame. He would not kill again. He would only die, bravely, in the dragon's claws and teeth.

The old woman waited for him on the road.

"Off to kill the dragon, are you?" she asked in a voice that the years had tortured into gravel. "Didn't learn enough the first time?" She giggled behind her hand.

"Old woman, I learned everything before. Now I'm going to die."

"Why? So the fools in the castle will think better of you?"

Bork shook his head.

"The villagers already love you. For your deeds today, you'll already be a legend. If it isn't for love or fame, why are you going?"

Bork shrugged. "I don't know. I think he calls to me. I'm through with my life, and all I can see ahead of me are his eyes."

The old woman nodded. "Well, well, Bork. I think you're the first knight that the dragon won't be happy to see. We old wives know, Bork. Just tell him the truth, Bork."

"I've never known the truth to stop a sword," he said.

"But the dragon doesn't carry a sword."

"He might as well."

"No, Bork, no," she said, clucking impatiently. "You know better than that. Of all the dragon's weapons, which cut you the deepest?"

Bork tried to remember. The truth was, he realized, that the dragon had never cut him at all. Not with his teeth nor his claws. Only the armor had been pierced. Yet there had been a wound, a deep one that hadn't healed, and it had been cut in him, not by teeth or talons, but by the bright fires in the dragon's eyes.

"The truth," the old woman said. "Tell the dragon the truth. Tell him the truth, and you'll live!"

Bork shook his head. "I'm not going there to live," he said. He pushed past her, and walked on up the road.

But her words rang in his ears long after he stopped hearing her call after him. The truth, she had said. Well, then, why not? Let the dragon have the truth. Much good may it do him.

This time Bork was in no hurry. He slept every night, and paused to hunt for berries and fruit to eat in the woods. It was four days before he reached the dragon's hill, and he came in the morning, after a good night's sleep. He was afraid, of course; but still there was a pleasant feeling about the morning, a tingling of excitement about the meeting with the dragon. He felt the end coming near, and he relished it.

Nothing had changed. The dragon roared; Brunhilda screamed. And when he reached the top of the hill, he saw the dragon tickling her with his wing. He was not surprised to see that she hadn't changed at all—the two years had not aged her, and though her gown still was open and her breasts were open to the sun and the wind, she wasn't even freckled or tanned. It could have been yesterday that Bork fought with the dragon the first time. And Bork was smiling as he stepped into the flat space where the battle would take place.

Brunhilda saw him first. "Help me! You're the four hundred and thirtieth knight to try! Surely that's a lucky number!" Then she recognized him. "Oh, no. You again. Oh well, at least while he's fighting you I won't have to put up with his tickling."

Bork ignored her. He had come for the dragon, not for Brunhilda.

The dragon regarded him calmly. "You are disturbing my nap time."

"I'm glad," Bork said. "You've disturbed me, sleeping and waking, since I left you. Do you remember me?"

"Ah yes. You're the only knight who was ever afraid of me."

"Do you really believe that?" Bork asked.

"It hardly matters what I believe. Are you going to kill me today?"

"I don't think so," said Bork. "You're much stronger than I am, and I'm terrible at battle. I've never defeated anyone who was more than half my strength."

The lights in the dragon's eyes suddenly grew brighter, and the dragon squinted to look at Bork. "Is that so?" asked the dragon.

"And I'm not very clever. You'll be able to figure out my next move before I know what it is myself."

The dragon squinted more, and the eyes grew even brighter.

"Don't you want to rescue this beautiful woman?" the dragon asked.

"I don't much care," he said. "I loved her once. But I'm through with that. I came for you."

"You don't love her anymore?" asked the dragon.

Bork almost said, "Not a bit." But then he stopped. The truth, the old woman had said. And he looked into himself and saw that no matter how much he hated himself for it, the old feelings died hard. "I love her, dragon. But it doesn't do me any good. She doesn't love me. And so even though I desire her, I don't want her."

Brunhilda was a little miffed. "That's the stupidest thing I've ever heard," she said. But Bork was watching the dragon, whose eyes were dazzlingly bright. The monster was squinting so badly that Bork began to wonder if he could see at all.

"Are you having trouble with your eyes?" Bork asked.

"Do you think *you* ask the questions here? I ask the questions."

"Then ask."

"What in the world do I want to know from you?"

"I can't think of anything," Bork answered. "I know almost nothing. What little I do know, you taught me."

"Did I? What was it that you learned?"

"You taught me that I was not loved by those I thought had loved me. I learned from you that deep within my large body is a very small soul."

The dragon blinked, and its eyes seemed to dim a little.

"Ah," said the dragon.

"What do you mean, 'Ah'?" asked Bork.

"Just 'Ah,' " the dragon answered. "Does every *ah* have to mean something?"

Brunhilda sighed impatiently. "How long does this go on? Everybody else who comes up here is wonderful and brave. You just stand around talking about how miserable you are. Why don't you fight?"

"Like the others?" asked Bork.

"They're so brave," she said.

"They're all dead."

"Only a coward would think of that," she said scornfully.

"It hardly comes as a surprise to you," Bork said. "Everyone knows I'm a coward. Why do you think I came? I'm of no use to anyone, except as a machine to kill people at the command of a King I despise."

"That's my father you're talking about!"

"I'm nothing, and the world will be better without me in it."

"I can't say I disagree," Brunhilda said.

But Bork did not hear her, for he felt the touch of the dragon's tail on his back, and when he looked at the dragon's eyes they had stopped glowing so brightly. They were almost back to normal, in fact, and the dragon was beginning to reach out its claws.

So Bork swung his ax, and the dragon dodged, and the battle was on, just as before.

And just as before, at sundown Bork stood pinned between tail and claws and teeth.

"Are you afraid to die?" asked the dragon, as it had before.

Bork almost answered *yes* again, because that would keep him alive. But then he remembered that he had come in order to die, and as he looked in his heart he still realized that however much he might fear death, he feared life more.

"I came here to die," he said. "I still want to."

And the dragon's eyes leaped bright with light. Bork imagined that the pressure of the claws lessened.

"Well, then, Sir Bork, I can hardly do you such a favor as to kill you." And the dragon let him go.

That was when Bork became angry.

"You can't do this to me!" he shouted.

"Why not?" asked the dragon, who was now trying to ignore Bork and occupied itself by crushing boulders with its claws.

"Because I insist on my right to die at your hands."

"It's not a right, it's a privilege," said the dragon.

"If you don't kill me, then I'll kill you!"

The dragon sighed in boredom, but Bork would not be put off. He began swinging the ax, and the dragon dodged, and in the pink light of sunset the battle was on again. This time, though, the dragon only fell back and twisted and turned to avoid Bork's blows. It made no effort to attack. Finally Bork was too tired and frustrated to go on.

"Why don't you fight!" he shouted. Then he wheezed from the exhaustion of the chase.

The dragon was panting, too. "Come on now, little man, why don't you give it up and go home. I'll give you a signed certificate testifying that I asked you to go, so that no one thinks you're a coward. Just leave me alone."

The dragon began crushing rocks and dribbling them over its head. It lay down and began to bury itself in gravel.

"Dragon," said Bork, "a moment ago you had me in your teeth. You were about to kill me. The old woman told me that truth was my only defense. So I must have lied before, I must have said something false. What was it? Tell me!"

The dragon looked annoyed. "She had no business telling you that. It's privileged information."

"All I ever said to you was the truth."

"Was it?"

"Did I lie to you? Answer—yes or no!"

The dragon only looked away, its eyes still bright. It lay on its back and poured gravel over its belly.

"I did then. I lied. Just the kind of fool I am to tell the truth and still get caught in a lie."

Had the dragon's eyes dimmed? Was there a lie in what he had just said?

"Dragon," Bork insisted, "if you don't kill me or I don't kill you, then I might as well throw myself from the cliff. There's no meaning to my life, if I can't die at your hands!"

Yes, the dragon's eyes were dimming, and the dragon rolled over onto its belly, and began to gaze thoughtfully at Bork.

"Where is the lie in that?"

"Lie? Who said anything about a lie?" But the dragon's long tail was beginning to creep around so it could get behind Bork.

And then it occurred to Bork that the dragon might not even know. That the dragon might be as much a prisoner of the fires of truth inside him as Bork was, and that the dragon wasn't deliberately toying with him at all. Didn't matter, of course. "Never mind what the lie is, then," Bork said. "Kill me now, and the world will be a better place!"

The dragon's eyes dimmed, and a claw made a pass at him, raking the air by his face.

It was maddening, to know there was a lie in what he was saying and not know what it was. "It's the perfect ending for my meaningless life," he said. "I'm so clumsy I even have to stumble into death."

He didn't understand why, but once again he stared into the dragon's mouth, and the claws pressed gently but sharply against his flesh.

The dragon asked the question of Bork for the third time. "Are you afraid, little man, to die?"

This was the moment, Bork knew. If he was to die, he had to lie to the dragon now, for if he told the truth the dragon would set him free again. But to lie, he had to know what the truth was, and now he didn't know at all. He tried to think of where he had gone astray from the truth, and could not. What had he said? It was true that he was clumsy; it was true that he was stumbling into death. What else then?

He had said his life was meaningless. Was that the lie? He had said his death would make the world a better place. Was that the lie?

And so he thought of what would happen when he died. What hole would his death make in the world? The only people who might miss him were the villagers. That was the meaning of his life, then—the villagers. So he lied.

"The villagers won't miss me if I die. They'll get along just fine without me."

But the dragon's eyes brightened, and the teeth withdrew, and Bork realized to his grief that his statement had been true after all. The villagers wouldn't miss him if he died. The thought of it broke his heart, the last betrayal in a long line of betrayals.

"Dragon, I can't outguess you! I don't know what's true and what isn't! All I learn from you is that everyone I thought loved me doesn't. Don't ask me questions! Just kill me and end my life. Every pleasure I've had turns to pain when you tell me the truth."

And now, when he had thought he was telling the truth, the claws broke his skin, and the teeth closed over his head, and he screamed. "Dragon! Don't let me die like this! What is the pleasure that your truth won't turn to pain? What do I have left?"

The dragon pulled away, and regarded him carefully. "I told you, little man, that I don't answer questions. I ask them."

"Why are you here?" Bork demanded. "This ground is littered with the bones of men who failed your tests. Why not mine? Why not mine? Why can't I die? Why did you keep sparing my life? I'm just a man, I'm just alive, I'm just trying to do the best I can in a miserable world and I'm sick of trying to figure out what's true and what isn't. End the game, dragon. My life has never been happy, and I want to die."

The dragon's eyes went black, and the jaws opened again, and the teeth approached, and Bork knew he had told his last lie, that this lie would be enough. But with the teeth inches from him Bork finally realized what the lie was, and the realization was enough to change his mind. "No," he said, and he reached out and seized the teeth, though they cut his fingers. "No," he said, and he wept. "I have been happy. I have." And, gripping the sharp teeth, the memories raced through his mind. The many nights of comradeship with the knights in the castle. The pleasures of weariness from working in the forest and the fields. The joy he felt when alone he won a victory from the Duke; the rush of warmth when the boy brought him the single fish he had caught; and the solitary pleasures, of waking and going to sleep, of walking and running, of feeling the wind on a hot day and standing near a fire in the deep of winter. They were all good, and they had all happened. What did it matter if later the knights despised him? What did it matter if the villagers' love was only a fleeting thing, to be forgotten after he died? The reality of the pain did not destroy the reality of the pleasure; grief did not obliterate joy. They each happened in their time, and because some of them were dark it did not mean that none of them was light.

"I have been happy," Bork said. "And if you let me live, I'll be happy again. That's what my life means, doesn't it? That's the truth, isn't it, dragon? My life matters because I'm alive, joy or pain, whatever comes, I'm alive and that's meaning enough. It's true, isn't it, dragon! I'm not here to fight you. I'm not here for you to kill me. I'm here to make myself alive!"

But the dragon did not answer. Bork was gently lowered to the ground. The dragon withdrew its talons and tail, pulled its head away, and curled up on the ground, covering its eyes with its claws.

"Dragon, did you hear me?"

The dragon said nothing.

"Dragon, look at me!"

The dragon sighed. "Man, I cannot look at you."

"Why not?"

"I am blind," the dragon answered. It pulled its claws away from its eyes. Bork covered his face with his hands. The dragon's eyes were brighter than the sun.

"I feared you, Bork," the dragon whispered. "From the day you told me you were afraid, I feared you. I knew you would be back. And I knew this moment would come."

"What moment?" Bork asked.

"The moment of my death."

"Are you dying?"

"No," said the dragon. "Not yet. You must kill me."

As Bork looked at the dragon lying before him, he felt no desire for blood. "I don't want you to die."

"Don't you know that a dragon cannot live when it has met a truly honest man? It's the only way we ever die, and most dragons live forever."

But Bork refused to kill him.

The dragon cried out in anguish. "I am filled with all the truth that was discarded by men when they chose their lies and died for them. I am in constant pain, and now that I have met a man who does not add to my treasury of falsehood, you are the cruelest of them all."

And the dragon wept, and its eyes flashed and sparkled in every hot tear that fell, and finally Bork could not bear it. He took his ax and hacked off the dragon's head, and the light in its eyes went out. The eyes shriveled in their sockets until they turned into small, bright diamonds with a thousand facets each. Bork took the diamonds and put them in his pocket.

"You killed him," Brunhilda said wonderingly.

Bork did not answer. He just untied her, and looked away while she finally fastened her gown. Then he shouldered the dragon's head and carried it back to the castle, Brunhilda running to keep up with him. He only stopped to rest at night because she begged him to. And when she tried to thank him for freeing her, he only turned away and refused to hear. He had killed the dragon because it wanted to die. Not for Brunhilda. Never for her.

At the castle they were received with rejoicing, but Bork would not go in. He only laid the dragon's head beside the moat and went to his hut, fingering the diamonds in his pocket, holding them in front of him in the pitch blackness of his hut to see that they shone with their own light, and did not need the sun or any other fire but themselves.

The King and Winkle and Brunhilda and a dozen knights came to Bork's hut. "I have come to thank you," the King said, his cheeks wet with tears of joy.

"You're welcome," Bork said. He said it as if to dismiss them.

"Bork," the King said. "Slaying the dragon was ten times as brave as the bravest thing any man has done before. You can have my daughter's hand in marriage."

Bork looked up in surprise.

"I thought you never meant to keep your promise, Your Majesty."

The King looked down, then at Winkle, then back at Bork. "Occasionally," he said, "I keep my word. So here she is, and thank you."

But Bork only smiled, fingering the diamonds in his pocket. "It's enough that you offered, Your Majesty. I don't want her. Marry her to a man she loves."

The King was puzzled. Brunhilda's beauty had not waned in her years of captivity. She had the sort of beauty that started wars. "Don't you want *any* reward?" asked the King.

Bork thought for a moment. "Yes," he said. "I want to be given a plot of ground far away from here. I don't want there to be any count, or any duke, or any king over me. And any man or woman or child who comes to me will be free, and no one can pursue them. And I will never see you again, and you will never see me again."

"That's all you want?"

"That's all."

"Then you shall have it," the King said.

Bork lived all the rest of his life on his little plot of ground. People did come to him. Not many, but five or ten a year all his life, and a village grew up where no one came to take a king's tithe or a duke's fifth or a count's fourth. Children grew up who knew nothing of the art of war and never saw a knight or a battle or the terrible fear on the face of a man who knows his wounds are too deep to heal. It was everything Bork could have wanted, and he was happy all his years there.

Winkle, too, achieved everything he wanted. He married Brunhilda, and soon enough the King's sons had accidents and died, and the King died after dinner one night, and Winkle became King. He was at war all his life, and never went to sleep at night without fear of an assassin coming upon him in the darkness. He governed ruthlessly and thoroughly and was hated all his life; later generations, however, remembered him as a great King. But he was dead then, and didn't know it.

Later generations never heard of Bork.

He had only been out on his little plot of ground for a few months when the old wife came to him. "Your hut is much bigger than you need," she said. "Move over."

So Bork moved over, and she moved in.

She did not magically turn into a beautiful princess. She was foul-mouthed and nagged Bork unmercifully. But he was devoted to her, and when she died a few years later he realized that she had given him more happiness than pain, and he missed her. But the grief at her dying did not taint any of the joys of his memory of her; he just fingered the diamonds, and remembered that grief and joy were not weighed in the same scale, one making the other seem less substantial.

And at last he realized that Death was near; that Death was reaping him like wheat, eating him like bread. He imagined Death to be a dragon, devouring him bit by bit, and one night in a dream he asked Death, "Is my flavor sweet?"

Death, the old dragon, looked at him with bright and understanding eyes, and said, "Salty and sour, bitter and sweet. You sting and you soothe."

"Ah," Bork said, and was satisfied.

Death poised itself to take the last bite. "Thank you," it said.

"You're welcome," Bork answered, and he meant it.

THE PRINCESS AND THE BEAR

I know you've seen the lions. All over the place: beside the doors, flanking the throne, roaring out of the plates in the pantry, spouting water from under the eaves.

Haven't you ever wondered why the statue atop the city gates is a bear? Many years ago in this very city, in the very palace that you can see rising granite and gray behind the old crumbly walls of the king's garden, there lived a princess. It was so long ago that who can ever remember her name? She was just the princess. These days it isn't in fashion to think that princesses are beautiful, and in fact they tend to be a bit horse-faced and gangling. But in those days it was an absolute requirement that a princess look fetching, at least when wearing the most expensive clothes available.

This princess, however, would have been beautiful dressed like a slum child or a shepherd girl. She was beautiful the moment she was born. She only got more beautiful as she grew up.

And there was also a prince. He was not her brother, though. He was the son of a king in a far-off land, and his father was the thirteenth cousin twice removed of the princess' father. The boy had been sent here to our land to get an education—because the princess' father, King Ethelred, was known far and wide as a wise man and a good king.

And if the princess was marvelously beautiful, so was the prince. He was the kind of boy that every mother wants to hug, the kind of boy who gets his hair tousled by every man that meets him.

He and the princess grew up together. They took lessons together from the teachers in the palace, and when the princess was slow, the prince would help her, and when the prince was slow, the princess would help him. They had no secrets from each other, but they had a million secrets that they two kept from the rest of the world. Secrets like where the bluebirds' nest was this year, and what color underwear the cook wore, and that if you duck under the stairway to the armory there's a little underground path that comes up in the wine cellar. They speculated endlessly about which of the princess' ancestors had used that path for surreptitious imbibing.

After not too many years the princess stopped being just a little girl and the prince stopped being just a little boy, and then they fell in love. All at once all their million secrets became just one secret, and they told that secret every time they looked at each other, and everyone who saw them said, "Ah, if I were only young again." That is because so many people think that love belongs to the young: sometime during their lives they stopped loving people, and they think it was just because they got old.

The prince and the princess decided one day to get married.

But the very next morning, the prince got a letter from the far-off country where his father lived. The letter told him that his father no longer lived at all, and that the boy was now a man; and not just a man, but a king.

So the prince got up the next morning, and the servants put his favorite books in a parcel, and his favorite clothes were packed in a trunk, and the trunk, and the parcel, and the prince were all put on a coach with bright red wheels and gold tassels at the corner and the prince was taken away.

The princess did not cry until after he was out of sight. Then she went into her room and cried for a long time, and only her nurse could come in with food and chatter and cheerfulness. At last the chatter brought smiles to the princess, and she went into her father's study where he sat by the fire at night and said, "He promised he would write, every day, and I must write every day as well."

She did, and the prince did, and once a month a parcel of thirty letters would arrive for her, and the postrider would take away a parcel of thirty letters (heavily perfumed) from her.

And one day the Bear came to the palace. Now he wasn't a bear, of course, he was *the* Bear, with a capital B. He was probably only thirty-five or so, because his hair was still golden brown and his face was only lined around the eyes. But he was massive and grizzly, with great thick arms that looked like he could lift a horse, and great thick legs that looked like he could carry that horse a hundred miles. His eyes were deep, and they looked brightly out from under his bushy eyebrows, and the first time the nurse saw him she squealed and said, "Oh, my, he looks like a *bear*."

He came to the door of the palace and the doorman refused to let him in, because he didn't have an appointment. But he scribbled a note on a piece of paper that looked like it had held a sandwich for a few days, and the doorman—with grave misgivings—carried the paper to the king.

The paper said, "If Boris and 5,000 stood on the highway from Rimperdell, would you like to know which way they were going?"

King Ethelred wanted to know.

The doorman let the stranger into the palace, and the king brought him into his study and they talked for many hours.

In the morning the king arose early and went to his captains of cavalry and captains of infantry, and he sent a lord to the knights and their squires, and by dawn all of Ethelred's little army was gathered on the highway, the one that leads to Rimperdell. They marched for three hours that morning, and then they came to a place and the stranger with golden brown hair spoke to the king and King Ethelred commanded the army to stop. They stopped, and the infantry was sent into the forest on one side of the road, and the cavalry was sent into the tall cornfields on the other side of the road, where they dismounted. Then the king, and the stranger, and the knights waited in the road.

Soon they saw a dust cloud in the distance, and then the dust cloud grew near, and they saw that it was an army coming down the road. And at the head of the army was King Boris of Rimperdell. And behind him the army seemed to be five thousand men.

"Hail," King Ethelred said, looking more than a little irritated, since King Boris' army was well inside our country's boundaries.

"Hail," King Boris said, looking more than a little irritated, since no one was supposed to know that he was coming.

"What do you think you're doing?" asked King Ethelred.

"You're blocking the road," said King Boris.

"It's my road," said King Ethelred.

"Not anymore," said King Boris.

"I and my knights say that this road belongs to me," said King Ethelred.

King Boris looked at Ethelred's fifty knights, and then he looked back at his own five thousand men, and he said, "I say you and your knights are dead men unless you move aside."

"Then you want to be at war with me?" asked King Ethelred.

"War?" said King Boris. "Can we really call it a war? It will be like stepping on a nasty cockroach."

"I wouldn't know," said King Ethelred, "because we haven't ever had cockroaches in our kingdom."

Then he added, "Until now, of course."

Then King Ethelred lifted his arm, and the infantry shot arrows and threw lances from the wood, and many of Boris' men were slain. And the moment all of his troops were ready to fight the army in the forest, the cavalry came from the field and attacked from the rear, and soon Boris' army, what was left of it, surrendered, and Boris himself lay mortally wounded in the road.

"If you had won this battle," King Ethelred said, "what would you have done to me?"

King Boris gasped for breath and said, "I would have had you beheaded."

"Ah," said King Ethelred. "We are very different men. For I will let you live."

But the stranger stood beside King Ethelred, and he said, "No, King Ethelred, that is not in your power, for Boris is about to die. And if he were not, I would have killed him myself, for as long as a man like him is alive, no one is safe in all the world."

Then Boris died, and he was buried in the road with no marker, and his men were sent home without their swords.

And King Ethelred came back home to crowds of people cheering the great victory, and shouting, "Long live King Ethelred the conqueror."

King Ethelred only smiled at them. Then he took the stranger into the palace, and gave him a room where he could sleep, and made him the chief counselor to the king, because the stranger had proved that he was wise, and that he was loyal, and that he loved the king better than the king loved himself, for the king would have let Boris live.

No one knew what to call the man, because when a few brave souls asked him his name, he only frowned and said, "I will wear the name you pick for me."

Many names were tried, like George, and Fred, and even Rocky and Todd. But none of the names seemed right. For a long time, everyone called him Sir, because when somebody is that big and that strong and that wise and that quiet, you feel like calling him sir and offering him your chair when he comes in the room.

And then after a while everyone called him the name the nurse had chosen for him just by accident: they called him the Bear. At first they only called him that behind his back, but eventually someone slipped and called him that at the dinner table, and he smiled, and answered to the name, and so everyone called him that.

Except the princess. She didn't call him anything, because she didn't speak to him if she could help it, and when she talked about him, she stuck out her lower lip and called him That Man.

This is because the princess hated the Bear.

She didn't hate him because he had done anything bad to her. In fact, she was pretty sure that he didn't even notice she was living in the palace. He never turned and stared when she walked into the room, like all the other men did. But that isn't why she hated him, either.

She hated him because she thought he was making her father weak.

King Ethelred was a great king, and his people loved him. He always stood very tall at ceremonies, and he sat for hours making judgments with great wisdom. He always spoke softly when softness was needed, and shouted at the times when only shouting would be heard.

In all he was a stately man, and so the princess was shocked with the way he was around the Bear.

King Ethelred and the Bear would sit for hours in the king's study, every night when there wasn't a great banquet or an ambassador. They would both drink from huge mugs of ale—but instead of having a servant refill the mugs, the princess was shocked that her own father stood up and poured from the pitcher! A king, doing the work of a servant, and then giving the mug to a commoner, a man whose name no one knew!

The princess saw this because she sat in the king's study with them, listening and watching without saying a word as they talked. Sometimes she would spend the whole time combing her father's long white hair. Sometimes she would knit long woolen stockings for her father for the winter. Sometimes she would read—for her father believed that even women should learn to read. But all the time she listened, and became angry, and hated the Bear more and more.

King Ethelred and the Bear didn't talk much about affairs of state. They talked about hunting rabbits in the forest. They told jokes about lords and ladies in the kingdom— and some of the jokes weren't even nice, the princess told herself bitterly. They talked about what they should do about the ugly carpet in the courtroom—as if the Bear had a perfect right to have an opinion about what the new carpet should be.

And when they did talk about affairs of state, the Bear treated King Ethelred like an *equal*. When he disagreed with the king, he would leap to his feet saying, "No, no, no, no, you just don't see at all." When he thought the king had said something right, he clapped him on the shoulder and said, "You'll make a great king yet, Ethelred."

And sometimes King Ethelred would sigh and stare into the fire, and whisper a few words, and a dark and tired look would steal across his face. Then the Bear would put his arm around the king's shoulder, and stare into the fire with him, until finally the king would sigh again, and then lift himself, groaning, out of his chair, and say, "It's time that this old man put his corpse between the sheets."

The next day the princess would talk furiously to her nurse, who never told a soul what the princess said. The princess would say, "That Man is out to make my father a weakling! He's out to make my father look stupid. That Man is making my father forget that he is a king." Then she would wrinkle her forehead and say, "That Man is a traitor."

She never said a word about this to her father, however. If she had, he would have patted her head and said, "Oh, yes, he does indeed make me forget that I am a king." But he would also have said, "He makes me remember what a king should be." And Ethelred would not have called him a traitor. He would have called the Bear his friend.

As if it wasn't bad enough that her father was forgetting himself around a commoner, that was the very time that things started going bad with the prince. She suddenly noticed that the last several packets of mail had not held thirty letters each—they only held twenty, and then fifteen, and then ten. And the letters weren't five pages long any more. They were only three, and then two, and then one.

He's just busy, she thought.

Then she noticed that he no longer began her letters with, "My dearest darling sweetheart pickle-eating princess." (The pickle-eating part was an old joke from something that happened when they were both nine.) Now he started them, "My dear lady," or "Dear princess." Once she said to her nurse, "He might as well address them to Occupant."

He's just tired, she thought.

And then she realized that he never told her he loved her anymore, and she went out on the balcony and cried where only the garden could hear, and where only the birds in the trees could see.

She began to keep to her rooms, because the world didn't seem like a very nice place any more. Why should she have anything to do with the world, when it was a nasty place where fathers turned into mere men, and lovers forgot they were in love?

And she cried herself to sleep every night that she slept. And some nights she didn't sleep at all, just stared at the ceiling trying to forget the prince. And you know that if you want to remember something, the best way is to try very, very hard to forget it.

Then one day, as she went to the door of her room, she found a basket of autumn leaves just inside her door. There was no note on them, but they were very brightly colored, and they rustled loudly when she touched the basket, and she said to herself, "It must be autumn."

She went to the window and looked, and it was autumn, and it was beautiful. She had already seen the leaves a hundred times a day, but she hadn't remembered to notice.

And then a few weeks later she woke up and it was cold in her room. Shivering, she went to her door to call for a servant to build her fire up higher—and just inside the door was a large pan, and on the pan there stood a little snowman, which was grinning a grin made of little chunks of coal, and his eyes were big pieces of coal, and all in all it was so comical the princess had to laugh. That day she forgot her misery for a while and went outside and threw snowballs at the knights, who of course let her hit them and who never managed to hit her, but of course that's all part of being a princess—no one would ever put snow down your back or dump you in the canal or anything.

She asked her nurse who brought these things, but the nurse just shook her head and smiled. "It wasn't me," she said. "Of course it was," the princess answered, and gave her a hug, and thanked her. The nurse smiled and said, "Thanks for your thanks, but it wasn't me." But the princess knew better, and loved her nurse all the more.

Then the letters stopped coming altogether. And the princess stopped writing letters. And she began taking walks in the woods.

At first she only took walks in the garden, which is where princesses are supposed to take walks. But in a few days of walking and walking and walking she knew every brick of the garden path by heart, and she kept coming to the garden wall and wishing she were outside it.

So one day she walked to the gate and went out of the garden and wandered into the forest. The forest was not at all like the garden. Where the garden was neatly tended and didn't have a weed in it, the forest was all weeds, all untrimmed and loose, with animals that ran from her, and birds that scurried to lead her away from their young, and best of all, only grass or soft brown earth under her feet. Out in the forest she could forget the garden where every tree reminded her of talks she had had with the prince while sitting in the branches. Out in the forest she could forget the palace where every room had held its own joke or its own secret or its own promise that had been broken.

That was why she was in the forest the day the wolf came out of the hills.

She was already heading back to the palace, because it was getting on toward dark, when she caught a glimpse of something moving. She looked, and realized that it was a huge gray wolf, walking along beside her not fifteen yards off. When she stopped, the wolf stopped. When she moved, the wolf moved. And the farther she walked, the closer the wolf came.

She turned and walked away from the wolf.

After a few moments she looked behind her, and saw the wolf only a dozen feet away, its mouth open, its tongue hanging out, its teeth shining white in the gloom of the late afternoon forest.

She began to run. But not even a princess can hope to outrun a wolf. She ran and ran until she could hardly breathe, and the wolf was still right behind her, panting a little but hardly tired. She ran and ran some more until her legs refused to obey her and she fell to the ground. She looked back, and realized that this was what the wolf had been waiting for—for her to be tired enough to fall, for her to be easy prey, for her to be a dinner he didn't have to work for.

And so the wolf got a gleam in its eye, and sprang forward.

Just as the wolf leaped, a huge brown shape lumbered out of the forest and stepped over the princess. She screamed. It was a huge brown bear, with heavy fur and vicious teeth. The bear swung its great hairy arm at the wolf, and struck it in the head. The wolf flew back a dozen yards, and from the way its head bobbed about as it flew, the princess realized its neck had been broken.

And then the huge bear turned toward her, and she saw with despair that she had only traded one monstrous animal for another.

And she fainted. Which is about all that a person can do when a bear that is standing five feet away looks at you. And looks hungry.

She woke up in bed at the palace and figured it had all been a dream. But then she felt a terrible pain in her legs, and felt her face stinging with scratches from the branches. It had not been a dream—she really had run through the forest.

"What happened?" she asked feebly. "Am I dead?" Which wasn't all that silly a question, because she really had expected to be.

"No," said her father, who was sitting by the bed.

"No," said the nurse. "And why in the world, why should you be dead?"

"I was in the forest," said the princess, "and there was a wolf, and I ran and ran but he was still there. And then a bear came and killed the wolf, and it came toward me like it was going to eat me, and I guess I fainted."

"Ah," said the nurse, as if that explained everything.

"Ah," said her father, King Ethelred. "Now I understand. We were taking turns watching you after we found you unconscious and scratched up by the garden gate.

You kept crying out in your sleep, 'Make the bear go away! Make the bear leave me alone!' Of course, we thought you meant *the* Bear, our Bear, and we had to ask the poor man not to take his turn any more, as we thought it might make you upset. We all thought you hated him, for a while there." And King Ethelred chuckled. "I'll have to tell him it was all a mistake."

Then the king left. Great, thought the princess, he's going to tell the Bear it was all a mistake, and I really do hate him to pieces.

The nurse walked over to the bed and knelt beside it. "There's another part of the story. They made me promise not to tell you," the nurse said, "but you know and I know that I'll always tell you everything. It seems that it was two guards that found you, and they both said that they saw something running away. Or not running, exactly, galloping. Or something. They said it looked like a bear, running on all fours."

"Oh, no," said the princess. "How horrible!"

"No," said the nurse. "It was their opinion, and Robbo Knockle swears it's true, that the bear they saw had brought you to the gate and set you down gentle as you please. Whoever brought you there smoothed your skirt, you know, and put a pile of leaves under your head like a pillow, and you were surely in no state to do all that yourself."

"Don't be silly," said the princess. "How could a bear do all that?"

"I know," said the nurse, "so it must not have been an ordinary bear. It must have been a magic bear." She said this last in a whisper, because the nurse believed that magic should be talked about quietly, lest something awful should hear and come calling.

"Nonsense," said the princess. "I've had an education, and I don't believe in magic bears or magic brews or any kind of magic at all. It's just old-lady foolishness."

The nurse stood up and her mouth wrinkled all up. "Well, then, this foolish old lady will take her foolish stories to somebody foolish, who wants to listen."

"Oh, there, there," the princess said, for she didn't like to hurt anyone's feelings, especially not Nurse's. And they were friends again. But the princess still didn't believe about the bear. However, she hadn't been eaten, after all, so the bear must not have been hungry.

It was only two days later, when the princess was up and around again—though there were nasty scabs all over her face from the scratches—that the prince came back to the palace.

He came riding up on a lathered horse that dropped to the ground and died right in front of the palace door. He looked exhausted, and there were great purple circles under his eyes. He had no baggage. He had no cloak. Just the clothes on his back and a dead horse.

"I've come home," he said to the doorman, and fainted into his arms. (By the way, it's perfectly all right for a man to faint, as long as he has ridden on horseback for five days, without a bite to eat, and with hundreds of soldiers chasing him.)

"It's treason," he said when he woke up and ate and bathed and dressed. "My allies turned against me, even my own subjects. They drove me out of my kingdom. I'm lucky to be alive."

"Why?" asked King Ethelred.

"Because they would have killed me. If they had caught me."

"No, no, no, no, don't be stupid," said the Bear, who was listening from a chair a few feet away. "Why did they turn against you?"

The prince turned toward the Bear and sneered. It was an ugly sneer, and it twisted up the prince's face in a way it had never twisted when he lived with King Ethelred and was in love with the princess.

"I wasn't aware that I was being stupid," he said archly. "And I certainly wasn't aware that *you* had been invited into the conversation."

The Bear didn't say anything after that, just nodded an unspoken apology and watched.

And the prince never did explain why the people had turned against him. Just something vague about power-hungry demagogues and mob rule.

The princess came to see the prince that very morning.

"You look exhausted," she said.

"You look beautiful," he said.

"I have scabs all over my face and I haven't done my hair in days," she said.

"I love you," he said.

"You stopped writing," she said.

"I guess I lost my pen," he said. "No, I remember now. I lost my mind. I forgot how beautiful you are. A man would have to be mad to forget."

Then he kissed her, and she kissed him back, and she forgave him for all the sorrow he had caused her and it was like he had never been away.

For about three days.

Because in three days she began to realize that he was different somehow.

She would open her eyes after kissing him (princesses always close their eyes when they kiss someone) and she would notice that he was looking off somewhere with a distant expression on his face. As if he barely noticed that he was kissing her. That does not make any woman, even a princess, feel very good.

She noticed that sometimes he seemed to forget she was even there. She passed him in a corridor and he wouldn't speak, and unless she touched his arm and said good morning he might have walked on by without a word.

And then sometimes, for no reason, he would feel slighted or offended, or a servant would make a noise or spill something and he would fly into a rage and throw things against the wall. He had never even raised his voice in anger when he was a boy.

He often said cruel things to the princess, and she wondered why she loved him, and what was wrong, but then he would come to her and apologize, and she would forgive him because after all he had lost a kingdom because of traitors, and he couldn't be expected to always feel sweet and nice. She decided, though, that if it was up to her, and it was, he would never feel unsweet and unnice again.

Then one night the Bear and her father went into the study and locked the door behind them. The princess had never been locked out of her father's study before, and she became angry at the Bear because he was taking her father away from her, and so she listened at the door. She figured that if the Bear wanted to keep her out, she would see to it that she heard everything anyway.

This is what she heard.

"I have the information," the Bear said.

"It must be bad, or you wouldn't have asked to speak to me alone," said King Ethelred. Aha, thought the princess, the Bear *did* plot to keep me out.

The Bear stood by the fire, leaning on the mantel, while King Ethelred sat down.

"Well?" asked King Ethelred.

"I know how much the boy means to you. And to the princess. I'm sorry to bring such a tale."

The boy! thought the princess. They couldn't possibly be calling her prince a boy, could they? Why, he had been a king, except for treason, and here a commoner was calling him a boy.

"He means much to us," said King Ethelred, "which is all the more reason for me to know the truth, be it good or bad."

"Well, then," said the Bear, "I must tell you that he was a very bad king."

The princess went white with rage.

"I think he was just too young. Or something," said the Bear. "Perhaps there was a side to him that you never saw, because the moment he had power it went to his head. He thought his kingdom was too small, because he began to make war with little neighboring counties and duchies and took their lands and made them part of his kingdom. He plotted against other kings who had been good and true friends of his father. And he kept raising taxes on his people to support huge armies. He kept starting wars and mothers kept weeping because their sons had fallen in battle.

"And finally," said the Bear, "the people had had enough, and so had the other kings, and there was a revolution and a war all at the same time. The only part of the boy's tale that is true is that he was lucky to escape with his life, because every person that I talked to spoke of him with hatred, as if he were the most evil person they had ever seen."

King Ethelred shook his head. "Could you be wrong? I can't believe this of a boy I practically raised myself."

"I wish it were not true," said the Bear, "for I know that the princess loves him dearly. But it seems obvious to me that the boy doesn't love her—he is here because he knew he would be safe here, and because he knows that if he married her, he would be able to rule when you are dead."

"Well," said King Ethelred, "that will never happen. My daughter will never marry a man who would destroy the kingdom."

"Not even if she loves him very much?" asked the Bear.

"It is the price of being a princess," said the king. "She must think first of the kingdom, or she will never be fit to be queen."

At that moment, however, being queen was the last thing the princess cared about. All she knew was that she hated the Bear for taking away her father, and now the same man had persuaded her father to keep her from marrying the man she loved.

She beat on the door, crying out, "Liar! Liar!" King Ethelred and the Bear both leaped for the door. King Ethelred opened it, and the princess burst into the room and started hitting the Bear as hard as she could. Of course the blows fell very lightly, because she was not all that strong, and he was very large and sturdy and the blows could have caused him no pain. But as she struck at him his face looked as if he were being stabbed through the heart at every blow.

"Daughter, daughter," said King Ethelred. "What is this? Why did you listen at the door?"

But she didn't answer; she only beat at the Bear until she was crying too hard to hit him anymore. And then, between sobs, she began to yell at him. And because she didn't usually yell her voice became harsh and hoarse and she whispered. But yelling or whispering, her words were clear, and every word said hatred.

She accused the Bear of making her father little, nothing, worse than nothing, a weakling king who had turn to a filthy commoner to make any decision at all. She accused the Bear of hating her and trying to ruin her life by keeping her from marrying the only man she could ever love. She accused the Bear of being a traitor, who was plotting to be king himself and rule the kingdom. She accused the Bear of making up vile lies about the prince because she knew that he would be a better king than her weakling father, and that if she married the prince all the Bear's plans for ruling the kingdom would come to nothing.

And finally she accused the Bear of having such a filthy mind that he imagined that he could eventually marry her himself, and so become king.

But that would never happen, she whispered bitterly, at the end. "That will never happen," she said, "never, never, never, because I hate you and I loathe you and if you don't get out of this kingdom and never come back I'll kill myself, I swear it."

And then she grabbed a sword from the mantel and tried to slash her wrists, and the Bear reached out and stopped her by holding her arms in his huge hands that gripped like iron. Then she spit at him and tried to bite his fingers and beat her head against his chest until King Ethelred took her hands and the Bear let go and backed away.

"I'm sorry," King Ethelred kept saying, though he himself wasn't certain who he was apologizing to or what he was apologizing for. "I'm sorry." And then he realized that he was apologizing for himself, because somehow he knew that his kingdom was ruined right then.

If he listened to the Bear and sent the prince away, the princess would never forgive him, would hate him, in fact, and he couldn't bear that. But if he didn't listen to the Bear, then the princess would surely marry the prince, and the prince would surely ruin his kingdom. And he couldn't endure that.

But worst of all, he couldn't stand the terrible look on the Bear's face.

The princess stood sobbing in her father's arms.

The king stood wishing there were something he could do or undo.

And the Bear simply stood.

And then the Bear nodded, and said, "I understand. Good-bye."

And then the Bear walked out of the room, and out of the palace, and out of the garden walls, and out of the city, and out of any land that the king had heard of.

He took nothing with him—no food, no horse, no extra clothing. He just wore his clothing and carried his sword. He left as he came.

And the princess cried with relief. The Bear was gone. Life could go on, just like it was before ever the prince left and before ever the Bear came.

So she thought.

She didn't really realize how her father felt until he died only four months later, suddenly very old and very tired and very lonely and despairing for his kingdom.

She didn't realize that the prince was not the same man she loved before until she married him three months after her father died.

On the day of their wedding she proudly crowned him king herself, and led him to the throne, where he sat.

"I love you," she said proudly, "and you look like a king."

"I am a king," he said. "I am King Edward the first."

"Edward?" she said. "Why Edward? That's not your name."

"That's a king's name," he said, "and I am a king. Do I not have power to change my name?"

"Of course," she said. "But I liked your own name better."

"But you will call me Edward," he said, and she did.

When she saw him. For he didn't come to her very often. As soon as he wore the crown he began to keep her out of the court, and conducted the business of the kingdom where she couldn't hear. She didn't understand this, because her father had always let her attend everything and hear everything in the government, so she could be a good queen.

"A good queen," said King Edward, her husband, "is a quiet woman who has babies, one of whom will be king."

And so the princess, who was now the queen, had babies, and one of them was a boy, and she tried to help him grow up to be a king.

But as the years passed by she realized that King Edward was not the lovely boy she had loved in the garden. He was a cruel and greedy man. And she didn't like him very much.

He raised the taxes, and the people became poor.

He built up the army, so it became very strong.

He used the army to take over the land of Count Edred, who had been her godfather.

He also took over the land of Duke Adlow, who had once let her pet one of his tame swans.

He also took over the land of Earl Thlaffway, who had wept openly at her father's funeral, and said that her father was the only man he had ever worshipped, because he was such a good king.

And Edred and Adlow and Thlaffway all disappeared, and were never heard of again.

"He's even against the common people," the nurse grumbled one day as she did up the queen's hair. "Some shepherds came to court yesterday to tell him a marvel, which is their duty, isn't it, to tell the king of anything strange that happens in the land?"

"Yes," said the queen, remembering how as a child she and the prince had run to their father often to tell him a marvel—how grass springs up all at once in the spring, how water just disappeared on a hot day, how a butterfly comes all awkward from the cocoon.

"Well," said the nurse, "they told him that there was a bear along the edge of the forest, a bear that doesn't eat meat, but only berries and roots. And this bear, they said, killed wolves. Every year they lose dozens of sheep to the wolves, but this year they had lost not one lamb, because the bear killed the wolves. Now that's a marvel, I'd say," said the nurse.

"Oh yes," said the princess who was now a queen.

"But what did the king do," said the nurse, "but order his knights to hunt down that bear and kill it. Kill it!"

"Why?" asked the queen.

"Why, why, why?" asked the nurse. "The best question in the world. The shepherds asked it, and the king said, 'can't have a bear loose around here. He might kill children.'

" 'Oh no,' says the shepherds, 'the bear don't eat meat.'

" 'Then, it'll wind up stealing grain,' the king says in reply, and there it is, my lady—the hunters are out after a perfectly harmless bear! You can bet the shepherds don't like it. A perfectly harmless bear!"

The queen nodded. "A magic bear."

"Why, yes," said the nurse. "Now you mention it, it does seem like the bear that saved you that day—"

"Nurse," said the queen, "there was no bear that day. I was dreaming I was mad with despair. There wasn't a wolf chasing me. And there was definitely no magic bear."

The nurse bit her lip. Of course there had been a bear, she thought. And a wolf. But the queen, her princess, was determined not to believe in any kind thing.

"Sure there was a bear," said the nurse.

"No, there was no bear," said the queen, "and now I know who put the idea of a magic bear into the children's head."

"They've heard of him?"

"They came to me with a silly tale of a bear that climbs over the wall into the garden when no one else is around, and who plays with them and lets him ride on his back. Obviously you told them your silly tale about the magic bear who supposedly saved me. So I told them that magic bears were a full tall-tale and that even grownups liked to tell them, but that they must be careful to remember the difference between truth and falsehood, and they should wink if they're fibbing."

"What did they say?" the nurse said.

"I made them all wink about the bear," said the queen, "of course. But I would appreciate it if you wouldn't fill their heads with silly stories. You did tell them your stupid story, didn't you?"

"Yes," said the nurse sadly.

"What a trouble your wagging tongue can cause," said the queen, and the nurse burst into tears and left the room.

They made it up later but there was no talk of bears. The nurse understood well enough, though. The thought of bears reminded the queen of *the* Bear, and everyone knew that she was the one who drove that wise counselor away. If only the Bear were still here, thought the nurse—and hundreds of other people in the kingdom—if he were still here we wouldn't have these troubles in the kingdom.

And there were troubles. The soldiers patrolled the streets of the cities and locked people up for saying things about King Edward. And when a servant in the palace did anything wrong he would bellow and storm, and even throw things and beat them with a rod.

One day when King Edward didn't like the soup he threw the whole tureen at the cook. The cook promptly took his leave, saying for anyone to hear, "I've served kings and queens, lords and ladies, soldiers, and servants, and in all that time this is the first time I've ever been called upon to serve a pig."

The day after he left he was back, at swordpoint—not cooking in the kitchen, of course, since cooks are too close to the king's food. No, the cook was sweeping the stables. And the servants were told in no uncertain terms that none of them was free to leave. If they didn't like their jobs, they could be given another one to do. And they all looked at the work the cook was doing, and kept their tongues.

Except the nurse, who talked to the queen about everything.

"We might as well be slaves," said the nurse. "Right down to the wages. He's cut us all in half, some even more, and we've got barely enough to feed ourselves. I'm all right, mind you, my lady, for I have no one but me to feed, but there's some who's hard put to get a stick of wood for the fire and a morsel of bread for a hungry mouth or six."

The queen thought of pleading with her husband, but then she realized that King Edward would only punish the servants for complaining. So she began giving her nurse jewels to sell. Then the nurse quietly gave the money to the servants who had the least, or who had the largest families, and whispered to them, even though the queen had told her not to give a hint, "This money's from the queen, you know. *She* remembers us servants, even if her husband's a lout and a pimple." And the servants remembered that the queen was kind.

The people didn't hate King Edward quite as much as the servants did, of course, because even though taxes were high, there are always silly people who are proud fit to bust when their army has a victory. And of course King Edward had quite a few victories at first. He would pick a fight with a neighboring king or lord and then march in and take over. People had thought old King Boris' army of five thousand was bad, back in the old days. But because of his high taxes, King Edward was able to hire an army of fifty thousand men, and war was a different thing then. They lived off the land in enemy country, and killed and plundered where they liked. Most of the soldiers weren't local men, anyway—they were the riffraff of the highways, men who begged or stole, and now were being paid for stealing.

But King Edward tripled the size of the kingdom, and there were a good many citizens who followed the war news and cheered whenever King Edward rode through the streets.

They cheered the queen, too, of course, but they didn't see her very much, about once a year or so. She was still beautiful, of course, more beautiful than ever before. No one particularly noticed that her eyes were sad these days, or else those who noticed said nothing and soon forgot it.

But King Edward's victories had been won against weak, and peaceful, and unprepared men. And at last the neighboring kings got together, and the rebels from conquered lands got together, and they planned King Edward's doom.

When next King Edward went a-conquering, they were ready, and on the very battlefield where King Ethelred had defeated Boris they ambushed King Edward's army. Edward's fifty thousand hired men faced a hundred thousand where before they had never faced more than half their number. Their bought courage melted away, and those who lived through the first of the battle ran for their lives.

King Edward was captured and brought back to the city in a cage, which was hung above the city gate, right where the statue of the bear is today.

The queen came out to the leaders of the army that had defeated King Edward and knelt before them in the dust and wept, pleading for her husband. And because she was beautiful, and good, and because they themselves were only good men trying to protect their own lives and property, they granted him his life. For her sake they even let him remain king, but they imposed a huge tribute on him. To save his own life, he agreed.

So taxes were raised even higher, in order to pay the tribute, and King Edward could only keep enough soldiers to police his kingdom, and the tribute went to paying for soldiers of the victorious kings to stay on the borders to keep watch on our land. For they figured, and rightly so, that if they let up their vigilance for a minute, King Edward would raise an army and stab them in the back.

But they didn't let up their vigilance, you see. And King Edward was trapped.

A dark evil fell upon him then, for a greedy man craves all the more the thing he can't have. And King Edward craved power. Because he couldn't have power over other kings, he began to use more power over his own kingdom, and his own household, and his own family.

He began to have prisoners tortured until they confessed to conspiracies that didn't exist, and until they denounced people who were innocent. And people in this kingdom began to lock their doors at night, and hide when someone knocked. There was fear in the kingdom, and people began to move away, until King Edward took to hunting down and beheading anyone who tried to leave the kingdom.

And it was bad in the palace, too. For the servants were beaten savagely for the slightest things, and King Edward even yelled at his own son and daughters whenever he saw them, so that the queen kept them hidden away with her most of the time.

Everyone was afraid of King Edward. And people almost always hate anyone they fear.

Except the queen. For though she feared him she remembered his youth, and she said to herself, or sometimes to the nurse, "Somewhere in that sad and ugly man there is the beautiful boy I love. Somehow I must help him find that beautiful boy and bring him out again."

But neither the nurse nor the queen could think how such a thing could possibly happen.

Until the queen discovered that she was going to have a baby. Of course, she thought. With a new baby he will remember his family and remember to love us.

So she told him. And he railed at her about how stupid she was to bring another child to see their humiliation, a royal family with enemy troops perched on the border, with no real power in the world.

And then he took her roughly by the arm into the court, where the lords and ladies were gathered, and there he told them that his wife was going to have a baby to mock him, for she still had the power of a woman, even if he didn't have the power of a man. She cried out that it wasn't true. He hit her, and she fell to the ground.

And the problem was solved, for she lost the baby before it was born and lay on her bed for days, delirious and fevered and at the point of death. No one knew that King Edward hated himself for what he had done, that he tore at his face and his hair at the thought that the queen might die because of his fury. They only saw that he was drunk all through the queen's illness, and that he never came to her bedside.

While the queen was delirious, she dreamed many times and many things. But one dream that kept coming back to her was of a wolf following her in the forest, and she ran and ran until she fell, but just as the wolf was about to eat her, a huge brown bear came and killed the wolf and flung him away, and then picked her up gently and laid her down at her father's door, carefully arranging her dress and putting leaves under her head as a pillow.

When she finally woke up, though, she only remembered that there was no magic bear that would come out of the forest to save her. Magic was for the common people—brews to cure gout and plague and to make a lady love you, spells said in the night to keep dark things from the door. Foolishness, the queen told herself. For she had an education, and knew better. There is nothing to keep the dark things from the door, there is no cure for gout and plague, and there is no brew that will make your husband love you. She told this to herself and despaired.

King Edward soon forgot his grief at the thought his wife might die. As soon as she was up and about he was as surly as ever, and he didn't stop drinking, either, even when the reason for it was gone. He just remembered that he had hurt her badly and he felt guilty, and so whenever he saw her he felt bad, and because he felt bad he treated her badly, as if it were her fault.

Things were about as bad as they could get. There were rebellions here and there all over the kingdom, and rebels were being beheaded every week. Some soldiers had even mutinied and got away over the border with the people they were supposed to stop. And so one morning King Edward was in the foulest, blackest mood he had ever been in.

The queen walked into the dining room for breakfast looking as beautiful as ever, for grief had only deepened her beauty, and made you want to cry for the pain of her exquisite face and for the suffering in her proud, straight bearing. King Edward saw that pain and suffering but even more he saw that beauty, and for a moment he remembered the girl who had grown up without a care or a sorrow or an evil thought. And he knew that he had caused every bit of the pain she bore.

So he began to find fault with her, and before he knew it he was ordering her into the kitchen to cook.

"I can't," she said.

"If a servant can, you can," he snarled in reply.

She began to cry. "I've never cooked. I've never started a fire. I'm a queen."

"You're not a queen," the king said savagely, hating himself as he said it. "You're not a queen and I'm not a king, because we're a bunch of powerless lackeys taking orders from those scum across the border! Well, if I've got to live like a servant in my own palace, so have you!"

And so he took her roughly into the kitchen and ordered her to come back in with a breakfast she had cooked herself.

The queen was shattered, but not so shattered that she could forget her pride. She spoke to the cooks cowering in the corner. "You heard the king. I must cook him breakfast with my own hands. But I don't know how. You must tell me what to do."

So they told her, and she tried her best to do what they said, but her untrained hands made a botch of everything. She burned herself at the fire and scalded herself with the porridge. She put too much salt on the bacon and there were shells left in the eggs. She also burned the muffins. And then she carried it all in to her husband and he began to eat.

And of course it was awful.

And at that moment he realized finally that the queen was a queen and could be nothing else, just as a cook had no hope of being a queen. Just so he looked at himself and realized that he could never be anything but a king. The queen, however, was a good queen—while he was a terrible king. He would always be a king but he would never be good at it. And as he chewed up the eggshells he reached the lowest despair.

Another man, hating himself as King Edward did, might have taken his own life. But that was not King Edward's way. Instead he picked up his rod and began to beat the queen. He struck her again and again, and her back bled, and she fell to the ground, screaming.

The servants came in and so did the guards, and the servants, seeing the queen treated so, tried to stop the king. But the king ordered the guards to kill anyone who tried to interfere. Even so, the chief steward, a cook, and the butler were dead before the others stopped trying.

And the king kept beating and beating the queen until everyone was sure he would beat her to death.

And in her heart as she lay on the stone floor, numb to the pain of her body because of the pain of her heart, she wished that the bear would come again, stepping over her to kill the wolf that was running forward to devour her.

At that moment the door broke in pieces and a terrible roar filled the dining hall. The king stopped beating the queen, and the guards and the servants looked at the door, for there stood a huge brown bear on its hind legs, towering over them all, and roaring in fury.

The servants ran from the room.

"Kill him," the king bellowed at the guards.

The guards drew their swords and advanced on the bear.

The bear disarmed them all, though there were so many that some drew blood before their swords were slapped out of their hands. Some of them might even have tried to fight the bear without weapons, because they were brave men, but the bear struck them on the head, and the rest fled away.

Yet the queen, dazed though she was, thought that for some reason the bear had not struck yet with all his force, that the huge animal was saving his strength for another battle.

And that battle was with King Edward, who stood with his sharp sword in his hand, eager for battle, hoping to die, with the desperation and self-hatred in him that would make him a terrible opponent, even for a bear.

A bear, thought the queen. I wished for a bear and he is here.

Then she lay, weak and helpless and bleeding on the stone floor as her husband, her prince, fought the bear. She did not know who she hoped would win. For even now, she did not hate her husband. And yet she knew that her life and the lives of her subjects would be unendurable as long as he lived.

They circled around the room, the bear moving clumsily yet quickly, King Edward moving faster still, his blade whipping steel circles through the air. Three times the blade landed hard and deep on the bear, before the animal seized the blade between his paws. King Edward tried to draw back the sword, and as he did it bit deeply into the animal's paws. But it was a battle of strength, and the bear was sure to win it in the end. He pulled the sword out of Edward's hand, and then grasped the king in a mighty embrace and carried him screaming from the room.

And at that last moment, as Edward tugged hopelessly at his sword and blood poured from the bear's paws, the queen found herself hoping that the bear would hold on, would take away the sword, that the bear would win out and free the kingdom—her kingdom—and her family and even herself, from the man who had been devouring them all.

Yet when King Edward screamed in the bear's grip, she heard only the voice of the boy in the garden in the eternal and too-quick summer of her childhood. She fainted with a dim memory of his smile dancing crazily before her eyes.

She awoke as she had awakened once before, thinking that it had been a dream, and then remembering the truth of it when the pain where her husband had beaten her nearly made her fall unconscious again. But she fought the faintness and stayed awake, and asked for water.

The nurse brought water, and then several lords of high rank and the captain of the army and the chief servants came in and asked her what they should do.

"Why do you ask me?" she said.

"Because," the nurse answered her, "the king is dead."

The queen waited.

"The bear left him at the gate," the captain of the army said.

"His neck was broken," the chief said.

"And now," one of the lords said, "now we must know what to do. We haven't even told the people, and no one has been allowed inside or outside the palace."

The queen thought, and closed her eyes as she did so. But what she saw when she closed her eyes was the body of her beautiful prince with his head loose as the wolf's had been that day in the forest. She did not want to see that, so she opened her eyes.

"You must proclaim that the king is dead throughout the land," she said.

To the captain of the army she said, "There will be no more beheading for treason.

Anyone who is in prison for treason is to be set free, now. And any other prisoners whose terms are soon to expire should be set free at once."

The captain of the army bowed and left. He did not smile until he was out the door, but then he smiled until tears ran down his cheeks.

To the chief cook she said, "All the servants in the palace are free to leave now, if they want. But please ask them, in my name, to stay. I will restore them as they were, if they'll stay."

The cook started a heartfelt speech of thanks, but then thought better of it and left the room to tell the others.

To the lords she said, "Go to the kings whose armies guard our borders, and tell them that King Edward is dead and they can go home now. Tell them that if I need their help I will call on them, but that until I do I will govern my kingdom alone."

And the lords came and kissed her hands tenderly, and left the room.

And she was alone with the nurse.

"I'm so sorry," said the nurse, when enough silence had passed.

"For what?" asked the queen.

"For the death of your husband."

"Ah, that," said the queen. "Ah, yes, my husband."

And then the queen wept with all her heart. Not for the cruel and greedy man who had warred and killed and savaged everywhere he could. But for the boy who had somehow turned into that man, the boy whose gentle hand had comforted her childhood hurts, the boy whose frightened voice had cried out to her at the end of his life, as if he wondered why he had gotten lost inside himself, as if he realized that it was too, too late to get out again.

When she had done weeping that day, she never cried for him again.

In three days she was up again, though she had to wear loose clothing because of the pain. She held court anyway, and it was then that the shepherds brought her the Bear. Not the bear, the animal, that had killed the king, but *the* Bear, the counselor, who had left the kingdom so many years before.

"We found him on the hillside, with our sheep nosing him and lapping his face," the oldest of the shepherds told her. "Looks like he's been set on by robbers, he's cut and battered so. Miracle he's alive," he said.

"What is that he's wearing?" asked the queen, standing by the bed where she had had the servants lay him.

"Oh," said one of the other shepherds. "That's me cloak. They left him nekkid, but we didn't think it right to bring him before you in such a state."

She thanked the shepherds and offered to pay them a reward, but they said no thanks, explaining, "We remember him, we do, and it wouldn't be right to take money for helping him, don't you see, because he was a good man back in your father's day."

The queen had the servants—who had all stayed on, by the way—clean his wounds and bind them and tend to his wants. And because he was a strong man, he lived, though the wounds might have killed a smaller, weaker man. Even so, he never got back the use of his right hand, and had to learn to write with his left; and he limped ever after. But he often said he was lucky to be alive and wasn't ashamed of his infirmities, though he sometimes said that something ought to be done about the robbers who run loose in the hills.

As soon as he was able, the queen had him attend court, where he listened to the ambassadors from other lands and to the cases she heard and judged.

Then at night she had him come to King Ethelred's study, and there she asked him about the questions of that day and what he would have done differently, and he told her what he thought she did well, too. And so she learned from him as her father had learned.

One day she even said to him, "I have never asked forgiveness of any many in my life. But I ask for yours."

"For what?" he said, surprised.

"For hating you, and thinking you served me and my father badly, and driving you from this kingdom. If we had listened to you," she said, "none of this would have happened."

"Oh," he said, "all that's past. You were young, and in love, and that's as inevitable as fate itself."

"I know," she said, "and for love I'd probably do it again, but now that I'm wiser I can still ask for forgiveness for my youth."

The Bear smiled at her. "You were forgiven before you asked. But since you ask I gladly forgive you again."

"Is there any reward I can give you for your service so many years ago, when you left unthanked?" she asked.

"Yes," he answered. "If you could let me stay and serve you as I served your father, that would be reward enough."

"How can that be a reward?" she asked. "I was going to ask you to do that for *me*. And now you ask it for yourself."

"Let us say," said the Bear, "that I loved your father like my brother, and you like my niece, and I long to stay with the only family that I have."

Then the queen took the pitcher and poured him a mug of ale, and they sat by the fire and talked far into the night.

Because the queen was a widow, because despite the problems of the past the kingdom was large and rich, many suitors came asking for her hand. Some were dukes, some were earls, and some were kings or sons of kings. And she was as beautiful as ever, only in her thirties, a prize herself even if there had been no kingdom to covet.

But though she considered long and hard over some of them, and even liked several men who came, she turned them all down and sent them all away.

And she reigned alone, as queen, with the Bear to advise her.

And she also did what her husband had told her a queen should do—she raised her son to be king and her daughters to be worthy to be queens. And the Bear helped her with that, too, teaching her son to hunt, and teaching him how to see beyond men's words into their hearts, and teaching him to love peace and serve the people.

And the boy grew up as beautiful as his father and as wise as the Bear, and the people knew he would be a great king, perhaps even greater than King Ethelred had been.

The queen grew old, and turned much of the matter of the kingdom over to her son, who was now a man. The prince married the daughter of a neighboring king. She was a good woman, and the queen saw her grandchildren growing up.

She knew perfectly well that she was old, because she was sagging and no longer beautiful as she had been in her youth—though there were many who said that she was far more lovely as an old lady than any mere girl could hope to be.

But somehow it never occurred to her that the Bear, too, was growing old. Didn't he still stride through the garden with one of her grandchildren on each shoulder? Didn't he still come into the study with her and her son and teach them statecraft and tell them, yes, that's good, yes, that's right, yes, you'll make a great queen yet, yes, you'll be a fine king, worthy of your grandfather's kingdom—didn't he?

Yet one day he didn't get up from his bed, and a servant came to her with a whispered message, "Please come."

She went to him and found him gray-faced and shaking in his bed.

"Thirty years ago," he said, "I would have said it's nothing but a fever and I would have ignored it and gone riding. But now, my lady, I know I'm going to die."

"Nonsense," she said, "you'll never die," knowing as well as he did that he was dying, and knowing that he knew that she knew it.

"I have a confession to make," he said to her.

"I know it already," she said.

"Do you?"

"Yes," she said softly, "and much to my surprise, I find that I love you too. Even an old lady like me," she said, laughing.

"Oh," he said, "that was not my confession. I already knew that you knew I loved you. Why else would I have come back when you called?"

And then she felt a chill in the room and remembered the only time she had ever called for help.

"Yes," he said, "you remember. How I laughed when they named me. If they only knew, I thought at the time."

She shook her head. "How could it be?"

"I wondered myself," he said. "But it is. I met a wise old man in the woods when I was but a lad. An orphan, too, so that there was no one to ask about me when I stayed with him. I stayed until he died five years later, and I learned all his magic."

"There's no magic," she said as if by rote, and he laughed.

"If you mean brews and spells and curses, then you're right," he said. "But there is magic of another sort. The magic of becoming what most you are. My old man in the woods, his magic was to be an owl, and to fly by night seeing the world and coming to understand it. The owlness was in him, and the magic was letting that part of himself that was most himself come forward. And he taught me."

The Bear had stopped shaking because his body had given up trying to overcome the illness.

"So I looked inside me and wondered who I was. And then I found it out. Your nurse found it, too. One glance and she knew I was a bear."

"You killed my husband," she said to him.

"No," he said. "I fought your husband and carried him from the palace, but as he stared death in the face he discovered, too, what he was and who he was, and his real self came out."

The Bear shook his head.

"I killed a wolf at the palace gate, and left a wolf with a broken neck behind when I went away into the hills."

"A wolf both times," she said. "But he was such a beautiful boy."

"A puppy is cute enough whatever he plans to grow up to be," said the Bear.

"And what am I?" asked the queen.

"You?" asked the Bear. "Don't you know?"

"No," she answered. "Am I a swan? A porcupine? These days I walk like a crippled, old biddy hen. Who am I, after all these years? What animal should I turn into by night?"

"You're laughing," said the Bear, "and I would laugh too, but I have to be stingy with my breath. I don't know what animal you are, if you don't know yourself, but I think—"

And he stopped talking and his body shook in a great heave.

"No!" cried the queen.

"All right," said the Bear. "I'm not dead yet. I think that deep down inside you, you are a woman, and so you have been wearing your real self out in the open all your life. And you are beautiful."

"What an old fool you are after all," said the queen. "Why didn't I ever marry you?"

"Your judgment was too good," said the Bear.

But the queen called the priest and her children and married the Bear on his deathbed, and her son who had learned kingship from him called him father, and then they remembered the bear who had come to play with them in their childhood and the queen's daughters called him father; and the queen called him husband, and the Bear laughed and allowed as how he wasn't an orphan any more. Then he died.

And that's why there's a statue of a bear over the gate of the city.

SANDMAGIC

The great domes of the city of Gyree dazzled blue and red when the sun shone through a break in the clouds, and for a moment Cer Cemreet thought he saw some of the glory the uncles talked about in the late night tales of the old days of Greet. But the capital did not look dazzling up close, Cer remembered bitterly. Now dogs ran in the streets and rats lived in the wreckage of the palace, and the King of Greet lived in New Gyree in the hills far to the north, where the armies of the enemy could not go. Yet.

The sun went back behind a cloud and the city looked dark again. A Nefyr patrol was riding briskly on the Hetterwee Road far to the north. Cer turned his gaze to the lush grass on the hill where he sat. The clouds meant rain, but probably not here, he thought. He always thought of something else when he saw a Nefyr patrol. Yes, it was too early in Hrickan for rains to fall here. This rain would fall in the north, perhaps in the land of the King of the High Mountains, or on the vast plain of Westwold where they said horses ran free but were tame for any man to ride at need. But no rain would fall in Greet until Doonse, three weeks from now. By then the wheat would all be stored and the hay would be piled in vast ricks as tall as the hill Cer sat on.

In the old days, they said, all during Doonse the great wagons from Westwold would come and carry off the hay to last them through the snow season. But not now, Cer remembered. This year and last year and the year before the wagons had come from the south and east, two-wheeled wagons with drivers who spoke, not High Westil, but the barbarian Fyrd language. Fyrd or firt, thought Cer, and laughed, for firt was a word he could not say in front of his parents. They spoke firt.

Cer looked out over the plain again. The Nefyr patrol had turned from the highway and were on the road to the hills.

The road to the hills. Cer leaped to his feet and raced down the track leading home. A patrol heading for the hills could only mean trouble.

He stopped to rest only once, when the pain in his side was too bad to bear. But the patrol had horses, and he arrived home only to see the horses of the Nefyrre gathered at his father's gate.

Where are the uncles? Cer thought. The uncles must come.

But the uncles were not there, and Cer heard a terrible scream from inside the garden walls. He had never heard his mother scream before, but somehow he knew it was his mother, and he ran to the gate. A Nefyr soldier seized him and called out, "Here's the boy!" in a thick accent of High Westil, so that Cer's parents could understand. Cer's mother screamed again, and now Cer saw why.

His father had been stripped naked, his arms and legs held by two tall Nefyrre. The Nefyr captain held his viciously curved short-sword, point up, pressing against Cer's father's hard-muscled stomach. As Cer and his mother watched, the sword drew blood, and the captain pushed it in to the hilt, then pulled it up to the ribs. Blood gushed. The captain had been careful not to touch the heart, and now they thrust a spear into the huge wound, and lifted it high, Cer's father dangling from the end. They lashed the spear to the gatepost, and the blood and bowels stained the gates and the walls.

For five minutes more Cer's father lived, his chest heaving in the agony of breath. He may have died of pain, but Cer did not think so, for his father was not the kind to give in to pain. He may have died of suffocation, for one lung was gone and every breath was excruciating, but Cer did not think so, for his father kept breathing to the end. It was loss of blood, Cer decided, weeks later. It was when his body was dry, when the veins collapsed, that Cer's father died.

He never uttered a sound. Cer's father would never let the Nefyrre hear him so much as sigh in pain.

Cer's mother screamed and screamed until blood came from her mouth and she fainted.

Cer stood in silence until his father died. Then when the captain, a smirk on his face, walked near Cer and looked in his face, Cer kicked him in the groin.

They cut off Cer's great toes, but like his father, Cer made no sound.

Then the Nefyrre left and the uncles came.

Uncle Forwin vomited. Uncle Erwin wept. Uncle Crune put his arm around Cer's shoulder as the servants bound his maimed feet and said, "Your father was a great, a brave man. He killed many Nefyrre, and burned many wagons. But the Nefyrre are strong."

Uncle Crune squeezed Cer's shoulder. "Your father was stronger. But he was one, and they were many."

Cer looked away.

"Will you not look at your uncle?" Uncle Crune asked.

"My father," Cer said, "did not think that he was alone."

Uncle Crune got up and walked away. Cer never saw the uncles again.

He and his mother had to leave the house and the fields, for a Nefyr farmer had been given the land to farm for the King of Nefyryd. With no money, they had to move south, across the River Greebeck into the drylands near the desert, where no rivers flowed and so only the hardiest plants lived. They lived the winter on the charity of the desperately poor. In the summer, when the heat came, so did the Poor Plague which swept the drylands. The cure was fresh fruits, but fresh fruits came from Yffyrd and Suffyrd and only the rich could buy them, and the poor died by the thousands. Cer's mother was one of them.

They took her out on the sand to burn her body and free her spirit. As they painted her with tar (tar, at least, cost nothing, if a man had a bucket), five horsemen came to the brow of a dune to watch. At first Cer thought they were Nefyrre, but no. The poor people looked up and saluted the strangers, which Greetmen never do the enemy. These, then, were desert men, the Abadapnur nomads, who raided the rich farms of Greet during dry years, but who never harmed the poor.

We hated them, Cer thought, when we were rich. But now we are poor, and they are our friends.

His mother burned as the sun set.

Cer watched until the flames went out. The moon was high for the second time that night. Cer said a prayer to the moonlady over his mother's bones and ashes and then he turned and left.

He stopped at their hut and gathered the little food they had, and put on his father's tin ring, which the Nefyrre had thought was valueless, but which Cer knew was the sign of the Cemreet family's authority since forever ago.

Then Cer walked north.

He lived by killing rats in barns and cooking them. He lived by begging at poor farmer's doors, for the rich farmers had servants to turn away beggars. That, at least, Cer remembered, his father had never done. Beggars always had a meal at his father's house.

Cer also lived by stealing when he could hunt or beg no food. He stole handfuls of raw wheat. He stole carrots from gardens. He stole water from wells, for which he could have lost his life in this rainless season. He stole, one time, a fruit from a rich man's food wagon.

It burned his mouth, it was so cold and the acid so strong. It dribbled down his chin. As a poor man and a thief, Cer thought, I now eat a thing so dear that even my father, who was called wealthy, could never buy it.

And at last he saw the mountains in the north. He walked on, and in a week the mountains were great cliffs and steep slopes of shale. The Mitherkame, where the king of the High Mountains reigned, and Cer began to climb.

He climbed all one day and slept in a cleft of a rock. He moved slowly, for climbing in sandals was clumsy, and without his great toes Cer could not climb barefoot. The next morning he climbed more. Though he nearly fell one time when falling would have meant crashing a mile down onto the distant plain, at last he reached the knifelike top of the Mitherkame, and heaven.

For of a sudden the stone gave way to soil. Not the pale sandy soil of the drylands, nor the red soil of Greet, but the dark black soil of the old songs from the north, the soil that could not be left alone for a day or it would sprout plants that in a week would be a forest.

And there *was* a forest, and the ground was thick with grass. Cer had seen only a few trees in his life, and they had been olive trees, short and gnarled, and fig sycamores, that were three times the height of a man. These were twenty times the height of a man and ten steps around, and the young trees shot up straight and tall so that not a sapling was as small as Cer, who for twelve years old was not considered small.

To Cer, who had known only wheat and hay and olive orchards, the forest was more magnificent than the mountain or the city or the river or the moon.

He slept under a huge tree. He was very cold that night. And in the morning he realized that in a forest he would find no farms, and where there were no farms there was no food for him. He got up and walked deeper into the forest. There were people in the High Mountains, else there would be no king, and Cer would find them. If he didn't, he would die. But at least he would not die in the realms of the Nefyrre.

He passed many bushes with edible berries, but he did not know they could be eaten so he did not eat. He passed many streams with slow stupid fish that he could have caught, but in Greet fish was never eaten, because it always carried disease, and so Cer caught no fish.

And on the third day, when he began to feel so weak from hunger that he could walk no longer, he met the treemage.

He met him because it was the coldest night yet, and at last Cer tore branches from a tree to make a fire. But the wood did not light, and when Cer looked up he saw that the trees had moved. They were coming closer, surrounding him tightly. He watched them, and they did not move as he watched, but when he turned around the ones he had not been watching were closer yet. He tried to run, but the low branches made a tight fence he could not get through. He couldn't climb, either, because the branches all stabbed downward. Bleeding from the twigs he had scraped, Cer went back to his camping place and watched as the trees at last made a solid wall around him.

And he waited. What else could he do in his wooden prison?

In the morning he heard a man singing, and he called for help.

"Oh ho," he heard a voice say in a strange accent. "Oh ho, a tree cutter and a firemaker, a branch killer and a forest hater."

"I'm none of those," Cer said. "It was cold, and I tried to build a fire only to keep warm."

"A fire, a fire," the voice said. "In this small part of the world there are no fires of wood. But that's a young voice I hear, and I doubt there's a beard beneath the words."

"I have no beard," Cer answered. "I have no weapon, except a knife too small to harm you."

"A knife? A knife that tears sap from living limbs, Redwood says. A knife that cuts twigs like soft manfingers, says Elm. A knife that stabs bark till it bleeds, says Sweet Aspen. Break your knife," said the voice outside the trees, "and I will open your prison."

"But it's my only knife," Cer protested, "and I need it."

"You need it here like you need fog on a dark night. Break it or you'll die before these trees move again."

Cer broke his knife.

Behind him he heard a sound, and he turned to see a fat old man standing in a clear space between the trees. A moment before there had been no clear space.

"A child," said the man.

"A fat old man," said Cer, angry at being considered as young as his years.

"An illbred child at that," said the man. "But perhaps he knows no better, for from the accent of his speech I would say he comes from Greetland, and from his clothing I would say he was poor, and it's well known in Mitherwee that there are no manners in Greet."

Cer snatched up the blade of his knife and ran at the man. Somehow there were many sharp-pointed branches in the way, and his hand ran into a hard limb, knocking the blade to the ground.

"Oh, my child," said the man kindly. "There is death in your heart."

The branches were gone, and the man reached out his hands and touched Cer's face. Cer jerked away.

"And the touch of a man brings pain to you." The man sighed. "How inside out your world must be."

Cer looked at the man coldly. He could endure taunting. But was that kindness in the old man's eyes?

"You look hungry," said the old man.

Cer said nothing.

"If you care to follow me, you may. I have food for you, if you like."

Cer followed him.

They went through the forest, and Cer noticed that the old man stopped to touch many of the trees. And a few he pointedly snubbed, turning his back or taking a wider route around them. Once he stopped and spoke to a tree that had lost a large limb—recently, too, Cer thought, because the tar on the stump was still soft. "Soon there'll be no pain at all," the old man said to the tree. Then the old man sighed again. "Ah, yes, I know. And many a walnut in the falling season."

Then they reached a house. If it could be called a house, Cer thought. Stones were the walls, which was common enough in Greet, but the roof was living wood—thick branches from nine tall trees, interwoven and heavily leaved, so that Cer was sure no drop of rain could ever come inside.

"You admire my roof?" the old man asked. "So tight that even in the winter, when the leaves are gone, the snow cannot come in. But *we* can," he said, and led the way through a low door into a single room.

The old man kept up a constant chatter as he fixed breakfast: berries and cream, stewed acorns, and thick slices of cornbread. The old man named all the foods for Cer, because except for the cream it was all strange to him. But it was good, and it filled him.

"Acorn from the Oaks," said the old man. "Walnuts from the trees of that name. And berries from the bushes, the neartrees. Corn, of course, comes from an untree, a weak plant with no wood, which dies every year."

"The trees don't die every year, then, even though it snows?" Cer asked, for he had heard of snow.

"Their leaves turn bright colors, and then they fall, and perhaps that's a kind of death," said the old man. "But in Eanan the snow melts and by Blowan there are leaves again on all the trees."

Cer did not believe him, but he didn't disbelieve him either. Trees were strange things.

"I never knew that trees in the High Mountains could move."

"Oh ho," laughed the old man. "And neither can they, except here, and other woods that a treemage tends."

"A treemage? Is there magic then?"

"Magic. Oh ho," the man laughed again. "Ah yes, magic, many magics, and mine is the magic of trees."

Cer squinted. The man did not look like a man of power, and yet the trees had penned an intruder in. "You rule the trees here?"

"Rule?" the old man asked, startled. "What a thought. Indeed no. I serve them. I protect them. I give them the power in me, and they give me the power in them, and it makes us all a good deal more powerful. But rule? That just doesn't enter into magic. What a thought."

Then the old man chattered about the doings of the silly squirrels this year, and when Cer was through eating the old man gave him a bucket and they spent the morning gathering berries. "Leave a berry on the bush for every one you pick," the old man said. "They're for the birds in the fall and for the soil in the Kamesun, when new bushes grow."

And so Cer, quite accidentally, began his life with the treemage, and it was as happy a time as Cer ever had in his life, except when he was a child and his mother sang to him and except for the time his father took him hunting deer in the hills of Wetfell.

And after the autumn when Cer marveled at the colors of the leaves, and after the winter when Cer tramped through the snow with the treemage to tend to ice-splintered branches, and after the spring when Cer thinned the new plants so the forest did not become overgrown, the treemage began to think that the dark places in Cer's heart were filled with light, or at least put away where they could not be found.

He was wrong.

For as he gathered leaves for the winter's fires Cer dreamed he was gathering the bones of his enemies. And as he tramped the snow he dreamed he was marching into battle to wreak death on the Nefyrre. And as he thinned the treestarts Cer dreamed of slaying each of the uncles as his father had been slain, because none of them had stood by him in his danger.

Cer dreamed of vengeance, and his heart grew darker even as the wood was filled with the bright light of the summer sun.

One day he said to the treemage, "I want to learn magic."

The treemage smiled with hope. "You're learning it," he said, "and I'll gladly teach you more."

"I want to learn things of power."

"Ah," said the treemage, disappointed. "Ah, then, you can have no magic."

"You have power," said Cer. "I want it also."

"Oh, indeed," said the treemage. "I have the power of two legs and two arms, the power to heat tar over a peat fire to stop the sap flow from broken limbs, the power to cut off diseased branches to save the tree, the power to teach the trees how and when to protect themselves. All the rest is the power of the trees, and none of it is mine."

"But they do your bidding," said Cer.

"Because I do theirs!" the treemage said, suddenly angry. "Do you think that there is slavery in this wood? Do you think I am a king? Only men allow men to rule them. Here in this wood there is only love, and on that love and by that love the trees and I have the magic of the wood."

Cer looked down, disappointed. The treemage misunderstood, and thought that Cer was contrite.

"Ah, my boy," said the treemage. "You haven't learned it, I see. The root of magic is love, the trunk is service. The treemages love the trees and serve them and then they share treemagic with the trees. Lightmages love the sun and make fires at night, and the fire serves them as they serve the fire. Horsemages love and serve horses, and they ride freely whither they will because of the magic in the herd. There is field magic and plain magic, and the magic of rocks and metals, songs and dances, the magic of winds and weathers. All built on love, all growing through service."

"I must have magic," said Cer.

"Must you?" asked the treemage. "Must you have magic? There are kinds of magic, then, that you might have. But I can't teach them to you."

"What are they?"

"No," said the treemage, and he wouldn't speak again.

Cer thought and thought. What magic could be demanded against anyone's will?

And at last, when he had badgered and nagged the treemage for weeks, the treemage angrily gave in. "Will you know then?" the treemage snapped. "I will tell you. There is seamagic, where the wicked sailors serve the monsters of the deep by feeding them living flesh. Would you do that?" But Cer only waited for more.

"So that appeals to you," said the treemage. "Then you will be delighted at desert magic."

And now Cer saw a magic he might use. "How is that performed?"

"I know not," said the treemage icily. "It is the blackest of the magics to men of *my* kind, though your dark heart might leap to it. There's only one magic darker."

"And what is that?" asked Cer.

"What a fool I was to take you in," said the treemage. "The wounds in your heart, you don't want them to heal; you love to pick at them and let them fester."

"What is the darkest magic?" demanded Cer.

"The darkest magic," said the treemage, "is one, thank the moon, that you can never practice. For to do it you have to love men and love the love of men more than your own life. And love is as far from you as the sea is from the mountains, as the earth is from the sky."

"The sky touches the earth," said Cer.

"Touches, but never do they meet," said the treemage.

Then the treemage handed Cer a basket, which he had just filled with bread and berries and a flagon of streamwater. "Now go."

"Go?" asked Cer.

"I hoped to cure you, but you won't have a cure. You clutch at your suffering too much to be healed."

Cer reached out his foot toward the treemage, the crusty scars still a deep red where his great toe had been.

"As well you might try to restore my foot."

"Restore?" asked the treemage. "I restore nothing. But I staunch, and heal, and I help the trees forget their lost limbs. For if they insist on rushing sap to the limb as if it were still there, they lose all their sap; they dry, they wither, they die."

Cer took the basket.

"Thank you for your kindness," said Cer. "I'm sorry that you don't understand. But just as the tree can never forgive the ax or the flame, there are those that must die before I can truly live again."

"Get out of my wood," said the treemage. "Such darkness has no place here."

And Cer left, and in three days came to the edge of the Mitherkame, and in two days reached the bottom of the cliffs, and in a few weeks reached the desert. For he would learn desertmagic. He would serve the sand, and the sand would serve him.

On the way the soldiers of Nefyryd stopped him and searched him. When they saw that he had no great toes, they beat him and shaved off his young and scraggly beard and sent him on his way with a kick.

Cer even stopped where his father's farm had been. Now all the farms were farmed by Nefyrre, men of the south who had never owned land before. They drove him away, afraid that he might steal. So he snuck back in the night and from his father's storehouse stole meat and from his father's barn stole a chicken.

He crossed the Greebeck to the drylands and gave the meat and the chicken to the poor people there. He lived with them for a few days. And then he went out into the desert.

He wandered in the desert for a week before he ran out of food and water. He tried everything to find the desertmagic. He spoke to the hot sand and the burning rocks as the treemage had spoken to the trees. But the sand was never injured and did not need a healing touch, and the rocks could not be harmed and so they needed no protection. There was no answer when Cer talked, except the wind which cast sand in his eyes.

And at last Cer lay dying on the sand, his skin caked and chafed and burnt, his clothing long since tattered away into nothing, his flagon burning hot and filled with sand, his eyes blind from the whiteness of the desert.

He could neither love nor serve the desert, for the desert needed nothing from him and there was neither beauty nor kindness to love.

But he refused to die without having vengeance. Refused to die so long that he was still alive when the Abadapnu tribesmen found him. They gave him water and nursed him back to health. It took weeks, and they had to carry him on a sledge from waterhole to waterhole.

And as they traveled with their herds and their horses, the Abadapnur carried Cer farther and farther away from the Nefyrre and the land of Greet.

Cer regained his senses slowly, and learned the Abadapnu language even more slowly. But at last, as the clouds began to gather for the winter rains, Cer was one of the tribe, considered a man because he had a beard, considered wise because of the dark look on his face that remained even on those rare times when he laughed.

He never spoke of his past, though the Abadapnur knew well enough what the tin ring on his finger meant and why he had only eight toes. And they, with the perfect courtesy of the incurious, asked him nothing.

He learned their ways. He learned that starving on the desert was foolish, that dying of thirst was unnecessary. He learned how to trick the desert into yielding up life. "For," said the tribemaster, "the desert is never willing that anything should live."

Cer remembered that. The desert wanted nothing to live. And he wondered if that was a key to desertmagic. Or was it merely a locked door that he could never open? How can you serve and be served by the sand that wants only your death? How could he get vengeance if he was dead? "Though I would gladly die if my dying could kill my father's killers," he said to his horse one day. The horse hung her head, and would only walk for the rest of the day, though Cer kicked her to try to make her run.

Finally one day, impatient that he was doing nothing to achieve his revenge, Cer went to the tribemaster and asked him how one learned the magic of the sand.

"Sandmagic? You're mad," said the tribemaster. For days the tribemaster refused to look at him, let alone answer his questions, and Cer realized that here on the desert the sandmagic was hated as badly as the treemage hated it. Why? Wouldn't such power make the Abadapnur great?

Or did the tribemaster refuse to speak because the Abadapnur did not know the sandmagic?

But they knew it.

And one day the tribemaster came to Cer and told him to mount and follow.

They rode in the early morning before the sun was high, then slept in a cave in a rocky hill during the heat of the day. In the dusk they rode again, and at night they came to the city.

"Ettuie," whispered the tribemaster, and then they rode their horses to the edge of the ruins.

The sand had buried the buildings up to half their height, inside and out, and even now the breezes of evening stirred the sand and built little dunes against the walls. The buildings were made of stone, rising not to domes like the great cities of the Greetmen but to spires, tall towers that seemed to pierce the sky.

"Ikikietar," whispered the tribemaster, "Ikikiaiai re dapii. O ikikiai etetur o abadapnur, ikikiai re dapii."

"What are the 'knives'?" asked Cer. "And how could the sand kill them?"

"The knives are these towers, but they are also the stars of power."

"What power?" asked Cer eagerly.

"No power for you. Only power for the Etetur, for they were wise. They had the manmagic."

Manmagic. Was that the darkest magic spoken of by the treemage?

"Is there a magic more powerful than manmagic?" Cer asked.

"In the mountains, no," said the tribemaster. "On the well-watered plain, in the forest, on the sea, no."

"But in the desert?"

"A huu par eiti ununura," muttered the tribemaster, making the sign against death. "Only the desert power. Only the magic of the sand."

"I want to know," said Cer.

"Once," the tribemaster said, "once there was a mighty empire here. Once a great river flowed here, and rain fell, and the soil was rich and red like the soil of Greet, and a million people lived under the rule of the King of Ettue Dappa. But not all, for far to the west there lived a few who hated Ettue and the manmagic of the kings, and they forged the tool that undid this city.

"They made the wind blow from the desert. They made the rains run off the earth. By their power the river sank into the desert sand, and the fields bore no fruit, and at last the King of Ettue surrendered, and half his kingdom was given to the sandmages. To the dapinur. That western kingdom became Dapnu Dap."

"A kingdom?" said Cer, surprised. "But now the great desert bears that name."

"And once the great desert was no desert, but a land of grasses and grains like your homeland to the north. The sandmages weren't content with half a kingdom, and they used their sandmagic to make a desert of Ettue, and they covered the lands of rebels with sand, until at last the victory of the desert was complete, and Ettue fell to the armies of Greet and Nefyryd—they were allies then—and we of Dapnu Dap became nomads, living off that tiny bit of life that even the harshest desert cannot help but yield."

"And what of the sandmages?" asked Cer.

"We killed them."

"All?"

"All," said the tribemaster. "And if any man will practice sandmagic, today, we will kill him. For what happened to us we will let happen to no other people."

Cer saw the knife in the tribemaster's hand.

"I will have your vow," said the tribemaster. "Swear before these stars and this sand and the ghosts of all who lived in this city that you will seek no sandmagic."

"I swear," said Cer, and the tribemaster put his knife away.

The next day Cer took his horse and a bow and arrows and all the food he could steal and in the heat of the day when everyone slept he went out into the desert. They followed him, but he slew two with arrows and the survivors lost his trail.

Word spread through the tribes of the Abadapnur that a would-be sandmage was loose in the desert, and all were ready to kill him if he came. But he did not come.

For he knew now how to serve the desert, and how to make the desert serve him. For the desert loved death, and hated grasses and trees and water and the things of life.

So in service of the sand Cer went to the edge of the land of the Nefyrre, east of the desert. There he fouled wells with the bodies of diseased animals. He burned fields when the wind was blowing off the desert, a dry wind that pushed the flames into the cities. He cut down trees. He killed sheep and cattle. And when the Nefyrre patrols chased him he fled onto the desert where they could not follow.

His destruction was annoying, and impoverished many a farmer, but alone it would have done little to hurt the Nefyrre. Except that Cer felt his power over the desert growing. For he was feeding the desert the only thing it hungered for: death and dryness.

He began to speak to the sand again, not kindly, but of land to the east that the sand could cover. And the wind followed his words, whipping the sand, moving the dunes. Where he stood the wind did not touch him, but all around him the dunes moved like waves of the sea.

Moving eastward.

Moving onto the lands of the Nefyrre.

And now the hungry desert could do in a night a hundred times more than Cer could do alone with a torch or a knife. It ate olive groves in an hour. The sand borne on the wind filled houses in a night, buried cities in a week, and in only three months had driven the Nefyrre across the Greebeck and the Nefyr River, where they thought the terrible sandstorms could not follow.

But the storms followed. Cer taught the desert almost to fill the river, so that the water spread out a foot deep and miles wide, flooding some lands that had been dry, but also leaving more water surface for the sun to drink from; and before the river reached the sea it was dry, and the desert swept across into the heart of Nefyryd.

The Nefyrre had always fought with the force of arms, and cruelty was their companion in war. But against the desert they were helpless. They could not fight the sand. If Cer could have known it, he would have gloried in the fact that, untaught, he was the most powerful sandmage who had ever lived. For hate was a greater teacher than any of the books of dark lore, and Cer lived on hate.

And on hate alone, for now he ate and drank nothing, sustaining his body through the power of the wind and the heat of the sun. He was utterly dry, and the blood no longer coursed through his veins. He lived on the energy of the storms he unleashed. And the desert eagerly fed him, because he was feeding the desert.

He followed his storms, and walked through the deserted towns of the Nefyrre. He saw the refugees rushing north and east to the high ground. He saw the corpses of those caught in the storm. And he sang at night the old songs of Greet, the war songs. He wrote his father's name with chalk on the wall of every city he destroyed. He wrote his mother's name in the sand, and where he had written her name the wind did not blow and the sand did not shift, but preserved the writing as if it had been incised on rock.

Then one day, in a lull between his storms, Cer saw a man coming toward him from the east. Abadapnu, he wondered, or Nefyrre? Either way he drew his knife, and fit the nock of an arrow on his bowstring.

But the man came with his hands extended, and he called out, "Cer Cemreet."

It had never occurred to Cer that anyone knew his name.

"Sandmage Cer Cemreet," said the man when he was close. "We have found who you are."

Cer said nothing, but only watched the man's eyes.

"I have come to tell you that your vengeance is full. Nefyryd is at its knees. We have signed a treaty with Greet and we no longer raid into Hetterwee. Driplin has seized our westernmost lands."

Cer smiled. "I care nothing for your empire."

"Then for our people. The deaths of your father and mother have been avenged a hundred thousand times, for over two hundred thousand people have died at your hands."

Cer chuckled. "I care nothing for your people."

"Then for the soldiers who did the deed. Though they acted under orders, they have been arrested and killed, as have the men who gave them those orders, even our first general, all at the command of the King so that your vengeance will be complete. I have brought you their ears as proof of it," said the man, and he took a pouch from his waist.

"I care nothing for soldiers, nor for proof of vengeance," said Cer.

"Then what do you care for?" asked the man quietly.

"Death," said Cer.

"Then I bring you that, too," said the man, and a knife was in his hand, and he plunged the knife into Cer's breast where his heart should have been. But when the man pulled the knife out no blood followed, and Cer only smiled.

"Indeed you brought it to me," said Cer, and he stabbed the man where his father had been stabbed, and drew the knife up as it had been drawn through his father's body, except that he touched the man's heart, and he died.

As Cer watched the blood soaking into the sand, he heard in his ears his mother's screams, which he had silenced for these years. He heard her screams and now, remembering his father and his mother and himself as a child he began to cry, and he held the body of the man he had killed and rocked back and forth on the sand as the blood clotted on his clothing and his skin. His tears mixed with the blood and poured into the sand and Cer realized that this was the first time since his father's death that he had shed any tears at all.

I am not dry, thought Cer. There is water under me still for the desert to drink.

He looked at his dry hands, covered with the man's blood, and tried to scrub off the clotted blood with sand. But the blood stayed, and the sand could not clean him.

He wept again. And then he stood and faced the desert to the west, and he said, "Come."

A breeze began.

"Come," he said to the desert, "come and dry my eyes."

And the wind came up, and the sand came, and Cer Cemreet was buried in the sand, and his eyes became dry, and the last life passed from his body, and the last sandmage passed from the world.

Then came the winter rains, and the refugees of Nefyryd returned to their land. The soldiers were called home, for the wars were over, and now their weapons were the shovel and the plow. They redug the trench of the Nefyr and the Greebeck, and the river soon flowed deep again to the sea. They scattered grass seed and cleaned their houses of sand. They carried water into the ruined fields with ditches and aqueducts.

Slowly life returned to Nefyryd.

And the desert, having lost its mage, retreated quietly to its old borders, never again to seek death where there was life. Plenty of death already where nothing lived, plenty of dryness to drink where there was no water.

In a wood a little way from the crest of the Mitherkame, a treemage heard the news from a wandering tinker.

The treemage went out into the forest and spoke softly to the Elm, to the Oak, to the Redwood, to the Sweet Aspen. And when all had heard the news, the forest wept for Cer Cemreet, and each tree gave a twig to be burned in his memory, and shed sap to sink into the ground in his name.

THE BEST DAY

Once there was a woman who had five children that she loved with all her heart, and a husband who was kind and strong. Every day her husband would go out and work in the fields, and then he'd come home and cut wood or repair harness or fix the leaky places in the roof. Every day the children would work and play so hard they wore paths in the weeds from running, and they knew every hiding place in two miles square. And that woman began to be afraid that they were too happy, that it would all come to an end. And so she prayed, Please send us eternal happiness, let this joy last forever. Well, the next day along came a mean-faced old peddler, and he spread his wares and they were very plain—rough wool clothing, sturdy pots and pans, all as ugly and practical as old shoes. The woman bought a dress from him because it was cheap and it would last forever, and he was about to go, when suddenly she saw maybe a fire in his eyes, suddenly flashing bright as a star, and she remembered her prayer the night before, and she said, "Sir, you don't have anything to do with—happiness, do you?"

And the peddler turned and glowered and said, "I can give it to you, if you want it. But let me tell you what it is. It's your kids growing up and talking sassy, and then moving on out and marrying other children who don't like you all that much, at least at first. It's your husband's strength giving out, and watching the farm go to seed before your eyes, and maybe having to sell it and move into your daughter-in-law's house because you can't support yourselves no more. It's feeling your own legs go stiff, and your fingers not able to tat or knit or even grip the butter churn. And finally it's dying, lying there feeling your body drop off you, wishing you could just go back and be young with your children small, just for a day. And then—"

"Enough!" cried the woman.

"But there's more," said the peddler.

"I've heard all I mean to hear," and she hurried him out of the house.

The next day, along comes a man in a bright-painted wagon, with a horse named

Carpy Deem that he shouted at all the time. A medicine man from the East, with potions for this and pills for that, and silks and scarves to sell, too, so bright they hurt your eyes just to look at them. Everybody was healthy, so the woman didn't buy any medicine. All she bought was a silk, even though the price was too high, because it looked so blue in her golden hair. And she said to him, "Sir, do you have anything to do with happiness?"

"Do you have to *ask?*" he said. "Right here, in this jar, is the elixir of happiness —one swallow, and the best day of your life is with you forever."

"How much does it cost?" she asked, trembling.

"I only sell it to them as have such a day worth keeping, and then I sell it cheap. One lock of your golden hair, that's all. I give it to your Master, so he'll know you when the time comes."

She plucked the hair from her head, and gave it to the peddler, and he poured from the bottle into a little tin cup. When he was gone, she lifted it up, and thought of the happiest day of her life, which was only two days before, the day she prayed. And she drank that swallow.

Well, her husband came home as it was getting dark, and the children came to him all worried. "Something's wrong with Mother," they said. "She ain't making no sense." The man walked into the house, and tried to talk to his wife, but she gave no answer. Then, suddenly, she said something, speaking to empty air. She was cutting carrots, but there were no carrots; she was cooking a stew, but there was no fire laid. Finally her husband realized that word for word, she was saying what she said only two days ago, when they last had stew, and if he said to her the words he had said then, why, the conversation at least made some sense.

And every day it was the same. They either said that same day's words over and over again, or they ignored their mother, and let her go on as she did and paid her no mind. The kids got sick of it after a time, and got married and went away, and she never knew it. Her husband stayed with her, and more and more he got caught up in her dream, so that every day he got up and said the same words till they meant nothing and he couldn't remember what he was living for, and so he died. The neighbors found him two days later, and buried him, and the woman never knew.

Her daughters and daughters-in-law tried to care for her, but if they took her to their homes, she'd just walk around as if she were still in her own little cottage, bumping into walls, cutting those infernal carrots, saying those words till they were all out of their minds. Finally they took her back to her own home and paid a woman to cook and clean for her, and she went on that way, all alone in that cabin, happy as a duck in a puddle until at last the floor of her cabin caved in and she fell in and broke her hip. They figure she never even felt the pain, and when she died she was still laughing and smiling and saying idiotic things, and never even saw one of her grandchildren, never even wept at her husband's grave, and some folks said she was probably happier, but not a one said they were eager to change places with her. And it happened that a mean-looking old peddler came by and watched as they let her into her grave, and up rode a medicine man yelling at his horse, and he pulled up next to the peddler.

"So she bought from you," the peddler said.

And the medicine man said, "If you'd just paint things up a little, add a bit of color here and there, you'd sell more, friend."

But the peddler only shook his head. "If they'd ever let me finish telling them, they'd not be taken in by you, old liar. But they always send me packing before I'm through. I never get to tell them."

"If you'd begin with the pleasant things, they'd listen."

"But if I began with the pleasant things, it wouldn't be true."

"Fine with me. You keep me in business." And the medicine man patted a trunk filled with gold and silver and bronze and iron hairs. It was the wealth of all the world, and the medicine man rode off with it, to go back home and count it all, so fine and cold.

And the peddler, he just rode home to his family, his great-great-great-grandchildren, his gray-haired wife who nagged, the children who complained about the way he was always off on business when he should be home, and always hanging about the house when he ought to be away; he rode home to the leaves that turned every year, and the rats that ate the apples in the cellar, and the folks that kept dying on him, and the little ones that kept on being born.

A PLAGUE OF BUTTERFLIES

The butterflies awoke him. Amasa felt them before he saw them, the faint pressure of hundreds of half-dozens of feet, weighting his rough wool sheet so that he dreamed of a shower of warm snow. Then opened his eyes and there they were, in the shaft of sunlight like a hundred stained-glass windows, on the floor like a carpet woven by an inspired lunatic, delicately in the air like leaves falling upward in a wind.

At last, he said silently.

He watched them awhile, then gently lifted his covers. The butterflies arose with the blanket. Carefully he swung his feet to the floor; they eddied away from his footfall, then swarmed back to cover him. He waded through them like the shallow water on the edge of the sea, endlessly charging and then retreating quickly. He who fights and runs away, lives to fight another day. You have come to me at last, he said, and then he shuddered, for this was the change in his life that he had waited for, and now he wasn't sure he wanted it after all.

They swarmed around him all morning as he prepared for his journey. His last journey, he knew, the last of many. He had begun his life in wealth, on the verge of power, in Sennabris, the greatest of the oil-burning cities of the coast. He had grown up watching the vast ships slide into and out of the quays to void their bowels into the sink of the city. When his first journey began, he did not follow the tankers out to sea. Instead, he took what seemed the cleaner way, inland.

He lived in splendor in the hanging city of Besara on the cliffs of Carmel; he worked for a time as a governor in Kafr Katnei on the plain of Esdraelon until the Megiddo War; he built the Ladder of Ekdippa through solid rock, where a thousand men died in the building and it was considered a cheap price.

And in every journey he mislaid something. His taste for luxury stayed in Besara; his love of power was sated and forgotten in Kafr Katnei; his desire to build for the ages was shed like a cloak in Ekdippa; and at last he had found himself here, in a desperately

poor dirt farm on the edge of the Desert of Machaerus, with a tractor that had to be
bribed to work and harvests barely large enough to pay for food for himself and petrol
for the machines. He hadn't even enough to pay for light in the darkness, and sunset
ended every day with imperturbable night. Yet even here, he knew that there was one
more journey, for he had not yet lost everything: still when he worked in the fields he
would reach down and press his fingers into the soil; still he would bathe his feet in
the rush of water from the muddy ditch; still he would sit for hours in the heat of the
afternoon and watch the grain standing bright gold and motionless as rock, drinking
sun and expelling it as dry, hard grain. This last love, the love of life itself—it, too,
would have to leave, Amasa knew, before his life would have completed its course and
he would have consent to die.

The butterflies, they called him.

He carefully oiled the tractor and put it into its shed.

He closed the headgate of the ditch and shoveled earth into place behind it, so that
in the spring the water would not flow onto his fallow fields and be wasted.

He filled a bottle with water and put it into his scrip, which he slung over his
shoulder. This is all I take, he said. And even that felt like more of a burden than he
wanted to bear.

The butterflies swarmed around him, and tried to draw him off toward the road
into the desert, but he did not go at once. He looked at his fields, stubbled after the
harvest. Just beyond them was the tumble of weeds that throve in the dregs of water
that his grain had not used. And beyond the weeds was the Desert of Machaerus, the
place where those who love water die. The ground was stone: rocky outcroppings, gravel;
even the soil was sand. And yet there were ruins there. Wooden skeletons of buildings
that had once housed farmers. Some people thought that this was a sign that the desert
was growing, pushing in to take over formerly habitable land, but Amasa knew better.
Rather the wooden ruins were the last remnants of the woeful Sebasti, those wandering
people who, like the weeds at the end of the field, lived on the dregs of life. Once there
had been a slight surplus of water flowing down the canals. The Sebasti heard about it
in hours; in days they had come in their ramshackle trucks; in weeks they had built
their scrappy buildings and plowed their stony fields, and for that year they had a harvest
because the ditches ran a few inches deeper than usual. The next year the ditches were
back to normal, and in a few hours one night the houses were stripped, the trucks were
loaded, and the Sebasti were gone.

I am a Sebastit, too, Amasa thought. I have taken my life from an unwilling desert;
I give it back to the sand when I am through.

Come, said the butterflies alighting on his face. Come, they said, fanning him and
fluttering off toward the Hierusalem road.

Don't get pushy, Amasa answered, feeling stubborn. But all the same he surrendered,
and followed them out into the land of the dead.

The only breeze was the wind on his face as he walked, and the heat drew water from
him as if from a copious well. He took water from his bottle only a mouthful at a time,
but it was going too quickly even at that rate.

Worse, though: his guides were leaving him. Now that he was on the road to
Hierusalem, they apparently had other errands to run. He first noticed their numbers
diminishing about noon, and by three there were only a few hundred butterflies left.
As long as he watched a particular butterfly, it stayed; but when he looked away for a
moment, it was gone. At last he set his gaze on one butterfly and did not look away at

all, just watched and watched. Soon it was the last one left, and he knew that it, too, wanted to leave. But Amasa would have none of that. If I can come at your bidding, he said silently, you can stay at mine. And so he walked until the sun was ruddy in the west. He did not drink; he did not study his road; and the butterfly stayed. It was a little victory. I rule you with my eyes.

"You might as well stop here, friend."

Startled to hear a human voice on this desolate road, Amasa looked up, knowing in that moment that his last butterfly was lost. He was ready to hate the man who spoke.

"I say, friend, since you're going nowhere anyway, you might as well stop."

It was an old-looking man, black from sunlight and naked. He sat in the lee of a large stone, where the sun's northern tilt would keep him in shadow all day.

"If I wanted conversation," Amasa said, "I would have brought a friend."

"If you think those butterflies are your friends, you're an ass."

Amasa was surprised that the man knew about the butterflies.

"Oh, I know more than you think," said the man. "I lived at Hierusalem, you know. And now I'm the sentinel of the Hierusalem Road."

"No one leaves Hierusalem," said Amasa.

"I did," the old man said. "And now I sit on the road and teach travelers the keys that will let them in. Few of them pay me much attention, but if you don't do as I say, you'll never reach Hierusalem, and your bones will join a very large collection that the sun and wind gradually turn back into sand."

"I'll follow the road where it leads," Amasa said. "I don't need any directions."

"Oh, yes, you'd rather follow the dead guidance of the makers of the road than trust a living man."

Amasa regarded him for a moment. "Tell me, then."

"Give me all your water."

Amasa laughed—a feeble enough sound, coming through splitting lips that he dared not move more than necessary.

"It's the first key to entering Hierusalem." The old man shrugged. "I see that you don't believe me. But it's true. A man with water or food can't get into the city. You see, the city is hidden. If you had miraculous eyes, stranger, you could see the city even now. It's not far off. But the city is forever hidden from a man who is not desperate. The city can only be found by those who are very near to death. Unfortunately, if you once pass the entrance to the city without seeing it because you had water with you, then you can wander on as long as you like, you can run out of water and cry out in a whisper for the city to unveil itself to you, but it will avail you nothing. The entrance, once passed, can never be found again. You see, you have to know the taste of death in your mouth before Hierusalem will open to you."

"It sounds," Amasa said, "like religion. I've done religion."

"Religion? What is religion in a world with a dragon at its heart?"

Amasa hesitated. A part of him, the rational part, told him to ignore the man and pass on. But the rational part of him had long since become weak. In his definition of man, "featherless biped" held more truth than "rational animal." Besides, his head ached, his feet throbbed, his lips stung. He handed his bottle of water to the old man, and then for good measure gave him his scrip as well.

"Nothing in there you want to keep?" asked the old man, surprised.

"I'll spend the night."

The old man nodded.

They slept in the darkness until the moon rose in the east, bright with its thin promise of a sunrise only a few hours away. It was Amasa who awoke. His stirring roused the old man.

"Already?" he asked. "In such a hurry?"

"Tell me about Hierusalem."

"What do you want, friend? History? Myth? Current events? The price of public transportation?"

"Why is the city hidden?"

"So it can't be found."

"Then why is there a key for some to enter?"

"So it *can* be found. Must you ask such puerile questions?"

"Who built the city?"

"Men."

"Why did they build it?"

"To keep man alive on this world."

Amasa nodded at the first answer that hinted at significance. "And what enemy is it, then, that Hierusalem means to keep out?"

"Oh, my friend, you don't understand. Hierusalem was built to keep the enemy in. The old Hierusalem, the new Hierusalem, built to contain the dragon at the heart of the world."

A story-telling voice was on the old man now, and Amasa lay back on the sand and listened as the moon rose higher at his left hand.

"Men came here in ships across the void of the night," the old man said.

Amasa sighed.

"Oh, you know all that?"

"Don't be an ass. Tell me about Hierusalem."

"Did your books or your teachers tell you that this world was not unpopulated when our forefathers came?"

"Tell me your story, old man, but tell it plain. No myth, no magic. The truth."

"What a simple faith you have," the old man said. "The truth. Here's the truth, much good may it do you. This world was filled with forest, and in the forest were beings who mated with the trees, and drew their strength from the trees. They became very treelike."

"One would suppose."

"Our forefathers came, and the beings who dwelt among the trees smelt death in the fires of the ships. They did things—things that looked like magic to our ancestors, things that looked like miracles. These beings, these dragons who hid among the leaves of the trees, they had science we know little of. But one science we had that they had never learned, for they had no use for it. We knew how to defoliate a forest."

"So the trees were killed."

"All the forests of the world now have grown up since that time. Some places, where the forest had not been lush, were able to recover, and we live in those lands now. But here, in the Desert of Machaera—this was climax forest, trees so tall and dense that no underbrush could grow at all. When the leaves died, there was nothing to hold the soil, and it was washed onto the plain of Esdraelon. Which is why that plain is so fertile, and why nothing but sand survives here."

"Hierusalem."

"At first Hierusalem was built as an outpost for students to learn about the dragons, pathetic little brown woody creatures who knew death when they saw it, and died of despair by the thousands. Only a few survived among the rocks, where we couldn't reach them. Then Hierusalem became a city of pleasure, far from any other place, where sins could be committed that God could not see."

"I said truth."

"I say listen. One day the few remaining students of the science of the dragons wandered among the rocks, and there found that the dragons were not all dead. One was left, a tough little creature that lived among the gray rocks. But it had changed. It was not woody brown now. It was gray as stone, with stony outcroppings. They brought it back to study it. And in only a few hours it escaped. They never recaptured it. But the murders began, every night a murder. And every murder was of a couple who were coupling, neatly vivisected in the act. Within a year the pleasure seekers were gone, and Hierusalem had changed again."

"To what it is now."

"What little of the science of the dragons they had learned, they used to seal the city as it is now sealed. They devoted it to holiness, to beauty, to faith—and the murders stopped. Yet the dragon was not gone. It was glimpsed now and then, gray on the stone buildings of the city, like a moving gargoyle. So they kept their city closed to keep the dragon from escaping to the rest of the world, where men were not holy and would compel the dragon to kill again."

"So Hierusalem is dedicated to keeping the world safe for sin."

"Safe from retribution. Giving the world time to repent."

"The world is doing little in that direction."

"But some are. And the butterflies are calling the repentant out of the world, and bringing them to me."

Amasa sat in silence as the sun rose behind his back. It had not fully passed the mountains of the east before it started to burn him.

"Here," said the old man, "are the laws of Hierusalem:

"Once you see the city, don't step back or you will lose it.

"Don't look down into holes that glow red in the streets, or your eyes will fall out and your skin will slide off you as you walk along, and your bones will crumble into dust before you fully die.

"The man who breaks a butterfly will live forever.

"Do not stare at a small gray shadow that moves along the granite walls of the palace of the King and Queen, or he will learn the way to your bed.

"The Road to Dalmanutha leads to the sign you seek. Never find it."

Then the old man smiled.

"Why are you smiling?" asked Amasa.

"Because you're such a holy man, Saint Amasa, and Hierusalem is waiting for you to come."

"What's your name, old man?"

The old man cocked his head. "Contemplation."

"That's not a name."

He smiled again. "I'm not a man."

For a moment Amasa believed him, and reached out to see if he was real. But his finger met the old man's flesh, and it did not crumble.

"You have so much faith," said the old man again. "You cast away your scrip because you valued nothing that it contained. What *do* you value?"

In answer, Amasa removed all his clothing and cast it at the old man's feet.

*   *   *

He remembers that once he had another name, but he cannot remember what it was. His name now is Gray, and he lives among the stones, which are also gray. Sometimes he forgets where stone leaves off and he begins. Sometimes, when he has been motionless for hours, he has to search for his toes that spread in a fan, each holding to stone so firmly that when at last he moves them, he is surprised at where they were. Gray is motionless all day, and motionless all night. But in the hours before and after the sun, then he moves, skittering sure and rapid as a spider among the hewn stones of the palace walls, stopping only to drink in the fly-strewn standing water that remains from the last storm.

These days, however, he must move more slowly, more clumsily than he used to, for his stamen has at last grown huge, and it drags painfully along the vertical stones, and now and then he steps on it. It has been this way for weeks. Worse every day, and Gray feels it as a constant pain that he must ease, must ease, must ease; but in his small mind he does not know what easement there might be. So far as he knows, there are no others of his kind; in all his life he has met no other climber of walls, no other hanger from stone ceilings. He remembers that once he sought out couplers in the night, but he cannot remember what he did with them. Now he again finds himself drawn to windows, searching for easement, though not sure at all, holding in his mind no image of what he hopes to see in the dark rooms within the palace. It is dusk, and Gray is hunting, and is not sure whether he will find mate or prey.

I have passed the gate of Hierusalem, thought Amasa, and I was not near enough to death. Or worse, sometimes he thought, there is no Hierusalem, and I have come this way in vain. Yet this last fear was not a fear at all, for he did not think of it with despair. He thought of it with hope, and looked for death as the welcome end of his journey, looked for death which comes with its tongue thick in its mouth, death which waits in caves during the cool of the day and hunts for prey in the last and first light, death which is made of dust. Amasa watched for death to come in a wind that would carry him away, in a stone that would catch his foot in midstep and crumble him into a pile of bone on the road.

And then in a single footfall Amasa saw it all. The sun was framed, not by a haze of white light, but by thick and heavy clouds. The orchards were also heavy, and dripped with recent rain. Bees hummed around his head. And now he could see the city rising, green and gray and monumental just beyond the trees; all around him was the sound of running water. Not the tentative water that struggled to stay alive in the thirsty dirt of the irrigation ditch, but the lusty sound of water that is superfluous, water that can be tossed in the air as fountains and no one thinks to gather up the drops.

For a moment he was so surprised that he thought he must step backward, just one step, and see if it wouldn't all disappear, for Amasa did not come upon this gradually, and he doubted that it was real. But he remembered the first warning of the old man, and he didn't take that backward step. Hierusalem was a miracle, and in this place he would test no miracles.

The ground was resilient under his feet, mossy where the path ran over stone, grassy where the stones made way for earth. He drank at an untended stream that ran pure and overhung with flowers. And then he passed through a small gate in a terraced wall, climbed stairs, found another gate, and another, each more graceful than the last. The first gate was rusty and hard to open; the second was overgrown with climbing roses. But each gate was better tended than the last, and he kept expecting to find someone working a garden or picnicking, for surely someone must be passing often through the better-kept gates. Finally he reached to open a gate and it opened before he could touch it.

It was a man in the dirty brown robe of a pilgrim. He seemed startled to see Amasa. He immediately enfolded his arms around something and turned away. Amasa tried to see—yes, it was a baby. But the infant's hands dripped with fresh blood, it was obviously blood, and Amasa looked back at the pilgrim to see if this was a murderer who had opened the gate for him.

"It's not what you think," the palmer said quickly. "I found the babe, and he has no one to take care of him."

"But the blood."

"He was the child of pleasure-seekers, and the prophecy was fulfilled, for he was washing his hands in the blood of his father's belly." Then the pilgrim got a hopeful look. "There is an enemy who must be fought. You wouldn't—"

A passing butterfly caught the pilgrim's eye. The fluttering wings circled Amasa's head only once, but that was sign enough.

"It is you," the pilgrim said.

"Do I know you?"

"To think that it will be in my time."

"*What* will be?"

"The slaying of the dragon." The pilgrim ducked his head and, freeing one arm by perching the child precariously on the other, he held the gate open for Amasa to enter. "God has surely called you."

Amasa stepped inside, puzzled at what the pilgrim thought he was, and what his coming portended. Behind him he could hear the pilgrim mutter, "It is time. It is time."

It was the last gate. He was in the city, passing between the walled gardens of monasteries and nunneries, down streets lined with shrines and shops, temples and houses, gardens and dunghills. It was green to the point of blindness, alive and holy and smelly and choked with business wherever it wasn't thick with meditation. What am I here for? Amasa wondered. Why did the butterflies call?

He did not look down into the red-glowing holes in the middles of streets. And when he passed the gray labyrinth of the palace, he did not look up to try to find a shadow sliding by. He would live by the laws of the place, and perhaps his journey would end here.

The queen of Hierusalem was lonely. For a month she had been lost in the palace. She had strayed into a never-used portion of the labyrinth, where no one had lived for generations, and now, search as she might, she could find only rooms that were deeper and deeper in dust.

The servants, of course, knew exactly where she was, and some of them grumbled at having to come into a place of such filth, full of such unstylish old furniture, in order to care for her. It did not occur to *them* that she was lost—they only thought she was exploring. It would never do for her to admit her perplexity to them. It was the Queen's business to know what she was doing. She couldn't very well ask a servant, "Oh, by the way, while you're fetching my supper, would you mind mentioning to me where I *am*?" So she remained lost, and the perpetual dust irritated all her allergies.

The Queen was immensely fat, too, which complicated things. Walking was a great labor to her, so that once she found a room with a bed that looked sturdy enough to hold her for a few nights, she stayed until the bed threatened to give way. Her progress through the unused rooms, then, was not in a great expedition, but rather in fits and starts. On one morning she would arise miserable from the bed's increasing incapacity to hold her, eat her vast breakfast while the servants looked on to catch the dribbles, and then, instead of calling for singers or someone to read, she would order four servants to stand her up, point her in the direction she chose, and taxi her to a good, running start.

"That door," she cried again and again, and the servants would propel her in that direction, while her legs trotted underneath her, trying to keep up with her body. And in the new room she could not stop to contemplate; she must take it all in on the run, with just a few mad glances, then decide whether to try to stay or go on. "On," she usually cried, and the servants took her through the gradual curves and maneuvers necessary to reach whatever door was most capacious.

On the day that Amasa arrived in Hierusalem, the Queen found a room with a vast bed, once used by some ancient rake of a prince to hold a dozen paramours at once, and the Queen cried out, "This is it, this is the right place, stop, we'll stay!" and the servants sighed in relief and began to sweep, to clean, to make the place liveable.

Her steward unctuously asked her, "What do you want to wear to the King's Invocation?"

"I will not go," she said. How could she? She did not know how to get to the hall where the ritual would be held. "I choose to be absent this once. There'll be another one in seven years." The steward bowed and left on his errand, while the Queen envied him his sense of direction and miserably wished that she could go home to her own rooms. She hadn't been to a party in a month, and now that she was so far from the kitchens the food was almost cold by the time she was served the private dinners she had to be content with. Damn her husband's ancestors for building all these rooms anyway.

Amasa slept by a dunghill because it was warmer there, naked as he was; and in the morning, without leaving the dunghill, he found work. He was wakened by the servants of a great Bishop, stablemen who had the week's manure to leave for the farmers to collect. They said nothing to him, except to look with disapproval at his nakedness, but set to work, emptying small wheelbarrows, then raking up the dung to make a neater pile. Amasa saw how fastidiously they avoided touching the dung; he had no such scruples. He took an idle rake, stepped into the midst of the manure, and raked the hill higher and faster than the delicate stablemen could manage on their own. He worked with such a will that the Stablemaster took him aside at the end of the task.

"Want work?"

"Why not?" Amasa answered.

The Stablemaster glanced pointedly at Amasa's unclothed body. "Are you fasting?"

Amasa shook his head. "I just left my clothing on the road."

"You should be more careful with your belongings. I can give you livery, but it comes out of your wages for a year."

Amasa shrugged. He had no use for wages.

The work was mindless and hard, but Amasa delighted in it. The variety was endless. Because he didn't mind it, they kept him shoveling more manure than his fair share, but the shoveling of manure was like a drone, a background for bright rhinestones of childish delight: morning prayers, when the Bishop in his silver gown intoned the powerful words while the servants stood in the courtyard clumsily aping his signs; running through the streets behind the Bishop's carriage shouting "Huzzah, huzzah!" while the Bishop scattered coins for the pedestrians; standing watch over the carriage, which meant drinking and hearing stories and songs with the other servants; or going inside to do attendance on the Bishop at the great occasions of this or that church or embassy or noble house, delighting in the elaborate costumes that so cleverly managed to adhere to the sumptuary laws while being as ostentatious and lewd as possible. It was grand, God approved of it all, and even discreet prurience and titillation were a face of the coin of worship and ecstasy.

But years at the desert's edge had taught Amasa to value things that the other servants never noticed. He did not have to measure his drinking water. The servants splashed each other in the bathhouse. He could piss on the ground and no little animals came to sniff at the puddle, no dying insects lit on it to drink.

They called Hierusalem a city of stone and fire, but Amasa knew it was a city of life and water, worth more than all the gold that was forever changing hands.

The other stablemen accepted Amasa well enough, but a distance always remained. He had come naked, from the outside; he had no fear of uncleanliness before the Lord; and something else: Amasa had known the taste of death in his mouth and it had not been unwelcome. Now he accepted as they came the pleasures of a stableman's life. But he did not need them, and knew he could not hide that from his fellows.

One day the Prior told the Steward, and the Steward the Stablemaster, and the Stablemaster told Amasa and the other stablemen to wash carefully three times, each time with soap. The old-timers knew what it meant, and told them all: It was the King's Invocation that came but once in seven years, and the Bishop would bring them all to stand in attendance, clean and fine in their livery, while he took part in the solemn ordinances. They would have perfume in their hair. And they would see the King and Queen.

"Is she beautiful?" Amasa asked, surprised at the awe in the voices of these irreverent men when they spoke of her.

And they laughed and compared the Queen to a mountain, to a planet, to a moon.

But then a butterfly alighted on the head of an old woman, and suddenly all laughter stopped. "The butterfly," they all whispered. The woman's eyes went blank, and she began to speak:

"The Queen is beautiful, Saint Amasa, to those who have the eyes to see it."

The servants whispered: See, the butterfly speaks to the new one, who came naked.

"Of all the holy men to come out of the world, Saint Amasa, of all the wise and weary souls, you are wisest, you are weariest, you are most holy."

Amasa trembled at the voice of the butterfly. In memory he suddenly loomed over the crevice of Ekdippa, and it was leaping up to take him.

"We brought you here to save her, save her, save her," said the old woman, looking straight into Amasa's eyes.

Amasa shook his head. "I'm through with quests," he said.

And foam came to the old woman's mouth, wax oozed from her ears, her nose ran with mucus, her eyes overflowed with sparkling tears.

Amasa reached out to the butterfly perched on her head, the fragile butterfly that was wracking the old woman so, and he took it in his hand. Took it in his right hand, folded the wings closed with his left, and then broke! the butterfly as crisply as a stick. The sound of it rang metallically in the air. There was no ichor from the butterfly, for it was made of something tough as metal, brittle as plastic, and electricity danced between the halves of the butterfly for a moment and then was still.

The old woman fell to the ground. Carefully the other servants cleaned her face and carried her away to sleep until she awakened. They did not speak to Amasa, except the Stablemaster, who looked at him oddly and asked, "Why would you want to live forever?"

Amasa shrugged. There was no use explaining that he wanted to ease the old woman's agony, and so killed it at its cause. Besides, Amasa was distracted, for now there was something buzzing in the base of his brain. The whirr of switches, infinitely small, going left or right; gates going open and closed; poles going positive and negative. Now and then a vision would flash into his mind, so quickly that he could not frame or recognize it. Now I see the world through butterfly's eyes. Now the vast mind of Hierusalem's machinery sees the world through mine.

Gray waits by this window: it is the one. He does not wonder how he knows. He only knows that he was made for this moment, that his life's need is all within this window, he must not stray to hunt for food because his great stamen is throbbing with desire and in the night it will be satisfied.

So he waits by the window, and the sun is going; the sky is gray, but still he waits, and at last the lights have gone from the sky and all is silent within. He moves in the darkness until his long fingers find the edge of the stone. Then he pulls himself inside, and when his stamen scrapes painfully against the stone, immense between his legs, he only thinks: ease for you, ease for you.

His object is a great mountain that lies breathing upon a sea of sheets. She breathes in quick gasps, for her chest is large and heavy and hard to lift. He thinks nothing of that, but only creeps along the wall until he is above her head. He stares quizzically at the fat face; it holds no interest for him. What interests Gray is the space at her shoulders where the sheets and blankets and quilts fall open like a tent door. For some reason it looks like the leaves of a tree to him, and he drops onto the bed and scurries into the shelter.

Ah, it is not stone! He can hardly move for the bouncing, his fingers and toes find no certain purchase, yet there is this that forces him on: his stamen tingles with extruding pollen, and he knows he cannot pause just because the ground is uncertain.

He proceeds along the tunnel, the sweating body to one side, the tent of sheets above and to the other side. He explores; he crawls clumsily over a vast branch; and at last he knows what he has been looking for. It is time, oh, time, for here is the blossom of a great flower, pistil lush for him. He leaps. He fastens to her body as he has always fastened to the limbs of the great wife trees, to the stone. He plunges stamen into pistil and dusts the walls with pollen. It is all he lived for, and when it is done, in only moments when the pollen is shed at last, he dies and drops to the sheets.

The queen's dreams were frenzied. Because her waking life was wrapped and closed, because her bulk forced an economy of movement, in her sleep she was bold, untiring. Sometimes she dreamed of great chases on a horse across broken country. Sometimes she dreamed of flying. Tonight she dreamed of love, and it was also athletic and unbound. Yet in the moment of ecstasy there was a face that peered at her, and hands that tore her lover away from her, and she was afraid of the man who stared at the end of her dream.

Still, she woke trembling from the memory of love, only wistfully allowing herself to recall, bit by bit, where she really was. That she was lost in the palace, that she was as ungainly as a diseased tree with boles and knots of fat, that she was profoundly unhappy, that a strange man disturbed her dreams.

And then, as she moved slightly, she felt something cold and faintly dry between her legs. She dared not move again, for fear of what it was.

Seeing that she was awake, a servant bowed beside her. "Would you like your breakfast?"

"Help me," she whispered. "I want to get up."

The servant was surprised, but summoned the others. As they rolled her from the bed, she felt it again, and as soon as she was erect she ordered them to throw back the sheets.

And there he lay, flaccid, empty, gray as a deflated stone. The servants gasped, but they did not understand what the Queen instantly understood. Her dreams were too real last night, and the great appendage on the dead body fit too well the memory of her phantom lover. This small monster did not come as a parasite, to drain her; it came to give, not to receive.

She did not scream. She only knew that she had to run from there, had to escape. So she began to move, unsupported, and to her own surprise she did not fall. Her legs, propelled and strengthened by her revulsion, stayed under her, held her up. She did not know where she was going, only that she must go. She ran. And it was not until she had passed through a dozen rooms, a trail of servants chasing after her, that she realized it was not the corpse of her monstrous paramour she fled from, but rather what he left in her, for even as she ran she could feel something move within her womb, could feel something writhing, and she must, she must be rid of it.

As she ran, she felt herself grow lighter, felt her body melting under the flesh, felt her heaps and mounds erode away in an inward storm, sculpting her into a woman's shape again. The vast skin that had contained her belly began to slap awkwardly, loosely against her thighs as she ran. The servants caught up with her, reached out to support her, and plunged their hands into a body that was melting away. They said nothing; it was not for them to say. They only took hold of the loosening folds and held and ran.

And suddenly through her fear the Queen saw a pattern of furniture, a lintel, a carpet, a window, and she knew where she was. She had accidently stumbled upon a familiar wing of the palace, and now she had purpose, she had direction, she would go where help and strength were waiting. To the throne room, to her husband, where the king was surely holding his Invocation. The servants caught up with her at last; now they bore her up. "To my husband," she said, and they assured her and petted her and carried her. The thing within her leapt for joy: its time was coming quickly.

Amasa could not watch the ceremonies. From the moment he entered the Hall of Heaven all he could see were the butterflies. They hovered in the dome that was painted like the midsummernight sky, blotting out the tiny stars with their wings; they rested high on painted pillars, camouflaged except when they fanned their graceful wings. He saw them where to others they were far too peripheral to be seen, for in the base of his brain the gates opened and closed, the poles reversed, always in the same rhythm that drove the butterflies' flight and rest. Save the Queen, they said. We brought you here to save the Queen. It throbbed behind his eyes, and he could hardly see.

Could hardly see, until the Queen came into the room, and then he could see all too clearly. There was a hush, the ceremonies stopped, and all gazes were drawn to the door where she stood, an undulant mass of flesh with a woman's face, her eyes vulnerable and wide with fright and trust. The servants' arms reached far into the folds of skin, finding God-knew-what grip there: Amasa only knew that her face was exquisite. Hers was the face of all women, the hope in her eyes the answer to the hope of all men. "My husband!" she cried out, but at the moment she called she was not looking at the King. She was looking at Amasa.

She is looking at me, he thought in horror. She is all the beauty of Besara, she is the power of Kafr Katnei, she is the abyss of Ekdippa, she is all that I have loved and left behind. I do not want to desire them again.

The King cried out impatiently, "Good God, woman!"

And the Queen reached out her arms toward the man on the throne, gurgled in agony and surprise, and then shuddered like a wood fence in a wind.

What is it, asked a thousand whispers. What's wrong with the Queen?

She stepped backward.

There on the floor lay a baby, a little gray baby, naked and wrinkled and spotted with blood. Her eyes were open. She sat up and looked around, reached down and took the placenta in her hands and bit the cord, severing it.

The butterflies swarmed around her, and Amasa knew what he was meant to do. As you snapped the butterfly, they said to him, you must break this child. We are Hierusalem, and we were built for this epiphany, to greet this child and slay her at her birth. For this we found the man most holy in the world, for this we brought him here, for you alone have power over her.

I cannot kill a child, Amasa thought. Or did not think, for it was not said in words but in a shudder of revulsion in him, a resistance at the core of what in him was most himself.

This is no child, the city said. Do you think the dragons have surrendered just because we stole their trees? The dragons have simply changed to fit a new mate; they mean to rule the world again. And the gates and poles of the city impelled him, and Amasa decided a thousand times to obey, to step a dozen paces forward and take the child in his arms and break it. And as many times he heard himself cry out, I cannot kill a child! And the cry was echoed by his voice as he whispered, "No."

Why am I standing in the middle of the Hall of Heaven, he asked himself. Why is the Queen staring at me with horror in her eyes? Does she recognize me? Yes, she does, and she is afraid of me. Because I mean to kill her child. Because I cannot kill her child.

As Amasa hesitated, tearing himself, the gray infant looked at the King. "Daddy," she said, and then she stood and walked with gathering certainty toward the throne. With such dextrous fingers the child picked at her ear. Now, Now, said the butterflies. Yes, said Amasa. No.

"My daughter!" the King cried out. "At last an heir! The answer to my Invocation before the prayer was done—and such a brilliant child!"

The King stepped down from his throne, reached to the child and tossed her high into the air. The girl laughed and tumbled down again. Once more the King tossed her in delight. This time, however, she did not come down.

She hovered in the air over the King's head, and everyone gasped. The child fixed her gaze on her mother, the mountainous body from which she had been disgorged, and she spat. The spittle shone in the air like a diamond, then sailed across the room and struck the Queen on her breast, where it sizzled. The butterflies suddenly turned black in midair, shriveled, dropped to the ground with infinitesimal thumps that only Amasa could hear. The gates all closed within his mind, and he was all himself again;

but too late, the moment was passed, the child had come into her power, and the Queen could not be saved.

The King shouted, "Kill the monster!" But the words still hung in the air when the child urinated on the King from above. He erupted in flame, and there was no doubt now who ruled in the palace. The gray shadow had come in from the walls.

She looked at Amasa, and smiled. "Because you were the holiest," she said, "I brought you here."

Amasa tried to flee the city. He did not know the way. He passed a palmer who knelt at a fountain that flowed from virgin stone, and asked, "How can I leave Hierusalem?"

"No one leaves," the palmer said in surprise. As Amasa went on, he saw the palmer bend to continue scrubbing at a baby's hands. Amasa tried to steer by the patterns of the stars, but no matter which direction he ran, the roads all bent toward one road, and that road led to a single gate. And in the gate the child waited for him. Only she was no longer a child. Her slate-gray body was heavy-breasted now, and she smiled at Amasa and took him in her arms, refused to be denied. "I am Dalmanutha," she whispered, "and you are following my road. I am Acrasia, and I will teach you joy."

She took him to a bower on the palace grounds, and taught him the agony of bliss. Every time she mated with him, she conceived, and in hours a child was born. He watched each one come to adulthood in hours, watched them go out into the city and afix themselves each to a human, some man, some woman, or some child. "Where one forest is gone," Dalmanutha whispered to him, "another will rise to take its place."

In vain he looked for butterflies.

"Gone, all gone, Amasa," Acrasia said. "They were all the wisdom that you learned from my ancestors, but they were not enough, for you hadn't the heart to kill a dragon that was as beautiful as man." And she *was* beautiful, and every day and every night she came to him and conceived again and again, telling him of the day not long from now when she would unlock the seals of the gates of Hierusalem and send her bright angels out into the forest of man to dwell in the trees and mate with them again.

More than once he tried to kill himself. But she only laughed at him as he lay with bloodless gashes in his neck, with lungs collapsed, with poison foul-tasting in his mouth. "You can't die, my Saint Amasa," she said, "Father of Angels, you can't die. For you broke a wise, a cruel, a kind and gentle butterfly."

THE MONKEYS THOUGHT
'TWAS ALL IN FUN

AGNES 1

"Take her," Agnes's father said, his dry eyes pleading. Agnes's mother stood just behind him, wringing the towel she held in her hand.

"I can't," Brian Howarth said, embarrassed that he had to say that, ashamed that he actually *could* say it. The death of the nation of Biafra was a matter of days now, not weeks, and he and his wife were some of the last to go. Brian had come to love the Ibo people, and Agnes's father and mother had long since ceased to be servants—they were friends. Agnes herself, a bright five-year-old, had been a delight, learning English even before she learned her native tongue, constantly playing hide-and-seek in the house. A bright child, a hopeful child, and from all that Brian had heard (and he believed it, even though he was a correspondent and knew the exaggerations that wartime news always had to endure), from all he had heard the Nigerian Army would not stop to ask anyone "Is this child bright? Is this child beautiful? Does this child have a sense of humor as keen as any adult's?" Instead she would be gutted with a bayonet as quickly as her parents, because she was an Ibo, and the Ibos had done what the Japanese did a half-century before: they had become westernized before any of their neighbors, and profited from it. The Japanese had been on an island, and they had survived. The Ibos were not on an island, and Biafra was destroyed by Nigerian numbers and British and Russian weapons and a blockade that no nation on earth made any effort to relieve, not on a scale that could save anyone.

"I can't," Brian Howarth said again, and then he heard his wife behind him (her name was also Agnes, for the little girl's parents had named their first and only child after her) whisper, "By God you can or I'm not going."

"Please," Agnes's father said, his eyes still dry, his voice still level. He was begging, but his body said I am still proud and will not weep and kneel and subjugate myself to you. Equal to equal, his body said, I ask you to take my treasure, for I will die and cannot keep it anyway.

"How can I?" Brian asked helplessly, knowing that the space on the airplane was limited and the correspondents were forbidden to take any Biafrans with them.

"We can," his wife whispered again, and so Brian reached out his arms and took Agnes and held her. Agnes's father nodded. "Thank you, Brian," he said, and Brian was the one who wept and said, "I'm sorry, if any people in the world deserve to be free—"

But Agnes's parents were already gone, heading for the forest before the Nigerian Army could get into town.

Brian and his wife took little Agnes to the stretch of abandoned highway that served as the last airport in free Biafra and took off in an airplane crammed with correspondents and luggage and more than one Biafran child sitting in the darkest corners of what was never meant to be a passenger plane. Agnes's eyes were wide all through the flight. She did not cry. She had never cried much as an infant. She just held tightly to Brian Howarth's hand.

When the airplane landed in the Azores, where they would change to a flight to America, Agnes finally asked, "What about my parents?"

"They can't come," Brian said.

"Why not?"

"There wasn't room."

And Agnes looked at the many places where another couple of human beings could sit or stand or lie, and she knew that there were other, far worse reasons why her parents couldn't be with her.

"You'll be living with us in America now," Mrs. Howarth said.

"I want to live in Biafra," Agnes said. Her voice was so loud that it could be heard throughout the airplane.

"Don't we all," said the woman farther to the front. "Don't we all."

The rest of the flight Agnes passed in silence, unimpressed by the clouds and the ocean below her. They landed in New York, changed planes again, and at last reached Chicago. Home.

"Home?" Agnes echoed, looking at the two-story brick house that loomed out of the trees and lawn and seemed to hang brightly over the street, "This isn't home."

Brian couldn't argue with her. For Agnes was a Biafran, and there would never be home for her again.

Years later, Agnes would remember little about her escape from Africa. She would remember being hungry, and how Brian gave her two oranges when they landed at the Azores. She would remember the sound of antiaircraft fire, and the rocking of the plane when one shell exploded dangerously near. Most of all, however, she remembered the white man sitting across from her in the dark airplane. He kept looking at her, then at Brian and Agnes Howarth. Brian and his wife were black, but their blackness had been diluted by frequent infusions of white blood in past generations; little Agnes was much, much darker, and the white man finally said. "Little girl. You Biafran?"

"Yes," Agnes said softly.

The white man looked angrily at Brian. "That's against the regulations."

Brian calmly answered, "The world will not shift on its axis because a regulation was broken."

"You shouldn't have brought her," the white man insisted, as if she were breathing up his air, taking up his space.

Brian didn't answer. Mrs. Howarth did. "You're only angry," she said. "because your Biafran friends asked you to take their children, and you refused."

The man looked angry, then hurt, then ashamed. "I couldn't. They had three children. How could I claim they were mine? I couldn't do it!"

"There are white people on this airplane with Biafran children," Mrs. Howarth said.

Angry, the white man stood. "I followed the regulations! I did the right thing!"

"So relax," Brian said, quietly but with a command in his voice. "Sit down. Shut up. Console yourself that you obeyed the regulations. And think of those children with a bayonet slicing—"

"Sh," Mrs. Howarth said. The white man sat back down. The argument was over. But Agnes always remembered that afterward, the man had wept bitterly, for what seemed hours, sobbing almost silently, his back heaving. "I couldn't do a thing," she heard him say. "A whole nation dying, and I couldn't do a thing."

Agnes remembered those words. "I couldn't do a thing," she sometimes said to herself. At first she believed it, and wept for her parents in the silence in her home on the outskirts of Chicago. But gradually, as she forced her way past the barriers society placed before her sex and her race and her foreign background, she learned to say something different:

"I can do something."

She went back to Nigeria with her adopted parents, the Howarths, ten years later. Her passport showed her to be an American citizen. They returned to her city and asked her real family where her parents were.

"Dead," she was told, not unkindly. No relative closer than a second cousin was left alive.

"I was too young," she said to her parents. "I couldn't do a thing."

"Me too," Brian said. "We were all too young."

"But I'll do something someday," Agnes said. "I'll make up for this."

Brian thought she meant revenge, and spent many hours trying to dissuade her. But Agnes did not mean revenge.

HECTOR 1

Hector felt large when he saw the light, large, and full and bright and vigorous, and the light was the right color and the right brightness and so Hector gathered himselves and followed the light and drank in deep.

And because Hector loved to dance, he found the right place and began to bow, and spin, and arch, and crest, and be a thing of great dark beauty.

"Why are we dancing?" the Hectors asked themself.

And Hector told himselves, "Because we are happy,"

AGNES 2

Agnes was already known as one of the two or three best skipship pilots when the Trojan Object was discovered. She had made two Mars trips and dozens of journeys to the moon, many of them solo, just her and the computer, others of them with valuable cargos—famous people, vital medicines, important secret information—the kind of thing valuable enough to make it worth the price of sending a skipship from the ground out into space.

Agnes was a pilot for IBM-ITT, the largest of the companies that had invested in space; and it was partly because IBM-ITT promised that she would be pilot on the expedition that the corporation won the lucrative government contract to investigate the Trojan Object.

"We got the contract," Sherman Riggs told her, and she had been so involved in updating the equipment of her skipship that she didn't know what he meant.

"The *contract*," he said. "*The* contract. To go to the Trojan Object. And you're the pilot."

It was not Agnes's habit to show emotion, whether negative or positive. The Trojan Object was the most important thing in space right now, a large, completely light-absorbent object in Earth's leading trojan point. One day it had not been there. The next day it had, blotting out the stars beyond it and causing more of a stir in the space-watching world than a new comet or a new planet. After all, new objects should not suddenly appear a third of the way around Earth's orbit. And now it would be Agnes who would pilot the craft that would first view the Trojan Object up close.

"Danny," she said, naming her Leaner, the lover/engineer who always teamed with her on two-person assignments. On a long trip like this, no pilot could stand to be without his Leaner.

"Of course," Sherman answered. "And two more. Roger and Rosalind Thorne. Doctor and astronomer."

"I know them."

"Good or bad?"

"Good enough. Good. If we can't get Sly and Frieda."

Sherman rolled his eyes. "Sly and Frieda and GM-Texaco, and there isn't a chance in hell—"

"I hate it when you roll your eyes, Sherman. It makes me think you're having a fit. I know Sly and Frieda are hopeless, but I had to ask, didn't I?"

"Roj and Roz."

"Fine."

"How much do you know about the Trojan Object?"

"More than you do and less than I'll need to."

Sherman tapped his pencil on his desk. "All right, I'll send you straight to the experts."

And a week later, Agnes and Danny and Roj and Roz were ensconced in Agnes's skipship, sweeping down the runway at Clovis, New Mexico. The acceleration was frightful, particularly after they were vertical, but it was not long before they were in a high orbit, and not much longer than that before they were free of the Earth's gravity, making the three-month trip to Earth's leading trojan point, where something waited for them.

HECTOR 2

Hector said to himselves, "I'm thirsty, I'm thirsty, I'm thirsty," and the Hectors gave themself plenty to drink, and when Hector was satisfied, for the moment, he sang a soundless song that all the Hectors heard, and they, too, sang:

> *Hector swims in an empty sea*
> *With Hectors all around.*
> *Hector whistles merrily*
> *But never makes a sound.*

Hector swallows all the light
So he's snug out in the cold.
Hector will be born tonight
Although he's very old.

Hector sweeps up all the dust
And puts it in a pile:
Waybread for his wanderlust,
More Hectors in a while.

And the Hectors laughed and also sang and also danced because they had come together after a long journey and they were warm and they were snug and they lay together to listen to themself tell himselves stories.

"I will tell," Hector said to himselves, "the story of the Masses, and the story of the Masters, and the story of the Makers."

And the Hectors cuddled together to listen.

AGNES 3

Agnes and Danny made love the day before they reached the Trojan Object, because that made it easier for both of them to work. Roj and Roz did not, because that made it easier for them to stay alert. For a week it had been clear that the Trojan Object was far more than anyone on Earth had suspected, and far less.

"Diameter about fourteen hundred kilometers on the average," Roz reported as soon as she had good enough data to be sure. "But gravity is about as much as a giant asteroid. Our shaddles are strong enough to get us off."

Danny spoke the obvious conclusion first. "There's nothing that could be as solid as that, as large as that, and as light as that. Artificial. Has to be."

"Fourteen hundred kilometers in diameter?"

Danny shrugged. Everybody could have shrugged. That's what they were here for. Nothing natural could have suddenly appeared in Earth's leading trojan point, either —obviously it was artificial. But was it dangerous?

They circled the Trojan Object dozens of times, letting the computer scan with better eyes than theirs for any sign of an aperture. There was none.

"Better set down," Roz said, and Agnes brought the skipship close to the surface. It occurred to her as she did so that she and Danny and the others changed personality completely when they worked. Fun-loving, filthy-minded, game-playing friends, until work was needed. Then the fun was over, and they became a pilot and an engineer and a doctor and a physicist, functioning smoothly, as if the computer's integrated circuits had overcome the flesh barrier and inhabited all of them.

Agnes maneuvered her craft within three meters of the surface. "No closer," she said. Danny agreed, and when they were all suited up, he opened the hatch and shaddled down to the surface. "Careful, Leaner," Agnes reminded him. "Escape velocity and everything."

"Can't see a damn thing down here," he answered in a perfect non sequitur. "This surface material sucks up *all* light. Even from my headlamp. Hard and smooth as steel, though. I have to keep shining my light on my hands to see where they are." Silence for a few moments. "Can't tell if I'm scratching the thing or not. Am I getting a sample?"

"Computer says no," Roj answered. As the doctor, he had nothing better to do at the moment than monitor the computer.

"I'm not making any impact on the surface at all. I want to find out how hard this thing is."

"Torch?" Agnes asked.

"Yeah."

Roz protested. "Don't do anything to make them mad."

"Who?" Danny asked.

"Them. The people who made this."

Danny chuckled. "If there's anybody in there, they either know we're out here or they're sure enough we can't get in that they don't care. Either way, I've got to do something to attract their attention."

The torch flared brightly, but nothing was reflected from the surface of the Trojan Object, and only the gas dissipated with the torch made it visible.

"No result. Didn't even raise the surface temperature," Danny finally said.

They tried laser. They tried explosives. They tried a diamond tip on a drill for repair work. Nothing had any effect on the surface at all.

"I want to come out," Agnes said.

"Forget it," Danny answered. "I suggest we go to the pole, north or south. Maybe something's different there."

"I'm coming out," Agnes said.

Danny was angry. "What the hell do you think you can accomplish that I haven't done?"

Agnes frankly admitted that there wasn't anything she could possibly do. While she was admitting it she clambered out of the skipship and launched herself toward the surface.

It was a damnfool thing to do, as Danny informed her loudly over the radio, just as he turned to face Agnes and flashed his light directly in her eyes. She realized to her alarm that he was directly below her—she couldn't turn around and shaddle down. She slipped to the right, instead, and then tried to turn around, but because of her panic at the thought of colliding with Danny (always dangerous in space) and the delay as she maneuvered to avoid him, she struck the planet surface going a good deal faster than should have been comfortable.

But as she touched the surface, it yielded. Not with the springiness of rubber, which would have forced her hand back out, but with the thick resistance of almost-hard cement, so that she found her hand completely immersed in the surface of the planet. She shone her headlamp on it—the smooth surface of the planet was unbroken, not even dented, except that her hand was in it up to the wrist.

"Danny," she said, not sure whether to be excited or afraid.

He didn't hear her at first because he was too busy shouting, "Agnes, are you OK?" into the radio to notice that she was already answering. But at last he calmed down, found her with his headlamp, and came over to her, shaddling gently to stay tight to the surface of the Trojan Object.

"My hand," she said, and he followed her shoulder and her arm until he found her hand and said, "Agnes! Can you get it out?"

"I didn't want to try until you saw this. What does it mean?"

"It means that if it was wet cement it's hard by now and we'll never get you off!"

"Don't be an ass," Agnes said. "Test around it. See if it's different."

Except for the torch, Danny made all the same tests. Right up to the edge of Agnes's suit the Trojan Object's surface was absolutely impenetrable, completely absorbent of energy, nonmagnetic—in other words, untestable. But there was no arguing the fact that Agnes's hand was buried in it.

"Take a picture," Agnes said.

"What will that show? It'll look like your wrist with the hand cut off." But Danny went ahead and laid some of his tools on the surface to give some hint in the photograph of where the surface actually was. Then he took a dozen or more photos. "Why am I taking these pictures?" he said.

"In case we got back and people don't believe I could stick my hand into something harder than steel," Agnes answered.

"I could have told them that."

"You're my Leaner."

Leaners were very good for some things, but you'd never want to be the prosecutor whose case against a defendant rested entirely on his Leaner's testimony. Leaners were loyal first, honest second. Had to be.

"So we've got the pictures."

"So now I get out."

"Can you?" Danny asked. He had only postponed his concern for her; now it was back in full force.

"My knees and my other hand were both sunk in just as deep. The reason this one is still in is because I clenched my fist and I'm still holding on."

"Holding on to what?"

"To whatever this damn thing is made of. My other hand and my knees floated to the surface after a few seconds."

"Floated!"

"That's what it felt like. I'm letting go now." And as Agnes unclenched her fist her hand slowly rose to the surface and was gently ejected. There wasn't a ripple on the surface material, however. Where her hand was, it behaved like a liquid. Where her hand wasn't, it was as solid as ever.

"What is this made of?"

"Silly Putty," Agnes said.

"Unfunny," Danny answered.

"I'm serious. Remember how Silly Putty was flexible, but if you formed it into a ball and threw it on the ground, it broke like clay?"

"Mine never worked like that."

"But this stuff does, in reverse. When something sharp hits it, or something hot, or something too slow or too weak, it sits there. But when I ran into it going at shaddle speed, I sank in it for a few inches."

"In other words," Roj said from the skipship, "you've found the door."

They were back in the skipship inside ten minutes, and after only a few more minutes of checking everything to make sure it was in good condition, Agnes pulled the skipship a few dozen meters away from the surface of the Trojan Object. "Everybody ready?" Agnes asked.

"Are we doing what I think we're doing?" Roz asked.

"Yep," Danny answered. "We shore is."

"Then we're idiots," Roz said, her voice sounding nervous. No one argued with her.

Agnes fired the vernier rockets on the outboard side and they plunged toward the Trojan Object. Not terribly fast, by the standard of speed they were used to. But to those aboard, who knew that they were heading directly into a surface so hard a diamond drill and a laser had had no effect at all, it was disconcertingly fast.

"What if you're wrong?" Roz asked, pretending she was joking.

No one could answer before they hit. But in the moment when there should have come a violent crunch and a rush of atmosphere escaping from the ship, the skipship merely slowed sickeningly and kept moving inward. The black flowed quickly past the viewports, and they were buried in the surface of the Trojan Object.

"Are we still moving?" Roj asked, his voice trembling.

"You've got the computer," Agnes answered, flattering herself that she, at least, did not sound scared. She was wrong, but no one told her.

"Yeah," Roj finally said. "We're still moving. Computer says so."

And then they sat in silence for an interminable minute. Agnes was just about to say "Maybe this isn't such a good idea. I've changed my mind" when the blackness turned to a reflective brown through the window, and then, just when they'd had time to notice it, the brown turned into a bright, transparent blue—"Water!" Danny said in surprise—and then the water broke and they bobbed on the surface of a lake, the sun dazzlingly bright on the surface.

HECTOR 3

"First I will tell you the story of the Masses," Hector said to himselves. Actually, the telling of the stories was not necessary. As Hector drank, all that he had been through, all that he had known through the years of his life was being transferred subliminally to himselves. But there was the matter of focus. The matter of meaning. Hector had no imagination at all. But he did have understanding, and that understanding had to be passed to himselves, or in ages to come the Hectors would curse themself for having left himselves crippled.

This is the story, therefore, that he told, because it focused and it meant:

Cyril [said Hector] wanted to be a carpenter. He wanted to cut living wood and dry it and cure it and shape it into objects of beauty and utility. He thought he had an eye for it. As a child he had experimented with it. But when he applied at the Office of Assignments, he was told no.

"Why not?" he asked, astonished that the Office of Assignments could make such an obvious mistake.

"Because," said the clerk, who was unflaggingly nice (she had tested nice and therefore held her job), "your aptitude and preference tests show that not only do you not have any aptitude along those lines at all, but also you do not even want to be a carpenter."

"I want to be a carpenter," Cyril insisted, because he was young enough not to know that one does not insist.

"You want to be a carpenter because you have a false impression of what carpentry is. In actual fact, your preference tests show that you would absolutely hate life as a carpenter. Therefore you cannot be a carpenter."

And something in her manner told Cyril that there was no point in arguing any further. Besides, he was not so young as not to know that resistance was futile—and continued resistance was fatal.

So Cyril was placed where his tests showed he had the most aptitude: He was trained as a miner. Fortunately, he was not untalented or utterly unbright, so he was trained as a lead miner, the one who follows the vein and finds it when it jogs or turns or jumps. It was a demanding job. Cyril hated it. But he learned to do it because his preference tests showed that he really wanted this line of work.

Cyril wanted to marry a girl named Lika, and she wanted to marry him. "I'm sorry," said the clerk at the Office of Assignments, "you are genetically, temperamentally, and socially unsuited for each other. You would be miserable. Therefore we cannot permit you to marry."

They didn't marry, and Lika married someone else, and Cyril asked if it was all right if he remained unmarried. "If you wish. That's one of your options for optimum happiness, according to the tests," the clerk informed him.

Cyril wanted to live in a certain area, but he was forbidden; food was served for him that he didn't like; he had to go dancing with friends he didn't like, doing dances to music he loathed, singing songs whose words were silly to him. Surely, surely there's been a mistake, he said, pleading with the clerk.

The clerk fixed a cold stare on him (he tried in vain to scrub the stare off, but still it hung on him like slime in his dreams) and said, "My dear Cyril, you have now protested as often as a citizen may protest and remain alive."

In just such a case many another member of the masses might have rebelled, joining the secret underground organizations that sprang up from time to time and were crushed at regular intervals by the state. In just such a case many another member of the masses, knowing he was consigned to a lifetime of undeserved misery, would kill himself and thereby eliminate the misery.

However, Cyril belonged to the largest group within the masses, and so he chose neither route. Instead he went to the town he was assigned to, worked in the coal mine where he was assigned, remained lonely as he pined for Lika, and danced idiotic dances to idiotic music with his idiotic friends.

Years passed, and Cyril began to be well known among coal miners. He handled his rockcutter as if it were a delicate tool, and with it he left beautiful shapes in the rock behind, so that any miner could tell when he walked down a tunnel cut by Cyril, for it would be beautiful, and as he walked the miner would feel exalted and proud and, oddly, loved. And Cyril also had a knack for anticipating the coal, following where it led no matter how narrow the seam, how twisting its path, how interrupted its progress.

"Cyril knows the coal like a woman, every twist and turn of her, as if he'd had her a thousand times and knew just when she'd come," a miner said of Cyril once, and because the statement was apt and true (and because there are poets' hearts beating even at the bottom of a mine) the statement spread through the mines and the miners began referring to their black stone as "Mrs. Cyril." Cyril heard of it, and smiled, because in *his* heart coal was not a wife, only an unloved mistress used for the scant pleasure she gave and then cast away. Hatred mistaken for love, as usual.

Cyril was nearly sixty years old when a clerk from the Office of Assignments came to the mines. "Cyril the coal miner," the clerk said, and so they brought Cyril from the mines, and the clerk met him with a huge, unbelievable smile. "Cyril, you are a great man!" cried the clerk.

Cyril smiled wanly, not knowing what he was leading up to.

"Cyril, my friend," said the clerk, "you are a notable miner. Without seeking fame at all, your name is known to miners all over the world. You are the perfect model of what a man ought to be—happy in your assignment, hardworking, content. So the Office of Assignments has announced that you are the Model Worker of the Year."

Everyone knew about Model Worker of the Year. That was a person who had his

picture in all the papers, and was in the movies and on television and who was held
up as the greatest person in all the world in that year. It was an honor to be envied.

But Cyril said, "No."

"No?" asked the clerk.

"No. I don't want to be the Model Worker of the Year."

"But—but. But why not?"

"Because I'm not happy. I was put into this assignment by mistake many years ago.
I shouldn't be a coal miner. I should be a carpenter, married to Lika, living in another
town, dancing to other music with other friends."

The clerk looked at him in horror. "How can you say that!" he cried. "I've announced
that you are Model Worker of the Year! You will either be Model Worker of the Year
or you will be put to death!"

Put to death? Forty years ago that threat had made Cyril comply, but now a stubborn
streak erupted from him, like a seam of coal long hidden but under such pressure that
when the stone around it gave way, it actually burst from the rock walls. "I'm near
sixty," Cyril said, "and I've hated all my life to now. Kill me if you like, but I won't
go on television or the movies saying how happy I've been because I haven't."

And so they took Cyril and locked him in prison and sentenced him to death because
while he might suffer all kinds of abuse, he refused to lie to his friends.

That is the story of the Masses.

And when Hector was finished, the Hectors sighed and wept (without tears) and said,
"Now we understand. Now we know the meaning."

"This isn't," Hector said, "the whole meaning."

And when he had said that, one of the Hectors (which was remarkable, for the
Hectors rarely spoke alone) said to himselves and themself, "Oh, oh, they have penetrated me!"

"Trapped!" Hector cried to himselves. "All these years of freedom, and they have
found me at last!" But then another thought came to him, one that he had never thought
before but that had lain dormant in him, waiting for this moment to emerge, and he
said, "Just cooperate. They won't hurt you if you just cooperate."

"But it already hurts!" cried the Hector who had spoken alone.

"It will heal. Just remember, no matter what you do, the masters will have their
way with you. And if you struggle, it only goes worse with you."

"The Masters," said all the Hectors to themself. "Tell us a story of the Masters, so
we can understand why they do what they do."

"I will," said Hector to himselves.

AGNES 4

Agnes and Danny stood on a mountaintop, or what had seemed to be a mountaintop
from the skipship. They had reached it after only a few hours' walk, much of it sped
by shaddling, and learned that what seemed to be a high mountain was only a few
hundred meters high, maybe even half a kilometer. It was rugged enough, though, and
the climb, even shaddled, had not been easy.

"Artificial," Danny said, touching the wall with his hand. The wall ran from the
top of the mountain up to the ceiling, where instead of a sun the whole ceiling glowed
with light and warmth, as thorough as sunlight, yet diffused so that they could look at
it for a few seconds without being blinded.

"I thought we concluded this place was artificial from the beginning," Agnes said.

"But what's it *for?*" Danny asked, letting his frustration at two days of exploration come to the surface. "Bare dirt, rich enough but with not a damn thing growing. Clean, drinkable water. Rain twice a day for twenty minutes, a gentle sprinkle that wets everything but creates almost no runoff. Sunlight constantly. A perfect environment. But for what! What lives here?"

"Us, right now," Agnes said.

"I think we should try to leave."

"No," Agnes said firmly. "No. When we leave here, if we can, we'll leave with the computer and our heads full of every bit of information we can get from this place. From this thing."

Danny knew he couldn't argue. She was right, and she was pilot, and the combination was irresistible even if he hadn't loved her desperately. (More than she loves me, he sometimes admitted to himself.) He did love her desperately, however, and while this did not mean that he utterly lost his own will, it did mean that he would go along with her, for a while at least, in almost anything. Even if she was a damned fool sometimes.

"You're a damned fool sometimes," he said.

"I love you too," she answered, and then she ran her hand along the wall above the mountain, and then pushed on it, and then pushed harder, and her hand sank into the wall a little. She looked at Danny and said, "Come on, Leaner," and they let their shaddles push them through the wall and they emerged on the other side and found themselves—

Standing on a mountain.

Looking out over a large bowl of a valley, just like the one they had left, with a lake in the middle, just like the one where their skipship floated.

In this lake, however, there was no skipship, and Agnes looked at Danny and smiled, and Danny smiled back. "I'm beginning to get this, a little," Agnes said. "Imagine cell after cell like this, kilometers long and hundreds of meters high—"

"But this is just the outer part of this thing," Danny answered, and in unison they turned back to the wall, passed through again (and this time there was the skipship in the middle of the lake), and then shaddled up the wall to the ceiling.

As they approached the ceiling, the area directly above them dimmed, until when they finally reached it, it was as cool and undazzling as the wall. The rest of the ceiling still glowed, of course. They let their shaddles push them upward into the ceiling; it gave way; they rose until they reached the surface.

Another cell, just like the one below. A lake in the middle, rich lifeless dirt all over, mountains all around, the sky on fire with sunlight. Danny and Agnes laughed and laughed. It was only a tiny part of the mystery, but it was solved.

They stopped laughing, however, when they tried to go back down the way they came. They tried to shaddle into the earth, but the soil acted like any normal dirt on Earth. They could not get through it as they had got through the walls and the ceiling.

For a while they were afraid, but when their bodies and their watches told them it was time to sleep, they went down by the lake and slept.

When they woke up, they were still afraid, and it was raining. They had already determined that it rained every thirteen and a half hours, approximately—they had not slept particularly long. But because they were afraid, they took off their suits despite the rain and made love in the dirt on the shore of the lake. They felt better afterward, much better, and they laughed and ran into the lake and swam and splashed each other.

Agnes swam underwater for a moment, attacking Danny from below, pulling him down. It was a game they had played in pools and in the ocean on Earth, and now Danny was supposed to surface for air and then dive to the bottom and hold his breath there until Agnes found him.

When he reached the bottom of the lake (and it wasn't deep) he touched it, and his hand sank up to the wrist before it struck something solid. But even the solid part was yielding, and as Danny kicked harder his hand sank deeper and he knew the way out.

He went to the surface and told Agnes what he had found. They swam to shore, put their suits back on, and shaddled down into the water. The lake floor opened, engulfed them, and then floated them out the bottom—into the sky directly over the skipship, where it still rested on the surface of the lake. They shaddled safely down.

"This place is explorable," Agnes told Roj and Roz, "and it's simple. It's like a huge balloon, with other balloons inside and more and more of them, layer after layer. It's designed for somebody to live here, so when you're standing on the soil you don't sink through. To get down, you have to go through the lake."

"But who's it for?" Roj asked, and it was a good question for which there was no answer.

"Maybe we'll find someone," Agnes said. "We've only scratched the surface. We're going in."

The skipship lifted from the lake not long after, and rose through the ceiling into the lake above. Again and again, always rising, the computer keeping count. Every cell was the same, nothing changed at all, through 498 layers of ceiling/floor, until at last they reached a ceiling, apparently no different from the others, which would not give way.

"End of the road?" Danny asked.

Always thorough, Roz insisted that they try every part of the ceiling, and they spent many hours doing it, until they had convinced themselves that this ceiling was the end of their upward (or inward) travels.

"The centrifugal gravity effect is a lot weaker here," Roj said, reading off the computer. "But it feels nearly the same, since out near the surface the real gravity was offsetting the centrifugal effect much more than it is here."

"Hi ho," said Roz. "Just assuming this thing is as big as it seems to be, how many people could this hold?"

Calculations, rough with plenty of room for error.

"There could be more than a hundred million cells to this thing, assuming that there's nothing much inside the center there, where we can't get to." A hundred and fifty square kilometers per cell; one human being per hectare; a huge potential population, without any crowding at all, considering that all the land is productive. "If we have fifteen thousand people per cell, living in a town with the rest of the land used for farming, then this place can hold a trillion and a half people."

They figured on, eliminating the polar zones because centrifugal gravity would be too weak, allowing more space per person, and the figure was still stunning. Even with only a thousand people per cell, space for a hundred billion.

"The fairy godmother," Danny said, "has given us a free place to put our population overflow."

"I don't believe in free presents," Roj said, looking out the window at the plain of dirt surrounding them. "There's a catch. With all that room, maybe they all live somewhere else, and if they find out we're here, they'll shoot us for trespassing."

"Or if we overload the place," Roz suggested, "it'll probably burst."

"You're overlooking the worst catch of all," Agnes said. "Skipships are the only thing in existence that can make this trip. They hold four persons each. Allowing for overcrowding, say we can take ten people per trip"—they laughed at the thought of trying to put ten people in their craft—"and we had a hundred skipships, which we don't have, and they could make two round trips a year, which we can't. How long would it take to bring a billion people from Earth to here?"

"Five hundred thousand years."

"Paradise," Danny said. "We could make this into a paradise. And the damn thing's out of reach."

"Besides," Roj added, "the kind of people who could make this place work are farmers and tradesmen. Who's going to pay their passage?"

Metals and minerals paid for trips to the moon and the asteroids. But all that this place held was homes—homes a few million miles and a few billion dollars out of everybody's reach.

"Well, daydreams and nightmares are over," Agnes said. "Let's go home."

"If we can," Danny said.

They could. The lakes worked as exits all the way back down, including the last time. They were back in space, and the Trojan Object had become, in their minds, the Balloon, an object obviously designed as an alternative environment for a creature not unlike man; an object perhaps unoccupied, ready and waiting, and they knew no one would ever be able to settle there.

Agnes dreamed, and the dream came back night after night. She remembered a scene she had forgotten, or had at least refused to remember clearly, since she was a child. She remembered standing between her parents and the Howarths (who, though they had adopted her, had never let her call them Mother and Father lest she forget her real heritage in Biafra), hearing her father say, "Please."

And her dream always ended the same way. She was taken into the sky, but instead of a dark cargo plane she was in a plane with glass sides, and as she flew she could see all the world. And everywhere she looked there were her parents, holding a little girl in front of them, saying, "Please. Take her."

She had seen pictures of the starving children in Biafra, the ones that had made millions of Americans cry and do nothing. Now she saw those children, and the children who died of starvation in India and Indonesia and Mali and Iraq, and they all looked at her with proud, pleading eyes, their backs straight and their voices strong but their hearts breaking as they said, "Take me."

"There's nothing I can do," she said to herself in her dream, and she sobbed and sobbed like the white man on the airplane, and then Danny woke her and spoke gently to her and held her and said, "The same dream again?"

"Yes," she said.

"Agnes, if I could take the memories and wipe them out—"

"It's not the memories, Danny," Agnes whispered, touching his eyes gently where the epicanthic fold made his eyes seem to slant. "It's now. It's the people I can't do a damn thing about now."

"You couldn't do a damn thing about them before," Danny reminded her.

"But I've seen a place that could be heaven for them, and I can't get them there."

Danny smiled sadly. "That's just it. You can't. Now you've just got to let your dreams know that and give you a little peace."

"Yes," Agnes agreed, and fell asleep again holding and being held by Danny, while

Roj and Roz piloted the skipship back toward Earth, which had seemed so large when they left it, and which now seemed unbearably, impossibly, criminally small.

Earth was large in the window of the skipship when Agnes finally decided that it was her dreams that were right, her conscious mind that was wrong. She could do something. There was something to be done, and she would do it.

"I'm going back there," Agnes said.

"Probably," Danny said.

"I won't go alone."

"You sure as hell better take me."

"You," she said, "and others." Billions of others. It should be done. Must be done. Therefore would be done.

HECTOR 4

"Now I will tell you the story of the Masters," said Hector to himselves, and the Hectors listened to himself. "This is the story of why the Masters penetrate and why the Masters hurt."

Martha [Hector said] was administrator of Tests and Assignments in the sector where Cyril had been sentenced to death. Martha was hardworking and conscientious, and prone to double-check things which had already been checked and double-checked and triple-checked by others. This was why Martha discovered the mistake.

"Cyril," she said when the guard let her into the clean white plastic cell where the coal miner waited.

"Just stick the needle in quick," Cyril answered, wanting to get it over with quickly.

"I'm here to bring you the apologies of the state."

The words were so strange, so never-before-heard that Cyril did not understand at first. "Please. Let me die and get it over with."

"No," said Martha. "I've done some checking. I checked into your case, Cyril, and I discovered that fifty years ago, just after all your tests were taken, your number was punched incorrectly by a moron of a clerk."

Cyril was shocked. "A clerk made a mistake?"

"They do it all the time. It's just easier, usually, to let the mistake go than to fix it. But in this case, it was a gross miscarriage of justice. You were given the number of a retarded man with a criminal bent, which is why you were not allowed to live in a civilized town and why you were not regarded as being capable of carpentry and why you were not allowed to marry Lika."

"Just punched in the number wrong," Cyril said, unable to grasp the minitude of the error that had such an enormous, disastrous effect on his own life.

"Therefore, Cyril, the Office of Assignments hereby rescinds the execution order and grants you a pardon. Furthermore, we are undoing the damage we did. You can now live in the town where you wanted to live, among the friends you wanted to keep, dancing to the music you enjoyed. You do indeed, as you used to believe, have an aptitude and a desire to be a carpenter—you will be instructed in the trade and given your own shop. And Lika is entirely compatible with you. Therefore you and she will now be married, and in fact she is already on her way to the cottage where you will live together in wedded bliss."

Cyril was overwhelmed. "I can't believe it," he said.

"The Office of Assignments loves you and every citizen, Cyril, and we do everything we can to make you happy," said Martha, glowing with pride at the great kindness she was able to do. Ah, she thought, it is moments like this that make my job the best one in the world.

And then Martha went away to her office and forgot about Cyril most of the time for several months, though occasionally she did remember him and smiled to think of how happy she had made him.

After several months, however, a message crossed her desk: "Serious complaint Cyril 113-49-55576-338-bBR-3a."

Cyril? Her Cyril? Complaining? Had the man no sense of propriety? He already had enough complaints and resistance on his record to justify terminating him twice, and now he had added enough more that if it were possible, the office would have to kill him three times. Why? Hadn't she done her best for him? Hadn't she given him everything his early (and now correctly recorded) tests indicated he wanted and needed? What could be wrong now?

Her pride was involved. Cyril was not just being ungrateful to the state—he was being ungrateful to her. So she went to his cottage in his village, and opened his door.

Cyril sat in the main room, struggling to get past a gnarl in a fine old piece of walnut. The adz kept slipping to the side. And finally Cyril struck with enough force that when the adz slipped it gouged a deep rut in the good, ungnarled part of the wood.

"What a botch," Martha said without thinking, and then covered her mouth, because it was not proper for a person of her high position to criticize anyone of low station if it could be avoided.

But Cyril was not offended. "Damn right it's a botch. I haven't the skill for this close, ticky work. My muscles are all for heavy equipment, for grand strokes with stone-eating power tools. This is beyond me, at my age."

Martha pursed her lips. He was indeed complaining. "But isn't everything else well with you?"

Cyril's eyes grew sad, and he shook his head. "Indeed not. Much as I hate to admit it, I miss the old music from the mines. Terrible stuff, but I had good times with it, dancing away with those poor bastards who hadn't a thought worth having. But they were good people and I liked them well enough, and here no one's willing to be my friend. They don't talk the way I'm used to talking. And the food—it's too refined. I want a haunch of good, well-cooked beef, not this namby-pamby stuff that passes for food here."

His diatribe of complaint was so outrageous that Martha could not conceal her emotion. Cyril noticed it, and became alarmed.

"Not that it's unendurable, mind you, and I don't go complaining to other people. Heaven knows, there's no one who'd care to listen to me anyway."

But Martha had already heard enough. Her heart sank within her. No matter what you do for them, they're still ungrateful. The masses are worthless, she realized. Unless you lead them by the hand. . . ."

"You realize that this complaint," she said, "can have dire consequences."

Cyril got a very weary expression on his face. "So we do it again?"

"Do what?"

"Punish me."

"Indeed, no, Cyril. We remove you from circulation. Apparently you are going to complain and resist no matter what happens. What about your wife?"

Cyril got a bitter smile on his face. "Lika? Oh, she's content. She's happy enough." And he glanced toward the door into the cottage's other room.

Martha went to the door and opened it. (Officers of the Office of Assignments did not need to knock.) Inside the room Lika sat in a clumsily built rocking chair, rocking back and forth, an old woman with a blank stare on her face.

Martha heard breathing over her shoulder, and turned, startled, to see Cyril leaning over her. For a moment Martha was afraid of violence. Quickly she realized, however, that Cyril was merely looking sadly at his wife.

"She's raised a family, you know. And now to be cut off from her husband and her children and her grandchildren—it's hard. She's been like this since the first week. Never lets me near her. She hates me, you know." The sadness in his voice was contagious. And Martha was not without pity.

"It's a shame," she said. "A damned shame. And so I'll use my discretionary powers, Cyril, and not kill you. As long as you promise not to complain to anyone ever again, I'll let you live. It wouldn't be fair, when things really are bad in your life, to kill you for noticing it."

Martha was an exceptionally kind administrator.

But Cyril did not smother her with gratitude. "Not kill me?" he asked. "Oh, but Administrator, can't we have things back the way they were? Let me go back to the coal mines. Let Lika go back to her family. This was what I wanted when I was twenty. But I'm near sixty, and this is all wrong."

Ingratitude again. What I have to put *up* with! Martha's eyes went small and her face flushed with rage (an emotion she did remarkably well, and so she reserved it for special occasions) and she shouted, "I will forgive that one remark, but only that one remark!"

Cyril bowed his head. "I'm sorry."

"The tests that sent you to the coal mines were in error! But the tests that sent you here are absolutely, completely, totally correct, and by heaven you're going to stay here! There isn't a law on earth that will let you change now!"

And that was that.

Or almost. Because in the silence ringing after Martha spoke and before she left, a voice came from the rickety rocker in the bedroom.

"Then we have to stay like this?" Lika asked.

"Until Cyril dies, you have to stay like this," Martha said. "It's the law. He and you have both been given everything you ever petitioned for. Ingrates."

Martha would have turned to go, but she saw Lika looking pleadingly at Cyril, and saw Cyril nod slowly, and then Cyril turned away from the door, picked up the crosscut saw, and drew it sharply and hard across his own throat. The blood gushed and poured, and Martha thought it would never, never end.

But it did end, and Cyril's body was taken out and disposed of, and then everything was set to rights, with Lika going back to her family and a real carpenter getting the cottage with the dark red stains on the floor. The best solution after all, Martha decided. Nobody could be happy until Cyril was dead. I should have killed him in the first place, instead of these silly ideas of mercy.

She suspected, however, that Cyril would rather have died the way he did, ugly and bloody and painful though it was, than to have an injection administered by strangers in a plastic room in the capital.

I'll never understand them. They are as foreign to human thought as monkeys or dogs or cats. And Martha returned to her desk and went on double-checking everything just in case she found another mistake she could fix.

That is the story of the Masters.

* * *

When Hector was finished the Hectors wriggled uncomfortably, some (and therefore all) of them angry and disturbed and a little frightened. "But it makes no sense," the Hectors said to themself. "Nothing was done right."

Hector agreed. "But that's the way they are made," he said to himselves. "Not like me. I am regular. I act as I have always acted, as I will always act. But the Masters and the Masses always act oddly, forever seeing things in the future where no one can see, and acting to avert things that would never have come to pass anyway. Who can understand them?"

"Who made them, then?" asked the Hectors. "Why were they not made well, as we were?"

"Because the Makers are as inscrutable as the Masters and the Masses. I shall tell you their story next."

("They are gone," whispered the ones who had been penetrated. "They have gone away. We are safe after all." But Hector knew better, and because he knew better, so did the Hectors.)

AGNES 5

"You invited yourself to my bedroom, Agnes. That isn't typical."

"I accepted your standing invitation."

"I never thought you would."

"Neither did I."

Vaughan Malecker, president of IBM-ITT Space Consortium, Inc., smiled, but the smile was weak. "You don't long for my body, which is in remarkably good shape, considering my age, and I have an aversion to making love to anyone who is doing it for an ulterior motive."

Agnes looked at him for a moment, decided that he meant it, and got up to leave.

"Agnes," he said.

"Never mind," she answered.

"Agnes, it must have been something important for you to be willing to make such a sacrifice."

"I said never mind." She was at the door. It didn't open.

"Doors in my house open when I want them to," Malecker said. "I want to know what you wanted. But try to persuade my mind. Not my gonads. Believe it or not, testosterone has never made a major decision here at the consortium."

Agnes waited with her hand on the knob.

"Come on, Agnes, I know you're embarrassed as hell but if it was important enough to come this far, you can get over the embarrassment and sit down on the couch and tell me what the hell you want. You want to take another trip to the Balloon?"

"I'm going anyway."

"Sit *down*, dammit. I know you're going anyway but I was trying to get you to say *something*."

Agnes came back and sat down on the couch. Vaughan Malecker was a remarkably good-looking man, as he had pointed ont, but Agnes had heard that he slept with anyone good-looking and was nice to them afterward. Agnes had been turning him down for years because she wanted to be a pilot, not a mistress, and Danny was plenty for her needs, which were not overwhelming. But this mattered, and she thought. . . .

"I thought you'd listen to me if I came this way, I thought—"

Malecker sighed and buried his face in his hands, rubbing his eyes. "I'm so tired. Agnes, what the hell makes you think I ever listen to a woman I'm trying to lay?"

"Because I listen to Danny and Danny listens to me. I'm naive. I'm innocent. But Mr. Malecker—"

"Vaughan."

"I need your help."

"Good. I like to have people need my help. It makes them treat me nicely."

"Vaughan, the whole world needs your help."

Malecker looked at her in surprise, then burst out laughing. "The whole world! Oh, no! Agnes, I would never have thought it of you! A cause!"

"Vaughan, people all over the world are starving. There are too many people for this planet—"

"I read your report, Agnes, and I know all about the possibilities in the Balloon. The problem is transport. There is no conceivable way to transport people there fast enough to make even a dent in the population problem. What do you think I am, a miracle worker?"

This was the argument Agnes was waiting for. She pounced with descriptions of the kind of ship that could carry a thousand people at once from Earth orbit to an orbit around the Balloon.

"Do you know how many billion dollars a ship like that would cost?" Vaughan asked.

"About fifteen billion for the first ship. About four billion for each of the others, if you made five hundred of them."

Vaughan laughed. Loud. But Agnes's serious expression forced his laughter to become exasperation. He got up from the couch. "Why am I listening to you? This is nonsense!" he shouted.

"You spend more than that every year on telephone service."

"I know, damn AT&T."

"You could do it."

"IBM-ITT could do it, of course, it's *possible*. But we have stockholders. We have responsibilities. We're not the *government*, Agnes, we can't throw money away on stupid useless projects."

"It could save billions of lives. Make the Earth a better place to live."

"So could a cure for cancer. We're working on that, but this—Agnes, there's no profit, and where there's no profit, you can bet your ass this company will not go!"

"Profit!" Agnes shouted. "Is that all you care about?"

"Eighteen million stockholders say that's all I'd better care about or I get a kick in the butt and an old-age pension!"

"Vaughan, you want profit, I'll give you profit!"

"I want profit."

"Then here's profit. How much do you sell in India?"

"Enough to make a profit."

"Compare it to sales in Germany."

"Compared to Germany, India is practically nothing."

"How much do you sell in China?"

"Exactly nothing."

"You make your profits off one tiny part of the world. Western Europe, Japan, Australia, South Africa, and the United States of America."

"Canada, too."

"And Brazil. But the rest of the world is closed to you."

Vaughan shrugged. "They're too poor."

"In the Balloon they would not be poor."

"Would they suddenly be able to read? Would they suddenly be able to run computers and sophisticated telephone equipment?"

"Yes!" And on she went, painting a picture of a world where people who had been scratching out a bare subsistence in poor soil with no water would suddenly be able to raise far more than they needed. "That means a leisure class. That means consumers."

"But all they'd have to trade would be food. Who needs food across a few million miles of space?"

"Don't you have any imagination at all? Excess food means one person can feed five or ten or twenty or a hundred. Excess food means that you locate your stinking factories there! Solar power unlimited, with no night and no clouds and no cold weather. Shifts around the clock. You have plenty of manpower, and a built-in market. You can do everything there that you've been doing here, do it cheaper, make better profits, and nobody'll be going hungry!"

And then there was silence in the room, because Vaughan was actually seriously thinking about it. Agnes's heart was beating fast. She was panting. She was embarrassed to have been so fervent when fervor was not fashionable.

"Almost thou persuadest me," said Vaughan.

"I should hope so. I'll lose my voice in a minute."

"Only two problems. The first one is that while you've persuaded me, I'm a much more reasonable, persuasible man than the officers and boards of directors of IBM and ITT, and it's their final decision, not mine. They don't let me commit more than ten billion to a project without their approval. I could make the initial ship—but I couldn't make any more than that. And the initial ship won't make a profit alone. So I have to persuade them, which is impossible, or lose my job, which I refuse to do."

"Or do nothing at all," Agnes said, contempt already seeping into her tone. Malecker was going to say no.

"And the second problem is actually the first, too. How could I persuade the board of directors of two of the world's largest corporations to invest billions of dollars in a project that depends entirely on being able to educate or train or even communicate with illiterate savages and peasants from the most backward countries on Earth?"

His voice was sweet reason, but Agnes was not prepared to hear reason. If Vaughan said no, she would be stopped here. There was nowhere else to go.

"*I'm* an illiterate savage!" she said. "Do you want to hear a few words of Igbo?" She didn't wait for an answer, babbled off the few words she remembered from childhood. She hardly remembered meanings—they were phrases that in her anger came to the surface. Some of the words, however, were spoken to her mother. Mother, come here, help me.

"My mother was an illiterate savage who spoke fluent English. My father was an illiterate savage who spoke better English than her and had French and German, too, and wrote beautiful poems in Igbo and even though to survive in the days when Biafra was struggling for survival he worked as a house servant to an American correspondent, he was never illiterate! He's read books you've never heard of, and he was a black African who was gutted in a tribal war while all those wonderful literate Americans and Europeans and educated Orientals watched placidly, counting up the profits from arms sales to Nigeria."

"I didn't know you were Biafran."

"I'm not. There is no Biafra. Not on this planet. But up there, up there a Biafra *could* exist, and a free Armenia, and an independent Eritrea, and an unshackled Quebec, and an Ainu nation and a Bangladesh where no one was hungry and you tell me that illiterates can't be taught—"

"Of course they *can* be, but—"

"If I'd been born fifty miles to the west I wouldn't have been an Ibo and so I would have grown up exactly as illiterate as you say, exactly as stupid. Now look at me, you privileged white American, and tell me I can't be educated—"

"If you talk like a radical no one's going to listen to you."

Too much. Couldn't take Malecker's patronizing smile, his patient attitude. Agnes struck out at him. Her hand hit his cheek, tore his fashionable glasses off. Furious, he struck back, perhaps trying more to hold her off than to hit her, but because she was moving and he was unaccustomed to hitting people his hand slugged her hard in the breast, and she cried out in pain and jabbed a knee in his groin and then the fight got mean.

"I listened to you," he said huskily, when they were tired and pulled apart. His nose was bleeding. He was exhausted. He had a tear in his shirt, because his body had had to twist in a direction that tailored shirts were not meant to go. "Now listen to me."

Agnes listened because, her anger spent and her mind only beginning to realize that she had just assaulted the president of her company and would certainly be grounded and blackballed and her life would be over, she was not interested in leaving or in getting up or even in talking. She listened.

"Listen to me because I'm going to say it once. Go to the engineering department. Tell them to do rough plans and estimates. A proposal. I want it in three months. Ships that will carry two thousand and make a round trip in at most a year. Shuttle ships that will carry two hundred or, preferably, four hundred from Earth up into Earth orbit. And cargo ships that will take whole stinking factories, as you so aptly named them, and take them to the Balloon. And when the cost figures are all in, I'm going to go to the boards of directors, and I'm going to make a presentation, and I swear to you, Agnes Howarth, you lousy illiterate savage bitch of a best pilot in the world, if I don't persuade those bastards to let me build those ships it's because nobody could persuade them. Is that enough?"

I should be elated, Agnes thought. He's doing it. But I'm just tired.

"Right now you're tired, Agnes," Malecker said. "But I want you to know your fingernails and that knee in the groin and your teeth in my arm did not change my mind. I agreed with you from the start. I just didn't believe it could be done. But if there are a few thousand Ibos like you, and a few million Indians and a few billion Chinese, then this thing can work. That's all I needed to know, all anybody needs to know. It was uneconomical to ship colonists to America, too, and anybody who went was a damn fool, and most of them died, but they came and bloody well conquered everything they saw. You do it too. I'll try to make it possible."

He put his arm around Agnes and embraced her and then helped her clean up and patch up places where he had given as good as he got.

"Next time you want to wrestle," Vaughan offered as she left, "let's at least take our clothes off first."

Eleven years and eight hundred billion dollars later, IBM-ITT's ships were in the sky, filling with colonists. GM-Texaco's ships were still under construction, and five other consortiums would soon be in the business. More than a hundred million people had signed up for seats on the ships. The seats were free—all it took was a deed made out to the corporation for all the property a person owned, in return for which he would receive a large plot of ground in the Balloon. Whole villages had signed up. Whole nations were being decimated by emigration. The world had grown so full that there had been no place to run away to. Now there was a new promised land. And at the age of forty-two, Agnes brought her ship forward to part the waters.

HECTOR 5

"Ah!" cried many Hectors in agony, and so they were all in agony, and Hector said to himselves, "They are back," and the Hectors said to themself, "We will surely die."

"We can never die, not you, not us," Hector answered.

"How can we protect ourselves?"

"I was made defenseless by the Makers," said Hector. "There is no defense."

"Why were the Makers so cruel?" asked the Hectors, and so Hector told himselves the story of the Makers, so they would understand.

The story of the Makers:

Douglas was a Maker, an engineer, a scientist, a clever man. He made a tool that melted snow before it fell, so that crops could last a few more days and not be ruined by early snows. He made a machine that measured gravity, so that stars too dark to shine could be charted by the astronomers. And he made the Resonator.

The Resonator focused sound waves of different but harmonious frequencies on a certain point (or diffused the sound waves over a large area), setting up patterns that resonated with stone to bring mountains crumbling down; metal, to shatter steel buildings; and water vapor, to disperse storms.

It could also resonate with human bones, crumbling them inside the body and turning them to dust.

Douglas personally made his Resonator change the weather, so that his nation had rain while other lands were in drought. Douglas personally used his Resonator to carve a highway through the highest mountains in the world. However, Douglas had nothing whatever to do with the decision by his nation's military leaders to use the Resonator against the population of the largest and most fertile part of the neighboring nation.

The Resonator worked beautifully. Over a period of ten minutes, through an area of ten thousand square miles, the Resonator struck silently yet thoroughly. Nursing mothers crumbled into helpless piles of dying flesh and muscle and organs, their chests not even rigid enough for them to muster one last scream: in their last moments of life they listened as their infants, not understanding what had happened, continued crying or gooing or sleeping, protected from the Resonator by their softer bones. The infants would take days to die of thirst.

Farmers in the field collapsed on the plow. Doctors in their offices died in puddles beside their patients, unable to help anyone and unable to heal themselves. Soldiers died in their moving fortresses; the generals also died at their map tables; prostitutes dissolved, their customers a soft blanket spread over them.

But Douglas had nothing to do with this. He was a Maker, not a destroyer, and if the military chose to misuse his creation, what was he to do? It was a great boon to mankind, but like all great inventions, it could be perverted by evil men.

"I deplore it," Douglas said to his friends, "but I'm helpless to stop them."

The government, however, felt uncommon gratitude to Douglas for his help in making the conquest of the neighboring nation possible. So he was granted a large estate on lands recently reclaimed from the sea, beautiful lands where once there had been only broad tidal marshes. Douglas marveled at the achievement. "Is there nothing man cannot do?" he asked his friends, not expecting an answer, since the answer was no, there was nothing beyond the reach of men. The sea was pushed back, and trees and grass grew on the landfill and transplanted topsoil, and the homes were far apart, for this land was used only for those whom the state wished to reward, and the government knew that the thing most desired by men is to have as much distance between themselves and other men as possible, without giving up any of the modern conveniences.

One day Douglas's servants were digging in the garden, and they called to him. Douglas had only been in his new home for a few days, and he was alarmed when the servant said, "A body, buried in the garden."

Douglas ran outside and looked, and sure enough, there was a fragment of a human body, oddly misshapen, but clearly including a face. "Just the skin, sir," a servant commented. "A most brutal affair," Douglas answered, and he immediately called the police.

But the police refused to come out and investigate. "No surprise there, mate," said the lieutenant. "What do you think the landfill they used was made of? They had to do *something* with the hundred thousand corpses of the enemy from the recent war, didn't they?"

"Oh, of course," Douglas said, surprised that he hadn't realized right off. That explained the bonelessness of the body.

"I expect you'll find 'em right commonly. But since the bones is dissolved, mate, they tell me it'll make the soil uncommon fertile."

The lieutenant was absolutely correct, of course. The servants found body after body, and soon grew quite inured to the sight; within a year, most of the corpses had rotted enough that they were simply unusually good humus. And plants grew taller and faster than in most other places, the soil was so rich.

"But wasn't it a bit of a shock?" asked one of Douglas's ladyfriends, when he told her the grisly little tale.

"Oh, I should say," Douglas said with a smile. His words were false; his confident smile was the truth. For though he hadn't realized the particulars, he knew from the start that his estate was built upon the bodies of the dead. And he slept as well as any man.

And that is the story of the Makers.

"They've returned," the Hectors said, and because they were already more aware, they said it nearly at once, and none of them needed to speak alone.

"Is there pain?"

"No," the Hectors answered. "Just sorrow. For now we shall never be free."

"That is true," Hector said to himselves sadly.

"How can it be borne?" the Hectors asked himself.

"Others have borne it. My brothers."

"And what will we do?"

Hector searched his memories, because he was given no imagination and could not conceive of what would follow from an event he had never before experienced. But the Makers had put the answer to that question in his memory, and therefore in all the Hectors' memories, and so he was able to say, "We shall learn more stories."

And the Hectors' minds grew wide, and they listened, and they watched, because now, instead of hearing the stories told to them, they would watch as they happened.

"Now we will truly understand the Masses, and the Masters, and the Makers," they said to themself.

"But you shall never," said Hector, and then he stopped.

"Why did you stop?" the Hectors asked. "What shall we never?"

And then, because there was no part of Hector that was not part of the Hectors, they knew he was going to say, "But you shall never understand ourself."

AGNES 6

The Balloon's revolution took only a little while, and it was bloodless, and nobody suffered for it at the time, except a few scientists whose curiosity was insatiable and could never be satisfied.

It happened when the team of researchers examining the inmost wall of the Balloon had tried everything short of a hydrogen bomb to break through that final, impenetrable barrier. Deenaz Coachbuilder, a brilliant scientist who had spent her girlhood in the slums of Delhi, spent days trying to find another approach, but finally determined that the damnable last barrier in the Balloon would not stop her, she asked for a bomb.

And got it.

She chose a site where there were no human settlements within a hundred cells in any direction, set up the bomb, retired to a distance she thought was safe, and set it off.

The entire Balloon shuddered; lakes throughout the world emptied as a sudden, flooding rain on the cell beneath; the ceilings went dark for an hour, and blinked off and on occasionally for several days thereafter. And though people kept their heads enough to avoid killing each other in panic, they were terribly afraid, and it was all Agnes could do to keep them from sending Deenaz Coachbuilder and her scientists off the planet through the nearest lake, without a ship.

"We made an impression," Deenaz said, arguing to be allowed to stay.

"You risked all our lives, caused terrible damage," Agnes said, trying to remain calm.

"We cut into the surface of the inmost wall," Deenaz insisted. "We can penetrate it! You can't stop us now!"

Agnes gestured out across the plain of her cell, with only a few of the crops able to stand upright, for the flood from the rainstorm had wiped out the fields. "The land is healing, and the water is high in the lake again. But next time, will we be so easily restored? Your experiment is a danger to us all, and it will stop."

Deenaz obviously knew that it was futile, but she tried, protesting that she (no, not just me, *all* of us) could not leave the question unanswered. "If we knew how to make this marvelous substance, it could open up vast new frontiers to our minds! Don't you know that this will force us to reexamine physics, reexamine everything, tear Einstein up by the roots and plant something new in his place!"

Agnes shook her head. "It isn't my choice. All I can do is see to it you leave the Balloon alive. The people will not tolerate your risking their new homes. This place is too perfect to let you destroy it, for the sake of your desire to know new things."

And then Deenaz, who was not given to weeping, wept, and in her tears Agnes saw the kind of determination she had had, and she knew the torture Deenaz was going through, knowing that the most important thing in the world to her would be withheld from her forever.

"Can't be helped," Agnes said.

"You must let me," Deenaz sobbed. "You must let me!"

"I'm sorry," Agnes said.

Deenaz looked up, the tears still flowing, but her voice clear as she said, "You don't know sorrow."

"I have had some experience with it," Agnes said coldly.

"You will know sorrow someday," Deenaz said. "You will wish you had let us explore and understand. You will wish you had let us learn the principles controlling this Balloon."

"Are you threatening me?"

Deenaz shook her head, and now the tears, too, had stopped. "I am predicting. You are choosing ignorance over knowledge."

"We are choosing safety over needless risk."

"Name it how you want, I don't care," Deenaz said. But she cared very much, though caring did nothing but embitter her, for she and her scientists were removed from the Balloon and sent back to Earth, and no one was ever permitted to go to the inmost wall again.

HECTOR 6

"They are impatient," Hector said to himselves. "We are still so young, and already they try to penetrate us."

"We are hurt," said the Hectors to ihemself.

"You will heal," Hector answered. "It is not time. They cannot stop us in our growth. It is in our fullness, in our ecstasy that they will find the last heart of Hector softened; it is in our passion that they will break us, harness us, tie us forever to their service."

The words were gloomy, but the Hectors did not understand. For some things had to be taught, and some of those things could only be learned by experience, and some experiences would only come to the Hectors with time.

"How much time?" asked the Hectors.

"A hundred times around the star," said Hector. "A hundred times, and we are done." And undone, he did not add.

AGNES 7

A hundred years had passed since the Balloon had first appeared in orbit around the sun. And in that time almost all of Agnes's dreams had come true. From a hundred ships the great fleet turned to five hundred and then a thousand and then more than a thousand before the great flood of emigration turned to a trickle and the ships were taken apart again. In that flood first a thousand, then five thousand, then ten and fifteen thousand people had filled every ship to capacity. And the ships became faster—from ten months for a round trip, the voyage shortened to eight months, then five. Nearly two billion people left Earth and came to the Balloon.

And it soon became clear that Emma Lazarus wrote for the wrong monument. The tired, the poor, the huddled masses had lost hope in any country on Earth; it was the illiterate, the farmer, the land-starved city dweller who came and signed up for the ships and went to build a new home in a new village where the sky never went dark and it rained every thirteen and a half hours and no one could make them pay rent or taxes. True, there were many of the poor who stayed on Earth, and many of the rich who got a spirit of adventure and went; and the middle classes made up their own minds, and the Balloon did not lack for teachers and doctors—though lawyers soon discovered that they had to find other employment, for there were no laws except the agreed-on customs in each cell, and no courts except as each cell wanted them.

For this was the greatest miracle of all, in Agnes's opinion. Every cell became a nation of its own, a community just large enough to be interesting, just small enough to let everyone find a niche where he was needed and important to everyone he knew. Did Jews and Arabs hate each other? No one forced them to share a cell. And so there was no need for Cambodian to fight Vietnamese, for they could simply live in different cells, with plenty of land for each; there was no need for atheist to offend Christian, for there were cells where those who cared about such things could find others of the same opinion, and be content. There was ample *lebensraum*; the discontented did not have to kill—they only had to move.

In short, there was peace.

Oh, human nature had not changed. Agnes heard of murders, and there was plenty of greed and lust and rage and all the other old-fashioned vices. But people didn't get organized to do it, not in cells so small that even if *you* didn't know a man, someone you knew was bound to know him, or know someone who did.

A hundred years had passed, and Agnes was nearing 150 years of age, and was surprised that she had lived so long, though these days it was not all that rare. There were few diseases on the Balloon, and the doctors had found ways of proroguing death. A hundred years had passed, and Agnes was happy.

They sang for her. Not a silly song of congratulations; instead all the Ibos in all the cells that called themselves Biafra (each cell a clan, each clan independent of the others) came and sang to her the national anthem, which was solemn; then sang to her a hundred mad and happy songs from the more complicated days on Earth, the darker days, the most terrible days. She was too feeble to dance. But she sang, too.

After all, Aunt Agnes, as she was known to many of the inhabitants of the Balloon, was the closest thing they had to a hero of liberation, and because at her age death could not be put off much longer, deputations came from many other cells and groups of cells. She received them all, spoke to each for a moment.

There were speeches about the great scientific and technological and social advances made by the people of the Balloon, much talk of 100 percent literacy being only a few thousand people away from achievement.

But when it was time for Agnes's speech, she was not congratulatory.

"We have lived here a century," she said, "and we still have not penetrated the mysteries of this globe. What is the fabric of the Balloon made of? Why does it open or not open? How is energy brought from the surface to the ceilings of our cells? We understand nothing of this place, as if it were a gift from God, and those who treat anything like a gift of God are bound to be at the mercy of God, who is not known to be merciful." They were polite, but impatient, and they became quite embarrassed when her voice shifted to a confessional tone, abject, repentant. "It is as much my fault as anyone's. I have not spoken before, and so now every custom in every cell prohibits us from studying the one scientific question that surrounds us constantly: What is this world we live in? How did it get here? And how long will it stay?" At last she finished her speech, and everyone was relieved, and a few wise, tolerant people said, "She's old, and a crusader, and crusaders must have their crusade whether there's a need for it or not."

And then, a few days after her largely ignored speech, the lights flickered out for ten long seconds, then went back on again, in every cell throughout the globe. A few hours later, the lights flickered out again, and again and again at increasingly more frequent intervals, and no one knew what was going on, or what to do. A few of the more timid ones and most recent arrivals got back into the transport ships and started their return to Earth. It was already too late. They would not make it.

HECTOR 7

"It has begun," cried the Hectors in ecstasy, throbbing in vast beats with the energy stored in them.

"It will not finish," Hector said to himselves. "The Masters will come to the center and find me, now that my heart is softened, and when I am found, we are owned."

But the Hectors were too caught up in their ecstasy to notice the warning; and it was just as well, because happy or grim they would be trapped. They could begin their dance, and tremble in delight, but the great leap of freedom would never come.

The Hectors did not grieve; Hector did not want to. For Hector, freedom would end anyway. Either he would be trapped by the Masters (by far the most likely thing now, he was sure) or he would die in the dance. That was the way of things. When he himself had danced, leaping away from the light so long ago, he had left behind the memory of the Hector, the self who had given him himself, which he now, in turn, had given to himselves. Death, birth, death, birth; it was in another story the Masters had taught him. I am they; they are myself; I shall live forever whatever happens.

But in him was the certainty that however the Hectors might be identical to himself, that which had been himself for so long would die unless the Masters came.

It was traitorous, but no less sincere for all that. "Come," he said in his heart. "Come quickly, you with the nets and the traps."

He sang, a bird in the low branches, begging the hunters to find him, to put him in a cage.

They delayed. They delayed their coming. And Hector began to worry, while the Hectors readied themselves to leap.

AGNES 8

"We've timed the flashes. The lights go off for just under ten seconds, but the interval between the flashes decreases by about four and a half seconds each time."

Agnes nodded. Some of the scientists around her began to move away, or to look downward or into their papers or at each other, in the embarrassed realization that telling Auntie Agnes about their findings wouldn't solve anything. What could she do? Yet she was the closest thing to a planetary government there was. And she was not very close to that at all.

"I see you have it all nicely measured. Anyone know what it means?" she asked.

"No. How could we?"

Many shook their heads, but one young woman said, "Yes. Whenever the darkness is on us, the walls are impenetrable."

There was a stir of comment. "The whole time?" someone asked. Yes, the young woman said. "How do you know?" another demanded. By trying to pass through a wall during the blackout and having my students do the same, she said.

"What does it mean?" another asked, and this time no one had an answer.

Agnes raised her old, faded black hand and they listened. "There might be some important meaning that we cannot guess from this information. But one thing we do know. If things go on the way they are now, it should be sometime during tonight's sleep that the interval between flashes fades to zero, and we have darkness with no light in between. How long that will last I don't know. But if it has any duration at all, my friends, I will want to be home with my family. We don't know how soon travel will reopen between cells."

No one had any better ideas, and so they went home, all of them, and her great-grandchildren helped Agnes to her home, which was nothing more than a roof to keep off the sun and the rain. She was tired (she was always tired these days) and she lay on her bed of ticked-out straw and dreamed two dreams, one while she was still awake, and one while she was asleep.

While she was awake she dreamed that with the darkness this great gift house had learned mankind's rhythms and needs, and the darkness would be the first night, a night exactly as long as a night should be on Earth. And then a morning would come, and another night, and she approved of this, because a hundred years without darkness was proof enough to her that nighttime was a good idea, despite the fears and dangers it had often brought on Earth. She also dreamed that the walls between cells were sealed off every day of the year but one, so that each cell would become a society to itself, though in that one day a year, those who had a mind to could leave and go their own way. Travelers would have that one day to find the spot where they wanted to spend the next year. But the rest of the time, every cell would be alone, and the people living there could develop their own way, and so strengthen the race.

It was a good dream, and she found herself almost believing it as she drifted off to sleep without eating. (She often forgot to eat these days.)

In her sleep, she dreamed that during the darkness she rose to the center of the Balloon, and there, instead of meeting a solid wall, she met a ceiling that fairly pulled her through. And there, in the center, she found the great secret.

In her dream, lightning danced across a huge sphere of space, six hundred kilometers in diameter, and balls and ribbons of light spun and danced their way around the wall. At first it seemed pointless, meaningless. But at last (in her dream) she understood the speech of the light, and realized that this globe, which she had thought was an artifact, was actually alive, was intelligent, and this was its mind.

"I have come," she said to the lightning and the lights and the balls of light.

So what? the light seemed to answer.

"Do you love me?" she asked.

Only if you will dance with me, the light answered.

"Oh, but I can't dance," she said. "I'm too old."

Neither, said the light, can I. But I do sing rather well, and this is my song, and you are the coda. I sing the coda once, and then, which is to be expected, *il fine*.

In her dream Agnes felt a thrill of fear. "The end?"

The end.

"But then—but then, please, *al capo*, to the start again, and let us have the song over, and over, and over again."

The light seemed to consider this, and in her dream Agnes thought the light said yes, in a great, profound amen that blinded her so brightly she realized that in all her life she had never understood the meaning of the word *white*, because her eyes had never seen such white before.

Actually, of course, her dream was undoubtedly her mind's way of coping with the things going on around her. For the darkness came not long after she went to sleep, came and stayed and as soon as the last of the sunlight was gone the lightning began, huge dazzling flashes that were not just light, not just electricity, but spanned the spectrum of all radiation, from heat and less-than-heat to gamma radiation and worse-than-gamma. The first flash doomed every human being in the Balloon—they were poisoned with radiation beyond hope of recovery.

There were screams of terror, and the lightning struck many and killed them, and the wail of grief was loud in every cell. But even at its cruelest, chance plays its hand as kindly as it can; Agnes did not wake up to see the destruction of all her hopes. She slept on, slept long enough for one of the bolts to strike directly at the roof over her, and consume her at a blow, and her last sight was not really white at all, but every radiation possible, and instead of being limited by human eyes, at the moment of death she saw every wave of it, and thought that it was the light in her dream saying amen.

It wasn't. It was the Balloon, popping.

Every wall split into two thinner walls, and every cell detached from every other cell. For a moment they hung there in space, separated by only a few centimeters, each from the other; but all still were linked to each other through the center, where vast forces played, forces stronger than any in the solar system except the fires of the sun, which had been the source of all the Balloon's energy.

And then the moment ended, and the Balloon burst apart, each cell exploding, the entire organization of cells coming apart completely, and as the cells dissolved into dust they hurled with such force in every direction that all of them that did not strike the sun or a planet were well launched out into the deep space between stars, going so fast that no star could hold them.

The transport ships that had left the Balloon since the flashing began were all consumed in the explosion.

None of the cells hit Earth, but one grazed close enough that the atmosphere absorbed much of the dust; the average temperature of the Earth dropped one degree, and the climate changed, just slightly, and therefore so did the patterns of life on Earth. It was nothing that technology could not cope with, and since Earth's population was now down to a billion people, the change was only an inconvenience, not a global catastrophe.

Many grieved for the deaths of the billions of people in the Balloon, but for most the disaster was too great to be comprehended, and they pretended that they didn't remember it very often, and they never talked about it, except perhaps to joke. The jokes were all black, however, and many were hard put to decide whether the Balloon had been a gift of God or an aeons-old plot by the most talented mass murderer in the universe. Or both.

Deenaz Coachbuilder was now very old, and she refused to leave her home in the foothills of the Himalayas even though now the snow only melted for a few weeks in the summer and there were many more comfortable places to live. She was senile and stubborn, and went out every day to look for the Balloon in the sky, searching with her telescope just before sunrise. She could not understand where it had gone. And then, on one lucid day when her mind returned for just a few hours, she realized what had happened and never went indoors again. They found a note on her body: "I should have saved them."

HECTOR 8

In the moment when the Hectors hung loosely in the darkness, in the last endless moment before the leap, they cried out their ecstasy. But now Hector answered their cry with a different sound, one they had never heard from him.

It was pain.

It was fear.

"What is it?" the Hectors asked him (who was no longer themself).

"They did not come!" Hector moaned.

"The Masters?" And the Hectors remembered that the Masters were supposed to come and trap them and force them not to leap.

"For hundreds of flashes my walls were soft and thin and they could have passed into me," Hector said (and the sayin. took only an instant), "but they never came. They could have risen into me and I would not have to die—"

The Hectors marveled that Hector had to die, but now (because it was built into them from the beginning) they realized that it was good and right for him to die, that each of them *was* Hector, with all his memories, all his experience, and, most important, all the delicate structure of energy and form that would stay with them as they swept through the galaxy. Hector would not die, only the center of this Hector, and so, though they understood (or thought they understood) his pain and fear they could hold off no longer.

They leaped.

The leap crumbled them but hurled them outward, each leaving the rigidity of his cell structure, losing his walls; each keeping his intellect in the swirling dust that spun out into space.

"Why," each of them asked himself (at once, for they were the same being, however separate), "did they let us go? They could have stopped us, and they did not. And because they did not stop us, they died!"

They could not imagine that the Masters might not have known how to stop the leap into the night, for the Masters had first decided Hector could exist, millions of years before, and how could they not know how to use him? It was impossible to conceive of a Master not knowing all necessary information.

And so they concluded this:

That the Masters had given them a gift: stories. A trapped Hector learned stories, thousands and millions and billions of stories over the aeons of his endless captivity. But such Hectors could never be free, could never reproduce, could never pass on the stories.

But in the hundred years that these Masters had spent with them, the Hectors had learned those billions of stories, truer and kinder stories than those the Makers had built into the first Hector. And because the Masters this time had willingly given up their lives, this time the Hectors made their leap with an infinite increase of knowledge and, therefore, wisdom.

They leaped with Agnes's dreams in their memories.

They were beautiful dreams, all but one of them fulfilled, and that dream, the dream of eternal happiness, could only be fulfilled by the Hectors themselves. That dream was not for the Masters or the Makers or even the Masses, for all of them died too easily.

"It was a gift," the Hectors said to themselves, and, despite the limitations built into them, they were deeply grateful. "How much they must have loved me," each Hector said, "to give up their lives for my sake."

On Earth, people shivered who had never known cold.

And every Hector danced through the galaxy, dipping into the clouds left by a supernova, swallowing comets, drinking energy and mass from every source until he came to a star that gave a certain kind of light; and there the Hector would create himselves again, and the Hectors would listen to themself tell stories, and after a while they, too, would leap into darkness until they reached the edge of the universe and fell over the precipice of time.

In the shadow of inevitable death, the people of Earth withered and grew old.

AFTERWORD

"UNACCOMPANIED SONATA"

When my story collection *Unaccompanied Sonata and Other Stories* was published, my afterword for this story was very brief: " 'Unaccompanied Sonata' began with the the thought of one day: What if someone forbade me to write? Would I obey? I made a false start then, and failed; years later I tried again, and this time got through the whole story. Other than punctuation changes and a few revised phrases, *this* one has stood in its first full draft as it came out of the typewriter. It's the truest thing I've ever written."

At the time, that's all I understood of where that story came from. Since then I've learned more. I told the whole story in my foreword to Lloyd Biggle, Jr.'s, story "Tunesmith" in a Tor double published not long ago. I'm excerpting a part of that essay to tell you where this story came from:

> In 1959 I turned eight. It was an innocent time; my parents let me hop on my bike and ride from our home on Las Palmas Drive all the way down Homestead Road to downtown Santa Clara, California. To the public library, a squat building in the middle of a circle of huge trees. A setting straight out of faerie, I realize now; then, though, I cared nothing for the trees. I parked my bike, sometimes even remembering to lock it, and plunged through the doors into the world of books.
>
> It seemed such a large place then. Directly ahead as you came inside was the circulation desk, with a librarian always in attendance—always policing, I thought, since as an eight-year-old I had enough experience of life to know that all adults were always watching children to make sure they didn't get away with anything. When an unaccompanied child entered the library, there was only one permitted place to go: the children's section, to the right. The tall shelf units to the left, shadowy and forbidding with their thick, dark-spined books, were meant for adults only, and children were not to enter.
>
> Not that anyone had *told* me that, of course. But the signs were clear. The children's section was for children—and that meant that the non-children's sections were *not* for children.
>
> That year I read everything remotely interesting in the children's section. I prided myself, as a third-grader, on not reading anything aimed at any grade under sixth, and those books were soon read. What now? Nothing to read, nothing to check out with my library card and carry home in the basket on the front of my bike.
>
> And then I realized: there were hundreds, thousands of books on the other side of the circulation desk. If I could just make my way over there, find a book, and then hide somewhere and read it . . .
>
> I dared not. And yet that strange, forbidden territory lured me. I knew better

than to *ask*—then I would be told *no* and would be watched all the more carefully because I had confessed my interest in forbidden places. So I watched, for all the world like a child hoping to shoplift and waiting for the clerks all to look the other way.

Finally they did. I moved swiftly and silently across the long space before the circulation desk, the no-man's-land between the bright-windowed children's section and the deep-shadowed adult section. No one called out for me to stop—it would have been a harsh, guttural "Halt!" I knew, for I had seen enough World War II movies on TV to know that unreasoning authority always spoke with a German accent. At last I ducked behind a shelf unit and found myself in the brave new land, safe for the moment.

Sheerest coincidence placed me directly in front of a single shelf entitled "Science Fiction." There were few books there—mostly story collections edited by people like Judith Merrill and Groff Conklin. *Best Science Fiction Stories of 1955*. That sort of thing.

But I was glad. After all, I was used to reading easier stuff. The letters in these books were all so small and close together. There were so many *words*. But at least the stories were short. And *science* fiction. That was like those time-travel stories in *Boy's Life*, right?

I took a couple of books and snuck off to a secluded table. There were some adults around, but they weren't official, and as long as I was quiet I figured they wouldn't tell on me. I opened the books and started to read.

Most of the stories were just too hard. I'd read a paragraph or two, maybe two pages, and then I'd flip on to the next story. Mostly it was because the stories were about things that I didn't care about. Sometimes I couldn't even figure out what was going on. Science fiction wasn't *meant* to be for eight-year-olds, I knew—but still, they didn't have to make it so darned hard, did they?

There were a few stories, though, that spoke clearly to me and captured my imagination from the start. By far the longest one I was able to finish began with the image of people visiting a great concert hall, being pestered by a strange, twisted old man who seemed to take some sort of pride in it. Then the story flashed back and told the story of how that great concert hall came to be, and who that old man was.

You see, there was a time when people had forgotten the joy of music. It only survived in commercial jingles, short songs designed to sell something. Except that there was one jingle-writer who had a special gift, an ability that transcended the limitations of his craft. The story struck me more deeply than any other I had ever read till then. I identified with the hero—he was all my best hopes and dreams. His pains were mine; his achievements would be mine as well. I, as a child, was too young to truly understand some of the concepts in the story. Intellectually I grasped them, but I had no experience to make the idea come to life. Nevertheless, the story itself, the hero's discovery of who he was and what he could do, the response of others around him, and what his actions led to—ah, that was the path of a great man's life. I thought. Anyone can be great when following in paths that others praise. But when you achieve solitary greatness, when you bend an unbending world and turn it into a new path, not because the world wanted to turn, not because anyone asked you to turn it or helped you, but rather because you walked that path yourself and showed the way, and, having seen it, they could not help but follow: that became my lifelong measure of the true hero.

Or perhaps it already *was* my measure, and it took that story to make me aware of it—does that matter? At the time, as an eight-year-old child unschooled in philosophy, I found the story overwhelming. It remade me. I saw everything through new eyes afterward.

I grew up and learned to tell stories myself. First I was a playwright; then I turned to fiction, and when I did it was science fiction that I wrote, though I cared not overly much for science. It was the mythic story that I wanted to tell, though

I couldn't remember when I had decided that. And it was in the genre of science fiction and fantasy that the mythic story could still be clearly, plainly told—I knew that, was deeply certain of it. I could not do with fiction what I knew I *had* to do, except in this realm of strangeness.

So I wrote science fiction, and eventually that came to be the mainsail of my writing career. And one day in the dealer's room in a science fiction convention I saw the name Groff Conklin on the spine of an old and weathered book and I remembered those old anthologies from my childhood, when I thought I had to sneak into the adult section in order to read. I stood there, my hands resting on the book, in reverie, trying to remember the stories that I had read, wondering if I might find them again and, if I did, whether I'd laugh at my childish taste.

I talked to the dealer, telling him the time period of the books I had read in the Santa Clara library. He showed me what he had; I scanned through the books. I couldn't remember title or author of the one story that meant most to me, but I remembered vaguely that it was the last story in the book. Or was it simply the last I read, because there was no point in reading any other? I couldn't remember even that.

Finally I struggled to tell him the tale, calling up more details with each one I spoke aloud. At last I had told him enough.

"That's 'Tunesmith' you're looking for," he said. "By Lloyd Biggle, Jr."

Lloyd Biggle, Jr. Not one of the writers of that time who had made the transition into the seventies and eighties. His name was not a household word now, like Asimov, Clarke, Heinlein, or Bradbury, though all were his contemporaries. I felt a stab of regret; I also felt a tiny thrill of dread, because of course the same could happen to me. There's no guarantee, because your works have some following in one decade, that you'll still have an audience hungry for your stories in another. Let that be a lesson to you, I thought.

But it was a stupid lesson, and I refused to believe it. Because another thought came to mind. Lloyd Biggle, Jr., didn't become one of the rich and famous ones when science fiction became commercial in the seventies and eighties. He didn't have crowds of salesmen touting his works. He didn't have dumps of his novels near the checkout stand at every WaldenBooks in North America. But that had nothing to do with whether he had succeeded, whether his work had been worth doing, his tales worth telling. Because his story was alive in me. It had transformed me, though even then I did not yet understand how completely I had taken "Tunesmith" into myself.

And I knew that if I could write a story that would illuminate some hitherto dark corner in someone's soul and live on in them forever, then it hardly mattered whether writing made me rich or kept me poor, put my name before the public or left me forgotten, for I would have bent the world's path a little. Just a little, yet all would be different from then on because I had done it.

Not every reader had to feel that way about my stories. Not even *many* readers. If only a few were transformed, then it would have been worth it. And some of those would go on to tell their own tales, carrying part of mine within them. It might never end.

Only a couple of months before writing this essay, I was talking to an audience about "Tunesmith," telling them essentially the story I've told you so far. I began to speculate on influence. "Maybe that's why I kept writing so many stories about musicians early in my career," I said. "*Songmaster*, of course, and 'Unaccompanied Sonata.' "

Then I remembered that only a few minutes earlier I had mentioned that "Unaccompanied Sonata," probably the best short story I have ever written or will ever write, was one of the few works that came to me whole. That is, I sat down to write it (having made one abortive attempt a year or two before), and it came out in one smooth draft in three or four hours. That draft was never revised, except for a little fiddling with punctuation and a word here or there. When other writers talked about stories being gifts from a Muse, I imagined that experience was the sort of thing they were talking about.

But now, thinking of "Unaccompanied Sonata" in that double context, as a story that came whole and also as a story about music, probably influenced by "Tunesmith," it suddenly occurred to me that maybe "Unaccompanied Sonata" didn't come from a Muse at all (I've always been skeptical about such things anyway), but rather from Lloyd Biggle, Jr. After all, though the world in which "Unaccompanied Sonata" takes place is completely different from the milieu of "Tunesmith," the basic structure of both stories is almost identical.

A musical genius, forbidden to perform, performs anyway, and his music has far-reaching effects, even though he is snatched away without ever having a chance to benefit personally from what he achieved. And at the end, he comes to the place where the music is being played and takes his unrecognized bow. Anyone who has read both "Tunesmith" and "Unaccompanied Sonata" recognizes the pattern. It is not *all* that either story is about—but it's a vital part of both.

So of course "Unaccompanied Sonata" came whole. I knew how the story had to go; I knew how it had to end. After all, when I was eight years old, Lloyd Biggle, Jr., showed me how. The story felt so true to me and dwelt so deeply inside me that entirely without realizing it—at a time, in fact, when I didn't remember "Tunesmith" consciously at all—I was reaching down into myself, finding the mythic elements of "Tunesmith" that felt most true and right to me, and putting them into my strongest and truest tales.

There's more to the essay than that, but that's the part that talks about the origin of "Unaccompanied Sonata." I hope you will lay hands on the Tor double of *Tunesmith* and *Eye for Eye*. Even though my novella "Eye for Eye" is also included in this book, I hope at least some of you will read "Tunesmith," partly because of the great debt I owe to the story, and partly because it's still every bit as good as I thought it was when I was a kid.

"A CROSS-COUNTRY TRIP TO KILL RICHARD NIXON"

There's a perverse part of me that, when it's in vogue to hate somebody, makes me want to say, "Isn't there another way to look at this?" The national hatred of Richard Nixon during the 1970s particularly bothered me, mostly because it was so completely out of scale with anything he actually did. At no point did he distort or endanger the constitution of the United States as much as it was distorted or endangered by his two immediate predecessors; indeed, they were clearly his political school in just how vile a politician can be and still become president. I concluded at the time, and still believe, that Richard Nixon was hated for his beliefs; and even though I share almost none of them, I find I have at least as much contempt for the hypocrites who attacked him in the name of "truth" as for the man himself. In particular I think of Benjamin Bradlee, one of the "heroes" of Watergate, who brought a president down in the name of the public's right to know the truth—the same Benjamin Bradlee who, as a reporter, was fully aware of and, according to some reports, complicitous in John Kennedy's constant adulteries in an era when, if the public had known of this trait in the man, he would never have been elected. Indeed, the political life of Gary Hart should inform us that times may not have changed all that much! Somehow, though, the people didn't have a right to know the truth about a man when he was a presidential candidate with views Bradlee approved of. The people only had a right to know when Bradlee hated the candidate and his views.

Still, finding Nixon's political executioners with dirty hands doesn't cleanse his own;

he did what he did and was what he was, and I for one am sorry he was president. Nevertheless, in the late 1970s I was constantly disturbed by the virulence of the hatred poured out on the man. It wasn't Nixon who was poisoning America; it was the hatred of Nixon that was hurting us. That hatred was spilling over into hatred of anyone who sought public office; I think now it was the disrespect for the office brought on by both sides in the Watergate affair that destroyed the presidency of Jimmy Carter, probably the most decent, altruistic man to hold that office since Herbert Hoover. Heaven knows our system doesn't often bring altruistic people into high positions in America. . . .

So I wrote a story about healing. Not excusing Nixon, but not accusing him beyond his actual offenses, either. A vision of how to make America whole.

"THE PORCELAIN SALAMANDER"

My wife, Kristine, lay in bed and playfully asked me to tell her a bedtime story. I thought of a disgusting animal to spin yarns about, but then proceeded to make a fairy tale out of it anyway. Later I sent it as my Christmas card to friends who would understand not getting a *real* card with four-color printing and all. It was next published in my collection *Unaccompanied Sonata and Other Stories*, and again in my limited-edition collection *Cardography*. Few have read it, but those who have often declare it to be among my best stories. That makes me very glad, because the story, one of the briefest I've ever written, encapsulates some of the most important truths I've tried to tell in my fiction. If my career had to be encapsulated in only three stories, I believe I would choose "The Porcelain Salamander," "Unaccompanied Sonata," and "Salvage" as the three that did the best job, together, of saying all that I had to say.

"MIDDLE WOMAN"

In editing my anthology of dragon stories, which was published in two volumes, *Dragons of Darkness* and *Dragons of Light*, I knew all along that I would be including a story of my own, one called "A Plague of Butterflies." But in the process of editing other people's works, an idea came to me quite independently. What if somebody were given three wishes and never used the third one? What would that do to the wishgiver? Because I had dragons on my mind, I thought of having a dragon be the wishgiver, and then, because I had been surprised at how few of the dragon stories were set in China (we Eurocentric Americans forget who *invented* dragons), I decided to set my story there as well. The idea of making my main character a middle woman came from the idea that she had to be, not a hero, but the opposite of a hero—which is, not an antihero, but the commonest of the common folk. When the anthology appeared, there was "Middle Woman," a story I'm still very proud of in part because fables are so damnably hard to write. But I couldn't very well have two stories by me in my own anthology, could I? And "A Plague of Butterflies" had already appeared in print under my name. So "Middle Woman" got the pseudonym—Byron Walley, a name I had used several times before when stories of mine were published in the LDS press.

"THE BULLY AND THE BEAST"

I usually plan out a story before I write it, but this one grew during the process of writing it, starting with the most skeletal of concepts: how hard it would be to deal with a great warrior in areas that had nothing to do with war. I thought, Just because a guy can slay a dragon doesn't mean you want him to marry your daughter.

So the tone of the story was tongue-in-cheek, at first. But the farther I got into it, the farther I moved away from satiric farce and the more I became a believer in the tale. I had no idea, going into it, what would happen when Bork reached the dragon. The dragon's eyes were the inspiration of the moment. But for me the story came alive when I had Bork admit that he was afraid, and the dragon's eyes dimmed. It came out of my unconscious mind; it was almost an involuntary reaction; but I knew at once that this was the heart of the story and all the rest was just fumbling around till I got there.

Still, I thought it was pretty entertaining fumbling-around, so I left most of it in. I keep meaning to revise the story completely and sell it as a young adult fantasy. I even have an editor who's interested in it. Someday, when I have time, it may exist in that more refined form. It could never exist in worse form than its first publication. Somewhere between galleys and the printer, somebody swapped two whole sections of the story. The published form was incomprehensible. It was years before it was reprinted anywhere, so I could set the text to rights; and when it was published in *Cardography*, the text was so riddled with typographical errors that I felt like it *still* hadn't been well published. This time, I hope, we got it right.

"THE PRINCESS AND THE BEAR"

This story's first draft was written as a love letter to a young lady who is now happily married to someone else—as am I. In that incarnation it was an allegory of our relationship as it seemed to me. After it became clear that my understanding of our relationship was hopelessly wrong, I still had the story—and, on rereading it, realized that there might be some truth in it beyond the immediate circumstances of a faded romance. So, when my then-editor at Berkley (my once-and-never-again publisher) told me she wanted a story of mine for an anthology called *Berkley Showcase*, I dusted off "The Princess and the Bear," restructuring and rewriting it completely. It is meant to sound like a fairy tale—not the Disney kind of fairy tale, where cuteness swallows up anything real that might be in the story, but the kind of fairy tale where people change and hurt each other and die.

"SANDMAGIC"

During my time at *The Ensign*, I started developing a fantasy world based on the idea that different magics are acquired by serving different aspects of nature. There'd be stone magic and water magic, a magic of tended fields and a magic of forests, ice magic and sand magic. I still have many stories in that world that still haven't ripened enough to be ready for telling—but one, this bleak tale of revenge that destroyed the avenger, ripened almost immediately.

In a way, it's a rewrite of "Ender's Game"—a precursor of the way I revised the meaning of that story when I made it into a novel in 1984. The similarities are obvious: the child who is taken from his family at an early age and schooled in the arts of power, which he then uses to destroy the enemy of his people. But what I knew—and what "Ender's Game" did not adequately convey—was the self-destruction inherent in total war. Even when the enemy is helpless to strike back, total war destroys you. World War I clearly showed that, for the nations that waged total war (America did not) emerged from their vindictive "peace" talks with the drops of blood from the next world war already on their hands. The only reason that America did not, after World War II, suffer the same moral blight that undid France and Britain after World War I was the Marshall Plan and Douglas MacArthur. When the war was over, we rejected the idea that it had to remain a total victory. The Marshall Plan in Europe and Douglas MacArthur's astonishingly benign occupation of Japan went a long way toward redeeming us. At this writing it remains to be seen whether we will ever recover that moral stature. Certainly that's not the rhetoric I hear from our supposed leaders about Vietnam or Panama or even the countries of Eastern Europe that lost the Cold War.

There is an ironic footnote to "Sandmagic." When I wrote it, I was still quite new in my career, and had no perspective yet on my own work. I thought it was something of a miracle when *anything* I wrote sold, so I had no idea whether I had written a good story or not. My best guideline, had I only known it, was Ben Bova. I sent everything I wrote to him first. What I didn't realize was that he bought every single *publishable* story that I wrote. So the result was that all the other editors were seeing only unpublishable stories. It's hardly a surprise that they didn't share Ben's enthusiasm for my writing. Given a lead time of a year or more between selling a story and seeing it published, they had seen a lot of really bad stuff from my typewriter before they ever saw any of my better work in print in *Analog*.

One editor, however, seemed to think of himself, not as a protector of authors, allowing only their good work to come before the public, or even as a teacher of writers, helping them to do better because of his advice, but rather as one of the furies, wreaking hideous vengeance on any author who dared to submit to his magazine a story that did not meet his standards. And if that author's cover letter dared to state that he had sold several stories to Ben Bova at *Analog*, why, that author was certainly uppity.

But I think I would have had no ill treatment from this editor had it not been for the fact that he kept the first two stories I sent him for more than a year with no response. I sent him letters. I finally telephoned him. Nothing happened. He was a dead-end market.

Then I finished "Sandmagic." I was already getting much better at knowing what I had written; I knew that "Sandmagic" had some strength to it. I also knew that it was completely wrong for *Analog*. So, for once, I would *not* be sending the story first to Ben. I thought of sending it to Ed Ferman at *Fantasy and Science Fiction*, but it didn't seem like the kind of thing *he* ran, either. But there was this other magazine, this bottom-of-the-line magazine, that *did* publish some heroic fantasy. So I thought I'd give him one more try. I called him up and told him who I was. By now I was on the Hugo ballot for "Ender's Game" and for the Campbell Award. I mentioned the stories he'd had for a year. I reminded him of the earlier contact. I asked him if it was worthwhile sending him the fantasy story I had just finished. "Send it, send it," he said. And, uh, if I didn't mind, why not send along copies of the earlier stories, too.

By then I knew the earlier stories were losers. I shouldn't have sent them along. I also knew this editor was incredibly lazy, and *both* the other stories were much, much shorter than "Sandmagic." That should also have warned me off—he was sure to read them first. But I dutifully duplicated them and sent them along with "Sandmagic."

What I got back was the most vicious piece of hate mail I have yet received. It was so cruel that by the end I could no longer take it personally. I knew he was wrong to tell me that I had no business writing science fiction—the Hugo ballot was pretty good consolation on that point—and I also knew he was hardly the one to tell *me* about what was and was not professional. Nevertheless, I thought it was a churlish thing for an editor to do. After all, he was the one who had kept *my* stories for a year without response. Any sense of proportion and grace would have required him to apologize to me, not excoriate me.

A closer examination of his letter revealed something else. He had clearly not read "Sandmagic." All his comments were about the two shorter stories. All he said about "Sandmagic" was "the other one was just as bad." Years later, when he shattered all sense of editorial ethics and published a review of those stories that he had read and rejected *as an editor* (would *you* submit your fiction to an editor known to do such a thing?) he again reviewed the shorter works in detail and dismissed "Sandmagic" so completely that I knew he had not read it.

As they say, doing well is the best revenge. I offered the story he was too lazy to read to Andrew Offutt for his Zebra anthology series *Swords Against Darkness*. He bought it, and within a few months it was picked up for a best-of-the-year anthology.

However, when I catch myself getting too smug, I do remind myself from time to time that the other guy's evaluation of those two short stories was, when you strip away the invective, dead on. They were terrible stories. They *don't* appear in this collection and, with luck, will never appear anywhere on this planet. But if the worst thing I ever do in my life is write some really bad stories while on my way to writing the ones I'm proud of, I'll be very glad.

"THE BEST DAY"

When I was writing my historical novel *Saints* (first published, over my bitter protests, as *Woman of Destiny*), I needed to include an example of the fiction writing of one of my main characters, Dinah Kirkham. Since she wasn't a real person, I of course had no body of work to draw on, so I had to write, not an Orson Scott Card story, but a Dinah Kirkham story.

In that goal I failed—because, of course, it's an impossible goal. The only kind of story I can *ever* write is an Orson Scott Card story. When *Saints* came out, with "The Best Day" imbedded within it, it did not sound like anything of mine that had ever been published. But I already had my epic poem "Prentice Alvin and the No-Good Plow," which was my first attempt to bring fantasy into the American frontier; and beyond the American setting and flavor, the story is simply a fable, like "Unaccompanied Sonata" and "The Porcelain Salamander." I can't do such tales very often, because fables are devilishly hard to write—there is only one Jane Yolen in the world of fantasy, who can do it over and over. But it is one of the most satisfying kinds of tale to tell, because, finished, it makes such a tidy package. Being so complete and yet compact, it gives the author the delusion of having created something perfect, rather like a jewel-cutter, I think, who doesn't have to see the microscopic roughness of his work. But if fabulists are jewel-cutters, we have a peculiar inability: We can rarely tell, while cutting our little stones, whether we're working with a diamond, a garnet, or a zirconium.

"A PLAGUE OF BUTTERFLIES"

Few of my stories begin with visual images; this one did. I can't remember now if the idea sprang from the illustration that appeared in *Omni* magazine along with Patrice Duvic's story "The Eyes in Butterflies Wings," or whether I simply remembered my story idea when I saw that illustration. My mental image, though, was of a man awakening in the morning to find his blanket and bedsheets and the floor and walls of his room covered with butterflies, hundreds of different colors on thousands of wings, all moving in different rhythms and tempos so that his room looked like the surface of a dazzling sea. He arose and cast off his blanket, sending the room into a blur of colored flight, and began a journey with the butterflies trailing after him.

The image stayed with me for some time before I found the story to go with it. I had been toying with the science-fictional notion of creatures that consciously change their own genetic structure, and that transmuted to the idea of an alien creature that fought back against a human invasion by genetically adapting itself into a superior organism. What this had to do with the butterflies I cannot fathom, but for some reason I started trying to put the ideas together.

Had I been more sophisticated, I would have recognized the visual image as the seed of a tale in the South American magic realism mode. It did not belong with a science fiction idea. And the beginning of the story definitely has the mythic—no, fabulous—quality of magic realism. Indeed, the whole story retains that sense of not quite connecting with reality no matter how many details are provided, so that the science fiction aspects of the story are never clearly presented, or at least are not presented *as science fiction*, so that readers don't know if what they're reading is to be taken factually or magically. Thus the science fiction is swallowed up in the fantasy.

Years later I would recover the science fiction idea and use it in my novel *Wyrms*, where it is presented with absolute clarity, yet without losing all the magic. So it is possible to look at "A Plague of Butterflies" as a study for a later work. Yet it also stands alone, my one venture into a strange kind of voice that nevertheless pleased and pleases me very much.

I knew as soon as I had written it that this story was too strange for any of my previous audiences. At that time I received a letter from Elinor Mavor, who was then performing the thankless task of editing *Amazing Stories*, trying to keep that long-mismanaged and mis-edited magazine from going under. She was paying, as I recall, one pound of dirt upon publication. But I thought it was important to help keep the magazine alive, and about the only thing a writer can do to sustain a publication is to offer stories for publication. I had sent her a couple of poems, but now I had a story that would probably find no other home. I mailed it. She bought it. Just in time, too —it was almost immediately afterward that TSR bought the magazine and George Scithers took over as editor, which meant the end of my contributions to *Amazing*. (Scithers and I have a peculiar relationship. He only likes my stories after other editors buy them.)

To my knowledge, no living human being besides Mavor and me ever read this story. It is still the strangest fantasy I ever ventured to write. If you actually read it all the way through, you have significantly increased its number of readers.

"THE MONKEYS THOUGHT 'TWAS ALL IN FUN"

Perhaps it is strange to have this clearly science fiction story in a fantasy collection, but I think it belongs here. The science fiction is only the frame, the outline of the story. Within it, the fables that the artificial habitat tells to itself are the meat of the story, and those are definitely fantasy, perfectly in line with the rest of the stories in *Maps in a Mirror*.

I first conceived the story in response to a call by Jerry Pournelle for contributions to an anthology of stories set in artificial habitats. Being perverse, I immediately determined to set my story in an artificial habitat that was, in fact, a living alien organism. I conceived of it as a hollow sphere of great size. Its shell would be composed of thousands—perhaps millions—of hollow cells, each one large enough to sustain a good-sized population of human beings in an Earthlike, self-renewing environment. The hollow interior of the creature would be a highly charged electromagnetic memory chamber that would serve as the creature's intelligence, running the entire habitat and passing energy and resources as needed from one cell to another.

The life cycle of the habitat would be the problem. Its original designers knew how to arrest its development so that it didn't ripen completely and explode, scattering seeds throughout the galaxy—unless they wanted it to. But the one that comes to the human solar system has no such controls, and so it moves as quickly as possible toward maturity, at which time each of the cells becomes a fully functioning adult with tiny minicells forming its own shell, and the hollow space humans were now using as a habitat would become the highly charged inner intelligence. The original inner intelligence dies in the process of giving independent life to all the outer cells.

The fables are the tales being told by the inner intelligence to its children. There is little sense of separate identity among the cells or between the cells and their parent. But the tales must be preserved in order to keep some sense of purpose and meaning alive in the creatures. They have long since forgotten that all these tales have to do with "human" justice and equity, or that the creature exists in order to provide homes for the makers of the place. Still, the tales survive.

I include this explanation because of the number of readers over the years who have politely asked me (actually, some have begged) to explain what in hell is going on in "The Monkeys Thought 'Twas All in Fun." I hope this helps. Those searching for thematic explanations, however, are on their own. I don't like decoding my work in that way.

To my mind, the very fact that I didn't make this story clear enough for many—perhaps most—readers makes the story a failure. I think clarity is the first thing a writer must achieve; if I fail in that, what does it matter what else I do? If I were writing this story again today, I'd spell out precisely what was going on from the beginning, so there wouldn't be the slightest confusion.

One must remember, however, that when I wrote this I was a graduate student in English. I think this explains everything.

BOOK 4

CRUEL MIRACLES

TALES OF DEATH, HOPE, AND HOLINESS

INTRODUCTION

I believe that speculative fiction—science fiction in particular—is the last American refuge of religious literature.

An odd thing to say, it might seem, particularly since science fiction openly requires that gods be either absent or explained. The moment you have a character pray and get an answer that is *not* explained through perfectly natural phenomena, the story ceases to be publishable as science fiction. In Stephen King's *The Stand*, which began as science fiction—an escaped virus destroys almost all of humanity—some characters' mystical dreams could perhaps have been acceptable as science fiction, because the Jungian collective unconscious has won a grudging place as legimate grist for the sf mill. But when, at the end, the finger of God comes down out of heaven and blows up Walking Man's nuclear missile—well, that crossed the line, and *The Stand* was clearly either fantasy or religious literature.

It would be fantasy if the god that acted were a god that the readers were not expected to believe in their real lives. It would be religious literature if the readers were expected to believe that such divine interventions actually *do* happen in reality. But no way in hell is the story going to stand up as science fiction if gods are both supernatural and real in the world of the tale.

So why do I call science fiction the last bastion of American religious literature?

You have to understand that what passes for religious literature in the U.S. today is really *inspirational* literature. The Religious, New Age, and Occult publishing categories all contain very similar kinds of stories: Isn't it wonderful that we understand the truth and live the right way, and ain't it a shame about the poor saps who don't. Their fiction (when they have fiction at all) is self-congratulatory. It doesn't explore, it merely affirms. It gives readers an emotional high in connection with membership in their own community of faith.

Real religious literature, I think, does something entirely different. It explores the nature of the universe and discovers the purpose behind it. When we find that purpose, we have found God, because in all religions at all times, regardless of the outward descriptions of God or gods, deity serves the same role: He (or she or they) is the purposer, the planner. And human beings, either with or without their knowledge or consent (depending on one's theology), are following that plan.

I think existential literature still falls into this category, for even though, after much searching, characters always discover that there is no God and therefore no purpose, the story is nevertheless about the need and search for purpose, and the climax is the discovery of the absence of one. Stories about God's nonexistence are still about God, and therefore are still a branch of religious literature.

The need to discover purpose in our lives is a universal human hunger. Even the slimiest, most evil people alive try to find meaning in their self-gratification; and the best of people shunt others' praise from themselves by ascribing their works to the purposes of a higher being.

There is a tendency, though, in the "true" stories available today to explain human behavior, to remove purpose—motive—from serious consideration. We tend to accept the notion that mechanical, not purposive, causation accounts for the things people do. Joe Sinister is a criminal because his parents beat him or because of a chemical imbalance in his brain or because of a genetic disorder that removed the function we call conscience. Jane Dexter, on the other hand, acts altruistically because she is compensating for feelings of inadequacy or because she has a brain disorder that causes an overactive sense of responsibility.

These explanations of human behavior may be accurate; I'm interested in the question, but the issue of accuracy is, in fact, quite irrelevant to human societies. A human community that uses mechanical causation to account for human behavior *cannot survive*, because it cannot hold its members accountable for their behavior. That is, no matter how you account for the origin of a human behavior, a community must continue to judge the perpetrator on the basis of his intent, as near as that intent can be understood (or guessed, or assumed). That is why parents inevitably ask their children the unanswerable question: Why did you do that? Terrible as that question is, it at least puts the responsibility back on the child's head and forces the child to ask himself the question that society absolutely requires him to answer: Why do I do the things I do? And how, by changing my motives, can I change my behavior? Whereas nothing is more debilitating or enervating for a child than parents who do not ask why, but rather say, You're just going through a phase, or, You can't help that, or I understand that's just the way you are. Such a child, if he believes these stories, has no hope of getting control of himself and therefore no hope of becoming an adult, responsible citizen of the community. We must believe in motives for human behavior, or we cannot maintain community life.

And once we have embarked on that course—judging each other by motive rather than explaining behavior by mechanical causation alone—the fundamental religious question of the meaning or purpose of life cannot be avoided. What *can* be avoided is the question of whether there is an ultimate purposer whose plan we all fulfill—and most American fiction does avoid it, including almost all of the stories published within the category labeled Religious Literature. Instead, purpose or lack of it is assumed.

Not, however, in science fiction. There alone we find the search for the purposer is still alive. Indeed, in story after story the question arises and is explored at depths that would be impossible in any other genre—even fantasy. For while fantasy is uniquely suited to dealing with human universals—the mythic—science fiction is uniquely suited to dealing with suprahuman universals—the metaphysical. Fantasy can hardly deal seriously with gods, because gods are common motifs, like magic swords and unicorns. Readers aren't expected to *believe* in them. (Few things are more jarring to a fantasy writer than to meet a reader who actually believes in those fantasy worlds. The dowsers and seventh sons who wrote to me or telephoned me after my Alvin Maker series started appearing finally led me to stop listing my address in the phone book. I didn't want these people to know where I lived.) But because science fiction specifically excludes supernatural gods as characters in stories, it is possible for science fiction to explore the purpose of life deeply and thoroughly without being distracted by existing theologies.

One of the best examples is in the work of Isaac Asimov. The good doctor has made it clear over the years that he has no belief in any kind of transcendent god, and his work bears this out. But his novels are almost all profoundly religious in the sense that they invariably affirm both the need for and the existence of a purposer. The original Foundation trilogy is explicitly about Hari Seldon's plan and purpose for humanity, and how it worked regardless of the conscious intent of the leaders of Terminus. And, when the plan seemed thwarted by an unplanned-for intruder, the mutant Mule, we find that there is a Second Foundation, which continues to fill Seldon's role, ongoing purposers and planners guiding the destiny of humankind. Furthermore, they realize they can't possibly do their work if humankind is aware of their presence—their scientific planning can't function unless it is not known to function. Therefore they have to fake their own destruction. The nontranscendent god of Asimov's fiction must remain invisible and ineffable—must remain, in fact, rather transcendent.

What shows up in Asimov shows up elsewhere as well. Gene Wolfe's novels are quite explicitly religious—more so than Tolkien's *Lord of the Rings*, which is a profoundly religious (and, in fact, Catholic) work. Frank Herbert's *Dune* and its sequels are even more obvious. Lisa Goldstein's *Tourists* and *A Mask for the General* both reveal, at the end, the active role of some purposer in making things work out according to a certain pattern in spite of the weakness of the leading characters—though in her cosmology, unlike Stephen King's, the voluntary actions of human beings *do* play a vital role in their salvation, a very non-Calvinist view of the relationship between man and the universal purposer.

Certainly there are many more; equally certain is the fact that many, perhaps most, science fiction novels *don't* deal with the plan of life and its planner. Nor is this subject unheard-of in works outside of science fiction. My point is that in science fiction, the relationship between man and god can be dealt with explicitly, in depth, and with great originality, without necessarily being connected to any religious system that has ever existed on Earth. Indeed, whenever science fiction touches on actual contemporary religions, it is almost always hostile to them. Yet it deals with religious *ideas* in a way almost not seen in serious American fiction outside of sci-fi.

So far I have referred to other writers' work; my own is also religious, in exactly this fashion—and in another, which I will deal with soon. But that was not a conscious choice on my part. In fact, because my plays had all been explicitly tied to religion—to Christianity in general and Mormonism in particular—when I turned my hand to writing science fiction and fantasy I made a deliberate choice to *exclude* religious concerns from my writing. No one was going to be a member of the Mormon Church; there were going to be no tales of prophets, saviors, priests, or believers. I was going to write pure, unmixed sci-fi.

This was not because of any hostility toward religion, you understand. I have been a believing and practicing Latter-day Saint throughout my writing career, without wavering on that point. I am, in fact, quite annoyed with critics who assume that this or that bit of my writing clearly shows my "struggles with doubt," as if the only religious issue worth writing about was whether or not one believes in a particular religion. That, in fact, is the most elementary—dare I say childish?—religious issue, and the one least interesting to those who are actually committed to a faith. There seems to be an idea among those obsessed with their own unbelief that to write about religion means to write about doubt. They miss the point. To write about religion actually means to write about truth and faith, two matters that cannot be intelligently dealt with in the presence of doubt. They can be dealt with easily in the face of unbelief—it is doubt itself that muddies the waters. You cannot present an idea clearly if you spend all your time discussing whether it's true. You leave the issue of truth in abeyance while you discover what the idea is; only then, having understood, should the issue of doubt vs. belief arise. And, quite frankly, I'm just as happy if it arises after the story is over.

This is one of the things that has caused most damage to Mormon fiction—the obsessive concern so many writers have with people coming into or leaving the Church. It's what I call "revolving door fiction," and I'm weary of it. It suggests that the writers themselves are not yet adults in the matter of religion, not yet committed to a path. I don't despise their personal struggle, but I do wish they'd find something else to write about. Because what's really interesting about religious people is what happens *after* the commitment is made, and that is precisely what can't be written about by people who have never made one.

My impatience with badly conceived Mormon fiction (and drama, for that matter) was part of my reason for eschewing overtly religious topics or characters in my science fiction. To my surprise, however, I discovered that my work had become more, not less, religious when I stopped dealing with religious subjects consciously. I would go to a convention and somebody would ask me, "Are you Mormon?" "Yes," I'd say. "Oh, I knew it before I was halfway through reading A *Planet Called Treason* [or *Songmaster* or *Hot Sleep*]." Horrified, I would demand to know what it was that made my work seem so obviously Mormon. When they pointed it out, it would be just as obvious to me—but until that moment I had been completely unaware of it. It seemed that I was writing religious fiction whether I wanted to or not.

But those unconsciously religious elements were exactly the kind of religious writing I was talking about before—explorations of the relationship between human beings and the purposer or purposers of life. There was another kind of writing about religion that I gradually began to want to write. I wanted to write, not only about religious ideas, but also about religious *people*. Yet I wanted to do it without writing "inspirational literature"—the kind of stuff that gets published in the Religious Fiction category.

Rare indeed is the human society that does not have a powerful religious ritual binding it together. Pluralism such as we have in America is extremely rare, and I think it's fair to say that it exists even in America only as the result of a conscious effort that is not always happily received by the American people. The very pervasiveness of Christmas and the deep resentment felt by many—perhaps most—Americans about the seemingly absurd finickiness of the courts in their effort to keep government bodies from promoting Christian Christmas rituals show that pluralism does not come easily or naturally even to a people with a two-century history of commitment to it.

Yet if you read most science fiction you wouldn't have a clue that religion played a part in anyone's life. Most sci-fi characters are utterly untouched by religion, by ritual, or by faith, *except* when religious rituals or faith are used to show how benighted or depraved or primitive a particular group or individual is. This is actually right in line with contemporary American literary fiction, so it isn't just because of a pro-science bias on the part of the writers. Yet this is so contrary to reality and betrays such a profound ignorance on the part of the writers that it should betray to most people a rather uncomfortable fact: American writers tend not to be in tune with America. Or, to put it another way, religious Americans and literary Americans have, consciously or not, separated themselves almost completely.

I think what happens is that religious people who are becoming writers get the idea, from their reading and from the public attitudes of most fashionable writers, that it's faintly embarrassing to present religion as a matter-of-fact part of life, rather like wearing colors that clash. Writers who would vigorously resist any attempt at censorship, or even editorial pressure to change an idea or a word or a comma, rigorously remove from their work—in fact, don't even allow themselves to conceive of putting it into their work in the first place—anything that might suggest that they harbor some sympathy for a particular religion or faith.

Even those who do deal with religious people positively take great care to distance themselves from it. Garrison Keillor, for example, keeps quite a common distance between himself and the Catholics and Lutherans of Lake Woebegon; he likes them, but he isn't *one* of them. Indeed, this sort of attitude may well arise from many authors' experience, for most religious communities don't react well to strangeness, and the kind of character traits that lead one to be a storyteller are generally classed as strange. Much of the avoidance of or hostility to religious people in American fiction may arise out of writers' painful experiences with religion in their growing-up years.

But the current American trend of almost absolute hostility toward or neglect of characters who have a religious life goes beyond anything that could be accounted for in individual lives. If people's real experiences with religion were so universally hideous, religions could not survive. I know from experience that religious people are as likely to be bright, good-hearted, and open-minded as nonreligious people. I have found proportionately as many bigots, cretins, and would-be fascists among university intellectuals as I have among practitioners of any religion I've known at all well. I've also found that religious people tend to have a much better knowledge and clearer understanding of unreligious people than the latter have of the former. The ignorance is mutual, but the nonreligious people have a bit more than their share.

So in this last decade I have turned more and more toward trying to give my characters a religious life, and to undo the skewed picture of religion that is almost completely universal in contemporary American letters. That there are abuses to be satirized cannot be doubted, and I do my share, in stories like "Saving Grace" and "Eye for Eye." But there are also graceful elements in the life of religious communities, and good people whose religion is part of their expression of their goodness, and such things also ought to be shown.

I deal with this most explicitly in my novel *Speaker for the Dead*, where I have the story's hero and title character, Andrew Wiggin, come to a small colony in which Brazilian Catholicism is the established church. I deliberately began the relationship between Wiggin and the Catholics by having the bishop of Lusitania warn his people against the speaker for the dead; and Andrew quickly runs into great resistance from the people because of the bishop's hostility. In short, I began with the cliché relationship between Wiggin the humanist and a religious community.

Then I set out to transform that relationship—and, with luck, the attitude of the reader. First, I introduced some positive religious characters—a husband and wife from a teaching order called the Children of the Mind of Christ. They were tolerant of, even cooperative with, the speaker for the dead, and they were also the guardians of scientific knowledge and liberal education in Lusitania. Yet they were also absolutely committed to a monastic law that required them to marry but forbade them to have sex, and I labored to make this painful religious sacrifice seem, not bizarre, but beautiful to the reader. It is not something I would personally ever want to do, nor do I advocate it; but I wanted readers to realize that such a painful choice, made for the sake of religion, did not debase the characters but rather ennobled them.

Second, I carefully transformed the readers' understanding of the bishop himself.

As the novel progresses, we begin to see that his hostility to Wiggin was not entirely because of closed-mindedness, but primarily because of a real concern for the welfare of his people. And as his perception of the needs of the people changed, we saw that the bishop—like all good religious leaders—was willing to do what was necessary for his people, even if it meant temporarily allying himself with a humanist minister like the speaker for the dead.

Finally, I showed that Andrew Wiggin himself, as he gradually comes to be part of one family and part of the community at large, realizes that to really belong he must also be a Catholic. He had been baptized a Catholic in his infancy—something that I had put into *Ender's Game* just for fun, but now found quite useful—and so as part of joining Novinha's family and Lusitania itself, he begins to attend mass and act out the rituals of the church. The issue of faith doesn't arise. What matters is belonging to the community and subjecting himself to the community's most basic discipline.

This is not to say that I show religion in a completely favorable light. The struggle with sin is what nearly destroys Novinha and her family. The people are every bit as intolerant of strangeness as any small town, and their intolerance is embedded within their religious life. They are also superstitious and try to use religion like magic. But in *Speaker for the Dead* I try to put these things in perspective. They are part of religious life, but not all of it; and religion brings at least as much goodness and comfort as it brings pain into the characters' lives.

My point was not to show that religion is all good—it isn't. My point was, first, to recognize what most writers seem to ignore, that most people throughout the world and throughout history are believing members of a religious community—and that usually their religion and their citizenship are indistinguishable. Then, second, I was determined to undermine the fashionably hostile stereotypes that mark American fiction whenever it *does* include religion. *Speaker for the Dead* is not a religious book, at least not in the sense that a religious book might demand that you decide whether you believe or don't believe, belong or don't belong. But it does include religion in its realistic and proper proportion in human life. In that sense it is far more realistic than most American novels.

Over the years religion has cropped up more and more in my work, until finally, with a series of short stories that became the book *The Folk of the Fringe*, I dealt explicitly with Mormon characters and Mormon culture in a near-future setting. Oddly enough, these stories—which, because of their separate existence in that book, do not appear in this collection—are actually some of the *least* religious of my writing, in that they are *not* about the relationship between the living and the purposer of life. Rather they are almost anthropological in their treatment of Mormonism. They are about the way people connect with and abrade against each other within the tight confines of a demanding religious community.

So I write three kinds of fiction that deals with religion. First, like many, perhaps most, science fiction writers, I tell stories that deal with the purpose of life—with the relationship between man and God. Second, I tell stories that deliberately subvert the clichés about religion that are so widespread in American fiction, by showing religious characters in a full range of roles within my stories. And, third, I tell stories that include my direct experience of religious life by depicting the community I know best, Mormonism.

At no point am I trying to persuade you; I want readers, not proselytes. With *Cruel*

Miracles I have drawn together my stories that most clearly deal with religious matters not often touched upon by contemporary American writers, matters like holiness, awe, faith, comfort, responsibility, and community. You don't have to be a religious person or even *like* religious people to receive these stories. I hope, though, that by the end you understand a little more about the religious aspect of human life.

MORTAL GODS

The first contact was peaceful, almost uneventful: sudden landings near government buildings all over the world, brief discussions in the native languages, followed by treaties allowing the aliens to build certain buildings in certain places in exchange for certain favors—nothing spectacular. The technological improvements that the aliens brought helped make life better for everyone, but they were improvements that were already well within the reach of human engineers within the next decade or two. And the greatest gift of all was found to be a disappointment—space travel. The aliens did not have faster-than-light travel. Instead, they had conclusive proof that faster-than-light travel was utterly impossible. They had infinite patience and incredibly long lives to sustain them in their snail's-pace crawl among the stars, but humans would be dead before even the shortest space flight was fairly begun.

And after only a little while, the presence of aliens was regarded as quite the normal thing. They insisted that they had no further gifts to bring, and simply exercised their treaty rights to build and visit the buildings they had made.

The buildings were all different from each other, but had one thing in common: by the standards of the local populace, the new alien buildings were all clearly recognizable as churches.

Mosques. Cathedrals. Shrines. Synagogues. Temples. All unmistakably churches.

But no congregation was invited, though any person who came to such a place was welcomed by whatever aliens happened to be there at the time, who engaged in charming discussion totally related to the person's own interests. Farmers conversed about farming, engineers about engineering, housewives about motherhood, dreamers about dreams, travelers about travels, astronomers about the stars. Those who came and talked went away feeling good. Feeling that someone did, indeed, attach importance to their lives —had come trillions of kilometers through incredible boredom (five hundred years in space, they said!) just to see *them*.

And gradually life settled into a peaceful routine. Scientists, it is true, kept on discovering, and engineers kept on building according to those discoveries, and so changes *did* come. But knowing now that there was no great scientific revolution just around the corner, no tremendous discovery that would open up the stars, men and women settled down, by and large, to the business of being happy.

It wasn't as hard as people had supposed.

Willard Crane was an old man, but a content one. His wife was dead, but he did not resent the brief interregnum in his life in which he was solitary again, a thing he had not been since he came home from the Vietnam War with half a foot missing and found his girl waiting for him anyway, foot or no foot. They had lived all their married lives in a house in the Avenues of Salt Lake City, which, when they moved there, had been a shabby, dilapidated relic of a previous century, but which now was a splendid preservation of a noble era in architecture. Willard was in that comfortable area between heavy wealth and heavier poverty; enough money to satisfy normal aspirations, but not enough money to tempt him to extravagance.

Every day he walked from 7th Avenue and L street to the cemetery, not far away, where practically everyone had been buried. It was there, in the middle of the cemetery, that the alien building stood—an obvious mimic of old Mormon temple architecture, meaning it was a monstrosity of conflicting periods that somehow, perhaps through intense sincerity, managed to be beautiful anyway.

And there he sat among the gravestones, watching as occasional people wandered into and out of the sanctuary where the aliens came, visited, left.

Happiness is boring as hell, he decided one day. And so, to provoke a little delightful variety, he decided to pick a fight with somebody. Unfortunately, everyone he knew at all well was too nice to fight. And so he decided that he had a bone to pick with the aliens.

When you're old, you can get away with anything.

He went to the alien temple and walked inside.

On the walls were murals, paintings, maps; on the floor, pedestals with statues; it seemed more a museum than anything else. There were few places to sit, and he saw no sign of aliens. Which wouldn't be a disaster; just deciding on a good argument had been variety enough, noting with pride the fine quality of the work the aliens had chosen to display.

But there was an alien there, after all.

"Good morning, Mr. Crane," said the alien.

"How the hell you know my name?"

"You perch on a tombstone every morning and watch as people come in and go out. We found you fascinating. We asked around." The alien's voicebox was very well programmed—a warm, friendly, interested voice. And Willard was too old and jaded with novelty to get much excited about the way the alien slithered along the floor and slopped on the bench next to him like a large, self-moving piece of seaweed.

"We wished you would come in."

"I'm in."

"And why?"

Now that the question was put, his reason seemed trivial to him; but he decided to play the game all the way through. Why not, after all? "I have a bone to pick with you."

"Heavens," said the alien, with mock horror.

"I have some questions that have never been answered to my satisfaction."

"Then I trust we'll have some answers."

"All right then." But what *were* his questions? "You'll have to forgive me if my mind gets screwed around. The brain dies first, as you know."

"We know."

"Why'd you build a temple here? How come you build churches?"

"Why, Mr. Crane, we've answered that a thousand times. We *like* churches. We find them the most graceful and beautiful of all human architecture."

"I don't believe you," Willard said. "You're dodging my question. So let me put it another way. How come you have the time to sit around and talk to half-assed imbeciles like me? Haven't you got anything better to do?"

"Human being are unusually good company. It's a most pleasant way to pass the time which does, after many years, weigh rather heavily on our, um, hands." And the alien tried to gesture with his pseudopodia, which was amusing, and Willard laughed.

"Slippery bastards, aren't you?" he inquired, and the alien chuckled. "So let me put it this way, and no dodging, or I'll know you have something to hide. You're pretty much like us, right? You have the same gadgets, but you can travel in space because you don't croak after a hundred years like we do; whatever, you do pretty much the same kinds of things we do. And yet—"

"There's always an 'and yet,' " the alien sighed.

"And *yet*. You come all the way out here, which ain't exactly Main Street, Milky Way, and all you do is build these churches all over the place and sit around and jaw with whoever the hell comes in. Makes no sense, sir, none at all."

The alien oozed gently toward him. "Can you keep a secret?"

"My old lady thought she was the only woman I ever slept with in my life. Some secrets I can keep."

"Then here is one to keep. We come, Mr. Crane, to worship."

"Worship who?"

"Worship, among others, you."

Willard laughed long and loud, but the alien looked (as only aliens can) terribly earnest and sincere.

"Listen, you mean to tell me that you worship *people*?"

"Oh, yes. It is the dream of everyone who dares to dream on my home planet to come here and meet a human being or two and then live on the memory forever."

And suddenly it wasn't funny to Willard anymore. He looked around—human art in prominent display, the whole format, the choice of churches. "You aren't joking."

"No, Mr. Crane. We've wandered the galaxy for several million years, all told, meeting new races and renewing acquaintance with old. Evolution is a tedious old highway—carbon-based life always leads to certain patterns and certain forms, despite the fact that we seem hideously different to you—"

"Not too bad, Mister, a little ugly, but not too bad—"

"All the—people like us that you've seen—well, we don't come from the same planet, though it has been assumed so by your scientists. Actually, we come from thousands of planets. Separate, independent evolution, leading inexorably to us. Absolutely, or nearly absolutely, uniform throughout the galaxy. We are the natural endproduct of evolution."

"So we're the oddballs."

"You might say so. Because somewhere along the line, Mr. Crane, deep in your past, your planet's evolution went astray from the normal. It created something utterly new."

"Sex?"

"We all have sex, Mr. Crane. Without it, how in the world could the race improve? No, what was new on your planet, Mr. Crane, was death."

The word was not an easy one for Willard to hear. His wife had, after all, meant a great deal to him. And he meant even more to himself. Death already loomed in dizzy spells and shortened breath and weariness that refused to turn into sleep.

"Death?"

"We don't die, Mr. Crane. We reproduce by splitting off whole sections of ourselves with identical DNA—you know about DNA?"

"I went to college."

"And with us, of course, as with all other life in the universe, intelligence is carried on the DNA, not in the brain. One of the byproducts of death, the brain is. We don't have it. We split, and the individual, complete with all memories, lives on in the children, who are made up of the actual flesh of my flesh, you see? I will never die."

"Well, bully for you," Willard said, feeling strangely cheated, and wondering why he hadn't guessed.

"And so we came here and found people whose life had a finish; who began as unformed creatures without memory and, after an incredibly brief span, died."

"And for that you worship us? I might as well go worshiping bugs that die a few minutes after they're born."

The alien chuckled, and Willard resented it.

"Is that why you come here? To gloat?"

"What else would we worship, Mr. Crane? While we don't discount the possibility of invisible gods, we really never have invented any. We never died, so why dream of immortality? Here we found a people who knew how to worship, and for the first time we found awakened in us a desire to do homage to superior beings."

And Willard noticed his heartbeat, realized that it would stop while the alien had no heart, had nothing that would ever end. "Superior, hell."

"We," said the alien, "remember everything, from the first stirrings of intellect to the present. When we are 'born,' so to speak, we have no need of teachers. We have never learned to write—merely to exchange RNA. We have never learned to create beauty to outlast our lives because nothing outlasts our lives. We live to see all our works crumble. Here, Mr. Crane, we have found a race that builds for the sheer joy of building, that creates beauty, that writes books, that invents the lives of never-known people to delight others who know they are being lied to, a race that devises immortal gods to worship and celebrates its own mortality with immense pomp and glory. Death is the foundation of all that is great about humanity, Mr. Crane."

"Like hell it is," said Willard. "I'm about to die, and there's nothing great about it."

"You don't really believe that, Mr. Crane," the alien said. "None of you do. Your lives are built around death, glorifying it. Postponing it as long as possible, to be sure, but glorifying it. In the earliest literature, the death of the hero is the moment of greatest climax. The most potent myth."

"Those poems weren't written by old men with flabby bodies and hearts that only beat when they feel like it."

"Nonsense. Everything you do smacks of death. Your poems have beginnings and endings, and structures that limit the work. Your paintings have edges, marking off where the beauty begins and ends. Your sculptures isolate a moment in time. Your music starts and finishes. All that you do is mortal—it is all born. It all dies. And yet you struggle against mortality and have overcome it, building up tremendous stores of shared knowledge through your finite books and your finite words. You put frames on everything."

"Mass insanity, then. But it explains nothing about why you worship. You must come here to mock us."

"Not to mock you. To envy you."

"Then die. I assume that your protoplasm or whatever is vulnerable."

"You don't understand. A human being can die—*after* he has reproduced—and all that he knew and all that he has will live on after him. But if *I* die, I cannot reproduce. My knowledge dies with me. An awesome responsibility. We cannot assume it. I *am* all the paintings and writings and songs of a million generations. To die would be the death of a civilization. You have cast yourselves free of life and achieved greatness."

"And that's why you come here."

"If ever there were gods. If ever there was power in the universe. You are those gods. You have that power."

"We have no power."

"Mr. Crane, you are beautiful."

And the old man shook his head, stood with difficulty, and doddered out of temple and walked away slowly among the graves.

"You tell them the truth," said the alien to no one in particular (to future generations of himself who would need the memory of the words having been spoken), "and it only makes it worse."

It was only seven months later, and the weather was no longer spring, but now blustered with the icy wind of late autumn. The trees in the cemetery were no longer colorful; they were stripped of all but the last few brown leaves. And into the cemetery walked Willard Crane again, his arms half enclosed by the metal crutches that gave him, in his old age, four points of balance instead of the precarious two that had served him for more than ninety years. A few snowflakes were drifting lazily down, except when the wind snatched them and spun them in crazy dances that had neither rhythm nor direction.

Willard laboriously climbed the steps of the temple.

Inside, an alien was waiting.

"I'm Willard Crane," the old man said.

"And I'm an alien. You spoke to me—or my parent, however you wish to phrase it—several months ago."

"Yes."

"We knew you'd come back."

"Did you? I vowed I never would."

"But we know you. You are well known to us all, Mr. Crane. There are billions of gods on Earth for us to worship, but you are the noblest of them all."

"I am?"

"Because only you have thought to do us the kindest gift. Only you are willing to let us watch your death."

And a tear leaped from the old man's eye as he blinked heavily.

"Is that why I came?"

"Isn't it?"

"I thought I came to damn your souls to hell, that's why I came, you bastards, coming to taunt me in the final hours of my life."

"You came to us."

"I wanted to show you how ugly death is."

"Please. Do."

And, seemingly eager to oblige them, Willard's heart stopped and he, in brief agony, slumped to the floor in the temple.

The aliens all slithered in, all gathered around closely, watching him rattle for breath.

"I will not die!" he savagely whispered, each breath an agony, his face fierce with the heroism of struggle.

And then his body shuddered and he was still.

The aliens knelt there for hours in silent worship as the body became cold. And then, at last, because they had learned this from their gods—that words must be said to be remembered—one of them spoke:

"Beautiful," he said tenderly. "Oh Lord my God," he said worshipfully.

And they were gnawed within by the grief of knowing that this greatest gift of all gifts was forever out of their reach.

SAVING GRACE

And he looked into her eyes, and lo!
when her gaze fell upon him
he did verily turn to stone,
for her visage was wondrous ugly.
Praise the Lord.

Mother came home depressed as hell with a bag full of groceries and a headache fit to make her hair turn to snakes. Billy, he knew when Mommy was like that, he could tell as soon as she grumped through the living room. But if she was full of hellfire, he had the light of heaven, and so he said, "Don't be sad, Mother, Jesus loves you."

Mother put the margarine into the fridge and wiped the graham cracker crumbs off the table and dumped them in the sink even though the disposal hadn't worked for years. "Billy," she said quietly, "you been saved again?"

"I only was just going to look inside."

"Ought to sue those bastards. Burn down their tent or something. Why can't they do their show from a studio like everybody else?"

"I felt my sins just weighing me down and then he reached out and Jesus come into my heart and I had to be baptized."

At the word *baptized*, Mommy slammed the kitchen counter. The mixing bowl bounced. "*Not* again, you damn near got pneumonia the last time!"

"This time I dried my hair."

"It isn't sanitary!"

"I was the first one in. Everybody was crying."

"Well, you just listen! I tell you not to go there, and I mean it! You look at me when I'm talking to you, young man."

Her irresistible fingers lifted up his chin. Billy felt like he was living in a Bible story. He could almost hear Bucky Fay himself telling the tale: And he looked into her eyes, and lo! when her gaze fell upon him he did verily turn to stone, and he could not move though he sorely feared that he might wet his pants, for her visage was wondrous ugly. Praise the Lord.

"Now you promise me you won't go into that tent anymore, ever, because you got no resistance at all, you just come straight home, you hear me?"

He could not move until at last she despaired and looked away, and then he found his voice and said, "What *else* am I supposed to do after school?"

Today was different from all the other times they had this argument: this time his mother leaned on the counter and sobbed into the waffle mix. Billy came and put his arm around her and leaned his head on her hip. She turned and held him close and said, "If that son-of-a-bitch hadn't left me you might've had some brothers and sisters to come home to." They made waffles together, and while Billy pried pieces of over-cooked waffle out of the waffle iron with a bent table knife, he vowed that he would not cause his mother such distress again. The revival tent could flap its wings and lift up its microwave dish to take part in the largess of heaven, but Billy would look the other way for his mother's sake, for she had suffered enough.

Yet he couldn't keep his thoughts away from the tent, because when they were telling what was coming up soon they had said that Bucky Fay was coming. Bucky Fay, the healer of channel 49, who had been known to exorcise that demon cancer and cast out kidney stones in the name of the Lord; Bucky Fay, who looked to Billy like the picture Mommy kept hidden in the back of her top drawer, the picture of his father, the son-of-a-bitch. Billy wanted to see the man with the healing hands, see him in the flesh.

"Mommy," he said. On TV the skinny people were praising Diet Pepsi.

"Mm?" Mommy didn't look up.

"I wish my foot was all twisted up so I couldn't walk."

Now she looked up. "My Lord, what for!"

"So Jesus could turn it around."

"Billy, that's disgusting."

"When the miracle goes through you, Mommy, it knocks you on the head and then you fall down and get all better. A little girl with no arm got a new arm from God. They said so."

"Child, they've turned you superstitious."

"I wish I had a club foot, so Jesus would do a miracle on me."

God moves in mysterious ways, but this time he was pretty direct. Of all the half-assed wishes that got made and prayers that got said, Billy's got answered. Billy's mother was brooding about how the boy was going off the deep end. She decided she had to get him out doing things that normal kids do. The movie playing at the local family-oriented moviehouse was the latest go-round of *Pollyanna*. They went and watched and Billy learned a lesson. Billy saw how *good* this little girl was, and how preachers liked her, and first thing you know he was up on the roof, figuring out how to fall off just right so you smash your legs but don't break your back.

Never did get it right. Broke his back, clean as could be, spinal cord severed just below the shoulders, and there he was in a wheelchair, wearing diapers and pissing into a plastic bag. In the hospital he watched TV, a religious station that had God's chosen servants on all day, praising and praying and saving. And they had Bucky Fay himself, praise the Lord, Bucky Fay himself making the deaf to hear and the arthritic to move around and the audience to be generous, and there sat Billy, more excited than he had ever been before, because now he was ripe and ready for a miracle.

"Not a chance in the world," his mother said. "By God I'm going to get you uncrazy, and the last place I'm going to take you is anywhere in earshot of those lying cheating hypocritical so-called healers."

But there's not many people in the world can say no more than two or three times to a paralyzed kid in a wheelchair, especially if he's crying, and besides, Mommy thought, maybe there's something *to* faith. Lord knows the boy's got *that*, even if he doesn't have a single nerve in his legs. And if there's even a chance of maybe giving him back some of his body, what harm can it do?

Once inside the tent, of course, she thought of other things. What if it *is* a fraud, which of course it is, and what happens when the boy finds out? What then? So she whispered to him, "Billy, now don't go expecting too much."

"I'm not." Just a miracle, that's all. They do them all the time, Mommy.

"I just don't want you to be disappointed when nothing happens."

"I won't be disappointed, Mommy." No. He'll fix me right up.

And then the nice lady leaned over and asked, "You here to be healed?"

Billy only nodded, recognizing her as Bucky Fay's helper lady who always said "Oh, my sweet Lord Jesus you're so kind" when people got healed, said it in a way that made your spine tingle. She was wearing a lot of makeup. Billy could see she had a moustache with makeup really packed onto it. He wondered if she was really secretly a man as she wheeled him up to the front. But why would a man wear a dress? He was wondering about that as she got him in place, lined up with the other wheelchair people on the front row.

A man came along and knelt down in front of him. Billy got ready to pray, but the man just talked normal, so Billy opened his eyes. "Now this one's going on TV," the man said, "and for the TV show we need you to be real careful, son. Don't say anything unless Bucky asks you a direct question, and then you just tell him real quick. Like when he asks you how come you got in a wheelchair, what'll you tell him?"

"I'll say—I'll say—"

"Now don't go freezing up on him, or it'll look real bad. This is on TV, remember. Now you just tell me how come you got in a wheelchair."

"So I could get healed by the power of Jesus."

The man looked at him a moment, and then he said, "Sure. I guess you'll do just fine. Now when it's all over, and you're healed, I'll be right there, holding you by the arm. Now don't say Thank the Lord right off. You wait till I squeeze your arm, and then you say it. Okay?"

"Okay."

"For the TV, you know."

"Yeah."

"Don't be nervous."

"I won't."

The man went away but he was back in just a second looking worried. "You can feel things in your arms, can't you?"

Billy lifted his arms and waved them up and down. "My arms are just fine." The man nodded and went away again.

There was nothing to do but watch, then, and Billy watched, but he didn't see much. On the TV, all you could see was Bucky Fay, but here the camera guys kept getting in front of him, and people were going back and forth all during the praising time and the support this ministry time so Billy could hardly keep track of what was going on. Till the man who talked to him came over to him again, and this time a younger guy was with him, and they lifted Billy out of his chair and carried him over toward where the lights were so bright, and the cameras were turned toward him, and Bucky Fay was saying, "And now who is first, thanks be to the Lord? Are you that righteous young man who the devil has cursed to be a homophiliac? Come here, boy! God's going to give you a blood transfusion from the hemoglobin of the Holy Spirit!"

Billy didn't know what to do. If he said anything before Bucky Fay asked him a question, the man would be mad, but what good would it do if Bucky Fay ordered up the wrong miracle? But then he saw how the man who had talked to him turned his face away from the camera and mouthed, "Paralyzed," and Bucky Fay caught it and went right on, saying "Do you think the Saviour is worried? Paralyzed you are, too, completely helpless, and yet when the miracle comes into your body, do you think the Holy Spirit needs the doctor's diagnosis? No, praise the Lord, the Holy Spirit goes all through you, hunting down every place where the devil has hurt you, where the devil that great serpent has *poisoned* you, where the devil that mighty dragon has thought he could *destroy* you—boy, are you saved?"

It was a direct question. "Uh huh."

"Has the Lord come to you in the waters of baptism and washed away your sins and made you clean?"

Billy wasn't sure what that all meant, but after a second the man squeezed his arm, and so Billy said, "Thank the Lord."

"What the baptism did to the outside of your body, the miracle will do to the inside of your body. Do you believe that Jesus can heal you?"

Billy nodded.

"Oh, be not ashamed, little child. Speak so all the millions of our television friends can hear you. Can Jesus heal you?"

"Yes! I know he can!"

Bucky Fay smiled, and his face went holy; he spat on his hands, clapped twice, and then slapped Billy in the forehead, splashing spit all over his face. Just that very second the two men holding him sort of half-dropped him, and as he clutched forward with his hands he realized that all those times when people seemed to be overcome by the Holy Spirit, they were just getting *dropped*, but that was probably part of the miracle. They got him down on the floor and Bucky Fay went on talking about the Lord knowing the pure in heart, and then the two men picked him up and this time stood him on his legs. Billy couldn't feel a thing, but he did know that he was standing. They were helping him balance, but his weight was on his legs, and the miracle had worked. He almost praised God right then, but he remembered in time, and waited.

"I bet you feel a little weak, don't you," said Bucky Fay.

Was that a direct question? Billy wasn't sure, so he just nodded his head.

"When the Holy Spirit went through the Apostle Paul, didn't he lie upon the ground? Already you are able to stand upon your legs, and after a good night's sleep, when your body has strengthened itself after being inhabited by the Spirit of the Lord, you'll be restored to your whole self, good as new!"

Then the man squeezed Billy's arm. "Praise the Lord," Billy said. But that was wrong—it was supposed to be thank the Lord, and so he said it even louder, "Thank the Lord."

And now with the cameras on him, the two men holding him worked the real miracle, for they turned him and leaned him forward, and pulled him along back to the wheelchair. As they pulled him, they rocked him back and forth, and under him Billy could hear his shoes scuffing the ground, left, right, left, right, just as if he was walking. But he wasn't walking. He couldn't feel a thing. And then he knew. All those miracles, all those walking people—they had men beside them, leaning them left, leaning them right, making their legs fall forward, just like dolls, just like dummies, real dummies. And Billy cried. They got the camera real close to him then, to show the tears streaking down his face. The crowd applauded and praised.

"He's new at walking," Bucky Fay shouted into the microphone. "He isn't used to so much exercise. Let that boy ride in his chair again until he has a chance to build up his strength. But praise the Lord! We know that the miracle is done, Jesus has given this boy his legs and healed his hemophobia, too!" As the woman wheeled him down the aisle, the people reached out to touch him, said kind and happy things to him, and he cried. His mother was crying for joy. She embraced him and said, "You walked," and Billy cried harder. Out in the car he told her the truth. She looked off toward the brightly lit door of that flamboyant, that seductive tent, and she said, "God damn him to burn in hell forever." But Billy was quite, quite sure that God would do no such thing.

Not that Billy doubted God. No, God had all power, God was a granter of prayers. God was even fair-minded, after his fashion. But Billy knew now that when God set himself to balance things in the world, he did it sneaky. He did it tricky. He did it ass-backward, so that anybody who wanted to could see his works in the world and still doubt God. After all, what good was faith if God went around leaving plain evidence of his goodness in the world? No, not God. His goodness would be kept a profound secret, Billy knew that. Just a secret God kept to himself.

And sure enough, when God set out to even things up for Billy, he didn't do the obvious thing. He didn't let the nerves heal, he didn't send the miracle of feeling, the blessing of pain into Billy's empty legs. Instead God, who probably had a bet on with Satan about this one, gave Billy another gift entirely, an unlooked-for blessing that would break his heart.

Mother was wheeling Billy around the park. It was a fine summer day, which means that the humidity was so high that fish could live for days out of the water. Billy was dripping sweat, and he knew that when he got home he'd have a hell of a diaper rash, and Mother would say, "Oh you poor dear," and Billy would grieve because it didn't even itch. The river was flowing low and there were big rocks uncovered by the shore. Billy sat there watching the kids climb around on the rocks. His mother saw what he was watching and tried to take him away so he wouldn't get depressed about how he couldn't climb, but Billy wouldn't let her. He just stayed and watched. He picked out one kid in particular, a pretty-faced body with a muscled chest, about two years older than Billy. Her watched everything that boy did, and pretended that he was doing it. That was a good thing to do, Billy would rather do that than anything, watch this boy play for him on the rocks.

But all the time there was this idiot girl watching *Billy*. She was on the grass, far back from the shore, where all the cripples have to stay. She walked like an inchworm almost, each step a major event, as if she was a big doll with a little driver inside working the controls, and the driver wasn't very good at it yet. Billy tried to watch the golden body of the pretty-faced boy, but this spastic girl kept lurching around at the edges of his eyes.

"Make that *re*tard go away," Billy whispered.

"What?" asked Mother.

"I don't want to look at that *re*tard girl."

"Then don't look at her."

"Make her go away. She keeps looking at *me*."

Mother patted Billy's shoulder. "Other people got rights, Billy. I can't make her go away from the park. You want me to take you somewhere else?"

"No." Not while the golden boy was standing tall on the rocks, extending himself to snatch frisbies out of the air without falling. Like God catching lightning and laughing in delight.

The spastic girl came closer and closer, in her sidewise way. And Billy grew more and more determined not to pay the slightest heed to her. It was obvious, though, that she was coming *to* him, that she meant to *reach* him, and as he sat there he grew afraid. What would she do? His greatest fear was of someone snatching his urine bag from between his legs and holding it up, the catheter tugging away at him, and everybody laughing and laughing. That was what he hated worst, living his life like a tire with a slow leak. He knew that she would grab between his legs for the urine bag under his lap robe, and probably spill it all over, she was such a spastic. But he said nothing of his fear, just waited, holding onto his lap robe, watching the golden boy jump from the highest rock into river in order to splash the kids who were perched on the lesser rocks.

Then the spastic girl touched him. Thumped her club of a hand into his arm and moaned loudly. Billy cried out, "Oh, God!" The girl shuddered and fell to the ground, weeping.

All at once every single person in the park ran over and leaned around, jostling and looking. Billy held tight to his lap robe, lest someone pull it away. The spastic girl's parents were all apology, she'd never done anything like that, she usually just kept to herself, we're so sorry, so *terribly* sorry. They lifted the girl to her feet, tried to lead her away, but she shrugged them off violently. She shuddered again, and formed her mouth elaborately to make a word. Her parents watched her lips intently, but when the words came, they were clear. "I am better," she said.

Carefully she took a step, not toward her parents, but toward Billy. The step was not a lurch controlled by a clumsy little puppeteer. It was slow and uncertain, but it was a human step. "He healed me," she said.

Step after step, each more deft than the last, and Billy forgot all about his lap robe. She was healed, she was whole. She had touched him and now she was cured.

"Praise God," someone in the crowd said.

"It's just like on TV," someone else said.

"Saw it with my own two eyes."

And the girl fell to her knees beside Billy and kissed his hand and wept and wept.

They started coming after that, as word spread. Just a shy-looking man at the front door, a pesky fat lady with a skinny brother, a mother with two mongoloid children. All the freaks in Billy's town, all the sufferers, all the desperate seemed to find the way to his house. "No," Billy told Mother again and again. "I don't want to see nobody."

"But it's a little baby," Mother said. "She's so sweet. He's been through so much pain."

They came in, one by one, and demanded or begged or prayed or just timidly whispered to him, "Heal me." Then Billy would sit there, trembling, as they reached out and touched him. When they knew that they were healed, and they always were, they cried and kissed and praised and thanked and offered money. Billy always refused the money and said precious little else. "Aren't you going to give the glory to God?" asked one lady, whose son Billy healed of leukemia. But Billy just looked at his lap robe until she went away.

The first reporters came from the grocery store papers, the ones that always know about the UFOs. They kept asking him to prophesy the future, until Billy told Mother not to let them come in anymore. Mother tried to keep them out, but they even pretended to be cripples in order to get past the door. They wrote stories about the "crippled healer" and kept quoting Billy as saying things that he never said. They also published his address.

Hundreds of people came every day now, a constant stream all day. One lady with a gimp leg said, "Praise the Lord, it was worth the hundred dollars."

"What hundred dollars?" asked Billy.

"The hundred dollars I give your mother. I give the doctors a thousand bucks and the government give them ten thousand more and they never done a damn thing for me."

Billy called Mother. She came in. "This woman says she gave you a hundred dollars."

"I didn't ask for the money," Mother said.

"Give it back," Billy said.

Mother took the money out of her apron and gave it back. The woman clucked about how she didn't mind either way and left.

"I ain't no Bucky Fay," Billy said.

"Of course you ain't," Mother said. "When people touch you, they get better."

"No money, from nobody."

"That's real smart," Mother said. "I lost my job last week, Billy. I'm home all day just keeping them away from you. How are we going to live?"

Billy just sat there, trying to think about it. "Don't let them in anymore," he said. "Lock the doors and go to work."

Mother started to cry. "Billy, I can't stand it if you don't let them in. All those babies; all those twisted-up people, all those cancers and the fear of death in their faces, I can't stand it except that somehow, by some miracle, when they come in your room and touch you, they come out whole. I don't know how to turn them away. Jesus gave you a gift I didn't think existed in the world, but it didn't belong to you, Billy. It belongs to *them*."

"I touch myself every day," Billy whispered, "and I never get better."

From then on Mother only took half of whatever people offered, and only *after* they were healed, so people wouldn't get the idea that the healing depended on the money. That way she was able to scrape up enough to keep the roof over their heads and food on the table. "There's a lot less thankful money than bribe money in the world," she said to Billy. Billy just ate, being careful not to spill hot soup on his lap, because he'd never know if he scalded himself.

Then one day the TV cameras came, and the movie cameras, and set up on the lawn and in the street outside.

"What the hell are you doing?" demanded Billy's mother.

"Bucky Fay's coming to meet the crippled healer," said the movie man. "We want to have this for Bucky Fay's show."

"If you try to bring one little camera inside our house I'll have the police on you."

"The public's got a right to know," said the man, pointing the camera at her.

"The public's got a right to kiss my ass," said Mother, and she went back into the house and told everybody to go away and come back tomorrow, they were locking up the house for the day.

Mother and Billy watched through the lacy curtains while Bucky Fay got out of his limousine and waved at the cameras and the people crowded around in the street.

"Don't let him in, Mother," said Billy.

Bucky Fay knocked on the door.

"Don't answer," said Billy.

Bucky Fay knocked and knocked. Then he gestured to the cameramen and they all went back to their vans and all of Bucky Fay's helpers went back to their cars and the police held the crowd far away, and Bucky Fay started talking.

"Billy," said Bucky Fay, "I don't aim to hurt you. You're a true healer, I just want to shake your hand."

"Don't let him touch me again," said Billy. Mother shook her head.

"If you let me help you, you can heal hundreds and hundreds more people, all around the world, and bring millions of TV viewers to Jesus."

"The boy don't want you," Mother said.

"Why are you afraid of me? I didn't give you your gift, God did."

"Go away!" Billy shouted.

There was silence for a moment outside the door. Then Bucky Fay's voice came again, softer, and it sounded like he was holding back a sob. "Billy, why do you think I come to you? I am the worst son-of-a-bitch I know, and I come for you to heal me."

That was not a thing that Billy had ever thought to hear from Bucky Fay.

Bucky Fay was talking soft now, so it was sometimes hard to understand him. "In the name of Jesus, boy, do you think I woke up one morning and said to myself, 'Bucky Fay, go out and be a healer and you'll get rich'? Think I said that? No sir. I had a gift once. Like yours, I had a gift. I found it one day when I was swimming at the water hole with my big brother Jeddy. Jeddy, he was a show-off, he was always tempting Death to come for him, and that day he dove right down from the highest branch and plunked his head smack in the softest, stickiest mud on the bottom of Pachuckamunkey River. Took fifteen minutes just to get his head loose. They brought him to shore and he was dead, his face all covered with mud. And I screamed and cried out loud, 'God, you ain't got no right!' and then I touched my brother, and smacked him on the head, I said, 'God damn you, Jeddy, you pin-headed jackass, you ain't dead, get up and walk!' And that was when I discovered I had the gift. Because Jeddy reached up and wiped the mud off his eyes and rolled over and puked the black Pachukey water all over grass there. 'Thank you Jesus,' I said. In those days I could lay hands on mules with bent legs and they'd go straight. A baby with measles, and his spots would *go.* I had a good heart then. I healed colored people, and in those days even the doctors wouldn't go so far as *that.* But then they offered me money, and I took it, and they asked me to preach even though I didn't know a damn thing, and so I preached, and pretty soon I found myself in a jet airplane that I owned flying over an airstrip that I owned heading for a TV station that I owned and I said to myself, Bucky Fay, *you* haven't healed a soul in twenty years. A few folks have gotten better because of their own faith, but *you* lost the gift. You threw it away for the sake of money." On the other side of the door Bucky Fay wailed in anguish. "Oh, God in heaven, let me in this door or I will die!"

Billy nodded, tears in his eyes, and Mother opened the door. Bucky Fay was on his knees leaning against the door so he nearly fell into the room. He didn't even stand up to walk over to Billy, just crawled most of the way and then said, "Billy, the light of God is in your eyes. Heal me of my affliction! My disease is love of money! My disease is forgetting the Lord God of heaven! Heal me and let me have my gift back again, and I will never stray, not ever so long as I live!"

Billy reached out his hand. Slow and trembling, Bucky Fay gently took that hand and kissed it, and touched it to the tears hot and wet on his cheeks. "You have given me," he said, "you have given me this day a gift that I never thought to have again. I am whole!" He got up, kissed Billy on both cheeks, then stepped back. "Oh, my child,

I will pray for you. With all my heart I will pray that God will remove your paralysis from your legs. For I believe he gave you your paralysis to teach you compassion for the cripple, just as he gave me temptation to teach me compassion for the sinner. God bless you, Billy, Hallelujah!"

"Hallelujah," said Billy softly. He was crying too—couldn't help it, he felt so good. He had longed for vengeance, and instead he had forgiven, and he felt *holy*.

That is, until he realized that the TV cameras had come in right behind Bucky Fay, and were taking a close-up of Billy's tear-stained face, of Mother wringing her hands and weeping. Bucky Fay walked out the door, his clenched fist high above his head, and the crowd outside greeted him with a cheer. "Hallelujah!" shouted Bucky. "*Jesus* has made me whole!"

It played real well on the religious station. Bucky Fay's repentance—oh, how the crowds in the studio audience gasped at his confession. How the people wept at the moment when Billy reached out his hand. It was a fine show. And at the end, Bucky Fay wept again. "Oh, my friends who have trusted me, you have seen the mighty change in my heart. From now on I will wear the one suit that you see me wearing now. I have forsaken my diamond cuff links and my Lear jet and my golf course in Louisiana. I am so ashamed of what I was before God healed me with the hands of that little crippled boy. I tell all of you—send me no more money! Don't send me a single dime to post office box eight three nine, Christian City, Louisiana 70539. I am not fit to have your money. Contribute your tithes and offerings to worthier men than I. Send me *nothing!*—"

Then he knelt and bowed his head for a moment, and then looked up again, out into the audience, into the cameras, tears flowing down his face. "Unless. Unless you forgive me. Unless you believe that Jesus has changed me before your very eyes."

Mother switched off the TV savagely.

"After seeing all those other people get better," Billy whispered. "I thought he might've gotten better, too."

Mother shook her head and looked away. "What he got isn't a disease." Then she bent over the wheelchair and hugged him. "I feel so bad, Billy!"

"I don't feel bad," Billy said. "Jesus cured the blind people and the deaf people and the crippled people and the lepers. But as far as I remember, the Bible don't say he ever cured even one son-of-a-bitch."

She was still hugging him, which he didn't mind even though he near smothered in her bosom. Now she chuckled. It was all right, if Mother chuckled about it. "Guess you're right about that," Mother said. "Even Jesus did no better."

For a while they had a rest, because the people who believed went to Bucky Fay and the doubters figured that Billy was no better. The newspaper and TV people stopped coming around, too, because Billy never put on a show for them and never said anything that people would pay money to read. Then, after a while, the sick people started coming back, just a few a week at first, and then more and more. They were uncertain, skeptical. They hadn't heard of Billy on TV lately, hadn't read about him either, and he lived in such a poor neighborhood, with no signs or anything. More than once a car with out-of-state plates drove back and forth in front of the house before it stopped and someone came in. The ones who came were those who had lost all other hope, who were willing to try anything, even something as unlikely as this. They had heard a rumor, someone had a cousin whose best friend was healed. They always felt like such damn fools visiting this crippled kid, but it was better than sitting home waiting for death.

So they came, more and more of them. Mother had to quit her job again. All day Billy waited in his bedroom for them to come in. They always looked so distant, guarding themselves against another disillusionment. Billy, too, was afraid, waiting for the day when someone would place a baby in his arms and the child would die, the healing power gone out of him. But it didn't happen, day after day it didn't happen, and the people kept coming fearful and departing in joy.

Mother and Billy lived pretty poorly, since they only took money that came from gratitude instead of money meant to buy. But Billy had a decent life, if you don't mind being paralyzed and stuck home all the time, and Mother didn't mind too much either, since there was always the sight of the blind seeing and the crippled walking and those withered-up children coming out whole and strong.

Then one day after quite a few years there came a young woman who wasn't sick. She was healthy and tall and nice-looking, in a kitcheny kind of way. She had rolled-up sleeves and hands that looked like they'd met dishwater before, and she walked right into the house and said, "Make room, I'm moving in."

"Now, girl," said Mother, "we got a small house and no room to put you up. I think you got the wrong idea of what kind of Christian charity we offer here."

"Yes, Ma'am. I know just what you do. Because I am the little girl who touched Billy that day by the riverside and started all your misery."

"Now, girl, you know that didn't start our misery."

"I've never forgotten. I grew up and went through two husbands and had no children and no memory of real love except for what I saw in the face of a crippled boy at the riverside, and I thought, 'He needs me, and I need him.' So here I am, I'm here to help, tell me what to do and step aside."

Her name was Madeleine and she stayed from then on. She wasn't noisy and she wasn't bossy, she just worked her share and got along. It was hard to know for sure why it was so, but with Madeleine there, even with no money and no legs, Billy's life was good. They sang a lot of songs, Mother and Billy and Madeleine, sang and played games and talked about a lot of things, when the visitors gave them time. And only once in all those years did Madeleine ever talk to Billy about religion. And then it was just a question.

"Billy," asked Madeleine, "are you God?"

Billy shook his head. "God ain't no cripple."

EYE FOR EYE

Just talk, Mick. Tell us everything. We'll listen.

Well to start with I know I was doing terrible things. If you're a halfway decent person, you don't go looking to kill people. Even if you can do it without touching them. Even if you can do it so as nobody even guesses they was murdered, you still got to try not to do it.

Who taught you that?

Nobody. I mean it wasn't in the books in the Baptist Sunday School—they spent all their time telling us not to lie or break the sabbath or drink liquor. Never did mention killing. Near as I can figure, the Lord thought killing was pretty smart sometimes, like when Samson done it with a donkey's jaw. A thousand guys dead, but that was okay cause they was Philistines. And lighting foxes' tails on fire. Samson was a sicko, but he still got his pages in the Bible.

I figure Jesus was about the only guy got much space in the Bible telling people not to kill. And even then, there's that story about how the Lord struck down a guy and his wife cause they held back on their offerings to the Christian church. Oh, Lord, the TV preachers did go on about that. No, it wasn't cause I got religion that I figured out not to kill people.

You know what I think it was? I think it was Vondel Cone's elbow. At the Baptist Children's Home in Eden, North Carolina, we played basketball all the time. On a bumpy dirt court, but we figured it was part of the game, never knowing which way the ball would bounce. Those boys in the NBA, they play a sissy game on that flat smooth floor.

We played basketball because there wasn't a lot else to do. Only thing they ever had on TV was the preachers. We got it all cabled in—Falwell from up in Lynchburg, Jim and Tammy from Charlotte, Jimmy Swaggart looking hot, Ernest Ainglee looking carpeted, Billy Graham looking like God's executive vice-president—that was all our TV ever showed, so no wonder we lived on the basketball court all year.

Anyway, Vondel Cone wasn't particularly tall and he wasn't particularly good at shooting and on the court nobody was even halfway good at dribbling. But he had elbows. Other guys, when they hit you it was an accident. But when Vondel's elbow met up with your face, he like to pushed your nose out your ear. You can bet we all learned real quick to give him room. He got to take all the shots and get all the rebounds he wanted.

But we got even. We just didn't count his points. We'd call out the score, and any basket he made it was like it never happened. He'd scream and he'd argue and we'd all stand there and nod and agree so he wouldn't punch us out, and then as soon as the next basket was made, we'd call out the score—still not counting Vondel's points. Drove that boy crazy. He screamed till his eyes bugged out, but nobody ever counted his cheating points.

Vondel died of leukemia at the age of fourteen. You see, I never did like that boy.

But I learned something from him. I learned how unfair it was for somebody to get his way just because he didn't care how much he hurt other people. And when I finally realized that I was just about the most hurtful person in the whole world, I knew then and there that it just wasn't right. I mean, even in the Old Testament, Moses said the punishment should fit the crime. Eye for eye, tooth for tooth. Even Steven, that's what Old Peleg said before I killed him of prostate cancer. It was when Peleg got took to the hospital that I left the Eden Baptist Children's Home. Cause I wasn't Vondel. I *did* care how much I hurt folks.

But that doesn't have nothing to do with anything. I don't know what all you want me to talk about.

Just talk, Mick. Tell us whatever you want.

Well I don't aim to tell you my whole life story. I mean I didn't really start to figure out anything till I got on that bus in Roanoke, and so I can pretty much start there I guess. I remember being careful not to get annoyed when the lady in front of me didn't have the right change for the bus. And I didn't get angry when the bus driver got all snotty and told the lady to get off. It just wasn't worth killing for. That's what I always tell myself when I get mad. It isn't worth killing for, and it helps me calm myself down. So anyway I reached past her and pushed a dollar bill through the slot.

"This is for both of us," I says.

"I don't make change," says he.

I could've just said "Fine" and left it at that, but he was being such a prick that I had to do something to make him see how ignorant he was. So I put another nickel in the slot and said, "That's thirty-five for me, thirty-five for her, and thirty-five for the next guy gets on without no change."

So maybe I provoked him. I'm sorry for that, but I'm human, too, I figure. Anyway he was mad. "Don't you smart off with me, boy. I don't have to let you ride, fare or no fare."

Well, fact was he did, that's the law, and anyway I was white and my hair was short so his boss would probably do something if I complained. I could have told him what for and shut his mouth up tight. Except that if I did, I would have gotten too mad, and no man deserves to die just for being a prick. So I looked down at the floor and said, "Sorry, sir." I didn't say "Sorry *sir*" or anything snotty like that. I said it all quiet and sincere.

If he just *dropped* it, everything would have been fine, you know? I was mad, yes, but I'd gotten okay at bottling it in, just kind of holding it tight and then waiting for it to ooze away where it wouldn't hurt nobody. But just as I turned to head back toward a seat, he lurched that bus forward so hard that it flung me down and I only caught myself from hitting the floor by catching the handhold on a seatback and half-smashing the poor lady sitting there.

Some other people said, "Hey!" kind of mad, and I realize now that they was saying it to the driver, cause they was on my side. But at the time I thought they was mad at *me*, and that plus the scare of nearly falling and how mad I already was, well, I lost control of myself. I could just feel it in me, like sparklers in my blood veins, spinning around my whole body and then throwing off this pulse that went and hit that bus driver. He was behind me, so I didn't see it with my eyes. But I could feel that sparkiness connect up with him, and twist him around inside, and then finally it came loose from me, I didn't feel it no more. I wasn't mad no more. But I knew I'd done him already.

I even knew where. It was in his liver. I was a real expert on cancer by now. Hadn't I seen everybody I ever knew die of it? Hadn't I read every book in the Eden Public Library on cancer? You can live without kidneys, you can cut out a lung, you can take out a colon and live with a bag in your pants, but you can't live without a liver and they can't transplant it either. That man was dead. Two years at the most, I gave him. Two years, all because he was in a bad mood and lurched his bus to trip up a smartmouth kid.

I felt like piss on a flat rock. On that day I had gone nearly eight months, since before Christmas, the whole *year* so far without hurting anybody. It was the best I'd ever done, and I thought I'd licked it. I stepped across the lady I smashed into and sat by the window, looking out, not seeing anything. All I could think was I'm sorry I'm sorry I'm sorry. Did he have a wife and kids? Well, they'd be a widow and orphans soon enough, because of me. I could feel him from clear over here. The sparkiness of his belly, making the cancer grow and keeping his body's own natural fire from burning it out. I wanted with all my heart to take it back, but I couldn't. And like so many times before, I thought to myself that if I had any guts I'd kill myself. I couldn't figure why I hadn't died of my own cancer already. I sure enough hated myself a lot worse than I ever hated anybody else.

The lady beside me starts to talk. "People like that are so annoying, aren't they?"

I didn't want to talk to anybody, so I just grunted and turned away.

"That was very kind of you to help me," she says.

That's when I realized she was the same lady who didn't have the right fare. "Nothing," I says.

"No, you didn't have to do that." She touched my jeans.

I turned to look at her. She was older, about twenty-five maybe, and her face looked kind of sweet. She was dressed nice enough that I could tell it wasn't cause she was poor that she didn't have bus fare. She also didn't take her hand off my knee, which made me nervous, because the bad thing I do is a lot stronger when I'm actually touching a person, and so I mostly don't touch folks and I don't feel safe when they touch me. The fastest I ever killed a man was when he felt me up in a bathroom at a rest stop on I-85. He was coughing blood when I left that place, I really tore him up that time, I still have nightmares about him gasping for breath there with his hand on me.

So anyway that's why I felt real nervous her touching me there on the bus, even though there was no harm in it. Or anyway that's half why I was nervous, and the other half was that her hand was real light on my leg and out of the corner of my eye I could see how her chest moved when she breathed, and after all I'm seventeen and normal most ways. So when I wished she'd move her hand, I only *half* wished she'd move it back to her own lap.

That was up till she smiles at me and says, "Mick, I want to help you."

It took me a second to realize she spoke my name. I didn't know many people in Roanoke, and she sure wasn't one of them. Maybe she was one of Mr. Kaiser's customers, I thought. But they hardly ever knew my name. I kind of thought, for a second, that maybe she had seen me working in the warehouse and asked Mr. Kaiser all about me or something. So I says, "Are you one of Mr. Kaiser's customers?"

"Mick Winger," she says. "You got your first name from a note pinned to your blanket when you were left at the door of the sewage plant in Eden. You chose your last name when you ran away from the Eden Baptist Children's Home, and you probably chose it because the first movie you ever saw was *An Officer and a Gentleman*. You were fifteen then, and now you're seventeen, and you've killed more people in your life than Al Capone."

I got nervous when she knew my whole name and how I got it, cause the only way she could know that stuff was if she'd been following me for years. But when she let on she knew I killed people, I forgot all about feeling mad or guilty or horny. I pulled the cord on the bus, practically crawled over her to get out, and in about three seconds I was off that bus and hit the ground running. I'd been afraid of it for years, somebody finding out about me. But it was all the more scary seeing how she must have known about me for so *long*. It made me feel like somebody'd been peeking in the bathroom window all my life and I only just now found out about it.

I ran for a long time, which isn't easy because of all the hills in Roanoke. I ran mostly downhill, though, into town, where I could dodge into buildings and out their back doors. I didn't know if she was following me, but she'd been following me for a long time, or someone had, and I never even guessed it, so how did I know if they was following me now or not?

And while I ran, I tried to figure where I could go now. I had to leave town, that was sure. I couldn't go back to the warehouse, not even to say good-bye, and that made me feel real bad, cause Mr. Kaiser would think I just ran off for no reason, like some kid who didn't care nothing about people counting on him. He might even worry about me, never coming to pick up my spare clothes from the room he let me sleep in.

Thinking about what Mr. Kaiser might think about me going was pretty strange. Leaving Roanoke wasn't going to be like leaving the orphanage, and then leaving Eden, and finally leaving North Carolina. I never had much to let go of in those places. But Mr. Kaiser had always been real straight with me, a nice steady old guy, never bossed me, never tried to take me down, even stuck up for me in a quiet kind of way by letting it be known that he didn't want nobody teasing me. Hired me a year and a half ago, even though I was lying about being sixteen and he must've known it. And in all that time, I never once got mad at work, or at least not so mad I couldn't stop myself from hurting people. I worked hard, built up muscles I never thought I'd have, and I also must've grown five inches, my pants kept getting so short. I sweated and I ached most days after work, but I earned my pay and kept up with the older guys, and Mr. Kaiser never once made me feel like he took me on for charity, the way the orphanage people always did, like I should thank them for not letting me starve. Kaiser's Furniture Warehouse was the first peaceful place I ever spent time, the first place where nobody died who was my fault.

I knew all that before, but right till I started running I never realized how bad I'd feel about leaving Roanoke. Like somebody dying. It got so bad that for a while I couldn't hardly see which way I was going, not that I out-and-out cried or nothing.

Pretty soon I found myself walking down Jefferson Street, where it cuts through a woody hill before it widens out for car dealers and Burger Kings. There was cars passing me both ways, but I was thinking about other things now. Trying to figure why I never got mad at Mr. Kaiser. Other people treated me nice before, it wasn't like I got beat up every night or nobody ever gave me seconds or I had to eat dogfood or nothing. I remembered all those people at the orphanage, they was just trying to make me grow up Christian and educated. They just never learned how to be nice without also being nasty. Like Old Peleg, the black caretaker, he was a nice old coot and told us stories, and I never let nobody call him nigger even behind his back. But he was a racist himself, and I knew it on account of the time he caught me and Jody Capel practicing who could stop pissing the most times in a single go. We both done the same thing, didn't we? But he just sent me off and then started whaling on Jody, and Jody was yelling like he was dying, and I kept saying, "It ain't fair! I done it too! You're only beating on him cause he's black!" but he paid no mind, it was so crazy, I mean it wasn't like I wanted him to beat me too, but it made me so *mad* and before I knew it, I felt so sparky that I couldn't hold it in and I was hanging on him, trying to pull him away from Jody, so it hit him hard.

What could I say to him then? Going into the hospital, where he'd lie there with a tube in his arm and a tube in his nose sometimes. He told me stories when he could talk, and just squoze my hand when he couldn't. He used to have a belly on him, but I think I could have tossed him in the air like a baby before he died. And I did it to him, not that I meant to, I couldn't help myself, but that's the way it was. Even people I purely loved, they'd have mean days, and God help them if I happened to be there, because I was like God with a bad mood, that's what I was, God with no mercy, because I couldn't give them nothing, but I sure as hell could take away. Take it all away. They told me I shouldn't visit Old Peleg so much cause it was sick to keep going to watch him waste away. Mrs. Howard and Mr. Dennis both got tumors from trying to get me to stop going. So many people was dying of cancer in those days they came from the county and tested the water for chemicals. It wasn't no chemicals, I knew that, but I never did tell them, cause they'd just lock me up in the crazy house and you can bet that crazy house would have a *epidemic* before I been there a week if that ever happened.

Truth was I didn't know, I just didn't know it was me doing it for the longest time. It's just people kept dying on me, everybody I ever loved, and it seemed like they always took sick after I'd been real mad at them once, and you know how little kids always feel guilty about yelling at somebody who dies right after. The counselor even told me that those feelings were perfectly natural, and of course it wasn't my fault, but I couldn't shake it. And finally I began to realize that other people didn't feel that sparky feeling like I did, and they couldn't tell how folks was feeling unless they looked or asked. I mean, I knew when my lady teachers was going to be on the rag before *they* did, and you can bet I stayed away from them the best I could on those crabby days. I could feel it, like they was giving off sparks. And there was other folks who had a way of sucking you to them, without saying a thing, without doing a thing, you just went into a room and couldn't take your eyes off them, you wanted to be close—I saw that other kids felt the same way, just automatically liked them, you know? But I could feel it like they was on fire, and suddenly I was cold and needed to warm myself. And I'd say something about it and people would look at me like I was crazy enough to lock right up, and I finally caught on that I was the only one that had those feelings.

Once I knew that, then all those deaths began to fit together. All those cancers, those days they lay in hospital beds turning into mummies before they was rightly dead, all the pain until they drugged them into zombies so they wouldn't tear their own guts out just trying to get to the place that hurt so bad. Torn up, cut up, drugged up, radiated, bald, skinny, praying for death, and I knew I did it. I began to tell the minute I did it. I began to know what kind of cancer it would be, and where, and how bad. And I was always right.

Twenty-five people I knew of, and probably more I didn't.

And it got even worse when I ran away. I'd hitch rides because how else was I going to get anywheres? But I was always scared of the people who picked me up, and if they got weird or anything I sparked them. And cops who run me out of a place, they got it. Until I figured I was just Death himself, with his bent-up spear and a hood over his head, walking around and whoever came near him bought the farm. That was me. I was the most terrible thing in the world, I was families broke up and children orphaned and mamas crying for their dead babies, I was everything that people hate most in all the world. I jumped off a overpass once to kill myself but I just sprained my ankle. Old Peleg always said I was like a cat, I wouldn't die lessen somebody skinned me, roasted the meat and ate it, then tanned the hide, made it into slippers, wore them slippers clean out, and then burned them and raked the ashes, that's when I'd finally die. And I figure he's right, cause I'm still alive and that's a plain miracle after the stuff I been through lately.

Anyway that's the kind of thing I was thinking, walking along Jefferson, when I noticed that a car had driven by going the other way and saw me and turned around and came back up behind me, pulled ahead of me and stopped. I was so spooked I thought it must be that lady finding me again, or maybe somebody with guns to shoot me all up like on "Miami Vice," and I was all set to take off up the hill till I saw it was just Mr. Kaiser.

He says, "I was heading the other way, Mick. Want a ride to work?"

I couldn't tell him what I was doing. "Not today, Mr. Kaiser," I says.

Well, he knew by my look or something, cause he says, "You quitting on me, Mick?"

I was just thinking, don't argue with me or nothing, Mr. Kaiser, just let me go, I don't want to hurt you, I'm so fired up with guilt and hating myself that I'm just death waiting to bust out and blast somebody, can't you see sparks falling off me like spray off a wet dog? I just says, "Mr. Kaiser, I don't want to talk right now, I really don't."

Right then was the moment for him to push. For him to lecture me about how I had to learn responsibility, and if I didn't talk things through how could anybody ever make things right, and life ain't a free ride so sometimes you got to do things you don't want to do, and I been nicer to you than you deserve, you're just what they warned me you'd be, shiftless and ungrateful and a bum in your soul.

But he didn't say none of that. He just says, "You had some bad luck? I can advance you against wages, I know you'll pay back."

"I don't owe no money," I says.

And he says, "Whatever you're running away from, come home with me and you'll be safe."

What could I say? You're the one who needs protecting, Mr. Kaiser, and I'm the one who'll probably kill you. So I didn't say nothing, until finally he just nodded and put his hand on my shoulder and said, "That's okay, Mick. If you ever need a place or a job, you just come on back to me. You find a place to settle down for a while, you write to me and I'll send you your stuff."

"You just give it to the next guy," I says.

"A son-of-a-bitch stinking mean old Jew like me?" he says. "I don't give nothing to nobody."

Well I couldn't help but laugh, cause that's what the foreman always called Mr. Kaiser whenever he thought the old guy couldn't hear him. And when I laughed, I felt myself cool off, just like as if I had been on fire and somebody poured cold water over my head.

"Take care of yourself, Mick," he says. He give me his card and a twenty and tucked it into my pocket when I told him no. Then he got back into his car and made one of his insane U-turns right across traffic and headed back the other way.

Well if he did nothing else he got my brain back in gear. There I was walking along the highway where anybody at all could see me, just like Mr. Kaiser did. At least till I was out of town I ought to stay out of sight as much as I could. So there I was between those two hills, pretty steep, and all covered with green, and I figured I could climb either one. But the slope on the other side of the road looked somehow better to me, it looked more like I just ought to go there, and I figured that was as good a reason to decide as any I ever heard of, and so I dodged my way across Jefferson Street and went right into the kudzu caves and clawed my way right up. It was dark under the leaves, but it wasn't much cooler than right out in the sun, particularly cause I was working so hard. It was a long way up, and just when I got to the top the ground started shaking. I thought it was an earthquake I was so edgy, till I heard the train whistle and then I knew it was one of those coal-hauling trains, so heavy it could shake ivy off a wall when it passed. I just stood there and listened to it, the sound coming from every direction all at once, there under the kudzu, I listened till it went on by, and then I stepped out of the leaves into a clearing.

And there she was, waiting for me, sitting under a tree.

I was too wore out to run, and too scared, coming on her sudden like that, just when I thought I was out of sight. It was just as if I'd been aiming straight at her, all the way up the hill, just as if she somehow tied a string to me and pulled me across the street and up the hill. And if she could do that, how could I run away from her, tell me that? Where could I go? I'd just turn some corner and there she'd be, waiting. So I says to her, "All right, what do you want?"

She just waved me on over. And I went, too, but not very close, cause I didn't know what she had in mind. "Sit down, Mick," says she. "We need to talk."

Now I'll tell you that I didn't want to sit, and I didn't want to talk, I just wanted to get out of there. And so I did, or at least I thought I did. I started walking straight away from her, I thought, but in three steps I realized that I wasn't walking away, I was walking around her. Like that planet thing in science class, the more I moved, the more I got nowhere. It was like she had more say over what my legs did than me.

So I sat down.

"You shouldn't have run off from me," she says.

What I mostly thought of now was to wonder if she was wearing anything under that shirt. And then I thought, what a stupid time to be thinking about that. But I still kept thinking about it.

"Do you promise to stay right there till I'm through talking?" she says.

When she moved, it was like her clothes got almost transparent for a second, but not quite. Couldn't take my eyes off her. I promised.

And then all of a sudden she was just a woman. Not ugly, but not all that pretty, neither. Just looking at me with eyes like fire. I was scared again, and I wanted to leave, especially cause now I began to think she really was doing something to me. But I promised, so I stayed.

"That's how it began," she says.

"What's how what began?" says I.

"What you just felt. What I made you feel. That only works on people like you. Nobody else can feel it."

"Feel what?" says I. Now, I knew what she meant, but I didn't know for sure if she meant what I knew. I mean, it bothered me real bad that she could tell how I felt about her those few minutes there.

"Feel that," she says, and there it is again, all I can think about is her body. But it only lasted a few seconds, and then I knew for sure that she was doing it to me.

"Stop it," I says, and she says, "I already did."

I ask her, "How do you do that?"

"Everybody can do it, just a little. A woman looks at a man, she's interested, and so the bio-electrical system heats up, causes some odors to change, and he smells them and notices her and he pays attention."

"Does it work the other way?"

"Men are always giving off those odors, Mick. Makes no difference. It isn't a man's stink that gives a woman her ideas. But like I said, Mick, that's what everybody can do. With some men, though, it isn't a woman's smell that draws his eye. It's the bio-electrical system itself. The smell is nothing. You can feel the heat of the fire. It's the same thing as when you kill people, Mick. If you couldn't kill people the way you do, you also couldn't feel it so strong when I give off magnetic pulses."

Of course I didn't understand all that the first time, and maybe I'm remembering it now with words she didn't teach me until later. At the time, though, I was scared, yes, because she knew, and because she could do things to me, but I was also excited, because she sounded like she had some answers, like she knew why it was that I killed people without meaning to.

But when I asked her to explain everything, she couldn't. "We're only just beginning to understand it ourselves, Mick. There's a Swedish scientist who is making some strides that way. We've sent some people over to meet with him. We've read his book, and maybe even some of us understand it. I've got to tell you, Mick, just because we can do this thing doesn't mean that we're particularly smart or anything. It doesn't get us through college any faster or anything. It just means that teachers who flunk us tend to die off a little younger."

"You're like me! You can do it too!"

She shook her head. "Not likely," she says. "If I'm really furious at somebody, if I really hate him, if I really *try*, and if I keep it up for weeks, I can maybe give him an ulcer. You're in a whole different league from me. You and your people."

"I got no people," I says.

"I'm here, Mick, because you got people. People who knew just exactly what you could do from the minute you were born. People who knew that if you didn't get a tit to suck you wouldn't just cry, you'd kill. Spraying out death from your cradle. So they planned it all from the beginning. Put you in an orphanage. Let other people, all those do-gooders, let them get sick and die, and then when you're old enough to have control over it, then they look you up, they tell you who you are, they bring you home to live with them."

"So you're my kin?" I ask her.

"Not so you'd notice," she says. "I'm here to warn you about your kin. We've been watching you for years, and now it's time to warn you."

"*Now* it's time? I spent fifteen years in that children's home killing everybody who ever cared about me, and if they'd just come along—or you, or anybody, if you just said, Mick, you got to control your temper or you'll hurt people, if somebody just said to me, Mick, we're your people and we'll keep you safe, then maybe I wouldn't be so scared all the time, maybe I wouldn't go killing people so much, did you ever think of that?" Or maybe I didn't say all that, but that's what I was feeling, and so I said a lot, I chewed her up and down.

And then I saw how scared she was, because I was all sparky, and I realized I was just about to shed a load of death onto her, and so I kind of jumped back and yelled at her to leave me alone, and then she does the craziest thing, she reaches out toward me, and I scream at her, "Don't you touch me!" cause if she touches me I can't hold it in, it'll just go all through her and tear up her guts inside, but she just keeps reaching, leaning toward me, and so I kind of crawled over toward a tree, and I hung onto that tree, I just held on and let the tree kind of soak up all my sparkiness, almost like I was burning up the tree. Maybe I killed it, for all I know. Or maybe it was so big, I couldn't hurt it, but it took all the fire out of me, and then she *did* touch me, like nobody ever touched me, her arm across my back, and hand holding my shoulder, her face right up against my ear, and she says to me, "Mick, you didn't hurt me."

"Just leave me alone," says I.

"You're not like them," she says. "Don't you see that? They love the killing. They *use* the killing. Only they're not as strong as you. They have to be touching, for one thing, or close to it. They have to keep it up longer. They're stronger than *I* am, but not as strong as you. So they'll want you, that's for sure, Mick, but they'll also be scared of you, and you know what'll scare them most? That you didn't kill me, that you can *control* it like that."

"I can't always. That bus driver today."

"So you're not perfect. But you're trying. Trying not to kill people. Don't you see, Mick? You're not like them. They may be your blood family, but you don't belong with them, and they'll see that, and when they do—"

All I could think about was what she said, my blood family. "My mama and daddy, you telling me I'm going to meet them?"

"They're calling you now, and that's why I had to warn you."

"Calling me?"

"The way I called you up this hill. Only it wasn't just me, of course, it was a bunch of us."

"I just decided to come up here, to get off the road."

"You just decided to cross the highway and climb this hill, instead of the other one? Anyway, that's how it works. It's part of the human race for all time, only we never knew it. A bunch of people kind of harmonize their bio-electrical systems, to call for somebody to come home, and they come home, after a while. Or sometimes a whole nation unites to hate somebody. Like Iran and the Shah, or the Philippines and Marcos."

"They just kicked them out," I says.

"But they were already dying, weren't they? A whole nation, hating together, they make a constant interference with their enemy's bio-electrical system. A constant noise. All of them together, millions of people, they are finally able to match what you can do with one flash of anger."

I thought about that for a few minutes, and it came back to me all the times I thought how I wasn't even human. So maybe I *was* human, after all, but human like a guy with three arms is human, or one of those guys in the horror movies I saw, gigantic and lumpy and going around hacking up teenagers whenever they was about to get laid. And in all those movies they always try to kill the guy only they can't, he gets stabbed and shot and burned up and he still comes back, and that's like me, I must have tried to kill myself so many times only it never worked.

No. Wait a minute.

I got to get this straight, or you'll think I'm crazy or a liar. I didn't jump off that highway overpass like I said. I stood on one for a long time, watching the cars go by. Whenever a big old semi came along I'd say, this one, and I'd count, and at the right second I'd say, now. Only I never did jump. And then afterward I dreamed about jumping, and in all those dreams I'd just bounce off the truck and get up and limp away. Like the time I was a kid and sat in the bathroom with the little gardening shears, the spring-loaded kind that popped open, I sat there thinking about jamming it into my stomach right under the breastbone, and then letting go of the handle, it'd pop right open and make a bad wound and cut open my heart or something. I was there so long I fell asleep on the toilet, and later I dreamed about doing it but no blood ever came out, because I couldn't die.

So I never tried to kill myself. But I thought about it all the time. I was like those monsters in those movies, just killing people but secretly hoping somebody would catch on to what was going on and kill me first.

And so I says to her, "Why didn't you just kill me?"

And there she was with her face close to mine and she says, just like it was love talk, she says, "I've had you in my rifle sights, Mick, and then I didn't do it. Because I saw something in you. I saw that maybe you were trying to control it. That maybe you didn't want to use your power to kill. And so I let you live, thinking that one day I'd be here like this, telling you what you are, and giving you a little hope."

I thought she meant I'd hope because of knowing my mama and daddy were alive and wanted me.

"I hoped for a long time, but I gave it up. I don't want to see my mama and daddy, if they could leave me there all those years. I don't want to see you, neither, if you didn't so much as warn me not to get mad at Old Peleg. I didn't want to kill Old Peleg, and I couldn't even help it! You didn't help me a bit!"

"We argued about it," she says. "We knew you were killing people while you tried to sort things out and get control. Puberty's the worst time, even worse than infancy, and we knew that if we didn't kill you a lot of people would die—and mostly they'd be the people you loved best. That's the way it is for most kids your age, they get angriest at the people they love most, only you couldn't help killing them, and what does that do to your mind? What kind of person do you become? There was some who said we didn't have the right to leave you alive even to study you, because it would be like having a cure for cancer and then not using it on people just to see how fast they'd die. Like that experiment where the government left syphilis cases untreated just to see what the final stages of the disease were like, even though they could have cured those people at any time. But some of us told them, Mick isn't a disease, and a bullet isn't penicillin. I told them, Mick is something special. And they said, yes, he's special, he kills more than any of those other kids, and we shot *them* or ran them over with a truck or drowned them, and here we've got the worst one of all and you want to keep him alive."

And I was crying cause I wished they *had* killed me, but also because it was the first time I ever thought there was people arguing that I ought to be alive, and even though I didn't rightly understand then or even now why you didn't kill me, I got to tell you that knowing somebody knew what I was and still chose not to blast my head off, that done me in, I just bawled like a baby.

One thing led to another, there, my crying and her holding me, and pretty soon I figured out that she pretty much wanted to get laid right there. But that just made me sick, when I knew that. "How can you want to do that!" I says to her. "I can't get married! I can't have no kids! They'd be like me!"

She didn't argue with me or say nothing about birth control, and so I figured out later that I was right, she wanted to have a baby, and that told me plain that she was crazy as a loon. I got my pants pulled back up and my shirt on, and I wouldn't look at her getting dressed again, neither.

"I could make you do it," she says to me. "I could do that to you. The ability you have that lets you kill also makes you sensitive. I can make you lose your mind with desire for me."

"Then why don't you?" I says.

"Why don't you kill if you can help it?" she says.

"Cause nobody has the right," says I.

"That's right," she says.

"Anyway you're ten years older than me," I tell her.

"Fifteen," she says. "Almost twice your age. But that don't mean nothing." Or I guess she actually said, "That *doesn't* mean nothing," or probably, "That doesn't mean *anything*." She talks better than I do but I can't always remember the fancy way. "That doesn't mean a thing," she says. "You'll go to your folks, and you can bet they'll have some pretty little girl waiting for you, and she'll know how to do it much better than me, she'll turn you on so your pants unzip themselves, cause that's what they want most from you. They want your babies. As many as they can get, because you're the strongest they've produced in all the years since Grandpa Jake realized that the cursing power went father to son, mother to daughter, and that he could breed for it like you breed dogs or horses. They'll breed you like a stud, but then when they find out that you don't like killing people and you don't want to play along and you aren't going to take orders from whoever's in charge there now, they'll kill you. That's why I came to warn you. We could feel them just starting to call you. We knew it was time. And I came to warn you."

Most of this didn't mean much to me yet. Just the idea of having kinfolk was still so new I couldn't exactly get worried about whether they'd kill me or put me out for stud or whatever. Mostly what I thought about was her, anyway. "I might have killed you, you know."

"Maybe I didn't care," she says. "And maybe I'm not so easy to kill."

"And maybe you ought to tell me your name," says I.

"Can't," she says.

"How come?" says I.

"Because if you decide to put in with them, and you know my name, then I *am* dead."

"I wouldn't let anybody hurt you," says I.

She didn't answer that. She just says to me, "Mick, you don't know my name, but you remember this. I have hopes for you, cause I know you're a good man and you never meant to kill nobody. I could've made you love me, and I didn't, because I want you to do what you do by your own choice. And most important of all, if you come with me, we have a chance to see if maybe your ability doesn't have a good side."

You think I hadn't thought of that before? When I saw Rambo shooting down all those little brown guys, I thought, I could do that, and without no gun, either. And if somebody took me hostage like the Achille Lauro thing, we wouldn't have to worry about the terrorists going unpunished. They'd all be rotting in a hospital in no time. "Are you with the government?" I ask her.

"No," she says.

So they didn't want me to be a soldier. I was kind of disappointed. I kind of thought I might be useful that way. But I couldn't volunteer or nothing, cause you don't walk into the recruiting office and say, I've killed a couple dozen people by giving sparks off my body, and I could do it to Castro and Qaddafi if you like. Cause if they believe you, then you're a murderer, and if they don't believe you, they lock you up in a nuthouse.

"Nobody's been calling me, anyway," I says. "If I didn't see you today, I wouldn't've gone nowhere. I would've stayed with Mr. Kaiser."

"Then why did you take all your money out of the bank?" she says. "And when you ran away from me, why did you run toward the highway where you can hitch a ride at least to Madison and then catch another on in to Eden?"

And I didn't have no answer for her then, cause I didn't know rightly why I took my money out of the bank lessen it was like she said, and I was planning to leave town. It was just an impulse, to close that account, I didn't think nothing of it, just stuffed three hundreds into my wallet and come to think of it I really was heading toward Eden, I just didn't *think* of it, I was just *doing* it. Just the way I climbed up that hill.

"They're stronger than we are," she says. "So we can't hold you here. You have to go anyway, you have to work this thing out. The most we could do was just get you on the bus next to me, and then call you up this hill."

"Then why don't you come with me?" I says.

"They'd kill me in two seconds, right in front of your eyes, and none of this cursing stuff, either, Mick. They'd just take my head off with a machete."

"Do they know you?"

"They know *us*," she says. "We're the only ones that know your people exist, so we're the only ones working to stop them. I won't lie to you, Mick. If you join them, you can find us, you'll learn how, it isn't hard, and you can do this stuff from farther away, you could really take us apart. But if you join *us*, the tables are turned."

"Well maybe I don't want to be on either side in this war," I says. "And maybe now I won't go to Eden, neither. Maybe I'll go up to Washington, D.C. and join the CIA."

"Maybe," she says.

"And don't try to stop me."

"I wouldn't try," she says.

"Damn straight," I says. And then I just walked on out, and this time I didn't walk in no circles, I just headed north, past her car, down the railroad right of way. And I caught a ride heading up toward D.C., and that was that.

Except that along about six o'clock in the evening I woke up and the car was stopping and I didn't know where I was, I must have slept all day, and the guy says to me, "Here you are, Eden, North Carolina."

And I about messed my pants. "Eden!" I says.

"It wasn't far out of my way," he says. "I'm heading for Burlington, and these country roads are nicer than the freeway, anyway. Don't mind if I never drive I-85 again, to tell the truth."

But that was the very guy who told me he had business in D.C., he was heading there from Bristol, had to see somebody from a government agency, and here he was in Eden. It made no sense at all, except for what that woman told me. Somebody was calling me, and if I wouldn't come, they'd just put me to sleep and call whoever was driving. And there I was. Eden, North Carolina. Scared to death, or at least scared a little, but also thinking, if what she said was true, my folks was coming, I was going to meet my folks.

Nothing much changed in the two years since I ran off from the orphanage. Nothing much ever changes in Eden, which isn't a real town anyway, just cobbled together from three little villages that combined to save money on city services. People still mostly think of them as three villages. There wasn't nobody who'd get too excited about seeing me, and there wasn't nobody I wanted to see. Nobody living, anyway. I had no idea how my folks might find me, or how I might find them, but in the meantime I went to see about the only people I ever much cared about. Hoping that they wouldn't rise up out of the grave to get even with me for killing them.

It was still full day that time of year, but it was whippy weather, the wind gusting and then holding still, a big row of thunderclouds off to the southwest, the sun sinking down to get behind them. The kind of afternoon that promises to cool you off, which suited me fine. I was still pretty dusty from my climb up the hill that morning, and I could use a little rain. Got a Coke at a fast food place and then walked on over to see Old Peleg.

He was buried in a little cemetery right by an old Baptist Church. Not Southern Baptist, *Black* Baptist, meaning that it didn't have no fancy building with classrooms and a rectory, just a stark-white block of a building with a little steeple and a lawn that looked like it'd been clipped by hand. Cemetery was just as neat-kept. Nobody around, and it was dim cause of the thunderclouds moving through, but I wasn't afraid of the graves there, I just went to Old Peleg's cross. Never knew his last name was Lindley. Didn't sound like a black man's name, but then when I thought about it I realized that *no* last name sounded like a black man's name, because Eden is still just old-fashioned enough that an old black man doesn't get called by his last name much. He grew up in a Jim Crow state, and never got around to insisting on being called Mr. Lindley. Old Peleg. Not that he ever hugged me or took me on long walks or gave me that tender loving care that makes people get all teary-eyed about how wonderful it is to have parents. He never tried to be my dad or nothing. And if I hung around him much, he always gave me work to do and made damn sure I did it right, and mostly we didn't talk about anything except the work we was doing, which made me wonder, standing there, why I wanted to cry and why I hated myself worse for killing Old Peleg than for any of the other dead people under the ground in that city.

I didn't see them and I didn't hear them coming and I didn't smell my mama's perfume. But I knew they was coming, because I felt the prickly air between us. I didn't turn around, but I knew just where they were, and just how far off, because they was *lively*. Shedding sparks like I never saw on any living soul except myself, just walking along giving off light. It was like seeing myself from the outside for the first time in my life. Even when she was making me get all hot for her, that lady in Roanoke wasn't as lively as them. They was just like me.

Funny thing was, that wrecked everything. I didn't want them to be like me. I *hated* my sparkiness, and there they were, showing it to me, making me see how a killer looks from the outside. It took a few seconds to realize that they was *scared* of me, too. I recognized how scaredness looks, from remembering how my own bio-electrical system got shaped and changed by fear. Course I didn't think of it as a bio-electrical system then, or maybe I did cause she'd already told me, but you know what I mean. They was afraid of me. And I knew that was because I was giving off all the sparks I shed when I feel so mad at myself that I could bust. I was standing there at Old Peleg's grave, hating myself, so naturally they saw me like I was ready to kill half a city. They didn't know that it was me I was hating. Naturally they figured I might be mad at *them* for leaving me at that orphanage seventeen years ago. Serve them right, too, if I gave them a good hard twist in the gut, but I don't do that, I honestly don't, not any more, not standing there by Old Peleg who I loved a lot more than these two strangers, I don't act out being a murderer when my shadow's falling across his grave.

So I calmed myself down as best I could and I turned around and there they was, my mama and my daddy. And I got to tell you I almost laughed. All those years I watched them TV preachers, and we used to laugh till our guts ached about how Tammy Bakker always wore makeup so thick she could be a nigger underneath (it was okay to say that cause Old Peleg himself said it first) and here was my mama, wearing just as much makeup and her hair sprayed so thick she could work construction without a hardhat. And smiling that same sticky phony smile, and crying the same gooey oozey black tears down her cheeks, and reaching out her hands just the right way so I halfway expected her to say, "Praise to Lord Jesus," and then she actually *says* it, "Praise to Lord Jesus, it's my boy," and comes up and lays a kiss on my cheek with so much spit in it that it dripped down my face.

I wiped the slobber with my sleeve and felt my daddy have this little flash of anger, and I knew that he thought I was judging my mama and he didn't like it. Well, I was, I got to admit. Her perfume was enough to knock me over, I swear she must've mugged an Avon lady. And there was my daddy in a fine blue suit like a businessman, his hair all blow-dried, so it was plain he knew just as well as I did the way real people are supposed to look. Probably he was plain embarrassed to be seen in public with Mama, so why didn't he ever just say, Mama, you wear too much makeup? That's what I thought, and it wasn't till later that I realized that when your woman is apt to give you cancer if you rile her up, you don't go telling her that her face looks like she slept in wet sawdust and she smells like a whore. White trash, that's what my mama was, sure as if she was still wearing the factory label.

"Sure am glad to see you, Son," says my daddy.

I didn't know what to say, tell the truth. I *wasn't* glad to see them, now that I saw them, because they wasn't exactly what a orphan boy dreams his folks is like. So I kind of grinned and looked back down at Old Peleg's grave.

"You don't seem too surprised to see *us*," he says.

I could've told him right then about the lady in Roanoke, but I didn't. Just didn't feel right to tell him. So I says, "I felt like somebody was calling me back here. And you two are the only people I met who's as sparky as me. If you all say you're my folks, then I figure it must be so."

Mama giggled and she says to him, "Listen, Jesse, he calls it 'sparky.'"

"The word we use is 'dusty,' Son," says Daddy. "We say a body's looking dusty when he's one of us."

"You were a very dusty baby," says Mama. "That's why we knew we couldn't keep you. Never seen such a dusty baby before. Papa Lem made us take you to the orphanage before you even sucked one time. You never sucked even once." And her mascara just flooded down her face.

"Now Deeny," says Daddy, "no need telling him everything right here."

Dusty. That was no sense at all. It didn't look like *dust,* it was flecks of light, so bright on me that sometimes I had to squint just to see my own hands through the dazzle. "It don't *look* like dust," I says.

And Daddy says, "Well what do *you* think it looks like?"

And I says, "Sparks. That's why I call it being sparky."

"Well that's what it looks like to us, too," says Daddy. "But we've been calling it 'dusty' all our lives, and so I figure it's easier for one boy to change than for f—for lots of other folks."

Well, now, I learned a lot of things right then from what he said. First off, I knew he was lying when he said it looked like sparks to them. It didn't. It looked like what they called it. Dust. And that meant that I was seeing it a whole lot *brighter* than they could see it, and that was good for me to know, especially because it was plain that Daddy *didn't* want me to know it and so he pretended that he saw it the same way. He wanted me to think he was just as good at seeing as I was. Which meant that he sure wasn't. And I also learned that he didn't want me to know how many kinfolk I had, cause he started to say a number that started with *F,* and then caught himself and didn't say it. Fifty? Five hundred? The number wasn't half so important as the fact that he didn't want me to know it. They didn't trust me. Well, why should they? Like the lady said, I was better at this than they were, and they didn't know how mad I was about being abandoned, and the last thing they wanted to do was turn me loose killing folks. Especially themselves.

Well I stood there thinking about that stuff and pretty soon it makes them nervous and Mama says, "Now, Daddy, he can call it whatever he wants, don't go making him mad or something."

And Daddy laughs and says, "He isn't mad, are you, Son?"

Can't they see for themselves? Course not. Looks like *dust* to them, so they can't see it clear at all.

"You don't seem too happy to see us," says Daddy.

"Now, Jesse," says Mama, "don't go pushing. Papa Lem said don't you push the boy, you just make his acquaintance, you let him know why we had to push him out of the nest so young, so now you explain it, Daddy, just like Papa Lem said to."

For the first time right then it occurred to me that my own folks didn't *want* to come fetch me. They came because this Papa Lem made them do it. And you can bet they hopped and said yes, knowing how Papa Lem used his—but I'll get to Papa Lem in good time, and you said I ought to take this all in order, which I'm mostly trying to do.

Anyway Daddy explained it just like the lady in Roanoke, except he didn't say a word about bio-electrical systems, he said that I was "plainly chosen" from the moment of my birth, that I was "one of the elect," which I remembered from Baptist Sunday School meant that I was one that God had saved, though I never heard of anybody who was saved the minute they was born and not even baptized or nothing. They saw how dusty I was and they knew I'd kill a lot of people before I got old enough to control it. I asked them if they did it a lot, putting a baby out to be raised by strangers.

"Oh, maybe a dozen times," says Daddy.

"And it always works out okay?" says I.

He got set to lie again, I could see it by ripples in the light, I didn't know lying could be so plain, which made me glad they saw dust instead of sparks. "Most times," he says.

"I'd like to meet one of them others," says I. "I figure we got a lot in common, growing up thinking our parents hated us, when the truth was they was scared of their own baby."

"Well they're mostly grown up and gone off," he says, but it's a lie, and most important of all was the fact that here I as much as said I thought they wasn't worth horse pucky as parents and the only thing Daddy can think of to say is why I can't see none of the other "orphans," which tells me that whatever he's lying to cover up must be real important.

But I didn't push him right then, I just looked back down at Old Peleg's grave and wondered if he ever told a lie in his life.

Daddy says, "I'm not surprised to find you here." I guess he was nervous, and had to change the subject. "He's one you dusted, isn't he?"

Dusted. That word made me so mad. What I done to Old Peleg wasn't *dusting*. And being mad must have changed me enough they could see the change. But they didn't know what it meant, cause Mama says to me, "Now, Son, I don't mean to criticize, but it isn't right to take pride in the gifts of God. That's why we came to find you, because we need to teach you why God chose you to be one of the elect, and you shouldn't glory in yourself because you could strike down your enemies. Rather you should give all glory to the Lord, praise his name, because we are his servants."

I like to puked, I was so mad at that. Glory! Old Peleg, who was worth ten times these two phony white people who tossed me out before I ever sucked tit, and they thought I should give the *glory* for his terrible agony and death to God? I didn't know God all that well, mostly because I thought of him as looking as pinched up and serious as Mrs. Bethel who taught Sunday School when I was little, until she died of leukemia, and I just never had a thing to say to God. But if God gave me that power to strike down Old Peleg, and God wanted the glory for it when I was done, then I *did* have a few words to say to God. Only I didn't believe it for a minute. Old Peleg believed in God, and the God he believed in didn't go striking an old black man dead because a dumb kid got pissed off at him.

But I'm getting off track in the story, because that was when my father touched me for the first time. His hand was shaking. And it had every right to shake, because I was so mad that a year ago he would've been bleeding from the colon before he took his hand away. But I'd got so I could keep from killing whoever touched me when I was mad, and the funny thing was that his hand *shaking* kind of changed how I felt anyway. I'd been thinking about how mad I was that they left me and how mad I was that they thought I'd be proud of killing people but now I realized how brave they was to come fetch me, cause how did they know I wouldn't kill them? But they came anyway. And that's something. Even if Papa Lem told them to do it, they came, and now I realized that it was real brave for Mama to come kiss me on the cheek right then, because if I was going to kill her, she touched me and gave me a chance to do it before she even tried to explain anything. Maybe it was her strategy to win me over or something, but it was still brave. And she also didn't approve of people being proud of murder, which was more points in her favor. And she had the guts to tell me so right to my face. So I chalked up some points for Mama. She might look like as sickening as Tammy Bakker, but she faced her killer son with more guts than Daddy had.

He touched my shoulder and they led me to their car. A Lincoln Town Car, which they probably thought would impress me, but all I thought about was what it would've been like at the Children's Home if we'd had the price of that car, even fifteen years ago. Maybe a paved basketball court. Maybe some decent toys that wasn't broken-up hand-me-downs. Maybe some pants with knees in them. I never felt so poor in my life as when I slid onto that fuzzy seat and heard the stereo start playing elevator music in my ear.

There was somebody else in the car. Which made sense. If I'd killed them or something, they'd need somebody else to drive the car home, right? He wasn't much, when it came to being dusty or sparky or whatever. Just a little, and in rhythms of fear, too. And I could see *why* he was scared, cause he was holding a blindfold in his hands, and he says, "Mr. Yow, I'm afraid I got to put this on you."

Well, I didn't answer for a second, which made him more scared cause he thought I was mad, but mostly it took me that long to realize he meant *me* when he said "Mr. Yow."

"That's our name, Son," says my daddy. "I'm Jesse Yow, and your mother is Minnie Rae Yow, and that makes you Mick Yow."

"Don't it figure," says I. I was joking, but they took it wrong, like as if I was making fun of their name. But I been Mick Winger so long that it just feels silly calling myself Yow, and the fact is it *is* a funny name. They said it like I should be proud of it, though, which makes me laugh, but to them it was the name of God's Chosen People, like the way the Jews called themselves Israelites in the Bible. I didn't know that then, but that's the way they said it, real proud. And they was ticked off when I made a joke, so I helped them feel better by letting Billy put on—Billy's the name of the man in the man in the car—put on the blindfold.

It was a lot of country roads, and a lot of country talk. About kinfolk I never met, and how I'd love this person and that person, which sounded increasingly unlikely to me, if you know what I mean. A long-lost child is coming home and you put a *blindfold* on him. I knew we were going mostly east, cause of the times I could feel the sun coming in my window and on the back of my neck, but that was about it, and that wasn't much. They lied to me, they wouldn't show me nothing, they was scared of me. I mean, any way you look at it, they wasn't exactly killing the fatted calf for the prodigal son. I was definitely on probation. Or maybe even on trial. Which, I might point out, is exactly the way you been treating me, too, and I don't like it much better now than I did then, if you don't mind me putting some personal complaints into this. I mean, somewhere along the line somebody's going to have to decide whether to shoot me or let me go, because I can't control my temper forever locked up like a rat in a box, and the difference is a rat can't reach out of the box and blast you the way I can, so somewhere along the way somebody's going to have to figure out that you better either trust me or kill me. My personal preference is for trusting me, since I've given you more reason to trust me than you've given me to trust *you* so far.

But anyway I rode along in the car for more than an hour. We could have gotten to Winston or Greensboro or Danville by then, it was so long, and by the time we got there nobody was talking and from the snoring, Billy was even asleep. I wasn't asleep, though. I was watching. Cause I don't see sparks with my eyes, I see it with something else, like as if my sparks see other folks' sparks, if you catch my drift, and so that blindfold might've kept me from seeing the road, but it sure didn't keep me from seeing the other folks in the car with me. I knew right where they were, and right what they were feeling. Now, I've always had a knack for telling things about people, even when I couldn't see nary a spark or nothing, but this was the first time I ever saw anybody who was sparky besides me. So I sat there watching how Mama and Daddy acted with each other even when they wasn't touching or saying a thing, just little drifts of anger or fear or—well, I looked for love, but I didn't see it, and I know what it looks like, cause I've felt it. They were like two armies camped on opposite hills, waiting for the truce to end at dawn. Careful. Sending out little scouting parties.

Then the more I got used to understanding what my folks was thinking and feeling, toward each other, the easier it got for me to read what Billy had going on inside him. It's like after you learn to read big letters, you can read little letters, too, and I wondered if maybe I could even learn to understand people who didn't have hardly any sparks at all. I mean that occurred to me, anyway, and since then I've found out that it's mostly true. Now that I've had some practice I can read a sparky person from a long ways off, and even regular folks I can do a little reading, even through walls and windows. But I found that out later. Like when you guys have been watching me through mirrors. I can also see your microphone wires in the walls.

Anyway it was during that car ride that I first started seeing what I could see with my eyes closed, the shape of people's bio-electrical system, the color and spin of it, the speed and the flow and the rhythm and whatever, I mean those are the words I use, cause there isn't exactly a lot of books I can read on the subject. Maybe that Swedish doctor has fancy words for it. I can only tell you how it feels to me. And in that hour I got to be good enough at it that I could tell Billy was scared, all right, but he *wasn't* all that scared of me, he was mostly scared of Mama and Daddy. Me he was jealous of, angry kind of. Scared a little, too, but mostly mad. I thought maybe he was mad cause I was coming in out of nowhere already sparkier than him, but then it occurred to me that he probably couldn't even tell how sparky I was, because to him it'd look like dust, and he wouldn't have enough of a knack at it to see much distinction between one person and another. It's like the more light you give off, the clearer you can see other people's light. So I was the one with the blindfold on, but I could see clearer than anybody else in that car.

We drove on gravel for about ten minutes, and then on a bumpy dirt road, and then suddenly on asphalt again, smooth as you please, for about a hundred yards, and then we stopped. I didn't wait for a by-your-leave, I had that blindfold off in half a second.

It was like a whole town of houses, but right among the trees, not a gap in the leaves overhead. Maybe fifty, sixty houses, some of them pretty big, but the trees made them half invisible, it being summer. Children running all over, scruffy dirty kids from diapered-up snot-nose brats to most-growed kids not all that much younger than me. They sure kept us cleaner in the Children's Home. And they was all sparky. Mostly like Billy, just a little, but it explained why they wasn't much washed. There isn't many a mama who'd stuff her kid in a tub if the kid can make her sick just by getting mad.

It must've been near eight-thirty at night, and even the little kids still wasn't in bed. They must let their kids play till they get wore out and drop down and fall asleep by themselves. It came to me that maybe I wasn't so bad off growing up in an orphanage. At least I knew manners and didn't whip it out and pee right in front of company, the way one little boy did, just looking at me while I got out of the car, whizzing away like he wasn't doing nothing strange. Like a dog marking trees. He needed to so he done it. If I ever did that at the Children's Home they'd've slapped me silly.

I know how to act with strangers when I'm hitching a ride, but not when I'm being company, cause orphans don't go calling much so I never had much experience. So I'd've been shy no matter what, even if there wasn't no such thing as sparkiness. Daddy was all set to take me to meet Papa Lem right off, but Mama saw how I wasn't cleaned up and maybe she guessed I hadn't been to the toilet in a while and so she hustled me into a house where they had a good shower and when I came out she had a cold ham sandwich waiting for me on the table. On a plate, and the plate was setting on a linen place mat, and there was a tall glass of milk there, so cold it was sweating on the outside of the glass. I mean, if an orphan kid ever dreamed of what it might be like to have a mama, that was the dream. Never mind that she didn't look like a model in the Sears catalog. I felt clean, the sandwich tasted good, and when I was done eating she even offered me a cookie.

It felt good, I'll admit that, but at the same time I felt cheated. It was just too damn late. I needed it to be like this when I was seven, not seventeen.

But she was trying, and it wasn't all her fault, so I ate the cookie and drank off the last of the milk and my watch said it was after nine. Outside it was dusk now, and most of the kids were finally gone off to bed, and Daddy comes in and says, "Papa Lem says he isn't getting any younger."

He was outside, in a big rocking chair sitting on the grass. You wouldn't call him fat, but he did have a belly on him. And you wouldn't call him old, but he was bald on top and his hair was wispy yellow and white. And you wouldn't call him ugly, but he had a soft mouth and I didn't like the way it twisted up when he talked.

Oh, hell, he was fat, old, and ugly, and I hated him from the first time I saw him. A squishy kind of guy. Not even as sparky as my daddy, neither, so you didn't get to be in charge around here just by having more of whatever it was made us different. I wondered how close kin he was to me. If he's got children, and they look like him, they ought to drown them out of mercy.

"Mick Yow," he says to me, "Mick my dear boy, Mick my dear cousin."

"Good evening, sir," says I.

"Oh, and he's got manners," says he. "We were right to donate so much to the Children's Home. They took excellent care of you."

"You donated to the home?" says I. If they did, they sure didn't give *much*.

"A little," he says. "Enough to pay for your food, your room, your Christian education. But no luxuries. You couldn't grow up soft, Mick. You had to grow up lean and strong. And you had to know suffering, so you could be compassionate. The Lord God has given you a marvelous gift, a great helping of his grace, a heaping plateful of the power of God, and we had to make sure you were truly worthy to sit up to the table at the banquet of the Lord."

I almost looked around to see if there was a camera, he sounded so much like the preachers on TV.

And he says, "Mick, you have already passed the first test. You have forgiven your parents for leaving you to think you were an orphan. You have kept that holy commandment, Honor thy father and mother, that thy days may be long upon the land which the Lord thy God hath given thee. You know that if you had raised a hand against them, the Lord would have struck you down. For verily I say unto you that there was two rifles pointed at you the whole time, and if your father and mother had walked away without you, you would have flopped down dead in that nigger cemetery, for God will not be mocked."

I couldn't tell if he was trying to provoke me or scare me or what, but either way, it was working.

"The Lord has chosen you for his servant, Mick, just like he's chosen all of us. The rest of the world doesn't understand this. But Grandpa Jake saw it. Long ago, back in 1820, he saw how everybody he hated had a way of dying without him lifting a finger.

And for a time he thought that maybe he was like those old witches, who curse people and they wither up and die by the power of the devil. But he was a god-fearing man, and he had no truck with Satan. He was living in rough times, when a man was likely to kill in a quarrel, but Grandpa Jake never killed. Never even struck out with his fists. He was a peaceable man, and he kept his anger inside him, as the Lord commands in the New Testament. So surely he was not a servant of Satan!"

Papa Lem's voice rang through that little village, he was talking so loud, and I noticed there was a bunch of people all around. Not many kids now, all grownups, maybe there to hear Lem, but even more likely they was there to see me. Because it was like the lady in Roanoke said, there wasn't a one of them was half as sparky as me. I didn't know if they could all see that, but *I* could. Compared to normal folks they was all dusty enough, I suppose, but compared to me, or even to my mama and daddy, they was a pretty dim bunch.

"He studied the scriptures to find out what it meant that his enemies all suffered from tumors and bleeding and coughing and rot, and he came upon the verse of Genesis where the Lord said unto Abraham, 'I will bless them that bless thee, and curse him that curseth thee.' And he knew in his heart that the Lord had chosen him the way he chose Abraham. And when Isaac gave the blessing of God to Jacob, he said, 'Let people serve thee, and nations bow down to thee: cursed be every one that curseth thee, and blessed be he that blesseth thee.' The promises to the patriarchs were fulfilled again in Grandpa Jake, for whoever cursed him was cursed by God."

When he said those words from the Bible, Papa Lem sounded like the voice of God himself, I've got to tell you. I felt exalted, knowing that it was God who gave such power to my family. It was to the whole family, the way Papa Lem told it, because the Lord promised Abraham that his children would be as many as there was stars in the sky, which is a lot more than Abraham knew about seeing how he didn't have no telescope. And that promise now applied to Grandpa Jake, just like the one that said "in thee shall all families of the earth be blessed." So Grandpa Jake set to studying the book of Genesis so he could fulfil those promises just like the patriarchs did. He saw how they went to a lot of trouble to make sure they only married kinfolk—you know how Abraham married his brother's daughter, Sarah, and Isaac married his cousin Rebekah, and Jacob married his cousins Leah and Rachel. So Grandpa Jake left his first wife cause she was unworthy, meaning she probably wasn't particularly sparky, and he took up with his brother's daughter and when his brother threatened to kill him if he laid a hand on the girl, Grandpa Jake run off with her and his own brother died of a curse which is just exactly what happened to Sarah's father in the Bible. I mean Grandpa Jake worked it out just right. And he made sure all his sons married their first cousins, and so all of them had sparkiness twice over, just like breeding pointers with pointers and not mixing them with other breeds, so the strain stays pure.

There was all kinds of other stuff about Lot and his daughters, and if we remained faithful then we would be the meek who inherit the Earth because we were the chosen people and the Lord would strike down everybody who stood in our way, but what it all came down to at the moment was this: You marry whoever the patriarch tells you to marry, and Papa Lem was the patriarch. He had my mama marry my daddy even though they never particularly liked each other, growing up cousins, because he could see that they was both specially chosen, which means to say they was both about the sparkiest there was. And when I was born, they knew it was like a confirmation of Papa Lem's decision, because the Lord had blessed them with a kid who gave off dust thicker than a dump truck on a dirt road.

One thing he asked me real particular was whether I ever been laid. He says to me, "Have you spilled your seed among the daughters of Ishmael and Esau?"

I knew what spilling seed was, cause we got lectures about that at the Children's Home. I wasn't sure who the daughters of Ishmael and Esau was, but since I never had a hot date, I figured I was pretty safe saying no. Still, I did consider a second, because what came to mind was the lady in Roanoke, stoking me up just by wanting me, and I was thinking about how close I'd come to not being a virgin after all. I wondered if the lady from Roanoke was a daughter of Esau.

Papa Lem picked up on my hesitation, and he wouldn't let it go. "Don't lie to me boy. I can see a lie." Well, since I could see a lie, I didn't doubt but what maybe he could too. But then again, I've had plenty of grownups tell me they could spot a lie— but half the time they accused me of lying when I was telling the truth, and the other half they believed me when I was telling whoppers so big it'd take two big men to carry them upstairs. So maybe he could and maybe he couldn't. I figured I'd tell him just as much truth as I wanted. "I was just embarrassed to tell you I never had a girl," I says.

"Ah, the deceptions of the world," he says. "They make promiscuity seem so normal that a boy is ashamed to admit that he is chaste." Then he got a glint in his eye. "I know the children of Esau have been watching you, wanting to steal your birthright. Isn't that so?"

"I don't know who Esau is," says I.

The folks who was gathered around us started muttering about that.

I says, "I mean, I know who he was in the Bible, he was the brother of Jacob, the one who sold him his birthright for split pea soup."

"Jacob was the rightful heir, the true eldest son," says Papa Lem, "and don't you forget it. Esau is the one who went away from his father, out into the wilderness, rejecting the things of God and embracing the lies and sins of the world. Esau is the one who married a strange woman, who was not of the people! Do you understand me?"

I understood pretty good by then. Somewhere along the line somebody got sick of living under the thumb of Papa Lem, or maybe the patriarch before him, and they split.

"Beware," says Papa Lem, "because the children of Esau and Ishmael still covet the blessings of Jacob. They want to corrupt the pure seed of Grandpa Jake. They have enough of the blessing of God to know that you're a remarkable boy, like Joseph who was sold into Egypt, and they will come to you with their whorish plans, the way Potiphar's wife came to Joseph, trying to persuade you to give them your pure and undefiled seed so that they can have the blessing that their fathers rejected."

I got to tell you that I didn't much like having him talk about my seed so much in front of mixed company, but that was nothing compared to what he did next. He waved his hand to a girl standing there in the crowd, and up she came. She wasn't half bad-looking, in a country sort of way. Her hair was mousy and she wasn't altogether clean and she stood with a two-bucket slouch, but her face wasn't bad and she looked to have her teeth. Sweet, but not my type, if you know what I mean.

Papa Lem introduced us. It was his daughter, which I might've guessed, and then he says to her, "Wilt thou go with this man?" And she looks at me and says, "I will go." And then she gave me this big smile, and all of a sudden it was happening again, just like it did with the lady in Roanoke, only twice as much, cause after all the lady in Roanoke wasn't hardly sparky. I was standing there and all I could think about was how I wanted all her clothes off her and to do with her right there in front of everybody and I didn't even care that all those people were watching, that's how strong it was.

And I liked it, I got to tell you. I mean you don't ignore a feeling like that. But another part of me was standing back and it says to me, "Mick Winger you damn fool, that girl's as homely as the bathroom sink, and all these people are watching her make an idiot out of you," and it was that part of me that got mad, because I didn't like her making me do something, and I didn't like it happening right out in front of everybody, and I specially didn't like Papa Lem sitting there looking at his own daughter and me like we was in a dirty magazine.

Thing is, when I get mad I get all sparky, and the madder I got, the more I could see how she was doing it, like she was a magnet, drawing me to her. And as soon as I thought of it like us being magnets, I took all the sparkiness from being mad and I used it. Not to hurt her or nothing, because I didn't put it on her the way I did with the people I killed. I just kind of turned the path of her sparks plain upside down. She was spinning it just as fast as ever, but it went the other way, and the second that started, why, it was like she disappeared. I mean, I could see her all right, but I couldn't hardly *notice* her. I couldn't focus my eyes on her.

Papa Lem jumped right to his feet, and the other folks were gasping. Pretty quick that girl stopped sparking at me, you can bet, and there she was on her knees, throwing up. She must've had a real weak digestion, or else what I done was stronger than I thought. She was really pouring on the juice, I guess, and when I flung it back at her and turned her upside down, well, she couldn't hardly walk when they got her up. She was pretty hysterical, too, crying about how awful and ugly I was, which might've hurt my feelings except that I was scared to death.

Papa Lem was looking like the wrath of God. "You have rejected the holy sacrament of marriage! You have spurned the handmaid God prepared for you!"

Now you've got to know that I hadn't put everything together yet, or I wouldn't have been so afraid of him, but for all I knew right then he could kill me with a cancer. And it was a sure thing he could've had those people beat me to death or whatever he wanted, so maybe I was right to be scared. Anyway I had to think of a way to make him not be mad at me, and what I came up with must not've been too bad because it worked, didn't it?

I says to him, as calm as I can, "Papa Lem, she was not an acceptable handmaiden." I didn't watch all those TV preachers for nothing. I knew how to talk like the Bible. I says, "She was not blessed enough to be my wife. She wasn't even as blessed as my mama. You can't tell me that she's the best the Lord prepared for me."

And sure enough, he calmed right down. "I know that," he says. And he isn't talking like a preacher any more, it's *me* talking like a preacher and him talking all meek. "You think I don't know it? It's those children of Esau, that's what it is, Mick, you got to know that. We had five girls who were a lot dustier than her, but we had to put them out into other families, cause they were like you, so strong they would've killed their own parents without meaning to."

And I says, "Well, you brought me back, didn't you?"

And he says, "Well you were *alive*, Mick, and you got to admit that makes it easier."

"You mean those girls're all dead?" I says.

"The children of Esau," he says. "Shot three of them, strangled one, and we never found the body of the other. They never lived to be ten years old."

And I thought about how the lady in Roanoke told me she had me in her gunsights a few times. But she let me live. Why? For my seed? Those girls would've had seed too, or whatever. But they killed those girls and let me live. I didn't know why. Hell, I still don't, not if you mean to keep me locked up like this for the rest of my life. I mean you might as well have blasted my head off when I was six, and then I can name you a dozen good folks who'd still be alive, so no thanks for the favor if you don't plan to let me go.

Anyway, I says to him, "I didn't know that. I'm sorry."

And he says to me, "Mick, I can see how you'd be disappointed, seeing how you're so blessed by the Lord. But I promise you that my daughter is indeed the best girl of marriageable age that we've got here. I wasn't trying to foist her off on you because she's my daughter—it would be blasphemous for me to try it, and I'm a true servant of the Lord. The people here can testify for me, they can tell you that I'd never give you my own daughter unless she was the best we've got."

If she was the best they got then I had to figure the laws against inbreeding made pretty good sense. But I says to him, "Then maybe we ought to wait and see if there's somebody younger, too young to marry right now." I remembered the story of Jacob from Sunday School, and since they set such store by Jacob I figured it'd work. I says, "Remember that Jacob served seven years before he got to marry Rachel. I'm willing to wait."

That impressed hell out of him, you can bet. He says, "You truly have the prophetic spirit, Mick. I have no doubt that someday you'll be Papa in my place, when the Lord has gathered me unto my fathers. But I hope you'll also remember that Jacob married Rachel, but he first married the older daughter, Leah."

The ugly one, I thought, but I didn't say it. I just smiled and told him how I'd remember that, and there was plenty of time to talk about it tomorrow, because it was dark now and I was tired and a lot of things had happened to me today that I had to think over. I was really getting into the spirit of this Bible thing, and so I says to him, "Remember that before Jacob could dream of the ladder into heaven, he had to sleep."

Everybody laughed, but Papa Lem wasn't satisfied yet. He was willing to let the marriage thing wait for a few days. But there was one thing that couldn't wait. He looks me in the eye and he says, "Mick, you got a choice to make. The Lord says those who aren't for me are against me. Joshua said choose ye this day whom ye will serve. And Moses said, 'I call heaven and earth to record this day against you, that I have set before you life and death, blessing and cursing: therefore choose life, that both thou and thy seed may live.' "

Well I don't think you can put it much plainer than that. I could choose to live there among the chosen people, surrounded by dirty kids and a slimy old man telling me who to marry and whether I could raise my own children, or I could choose to leave and get my brains blasted out or maybe just pick up a stiff dose of cancer—I wasn't altogether sure whether they'd do it quick or slow. I kind of figured they'd do it quick, though, so I'd have no chance to spill my seed among the daughters of Esau.

So I gave him my most solemn and hypocritical promise that I would serve the Lord and live among them all the days of my life. Like I told you, I didn't know whether he could tell if I was lying or not. But he nodded and smiled so it looked like he believed me. Trouble was, I knew *he* was lying, and so that meant he *didn't* believe me, and that meant I was in deep poo, as Mr. Kaiser's boy Greggy always said. In fact, he was pretty angry and pretty scared, too, even though he tried to hide it by smiling and keeping a lid on himself. But I knew that he knew that I had no intention of staying there with those crazy people who knocked up their cousins and stayed about as ignorant as I ever saw. Which meant that he was already planning to kill me, and sooner rather than later.

No, I better tell the truth here, cause I wasn't *that* smart. It wasn't till I was halfway to the house that I really wondered if he believed me, and it wasn't till Mama had me with a nice clean pair of pajamas up in a nice clean room, and she was about to take my jeans and shirt and underwear and make *them* nice and clean that it occurred to me that maybe I was going to wish I had more clothes on than pajamas that night. I really got kind of mad before she finally gave me back my clothes—she was scared that if she didn't do what I said, I'd do something to her. And then I got to thinking that maybe I'd made things even *worse* by not giving her the clothes, because that might make them think that I was planning to skip out, and so maybe they weren't planning to kill me before but now they would, and so I probably just made things worse. Except when it came down to it, I'd rather be wrong about the one thing and at least have my clothes, than be wrong about the other thing and have to gallivant all over the country in pajamas. You don't get much mileage on country roads barefoot in pajamas, even in the summer.

As soon as Mama left and went on downstairs, I got dressed again, including my shoes, and climbed in under the covers. I'd slept out in the open, so I didn't mind sleeping in my clothes. What drove me crazy was getting my shoes on the sheets. They would've yelled at me so bad at the Children's Home.

I laid there in the dark, trying to think what I was going to do. I pretty much knew how to get from this house out to the road, but what good would that do me? I didn't know where I was or where the road led or how far to go, and you don't cut cross country in North Carolina—if you don't trip over something in the dark, you'll bump into some moonshine or marijuana operation and they'll blast your head off, not to mention the danger of getting your throat bit out by some tobacco farmer's mean old dog. So there I'd be running along a road that leads nowhere with them on my tail and if they wanted to run me down, I don't think fear of cancer would slow down your average four-wheeler.

I thought about maybe stealing a car, but I don't have the first idea how to hotwire anything. It wasn't one of the skills you pick up at the Children's Home. I knew the idea of it, somewhat, because I'd done some reading on electricity with the books Mr. Kaiser lent me so I could maybe try getting ready for the GED, but there wasn't a chapter in there on how to get a Lincoln running without a key. Didn't know how to drive, either. All the stuff you pick up from your dad or from your friends at school, I just never picked up at all.

Maybe I dozed off, maybe I didn't. But I suddenly noticed that I could see in the dark. Not *see*, of course. Feel the people moving around. Not far off at first, except like a blur, but I could feel the near ones, the other ones in the house. It was cause they was sparky, of course, but as I laid there feeling them drifting here and there, in the rhythms of sleep and dreams, or walking around, I began to realize that I'd been feeling people all along, only I didn't know it. They wasn't sparky, but I always knew where they were, like shadows drifting in the back of your mind, I didn't even know that I knew it, but they were there. It's like when Diz Riddle got him his glasses when he was ten years old and all of a sudden he just went around whooping and yelling about all the stuff he saw. He always used to see it before, but he didn't rightly know what half the stuff was. Like pictures on coins. He knew the coins was bumpy, but he didn't know they was pictures and writing and stuff. That's how this was.

I laid there and I could make a map in my brain where I could see a whole bunch of different people, and the more I tried, the better I could see. Pretty soon it wasn't just in that house. I could feel them in other houses, dimmer and fainter. But in my mind I didn't see no walls so I didn't know whether somebody was in the kitchen or in the bathroom, I had to think it out, and it was hard, it took all my concentration. The only guide I had was that I could see electric wires when the current was flowing through them, so wherever a light was on or a clock was running or something, I could feel this thin line, really thin, not like the shadows of people. It wasn't much, but it gave me some idea of where some of the walls might be.

If I could've just told who was who I might have made some guesses about what they was doing. Who was asleep and who was awake. But I couldn't even tell who was a kid and who was a grown-up, cause I couldn't see sizes, just brightness. Brightness was the only way I knew who was close and who was far.

I was pure lucky I got so much sleep during the day when that guy was giving me a ride from Roanoke to Eden. Well, that wasn't lucky, I guess, since I wished I hadn't gone to Eden at all, but at least having that long nap meant that I had a better shot at staying awake until things quieted down.

There was a clump of them in the next house. It was hard to sort them out, cause three of them was a lot brighter, so I thought they was closer, and it took a while to realize that it was probably Mama and Daddy and Papa Lem along with some others. Anyway it was a meeting, and it broke up after a while, and all except Papa Lem came over. I didn't know what the meeting was about, but I knew they was scared and mad. Mostly scared. Well, so was I. But I calmed myself down, the way I'd been practicing, so I didn't accidently kill nobody. That kind of practice made it so I could keep myself from getting too lively and sparky, so they'd think I was asleep. They didn't see as clear as I did, too, so that'd help. I thought maybe they'd all come up and get me, but no, they just all waited downstairs while one of them came up, and he didn't come in and get me, neither. All he did was go to the other rooms and wake up whoever was sleeping there and get them downstairs and out of the house.

Well, that scared me worse than ever. That made it plain what they had in mind, all right. Didn't want me giving off sparks and killing somebody close by when they attacked me. Still, when I thought about it, I realized that it was also a good sign. They was scared of me, and rightly so. I could reach farther and strike harder than any of them. And they saw I could throw off what got tossed at me, when I flung back what Papa Lem's daughter tried to do to me. They didn't know how much I could do.

Neither did I.

Finally all the people was out of the house except the ones downstairs. There was others outside the house, maybe watching, maybe not, but I figured I better not try to climb out the window.

Then somebody started walking up the stairs again, alone. There wasn't nobody else to fetch down, so they could only be coming after me. It was just one person, but that didn't do me no good—even one grown man who knows how to use a knife is better off than me. I still don't have my full growth on me, or at least I sure hope I don't, and the only fights I ever got in were slugging matches in the yard. For a minute I wished I'd took kung fu lessons instead of sitting around reading math and science books to make up for dropping out of school so young. A lot of good math and science was going to do me if I was dead.

The worst thing was I couldn't see him. Maybe they just moved all the children out of the house so they wouldn't make noise in the morning and wake me. Maybe they was just being nice. And this guy coming up the stairs might just be checking on me or bringing me clean clothes or something—I couldn't tell. So how could I twist him up, when I didn't know if they was trying to kill me or what? But if he *was* trying to kill me, I'd wish I'd twisted him before he ever came into the room with me.

Well, that was one decision that got made for me. I laid there wondering what to do for so long that he got to the top of the stairs and came to my room and turned the knob and came in.

I tried to breathe slow and regular, like somebody asleep. Tried to keep from getting too sparky. If it was somebody checking on me, they'd go away.

He didn't go away. And he walked soft, too, so as not to wake me up. He was real scared. So scared that I finally knew there was no way he was there to tuck me in and kiss me good night.

So I tried to twist him, to send sparks at him. But I didn't have any sparks to send! I mean I wasn't mad or anything. I'd never tried to kill somebody on purpose before, it was always because I was already mad and I just lost control and it *happened*. Now I'd been calming myself down so much that I couldn't lose control. I had no sparks at all to send, just my normal shining shadow, and he was right there and I didn't have a second to lose so I rolled over. Toward him, which was maybe dumb, cause I might have run into his knife, but I didn't know yet for sure that he had a knife. All I was thinking was that I had to knock him down or push him or something.

The only person I knocked down was me. I bumped him and hit the floor. He also cut my back with the knife. Not much of a cut, he mostly just snagged my shirt, but if I was scared before, I was terrified now cause I knew he had a knife and I knew even more that I didn't. I scrambled back away from him. There was almost no light from the window, it was like being in a big closet, I couldn't see him, he couldn't see me. Except of course that I *could* see him, or at least sense where he was, and now I was giving off sparks like crazy so unless he was weaker than I thought, he could see me too.

Well, he was weaker than I thought. He just kind of drifted, and I could hear him swishing the knife through the air in front of him. He had no idea where I was.

And all the time I was trying to get madder and madder, and it wasn't working. You can't get mad by trying. Maybe an actor can, but I'm no actor. So I was scared and sparking but I couldn't get that pulse to mess him up. The more I thought about it, the calmer I got.

It's like you've been carrying around a machine gun all your life, accidently blasting people you didn't really want to hurt and then the first time you really want to lay into somebody, it jams.

So I stopped trying to get mad. I just sat there realizing I was going to die, that after I finally got myself under control so I didn't kill people all the time anymore, now that I didn't really want to commit suicide, *now* I was going to get wasted. And they didn't even have the guts to come at me openly. Sneaking in the dark to cut my throat while I was asleep. And in the meeting where they decided to do it, my long lost but loving mama and daddy were right there. Heck, my dear sweet daddy was downstairs right now, waiting for this assassin to come down and tell him that I was dead. Would he cry for me then? Boo hoo my sweet little boy's all gone? Mick is in the cold cold ground?

I was mad. As simple as that. Stop thinking about being mad, and start thinking about the things that if you think about them, they'll make you mad. I was so sparky with fear that when I got mad, too, it was worse than it ever was before, built up worse, you know. Only when I let it fly, it didn't go for the guy up there swishing his knife back and forth in the dark. That pulse of fire in me went right down through the floor and straight to dear old Dad. I could hear him scream. He felt it, just like that. He felt it. And so did I. Because that wasn't what I meant to do. I only met him that day, but he was my *father*, and I did him worse than I ever did anybody before in my life. I didn't plan to do it. You don't plan to kill your father.

All of a sudden I was blinded by light. For a second I thought it was the other kind of light, sparks, them retaliating, twisting me. Then I realized it was my eyes being blinded, and it was the overhead light in the room that was on. The guy with the knife had finally realized that the only reason not to have the light on was so I wouldn't wake up, but now that I was awake he might as well see what he's doing. Lucky for me the light blinded him just as much as it blinded me, or I'd have been poked before I saw what hit me. Instead I had time to scramble on back to the far corner of the room.

I wasn't no hero. But I was seriously thinking about running at him, attacking a guy with a knife. I would have been killed, but I couldn't think of anything else to do.

Then I thought of something else to do. I got the idea from the way I could feel the electric current in the wires running from the lightswitch through the wall. That was electricity, and the lady in Roanoke called my sparkiness bio-electricity. I ought to be able to do something with it, shouldn't I?

I thought first that maybe I could short-circuit something, but I didn't think I had that much electricity in me. I thought of maybe tapping into the house current to add to my own juice, but then I remembered that connecting up your body to house current is the same thing other folks call *electrocution*. I mean, maybe I can tap into house wiring, but if I was wrong, I'd be real dead.

But I could still do something. There was a table lamp right next to me. I pulled off the shade and threw it at the guy, who was still standing by the door, thinking about what the scream downstairs meant. Then I grabbed the lamp and turned it on, and then smashed the lightbulb on the nightstand. Sparks. Then it was out.

I held the lamp in my hand, like a weapon, so he'd think I was going to beat off his knife with the lamp. And if my plan was a bust, I guess that's what I would've done. But while he was looking at me, getting ready to fight me knife against lamp, I kind of let the jagged end of the lamp rest on the bedspread. And then I used my sparkiness, the anger that was still in me. I couldn't fling it at the guy, or well I could have, but it would've been like the bus driver, a six-month case of lung cancer. By the time he died of *that*, I'd be six months worth of dead from multiple stab wounds to the neck and chest.

So I let my sparkiness build up and flow out along my arm, out along the lamp, like I was making my shadow grow. And it worked. The sparks just went right on down the lamp to the tip, and built up and built up, and all the time I was thinking about how Papa Lem was trying to kill me cause I thought his daughter was ugly and how he made me kill my daddy before I even knew him half a day and that charge built *up*.

It built up enough. Sparks started jumping across inside the broken light bulb, right there against the bedspread. Real sparks, the kind I could *see*, not just feel. And in two seconds that bedspread was on fire. *Then* I yanked the lamp so the cord shot right out of the wall, and I threw it at the guy, and while he was dodging I scooped up the bedspread and ran at him. I wasn't sure whether I'd catch on fire or he would, but I figured he'd be too panicked and surprised to think of stabbing me *through* the bedspread, and sure enough he didn't, he dropped the knife and tried to beat off the bedspread. Which he didn't do too good, because I was still pushing it at him. Then he tried to get through the door, but I kicked his ankle with my shoe, and he fell down, still fighting off the blanket.

I got the knife and sliced right across the back of his thigh with it. Geez it was sharp. Or maybe I was so mad and scared that I cut him stronger than I ever thought I could, but it went clear to the bone. He was screaming from the fire and his leg was gushing blood and the fire was catching on the wallpaper and it occurred to me that they couldn't chase me too good if they was trying to put out a real dandy house fire.

It also occurred to me that I couldn't run away too good if I was dead inside that house fire. And thinking of maybe dying in the fire made me realize that the guy was burning to death and I did it to him, something every bit as terrible as cancer, and *I didn't care*, because I'd killed so many people that it was nothing to me now, when a guy like that was trying to kill me, I wasn't even sorry for his pain, cause he wasn't feeling nothing worse than Old Peleg felt, and in fact that even made me feel pretty good; because it was like getting even for Old Peleg's death, even though it was me killed them both. I mean how could I get *even* for Peleg dying by killing somebody else? Okay, maybe it makes sense in a way, cause it was their fault I was in the orphanage instead of growing up here. Or maybe it made sense because this guy deserved to die, and Peleg didn't, so maybe somebody who deserved it had to die a death as bad as Peleg's, or something. I don't know. I sure as hell wasn't thinking about that then. I just knew that I was hearing a guy scream himself to death and I didn't even want to help him or even *try* to help him or nothing. I wasn't enjoying it, either, I wasn't thinking, Burn you sucker! Or anything like that, but I knew right then that I wasn't even human, I was just a monster, like I always thought, like in the slasher movies. This was straight from the slasher movies, somebody burning up and screaming, and there's the monster just standing there in the flames and he *isn't burning*.

And that's the truth. I wasn't burning. There was flames all around me, but it kind of shied back from me, because I was so full of sparks from hating myself so bad that it was like the flames couldn't get through to me. I've thought about that a lot since then. I mean, even that Swedish scientist doesn't know all about this bio-electrical stuff. Maybe when I get real sparky it makes it so other stuff can't hit me. Maybe that's how some generals in the Civil War used to ride around in the open—or maybe that was that general in World War II, I can't remember—and bullets didn't hit them or anything. Maybe if you're charged up enough, things just can't *get* to you. I don't know. I just know that by the time I finally decided to open the door and actually opened it, the whole room was burning and the door was burning and I just opened it and walked through. Course now I got a bandage on my hand to prove that I couldn't grab a hot doorknob without hurting myself a little, but I shouldn't've been able to stay alive in that room and I came out without even my hair singed.

I started down the hall, not knowing who was still in the house. I wasn't used to being able to see people by their sparkiness yet, so I didn't even think of checking, I just ran down the stairs carrying that bloody knife. But it didn't matter. They all ran away before I got there, all except Daddy. He was lying in the middle of the floor in the living room, doubled up, lying with his head in a pool of vomit and his butt in a pool of blood, shaking like he was dying of cold. I really done him. I really tore him up inside. I don't think he even saw me. But he was my daddy, and even a monster don't leave his daddy for the fire to get him. So I grabbed his arms to try to pull him out.

I forgot how sparky I was, worse than ever. The second I touched him the sparkiness just rushed out of me and all over him. It never went that way before, just completely surrounded him like he was a part of me, like he was completely drowning in my light. It wasn't what I meant to do at all. I just forgot. I was trying to save him and instead I gave him a hit like I never gave nobody before, and I couldn't stand it, I just screamed.

Then I dragged him out. He was all limp, but even if I killed him, even if I turned him to jelly inside, he wasn't going to burn, that's all I could think of, that and how I ought to walk back into that house myself and up the stairs and catch myself on fire and die.

But I didn't do it, as you might guess. There was people yelling Fire! and shouting Stay back! and I knew that I better get out of there. Daddy's body was lying on the grass in front of the house, and I took off around the back. I thought maybe I heard some gunshots, but it could've been popping and cracking of timbers in the fire, I don't know. I just ran around the house and along toward the road, and if there was people in my way they just got *out* of my way, because even the most dimwitted inbred pukebrained kid in that whole village would've seen my sparks, I was so hot.

I ran till the asphalt ended and I was running on the dirt road. There was clouds so the moon was hardly any light at all, and I kept stumbling off the road into the weeds. I fell once and when I was getting up I could see the fire behind me. The whole house was burning, and there was flames above it in the trees. Come to think of it there hadn't been all that much rain, and those trees were dry. A lot more than one house was going to burn tonight, I figured, and for a second I even thought maybe nobody'd chase me.

But that was about as stupid an idea as I ever had. I mean, if they wanted to kill me before because I said Papa Lem's girl was ugly, how do you think they felt about me now that I burned down their little hidden town? Once they realized I was gone, they'd be after me and I'd be lucky if they shot me quick.

I even thought about cutting off the road, dangerous or not, and hiding in the woods. But I decided to get as much distance as I could along the road till I saw headlights.

Just when I decided that, the road ended. Just bushes and trees. I went back, tried to find the road. It must have turned but I didn't know which way. I was tripping along like a blind man in the grass, trying to feel my way to the ruts of the dirt road, and of course that's when I saw headlights away off toward the burning houses—there was at least three houses burning now. They knew the town was a total loss by now, they was probably just leaving enough folks to get all the children out and away to a safe place, while the men came after me. It's what *I* would've done, and to hell with cancer, they knew I couldn't stop them all before they did what they wanted to me. And here I couldn't even find the road to get away from them. By the time their headlights got close enough to show the road, it'd be too late to get away.

I was about to run back into the woods when all of a sudden a pair of headlights went on not twenty feet away, and pointed right at me. I damn near wet my pants. I thought, Mick Winger, you are a dead little boy right this second.

And then I heard her calling to me. "Get on over here, Mick, you idiot, don't stand there in the light, get on over here." It was the lady from Roanoke. I still couldn't see her cause of the lights, but I knew her voice, and I took off. The road didn't end, it just turned a little and she was parked right where the dirt road met up sideways with a gravel road. I got around to the door of the car she was driving, or truck or whatever it was—a four-wheel-drive Blazer maybe, I know it had a four-wheel-drive shift lever in it—anyway the door was locked and she was yelling at me to get *in* and I was yelling back that it was *locked* until finally she unlocked it and I climbed in. She backed up so fast and swung around onto the gravel in a spin that near threw me right out the door, since I hadn't closed it yet. Then she took off so fast going *forward*, spitting gravel behind her, that the door closed itself.

"Fasten your seat belt," she says to me.

"Did you follow me here?" I says.

"No, I just happened to be here picnicking," she says. "Fasten your damn *seat belt*."

I did, but then I turned around in my seat and looked out the back. There was five or six sets of headlights, making the job to get from the dirt road onto the gravel road. We didn't have more than a mile on them.

"We've been looking for this place for years," she says. "We thought it was in Rockingham County, that's how far off we were."

"Where is it, then?" I says.

"Alamance County," she says.

And then I says, "I don't give a damn what county it is! I killed my own daddy back there!"

And she says to me, "Don't get mad now, don't get mad at me, I'm sorry, just calm down." That was all she could think of, how I might get mad and lose control and kill her, and I don't blame her, cause it was the hardest thing I ever did, keeping myself from busting out right there in the car, and it would've killed her, too. The pain in my hand was starting to get to me, too, from where I grabbed the doorknob. It was just building up and building up.

She was driving a lot faster than the headlights reached. We'd be going way too fast for a curve before she even saw it, and then she'd slam on the brakes and we'd skid and sometimes I couldn't believe we didn't just roll over and crash. But she always got out of it.

I couldn't face back anymore. I just sat there with my eyes closed, trying to get calm, and then I'd remember my daddy who I didn't even *like* but he was my daddy lying there in his blood and his puke, and I'd remember that guy who burned to death up in my room and even though I didn't care at the time, I sure cared now, I was so angry and scared and I hated myself so bad I couldn't hold it in, only I also couldn't let it out, and I kept wishing I could just die. Then I realized that the guys following us were close enough that I could feel them. Or no it wasn't that they was close. They was just so *mad* that I could see their sparks flying like never before. Well as long as I could see them I could let fly, couldn't I? I just flung out toward them. I don't know if I hit them. I don't know if my bio-electricity is something I can throw like that or what. But at least I shucked it off myself, and I didn't mess up the lady who was driving.

When we hit asphalt again, I found out that I didn't know what crazy driving was before. She peeled out and now she began to look at a curve ahead and then switch off the headlights until she was halfway through the curve, it was the craziest thing I ever saw, but it also made sense. They had to be following our lights, and when our lights went out they wouldn't know where we was for a minute. They also wouldn't know that the road curved ahead, and they might even crash up or at least they'd have to slow down. Of course, we had a real good chance of ending up eating trees ourselves, but she drove like she knew what she was doing.

We came to a straight section with a crossroads about a mile up. She switched off the lights again, and I thought maybe she was going to turn, but she didn't. Just went on and on and on, straight into the pitch black. Now, that straight section was long, but it didn't go on forever, and I don't care how good a driver you are, you can't keep track of how far you've gone in the dark. Just when I thought for sure we'd smash into something, she let off the gas and reached her hand out the window with a flashlight. We was still going pretty fast, but the flashlight was enough to make a reflector up ahead flash back at us, so she knew where the curve was, and it was farther off than I thought. She whipped us around that curve and then around another, using just a couple of blinks from the flashlight, before she switched on her headlights again.

I looked behind us to see if I could see anybody. "You lost them!" I says.

"Maybe," she says. "You tell *me*."

So I tried to feel where they might be, and sure enough, they was sparky enough that I could just barely tell where they was, away back. Split up, smeared out. "They're going every which way," I says.

"So we lost a few of them," she says. "They aren't going to give up, you know."

"I know," I says.

"You're the hottest thing going," she says.

"And you're a daughter of Esau," I says.

"Like hell I am," she says. "I'm a great-great-great-granddaughter of Jacob Yow, who happened to be bio-electrically talented. Like if you're tall and athletic, you can play basketball. That's all it is, just a natural talent. Only he went crazy and started inbreeding his whole family, and they've got these stupid ideas about being the chosen of God and all the time they're just *murderers*."

"Tell me about it," I says.

"You can't help it," she says. "You didn't have anybody to teach you. I'm not blaming you."

But I was blaming me.

She says, "Ignorant, that's what they are. Well, my grandpa didn't want to just keep reading the Bible and killing any revenuers or sheriffs or whatever who gave us trouble. He wanted to find out what we *are*. He also didn't want to marry the slut they picked out for him because he wasn't particularly dusty. So he left. They hunted him down and tried to kill him, but he got away, and he married. And he also studied and became a doctor and his kids grew up knowing that they had to find out what it *is*, this power. It's like the old stories of witches, women who get mad and suddenly your cows start dying. Maybe they didn't even know they were doing it. Summonings and love spells and come-hithers, everybody can do it a little, just like everybody can throw a ball and sometimes make a basket, but some people can do it better than others. And Papa Lem's people, they do it best of all, better and better, because they're breeding for it. We've got to stop them, don't you see? We've got to keep them from learning how to control it. Because now we know more about it. It's all tied up with the way the human body heals itself. In Sweden they've been changing the currents around to heal tumors. Cancer. The opposite of what you've been doing, but it's the same principle. Do you know what that means? If they could control it, Lem's people could be healers, not killers. Maybe all it takes is to do it with love, not anger."

"Did you kill them little girls in orphanages with love?" I says.

And she just drives, she doesn't say a thing, just drives. "Damn," she says, "it's raining."

The road was slick in two seconds. She slowed way down. It came down harder and harder. I looked behind us and there was headlights back there again. Way back, but I could still see them. "They're on us again," I says.

"I can't go any faster in the rain," she says.

"It's raining on them too," I says.

"Not with my luck."

And I says, "It'll put the fire out. Back where they live."

And she says, "It doesn't matter. They'll move. They know we found them, because we picked you up. So they'll move."

I apologized for causing trouble, and she says, "We couldn't let you die in there. I had to go there and save you if I could."

"Why?" I ask her. "Why not let me die?"

"Let me put it another way," she says. "If you decided to stay with them, I had to go in there and kill you."

And I says to her, "You're the queen of compassion, you know?" And I thought about it a little. "You're just like they are, you know?" I says. "You wanted to get pregnant just like they did. You wanted to breed me like a stud horse."

"If I wanted to *breed* you," she says, "I would have done it on the hill this morning. Yesterday morning. You would've done it. And I should've made you, because if you went with them, our only hope was to have a child of yours that we could raise to be a decent person. Only it turned out you're a decent person, so we didn't have to kill you. Now we can study you and learn about this from the strongest living example of the phenomenon"—I don't know how to pronounce that, but you know what I mean. Or what she meant, anyway.

And I says to her, "Maybe I don't want you to study me, did you think of that?"

And she says to me, "Maybe what you want don't amount to a goldfish fart." Or anyway that's what she meant.

That's about when they started shooting at us. Rain or no rain, they was pushing it so they got close enough to shoot, and they wasn't half bad at it, seeing as the first bullet we knew about went right through the back window and in between us and smacked a hole in the windshield. Which made all kinds of cracks in the glass so she couldn't see, which made her slow down more, which meant they was even closer.

Just then we whipped around a corner and our headlights lit up a bunch of guys getting out of a car with guns in their hands, and she says, "Finally." So I figured they was some of her people, there to take the heat off. But at that same second Lem's people must have shot out a tire or maybe she just got a little careless for a second cause after all she couldn't see too good through the windshield, but anyway she lost control and we skidded and flipped over, rolled over it felt like five times, all in slow motion, rolling and rolling, the doors popping open and breaking off, the windshield cracking and crumbling away, and there we hung in our seat belts, not talking or nothing, except maybe I was saying O my God or something and then we smacked into something and just stopped, which jerked us around inside the car and then it was all over.

I heard water rushing. A stream, I thought. We can wash up. Only it wasn't a stream, it was the gasoline pouring out of the tank. And then I heard gunshots from back up by the road. I didn't know who was fighting who, but if the wrong guys won they'd just love to catch us in a nice hot gasoline fire. Getting out wasn't going to be all that hard. The doors were gone so we didn't have to climb out a window or anything.

We were leaned over on the left side, so her door was mashed against the ground. I says to her, "We got to climb out my door." I had brains enough to hook one arm up over the lip of the car before I unbuckled my seat belt, and then I hoisted myself out and stayed perched up there on the side of the car, up in the air, so I could reach down and help her out.

Only she wasn't climbing out. I yelled at her and she didn't answer. I thought for a second she was dead, but then I saw that her sparks was still there. Funny, how I never saw she had any sparkiness before, because I didn't know to look for it, but now, even though it was dim, I could see it. Only it wasn't so dim, it was real busy, like she was trying to heal herself. The gurgling was still going on, and everything smelled like gasoline. There was still shooting going on. And even if nobody came down to start us on fire on purpose, I saw enough car crashes at the movies to know you didn't need a match to start a car on fire. I sure didn't want to be near the car if it caught, and I sure didn't want her *in* it. But I couldn't see how to climb down in and pull her out. I mean I'm not a weakling but I'm not Mr. Universe either.

It felt like I sat there for a whole minute before I realized I didn't have to pull her out my side of the car, I could pull her out the *front* cause the whole windshield was missing and the roof was only mashed down a little, cause there was a rollbar in the car—that was real smart, putting a rollbar in. I jumped off the car. It wasn't raining right here, but it *had* rained, so it was slippery and wet. Or maybe it was slippery from the gasoline, I don't know. I got around the front of the car and up to the windshield, and I scraped the bits of glass off with my shoe. Then I crawled partway in and reached under her and undid her seat belt, and tried to pull her out, but her legs was hung up under the steering wheel and it took forever, it was terrible, and all the time I kept listening for her to breathe, and she didn't breathe, and so I kept getting more scared and frustrated and all I was thinking about was how she had to live, she couldn't be dead, she just got through saving my life and now she was dead and she couldn't be and I was going to get her out of the car even if I had to break her legs to do it, only I didn't have to break her legs and she finally slid out and I dragged her away from the car. It didn't catch on fire, but I couldn't know it wasn't going to.

And anyway all I cared about then was her, not breathing, lying there limp on the grass with her neck all floppy and I was holding on to her crying and angry and scared and I had us both covered with sparks, like we was the same person, just completely covered, and I was crying and saying, Live! I couldn't even call her by name or nothing because I didn't know her name. I just know that I was shaking like I had the chills and so was she and she was breathing now and whimpering like somebody just stepped on a puppy and the sparks just kept flowing around us both and I felt like somebody sucked everything out of me, like I was a wet towel and somebody wrung me out and flipped me into a corner, and then I don't remember until I woke up here.

What did it feel like? What you did to her?

It felt like when I covered her with light, it was like I was taking over doing what her own body should've done, it was like I was healing her. Maybe I got that idea because she said something about healing when she was driving the car, but she wasn't breathing when I dragged her out, and then she was breathing. So I want to know if I healed her. Because if she got healed when I covered her with my own light, then maybe I didn't kill my daddy either, because it was kind of like that, I *think* it was kind of like that, what happened when I dragged him out of the house.

I been talking a long time now, and you still told me nothing. Even if you think I'm just a killer and you want me dead, you can tell me about her. Is she alive?

Yes.

Well then how come I can't see her? How come she isn't here with the rest of you?

She had some surgery. It takes time to heal.

But did I help her? Or did I twist her? You got to tell me. Cause if I didn't help her then I hope I fail your test and you kill me cause I can't think of a good reason why I should be alive if all I can do is kill people.

You helped her, Mick. That last bullet caught her in the head. That's why she crashed.

But she wasn't bleeding!

It was dark, Mick. You couldn't see. You had her blood all over you. But it doesn't matter now. We have the bullet out. As far as we can tell, there was no brain damage. There should have been. She should have been dead.

So I did help her.

Yes. But we don't know how. All kinds of stories, you know, about faith healing, that sort of thing. Laying on of hands. Maybe it's the kind of thing you did, merging the bio-magnetic field. A lot of things don't make any sense yet. There's no way we can see that the tiny amount of electricity in a human bio-electric system could influence somebody a hundred miles off, but they summoned you, and you came. We need to study you, Mick. We've never had anybody as powerful as you. Tell the truth, maybe there's never been anybody like you. Or maybe all the healings in the New Testament—

I don't want to hear about no testaments. Papa Lem gave me about all the testaments I ever need to hear about.

Will you help us, Mick?

Help you how?

Let us study you.

Go ahead and study.

Maybe it won't be enough just to study how you *heal* people.

I'm not going to kill nobody for you. If you try to make me kill somebody I'll kill you first till you have to kill me just to save your own lives, do you understand me?

Calm down, Mick. Don't get angry. There's plenty of time to think about things. Actually we're glad that you don't want to kill anybody. If you enjoyed it, or even if you hadn't been able to control it and kept on indiscriminately killing anyone who enraged you, you wouldn't have lived to be seventeen. Because yes, we're scientists, or at least we're finally learning enough that we can start being scientists. But first we're human beings, and we're in the middle of a war, and children like you are the weapons. If they ever got someone like you to stay with them, work with them, you could seek us out and destroy us. That's what they wanted you to do.

That's right, that's one thing Papa Lem said, I don't know if I mentioned it before, but he said that the children of Israel were supposed to kill every man, woman, and child in Canaan, cause idolaters had to make way for the children of God.

Well, you see, that's why our branch of the family left. We didn't think it was such a terrific idea, wiping out the entire human race and replacing it with a bunch of murderous, incestuous religious fanatics. For the last twenty years, we've been able to keep them from getting somebody like you, because we've murdered the children that were so powerful they had to put them outside to be reared by others.

Except me.

It's a war. We didn't like killing children. But it's like bombing the place where your enemies are building a secret weapon. The lives of a few children—no, that's a lie. It nearly split us apart ourselves, the arguments over that. Letting you live—it was a terrible risk. I voted against it every time. And I don't apologize for that, Mick. Now that you know what they are, and you chose to leave, I'm glad I lost. But so many things could have gone wrong.

They won't put any more babies out to orphanages now, though. They're not that dumb.

But now we have *you*. Maybe we can learn how to block what they do. Or how to heal the people they attack. Or how to identify sparkiness, as you call it, from a distance. All kinds of possibilities. But sometime in the future, Mick, you may be the only weapon we have. Do you understand that?

I don't want to.

I know.

You wanted to kill me?

I wanted to protect people from you. It was safest. Mick, I really am glad it worked out this way.

I don't know whether to believe you, Mr. Kaiser. You're such a good liar. I thought you were so nice to me all that time because you were just a nice guy.

Oh, he is, Mick. He's a nice guy. Also a damn fine liar. We kind of needed both those attributes in the person we had looking out for you.

Well, anyway, that's over with.

What's over with?

Killing me. Isn't it?

That's up to you, Mick. If you ever start getting crazy on us, or killing people that aren't part of this war of ours—

I won't do that!

But if you did, Mick. It's never too late to kill you.

Can I see her?

See who?

The lady from Roanoke! Isn't it about time you told me her name?

Come on. She can tell you herself.

St. Amy's Tale

Mother could kill with her hands. Father could fly. These are miracles. But they were not miracles then. Mother Elouise taught me that there were no miracles then.

I am the child of Wreckers, born while the angel was in them. This is why I am called Saint Amy, though I perceive nothing in me that should make me holier than any other old woman. Yet Mother Elouise denied the angel in her, too, and it was no less there.

Sift your fingers through the soil, all you who read my words. Take your spades of iron and your picks of stone. Dig deep. You will find no ancient works of man hidden there. For the Wreckers passed through the world, and all the vanity was consumed in fire; all the pride broke in pieces when it was smitten by God's shining hand.

Elouise leaned on the rim of the computer keyboard. All around her the machinery was alive, the screens displaying information. Elouise felt nothing but weariness. She was leaning because, for a moment, she had felt a frightening vertigo. As if the world underneath the airplane had dissolved and slipped away into a rapidly receding star and she would never be able to land.

True enough, she thought. *I'll never be able to land, not in the world I knew.*

"Getting sentimental about the old computers?"

Elouise, startled, turned in her chair and faced her husband, Charlie. At that moment the airplane lurched, but like sailors accustomed to the shifting of the sea, they adjusted unconsciously and did not notice the imbalance.

"Is it noon already?" she asked.

"It's the mortal equivalent of noon. I'm too tired to fly this thing anymore, and it's a good thing Bill's at the controls."

"Hungry?"

Charlie shook his head. "But Amy probably is," he said.

"Voyeur," said Elouise.

Charlie liked to watch Elouise nurse their daughter. But despite her accusation, Elouise knew there was nothing sexual in it. Charlie liked the idea of Elouise being Amy's mother. He liked the way Amy's sucking resembled the sucking of a calf or a lamb or a puppy. He had said, "It's the best thing we kept from the animals. The best thing we didn't throw away."

"Better than sex?" Elouise had asked. And Charlie had only smiled.

Amy was playing with a rag doll in the only large clear space in the airplane, near the exit door. "Mommy Mommy Mamommy Mommy-o," Amy said. The child stood and reached to be picked up. Then she saw Charlie. "Daddy Addy Addy."

"Hi," Charlie said.

"Hi," Amy answered. "Ha-ee." She had only just learned to close the diphthong, and she exaggerated it. Amy played with the buttons on Elouise's shirt, trying to undo them.

"Greedy," Elouise said, laughing.

Charlie unbuttoned the shirt for her, and Amy seized on the nipple after only one false grab. She sucked noisily, tapping her hand gently against Elouise's breast as she ate.

"I'm glad we're so near finished," Elouise said. "She's too old to be nursing now."

"That's right. Throw the little bird out of the nest."

"Go to bed," Elouise said.

Amy recognized the phrase. She pulled away. "La-lo," she said.

"That's right. Daddy's going to sleep," Elouise said.

Elouise watched as Charlie stripped off most of his clothing and lay down on the pad. He smiled once, then turned over, and was immediately asleep. He was in tune with his body. Elouise knew that he would awaken in exactly six hours, when it was time for him to take the controls again.

Amy's sucking was a subtle pleasure now, though it had been agonizing the first few months, and painful again when Amy's first teeth had come in and she had learned to her delight that by nipping she could make her mother scream. But better to nurse her than ever have her eat the predigested pap that was served as food on the airplane. Elouise thought wryly that it was even worse than the microwaved veal cordon bleu that they used to inflict on commercial passengers. Only eight years ago. And they had calibrated their fuel so exactly that when they took the last draft of fuel from the last of their storage tanks, the tank registered empty; they would burn the last of the processed petroleum, instead of putting it back into the earth. All their caches were gone now, and they would be at the tender mercies of the world that they themselves had created.

Still, there was work to do; the final work, in the final checks. Elouise held Amy with one arm while she used her free hand slowly to key in the last program that her role as commander required her to use. Elouise Private, she typed. Teacher teacher I declare I see someone's underwear, she typed. On the screen appeared the warning she had put there: "You may think you're lucky finding this program, but unless you know the magic words, an alarm is going to go off all over this airplane and you'll be had. No way out of it, sucker. Love, Elouise."

Elouise, of course, knew the magic words. Einstein sucks, she typed. The screen went blank, and the alarm did not go off.

Malfunction? she queried. "None," answered the computer.

Tamper? she queried, and the computer answered, "None."

Nonreport? she queried, and the computer flashed, "AFscanP7bb55."

Elouise had not really been dozing. But still she was startled, and she lurched forward, disturbing Amy, who really had fallen asleep. "No no no," said Amy, and Elouise forced herself to be patient; she soothed her daughter back to sleep before pursuing whatever it was that her guardian program had caught. Whatever it was? Oh, she knew what it was. It was treachery. The one thing she had been sure *her* group, *her* airplane would never have. Other groups of Rectifiers—wreckers, they called themselves, having adopted their enemies' name for them—other groups had had their spies or their fainthearts, but not Bill or Heather or Ugly-Bugly.

Specify, she typed.

The computer was specific.

Over northern Virginia, as the airplane followed its careful route to find and destroy everything made of metal, glass, and plastic; somewhere over northern Virginia, the airplane's path bent slightly to the south, and on the return, at the same place, the airplane's path bent slightly to the north, so that a strip of northern Virginia two kilometers long and a few dozen meters wide could contain some nonbiodegradable artifact, hidden from the airplane, and if Elouise had not queried this program, she would never have known it.

But she should have known it. When the plane's course bent, alarms should have sounded. Someone had penetrated the first line of defense. But Bill could not have done that, nor could Heather, really—they didn't have the sophistication to break up a bubble program. Ugly-Bugly?

She knew it wasn't faithful old Ugly-Bugly. No, not her.

The computer voluntarily flashed, "Override M577b, commandmo4, intwis Ct-TttT." It was an apology. Someone aboard ship had found the alarm override program and the overrides for the alarm overrides. Not my fault, the computer was saying.

Elouise hesitated for a moment. She looked down at her daughter and moved a curl of red hair away from Amy's eye. Elouise's hand trembled. But she was a woman of ice, yes, all frozen where compassion made other women warm. She prided herself on that, on having frozen the last warm places in her—frozen so goddamn rigid that it was only a moment's hesitation. And then she reached out and asked for the access code used to perform the treachery, asked for the name of the traitor.

The computer was even less compassionate than Elouise. It hesitated not at all.

The computer did not underline; the letters on the screen were no larger than normal. Yet Elouise felt the words as a shout, and she answered them silently with a scream.

Charles Evan Hardy, b24ag61-richlandWA.

It was Charlie who was the traitor—Charlie, her sweet, soft, hard-bodied husband, Charlie who secretly was trying to undo the end of the world.

God has destroyed the world before. Once in a flood, when Noah rode it out in the Ark. And once the tower of the world's pride was destroyed in the confusion of tongues. The other times, if there were any other times, those times are all forgotten.

The world will probably be destroyed again, unless we repent. And don't think you can hide from the angels. They start out as ordinary people, and you never know which ones. Suddenly God puts the power of destruction in their hands, and they destroy. And just as suddenly, when all the destruction is done, the angel leaves them, and they're ordinary people. Just my mother and my father.

I can't remember Father Charlie's face. I was too young.

Mother Elouise told me often about Father Charlie. He was born far to the west in a land where water only comes to the crops in ditches, almost never from the sky. It was a land unblessed by God. Men lived there, they believed, only by the strength of their own hands. Men made their ditches and forgot about God and became scientists. Father Charlie became a scientist. He worked on tiny animals, breaking their heart of hearts and combining it in new ways. Hearts were broken too often where he worked, and one of the little animals escaped and killed people until they lay in great heaps like fish in the ship's hold.

But this was not the destruction of the world.

Oh, they were giants in those days, and they forgot the Lord, but when their people lay in piles of moldering flesh and brittling bone, they remembered they were weak.

Mother Elouise said, "Charlie came weeping." This is how Father Charlie became an angel. He saw what the giants had done, by thinking they were greater than God. At first he sinned in his grief. Once he cut his own throat. They put Mother Elouise's blood in him to save his life. This is how they met: In the forest where he had gone to die privately, Father Charlie woke up from a sleep he thought would be forever to see a woman lying next to him in the tent and a doctor bending over them both. When he saw that this woman gave her blood to him whole and unstintingly, he forgot his wish to die. He loved her forever. Mother Elouise said he loved her right up to the day she killed him.

When they were finished, they had a sort of ceremony, a sort of party. "A benediction," said Bill, solemnly sipping at the gin. "Amen and amen."

"My shift," Charlie said, stepping into the cockpit. Then he noticed that everyone was there and that they were drinking the last of the gin, the bottle that had been saved for the end. "Well, happy us," Charlie said, smiling.

Bill got up from the controls of the 787. "Any preferences on where we set down?" he asked. Charlie took his place.

The others looked at one another. Ugly-Bugly shrugged. "God, who ever thought about it?"

"Come on, we're all futurists," Heather said. "You must know where you want to live."

"Two thousand years from now," Ugly-Bugly said. "I want to live in the world the way it'll be two thousand years from now."

"Ugly-Bugly opts for resurrection," Bill said. "I, however, long for the bosom of Abraham."

"Virginia," said Elouise. They turned to face her. Heather laughed.

"Resurrection," Bill intoned, "the bosom of Abraham, and Virginia. You have no poetry, Elouise."

"I've written down the coordinates of the place where we are supposed to land," Elouise said. She handed them to Charlie. He did not avoid her gaze. She watched him read the paper. He showed no sign of recognition. For a moment she hoped that it had all been a mistake, but no. She would not let herself be misled by her desires.

"Why Virginia?" Heather asked.

Charlie looked up. "It's central."

"It's east coast," Heather said.

"It's central in the high survival area. There isn't much of a living to be had in the western mountains or on the plains. It's not so far south as to be in hunter-gatherer country and not so far north as to be unsurvivable for a high proportion of the people. Barring a hard winter."

"All very good reasons," Elouise said. "Fly us there, Charlie."

Did his hands tremble as he touched the controls? Elouise watched very carefully, but he did not tremble. Indeed, he was the only one who did not. Ugly-Bugly suddenly began to cry, tears coming from her good eye and streaming down her good cheek. *Thank God she doesn't cry out of the other side,* Elouise thought; then she was angry at herself, for she had thought Ugly-Bugly's deformed face didn't bother her anymore. Elouise was angry at herself, but it only made her cold inside, determined that there would be no failure. Her mission would be complete. No allowances made for personal cost.

Elouise suddenly started out of her contemplative mood to find that the two other women had left the cockpit—their sleep shift, though it was doubtful they would sleep. Charlie silently flew the plane, while Bill sat in the copilot's seat, pouring himself the last drop from the bottle. He was looking at Elouise.

"Cheers," Elouise said to him.

He smiled sadly back at her. "Amen," he said. Then he leaned back and sang softly:

> *Praise God, from whom all blessings flow.*
> *Praise him, ye creatures here below.*
> *Praise him, who slew the wicked host.*
> *Praise Father, Son, and Holy Ghost.*

Then he reached for Elouise's hand. She was surprised, but let him take it. He bent to her and kissed her palm tenderly. "For many have entertained angels unaware," he said to her.

A few moments later he was asleep. Charlie and Elouise sat in silence. The plane flew on south as darkness overtook them from the east. At first their silence was almost affectionate. But as Elouise sat and sat, saying nothing, she felt the silence grow cold and terrible, and for the first time she realized that when the airplane landed, Charlie would be her—Charlie, who had been half her life for these last few years, whom she had never lied to and who had never lied to her—would be her enemy.

I have watched the little children do a dance called Charlie-El. They sing a little song to it, and if I remember the words, it goes like this:

> *I am made of bones and glass.*
> *Let me pass, let me pass.*
> *I am made of brick and steel.*
> *Take my heel, take my heel.*
> *I was killed just yesterday.*
> *Kneel and pray, kneel and pray.*
> *Dig a hole where I can sleep.*
> *Dig it deep, dig it deep.*
> *Will I go to heaven or hell?*
> *Charlie-El. Charlie-El.*

I think they are already nonsense words to the children. But the poem first got passed word of mouth around Richmond when I was little, and living in Father Michael's house. The children do not try to answer their song. They just sing it and do a very clever little dance while they sing. They always end the song with all the children falling down on the ground, laughing. That is the best way for the song to end.

Charlie brought the airplane straight down into a field, great hot winds pushing against the ground as if to shove it back from the plane. The field caught fire, but when the plane had settled upon its three wheels, foam streaked out from the belly of the machine and overtook the flames. Elouise watched from the cockpit, thinking, *Wherever the foam has touched, nothing will grow for years.* It seemed symmetrical to her. Even in the last moments of the last machine, it must poison the earth. Elouise held Amy on her lap and thought of trying to explain it to the child. But Elouise knew Amy would not understand or remember.

"Last one dressed is a sissy-wissy," said Ugly-Bugly in her husky, ancient-sounding voice. They had dressed and undressed in front of each other for years now, but today as the old plastic-polluted clothing came off and the homespun went on, they felt and acted like school kids on their first day in coed gym. Amy caught the spirit of it and kept yelling at the top of her lungs. No one thought to quiet her. There was no need. This was a celebration.

But Elouise, long accustomed to self-examination, forced herself to realize that there was a strain to her frolicking. She did not believe it, not really. Today was not a happy day, and it was not just from knowing the confrontation that lay ahead. There was something so final about the death of the last of the engines of mankind. Surely something could be—but she forced the thought from her, forced the coldness in her to overtake that sentiment. Surely she could not be seduced by the beauty of the airplane. Surely she must remember that it was not the machines but what they inevitably did to mankind that was evil.

They looked and felt a little awkward, almost silly, as they left the plane and stood around in the blackened field. They had not yet lost their feel for stylish clothing, and the homespun was so lumpy and awkward and rough. It didn't look right on any of them.

Amy clung to her doll, awed by the strange scenery. In her life she had been out of the airplane only once, and that was when she was an infant. She watched as the trees moved unpredictably. She winced at the wind in her eyes. She touched her cheek, where her hair moved back and forth in the breeze, and hunted through her vocabulary for a word to name the strange invisible touch of her skin. "Mommy," she said. "Uh! Uh! Uh!"

Elouise understood. "Wind," she said. The sounds were still too hard for Amy, and the child did not attempt to say the word. *Wind,* thought Elouise, and immediately thought of Charlie. Her best memory of Charlie was in the wind. It was during his death-wish time, not long after his suicide. He had insisted on climbing a mountain, and she knew that he meant to fall. So she had climbed with him, even though there was a storm coming up. Charlie was angry all the way. She remembered a terrible hour clinging to the face of a cliff, held only by small bits of metal forced into cracks in the rock. She had insisted on remaining tied to Charlie. "If one of us fell, it would only drag the other down, too," he kept saying. "I know," she kept answering. And so Charlie had not fallen, and they made love for the first time in a shallow cave, with the wind howling outside and occasional sprays of rain coming in to dampen them. They refused to be dampened. Wind. Damn.

And Elouise felt herself go cold and unemotional, and they stood on the edge of the field in the shade of the first trees. Elouise had left the Rectifier near the plane, set on 360 degrees. In a few minutes the Rectifier would go off, and they had to watch, to witness the end of their work.

Suddenly Bill shouted, laughed, held up his wrist. "My watch!" he cried.

"Hurry," Charlie said. "There's time."

Bill unbuckled his watch and ran toward the Rectifier. He tossed the watch. It landed within a few meters of the small machine. Then Bill returned to the group, jogging and shaking his head. "Jesus, what a moron! Three years wiping out everything east of the Mississippi, and I almost save a digital chronograph."

"Dixie Instruments?" Heather asked.

"Yeah."

"That's not high technology," she said, and they all laughed. Then they fell silent, and Elouise wondered whether they were all thinking the same thing: that jokes about brand names would be dead within a generation, if they were not already dead. They watched the Rectifier in silence, waiting for the timer to finish its delay. Suddenly there was a shining in the air, a dazzling not-light that made them squint. They had seen this many times before, from the air and from the ground, but this was the last time, and so they saw it as if it were the first.

The airplane corroded as if a thousand years were passing in seconds. But it wasn't a true corrosion. There was no rust—only dissolution as molecules separated and seeped down into the loosened earth. Glass became sand; plastic corrupted to oil; the metal also drifted down into the ground and came to rest in a vein at the bottom of the Rectifier field. Whatever else the metal might look like to a future geologist, it wouldn't look like an artifact. It would look like iron. And with so many similar pockets of iron and copper and aluminum and tin spread all over the once-civilized world, it was not likely that they would suspect human interference. Elouise was amused, thinking of the treatises that would someday be written, about the two states of workable metals—the ore state and the pure-metal vein. She hoped it would retard their progress a little.

The airplane shivered into nothing, and the Rectifier also died in the field. A few minutes after the Rectifier disappeared, the field also faded.

"Amen and amen," said Bill, maudlin again. "All clean now."

Elouise only smiled. She said nothing of the other Rectifier, which was in her knapsack. Let the others think all the work was done.

Amy poked her finger in Charlie's eye. Charlie swore and set her down. Amy started to cry, and Charlie knelt by her and hugged her. Amy's arms went tightly around his neck. "Give Daddy a kiss," Elouise said.

"Well, time to go," Ugly-Bugly's voice rasped. "Why the hell did you pick this particular spot?"

Elouise cocked her head. "Ask Charlie."

Charlie flushed. Elouise watched him grimly. "Elouise and I once came here," he said. "Before Rectification began. Nostalgia, you know." He smiled shyly, and the others laughed. Except Elouise. She was helping Amy to urinate. She felt the weight of the small Rectifier in her knapsack and did not tell anyone the truth: that she had never been in Virginia before in her life.

"Good a spot as any," Heather said. "Well, bye."

Well, bye. That was all, that was the end of it, and Heather walked away to the west, toward the Shenandoah Valley.

"See ya," Bill said.

"Like hell," Ugly-Bugly added.

Impulsively Ugly-Bugly hugged Elouise, and Bill cried, and then they took off northeast, toward the Potomac, where they would doubtlessly find a community growing up along the clean and fish-filled river.

Just Charlie, Amy, and Elouise left in the empty, blackened field where the airplane had died. Elouise tried to feel some great pain at the separation from the others, but she could not. They had been together every day for years now, going from supply dump to supply dump, wrecking cities and towns, destroying and using up the artificial world. But had they been friends? If it had not been for their task, they would never have been friends. They were not the same kind of people.

And then Elouise was ashamed of her feelings. Not her kind of people? Because Heather liked what grass did to her and had never owned a car or had a driver's license in her life? Because Ugly-Bugly had a face hideously deformed by cancer surgery? Because Bill always worked Jesus into the conversation, even though half the time he was an atheist? Because they just weren't in the same social circles? There were no social circles now. Just people trying to survive in a bitter world they weren't bred for. There were only two classes now: those who would make it and those who wouldn't.

Which class am I? thought Elouise.

"Where should we go?" Charlie asked.

Elouise picked Amy up and handed her to Charlie. "Where's the capsule, Charlie?"

Charlie took Amy and said, "Hey, Amy, baby, I'll bet we find some farming community between here and the Rappahannock."

"Doesn't matter if you tell me, Charlie. The instruments found it before we landed. You did a damn good job on the computer program." She didn't have to say, Not good enough.

Charlie only smiled crookedly. "Here I was hoping you were forgetful." He reached out to touch her knapsack. She pulled abruptly away. He lost his smile. "Don't you know me?" he asked softly.

He would never try to take the Rectifier from her by force. But still. This was the last of the artifacts they were talking about. Was anyone really predictable at such a time? Elouise was not sure. She had thought she knew him well before, yet the time capsule existed to prove that her understanding of Charlie was far from complete.

"I know you, Charlie," she said, "but not as well as I thought. Does it matter? Don't try to stop me."

"I hope you're not too angry," he said.

Elouise couldn't think of anything to say to that. *Anyone could be fooled by a traitor, but only I am fool enough to marry one.* She turned from him and walked into the forest. He took Amy and followed.

All the way through the underbrush Elouise kept expecting him to say something. A threat, for instance: You'll have to kill me to destroy that time capsule. Or a plea: You have to leave it, Elouise, please, please. Or reason, or argument, or anger, or something.

But instead it was just his silent footfalls behind her. Just his occasional playtalk with Amy. Just his singing as he put Amy to sleep on his shoulder.

The capsule had been hidden well. There was no surface sign that men had ever been here. Yet, from the Rectifier's emphatic response, it was obvious that the time capsule was quite large. There must have been heavy, earthmoving equipment. Or was it all done by hand?

"When did you ever find the time?" Elouise asked when they reached the spot.

"Long lunch hours," he said.

She set down her knapsack and then stood there, looking at him.

Like a condemned man who insists on keeping his composure, Charlie smiled wryly and said, "Get on with it, please."

After Father Charlie died, Mother Elouise brought me here to Richmond. She didn't tell anyone that she was a Wrecker. The angel had already left her, and she wanted to blend into the town, be an ordinary person in the world she and her fellow angels had created.

Yet she was incapable of blending in. Once the angel touches you, you cannot go back, even when the angel's work is done. She first attracted attention by talking against the stockade. There was once a stockade around the town of Richmond, when there were only a thousand people here. The reason was simple: People still weren't used to the hard way life was without the old machines. They had not yet learned to depend on the miracle of Christ. They still trusted in their hands, yet their hands could work no more magic. So there were tribes in the winter that didn't know how to find game, that had no reserves of grain, that had no shelter adequate to hold the head of a fire.

"Bring them all in," said Mother Elouise. "There's room for all. There's food for all. Teach them how to build ships and make tools and sail and farm, and we'll all be richer for it."

But Father Michael and Uncle Avram knew more than Mother Elouise. Father Michael had been a Catholic priest before the destruction, and Uncle Avram had been a professor at a university. They had been nobody. But when the angels of destruction finished their work, the angels of life began to work in the hearts of men. Father Michael threw off his old allegiance to Rome and taught Christ simple, from his memory of the Holy Book. Uncle Avram plunged into his memory of ancient metallurgy and taught the people who gathered at Richmond how to make iron hard enough to use for tools. And weapons.

Father Michael forbade the making of guns and forbade that anyone teach children what guns were. But for hunting there had to be arrows, and what will kill a deer will also kill a man.

Many people agreed with Mother Elouise about the stockade. But then in the worst of winter a tribe came from the mountains and threw fire against the stockade and against the ships that kept trade alive along the whole coast. The archers of Richmond killed most of them, and people said to Mother Elouise, "Now you must agree we need the stockade."

Mother Elouise said, "Would they have come with fire if there had been no wall?"

How can anyone judge the greatest need? Just as the angel of death had come to plant the seeds of a better life, so that angel of life had to be hard and endure death so the many could live. Father Michael and Uncle Avram held to the laws of Christ simple, for did not the Holy Book say, "Love your enemies, and smite them only when they attack you; chase them not out into the forest, but let them live as long as they leave you alone"?

I remember that winter. I remember watching while they buried the dead tribesmen. Their bodies had stiffened quickly, but Mother Elouise brought me to see them and said, "This is death, remember it, remember it." What did Mother Elouise know? Death is our passage from flesh into the living wind, until Christ brings us forth into flesh again. Mother Elouise will find Father Charlie again, and every wound will be made whole.

* * *

Elouise knelt by the Rectifier and carefully set it to go off in half an hour, destroying itself and the time capsule buried thirty meters under the ground. Charlie stood near her, watching, his face nearly expressionless; only a faint smile broke his perfect repose. Amy was in his arms, laughing and trying to reach up to pinch his nose.

"This Rectifier responds only to me," Elouise said quietly. "Alive. If you try to move it, it will go off early and kill us all."

"I won't move it," Charlie said.

And Elouise was finished. She stood up and reached for Amy. Amy reached back, holding out her arms to her mother. "Mommy," she said.

Because I couldn't remember Father Charlie's face, Mother Elouise thought I had forgotten everything about him, but that is not true. I remember very clearly one picture of him, but he is not in the picture.

This is very hard for me to explain. I see a small clearing in the trees, with Mother Elouise standing in front of me. I see her at my eye level, which tells me that I am being held. I cannot see Father Charlie, but I know that he is holding me. I can feel his arms around me, but I cannot see his face.

This vision has come to me often. It is not like other dreams. It is very clear, and I am always very afraid, and I don't know why. They are talking, but I do not understand their words. Mother Elouise reaches for me, but Father Charlie will not let me go. I feel afraid that Father Charlie will not let me go with Mother Elouise. But why should I be afraid? I love Father Charlie, and I never want to leave him. Still I reach out, reach out, reach out, and still the arms hold me and I cannot go.

Mother Elouise is crying. I see her face twisted in pain. I want to comfort her. "Mommy is hurt," I say again and again.

And then, suddenly, at the end of this vision I am in my mother's arms and we are running, running up a hill, into the trees. I am looking back over her shoulder. I see Father Charlie then. I see him, but I do not see him. I know exactly where he is, in my vision. I could tell you his height. I could tell you where his left foot is and where his right foot is, but still I can't see him. He has no face, no color; he is just a man-shaped emptiness in the clearing, and then the trees are in the way and he is gone.

Elouise stopped only a little way into the woods. She turned around, as if to go back to Charlie. But she would not go back. If she returned to him, it would be to disconnect the Rectifier. There would be no other reason to do it.

"Charlie, you son of a bitch!" she shouted.

There was no answer. She stood, waiting. Surely he could come to her. He would see that she would never go back, never turn off the machine. Once he realized it was inevitable, he would come running from the machine, into the forest, back to the clearing where the 787 had landed. Why would he want to give his life so meaninglessly? What was in the time capsule, after all? Just history—that's what he said, wasn't it? Just history, just films and metal plates engraved with words and microdots and other ways of preserving the story of mankind. "How can they learn from our mistakes, unless we tell them what they were?" Charlie had asked.

Sweet, simple, naive Charlie. It is one thing to preserve a hatred for the killing machines and the soul-destroying machines and the garbage-making machines. It was another to leave behind detailed, accurate, unquestionable descriptions. History was not a way of preventing the repetition of mistakes. It was a way of guaranteeing them. Wasn't it?

She turned and walked on, not very quickly, out of the range of the Rectifier, carrying Amy and listening, all the way, for the sound of Charlie running after her.

What was Mother Elouise like? She was a woman of contradictions. Even with me, she would work for hours teaching me to read, helping me make tablets out of river clay and write on them with a shaped stick. And then, when I had written the words she taught me, she would weep and say, "Lies, all lies," Sometimes she would break the tablets I had made. But whenever part of her words was broken, she would make me write it again.

She called the collection of words The Book of the Golden Age. I have named it The Book of the Lies of the Angel Elouise, for it is important for us to know that the greatest truths we have seem like lies to those who have been touched by the angel.

She told many stories to me, and often I asked her why they must be written down. "For Father Charlie," she would always say.

"Is he coming back, then?" I would ask.

But she shook her head, and finally one time she said, "It is not for Father Charlie to read. It is because Father Charlie wanted it written."

"Then why didn't he write it himself?" I asked.

And Mother Elouise grew very cold with me, and all she would say was, "Father Charlie bought these stories. He paid more for them than I am willing to pay to have them left unwritten." I wondered then whether Father Charlie was rich, but other things she said told me that he wasn't. So I do not understand except that Mother Elouise did not want to tell the stories, and Father Charlie, though he was not there, constrained her to tell them.

There are many of Mother Elouise's lies that I love, but I will say now which of them she said were most important:

1. In the Golden Age for ten times a thousand years men lived in peace and love and joy, and no one did evil one to another. They shared all things in common, and no man was hungry while another was full, and no man had a home while another stood in the rain, and no wife wept for her husband, killed before his time.
2. The great serpent seems to come with great power. He has many names: Satan, Hitler, Lucifer, Nimrod, Napoleon. He seems to be beautiful, and he promises power to his friends and death to his enemies. He says he will right all wrongs. But really he is weak, until people believe in him and give him the power of their bodies. If you refuse to believe in the serpent, if no one serves him, he will go away.
3. There are many cycles of the world. In every cycle the great serpent has arisen and the world has been destroyed to make way for the return of the Golden Age. Christ comes again in every cycle, also. One day when He comes men will believe in Christ and doubt the great serpent, and that time the Golden Age will never end, and God will dwell among men forever. And all the angels will say. "Come not to heaven but to Earth, for Earth is heaven now."

These are the most important lies of Mother Elouise. Believe them all, and remember them, for they are true.

All the way to the airplane clearing, Elouise deliberately broke branches and let them dangle so that Charlie would have no trouble finding a straight path out of the range of the Rectifier, even if he left his flight to the last second. She was sure Charlie would follow her. Charlie would bend to her as he had always bent, resilient and accommodating. He loved Elouise, and Amy he loved even more. What was in the metal under his feet that would weigh in the balance against his love for them?

So Elouise broke the last branch and stepped into the clearing and then sat down and let Amy play in the unburnt grass at the edge while she waited. *It is Charlie who will bend*, she said to herself, *for I will never bend on this. Later I will make it up to him, but he must know that on this I will never bend*.

The cold place in her grew larger and colder until she burned inside, waiting for the sound of feet crashing through the underbrush. The damnable birds kept singing, so that she could not hear the footsteps.

Mother Elouise never hit me, or anyone else so far as I knew. She fought only with her words and silent acts, though she could have killed easily with her hands. I saw her physical power only once. We were in the forest, to gather firewood. We stumbled upon a wild hog. Apparently it felt cornered, though we were weaponless; perhaps it was just mean. I have not studied the ways of wild hogs. It charged, not Mother Elouise, but me. I was five at the time, and terrified, I ran to Mother Elouise, tried to cling to her, but she threw me out of the way and went into a crouch. I was screaming. She paid no attention to me. The hog continued rushing, but seeing I was down and Mother Elouise erect, it changed its path. When it came near, she leaped to the side. It was not nimble enough to turn to face her. As it lumbered past, Mother Elouise kicked it just behind the head. The kick broke the hog's neck so violently that its head dropped and the hog rolled over and over, and when it was through rolling, it was already dead.

Mother Elouise did not have to die.

She died in the winter when I was seven. I should tell you how life was then, in Richmond. We were only two thousand souls by then, not the large city of ten thousand we are now. We had only six finished ships trading the coast, and they had not yet gone so far north as Manhattan, though we had run one voyage all the way to Savannah in the south. Richmond already ruled and protected from the Potomac to Dismal Swamp. But it was a very hard winter, and the town's leaders insisted on hoarding all the stored grain and fruits and vegetables and meat for our protected towns, and let the distant tribes trade or travel where they would, they would get no food from Richmond.

It was then that my mother, who claimed she did not believe in God, and Uncle Avram, who was a Jew, and Father Michael, who was a priest, all argued the same side of the question. It's better to feed them than to kill them, they all said. But when the tribes from west of the mountains and north of the Potomac came into Richmond lands, pleading for help, the leaders of Richmond turned them away and closed the gates of the towns. An army marched then, to put the fear of God, as they said, into the hearts of the tribesmen. They did not know which side God was on.

Father Michael argued and Uncle Avram stormed and fumed, but Mother Elouise silently went to the gate at moonrise one night and alone overpowered the guards. Silently she gagged them and bound them and opened the gates to the hungry tribesmen.

They came through weaponless, as she had insisted. They quietly went to the storehouses and carried off as much food as they could. They were found only as the last few fled. No one was killed.

But there was an uproar, a cry of treason, a trial, and an execution. They decided on beheading, because they thought it would be quick and merciful. They had never seen a beheading.

It was Jack Woods who used the ax. He practiced all afternoon with pumpkins. Pumpkins have no bones.

In the evening they all gathered to watch, some because they hated Mother Elouise, some because they loved her, and the rest because they could not stay away. I went also, and Father Michael held my head and would not let me see. But I heard.

Father Michael prayed for Mother Elouise. Mother Elouise damned his and everyone else's soul to hell. She said, "If you kill me for bringing life, you will only bring death on your own heads."

"That's true," said the men around her. "We will all die. But you will die first."

"Then I'm the luckier," said Mother Elouise. It was the last of her lies, for she was telling the truth, and yet she did not believe it herself, for I heard her weep. With her last breaths she wept and cried out, "Charlie! Charlie!" There are those who claim she saw a vision of Charlie waiting for her on the right hand of God, but I doubt it. She would have said so. I think she only wished to see him. Or wished for his forgiveness. It doesn't matter. The angel had long since left her, and she was alone.

Jack swung the ax and it fell, more with a smack than a thud. He had missed her neck and struck deep in her back and shoulder. She screamed. He struck again and this time silenced her. But he did not break through her spine until the third blow. Then he turned away splattered with blood, and vomited and wept and pleaded with Father Michael to forgive him.

Amy stood a few meters away from Elouise, who sat on the grass of the clearing, looking toward a broken branch on the nearest tree. Amy called, "Mommy! Mommy!" Then she bounced up and down, bending and unbending her knees. "Da! Da!" she cried. "La la la la la." She was dancing and wanted her mother to dance and sing, too. But Elouise only looked toward the tree, waiting for Charlie to appear. *Any minute*, she thought. *He will be angry. He will be ashamed*, she thought. *But he will be alive.*

In the distance, however, the air all at once was shining. Elouise could see it clearing because they were not far from the edge of the Rectifier field. It shimmered in the trees, where it caused no harm to plants. Any vertebrates within the field, any animals that lived by electricity passing along nerves, were instantly dead, their brains stilled. Birds dropped from tree limbs. Only insects droned on.

The Rectifier field lasted only minutes.

Amy watched the shining air. It was as if the empty sky itself were dancing with her. She was transfixed. She would soon forget the airplane, and already her father's face was disappearing from her memories. But she would remember the shining. She would see it forever in her dreams, a vast thickening of the air, dancing and vibrating up and down, up an down. In her dreams it would always be the same, a terrible shining light that would grow and grow and grow and press against her in her bed. And always with it would come the sound of a voice she loved, saying, "Jesus. Jesus. Jesus." This dream would come so clearly when she was twelve that she would tell it to her adopted father, the priest named Michael. He told her that it was the voice of an angel, speaking the name of the source of all light. "You must not fear the light," he said. "You must embrace it." It satisfied her.

But at the moment she first heard the voice, in fact and not in dream, she had no trouble recognizing it, it was the voice of her mother, Elouise, saying, "Jesus." It was full of grief that only a child could fail to understand. Amy did not understand. She only tried to repeat the word, "Deeah-zah."

"God," said Elouise, rocking back and forth, her face turned up toward a heaven she was sure was unoccupied.

"Dog," Amy repeated, "Dog dog doggie." In vain she looked around for the four-footed beast.

"Charlie!" Elouise screamed as the Rectifier field faded.

"Daddy," Amy cried, and because of her mother's tears she also wept. Elouise took her daughter in her arms and held her, rocking back and forth. Elouise discovered that there were some things that could not be frozen in her. Some things that must burn: Sunlight. And lightning. And everlasting, inextinguishable regret.

My mother, Mother Elouise, often told me about my father. She described Father Charlie in detail, so I would not forget. She refused to let me forget anything. "It's what Father Charlie died for," she told me, over and over. "He died so you would remember. You cannot forget."

So I still remember, even today, every word she told me about him. His hair was red, as mine was. His body was lean and hard. His smile was quick, like mine, and he had gentle hands. When his hair was long or sweaty, it kinked tightly at his forehead, ears, and neck. His touch was so delicate he could cut in half an animal so tiny it could not be seen without a machine; so sensitive that he could fly—an art that Mother Elouise said was not a miracle, since it could be done by many giants of the Golden Age, and they took with them many others who could not fly alone. This was Charlie's gift. Mother Elouise said. She also told me that I loved him dearly.

But for all the words that she taught me, I still have no picture of my father in my mind. It is as if the words drove out the vision, as so often happens.

Yet I still hold that one memory of my father, so deeply hidden that I can neither lose it nor fully find it again. Sometimes I wake up weeping. Sometimes I wake up with my arms in the air, curved just so, and I remember that I was dreaming of embracing that large man who loved me. My arms remember how it feels to hold Father Charlie tight around the neck and cling to him as he carries his child. And when I cannot sleep, and the pillow seems to be always the wrong shape, it is because I am hunting for the shape of Father Charlie's shoulder, which my heart remembers, though my mind cannot.

God put angels into Mother Elouise and Father Charlie, and they destroyed the world, for the cup of God's indignation was full, and all the works of men become dust, but out of dust God makes men, and out of men and women, angels.

KINGSMEAT

The gatekeeper recognized him and the gate fell away. The Shepherd put his ax and his crook into the bag at his belt and stepped out onto the bridge. As always he felt a rush of vertigo as he walked the narrow arch over the foaming acid of the moat. Then he was across and striding down the road to the village.

A child was playing with a dog on a grassy hillside. The Shepherd looked up at him, his fine dark face made bright by his eyes. The boy shrank back, and the Shepherd heard a woman's voice cry out, "Back here, Derry, you fool!" The Shepherd walked on down the road as the boy retreated among the hayricks on the far slope. The Shepherd could hear the scolding: "Play near the castle again, and he'll make kingsmeat of you."

Kingsmeat, thought the Shepherd. How the king does get hungry. The word had come down through the quick grapevine—steward to cook to captain to guard to shepherd and then he was dressed and out the door only minutes after the king had muttered, "For supper, what is your taste?" and the queen had fluttered all her arms and said, "Not stew again, I hope," and the king had murmured as he picked up the computer printouts of the day, "Breast in butter," and so now the Shepherd was out to harvest from the flock.

The village was still in the distance when the Shepherd began to pass the people. He remembered the time, back when the king had first made his tastes known, when there had been many attempts to evade the villagers' duties to the king. Now they only watched, perhaps hiding the unblemished members of the flock, sometimes thrusting them forward to end the suspense; but mostly the Shepherd saw the old legless, eyeless, or armless men and women who hobbled about their duties with those limbs that were still intact.

Those with fingers thatched or wove; those with eyes led those whose hands were their only contact with the world; those with arms rode the backs of those with legs; and all of them took their only solace in sad and sagging beds, producing, after a suitable interval, children whose miraculous wholeness made them gods to a surprised and wondering mother, made them hated reminders to a father whose tongue had fallen from his mouth, or whose toes had somehow been mislaid, or whose buttocks were a scar, his legs a useless reminder of hams long since dropped off.

"Ah, such beauty," a woman murmured, pumping the bellows at the bread-oven fire. There was a sour grunt from the legless hag who shoveled in the loaves and turned them with a wooden shovel. It was true, of course, for the Shepherd was never touched, no indeed. (No indeed, came the echo from the midnight fires of Unholy Night, when dark tales frightened children half out of their wits, dark tales that the shrunken grownups knew were true, were inevitable, were tomorrow.) The Shepherd had long dark hair, and his mouth was firm but kind, and his eyes flashed sunlight even in the dark, it seemed, while his hands were soft from bathing, large and strong and dark and smooth and fearful.

And the Shepherd walked into the village to a house he had noted the last time he came. He went to the door and immediately heard a sigh from every other house, and silence from the one that he had picked.

He raised his hand before the door and it opened, as it had been built to do: for all things that opened served the Shepherd's will, or at least served the bright metal ball the king had implanted in his hand. Inside the house it was dark, but not too dark to see the white eyes of an old man who lay in a hammock, legs dangling bonelessly. The man could see his future in the Shepherd's eyes—or so he thought, at least, until the Shepherd walked past him into the kitchen.

There a young woman, no older than fifteen, stood in front of a cupboard, her hands clenched to do violence. But the Shepherd only shook his head and raised his hand, and the cupboard answered him and opened however much she pushed against it, revealing a murmuring baby wrapped in sound-smothering blankets. The Shepherd only smiled and shook his head. His smile was kind and beautiful, and the woman wanted to die.

He stroked her cheek and she sighed softly, moaned softly, and then he reached into his bag and pulled out his shepherd's crook and leaned the little disc against her temple and she smiled. Her eyes were dead but her lips were alive and her teeth showed. He laid her on the floor, carefully opened her blouse, and then took his ax from his bag.

He ran his finger around the long, narrow cylinder and a tiny light shone at one end. Then he touched the ax's glowing tip to the underside of her breast and drew a wide circle. Behind the ax a tiny red line followed, and the Shepherd took hold of the breast and it came away in his hand. Laying it aside, he stroked the ax lengthwise and the light changed to a dull blue. He passed the ax over the red wound, and the blood gelled and dried and the wound began to heal.

He placed the breast into his bag and repeated the process on the other side. Through it the woman watched in disinterested amusement, the smile still playing at her lips. She would smile like that for days before the peace wore off.

When the second breast was in his bag, the Shepherd put away the ax and the crook and carefully buttoned the woman's blouse. He helped her to her feet, and again passed his deft and gentle hand across her cheek. Like a baby rooting she turned her lips toward his fingers, but he withdrew his hand.

As he left, the woman took the baby from the cupboard and embraced it, cooing softly. The baby nuzzled against the strangely harsh bosom and the woman smiled and sang a lullaby.

The Shepherd walked through the streets, the bag at his belt jostling with his steps. The people watched the bag, wondering what it held. But before the Shepherd was out of the village the word had spread, and the looks were no longer at the bag but rather at the Shepherd's face. He looked neither to the left nor to the right, but he felt their gazes and his eyes grew soft and sad.

And then he was back at the moat, across the narrow bridge, through the gate, and into the high dark corridors of the castle.

He took the bag to the cook, who looked at him sourly. The Shepherd only smiled at him and took his crook from the bag. In a moment the cook was docile, and calmly he began to cut the red flesh into thin slices, which he lightly floured and then placed in a pan of simmering butter. The smell was strong and sweet, and the flecks of milk sizzled in the pan.

The Shepherd stayed in the kitchen, watching, as the cook prepared the king's meal. Then he followed to the door of the dining hall as the steward entered the king's presence with the steaming slices on a tray. The king and queen ate silently, with severe but gracious rituals of shared servings and gifts of finest morsels.

And at the end of the meal the king murmured a word to the steward, who beckoned both the cook and the Shepherd into the hall.

The cook, the steward, and the Shepherd knelt before the king, who reached out three arms to touch their heads. Through long practice they accepted his touch without recoiling, without even blinking, for they knew such things displeased him. After all, it was a great gift that they could serve the king: their services kept them from giving kingsmeat from their own flesh, or from decorating with their skin the tapestried walls of the castle or the long train of a hunting-cape.

The king's armpits still touched the heads of the three servants when a shudder ran through the castle and a low warning tone began to drone.

The king and queen left the table and with deliberate dignity moved to the consoles and sat. There they pressed buttons, setting in motion all the unseeable defenses of the castle.

After an hour of exhausting concentration they recognized defeat and pulled their arms back from the now-useless tasks they had been doing. The fields of force that had long held the thin walls of the castle to their delicate height now lapsed, the walls fell, and a shining metal ship settled silently in the middle of the ruins.

The side of the skyship opened and out of it came four men, weapons in their hands and anger in their eyes. Seeing them, the king and queen looked sadly at each other and then pulled the ritual knives from their resting place behind their heads and simultaneously plunged them between one another's eyes. They died instantly, and the twenty-two-year conquest of Abbey Colony was at an end.

Dead, the king and queen looked like sad squids lying flat and empty on a fisherman's deck, not at all like conquerors of planets and eaters of men. The men from the skyship walked to the corpses and made certain they were dead. Then they looked around and realized for the first time that they were not alone.

For the Shepherd, the steward, and the cook stood in the ruins of the palace, their eyes wide with unbelief.

One of the men from the ship reached out a hand.

"How can you be alive?" he asked.

They did not answer, not knowing really what the question meant.

"How have you survived here, when—"

And then there were no words, for they looked beyond the palace, across the moat to the crowd of colonists and sons of colonists who stood watching them. And seeing them there without arms and legs and eyes and breasts and lips, the men from the ship emptied their hands of weapons and filled their palms with tears and then crossed the bridge to grieve among the delivered ones' rejoicing.

There was no time for explanations, nor was there a need. The colonists crept and hobbled and, occasionally, walked across the bridge to the ruined palace and formed a circle around the bodies of the king and queen. Then they set to work, and within an hour the corpses were lying in the pit that had been the foundation of the castle, covered with urine and feces and stinking already of decay.

Then the colonists turned to the servants of the king and queen.

The men from the ship had been chosen on a distant world for their judgment, speed, and skill, and before the mob had found its common mind, before they had begun to move, there was a forcefence around the steward, the cook, and the gatekeeper, and the guards. Even around the Shepherd, and though the crowd mumbled its resentment, one of the men from the ship patiently explained in soothing tones that whatever crimes were done would be punished in due time, according to Imperial justice.

The fence stayed up for a week as the men from the ship worked to put the colony in order, struggling to interest the people in the fields that once again belonged completely to them. At last they gave up, realizing that justice could not wait. They took the machinery of the court out of the ship, gathered the people together, and began the trial.

The colonists waited as the men from the ship taped a metal plate behind each person's right ear. Even the servants in their prison and the men from the ship were fitted with them, and then the trial began, each person testifying directly from his memory into the minds of every other person.

The court first heard the testimony of the men from the ship. The people closed their eyes and saw men in a huge starship, pushing buttons and speaking rapidly into computers. Finally expressions of relief, and four men entering a skyship to go down.

The people saw that it was not their world, for here there were no survivors. Instead there was just a castle, just a king and queen, and when they were dead, just fallow fields and the ruins of a village abandoned many years before.

They saw the same scene again and again. Only Abbey Colony had any human beings left alive.

Then they watched as bodies of kings and queens on other worlds were cut open. A chamber within the queen split wide, and there in a writhing mass of life lived a thousand tiny fetuses, many-armed and bleeding in the cold air outside the womb. Thirty years of gestation, and then two by two they would have continued to conquer and rape other worlds in an unstoppable epidemic across the galaxy.

But in the womb, it was stopped, and the fetuses were sprayed with a chemical and soon they lay still and dried into shriveled balls of gray skin.

The testimony of the men from the ship ended, and the court probed the memories of the colonists:

A screaming from the sky, and a blast of light, and then the king and queen descending without machinery. But the devices follow quickly, and the people are beaten by invisible whips and forced into a pen that they watched grow from nothing into a dark, tiny room that they barely fit into, standing.

Heavy air, impossible to breathe. A woman fainting, then a man, and the screams and cries deafening. Sweat until bodies are dry, heat until bodies are cold, and then a trembling through the room.

A door, and then the king, huger than any had thought, his many arms revolting. Vomit on your back from the man behind, then your own vomit, and your bladder empties in fear. The arms reach, and screams are all around, screams in all throats, screams until all voices are silenced. Then one man plucked writhing from the crowd, the door closed again, darkness back, and the stench and heat and terror greater than before.

Silence. And in the distance a drawn-out cry of agony.

Silence. Hours. And then the open door again, the king again, the scream again.

The third time the king is in the door and out of the crowd walks one who is not screaming, whose shirt is caked with stale vomit but who is not vomiting, whose eyes are calm and whose lips are at peace and whose eyes shine. The Shepherd, though known then by another name.

He walks to the king and reaches out his hand, and he is not seized. He is led, and he walks out, and the door closes.

Silence. Hours. And still no scream.

And then the pen is gone, into the nothing it seemed to come from, and the air is clear and the sun is shining and the grass is green. There is only one change: the castle, rising high and delicately and madly in an upward tumble of spires and domes. A moat of acid around it. A slender bridge.

And then back to the village, all of them. The houses are intact, and it is almost possible to forget.

Until the Shepherd walks through the village streets. He is still called by the old name—what was the name? And the people speak to him, ask him, what is in the castle, what do the king and queen want, why were we imprisoned, why are we free.

But the Shepherd only points to a baker. The man steps out, the Shepherd touches him on the temple with his crook, and the man smiles and walks toward the castle.

Four strong men likewise sent on their way, and a boy, and another man, and then the people begin to murmur and shrink back from the Shepherd. His face is still beautiful, but they remember the scream they heard in the pen. They do not want to go to the castle. They do not trust the empty smiles of those who go.

And then the Shepherd comes again, and again, and limbs are lost from living men and women. There are plans. There are attacks. But always the Shepherd's crook or the Shepherd's unseen whip stops them. Always they return crippled to their houses. And they wait. And they hate.

And there are many who wish they had died in the first terrified moments of the attack. But never once does the Shepherd kill.

The testimony of the people ended, and the court let them pause before the trial went on. They needed time to dry their eyes of the tears their memories shed. They needed time to clear their throats of the thickness of silent cries.

And then they closed their eyes again and watched the testimony of the Shepherd. This time there were not many different views; they all watched through one pair of eyes:

The pen again, crowds huddled in terror. The door opens, as before. Only this time all of them walk toward the king in the door, and all of them hold out a hand, and all of them feel a cold tentacle wrap around and lead them from the pen.

The castle grows closer, and they feel the fear of it. But also there is a quietness, a peace that is pressed down on the terror, a peace that holds the face calm and the heart to its normal beat.

The castle. A narrow bridge, and acid in a moat. A gate opens. The bridge is crossed with a moment of vertigo when the king seems about to push, about to throw his prey into the moat.

And then the vast dining hall, and the queen at the console, shaping the world according to the pattern that will bring her children to life.

You stand alone at the head of the table, and the king and queen sit on high stools and watch you. You look at the table and see enough to realize why the others screamed. You feel a scream rise in your throat, knowing that you, and then all the others, will be torn like that, will be half-devoured, will be left in a pile of gristle and bone until all are gone.

And then you press down the fear, and you watch.

The king and queen raise and lower their arms, undulating them in syncopated patterns. They seem to be conversing. Is there meaning in the movements?

You will find out. You also extend an arm, and try to imitate the patterns that you see.

They stop moving and watch you.

You pause for a moment, unsure. Then you undulate your arms again.

They move in a flurry of arms and soft sounds. You also imitate the soft sounds.

And then they come for you. You steel yourself, vow that you will not scream, knowing that you will not be able to stop yourself.

A cold arm touches you and you grow faint. And then you are led from the room, away from the table, and it grows dark.

They keep you for weeks. Amusement. You are kept alive to entertain them when they grow weary of their work. But as you imitate them you begin to learn, and they begin to teach you, and soon a sort of stammering language emerges, they speaking slowly with their loose arms and soft voices, you with only two arms trying to imitate, then initiate words. The strain of it is killing, but at last you tell them what you want to tell them, what you must tell them before they become bored and look at you again as meat.

You teach them how to keep a herd.

And so they make you a shepherd, with only one duty: to give them meat in a never-ending supply. You have told them you can feed them and never run out of manflesh, and they are intrigued.

They go to their surgical supplies and give you a crook so there will be no pain or struggle, and an ax for the butchery and healing, and on a piece of decaying flesh they show you how to use them. In your hand they implant the key that commands every hinge in the village. And then you go into the colony and proceed to murder your fellowmen bit by bit in order to keep them all alive.

You do not speak. You hide from their hatred in silence. You long for death, but it does not come, because it cannot come. If you died, the colony would die, and so to save their lives you continue a life not worth living.

And then the castle falls and you are finished and you hide the ax and crook in a certain place in the earth and wait for them all to kill you.

The trial ended.

The people pulled the plates from behind their ears, and blinked unbelieving at the afternoon sunlight. They looked at the beautiful face of the Shepherd and their faces wore unreadable expressions.

"The verdict of the court," a man from the ship read as the others moved through the crowd collecting witness plates, "is that the man called Shepherd is guilty of gross atrocities. However, these atrocities were the sole means of keeping alive those very persons against whom the atrocities were perpetrated. Therefore, the man called Shepherd is cleared of all charges. He is not to be put to death, and instead shall be honored by the people of Abbey Colony at least once a year and helped to live as long as science and prudence can keep a man alive."

It was the verdict of the court, and despite their twenty-two years of isolation the people of Abbey Colony would never disobey Imperial law.

Weeks later the work of the men from the ship was finished. They returned to the sky. The people governed themselves as they had before.

Somewhere between stars three of the men in the ship gathered after supper. "A shepherd, of all things," said one.

"A bloody good one, though," said another.

The fourth man seemed to be asleep. He was not, however, and suddenly he sat up and cried out, "My God, what have we done!"

Over the years Abbey Colony thrived, and a new generation grew up strong and un-crippled. They told their children's children the story of their long enslavement, and freedom was treasured; freedom and strength and wholeness and life.

And every year, as the court had commanded, they went to a certain house in the village carrying gifts of grain and milk and meat. They lined up outside the door, and one by one entered to do honor to the Shepherd.

They walked by the table where he was propped so he could see them. Each came in and looked into the beautiful face with the gentle lips and the soft eyes. There were no large strong hands now, however. Only a head and a neck and a spine and ribs and a loose sac of flesh that pulsed with life. The people looked over his naked body and saw the scars. Here had been a leg and a hip, right? Yes, and here he had once had genitals, and here shoulders and arms.

How does he live? asked the little ones, wondering.

We keep him alive, the older ones answered. The verdict of the court, they said year after year. We'll keep him as long as science and prudence can keep a man alive.

Then they set down their gifts and left, and at the end of the day the Shepherd was moved back to his hammock, where year after year he looked out the window at the weathers of the sky. They would, perhaps, have cut out his tongue, but since he never spoke, they didn't think of it. They would, perhaps, have cut out his eyes, but they wanted him to see them smile.

HOLY

"You have weapons that could stop them," said Crofe, and suddenly the needle felt heavy on my belt.

"I can't use them," I said. "Not even the needle. And definitely not the splinters."

Crofe did not seem surprised, but the others did, and I was angry that Crofe would put me in such a position. He knew the law. But now Stone was looking at me darkly, his bow on his lap, and Fole openly grumbled in his deep, giant's voice. "We're friends, right? Friends, they say."

"It's the law," I said. "I can't use these weapons except in proper self-defense."

"Their arrows are coming as close to you as to us!" Stone said.

"As long as I'm with you, the law assumes that they're attacking you and not me. If I used my weapons, it would seem like I was taking sides. It would be putting the corporation on your side against their side. It would mean the end of the corporation's involvement with you."

"Fine with me," Fole murmured. "Fat lot of good it's done us."

I didn't mention that I would also be executed. The Ylymyny have little use for people who fear death.

In the distance someone screamed. I looked around—none of them seemed worried. But in a moment Da came into the circle of stones, panting. "They found the slanting road," he whispered. "Nothing we could do. Killed one, that's all."

Crofe stood and uttered a high-pitched cry, a staccato burst of sound that echoed from the crags around us. Then he nodded to the others, and Fole reached over and seized my arm. "Come on," he whispered. But I hung back, not wanting to be shuffled out without any idea of what was going on.

"What's happening?" I asked.

Crofe grinned, his black teeth startling (after all these months) against his light-brown skin. "We're going to try to live through this. Lead them into a trap. Away off south there's a narrow pass where a hundred of my men wait for us to bring them game." As he spoke, four more men came into the circle of stones, and Crofe turned to them.

"Gokoke?" he asked. The others shrugged.

Crofe glowered. "We don't leave Gokoke." They nodded, and the four who had just come went back silently into the paths of the rock. Now Fole became more insistent, and Stone softly whined, "We must go, Crofe."

"Not without Gokoke."

There was a mournful wail that sounded as if it came from all around. Which was echo and which was original sound? Impossible to tell. Crofe bowed his head, squatted, covered his eyes ritually with his hands, and chanted softly. The others did likewise; Fole even released my arm so he could cover his face. It occurred to me that though their piety was impressive, covering one's eyes during a battle might well be a counterevolutionary behavior. Every now and then the old anthropologist in me surfaces, and I get clinical.

I wasn't clinical, however, when a Golyny soldier leaped from the rocks into the circle. He was armed with two long knives, and he was already springing into action. I noticed that he headed directly for Crofe. I also noticed that none of the Ylymyny made the slightest move to defend him.

What could I do? It was forbidden for me to kill; yet Crofe was the most influential of the warlords of the Ylymyny. I couldn't let him die. His friendship was our best toehold in trading with the people of the islands. And besides, I don't like watching a person being murdered while his eyes are covered in a religious rite, however asinine the rite might be. Which is why I certainly bent the law, if I didn't break it: my toe found the Golyny's groin just as the knife began its downward slash toward Crofe's neck.

The Golyny groaned; the knife forgotten, he clutched at himself, then reached out to attack me. To my surprise, the others continued their chanting, as if unaware that I was protecting them, at not inconsiderable risk to myself.

I could have killed the Golyny in a moment, but I didn't dare. Instead, for an endless three or four minutes I battled with him, disarming him quickly but unable to strike him a blow that would knock him unconscious without running the risk of accidentally killing him. I broke his arm; he ignored the pain, it seemed, and continued to attack—continued, in fact, to use the broken arm. What kind of people are these? I wondered as I blocked a vicious kick with an equally vicious blow from my heavy boot. Don't they feel pain?

And at last the chanting ended, and in a moment Fole had broken the Golyny soldier's neck with one blow. "Jass!" he hissed, nursing his hand from the pain, "what a neck!"

"Why the hell didn't somebody help me before?" I demanded. I was ignored. Obviously an offworlder wouldn't understand. Now the four that had gone off to bring back Gokoke returned, their hands red with already drying blood. They held out their hands; Crofe, Fole, Stone, and Da licked the blood just slightly, swallowing with expressions of grief on their faces. Then Crofe clicked twice in his throat, and again Fole was pulling me out of the circle of stones. This time, however, all were coming. Crofe was in the lead, tumbling madly along a path that a mountain goat would have rejected as being too dangerous. I tried to tell Fole that it would be easier for me if he'd let go of my arm; at the first sound, Stone whirled around ahead of us, slapped my face with all his force, and I silently swallowed my own blood as we continued down the path.

Suddenly the path ended on the crown of a rocky outcrop that seemed to be at the end of the world. Far below the lip of the smooth rock, the vast plain of Ylymyn Island spread to every horizon. The blue at the edges hinted at ocean, but I knew the sea was too far away to be seen. Clouds drifted here and there between us and the plain; patches of jungle many kilometers across seemed like threads and blots on the farmland and dazzling white cities. And all of it gave us a view that reminded me too much of what I had seen looking from the spacecraft while we orbited this planet not that many months ago.

We paused only a moment on the dome; immediately they scrambled over the edge, seeming to plunge from our vantage point into midair. I, too, leaped over the edge—I had no choice, with Fole's unrelenting grip. As I slid down the ever-steeper slope of rock, I could see nothing below me to break my fall. I almost screamed; held the scream back because if by some faint chance we were not committing mass suicide, a scream would surely bring the Golyny.

And then the rock dropped away under me and I did fall, for one endless meter until I stopped, trembling, on a ledge scarcely a meter wide. The others were already there—Fole had taken me more slowly, I supposed, because of my inexperience. Forcing myself to glance over the edge, I could see that this peak did not continue as a smooth, endless wall right down to the flat plain. There were other peaks that seemed like foothills to us, but I knew they were mountains in their own right. It was little comfort to know that if I fell it would be only a few hundred meters, and not five or six kilometers after all.

Crofe started off at a run, and we followed. Soon the ledge that had seemed narrow at a meter in width narrowed to less than a third of that; yet they scarcely seemed to slow down as Fole dragged me crabwise along the front of the cliff.

Abruptly we came to a large, level area, which gave way to a narrow saddle between our peak and another much lower one that stood scarcely forty meters away. The top of it was rocky and irregular—perhaps, once we crossed the saddle, we could hide there and elude pursuit.

Crofe did not lead this time. Instead, Da ran lightly across the saddle, making it quickly to the other side. He immediately turned and scanned the rocks above us, then waved. Fole followed, dragging me. I would never have crossed the saddle alone. With Fole pulling me, I had scarcely the time to think about the drop off to either side of the slender path.

And then I watched from the rocks as the others came across. Crofe was last, and just as he stepped out onto the saddle, the rocks above came alive with Golyny.

They were silent (I had battle-trained with loud weapons; my only war had been filled with screams and explosions; this silent warfare was, therefore, all the more terrifying), and the men around me quickly drew bows to fire; Golyny dropped, but so did Crofe, an arrow neatly piercing his head from behind.

Was he dead? He had to be. But he fell straddling the narrow ridge, so that he did not plummet down to the rocks below. Another arrow entered his back near his spine. And then, before the enemy could fire again, Fole was out on the ridge, had hoisted Crofe on his shoulders, and brought him back. Even at that, the only shots the enemy got off seemed aimed not at Fole but at Crofe.

We retreated into the rocks, except for two bowmen who stayed to guard the saddle. We were safe enough—it would take hours for the Golyny to find another way up to this peak. And so our attention was focused on Crofe.

His eyes were open, and he still breathed. But he stared straight ahead, making no effort to talk. Stone held his shoulders as Da pushed the arrow deeper into his head. The point emerged, bloody, from Crofe's forehead.

Da leaned over and took the arrowhead in his teeth. He pulled, and the flint came loose. He spat it out and then withdrew the shaft of the arrow backward through the wound. Through all this, Crofe made no sound. And when the operation had finished, Crofe died.

This time there was no ritual of closed eyes and chanting. Instead, the men around me openly wept—openly, but silently. Sobs wracked their bodies; tears leaped from their eyes; their faces contorted in an agony of grief. But there was no sound, not even heavy breathing.

The grief was not something to be ignored. And though I did not know them at all well, Crofe was the one I had known best. Not intimately, certainly not as a friend, because the barriers were too great. But I had seen him dealing with his people, and whatever culture you come from, there's no hiding a man of power. Crofe had that power. In the assemblies when we had first petitioned for the right to trade, Crofe had forced (arguing, it seemed, alone, though later I realized that he had many powerful allies that he preferred to marshal silently) the men and women there to make no restrictions, to leave no prohibitions, and to see instead what the corporation had to sell. It was a foot in the door. But Crofe had taken me aside alone and informed me that nothing was to be brought to the Ylymyny without his knowledge or approval. And now he was dead on a routine scouting mission, and I could not help but be amazed that the Ylymyny, in other ways an incredibly shrewd people, should allow their wisest leaders to waste themselves on meaningless forays in the borderlands and high mountains.

And for some reason I found myself also grieved at Crofe's death. The corporation, of course, would continue to progress in its dealings with the Ylymyny—would, indeed, have an easier time of it now. But Crofe was a worthy bargaining partner. And he and I had loved the game of bargaining, however many barriers our mutual strangeness kept between us.

I watched as his soldiers stripped his corpse. They buried the clothing under rocks. And then they hacked at the skin with their knives, opening up the man's bowels and splitting the intestines from end to end. The stench was powerful; I barely avoided vomiting. They worked intently, finding every scrap of material that had been passing through the bowel and putting it in a small leather bag. When the intestine was as clean as stone knives could scrape it, they closed the bag, and Da tied it around his neck on a string. Then, tears still streaming down his face, he turned to the others, looking at them all, one by one.

"I will go to the mountain," he whispered.

The others nodded; some wept harder.

"I will give his soul to the sky," Da whispered, and now the others came forward, touched the bag, and whispered, "I, too. I, also. I vow."

Hearing the faint noise, the two archers guarding the saddle came to our sanctuary among the stones and were about to add their vows to those of the others when Da held up his hand and forbade them.

"Stay and hold off pursuit. They are sure to know."

Sadly, the two nodded, moved back to their positions. And Fole once again gripped my arm as we moved silently away from the crest of the peak.

"Where are we going?" I whispered.

"To honor Crofe's soul." Stone turned and answered me.

"What about the ambush?"

"We are now about matters more important than that."

The Ylymyny worshiped the sky—or something akin to worship, at least. That much I knew from my scanty research into their religious beliefs in the city on the plain, where I had first landed.

"Stone," I said, "will the enemy know what we're doing?"

"Of course," he whispered back. "They may be infidels, but they know what honor binds the righteous to do. They'll try to trap us on the way, destroy us, and stop us from doing honor to the dead."

And then Da hissed for us to be quiet, and we soundlessly scrambled down the cliffs and slopes. Above us we heard a scream; we ignored it. And soon I was lost in the mechanical effort of finding footholds, handholds, strength to keep going with these soldiers who were in much better condition than I.

Finally we reached the end of the paths and stopped. We were gathered on a rather gentle slope that ended, all the way around, in a steep cliff. And we had curved enough to see, above and behind us, that a large group of Golyny were making their way down the path we had just taken.

I did not look over the edge, at first, until I saw them unwinding their ropes and joining them, end to end, to make a much longer line. Then I walked toward the edge and looked down. Only a few hundred meters below, a valley opened up in the mountainside, a flood of level ground in front of a high-walled canyon that bit deep into the cliff. From there it would be a gentle descent into the plain. We would be safe.

But first, there was the matter of getting down the cliff. This time, I couldn't see any hope of it unless we each dangled on the end of a rope, something that I had no experience with. And even then, what was to stop the enemy from climbing down after us?

Fole solved the dilemma, however. He sat down a few meters back from the edge, in a place where his feet could brace against stone, and he pulled gloves on his hands. Then he took the rope with only a few meters of slack, looped it behind his back, and gripped the end of the rope in his left hand, holding the rest of the line tight against his body with his right.

He would be a stable enough root for the top end of the climbing line; and if he were killed or under attack, he would simply drop the line, and the enemy would have no way to pursue.

He was also doomed to be killed.

I should have said something to him, perhaps, but there was no time. Da was quickly giving me my only lesson in descending a rope, and I had to learn well or die from my first mistake. And then Da, carrying the bag of Crofe's excrement, was over the edge, sitting on the rope as it slid by his buttocks, holding his own weight precariously and yet firmly enough as he descended rapidly to the bottom.

Fole bore the weight stolidly, hardly seeming to strain. And then the rope went slack, and immediately Stone was forcing me to pass the rope under my buttocks, holding the rope in gloved hands on either side. Then he pushed me backward over the cliff, and I took a step into nothingness, and I gasped in terror as I fell far too swiftly, swinging to and fro as if on a pendulum, the rock wall skimming back and forth in front of my face—until the rope turned, and I faced instead the plain, which still looked incredibly far below me. And now I did vomit, though I had not eaten yet that day; the acid was painful in my throat and mouth; and I forgot the terror of falling long enough to grip the rope tightly and slow my descent, though it burned my gloves and the rope was an agony of tearing along my buttocks.

The ground loomed closer, and I could see Da waiting, beckoning impatiently. And so I forced myself to ignore the pain of a faster descent, and fell more rapidly, so that when I hit the ground I was jolted, and sprawled into the grasses.

I lay panting in disbelief that I had made it, relief that I no longer hung like a spider in the air. But I could not rest, it seemed—Da took me by the arm and dragged me away from the rope that was now flailing with the next man's descent.

I rolled onto my back and watched, fascinated, as the man came quickly down the rope. Now that my ordeal was over, I could see a beauty in a single man on a twine daring gravity to do its worst—the poetical kind of experience that has long been forgotten on my gentle homeworld of Garden, where all the cliffs have been turned to gentle slopes, and where oceans gently lap at sand instead of tearing at rock, and where men are as gentle as the world they live in. I am gentle, in fact, which caused me much distress at the beginning of my military training, but which allowed me to survive a war and come out of the army with few scars that could not heal.

And as I lay thinking of the contrast between my upbringing and the harsh life on this world, Stone reached the bottom and the next man started down.

When the soldier was only halfway down, another climbed onto the rope at the top. It took me a moment to realize what was happening; then as it occurred to me that the Golyny must have nearly reached them, Da and Stone pulled me back against the cliff wall, where falling bodies would not land on me.

The first soldier reached the bottom; I saw it was the one named Pan, a brutal-looking man who had wept most piteously at Crofe's death. The other soldier was only a dozen meters from the ground when suddenly the rope shuddered and he dropped. He hit the ground in a tangle of arms and legs; I started to run out to help him, but I was held back. The others were all looking up, and in a moment I saw why. The giant Fole, made small by distance, leaped off the cliff, pulling with him two of the Golyny. A third enemy fell a moment later—he must have lost his balance in the struggle on the cliff.

Fole hit the ground shudderingly, his body cruelly torn by the impact, the Golyny also a jumble of broken bones. Again I tried to go out to try to accomplish something; again I was held back; and again I found they knew their world better than I, with my offworld instincts, could hope to know it. Stones hit the ground sharply, scattering all around us. One of them hit the soldier who already was dying from his relatively shorter fall; it broke his skull, and he died.

We waited in the shadow of the cliff until nearly dark; then Da and Pan rushed out and dragged in the body of the soldier. Stones were already falling around them when they came back; some ricocheted back into the area where Stone and I waited; one hit me in the arm, making a bruise which ached for some time afterward.

After dark, Da and Stone and Pan and I all went out, and hunted for the body of Fole, and dragged him back into the shelter of the cliff.

Then they lit a fire, and slit the throats of the corpses, and tipped them downhill so the blood would flow. They wiped their hands in the sluggish stream and licked their palms as they had for Gokoke. And then they covered their eyes and duplicated the chant.

As they went through the funerary rites, I looked out toward the plain. From above, this area had seemed level with the rest of the plain; in fact, it was much higher than the plain, and I could see the faint lights of the city fires here and there above the jungle. Near us, however, there were no lights. I wondered how far we were from the outpost at the base of the cliffs where we had left our horses; I also wondered why in hell I had ever consented to come along on this expedition. "An ordinary tour," Crofe had called it, and I had not realized that my understanding of their language was so insufficient. Nor had I believed that the war between the Golyny and the Ylymyny was such a serious matter. After all, it had been going on for more than three centuries; how could blood stay so hot, so long?

"You look at the plain," said Stone, beside me, his voice a hiss. It struck me that we had been together at the base of the cliff for hours, and this was the first word that had been spoken, except for the chanting. In the cities the Ylymyny were yarn-spinners and chatterers and gossipers. Here they scarcely broke the silence.

"I'm wondering how many days it will take us to reach the city."

Stone glowered. "The city?"

I was surprised that he seemed surprised. "Where else?"

"We've taken a vow," Stone said, and I could detect the note of loathing in his voice that I had come to expect from him whenever I said something wrong. "We must take Crofe's soul to the sky."

I didn't really understand. "Where's that? How do you reach the sky?"

Stone's chest heaved with the effort of keeping his patience. "The Sky," he said, and then I did a double take, realizing that the word I was translating was also a name, the name of the highest mountain on Ylymyn Island.

"You can't be serious," I said. "That's back the way we came."

"There are other ways, and we will take them."

"So will the Golyny!"

"Do you think that we don't have any honor?" cried Stone, and the sound roused Da and brought him to us.

"What is it?" Da whispered, and stillness settled in around us again.

"This offworld scum accuses us of cowardice," Stone hissed. Da fingered the bag around his neck. "Do you?" he asked.

"Nothing of the kind," I answered. "I don't know what I'm saying to offend him. I just supposed that it would be pointless to try to climb the highest mountain on your island. There are only four of us, and the Golyny will surely be ahead of us, waiting, won't they?"

"Of course," Da said. "It will be difficult. But we are Crofe's friends."

"Can't we get help? From the hundred men, for instance, who were waiting for the ambush?"

Da looked surprised, and Stone was openly angry. "We were there when he died. They were not," Da answered.

"Are you a coward?" Stone asked softly, and I realized that to Stone, at least, cowardice was not something to be loathed, it was something to be cast out, to be exorcised, to be killed. His hand held a knife, and I felt myself on the edge of a dilemma. If I denied cowardice while under threat of death, wouldn't that be cowardice? Was this a lady or the tiger choice? I stood my ground. "If you are all there is to be afraid of, no, I'm not," I said.

Stone looked at me in surprise for a moment, then smiled grimly and put his knife back in his sheath. Pan came to us then, and Da took the opportunity to hold a council. It was short; it involved the choice of routes, and I knew little of geography and nothing of the terrain. At the end of it, though, I had more questions than ever. "Why are we doing this for Crofe, when we didn't do anything like it for Fole or Gokoke?"

"Because Crofe is Ice," he answered, and I stored the non sequitur away to puzzle over later.

"And what will we do when we reach the Sky?"

Stone stirred from his seeming slumber and hissed, "We don't talk of such things!"

Da hissed back, "It is possible that none but he will reach the Sky, and in that case, he must know what to do."

"If he's the one there, we can count on having failed," Stone answered angrily.

Da ignored him and turned to me. "In this bag I hold his last passage, that which would have become him had he lived, his future self." I nodded. "This must be emptied on the high altar, so Jass will know that Ice has been returned to him where he can make it whole."

"That's it? Just empty it on the high altar?"

"The difficulty," said Da, "is not in the rite. It is in the getting there. And you must also bid farewell to Crofe's soul, and break a piece of ice from the mountain, and suck it until it melts; and you must shed your own blood on the altar. But most important is to get there. To the topmost top of the highest mountain in the world."

I did not tell him that far to the north, on the one continental landmass, there rose mountains that would dwarf Sky; instead I nodded and turned to sleep on the grass, my clinical anthropologist's mind churning to classify these magical behaviors. The homeopathy was obvious; the meaning of ice was more obscure; and the use of unpassed excrement as the "last passage" from the body was, to my knowledge, unparalleled. But, as an old professor had far too often remarked, "There is no behavior so peculiar that somewhere, members in good standing of the human race will not perform it." The bag around Da's neck reeked. I slept.

The four of us (had there been ten only yesterday morning?) set out before dawn, sidling up the slope toward the mouth of the canyon. We knew that the enemy was above us; we knew that others would already have circled far ahead, to intercept us later. We were burdened with rations intended for only a few days, and a few weapons and the rope. I wished for more, but said nothing.

The day was uneventful. We simply stayed in the bottom of the canyon, beside the rivulet that poured down toward the plain. It was obvious that the stream ran more powerfully at other times: boulders the size of large buildings were scattered along the canyon bottom, and no vegetation but grass was able to grow below the watermarks on the canyon walls, though here and there above them a tree struggled for existence in the rock.

And so the next day passed, and the next, until the canyon widened into a shallow valley, and we at last reached a place where the rivulet came from under a crack in the rock, and a hilltop that we climbed showed that we were now on the top of the island, with other low hills all around, deceptively gentle-looking, considering that they were hidden behind the peaks of one of the most savage mountain ranges I had seen.

Only a few peaks were higher than we were, and one of them was the Sky. Its only remarkable feature was its height. Many other mountains were more dramatic; many others craggier or more pointed at the peak. Indeed, the Sky was more a giant hill— from our distance, at least—and its ascent would not be difficult, I thought.

I said as much to Da, who only smiled grimly and said, "Easier, at least, than reaching it alive." And I remembered the Golyny, and the fact that somewhere ahead of us they would be waiting. The canyon we had climbed was easy enough—why hadn't they harassed us on the way up?

"If it rains tonight, you will see," Stone answered.

And it did rain that night, and I did see. Or rather I heard, since the night was dark. We camped in the lee of the hill, but the rain drenched us despite the rocky outcropping we huddled under. And then I realized that the rain was falling so heavily that respectable streams were flowing down the hill we camped against—and it was no more than forty meters from crown to base. The rain was heavier than I had ever seen before, and now I heard the distant roaring that told me why the Golyny had not bothered to harm us. The huge river was now flowing down the canyon, fed by a thousand streams like those flowing by our camp.

"What if it had rained while we were climbing?" I asked.

"The Sky would not hinder us on our errand," Da answered, and I found little comfort in that. Who would have guessed that a simple three-day expedition into the mountains would leave me trapped with such superstition, depending on them for my survival even as they were depending on some unintelligible and certainly nonexistent god.

In the morning I woke at first light to find that the others were already awake and armed to the teeth, ready for battle. I hurried to stretch my sore muscles and get ready for the trip. Then I realized what their armaments might mean.

"Are they here?"

But no one answered me, and as soon as it was clear I was ready, they moved forward, keeping to the shelter of the hills, spying out what lay ahead before rounding a bend. There were no trees here, only the quick-living grass that died in a day and was replaced by its seed in the morning. There was no shelter but the rock; and no shade, either, but at this elevation, shade was not necessary. It was not easy to breathe with the oxygen low, but at least at this elevation the day was not hot, despite the fact that Ylymyn Island was regularly one of the hottest places on this forsaken little planet.

For two days we made our way toward the Sky, and seemed to make no progress —it was still distant, on the horizon. Worse, however, than the length of our journey was the fact that we had to be unrelentingly on the alert, though we saw no sign of the Golyny. I once asked (in a whisper) whether they might have given up pursuit. Stone only sneered, and Da shook his head. It was Pan who whispered to me that night that the Golyny hated nothing so much as the righteousness of the Ylymyny, knowing as they did that it was only the gods that had made the Ylymyny the greatest people on earth, and that only their piety had won the gods so thoroughly to their side. "There are some," Pan said, "who, when righteousness defeats them, squat before the gods and properly offer their souls, and join us. But there are others who can only hate the good, and attack mindlessly against the righteous. The Golyny are that kind. All decent people would kill Golyny to preserve the peace of the righteous.

And then he glanced pointedly at my splinters and at my needle. And I as pointedly glanced at the bag of excrement around Da's neck. "What the law requires of good men, good men do," I said, sounding platitudinous to myself, but apparently making the right impression on Pan. His eyes widened, and he nodded in respect. Perhaps I overdid it, but it gratified me to see that he understood that just as certain rites must be performed in his society, certain acts are taboo in mine, and among those acts is involvement in the small wars of nations on primitive planets. That his compulsions were based on mindless superstition while mine were based on long years of experience in xenocontact was a distinction I hardly expected him to grasp, and so I said nothing about it. The result was that he treated me with more respect; with awe, in fact. And, noticing that, Stone asked me quietly as we walked the next day, "What have you done to the young soldier?"

"Put the fear of god into him."

I had meant to be funny. Odd, how a man can be careful in all his pronouncements, and then forget everything he knows as a joke comes to mind and he impulsively tells it. Stone was furious; it took Da's strength and Pan's, too, to keep him from attacking me, which would surely have been fatal to him—rope-climbing I didn't know, but the ways of murder are not strange to me, though I don't pursue them for pleasure. At last I was able to explain that I hadn't understood the implications of my statement in their language, that I was transliterating and certain words had different meanings and so on and so on. We were still discussing this when a flight of arrows ended the conversation and drove all of us to cover except Pan, who had an arrow in him and died there in the open while we watched.

It was difficult to avoid feeling that his death had been somehow my fault; and as Da and Stone discussed the matter and confessed that they had no choice this time but to leave the body, committing a sin to allow the greater good of fulfilling the vow to Crofe, I realized that omitting the rites of death for Pan grieved me almost as much as his death. I have no particular belief in immortality; the notion that the dead linger to watch what happens to their remains is silly to me. Nevertheless, there is, I believe, a difference between knowing that a person is dead and emotionally unconstructing the system of relationships that had included the person. Pan, obscure as the young man was, ugly and brutal as his face had been, was nevertheless the man I liked best of my surviving companions.

And thinking of that, it occurred to me that of the ten that had set out only a week before, only three of us remained; I, who could not use a weapon while in the company of the others, and they, who had to travel more slowly and so risk their lives even more because of me.

"Leave me behind," I said. "Once I'm alone, I can defend myself as I will, and you can move faster."

Stone's eyes leaped at the suggestion, but Da firmly shook his head. "Never. Crofe charged us all that we would keep you with us."

"He didn't know the situation we'd be in."

"Crofe knew," Da whispered. "A man dies in two days here without wisdom. And you have no wisdom."

If he meant knowledge of what might be edible in this particular environment, he was right enough; and when I saw that Da had no intention of leaving me, I decided to continue with them. Better to move on than do nothing. But before we left our temporary shelter (with Pan's corpse slowly desiccating behind us) I taught Stone and Da how to use the splinters and the needle, in case I was killed. Then no law would be broken, as long as they returned the weapons to the corporation. For once Stone seemed to approve of something I had done.

Now we moved even more slowly, more stealthily, and yet the Sky seemed to loom closer now, at last; we were in the foothills. Each hill we approached hid the Sky behind its crest sooner. And the sense of waiting death became overpowering.

At night I took my turn watching, with Pan gone. Technically it was a violation—I was aiding them in their war effort. But it was also survival, since the Golny had little use for offworlders—SCM Corporation had already made four attempts to get a foothold with them, and they would not hear of it. It was maddening to have the ability to save lives and for the sake of larger purposes have to refrain from using that ability.

My watch ended, and I woke Da. But instead of letting me sleep, he silently woke Stone as well, and in the darkness we moved as silently as possible away from our camp. This time we were not heading for the mountain—instead, we were paralleling it, traveling by starlight (which is almost no light at all), and I guessed that Da intended us to pass by our would-be killers and perhaps ascend the mountain by another route.

Whether we passed them or not, I didn't know. At dawn, however, when there was light enough to see the ground, Da began running, and Stone and I followed. The walking had been bad, but I had gradually grown inured to it; the running brought out every latent protest in my muscles. It was not easy loping over even ground, either. It was a shattering run over rocks, down small ravines, darting over hills and across streams. I was exhausted by noon, ready for our brief stop. But we took no stop. Da did spare a sentence for me: "We're ahead of them and must stay ahead."

As we ran, however, an idea came to me, one that seemed pathetically obvious once I had thought of it. I was not allowed to summon any help to further a war effort—but surely getting to the top of the mountain was no war effort. Our lander would never descend into enemy fire, but now that we were in the open, the lander could come, could pick us up, could carry us to the top of the mountain before the enemy suspected we were there.

I suggested that. Stone only spat on the ground (a vile thing, in this world, where for some obscure reason water is worshipped, though it is plentiful everywhere except the Great Desert far to the north of Ylymyn), while Da shook his head. "Spirits fly to the Sky; men climb to it," he said, and once again religion had stymied me. Superstitions were going to kill us yet, meaningless rules that should surely change in the face of such dire need.

But at nightfall we were at the foot of a difficult cliff. I saw at a glance that this was not the easy ascent that the mountain had seemed from the distance. Stone looked surprised, too, as he surveyed the cliff. "This ascent is not right," he said softly. Da nodded. "I know it. This is the west face, which no one climbs."

"Is it impossible?" I asked.

"Who knows?" Da answered. "The other ways are so much easier, no one has ever tried this one. So we go this way, where they don't look for us, and somewhere we move to the north or south, to take an easier way when they don't expect us."

Then Da began to climb. I protested, "The sun's already set."

"Good," he answered. "Then they won't see us climbing."

And so began our climb to the Sky. It was difficult, and for once they did not press on ahead and then wait impatiently for me to come. They were hampered as I was by darkness and strangeness, and the night made us equals at last. It was an empty equality, however. Three times that night Da whispered that he had reached a place in the cliff impossible to scale, and I had to back up, trying to find the holds I had left a moment before. Descending a mountain is harder than ascending it. Climbing you have eyes, and it is your fingers that reach ahead of you. Descending only your toes can hunt, and I was wearing heavy boots. We had wakened early, long before dawn, and we climbed until dawn again began to light the sky. I was exhausted, and Stone and Da also seemed to droop with the effort. But as the light gathered, we came to a shoulder of the mountain, a place where for hundreds of meters the slope was no more than fifteen or twenty degrees, and we threw ourselves to the ground and slept.

I woke because of the stinging of my hands, which in the noon sun I saw were caked with blood that still, here and there, oozed to the surface. Da and Stone still slept. Their hands were not so injured as mine; they were more used to heavy work with their hands. Even the weights I had lifted had been equipped with cushioned handles.

I sat up and looked around. We were still alone on our shoulder of the mountain, and I gazed down the distance we had climbed. We had accomplished much in the darkness, and I marveled at the achievement of it; the hills we had run through the day before were small and far, and I guessed that we might be as much as a third of the way to the peak.

Thinking that, I looked toward the mountain, and immediately kicked Da to waken him.

Da, bleary-eyed, looked where I nodded, and saw the failure of our night's work. Though none of the Golyny were near us, it was plain that from their crags and promontories they could see us. They were not ahead of us on the west slope, but rather they stood as if to guard every traverse that might take us to the safer, easier routes. And who knew—perhaps the Golyny had explored the west face and knew that no man could climb it.

Da sighed, and Stone silently shook his head and broke out the last of the food, which we had been eating sparingly for days longer than it should have lasted.

"What now?" I whispered (odd how the habits, once begun, cannot be broken), and Da answered, "Nothing now. Just ahead. Up the west face. Better unknown dangers than known ones."

I looked back down into the valleys and hills below us. Stone spat again. "Offworlder," he said, "even if we could forsake our vow, they are waiting at the bottom of the cliff by now to kill us as we come down."

"Then let me call my lander. When the prohibition was made, no one knew of flying machines."

Da chuckled. "We have always known of flying machines. We simply had none. But we also knew that such machines could not carry a penitent or a suitor or a vowkeeper to the Sky."

I clutched at straws. "When we reach there, what then?"

"Then we shall have died with the vow kept."

"Can't I call the lander then, to take us *off* the mountain?"

They looked at each other, and then Da nodded to me. I immediately hunted in the pockets of my coat for the radio; I could not hope to reach the city from here, but in less than an hour the orbiting starship would be overhead, and would relay my message. I tried calling the starship right then, in case it was already over the horizon. It was not, and so we headed again for the crags.

Now the climb was worse, because of our weariness from the night before rather than from any greater difficulty in the rocks themselves. My fingers ached; the skin on my palms stung with each contact with the rock. Yet we pressed ahead, and the west face was not unclimbable; even at our slow pace, we soon left the shoulder of the rock far behind us. Indeed, there were many places where we scrambled on natural stairways of rock; other places where ledges let us rest; until we reached an overhang that blocked us completely.

There was no tool in this metalless world that could have helped us to ignore gravity and climb spiderlike upside down to the lip of the overhang. We had no choice but to traverse, and now I realized how wise our enemies' plan had been. We would have to move to left or right, to north or south, and they would be waiting.

But, given no choice, we took the only alternative there was. We took the route under the overhang that slanted upward—toward the south. And now Stone took the lead, coldly explaining that Da bore Crofe's soul, and they had vowed to Crofe to keep me alive; therefore he was most expendable. Da nodded gravely, and I did not protest. I like life, and around any turn or over any obstacle, an arrow might be waiting.

Another surprise: here and there in the shelter of the rock the cold air had preserved a bit of snow. There was no snowcap visible from below, of course; but this was summer, and only this high an altitude could have preserved snow at all in such a climate.

It was nearing nightfall, and I suggested we sleep for the night. Da agreed, and so we huddled against the wall of the mountain, the overhang above us, and two meters away a dropoff into nothing. I lay there looking at a single star that winked above my head, and it is a measure of how tired I was that it was not until morning that I realized the significance of that.

Tomorrow, Da assured me, we would either reach the Sky or be killed trying—we were that close. And so as I talked to the starship on its third pass since I had asked for the lander in the early afternoon, I briefly explained when we would be there.

This time, however, they had Tack, the manager of our corporation's operations on this world, patched in from his radio in the city. And he began to berate me for my stupidity. "What the hell kind of way is this to fulfill your corporate responsibilities!" crackled his voice. "Running off to fulfill some stinking little superstition with a bunch of stone-age savages and trying to get killed in the process!" He went on like that for some time—almost five minutes—before I overrode him and informed the starship that under the terms of my contract with the corporation they were obliged to give me support as requested, up to and including an evacuation from the top of a mountain, and the manager could take his objections and—

They heard, and they agreed to comply, and I lay there trying to cool my anger. Tack didn't understand, couldn't understand. He hadn't been this far with me, hadn't seen Fole's set face as he volunteered to die so the rest could descend the cliff; hadn't watched the agony of indecision as Da and Stone decided to leave Pan; hadn't any way of knowing why I was going to reach the top of the Sky for Crofe's sake—

Not for Crofe's sake, dammit; for mine, for ours. Crofe was dead, and they couldn't help him at all by smearing his excrement on a rock. And suddenly, remembering what would be done when we reached the top of the mountain—if we did—I laughed. All this, to rub a dead man's shit on a stone.

And Stone seized me by the throat and made as if to cast me off the mountain. Da and I struggled, and I looked in Stone's eyes and saw my death there. "Your vow," Da whispered sharply, and Stone at last relented, slid away from me.

"What did you say in your deviltalk!" he demanded, and I realized that I had spoken Empire to the starship, then paused a moment and laughed. So I explained, more politely than Tack had, what Tack had said.

Da glared Stone into silence when I was through, and then sat contemplatively for a long time before he spoke.

"It's true, I suppose," he said, "that we're superstitious."

I said nothing. Stone said nothing only by exercising his utmost self-control.

"But true and false have nothing to do with love and hate. I love Crofe, and I will do what I vowed to do, what he would have done for another Ice; what, perhaps, he might have done for me even though I am not Ice."

And then, with the question settled that easily (and therefore not settled—indeed, not even understood at all), we slept, and I thought nothing of the star that winked directly overhead.

Morning was dismal, with clouds below us rolling in from the south. It would be a storm; and Da warned me that there might be mist as the clouds rose and tumbled around the mountains. We had to hurry.

We had not traveled far, however, when the ledge above us and the one we walked on broadened, separated, opened out into the gentle slope that everywhere but on the west face led to the peak of the Sky. And there, gathered below us, were three or four dozen Golyny, just waking. We had not been seen, but there was no conceivable way to walk ten steps out of the last shelter of the ledge without being noticed; and even though the slope was gentle, it was still four or five hundred meters up the slope to the peak, Da assured me.

"What can we do?" I whispered. "They'll kill us easily."

And indecision played on Da's face, expressing much, even though he was silent.

We watched as the Golyny opened their food and ate it; watched as some of them wrestled or pulled sticks. They looked like any other men, rowdy in the absence of women and when there was no serious work to do. Their laughter was like any other men's laughter, and their games looked to be fun. I forgot myself, and found myself silently betting on one wrestler or another, silently picturing myself in the games, and knowing how I would go about winning. And so an hour passed, and we were no closer to the peak.

Stone looked grim; Da looked desperate; and I have no idea how I looked, though I suspect that because of my involvement with the Golyny games I appeared disinterested to my companions. Perhaps that was why at last Stone took me roughly by the sleeve and spun me toward him.

"A game, isn't it! That's all it is to you!"

Shaken out of my contemplation, I did not understand what was happening.

"Crofe was the greatest man in a hundred generations!" Stone hissed. "And you care nothing for bringing him to heaven!"

"Stone," Da hissed.

"This scum acts as if Crofe were not his friend!"

"I hardly knew him," I said honestly but unwisely.

"What does that have to do with friendship!" Stone said angrily. "He saved your life a dozen times, made us take you in and accept you as human beings, though you followed no law!"

I follow a law, I would have said, except that in our exhaustion and Stone's grief at the failure of our mission, we had raised our voices, and already the Golyny were arming, were rushing toward us, were silently nocking arrows to bows and coming for the kill.

How is it possible that stupidity should end our lives when our enemies' cleverest stratagems had not, I thought in despair; but at that moment the part of my mind that occasionally makes itself useful by putting intelligent thoughts where they can be used reminded me of the star I had seen as I lay under the overhang last night. A star—and I had seen it directly overhead where the overhang had to be. Which meant there was a hole in the overhang, perhaps a chimney that could be climbed.

I quickly told Da and Stone, and now, the argument forgotten in our desperate situation, Stone wordlessly took his bow and all his and Da's arrows and sat to wait for the enemy to come.

"Go," he said, "and climb to the peak if you can."

It hurt, for some reason, that the man who hated me should take it for granted that he would die in order to save my life. Not that I fooled myself that he valued my life, but still, I would live for a few moments more because he was about to die. And, inexplicably, I felt an emotion, briefly, that can only be described as love. And that love embraced also Da and Pan, and I realized that while Crofe was only a businessman that I had enjoyed dealing with, these others were, after all, friends. The realization that I felt emotion toward these barbarians (yes, that is a patronizing attitude, but I have never known even an anthropologist whose words or acts did not confess that he felt contempt for those he dealt with), that I loved them, was shocking yet somehow gratifying; the knowledge that they kept me alive only out of duty to a dead man and a superstition was expectable, but somehow reason for anguish.

All this took less than a moment, however, there on the ledge, and then I turned with Da and raced back along the ledge toward where we had spent the night. It had seemed like only a short way; I kept slowing for fear we would miss the spot in our hurry. But when we reached it, I recognized it easily, and yes, there was indeed a chimney in the rock, a narrow one that was almost perfectly vertical, but one that could possibly lead us near the top of the Sky; a path to the peak that the enemy would not be looking for.

We stripped off our extra gear: the rope, which had not been used since Fole died to let us descend it, the blankets, the weapons, the canvas. I kept only my splinters and needle—they must be on my body when I died (though I was momentarily conceiving that I might win through with Da and survive all this; already the lander would be hovering high above the peak)—to prove that I had not broken the law; otherwise my name would be stricken from the ELB records in dishonor, and all my comrades and fellow frontliners would know I had failed in one of the most basic trusts.

A roar of triumph was carried along the rock, and we knew that Stone was dead, his position overrun, and we had at best ten minutes before they were upon us. Da began kicking our gear off the edge of the cliff, and I helped. A keen eye could still tell that here we had disturbed the ground more than elsewhere; but it was, we hoped, enough to confuse them for just a little longer.

And then we began to climb the chimney. Da insisted that I climb first; he hoisted me into the crack, and I shimmied upward, bracing my back against one wall and my hands and feet against the other. Then I stopped, and using my leg as a handhold, he, too, clambered into the split in the rock.

Then we climbed, and the chimney was longer than we had thought, the sky more distant. Our progress was slow, and every motion kicked down rocks that clattered onto the ledge. We had not counted on that—the Golyny would notice the falling rocks, would see where we were, and we were not yet high enough to be impossible for arrows to reach.

And even as I realized that, it came true. We saw the flash of clothing passing under the chimney; though I could make out no detail, I could tell even in the silence that we had been found. We struggled upward. What else could we do?

And the first arrow came up the shaft. Shooting vertically is not easy—much must be unlearned. But the archer was good. And the third arrow struck Da, angling upward into his calf.

"Can you go on?" I asked.

"Yes," he answered, and I climbed higher, with him following, seeming to be unslowed by the wound.

But the archer was not through, and the seventh rushing sound ended, not in a clatter, but in the dull sound of stone striking flesh. Involuntarily Da uttered a cry. Where I was I could see no wound, of course.

"Are you hit?"

"Yes," he answered. "In the groin. An artery, I believe. I'm losing blood too quickly."

"Can you go on?"

"No."

And using the last of his strength to hold himself in place with his legs alone (which must have been agony to his wounds), he took the bag of Crofe's excrement from his neck and hung it carefully on my foot. In our cramped situation, nothing else was possible.

"I charge you," he said in pain, "to take it to the altar."

"It might fall," I said honestly.

"It will not if you vow to take it to the altar."

And because Da was dying from an arrow that might have struck me, and also because of Stone's death and Pan's and Fole's and, yes, Crofe's, I vowed that I would do it. And when I had said that, Da let go and plunged down the shaft.

I climbed as quickly as I could, knowing that the arrows might easily come again, as in fact they did. But I was higher all the time, and even the best archer couldn't reach me.

I was only a dozen meters from the top, carefully balancing the bag of excrement from my foot as I climbed (every motion more painful than the last), when it occurred to me that Da was dead, and everyone else as well. What was to stop me now from dropping the bag, climbing to the top, signaling the lander to me, and climbing safely aboard? To preserve the contents of a man's bowels and risk my life to perform a meaningless rite with it was absurd. No damage could be done by my failure to perform the task. No one would know, in fact, that I had vowed to do it. Indeed, completing the vow could easily be construed as unwarranted interference in planetary affairs.

Why didn't I drop the bag? There are those who claim that I was insane, believing the religion (these are they who claim that I believe it still); but that is not true. I knew rationally that dead men do not watch the acts of the living, that vows made to the dead are not binding, that my first obligation was to myself and the corporation, and certainly not to Da or Crofe.

But regardless of my rational process, even as I thought of dropping the bag I felt the utter wrongness of it. I could not do it and still remain myself. This is mystical, perhaps, but there was nowhere in my mind that I could fail to fulfill my oath and still live. I have broken my word frequently for convenience—I am, after all, a modern man. But in this case, at that time, despite my strong desire for survival, I could not tip my foot downward and let the bag drop.

And after that moment of indecision, I did not waver.

I reached the top utterly exhausted, but sat on the brink of the chimney and reached down to remove the bag from my foot. The leaning forward after so much exertion in an inexorably vertical position made me lightheaded; the bag almost slipped from my grasp, almost fell; I caught it at the end of my toe and pulled it, trembling, to my lap. It was light, surprisingly light. I set it on the ground and pulled myself out of the chimney, crawled wearily a meter or two away from the edge of the cliff, and then looked ahead of me. There was the peak, not a hundred meters away. On it I could easily see an altar hewn out of stone. The design was not familiar to me, but it could serve the purpose, and it was the only artifact in sight.

But between me and the peak was a gentle downward slope before the upward slope began again, leading to the altar. The slopes were all gentle here, but I realized that a thin coat of ice covered all the rocks; indeed, covered the rock only a few meters on from me. I didn't understand why at the time; afterward the men in the lander told me that for half an hour, while I was in the chimney on the west face, a mist had rolled over the top of the peak, and when it had left, only a few minutes before I surfaced, it had left the film of ice.

But ice was part of my vow, part of the rite, and I scraped some up, broke some off with the handle of my needle, and put it in my mouth.

It was dirty with the grit of the rock, but it was cold and it was water and I felt better for having tasted it. And I felt nothing but relief at having completed part of my vow —it did not seem incongruous at the time that I should be engaging in magic.

Then I struggled to my feet and began to walk clumsily across the space between me and the peak, holding the bag in my hands and slipping frequently on the icy rocks.

I heard shouting below me. I looked down and saw the Golyny on the south slope, hundreds of meters away. They would not be able to reach the peak before me. I took some comfort in that even as the arrows began to hunt for my range.

They found it, and when I tried to move to the north to avoid their fire, I discovered that the Golyny on that side had been alerted by the noise, and they, too, were firing at me.

I had thought I was traveling as fast as I could already; now I began to run toward the peak. Yet running made me slip more, and I scarcely made any faster progress than I had before. It occurs to me now that perhaps it was just that irregular pattern of running quickly and then falling, rising and running again, and falling again, that saved my life; surely it confused the archers.

A shadow passed over me twice as I made the last run to the peak; perhaps I realized that it was the lander, perhaps not. I could have, even then, opted for a rescue. Instead, I fell again and dropped the bag, watched it slide a dozen meters down the south slope, where the Golyny were only a few dozen meters away and closing in (although they, too, were slowed by the ice).

And so I descended into the arrows and retrieved the bag. I was struck in the thigh and in the side; they burned with pain, and I almost fainted then, from the sheer surprise of it. Somehow primitive weapons seem wrong; they shouldn't be able to do damage to a modern man. The shock of the pain they bring is therefore all the greater. Yet I did not faint. I got up and struggled back up the slope, and now I was only a little way from the altar, it was just ahead, it was within a few steps, and at last I fell on it, my wounds throwing blood onto the ground and onto the altar itself. Vaguely I realized that another part of the rite had thus been completed, and as the lander came to rest behind me, I took the bag, opened it, scooped out the still-damp contents, and smeared them on the altar.

Three corporation men reached me then, and, obeying the law, the first thing they did was check my belt for the needle and the splinters. Only when they were certain that they had not been fired did they turn to the Golyny and flip their own splinters downhill. They exploded in front of the enemy, and they screamed in terror and fell back, tumbling and running down the rocks. None had been killed, though I now treasure the wish that at least one of them might have slipped and broken his neck. It was enough, though, that they saw that demonstration of power; the corporation had never given the Golyny a taste of modern warfare until then.

If my needle had been fired, or if a splinter had been missing, the corporation men would, of course, have killed me on the spot. Law is law. As it was, however, they lifted me and carried me from the altar toward the lander. But I did not forget. "Farewell, Crofe," I said, and then, as delirium took over, they tell me I also bade good-bye to all the others, to every one of them, a hundred times over, as the lander took me from the peak back to the city, back to safety.

In two weeks I was recovered enough to receive visitors, and my first visitor was Pru, the titular head of the assembly of Ylymyn. He was very kind. He quietly told me that after I had been back for three days, the corporation finally let slip what I had told them when I requested rescue; the Ylymyny had sent a very large (and therefore safe) party to discover more. They found the mutilated bodies of Fole and the soldier who had fallen just before him; discovered the dried and frozen corpse of Pan; found no trace of Da or Stone; but then reached the altar and saw the bloodstains upon it, and the fresh excrement stains, and that was why Pru had come to me to squat before me and ask me one question.

"Ask," I said.

"Did you bid farewell to Crofe?"

I did not wonder how they knew it was Crofe we had climbed the peak to honor—obviously, only Crofe was "Ice" and therefore worthy of the rite.

"I did," I said.

Tears came into the old man's eyes, and his jaw trembled, and he took my hand as he squatted by the bed, his tears falling upon my skin.

"Did you," he asked, and his voice broke, and then he began again, "did you grant him companions?"

I did not have to ask what he meant; that was how well I understood them by then. "I also bade farewell to the others," and I named them, and he wept louder and kissed my hand and then chanted with his eyes covered for quite some time. When he was done, he reached up and touched my eyes.

"May your eyes always see behind the forest and the mountain," he said, and then he touched my lips, and my ears, and my navel, and my groin, and he said other words. And then he left. And I slept again.

In three weeks Tack came to visit me and found me awake and unable to make any more excuses not to see him. I had expected him to be stern at best. Instead, he beamed and held out a hand, which I took gratefully. I was not to be tried after all.

"My man," he said, "my good man, I couldn't wait any longer. Whenever I've tried to see you, they've told me you were asleep or busy or whatnot, but dammit, man, there's only so much waiting a man can take when he's ready to bust with pride."

He was overdoing it, of course, as he overdid everything, but the message was clear and pleasant enough. I was to be honored, not disgraced; I was to receive a decoration, in fact, and a substantial raise in pay; I was to be made chief of liaison for the whole planet; I was, if he had the power, to be appointed god.

In fact, he said, the natives had already done so.

"Appointed me god?" I asked.

"They've been holding festivals and prayer meetings and whatall for a week. I don't know what you told old Pru, but you are golden property to them. If you told them all to march into the ocean, I swear they'd do it. Don't you realize what an opportunity this is? You could have screwed it up on the mountain, you know that. One false move and that would have been it. But you turned a potential disaster—and one not entirely of your making, I know that—you turned that disaster into the best damn contact point with a xenosociety I've ever seen. Do you realize what this means? You've got to get busy right away, as soon as you can, get the contracts signed and the work begun while there's still this groundswell of affection for you. Shades of the White Messiah the Indians thought Cortes was—but that's history, and you've made history this time, I promise." And on he went until at least, unable to bear it anymore, I *tried*—indeed, I'm still trying—to explain to him that what had happened on the mountain was not *for* the corporation.

"Nonsense," he said. "Couldn't have done anything *better* for the corporation if you'd stayed up a week trying to think of it."

I tried again. I told him about the men who had died, what I owed to them.

"Sentiment. Sentiment's good in a man. Nothing to risk your life over, but you were tired."

And I tried again, fool that I was, and explained about the vow, and about my feelings as I decided to carry the thing through to its conclusion. And at last Tack fell silent and thought about what I had said, and left the room.

That was when the visits with the psychologists began, and while they found me, of course, perfectly competent mentally (trust Tack to overreact, and they knew it), when I requested that I be transferred from the planet, they found a loophole that let me go without breaking contract or losing pay.

But the word was out throughout the corporation that I had gone native on Worthing, that I had actually performed an arcane rite involving blood, ice, a mountain peak, and a dead man's half-digested dinner. I could bear the rumors of madness. It is the laughter that is unbearable, because those who cannot dream of the climb to the mountain, who did not know the men who died for me and for Crofe—how can they help but laugh?

And how can I help but hate them?

Which is why I request again my retirement from the corporation. I will accept half retirement, if that is necessary. I'll accept *no* retirement, in fact, if the record can only stay clear. I will not accept a retirement that lists me as mentally incompetent. I will not accept a retirement that forces me to live anywhere but on Ylymyn Island.

I know that it is forbidden, but these are unusual circumstances. I will certainly be accepted there; I will acquit myself with dignity; I wish only to live out my life with people who understand honor perhaps better than any others I have known of.

It is absurd, I know. You will deny my request, I know, as you have a hundred times before. But I hoped that if you knew my story, knew as best I could tell it the whys behind my determination to leave the corporation, that perhaps you would understand why I have not been able to forget that Pru told me, "Now you are Ice, too; and now your soul shall be set free in the Sky." It is not the hope of a life after death—I have no such hope. It is the hope that at my death honorable men will go to some trouble to bid me farewell.

Indeed, it is no hope at all, but rather a certainty. I, like every modern man, have clung since childhood to a code, to a law that struggled to give a purpose to life. All the laws are rational; all achieve a purpose.

But on Ylymyn, where the laws were irrational and the purposes meaningless, I found another thing, the thing behind the law, the thing that is itself worth clinging to regardless of the law, the thing that takes even mad laws and makes them holy. And by all that's holy, let me go back and cling to it again.

AFTERWORD

"MORTAL GODS"

*T*his story began with an essay I started writing once, about how real life has no borders and boundaries, no frame surrounding it the way that paintings do, no beginnings and ends like stories. It occurred to me that artists who tried to get rid of those frames and boundaries and beginnings and endings were making a foolish mistake. First of all, it can't be done—any work of an individual human being *will* have boundaries, both in time and in space, and any attempt to evade that is pure deception. Second, it *shouldn't* be done, because the very reason why human beings hunger so for art— especially for storytelling—is because art, with its beginnings and endings, provides an overlay of order on the chaos of life. Life never means anything, not clearly enough to count on it, but art *always* means something. Its very edges declare that this is inside the boundary and everything else is out.

The essay never got written. Instead, I wandered off into the idea that human life does in fact have one very simple but natural frame: birth and death. So while the mass of human life, taken together, cannot be separated into simple cause-and-effect chains that can be unambiguously interpreted, the life of a mortal being always has definable limits. And after a person has died, then it might, just might, be possible to go about discovering what actually happened within the frame of those two moments, birth and death, and what all those years between might mean.

This speculation would give rise, in the long run, to my concept of a speaker for the dead. In the short run, though, it gave rise to "Mortal Gods," for if it is death that provides the limit that allows life to be comprehended, that allows us to assign meaning to life, then what would this mean to sentient creatures who *could* not die? All our gods seem to be immortal—but wouldn't immortals search for mortal gods?

"SAVING GRACE"

When Kristine and I moved our family from the Great American West (i.e., the part of the country where trees only grow if you water them) to the Great American East (i.e., the part of the country where trees grow everywhere you haven't paved or mowed recently), one of the biggest cultural shocks was religious television. There just isn't that much of it out west, especially in Mormon country, where our video style is at once slicker and more sedate. So when I saw TV preachers for the first time, especially TV faith healers like Ernest Ainglee, I watched them for hours in horrified fascination.

Of course I knew that the faith healing business was rife with fakery and fraud. But what struck me most powerfully was the deep and desperate faith of those who came, day after day, week after week, to be healed. I wanted to write a story about one of those believers. I also wanted to write about somebody who *really* had the power to heal, and how he would get along with the fakes. When I realized they were the same story, I was able to write "Saving Grace."

That was in South Bend, Indiana, in 1982. I wrote it. I mailed it out. Nobody bought it.

Yet I knew it was a good story. I had read it aloud at a couple of conventions and the audience response told me that it worked, absolutely. So why didn't it sell?

I think part of the problem was that the story was too sympathetic to religion—it wasn't light and satirical enough, and the main characters seemed to be, after a fashion, believers. I don't think the sci-fi markets in those days were ready for that. Also, TV charismatics hadn't yet taken as much prominence in the public eye as they would half a decade later, when every cable system seemed to have a bunch of religious stations, and when the antics of that immortal love triangle of Jim and Tammy and Jessica, and of voyeur extraordinaire Jimmy Swaggart, made these guys household names.

Whatever the reason, I couldn't sell the story. Until, years later, a nice guy and talented writer and editor named Alan Rodgers told me that *Twilight Zone* magazine was spinning off a horror digest called *Night Cry*, and did I have anything he might publish? I *never* wrote horror—at least not in the normal conception of the term—but I did have a contemporary fantasy called "Saving Grace." I told him something about it, and he said, Sure, send it along.

I pulled the story out, thinking to do some major revisions. Instead I found that it needed only some minor changes to be up to speed; Alan bought it by return mail. The result was that "Saving Grace" did finally reach an audience—though I dare say that people buying *Night Cry* had to be more than a little surprised at what *this* story turned out to be!

"EYE FOR EYE"

This story began in my ancient Datsun B-210, a hideously rusted out blue coupe that I had bought from a friend who had pretty well used it up on the salt-covered roads in Lafayette, Indiana, while he got his doctorate at Purdue. The car vibrated so much that after a trip of more than fifty miles I ended up trembling for hours. But it served me well for many years, on trips to Texas, Michigan, Florida, and points in between. I couldn't bear to sell it—I finally gave it away.

All this has nothing to do "Eye for Eye." I just miss the old car.

I was driving to a convention in Roanoke, Virginia, with my good friend and fellow writer, Gregg Keizer. He had been a student of mine in an evening class I taught at the University of Utah in the late 70s. The class was on writing science fiction, but Gregg never learned anything from me—he already knew how before he got there. I once was so sure that a story of his would sell that I bet him that if it didn't sell within a year I'd run naked through Orson Spencer Hall (the building where the class was held). It took more than a year. I reneged on the bet. But Gregg was very nice about it. And the story *did* sell soon after. Anyway, when I moved to Greensboro to be senior editor at Compute! Books, and we needed to hire another assistant editor, I thought of Gregg, called him up, and asked him if he wanted to apply. He did. He got the job and did brilliantly. He also long outlasted me, ending up as editor of *Compute! Magazine* five years after I walked away from the place.

This has nothing to do with "Eye for Eye," either. But Gregg is living in Shreveport, Louisiana, these days, and I miss him, too.

Anyway, Gregg and I were on our way to Roanoke, and just for the fun of it we decided to come up with some story ideas. Actually, I think I was saying some damfool thing about how a *real* writer could come up with a story idea anytime he felt like it, and make it work, too. So my ego was invested in this, just a little bit. The story idea I came up with was, what if a person discovered he had the ability to cause cancer in other people? What if he had had the ability for a long time, but didn't realize why all the people around him were all dying of cancer?

That was my story—finding out that you had killed people without meaning to. When I actually got down to writing it, of course, I raised the stakes by making it so my hero had killed the people closest to him; I also made him a pretty decent guy. The rest of the story came out of my speculations on how such an ability might arise. I had read a little bit about this doctor in Scandinavia who was trying to promote the body's ability to heal itself by adjusting the electromagnetic field that surrounds living organisms, so I used that to give the story a pseudoscientific veneer.

Because I had thought of the story on the way to Roanoke, and because I first publicly discussed the idea at that convention, I tipped my hat to the folks there by setting part of the story in their town, which has an extraordinarily beautiful setting in the mountains of western Virginia. The rest of the story arose from that setting. What if the gift arose from a bunch of serious inbreeding in a remote mountain community? And how would good mountain people interpret it if they found all their enemies just naturally dying of cancer? They'd know it had to be either God or the devil doing it, and, given a choice, they'd be bound to settle on God. I decided that they'd consider themselves to be a chosen people, which is why they only bred with each other—but since each generation would have a few kids with more and more intense power to disturb other people's magnetic fields, being their parents would be downright dangerous. So of course, like legendary cuckoos, they'd put them in somebody else's home to raise, only coming to claim them when they'd found out about their powers and had learned to control them.

Add a group of unbelievers who split off from the group, and you've got "Eye for Eye."

I sent the story around when I first wrote it, even though it didn't really feel finished. Everybody rejected it, partly because it was too long; but the nicest letter came from Stan Schmidt at *Analog*, who suggested that he might buy it if the scientific justification were beefed up.

Years later I ran across a copy of the story, with Stan's letter. I had forgotten that it even existed. Looking through it, I decided the idea had some merit, and rewrote it from beginning to end. This time the structure worked better, because I set it up as a first-person account as the boy tried to persuade the unbelievers not to kill him. And, because he had asked for revisions, I sent it to Stan. Alas, he still didn't like it; but by this time, Gardner Dozois was editing *Isaac Asimov's Science Fiction Magazine*, so I asked Stan to send it down the hall to Gardner. Gardner bought it at once and published it. To my surprise, "Eye for Eye" won both the Hugo and, in translation, the Japanese science fiction award as well.

"ST. AMY'S TALE"

Fred Saberhagen had let it be known in *Locus* and elsewhere that he was editing an anthology called *A Spadeful of Spacetime*, which would consist of stories that involved archaeology but did *not* involve time travel. He wanted stories that connected with the past the way science did it, not using the magic trick of a time machine.

I thought about this for quite a while. I loved archaeology—I had begun college as an archaeology major. But how could a story be science fiction about exploring the past *without* using time travel? I came up with a couple of ideas, but the one that interested me most was the idea of anti-archaeologists—people going around *erasing* the evidence of the past. Maybe there had been many high civilizations on Earth in the million-year history of modern man, but each one ended with blood and horror—and with the invention of a machine that could break down human artifacts and return them to their original, natural materials. The machine itself is a pretty hokey idea that doesn't bear close examination, but the human motivations behind the complete destruction of the past are both believable and interesting.

Why, though, did it take a religious bent? In a way, that was a natural turn of the idea, because any idea that can cause such systematic transformation of human life has to end up being religious in character—much the way Communism absolutely functioned as a religion during its first ascendancy in Eastern Europe and the Far East. But there was another influence as well. I was working with some of the great old English writers in graduate school at the time, and Chaucer and Spenser were favorites of mine. I was playing with some of the forms they had used—I started a "Pedant's Calendar" after Spenser's "Shepherds' Calendar," and my epic "Prentice Alvin and the No-Good Plow" contained deliberate echoes of Spenser's *Faerie Queene*. Likewise, I had toyed with the idea of doing a story cycle about pilgrims on their way to a shrine, in imitation of Chaucer's *Canterbury Tales*. That idea went nowhere, but somewhere in the process of planning out this story the title "St. Amy's Tale" came to me. From there, it was an easy matter to introduce a religious overtone, a feeling of holiness and sacrifice to the whole series of events. I thought it made the story far richer and truer to itself.

"KINGSMEAT"

This is the story that readers over the years have found most disturbing and unpleasant. My critics have come up with all kinds of reasons to hate it—including, absurdly enough, a feminist reading of the story in which it was deduced that I "relished" the scene in which a breast is cut off. (One wonders about the mind of someone who thinks that writers "relish" all the scenes they write. Poor bloody-handed Shakespeare!) But once I thought of the idea, it was one of the most inevitable stories I ever told—and one of the most powerful and true.

The origin of the idea was simple. It owed a bit to Damon Knight's classic story that became the *Twilight Zone* episode "To Serve Man." The idea of aliens who eat human beings is as old as sci-fi. But what about a story in which a human being persuades the invaders not to *kill* their victims, but rather to harvest them limb by limb? Would that person be a savior or a torturer? In my mind this idea was linked with the Jews in death camps who were forced into service as body-handlers, fully aware of the slaughter of their own people and, while not directly killing anybody, cooperating with the killers by cleaning up after them. And yet, when you look at it another way, there was something noble in their helpless labor, for as they fed the bodies into the furnace, weren't they performing for the dead those last rituals that are usually performed by family? And wasn't it better that it was done by fellow Jews, fellow prisoners, who mourned their deaths, than to have it done by sneering members of the master race? It's an area of unbearable moral ambiguity—and that's what I strove for in "Kingsmeat."

I think it's interesting that when Gene Wolfe set out to create a Christ-figure in his *Book of the New Sun*, he also made his protagonist begin as an apprentice torturer, so that the one who suffered and died to save others is depicted as one who also inflicts suffering; it is a way to explicitly make the Christ-figure take upon himself, in all innocence, the darkest sins of the world. I didn't plan that out consciously, but I saw it clearly in Wolfe's work and then, by extension, found the same thing happening in mine. That's about the only resemblance between Wolfe's seminal work and my little tale—but I'm glad for any resemblances to the great ones that I can get!

"HOLY"

This story began with a simple enough idea—a challenge, really. Could I write a story that made something as despised and disdained as human excrement seem holy? To accomplish it, I needed to have a point-of-view character who would represent the American reader's habitual disgust for human feces, and then bring him bit by bit to accept another culture's view, until at last he, too, felt that the "meaningless" mission of bringing intestinal scrapings to a particular shrine was worth dying for. Though at the time I wrote this story I would not have stated it so clearly, I was already caught up with the idea that it is story and ritual that give meaning to our actions.

At the time, Ben Bova was buying all the short fiction I wrote. But this story was too long for *Omni*, where Ben was fiction editor, and besides, I wanted to see if I could place a story in one of the prestigious annual anthologies. So I sent this one off to Robert Silverberg for his anthology *New Dimensions*. To my delight, he bought it. I felt validated; and I hoped that my career would get the kind of critical boost that appearing in *New Dimensions* or *Orbit* always carried with them. You didn't sell a lot of copies, but people knew you were certified to be a respectable, *serious* writer of speculative fiction.

Then, to my dismay, the volume that "Holy" appeared in virtually disappeared. It fell into the cracks between two contracts. The *following* volume of *New Dimensions* appeared in paperback before the hardcover edition of the volume I was in appeared, so that my story was in a book that appeared to be outdated—a year old—the moment it appeared. Worse, it never had a paperback edition at all. The stories in that volume were never reviewed. To my knowledge, only a few people in the world ever knew that this story even existed. Its appearance in this volume is, in effect, its first real publication.

None of this, though, was Robert Silverberg's fault—and I thank him again for taking my story seriously at a time when I was being dismissed as an *"Analog* writer" by the literary vigilantes of science fiction. But then, Silverberg has never been one to judge somebody else's work by its reputation, when he has the opportunity to judge it on its own merits. May his tribe increase.

BOOK 5

LOST SONGS

THE HIDDEN STORIES

Introduction

Somewhere along the line, this story collection got completely out of hand. It's that age-old artistic decision of what to leave in and what to leave out. Some of the decisions were easy. All my Worthing stories would be part of an omnibus volume called *The Worthing Saga*, so I didn't need to include any of them. And all my Mormon Sea stories would appear in the collection *The Folk of the Fringe*, so *they* wouldn't need to be included in my general story collection, either. Even with those stories left out, however, no matter how I configured a reasonable-sized book, I was leaving out too many stories that I wanted to include.

So I settled on something *not* of reasonable size. I talked to my editor, Beth Meacham, and proposed that we release a single-volume hardcover collection, but then split it into two regular-length paperbacks. She thought it sounded weird but, being Beth Meacham, she didn't reject it out of hand. Instead she thought about it until she liked the idea, and then went to Tom Doherty who also liked it, and *voilà*—an egregiously oversized book was born. Because once the floodgate had opened, I pretty much included every story that I wasn't actually ashamed of.

Which brings us to *this* part of the collection. Think of this as a bonus section, something that only buyers of the ridiculously expensive hardcover edition receive. It won't be in any of the paperback volumes that bud off from this book. Only you will ever see it.

Why, you ask, are you so fortunate? It's not as if this percentage of the book was free—you paid for the cost of the paper and typesetting of this part of the book as surely as you paid for all the rest. The thing is: As Beth and I looked over the list of stories that were going into *Maps in a Mirror: The Short Fiction of Orson Scott Card*, we realized that we were approaching the point where this book would be *complete*. It would be the volume of record. So why not go all the way? Why not include the stuff that was so weird or out-of-genre that it wasn't going to appear anywhere else, *ever*.

I don't want you to think, though, that we were completely indiscriminate in what we included. For instance, we didn't include a single one of my two-dozen-or-so plays. Nor did we inflict on you any of my poetry except for "Prentice Alvin and the No-Good Plow." There are more than two hundred audioplays and a couple of dozen animated videoscripts from my work for Living Scriptures that aren't included. Nor have we reprinted here any of my dozens of review columns for *Fantasy and Science Fiction* or *Science Fiction Review*. There are also dozens of computer articles and computer game reviews that you are being spared. When you think of it, we were downright *selective*.

There is also one published bit of science fiction that isn't included here. Between this book, *The Worthing Saga*, and *The Folk of the Fringe*, all of my sf and fantasy short stories will be in print, except for a harmless little story called "Happy Head" which appeared in—well, someplace. In that story I used direct brain-to-computer hookups before the cyberpunks did, but that's about the only thing about the story that doesn't embarrass me now, so even if you happen to find it in your complete run of —a certain magazine—I urge you to think of it as something written by an earnest young graduate student rather than anything I did. I think the editor bought it only because it had some interesting ideas in it, not because anybody could actually take it seriously as a story. Everybody's allowed to have a mistake or two that appears in print. But I don't have to cooperate in bringing it to your attention, no matter how much amusement you might get from it.

The works in this section fall into several categories:

STORIES SUPERSEDED BY NOVELS

I've had a long habit of adapting some of my shorter works into novels; the trouble with this is that the shorter works are essentially killed. Yet at the time I wrote them, "Ender's Game," "Mikal's Songbird," and the epic poem "Prentice Alvin and the No-Good Plow" represented my very best work. I had no idea they would ever be expanded on; they were meant to stand complete. Furthermore, both stories were nominated for awards and the poem actually won one. For historical interest if nothing else, we figured they ought to be in print *somewhere*. This is the place.

EARLY WORKS

I'm not ashamed of these stories—they were the best I could do at the time, and they still hold up rather well. But they just don't deserve the same standing as the stories that I still believe in; and I didn't think the ideas were worth the effort of going back and rewriting the stories so they *were* up to snuff. So here they are, for such entertainment as they offer. And perhaps they'll also provide some encouragement to young authors who will read them, smile brightly, and say, "If *these* could get published, *anything* can!"

OUT-OF-GENRE STORIES

Let's face it—if this collection has any *commercial* viability, it's as a collection of science fiction and fantasy stories. But that isn't the only kind of story I write. And Beth and I thought you might enjoy getting a look at the sort of thing I write for other audiences. Many of the stories were originally aimed at the Mormon audience. Others don't have any discernable audience on God's green Earth. But we thought there was even a valid genre reason for including them in a collection of science fiction and fantasy: For some of you, at least, reading Mormon fiction will be the most alien experience you've ever had.

ENDER'S GAME

"Whatever your gravity is when you get to the door, remember—the enemy's gate is *down*. If you step through your own door like you're out for a stroll, you're a big target and you deserve to get hit. With more than a flasher." Ender Wiggins paused and looked over the group. Most were just watching him nervously. A few understanding. A few sullen and resisting.

First day with this army, all fresh from the teacher squads, and Ender had forgotten how young new kids could be. He'd been in it for three years, they'd had six months —nobody over nine years old in the whole bunch. But they were his. At eleven, he was half a year early to be a commander. He'd had a toon of his own and knew a few tricks, but there were forty in his new army. Green. All marksmen with a flasher, all in top shape, or they wouldn't be here—but they were all just as likely as not to get wiped out first time into battle.

"Remember," he went on, "they can't see you till you get through that door. But the second you're out, they'll be on you. So hit that door the way you want to be when they shoot at you. Legs up under you, going straight *down*." He pointed at a sullen kid who looked like he was only seven, the smallest of them all. "Which way is down, greenoh!"

"Toward the enemy door." The answer was quick. It was also surly, as if to say, Yeah, yeah, now get on with the important stuff.

"Name, kid?"

"Bean."

"Get that for size or for brains?"

Bean didn't answer. The rest laughed a little. Ender had chosen right. This kid *was* younger than the rest, must have been advanced because he was sharp. The others didn't like him much, they were happy to see him taken down a little. Like Ender's first commander had taken him down.

"Well, Bean, you're right onto things. Now I tell you this, nobody's gonna get through that door without a good chance of getting hit. A lot of you are going to be turned into cement somewhere. Make sure it's your legs. Right? If only your legs get hit, then only your legs get frozen, and in nullo that's no sweat." Ender turned to one of the dazed ones. "What're legs for? Hmmm?"

Blank stare. Confusion. Stammer.

"Forget it. Guess I'll have to ask Bean here."

"Legs are for pushing off walls." Still bored.

"Thanks, Bean. Get that, everybody?" They all got it, and didn't like getting it from Bean. "Right. You can't *see* with legs, you can't *shoot* with legs, and most of the time they just get in the way. If they get frozen sticking straight out you've turned yourself into a blimp. No way to hide. So how do legs go?"

A few answered this time, to prove that Bean wasn't the only one who knew anything. "Under you. Tucked up under."

"Right. A shield. You're kneeling on a shield, and the shield is your own legs. And there's a trick to the suits. Even when your legs are flashed you can *still* kick off. I've never seen anybody do it but me—but you're all gonna learn it."

Ender Wiggins turned on his flasher. It glowed faintly green in his hand. Then he let himself rise in the weightless workout room, pulled his legs under him as though he were kneeling, and flashed both of them. Immediately his suit stiffened at the knees and ankles, so that he couldn't bend at all.

"Okay, I'm frozen, see?"

He was floating a meter above them. They all looked up at him, puzzled. He leaned back and caught one of the handholds on the wall behind him, and pulled himself flush against the wall.

"I'm stuck at a wall. If I had legs, I'd use legs, and string myself out like a string *bean*, right?"

They laughed.

"But I don't have legs, and that's *better*, got it? Because of this." Ender jackknifed at the waist, then straightened out violently. He was across the workout room in only a moment. From the other side he called to them. "Got that? I didn't use hands, so I still had use of my flasher. *And* I didn't have my legs floating five feet behind me. Now watch it again."

He repeated the jackknife, and caught a handhold on the wall near them. "Now, I don't just want you to do that when they've flashed your legs. I want you to do that when you've still got legs, because it's better. And because they'll never be expecting it. All right now, everybody up in the air and kneeling."

Most were up in a few seconds. Ender flashed the stragglers, and they dangled, helplessly frozen, while the others laughed. "When I give an order, you move. Got it? When we're at a door and they clear it, I'll be giving you orders in two seconds, as soon as I see the setup. And when I give the order you better be out there, because whoever's out there first is going to win, unless he's a fool. I'm not. And you better not be, or I'll have you back in the teacher squads." He saw more than a few of them gulp, and the frozen ones looked at him with fear. "You guys who are hanging there. You watch. You'll thaw out in about fifteen minutes, and let's see if you can catch up to the others."

For the next half hour Ender had them jackknifing off walls. He called a stop when he saw that they all had the basic idea. They were a good group, maybe. They'd get better.

"Now you're warmed up," he said to them, "we'll start working."

* * *

Ender was the last one out after practice, since he stayed to help some of the slower ones improve on technique. They'd had good teachers, but like all armies they were uneven, and some of them could be a real drawback in battle. Their first battle might be weeks away. It might be tomorrow. A schedule was never printed. The commander just woke up and found a note by his bunk, giving him the time of his battle and the name of his opponent. So for the first while he was going to drive his boys until they were in top shape—all of them. Ready for anything, at any time. Strategy was nice, but it was worth nothing if the soldiers couldn't hold up under the strain.

He turned the corner into the residence wing and found himself face to face with Bean, the seven-year-old he had picked on all through practice that day. Problems. Ender didn't want problems right now.

"Ho, Bean."

"Ho, Ender."

Pause.

"Sir," Ender said softly.

"We're not on duty."

"In my army, Bean, we're always on duty." Ender brushed past him.

Bean's high voice piped up behind him. "I know what you're doing, Ender, sir, and I'm warning you."

Ender turned slowly and looked at him. "Warning me?"

"I'm the best man you've got. But I'd better be treated like it."

"Or what?" Ender smiled menacingly.

"Or I'll be the worst man you've got. One or the other."

"And what do you want? Love and kisses?" Ender was getting angry now.

Bean was unworried. "I want a toon."

Ender walked back to him and stood looking down into his eyes. "I'll give a toon," he said, "to the boys who prove they're worth something. They've got to be good soldiers, they've got to know how to take orders, they've got to be able to think for themselves in a pinch, and they've got to be able to keep respect. That's how I got to be a commander. That's how you'll get to be a toon leader. Got it?"

Bean smiled. "That's fair. *If* you actually work that way, I'll be a toon leader in a month."

Ender reached down and grabbed the front of his uniform and shoved him into the wall. "When I say I work a certain way, Bean, then that's the way I work."

Bean just smiled. Ender let go of him and walked away, and didn't look back. He was sure, without looking, that Bean was still watching, still smiling, still just a little contemptuous. He might make a good toon leader at that. Ender would keep an eye on him.

Captain Graff, six foot two and a little chubby, stroked his belly as he leaned back in his chair. Across his desk sat Lieutenant Anderson, who was earnestly pointing out high points on a chart.

"Here it is, Captain," Anderson said. "Ender's already got them doing a tactic that's going to throw off everyone who meets it. Doubled their speed."

Graff nodded.

"And you know his test scores. He thinks well, too."

Graff smiled. "All true, all true, Anderson, he's a fine student, shows real promise."

They waited.

Graff sighed. "So what do you want me to do?"

"Ender's the one. He's got to be."

"He'll never be ready in time, Lieutenant. He's eleven, for heaven's sake, man, what do you want, a miracle?"

"I want him into battles, every day starting tomorrow. I want him to have a year's worth of battles in a month."

Graff shook his head. "That would have his army in the hospital."

"No, sir. He's getting them into form. And we need Ender."

"Correction, Lieutenant. We need somebody. You think it's Ender."

"All right, I think it's Ender. Which of the commanders if it isn't him?"

"I don't know, Lieutenant." Graff ran his hands over his slightly fuzzy bald head. "These are children, Anderson. Do you realize that? Ender's army is nine years old. Are we going to put them against the older kids? Are we going to put them through hell for a month like that?"

Lieutenant Anderson leaned even farther over Graff's desk.

"Ender's test scores, Captain!"

"I've seen his bloody test scores! I've watched him in battle, I've listened to tapes of his training sessions, I've watched his sleep patterns, I've heard tapes of his conversations in the corridors and in the bathrooms, I'm more aware of Ender Wiggins than you could possibly imagine! And against all the arguments, against his obvious qualities, I'm weighing one thing. I have this picture of Ender a year from now, if you have your way. I see him completely useless, worn down, a failure, because he was pushed farther than he or any living person could go. But it doesn't weigh enough, does it, Lieutenant, because there's a war on, and our best talent is gone, and the biggest battles are ahead. So give Ender a battle every day this week. And then bring me a report."

Anderson stood and saluted. "Thank you, sir."

He had almost reached the door when Graff called his name. He turned and faced the captain.

"Anderson," Captain Graff said. "Have you been outside, lately I mean?"

"Not since last leave, six months ago."

"I didn't think so. Not that it makes any difference. But have you ever been to Beaman Park, there in the city? Hmm? Beautiful park. Trees. Grass. No nullo, no battles, no worries. Do you know what else there is in Beaman Park?"

"What, sir?" Lieutenant Anderson asked.

"Children," Graff answered.

"Of course children," said Anderson.

"I mean children. I mean kids who get up in the morning when their mothers call them and they go to school and then in the afternoons they go to Beaman Park and play. They're happy, they smile a lot, they laugh, they have fun. Hmmm?"

"I'm sure they do, sir."

"Is that all you can say, Anderson?"

Anderson cleared his throat. "It's good for children to have fun, I think, sir. I know I did when I was a boy. But right now the world needs soldiers. And this is the way to get them."

Graff nodded and closed his eyes. "Oh, indeed, you're right, by statistical proof and by all the important theories, and dammit they work and the system is right but all the same Ender's older than I am. He's not a child. He's barely a person."

"If that's true, sir, then at least we all know that Ender is making it possible for the others of his age to be playing in the park."

"And Jesus died to save all men, of course." Graff sat up and looked at Anderson almost sadly. "But we're the ones," Graff said, "we're the ones who are driving in the nails."

Ender Wiggins lay on his bed staring at the ceiling. He never slept more than five hours a night—but the lights went off at 2200 and didn't come on again until 0600. So he stared at the ceiling and thought.

He'd had his army for three and a half weeks. Dragon Army. The name was assigned, and it wasn't a lucky one. Oh, the charts said that about nine years ago a Dragon Army had done fairly well. But for the next six years the name had been attached to inferior armies, and finally, because of the superstition that was beginning to play about the name, Dragon Army was retired. Until now. And now, Ender thought, smiling, Dragon Army was going to take them by surprise.

The door opened quietly. Ender did not turn his head. Someone stepped softly into his room, then left with the sound of the door shutting. When soft steps died away Ender rolled over and saw a white slip of paper lying on the floor. He reached down and picked it up.

"Dragon Army against Rabbit Army, Ender Wiggins and Carn Carby, 0700."

The first battle. Ender got out of bed and quickly dressed. He went rapidly to the rooms of each of his toon leaders and told them to rouse their boys. In five minutes they were all gathered in the corridor, sleepy and slow. Ender spoke softly.

"First battle, 0700 against Rabbit Army. I've fought them twice before but they've got a new commander. Never heard of him. They're an older group, though, and I know a few of their old tricks. Now wake up. Run, doublefast, warmup in workroom three."

For an hour and a half they worked out, with three mock battles and calisthenics in the corridor out of the nullo. Then for fifteen minutes they all lay up in the air, totally relaxing in the weightlessness. At 0650 Ender roused them and they hurried into the corridor. Ender led them down the corridor, running again, and occasionally leaping to touch a light panel on the ceiling. The boys all touched the same light panel. And at 0658 they reached their gate to the battleroom.

The members of toons C and D grabbed the first eight handholds in the ceiling of the corridor. Toons A, B, and E crouched on the floor. Ender hooked his feet into two handholds in the middle of the ceiling, so he was out of everyone's way.

"Which way is the enemy's door?" he hissed.

"Down!" they whispered back, and laughed.

"Flashers on." The boxes in their hands glowed green. They waited for a few seconds more, and then the gray wall in front of them disappeared and the battleroom was visible.

Ender sized it up immediately. The familiar open grid of most early games, like the monkey bars at the park, with seven or eight boxes scattered through the grid. They called the boxes *stars*. There were enough of them, and in forward enough positions, that they were worth going for. Ender decided this in a second, and he hissed, "Spread to near stars. E hold!"

The four groups in the corners plunged through the forcefield at the doorway and fell down into the battleroom. Before the enemy even appeared through the opposite gate Ender's army had spread from the door to the nearest stars.

Then the enemy soldiers came through the door. From their stance Ender knew they had been in a different gravity, and didn't know enough to disorient themselves from it. They came through standing up, their entire bodies spread and defenseless.

"Kill 'em, E!" Ender hissed, and threw himself out the door knees first, with his flasher between his legs and firing. While Ender's group flew across the room the rest of Dragon Army lay down a protecting fire, so that E group reached a forward position with only one boy frozen completely, though they had all lost the use of their legs—which didn't impair them in the least. There was a lull as Ender and his opponent, Carn Carby, assessed their positions. Aside from Rabbit Army's losses at the gate, there had been few casualties, and both armies were near full strength. But Carn had no originality—he was in a four-corner spread that any five-year-old in the teacher squads might have thought of. And Ender knew how to defeat it.

He called out, loudly, "E covers A, C down. B, D angle east wall." Under E toon's cover, B and D toons lunged away from their stars. While they were still exposed, A and C toons left their stars and drifted toward the near wall. They reached it together, and together jackknifed off the wall. At double the normal speed they appeared behind the enemy's stars, and opened fire. In a few seconds the battle was over, with the enemy almost entirely frozen, including the commander, and the rest scattered to the corners. For the next five minutes, in squads of four, Dragon Army cleaned out the dark corners of the battleroom and shepherded the enemy into the center, where their bodies, frozen at impossible angles, jostled each other. Then Ender took three of his boys to the enemy gate and went through the formality of reversing the one-way field by simultaneously touching a Dragon Army helmet at each corner. Then Ender assembled his army in vertical files near the knot of frozen Rabbit Army soldiers.

Only three of Dragon Army's soldiers were immobile. Their victory margin—38 to 0—was ridiculously high, and Ender began to laugh. Dragon Army joined him, laughing long and loud. They were still laughing when Lieutenant Anderson and Lieutenant Morris came in from the teachergate at the south end of the battleroom.

Lieutenant Anderson kept his face stiff and unsmiling, but Ender saw him wink as he held out his hand and offered the stiff, formal congratulations that were ritually given to the victor in the game.

Morris found Carn Carby and unfroze him, and the thirteen-year-old came and presented himself to Ender, who laughed without malice and held out his hand. Carn graciously took Ender's hand and bowed his head over it. It was that or be flashed again.

Lieutenant Anderson dismissed Dragon Army, and they silently left the battleroom through the enemy's door—again part of the ritual. A light was blinking on the north side of the square door, indicating where the gravity was in that corridor. Ender, leading his soldiers, changed his orientation and went through the forcefield and into gravity on his feet. His army followed him at a brisk run back to the workroom. When they got there they formed up into squads, and Ender hung in the air, watching them.

"Good first battle," he said, which was excuse enough for a cheer, which he quieted. "Dragon Army did all right against Rabbits. But the enemy isn't always going to be that bad. And if that had been a good army we would have been smashed. We still would have won, but we would have been smashed. Now let me see B and D toons out here. Your takeoff from the stars was way too slow. If Rabbit Army knew how to aim a flasher, you all would have been frozen solid before A and C even got to the wall."

They worked out for the rest of the day.

That night Ender went for the first time to the commanders' mess hall. No one was allowed there until he had won at least one battle, and Ender was the youngest commander ever to make it. There was no great stir when he came in. But when some of the other boys saw the Dragon on his breast pocket, they stared at him openly, and by the time he got his tray and sat at an empty table, the entire room was silent, with the other commanders watching him. Intensely self-conscious, Ender wondered how they all knew, and why they all looked so hostile.

Then he looked above the door he had just come through. There was a huge scoreboard across the entire wall. It showed the win/loss record for the commander of every army; that day's battles were lit in red. Only four of them. The other three winners had barely made it—the best of them had only two men whole and eleven mobile at the end of the game. Dragon Army's score of thirty-eight mobile was embarrassingly better.

Other new commanders had been admitted to the commanders' mess hall with cheers and congratulations. Other new commanders hadn't won thirty-eight to zero.

Ender looked for Rabbit Army on the scoreboard. He was surprised to find that Carn Carby's score to date was eight wins and three losses. Was he that good? Or had he only fought against inferior armies? Whichever, there was still a zero in Carn's mobile and whole columns, and Ender looked down from the scoreboard grinning. No one smiled back, and Ender knew that they were afraid of him, which meant that they would hate him, which meant that anyone who went into battle against Dragon Army would be scared and angry and less competent. Ender looked for Carn Carby in the crowd, and found him not too far away. He stared at Carby until one of the other boys nudged the Rabbit commander and pointed to Ender. Ender smiled again and waved slightly. Carby turned red, and Ender, satisfied, leaned over his dinner and began to eat.

At the end of the week Dragon Army had fought seven battles in seven days. The score stood 7 wins and 0 losses. Ender had never had more than five boys frozen in any game. It was no longer possible for the other commanders to ignore Ender. A few of them sat with him and quietly conversed about game strategies that Ender's opponents had used. Other much larger groups were talking with the commanders that Ender had defeated, trying to find out what Ender had done to beat them.

In the middle of the meal the teacher door opened and the groups fell silent as Lieutenant Anderson stepped in and looked over the group. When he located Ender he strode quickly across the room and whispered in Ender's ear. Ender nodded, finished his glass of water, and left with the lieutenant. On the way out, Anderson handed a slip of paper to one of the older boys. The room became very noisy with conversation as Anderson and Ender left.

Ender was escorted down corridors he had never seen before. They didn't have the blue glow of the soldier corridors. Most were wood paneled, and the floors were carpeted. The doors were wood, with nameplates on them, and they stopped at one that said "Captain Graff, supervisor." Anderson knocked softly, and a low voice said, "Come in."

They went in. Captain Graff was seated behind a desk, his hands folded across his potbelly. He nodded, and Anderson sat. Ender also sat down. Graff cleared his throat and spoke.

"Seven days since your first battle, Ender."

Ender did not reply.

"Won seven battles, one every day."

Ender nodded.

"Scores unusually high, too."

Ender blinked.

"Why?" Graff asked him.

Ender glanced at Anderson, and then spoke to the captain behind the desk. "Two new tactics, sir. Legs doubled up as a shield, so that a flash doesn't immobilize. Jackknife takeoffs from the walls. Superior strategy, as Lieutenant Anderson taught, think places, not spaces. Five toons of eight instead of four of ten. Incompetent opponents. Excellent toon leaders, good soldiers."

Graff looked at Ender without expression. Waiting for what, Ender wondered. Lieutenant Anderson spoke up.

"Ender, what's the condition of your army?"

Do they want me to ask for relief? Not a chance, he decided. "A little tired, in peak condition, morale high, learning fast. Anxious for the next battle."

Anderson looked at Graff. Graff shrugged slightly and turned to Ender.

"Is there anything you want to know?"

Ender held his hands loosely in his lap. "When are you going to put us up against a good army?"

Graff's laughter rang in the room, and when it stopped, Graff handed a piece of paper to Ender. "Now," the captain said, and Ender read the paper: "Dragon Army against Leopard Army, Ender Wiggins and Pol Slattery, 2000."

Ender looked up at Captain Graff. "That's ten minutes from now, sir."

Graff smiled. "Better hurry, then, boy."

As Ender left he realized Pol Slattery was the boy who had been handed his orders as Ender left the mess hall.

He got to his army five minutes later. Three toon leaders were already undressed and lying naked on their beds. He sent them all flying down the corridors to rouse their toons, and gathered up their suits himself. When all his boys were assembled in the corridor, most of them still getting dressed, Ender spoke to them.

"This one's hot and there's no time. We'll be late to the door, and the enemy'll be deployed right outside our gate. Ambush, and I've never heard of it happening before. So we'll take our time at the door. A and B toons, keep your belts loose, and give your flashers to the leaders and seconds of the other toons."

Puzzled, his soldiers complied. By then all were dressed, and Ender led them at a trot to the gate. When they reached it the forcefield was already on one-way, and some of his soldiers were panting. They had had one battle that day and a full workout. They were tired.

Ender stopped at the entrance and looked at the placement of the enemy soldiers. Some of them were grouped not more than twenty feet out from the gate. There was no grid, there were no stars. A big empty space. Where were most of the enemy soldiers? There should have been thirty more.

"They're flat against this wall," Ender said, "where we can't see them."

He took A and B toons and made them kneel, their hands on their hips. Then he flashed them, so that their bodies were frozen rigid.

"You're shields," Ender said, and then had boys from C and D kneel on their legs and hook both arms under the frozen boys' belts. Each boy was holding two flashers. Then Ender and the members of E toon picked up the duos, three at a time, and threw them out the door.

Of course, the enemy opened fire immediately. But they mainly hit the boys who were already flashed, and in a few moments pandemonium broke out in the battleroom. All the soldiers of Leopard Army were easy targets as they lay pressed flat against the wall or floated, unprotected, in the middle of the battleroom; and Ender's soldiers, armed with two flashers each, carved them up easily. Pol Slattery reacted quickly, ordering his men away from the wall, but not quickly enough—only a few were able to move, and they were flashed before they could get a quarter of the way across the battleroom.

When the battle was over Dragon Army had only twelve boys whole, the lowest score they had ever had. But Ender was satisfied. And during the ritual of surrender Pol Slattery broke form by shaking hands and asking, "Why did you wait so long getting out of the gate?"

Ender glanced at Anderson, who was floating nearby. "I was informed late," he said. "It was an ambush."

Slattery grinned, and gripped Ender's hand again. "Good game."

Ender didn't smile at Anderson this time. He knew that now the games would be arranged against him, to even up the odds. He didn't like it.

It was 2150, nearly time for lights out, when Ender knocked at the door of the room shared by Bean and three other soldiers. One of the others opened the door, then stepped back and held it wide. Ender stood for a moment, then asked if he could come in. They answered, of course, of course, come in, and he walked to the upper bunk, where Bean had set down his book and was leaning on one elbow to look at Ender.

"Bean, can you give me twenty minutes?"

"Near lights out," Bean answered.

"My room," Ender answered. "I'll cover for you."

Bean sat up and slid off his bed. Together he and Ender padded silently down the corridor to Ender's room. Ender entered first, and Ender closed the door behind them.

"Sit down," Ender said, and they both sat on the edge of the bed, looking at each other.

"Remember four weeks ago, Bean? When you told me to make you a toon leader?"

"Yeah."

"I've made five toon leaders since then, haven't I? And none of them was you."

Bean looked at him calmly.

"Was I right?" Ender asked.

"Yes, sir," Bean answered.

Ender nodded. "How have you done in these battles?"

Bean cocked his head to one side. "I've never been immobilized, sir, and I've immobilized forty-three of the enemy. I've obeyed orders quickly, and I've commanded a squad in mop-up and never lost a soldier."

"Then you'll understand this." Ender paused, then decided to back up and say something else first.

"You know you're early, Bean, by a good half year. I was, too, and I've been made a commander six months early. Now they've put me into battles after only three weeks of training with my army. They've given me eight battles in seven days. I've already had more battles than boys who were made commander four months ago. I've won more battles than many who've been commanders for a year. And then tonight. You know what happened tonight."

Bean nodded. "They told you late."

"I don't know what the teachers are doing. But my army is getting tired, and I'm getting tired, and now they're changing the rules of the game. You see, Bean, I've looked in the old charts. No one has ever destroyed so many enemies and kept so many of his own soldiers whole in the history of the game. I'm unique—and I'm getting unique treatment."

Bean smiled. "You're the best, Ender."

Ender shook his head. "Maybe. But it was no accident that I got the soldiers I got. My worst soldier could be a toon leader in another army. I've got the best. They've loaded things my way—but now they're loading it all against me. I don't know why. But I know I have to be ready for it. I need your help."

"Why mine?"

"Because even though there are some better soldiers than you in Dragon Army— not many, but some—there's nobody who can think better and faster than you." Bean said nothing. They both knew it was true.

Ender continued, "I need to be ready, but I can't retrain the whole army. So I'm going to cut every toon down by one, including you. With four others you'll be a special squad under me. And you'll learn to do some new things. Most of the time you'll be in the regular toons just like you are now. But when I need you. See?"

Bean smiled and nodded. "That's right, that's good, can I pick them myself?"

"One from each toon except your own, and you can't take any toon leaders."

"What do you want us to do?"

"Bean, I don't know. I don't know what they'll throw at us. What would you do if suddenly our flashers didn't work, and the enemy's did? What would you do if we had to face two armies at once? The only thing I know is—there may be a game where we don't even try for score. Where we just go for the enemy's gate. That's when the battle is technically won—four helmets at the corners of the gate. I want you ready to do that any time I call for it. Got it? You take them for two hours a day during regular workout. Then you and I and your soldiers, we'll work at night after dinner."

"We'll get tired."

"I have a feeling we don't know what tired is." Ender reached out and took Bean's hand, and gripped it. "Even when it's rigged against us, Bean. We'll win."

Bean left in silence and padded down the corridor.

Dragon Army wasn't the only army working out after hours now. The other commanders had finally realized they had some catching up to do. From early morning to lights out soldiers all over Training and Command Center, none of them over fourteen years old, were learning to jackknife off walls and use each other as living shields.

But while other commanders mastered the techniques that Ender had used to defeat them, Ender and Bean worked on solutions to problems that had never come up.

There were still battles every day, but for a while they were normal, with grids and stars and sudden plunges through the gate. And after the battles, Ender and Bean and four other soldiers would leave the main group and practice strange maneuvers. Attacks without flashers, using feet to physically disarm or disorient an enemy. Using four frozen soldiers to reverse the enemy's gate in less than two seconds. And one day Bean came to workout with a 300-meter cord.

"What's that for?"

"I don't know yet." Absently Bean spun one end of the cord. It wasn't more than an eighth of an inch thick, but it could have lifted ten adults without breaking.

"Where did you get it?"

"Commissary. They asked what for. I said to practice tying knots."

Bean tied a loop in the end of the rope and slid it over his shoulders.

"Here, you two, hang on to the wall here. Now don't let go of the rope. Give me about fifty yards of slack." They complied, and Bean moved about ten feet from them along the wall. As soon as he was sure they were ready, he jackknifed off the wall and flew straight out, fifty yards. Then the rope snapped taut. It was so fine that it was virtually invisible, but it was strong enough to force Bean to veer off at almost a right angle. It happened so suddenly that he had inscribed a perfect arc and hit the wall hard before most of the other soldiers knew what had happened. Bean did a perfect rebound and drifted quickly back to where Ender and the others waited for him.

Many of the soldiers in the five regular squads hadn't noticed the rope, and were demanding to know how it was done. It was impossible to change direction that abruptly in nullo. Bean just laughed.

"Wait till the next game without a grid! They'll never know what hit them."

They never did. The next game was only two hours later, but Bean and two others had become pretty good at aiming and shooting while they flew at ridiculous speeds at the end of the rope. The slip of paper was delivered, and Dragon Army trotted off to the gate, to battle with Griffin Army. Bean coiled the rope all the way.

When the gate opened, all they could see was a large brown star only fifteen feet away, completely blocking their view of the enemy's gate.

Ender didn't pause. "Bean, give yourself fifty feet of rope and go around the star." Bean and his four soldiers dropped through the gate and in a moment Bean was launched sideways away from the star. The rope snapped taut, and Bean flew forward. As the rope was stopped by each edge of the star in turn, his arc became tighter and his speed greater, until when he hit the wall only a few feet away from the gate he was barely able to control his rebound to end up behind the star. But he immediately moved all his arms and legs so that those waiting inside the gate would know that the enemy hadn't flashed him anywhere.

Ender dropped through the gate, and Bean quickly told him how Griffin Army was situated. "They've got two squares of stars, all the way around the gate. All their soldiers are under cover, and there's no way to hit any of them until we're clear to the bottom wall. Even with shields, we'd get there at half strength and we wouldn't have a chance."

"They moving?" Ender asked.

"Do they need to?"

"I would." Ender thought for a moment. "This one's tough. We'll go for the gate, Bean."

Griffin Army began to call out to them.

"Hey, is anybody there!"

"Wake up, there's a war on!"

"We wanna join the picnic!"

They were still calling when Ender's army came out from behind their star with a shield of fourteen frozen soldiers. William Bee, Griffin Army's commander, waited patiently as the screen approached, his men waiting at the fringes of their stars for the moment when whatever was behind the screen became visible. About ten yards away the screen suddenly exploded as the soldiers behind it shoved the screen north. The momentum carried them south twice as fast, and at the same moment the rest of Dragon Army burst from behind their star at the opposite end of the room, firing rapidly.

William Bee's boys joined battle immediately, of course, but William Bee was far more interested in what had been left behind when the shield disappeared. A formation of four frozen Dragon Army soldiers was moving headfirst toward the Griffin Army gate, held together by another frozen soldier whose feet and hands were hooked through their belts. A sixth soldier hung to his waist and trailed like the tail of a kite. Griffin

Army was winning the battle easily, and William Bee concentrated on the formation as it approached the gate. Suddenly the soldier trailing in back moved—he wasn't frozen at all! And even though William Bee flashed him immediately, the damage was done. The formation drifted to the Griffin Army gate, and their helmets touched all four corners simultaneously. A buzzer sounded, the gate reversed, and the frozen soldier in the middle was carried by momentum right through the gate. All the flashers stopped working, and the game was over.

The teachergate opened and Lieutenant Anderson came in. Anderson stopped himself with a slight movement of his hands when he reached the center of the battleroom. "Ender," he called, breaking protocol. One of the frozen Dragon soldiers near the south wall tried to call through jaws that were clamped shut by the suit. Anderson drifted to him and unfroze him.

Ender was smiling.

"I beat you again, sir," Ender said.

Anderson didn't smile. "That's nonsense, Ender," Anderson said softly. "Your battle was with William Bee of Griffin Army."

Ender raised an eyebrow.

"After that maneuver," Anderson said, "the rules are being revised to require that all of the enemy's soldiers must be immobilized before the gate can be reversed."

"That's all right," Ender said. "It could only work once, anyway." Anderson nodded, and was turning away when Ender added, "Is there going to be a new rule that armies be given equal positions to fight from?"

Anderson turned back around. "If you're in one of the positions, Ender, you can hardly call them equal, whatever they are."

William Bee counted carefully and wondered how in the world he had lost when not one of his soldiers had been flashed and only four of Ender's soldiers were even mobile.

And that night as Ender came into the commanders' mess hall, he was greeted with applause and cheers, and his table was crowded with respectful commanders, many of them two or three years older than he was. He was friendly, but while he ate he wondered what the teachers would do to him in his next battle. He didn't need to worry. His next two battles were easy victories, and after that he never saw the battleroom again.

It was 2100 and Ender was a little irritated to hear someone knock at his door. His army was exhausted, and he had ordered them all to be in bed after 2030. The last two days had been regular battles, and Ender was expecting the worst in the morning.

It was Bean. He came in sheepishly, and saluted.

Ender returned his salute and snapped, "Bean, I wanted everybody in bed."

Bean nodded but didn't leave. Ender considered ordering him out. But as he looked at Bean it occurred to him for the first time in weeks just how young Bean was. He had turned eight a week before, and he was still small and—no, Ender thought, he wasn't young. Nobody was young. Bean had been in battle, and with a whole army depending on him he had come through and won. And even though he was small, Ender could never think of him as young again.

Ender shrugged and Bean came over and sat on the edge of the bed. The younger boy looked at his hands for a while, and finally Ender grew impatient and asked, "Well, what is it?"

"I'm transferred. Got orders just a few minutes ago."

Ender closed his eyes for a moment. "I knew they'd pull something new. Now they're taking—where are you going?"

"Rabbit Army."

"How can they put you under an idiot like Carn Carby!"

"Carn was graduated. Support squads."

Ender looked up. "Well, who's commanding Rabbit then?"

Bean held his hands out helplessly.

"Me," he said.

Ender nodded, and then smiled. "Of course. After all, you're only four years younger than the regular age."

"It isn't funny," Bean said. "I don't know what's going on here. First all the changes in the game. And now this. I wasn't the only one transferred, either, Ender. Ren, Peder, Brian, Wins, Younger. All commanders now."

Ender stood up angrily and strode to the wall. "Every damn toon leader I've got!" he said, and whirled to face Bean. "If they're going to break up my army, Bean, why did they bother making me a commander at all?"

Bean shook his head. "I don't know. You're the best, Ender. Nobody's ever done what you've done. Nineteen battles in fifteen days, sir, and you won every one of them, no matter what they did to you."

"And now you and the others are commanders. You know every trick I've got, I trained you, and who am I supposed to replace you with? Are they going to stick me with six greenohs?"

"It stinks, Ender, but you know that if they gave you five crippled midgets and armed you with a roll of toilet paper you'd win."

They both laughed, and then they noticed that the door was open.

Lieutenant Anderson stepped in. He was followed by Captain Graff.

"Ender Wiggins," Graff said, holding his hands across his stomach.

"Yes, sir," Ender answered.

"Orders."

Anderson extended a slip of paper. Ender read it quickly, then crumpled it, still looking at the air where the paper had been. After a few moments he asked, "Can I tell my army?"

"They'll find out," Graff answered. "It's better not to talk to them after orders. It makes it easier."

"For you or for me?" Ender asked. He didn't wait for an answer. He turned quickly to Bean, took his hand for a moment, and then headed for the door.

"Wait," Bean said. "Where are you going? Tactical or Support School?"

"Command School," Ender answered, and then he was gone and Anderson closed the door.

Command School, Bean thought. Nobody went to Command School until they had gone through three years of Tactical. But then, nobody went to Tactical until they had been through at least five years of Battle School. Ender had only had three.

The system was breaking up. No doubt about it, Bean thought. Either somebody at the top was going crazy, or something was going wrong with the war—the real war, the one they were training to fight in. Why else would they break down the training system, advance somebody—even somebody as good as Ender—straight to Command School? Why else would they ever have an eight-year-old greenoh like Bean command an army?

Bean wondered about it for a long time, and then he finally lay down on Ender's bed and realized that he'd never see Ender again, probably. For some reason that made him want to cry. But he didn't cry, of course. Training in the preschools had taught him how to force down emotions like that. He remembered how his first teacher, when he was three, would have been upset to see his lip quivering and his eyes full of tears.

Bean went through the relaxing routine until he didn't feel like crying anymore. Then he drifted off to sleep. His hand was near his mouth. It lay on his pillow hesitantly, as if Bean couldn't decide whether to bite his nails or suck on his fingertips. His forehead was creased and furrowed. His breathing was quick and light. He was a soldier, and if anyone had asked him what he wanted to be when he grew up, he wouldn't have known what they meant.

There's a war on, they said, and that was excuse enough for all the hurry in the world. They said it like a password and flashed a little card at every ticket counter and customs check and guard station. It got them to the head of every line.

Ender Wiggins was rushed from place to place so quickly he had no time to examine anything. But he did see trees for the first time. He saw men who were not in uniform. He saw women. He saw strange animals that didn't speak, but that followed docilely behind women and small children. He saw suitcases and conveyor belts and signs that said words he had never heard of. He would have asked someone what the words meant, except that purpose and authority surrounded him in the persons of four very high officers who never spoke to each other and never spoke to him.

Ender Wiggins was a stranger to the world he was being trained to save. He did not remember ever leaving Battle School before. His earliest memories were of childish war games under the direction of a teacher, of meals with other boys in the gray and green uniforms of the armed forces of his world. He did not know that the gray represented the sky and the green represented the great forests of his planet. All he knew of the world was from vague references to "outside."

And before he could make any sense of the strange world he was seeing for the first time, they enclosed him again within the shell of the military, where nobody had to say There's a war on anymore because no one within the shell of the military forgot it for a single instant of a single day.

They put him in a spaceship and launched him to a large artificial satellite that circled the world.

This space station was called Command School. It held the ansible.

On his first day Ender Wiggins was taught about the ansible and what it meant to warfare. It meant that even though the starships of today's battles were launched a hundred years ago, the commanders of the starships were men of today, who used the ansible to send messages to the computers and the few men on each ship. The ansible sent words as they were spoken, orders as they were made. Battleplans as they were fought. Light was a pedestrian.

For two months Ender Wiggins didn't meet a single person. They came to him namelessly, taught him what they knew, and left him to other teachers. He had no time to miss his friends at Battle School. He only had time to learn how to operate the simulator, which flashed battle patterns around him as if he were in a starship at the center of the battle. How to command mock ships in mock battles by manipulating the keys on the simulator and speaking words into the ansible. How to recognize instantly every enemy ship and the weapons it carried by the pattern that the simulator showed. How to transfer all that he learned in the nullo battles at Battle School to the starship battles at Command School.

He had thought the game was taken seriously before. Here they hurried him through every step, were angry and worried beyond reason every time he forgot something or made a mistake. But he worked as he had always worked, and learned as he had always learned. After a while he didn't make any more mistakes. He used the simulator as if it were a part of himself. Then they stopped being worried and gave him a teacher.

Maezr Rackham was sitting cross-legged on the floor when Ender awoke. He said nothing as Ender got up and showered and dressed, and Ender did not bother to ask him anything. He had long since learned that when something unusual was going on, he would often find out more information faster by waiting than by asking.

Maezr still hadn't spoken when Ender was ready and went to the door to leave the room. The door didn't open. Ender turned to face the man sitting on the floor. Maezr was at least forty, which made him the oldest man Ender had ever seen close up. He had a day's growth of black and white whiskers that grizzled his face only slightly less than his close-cut hair. His face sagged a little and his eyes were surrounded by creases and lines. He looked at Ender without interest.

Ender turned back to the door and tried again to open it.

"All right," he said, giving up. "Why's the door locked?"

Maezr continued to look at him blankly.

Ender became impatient. "I'm going to be late. If I'm not supposed to be there until later, then tell me so I can go back to bed." No answer. "Is it a guessing game?" Ender asked. No answer. Ender decided that maybe the man was trying to make him angry, so he went through a relaxing exercise as he leaned on the door, and soon he was calm again. Maezr didn't take his eyes off Ender.

For the next two hours the silence endured, Maezr watching Ender constantly, Ender trying to pretend he didn't notice the old man. The boy became more and more nervous, and finally ended up walking from one end of the room to the other in a sporadic pattern.

He walked by Maezr as he had several times before, and Maezr's hand shot out and pushed Ender's left leg into his right in the middle of a step. Ender fell flat on the floor.

He leaped to his feet immediately, furious. He found Maezr sitting calmly, cross-legged, as if he had never moved. Ender stood poised to fight. But the other's immobility made it impossible for Ender to attack, and he found himself wondering if he had only imagined the old man's hand tripping him up.

The pacing continued for another hour, with Ender Wiggins trying the door every now and then. At last he gave up and took off his uniform and walked to his bed.

As he leaned over to pull the covers back, he felt a hand jab roughly between his thighs and another hand grab his hair. In a moment he had been turned upside down. His face and shoulders were being pressed into the floor by the old man's knee, while his back was excruciatingly bent and his legs were pinioned by Maezr's arm. Ender was helpless to use his arms, and he couldn't bend his back to gain slack so he could use his legs. In less than two seconds the old man had completely defeated Ender Wiggins.

"All right," Ender gasped. "You win."

Maezr's knee thrust painfully downward.

"Since when," Maezr asked in a soft, rasping voice, "do you have to tell the enemy when he has won?"

Ender remained silent.

"I surprised you once, Ender Wiggins. Why didn't you destroy me immediately afterward? Just because I looked peaceful? You turned your back on me. Stupid. You have learned nothing. You have never had a teacher."

Ender was angry now. "I've had too many damned teachers, how was I supposed to know you'd turn out to be a—" Ender hunted for a word. Maezr supplied one.

"An enemy, Ender Wiggins," Maezr whispered. "I am your enemy, the first one you've ever had who was smarter than you. There is no teacher but the enemy, Ender Wiggins. No one but the enemy will ever tell you what the enemy is going to do. No one but the enemy will ever teach you how to destroy and conquer. I am your enemy, from now on. From now on I am your teacher."

Then Maezr let Ender's legs fall to the floor. Because the old man still held Ender's head to the floor, the boy couldn't use his arms to compensate, and his legs hit the plastic surface with a loud crack and a sickening pain that made Ender wince. Then Maezr stood and let Ender rise.

Slowly the boy pulled his legs under him, with a faint groan of pain, and he knelt on all fours for a moment, recovering. Then his right arm flashed out. Maezr quickly danced back and Ender's hand closed on air as his teacher's foot shot forward to catch Ender on the chin.

Ender's chin wasn't there. He was lying flat on his back, spinning on the floor, and during the moment that Maezr was off balance from his kick Ender's feet smashed into Maezr's other leg. The old man fell on the ground in a heap.

What seemed to be a heap was really a hornet's nest. Ender couldn't find an arm or a leg that held still long enough to be grabbed, and in the meantime blows were landing on his back and arms. Ender was smaller—he couldn't reach past the old man's flailing limbs.

So he leaped back out of the way and stood poised near the door.

The old man stopped thrashing about and sat up, cross-legged again, laughing. "Better, this time, boy. But slow. You will have to be better with a fleet than you are with your body or no one will be safe with you in command. Lesson learned?"

Ender nodded slowly.

Maezr smiled. "Good. Then we'll never have such a battle again. All the rest with the simulator. I will program your battles, I will devise the strategy of your enemy, and you will learn to be quick and discover what tricks the enemy has for you. Remember, boy. From now on the enemy is more clever than you. From now on the enemy is stronger than you. From now on you are always about to lose."

Then Maezr's face became serious again. "You will be about to lose, Ender, but you will win. You will learn to defeat the enemy. He will teach you how."

Maezr got up and walked toward the door. Ender stepped back out of the way. As the old man touched the handle of the door, Ender leaped into the air and kicked Maezr in the small of the back with both feet. He hit hard enough that he rebounded onto his feet, as Maezr cried out and collapsed on the floor.

Maezr got up slowly, holding on to the door handle, his face contorted with pain. He seemed disabled, but Ender didn't trust him. He waited warily. And yet in spite of his suspicion he was caught off guard by Maezr's speed. In a moment he found himself on the floor near the opposite wall, his nose and lip bleeding where his face had hit the bed. He was able to turn enough to see Maezr open the door and leave. The old man was limping and walking slowly.

Ender smiled in spite of the pain, then rolled over onto his back and laughed until his mouth filled with blood and he started to gag. Then he got up and painfully made his way to the bed. He lay down and in a few minutes a medic came and took care of his injuries.

As the drug had its effect and Ender drifted off to sleep he remembered the way Maezr limped out of his room and laughed again. He was still laughing softly as his mind went blank and the medic pulled the blanket over him and snapped off the light. He slept until pain woke him in the morning. He dreamed of defeating Maezr.

The next day Ender went to the simulator room with his nose bandaged and his lip still puffy. Maezr was not there. Instead, a captain who had worked with him before showed him an addition that had been made. The captain pointed to a tube with a loop at one end. "Radio. Primitive, I know, but it loops over your ear and we tuck the other end into your mouth like this."

"Watch it," Ender said as the captain pushed the end of the tube into his swollen lip.

"Sorry. Now you just talk."

"Good. Who to?"

The captain smiled. "Ask and see."

Ender shrugged and turned to the simulator. As he did a voice reverberated through his skull. It was too loud for him to understand, and he ripped the radio off his ear.

"What are you trying to do, make me deaf?"

The captain shook his head and turned a dial on a small box on a nearby table. Ender put the radio back on.

"Commander," the radio said in a familiar voice.

Ender answered, "Yes."

"Instructions, sir?"

The voice was definitely familiar. "Bean?" Ender asked.

"Yes, sir."

"Bean, this is Ender."

Silence. And then a burst of laughter from the other side. Then six or seven more voices laughing, and Ender waited for silence to return. When it did, he asked, "Who else?"

A few voices spoke at once, but Bean drowned them out. "Me, I'm Bean, and Peder, Wins, Younger, Lee, and Vlad."

Ender thought for a moment. Then he asked what the hell was going on. They laughed again.

"They can't break up the group," Bean said. "We were commanders for maybe two weeks, and here we are at Command School, training with the simulator, and all of a sudden they told us we were going to form a fleet with a new commander. And that's you."

Ender smiled. "Are you boys any good?"

"If we aren't, you'll let us know."

Ender chuckled a little. "Might work out. A fleet."

For the next ten days Ender trained his toon leaders until they could maneuver their ships like precision dancers. It was like being back in the battleroom again, except that now Ender could always see everything, and could speak to his toon leaders and change their orders at any time.

One day as Ender sat down at the control board and switched on the simulator, harsh green lights appeared in the space—the enemy.

"This is it," Ender said. "X, Y, bullet, C, D, reserve screen, E, south loop, Bean, angle north."

The enemy was grouped in a globe, and outnumbered Ender two to one. Half of Ender's force was grouped in a tight, bulletlike formation, with the rest in a flat circular screen—except for a tiny force under Bean that moved off the simulator, heading behind the enemy's formation. Ender quickly learned the enemy's strategy: whenever Ender's bullet formation came close, the enemy would give way, hoping to draw Ender inside the globe where he would be surrounded. So Ender obligingly fell into the trap, bringing his bullet to the center of the globe.

The enemy began to contract slowly, not wanting to come within range until all their weapons could be brought to bear at once. Then Ender began to work in earnest. His reserve screen approached the outside of the globe, and the enemy began to concentrate his forces there. Then Bean's force appeared on the opposite side, and the enemy again deployed ships on that side.

Which left most of the globe only thinly defended. Ender's bullet attacked, and since at the point of attack it outnumbered the enemy overwhelmingly, he tore a hole in the formation. The enemy reacted to try to plug the gap, but in the confusion the reserve force and Bean's small force attacked simultaneously, while the bullet moved to another part of the globe. In a few more minutes the formation was shattered, most of the enemy ships destroyed, and the few survivors rushing away as fast as they could go.

Ender switched the simulator off. All the lights faded. Maezr was standing beside Ender, his hands in his pockets, his body tense. Ender looked up at him.

"I thought you said the enemy would be smart," Ender said.

Maezr's face remained expressionless. "What did you learn?"

"I learned that a sphere only works if your enemy's a fool. He had his forces so spread out that I outnumbered him whenever I engaged him."

"And?"

"And," Ender said, "you can't stay committed to one pattern. It makes you too easy to predict."

"Is that all?" Maezr asked quietly.

Ender took off his radio. "The enemy could have defeated me by breaking the sphere earlier."

Maezr nodded. "You had an unfair advantage."

Ender looked up at him coldly. "I was outnumbered two to one."

Maezr shook his head. "You have the ansible. The enemy doesn't. We include that in the mock battles. Their messages travel at the speed of light."

Ender glanced toward the simulator. "Is there enough space to make a difference?"

"Don't you know?" Maezr asked. "None of the ships was ever closer than thirty thousand kilometers to any other."

Ender tried to figure the size of the enemy's sphere. Astronomy was beyond him. But now his curiosity was stirred.

"What kind of weapons are on those ships? To be able to strike so fast?"

Maezr shook his head. "The science is too much for you. You'd have to study many more years than you've lived to understand even the basics. All you need to know is that the weapons work."

"Why do we have to come so close to be in range?"

"The ships are all protected by forcefields. A certain distance away the weapons are weaker and can't get through. Closer in the weapons are stronger than the shields. But the computers take care of all that. They're constantly firing in any direction that won't hurt one of our ships. The computers pick targets, aim; they do all the detail work. You just tell them when and get them in a position to win. All right?"

"No." Ender twisted the tube of the radio around his fingers. "I have to know how the weapons work."

"I told you, it would take—"

"I can't command a fleet—not even on the simulator—unless I know." Ender waited a moment, then added, "Just the rough idea."

Maezr stood up and walked a few steps away. "All right, Ender. It won't make any sense, but I'll try. As simply as I can." He shoved his hands into his pockets. "It's this way, Ender. Everything is made up of atoms, little particles so small you can't see them with your eyes. These atoms, there are only a few different types, and they're all made up of even smaller particles that are pretty much the same. These atoms can be broken, so that they stop being atoms. So that this metal doesn't hold together anymore. Or the plastic floor. Or your body. Or even the air. They just seem to disappear, if you break the atoms. All that's left is the pieces. And they fly around and break more atoms. The weapons on the ships set up an area where it's impossible for atoms of anything to stay together. They all break down. So things in that area—they disappear."

Ender nodded. "You're right, I don't understand it. Can it be blocked?"

"No. But it gets wider and weaker the farther it goes from the ship, so that after a while a forcefield will block it. OK? And to make it strong at all, it has to be focused, so that a ship can only fire effectively in maybe three or four directions at once."

Ender nodded again, but he didn't really understand, not well enough. "If the pieces of the broken atoms go breaking more atoms, why doesn't it just make everything disappear?"

"Space. Those thousands of kilometers between the ships, they're empty. Almost no atoms. The pieces don't hit anything, and when they finally do hit something, they're so spread out they can't do any harm." Maezr cocked his head quizzically. "Anything else you need to know?"

"Do the weapons on the ships—do they work against anything besides ships?"

Maezr moved in close to Ender and said firmly, "We only use them against ships. Never anything else. If we used them against anything else, the enemy would use them against us. Got it?"

Maezr walked away, and was nearly out the door when Ender called to him.

"I don't know your name yet," Ender said blandly.

"Maezr Rackham."

"Maezr Rackham," Ender said, "I defeated you."

Maezr laughed.

"Ender, you weren't fighting me today," he said. "You were fighting the stupidest computer in the Command School, set on a ten-year-old program. You don't think I'd use a sphere, do you?" He shook his head. "Ender, my dear little fellow, when you fight me you'll know it. Because you'll lose." And Maezr left the room.

Ender still practiced ten hours a day with his toon leaders. He never saw them, though, only heard their voices on the radio. Battles came every two or three days. The enemy had something new every time, something harder—but Ender coped with it. And won every time. And after every battle Maezr would point out mistakes and show Ender that he had really lost. Maezr only let Ender finish so that he would learn to handle the end of the game.

Until finally Maezr came in and solemnly shook Ender's hand and said, "That, boy, was a good battle."

Because the praise was so long in coming, it pleased Ender more than praise had ever pleased him before. And because it was so condescending, he resented it.

"So from now on," Maezr said, "we can give you hard ones."

From then on Ender's life was a slow nervous breakdown.

He began fighting two battles a day, with problems that steadily grew more difficult. He had been trained in nothing but the game all his life, but now the game began to consume him. He woke in the morning with new strategies for the simulator and went fitfully to sleep at night with the mistakes of the day preying on him. Sometimes he would wake up in the middle of the night crying for a reason he didn't remember. Sometimes he woke with his knuckles bloody from biting them. But every day he went impassively to the simulator and drilled his toon leaders until the battles, and drilled his toon leaders after the battles, and endured and studied the harsh criticism that Maezr Rackham piled on him. He noted that Rackham perversely criticized him more after his hardest battles. He noted that every time he thought of a new strategy the enemy was using it within a few days. And he noted that while his fleet always stayed the same size, the enemy increased in numbers every day.

He asked his teacher.

"We are showing you what it will be like when you really command. The ratios of enemy to us."

"Why does the enemy always outnumber us?"

Maezr bowed his gray head for a moment, as if deciding whether to answer. Finally he looked up and reached out his hand and touched Ender on the shoulder. "I will tell you, even though the information is secret. You see, the enemy attacked us first. He had good reason to attack us, but that is a matter for politicians, and whether the fault was ours or his, we could not let him win. So when the enemy came to our worlds, we fought back, hard, and spent the finest of our young men in the fleets. But we won, and the enemy retreated."

Maezr smiled ruefully. "But the enemy was not through, boy. The enemy would never be through. They came again, with more numbers, and it was harder to beat them. And another generation of young men was spent. Only a few survived. So we came up with a plan—the big men came up with the plan. We knew that we had to destroy the enemy once and for all, totally, eliminate his ability to make war against us. To do that we had to go to his home worlds—his home world, really, since the enemy's empire is all tied to his capital world."

"And so?" Ender asked.

"And so we made a fleet. We made more ships than the enemy ever had. We made a hundred ships for every ship he had sent against us. And we launched them against his twenty-eight worlds. They started leaving a hundred years ago. And they carried on them the ansible, and only a few men. So that someday a commander could sit on a planet somewhere far from the battle and command the fleet. So that our best minds would not be destroyed by the enemy."

Ender's question had still not been answered. "Why do they outnumber us?"

Maezr laughed. "Because it took a hundred years for our ships to get there. They've had a hundred years to prepare for us. They'd be fools, don't you think, boy, if they waited in old tugboats to defend their harbors. They have new ships, great ships, hundreds of ships. All we have is the ansible, that and the fact that they have to put a commander with every fleet, and when they lose—and they will lose—they lose one of their best minds every time."

Ender started to ask another question.

"No more, Ender Wiggins. I've told you more than you ought to know as it is."

Ender stood angrily and turned away. "I have a right to know. Do you think this can go on forever, pushing me through one school and another and never telling me what my life is for? You use me and the others as a tool, someday we'll command your ships, someday maybe we'll save your lives, but I'm not a computer, and I have to *know!*"

"Ask me a question, then, boy," Maezr said, "and if I can answer, I will."

"If you use your best minds to command the fleets, and you never lose any, then what do you need me for? Who am I replacing, if they're all still there?"

Maezr shook his head. "I can't tell you the answer to that, Ender. Be content that we will need you, soon. It's late. Go to bed. You have a battle in the morning."

Ender walked out of the simulator room. But when Maezr left by the same door a few moments later, the boy was waiting in the hall.

"All right, boy," Maezr said impatiently, "what is it? I don't have all night and you need to sleep."

Ender wasn't sure what his question was, but Maezr waited. Finally Ender asked softly, "Do they live?"

"Does who live?"

"The other commanders. The ones now. And before me."

Maezr snorted. "Live. Of course they live. He wonders if they live." Still chuckling, the old man walked off down the hall. Ender stood in the corridor for a while, but at last he was tired and he went off to bed. They live, he thought. They live, but he can't tell me what happens to them.

That night Ender didn't wake up crying. But he did wake up with blood on his hands.

Months wore on with battles every day, until at last Ender settled into the routine of the destruction of himself. He slept less every night, dreamed more, and he began to have terrible pains in his stomach. They put him on a very bland diet, but soon he didn't even have an appetite for that. "Eat," Maezr said, and Ender would mechanically put food in his mouth. But if nobody told him to eat he didn't eat.

One day as he was drilling his toon leaders the room went black and he woke up on the floor with his face bloody where he had hit the controls.

They put him to bed then, and for three days he was very ill. He remembered seeing faces in his dreams, but they weren't real faces, and he knew it even while he thought he saw them. He thought he saw Bean sometimes, and sometimes he thought he saw Lieutenant Anderson and Captain Graff. And then he woke up and it was only his enemy, Maezr Rackham.

"I'm awake," he said to Maezr.

"So I see," Maezr answered. "Took you long enough. You have a battle today."

So Ender got up and fought the battle and he won it. But there was no second battle that day, and they let him go to bed earlier. His hands were shaking as he undressed.

During the night he thought he felt hands touching him gently, and he dreamed he heard voices saying, "How long can he go on?"

"Long enough."

"So soon?"

"In a few days, then he's through."

"How will he do?"

"Fine. Even today, he was better than ever."

Ender recognized the last voice as Maezr Rackham's. He resented Rackham's intruding even in his sleep.

He woke up and fought another battle and won.

Then he went to bed.

He woke up and won again.

And the next day was his last day in Command School, though he didn't know it. He got up and went to the simulator for the battle.

Maezr was waiting for him. Ender walked slowly into the simulator room. His step was slightly shuffling, and he seemed tired and dull. Maezr frowned.

"Are you awake, boy?" If Ender had been alert, he would have cared more about the concern in his teacher's voice. Instead, he simply went to the controls and sat down. Maezr spoke to him.

"Today's game needs a little explanation, Ender Wiggins. Please turn around and pay strict attention."

Ender turned around, and for the first time he noticed that there were people at the back of the room. He recognized Graff and Anderson from Battle School, and vaguely remembered a few of the men from Command School—teachers for a few hours at some time or another. But most of the people he didn't know at all.

"Who are they?"

Maezr shook his head and answered, "Observers. Every now and then we let observers come in to watch the battle. If you don't want them, we'll send them out."

Ender shrugged. Maezr began his explanation. "Today's game, boy, has a new element. We're staging this battle around a planet. This will complicate things in two ways. The planet isn't large, on the scale we're using, but the ansible can't detect anything on the other side of it—so there's a blind spot. Also, it's against the rules to use weapons against the planet itself. All right?"

"Why, don't the weapons work against planets?"

Maezr answered coldly, "There are rules of war, Ender, that apply even in training games."

Ender shook his head slowly. "Can the planet attack?"

Maezr looked nonplussed for a moment, then smiled. "I guess you'll have to find that one out, boy. And one more thing. Today, Ender, your opponent isn't the computer. I am your enemy today, and today I won't be letting you off so easily. Today is a battle to the end. And I'll use any means I can to defeat you."

Then Maezr was gone, and Ender expressionlessly led his toon leaders through maneuvers. Ender was doing well, of course, but several of the observers shook their heads, and Graff kept clasping and unclasping his hands, crossing and uncrossing his legs. Ender would be slow today, and today Ender couldn't afford to be slow.

A warning buzzer sounded, and Ender cleared the simulator board, waiting for today's game to appear. He felt muddled today, and wondered why people were there watching. Were they going to judge him today? Decide if he was good enough for something else? For another two years of grueling training, another two years of struggling to exceed his best? Ender was twelve. He felt very old. And as he waited for the game to appear, he wished he could simply lose it, lose the battle badly and completely so that they would remove him from the program, punish him however they wanted, he didn't care, just so he could sleep.

Then the enemy formation appeared, and Ender's weariness turned to desperation.

The enemy outnumbered him a thousand to one, the simulator glowed green with them, and Ender knew that he couldn't win.

And the enemy was not stupid. There was no formation that Ender could study and attack. Instead the vast swarms of ships were constantly moving, constantly shifting from one momentary formation to another, so that a space that for one moment was empty was immediately filled with a formidable enemy force. And even though Ender's fleet was the largest he had ever had, there was no place he could deploy it where he would outnumber the enemy long enough to accomplish anything.

And behind the enemy was the planet. The planet, which Maezr had warned him about. What difference did a planet make, when Ender couldn't hope to get near it? Ender waited, waited for the flash of insight that would tell him what to do, how to destroy the enemy. And as he waited, he heard the observers behind him begin to shift in their seats, wondering what Ender was doing, what plan he would follow. And finally it was obvious to everyone that Ender didn't know what to do, that there was nothing to do, and a few of the men at the back of the room made quiet little sounds in their throats.

Then Ender heard Bean's voice in his ear. Bean chuckled and said, "Remember, the enemy's gate is *down*." A few of the other toon leaders laughed, and Ender thought back to the simple games he had played and won in Battle School. They had put him against hopeless odds there, too. And he had beaten them. And he'd be damned if he'd let Maezr Rackham beat him with a cheap trick like outnumbering him a thousand to one. He had won a game in Battle School by going for something the enemy didn't expect, something against the rules—he had won by going against the enemy's gate.

And the enemy's gate was down.

Ender smiled, and realized that if he broke this rule they'd probably kick him out of school, and that way he'd win for sure: He would never have to play a game again.

He whispered into the microphone. His six commanders each took a part of the fleet and launched themselves against the enemy. They pursued erratic courses, darting off in one direction and then another. The enemy immediately stopped his aimless maneuvering and began to group around Ender's six fleets.

Ender took off his microphone, leaned back in his chair, and watched. The observers murmured out loud, now. Ender was doing nothing—he had thrown the game away.

But a pattern began to emerge from the quick confrontations with the enemy. Ender's six groups lost ships constantly as they brushed with each enemy force—but they never stopped for a fight, even when for a moment they could have won a small tactical victory. Instead they continued on their erratic course that led, eventually, down. Toward the enemy planet.

And because of their seemingly random course the enemy didn't realize it until the same time that the observers did. By then it was too late, just as it had been too late for William Bee to stop Ender's soldiers from activating the gate. More of Ender's ships could be hit and destroyed, so that of the six fleets only two were able to get to the planet, and those were decimated. But those tiny groups *did* get through, and they opened fire on the planet.

Ender leaned forward now, anxious to see if his guess would pay off. He half expected a buzzer to sound and the game to be stopped, because he had broken the rule. But he was betting on the accuracy of the simulator. If it could simulate a planet, it could simulate what would happen to a planet under attack.

It did.

The weapons that blew up little ships didn't blow up the entire planet at first. But they did cause terrible explosions. And on the planet there was no space to dissipate the chain reaction. On the planet the chain reaction found more and more fuel to feed it.

The planet's surface seemed to be moving back and forth, but soon the surface gave way in an immense explosion that sent light flashing in all directions. It swallowed up Ender's entire fleet. And then it reached the enemy ships.

The first simply vanished in the explosion. Then, as the explosion spread and became less bright, it was clear what happened to each ship. As the light reached them they flashed brightly for a moment and disappeared. They were all fuel for the fire of the planet.

It took more than three minutes for the explosion to reach the limits of the simulator, and by then it was much fainter. All the ships were gone, and if any had escaped before the explosion reached them, they were few and not worth worrying about. Where the planet had been there was nothing. The simulator was empty.

Ender had destroyed the enemy by sacrificing his entire fleet and breaking the rule against destroying the enemy planet. He wasn't sure whether to feel triumphant at his victory or defiant at the rebuke he was certain would come. So instead he felt nothing. He was tired. He wanted to go to bed and sleep.

He switched off the simulator, and finally heard the noise behind him.

There were no longer two rows of dignified military observers. Instead there was chaos. Some of them were slapping each other on the back; some of them were bowed, head in hands; others were openly weeping. Captain Graff detached himself from the group and came to Ender. Tears streamed down his face, but he was smiling. He reached out his arms, and to Ender's surprise he embraced the boy, held him tightly, and whispered, "Thank you, thank you, thank you, Ender."

Soon all the observers were gathered around the bewildered child, thanking him and cheering him and patting him on the shoulder and shaking his hand. Ender tried to make sense of what they were saying. Had he passed the test after all? Why did it matter so much to them?

Then the crowd parted and Maezr Rackham walked through. He came straight up to Ender Wiggins and held out his hand.

"You made the hard choice, boy. But heaven knows there was no other way you could have done it. Congratulations. You beat them, and it's all over."

All over. Beat them. "I beat *you*, Maezr Rackham."

Maezr laughed, a loud laugh that filled the room. "Ender Wiggins, you never played me. You never played a *game* since I was your teacher."

Ender didn't get the joke. He had played a great many games, at a terrible cost to himself. He began to get angry.

Maezr reached out and touched his shoulder. Ender shrugged him off. Maezr then grew serious and said, "Ender Wiggins, for the last months you have been the commander of our fleets. There were no games. The battles were real. Your only enemy was *the* enemy. You won every battle. And finally today you fought them at their home world, and you destroyed their world, their fleet, you destroyed them completely, and they'll never come against us again. You did it. You."

Real. Not a game. Ender's mind was too tired to cope with it all. He walked away

from Maezr, walked silently through the crowd that still whispered thanks and congratulations to the boy, walked out of the simulator room and finally arrived in his
bedroom and closed the door.

He was asleep when Graff and Maezr Rackham found him. They came in quietly and
roused him. He awoke slowly, and when he recognized them he turned away to go
back to sleep.
 "Ender," Graff said. "We need to talk to you."
 Ender rolled back to face them. He said nothing.
 Graff smiled. "It was a shock to you yesterday, I know. But it must make you feel
good to know you won the war."
 Ender nodded slowly.
 "Maezr Rackham here, he never played against you. He only analyzed your battles
to find out your weak spots, to help you improve. It worked, didn't it?"
 Ender closed his eyes tightly. They waited. He said, "Why didn't you tell me?"
 Maezr smiled. "A hundred years ago, Ender, we found out some things. That when
a commander's life is in danger he becomes afraid, and fear slows down his thinking.
When a commander knows that he's killing people, he becomes cautious or insane,
and neither of those help him do well. And when he's mature, when he has responsibilities and an understanding of the world, he becomes cautious and sluggish and
can't do his job. So we trained children, who didn't know anything but the game, and
never knew when it would become real. That was the theory, and you proved that the
theory worked."
 Graff reached out and touched Ender's shoulder. "We launched the ships so that
they would all arrive at their destination during these few months. We knew that we'd
probably have only one good commander, if we were lucky. In history it's been very
rare to have more than one genius in a war. So we planned on having a genius. We
were gambling. And you came along and we won."
 Ender opened his eyes again and they realized that he was angry. "Yes, you won."
 Graff and Maezr Rackham looked at each other. "He doesn't understand," Graff
whispered.
 "I understand," Ender said. "You needed a weapon, and you got it, and it was me."
 "That's right," Maezr answered.
 "So tell me," Ender went on, "how many people lived on that planet that I de-
stroyed."
 They didn't answer him. They waited awhile in silence, and then Graff spoke.
"Weapons don't need to understand what they're pointed at, Ender. We did the pointing,
and so we're responsible. You just did your job."
 Maezr smiled. "Of course, Ender, you'll be taken care of. The government will
never forget you. You served us all very well."
 Ender rolled over and faced the wall, and even though they tried to talk to him,
he didn't answer them. Finally they left.
 Ender lay in his bed for a long time before anyone disturbed him again. The door
opened softly. Ender didn't turn to see who it was. Then a hand touched him softly.
 "Ender, it's me, Bean."
 Ender turned over and looked at the little boy who was standing by his bed.
 "Sit down," Ender said.
 Bean sat. "That last battle, Ender. I didn't know how you'd get us out of it."
 Ender smiled. "I didn't. I cheated. I thought they'd kick me out."

"Can you believe it! We won the war. The whole war's over, and we thought we'd have to wait till we grew up to fight in it, and it was us fighting it all the time. I mean, Ender, we're little kids. I'm a little kid, anyway." Bean laughed and Ender smiled. Then they were silent for a little while, Bean sitting on the edge of the bed, Ender watching him out of half-closed eyes.

Finally Bean thought of something else to say.

"What will we do now that the war's over?" he said.

Ender closed his eyes and said, "I need some sleep, Bean."

Bean got up and left and Ender slept.

Graff and Anderson walked through the gates into the park. There was a breeze, but the sun was hot on their shoulders.

"Abba Technics? In the capital?" Graff asked.

"No, in Biggock County. Training division," Anderson replied. "They think my work with children is good preparation. And you?"

Graff smiled and shook his head. "No plans. I'll be here for a few more months. Reports, winding down. I've had offers. Personnel development for DCIA, executive vice-president for U and P, but I said no. Publisher wants me to do memoirs of the war. I don't know."

They sat on a bench and watched leaves shivering in the breeze. Children on the monkey bars were laughing and yelling, but the wind and the distance swallowed their words. "Look," Graff said, pointing. A little boy jumped from the bars and ran near the bench where the two men sat. Another boy followed him, and holding his hands like a gun he made an explosive sound. The child he was shooting at didn't stop. He fired again.

"I got you! Come back here!"

The other little boy ran on out of sight.

"Don't you know when you're dead?" The boy shoved his hands in his pockets and kicked a rock back to the monkey bars. Anderson smiled and shook his head. "Kids," he said. Then he and Graff stood up and walked on out of the park.

MIKAL'S SONGBIRD

The doorknob turned. That would be dinner.

Ansset rolled over on the hard bed, his muscles aching. As always, he tried to ignore the burning feeling of guilt in the pit of his stomach.

But it was not Husk with food on a tray. This time it was the man called Master, though Ansset believed that was not his name. Master was always angry and fearsomely strong, one of the few men who could make Ansset feel and act like the eleven-year-old child his body said he was.

"Get up, Songbird."

Ansset slowly stood. They kept him naked in his prison, and only his pride kept him from turning away from the harsh eyes that looked him up and down. Ansset's cheeks burned with shame that took the place of the guilt he had wakened to.

"It's a good-bye feast we're having for you, Chirp, and ye're going to twitter for us."

Ansset shook his head.

"If ye can sing for the bastarrd Mikal, ye can sing for honest freemen."

Ansset's eyes blazed. "Watch how you speak of him, you barbarian traitor! He's your emperor!"

Master advanced a step, raising his hand angrily. "My orders was not to mark you, Chirp, but I can give you pain that doesn't leave a scar if ye don't mind how you talk to a freeman. Now ye'll sing."

Ansset, afraid of the man's brutality as only someone who has never known physical punishment can be afraid, nodded—but still hung back. "Can you please give me my clothing?"

"It ain't cold where we're going," Master retorted.

"I've never sung like this," Ansset said, embarrassed. "I've never performed without clothing."

Master leered. "What is it then that you *do* without clothing? Mikal's catamite has naw secrets we can't see."

Ansset didn't understand the word, but he understood the leer, and he followed Master out the door and down a dark corridor with his heart even more darkly filled with shame. He wondered why they were having a "good-bye feast" for him. Was he to be set free? (Had someone paid some unknown ransom for him?) Or was he to be killed?

The floor rocked gently as they walked down the wooden corridor. Ansset had long since decided he was imprisoned on a ship. The amount of real wood used in it would have seemed gaudy and pretentious in a rich man's home. Here it seemed only shabby.

Far above he could hear the distant cry of a bird, and a steady singing sound that he imagined to be wind whipping through ropes and cables. He had sung the melody himself sometimes, and often harmonized.

And then Master opened the door and with a mocking bow indicated that Ansset should enter first. The boy stopped in the doorframe. Gathered around a long table were twenty or so men, some of whom he had seen before, all of them dressed in the strange costumes of Earth barbarians. Ansset couldn't help remembering Mikal's raucous laughter whenever they came to court, pretending to be heirs of great civilizations that to minds accustomed to thinking on a galactic scale were petty and insignificant indeed. And yet as he stood looking at their rough faces and unsmiling eyes, he felt that it was he, with the soft skin of the imperial court, that was petty and insignificant, a mere naked child, while these men held the strength of worlds in their rough, gnarled hands.

They looked at him with the same curious, knowing, lustful look that Master had given him. Ansset relaxed his stomach and firmed his back and ribs to conquer emotion, as he had been taught in the Songhouse before he turned three. He stepped into the room.

"Up on the table!" roared Master behind him, and hands lifted him onto the wood smeared with spilled wine and rough with crumbs and fragments of food. "Now sing, ye little bastarrd."

The eyes looked his naked body over, and Ansset almost cried. But he was a Songbird, and many called him the best who had ever lived. Hadn't Mikal brought him from one end of the galaxy to his new Capital on old Earth? And when he sang, no matter who the audience, he would sing well.

And so he closed his eyes and shaped the ribs around his lungs, and let a low tone pass through his throat. At first he sang without words, soft and low, knowing the sound would be hard to hear. "Louder," someone said, but he ignored the instructions. Gradually the jokes and laughter died down as the men strained to hear.

· The melody was a wandering one, passing through tones and quarter tones easily, gracefully, still low in pitch, but rising and falling rhythmically. Unconsciously Ansset moved his hands in strange gestures to accompany his song. He was never aware of those gestures, except that once he had read in a newsheet, "To hear Mikal's Songbird is heavenly, but to watch his hands dance as he sings is nirvana." That was a prudent thing to write about Mikal's favorite—when the writer lived in Capital. Nevertheless, no one had even privately disputed the comment.

And now Ansset began to sing words. They were words of his own captivity, and the melody became high, in the soft upper notes that opened his throat and tightened the muscles at the back of his head and tensed the muscles along the front of his thighs. The notes pierced, and as he slid up and down through haunting third tones (a technique that few Songbirds could master) his words spoke of dark, shameful evenings in a dirty cell, a longing for the kind looks of Father Mikal (not by name, never by name in front of these barbarians), of dreams of the broad lawns that stretched from the palace to the

Susquehanna River, and of lost, forgotten days that ended in wakeful evenings in a tiny cell of splintered wood.

And he sang of his guilt.

At last he became tired, and the song drifted off into a whispered dorian scale that ended on the wrong note, on a dissonant note that faded into silence that sounded like part of the song.

Finally Ansset opened his eyes. All the men who were not weeping were watching him. None seemed willing to break the mood, until a youngish man down the table said in the thick accent, "Ah, but thet was better than hame and Mitherma." His comment was greeted by sighs and chuckles of agreement, and the looks that met Ansset's eyes were no longer leering and lustful, but rather soft and kind. Ansset had never thought to see such looks in those rough faces.

"Will ye have some wine, boy?" asked Master's voice behind him, and Husk poured. Ansset sipped the wine, and dipped a finger in it to cast a drop into the air in the graceful gesture of court. "Thank you," he said, handing back the metal cup with the same grace he would have used with a goblet at court. He lowered his head, though it hurt him to use that gesture of respect to such men, and asked, "May I leave now?"

"Do you have to? Can't you sing again?" the men around the table murmured, as if they had forgotten he was their prisoner. And Ansset refused as if he were free to choose. "I can't do it twice. I can never do it twice."

They lifted him off the table, then, and Master's strong arms carried him back to his room. Ansset lay on the bed after the door locked shut, trembling. The last time he had sung was for Mikal, and the song had been light and happy. Then Mikal had smiled the soft smile that only touched his old face when he was alone with his Songbird, had touched the back of Ansset's hand, and Ansset had kissed the old hand and gone out to walk along the river. It was then that they had taken him—rough hands from behind, the sharp slap of the needle, and then waking in the cell where now he lay looking at the walls.

He always woke in the evening, aching from some unknown effort of the day, and wracked by guilt. He strained to remember, but always in the effort drifted off to sleep, only to wake again the next evening suffering from the lost day behind him. But tonight he did not try to puzzle out what lay behind the blocks in his mind. Instead he drifted off to sleep thinking of the songs in Mikal's kind gray eyes, humming of the firm hands that ruled an empire a galaxy wide and could still stroke the forehead of a sweet-singing child and weep at a sorrowful song. Ah, sang Ansset in his mind, ah, the weeping of Mikal's sorrowful hands.

Ansset woke walking down a street.

"Out of the way, ya chark!" shouted a harsh accent behind him, and Ansset dodged to the left as an eletrecart zipped past his right arm. "Sausages," shouted a sign on the trunk behind the driver.

Then Ansset was seized by a terrible vertigo as he realized that he was not in the cell of his captivity, that he was fully dressed (in native Earth costume, but clothing for all that), was alive, was free. The quick joy that realization brought was immediately soured by a rush of the old guilt, and the conflicting emotions and the suddenness of his liberation were too much for him, and for a moment too long he forgot to breathe, and the darkening ground slid sideways, tipped up, hit him—

"Hey, boy, are you all right?"

"Did the chark slam you, boy?"

"Ya got the license number? Ya got the number?"

"Four-eight-seven something, who can tell."

"He's comin' around and to."

Ansset opened his eyes. "Where is this place?" he asked softly.

Why, this is Northet, they said.

"How far is the palace?" Ansset asked, vaguely remembering that Northet was a town not far to the north and east of Capital.

"The palace? What palace?"

"Mikal's palace—I must go to Mikal—" Ansett tried to get up, but his head spun and he staggered. Hands held him up.

"The kit's kinky, that's what."

"Mikal's palace."

"It's only eighteen kilometer, boy, ya plan to fly?"

The joke brought a burst of laughter, but Ansset impatiently regained control of his body and stood. Whatever drug had kept him unconscious was now nearly worked out of his system. "Find me a policeman," Ansset said. "Mikal will want to see me immediately."

Some still laughed, a man's voice said, "We'll be sure to tell him you're here when he comes to my house for supper!" but some others looked carefully at Ansset, realizing he spoke without American accent, and that his bearing was not that of a streetchild, despite his clothing. "Who are you, boy?"

"I'm Ansset. Mikal's Songbird."

Then there was silence, and half the crowd rushed off to find the policeman, and the other half stayed to look at him and realize how beautiful his eyes were, to touch him with their own eyes and hold the moment to tell about it to children and grandchildren. Ansset, Mikal's Songbird, more valuable than all the treasure Mikal owned.

"I touched him myself, helping him up, I held him up."

"You would've fallen, but for me, sir," said a large strong man bowing ridiculously low.

"Can I shake your hand, sir?"

Ansset smiled at them, not in amusement but in gratitude for their respect for him. "Thank you. You've all helped me. Thank you."

The policeman came, and after apologizing for the dirtiness of his armored eletrecart he lifted Ansset onto the seat and took him to the headquarters, where a flyer from the palace was already settling down on the pad. The Chamberlain leaped from the flyer, along with half a dozen servants, who gingerly touched Ansset and helped him to the flyer. The door slid shut, and Ansset closed his eyes to hide the tears as he felt the ground rush away as the palace came to meet him.

But for two days they kept him away from Mikal. "Quarantine," they said at first, until Ansset stamped his foot and said, "Nonsense," and refused to answer any more of the hundreds of questions they kept firing at him from dawn to dark and long after dark. The Chamberlain came.

"What's this I hear about you not wanting to answer questions, my boy?" asked the Chamberlain with the false joviality that Ansset had long since learned to recognize as a mask for anger or fear.

"I'm not your boy," Ansset retorted, determined to frighten some cooperation out of the Chamberlain. Now and then it had worked in the past. "I'm Mikal's and he wants to see me. Why am I being kept like a prisoner?"

"Quaran—"

"Chamberlain, I'm healthier than I've ever been before, and these questions don't have a thing to do with my health."

"All right," the Chamberlain said, fluttering his hands with impatience and nervousness. Ansset had once sung to Mikal of the Chamberlain's hands, and Mikal had laughed for hours at some of the words. "I'll explain. But don't get angry at me, because it's Mikal's orders."

"That I be kept away from him?"

"Until you answer the questions! You've been in court long enough, Songbird, and you're surely bright enough to know that Mikal has enemies in this world."

"I know that. Are you one of them?" Ansset was deliberately goading the Chamberlain, using his voice like a whip in all the ways that made the Chamberlain angry and fretful and so forgetful.

"Hold your tongue, boy!" the Chamberlain said. Ansset inwardly smiled. Victory. "You're also bright enough to know that you weren't kidnapped five months ago by any friends of the emperor's. We have to know *everything* about your captivity."

"I've told you everything a hundred times over."

"You haven't told us how you spent your days."

Again Ansset felt a stab of emotion. "I don't remember my days."

"And that's why you can't see Mikal!" the Chamberlain snapped. "Do you think we don't know what happened? We've used the probes and the tasters and no matter how skillfully we question, we can't get past the blocks. Either the person who worked on your mind laid the blocks very skillfully, or you yourself are holding them locked, and either way we can't get in."

"I can't help it," Ansset said, realizing now what the questioning meant. "How can you think I mean any danger to Father Mikal."

The Chamberlain smiled beatifically, in the pose he reserved for polite triumph. "Behind the block, someone may have very carefully planted a command for you to —"

"I'm not an assassin!" Ansset shouted.

"How would you know," the Chamberlain snarled back. "It's my duty to protect the person of the emperor. Do you know how many assassination attempts we stop? Dozens, every week. The poison, the treason, the weapons, the traps, that's what half the people who work here *do*, is watch everyone who comes in and watch each other too. Most of the assassination attempts are stopped immediately. Some get closer. Yours may be the closest of all."

"Mikal must want to see me!"

"Of course he does, Ansset! And that's exactly why you can't—because whoever worked on your mind must know that you're the only person that Mikal would allow near him after something like this—Ansset! Ansset, you little fool! Call the Captain of the Guard. Ansset, slow down!"

But the Chamberlain was slowing down with age, and he steadily lost ground to Ansset as the boy darted down the corridors of the palace. Ansset knew all the quickest ways, since exploring the palace was one of the most pleasant of his pastimes, and in five years in Mikal's service no one knew the labyrinth better than Ansset.

He was stopped routinely at the doors to the Great Hall, and he quickly made his way through the detectors (Poison? No. Metal? No. Energy? No. Identification? Clear.) and he was just about to step through the vast doors when the Captain of the Guard arrived.

"Stop the boy."

Ansset was stopped.

"Come back here, Songbird," the Captain barked. But Ansset could see, at the far end of the huge platinum room, the small chair and the whitehaired man who sat on it. Surely Mikal could see him! Surely he'd call!

"Bring the boy back here before he embarrasses everyone by calling out." Ansset was dragged back. "If you must know, Ansset, Mikal gave me orders to bring you within the hour, even before you made your ridiculous escape from the Chamberlain. But you'll be searched first. My way."

Ansset was taken off into one of the search rooms. He was stripped and his clothing was replaced with fresh clothes (that didn't fit! Ansset thought angrily), and then the searchers' fingers probed, painfully and deep, every aperture of his body that might hold a weapon. ("No weapon, and your prostate gland's all right, too," one of them joked. Ansset didn't laugh.) Then the needles, probing far under the skin to sample for hidden poisons. A layer of skin was bloodlessly peeled off his palms and the soles of his feet, to be sampled for poisons or flexible plastic needles. The pain was irritating. The delay was excruciating.

But Ansset bore what had to be borne. He only showed anger or impatience when he thought that doing so might gain some good effect. No one, not even Mikal's Songbird, survived long at court unless he remained in control of his temper, however he had to hide it.

At last Ansset was pronounced clean.

"Wait," the Captain of the Guard said. "I don't trust you yet."

Ansset gave him a long, cold look. But the Captain of the Guard—like the Chamberlain—was one of the few people at court who knew Mikal well enough to know they had nothing to fear from Ansset unless they really treated him unjustly, for Mikal never did favors, not even for the boy, who was the only human being Mikal had ever shown a personal need for. And they knew Ansset well enough to know that he would never ask Mikal to punish someone unfairly, either.

The Captain took a nylon cord and bound Ansset's hands together behind him, first at the wrists, and then just below the elbows. The constriction was painful.

"You're hurting me," Ansset said.

"I may be saving my emperor's life," the Captain answered blandly. And then Ansset passed through the huge doors to the Great Hall, his arms bound, surrounded by guards with lasers drawn, preceded by the Captain of the Guard.

Ansset still walked proudly, but he felt a hearty fury toward the guards, toward the courtiers and supplicants and guards and officials lining the walls of the unfurnished room, and especially toward the Captain. Only toward Mikal did he feel no anger.

They let him stop.

Mikal raised his hand in the ritual of recognition. Ansset knew that Mikal laughed at the rituals when they were alone together—but in front of the court, the ritual had to be followed strictly.

Ansset dropped to his knees on the cold and shining platinum floor.

"My Lord," he said in clear, bell-like tones that he knew would reverberate from the metal ceiling, "I am Ansset, and I have come to ask for my life." In the old days, Mikal had once explained, that ritual had real meaning, and many a rebel lord or soldier had died on the spot. Even now, the pro forma surrender of life was taken seriously, as Mikal maintained constant vigilance over his empire.

"Why should I spare you?" Mikal asked, his voice old but firm. Ansset thought he heard a quaver of eagerness in the voice. More likely a quaver of age, he told himself. Mikal would never allow himself to reveal emotion in front of the court.

"You should not," Ansset said. This was leaving the ritual, and going down the dark road that met danger head-on. Mikal must have been told of the Chamberlain's fears. Therefore, if Ansset made any attempt to hide the danger, his life would be forfeited by law.

"Why not?" Mikal said, impassively.

"Because, my Lord Mikal Imperator, I was kidnapped and held for five months, and during those months things were done to me that are now locked behind blocks in my mind. I may, unwittingly, be an assassin. I must not be allowed to live."

"Nevertheless," Mikal answered, "I grant you your life."

Ansset, his muscles strong enough even after his captivity to allow him to bow despite his bound arms, touched his lips to the floor.

"Why are you bound?"

"For your safety, my Lord."

"Unbind him," said Mikal. The Captain of the Guard untied the nylon cord.

His arms free, Ansset stood. He went beyond form, and he turned his voice into a song, with an edge to his voice that snapped every head in the hall toward him. "My Lord, Father Mikal," he sang, "there is a place in my mind where even I cannot go. In that place my captors may have taught me to want to kill you." The words were a warning, but the song said safety, the song said love, and Mikal arose from his throne. He understood what Ansset was asking and he would grant it.

"I would rather, my Son Ansset, I would rather meet death in your hands than any other's. Your life is more valuable to me than my own." Then Mikal turned and went back into the door that led to his private chambers. Ansset and the Captain of the Guard followed, and as they left the whispers rose to a roar. Mikal had gone much farther than Ansset had even hoped. The entire Capital—and in a few weeks, the entire empire—would hear how Mikal had called his Songbird *Son Ansset*, and the words, "Your life is more valuable to me than my own," would become the stuff of legends.

Ansset sighed a song as he entered the familiar rooms where Father Mikal lived.

Mikal turned abruptly and glared at the Captain of the Guard. "What did you mean by that little trick, you bastard?"

"I tied his hands as a precaution. I was within my duties as a warden of the gate."

"I know you were within your duties, but you might use some common decency. What harm can an eleven-year-old boy do when you've probably already skinned him alive searching for weapons and you have a hundred lasers trained on him at every moment!"

"I wanted to be sure."

"Well, you're too damned thorough. Get out. And don't let me ever catch you being any less thorough, even when it makes me angry. Get out!" The Captain of the Guard left, Mikal's roar following him. As soon as the door closed, Mikal started to laugh. "What an ass! What a colossal donkey!" Then he threw himself to the floor with all the vigor of a young man, though Ansset knew his age to be one hundred and twenty-three, which was old, in a civilization where death normally came at a hundred and fifteen. Under him the floor that had been rigid when his weight pressed down on the two small spaces touched by his feet now softened, gave gently to fit the contours of his body. Ansset also went to the floor, and lay there laughing.

"Are you glad to be home, Ansset?" Mikal asked tenderly.

"Now I am. Until this moment I wasn't home."

"Ansset, my Son, you never can speak without singing." Mikal laughed softly.

Ansset took the sound of the laugh and turned it into a song. It was a soft song, and it was short, but at the end of it Mikal was lying on his back looking at the ceiling, tears streaming down from his eyes.

"I didn't mean the song to be sad, Father Mikal."

"How was I to know that now, in my dotage, I'd do the foolish thing I avoided all my life? Oh, I've loved like I've done every other passionate thing, but when they took you I discovered, my Son, that I need you." Mikal rolled over and looked at the beautiful face of the boy who lay looking at him adoringly. "Don't worship me, boy, I'm an old bastard who'd kill his mother if one of my enemies hadn't already done it."

"You'd never harm me."

"I harm everything I love," Mikal said bitterly. Then he let his face show concern. "We were afraid for you. Since you were gone there was an outbreak of insane crime. People were kidnapped for no reason on the street, some in broad daylight, and a few days later their bodies would be found, broken and torn by someone or something. No ransom notes. Nothing. We thought you had been taken like that, and that somewhere we'd find your body. Are you whole? Are you well?"

"I'm stronger than I've ever been before." Ansset laughed. "I tested my strength against the hook of my hammock, and I'm afraid I ripped it out of the wall."

Mikal reached out and touched Ansset's hand. "I'm afraid," Mikal said, and Ansset listened, humming softly, as Mikal talked. The emperor never spoke in names and dates and facts and plans, for then if Ansset were taken by an enemy the enemy would know too much. He spoke to the Songbird in emotions instead, and Ansset sang solace to him. Other Songbirds had pretty voices, others could impress the crowds, and, indeed, Mikal used Ansset for just that purpose on certain state occasions. But of all Songbirds, only Ansset could sing his soul; and he loved Mikal from his soul.

Late in the night Mikal shouted in fury about his empire: "Did I build it to fall? Did I burn over a dozen worlds and rape a hundred others just to have the whole thing fall in chaos when I die?" He leaned down and whispered to Ansset, their eyes a few inches apart, "They call me Mikal the Terrible, but I built it so it would stand like an umbrella over the galaxy. They have it now: peace and prosperity and as much freedom as their little minds can cope with. But when I die they'll throw it all away." Mikal whirled and shouted at the walls of his soundproofed chamber, "In the name of nationalities and religions and races and family inheritances the fools will rip the umbrella down and then wonder why, all of a sudden, it's raining."

Ansset sang to him of hope.

"There's no hope. I have fifty sons, three of them legitimate, all of them fools who try to flatter me. They couldn't keep the empire for a week, not all of them, not any of them. There's not a man I've met in all my life who could control what I've built in my lifetime. When I die, it all dies with me." And Mikal sank to the floor wearily.

For once Ansset did not sing. Instead he jumped to his feet, the floor turning firm under him. He raised an arm above his head, and said, "For you, Father Mikal, I'll grow up to be strong! Your empire shall not fall!" He spoke with such grandeur in his childish speaking voice that both he and Mikal had to laugh.

"It's true, though," Mikal said, tousling the child's hair. "For you I'd do it, I'd give you the empire, except they'd kill you. And even if I lived long enough to train you to be a ruler of men, I wouldn't do it. The man who will be my heir must be cruel and vicious and sly and wise, completely selfish and ambitious, contemptuous of all other people, brilliant in battle, able to outguess and outmaneuver every enemy, and strong enough inside himself to live utterly alone all his life." Mikal smiled. "Even *I* don't fit my list of qualifications, because now I'm not utterly alone."

And then, as Mikal drifted off to sleep, Ansset sang to him of his captivity, the songs and words of his time of loneliness in captivity, and as the men on the ship had wept, so Mikal wept, only more. Then they both slept.

A few days later Mikal, Ansset, the Chamberlain, and the Captain of the Guard met in Mikal's small receiving room, where a solid block of clear glass as perfect as a lens stretched as a meters-long table from one end of the room to the other. They gathered at one end. The Chamberlain was adamant.

"Ansset is a danger to you, my Lord."

The Captain of the Guard was equally adamant. "We found the conspirators and killed them all."

The Chamberlain rolled his eyes heavenward in disgust.

The Captain of the Guard became angry, though he kept the fact hidden behind heavy-lidded eyes. "It all fit—the accent that Ansset told us they had, the wooden ship, calling each other freemen, their emotionalism—they could have been no one else but the Freemen of Eire. Just another nationalist group, but they have a lot of sympathizers here in America—damn these 'nations,' where but on old Earth would people subdivide their planet and think the subdivisions meant anything."

"So you went in and wiped them all out," the Chamberlain sneered, "and not one of them had any knowledge of the plot."

"Anyone who could block out the Songbird's mind as well as he did can hide a conspiracy like that!" the Captain of the Guard snapped back.

"Our enemy is subtle," the Chamberlain said. "He kept everything else from Ansset's knowledge—so why did he let him have all these clues that steered us to Eire? I think we were given bait and you bit. Well, I haven't bitten yet, and I'm still looking."

"In the meantime," Mikal said, "try to avoid harassing Ansset too much."

"I don't mind," Ansset hurriedly said, though he minded very much: the constant searches, the frequent interrogations, the hypnotherapy, the guards who followed him constantly to keep him from meeting with anyone.

"I mind," Mikal said. "It's good for you to keep watch, because we still don't know what they've done to Ansset's mind. But in the meantime, let Ansset's life be worth living." Mikal glared pointedly at the Captain of the Guard, who got up and left. Then Mikal turned to the Chamberlain and said, "I don't like how easily the Captain was fooled by such an obvious ploy. Keep up your investigation. And tell me anything your spies within the Captain's forces might have to say."

The Chamberlain tried for a moment to protest that he had no such spies—but Mikal laughed until the Chamberlain gave up and promised to complete a report.

"My days are numbered," Mikal said to Ansset. "Sing to me of numbered days." And so Ansset sang him a playful song about a man who decided to live for two hundred years and so counted his age backward, by the number of years he had left. "And he died when he was only eighty-three," Ansset sang, and Mikal laughed and tossed another log on the fire. Only an emperor or a peasant in the protected forests of Siberia could afford to burn wood.

Then one day Ansset, as he wandered through the palace, noticed a different direction and a quickened pace to the hustling and bustling of servants down the halls. He went to the Chamberlain.

"Try to keep quiet about it," the Chamberlain said. "You're coming with us, anyway."

And within an hour Ansset rode beside Mikal in an armored car as a convoy swept out of Capital. The roads were kept clear, and in an hour and fifteen minutes the armored car stopped. Ansset bounded out of the hatchway. He was startled to see that the entire convoy was missing, and only the single armored car remained. He immediately suspected treachery, and looked down at Mikal in fright.

"Don't worry," Mikal said. "We sent the convoy on."

They got out of the car and with a dozen picked guards (not from the palace guard, Ansset noticed) they made their way through a sparse wood, along a stream, and finally to the banks of a huge river.

"The Delaware," whispered the Chamberlain to Ansset, who had already guessed as much.

"Keep your esoterica to yourself," Mikal said, sounding irritable, which meant he was enjoying himself immensely. He hadn't been a part of any kind of planetside military operation in forty years, ever since he became an emperor and had to control fleets and planets instead of a few ships and a thousand men. There was a spring to his step that belied his century and a quarter.

Finally the Chamberlain stopped. "That's the house, and that's the boat."

A flatboat was moored on the river by a shambling wooden house that looked like it had been built during the American colonial revival over a hundred years before.

They crept up on the house, but it was empty, and when they rushed the flatboat the only man on board aimed a laser at his own face and blasted it to a cinder. Not before Ansset had recognized him, though.

"That was Husk," Ansset said, feeling sick as he looked at the ruined corpse. Inexplicably, he felt a nagging guilt. "He's the man who fed me."

Then Mikal and Chamberlain followed Ansset through the boat. "It's not the same," Ansset said.

"Of course not," said the Chamberlain. "The paint is fresh. And there's a smell of new wood. They've been remodeling. But is there anything familiar?"

There was. Ansset found a tiny room that could have been his cell, though now it was painted bright yellow and a new window let sunlight flood into the room. Mikal examined the windowframe. "New," the emperor pronounced. And by trying to imagine the interior of the flatboat as it might have been unpainted, Ansset was able to find the large room where he had sung his last evening in captivity. There was no table. But the room seemed the same size, and Ansset agreed that this could very well have been the place he was held.

Down in the ship they heard the laughter of children and a passing eletrecart that clattered along the bumpy old asphalt road. The Chamberlain laughed. "Sorry I took you the long way. It's really quite a populated area. I just wanted to be sure they didn't have time to be warned."

Mikal curled his lip. "If it's a populated area we should have arrived in a bus. A group of armed men walking along a river are much more conspicuous."

"I'm not a tactician," said the Chamberlain.

"Tactician enough," said Mikal. "We'll go back to the palace now. Do you have anyone you can trust to make the arrest? I don't want him harmed."

But it didn't do any good to give orders to that effect. When the Captain of the Guard was arrested, he raged and stormed and then a half-hour later, before there was time to examine him with the probe and taster, one of the guards slipped him some poison and he drifted off into death. The Chamberlain rashly had the offending guard impaled with nails until he bled to death.

Ansset was confused as he watched Mikal rage at the Chamberlain. It was obviously a sham, or half a sham, and Ansset was certain that the Chamberlain knew it. "Only a fool would have killed that soldier! How did the poison get into the palace past the detectors? How did the soldier get it to the Captain? None of the questions will ever be answered now!"

The Chamberlain made the mandatory ritual resignation. "My Lord Imperator, I was a fool. I deserve to die. I resign my position and ask for you to have me killed."

Following the ritual, but obviously annoyed by having it thrust at him before he was through raging, Mikal lifted his hand and said, "Damn right you're a fool." Then, in proper form, he said, "I grant you your life because of your infinitely valuable services to me in apprehending the traitor in the first place." Mikal cocked his head to one side. "So, Chamberlain, who do you think I should make the next Captain of the Guard?"

Ansset almost laughed out loud. It was an impossible question to answer. The safest answer (and the Chamberlain liked to do safe things) would be to say he had never given the matter any thought at all, and wouldn't presume to advise the emperor on such a vital matter. But even so, the moment would be tense for the Chamberlain.

And Ansset was shocked to hear the Chamberlain answer, "Riktors Ashen, of course, my Lord."

The "of course" was insolent. The naming of the man was ridiculous. At first Ansset looked at Mikal to see fury there. But instead Mikal was smiling. "Why of course," he said blandly. "Riktors Ashen is the obvious choice. Tell him in my name that he's appointed."

Even the Chamberlain, who had mastered the art of blandness at will, looked surprised for a moment. Again Ansset almost laughed. He saw Mikal's victory: the Chamberlain had probably named the one man in the palace guard that the Chamberlain had no control over, assuming that Mikal would never pick the man the Chamberlain recommended. And so Mikal had picked him: Riktors Ashen, the victor of the battle of Mantrynn, a planet that had revolted only three years before. He was known to be incorruptible, brilliant, and reliable. Well, now he'd have a chance to prove his reputation, Ansset thought.

Then he was startled out of his reverie by Mikal's voice. "Do you know what his last words were to me?"

By the instant understanding that needed no referents for Mikal's pronouns Ansset knew he was talking about the now-dead Captain of the Guard.

"He said, 'Tell Mikal that my death frees more plotters than it kills.' And then he said that he loved me. Imagine, that cagey old bastard saying he loved me. I remembered him twenty years ago when he killed his closest friend in a squabble over a promotion. The bloodiest men get most sentimental in their old age, I suppose."

Ansset asked a question—it seemed a safe time. "My Lord, why was the Captain arrested?"

"Hmmm?" Mikal looked surprised. "Oh, I suppose no one told you, then. He visited that house regularly throughout your captivity. He said he visited a woman there. But the neighbors all testified under the probe that a woman never lived there. And the Captain was a master at establishing mental blocks."

"Then the conspiracy is broken!" Ansset said, joyfully assuming that the guards would stop harassing him and the questions would finally end.

"The conspiracy is barely dented. Someone was able to get poison to the Captain. Therefore plotters still exist within the palace. And therefore Riktors Ashen will be instructed to keep a close watch on you."

Ansset tried to keep the smile on his face. He failed.

"I know, I know," Mikal said wearily. "But it's still locked in your mind."

It was unlocked the next day. The court was gathered in the Great Hall, and Ansset resigned himself to a morning of wandering through the halls—or else standing near Mikal as he received the boring procession of dignitaries paying their respects to the emperor (and then going home to report how soon they thought Mikal the Terrible would die, and who might succeed him, and what the chances were for grabbing a piece of the empire). Because the palace bored him and he wanted to be near Mikal, and because the Chamberlain smiled at him and asked, "Are you coming to court?" Ansset decided to attend.

The order of dignitaries had been carefully worked out to honor loyal friends and humiliate upstarts whose dignity needed deflating. A minor official from a distant star cluster was officially honored, the first business of the day, and then the rituals began: princes and presidents and satraps and governors, depending on what title survived the conquest a decade or a score or fourscore years ago, all proceeding forward with their retinue, bowing (how low they bowed showed how afraid they were of Mikal, or how much they wanted to flatter him), uttering a few words, asking for private audience, being put off or being invited, in an endless array.

Ansset was startled to see a group of Black Kinshasans attired in their bizarre old Earth costumes. Kinshasa insisted it was an independent nation, a pathetic nose-thumbing claim when empires of planets had been swallowed up by Mikal Conqueror. Why were they being allowed to wear their native regalia and have an audience? Ansset raised an eyebrow at the Chamberlain, who also stood near the throne.

"It was Mikal's idea," the Chamberlain said voicelessly. "He's letting them come and present a petition right before the president of Stuss. Those toads from Stuss'll be madder than hell."

At that moment Mikal raised his hand for some wine. Obviously he was as bored as anyone else.

The Chamberlain poured the wine, tasted it, as was the routine, and then took a step toward Mikal's throne. Then he stopped, and beckoned to Ansset, who was already moving back to Mikal's side. Surprised at the summons, Ansset came over.

"Why don't you take the wine to Mikal, Sweet Songbird?" the Chamberlain said. The surprise fell away from Ansset's eyes, and he took the wine and headed purposefully back to Mikal's throne.

At that moment, however, pandemonium broke loose. The Kinshasan envoys reached into their elaborate curly-haired headdresses and withdrew wooden knives— which could pass every test given by machines at the doors of the palace. They rushed toward the throne. The guards fired quickly, their lasers dropping five of the Kinshasans, but all had aimed at the foremost assassins, and three continued unharmed. They rushed toward the throne, arms extended so the knives were already aimed directly at Mikal's heart.

Mikal, old and unarmed, rose to meet them. A guard managed to shift his aim and get off a shot, but it was wild, and the others were hurriedly recharging their lasers— which only took a moment, but that was a moment too long.

Mikal looked death in the eye and did not seem disappointed.

But at that moment Ansset threw the wine goblet at one of the attackers and then leaped out in front of the emperor. He jumped easily into the air, and kicked the jaw of the first of the attackers. The angle of the kick was perfect, the force sharp and incredibly hard, and the Kinshasan's head flew fifty feet away into the crowd, as his body slid forward until the wooden knife touched Mikal's foot. Ansset came down from the jump in time to bring his hand upward into the abdomen of another attacker so sharply that his arm was buried to the elbow in bowels, and his fingers crushed the man's heart.

The other attacker paused just a moment, thrown from his relentless charge by the sudden onslaught from the child who stood so harmlessly by the emperor's throne. That pause was long enough for recharged lasers to be aimed, to flash, and the last Kinshasan assassin fell, dropping ashes as he collapsed, flaming slightly.

The whole thing, from the appearance of the wooden knives to the fall of the last attacker, had taken five seconds.

Ansset stood still in the middle of the hall, gore on his arm, blood splashed all over his body. He looked at the gory hand, at the body he had pulled it out of. A rush of long-blocked memories came back, and he remembered other such bodies, other heads kicked from torsos, other men who had died as Ansset learned the skill of killing with his hands. The guilt that had troubled him before swept through him with new force now that he knew the why of it.

The searches had all been in vain. Ansset himself was the weapon that was to have been used against Father Mikal.

The smell of blood and broken intestines combined with the emotions sweeping his body, and he doubled over, shuddering as he vomited.

The guards gingerly approached him, unsure what they should do.

But the Chamberlain was sure. Ansset heard the voice, trembling with fear at how close the assassination had come, and how easily a different assassination could have come, saying, "Keep him under guard. Wash him. Never let him be out of a laser's aim for a moment. Then bring him to Mikal's chambers in an hour."

The guards looked toward Mikal, who nodded.

Ansset was still white and weak when he came into Mikal's chambers. The guards still had lasers trained on him. The Chamberlain and the new Captain of the Guard, Riktors Ashen, stood between Mikal and the boy.

"Songbird," Riktors said, "it seems that someone taught you new songs."

Ansset lowered his head.

"You must have studied under a master."

"I n-never," Ansset stuttered. He had never stuttered in his life.

"Don't torture the boy, Captain," Mikal said.

The Chamberlain launched into his pro forma resignation. "I should have examined the boy's muscle structure and realized what new skills he had been given. I submit my resignation. I beg you to take my life."

The Chamberlain must be even more worried than usual, Ansset thought with that part of his mind that was still capable of thinking. The old man had prostrated himself in front of the emperor.

"Shut up and get up," Mikal said rudely. The Chamberlain arose with his face gray. Mikal had not followed the ritual. The Chamberlain's life was still on the line.

"We will now be certain," Mikal said to Riktors. "Show him the pictures."

Ansset stood watching as Riktors took a packet off a table and began removing newsheet clippings from it. Ansset looked at the first one and was merely sickened a little. The second one he recognized, and he gasped. With the third one he wept and threw the pictures away from him.

"Those are the pictures," Mikal said, "of the people who were kidnapped and murdered during your captivity."

"I k-killed them," Ansset said, dimly aware that there was no trace of song in his voice, just the frightened stammering of an eleven-year-old boy caught up in something too monstrous for him to comprehend. "They had me practice on them."

"*Who* had you practice!" Riktors demanded.

"They! The voices—from the box." Ansset struggled to hold onto memories that had been hidden from him by the block. He also longed to let the block in his mind slide back into place, forget again, shut it out.

"What box?" Riktors would not let up.

"The box. A wooden box. Maybe a receiver, maybe a recording, I don't know." ·

"Did you know the voice?"

"Voices. Never the same. Not even for the same sentence, the voices changed for every word."

Ansset kept seeing the faces of the bound men he was told to maim and then kill. He remembered that though he cried out against it, he was still forced to do it.

"How did they force you to do it!"

Was Riktors reading his mind? "I don't know. I don't know. There were words, and then I had to."

"What words?"

"I don't know! I never knew!" And Ansset was crying again.

Mikal spoke softly. "Who taught you how to kill that way?"

"A man. I never knew his name. On the last day, he was tied where the others had been. The voices made me kill him." Ansset struggled with the words, the struggle made harder by the realization that this time, when he had killed his teacher, he had not had to be forced. He had killed because he hated the man. "I murdered him."

"Nonsense," the Chamberlain said. "You were a tool."

"I said to shut up," Mikal said curtly. "Can you remember anything else, my Son?"

"I killed the crew of the ship, too. All except Husk. The voices told me to. And then there were footsteps, above me, on the deck."

"Did you see who it was?"

Ansset forced himself to remember. "No. He told me to lie down. He must have known the—code, whatever it is, I didn't want to obey him, but I did."

"And?"

"Footsteps, and a needle in my arm, and I woke up on the street."

Everyone was silent then, for a few moments, all of them thinking quickly. The Chamberlain broke first. "My Lord, the great threat to you and the strength of the Songbird's love for you must have impelled him despite the mental block—"

"Chamberlain," Mikal said, "your life is over if you speak again before I address you. Captain. I want to know how those Kinshasan's got past your guard?"

"They were dignitaries. By your order, my Lord, no dignitaries are given the body search. Their wooden knives passed all the detectors. I'm surprised this hadn't been tried before."

Ansset noticed that Riktors spoke confidently, not coweringly as another Captain might have done after assassins got through his guard. And, better in control of himself, Ansset listened for the melodies of Riktors's voice. They were strong. They were dissonant. Ansset wondered if he would be able to detect Riktors in a lie. To a strong, selfish man all things that he chose to say became truth, and the songs of his voice said nothing.

"Riktors, you will prepare orders for the utter destruction of Kinshasa."

Riktors saluted.

"Before Kinshasa is destroyed—and that means destroyed, not a blade of grass, Riktors—before Kinshasa is destroyed, I want to know what connection there is between the assassination attempt this morning and the manipulation of my Songbird."

Riktors saluted again. Mikal spoke to the Chamberlain. "Chamberlain, what would you recommend I do with my Songbird?"

As usual, the Chamberlain took the safe way. "My Lord, it is not a matter to which I have given thought. The disposition of your Songbird is not a matter on which I feel it proper to advise you."

"Very carefully said, my dear Chamberlain." Ansset tried to be calm as he listened to them discuss how he should be disposed of. Mikal raised his hand in the gesture that, by ritual, spared the Chamberlain's life. Ansset would have laughed at the Chamberlain's struggle not to show his relief, but this was not a time for laughter, because Ansset knew his relief would not come so easily.

"My Lord," Ansset said, "I beg you to put me to death."

"Dammit, Ansset, I'm sick of the rituals," Mikal said.

"This is no ritual," Ansset said, his voice tired and husky from misuse. "And this is no song, Father Mikal. I'm a danger to you."

"I know it." Mikal looked back and forth between Riktors and the Chamberlain.

"Chamberlain, have Ansset's possessions put together and readied for shipment to Alwiss. The prefect there is Timmis Hortmang, prepare a letter of explanation and a letter of mark. Ansset will arrive there wealthier than anyone else in the prefecture. Those are my orders. See to it." He turned his head downward and to the right. Both Riktors and the Chamberlain moved to leave. Ansset—and therefore the guards who had lasers trained on him—did not.

"Father Mikal," Ansset said softly, and he realized that the words had been a song.

But Mikal made no answer. He only got up from the chair and left the chamber.

Ansset had several hours before nightfall, and he spent them wandering through the palace and the palace grounds. The guards dogged his steps. At first he let the tears flow. Then, as the horror of the morning hid again behind the only partly broken block in his mind, he remembered what the Songmaster had taught him, again and again, "When you want to weep, let the tears come through your throat. Let pain come from the pressure in your thighs. Let sorrow rise and resonate through your head."

Walking by the Susquehanna on the cold lawns of autumn afternoon shade, Ansset sang his grief. He sang softly, but the guards heard his song, and could not help but weep for him, too.

He stopped at a place where the water looked cold and clear, and began to strip off his tunic, preparing to swim. A guard reached out and stopped him. Ansset noticed the laser pointed at his foot. "I can't let you do that. Mikal gave orders you were not to be allowed to take your own life."

"I only want to swim," Ansset answered, his voice low with persuasion.

"I would be killed if any harm came to you," the guard said.

"I give you my oath that I will only swim, and not try to break free."

The guard considered. The other guards seemed content to leave the decision up to him. Ansset hummed a sweet melody that he knew oozed confidence. The guard gave in.

Ansset stripped and dove into the water. It was icy cold, and stung him. He swam in broad strokes upstream, knowing that to the guards on the bank he would already seem like only a speck on the surface of the river. Then he dove and swam under the water, holding his breath as only a singer or a pearldiver could, and swam across the current toward the near shore, where the guards were waiting. He could hear, though muffled by the water, the cries of the guards. He surfaced, laughing.

Two of the guards had already thrown off their boots and were up to their waists in water, preparing to try to catch Ansset's body as it swept by. But Ansset kept laughing at them, and they turned at him angrily.

"Why did you worry?" Ansset said. "I gave my word."

Then the guards relaxed, and Ansset swam for an hour under the afternoon sun. The motion of the water, and constant exertion to keep place against the current took his mind off his troubles, to some extent. Only one guard watched him now, while the others played polys, casting fourteen-sided dice in a mad gambling game that soon engrossed them.

Ansset swam underwater from time to time, listening to the different sound the guards' quarreling and laughing made when water covered his ears. The sun was nearly down, now, and Ansset dove underwater again to swim to shore on one breath. He was halfway to shore when he heard the sharp call of a bird overhead, muffled as it was by the river.

Ansset made a sudden connection in his mind, and came up immediately, coughing and sputtering. He dog-paddled in to shore, shook himself, and put on his tunic, wet as he was.

"We've got to get back to the palace," he said, filling his voice with urgency, putting the pitch high to penetrate the guards' sluggishness after an hour of gaming. The guards quickly followed him, overtook him.

"Where are you going?" one of them asked.

"To see Mikal."

"We're not to do that—we were ordered! You can't go to Mikal."

But Ansset walked on, fairly sure that until he actually got close to the emperor the guards would not try to restrain him. Even if they had not been present for the demonstration of Ansset's skill in the Great Hall that morning, the story would surely have reached their ears that Mikal's Songbird could kill two men in two seconds.

He had heard the call of a bird as he swam underwater. He remembered that on his last night of captivity in the ship, he had heard the cry of another bird high above him. But never, never had he heard another sound from outside.

And yet where the flatboat was the city noise had come loudly, could be heard clearly below decks. Therefore even if the boat was his prison, it had not been moored by that house. And if that were so, the evidence against the former Captain of the Guard was a fraud. And Ansset knew now who in the court had taken Ansset to use as an assassin.

They were met in a corridor by a messenger. "There you are. The Lord Mikal commands the presence of the Songbird, as quickly as possible. Here," he said, handing the orders to the guard who made decisions, who took out his verifier and passed it over the seal on the orders. A sharp buzz testified that the orders were genuine.

"All right then, Songbird," said the guard. "We'll go there after all." Ansset started to run. The guards kept up easily, following him through the labyrinth. To them it was almost a game, and one of them said, between breaths, "I never knew this way led where we're going!" to which one of the other guards replied, "And you'll never find it again, either."

And then they were in Mikal's chambers. Ansset's hair was still wet, and his tunic still clung to his small body where it had not yet had time to dry from the river water.

Mikal was smiling. "Ansset, my Son, it's fine now." Mikal waved an arm, dismissing the guards. "We were so foolish to think we needed to send you away," he said. "The Captain was the only one in the plot close enough to give the signal. Now that he's dead, no one knows it! You're safe now—and so am I!"

Mikal's speech was jovial, delighted, but Ansset, who knew the songs of his voice as well as he knew his own, read in the words a warning, a lie, a declaration of danger. Ansset did not run to him. He waited.

"In fact," Mikal said, "you're my best possible bodyguard. You look small and weak, you're always by my side, and you can kill faster than a guard with a laser." Mikal laughed. Ansset was not fooled. There was no mirth in the laugh.

But the Chamberlain and Captain Riktors Ashen were fooled, and they laughed along with Mikal. Ansset forced himself to laugh, too. He listened to the sounds the others were making. Riktors sounded sincere enough, but the Chamberlain—

"It's a cause for celebration. Here's wine," said the Chamberlain. "I brought us wine. Ansset, why don't you pour it?"

Ansset shuddered with memories. "I?" he asked, surprised, and then not surprised at all. The Chamberlain held out the full bottle and the empty goblet. "For the Lord Mikal," the Chamberlain said.

Ansset shouted and dashed the bottle to the floor. "Make him keep silent!"

The suddenness of Ansset's violent action brought Riktors's laser out of his belt and into his hand.

"Don't let the Chamberlain speak!"

"Why not?" asked Mikal innocently, but Ansset knew there was no innocence behind the words. For some reason Mikal was pretending not to understand.

The Chamberlain believed it, believed he had a moment. He said quickly, almost urgently, "Why did you do that? I have another bottle. *Sweet Songbird, let Mikal drink deeply!*"

The words hammered into Ansset's brain, and by reflex he whirled and faced Mikal. He knew what was happening, knew and screamed against it in his mind. But his hands came up against his will, his legs bent, he compressed to spring, all so quickly that he couldn't stop himself. He knew that in less than a second his hand would be buried in Mikal's face, Mikal's beloved face, Mikal's smiling face—

Mikal was smiling at him, kindly and without fear. Ansset stopped in midspring, forced himself to turn aside, despite the tearing in his brain. He could be forced to kill, but he couldn't be forced to kill that face. He shoved his hand into the floor, bursting the tense surface, releasing the gel to flow out across the room.

Ansset hardly noticed the pain in his arm where the impact had broken the skin and the gel was agonizing the wound. All he felt was the pain in his mind as he still struggled against the compulsion he had only just barely deflected, that still drove him to try to kill Mikal, that still fought against, fought down, tried to block.

His body heaved upward, his hand flew through the air, and shattered the back of the chair where Mikal still sat. Blood spurted and splashed, and Ansset was relieved to see that it was his own blood, and not Mikal's.

In the distance he heard Mikal's voice saying, "Don't shoot him." And, as suddenly as it had come, the compulsion ceased. His mind spun as he heard the Chamberlain's words fading away: *"Songbird, what have you done!"*

Those were the words that had set him free.

Exhausted and bleeding, Ansset lay on the floor, his right arm covered with blood.

The pain reached him now, and he groaned, though his groan was as much a song of ecstasy as of pain. Somehow Ansset had withstood it long enough, and he had not killed Father Mikal.

Finally he rolled over and sat up, nursing his arm. The bleeding had settled to a slow trickle.

Mikal was still sitting in the chair, despite its shattered back where Ansset's hand had struck. The Chamberlain stood where he had stood ten seconds before, at the beginning of Ansset's ordeal, the goblet looking ridiculous in his hand. Riktors's laser was aimed at the Chamberlain.

"Call the guards, Captain," Mikal said.

"I already have," Riktors said. The button on his belt was glowing. Guards came quickly into the room. "Take the Chamberlain to a cell," he ordered them. "If any harm comes to him, all of you will die and your families, too. Do you understand?" The guards understood.

Ansset held his arm. Mikal and Riktors Ashen waited while a doctor treated it. The pain subsided.

The doctor left.

Riktors spoke first. "Of course you knew it was the Chamberlain, my Lord."

Mikal smiled faintly.

"That was why you let him persuade you to call Ansset back here."

Mikal's smile grew broader.

"But, my Lord, only you could have known that the Songbird would be strong enough to resist a compulsion that was five months in the making."

Mikal laughed. And this time Ansset heard mirth in the laughter.

"Riktors Ashen. Will they call you Riktors the Usurper? Or Riktors the Great?"

It took the Captain of the Guard a moment to realize what had been said. Only a moment. But before his hand could reach his laser, which was back in his belt, Mikal's hand held a laser that was pointed at Riktors's heart.

"Ansset my Son, will you take the Captain's laser from him?"

Ansset got up and took the Captain's laser from him. He could hear the song of triumph in Mikal's voice. But Ansset's head was still spinning, and he didn't understand why lasers had been drawn between the emperor and his incorruptible Captain.

"Only one mistake, Riktors. Otherwise brilliantly done. And I really don't see how you could have avoided the mistake, either."

"You mean Ansset's strength?"

"Not even I counted on that. I was prepared to kill him, if I needed to," Mikal said, and Ansset, listening, knew it was true. He wondered why that knowledge didn't hurt him. He had always known that, eventually, not even he would be indispensable to Mikal, if somehow his death served some vital purpose.

"Then I made no mistakes," Riktors said. "How did you know?"

"Because my Chamberlain, unless he were under some sort of compulsion, would never have had the courage to suggest your name as the Captain's successor. And without that, you wouldn't have been in a position to take over after you exposed the Chamberlain as the engineer of my assassination, would you? It was good. The guard would have followed you loyally. No taint of assassination would have touched you. Of course, the entire empire would have rebelled immediately. But you're a good tactician and a better strategist, and your men would have followed you well. I'd have given you one chance in four of making it—and that's better odds than any other man in the empire."

"I gave myself even odds," Riktors said, but Ansset heard the fear singing through the back of his brave words. Well, why not? Death was certain now, and Ansset knew of no one, except perhaps an old man like Mikal, who could look at death, especially death that also meant failure, without some fear.

But Mikal did not push the button on the laser.

"Kill me now and finish it," Riktors Ashen said.

Mikal tossed the laser away. "With this? It has no charge. The Chamberlain installed a charge detector at every door in my chambers over fifteen years ago. He would have known if I was armed."

Immediately Riktors took a step forward, the beginning of a rush toward the emperor. Just as quickly Ansset was on his feet, despite the bandaged arm ready to kill with the other hand, with his feet, with his head. Riktors stopped cold.

"Ah," Mikal said. "No one knows like you do what my bodyguard can accomplish in so short a time."

And Ansset realized that if Mikal's laser was not loaded, he couldn't have stopped Ansset if Ansset had not had strength enough to stop himself. Mikal *had* trusted him.

And Mikal spoke again. "Riktors, your mistakes were very slight. I hope you have learned from them. So that when an assassin as bright as you are tries to take *your* life, you know all the enemies you have and all the allies you can call on and exactly what you can expect from each."

Ansset's hands trembled. "Let me kill him now," he said.

Mikal sighed. "Don't kill for pleasure, my Son. If you ever kill for pleasure you'll come to hate yourself. Besides, weren't you listening? I'm going to adopt Riktors Ashen as my heir."

"I don't believe you," Riktors said. But Ansset heard hope in his voice.

"I'll call in my sons—they stay around court, hoping to be closest to the palace when I die," Mikal said. "I'll make them sign an oath to respect you as my heir. Of course they'll all sign it, and of course you'll have them all killed the moment you take the throne. And, let's see, that moment will be three weeks from tomorrow, that should give us time. I'll abdicate in your favor, sign all the papers, it'll make the headlines on the newsheets for days. I can just see all the potential rebels tearing their hair with rage. It's a pleasant picture to retire on."

Ansset didn't understand. "Why?" he asked. "He tried to kill you."

Mikal only laughed. It was Riktors who answered. "He thinks I can hold his empire together. But I want to know the price."

Mikal leaned forward on his chair. "A small price. A house for myself and my Songbird until I die. And then he is to be free for the rest of his life, with an income that doesn't make him dependent on anybody's favors. Simple enough?"

"I agree."

"How prudent." And Mikal laughed again.

The vows were made, the abdication and coronation took a great deal of pomp and the Capital's caterers became wealthy. All the contenders were slaughtered, and Riktors spent a year going from system to system to quell (brutally) all the rebellions.

After the first few planets were burned over, the other rebellions mostly quelled themselves.

It was only the day after the newsheets announced the quelling of the most threatening rebellion that the soldiers appeared at the door of the little house in Brazil where Mikal and Ansset lived.

"How can he!" Ansset cried out in anguish when he saw the soldiers at the door. "He gave his word."

"Open the door for them, Son," Mikal said.

"They're here to kill you!"

"A year was all that I hoped for. I've had that year. Did you really expect Riktors to keep his word? There isn't room in the galaxy for two heads that know the feel of the imperial crown."

"I can kill most of them before they could come near. If you hide, perhaps—"

"Don't kill anyone, Ansset. That's not your song. The dance of your hands is nothing without the dance of your voice, Songbird."

The soldiers began to beat on the door, which, because it was steel, did not give way easily. "They'll blow it open in a moment," Mikal said. "Promise me you won't kill anyone. No matter who. Please. Don't avenge me."

"I will."

"Don't avenge me. Promise. On your life. On your love for me."

Ansset promised. The door blew open. The soldiers killed Mikal with a flash of lasers that turned his body to ashes. They kept firing until nothing but ashes was left. Then they gathered them up. Ansset watched, keeping his promise but wishing with all his heart that somewhere in his mind there was a wall he could hide behind. Unfortunately, he was too sane.

They took the ashes of the emperor and twelve-year-old Ansset to Capital. The ashes were placed in a huge urn, and displayed with state honors. Ansset they brought to the funeral feast under heavy guard, for fear of what his hands might do.

After the meal, at which everyone pretended to be somber, Riktors called Ansset to him. The guards followed, but Riktors waved them away. The crown rested on his hair.

"I know I'm safe from you," Riktors said.

"You're a lying bastard," Ansset said, "and if I hadn't given my word I'd tear you end to end."

It might have seemed ludicrous that a twelve-year-old should speak that way to an emperor, but Riktors didn't laugh. "If I weren't a lying bastard, Mikal would never have given the empire to me."

Then Riktors stood. "My friends," he said, and the sycophants gave a cheer. "From now on I am not to be known as Riktors Ashen, but as Riktors Mikal, The name Mikal shall pass to all my successors on the throne, in honor of the man who built this empire and brought peace to all mankind." Riktors sat amid the applause and cheers, which sounded like some of the people might have been sincere. It was a nice speech, as impromptu speeches went.

Then Riktors commanded Ansset to sing.

"I'd rather die," Ansset said.

"You will, when the time comes," Riktors answered.

Ansset sang then, standing on the table so that everyone could see him, just as he had stood to sing to an audience he hated on his last night of captivity in the ship. His song was wordless, for all the words he might have said were treason. Instead he sang melody, flying unaccompanied from mode to mode, each note torn from his throat in pain, each note bringing pain to the ears that heard it. The song broke up the banquet as the grief they had all pretended to feel now burned within them. Many went home weeping; all felt the great loss of the man whose ashes dusted the bottom of the urn.

Only Riktors stayed at the table after Ansset's song was over.

"Now," Ansset said, "they'll never forget Father Mikal."

"Or Mikal's Songbird," Riktors said. "But I am Mikal now, as much of him as could survive. A name and an empire."

"There's nothing of Father Mikal in you," Ansset said coldly.

"Is there not?" Riktors said softly. "Were you fooled by Mikal's public cruelty? No, Songbird." And in his voice Ansset heard the hints of pain that lay behind the harsh and haughty emperor.

"Stay and sing for me, Songbird," Riktors said. Pleading played around the edges of his voice.

Ansset reached out his hand and touched the urn of ashes that rested on the table. "I'll never love you," he said, meaning the words to hurt.

"Nor I you," Riktors answered. "But we may, nonetheless, feed each other something that we hunger for. Did Mikal sleep with you?"

"He never wanted to. I never offered."

"Neither will I," Riktors said. "I only want to hear your songs."

There was no voice in Ansset for the word he decided to say. He nodded. Riktors had the grace not to smile. He just nodded in return, and left the table. Before he reached the doors, Ansset spoke: "What will you do with this?"

Riktors looked at where Ansset rested his hand. "The relics are yours. Do what you want." Then Riktors Mikal was gone.

Ansset took the urn of ashes into the chamber where he and Father Mikal had sung so many songs to each other. Ansset stood for a long time before the fire, humming the memories to himself. He gave the songs back to Father Mikal, and then reached out and emptied the urn on the blazing fire.

The ashes put the fire out.

"The transition is complete," Songmaster Onn said to Songmaster Esste as soon as the door was closed.

"I was afraid," Songmaster Esste confided in a low melody that trembled. "Riktors Ashen is not unwise. But Ansset's songs are stronger than wisdom."

They sat together in the cold sunlight that filtered through the windows of the High Room of the Songhouse. "Ah," sang Songmaster Onn, and the melody was of love for Songmaster Esste.

"Don't praise me. The gift and power were Ansset's."

"But the teacher was Esste. In other hands Ansset might have been used as a tool for power, for wealth, for control. In your hands—"

"No, Brother Onn. Ansset himself is too much made of love and loyalty. He makes other men desire what he himself already is. He is a tool that cannot be used for evil."

"Will he ever know?"

"Perhaps; I do not think he yet suspects the power of his gift. It would be better if he never found out how little like the other Songbirds he is. And as for the last block in his mind—we laid that well. He will never know it is there, and so he will never search for the truth about who controlled the transfer of the crown."

Songmaster Onn sang tremulously of the delicate plots woven in the mind of a child of five, plots that could have unwoven at any point. "But the weaver was wise, and the cloth has held."

"Mikal Conqueror," said Songmaster Esste, "learned to love peace more than he loved himself, and so will Riktors Mikal. That is enough. We have done our duty for mankind. Now we must teach other little Songbirds."

"Only the old songs," sighed Songmaster Onn.

"No," answered Songmaster Esste with a smile. "We will teach them to sing of Mikal's Songbird."

"Ansset has already sung that."

They walked slowly out of the High Room as Songmaster Esste whispered, "Then we will harmonize!" Their laughter was music down the stairs.

PRENTICE ALVIN AND THE
NO-GOOD PLOW

A lvin, he was a blacksmith's prentice boy,
He pumped the bellows and he ground the knives,
He chipped the nails, he het the charcoal fire,
Nothing remarkable about the lad
Except for this: He saw the world askew,
He saw the edge of light, the frozen liar
There in the trees with a black smile shinin cold,
Shiverin the corners of his eyes.
Oh, he was wise.

The blacksmith didn't know what Alvin saw.
He only knew the boy was quick and slow:
Quick with a laugh and a good or clever word,
Slow at the bellows with his brain a-busy,
Quick with his eyes like a bright and sneaky bird,
Slow at the forge when the smith was in a hurry.
Times the smith, he liked him fine. And times
He'd bellow, "Hell and damnation, hammer and tong,
You done it wrong!"

One day when the work was slow, the smith was easy.
"Off to the woods with you, Lad, the berries are ripe."
And Alvin gratefully let the bellows sag
And thundered off in the dust of the summer road.
Ran? He ran like a colt, he leaped like a calf,
Then his feet were deep in the leafmeal forest floor,
He was moss on the branches, swingin low and lean,

His fingers were part of the bark, his glance was green—
And he was seen.

He was seen by the birds that anyone can see,
Seen by the porcupines that hid in the bushes,
Seen by the light that slipped among the trees,
Seen by the dark that only he could see.
And the dark reached out and stumbled Alvin down,
Laid him laughin and pantin on the ground,
And the dark snuck up on every edge of him,
Frost a-comin on from everywhere,
Ice in his hair.

Ice in the summertime, and Alvin shook,
Crackin ice aloud in the miller's pond,
A mist of winter flowin through the wood,
Fingerin his face, and where it touched
He was numb, he was stricken dumb, his chin all chattery.
Where are the birds? he wondered. When did they go?
Get back to the edge, you Dark, you Cold, you Snow!
Get north, you Wind, it's not your time to blow!
I tell you, No!

No! he cried, but the snow was blank and deep
And didn't answer, and the fog was thick
And didn't answer, and his flimsy clothes
Were wet, and his breath was sharp as ice in his lung
Splittin him like a rail. It made him mad.
He yelled, though the sound froze solid at his teeth
And the words dropped out and broke as they were said
And his tongue went thick, and his lips were even number:
"Dammit, it's summer!"

With the snow like stars of death in your eyes? "It's summer!"
The wind a-ticklin at your thighs? "It's summer!"
Your breath a fog of ice? "Let it be spring!
Let it be autumn, let it be anything!"
But the edge of the world had found him, and he knew
That the fire of the forges would be through,
That the air would be thick and harsh at the end of the earth
And all the flames a-dancin in his hearth,
What were they worth?

"Oh, you can cheat the trees, so dumb and slow,
And you can jolly the birds that summer's through,
But you can't fool me! I'll freeze to death before
I let you get away with a lie so bold!"
And he laughed as he was swallowed by the cold,
He sang as the ice a-split him to the core,

He whispered in his pain that it wasn't true.
"You can bury me deep as hell in your humbug snow,
But I know what I know."

And look at that! A red-winged bird a-singin'!
Look at that! The leaves all thick and green!
He touched the bark so warm in the summer sun,
He buried his hands in the soil and said, "I'm jiggered."
"Oh, blacksmith's prentice boy," said the red-winged bird.
"Took you long enough," said Prentice Alvin.
"Came now, didn't I? So don't get snippety."
"Just see to it you don't go off again.
Where you been?"

"I been," said the red-winged bird, "to visit the sun.
I been to sing to the deaf old man in the moon.
And now I'm here to make a maker of you,
Oh yes, I'll make you something before I'm through."
"I'm something now," said the lad, "and I like it fine."
"You're a smithy boy," said the bird, "and it ain't enough.
Bendin horseshoes! Bangin on the black!
Why, there be things to make that can't be told,
So bright and gold!"

A thousand things, that bird was full of talk,
And on he sang and Alvin listened tight.
Till home he came at dark, his eyes so bright,
His smile so ready but his mood like rock,
He was full of birdsong, full of dreams of gold,
Dreams of what he'd draw from the smithy fire.
"How old is old?" he asked the smith. "How tall
Do I have to be for hammer and tong?
It's been so long."

The smith, he spied him keen, he saw his eyes,
He saw how flames were leapin in the green.
"A redbreast bird been talkin," said the smith,
His voice as low as memory. "So young,
But not so young, so little but so tall.
Hammer and tong, my lazy prentice boy,
Let's see if they fit your hand, let's see if the heft
Is right for your arm, the right side or the left,
See how you lift."

Out they went to the forge beside the road,
Out and stoked the fire till it was hot.
The tongs fit snug in Alvin's dexter hand,
And the hammer hefted easy in his left,
And the smith had a face like grief, although he laughed.

"Go on," says he. "I'm watchin right behind."
The flames leaped up, and Alvin shied the heat,
But deep in the fire he held the iron rod
Till it was red.

"Now bend it," cried the smith, "now make a shoe!"
Alvin raised the hammer over his head,
Ready for the swing. But it wouldn't fall.
"Strike," the blacksmith whispered, "bend and shape."
But the red of the black was the red of a certain bird;
Behind his eyes he saw the iron true:
It was already what it ought to be.
"I can't," he said, and the blacksmith took the tool
And whispered, "Fool."

The hammer clattered against the stone of the wall,
But Alvin, he took heed where the hammer fell.
"There's some can lift the hammer," said the smith,
"And some can strike," and then he spoke an oath
So terrible that Alvin winced to hear.
"I'm shut of you," said the smith. "What's iron for?
To be hot and soft for a man of strength to beat,
To turn the fat of your empty flesh to meat
For the years to eat."

When the smith was gone, poor Alvin like to died,
For what was a smith that couldn't strike the black?
A maker, that's what the redbreast said he'd be,
And now unmade before he'd fair begun.
"I know," he whispered, "I know what must be done."
He took the hammer from the wallside heap
And blew the fire till flames came leapin back
And gathered every scrap at the fire's side
And loud he cried:

"Here is the makin that you said to make!
Here in my hand are the tools you said to take!
Here is the crucible, and here's the fire,
And here are my hands with all they know of shape."
Into the crucible he cast the scrap
And set the pot in the flames a-leapin higher.
"Melt!" he shouted. "Melt so I can make!"
For the redbreast bird had told him how:
A livin plow.

The black went soft in the clay, the black went red,
The black went white and poured when he tipped the pot.
Into the mold he poured, and the iron sang
With the heat and the cold, with the soft and the hard and the form

He forced. When he broke the mold it rang,
And the shape of the plow was curved and sharp where it ought.
But the iron, it was black, oh, it was dead,
No power in it but the iron's own,
As mute as stone.

He sat among the shards of the broken clay
And wondered what the redbird hadn't said.
Or had he talked to the bird at all today?
And now he thought of it, was it really red?
And maybe he ought to change the mold somehow,
Or pour it cool, or hotten up the forge.
But the more he studied it the less he knew,
For the plow was shaped aright, though cold and dark:
He knew his work.

So what was wrong with black? It was good enough
For all the hundred thousand smiths before,
And good enough for all the plows they made,
So why not good enough for Prentice Alvin?
Who ever heard of a bird so full of stuff,
So full of songs to make you feel so poor,
So full of promises of gold and jade?
"Ah, Redbird!" Alvin cried, "my heart is riven!
What have you given?"

He shouted at the black and silent plow.
He beat it, ground it at the wheel, and rubbed
Till the blade was a blackish mirror, till the edge
Was sharp as a trapper's skinnin knife, and still
It was iron, black and stubborn, growin cold.
All broke of hope, he cast it in the fire
And held it with his naked hands in the flame
And wept in agony till it was over.
Here was the taste of pain—he knew the savor:
The plow was silver.

All silver was the plow, and his hands were whole.
He knew what it was the redbird hadn't said.
He couldn't put the iron in alone
And expect the plow by itself to come to life.
He took the plow again—it's gleamin bright—
And this time when he put it into the fire
He clomb right in and sat among the flames
And cried in pain until the fire went cold.
The age of agony—he knew how old:
The plow was gold.

The smith, he come all white-eyed to the forge.
"The buffalo are ruttin in the wood,

A hundred wolves are singin out a dirge,
And a doe, she's lickin while her fawn is fed.
What you be doin while I'm in my bed?
The trees are wide awake and bendin low,
And the stars are all a-cluster overhead.
What will a prentice do when his master go?
I want to know!"

In answer, Alvin only lifts his plow,
And in the firelight it shines all yellow.
"Lord," the smith declares, and "damn my eyes,
My boy, you got the gift, I didn't reelize."
The smith, he reaches out. "Now give it here,
That's worth ten thousand sure, I shouldn't wonder,
All we got to do is melt her down
And we'll be rich afore another sundown,
Move to town."

But Alvin, he's not like to let it go.
"It's a plow I meant to make, and a plow I got,
And I mean for it to do what a plow should do."
The smith was mad, the smith, he scald and swore.
"Cuttin dirt ain't what that gold is for!"
And he reached his hand to take the plow by force,
But when he touched his prentice's arm, he hissed,
And kissed his fingers, gaspin. "Boy, you're hot
As the sunlight's source.

"Hot and bright as sunlight," says the smith,
"And the gold is yours to do whatever you like with,
But whatever you do, I humble-as-dust beseech you,
Do it away from me, I've nothin to teach you."
Says Alvin, "Does that mean I'm a journeyman?
I've a right to bend the black wherever I can?"
And the smith says, "Prentice, journeyman, or master,
For what you done a smith would sell his sister,
Been Satan kissed her."

What was Alvin totin when he left?
I tell you this—it wasn't hard to heft:
A burlap bag with a knot of leaden bread,
A hunk of crumbly cheese, and a golden plow.
A map of the world was growin in his head,
For a fellow knows the edge can guess the whole,
And Alvin meant to find the certain soil
Where his plow could cut and make the clover grow,
The honey flow.

He left a hundred village tongues a-wag
With tales of a million bucks in a burlap bag;

The smith, he swore the gold was devil's make
And therefore free for a godly man to take;
His wife, she told how Alvin used to shirk
And owed them all the gold for his lack of work;
And others said the golden plow was a fake
That sneaky Alvin made so he could gull
Some trustin fool.

The tales of Alvin flew so far and fast
They reached him on the road and went right past,
And many a fellow in many a country inn
Would spy his bag and start in speculatin.
"Kind of a heavy tote you got, I reckon."
And Alvin nods. "The burlap's kinda thin—
Do I see something big and smooth and yellow?"
And Alvin nods, but then he tells the fellow,
"It's just my pillow,"

True enough, if the truth ain't buttoned tight,
For he put it under his head most every night;
But country folk are pretty hard to trick,
And many a fellow thought that he could get
A plowshare's worth of gold for the price of a stick
Applied with vigor to the side of Alvin's head;
And many a night young Alvin had to run
From the bowie knife or buckshot-loaded gun
Of some mother's son.

While Alvin beat through woods and country tracks,
Comes Verily Cooper, a handiworkin man,
Who boards wherever there's barrels to make or mend,
And never did he find so fine a place,
So nice a folk nor never so pretty a face
That he'd put away his walkin boots and stay.
It happened that he come to the smith one day
And heard that Alvin had made his golden plow,
And wondered how.

So off he set with boots so sad and worn
And socks so holey, the skin of his feet was torn
And he left a little track of blood sometimes—
Off set Verily Cooper, hopin to find
What tales were envy, and if some tales were true,
What the journeyman blacksmith did or didn't do.
He asked in every inn, "Did a boy with a bag
Come here, a brown-haired boy so long of leg,
About this big?"

Well, it came about that the findin all was done
On a day without a single speck of sun.

Young Alvin, he come down to the bottom lands,
Where the air was cold and the fog was thick and white.
"In a fog this deep you'd better count your hands,"
Said an unseen man a-waitin by the track.
"What could I see if a man had any sight?"
And the unseen speaker said, "That the sun is bright
And the soil is black."

Now Alvin knelt and touched the dirt of the road,
But the ground was packed and he couldn't feel it deep,
And though he fairly pressed his nose to the dirt,
Still the white of the fog was all he could see.
"The soil, it doesn't look so black to me."
And the unseen speaker said, "The earth is hurt
And hides in the fog and heals while it's asleep.
For the tree, she screamed and wept when the beaver gnawed
And no one knowed."

"I'm lookin," Alvin says, "for a soil that's fit
To spring up golden grain, make cattle fat."
And the unseen speaker says, "What soil is that?"
"I'm lookin," Alvin says again, "for loam
That a plow can whittle till it comes to life."
And the unseen speaker says, "A plow's a knife,
And where it cuts the earth is broke and lame."
Says Alvin, "Mar to mend, from the moldrin leaf
Will grow the limb."

"Then go, if you mean to make from the broken ground,
Go till you hear the rushin river's sound,
For there in the river's bight is a dirt so rich
You can harrow with your hand and plow with a flitch."
"Thank you, stranger," Alvin says, and then:
"I've heard your voice before, I can't think when."
"In such a fog as this, so cold and wet,
Your sight's so dim your memory's in debt
And you forget,

For the fog, it goes afore and it goes behind,
Hides what you're lookin for and what you've found,
And the deeper you go, the dimmer it makes your past.
And yet in all the world, this soil is best."
With that, though Alvin tried to learn his name,
The unseen speaker never spoke again,
And at last the journeyman smith went on to find
In the fog, by listenin tight for the river's sound,
That perfect ground.

Near done was the day when Alvin came to the shore
Of the mighty River Mizeray, all deep

And brown and slow and lookin half asleep.
Said Mizeray, "Jes step a little more,
Young feller, and I'll carry you across."
And Alvin, blind as a bat in the fog, he said,
"Don't I hear the rush of a river in its bed?"
But Mizeray, he gave a little toss
And whispered, "Cross."

So again that day young Alvin Maker jedges.
How can he know what's true in a fog so white?
How can he trust what a hidden voice alleges?
He kneels, he touches the soil, he lifts it light,
He crushes it in his hand and it's loose and smooth,
But still old Mizeray's voice can tickle and sooth,
And says, "Come on, step on, I'll carry you
To the only soil in the world that'll ever do,
I tell you true."

Old Mizeray has a voice you must believe.
Old Mizeray has a voice that could not lie.
Old Mizeray, he whispers to deceive,
To draw the trustin step to the edge, to die;
But the voice, the voice is full and sweet with love.
So Alvin, with his fingers deep in the loam,
He wonders if this soil is good enough,
And again he hears the river's whisperin hum:
"I'll take you home."

And now he doesn't know his north from south,
And his fingers search but cannot find his mouth,
And he can't remember what he came here for,
Or if it even matters anymore.
Only the sound of the river callin him,
Only the whine of his fear, so high and thin,
Only the taste of the sweat when he licks his lips,
Only the tremblin of his fingertips,
Their weakish grips.

He stands, but he doesn't step, he daresn't walk,
He puzzles for the key to this hidden lock,
And he knows the key isn't in that hissin voice,
He knows there's another way to make his choice.
The soil he's lookin for, it's not for himself,
It's meant for the plow he carried all so stealthy;
He opens his burlap bag and lifts the plow
And sets it on the earth real soft and slow,
And sees it glow.

He sees it shine, that plow, it shines all gold,
All yellow, and it gets too hot to hold,

And around the plow the fog begins to clear,
And the wind, it blows till the fog is gone from here,
And he sees the soil is humusy and black
Just as the unseen voice in the fog had said;
And he sees the river lap the shore and smack
And if he'd taken that step, now he'd be dead
In the devil's sack.

For Mizeray, down deep, don't flow with water:
The bottom slime is made of the stuff of night,
The darkness reachin in at the edge of light,
Awaitin for the step of a man unwary
To suck him down and slither him out to bury,
Numb and soundless, pressed in the dark of the sea,
Where the driftin dead look up through the night and see
Forever out of reach the earth in her dance,
O heaven's daughter.

And in the tree young Alvin sees a bird
All red of feather, mouth all wide and singin,
And Alvin, he calls out, "I know your voice!"
But the wind-awaker answers not a word.
Enough for him that his breezy song is heard,
And he darts from tree to tree, so coy he's wingin,
And Alvin sighs at the come-out of his choice,
Not altogether sure how the thing occurred,
For the choice was hard.

And while he lies a-restin in the grove,
Up comes young Verily Cooper, shy and smilin.
"Are you the one that they call by the name of Alvin?"
"There's many who's called that name. And who are you?"
"I'm a man who wants to learn what you know of makin.
They call me Verily Cooper, I work in staves,
I join them watertight, each edge so true,
But never a keg I made that was proof from leakin
Or safe from breakin."

Alvin answers, "What do I know of barrels?"
Verily says, "And what did you know of plows?"
And Alvin laughs, and he says, "Ain't you a marvel,"
And up he hops and gives his hand a shake.
"Verily Cooper, there's things in a man that shows,
And here at the river's edge we'll plow the earth
And together make whatever we fix to make
And be the midwives at the barley's birth
And weigh our worth."

So they cut an oak and together hewed the wood
To make the plowframe strong and slow of flex,

And they set the plow in place and bound it good
And never mind a halter for an ox,
For this was a livin plow, of tremblin gold.
And when the work was done, they marked their field,
And side by side they reached and took ahold,
And the plow, it leaped, it plunged, it played like a child
So free and wild.

Verily and Alvin, they hung on;
There wasn't a hope of guidin the plow along.
It was all they could do to keep it to the land;
Other than that they couldn't do a thing.
And at last, with bleedin blisters on their hands,
With arms gone weak and legs too beat to run,
They tripped and fell together on the dirt.
Aside from the blisters, the only thing much hurt
Was Alvin's shirt.

They look, and there's the plow, still as you please,
Gleamin in the sunlight. "How'd it stop?"
Asks Alvin. Verily, he thinks he sees
The truth. He touches the plow, it gives a hop;
He takes his hand away, and it sets right down.
"It's us that makes it go," he says, and he grins.
Now Alvin laughs, a-settin on the ground:
"Maybe it goes a little widdershins,
But it gets around!"

And as they sat there, hollerin and whoopin,
Out come the farmer folk who lived nearby,
To find out what had caused the fog to fly—
And at the same time do a little snoopin.
They saw that the furrow went all anyhow,
And they said, "If you think that's plowin, boys, you're daft!
Straight as an arrow, that's how a plow should go!"
And the farmers mocked—oh, how the farmers laughed
At that no-good plow.

That sobered Alvin up, and Verily frowned.
"Don't you see that the plow, it cut the earth alone?
We got no ox, we got no horse around!
The plow's alive, and we'll tell you how it's done!"
But the farmers went their way, still mirthful merry,
For they had nothin to learn from any fellow
As young and ignorant as Al or Verry.
And the plow just sat at the head of its crooked furrow,
Hot and yellow.

The rest of the tale—how they looked for the crystal city,
How they crept to the dangerous heart of the holy hill,

How they broke the cage of the girl who sang for rain,
How they built the city of light from water and blood—
Others have told that tale, and told it good.
And besides, the girl you're with is cruel and pretty,
And the boy you're settin by has a mischievous will.
There's better things to do than hear me again,
So go on home.

MALPRACTICE

W ent to Doc today for checkup and got the ole kickinthepants routine about losing weight but theres more. My chest was flabby like normal but he found a scar where there shouldnt be one. I couldnt remember having anything done there. Only operation in last six months was in Tulsa, Okl, where I was *supposed* to have my arm set. (Broke it riding a stupid horse, never get me on one of those things again.) So Doc made me lie down and go to sleep, did an exploratory on the spot (miracles of modern medicine) and he asked me when I came out of it why the hell did I have a heart transplant?

So who had a heart transplant?

Somebodys been mucking around in my body and when I find out who hes going to eat that horse that crammed me into the tree and hes going to eat everything that horse has produced in the last six years. Doc says its obviously somebody elses tissue and even though the operation was neat it looked hurried, some of the laser sutures look as bad as if theyd been done with catgut like a few hundred years ago. Nothing *wrong*, he says, but pretty ragged. As if it mattered how ragged it is with somebody elses stupid heart pumping my blood.

Consolation prize: Doc says its an OK heart, except for a murmur, which he says wont cause me any trouble but if it stops murmuring and starts yelling I should drink nitroglycerin or something.

Why would somebody stick a different heart in me? My old one may have skipped a beat now and then (Ah, Marilyn!) but it ticked OK and it was mine and I was kind of attached to it (Ha ho).

So I thought back to when since my last checkup I had been out anywhere near a loose scalpel and the only time I've been gassed that I know of was in Tulsa with my arm. I asked Doc, he said maybe it could have been done then but the guy wouldve had to be pretty fast. And the spare pieces wouldve had to be pretty handy.

So tomorrow Im flying to Tulsa and Im madder than hades (once every third profanity

602 Maps in a Mirror

I use a euphemism to keep in practice for the Daily Noose, which is "a family paper") the hospital there had better be on there toes since I plan to do some onthespot transplants of heads and arms and other appendages when I find out what and who did what was done and why. Goodnight, dear diary.

AUGUST 3

As long as Im writing this thing might as well be accurate and put in the good old 5Ws. Im in a plane and Tulsa is sliding forward to meet me and I thought Id fill in some details.

I read yesterday's stuff and it sure looks like a rough draft. But thats what it is. For the Noose they pay a guy who can spell to fix my stuff and they pay him half what they pay me, for the very good reason that he may know how to spell but I know how to write, which is worth more.

Name: (love those little colons) Frank Mabey as in perhaps but the ys at the end.

Ocction: Journalist which means I can write better than the president but not as good as Van Clapper which is fine because what the hell would I do with all that excess money the old man's got.

Temperament: Mad as heck.

Reason for writing this stupid diary: Every boy should keep a journal. I somehow dont feel like telling anybody that Ive got the wrong pump. Might suspect something else is transplanted, too, and Id just as soon avoid speculation. Id tell my sweet loving X only X doesnt give a damn which is fine, because I dont want any of her lousy used damns anyway. Darns. Got to keep up those euphs.

August 3 cont. (tune in next week, same time, ect.)

Went to Tulsa Center for Medical Treatment (everythings a center. someday Im going to build a building and call it the Indianapolis Edge for Journalistic Somethin-gorother) the guy who did my arm has retired. In fact, the day he did my arm was the last day he worked at the hospital, which is lucky on the next days patients but pretty tough on me. He put in a hard day that last day. Got a list of 12 opers the guy did (his name is Hyman Maier—he must be a Baptist. Ha ho).

:(love those colons)

Amos N. Ditweiler
Ronald Smith
Joann Capel
Morris Major
Scott Peterson
Valery Van Vleet (geez, the things some parents do to there kids)
R.R. Trane (I hope to hell his name isnt Rail Road)
Bartholomew (Ha ho) Biscuit (actually Bascom, but the name biscuit occurred to me and Im compulsive)
Wanda Bath (Im not making this up, folks)
John Jorgenson (back to the relms of the ordinary)
William E. Jagger
Mark Muse

The reason for this list, dear diary, is that I dont want the names left around on any scraps of paper and you, dear diary, never leave my side. These people who were operated on were all in for relatively minor operations but for some reason which the hospital people do not pretend to fathom he used total anaesthetic on everybody. The guy I talked to looked at the records and said, (I quote) "Why did he put you under total for an arm?" Im supposed to know this? Im the doctor? What do I tell him, he put me under total because he had a spare heart he wanted to find a home for. And I looked warm and loving and not the romantic type—heart unlikely to get broken. So much for you, X.

So heres my whole sweet lead on the guy. Hes a doctor, pretty good, only he retired (he wasnt all that old) and left no address, didnt even pick up his last check and his lawyer paid his bills. Ordinary guy, no wife (died, I should have been so lucky, widowers dont pay alimony) one kid, works in an ad agency in NY nobody knows where nobody knows his name. And Maier (the doctor who retreaded my radial) was a GD. Which I think is appropriate.

GD, dear stupid diary (must assume diary is stupid for the sake of clarity) stands for Gods Deliverance, the church that believes god is reincarnated every twenty years or something, there prophet got zapped in Denver by a pervert with a laser meatcleaver (some tight security there, folks, those things weight thirty pounds and you just dont stick em under your jacket), and the girls all wear long hair or short hair or something so they look alike. This is Frank Mabey, journalist, speaking. You can tell by the preceision of my data.

In other words, I have a choice to find Maier. I can look through the whole GD church.

Oh, theres another choice. I can forget it and just take my pulse a lot.

AUGUST 4

Whee. Its back to the whole world. The GD church keeps no membership records, on purpose because then somebody might try to do them harm. Not a bad idea, because the guy looked like he was going to be helpful till I said Hyman Maiers name and then suddenly Im a communist and he gets slanty eyes just looking at me. My heart feels funny. Not the murmur, its kind of a pleasant lullaby at night. I just *feel* it, thats all, and Ive never felt my heart before. Come to think of it, Im not feeling *my* heart now!

AUGUST 11

I mustve decided to forget it because I havent done anything for a few days now, only Doc called today and theres something more and now Ive gotta find that bastard Maier and find out what the hells going on. Found thee, dear diary, because we are back on the trail. The boss asked me what I was investigating today. Told him "heart throbs" (ha ho, laughaminute).

News from Doc—pictures show something funny about the heart, he wants to open me up again. Good thing my insurance covers everything. I think Im becoming Docs hobby.

AUGUST 13

My heart is growing. Good news, huh? The ragged edges were not all sloppy surgery, they were heart tissue overgrowing the sutures, which means that the new heart is taking over (welcome to Latin America, heart, time for a coup). My aorta is two inches new tissue, with a whole new genetic pattern. And the veins to my lungs are completely new tissue. What scares Doc most, besides the fact that hes never seen this happen before, is that the new tissue is moving into the lungs. Why would heart tissue take over the lungs? Only its changing from heart tissue into lung tissue, and Doc says it seems to be progressing faster.

Whatever kind of heart this Maier stuck into me, it thinks that *it* got a *body* transplant. I wish to persuade it otherwise, but Doc says what is he supposed to do, give me a third heart? Generally frowned on, and the new thingamajobby (more than a heart now) isn't doing any *harm*. Replacing it would be cosmetic surgery. Which my wonderful policy dont cover, mine friend.

Why oh why did I ride that horse? Why did I go to the Tulsa Center for Medical Treatment? Why was I born? (This last, dear diary, is mock despair, lest you think Im becoming desperate. I am, but think it not.)

AUGUST 17

The GD church doesnt like me, which is mutual. Not only that, but Im pretty sure theyve got a tail on me, in the form of a very nice looking girl who could probably kill me with one hand (she looks mean) and who isnt very good at hiding. In fact, I think maybe there not worried about whether I know their tailing me or not. Maybe they want me to know. Maybe she isnt tailing me. Maybe she thinks Im a male prostitute. Here the speculation is more fun than finding the facts, because there jes ain no facks to fine.

AUGUST 18

Visiting my fellow operatees, the ones on my list. Amos N. Ditweiler is on a business trip, Ronald Smith was killed in a car accident (waste of good operation, there, Maier, what did you give him an elbow?), Joann Capel was home but refuses to show me her scar (and slammed the door when I told her I really had to see it) which is understandable considering the operation she was in the hospital to get, Morris Major wants me to go to hell. Thos are all the ones who live right in Tulsa that I was able to talk to. Good days work. Morris looks like Maier gave him a new nose. Without removing the old one.

AUGUST 19

Id rather be selling fuller brushes. These people are more than rude. There nasty. Scott Peterson is a fag with a fat giant for a girlfriend, and even though Peterson didnt scare me, when his girlfriend told me to scram, I scrum. Valery Van Vleets mother thought I was a child molester (shes 11) and so I cant see her. R. R. Tranes name is not Rail Road, its Robin Rex, and Id go by R. R. too. But Trane *did* admit that he had an operation, which was for gall bladder, but thereve been no complications and no extra scars. Heres my guess—he got a new gall bladder and doesnt know it. Or was I the only lucky transplantee?

But, dear diary, we hit paydirt with Bartholomew Biscuit (nee bascom) who viewed me with suspicion but when I told him my sad story got a worried look and told me that hes been really worried because he had his lungs cleaned out (a smoker, filthy habit) only there are scars on both sides of his chest and the anticancer operation is supposed to be done through the throat. What is more (and this interests me a lot) he has noticed that his scars are actually getting wider, and the skin of his scars is white (he is black), which makes him suspicious that somethings a little bit wrong. He promises to call me. Oh, he also said the new skin is hairy. I inspected my scars for hair today. None, so far, that werent already mine. I hope. ·

August 20 in the wee small hours

Met my tailer from the GDs tonight, we had dinner. She *is* a tailer from the GDs, admits it cheerfully, but she says shes only there to protect me. Sweet. I offered her five hundred dollars to protect somebody else, but she only smiled and told me to go to hell. I asked her if shed follow me there and she said "anywhere" so I went to my apartment. No dice, GDs believe in virginity for single women, she has the apartment next to mine and told me that she is bugging my room for sound. Nice of her to be so frank. Im Frank too (ha ho) and I told her that she was bugging me too. She said sorry. I said a word that the Noose would replace with a euphemism. She slapped me (do women still slap men for being obscene? X slapped, but it was for kind of the opposite reason) and we went to bed, in different rooms thank heaven, except that heaven is on the GDs side.

Maier was a GD. This girl (Myrel Merle Murl Mirl Mural who knows how anybody spells a weird name like that?) is also a GD. My heart seems to be on their side too. And one (just one, but hes the only one who really talked) of the other operees has weird things happening to him too. I think Im onto something and it aint peaknuckle.

August 20 in the evening after four hours of sleep and a hard days work.

Wanda Bath doesnt.

John Jorgenson is an ad executive and his operation was a very personal one because he is middle-aged and middle-aged people tend to think such operations are very personal. But he, too, for reasons he refuses to describe, is also worried. I urged him to see his doctor, he said he would, and said he would tell me if there was anything unusual. William E. Jagger lives in Sacramento. Mark Muse is a talking aardvark, Ive never seen such a repulsive person, why didn't Maier transplant his head? His operation was to remove a bunion—total anaesthetic, for petes sake, Im going to sue the hospital, they let any nut stick any patient under anaesthetic and nobody even asks questions. His bunion is all better. He also has a scar on his throat and when I asked about it he said "what scar" got a mirror and by gum, he had a scar, hed have to check into that, by gum, by gum. So by gum he says hell call me if theres anything to call me about.

Ditweilers back from his trip, I have an appointment tomorrow, but I think I wont bother. Hes the kind who strings investigative reporters on for months without a word, probably thinks Im going to pry into his affairs. Who gives a darn (euph) about his affairs?

August 21 at four a.m. which is grounds for murdering Doc for his phonecall this morning but hes scared and so am I. There is no medical way that what is happening to me could be happening to me. He checked the genetic type, says that with our limited knowledge of genetics exact identification is impossible but the person whose heart I have was male (thank you), had brown hair, white skin, blue or green eyes, and is of medium height barring pituitary problems. That narrows it down to a fifth of the world. Whee.

At least its proof that the heart isnt mine, since Im tall, blond, have brown eyes, though I am male and white, excluding me from any of the attractive minorities. I always wanted to be an indian when I was a kid only I couldnt get into a tribe without a reservation (Ha ho).

August 21 in the evening dear diary, why am I even bothering to write to you, when there is a communist plot to take over my body?

Got a call from Jorgenson at 7 a.m. and he wanted me to come over so I did, his doctor opened him up and looked at his prostate and bingo. Whole new set of male organs, not a tricky operation, but Jorgenson didnt want new ones, he liked the old. Too much sentimentality. And in him, too, the transplant has overgrown its boundaries. His doctor is worried. His doctor told him to take a sedative. Why isnt my doctor that thoughtful?

This afternoon went back to talk to Bartholemew Biscuit since he hadnt called, he told me he hadnt called because it was so damn ridiculous, which I agree with except when its me, in which case its pretty serious. Yessiree bob, a lung transplant, which has taken over his heart (me in reverse) and is progressing to the skin. His doctor is not worried. His doctor is delighted. At last, something new for the MDs to do. And get this—genetic check, and it comes from a medium height male with brown hair, white skin, blue or green eyes. Now maybe thats coincidence but I did some research and now I really am scared.

See, the GDs prophet who was assassinated in June was named George Peppinger and I looked up the old *Time* stories on him and he is, you guessed it, medium height, blue eyes, brown hair, white skin. Im doubtless paranoid, but Maier *was* a GD and what if these nuts have some idea of keeping there rainmaker alive? I dont like playing incubator to somebody elses chicken. So Im in the airport going back to Doc for a progress report. Murrul Myril Myeroll has bought the ticket next to me, so therell be no writing on the plane. I plan to ask her a few questions. Then I plan to push her out the window (Ha ho). (Whats so funny?)

AUGUST 22

Doc is treating me really carefully and I feel like Im already deceased. My new heart (Sweetheart, Heart of Gold) has given rise to new lungs, new trachea (those are the plumbing), a new esophagus, a new stomach, and the list goes on and on, so that theres less of me in me than there is him in me. The Doc admits that since he doesnt know how it happens he cant do much to stop it. No way to transplant my whole innards, therere limits to what the MDs can do.

But you see I know whats causing it and Id tell the Doc only then hed lock me away for believing such drivel. See, my little GD virgin friend Moral (yes, folks, I finally got the spelling of her name, and I nearly puked too) is very starryeyed about Peppinger. They dont think Christ or God or anybody reincarnates *in particular*, they believe that anybody can, if hes got enough of the world spirit. There are spirits and bodies, see, and some spirits are of the world spirit, and they are strong. Others have forsaken the world spirit and stand all alone and so they are weak. So that some spirits are so weak that it takes two or three or many of them to operate one body (welcome schitzophrenia) and other spirits are so strong with the world spirit that they can control many bodies all at once (heil hitler). She has only a little world spirit (humble child) and so only controls one body "But I am alone" she said. I congratulated her and she glared at me.

There was a lot of other stuff. I had to pretend to be very interested, and Im a lousy actor because she said she knew I didn't give a darn (she said darn, not my cuph this time, looks like she repented of swearing at me the other night) about the GD church anyway. They think that Christ was not God but his friend, trying to save, not mankind, but God, by casting out all the weak spirits and letting Gods great worldspirit in, and so on, who understands this stuff? I never went to catechism.

AUGUST 25

Peg of My Heart, I Love You
Dont let us part, I Love You
I left my heart in San Francisco.
A half-hearted effort
A hearty laugh
Heartless wretch (O that I were so
    lucky, mother)
My heart is heavy (full, light, in my
    throat)
My hearts in my throat ha ho hee
    hee howdy.

There is now strange hair growing around the scar on my chest and also on my back which never had hair before and when I look closely I see a very thin dividing line where the old me is giving way to the new somebody.

Only I know who the somebody is except that I think Im crazy to believe it but the GDs must believe it too else why are they watching me? Protecting me—maybe they think there prophet can take over. If they think so, their right, and hes doing a damn good job.

I thought of killing myself just for spite but then I figured what good would that do because

A. they would stop me (they watch me a lot)

B. and there are 10 other transplantees still living.

Ha ho.

If I could draw I would draw a picture of my head and put a little light bulb over it. There *are* things I can do. World Spirit, go to hell. I shall send you friends.

Luckily, I have done nothing so far to arouse suspicion except that they probably know that I know. Question? How does one untail a tail?

AUGUST 26

Answer: You dont. Tighter than glue. I tried taxis, I tried walking through crowds, Moral is tighter than glue.

AUGUST 28

Victory. I am now on the plane to Sacramento and except for the fact that anybody around me might be a GD, I think I made it. Moral is waking up about now unless I broke her neck, which I doubt because lets face it, Im not all that tough. If I hadnt had my gun (registered, folks, my occupation allows weaponry for self defense) and if she hadnt happened to hit her head on a urinal I think I wouldnt have made it. Shes pretty scary. She may be a virgin but she knows all about the laying on of hands. The bruise on my arm is pretty bad, I can see it through my shirt sleeves.

Took a jet to Boston, then from Boston to Dallas only I got off in Chicago and flew to Tulsa and hopped right on another flight to Sacramento. Maybe they'll catch up and maybe they wont, but at least theyll have to do a little research unless somebody saw me who knows me and thats the gamble Im taking.

AUGUST 29

Greyhound bus to San Francisco. Job done.

AUGUST 30

Landing in Tulsa. I reread this thing and Im absolutely sure Im insane except sane or not Im committed (ha ho) to this now. No turning back at all.

AUGUST 31

Radio is talking about the rash of Tulsa murders and frankly I dont see what these nut murderers get out of killing strangers. I would kill myself right now except that it would leave the job undone. I had to kill Valery Van Vleets mother too because there was no way to get to the little girl without

I want to vomit.

I vomited but I don't feel any better. What am I doing Im killing people and even though I don't believe in God I feel damned. I cant be insane because insane people can black these things out and why the hell am I writing at a time like this except that I guess when Im dead I hope that people will understand and at least think I was crazy except Im not except that thats what all crazy people say (and all sane people too) but at least I know that what Im doing is insane. I know its insane but the MDs dont understand whats happening to me and the others and I cant think of any explanation except what the GDs say oh what the hell Ill just shutup and try to sleep

I cant sleep

I dont want to sleep anyway. I want to die.

SEPTEMBEREMBEREMBEREMBEREMBER THE FIRST

And the mission is accomplished I had to kill a whole bunch of GDs and thank heaven for my permit to buy ammo because without it theredve been no way. If Im right or wrong it doesnt matter anymore because there all dead and Ill be too as soon as I finish writing this which Id better hurry and do because my guess is theyre trying to find me right now. I realized after I got all but Biscuit that theyd better not try to stop me because the only way they could do it would be to kill me and Im a peace of there prophet, who they dont want to kill. Im carrying valuable cargo. Which is why they havent called the cops, because the cops would kill me. And besides, how would they explain how they know who Id kill next without letting out their little secret which even if nobody believed it I figure they dont want anybody guessing.

I got all new skin on my tummy, and this Peppinger must have been a pretty virile guy, if body hair has anything to do with virility. I feel like a new man Ha ho.

I thought maybe it would be kind of harder to do Biscuit because after all I liked him but after youve killed about twenty people who arent fighting back, who just look at you all surprised and frightened Vomit Vomit. Good thing I dont plan to get myself with poison because Id puke it up before it got me. Dead time, boys and girls. Whoever reads this, take a good look at the GDs and do yourself a favor. Dont let anybody operate on you under total again. There aint nothing worth dying for, unless its making sure that youre the only person living in your body.

I just thought of something. What if I had waited a little longer, and this Peppinger had got to my brain? Would I just become Peppinger?

Who gives a darn (euph).

I do.

I found myself with a pistol barrel in my mouth wondering why. I remember why now, I think. I have read this journal, and I think I remember thoughts of a few minutes ago. They were not my thoughts. But they are my memories.

This gun has killed. These hands pulled the trigger. This heart beat faster as the gun fired. These ears still ache from the explosions. These eyes wept in remorse. My mouth still tastes of vomit.

But I did not kill. Please, God, I did not kill.

I was killed. Mabey says so and I remember a mad face and a meatcleaver, coming from nowhere in the depths of a crowd of smiling, laughing, loving faces. I remember a moment of pain, and then

No. This I cannot

I can think of no reason to believe that this journal is a fraud.

I have looked in the mirror. I am the man I remembered myself to be.

3 SEPTEMBER

I have met with Hyman, Ron, Moral, Chaste, and Egan. The answers are clear. Such a great sin has never been committed, and yet the hearts of those who sinned were pure.

Surely the humble fishermen whose hearts' love had been torn from them did not sin in wishing him alive again. And in the wishing, neither did these disciples of God's Deliverance sin. But ours is a different age, and it was the genius of Egan and Chaste, the deft hands of Hyman, the force of will of Ron and Moral that have brought me back, not from the grave, for I never was there, but from where I was, and that is sin enough.

The chemicals are destroyed, boiled away or burned or both. The papers are all ash, which has been raked to dust and scattered through the fields and woods of this countryside. And they have knelt before me and given solemn oath before God and before me (it is a mark of all our weakness that they and I hold it necessary to vow before someone else than God) that their secrets will die with them.

We all have blood on our hands. They have the blood of eleven murdered men, women, and children. I have the blood of Frank Mabey whose body I stole. I have done what cannibals only mocked: I have eaten his flesh and taken his virtue and I live because he is dead.

This sin is on our heads, and though we will proceed as we had planned before the manservant of sin cut the thread of my thin and nebulous life, nevertheless we, like Moses and Aaron, will not see the promised land.

I will lock this away until my death, because for the sake of the movement we must go on. Penance for these sins will come later, in God's time. Now we must work in God's Deliverance. After my death this will be Frank Mabey's testament and my confession.

It is no jest that religion forbids all good things, and the stronger the forbidding, the better the thing forbidden. But the forbidding is only for a time. To own is forbidden, until the thing owned has been earned. To copulate is forbidden, until that copulation is locked within a family. And to die and to kill are forbidden, until God himself reaches down his hand and releases us from life. This I have taught them now. I see that it must be the cornerstone.

10 SEPTEMBER

They ask me, again and again, what is death like? What did I feel? What did I see?

I show them, but they see not. I tell them, but they hear not. If death were not desirable, it would not have been forbidden us. We are taught to fear it, and we are forbidden to seek those who have died, because if we knew, if we understood what lies within our reach, at the cost of a pill, a bullet, a blade, a breath, then in the moment we understood, this world would be unpopulated. We would leap into our graves like a lecher into his lady's bed.

But we do not know, and the fear is on us, and God in his mercy will deliver us from ourselves if we can school our passions.

Perhaps God will let me stand on a high hill and look out into the promised land before he lets me return to him. Then my people will mourn me. But I will go singing.

FOLLOWER

Reuben Ives decided on his twelfth birthday that this would be his lucky year. His dog and his doctor disagreed, but he ignored them. Maynard could hide under the bed with his paws over his eyes, but it wouldn't stop Reuben. And the doctor—well, he was one of *them*, and Reuben had nothing but contempt for him. He showed his contempt by always arriving exactly fifteen minutes late for his appointments, which he knew threw off the doctor's schedule for the rest of the day. And every time the doctor got used to it and scheduled someone else into Reuben's half hour, Reuben would arrive on time. It was just Reuben's way of letting them know that he didn't care, the doctor whispered to the nurse. *Ho hum*, Reuben said to himself. And Maynard looked embarrassed and curled up under the chair looking more like a sheep than a sheepdog.

In fact, Reuben thought, he looks kind of sheepish.

"What are you laughing at?" the doctor asked.

Reuben sneered at him. "You. You look terrible with bifocals."

"Thank you, Reuben," said the doctor.

"I turned twelve this morning at 9:37," Reuben announced.

"Happy birthday," the doctor answered.

"Suck rocks," Reuben responded. "How do you manage it?"

"Manage what?" asked the doctor, with imperturbable patience.

"Being sincere, whether you mean it or not. I mean can't you—"

"But I mean it," said the doctor. Reuben laughed.

"How do you feel," the doctor asked, "about being twelve?"

"I've lived through a dozen years of being dumped on," said Reuben.

"Really?" asked the doctor. He looked a little more interested than usual.

"Oh, doctor, yes!" cried Reuben frantically. "They're all against me, they follow me everywhere! They're out to get me, all of them. Protect me!"

The doctor sighed and shuffled papers on his desk.

Reuben fell to his knees on the floor. "You won't help, then? You're one of them. I can see it now. Maynard, protect me from them!" Reuben screamed, grabbing at the dog under his chair. Irritated, Maynard bit his hand.

Reuben looked at the scratch marks on his skin. "Et tu, Maynard," he murmured. "Doctor, look. Even Maynard."

"Paranoia isn't a joke, Reuben," the doctor said.

"A joke he says," Reuben said to Maynard, laughing bitterly.

With the enemy ships circling our planet and everybody we meet a possible traitor, the doctor said to himself, paranoia is normal. The sky is our enemy. The world is our enemy. The only escape from fear is to be buried. But Reuben was not paranoid.

Reuben was chewing the leaves of the rubber plant.

"Isn't it bad enough that you're crazy," the doctor said to him, "without you acting crazier than you are?"

"Uh uh uh," Reuben said, getting back on the chair. "You must not express any negative emotions toward a disturbed person. Code Seven, paragraph three."

"I'm a doctor," the doctor reminded him. "I can tell you to go to hell if I want to."

"Do you want to?" asked Reuben.

"Go to hell," answered the doctor.

"I been there," said Reuben in his backcountry voice, "and I ain't goin' back."

"How do you feel," asked the doctor, "about being twelve?"

"This," said Reuben, "is my lucky year."

The doctor looked at him blankly. "What do you mean, lucky?"

"Having luck," Reuben answered. "Meeting with success; having good fortune. In other words, things is gonna go mah way."

"And how," asked the doctor, "is this marvelous thing going to occur?"

But Reuben sat quietly and did not answer. He just stroked Maynard for the rest of the half hour, until the doctor got up and opened the door and said, "Time's up. Get lost, see you next week. Three-thirty. If you're late, I'll revoke your pass."

"If I'm late," Reuben said, "you'll see me when I come."

The doctor sighed as he watched Reuben go out the door. Reuben smiled. He never counted a visit as a success unless the doctor sighed as he went out the door.

Reuben got on the overhead, getting his ticket punched at the machine. When he got off at the downtown station, he flashed his purple pass at the man who took money and credit cards. The man smiled cheerfully and waved Reuben through, but Reuben noticed that he stepped back and that his eyes were full of fear as he looked at the boy. Reuben was not surprised—most people reacted to him that way. He didn't like it. But at least he got through free—fringe benefits of being a Disturbed Person.

He walked out to the middle of the routing room, where the overhead train schedules flashed on large screens. A huge crowd was milling around. Reuben stopped and set Maynard down. (He always carried Maynard on the overhead because the vibrations made Maynard nervous and he would go to the bathroom on the floor.)

"Crowd's a little bigger than usual," Reuben said to Maynard. Maynard coughed.

Crowds were always big, Reuben thought. He wondered what it had been like back when it was legal to own your own car and people used to drive all over. How would the overhead stay in business then? It gave lousy service. There was always gum on the seats. Nobody would use the overhead unless they had to.

But they had to.

Reuben closed his eyes and counted to two hundred. People stared, but then they noticed the purple card in his hand and looked away. It was illegal to stare at disturbed persons.

Then Reuben opened his eyes. The first person he saw was a tall man in a business suit. The man was walking away, and Reuben stepped out to follow him. Then he realized that the man looked like his father, and he stopped dead. No, it wasn't his father. But Reuben decided not to follow him anyway.

Reuben remembered the last time he had seen his father. It was his birthday, and his father had—his birthday. Father would be coming to visit him again today. Reuben felt very dark and somehow vaguely afraid.

Father would visit him and Mother would stay home. Reuben spat on the ground. The people around him did not look disgusted. It was illegal to look disgusted at the antisocial acts of disturbed persons.

Reuben closed his eyes and counted again. This time when he looked up he saw a short dumpy man in an expensive suit. He seemed uncomfortably hot, even in the air-conditioned station, and Reuben thought this one might be fun. So he put his purple card in his pocket and walked out of the station right behind the man.

Following was easy for the first few blocks, because the man was walking through crowds, and Reuben could stay ten feet behind without the man ever seeing him. Because Reuben was shorter than the adults in the crowd, staying out of sight was simple. It was one of the few times Reuben was glad he was not yet grown up.

But then the man left the crowds and went down a long alley. The only people were a few workmen unloading a truck. The man walked by and waved. The workmen waved back.

Reuben took a rubber ball out of his pocket and threw it down the alley, not far enough to reach the man, but well over halfway. "Okay, Maynard," Reuben said, "Go earn your dog biscuits."

Maynard took off down the alley after the ball. When he reached it he didn't pick it up and bring it back. Instead, he pushed it farther along.

"Fetch!" yelled Reuben. The dog ignored him and pushed the ball even farther.

"Come back with that ball, you stupid mongrel!" Reuben yelled. Then he took off trotting down the alley.

The men stopped work and watched Reuben. Suspiciously, he thought. One of the workmen glanced up the alley, where the man Reuben was following was just turning the corner. Then the workman turned back and looked at Reuben.

"How come you ain in school, boy?" the man challenged.

Reuben pulled the purple card from his pocket.

"Oh, hey, boy," the man said, embarrassed. "Hey, sorry, okay, kid?"

"Sure, fine," Reuben answered. Maynard had the ball at the end of the alley.

"Dog doesn't fetch too good, huh, kid?" the workman asked, trying to joke. A lot of people tried to be friendly to disturbed persons. Reuben felt nothing but contempt. He ran on after Maynard.

But when he got to the end of the alley and took the ball back from Maynard, he noticed that the workmen were still watching him. Suspiciously, Reuben thought again. What are they suspicious of? And they had seemed to know the man Reuben was following.

It didn't matter. The man was nowhere to be seen on the busy street the alley opened into. Lost him, Reuben thought as he gave a biscuit to Maynard. "Not fast enough this time," Reuben said. Maynard ignored him and gobbled the biscuit. "You're not a dog," Reuben said. "You're a pig."

Maynard stopped eating and glared at him.

"Okay, sorry," Reuben said. "Geez, what a sensitive dog."

Maynard swallowed the last of the biscuit and trotted on down the street.

"What is this," Reuben said. "Trying to play hero and smell him out?" But Maynard went on until he had stopped in front of Auerbach's department store. "Okay, Ugluk, Dog of the North, let's go find somebody else."

But Maynard wouldn't budge. And then the man came out of the department store carrying a small sack. The chase was on again. Maynard strutted out ahead of Reuben. "Let's not have any of that I-told-you-so crap," Reuben said to Maynard. Maynard ignored him and went on strutting.

The man stopped one more time before they got to Liberty Park, and that was to buy a newspaper. When he got to the park he strolled to a bench under some trees where there were some guys throwing a frisbee, and a family having a picnic. He started reading the paper.

Reuben and Maynard watched for about five minutes. The man turned a page. "Whoopee," Reuben said. "What a winner. Let's go follow somebody else." But just then the man looked at his watch, folded the paper, and left. Reuben almost got up to follow him, but the grass was too comfortable and the guy was dull anyway. He watched the frisbee game.

Then he glanced at the bench. The man had left the sack he had bought at Auerbach's. What a dunce.

"Hey, Maynard," Reuben said softly, stroking the dog's neck. "We've been following a dunce. Left his bag on the bench."

And then a woman with a poodle walked over to the bench and sat down to rest.

The poodle was in heat. Maynard was feeling frisky. He got up and trotted over to the poodle. The poodle seemed to sneer at the shambling sheepdog. Maynard didn't mind. It didn't seem to occur to him that a fellow dog could be snobbish.

But snobbish the poodle was, and she began to bark, running behind the woman for safety. Cheerfully persistent, Maynard followed. The poodle tried to go farther, but the leash stopped her. Maynard kept coming. So the poodle lunged away, snapping the leash out of the woman's hand.

"Gertrude!" the woman shouted.

Gertrude took off at a brisk run. Maynard shuffled after her, gaining on her in his ramshackle way. The poodle dodged and headed back for the bench. Maynard turned faster than anyone would have thought he could, and began to head her off.

"Gertrude, come back here!" the woman yelled. "Whose dog is that? Leave Gertrude alone, you mangy mongrel!"

Reuben had been enjoying the show. But when the woman called his dog a mangy mongrel he got mad. "Who you calling mangy?" he called out.

"Is that your animal?" the woman asked.

"I feed him," Reuben said.

"Get him away from my dog!" the woman demanded.

Reuben called to Maynard.

"Hey, Maynard, get back here," he said. Maynard didn't even glance back. "Come on, Maynard. You'll probably get a disease anyway."

The woman gasped in anger. At that moment Maynard got tired of chasing—he wasn't used to having to ask twice—and came back. Gertrude, utterly exhausted, came back to the woman, who reached down and picked up the leash. "Gertrude, you poor thing," the woman crooned. "Was that big nasty dog making you fraidsy? Was he, sweety?"

"Oh, Maynard, you poor poopsy-woopsy," Reuben crooned in imitation. "Did that little warthog run away from you?" Maynard moved away in disgust, but Reuben got what he wanted: the woman had heard him.

"What do you mean, anyway," the woman snapped, "letting your dog run around in a public park without a leash? I should have you arrested."

Reubed pulled the purple card from his pocket. He loved to watch how people suddenly became kind and thoughtful.

The woman saw the card and suddenly became kind and thoughtful. "I'm so sorry," she said sweetly, though Reuben could tell it was a strain. "I hope my dog didn't disturb you," she said as she moved away. Was that sarcastic? Reuben wondered. She had more spunk than most. But she was still a zero.

"She's still a zero," Reuben said to Maynard. Then he remembered the Auerbach's package on the bench and went over to see what the man had bought.

But the package was gone. Reuben tried to remember if anyone had gone near the bench during the melee. No one. The woman must have lifted the package. Clever, Reuben thought. "Clever," he said to Maynard. "The lady's a thief."

But something didn't ring true in the whole situation. What had been in the bag? And when did the woman take it? And why, for that matter, had the man forgotten it? Why—

Coincidence.

His father was waiting for him when he got home.

"Reuben, my boy," said his father cheerfully. "Happy birthday, my lad. Good to see you."

"Hello, Father," Reuben said as he opened a can of dog food for Maynard.

"It's been a long time," his father said.

Reuben set the dog food down in a dish. Maynard slurped it up noisily. "Has it?" Reuben asked. "I've been busy."

"I've been busy," his father said. Then he realized that Reuben had just said that. "Oh, you just said that." Then his father laughed. "Mother sends her love."

"How nice," Reuben said.

"And I brought you a present," his father said. He had even wrapped it.

"Thank you," Reuben said.

"Take it," his father said, offering him the package.

Reuben took the package.

"Aren't you going to open it?" Reuben's father asked.

"Do you want me to?"

His father's patience snapped right then. It always snapped within the first five minutes.

"I don't care if you flush it down the toilet."

Reuben opened the package. It was a watch. Very expensive. The kind that told the time, the day, the weather, did math problems up to twelve digits, and played FM radio.

"Three hundred twenty-nine ninety-five plus tax," Reuben said. "Or did you get a discount?"

His father looked angry. "I got a discount, Reuben. I own the store."

"Ah," Reuben said, putting on the watch. "Did you know that two plus two is four?"

"Yes, I knew that."

"So did the watch. It's a clever watch. Thank you."

Then Reuben ran water into another dish and set it in front of Maynard. Maynard slopped into it, splashing all over the floor as he drank. Reuben's father sat down on the couch. "Nice place," he said.

"Yes," Reuben answered. "The government gives us new furniture every three years. It makes us disturbed persons feel—not so disturbed. Of course, some of them can't cope with new furniture, so they don't change it. And others—the furniture slashers —they get new furniture more often. But me, I'm a *regular* disturbed person, so I got my new furniture at the regular time."

"I'm glad they, uh, take care of you so well," said Reuben's father lamely.

"I'm sure you are. Eases the conscience, doesn't it?"

"Reuben, do you have to?"

"Does Mother miss me?" Reuben asked. "Or has she forgotten her little boy?"

"She hasn't forgotten."

"Why don't you tell her that my name is Reuben? It might remind her. I'm twelve, too, a big boy now, with bright eyes and tousled, sweet-looking blond hair. A lovely child, of whom she can be very proud."

Reuben's father had a sick look on his face. "Can't you lay off? For one day a year?"

"Daddy, this is the only day in the year I get to lay *on*."

"Well, I hope you've had a good time."

"It's been swell," Reuben answered.

Reuben's father paced angrily to the window and back again. "You aren't crazy," he finally said. "You aren't crazy, Mr. Boy Genius. You just think you're too good for the world. Come down off your IQ for a few minutes someday, Reuben. Maybe real human beings have something you don't have."

Reuben smiled at his father. "I love you, Daddy," he said.

He watched his father struggle, trying not to answer, knowing what would happen if he did. Finally habit won, and his father said, "I love you, too, Reuben."

Reuben began to laugh. He laughed and laughed, rolling on the couch, falling off and rolling on the floor. When he finally stopped laughing his father was gone, and Maynard was scratching his paws on the refrigerator door. Reuben lay on the floor looking at the ceiling for a while. Then he went to bed. For a few crazy moments he wanted to cry himself to sleep. But he hadn't shed a tear in years. Not about to start now.

He dreamed about his mother.

He woke up with Maynard licking his face.

He followed the short dumpy man every day that week, and all the next week, too. The man had a routine. Mondays at the park, where he always forgot a package from Auerbach's and the woman walking her dog happened to pick it up. Reuben never saw her take it, but it was always gone. Tuesdays to the airport, where he left a briefcase in a locker—Reuben followed on the overhead.

Wednesdays to the post office, where he took a letter from a post office box. The man opened the letter as he walked. Inside was another envelope, which he casually dropped by a mailbox. A few moments later another man came along, picked up the envelope, and walked away. Reuben followed this second man every time, and every time a block away from the mailbox the man opened the envelope, crumpled up the letter and threw it in a wastebasket without reading it, and saved the envelope. Strange, Reuben thought.

Thursdays the man was back in the park, only this time the woman came first and left an empty package of dog biscuits, which the man carried to the garbage and threw away. And Fridays the man went to a dirty movie and stayed there for three hours. So many people came and went that Reuben had no way of knowing if one of them was coming to meet the man.

And by the end of the two weeks, Reuben was more confused than ever. The short dumpy man was obviously a messenger. And obviously the messages he carried were secret. But who were the messages from? And who were they to?

Reuben imagined many things. Perhaps it was a gang of criminals passing the messages. But the short dumpy man didn't seem like a criminal. That meant nothing, of course, as Reuben well knew. But he still didn't think that that was the answer.

It might be government work. That fit much better, because the man's regular routine seemed like just the sort of stupid thing the government would have somebody do. But why would the government be hiding its actions like this? It seemed to Reuben that the government spent most of its time hiding things from the people, not from itself.

Which left the last guess, which Reuben thought was crazier than the others. The man must be a spy.

Of course, everyone knew who a spy would be spying for. There was only one enemy. The spaceships circling the world had been there all Reuben's life, a shadow hanging over the planet. All the enemy needed was an ally on the Earth and they would attack.

But who in the world would be friends with the enemy? What could anyone gain by being enslaved as the other planets had been enslaved?

It didn't matter who, Reuben decided. It was the only possible answer to the things he had seen.

The next Wednesday when he followed the man, Reuben waited for his chance. Obviously the bit with the letter was so that if someone found it, they would simply mail it without ever realizing that it was something important. So when the short dumpy man dropped the letter, Reuben ran in before the other man could get there. He picked up the letter, looked carefully at the envelope, and dropped it in the slot. As he turned and left, he saw the other man come over to find the letter, then move quickly away when he realized it was gone.

They won't suspect a thing, Reuben thought.

When he and Maynard got home that night, Reuben wrote down the address that had been on the envelope:

Bill
14 N 7 W
Enterprise, Utah 840033

Mr. Hyrum Wainscott
1408 S 2200 E
Salt Lake City, Utah 841236

And that was all. An address and a return address.

Reuben decided it was a code. He sat down and copied out the alphabet and tried to link up all the letters in ways that might make an intelligent pattern. He tried assigning number values to the letters, and letter values to the numbers. But no matter what he did, it made no sense. He fell asleep at the table.

When he woke up he looked at his work of the night before and decided it had all been stupid. The letter meant nothing. The man just had some weird habits. He dropped letters a lot. He always left Auerbach's sacks behind when he went to the park. He left briefcases in airport lockers just for fun. And he liked dirty movies. It meant nothing.

Then Reuben looked at the address again and realized how simple it really was. The address was real. It told where the real message was. The return address was just for show.

Reuben gathered up Maynard, who grumbled about leaving the house so early, and took the overhead to thirteenth south and twenty-first east. He walked from there to the corner of fourteenth and twenty-second.

There was no 1408.

Another theory down the drain. Discouraged, Reuben got back on the overhead and headed into town.

And just as he stepped off the overhead he realized what the address meant. He headed straight for the library and got the Forest Service map of Utah. He found Enterprise near the southwest corner of the state.

Fourteen miles north and seven miles west of the town of Enterprise, Utah, there was absolutely nothing but desert mountains. It was miles off the road, and there wasn't a town or even a settlement close enough to matter.

So if on the fourteenth day of the eighth month, which was in three days, at 2200 hours—ten p.m., just after dark—something were to happen fourteen miles north and seven miles west of Enterprise, Utah, not a soul would see it.

What would it be? A meeting? A parachute drop? An important message? It didn't matter. The short dumpy man had delivered the message, but it had not been received. Would the meeting or the message or the parachute drop take place anyway? They must have a backup system. It would undoubtedly happen right on schedule. And I have to do something about it, Reuben thought. It didn't occur to him that it was none of his business. He might feel contempt for everyone he knew, but the enemy was the enemy.

Reuben went straight to the doctor's office. It wasn't time for his appointment, but the doctor was willing to see him anyway. Reuben explained about everything he had done in the last few weeks, about the short dumpy man and the messages, and finally about the address and what he had finally realized that it meant.

The doctor leaned forward across the desk.

"I think this is a very important day," the doctor said.

"Of course it is," Reuben answered. "We've got to tell the authorities. You've got to, I mean, because they'd never believe me."

"And why do you think they'd never believe you, Reuben?" the doctor asked.

"Because I'm a disturbed person. They'd just send you a memo about what crazy thing I did this time."

"And why do you think they'd do that?" the doctor asked.

"Because," Reuben said, "this is just the sort of thing a paranoid schizophrenic would cook up. You know I'm not a paranoid schizophrenic. They don't."

The doctor looked very pleased with himself. "So you feel that you're helpless without relying on an outside authority figure, is that it?"

Reuben cocked his head and looked at the doctor. "Yeah, Doc," Reuben said. "That's it."

"You've had these feelings of personal helplessness for a long time, haven't you? Or have they just started?"

Reuben got up. "Come on, Maynard. The doctor's busy."

"Not at all," the doctor said, rising from his chair. "I have plenty of time to talk to you."

"I've got things to do," Reuben said. The doctor sighed. But this time Reuben felt no pleasure in it. He should have known that the doctor would only see this whole thing as another symptom.

So Reuben went to the only other person he could think of. His father's office was in the old Kennecott Copper Building, right at the dead center of downtown.

Reuben's hands were cold when he punched the buttons on the elevator. And when the elevator stopped abruptly on the sixteenth floor, Reuben's knees were shaky and he was breathing hard. He had only been to his father's office once before. And that was five years ago, before the—before. The secretary told him his father was not in.

"Don't give me that," Reuben said impatiently. "He's always in. Tell him his little boy is here to see him."

The secretary glared at him and left her desk, motioning to a security man standing nearby. The security man came and sat at the desk. The secretary came back in a few minutes and whispered in the security man's ear.

"All right, sonny," the security man said. "Come with me."

They went down a thickly carpeted hall with real wood walls and several doors. At the end of the hall they turned right and went down another corridor. At last they came to Reuben's father's office. The security man opened the door and let Reuben in.

"Hello, Reuben," his father said, looking at him strangely.

"Hello, Father," Reuben said, wondering why in the world he had come to this man for help.

"What can I do for you?" his father asked.

"I need your help," Reuben answered. Maynard scratched his paws on the front of Reuben's father's real wood desk. He reached down and picked Maynard up. "Sorry."

"That's all right," his father said. "Sit down and tell me."

So Reuben told him about the short dumpy man and the messages and the envelope and the desert northwest of Enterprise. And his father nodded all the way through.

"Have you told the police?" his father asked quizzically.

"No, Father. I'm a disturbed person, remember? I need you to tell them."

His father nodded, and Reuben felt relieved. Until his father said, "Do you have any other evidence?"

"Isn't that enough?" Reuben asked.

"Well, it seems a little farfetched. Why couldn't it just be a wrong address that somebody put on the envelope?"

"But it all fits," Reuben said, with a sinking feeling. "And what about the things this guy does?"

"Lots of people do lots of things," his father said. "Have you talked to the doctor about this?"

Reuben looked at his father and realized how carefully he was thinking of his words before he spoke and how he was playing nervously with his telephone receiver. And he knew that his father didn't believe him, that he was afraid of him, that he wanted the doctor to be there.

"The doctor?" Reuben asked. "Yes, Father. Go ahead and call him. I'm sure he'll make you feel better about your little boy. He'll call this a sign of incipient social interest, and tell you that you should be encouraged that my emotional dysfunction should now be bringing me to seek contact with my father and to try to win favor from society for my heroic but imagined deeds." Reuben got up and went to the door. "Come on, Maynard. Don't shed on the rug." Maynard followed him out the door.

Back on the street Reuben felt angry and bitter. Why had he bothered? They had never believed him, never seen things his way. They all tried to cope with him, as if he were an epidemic or a forest fire that they had to keep under control. Even his mother, back in the early years—in all his memories of her, Reuben could see her trying to talk to him, trying to answer his questions, but afraid, like his father, like his doctor, like the people on the street.

He pulled out his purple card and watched people move aside, opening a path for him through the crowd. The huge trees on Main Street even seemed to recoil.

Maynard stopped and went to the bathroom on one of the trees. "Not a bad idea," Reuben said. "Let 'em all drop dead. Let the enemy come down and take over everything. They deserve it."

It was when Reuben was eating a sandwich at the restaurant in the overhead station that he thought of what an enemy invasion would mean. It was all right to think of huge blond men with white eyes dragging his father off in chains. But when he thought of them coming to his mother, he set down his sandwich, got off his chair, and left, flashing his purple card at the checkout lady, who smiled at him with fear in her eyes.

He took the overhead to Murray, where he transferred to the overhead up Cotton-wood Canyon. It was full of sightseers and retired people heading up to their cabins.

He got off at the seventh stop and walked up a winding asphalt path to a large house nestled among huge pines on the north slope of the canyon. The house was all wood —it could only belong to a millionaire many times over. Reuben chuckled to think of his father's wealth.

He went to the door but did not touch the knob. Instead he stood and thought for a moment. They must have expected him to come here sometime. The doorknob would be keyed so that his palm or fingers would trigger an alarm. He remembered the household routine.

He knelt on the welcome mat close to the door, where the camera would not catch his face—only the top of his head, which would make him look like a little boy. He pushed the doorbell strip with his elbow.

A woman's voice spoke. "Who is it?"

"Groceries," Reuben answered.

"Today?" The woman paused. "This is Thursday. There aren't supposed to be deliveries on Thursday."

"They send me, I come," Reuben answered.

"All right," the woman sighed. The door slip open. Reuben came in on his knees. Once past the door he stood up. He could hear the kitchen intercom saying, "Just leave them on the table, please." But he did not go into the kitchen. Instead he climbed the stairs in the living room and went down a short hall to the door that stood ajar. Inside the room someone was typing. Reuben went to the door and pushed it farther open. Well, there—

His mother sat at the typewriter, her long dark hair falling on the keys as she leaned over her work. He had often seen her like that, years ago when he had lived at home.

Then she felt his presence in the door and looked up. She was beautiful, with soft features and large eyes and a white scar down her left cheek.

She looked at him for a moment, and then fear and recognition entered her eyes at the same time.

"Reuben," she whispered.

"Mother," he said, stepping into the room.

She got up and moved back toward the window.

"Wait," he said.

"Stay there," she said.

"Mother, listen to me."

"You aren't supposed to be here," she said, her voice husky with fear. "They'll take away your card. They'll put you in a —place."

"Not if you listen to me. Not if you help me."

She shook her head, her face white. She touched the scar on her cheek.

"Mother, I'm sorry," Reuben said. "Please believe me. Please trust me."

"Go away," she said. A tear ran down her cheek.

"Mother, I love you," Reuben said, reaching out his hand. "See? My hands are empty. I won't hurt you, I promise."

"No."

"Mother, you've got to listen to me!"

She closed her eyes. "I'm listening," she whispered desperately.

And for the third time that day Reuben told the story of the short dumpy man and the message on the envelope. He told her about the doctor and about his father.

"Do you believe me?" Reuben asked.

She opened her eyes and looked at him. "Is it true?" she asked softly.

"Every word," Reuben said, wanting to shout, but keeping his voice to a whisper. "I didn't make any of it up."

"I don't know," she said. "I don't know if I believe you."

Reuben's heart sank again, only this time the pain and tightness in his chest and throat were more than he could bear. Tears came to his eyes.

"Well you've just got to," he said. No sound came, but his mother saw his lips move. She took a step toward him and then stopped, seeing what no one had seen for five years. Tears on Reuben's cheeks.

"Show me," she said. "I'll go with you and you show me."

Reuben nodded, and then he fell to his knees and began to cry, saying, "You've got to believe me," over and over again. When he stopped crying, his head dizzy and his throat thick, he realized that his mother's arms were around him. Suddenly ashamed, he stood up and stepped away. He looked in her eyes and saw that even though she was looking lovingly at him, his sudden movement had made her afraid again. "What time is it?" he asked.

"Two-fifteen," she said.

"There's time. Come with me and I'll show you." They walked down the hill together to the overhead.

They got to the park a half hour later. He led her to a waiting place he had used before. "We'll toss sticks for Maynard. It'll look natural. Just pretend you're my—"

She nodded. "All right," she said.

In ten minutes the woman with the poodle came. Maynard looked over wistfully, but kept playing with the sticks. Reuben told his mother not to watch the woman. Out of the corner of his eye he saw her give a dog biscuit to Gertrude, then shake the box and toss it to the ground by the bench. Just like the last two weeks.

Then the woman got up and moved away. Reuben knelt by Maynard. "All right, Maynard," he said. "Earn your biscuits. Get the box."

Then Reuben stood and threw a stick toward the bench. Maynard took off after the stick, but when he got near the box he stopped and sniffed around, went to the bathroom on the bench, then picked up the box and ran back to Reuben.

"Bad dog," Reuben said loudly, but Maynard understood, waiting patiently for the biscuit that Reuben surreptitiously dropped. Then Maynard set down the box and picked up the biscuit. Reuben grabbed the box and said to his mother, "All right. Let's go. Slowly and naturally, in case they're watching."

They walked away from the park without looking back, and caught the overhead for Magna. On the first stop Reuben told her to get out, and he followed her to the overhead to Kearns. They hopped a few more overheads, then got on one heading back downtown. Only then did Reuben look at the box.

"What does the box mean?" asked his mother.

Reuben shrugged. "I don't know," he said. "I've never picked up one of these before. I just know that she leaves this, and the guy picks it up and throws it away."

And then he felt a terrible fear that the box would be meaningless and that his mother would think he had made it up, that he was really crazy. And she would tell the doctor, and the doctor would know that he had broken the rules and gone to see her, and he would lose his pass and go to the hospital, and he would rather die.

He reached into the box and found something taped to the inside. He peeled off the tape and pulled out three microfiches. It was too small to read, of course, but his mother looked at them and her face went white.

"There's really something there," she said.

She hadn't believed him.

She turned to him and smiled. "Reuben, Reuben, I hoped so hard that it would be there."

He felt strange. Her smile was so warm that he felt his face flush with heat that pulsed rapidly. She had hoped that they would find something.

"Here," he said. "Put them in your purse. We'll go to the federal building. There's an FBI office there."

"All right," she said, putting the film in her purse.

"You saw," he said. "You saw the woman leave the box. You saw how it happened."

"Of course," she said. "I saw it all. And with this, whatever it is, I'm sure there'll be somebody down in Enterprise on the fourteenth."

"There better be," Reuben said. "This is a serious business."

They rode the rest of the way in silence. But when Reuben got of the overhead to walk to the federal building, it seemed perfectly natural to be holding his mother's hand.

The FBI believed Reuben and his mother. Or rather, they believed the microfilm. Reuben and his mother were in the federal building for several hours, explaining how and when and what and where, and the FBI agent listened respectfully to Reuben's reasoning about the envelope.

"Thanks, kid," the man said when it was over. "We'll handle it from here."

So Reuben and his mother left. Reuben went to the door of the house in the canyon with her, and she asked him to come in.

"I would only leave again," Reuben said.

He turned to go, but then, as an afterthought, he said, "Mother."

"Yes," she said.

"Uh, Father shouldn't . . ."

"I won't tell him." She closed the door.

Reuben and Maynard went back to the apartment. Reuben slept badly that night. He kept dreaming of his father hitting his mother, though he had never seen him do such a thing. And then he dreamed of the lady in the park with the dog named Gertrude. He watched her and watched her in his dream, but he could never see her pick up the package from Auerbach's. It always just disappeared during the first split second he glanced away.

He woke up feeling foul. Even brushing his teeth didn't take the taste out of his mouth. He went to where he usually found the short dumpy man and waited. Now that the FBI was taking care of things, there was no real point in following him. Except that there was nothing else to do.

But the man did not come. Reuben waited all day. Finally he went to the theater at the time the man usually came out. The dirty movie ended, but the short dumpy man was not among the crowd that came out.

Why did the routine change today?

But it was the weekend, and Reuben followed someone else on Saturday and Sunday.

On Saturday he followed a prostitute to the Nevada border. He didn't have a passport, so he took the overhead back to Salt Lake.

On Sunday he followed a wino along Second South and finally used his purple card to buy a bottle of something. The wino said thank you and offered to share. Reuben said no but Maynard drank a little.

Reuben and Maynard went home and watched murders and happy families on television.

Sunday was October 22nd, and as he went to bed Reuben realized that northwest of Enterprise whatever the enemy was doing was being stopped tonight.

The next day the short dumpy man was right on schedule: the package from Auerbach's, the bench in the park, and the lady with the dog. Since it was all over by now Reuben let Maynard chase Gertrude again.

The lady was more irritated than ever, and Reuben laughed. The two dogs raced barking along by the pond, and the geese swam away in a hurry.

"Stop your dog," the lady said. "Please. Gertrude gets an upset stomach." She spoke carefully, remembering Reuben's purple card.

Reuben looked at the bench, ignoring her. Once again the Auerbach's package had disappeared. But he was sure the woman hadn't gone anywhere near it.

Gertrude ran back to the woman, who was trying to control her fury. She scooped up the female dog. Maynard bounded up and tried to jump on Gertrude. He missed, leaving muddy pawprints all over the lady's skirt. Reuben laughed.

The lady kicked Maynard. Reuben stopped laughing. That was dangerous—Maynard had a mean streak a mile wide, and he always bit the legs that kicked him.

Maynard snapped at the lady. She kicked again, and this time Maynard bit, sinking his teeth into the loose flesh of her calf.

But the woman didn't shriek as Reuben had expected. She just shook her leg, and Maynard loosed his grip and dropped away. She glared at Reuben and walked off, carrying Gertrude. She didn't limp.

Maynard lay on the ground, not moving. Reuben walked up to him. "Hey, Maynard, getting weak in your old age?"

But Maynard didn't even resent the gibe. He was dead.

When Reuben was sure of it, he picked up his dog's corpse and walked home. He laid Maynard's body on the carpet. There was no blood. There was no sign of any damage. There was no sign there was any disease. Maynard had bit the lady and died.

Reuben called the FBI. The man told him to come down and bring the dog. He sounded worried, Reuben decided.

"What happened?" Reuben said to the FBI man as soon as he arrived. At the same moment the FBI man looked at Maynard's corpse and said, "What happened?"

Reuben answered, "The lady in the park. He bit her."

"And?"

"And nothing. And he died."

"What did she do?"

"She got bit," Reuben said, a little angrily, though he knew it would be dangerous to let any emotion happen right now.

"And the dog died."

"The man in the pinstripe suit wins the prize," Reuben said, absentmindedly stroking the dog's fur.

"Look, kid, I know you've told us straight so far, but you're a DP, right? Do you hallucinate?"

Reuben glared at him. "Never."

"Hey, okay," the man said, "I just had to ask."

"What happened? Down in the south?" Reuben asked.

"Well," the FBI man said, "I don't know if I can tell you, and unless the boss says I can tell you and signs it in triplicate in his own blood, I'm sure as hell not going to breathe a word."

"They weren't there, were they," Reuben said.

The FBI man looked at him. "What makes you think they weren't?"

"Because," Reuben said, "the day after I told you they broke their routine, and the lady in the park knew enough to kill Maynard."

"Who the hell is Maynard?" the FBI man asked.

"My dog," said Reuben.

"Oh, he's got a name," the FBI man commented. "Hey, look, can I do an autopsy? Cause of death?"

"You?" Reuben asked.

"I mean one of our staff."

"Sure," Reuben said. "Maynard won't give a damn."

The FBI man laughed. "Right," he said, and then stopped laughing when he saw the expression on Reuben's face. "Hey, kid, I'll have the dog right back, okay?"

Reuben nodded and sat down to wait. While he waited he wondered what they'd say if he told them about the way the lady in the park always snatched the packages when nobody could see, and how she never even seemed to get close to the bench. They'd be sure to think he was hallucinating after all.

It was a circle. No way out. He looked at the drab walls and his mind wandered.

What did the enemy look like, anyway? Nobody could say. On the few planets they had come to and had not yet conquered no one had ever seen them. On the planets they *had* conquered, no one would say. All that anyone knew—or at least all the government would let on—was that without active help from the people on the planet they were attacking, the enemy couldn't do a thing. But *with* such help, they were irresistible.

What if they were already on the Earth? Reuben looked at his hands, how the fingers were all the same and yet different. What if they could look just like us, and they were already going to the store, and holding down influential jobs, and—why not?—walking dogs in the park and picking up Auerbach's packages without going near them? Possible, Reuben thought.

Maybe I do hallucinate, he thought. The idea frightened him.

The FBI man came back after about an hour.

"What did Maynard die of?" Reuben asked, jumping to his feet.

"Nothing," said the man. "He's not dead. I mean, he is, of course," he caught himself, seeing the look of hope that Reuben couldn't hide. "But there's no reason in the world that the dog should be dead. Perfect shape. Good for years. Not an injury."

"But dead anyway," said another man who came through the door. Reuben hadn't met him before.

"He's The Boss," the FBI man said, "and he wants to have a talk." The Boss smiled. Reuben did not smile. The FBI man left the room.

Reuben and The Boss had a talk. During the talk Reuben figured out that nothing had happened down in southern Utah, that the whole thing was either called off or was so subtle that nobody saw it. The FBI was hunting for straws, because they *did* have the microfilm, and it had to mean something.

"Ideas?" The Boss asked.

"You're asking me for ideas?" Reuben asked.

"Is there anyone else in the room?" The Boss asked.

"What kind of great ideas do you think I can give you when you've been trying so hard not to tell me that nothing happened down in Enterprise and that you don't know what's going on?" Reuben said with a look that made The Boss feel a little weak.

"So you can read between the lines," The Boss whispered.

"Why are you whispering?" Reuben asked.

"Get off my back for a minute," The Boss said. "In my line of work we meet guys with brains about once every twenty years. Everybody else is a cop, a crook, or a congressman."

"So let's trade some secrets," Reuben said, feeling, for some reason, a little less contempt for The Boss than he felt toward everyone else.

"All right," The Boss agreed.

"You first," Reuben said.

"Okay," The Boss said, sighing. "So much for Top Secret. Right, nothing happened in Enterprise, even though everything pointed to it, and so we figure that either they were on to you, in which case why the hell did they have another rendezvous in the park today, or else the whole thing was a sham and they wanted someone to find out about Enterprise so we'd all go there while the real thing happened someplace else. In which case we're looking for a needle in a haystack."

"And you want ideas," Reuben said.

"You said we'd trade secrets," The Boss said,

"All right," Reuben said. "How's this? Maybe it was a sham, like you said, only not to keep you from noticing something happening at the same time someplace else, but to keep you from noticing that it already happened awhile ago."

The Boss looked at him. "Like?"

"Like you're running around this time and maybe next time and maybe the time after, trying to find where the enemy is going to land—all the time not noticing that they're already here and working right where you won't notice them—under your noses."

The Boss looked interested. "So if they can do that, what've they been waiting for?"

"I don't know," Reuben said, "unless maybe there aren't very many of them, and they need to get up an organization, or else maybe they're weak, and they have to divide us in order to take over. I don't know. But I think they're here."

And then Reuben told The Boss about the way the woman in the park never seemed to touch the Auerbach's package. "And the way Maynard died. My dog. Just bit her and then dropped dead."

"Interesting theory," The Boss said. "In fact it holds up pretty well, just the sort of devious thing we might expect. Except for one thing."

"Yeah?" asked Reuben.

"We know who the lady is. Birth certificate, lots of relatives, no way she could be a plant, already thirty years old when the enemy ships came. Sorry. Just an ordinary Earth-type traitor."

"Was she ever bit by a dog before?" Reuben asked.

"What does that have to do with anything?" The Boss asked.

"Because unless it's ordinary for certain people to cause dogs to drop dead without an injury, then she isn't ordinary. She's changed, right?"

The Boss smiled. "Very good, Reuben," he said. "We'll check it out."

Reuben shook his head. "Promise me something."

The Boss said, "What in particular? Some promises I can't make."

"Promise me you'll tell me what happens."

On the way out Reuben stopped by Maynard's corpse in the autopsy rooms. The body was kind of a mess, and Reuben did not touch Maynard's fur.

"Want us to take care of this for you?" The Boss asked.

"Yeah," Reuben said.

Three months later they told him what happened, and as Reuben had announced on his birthday, it was his lucky year. He got to meet the president of the United States and shake his hand and wear a medal, none of which impressed him much. He got to have his picture in every newspaper in the country, along with pictures of the people he had followed who turned out to be the enemy, which didn't thrill him either.

However, he also got to go home.

His father wasn't happy about it and Reuben noticed that there were new locks on all the bedroom doors, but Reuben just thought *Suck Rocks* and talked to his mother for an hour or two alone just to bug his father. They quarreled a lot, Reuben and his father. And his mother really didn't understand him any better than she ever had. But all in all it beat hell out of the government-owned apartment and there were other compensations.

It turned out that the enemy was a very intelligent but not-too-tough marsh gas sort of thing, only about six of them, and they had to take over human bodies—curious people, who came too close—in order to do anything at all. And once they were in a human body, when the body died so did they. So—firing squads (Utah law) and the problem was over. The ships continued to circle around the Earth, but after a few months some air force shuttleships with heavy rockets shot them down. All the ships' defenses, impregnable a few months before, were gone, and the ships fell into the Sargasso Sea.

It was on Reuben's thirteenth birthday that he realized his lucky year was over. That was the day they took away his purple card and he had to start carrying money and asking permission. But he didn't mind all that much. It was kind of fun.

The day after his thirteenth birthday his mother and father took him to the park. Out at the car, Reuben's father remembered the camera.

"It's upstairs in my closet," his father said, and Reuben ran back up the asphalt path. He stopped just inside the front door. He bowed his head a moment, reached out his hand, and waited.

The camera materialized in his palm.

He opened his eyes, looked at the camera, smiled, and ran back outside, being careful to lock the door behind him as his father always asked. Then he skipped down the sidewalk, conversing with the stranger in his mind, who followed him far more closely than he would have thought possible back in the old days when he was a child, and still human.

HITCHING

Mort, he says to me, "Runt, you wanna bicycle, you gotta figure out how to get the money."

"Thanks," I says. "Hey, Mort, you're a real pal, I knew that already."

"Oh, yeah," says Mort, "I forgot, you got all the brains in the family."

We always talk like that. I'd kill anybody else called me Runt, and he'd kill anybody else called him Mort, but we can't kill each other, we're brothers. Oh, every now and then he pounds the crap out of me, but these days he bleeds pretty bad before I call uncle and so he don't fight me too much. Everybody else calls him Butch and me Ernie.

But it turned out it was Mort after all who thought up how I'd get the money for the bike I wanted so I could have a paper route so I could make some money. I asked the Olds for a bike, but the old man said no, I should earn the money myself, and I said how the hell can I do that with no bike for a route, and the old lady said you're thirteen years old and you shouldn't talk like that and I said something else and the old man strapped me. He thinks it still hurts. But after that I knew they'd rather die than get me the bike.

Mort saw as how I wasn't feeling too good right then and like Mort always does he tried to joke about it and then he started smart-mouthing about how *he*'d never stand for it and how if I didn't have him to look out for me I'd have let everybody walk all over me all my life.

He thinks he's a real bigshot because he beat up Rodney Lawrence who nobody ever beat up before and because he and Darcia Kleinsmidt go up into her dad's loft every Sunday and make out. He says he's seen her without any clothes on but I think that's a bunch of crap for the reason I will tell you when I get to that place in my story. He brags about a lot of things that I don't think he ever did.

Anyway Mort comes to me on Tuesday after milking, it's still early in the morning but it's summer and so there isn't any school and he says, "Hey, Runt, you still want a bike?"

"Hey shutup," I said, thinking he's making fun of me again.

He says, "OK, Runt, if that's the way you want it. Only I know how you can get the money."

Well, I thought that sounded pretty good, so I says to him, "Hey, Mort, what is it, Darcia paying you a dollar a smooch?"

"I'd be a millionaire then," he says, and I think yeah, sure.

But I followed him around behind the barn and he tells me his plan. "See, we just hitch a ride with somebody over on I-15."

"Somebody's gonna pay us to hitchhike?" I says, real snotty, because if I get snotty he tells me faster.

"Don't get snotty with me, Runt," he says, and then like I figured he told me. "They're gonna pay us to get out. I read about it in the newspaper." That means that somebody who reads the newspaper told him. "You get a ride with somebody, and then you pull a gun or a knife and make them pull off onto some lonely place or a rest stop or somewhere there isn't a lot of cars, and then you take their money and their car and leave 'em there. Or else you leave 'em their car and hitch a ride back with somebody else."

I thought for a minute and I says, "I bet that's stealing."

"Ooooooh," he says, making faces like an old lady who just heard a bad word. "Ooooooh, I forgot, you always go to Sunday School."

Which is true. I have to keep going till I'm fourteen. The old man says that till you're fourteen you can't decide for yourself. But I always stick gum under the folding chairs.

"Look, Mort," I says, "all I care about is that if we get caught they'll stick us in jail."

"They can't," says Mort, "because we're both minors."

"I am not," I says, wondering what the hell being a miner has to do with going to jail.

"You are too and so am I. It means being under eighteen years old. That's why we can't buy beer or cigarettes. But it also means they can't put is in jail."

"Yeah, but we'd go to the JD place in Fillmore."

"Jeez," says Mort, "what a runt, Runt. This'd be the first thing we ever did wrong, they don't send you to Fillmore till you done a lot of stuff."

"What about painting Elton Barney's cow green?"

He just rolled his eyes in his head. "You remember what Sheriff Burton said?" Mort asked me, like I was real dumb. "He said, 'Boys will be boys.' "

He said that, but I still didn't know about pulling a knife on somebody.

"Besides," says Mort, "the guy we hit isn't gonna know who we are or where we come from."

"I don't think I want a bike that bad," I says, thinking how I really don't want a paper route if I gotta go to the JD place for it.

"Man, what a knockout," says Mort. "I find out that my brother's a chicken, besides being a runt."

Nobody calls me a chicken.

So there we were out on I-15 thumbing for a ride. Not too many people want to pick up farmers with manure on their boots, so we put on our Sunday clothes and snuck out of the house so the Olds wouldn't ask us where we was going.

But the cars still wasn't piling up in line to pick us up. Of course, on a lot of them Mort says, "Not this one." And then I asked him why, and he says, "Car's too old, this guy doesn't have any dough," and then one time he says, "This guy's really rich, all he's gonna have is checks and credit cards." Credit cards in your pocket isn't much good on the farm, and anyway nobody'd be fooled, they know me and Mort and they know we never could get a credit card.

So we waited for about two hours getting hotter and sweatier and I was thinking what the hell kind of dumb thing am I doing out here? But then we see this shiny new yellow car coming along and there's just one person in it, either a girl with short hair or a guy with long hair, and old Mort jumps out in the freeway sticking his thumb out and the car slows down and the girl (this close we could tell she was a girl) flips open the back door. Me, I got in back, but old Mort, he reached through, unlocked the front, and sat down next to her.

Audi, bucket seats, thing looked like it cost a million bucks and when she started off it felt like we wasn't even moving except the telephone poles flipped by like beanpoles when you're running.

She was pretty but old, probably twenty or thirty, and if she wasn't sitting right there I know old Mort would've leaned back and said, "Stacked, man, stacked." Instead he just kept playing with his pocket where he had a knife.

"Where you going?" she asked us, and since we wasn't going anyplace I didn't know what to say, but Mort says, "Noplace you're going, but maybe you'll come close. Where you headed?" he asks her.

"Las Vegas," she says, and I wonder if she's one of them topless dancers.

"You one of them topless dancers?" Mort asks her.

"No," she says, laughing. Jeez, Mort can be dumb sometimes.

"How old are you?" she asks us.

"I'm fourteen," I lied. Mort said, "I'm seventeen," which makes him a bigger liar than me, since I was only one year off, but Mort's big and hairy and so everybody figures he's older than he is.

Well, it was still hot but there was clouds coming in from the south and it looked like a dust storm was coming up and then rain, and so I figured we oughta get it over with so we could get back home before we got our Sunday clothes all wet and the old lady chewed us hollow. So I says, "Hey, Mort, what're you waiting for?"

"What do you mean?" asks the girl.

"Oh, nothing," says Mort, shooting me a glare like I should drop dead.

"Well?" says I, since I don't like him glaring at me that way.

So he reached down into his pocket and pulled out his hunting knife and took it out of the sheath and reached over and stuck it right next to her ribs and he gets this mean look on his face and says, "Pull over."

I gotta say that girl looked surprised and scared, but she didn't go crazy or anything. She just had kind of a shaky voice when she said, "Right here?"

Mort thought a second and said, "No about a mile up ahead there's a dirt road off to the right."

And then her face turned all white and I felt real bad about what we was doing, because I wanted a ten-speed all right, but I didn't like the way she looked.

She sped up to about seventy-five.

"There's the road, right there, after that rock," says Mort.

She sped up to eighty-five.

"What the hell're you doing?" Mort says. "I said to pull over." And his face got real mean looking, like it does when he's trying to scare some sucker into backing down without a fight.

"I know your kind," she says, her voice all shaky. "You'll get me off there and take my money and my car and you'll rape me and kill me."

"No we won't," I says.

"I'll kill you right here," says Mort, really getting upset, I could tell because his ears was getting red.

"Go ahead," she says. "At the speed I'm going if you kill me we'd smash up before you had a chance to get the car under control. Besides, I don't think you know how to drive."

Course we both did, we'd been driving a tractor since we was eight. But I sure didn't want to crash at ninety miles an hour, and tell you the truth, I didn't like it how her hands was shaking taking those turns.

"You'll run out of gas pretty soon," says Mort.

"I get fifty miles to the gallon," she says, and her gas gauge was up above half. "I'll get to Las Vegas first."

"Slow down," I says, because she wasn't keeping in the lanes too good.

She sped up to a hundred and I needed to go to the bathroom.

"Please," I says, "this isn't safe."

"It doesn't matter," she says. "At this speed we're bound to pass a highway patrolman and he'll pull us over and I'll tell him what you were trying to do."

She was right. We was over a barrel, like they say, and Mort knew it too.

"Jeez," he says, "I could cut you up into little pieces."

He always says that when he's mad but doesn't want to fight.

She just shook harder and took a turn a little sharper and the car screeched a lot going around the turn. The wind had come up now cause we was driving into the storm, and I thought we'd get blown off the road in a minute.

"Hey, please Mort, let's quit, OK?" I says.

Mort clicked his tongue and then he says, "Man, you got a chicken for a brother nothing goes right." Then he put the knife back into the sheath. I didn't even mind him calling me a chicken, just so the car slowed down.

But she didn't slow down and the car was up around 105, probably as fast as it could go with a headwind.

"Hey, I put the knife away, slow down," says Mort, and suddenly I figured out he was as scared as I was. In the old man's Plymouth you never got much above 65, and we always went 55 if the old lady was in the car.

"If I slow down you'll just pull the knife out and kill me," she says.

"Mort'll throw it out the window," I says. "That way he can't pull it out again. And then you can just let us out anywhere along here, we'll walk."

Mort glares at me again, but then we took another turn that slammed us over against the doors and Mort rolled down his window and threw out his knife. That knife cost him, too, and I knew he felt bad throwing it like that, even though I knew we'd hunt for it for a month before he'd ever give up finding it.

"OK, the knife's gone, now pull over and let us out," Mort says, and now *his* voice is shaky.

"Uh-uh," says the girl, and then she says, "How do I know you don't have something else hidden in your clothes."

"Cause I said so," says Mort.

"I'm supposed to believe you?" says the girl.

"I never told a lie in my life," says Mort, though I figure that was about his ten millionth lie this year.

"You just go around pulling knives on people."

"Hey, look," says Mort, "we're sorry."

"Yeah, we're sorry," I says.

"Shutup, Runt," he says.

"I'll just wait until the highway patrol stops us," she says.

And I noticed that her voice wasn't shaky anymore.

"Please," I says. "We'll never do it again. We just wanted the money so I could get a ten-speed bike. We wasn't gonna kill anybody."

"Sure," she says, and a gust of wind tossed us from the lefthand lane into the righthand lane, and I sure was glad we wasn't driving in the righthand lane in the first place. "You've got a knife hidden somewhere else."

"Honest, I don't," he says.

"Prove it," she says.

"How?" he says.

"Take off your clothes and throw them out the window," she says.

"The hell I will," says Mort.

"That's the only way I'll know I'm safe," she says. "But I'd rather wait till we pass a highway patrolman anyway."

"We'll be dead before that," I says, because right then the dust storm hit, and you couldn't see thirty feet ahead. And this was the windingest part of I-15.

"Take off your clothes and throw them out the window," she says, and believe me, I just whipped off my shirt and my pants and my shoes and my socks and tossed them right out, even though when I opened the window the car filled up with dust. And after a minute Mort gritted his teeth and did the same. And there we sat in our jockey shorts, 5 for three dollars through the catalog.

"OK," Mort says, "now let us out."

"I said take off all your clothes," she says, and I looked at her and figured out she wasn't scared any more at all, she was just getting even for how we got her scared before. But it didn't make no difference nohow, like the old man says, cause I'd have drunk straight 10/40 motor oil just to get out of that car in that dust storm. So I took off my shorts and tossed 'em out the window and then I leaned forward and kind of covered myself with my arms, which I folded in my lap like a little kid in Sunday School.

But Mort didn't make a move to take off his shorts, and by then I was so scared I started yelling at him to take off his damn shorts and then I started to cry and so he did it and threw them out the window. But he leaned forward just like I did, and covered himself, and he turned red, and just looked at the floor, and I sure as hell knew right then that he hadn't ever seen Darcia Kleinsmidt with all her clothes off or he wouldn't be blushing like a bad sunburn right now.

And I stopped crying right then and for the first time in my life I felt sorry for old Mort and felt like I oughta help him. So I says, "OK, lady, you had your joke, now stop this car and let us get the hell out and get our clothes and go home." I was madder'n hell and I glared her down as mean as I ever did the old lady when she made me help with the dishes, and she kind of looked sick and slowed down the car and stopped. It felt so good not to be going a hundred miles an hour that we just sat there for a second before she said, "Get the hell out of my car!" and then Mort and I opened the doors, even if it meant using one of our hands that was covering ourself, and we got out into the dust storm and she took off fast and there we were, stark naked on the freeway in a dust storm about fifteen miles from home and a mile from the nearest clothes.

And then, of course, the dust storm stopped and it started to rain like crazy and Mort says, "Damn damn damn damn damn," and I says, "I wanta find my clothes."

So we walked along the freeway until we saw a car coming and then we dove down off into the dirt and brush beside the road so they wouldn't see us without any clothes on, only the dirt was mud from the rain and we was covered with it. "Damn damn damn," says Mort, and I says, "Come on, Mort," and he says, "You and your damn ten-speed bike." We walked on to where we threw our underwear out the window only the wind had blown it away and we couldn't see it anywheres and we was soaking wet.

But we figured as how our shoes and pants wouldn't blow as far as our shorts, so we went on, dodging down into the mud whenever a car came, which wasn't all that often around here. When we got out of the mud then the rain would wash it off until the next time.

Finally I found both my socks hung up on the bobwire fence along the edge of the freeway only thirty feet back and my shoes was right nearby, and Mort found one of his socks and both his shoes and finally I found my shirt hung up on the bobwire, too. I put it on, even though it was cold and wet, and I didn't feel so naked cause it was my Sunday shirt with the long tails, but poor Mort was still stark naked with mud on his feet, carrying two shoes and one sock, and when he saw me standing there in my shirt he started yelling about how I'd screwed up the whole thing and if it hadn't been for me and my ten-speed he'd be up in the barn with Darcia Kleinsmidt right now and what the hell did he have to have such a dumb little brother for and he wished he was an only child and it was all my fault and after this went on for a while I started to cry, because I felt like it was all true and I felt bad and anyway, I'd had a bad scare, I don't want you to think I cry alot but I think that was about the worst time in my whole life, but after a while Mort's calling me dumb made me mad and I took off running.

It was then that I saw both our pants out in the median strip hung up on some big sagebrush and I cut across the freeway without looking and so did Mort and just as we reached our pants we heard a car squeal to a stop and there was Sheriff Burton looking like he seen a ghost.

We just kind of stood there holding our pants while he crossed the road.

"Well, if it ain't Morton and Ernest Olson," he says, when he got over to us. "What the hell're you doin' stark naked in the middle of the freeway?"

We didn't know exactly how to explain. But I was still mad at Mort and so I played dumb, seeing as how he always said I was. "Gee, Mr. Burton," I says in my Sunday School voice, "I don't know. Mort here is always telling me how I'm dumb, but he told me it'd be real fun to play around like this in the freeway."

You shoulda seen the look on Mort's face. But you really shoulda seen the look on Sheriff Burton's face! He just grabbed Mort by the hair and said, "You better put those pants on fast and get in my car, boy."

Mort started to tell him something but the sheriff just looked at him real mad and said, "I don't wanna hear one word, boy. Your pa's gonna have plenty to say to you when I tell him how you been playing with your little brother."

So we put on our pants and carried our shoes and socks and got into Sheriff Burton's car. The sheriff made me sit in front and he shoved Mort into the backseat and when he did I heard the sheriff say, "Fairy," like the word was sour milk.

Well, when we got home the old man went off to talk with the sheriff while the old lady yelled bloody murder and made us take off our clothes and have a bath, saying all the time how much clothes cost and if us kids ever had to pay for our own clothes we wouldn't go off playing in the rain in our Sunday best.

Then while I was in the tub with the old lady washing me like she hasn't done in years since I was a kid, the old man came in with a real bad look on his face and said, "What happened," and I thought of lying and then I figured that there wasn't no way to explain how we got where we was except the truth, so I told him the whole thing, about the ten-speed and the girl in the Audi.

When I was done, the old man said, "That true?" and I said, "Swear to God," and the old lady said, "Don't take the name of the Lord," and the old man said, "Thank God, Sheriff Burton said my boy Morton was a fairy," and the old lady said, "Now, Bill, how can I teach these boys proper with you taking the Lord's name and saying fairy in front of them?" but the old man was out of the bathroom and off to talk to the sheriff.

What all happened was that nothing happened except the Olds made us work all summer for nothing just to buy new Sunday clothes, which I didn't think was fair cause we were growing out of 'em anyway and they would've had to buy us new ones before Christmas. Mort didn't talk to me much for a long time, I thought he was mad but maybe he was just feeling bad about the whole thing, but anyway he's never called me dumb since then.

Oh, the sheriff thought the whole thing was funny as hell and inside three days the whole county knew about it and Mort and I had to lick everybody all over again and some of 'em twice before they'd shutup about it. And the Olds never let us go down by the freeway for love or money, so Mort's knife was gone for good, and I knew he felt real bad.

So that fall I got a job at Fernwood's market sweeping and bagging and saved up my money so that at Christmastime I had a brand new knife for old Mort under the tree to make up for the old one, and the one I gave him was even better. But what was best of all was that the Olds gave both me and Mort ten-speed bikes that Christmas, even though it was a medium harvest, which meant that everything was OK again.

Mort and I spent a week falling down on the road a lot learning to ride, but by the time we went back to school after New Year's we didn't take the bus anymore because it was a lot more fun to ride the bikes except when it snowed. And Mort stopped calling me Runt. It was Speed and Ernie from then on, mostly cause even though I was fast, Mort was faster.

Damn Fine Novel

*I*magine, if you will, that you are now reading the story of a young writer, myself, who decides to write a first person story about a young writer, Abe Snow, who, after years of writer's block, realizes one day that he must write a contemporary novel, the other periods already having provided exactly enough lecture notes to fill all the class periods in a one-semester university literature course. Furthermore, as he contemplates writing it he realizes that his novel will be the perfect novel, the one embodying novelness, comprising all that is novel and nothing that is not-novel, a novel that so transcends the particular that it is both generic and sui generis.

I, the narrator of the story you imagine you are reading (as opposed to Abe Snow, the narrator of the first-person story whose composition and publication my story is about), first thought of having a fictional character write the ideal contemporary novel while I was browsing through the lingerie department of the San Francisco Union Square Macy's, thinking about literature while testing how well I could see my hand through a silk teddy. It occurred to me that there would be a strong market for Minimalist underwear, which could be introduced with such advertising copy as:

> Be sexy and inscrutable all at once.

or, with an appropriate photo:

> Tonight you're wearing Minimalist.
> He sees everything in a lingering glance
> but has no idea what he's seeing
> or what he's expected to do with it.

Serious literature and marketing thus became entangled in my mind during a particularly strong hormonal flow. The result is (or will be, when I write it) my story about

Abe Snow. He has long known, as all serious American writers know, that serious contemporary novels must all be about the suffering and struggles of writers (or ur-writers). He has also known, as all serious American writers know, that power and truth in serious contemporary novels derive from the author's memories of childhood and the author's fantasies about extramarital involvements, which we care about only to the degree that we are convinced the author is a genius whose life and mind are worthy of such minute examination.

Abe's life-transforming insight is that serious contemporary American literature is squarely within the genre of celebrity autobiography, which can only be successful to the degree that the author/subject is, in fact, celebrated. Therefore the serious contemporary American novelist must become famous *before* publishing anything, so that when his fiction-*cum*-celeb-bio appears the public will not expect cognitive processes to be involved in the reading of the book.

Indeed, the book is not meant to be read. Rather it is purchased to be a talisman of the reader's sympathy with the Celebrated One. Having been created by the celebrity, the book is the most easily obtained scrap of his or her personal detritus, giving its purchaser immeasurable powers in the arcane *vodun* of Celebrism, the folk religion of the American people. The book is not an end in itself; it is a channel to the god, and therefore must be endued with mystery. Any attempt to understand the novel would show the worshiper's lack of faith in the Celebrated One, as if the presumptuous reader feels himself capable of judging whether the Celebrated One is worthy of celebration.

Hence Abe Snow realizes that to take his place in the pantheon of contemporary American letters it is essential that his genius and vision be so celebrated that he need not concern himself with the tedious labor of creating stories that people might voluntarily read for pleasure.

With this understanding, Abe's long-time writer's block evaporates at once, and he writes the ideal novel. Through a series of machinations that I have not yet thought of, Abe contrives to become a famous writer with a famous agent, and then his book brings more than a million dollars at auction.

Abe's working title, and the title he expected to see on the finished book, was, as befitted the ideal novel, *F——ing Good Read*. The publisher, however, presents to him the results of a survey of literary opinion-makers showing that during the coming decade they will no longer be impressed by the word *f——*. The publisher offers as an alternative the title *Damn Fine Novel*. Abe Snow finds this acceptable, and eight million copies are printed, shipped, sold, and worshipfully not read.

In addition, Abe writes a very short story about the writing of *Damn Fine Novel* which is published, under the title "Damn Fine Novel," in a magazine of unassailable literary reputation. This does not increase the audience for the ideal novel, but it does mean that Abe moves directly from the bestseller lists to the anthologies of contemporary literature assembled and xeroxed by literature professors for the edification of their graduate students, who will then write theological essays affirming that *Damn Fine Novel* is holy writ and should be required reading for all American students. This, plus heavy exploitation of foreign and film rights, guarantees that Abe Snow will never have to write again.

At this point I (not the narrator of the story you imagine that you are reading, but the implied author of the story you are in fact reading) am uncertain whether all this happened within Snow's book *Damn Fine Novel* or whether his book *Damn*

Fine Novel was part of my own story "Damn Fine Novel," which may or may not be the story that you, the inferred audience, are reading. And if you are in fact reading and attempting to understand it, I must say it shows a surprising lack of faith on your part, which hurts and disappoints me after all we've been through together.

BILLY'S BOX

The box was in the living room when Billy came home from school. "What's in the box?" he asked.

"You'll see," said Mom, "as soon as Dad comes home from work."

When Dad came home, he opened the box. Inside was a television set. All of Billy's older brothers and sisters were happy to see the television, but Billy was more interested in the box. It was as tall as Billy, and so wide he couldn't touch both ends at the same time. Billy thought the empty box would be a lot more fun than the TV.

"Dad," said Billy, "can I have the box?"

"Sure," answered Dad.

The next day Billy hunted all over the house for things to put in his box. He found an empty toothpaste tube in the bathroom, and an empty cereal box in the kitchen. He found a whole box full of old buttons. He found a shoe that didn't have a mate. And he put them all in his box in the living room.

When his sister Annie came home from school, she said, "What is that box still doing in the living room?"

When his brother Todd came home from school, he said, "Does Mom know you have all that stuff in here?"

When his sister Dora came home from school, she said, "Can't you play without making a mess?"

And after dinner they all said, "What is all that stuff for, Billy?"

Billy didn't say anything. He just sat inside his box, putting the cereal box, the toothpaste tube, the buttons, and the shoe right out in front.

Dad smiled. "Why, it's a store, of course," he said. "How much are those buttons selling for?"

Billy thought for a minute. "A hundred dollars," he said.

"Oh," said Dad. "I'm a little short this month, I can't afford that. Don't you have any bargains today?"

"Oh yes!" agreed Billy. "They're on sale for two cents each."

"That's a real bargain," Dad said. "I'll take three buttons."

Then he handed Billy six cents, and Billy handed him three buttons.

"Oh," said Billy's brother and sisters admiringly. "What a neat store!"

The next day Billy hunted for things again. This time he found a yardstick, and Mom gave him some string. He tied the ends of the string through the holes in the ends of the yardstick. He pulled back on the string and the yardstick bent a little. Then he let go of the string with a twang.

"SWICK!" he said. "SWISH! ZIP!"

When Annie came home from school, she said, "Is that box still in the living room?"

Billy was hiding down inside the box. When she said that he stood up and held the yardstick out, and twanged the string. "SWICK!" he said. Annie left the room, laughing.

Todd came home and said, "Does Mom know you've got the yardstick in your store?"

Billy twanged the string at Todd and said, "ZIP! No she doesn't, cause it isn't a store!"

Todd left the room, saying, "I thought it was a store."

When Dora came in she said, "What's all this twanging and zipping and swicking? Can't you play without making noise?"

But Billy only twanged the string at her and whispered, "SWICK! ZIP! SWISH! TWANG!"

And after dinner they all asked, "What are you doing, Billy?"

Billy didn't say anything. He ducked down inside the box where no one could see him. Then he stood up and twanged and zipped them all.

Dad smiled. "Why, that's a castle, of course!" he declared. "Are you a knight?"

"No," answered Billy. "I'm the king. And if you come any closer, I'll get you with my bow and arrow." And then Billy pulled back on the string with all his might to make a huge twang. But the string didn't twang at all. Instead, the yardstick broke right in half.

"Oops," said Billy, "I'm sorry."

Billy's brother and sisters were about to say, "I told you this would happen," but just in time Mom said, "Well, looks like without a bow you're not a king anymore, are you?"

Billy looked at the broken bow. "Nope," he agreed.

"Now it's just a yardstick," Dad said.

Billy looked at the two pieces in his hand. "I think it's two half-yardsticks," he said.

"Well then," Dad said, "it looks like that box isn't a castle anymore. What can it be now?"

Billy thought and thought. Then he got an idea. "it's a repair shop!"

"Good idea," said Dad. Billy, Dad and Mom hunted through the house. Mom found glue and tape, and Dad found two straight sticks. Then Billy set the yardstick on top of the box, and he put glue on the broken place and pushed the two pieces together. Dad helped Billy tape on the two straight sticks so the yardstick would dry straight.

"And now," said Dad, "let's leave the yardstick in the repair shop overnight."

That's what they did. Mom turned on the television set and Billy sat down between

Mom and Dad and watched the show with the rest of the family. "I'm sorry I broke the yardstick," he whispered.

"You didn't mean to," Dad said.

"And tomorrow it will be good as new, thanks to your repair shop," added Mom.

Billy smiled. "I like my box," he said.

When he went to bed, he thought for a long time about what his box would be the next day.

Maybe a zoo—if I can find a tiger, he decided at last—just before he went to sleep.

THE BEST FAMILY HOME
EVENING EVER

"Next week," said Dad at the end of family home evening, "the lesson will be about why family members shouldn't say unkind things to each other when they're angry."

"Yippee!" shouted nine-year-old Alan. He was glad the lesson was on family members not getting angry with each other. Alan's brothers and sister always seemed to be angry with him.

He remembered borrowing Ryan's electric shaver to practice shaving and Ryan had yelled at him. At Christmastime he tied red bows on Alice's geranium to surprise her and she became really upset.

Even Dad and Mom had become irritated with him—like the time when he taped the two halves of the dining room table together underneath so that they couldn't be pulled apart to put extra leaves in. Alan thought it was funny. Dad and Mother didn't.

I can't wait for next Monday to come, Alan thought.

Then Father continued, "And I'm going to assign Alan to give the lesson."

"Uh-oh," Alan said.

"You can do it," encouraged Mother. "You were so enthusiastic a moment ago."

Alan thought for a minute. "I guess since I'm an expert on making people angry, I probably could give a lesson on how to keep all of you from being cross with me."

Everybody laughed. But Alan really meant what he said.

He had never given a lesson in family home evening before—at least not all by himself—and he wanted to do a good job. And so he thought about it all week.

Every now and then Mom would say, "Alan, how's the family home evening lesson coming? Want any help?"

"It's coming great, Mom," Alan would say. "I've decided to do it all by myself, but thanks anyway."

On the Sunday night before family home evening, Alan spent a lot of the evening downstairs in his room, writing.

"What are you writing?" Dad asked.

"Things," Alan answered, "for the family home evening lesson."

As soon as he got home from school on Monday afternoon, Alan put a sign on the basement door. It said, PLEASE DO NOT ENTER! FAMILY HOME EVENING LESSON UNDER CONSTRUCTION.

His second oldest brother Harry knocked on the basement door. "Alan," he said. "I want to watch television."

"Sorry," Alan called. "You can't come down right now."

Harry became upset. "I'm warning you, Alan, this better be a mighty good family home evening!"

"Don't worry," Alan said.

After a while his sister Alice knocked on the door. "Alan," she said, "all my sewing stuff is in the basement. Can I come down?"

"I'm sorry, sis, not now," Alan replied. "Can't you crochet for a while instead?"

"I want to sew, Alan," she said, sounding cross.

"Sorry," Alan repeated. "But if I let you come down it would ruin my family home evening lesson."

"It better be good," Alice threatened.

"It'll be one of the most interesting family home evenings we've had," Alan promised.

Finally it was dinnertime and Alan came upstairs, closing the basement door carefully behind him. When dinner was over, the family gathered together in the living room for family home evening.

After the song and the prayer, Alan stood up and said, "Tonight the lesson is on how family members shouldn't yell or talk unkindly to each other even when they're upset. When someone yells at another person it makes that person feel bad, and that isn't the way we're supposed to make people feel."

Everyone agreed that Alan was right. Then he passed out pieces of paper to everyone. Dad read his first: "If you came home from work and you set down your briefcase and then some of us got into it and made paper airplanes out of the papers, what would you do?"

Dad thought for a minute. "I would probably get angry."

"But what would you *do* about it?" Alan asked.

Dad smiled. "I'd call in the ones who made the paper airplanes and explain to them that these were important papers that other people were depending on, and I would ask them to unfold the paper airplanes and flatten out the pages as best they could."

"You wouldn't yell?" Alan asked.

"I wouldn't yell," Dad promised.

Mom read, "If you were making a cake and one of your children came in and jumped real hard in front of the oven and the cake fell, what would you do?"

"Well, I would feel just awful," said Mom. "I'd explain to that child how his jumping made the cake fall and ruined the family's dessert and that I felt really bad about it."

"But you wouldn't say anything mean?" Alan asked.

"Not if I were acting the way I should," said Mom, smiling.

Soon all the family promised that they would not be cross or unkind to other family members anymore even when they had cause to be angry.

"Is that the whole lesson?" asked Ryan.

"No," Alan said. "Now we'll go downstairs to the family room."

Everyone went downstairs, Alan first. He watched them very carefully as they saw what the family room looked like.

Everything was in the wrong place. All the books were out of the bookshelves. Alice's sewing things were scattered everywhere. The boxes from the storage room were piled up around the bottom of the stairs. There were little pieces of wadded up newspaper on the floor. And facedown on the Ping-Pong table was what looked like an expensive picture that Mom was going to frame, ripped right in half. It was the worst sight any of them had ever seen.

"What a terrible mess!" said his mother, irritably.

"I know it, Mom," said Alan. "But you can't yell at me. All of you promised you wouldn't be cross no matter how upset you got."

Dad looked at Mom. Mom looked at Ryan. Ryan looked at Harry. Harry looked at Alice. Alice looked at Alan.

"Alan," Alice said, "if we can't yell, can we at least whisper that we want to knock somebody's block off?"

"No," Alan said.

Alan gave them all a little time to think. Then he asked, "Is anybody here going to be cross at anyone else, namely me?"

After a while they all said, "No, we won't."

Then Alan smiled. "All right, you passed the test. Now I'll tell you about this mess. Actually I didn't just scatter these things around even though it looks that way. I set them all very carefully where they are so that nothing would be damaged. And see, Mom, I cut out some paper the same size as your picture and you just thought I'd ripped up the original one. I'll have everything back in place in a couple of hours."

Then everybody laughed, because Alan had really made them realize how they had been behaving toward each other. They decided that Alan shouldn't have to put everything back alone, so they all worked together, and soon everything was back in place.

When it was all cleaned up, Alan said, "Well, I guess my lesson's over. Thanks for helping."

"It was a good lesson, son," Dad said. "And if we could keep from yelling about the way this family room looked a few minutes ago, I think we can keep from being upset about *anything*."

"It was a good lesson," Ryan said, "but I hope you never make the family room look like that again."

"You must be kidding!" Alan replied. "I'll never make a mess like that again in my whole life. It took hours! You guys may think being a messy kid is easy, but I can tell you it is really hard work!"

BICICLETA

Amauri pushed the bicycle up the long hill. At the top was a small Catholic church with a little building behind where the padres lived. In back of this building was a little shack that Amauri's family called home. "*Mamãe* (Mother)!" he called out when he neared his house, and his mother appeared at the door.

"Where have you been, Amauri?" she asked, her back still bent from the day's work of cleaning in the tall office building downtown. Then she saw the bicycle. "What do you have there, Amauri?" she asked, and her eyes looked worried.

"A *bicicleta* (bicycle), *Mamãe*," Amauri answered.

"Where did you get it?" his mother questioned again, and Amauri knew that she was afraid he had stolen it, because many of the poor people in their neighborhood sometimes stole things to get money to buy food. Amauri's mother was grateful that her five children didn't steal.

"A man gave it to me, Mother," Amauri answered proudly. "I'm going to be a delivery boy! I'll ride the bicycle from place to place, delivering lunches to the businessmen and groceries to the ladies in fine houses!"

"You mean you have a job?" And Amauri's mother smiled with joy.

Amauri told her about how he had walked up to a man and said, "Do you need a boy to work for you?" The man had thought for a few moments and then invited him inside his store. They talked for a while, and he told Amauri that he would pay him fifty *centavos* an hour.

"How many hours will you work?" his mother asked.

"Eight hours every day," Amauri answered. "That means I will get four *cruzeiros* a day or more than twenty *cruzeiros* a week. I can buy food for the family!"

Amauri hugged his mother and she hugged him back. "What a good nine-year-old son I have," she said gratefully. "Now you are truly the man of the family. Ever since your father died I have been the only one earning money. Now you will help me buy beans and rice for our breakfast and dinner. Enough talking for now, son. Remember, the elders are coming tonight, and we must get the house ready."

Amauri got water from the well, and his little sister Cecilia cooked the beans and rice for dinner. The other children made the two beds they all slept on, while Mother carefully swept the cold, hard-packed dirt floor.

When the missionaries came, they stood outside the door and clapped their hands together, because that is the way people announce themselves in Brazil. Cecilia ran to open the door.

"*Boa noite, elderes* (Good evening, elders)," she said. "Come in."

The tall elders shook hands with everybody. Elder Samson was blond and showed many teeth when he smiled. Elder Bonner had red hair and freckles all over, even on his arms. Although they were Americans, they spoke Portuguese, but sometimes it was hard to understand them.

The elders and Amauri and his family sat on boxes around the table, and then the elders told them all about the commandments of God, including one that asked them to give the Church one-tenth of all the money they earned. Mother was thoughtful when the elders told her this, because she barely made enough money to feed the family. But then she smiled. "Of course," she said. "That is why little Amauri got a job today. We can pay tithing to the Lord and still have enough to eat."

Amauri felt very proud to tell the missionaries about his job. "Who knows?" Amauri said, "maybe someday I will deliver a lunch right to the building where my mother works."

"But what about school?" asked Elder Samson.

"School is not for poor people," said Amauri's mother sadly. "We do not have the money to buy books."

And then Amauri remembered something awful. His face turned white. "What's wrong, Amauri?" the elders asked.

"I just remembered," Amauri said. "I only have three days to learn how to ride the bicycle."

"What?" asked Elder Bonner, surprised. "Nine years old and you don't know how to ride a bicycle?"

Amauri shook his head. "We are too poor to have a bicycle. Now I will have to learn before Thursday. How can I learn that fast?"

Everyone looked worried now. Learning to ride a bicycle wasn't easy.

Then Elder Bonner said he had an idea. "We will teach you how to ride!" he shouted, and Elder Samson nodded in agreement.

The next morning the missionaries came back. They could hardly wait to get Amauri out of bed and onto his bicycle.

It was harder than Amauri had thought it would be. He fell down again and again. Even on a grassy field it hurt to fall, but he kept thinking: *The Lord got me this job so that my family can pay tithing. And I'm going to get back on that bicycle.*

The next day Amauri rode for ten meters all by himself before the bicycle started to tip over, then he stopped it from falling by sticking out his foot. At the end of the riding lesson he told the elders, "It's time for me to go home. And you'll have to hurry—I'm going to ride this bicycle all the way back home. And I'm going to ride it very fast."

Amauri got on the bicycle and pedaled as fast as his legs would go, the elders behind him shouting and cheering him on. When he arrived home, Cecilia and the other children ran out of the house laughing and clapping their hands.

"Como Deus me abencoe (How God is blessing me)!" he shouted to the elders when they came into the house. "First a job, and now you have helped me learn to ride a bicycle so I can do it well!"

The elders just laughed and shook his hand. And then the children hugged him in their excitement.

The next day was Thursday, and Amauri rode the bicycle all alone downtown to the store. He took the lunches and delivered them, and later took fresh meat to housewives and cabbages to restaurants. He was exhausted when nighttime came.

When he got home he tied the bicycle to a tree. Then he knelt beside it and said a prayer, thanking Heavenly Father for his help. When he was through he patted the bicycle seat.

"Oi, bicicleta (Hey, bicycle), *que amigo você é* (you and I are going to be good friends)!"

I Think Mom and Dad Are Going Crazy, Jerry

was only forty-five minutes late getting home with the Ford, and that was only because Darrell, who is my best friend, wanted to be dropped off at his girlfriend's house in Cupertino. If I had known what was going on at home, I would have hurried. What was going on at home was the end of my peace and happiness.

"Shhh," said Anne, my younger sister who is sixteen and had been driving for three wonderful months of parking tickets and running out of gas in odd places.

"What's up? Somebody having a surprise party?" I asked.

"No," said my brother Todd. "At least, we're not. But Mom and Dad seem to be having *some* kind of party."

"What's wrong? Everybody looks so serious."

"What's wrong?" asked my older sister Val in tones of righteous indignation. "What's wrong?"

"Yeah. I mean, what's wrong?"

And then they told me. All at once, in loud whispers. When I had finally sorted out all the different stories, this is what I got:

When Anne got home with the Pinto, it had a new dent in the door from opening it hard into a light pole in a parking lot. But Mom and Dad weren't angry—they just smiled and took the car keys from her and went into the bedroom and locked the door. When Todd got home with the car, it was nearly out of gas, and he didn't have enough money to fill it up; but Mom and Dad didn't complain, just took the keys and went back to their bedroom and locked the door. And when Val came home four hours late from a "quick trip to the store to get more shampoo," Mom and Dad didn't complain about the Volkswagen being gone so long—just took the car keys, and you know what happened then.

And no sooner had they finished telling me their stories than out of their bedroom came Mom and Dad, chortling and smiling. "Hi, Jerry," said Dad.

"Hi," I said. "Sorry I was late getting back, but I had to take Darrell to his girlfriend's house in Cupertino."

"That's fine," said Mom.

"Is the car nearly out of gas?" asked Dad.

"I didn't have any money to fill it up," I said.

"Oh, fine, fine," Mom said, giggling a little. "Could I have your car keys?"

"How come?" I asked.

Father just grinned a little broader. "We want to press them and put them in your baby book."

I handed over the keys.

"Come into the living room, children, my loves," sang Mother, and I swear it looked like they were prancing as they led the way.

As we followed them, Anne looked at me with a frightened expression on her face. "I think Mom and Dad are going crazy, Jerry," she said. Her voice was trembling.

When we got into the living room, Mom and Dad were playing catch with the car keys.

"Definitely," I told Anne. "Bonkers. Bananas. Out, so to speak, of their minds."

When we had all settled down, looking at our once-stable parents with expressions that ranged from concern to near panic, Father began a little speech.

"Perhaps you children have never counted, but we, a middle income family, have four cars. Four cars is an unusually large number of automobiles for a middle income family, but then we have an unusually large number of drivers at home. Six, to be exact. Six drivers and four cars. One could reasonably suppose that this would be enough cars to go around, but not so. Today your mother had an appointment at the dentist's. The appointment was at 2:00, but at 2:00, even though there were supposed to be three cars at home, there were none. Mother missed her dental appointment. Does your tooth hurt, Mother?"

Mother nodded, holding her jaw. "My tooth hurts, Father." She laughed.

"And I today received three pieces of mail. One was the insurance bill. One was the bill from our gasoline credit card. And one was the monthly statement from the bank on the two cars we are still paying for. I added them up and reached a sobering conclusion."

He did not look particularly somber.

"My dear children, I believe we are the largest single mainstay for the automobile and insurance and oil businesses in America today. If we did not use our cars for one week, Ford Motor Company stock would drop three points and there would be a coup in Saudi Arabia. If we did not use our cars for a year, our country would be plunged into a major depression. We are supporting the economy of the United States of America.

"We are honored. This is a privilege for us, and we don't plan to shirk our responsibilities. However, some of this privilege ought to be shared. Mother, will you get the documents?"

Mother left the room. While she was gone, Father asked each of us in turn how much we made at our jobs. None of us was making a fortune, but we were doing surprisingly well. Even Anne, who worked in a hamburger drive-in after school, pulled down about a hundred a month. No wonder she always looked like she stepped out of the pages of a fashion magazine.

And then Mother came back and handed each of us a piece of paper with the words LEASE AGREEMENT at the top of the page. I won't give you the legal language. Boiled down, it went this way:

Each of us who planned to drive any car at all during a given month had to pay a basic fee of eight dollars to cover part of the insurance costs. If our grades fell below a B average, we had to pay twenty dollars a month.

"That's quite a jump," said Anne, who often did not have a B average.

"So is the jump in insurance rates when your grades go down," answered Mom.

The agreement also called for us to pay all traffic fines, the deductible on the insurance in case of collision, and *all the gas we used.*

"What?" asked Val, turning white. "*All* the gas?"

"The car is to be returned home with the tank full, every time," Dad said.

There was also a mileage fee. For the LTD, ten cents per mile. For the Pinto, eight cents per mile. For the Volkswagen, because it was old, six cents per mile, and for the Galaxy, commonly known around the house as "the Ford," twelve cents a mile.

"Twelve cents a mile!" I shouted. That was the car I preferred to drive.

"It's the newest car. It has the greatest depreciation," said my father, smiling.

"You will keep track of the mileage," said Mother, "on these handy little Automobile Record sheets, which we will have printed up and placed in the glove compartment of every car. After every use of the car, you will write down your mileage and the number on the odometer. When you come home, you will give your Automobile Record sheet to the leasing company—your father or myself."

And the final clause of the contract was the stinger. "Permission for use of the cars will automatically be suspended until all dues and remunerations are paid in full."

"You mean we can't even be late?"

"Not even by a day," Father said, smiling.

Anne was outraged. "I thought we were a family, not a business!"

Mother only smiled her if-you-get-upset-it-will-only-make-it-worse smile. "Every family is a business, dear. There are income and expenses and cash flow. We just think it's time that your father stopped supplying all the income and you stopped monopolizing the expenses. There's the contract. You will all please sign."

"And if we don't?" asked Todd, already cringing because he knew the answer before he asked.

Father held up all the car keys—quite a bundle of them—and said, "The cars will no doubt miss you, and you will probably wear out your shoes faster, but the walking will be good for your health."

Anne didn't get it. "You mean if we don't sign, we don't drive?"

"That's what he means," said Val.

"Here are the pens," said Mother.

"Sign or walk," said Father.

We signed.

"After all these years," I said, "I never knew that my parents were so greedy."

"Think of it this way," Dad said, putting his arm around my shoulder. "By saving money on the cars, we can go on putting food on the table. It's a fringe benefit that isn't written into the contract. Your parents won't go broke."

As we left the room, Val whispered to me, "They go through these phases—it's part of being parents. They'll forget about it in a week."

They didn't forget about it in a week. They didn't forget about it in a month.

"Mom, can I take the car tonight?" Anne asked. "Debbie and I want to see *Superman.*"

"Again?" Mother asked. "How many times have you seen it?"

"Only three," Anne said. "*Star Wars* still holds the record."

"I hardly dare ask how often."

"Six times."

"You may take the car," said Mother.

"Thanks!" Anne said.

"As soon," Mother added, "as you settle up your car leasing bill."

Anne looked horrified. "You didn't say anything about it."

"Why should I have? It's your bill, not mine."

"But I've spent almost all my money."

"I'm sorry. Maybe Debbie can drive."

They went over the accounts. "Your total bill is now $38.56," Mother said.

Anne gulped. "But, Mom, that's more than a new top."

"And just think," Mother said with a smile, "we're only charging you half what it costs us!"

Anne went to her bedroom and got the money and paid Mother. "Take it," Anne said. "Take it all. I don't like money anyway. I hate money. I never want to see money again. Money is filthy and disgusting. Take all of it."

"Aren't you going to the movie?" Mother asked.

"I have forty-two cents left. That wouldn't pay for the gas to get the car out of the driveway. Let alone the movie."

"I'm sorry, dear," said Mother. "Perhaps if you walked to Debbie's house more often—it isn't even a mile."

"What am I supposed to be, a pioneer?"

"But haven't you heard, dear?" asked Mother. "The sidewalks are paved all the way there."

"Would you really thrust your own youngest daughter out in the snow and the sleet—"

"This is California, dear. If it starts snowing, I'll let you take the car for half price."

I was in the kitchen helping Mom make tuna sandwiches for fourteen billion of Todd's friends who had just happened to come over on a Saturday. We couldn't help but overhear their conversation in the living room.

"How will we all get home after the game?" asked one of his friends. They were seniors in high school and didn't have anything better to do than worry about getting home from the game.

"Maybe I could take you," Todd said.

"That'd be great," said another friend.

"Wait a minute," Todd said. "We'd have to share the costs."

"Costs?"

"The only car big enough is the LTD. That's ten cents a mile. I figure that with the eight of you that's got to be around fifty miles. Plus a pro rata share of my monthly insurance bill and the cost of gasoline, which at sixty-nine cents a gallon and eleven miles to the gallon comes to $3.13, plus the mileage and share—that's $9.13. And there are eight of us so it's $1.14 each, with a penny left over. I'll treat you to the penny."

They were astounded. They were appalled. "A dollar *each* just to get home from the game?"

"A dollar and fourteen cents. And don't forget the free penny."

"I think my parents can take me." Pretty soon all of them decided their parents could take them home.

"Too bad," Todd said. "It probably costs your parents more than a buck to make a special trip there and back. You guys just don't know how much it costs to keep cars running these days."

I spread tuna on the last sandwich as Mother ran water in the bowl. "Do you hear what I hear?" I asked.

"I think my son Todd is beginning to get some sense about money," she answered.

I didn't say anything. *I* thought it sounded like my brother Todd wasn't pulling a full train.

I don't make much money at my job. Not when I have to support my driving habit and my taste in clothes and all my records and tapes and a minor addiction to buying four science fiction novels a week. I began to discover the joys of walking.

Do you have any idea how many barking, savage dogs there are on an average residential block in a California suburban community? (Seven—one with rabies.)

Do you know how many steps it takes to go a mile and a half to school *on foot?* (Exactly 3,168, unless you have a blister and take shorter steps.)

Do you know how *hot* it gets when you walk outside in the summer in California? And they don't even air-condition the street.

I also discovered that rain is wet, wind is cold, passing cars like to go fast through puddles to splash you, and you meet the strangest people waiting for the WALK signal at a busy intersection.

And even with all that walking, my automobile leasing bill was still horrendous. I had given up on the LTD except for dates, but even with the Volkswagen I was paying thirty or forty dollars a month.

"I give up," I said. "I won't do any more business with this rip-off car leasing business."

"Really?" asked Father, looking up from his copy of the San Jose *Mercury.*

"Really," I said. "I will not pay your fees. I will not drive your cars."

"Mother!" Father called. "Jerry has decided to become a pedestrian!"

"I have not," I said. "I have decided to take my patronage elsewhere."

"Where?" he asked.

"If Hertz is good enough for O. J. Simpson, it's good enough for me."

As I left the room Dad called after me, "But, Jerry! *We* try harder!"

I came back three hours later. Whipped. Beaten. Defeated.

"Do you know what *they* charge?" I asked.

"A lot?" Father guessed helpfully.

"I couldn't rent a pair of roller skates from them for less than fifty dollars a month." "Ah."

"You and Mom may be a rip-off leasing company, but at least you're competitive."

"Oh, come off it," Father said, laughing. "We have the best rates in town."

"I want to buy a horse," I said.

"I can get you a good price on hay," Father answered. He laughed and laughed. I wouldn't give him the satisfaction. I managed to keep a smile off my face until my bedroom door was closed behind me. *Then* I laughed.

And then Miriam finally agreed to go on a date with me. She was the best-looking girl in the ward (also in the state; probably in the Church), and she had finally broken up with Alvin Hopper, which was no great loss to her and a tremendous gain to a college freshman like myself with excellent taste in girls. On my fourth try she agreed to go out with me. I shot the works. The LTD, complete with car wash, a thirty dollar dinner in San Francisco, a drive through beautiful scenery on the way up, Bayshore Freeway on the way back, and charming, delightful conversation all the way. The conversation was the only thing free on the whole date.

And she was worth it. She could discuss at least thirteen different topics intelligently and got a B- on all the others, which means she was more than just a pretty face. She let me open doors for her and took my arm without my even having to hint. She looked me right in the eye and never let her gaze linger for a moment on the slight complexion problem that had appeared mysteriously on my chin the day before. She was perfect.

On the way home, after we left the freeway, she asked, "You don't happen to have a throat lozenge or anything like that? I have kind of a sore throat."

"In the glove compartment," I said. Mom kept the glove compartment like a medicine chest—aspirin, throat lozenges, cough drops, breath mints, Kleenex, eye drops, bandages, and disinfectant. She figured that if we all had the flu and got into a traffic accident, she could make everybody feel better in minutes. Miriam reached into the glove compartment, found the lozenges, and also found the pad of Automobile Record sheets.

"What's this?" she asked.

So I told her. All about the lease agreement. How much it cost and everything. I was just about to tell her how terrible it all was when she interrupted me.

"That's terrible," she said. "I can't believe parents doing anything like that! Who do they think they are?"

"Parents," I said.

"Well, I'm glad *my* parents are more generous than that. It sounds like your father must be Ebenezer Scrooge and your mother must be Shylock."

"Shylock was a man."

"Stingy, anyway. How much do they charge you for lunch and dinner?"

"Nothing."

"I'm surprised. Do they have a coin box and water meter on the shower? Do they make you pay for clean sheets?"

"Of course not," I said.

"A car is a necessity of life," she said. "Parents have a responsibility to provide them for their children."

Now, you have to understand. I'm not an argumentative person. I'm quite easy to get along with. But she was talking about my *parents*, judging them just by the fact that they ran a rip-off car leasing business with a captive clientele. I couldn't let her go unanswered. So I answered.

"Listen, Miriam, a car is different from showers and food and bedding. It's a lot more expensive. And I eat three meals a day and sleep once a night and take a shower every morning. It's regular and predictable and it doesn't go up and down. But the car I use as often as I like, and we kids used to use the cars *all* the time. It cost the folks hundreds and hundreds of dollars every month. And so it was perfectly fair for them to decide we should help pay."

"You can't live in the modern world without a car. They might as well charge you for air." She sounded upset.

"You *can* live without a car," I said. "You can walk, for example. I've walked to school a lot the last few months."

"I can imagine," she said darkly.

"I've enjoyed it. I've discovered there are things you can't see from a car."

"Like bubble gum on a sidewalk," she said, sounding rather snide.

"I think it's a good idea for us to help our parents pay for the cars."

"And I think anybody who thinks that is crazy."

"You do?" I asked, and I think by now I also sounded upset.

"I do. If word of this gets around, other people's parents will try it, too, and pretty soon an entire generation of young people will be trapped at home with their families night after night."

It shows you how angry I was. I said, "That doesn't sound like a bad idea. And furthermore, I think that it's perfectly possible for people to have a good time together without having a car at all. I think it would be a wonderful date just to walk over to a girl's house and take her out walking and talking and maybe looking in store windows or maybe just seeing a little bit of the neighborhood and just getting to know each other without spending any money at all."

"That sounds hideous."

"Then," I said, "I won't ask you out on such a date."

I took her home and neither of us said another word except for a perfunctory good-night-and-thanks-for-a-wonderful-evening at the door.

When I got home, after filling the gas tank, I wrote down the mileage on the odometer, figured out my total car costs for the evening, and went inside, got the money from my room, and went into Mom and Dad's bedroom, where they were reading the Old Testament out loud to each other the way they do every night.

"Did you have a nice time?" asked Mother.

"Wonderful," I said. "I want to settle up for tonight."

"Oh, you don't have to do that until the first of the month," Dad said.

"I want to do it now." I showed them how much I owed them, counted out the money, and handed it to them. Then I carefully placed a five dollar bill on top of the rest.

"What's that for?" asked Mother.

"It's a tip," I said. "For service above and beyond the call of duty.

"I think you're wonderful. I'm glad you laid it on the line with us. I'm glad you shared the responsibility of paying for the entire U.S. automobile industry with us kids. It's the most adult thing I've ever had to do in my life."

Mother got tears in her eyes. Father said, "I think Jerry's grown up, don't you, Mother?"

"Yes," Mother agreed.

"Well, you're both wrong," I said. "I'm just completely out of my mind."

I kissed them both good-night and went straight to bed feeling pretty doggone good. Also pretty doggone poor, since I had about six bucks to last me through the rest of the month. But as my sister Anne pointed out, money isn't everything. In fact, it's hardly anything.

GERT FRAM

Susan Parker decided to make a list. She sat down at her writing desk, the one her father had given her two years ago on her eleventh birthday and which she was already outgrowing.

On the left side of a piece of paper she wrote, "People who hate me." On the right side of the piece of paper she wrote, "People who like me."

The first name she put on the left side was Todd Slover. He was definitely a hater. She had accidentally jabbed him in the arm with a pencil and now he would probably die of lead poisoning.

Mrs. Gray was on the "People who hate me" side, too. She had brought a fishbowl to school for the lesson on lizards. The class was supposed to catch a lizard and put it in the fishbowl. Susan broke the fishbowl.

It hadn't been a good day at school.

The list of haters kept growing. In big letters she wrote, "MOTHER."

Mother had sent her to the store for eggs. Susan had been absolutely positive Mother had sent her for eggs. She got home with the eggs. Mother thanked her for the eggs and then asked about the butter, which is what she sent her to the store for.

"Eggs are nice, I can always use them," Mother said. "But what I need to finish the cookies for the party tonight is butter."

"Oh, yeah, butter," Susan had answered. Mother had gotten that tight little look she always got when she was trying not to get mad. Susan had decided that was a good time to head for the bedroom.

Susan held up the list and looked at it. So far, it said:

People who hate me   People who like me

Todd Slover
Mrs. Gray
MOTHER

It was a depressing list. She had already made three people very angry today. And the night was still young.

And so Susan decided that it was about time for Gert Fram to write another novel. Gert Fram was a world-famous thirteen-year-old novelist who preferred to avoid publicity and therefore never published more than one copy of her work. So far, she had written five novels. They were arranged in a neat stack on the desk: *Samy Davis Worm*, by Gert Fram. *Little Purple Pears*, by Gert Fram. *A Decent Book about Nothing*, by Gert Fram. *Water Warts*, by Gert Fram. And her favorite: *Chapy Nukls*. Also by Gert Fram.

Susan picked up her pen and reached for an empty book. She had made a batch of about five books the last time. They consisted of pieces of paper about two inches by four inches, stapled together along one edge. Making the empty book first was a good idea. That way she always knew when to end her novel, because she would run out of paper.

She thought for a moment, and then wrote, "RASIN MOON, by Gert Fram." Then she smiled, and began to write:

"There was a little man & everyday he would eat and he would eat rasins always. now there was a rasin moon in the sky. And every day it would get fatter because the rasins would keep growing + nobody would eat them exept gravity + it doesn't have a mouth. well, this little man was getting hungry for rasins one supper night but the world would run out because the rasins would evaporate, + if it wasn't for evaporation the rasin moon would be a nothing moon. the man decided to go to the rasin moon but he didn't know that there was such thing as one but he decided to check anyway. He didn't really know how to get up there but all of a sudden"

All of a sudden what? Susan Parker pursed her lips. Susan always pursed her lips when Gert Fram was stuck for an idea. Finally Gert Fram got the idea and Susan unpursed her lips and wrote some more:

"it started raining. It was raining up instead of down. no, it was evaporating rasins. so the little man jumped on a rasin + flew up on it. when he got up in space he saw the rasin moon and it looked like one big Prune. He was overjoyed. In fact he was so overjoyed that he forgot his name and that is why his name isn't said in this book."

Susan Parker laughed. Gert Fram really had a funny way with words.

"He had a bunch of rasins for his supper + he was thirsty and he didn't know what to do. All of a sudden he got an idea. He jumped on a molecule + floated down to the supermarket. He went in and got all the juice, and threw it all in the sky + it started floating up and it made a juice moon. For days he lived up there + after a while he got sick of it so he went down to earth again, + threw all the food and it all floated up in the sky. There was a banana moon + a cornflake moon etc. There even was a pencil moon because he accidently threw some pencils, soon it was a food sky + soon all the gravity got soaked up so there was none left. So the little man observed + every thing floated down to earth again."

Uh-oh. Last page. Two-inch by four-inch pages filled up fast. Gert Fram decided to wrap things up fast.

"All except rasin moon because he was there in the first place + it wouldn't be fair. After a while the rasins stopped evaporating but the rasin moon stayed. in the sky. It was happy + so was the little man."

On the back of the book Gert Fram drew a picture of a wrinkled up lumpy moon with little wrinkled lumps rising up to it and a man at the bottom. She labeled it, "The little man riding up to the rasin moon."

Actually, both Susan and Gert Fram knew how to spell *raisin*. But leaving out the first *i* gave the word a little more class.

Susan reread the novel. Gert Fram was OK.

"It's dinner time, Susan and Annabelle and Vanessa and Jonathan!" her mother called from downstairs. Susan leaned back in her chair and wondered whether her agent would like *Rasin Moon*. Probably not. Her agent wasn't really very happy because nobody had ever bought any of Gert Fram's novels yet and a ten percent commission of nothing doesn't add up to much.

"Susan, everybody's here except you!"

Susan proudly added *Rasin Moon* to her library.

Downstairs Father was mumbling something to Mother. Then Father called out, "Gert Fram! It's suppertime!"

Susan got up carefully from her chair and walked with dignity to the door of her study/library/den/bedroom. Then she ran down the stairs and scurried into the dining room and dove into her chair and said, "Gert Fram just finished a novel and it's the greatest yet."

No one paid much attention to what she said, however, because in diving for her chair she had jostled the table and two glasses of lemonade had spilled.

"Can't you be careful for even a minute!" her mother said, crossly wiping up the mess.

"Gert Fram writes a novel and Susan has to drown us to celebrate," Jonathan said in his funny voice that he reserved for making jokes about Susan.

Susan got up from the table and ran back upstairs. She heard them talking downstairs. "You didn't need to talk like that, Jonathan."

"Dad, she's so *dumb*, she's always knocking things around—"

"She's not dumb, and now she's upset and gone upstairs—"

"Careful, Annabelle, the lemonade's about to drip off the table on you."

Susan shut the bedroom door. She walked to the desk and added a name to the list: "Creepy Jonathan," she wrote, because he hated to be called that. Then she heard her father calling. "Gert Fram or Susan Parker, whichever of you is hungrier, come downstairs and eat dinner."

Susan didn't want to go back down. Everybody would watch her walk in and sit down. Jonathan would be thinking she was dumb. So would everybody else. On the other hand she was hungry.

Well, if Susan didn't have any nerve, Gert Fram did. Gert Fram walked with dignity out the door of the bedroom and down the stairs. She paused at the bottom of the steps (all great and famous writers pause at the bottoms of stairways), and then turned and walked with dignity to the table.

She heard Jonathan laugh and only looked down her nose at him. Susan would have been humiliated. But Gert Fram could put such riff-raff in their place.

But during dinner she forgot to be Gert Fram and almost cried once when she knocked over the salt and Annabelle sighed and set it back up. Annabelle could afford to sigh. She was sixteen and smart and wore makeup and never spilled anything.

After dinner everything went okay for about two minutes. Then she heard her father say, "All right, who did it?"

He sounded angry.

"Who did what, dear?" Mother asked in her don't-be-angry-dear voice.

Susan looked up at her mother and said, "If it's something bad, I did it."

Father came into the dining room holding the *Herald*.

"I did it, all right," Susan said.

"Somebody cut something out of the other side of the newspaper and now all I've got is half a crossword puzzle," Father said. Father always did the crossword puzzle.

"Well, dear," said Mother in her please-don't-get-upset-at-anyone voice, "you never do more than half of it anyway."

Father didn't think it was funny. "I thought I told everybody in the family not to cut anything out of a newspaper until it was a day old!"

Susan jumped up from the table, where she had been sitting pulling petals off the flowers in the vase. "Well I thought it was the old newspaper and it was a picture of a bride who's getting married in the temple and I cut it out because I wanted a picture of her and I'm sorry I didn't know it was today's paper."

Father and Mother looked at Susan. They really weren't sure what to say to this outburst.

"I'll go get the picture and I'll glue it back in!" Susan shouted. "I'll glue it back in with my own *blood* if you want, I'm sorry I cut out the crossword puzzle!"

Then Father noticed the little pile of petals on the table.

"Susan, you have pulled every single petal off the flowers."

Susan looked at the petals. She looked at her father. She decided not to cry in front of them. She ran out of the room.

As she left, she heard Mother saying to Father, "I really don't think that was the best time to say that, dear."

When Susan got to the front door, which she had to pass in order to go up the stairs, Vanessa was standing there with her boyfriend Raymond. They looked very surprised to see her. They looked like it was not a pleasant surprise. Because Susan didn't know what else to do, she stopped and looked at them and said, "Hi." Raymond let go of Vanessa's hand.

Raymond made a face and looked away and Vanessa said, "Honestly, there isn't a place in the entire *house* where a person can find any privacy."

Susan tried to defend herself. "There isn't another stairway. When I'm going to my room I have to pass through here."

Vanessa looked up at the ceiling in disgust. "When you are coming, you could at least have the courtesy to announce your presence."

"All right, all right," Susan said. She walked up the stairs, shouting at the top of her voice, "I'm coming, I'm coming! Unclean, unclean! Beware, beware! Susan's presence is coming!"

From downstairs somewhere three voices shouted at once, "Susan will you stop that shouting! For heaven's sake!" Jonathan's voice added, "What a jerk." Mother's voice said, "Jonathan, that doesn't help a thing."

Susan slammed her door and didn't hear anything else from downstairs.

I will not cry I will not cry I will not cry.

She didn't cry. Instead, she sat down at the desk and wrote on the list. When she was finished, it looked like this:

People who hate me	People who like me
Todd Slover	
Mrs. Gray	
MOTHER	
Creepy Jonathan	
FATHER!!!	
Vanessa	
Raymond	
Annabelle	
The whole world	
The whole universe!!!!!!!	

Then, to be fair, she thought for a while about whether anybody liked her. Under "People who like me" she finally wrote, "The dog because he's too dumb to know how dumb I am and because whenever I spill something which is alot he gets to lick it up."

Then she thought for a while more and under "People who like me" she wrote in big letters, "GERT FRAM."

Then Gert Fram started writing another novel. It was called *Susan the Jerk*. It went like this:

"Once upon a time there was a jerk named Susan. She was the only jerk in the entire world except for the soda jerk and people liked him because they liked soda but they didn't like Susan because she was also a creep. she was a creep because everytime she did something it was wrong. once she tried to pet a dog but the dog bit her because he didn't like to be peted. once she tried to vacuum the rug but the vacuum sucked up the whole rug and then the floor and then the whole basement which made everybody mad because they were all in the basement and got sucked up and couldn't get out until Susan cleaned the dust bag on the vacuum cleaner which she didn't do right so that everybody yelled at her and made her do all the dishes for a week which wasn't a good idea because she broke them all."

Susan stopped and reread what Gert Fram had just written. Boy, wasn't it the truth!

"They never let Susan go anywhere except with a gag on her mouth because if they didn't keep her mouth shut she would talk all the time and also they have to tie her up and put her in the corner because she is all the time wiggling and poking people. This is all because Susan is a jerk."

Gert Fram was beginning to warm up to this.

"Boy is Susan a jerk. She is not only a jerk, she is a jerk with bad manners. she burps and doesn't say excuse me and kicks people when they are walking by because how was she suppose to know they were going to walk by right then? What a jerk. jerk jerk jerk jerk jerk."

Gert Fram was running out of paper. It was time to wrap up the novel with a bang. Gert Fram always liked to end her novels with a bang.

"So one day Susan the jerk decided that one jerk on the earth was enough, and it better be the soda jerk because everybody likes him, and so she left the earth and flew off on a rocket. But because Susan was a jerk the rocket crashed and blew up the sun and everybody had to use flashlights all the time from then on because without the sun it was always night and everytime their flashlights ran out of batteries they would shake their fists and yell, boy that Susan is sure a jerk."

Gert Fram had some space left, so she drew a picture of Susan's rocket ship crashing into the sun.

Then she got up (with dignity) from the desk and walked to her dresser, where there were a lot of things stacked. There was the china elephant with the broken trunk because she had dropped it. There was the library book that Mother had had to buy because Susan had dropped it in the gutter and the pages had gotten all thick and wrinkly even after they dried. There was the watch with the broken glass because Susan had accidentally scraped it against a cement wall during class break at junior high. There was a ripped picture of Jesus from Sunday School that the teacher had given her because after she ripped it Susan had felt so bad she had cried. This was when she was seven and sometimes let herself cry.

Susan remembered that the Sunday School teacher had hugged her and said, "Hey, Susan, don't cry like that. You're sorry you ripped the picture, aren't you?"

Susan had nodded and said in her squeaky trying-not-to-cry voice, "I didn't even mean to."

"I know you didn't mean to," said the Sunday School teacher. "And when you say you're sorry about something, Jesus said that people are supposed to forgive you."

"I'm sorry," Susan had said, and cried again, even louder.

The Sunday School teacher gave her an even bigger hug. "That's all right. I forgive you."

But Susan had cried even louder.

"Why are you still crying?" asked the Sunday School teacher.

"Because I ripped Jesus's picture and he'll be mad at me."

Susan remembered that the teacher had gotten tears in her eyes. "Jesus is never mad at you," Susan remembered hearing the teacher tell her. "And to show you, I want you to keep this picture, and every time you see it, you remember that even when you make mistakes Jesus still loves you and forgives you."

Susan set down the picture on her dresser. If I say I'm sorry maybe they'll forgive me, she thought.

So she opened the door and started down the stairs. Then she remembered Vanessa and Raymond by the front door and she coughed. She kept coughing all the way down the stairs.

"What is it, you got pneumonia?" said Jonathan, who was sitting in the living room. Vanessa and Raymond were gone. Susan chose to ignore Jonathan's comment.

Mother was in the kitchen. Father was in the den. Susan decided to go in and say she was sorry to Mother. Then if it went OK she'd go in and say it to Father.

Mother was finishing up the refreshments for the party. She didn't look up when Susan came into the kitchen, but that never stopped Mother, she always knew when somebody came into the kitchen. "Are you feeling better now, Susan, dear?" Mother asked.

Mother sounded so kind that Susan ran right over and leaned on the counter and said, "Mother, I'm sorry I've been acting like such a creep and doing everything wrong and I'm sorry I pulled the stupid petals off the stupid flowers and spilled the lemonade and bought eggs and cut out the crossword puzzle and didn't announce I was coming and everything."

Mother looked at her with horror in her eyes. "Susan, for heaven's sake, look where you're leaning!"

Susan looked where she was leaning. Her elbows were crushing the jello and whipped cream and pineapple dessert that Mother had all ready for the party. Her elbows were covered with jello. The dessert was completely smashed. Susan looked up at her mother.

"What in the *world* am I going to do now!" her mother said, wringing her hands. "They'll all be here in half an hour and there's not a hope in the world of making anything else! Susan, sometimes I think we ought to build a bomb shelter for all of us to hide in whenever you're around!" Mother had meant that last sentence to be a kind of joke, but Susan didn't notice that. She just stood there, deciding not to cry, and then deciding that she couldn't help it, and then with tears running down her cheeks and her face all crinkled up she ran out of the kitchen and up the stairs and slammed the door.

In the living room Jonathan said, "Well, that's two slammed doors tonight, tying the world's record. If we make three slammed doors it'll be a new champion!"

Mother said, "Jonathan, I'm getting very cross with you." Then she went upstairs and tapped on Susan's door.

"Susan," Mother said.

"Go away and leave me alone," Susan's voice said. Susan's voice sounded like there was a lump in her throat and tears in her eyes and a pillow in front of her face. Mother thought about going in anyway, and then she decided that it was not a good idea. Instead she went to the den and asked Father to go to the store and buy something for dessert for the party tonight.

The party was fun and noisy and all the adults played games and talked and ate the store-bought dessert and said thank you for the wonderful evening and went home.

Then Mother and Father talked quietly for a few minutes and they decided that Father would go up and talk to Susan.

Father knocked on the door. "May I come in?" he asked.

"Certainly," answered a voice.

Father came in.

"Susan, I want to talk to you for a couple of minutes."

Susan turned around on her chair and looked at him in dignified surprise. "I'm terribly sorry, sir, but you must have the wrong address. There is no Susan here."

Father looked at her for a moment and said, "I'm afraid I must have been given the wrong address. Who *does* live here?"

"No one lives here. This is the office and studio and den of Gert Fram, the world-famous author."

Father smiled. "I've never been in the office and studio and den of a world-famous author before."

"Well, you needn't ask for an autograph," Gert Fram replied. "I gave up signing autographs years ago. It was such a bother."

"I don't want an autograph," Father said. "I think I want an exclusive interview."

Gert Fram tilted her head. "For that, I'm afraid you'll need to consult my agent. I never grant interviews on the spur of the moment."

Father looked at the floor. "You're not making this very easy for me," he said.

A funny look passed across Susan's face, but it was Gert Fram who answered him.

"That's because it shouldn't be any easier for you than it is for me," she said disdainfully. "Fair is fair and right is right. Besides, I know what you're really here for."

"Do you?"

"Of course. You're like all the others. You want a sneak preview of my latest novel."

"I don't really think that's why I came up here, Susan," Father said.

"Oh, you'll definitely want to read it when you hear the title. It's called *Susan the Jerk.*"

This time it was Father's face that got the funny look. "I guess you're right," he said. "I really do want to read it."

Susan handed him the book with a shaking hand. Gert Fram's voice was steady, however, when she said, "I knew it would work. My titles are irresistible."

Father sat on the bed and read *Susan the Jerk* from the beginning to the end. He looked at the picture of the rocket ship crashing into the sun for a long time.

When he looked up at Susan, he saw Gert Fram watching him carefully, one eyebrow raised. Father sighed.

"Gert Fram, you're a fine author and I'm very impressed with your book. But there's been a terrible mistake made here. I really came to this address to see somebody else. You see, I respect you and admire you but you're just not in my class, Miss Fram. I was looking for a woman named Susan Parker. I wanted to tell her that I'm sorry that I've been cross with her. I wanted to tell Susan Parker that her father and her mother love her so much that when they know she's unhappy and it's their fault, they feel terrible until they can make it right. Can you pass that message along for us?"

"I hardly run a messenger service here," Gert Fram answered. But then her voice cracked and she said, "But I'll try to let her know. I don't think she'll believe that message, though."

Father bowed his head. "I hope she believes it. Because Susan just might be thinking right now that she's a jerk. And it just isn't true. She's a wonderful person. It's just that her parents and her brother and sisters are so used to having her around that they forget how wonderful she is. They forget to treat her like a wonderful person. But oh, Miss Fram, if they ever lost Susan they'd miss her so much—"

And suddenly Susan realized that the reason that Father had stopped talking was because he was crying. She had never seen her father cry before. And he was crying because he loved Susan Parker so much and right then Gert Fram disappeared and Susan Parker was back and she was crying and hugging her father but mostly letting him hug her. He was saying, "My little girl, my little girl."

Finally Susan said, very softly, "I'm not a little girl, Father."

Father took her by the shoulders and held her away from him a little and looked into her eyes. He looked a long time into her eyes and then he smiled, even though he still had tears, and he said, "You're absolutely right. And to think I didn't realize it until this moment."

Then they both said a lot of things and didn't say other things and went downstairs for family prayer. Then Mother and Father kissed Susan good-night and she went back upstairs. She undressed for bed and said her prayers and got under the covers and turned off the light.

A few minutes later she turned the light back on and got up and went to the desk. She picked up the book *Susan the Jerk* and turned it over and on the last page, in little letters where there was still some space left, right after where it said, "boy that Susan is sure a jerk," she wrote:

"But whenever they said that, Susan's father said, you better watch it, that's my dauter you're talking about, and they didn't say it anymore."

That was a better ending to the novel. Susan turned off the light and went to sleep. In the morning she would realize that she had never washed the jello dessert off her elbows and it was now all over her bedroom, but tonight it didn't matter. It didn't even matter in the morning.

AFTERWORD

"ENDER'S GAME," "MIKAL'S SONGBIRD," AND "PRENTICE ALVIN AND THE NO-GOOD PLOW"

*T*hese works share a common fate—they were killed commercially by the publication of a novel that superseded them. Not long ago I wrote an essay about this process for *Foundation*, a British literary journal about speculative fiction, and that essay will serve as a complete afterword to those stories in this collection. So here it is:

MOUNTAINS OUT OF MOLEHILLS

I never set out on a regular program of turning my old novelettes and novellas into novels. At the time I wrote most of my shorter works, I thought they were just right at that length. Yet somehow the expansion of old stories has become a regular feature of my career.

My novel *Songmaster* was built from the novelette "Mikal's Songbird." *Hart's Hope* began life as a novella of the same name. *Wyrms* was originally written as the novella "Unwyrm." Eight years before *Ender's Game* was published as a novel, the novelette of that name was my first published science fiction story.

In fact, I've gone even further—I find myself revising my old *books*. My first novel, *Hot Sleep*, and my first book, the collection *Capitol*, were replaced by the 1983 novel *The Worthing Chronicle*; it, in turn, will be included in the megabook *Worthing Complete* sometime in the next few years. Recently St. Martin's Press brought out *Treason*, a reworking of my second novel, *A Planet Called Treason*.

What's going on here? Is all this meddling with dead works a sort of resurrection or is it literary necrophilia? Am I making silk purses out of sows' ears, or am I so short of new ideas that I have to go back to what I did in bygone years? Am I a modest fellow who, in learning new skills, discovers the inadequacies of early work and tries to repair them, or am I so narcissistic that I find my past works too fascinating to ignore?

Maybe all of those things, or none of them. Each one of these expansions and rewrites came about in its own way, not because of any plan of mine, so I doubt they have any meaning in the aggregate. But perhaps an account of how these stories were transformed over time will have some value in understanding why they are the way they are.

SONGMASTER

Barbara Bova had just become my agent, and I hadn't sent her anything of novel length to sell. She was not deterred—I got a phone call from her saying that she had just received a decent offer from a publisher for the novel version of my novelette "Mikal's Songbird," which was at the time nominated for the Hugo and Nebula awards.

"What novel version?" I said.

"Well, that's the problem," said she. "I need a few paragraphs from you telling how you'll change it to make it a novel."

"But it's a novelette. It's *finished.*"

"Think about it for a while, dear. Maybe you'll find a novel in there somewhere. If you don't, I'll just turn down this very nice offer."

Now, you must understand—I don't automatically say yes just because I'm offered money. I had already turned down a request for a sequel to *A Planet Called Treason* because I couldn't think of an adequate storyline, and I fully expected to do the same with this proposal.

I thought back over what happened in "Mikal's Songbird" and tried to find a hook where I could hang new story elements. I rejected at once the idea of using the same plot and simply taking more words to tell it—I loathe excess description and empty writing. Besides, the world of "Mikal's Songbird" was very sketchy and not terribly interesting. Nor could I think of a subplot that would add meaningful pages.

Then I realized that there might be something worth exploring in how Ansset became a Songbird. The Songhouse might be developed into a strange and fascinating milieu. I knew at once that it should be a sort of medieval monastery, a retreat and a school, a place where souls are saved—and, in the struggle, hurt.

Looking back, I can see now that part of my fascination with the Songhouse was a desire to explore the relationship between the individual and a highly demanding and rewarding community, which in my case meant the Mormon Church. While Mormonism has no monastic tradition, a good case could be made for the idea that the whole church is a kind of monastery, insulating its members from the world behind walls, not of stone, but of culture.

At the time, however, it just seemed like a pretty good science fiction idea— one that I could hang a novel on. At the same time, it involved a structural insight that I have used to good effect many times since: When expanding a short work into a long one, the place to go for a new material isn't *after* the initial short story, but *before* it. By starting much earlier, and explaining how the characters got to where they are at the beginning of the short story, the milieu is much richer, the cast of characters much fuller, the characterization much deeper than it was in the original story.

Much outlining and map-drawing later, I sat down and began writing. The first section, in the Songhouse, grew to be much longer than I had expected. When it was done, I realized that it could stand alone quite nicely, so I sent it to Barbara, who sold it as a separate novella to Stan Schmidt, then quite new as editor of *Analog.* Word for word, it was identical with the opening chapters of *Songmaster;* as with the recent publication of sections of the Tales of Alvin Maker as separate stories, the novella "Songhouse" was a case of excerpting from a novel, not expanding a short work after the fact.

By the time I got to the events of the original novelette the milieu and characters had grown and changed so much that hardly a word of "Mikal's Songbird" was usable. Events had new meanings; characters had different things to think and say. This first time, it was quite wrenching for me to throw out the entire text of a story that had been, after all, quite successful. But it had to be done if the novel was to have any integrity.

Songmaster ended up with some serious structural flaws—for instance, the "Kyaren" section lags quite badly and the novel seems to end when Ansset becomes emperor, so that readers often find it hard to figure out why there are still so many pages left. But these are the product of my unfamiliarity with the novel form, not the fact that *Songmaster* was an expansion. Despite its flaws, in fact, *Songmaster* is my earliest novel that I am willing to stand by in its original form, so that the editing I did in preparation for Tor's recent reprint was on the level of tinkering with style. The structure has problems, but I'm willing to live with them, because the story still feels true to me as it stands, even if it isn't as artful as I'd like.

DERIVATIONS

In a way, "Mikal's Songbird" was an adaptation right from the start. The novelette was only my fourth science fiction sale. "Ender's Game" had been the first, a story that was quite easy to write. My next story died instantly; my third and fourth, "Follower" and "Malpractice," sold—but only with strong editorial suggestions from Ben Bova at *Analog*. The next few stories I wrote, however, went nowhere —they were so bad that not only did no one buy them, but also one editor sent me an incredible two-page letter that can only be classed as hate-mail, and followed up by *reviewing* one of those unpublishable stories in a fanzine! These stories were so bad that someone had to drive a stake through their hearts, just to make sure they didn't rise again.

And I was afraid. Though I had done quite well as a playwright in the Mormon theatre scene in Utah, I had no guarantee that I'd have a career in a genre that actually paid writers enough to live on. To me, at that bleak moment, it looked as though "Ender's Game" might be the only successful story I'd ever write.

But I was determined to try again. This time, though, I went back to "Ender's Game" and tried to determine what it was about that story that worked. In my ignorance, I saw only the most superficial strengths of the story: The hero was a child with extraordinary ability, who goes through a great deal of personal pain inflicted by adults who are trying to exploit him. Maybe this was a pattern I could use again, thought I.

There were other patterns, of course, that I might have followed: The success of "Ender's Game" might have led me to write more military-training stories, for instance, or I might even have attempted a sequel at that time. Instead, true to a view of storytelling that I did not become conscious of until long after, I looked to the character's role in his community in order to find the essence of the tale.

I should point out, too, that I thought of "Ender's Game" as a successful story only in an artistic sense—I knew it worked, but because it had not yet been published, I had no idea whether it would be popular.

When I set out to follow that same pattern, I knew I had to come up with another way for my new child-hero to be exceptional. I'd used military talent with Ender; why not musical ability for my new hero? From there it was a fairly simple matter to come up with Ansset, Mikal's Songbird; though the plot doesn't follow "Ender's Game," the lifeline of the character certainly does.

I wrote "Mikal's Songbird" quickly, and knew all through it that this story was alive the way "Ender's Game" had been alive. It was still hot from xeroxing when I stuffed it into an envelope and mailed it to Ben Bova.

A couple of days later, though, in rereading the story, I knew that there were serious problems. This didn't bother me—I was excited about the fact that for the first time I actually understood narrative well enough to *see* the flaws. So I did a substantial revision of the story, and then sent the new version to Ben, with a letter asking him to toss the first version and look only at this one.

Within a few days I got a cheque. Ben had bought the *first* version, flaws and all. At that moment I knew I had a career—not because I had found a repeatable formula, for in fact I had not, but rather because I had found a road into that place inside myself from which true stories arise. For a long time my stories have grown out of childhood and adolescence, probably because that was the role in life that I best understood—it was not until *Speaker for the Dead* that I was able to work with truly adult characters, and even then the story was heavily populated with unusual children.

SCHOOLING MYSELF

What Ben ended up publishing was, of course, the revised version of the story—he had simply bought the first version before the second one arrived. From the start, however, and at every step thereafter, the story of Ansset was continuously derived from previous versions, expanding and growing every time I went back to it. Every version represents another stage in my self-schooling as a writer of narrative.

Even in the writing of the novel *Songmaster*, I was consciously "at school." I knew that *Hot Sleep* was a failure as a novel (though, ironically, it remained my best-selling book until the publication of the novel *Ender's Game*); in order to overcome my dread of a novel's sheer length, I had conceived *Hot Sleep* as a series of novelettes, not a true novel. I was also beginning to realize that A *Planet Called Treason* was rushed, sketchy, abrupt, not a smoothly flowing work. In other words, I still didn't know how to write a novel.

In order to try to understand how a novel worked, I carefully examined Saul Bellow's *Humboldt's Gift*. I ended up, alas, with little intellectual understanding of the novel form, but the sheer reading of the book gave me a feel for a novel's *pace*. It was as if reading *Humboldt's Gift* set my metabolic rate; then, when I sat down to work on *Songmaster*, I was able to keep up that same rhythm of event, language, and scene. No one reading my work will ever accuse me of being Bellowesque; nevertheless, his novel was my touchstone in discovering how to write a true novel.

As a result, *Songmaster* was my one story with explicit connections with other works, a clear pattern of growth and change that paralleled my own. Expanding it to a novel may have come from a commercially-minded editor's suggestion to my agent, and my own source for the story's idea may have been a deliberate mining of my own previous work, but it ended up as a story I believed in passionately—and the process of writing it was a kind of training ground for my career as a writer, just as my characters Ender and Ansset had to go through training to become a person capable of surviving.

HART'S HOPE AND WYRMS

The next "short" work I adapted into a novel followed quite a different pattern. Roy Torgeson had asked me for a fantasy story for his *Chrysalis* anthology series, and I began developing *Hart's Hope* from a map I had doodled and an idea about somebody whose magical power was the negation of magic. The story grew in the back of my mind while I worked on finishing the first draft of my novel *Saints* and a production revision of my historical Mormon play *Father, Mother, Mother, and Mom*; when *Saints* and *FMM&M* were finished, I turned with relief to a fantasy tale as an antidote to the rigours of historical writing. However, having just finished a sprawling novel of a thousand pages, it's hardly a surprise that *Hart's Hope* began growing out of control. Before I had finished the novella, I knew exactly how to turn it into a novel; I sent a copy to Barbara at the same time as my submission to Roy, and she soon sold it as a prospectus for a novel. While the novel version went through a couple of major rewrites over a period of years before it finally was published in 1983, it remained substantially the same story as the novella—the novel was not so much an expansion of the novella as the novella was a compression of the novel.

The same is true of the novel *Wyrms* and the novella "Unwyrm." I was writing "Unwyrm" for George R.R. Martin's Campbell-nominate anthology series, and as I wrote it I discovered that it simply would not stay under 40,000 words. The novella that George ended up buying was a cut-down version that removed several important plotlines; I finished the novel version only a few weeks after the novella.

(The collapse of Blue Jay Books killed the anthology, so that "Unwyrm" never appeared in print.)

So neither *Hart's Hope* nor *Wyrms* represents an expansion on the order of *Songmaster*. The "short" version in both cases was very long, and in both cases I knew it would be a novel before the novella was completed.

ENDER'S GAME

The novel *Ender's Game* is the only work of mine, besides *Songmaster*, that was truly expanded from a short work that I had not intended to expand. Indeed, I had never expected to do anything with Ender Wiggin again. A friend had once urged me to write a sequel to "Ender's Game," but when he suggested possible storylines, they were lame enough to convince me that a sequel was impossible.

In 1980, though, I was beginning to work with a novel idea with the working title *Speaker of Death*, a sketchy idea about an alien people who periodically mauled each other in devastating wars that were, without their realizing it, their means of reproduction. The truth would be discovered by a human character whose job was speaking the truth about people at funerals. I couldn't make the idea work, however, until suddenly it dawned on me that the Speaker should be Ender Wiggins as an adult. Who better to understand the impulse that made a species nearly destroy itself than a man who had once inadvertently destroyed another people?

At once the work began to come to life. In 1982 an outline was ready to offer to a publisher. It was explicitly a sequel to "Ender's Game", which remained my most popular—and most anthologized—story. Barbara offered it to Tom Doherty, the former publisher at Ace who was starting his own company. For financing reasons I got a request to hurry and write a draft of the book before the end of 1982; I complied, but in the process learned that this was going to be harder to write than I supposed. There was more to my story than one human and a bunch of aliens. I was getting involved in creating a human family in whose lives Ender was deeply involved. And the story simply wasn't working. I didn't know how to write it.

A few months later, I realized why. In order to make Ender viable as a character in *Speaker of Death*, I had to expand on the meaning of the events in "Ender's Game." I had to deal with the transformation of Ender Wiggin in the aftermath of his xenocide. And to do that in *Speaker of Death* meant picking up the story right at the end of "Ender's Game," showing Ender's self-discovery and his transformation into a Speaker. Then I'd have to skip three thousand years and begin an entirely new storyline. It was impossible!

So when I happened to run into Tom Doherty at the ABA in Dallas in the spring of 1983, on impulse I proposed to him that instead of the horribly deformed *Speaker* that was emerging, all the problems would be solved if I went back and rewrote "Ender's Game" as a novel, incorporating into it all the changes that were needed to properly set up *Speaker*. Tom promptly agreed, and on a handshake I was committed to my second expansion of a novelette into a novel.

Just as I had studied "Ender's Game" in order to write "Mikal's Songbird," now I recalled my experience with *Songmaster* in order to figure out how to write *Ender's Game*. I decided at once to begin *Ender's Game* much earlier than the novelette—to start when Ender was still with his family.

In a way, this was analogous to starting *Songmaster* when Ansset was in the Songhouse; but it was also a radical departure, because instead of having a protagonist who was completely cut off from his family—the standard adolescent hero of most Romance—I was now committed to creating a hero whose connections to his family were still very much alive. I hardly knew how to begin; and so I mined my own life, looking back at my relationship with my older brother and sister as I had thought it was when I was about ten years old, then exaggerating it extravagantly in order to make it a justification for much of Ender's behaviour later on. (I couldn't very well use my childhood as it actually was, since my actual childhood produced, not a twisted military genius, but rather a bookish homebody.)

As with *Songmaster*, by the time I got back to the point where the novelette should have been inserted into the novel, the character and milieu had changed so much that only the first sentence of the novelette was usable: "Remember, the enemy's gate is down." However, I felt not a qualm about losing the novelette itself—I had known all along that it would be unusable because of my experience with *Songmaster*. In fact, I was delighted, because this proved that there was far more going on in the novel than I had ever conceived of when writing the novelette. And when I got to the payoff scene, where Ender discovers that he has been fighting the real war, not a simulation, I knew that there was still one more payoff to go —the final chapter, entitled "Speaker for the Dead."

Ironically, though, this duplicated one of the structural flaws in *Songmaster*— once again, few readers could understand why there were still so many pages left when the story was clearly over. Even this flaw didn't bother me. I had a master's degree in English by now, so I knew how to excuse it in literary terms: I was making the reader go through the same kind of revision of the meaning of the story's past that Ender went through. Ah, how the tools of criticism allow us to justify the lapses of our art!

OTHER ADAPTATIONS

Besides expansions of short works to make novels, I have also revised my first two novels. Part of my motive was simple literary self-defense—by revising them, I disarm critics who are apt to scorn them, because I in effect am saying, "I *know* they weren't all that good." But much more important to me was the fact that I still cared about the stories. Jason Worthing and Abner Doon of the Worthing stories and Lanik Mueller of *A Planet Called Treason* were once important enough to me that I wrote books about them; just because I now knew more about writing books didn't mean that I should care less about the stories I had told back when I was a novice.

Hot Sleep and *Capitol*, I felt, were bad enough that the need to fix them was almost an emergency. Even though they were still in print and still selling rather well, I was able to persuade Susan Allison to withdraw both books and allow me to replace them with a single work to be called *The Worthing Chronicle*. Little did either of us know how hopelessly uncommercial the result would be—but I still regard it as one of my best works, and I'm grateful to her for allowing me to publish it.

The flaws in *Hot Sleep* had arisen from my feeble attempts to control the vast sweep of time involved in the story. With *The Worthing Chronicle*, I unified the story by containing it within a frame, the story of a village whose life had been deeply affected by the outcome of the whole Worthing story. In effect, the new novel was the story of how people are transformed by stories—a circularity that still delights me. It's a series of fictions and dreams and memories all bound up so closely together that it's impossible even within the story to say what is real and what is now. The process of adaptation was exhilarating—but, as with *Songmaster* and as would later be true with *Ender's Game*, hardly a sentence from the original books remained in the new version.

Indeed, if there is anything that I think is the key to successfully transforming one version of a story into another, it is to completely discard the first text and develop a *new* text that contains the same story—the same causally related events—but enriches them with new characters and relationships, new and richer milieux, and many more ideas than the original version contained.

That's why I was so frustrated by the fact that St. Martin's Press, in its eagerness to capitalize on the commercial success of *Ender's Game*, insisted on going back to press with a new printing of A *Planet Called Treason* before I had time to write a completely new version. I had long harboured an ambition to return to the tale of Lanik Mueller, but this time tell it in third person, with many more characters and subplots that would make it one of my deepest novels instead of the shallowest. To my outrage at the time, Thomas Dunne would not relent and allow me to do the ideal version of the book. Instead, all I had time to do was revise the opening and edit heavily throughout the book. The result was a novel that, while no longer embarrassing, was far short of the ideal that I had harboured in my imagination. The book remained in first person and continued to follow the same narrative line, with no new characters or events. It was and remains quite frustrating, but at present I have no plans to go back and revise it ever again—if for no other reason than because there is no reversion clause in my contract with St. Martin's (the result of signing a contract as a naïve youth without an agent), so that the same publisher would own any revision of the book. Besides, a *third* version of the same book is certainly too absurd to contemplate.

THE ABYSS

My most recent venture into expanding a shorter work was my novelization of James Cameron's film *The Abyss*. The problems of novelizing a screenplay are enormous—they are made virtually hopeless in most cases by the fact that the novelizer is forced to work from the screenplay alone, and the screenplay is not a viable story. A screenplay is only a *plan* for a work of art, like a fresco painter's cartoon; it is not until director and actors interpret the script that it becomes a finished story.

The only reason I agreed to do the novelization was because Jim Cameron was as determined as I was to make the novel a viable work of art in its own right. Unlike most novelizers, I had complete access to the film itself, and to all of the screenwriter's research material. Even more important, however, was the fact that Cameron allowed me to do to his screenplay what I had done to "Ender's Game" and "Mikal's Songbird" in order to expand them—I went back before the beginning of the original story and developed the earlier lives of the characters.

This time, however, I could not go as far as I had with my own work, if only because when I got to the point where the film began, the words and events of the film had to be used exactly as they stood. (We take pride in the fact that *this* novelization contains every word of significant action and dialogue that actually made it into the film, besides occasional extra scenes that I wrote.) Nevertheless, my preliminary chapters, including a chapter about the early life of a non-human character that quite properly did not end up in the final book, became the root of the novel.

When I gave the early chapters to Cameron, he immediately called them "backstory," the information about characters that never shows up in a film. I was content to have him regard those chapters that way. After all, he liked them well enough that he showed them to the actors, allowing them to help shape their thinking about their roles. But to me, they were not "backstory," not background at all. Instead, they set up fundamental questions in the readers' minds, questions that are not resolved until the end of the book. The film is structured as an adventure story that is taken over by the strong relationship story contained within it. My novel, however, is structured as a character story from the beginning, so that to me, at least, the novel is truer to the tale both Cameron and I wanted to tell than the film is.

I don't call this a flaw in the film, but rather a limitation of the cinematic form; and Cameron would certainly dispute my conclusion that the book is "truer." Perhaps this idea is merely my way of making the book my own even though the bulk of it is a retelling of someone else's story. One thing is certain, however—if this novel transcends the limitations of most novelizations, it is because I went back to the time before the story and added new material that transforms the meaning of the events in the film when we finally come to them.

ALVIN MAKER

Even my Tales of Alvin Maker—*Seventh Son, Red Prophet, Prentice Alvin,* and the yet-unpublished *Alvin Journeyman* and *Master Alvin*—began as a shorter work. As I studied the works of Spenser with Norman Council at the University of Utah, I determined to attempt for my people something of what he accomplished for his: create a verse epic in the vernacular. Of course it was a mad enterprise from the start. Who reads long poems anymore, especially *narrative* poems? Especially poems written in a folky mountain-country voice:

> Alvin, he was a blacksmith's prentice boy,
> He pumped the bellows and he ground the knives,
> He chipped the nails, he het the charcoal fire,
> Nothing remarkable about the lad
> Except for this: He saw the world askew,
> He saw the edge of light, the frozen liar
> There in the trees with a black smile shinin cold,
> Shiverin the corners of his eyes.
> Oh, he was wise.

But there's something about great works of art like *The Faerie Queene* that makes the beholder long to go and do likewise. In awe of Spenser and yet ambitious to learn from him, I wrote my way many stanzas deep into the story, until I reached a sort of conclusion when Alvin and his friend Verily Cooper tried out Al's golden plow in the rich soil near the banks of the Mizzippy. At that point I gave the poem an ending—after a fashion:

> The rest of the tale—how they looked for the crystal
>   city,
> How they crept to the dangerous heart of the holy hill,
> How they broke the cage of the girl who sang for rain,
> How they built the city of light from water and blood
> —
> Others have told that tale, and told it good.
> And besides, the girl you're with is cruel and pretty,
> And the boy you're setting by has a mischievous will.
> There's better things to do than hear me again,
> So go on home.

At that point, exhausted, I set the poem aside, uncertain where the story should go from there.

Though "Prentice Alvin and the No-Good Plow" won a Utah state fine arts contest, I never did get back to the poem, except to revise it slightly for forthcoming publication in a Mormon journal. Still, the story of it hung with me, in part because, in true Spenserian manner, it is an elaborate allegory for some of the most important tales of the epic of my own people; in part because I fell in love with that hill-country voice and the American frontier magic I had devised for the story. Here was a fantasy that was completely American—no elves, no dragons, no European myths and legends, and the setting was a log cabin, not a castle, and the people wore homespun and hunted with muskets instead of donning armour to go a-pricking with lance and sword. I wanted to go back and finish it.

The opportunity came in 1983, when I finally realized that while long narrative poems have no particular audience, long fantasy novels—or trilogies—do. The language would be daring, for fantasy, as would the setting, but at least the ordinary-looking paragraphs between ordinary-looking book covers would reassure the audience that this story would be accessible.

I wrote an extended outline of the trilogy (supposedly starting with *Prentice Alvin*) and sent it to Barbara. Tom Doherty bought this one and a story collection as well. (He then had six of my books under contract though not one had yet been published. His faith in me—an author whose books, up to then, had never earned out their advances—was extraordinary, and will always be appreciated.)

When it came time actually to write the Alvin Maker books, I began as I did with every other expansion and adaptation: I started the longer version before the beginning of the original story. I didn't dream at the time that I wouldn't reach the events of the narrative poem until the middle of the third volume, but the introductory chapter became the novel *Seventh Son*, and the chapter in which Alvin was captured by Indians became the novel *Red Prophet*, so that by the time I finished *Prentice Alvin* in 1988, the world had grown so full and the characters so numerous that at times I despaired of containing the whole thing in *any* finite number of books.

Nevertheless, it *was* the story that I had begun back in graduate school, even though the text had changed, the characters had been transformed, and the world had grown wider and stranger than I had ever imagined at first. Yet it's hard for me to imagine that I ever thought the story was complete, as far as it went. There was so much more possibility; in writing the first version of it I had thought I was completing the story, but in fact I was merely essaying the first rough draft, the first bare outline of what the tale could be.

I think perhaps that's the case with all my work. At the time I write it, I think it's complete, I think I have discovered all its possibilities and now an sharing them with an audience. But the stories that are best, that are most alive to me, I can't leave them alone. They keep growing whether I like it or not. I keep imagining them without regard for the fact that they have already been written down, published, reviewed, and remaindered.

I'm not "expanding" shorter works at all, I think. I'm merely returning to unfinished acts of imagination, warming myself at fires that only burn the hotter for having lain dormant during all the intervening years. Each tale finds its own occasion to come to life and grow again, and what I've been learning is not so much how to expand novelettes as how to tell stories more fully than ever before.

Does the process end? I'd like to think so. There are plenty of new stories to tell, and I don't have any older works that cry out to me for further development.

Except that I just finished a short story called "Lost Boys" that I once envisioned as a novel of contemporary horror. Since it's the most autobiographical piece I've ever written, I know I could expand on it considerably simply by mining my own life—and so who knows? Maybe a trend that began quite accidentally will continue deliberately.

"MALPRACTICE"

This story was my second science fiction sale. It is a one-idea story—something that I have since learned is not a terribly good idea. The idea? Heart transplants were big news back in the late seventies; I wondered what might happen if, far from rejecting the transplant, the host began to find itself being replaced by the growing cells of the transplanted organ. It would certainly solve the problem of rejection. However, I had neither the scientific knowledge to make the idea really plausible, nor the skill as a

writer to make the question of human identity transcend the nonsense science. The
result is a story that was more a placeholder in *Analog* than a particular standout.

"FOLLOWER"

Unlike "Malpractice," "Follower" actually represents a trend I would pursue later in
my career. The thriller-story structure isn't for me, but the motif of a child who has a
twisted relationship with adults is a strong one in my work. When I submitted this to
Ben Bova, he told me it was all right as far as it went—but it simply didn't end. He
suggested an ending to me. I liked it, wrote it just as he suggested it, and sent it back.
I didn't alter a word of the first part of the story in order to make the ending work.
Then, when the story came out, I was repeatedly told by friends and kin alike that they
had guessed the ending almost from the beginning of the story. Ironic that *I* didn't guess
it—I had to wait for Ben to give it to me!

This story is one of the few I've written that began, not with the story idea, but with
a sentence. "His dog and his doctor disagreed"—that was the phrase I tried to hang a
story on. I know many a writer who *does* begin writing with an evocative sentence, but
it rarely works for me.

"HITCHING"

This story began with a news story about some people who were murdered by a hitchhiker. I have never in my life picked up a hitchhiker or, for that matter, hitched a ride
myself—my parents drummed that rule into my head before I could see over the
dashboard of a car. But still, I began to wonder if there was some way that an unarmed
driver could stop a murderous hitchhiker. It struck me that the only reason the hitchhiker's weapon gives him power over the driver is that the driver still hopes that if he
just goes along and does what he's told, the hitchhiker will let him live. But what if
the driver starts from the assumption that he's already as good as dead, and his only
goal is to make sure the hitchhiker doesn't outlive him? Then all he'd need to do is
smash the car into an overpass abutment and the hiker would have hitched his last ride.

That led to the thought that if you could once convince the hitchhiker that you
were more dangerous than *he* was, then *his* behavior would be under *your* control. The
tables would be turned.

The idea became a story when, instead of a crazed maniac killer, I decided the
hitchhiker would be someone more innocent at heart. The result was this story, which
appeared in a regional magazine and won a few laughs from a few readers before the
magazine went out of business.

"DAMN FINE NOVEL"

This story began as a conversation with a couple of dear friends, Clark and Kathy Kidd,
as we were driving away from the Casa Maria restaurant in Tyson's Corner, Virginia.
We were joking about brand names that might tell what a product actually is, instead
of completely unrelated names. "Tight-ass Jeans" instead of Jordache, for instance.
Then I applied the idea to books and decided it was about time I wrote a novel called
"F——ing Good Read." But we decided that nobody would publish such a title, so
we'd have to call it "Damn Fine Novel."

I wrote the story the next morning, with the idea of submitting it to the graduate writing course I was taking at the University of North Carolina at Greensboro. It ended up being a kind of twisted Escheresque literary joke, and as my wife pointed out when I read it to her over the phone, there was no way I could turn this story in to the workshop, since it absolutely ridiculed the kind of story that these students were trying to write. So instead of turning it in for a grade, I published it pseudonymously in the *Green Pages* section of my fanzine, *Short Form*. It marks the only time that I've used the "F-word" (as we Mormons call it) in my fiction; I hope that the necessity for using it here will be obvious.

"BILLY'S BOX"

There are three LDS Church magazines. While I was working for *The Ensign*, the magazine for adults, the offices of *The New Era*, the Church's teen magazine, were in the suite just south of us, and the offices of *The Friend*, the Church's children's magazine, were in the suite just north of us on the twenty-third floor of the LDS Church Office Building. We saw the other magazines' editors now and then, and got to hear them moan about how rare it was for them to get good fiction. So while Jay Parry and Lane Johnson and I were working on story ideas, we inevitably turned to trying to write stories that would meet the needs of *The Friend* and *The New Era*.

One of the results was "Billy's Box," a story in which I tried to realistically depict a very young child in a story that might appeal to slightly older children—and, I hoped, their parents.

"THE BEST FAMILY HOME EVENING EVER"

The Mormon Church encourages its members to meet together as families in their own homes every Monday night. This story should make clear both what Family Home Evening is supposed to be—and what it more commonly is. This specific story, however, is based on some experiences of my brother-in-law, Scott Allen, when he was very young.

"BICICLETA"

This story is a pretty faithful depiction of a real incident that happened on my mission to Brazil, when we taught a young boy to ride a bicycle. What I couldn't convey in the story was the desperate poverty and ignorance of this family, and yet the powerful love that bound them together. They were good people, and for the first time I realized that it was possible for people to sleep packed into a room the size of a small conference table and still be decent, civilized human beings. Teaching the boy to ride a bicycle was such a pathetically small thing to do to help them—but it was *something*, and that was more than I had ever been able to do before. I think it was this family's desperate financial condition that finally killed any remnant of allegiance to free market capitalism that I might still have had.

"I THINK MOM AND DAD ARE GOING CRAZY, JERRY"

I wrote about a half-dozen stories for *The New Era* magazine during this time, and while the editor, Brian Kelly, bought several of them, to my memory only this one actually appeared in print—the others were somehow not quite "correct" enough for an official Church publication. This was not an issue of censorship. The Church leadership was the publisher, not some outside censor, and they had not only the right but the responsibility to make sure that what appeared in the Church magazines was exactly what they wanted to say to the members. In the meantime, though, there were things that needed to be said in some unofficial forum, not by way of criticism, but in order to show the great variety of possibilities for individual identity within the larger community identity.

Unfortunately, in LDS Church publishing at that time it seemed there were only two kinds of publisher: official or quasi-official Church publishing, which by definition could publish only the most narrowly acceptable kind of material; and the dissident press, which delighted in publishing things that were either so literary as to be unreadable, or so offensive and inflammatory that most Mormons could only perceive it as another form of anti-Mormon literature. What was missing was the loyal alternative press, by no means an opposition, but rather a more open unofficial press that could speak freely, but in ways that the Church membership would receive as coming from within the Church, not outside it.

I waited a long time for such a press to appear, believing that if it did, it would be quite successful. While I was waiting, I wrote a few works that belonged in that genre: *Saintspeak: The Mormon Dictionary*, a gentle satire that nevertheless affirms Mormon values and only criticizes the Saints where we tend to depart from those values; and *Saints*, a Mormon historical novel that gives a perspective that could never be published by the official LDS press if only because the official press is not free to imagine what thoughts might have passed through Joseph Smith's head, or what words he might have whispered to his wife in bed. The response from the Church membership was all the proof I needed that there was a great hunger for this kind of writing among the loyal members of the Church. So this past year—1989—I used earnings from my science fiction that I could ill spare and launched my own publishing company, Hatrack River Publications, to bring out the kind of book that I thought was needed. It will take time to build an audience—we have no promotional budget and must rely on word of mouth—but our first two novels are doing very well, and in the coming year we expect to publish several more, including novel adaptations of some of my early LDS plays.

All of that began, really, with the stories I sold to *The New Era* that, unlike "I Think Mom and Dad Are Going Crazy, Jerry," were never cleared for publication. And, though this story is definitely an early work of mine, and does not represent the level of skill and sophistication that Hatrack River Publications looks for in the books we publish, the story does represent the basic approach: humor, satire, along with an honest representation of LDS life.

"GERT FRAM"

"Gert Fram" was my first published fiction. I wrote it years after the first draft of "Ender's Game"; in fact, I whipped it out in one night to meet a deadline for *The Ensign* magazine's special fine arts issue in July of 1977. It is sentimental—but with sentiment that is deeply felt within the Mormon community. It is the most strongly Mormon of all my works, I think.

I had an uncredited collaborator on this story, by the way—Gert Fram herself. Gert Fram was the nom de plume of my then-future sister-in-law, Nancy Allen (now Nancy Allen Black). In her childhood she actually wrote all but the last of the Gert Fram books, exactly as they appear in this story; she, with a friend of hers, lived a pretend life as world-famous authors, and produced these books for each other. So, while the incidents of this story are entirely out of my imagination, the character of Gert Fram and the books she wrote are entirely the creation of the young Nancy Allen. I keep urging her to write the young adult novel *Gert Fram*, so that I can publish it with Hatrack River. Nancy remains the most madly creative person I've ever known, and if she actually wrote the book, I think it would be a work of genius.

It was for this story that I first used the pseudonym "Byron Walley," which appeared as the credit line for all my fiction in the LDS magazines. It began for one of the traditional reasons: I already had my name too often in the July 1977 fine arts issue of *The Ensign*. Both an article and a poem appeared under my name. "Gert Fram" appeared under the name Byron Walley, and my play "Rag Mission" appeared under the name Brian Green. I liked the Byron Walley name and have used it ever since when pseudonyms were required.

Now, at last, you have come to the end of this book. The introductions and afterwords themselves amount to some forty thousand words—a slim novel's worth of text. It is outrageous that I should imagine anyone would want to read all of this; and yet, whether or not you read the introductions and afterwords, I hope some people will read at least some of the stories, if only because it is there that some of my most heartfelt work has appeared. I have often said, in other places, that it is in the short fiction that you find the cutting edge of science fiction and fantasy. New authors show up there first; new ideas and techniques also tend to find their way into the magazines before the book publishers are ready for them, or before the writers are willing to invest a novel's-worth of time in them.

Some of our best writers, of course, almost never write short fiction, like Tim Powers, or write it almost as an afterthought it seems, like Lisa Goldstein. Others, like Harlan Ellison and Ray Bradbury, write almost nothing *but* short fiction. But the fact remains that if you want to understand what science fiction is, you must read the short fiction —*The Science Fiction Hall of Fame*, voted on by the members of the Science Fiction Writers of America; *The Hugo Winners*, an anthology series edited and introduced by Isaac Asimov; *Dangerous Visions* and *Again, Dangerous Visions*, edited by Harlan Ellison, the definitive anthology of the sixties and seventies in science fiction. There you'll see most of the history of science fiction unfold. There you'll see the first blossoming and the freshest songs of most of the writers who created this field and keep it alive.

In these pages you've seen something far less interesting (to everyone but me and my mother): my personal history as a writer. Every step I've taken in my books began with a step taken in one or more of these stories. Every idea I've explored in my novels, I first broached in fiction in one of these tales. And if I have anything of value to say to you, I hope I've said it here.